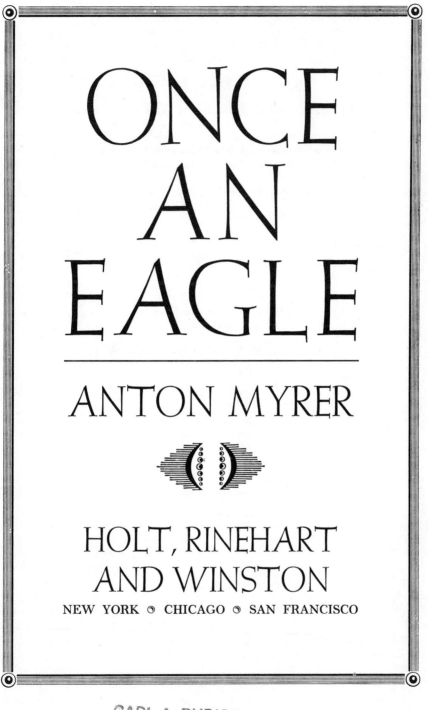

ONCE AN EAGLE

ANTON MYRER

HOLT, RINEHART AND WINSTON

NEW YORK ⌾ CHICAGO ⌾ SAN FRANCISCO

August, 1968

Published simultaneously in Canada by Holt, Rinehart
and Winston of Canada, Limited.

Library of Congress Catalog Card Number: 68-21746

DESIGNER: RONALD FARBER
8723058

Printed in the United States of America

FOR

PATRICIA SCHARTLE

grates persolvere dignas non opis est nostrae

"So in the Libyan fable it is told
That once an eagle, stricken with a dart,
Said, when he saw the fashion of the shaft,
'With our own feathers, not by others' hands,
Are we now smitten.'"

—AESCHYLUS

The average general envies the buck private; when things go wrong, the private can blame the general, but the general can blame only himself. The private carries the woes of one man; the general carries the woes of all. He is conscious always of the responsibility on his shoulders, of the relatives of the men entrusted to him, and of their feelings. He must act so that he can face those fathers and mothers without shame or remorse. How can he do this? By constant care, by meticulous thought and preparation, by worry, by insistence on high standards in everything, by reward and punishment, by impartiality, by an example of calm and confidence. It all adds up to character.

Q: If a man has enough character to be a good commander, does he ever doubt himself? He should not. In my case, I doubt myself. Therefore, I am in all probability not a good commander.

—GENERAL JOSEPH STILWELL

I
ORCHARD

"It all seems so faraway," Celia Harrodsen said. "Paris and Berlin. And poor little Belgium. Sam, do you honestly think we'll get mixed up in it?"

"I told you I do."

"Well, nobody else seems to think so."

"I can't help that."

Celia put her teeth on her lower lip. "You're just saying that because you want to go over there and see the world. Don't you try and fool *me*, Sam Damon." She shifted her position on the weatherbeaten bench and gazed across the front yard to the Damons' house, which looked pale and shabby in the soft June twilight, its clapboards peeling, troubled with shadows. From the porch the sound of voices reached them intermittently, and the occasional dry clink of a bottle touching a glass. "Anyway," she went on, "Father says we aren't so foolish as to get involved in futile European conflicts."

"Maybe," Sam Damon answered. He was sitting near her on the lawn, his big hands locked around his knees. "Only sometimes you get involved in something whether you want to or not."

"Oh, you're so sure of yourself." He made no reply to this, which irritated her still more. She was a tall, slender girl with blond hair and deep blue eyes that looked at everything with piercing candor, and she stared at him for a moment, hard, then tossed her head. "You don't know everything."

"Don't I?" he said, and grinned.

From down the street near Clausen's Forge there came a loud popping noise that swelled into a high, sustained roar, and in a few seconds a Packard touring car came by, majestic and maroon, churning up dust in clouds. Its driver, a slim young man in a white duster and maroon cloth cap, lifted one hand from the shiny wooden wheel and waved, calling out something to them, inaudible in the engine's clamor. The car swerved suddenly and the driver clutched the wheel again with both hands. Celia waved back. Fritz Clausen's dog, a bigheaded, shaggy animal, raced after it, yapping frantically, its tail thrashing round and round, and behind the dog came two children brandishing sticks and hooting in the golden dust.

"Look at him," Sam said. "Scared to death it'll run away with him."

"Well I never—! You can't even *drive* an automobile," she retorted.

"You want to bet?"

She stared at him. "Where would you have learned?"

"The truck. Down at the switchyard."

"Oh—a *truck* . . . I'm going to have one of my own when I'm twenty-one. An Olds Runabout. Have you seen them? There was a colored picture in *The Saturday Evening Post.* With yellow fenders and green leather upholstery. It's just the pezazz. Don't you want to own one, Sam?"

He turned and looked at her for a moment. He was tall and solidly muscled, with a rather long, angular face and steady gray eyes that could unsettle her completely. She had watched him play football and baseball and had gone to three dances with him, one formal. She'd had a crush on him ever since she'd been thirteen, and his brooding silences drove her wild.

"—Well, don't be so inscrutable!" she burst out. "Of course you want one . . ."

"Sure," he said simply. "Someday."

"Well, there's no earthly reason why you shouldn't." She looked around her, exasperated. From the massive old tree beside them a green apple fell with a thick, solid sound.

"July drop," Sam murmured.

"July drop," she mimicked. "It's still June." She spurned the apple with her foot. "Father says you could have a tremendous future ahead of you—he says you've got a lot of the necessary qualities: mental aptitude and self-discipline . . ." She paused, watching Sam, who seemed to be studying the trunk of the apple tree where the sapsuckers had stitched it with rows of neat round black holes. "He says you're too impulsive, too dreamy, your head in the clouds. He says"—and she leaned forward so that her face was close to his—"you're wasting the most important years of your life, Sam. Farm jobs and playing baseball, and that ridiculous night-clerk job at the hotel . . . Why on earth did you take it? Look at the rings under your eyes."

"It pays twelve-fifty a week, that's why," he answered shortly.

"You could be making a lot more than that, if you weren't so stubborn . . ."

There was a burst of laughter from the screen porch, and a lively voice with a trace of brogue cried, "No no no—they'll break through this summer and come goose-stepping down the Paris boulee-vards with the bands blaring and the glockenspiels twirling their wolf tails in a fine frenzy, just the way they did last time. They're *professionals,* Mr. Verney—they know soldiering from muzzle to butt plate, and that's where you want to put your money. I saw them in Peking. They never make a mistake."

"*Somebody* made a mistake at the Marne," old George Verney retorted in his hoarse, muffled monotone.

"A temporary setback, nothing more."

"If you call nearly two years—"

"You wait. They'll let the murdering sods of British bleed themselves white this season and then it'll be 'Hoch der Kaiser and on to Paris!' You mark my words . . ."

"Peg told me your Uncle Bill's come back to stay this time," Celia said. "Has he really?"

"I don't know. He never has before."

She frowned, scratching at the worn wood of the bench with her nails. The Damons were poor: that was half the trouble. The Damons were poor and the Harrodsens were well off. Her father was president of the Platte and Midland Bank, and a past president of the Grange. They had the biggest house in town, and she and her sister were the best-dressed girls; her mother was head of the Eastern Star and ran the charity bazaar at the county fair every September. The Damons on the other hand were a hard-luck family. Sam's father had started the hard-ware store that the Harlan brothers owned now, and had failed because of a panic; and then he'd been hurt in a harvesting accident and had to have his right leg amputated at the thigh, and had died five months later. Celia remembered him: a quiet, genial, unassuming man who would give her an all-day sucker from a crumpled paper bag in his shirt pocket and pass his hard hand gently over her hair . . . For six years now Sam and his mother had been supporting the family, with sporadic help from Sam's Uncle Bill Hanlon, who was what her father called a drifter, a man with no sand.

Aloud she said: "Father says he drinks. Your Uncle Bill."

Sam shrugged. "He has a few now and then, I guess. He's Irish, you know."

"So is your mother—she's his sister, for heaven's sake!"

"Well. She's a woman." He grinned at her. "There's nothing wrong with a man taking a drink once in a while. Uncle Bill was a sergeant in the Army."

"What difference does that make? Honestly, sometimes you don't make any sense at all . . ." A green apple struck the bench close beside her and she jumped, and then said suddenly: "Oh Sam, why don't you take it?"

"Take what?"

"The job at the bank, the bank! Haven't you even been *listening?*"

He stuck a blade of grass between his teeth. "Oh, that."

"Yes, that! Goodness! Half the boys in town would give their eye-teeth for a chance like that. And you—you act as if you don't even care . . ."

He kept gazing off at the willows at the end of the long field behind the house. "It's all right for some people," he said. "But not for me."

"Why not?"

"Because I've got something else on my mind."

"Well, you needn't give yourself such airs," she said crossly. "It's certainly better than going around playing baseball and being a night clerk . . ." She put her feet together and leaned back, watching him covertly out of the tail of her eye. "Who are you to be so toplofty? Just because you've got this silly idea about your destiny—"

His head snapped around at this and she couldn't help grinning: she knew she'd reached him. When he was aroused his eyes became darker and deeper until they were like slate; his face was very solemn. I wouldn't like to have him mad at me, she thought with a little shiver. Then to her surprise she giggled between her teeth.

"Where'd you get that idea?" he was saying in a very flat voice.

"Never mind." But she couldn't resist it and said: "You don't think girls have secrets between them, do you? Secrets are only between girls and *boys*."

"Peg," he said with finality.

"She says you've got all kinds of soupy ideas about saving your country in a moment of great peril. Like George Washington. Is that true?" He stared back at her a few seconds, his face very long and determined in the gathering twilight, and for an instant she thought, Maybe he could: maybe he could really do something just like that. Filled with a horde of conflicting thoughts, she cried: "Well, is it?"

He looked down then and blew on the blade of grass, which emitted a high, reedy squawk. "Something like that," he said.

"But that's crazy! Here you are"—she swung an arm airily—"in this little long-lost town a million miles from nowhere at all. You've never been east—you've never even been to *Omaha* . . ."

"I'll get there."

"Well, I can't for the life of me see how." He was studying the grass between his knees and she decided to be artful. "Sam . . ."

"Yes?"

"What would you do? with your life? If you had your choice—anything at all—and all you had to do was snap your fingers. What would you choose?"

"That'd be telling." He blew on the grass blade again, and his eyes rolled up at her. "But I'll tell you one thing: you'll hear about it when I do it."

"Don't be a tease . . . I won't tell a soul, Sam."

"Like Peg."

"Not like Peg. I promise."

He was silent for a moment, chewing on the grass stem. Then he looked up and said: "All right. I'm going to go to West Point."

Her head went back. "West Point! The *Army?*"

"That's right."

"But why—?"

"Well, for one thing there's no tuition. They pay your way through."

". . . But you can't just *go* there," she cried, exasperated at him all over again. "You have to be appointed or something."

"Then I'll get myself appointed."

"Well, I don't see how. And the exams—you'll never pass the exams . . ."

"I'm not so sure of that."

She gave a hoot of incredulity and stamped her foot. "That's the most fantastic thing I've ever heard of. Nobody with any ambition, any—any gumption, goes into the *Army* . . . It'll be years and years—barracks and fiendishly strict rules, and marching—Harriet Ebersen knew a boy from Council Bluffs who went there for a year—and then you'll get sent away to Slambangtokanga or some place, mangrove swamps full of snakes and alligators. And there you'll sit and sit, and wish you were never born . . . What on earth *for*, Sam?"

"Look, you asked me and I told you," he said with a trace of impatience. "There it is."

She flounced back on the bench. It infuriated her that he'd nursed this idea for so long and she'd never known about it. He will, she thought crossly; that's just what he'll do—he's just silly enough and stubborn enough. She was in love with him, she was sure she was in love with him—and he wasn't even listening to her half the time; his head was all awhirl with ideas like this!

"All because of your loony destiny," she mourned. Then her chin came up. "I won't wait for you, you know."

"That's a shame."

She shot a glance at him, her eyes wide with astonishment—saw he was grinning at her. "Oh, you! You think I'm joking, you'll find out I'm not. You can go off to—Manila, for all I care . . ." She proclaimed: "Fred Shurtleff is an outstanding young man!"

"He certainly is outstanding."

"You can make fun of him all you want. He owns a Packard automobile."

"His father gave it to him."

"He's going to be mayor of this town someday, governor of the state of Nebraska."

"Politics," Sam said scornfully.

"What's so dreadful about politics?"

"You spend half your life telling people things you don't believe yourself."

"Oh—you're impossible! . . . Why won't you face up to things?"

"No fun in that."

"You're unregenerate!—" With a sudden swift movement she flicked a hand at his head—and even more quickly he ducked away and caught her by the ankles. She let out a squeal and clung to the bench with all her might.

"Don't you pull me off, Sam Damon, I'll get my skirts all over grass stains—*don't!*"

"*You're* no fun anymore." With a show of disgust he released her.

"Remember the picnic at Hart's Island? when we were playing Desperadoes and Ollie Banning's prize bull got loose and Shellie Kimball tried to lasso it with a clothesline?"

"Uh-huh." She smoothed her skirts and passed a hand beneath her hair. "We're too old to play like that now," she declared. "Now we ought to think of the future."

"That's right. But the future hangs on the past."

"No, it doesn't."

"Yes, it does. That's the only way you learn to deal with the future."

"Maybe." He was always saying things like that, out of the blue; it was one of the reasons Miss Cincepaugh said at graduation that Sam was the brightest boy she'd ever taught . . .

"—six feet deep!" Uncle Bill Hanlon was saying, his voice near hilarity. "Yes! Spang in the middle of your back yard and fill it with water, and stand in it for three days and nights on an empty belly. Then hire a raving maniac to skulk around in the shrubbery taking potshots at you with a revolver whenever it happens to strike his happy fancy. Sure! That way you'll save yourself the trouble of going across the water and engulfing yourself in the doithering Donnybrook at all . . ."

The bell in the steeple of the Congregational Church on Main Street began to strike with measured care, and Celia jumped to her feet. "Oh! Eight. I've got to go home. I promised Mother I'd help her sort for the rummage. Walk me home, Sam. It's still early."

"All right."

Holding hands, they crossed the lawn and went out through the wooden gate and along Merivale Street; the elms made a still, lush canopy in the twilight. Lamps were coming on at kitchen windows, on porches, shining inside their frosted globes like tender yellow blooms of light. The town—its name was Walt Whitman and it had been incorporated only a bare sixteen years before—lay on the great south bend of the Platte River between Kearney and Lexington. Good farming country, the land ran back into gentle hills to the north or petered out in the cottonwoods along the river, where the Union Pacific switchyards were. A farm wagon went by, its two occupants sitting on the buckboard, swaying with the easy rocking motion of the axles. The driver, a heavy, red-faced man with a big nose, nodded to Sam, who murmured, "Good evening"; and the wagon creaked evenly away into the deepening dusk.

"Who's that?" Celia asked him.

"Cyrus Timrud. I've helped him with the harvest for years."

That made her think of Isobelle Timrud and she clucked in irritation. Miserable little red-haired tomboy hussy. At her own Halloween party the year before, Sam had spent so much time ducking for apples with Isobelle the front of his hair had got soaked and stuck up like a rooster's comb; and when they played that game of eating the licorice she could swear he'd deliberately held back so he and Isobelle got to the knot at the same moment. Well, that was silly, everybody did that a little; but the *point* was, Sam should only have done it with her . . .

At her front gate they stopped, and she turned toward him. "Do you want to come in?" She watched him run his eyes over the huge white structure with its two slender columns flanking the front door, the high hip roof of slate, the greenhouse on the southeast corner. It was the only house with a slate roof and a greenhouse for miles around.

"I guess not," he said. "There are a couple of things I've got to do."

She swung his big hand back and forth, her fingers interlocked in his, wishing it weren't quite so dark out—twenty minutes ago she would have looked more alluring, and she would have been able to read his expression better. She raised her eyes to his. "You think about it, Sam. I meant what I said. About not waiting. If you go cartwheeling off to some palm-tree island somewhere . . ."

"Of course you meant it."

"Stop laughing!" she said, peering up at him.

"I'm not laughing."

"Yes, you are. Honestly, you're incorrigible."

"I tell you I wasn't, Cele." But his voice still seemed to her near laughter.

In her most imperious tone she declared, "I fail to see where humor is involved . . . Don't you want to—become somebody, *be* somebody?"

"—You bet I do," he answered, and now his voice was as serious as it could be. "You just watch my dust."

He stood staring down at her. Big and lithe, capable of standing the world on its beam ends and giving it an extra spin if he chose, he looked immeasurably romantic and wild in the near dark. He's so handsome and intelligent and he won't do what I want, she inwardly wailed. He's so stubborn!

". . . Oh, Celia," he murmured all at once, "don't you see—life is so many things, it can roll out in so many ways from what you expect, what you plan on . . ." He threw out one hand, a rare gesture for him. "My God—there's all of *life*, over there somewhere—" He stopped, said: "That isn't what I mean."

"Destiny," she answered slyly, drawling out the word. But this time he didn't laugh or reach out to grab her. A train down at the switch-yards started up—a series of swift, chuffing bursts, stopped abruptly; and a child shrilly called to end a game of hide-and-seek. "All-ee—all-ee—in freeeeeee . . ." She sighed; she found herself gazing up at Sam, half-mesmerized. All at once he seemed part of the town, the very measure of it—slumbering, wide-flung land of cornfields and prairie, reaching west under a bold, starry sky, rooted and restless both; the sense of certainty, of unalterable promise hovered around him like heat in forged iron . . . He will be great and grand, she thought, rapt in the very contemplation of it; he will do something fine and noble and earth-shaking, and I will be standing there behind him while they all cheer.

"Mr. Destiny," she said, but softly this time, almost entreatingly, and raised her cheek to his. His lips brushed it solemnly, as though he were almost afraid to touch her. And then to her own great surprise—for she had never done anything like this before—she reached up and locked her arms around his neck and gave herself to him in a passionate kiss. But instead of captivating him as she had intended, she herself was swept with a delicious, singing tension that tightened and released and tightened again in fiery golden bands; she felt as if she were falling backward through a hundred miles of capering, streaming stars. She was slipping away, melting like wax in fire . . .

She tore her arms from his neck and pushed him away with a violent strength she did not know she possessed. She had staggered back against the fence, whose wrought-iron finials gouged her under the shoulder-blades; her breath was coming in thick little gasps and she could hardly see. He murmured something but she couldn't hear him.

"There," she said, panting, filled with a wild defiance. That'll hold him. There. She was inside the gate and moving up the walk with no knowledge of how she had got there. "That'll hold him," she breathed aloud. But turning now, watching his tall figure move quickly away under the elms, she wasn't so sure.

The lamp on the big round oak table was lighted when he came in. His mother was seated next to it, sewing. Uncle Bill was pouring old George Verney a beer from the big blue stoneware pitcher Sam's grandfather had brought with him from the Werratal, and little Ty was playing on the floor, listening to them. Sam smiled, watching their faces turn toward him, swimming in the lamp's golden aureole, as though he were some kind of magnet: his mother's face lined and sharp-featured, her chestnut hair loose around her brows, the blue in her pupils so intense it seemed to fill up her eyes; George Verney's expression remote, like some centennial statue; Uncle Bill's face round and red and convivial.

"Hello, Ma," he said, and on an impulse—borne perhaps on the memory of the moment at the gate with Celia—he went up to her and kissed her on the forehead.

"Why, Sam," she said in surprise, smiling up at him. "To what do I owe that?"

"A way with the girls, he has," Bill Hanlon said. "It runs in the family. Will you join us in a bucket of suds, lad?"

Sam shook his head. "I've got to go to work pretty soon." He sat down on the bench at the far end of the porch.

"And wants a clear head for his responsibilities." Bill Hanlon tilted his stein toward George Verney, who boarded with the Damons. "Ever see the like of it? And just turned eighteen years of age.—That's Carl, God rest his soul," he said to his sister. "That's the German discipline. He never got it from our side."

"And then what?" Little Ty broke in on him impatiently. "What happened then, Uncle Bill?"

"Ah, *then* . . ." Bill Hanlon raised a short, powerful arm on which was tattooed a soaring eagle holding in its beak a banner that proclaimed *For Mother, God & Country* in red and blue letters. Sam couldn't read the inscription at this moment but he knew that was what it said because when he'd been Ty's age he'd been allowed to inspect it in detail. "*Then* the very heavens came crashing down around our heads. Old Barnard had just slapped a dipper full of hash in my kit and was saying something, I can't recall just what, and I looked over his shoulder and there they were, thousands of 'em, the yellow devils." Grinning, he glared down at Ty and his eyebrows went up at the ends, giving him the look of a malevolent Santa. "Pouring into the tent from all sides."

"Thousands?" George Verney echoed drily.

"God's truth!" Billy Hanlon spun around. "All trussed up in those gaily colored wraparounds of theirs, swinging their bolo knives as sharp as razors. Ripping and slashing and screaming like banshees. And the lot of us standing there half asleep and nothing but our mess kits in our hands. The most horrible sight you'd ever want to see on a steaming Sunday morning at the far end of the world."

"Caught napping, sounds to me."

"Napping! And so would you be. On an errand of pacification we were! Who was to know the bloody Googoos were plotting death and destruction—and from the heart of Holy Mother Church at that . . ."

"Pacification." The old man had pounced on the word. His eyes slitted with secret amusement; in the lamplight his beard was like a soft silver thicket over his collar. "I know all about your pacification. Tying the poor beggars down and putting a funnel in their mouths—"

"Yes, and I'd do it again if I had to. Treacherous little devils, each and every one of them." Billy Hanlon waggled a finger back and forth earnestly. "Your native has no morals, you know. He's half animal, half child, half devil from hell."

"I believe that's three halves, Billy."

"Yes, and that's just about the cut of it. They're something strange. I could tell you stories about island girls that would amaze you beyond all bounds—"

"Well you won't, Billy," Kitty Damon said in her tart, clear voice.

"Of course I wouldn't. With innocent children present. That's just as a mere figuration."

"But what did you *do*, Uncle Billy?" Ty cried, and Sam, watching the boy's eyes, smiled faintly. Wild Bill Hanlon hadn't been home in four years and the story was new to him.

"*Do?* I acted with the speed of light. In a situation such as that, lad, one moment's cerebration and you're a corpus delict-eye. I threw my hash in the first devil's face, kit and all, scalding him nicely, grabbed up a stool and swung it like a ball bat and laid out the hellion behind him. By now the tent was full of Googoos, screaming and howling. My God, what a din! Somebody, I think it was Sergeant Markley, kept yelling, 'Get to the racks, boys! Get to the racks!' It was awful. There was Hutch, my old buddy from Peking, holding onto a bolo blade in his bare hand, and his throat squirting blood like a full head on Pumper Number Five—"

"Billy," Kitty Damon said warningly.

"God's truth. Holding a bolo blade in his bare hand while he jabbed his mess fork—*unh! anh!*—into his man like a kid punching his jack-knife into a barn door. And then the far end of the tent came down with a crash, the devils had cut the ropes. Poor lads, they were butchered like pigs in a sack. Well, I says to myself, another few bars of this waltz and they'll have our end down too, and I lit out for the squad hut. And there were two of 'em rushing at me like wolves, thirsting for my very blood. I busted one in the noggin with my stool and dodged around the other and kept going, with a banshee horde of them hot on my tracks.

"Now your nipa hut is up on stilts because of the terrible rains they have, and you reach the door through a bamboo ladder. Well, there I was three steps up the ladder and climbing like a St. Jago's monkey and *whomp!* one of the Googoos hit me with a club and then another one jumped on my back—and the ladder broke and down we all went. And I couldn't move a muscle. Flat on my back, all the wind knocked out of me. Paralyzed within an inch of my life. And right above me was one of the infernal devils, a scrawny little joker with his face all jungle sores and damp rot, with a naked bolo in his two hands . . ."

He broke off and took a drink of beer.

"And what happened *then*, Uncle Bill?" Ty cried in a frenzy.

"Then?" Billy Hanlon took another sip of beer and wiped his mouth, watching his youngest nephew out of one eye. "Ah, it was a bad moment, lad. I raised my arm, foolish as it was, and up that bolo went, up, up like the great, blue scimitar of Mohammed and all his prophets, and I could see it, the words clear as if you'd read them on a pallodium: *Wild Bill Hanlon's marked for death, his Sligo luck's run out at last*—and all at once that scru-ofulous-looking Googoo's eyes opened wide as a new-born babe's and over he went and gone. Vanished into thin air. And I looked straight up and there was Sergeant Markley, big as a bear and twice as hairy, standing in the squad-room door with his smoking rifle in his hands. 'Get in out of that, Hanlon!' he says, or words to that effect. And up I got, all over my paralysis, and shinnied up one of the posts and crawled inside and got my Krag, which was loaded in chamber and magazine . . ."

Idly watching his uncle's fiery face, half-listening to the many-times-told tale, Sam Damon frowned, thinking of the talk with Celia. He had surprised himself. The decision to apply for West Point had never been that clear to him: he was mildly astonished that he had said it right out, plain as day. That was Celia: she'd always been able to make him say things he'd never intended to voice to anyone. Now it'd be all over town. Winnott's Spa, Clausen's Forge, the livery stables behind town hall. *Did you hear? Sam Damon thinks he's going to West Point. No! That's what I heard. Well of all the nerve. Everyone knows the Damons haven't got a pot to piss in.* Scowling, he scratched his chin, gazing at Ty's rapt, eager face, his mother bent over her sewing. Well, they might be wrong, all of them. They just might be wrong. All a good man needed was one opening, one solid chance to show what he could do: if he was any good he'd make it the rest of the way on his own . . . But the amusement, the incredulity in Celia's face troubled him. Yes, and *she* just might be wrong too, he thought crossly, fretting. What did she know about the world?

He thought of the bank, her father's square white face, the steel-rimmed spectacles, the dark suit and high starched collar. He'd been enraged when Wilson beat Hughes, Sam had heard him on the steps of the town hall. "This country is in a bad way when we're obliged to trust our future to a college president." It had been a dazzling fall day, northwest, the sky an aching deep blue and the elm leaves on Main Street a million shimmering flakes of gold; and Mr. Harrodsen had looked like a stand of pine in the dead of winter. He always seemed to move in shadow . . .

It was a lot pleasanter dwelling on Celia. That kiss. That kiss! She'd never done anything like that before. The time at the Hart's Island picnic when he'd sneaked up behind her and grabbed her she'd let out a yelp and shot off like a yearling deer. What had got into her tonight? Idly he wondered if he was in love. She was beautiful, she was lively, she had a will of her own—it was fun walking and dancing and drinking cherry phosphates with her at Winnott's Drug Store. He tried to imagine himself married to her, sprawled on the lawn in front of their own home on High Street—but there the vision abruptly ended. There was nothing more. There rose in its place those dreams of foreign lands, piling one upon another like monsoon thunderheads—a cascading diorama of alabaster cities and jungles and gaunt castle towns, of moments lurid with crises so desperate the very stoutest hearts would blanch; and finally, pressed beyond endurance, overwhelmed, all would quail but Samuel A. Damon of Walt Whitman, Nebraska and the 6th Cavalry Regiment . . .

". . . Ah, it was a sight to wake the dead." Billy Hanlon's voice was louder now, and hoarser. "There was Voybada with his throat laid open like a butchered calf, the blood running in a Niagara between the cots, and little Jerry Driscoll on his hands and knees, his head split open like a cassava melon and his brains—"

"All right, Billy," Kitty Damon said in the sharp, forbidding tone none of them ever disputed. "That's more than enough of such sights."

"That's *war*, my girl," he retorted, and rubbed his mouth with the back of his hand. "What are you suggesting—that I boodle-ize it all for the boy? That's what war is . . ."

". . . War." Old George Verney clucked softly in his beard. "War . . . Why, you don't know what battle is, Billy Hanlon. You should have stood on the bluff at Shiloh, with the Johnny Rebs coming at you thick as Spanish needles in a fence corner, with their *Yip! Yip! Ya-hoooo!* war cry that would freeze your blood in your bones. First time you heard it, that is. After that you paid it no mind. And the minnie balls coming overhead in a sleet storm, and the canister whizzing and whining till you could hardly think or feel or see . . . *That* was war, Billy Hanlon."

The younger man nodded, irritated and out of countenance. "Ah, well. Shiloh . . ."

"You bet, Shiloh. None of this skulking around in swamps flushing little brown-skinned boys out of their bamboo huts and giving them the water cure—"

"Brown-skinned boys—they were devils incarnate, slashers and stabbers born with a machete in their hands . . . millions of 'em, I tell you, deep in a thousand miles of Godforsaken jungle and living by the light of your wits and a good Krag-Jorgensen rifle and a Hail Mary, full of grace. And malaria and yellow jack, don't you forget that, the hot-and-cold chills—we walked in the rain and heat until we dropped . . ."

But the old man wasn't listening. Tilted dangerously far back in the slat-backed rocker he was launched now, living it again. "Why, at the Peach Orchard the Johnnies—"

Hanlon rubbed his eyes, exasperated. "You going to tell us about that Peach Orchard again?"

"You wouldn't have lasted long at the Peach Orchard. Bushwhacker. Like to see you try to give the Johnny Rebs the water cure." George Verney emitted a high, dry cackle that was like retching, and chewed hard at the edge of his beard. Saliva lay in little foamy chains at the corners of his mouth. "They came on and they came on, as though no power on earth or under it was going to stop them. And Johnston riding out front of them, whipping them on, couldn't none of us hit him, with a shiny bright mess cup in his hand."

"A cup, Mr. Verney?" Ty asked. "A drinking cup?"

"That's right, boy. That's what he was waving. He'd picked it up in the tents of the Fifty-third Ohio when they came through."

"But didn't he have a sword? Why wasn't he waving his sword?"

"I don't know, boy . . . The bravest of the brave. I could hear him plain as day, swinging his big horse Fire-eater back and forth along the line. We were in two lines, first row prone, the second kneeling, the way they did in Wellington's army long ago. And on they came again, and we shot them down as though every bullet was a scythe blade at haying time, and still they came. And then they were on us and we rose up to meet them. I remember a short man with a black beard and a broken nose there in front of me, and we locked weapons, and I struck him down with the butt and bayoneted him through the heart . . . and right behind him was a slim young fellow with a handsome face and golden hair, he'd lost his cap somewhere along the line and his mouth was smeared with powder, he looked like the villain in a vaudeville show, comical with all that blond hair and that black powder mustache . . . he raised his rifle like a club and I couldn't get my weapon free of the other one. I kept twisting and yanking, twisting and yanking, and I couldn't take my eyes off that bayonet of his . . . and then, I don't know why, I let go my weapon and grabbed him around the waist and we wrestled around like two schoolboys quarreling over a fishing rod. And all at once I felt him sink against me soft as a cow's muzzle, and when I stepped back he fell dead at my feet . . ." He paused; his eyes were so narrowed it was impossible to see the pupils.

"What happened, Mr. Verney?" Ty pressed him.

"I don't know," the old man answered with sudden indifference. "Somebody shot him, I suppose. Old Hurlbut told us to fall back then, and we did, what were left of us, and tried to re-form. And on they came. It wasn't five minutes later I got my wound. No more Shiloh for me."

"How did you get wounded, Mr. Verney?"

"I don't know, boy. I don't rightly know. I've often wondered about it. Later I asked some of the boys and none of them could tell me." George Verney wagged his head. "There's an old saying you never see the ball that's marked for you, and there's a lot of truth in it. I remember I'd stopped to reload, I was tumping away with my ramrod—and next thing I knew I was laying on the ground without rifle or cartridge belt either, and everything was ringing and gray and faraway feeling. It was right near the Bloody Pool."

"Why'd they call it the Bloody Pool?" Ty asked him.

"They called it that, boy, because that's what it became. That day and night and most of the next day, too. The sun beat down on us hour after hour and we crawled to the pool, those of us that could crawl, friend and foe, and we put our heads in it and drank in the heat. And the water of that pool turned red . . ."

He paused. The night breeze seethed again in the trees on the lawn. Sam Damon was aware that he was scarcely breathing. The crucial moment, with the fate of the Northwest at stake. But Hurlbut had held beyond the Bloody Pool; Sherman had kept the lines from cracking open; and Grant had massed his cannon on the high ground near the Landing and made his plans for an attack at dawn on the 7th . . .

"*That* was the elephant and no mistake, Billy Hanlon," George Verney went on, his voice clearer now, as though the recollection had roused him. "You could have walked all over the Peach Orchard on

the bodies of the fallen and never once touched ground. Not once . . .
Whiskey and chloroform, that was all we had for wounds."

"Tell us about Sherman, Mr. Verney," Sam heard himself say, with
the eagerness of ten years past.

"Old Cump," George Verney said, and smiled. "Well, we'd never
cared much for him before that day—there were all those stories of his
having lost the knot in his thread, pure unadulterated drivel put out by
good-for-nothing journalists but we didn't know that, of course . . . but
that day he was a marvel. I remember him once leaning against a tree
right under the cannonading, smoking one of his ragged cigars, his wild
red beard black with powder and smeared with his own blood, the brim
of his hat torn to tatters by a ball and his wounded hand wrapped in a
crazy blue rag. Cool as a cucumber in deep shade. Couldn't nothing faze
him. That was his greatness, Sam: the critical moment. He could feel it
the way you can feel weather breaking. And he never flinched, even
after he was hit. Just to look at him was to have all your courage back
again. And there were braver men than he who threw down their rifles
and ran away that day. Yes, and repented of it and found themselves a
weapon and came back and fought like lions. Because of Sherman . . . I
recall a skinny preacher who'd euchered the governor into giving him a
uniform and a commission, came up to us waving his long arms and
calling, 'Rally for God and country, oh rally, men, for God and country!' and old Sherman ran into him and roared: 'Shut your mouth, you
God damned old fool! Shut your mouth and get out of the way!' "

George Verney chuckled softly in the silence, his bony frame shaking;
the corners of his eyes glowed with moisture. He took a slow, hesitant
sip of beer. Bill Hanlon had finished his stein and sat with his arms
folded, disgruntled and cross, staring at nothing. Sam Damon watched
them. They had met the elephant on fields half a world away, they had
both been wounded and had acquitted themselves with honor; and now
they sat on this porch in the Nebraska town of Walt Whitman and
drank beer and talked of those days of peril and triumph, those fiery
moments when they had taken their destinies like an apple in their two
hands . . .

Ty was asking Uncle Billy something about the Philippines and Sam
shifted his feet, gazing at the ivory porcelain globe of the lamp, where a
gray-blue moth bumped and fluttered clumsily. Destiny . . . He remembered when he'd first felt it. He had been lying in the field behind
Clausen's, a glittering July afternoon, watching clouds soar by in the
shapes of bears and warriors and rearing stallions, the wheat stalks swaying above him in the puffs of breeze . . . and the idea had started up in
his mind like a bugle call, piercing and sweet and infinitely insistent: a
clarion born of the hours of poring over Fanchett's *Pictorial History of
the World for Boys*—a massive tome laced with fine old engravings:
Wolfe dying on the heights of Quebec, Alexander's cavalry charge at
Arbela, Frederick the Great at Rossbach, Bonaparte rallying his men at

the bridge of Arcola . . . a roll call glorious and stern that had set his mind dancing; but what excited him most of all were the stories of Cincinnatus and Dumouriez and Prescott, of farmers and citizens who took arms to confound tyranny and crush it, who stepped into the mortal breach to save their native lands . . .

"It must be nearly nine, Sam," his mother said.

"Right." He drew out his father's gold watch with its slender black roman numerals: quarter to. As he started up to his room he met Peg coming down. Putting his hand on the railing, he blocked the stairs. "I hear you girls have been exchanging confidences."

Her homely, boyish face went blank with surprise—then she grinned mischievously. "Oh, she can't keep *anything* to herself! I should have known better."

"I ought to spank you good—" He lunged out for her but she danced away up the steps, swinging about on the newel post.

"She try to talk you out of it?"

"Yes."

"Good! It'll strengthen your character."

"Peg, now it'll be all over town," he complained.

"Of course it will!—if you want to be different from everybody else you've got to pay the price . . ." Laughing, she ran back into her room and banged the door shut.

He stared after her, smiling faintly; then he turned and went back down the stairs. As he left the porch Uncle Bill was regaling Ty and a sleepy, skeptical George Verney about the 9th Infantry's heroic storming of Tung P'en.

At nine thirty a hardware drummer from Chicago came in, and Sam Damon put him in Fourteen; and ten minutes later a couple named Ormsby, also off the Omaha train, who were on their way to visit relatives in Sheridan Forks.

Sam took them up to the large double room, Twenty-seven, and got them settled in. Then he went back to Mr. Thornton's desk at the head of the landing on the second floor and wrote down the times they wished to be awakened and their breakfast orders, to leave for Malvern Leach, the cook, when he came in at five thirty. Then it was quiet again; there was only an occasional horse clop-clopping by outside, and the low, uneven murmur of voices in the bar to the left of the front door downstairs. Sam sat for a few moments listening to the night sounds; then he reopened the big worn leatherbound volume at its place mark and began to read:

The din of the battle now grew by leaps and bounds, while Arnold, who as has been noted had been removed from his command as the result of the violent altercation with Gates on the 20th, paced up and down before his tent like a caged lion. The firing on the British right reached a crescendo, and at length Arnold could stand this helpless activity no longer. Turning to his aide-de-camp he exclaimed: "No power on earth shall hold me in this tent today! If I am to be without a command, then I will fight in the ranks like a common soldier. But the men, God bless them, will follow me wherever I shall lead them."

He then called for his horse, a powerful dun charger, and vaulting into the saddle galloped furiously toward the fray. General Gates observed his departure and cried for an aide to recall him; but Arnold put spurs to his horse, crossed the marshy ground at Mills Creek and hastened up the slope, where he came upon his old regiments, who recognized their former commander with joyous shouts and cheers. Drawing his sword Arnold led them forward in a violent onslaught upon the German center under Baron Reidesel; the Hessians however held firm. Arnold then hastened to the American left wing and incited Morgan's redoubtable riflemen in their attack against Balcarres' Light Infantry, who fell back in good order upon their fortifications near Freeman's Farm.

It was at this point that Arnold, traversing the length of the front line for the third time that morning and exposed to the extremely hazardous crossfire of the contending armies, perceived that the battle had attained its crucial stage; that the key to the situation lay in Breyman's Redoubt, and that, if it could be forced, Burgoyne's entire position would be turned, and so untenable. Once more encountering his old brigade, he led them in a savage assault upon the works, himself setting an example of the utmost valor, repeatedly riding, sword in hand, into the British ranks, until wounded in that same leg that had sustained injury—

The front door opened softly below; and looking down—Mr. Thornton had placed the desk so near the landing that its occupant could observe all comings and goings at a glance—Sam could see Ted Barlow's red hair in the light from the gas jet. He leaned into the bar and replied to a low chorus of greetings; leaned out again and came up the stairs two at a time and said: "Hello, Ace. What you reading there?"

Sam closed the book on its place mark. "Oh, little history. Revolutionary War history."

"All that fine print. Ruin your eyes and then where'll we be?" Barlow clucked his tongue and sat down in the hard black horsehair chair to the right of the desk. He was several years older than Sam; short and

stocky, with a button nose and a low, bulging forehead from which the hair had already begun to recede. Pulling a piece of paper from his shirt pocket he unfolded it and tossed it on the desk. "Here's their lineup."

Sam studied it intently. "Harrison's a sucker for low stuff. We got Galder on curves. Who's this Burchall?"

"I don't know. A big new guy, Wally says. Two doubles and a home run against Tyson Park."

Sam whistled once. "Well. We'll keep it low and away from him, see what he does. All right?"

"I guess so."

"And if he hits that—why then we'll just play deep and cut across."

The two men laughed, then bent over the list and went down it carefully, discussing the positioning of outfielders and other tactical problems in great detail. Ted worked in the Union Pacific yards but his passion was baseball. He was catcher, coach and general manager for the Walt Whitman Warriors, an aggregation that played teams from other towns every Sunday afternoon at the town field. His hopes of a big league tryout had faded as the years passed and the fat began to set in his muscles; but he continued to dream nonetheless—a perfect season, a shutout against Josselyn; there was even the possibility of becoming a scout for a major league team. Why not? If the Warriors could win all their games this year there was no telling where it might end. His enthusiasm was infectious. When Sam Damon had finished high school as their star pitcher and clean-up hitter Ted had talked him into pitching for the Warriors; and Sam was still winning.

"I've been thinking about a play," Sam said.

"Bit of deep strategy?"

The younger man nodded and grinned. "With a man on third and none or one out. You pretend you're defending against the squeeze. The third and first basemen charge the plate. The pitcher of course takes his full windup."

"What about the runner on third?"

"That's just it. *You* call for a pitch-out. And as I start my windup, the shortstop breaks for third. I throw a fast ball, way outside, and you fire back to the bag without any hesitation. With Stevie charging the plate the runner comes down the line a lot farther than he would ordinarily, and so we've got a chance to nail him. It's a matter of timing."

Barlow blinked, and ducked his head. "I remember that play—something like it . . . Where'd you hear of it?"

"I didn't. I made it up, the other night."

The catcher frowned. "They won't fall for it. It's bush league."

"We're bush league."

"You can't use it very often, I'll tell you that."

"Only once." Sam smiled. "The crucial place in a game."

Barlow watched him, his blue eyes twinkling. "You're pretty slick. All right. We'll give it a try."

"You'd better put your glove over your knee—something good and distinct. If I ever missed the sign and the batter swung away, poor Stevie could get killed."

"That's right, too . . . You never heard of that play?" Sam shook his head. "You beat everything, fella. You ought to go over to Flanders and show them how to fight that war." He picked up the sheet of paper. "You want a copy of this?"

"No. I've got it in my head."

Barlow nodded. He'd been incredulous and had said so sarcastically when Sam had first made that reply the year before—and then to his amazement Sam had repeated the line-up and every batter's weakness in perfect detail. "Mind like a photographic plate," he would boast of Sam to his friends or his wife, who had heard all she wanted to about Sam Damon.

"I wrote Hap Donnally," he said aloud. "I haven't had an answer yet but I will. He always answers my letters. I told him I want him to see you work."

"Do you think he'll come? way out here?" Hap Donnally was a celebrated scout for the Chicago Cubs.

"Sure he will. They've got expense accounts, those fellows. They go anywhere they want to, and the club picks up the tab." Barlow had been east once, to Chicago. "They're big spenders."

There was a little silence, punctuated by a low rumble of laughter down in the bar. Sam thought of Hap Donnally, of the great green diamonds and looming stadia of the major leagues, and chewed at the inside of his cheek. Ted Barlow got up, sat down again, pushed his stocky legs out, crossed them, and jammed his hands deep in his trouser pockets. "Hot this evening."

"Not bad."

Barlow fiddled some more, and said finally: "You seen Tim Riley?"

Sam shook his head, watching the coach without expression.

"I heard him down at the shop. He says he's going to come in here and have a few drinks tonight. As many as he wants. And that he's going to engage himself a room for good measure."

"Not here, he isn't," Sam said.

The manager puffed out his lips and scowled. "He was telling it all around. He won't back down after all that."

"I know."

"He gets off at quarter of eleven."

Sam glanced at Barlow but made no reply. Big Tim Riley was an ex-lumberjack, ex-sailor, ex-stevedore with a legendary past. He stood six feet five in his socks, a mountain of a man, uproarious and ungovernable. The week before he had got into a fight down in the bar with three patrons over the merits of the left-hander Rube Waddell, and caught up in the passion of the argument and the delights of destruction, had smashed to pieces four chairs, innumerable glasses and bottles and finally

the large painted mirror behind the bar before roaring out into the warm Nebraska night, where the law had caught up with him. He'd paid the damages readily enough and no one had pressed charges; but Mr. Thornton had explicitly told everyone at the Grand Western that Riley was not to be served if he came in again.

The only trouble with that was that Mr. Thornton, who was fifty-seven and who wore a pin-stripe suit and pince-nez and hummed loudly to himself while he worked, was in bed fast asleep right now.

"He claims he got a raw deal, Sam," Barlow was saying cautiously. "He's something when he gets going."

"I know."

"What are you going to do?"

Damon shrugged. "I guess I'll think of something when the time comes."

"It better be awful good." Barlow looked distressed and locked his hands. "Look, I—you know, I could hang around a little while. If you'd like. I'm no Jack Johnson but I'd be some help."

Sam shook his head again, firmly. "If I can't handle him alone then I'm not fit to sit at this desk."

"Jesus, Sam, he weighs two hundred and forty-five pounds. And he's not fat. There isn't a man in this county who could lick him in a fair fight."

"That's true."

". . . You're pretty damn cool, it seems to me." Barlow stared at the night clerk a moment longer, then got reluctantly to his feet. "Well. It's your funeral. Good-bye and good luck. As they say. I still think you're making one whale of a mistake."

"We'll see."

Ted Barlow's steps faded away down the stairs. Pop Ainslie, the crusty little old bartender, said something to him, and for a moment Sam Damon found himself hoping Barlow would go inside for a drink and stay on. But he said good night and went out, closing the big door carefully behind him. For a few minutes Sam listened to the desultory talk in the bar, which did seem more subdued than usual. Down in the swamp behind Clausen's Forge the tree toads were shrilling softly, and from far away, probably at Hart's Island, came the rhythmic clang of iron on iron. He stared out at the elms' dense leafy mass against the night sky, dreaming for a moment of Celia Harrodsen, and big-league baseball, and brooding, savage coasts under a blazing copper sky . . .

He opened the big leatherbound book again and went on reading for ten minutes or so; then reaching into the bottom drawer of the desk, took out a loose-leaf notebook with a soft black leather cover and big brass rings and began to write in a small, nicely formed hand:

Second Battle of Freeman's Farm, Saratoga, October 7, 1777. *Analysis:* Benedict Arnold won Battle of Saratoga—& possibly War of Inde-

pendence—when Gates would have lost it. Arnold's effectiveness lay in
(1) flexibility & tactical sense, (2) calm under fire, (3) ability to inspire
loyalty & confidence in men through force of personal example.

Key points: (a) when Reidesel's troops held firm, he did not waste
men & time in fruitless additional assaults, but shifted attack to Balcarres; (b) when he realized tactical importance of Breyman's Redoubt he
threw weight against it w/o delay, pressed assault relentlessly until position taken; (c) "But the soldiers . . . will follow me wherever I shall lead
them." Knew he must lead—& had complete confidence that Brigade
would follow him. Fact that he could inspire them to 3 successive assaults, each more severe, is crux of whole matter.

Problems: Gates pompous, vain, stupid man, continually confused
trivial with important. Through either fear or incompetence, incapable
of decisive action. Arnold knew Gates was incompetent. He had had
ample opportunity to gauge him in 1st Battle of Freeman's Farm, Sept.
19th. He probably realized battle would be lost if Burgoyne were permitted to force action, turn American position on Bemis Heights & open
door to Albany . . . So Arnold disobeyed orders, dominated action, won
battle & perhaps war. Should he have been court-martialled or decorated? or both? Apparently he was neither. Can direct disobedience of
orders be justified by circumstances? & if so, when, and for what reasons? Compare and contrast: Stuart at Gettysburg, Grouchy at Waterloo, Grant at Vicksburg.

Conclusions: If your leadership & tactical sense is better than your
superior's & if you are certain a battle would be lost if orders of that
superior allowed to stand, you MIGHT be justified in seizing initiative
yourself; BUT you must be prepared to accept consequences, in either
victory or defeat. Arnold was not. Is there a foreshadowing of his later
defection & treason in refusal to obey orders here? or was it more a
matter of outrage at lack of personal recognition? Was Arnold guilty of
excessive pride? Could he perhaps have handled that idiot Gates more
effectively, avoided violent quarrel after action of Sept. 19th? Or did he
lack—

The front door swung open and banged shut with a thump that
shivered the building. A large shadow passed across the threshold into
the entrance to the bar and a voice roared: "Hello, one and all! Fancy
meeting up with you once again." And listening intently, Sam Damon
thought: He's already had something. Plenty.

The deep voice went on: "I've decided to stop by for a little cheer
before retiring. Just a nip in good fellowship. Right?"

For a long moment there was no other sound in the bar. Then Pop
Ainslie's voice said hesitantly: "Now, Tim, you know Mr. Thornton
said—"

"*Mr.* Thornton!" Big Tim Riley crowed. "*Mr.* Thornton! I knew
Scratchy Thornton when he was selling yard goods at Nisbet's . . ."

There was the sound of jostled chairs—Riley was obviously making his ponderous, unsteady progress toward the bar—and then his voice came again, deceptively soft and wheedling. "And where would Mr. Thornton be this fine June evening?"

"Now he's not here, Tim, he's home in bed like most sensible folks. Young Sam Damon's at the desk now. You know that, Tim. Now, please try—"

"Young Sam Damon." This was uttered with strange, almost reflective care, and the owner of the name, bent forward over the big oak desk, scarcely breathing, could follow the big man's thoughts. "Poor Carl Damon's oldest boy, is it? God rest his soul . . . One that feels he's such a ballplayer?" There was another short pause in which Riley might have been surveying the room's few occupants. "Well, I wouldn't think young Sam Damon would mind my having a little sociable drink now, would you?"

"Sam told me you're not to be served." Pop Ainslie's voice sounded querulous and insubstantial in the cavernous silence. "He said so this evening when he came on."

"Did he now? Did he now? And he didn't hear Big Tim Riley was planning to stop by tonight? I'd have thought he might have heard about it. Wouldn't you, Pop?"

"Now Tim, don't you compel me to use force . . ."

"*Force!*" There was a thunderous guffaw, as though Riley found this immeasurably comical. "Force! Of course not, Pop. Of *course* not." Then the flat slap of an open hand striking the smooth mahogany plate of the bar. "Isn't that the crowning glory of a shame. Well, I'll just have to go up and *see* young Mr. Damon for a moment. Have a few easy words with him." The chairs jostled and scraped again.

"Now Tim, if you go up there I'll have to send for Charlie Bascom."

Tim Riley roared with laughter. "Charlie Bascom! Charlie Bascom's over at Hart's Island investigating the theft of a palomino mare named Marigold," he proclaimed with gusto. "And Chief Johansen is playing poker in Sheridan Forks. Yes! You go get him, you do that thing . . ."

He came around the corner into the little corridor and stood there, gazing upward, his face red under its shock of thick black hair, barbaric in the pale glow of the gas jet high on the wall. He filled up the corridor entirely. Catching sight of Sam, he grinned—a slow, delighted grin.

"Hello, sonny."

"Hello, Mr. Riley," Sam answered. His voice sounded steady. That was good. That was half the battle. He watched Riley scratch his collarbone with one enormous hand.

"Well, sonny . . ." The big man was still gazing up at him, his mouth distended in soundless laughter. Then apparently he didn't like what he saw, for his jaws came together again; his face darkened and grew solemn.

"Look, kid. Let's get each other straight." He pointed. "I'm going back into that bar, and Pop there is going to pour me out a little shot or two, and then I'm coming back out here in my good time and you're going to give me Room Seventeen. Now you got that?"

In a level voice Sam said: "You're not to be served in this hotel, Mr. Riley, and that's final. I'll have to ask you to clear out."

Riley's eyes opened until they were light blue discs rimmed with porcelain. "No sniveling YMCA kid fresh out of high school is going to tell Big Tim *Riley* what to do in this town or any other, from here to Seattle . . . Come on down here!" he roared. Sam Damon sat still as death. "All right. If that's how it is—I'll go up there and get you."

He started up the stairs. There were twenty-two risers—the main floor of the hotel had been built on a grand scale—and he grew bigger with each step he took. His shirt was open at the throat and hair in a burly black mat pushed out over the blue cotton. He was immense. Sam, who had seen him perhaps ten times over the past two years, had never realized how huge he was.

As Riley reached the top step Sam came to his feet, his hands flat on the desk top, and thrust at the big swivel chair with one foot; it glided away on its big casters and bumped softly against the wall. What was curious was that now he felt no fear. It was like the afternoon they'd been playing on the ice and Jimmy Wright had fallen through. The others had been helpless—they'd milled around or started yelling or stood gazing paralyzed at Jimmy's stocking cap bobbing at the edge of the hole—but he had felt no hesitation at all. He'd tied two hockey sticks together and crept out there, farther and farther, crawling finally, trying to calm Jimmy who was uttering short, high screams. The ice kept cracking under him like great hollow sheets of iron. "Hang on, Jimmy!" he'd shouted. "I'm coming, Jimmy, hang on! . . ." And finally Jimmy had hold of the end of the sticks and had one knee up, and then he was on the ice and floundering and he'd cried, "No, Jimmy, no! Stay flat! Stay flat, now . . ." and bit by bit he'd dragged him back from the long, hollow, shivering groans of the ice to where the other kids were shouting and dancing up and down.

It was like that now. In place of the earlier heart-leaping fear there was nothing but an emerald calm, cold as the river ice that February afternoon, hard at the edges and utterly clear. His senses were preternaturally, almost painfully, alive, and that was all. He noticed the way Riley's right eyelid drooped, the scar that ran through the eyebrow above it in a staggered white crescent. Outside, the tree toads shrilled softly and the wind sighed in the elms. He was waiting, that was all. Waiting for the moment: that inner monitor he'd learned to obey would throw a series of switches and then he would move, do what was needed. He wasn't even conscious of thinking this: it was simply *there*, trembling in its emerald immanence. He looked up at Riley, who towered above him—though he himself was over six feet—and waited.

The lumberjack came up to the desk; he was breathing thickly through his nose and Sam saw he was quite drunk. Drunk but fully coherent. And agile. Yes. Agile.

Riley said: "I'm going to whale the tar out of you. And then I'm going to drag you out and leave you in the square in front of the town hall, for everybody to see. Your pants need pressing, kid . . . Now are you going to come out from behind that desk or am I going to walk around and haul you out?"

I can't hit him hard enough, Sam found himself thinking. Nobody could. There won't be time to pick up a chair. I've got to knock him down those stairs. All the way down those stairs. He was conscious that his body was tensing, suspended, in wait for the moment. Riley was glaring at him, his eyes glittering with the thirst for battle. The big man shifted his weight, then his glance flicked to the side, to the open side of the desk and the stiff horsehair chair where Ted Barlow had been sitting. In the instant of that sidewise glance the monitor said *now*—and without thought Sam vaulted high over the desk, pivoting swiftly on his hands, and his shoes slammed full force into Riley's jaw. He felt a shock that drove from the soles of his feet to the top of his head; then nothing at all. One instant the giant was there, in the next he was gone—in a thundering series of bumps and crashes, as if a cartload of furniture had been dumped from a barn roof. He watched Riley tumbling down —head, feet, rump, head again, arms and legs flailing—brought up at last against the front door in one terrific final crepitation, and a shiver and tinkling of glass. Then there was complete silence; and Sam Damon, standing now in front of the desk, thought: My God. I've killed him.

He heard a laborious scraping and scuffling, and Tim Riley got very slowly and unsteadily to his feet, shaking his head like a dog out of water. His great shoulders hulking he shuffled forward into the light again, and Sam's heart sank. He was all right; he was unhurt. The man was indestructible. That was all there was to it. What'll you do now? he wondered hollowly. What now? You can't do it twice. His eyes fell on the chair beside the desk.

"—*One punch*," Big Tim Riley breathed. Then roared at the top of his lungs: "*ONE—PUNCH!*—" Impetuously he started up the stairs again . . . but this time the inner monitor ordered nothing, nothing at all. I'll brain him with that chair, the night clerk thought, belt him with that and then jump him, dive on him. It's my only chance. Riley kept coming up the long flight, staggering now: blood was running down the side of his head from a cut in his scalp, the bridge of his nose was scraped raw and sweat was streaking his eyebrows and cheeks. He looked unutterably fearsome. Sam started to reach toward the chair—then stopped, carried beyond amazement as Riley's face below him broke into a broad and merry grin. Leaning against the wall he extended one mammoth hand.

"Kid, you're all right. I mean it. I want to shake your hand." He shook his head again. "No, don't swing on me again. I mean it." Apparently he did. While Sam watched him warily he reached the landing again, took the night clerk's hand and pumped it up and down with ponderous solemnity. "You're the nonpareil. The only man in the state of Nebraska that could knock Big Tim Riley down a flight of stairs with one punch." He flipped Sam's hand over and examined it. "Never even skinned his knuckles!" he exclaimed in beaming wonder. "Jesus, think of that! Kid, you're all right. You'll go far, you mark my words." He released the younger man's hand. "You'll go far in this world."

"What I said goes, Mr. Riley," Sam Damon said quietly.

The lumberjack laughed then. "Right you are, kid. Right you are." For another moment he stood there, still grinning uncertainly, peering into Sam's face, as if he could actually read there a host of future triumphs emblazoned on the night clerk's forehead in letters of burnished gold. "Well, well," he muttered; slapping Sam on the back he started slowly down the stairs again, holding to the wall with one hand. At the little foyer he stopped and peered into the bar, where the silence had been funereal. Swaying he gazed at its occupants, unmindful of the blood now streaming into his shirt collar and lacing his nose and mouth. He grinned again, slowly, his lips curled in derision. "I believe I'll go along home and get some rest." Then, pointing back upstairs toward a still immobile Sam Damon: "Now listen: from now on, anybody gives this kid any trouble at all has got to reckon with Big Tim Riley. And that's my last word for the evening . . ."

He was gone. The big front door crashed shut with a final soft tinkle of glass. The silence was so vast Sam could hear the grandfather clock in the hall below stalking the solemn seconds one by one. Perspiration was sliding down his back and sides and through his scalp. Pop Ainslie's face swung into view around the corner, and then behind and above it the faces of Hobart Marsh and George Smith and Henry Vollmer, all of them goggling up at him.

"Hello, Pop," he said.

The little man came up two or three steps, blinking and staring as though he couldn't believe his eyes. His bow tie and armbands were a matching blue with a fine red stripe. "How on earth . . ." he began and stopped, his mouth working. "How'd you ever manage it?"

"Hit him first," Sam answered easily. "Hit him before he hit me. That's the object of the game, isn't it?" Pop and the others were still gazing at him open-mouthed and idiotic, so he added: "And remember now: Mr. Riley is not to be served in this hotel in any capacity until Mr. Thornton gives express instructions to the contrary." Still they gazed up at him speechless; Henry Vollmer's glasses flashed in vacant discs of light. The temptation to laugh was enormous, but he beat it down. "You'd better get back to the bar, hadn't you, Pop?"

"Yes, of course—right you are, son." Pop turned around like a little snow-haired tin toy, bumping into the others, and began herding them

on ahead of him. Back in the bar there was a muffled exclamation and
then the voices:

"Cool as an icicle—"

"Can you beat it!"

"Nerves of steel, that boy . . ."

"Never even got up a sweat. Can you *beat* it!"

Then Pop Ainslie said loudly and reverently: "Boys, the next round is
on me. Not on the Grand Western. Not on Mr. Thornton. On me."
There was low laughter and then the delicate clink of a bottle neck
against glass.

Sam Damon went around behind the desk and sat down; took his
handkerchief out of a hip pocket and mopped at his face and neck.
From the open windows came the abortive crow of a rooster wakened
prematurely. The air was redolent with spruce and roses and new-mown
hay—a summer scent as heavy as wine, and at whose center lay the
curious crystal calm evoked by the encounter. He'd done it; he'd
obeyed that fierce inner voice, followed its first impulse and it had been
exactly and solely the right move to make. He gripped his hands together; the sense of exultancy rose still higher. Down in the switchyard
behind Clausen's he could hear the soft chafing whine of steel rolling on
steel, then the bumping concatenation as the empty car was coupled;
and the hiss of released steam.

. . . I'll go to Lincoln, he decided abruptly, borne on the flushed
certainty of the moment. First chance I get. I'll ask Ted for a company
pass and take the train to Lincoln. And then by God we'll see.

Lincoln was a big city with sidewalks and colored advertisements and
department stores. There was a Civil War memorial in the middle of the
square with a tall young infantryman standing at parade rest; he was
wearing a full mustache like Mr. Verney's, but no beard. There was a
brand-new fire engine, all bright red and gleaming nickel; and Sam
Damon could see two other engines through the open doors. There
were fine houses every bit as grand as the Harrodsens', set back from the
street and bordered by hedges of privet clipped in the shape of battlements or lozenges and cones, or by shiny black wrought-iron fences of
spearheads and fleurs-de-lis. Lincoln had high curbs of granite. There
were automobiles, many of them; they raised clouds of dust that fell on
his suit like powder. If this was Lincoln, imagine what Chicago was like.
Or—or New York City . . .

It was very hot, and he didn't know where to go. The streets all
looked alike, and cars and wagons kept tearing by in a steady stream. He
came to a big plate-glass window and wandered up to it, pretending to
look at the chairs and chests of drawers inside but actually studying
his own reflection. He didn't look very prepossessing, and it bothered

him. He was wearing his father's blue serge suit. Carl Damon had been heavier and a good two inches shorter than his son, and his mother had lengthened the sleeves and cuffs and taken in the trousers; but the outfit looked bulky and loose on him, and it was no day to be wearing anything this heavy, with the temperature up in the nineties. The shirt with its detachable collar had been his father's too, but the tie, a navy blue with maroon and scarlet stripes, was his own: Peg had given it to him that past Christmas. He pulled down on the coat at the back so the collar wouldn't ride up so far on his neck—then bending over ran thumb and forefinger down his trousers, pinching hard at the knee to reinforce the crease. None of the passersby seemed to have noticed.

His father's gold watch said 2:14. Time was sliding along, slipping away, and he hadn't done anything yet. He stood at a street corner, befuddled by the crush of traffic. Then on the other side he saw a policeman talking to a fat man in a straw boater. He timed the gap between a Pierce Arrow touring car and a produce wagon and sprinted across. The two men turned to him as he came up.

"Well, young fellow," the policeman said. "Where'd you learn to run like that?"

"Just picked it up, I guess."

"You want to watch out, with all this heavy traffic here." The policeman's eyes under the visor were the palest gray. "Where do you hail from?"

"Walt Whitman, sir."

"And where is that?"

"Well, it's about fifteen miles from—" He saw they were having fun with him then, and broke off, grinning. "It's the first time I've ever been to Lincoln."

"I'd never have guessed it."

"Can you tell me where Congressman Bullen's office is?"

"Sure." The officer pointed past his shoulder. "Back where you came from. See that building there? with the bright yellow border?"

"Yes."

"That's his office. Second floor. You'll see the shingle." The policeman's gray eyes sparkled again. "Thinking of going into politics, are you?"

"Oh no, sir. I'm going to get me an appointment to West Point."

"I see." Both men laughed, and the policeman waved him along with a little flourish and called: "All right. Good luck to you."

He found the place easily. There was a sign in shiny black stone with gold letters that said *MATTHEW T. BULLEN, Attorney at Law*. He climbed the stairs and encountered the legend again on the frosted panel of the door. He paused a few seconds in indecision; he could hear a typewriter clacking along, then the clear high ting of the bell and the muffled slam of the carriage. Mr. Thornton said you should never barge in anywhere. If in doubt, knock, then enter. Mr. Bullen was a busy man.

He waited another moment, then gave a tug to his coattail, knocked twice lightly and opened the door and went in.

It was an office all right, but Congressman Bullen wasn't there. There was only a desk where a girl was typing and two oak filing cabinets and a long bench where a farmer was patiently sitting, his hat in his lap and a hand on each knee. The farmer gazed at him vacantly. The girl hadn't even looked up when he'd entered. Confused, a little irritated, he walked up to the desk and stood there. After a few seconds she gave a muttered exclamation and flipped up the paper-lock bar. She glanced up at him; she had a narrow face and bulging brown eyes.

"Yes?" she said crossly.

"I'd like to see Congressman Bullen."

"On what business?"

"It's about West Point."

"Do you have an appointment?"

An appointment. That stopped him. He paused, said, "No—I don't. I'm from near Kearney" (he would not make *that* mistake again). "I just got here a few minutes ago. On the train."

She threw him a glance of unbridled scorn and began to make the erasure. "Well. You'll have to take a seat. Over there."

He frowned. He wanted to tell her he had to get the 3:47 back, that it was important he see Mr. Bullen as soon as possible; but he couldn't think of any way to put it without making her really angry with him. Personal secretaries wielded a lot of power: you had to handle them with kid gloves. He'd heard drummers and businessmen at the hotel discussing the matter.

Reluctantly he went over and sat down near the old farmer, who nodded and went on staring into space. The girl took no further notice of him. There was a door beyond her to the right, and he knew without having to think it out that Congressman Bullen was in there. Once he heard a low burst of laughter, several men together, and then a single voice, slow and declamatory, the words drowned out by the crashing of the typewriter.

He opened his coat and lifted his arms to let some air in, and surreptitiously pulled the cloth away from his skin. There was an electric fan on a window ledge, a bright copper hoop with lots of scroll work, that turned slowly, whirring in a bass *thrum*, playing over the secretary's head and ruffling her hair, and he studied it with interest; he'd never seen an electric fan before. But none of its cooling breezes reached the bench. Perspiration began to run down his forehead and neck; he forced himself to wait a full five minutes before he took out his handkerchief. Time crawled along and he sat there, miserable and impatient, a slave to its whims; it was the feeling he hated more than all others. As he was mopping his face the girl suddenly pulled the letter out of the carriage and went into the other room; Sam caught a quick little glimpse of two men's heads bent over a square of light, and that was all. He could hear nothing that was said. In a few seconds the girl came out again, picked up some official-looking papers from her desk and left the office.

More minutes passed. Minutes of gold, of ivory, of steel. He was at the edge of the world—that fierce and glittering realm where men traveled for days in Pullman cars or rode up grand avenues in carriages or sat in oak-paneled board rooms and decided, in crisp, concise strokes, the world's affairs. This was that world—an edge of it, anyway—and here he sat, on the edge of this edge, waiting, sticky with sweat, his hands in his lap; ineffectual. The thought lent a furious heat to his blood. When he looked at his watch again he was horrified to find it was nearly three; he'd never make it to the train. As he put the thin gold case back in his pocket the old farmer heaved himself to his feet with a grunt and lumbered by him, his heavy boots creaking on the worn floor, and went out.

Sam waited until it was exactly three o'clock. Then he rose, and pulling down his coat again walked over to the private door, knocked smartly once and entered.

Three men were sitting around a big mahogany desk, a much grander desk than Mr. Thornton's, with legs like a lion's claws sitting in glass gliders. There were two shiny brass cuspidors, one at each end of the desk. Two men were sitting in chairs at each side, the third was standing behind the desk and tapping with a pencil a huge map scored with intersecting roads and dotted with bright blue and yellow patches. All three men were in their shirt sleeves with the cuffs rolled back and they were all smoking Pittsburgh stogies. The windows were open but cigar smoke hung in the room in fragrant blue clouds.

The man standing behind the desk was big and broad-shouldered, with a tough, craglike face as if poorly cut from some coarse-grained stone, and black wiry brows. Sam Damon recognized him at once. There had been posters up in Walt Whitman the year before, and Representative Bullen had stopped over once at the Grand Western. Sam had given him Number Fourteen, the best of the singles.

"Congressman Bullen?" he said.

The harsh face stared at him, irritated and expectant. "What is it, son?"

"I'd like to see you about an appointment to West Point."

"Look, I'm pretty busy right now. You go talk to Miss Millner."

"I did, sir. But she's been out of the office for some time, and I've got to catch the three forty-seven back to Walt Whitman or I'll be late for work this evening."

Matt Bullen glanced at the other two men, then thrust out his lower lip and tossed the pencil on to the map in front of him. Sam couldn't read his expression at all. "What's your name, son?"

"Samuel A. Damon."

"And you want to go to West Point, do you?"

"That's right, sir."

"You one of Albert Damon's boys?"

"No, sir. He's my uncle, he lives over in Sheridan Forks. Carl Damon was my father. He died some years ago."

"Oh, yes. I remember."

"They never got along very well, my father and my uncle." Sam felt all at once embarrassed at having said this, and added: "I didn't know you knew my Uncle Albert."

"I know a lot of things folks don't think I do," Matt Bullen said, and one of the other men laughed. "That's part of my business. Albert Damon votes the Democratic ticket, don't he?"

Sam paused. The room all at once seemed quieter. The other two men had turned in their chairs to watch him.

"Yes, sir," he answered. "My father did, too."

Matt Bullen leaned forward on his hands and bit into his cigar. "Son, how old are you?"

"Eighteen."

"You still got to learn what the world runs on." He picked up the pencil again and tapped the stiff paper of the map. "Now you give me three good reasons why I ought to recommend the nephew of a man who's always voted against me, for an appointment to the United States Military Academy at West Point on the Hudson River."

Sam placed his hands behind his back and clasped them tightly. All three men were looking at him now; the Congressman's face was particularly forbidding. He said in a quiet voice: "Mr. Bullen, when I serve my country as a soldier I'm not going to serve her as a Democrat or as a Republican, I'm going to serve her as an American. To my last breath."

Matt Bullen's expression remained unchanged. "All right. Two."

"Two," Sam echoed. "I'm my own man and not my father's or my uncle's. It's true I can't vote just yet, but when I do I intend to vote for the best man, regardless of his party. I can promise you that."

The Congressman's eyelid flickered. "Fair enough. Three."

"Three," Sam Damon said. He had no idea what he was going to say until he'd said it. "Because I'm the best man you'll get for the job."

Matt Bullen started at that; he threw the pencil on the map again. "That's a pretty broad statement. You prepared to back it up?"

"Yes."

"Just what makes you think so?"

"Try me out, sir. I'll outhike, outfight, outshoot, outthink any man you can put up. And I know my military history into the bargain."

Matt Bullen stared hard at him. "You're pretty salty for a young fella."

The man who had chuckled earlier, a sandy-haired man with a big red nose, said, "You better treat him gently, Matt. He's the kid that knocked out Big Tim Riley with one punch and never skinned his knuckles."

Bullen took the cigar out of his mouth. "He did? Who told you?"

"George Malden," the red-nosed man said affably. "Said it was all over the county. Said Riley swore he wouldn't touch another drop of red-eye for a month of Sundays if the kid wouldn't hit him again." He said to Sam, "Aren't you the Damon?"

Sam hesitated. "Well. I didn't knock him *out* . . ."

"By thunder, you look as if you could do it, too," Matt Bullen said as though he hadn't heard him; he started pacing up and down behind the desk. The red-nosed man looked at Sam and winked solemnly. So it had got here. All the way to Lincoln. That was the way the world was: whatever you did was magnified—if you did something bold you were a hero of Homeric proportions; if you did something cowardly . . .

"That's a mighty tough course of sprouts at the Point," Bullen was saying. "You know about that?"

"I know it is, sir. But when I put my mind to something I usually finish it."

"What makes you think you can pass the entrance examinations?"

"I graduated from Walt Whitman High with the highest grades in six years. And I've been studying on my own since then."

Matt Bullen stopped pacing and looked at him again, his hands in his pockets. The red-nosed man said, "Oh, give him a shot at it, Matt. He's convinced me, even if *you're* too damned stubborn."

"You keep out of this, Harry," Bullen retorted genially. He was studying the applicant shrewdly. "Maybe you can, son. Maybe you can at that. Now, who can you give me for personal recommendations? Character testimonials, that kind of thing."

"Well, there's Mr. Thornton, Mr. Herbert Thornton, who's manager of the Grand Western Hotel. He's my boss, I'm night clerk there. And Walter Harrodsen—he runs the Platte and Midland Bank in town . . ."

"Walt Harrodsen, yes. I mean someone who pulls weight. Someone with influence."

Sam stopped. He couldn't think of anyone. Then the inner monitor, the swift and irresistible voice, spoke and he looked up again and said: "To tell you the truth, I thought maybe you would, Mr. Bullen."

Matt Bullen gaped at him. "*I* would? . . ."

"That's right, sir."

"—But I don't know you from Adam's off ox, boy . . ."

"Well, I'm standing right here in front of you," Sam said simply.

". . . You mean you want *me* to—to give a character reference . . ." For another moment the Congressman stared at Damon, his deep blue eyes round with amazement; then all at once threw back his big craggy head and roared with laughter, in which the other two men joined. "Well, if that don't beat everything I ever heard in all my life. Everything!" He kept wagging his head, laughing, tears hanging in his eyes. "You want *me* to give you a character reference so that *I* can recommend you on the basis of that reference for an appointment to West Point . . . you want *me* to—" And he and the others dissolved again in mirth.

Sam felt bewildered and vaguely pleased. You never knew what would do it in this world. He saw the humor of his request, but persisted nevertheless, "Well, I only figured you've had a chance here to gauge me as a man—"

"Yes, I have," Matt Bullen cried, still laughing. "Indeed I have. I give up, son. I give up in a walk." He came around the desk, wiping his eyes, and clapped Sam on the shoulder. "All right, boy," he said, "you've got it. On the strength of that irrefutable logic alone you've got it." He walked toward the door. "Now I have to tell you that a principal has already been named for this year. But I'll put you down as alternate appointee and you can take the exams. The principal may fail his exams or withdraw for some reason. That's the best I can do for you."

"Thanks, Mr. Bullen. That's all I ask."

"You're all right, son. You're just what the doctor ordered." He swung open the door, and the thin-faced girl, now back at her desk, saw Sam and rose to her feet in an angry fluster.

"Mr. Bullen, I'm sorry, I had to go down the hall and I thought he'd left—"

"That's all right, Arlene. I wouldn't have missed this unscheduled interview for worlds. Not for worlds. You just take down this young feller's name and other pertinent data for the military examinations, will you?"

"Certainly, Mr. Bullen."

"That's a good girl." Turning again to Damon he shook his hand and clapped him on the shoulder again, smiling. "You're okay, son. You take those exams. And I'll be rooting for you." He went back inside and closed the door.

Standing by the desk and looking down into the girl's resentful face, answering her questions, Sam could hear voices and laughter from the private office. He had his chance! The chance he needed. You couldn't keep a good man down, as they said. But even then you needed a shot of luck. He stole a glance at his watch: he still had nine minutes to make the train.

The wind came up again and the dust lifted, swirling in baby twisters across the diamond from first to third; and Sam Damon put his glove to the side of his face. When it cleared again Sergeant Kintzelman, known to his intimates as Jumbo, went into his ponderous, pumping motion, rocked and threw. The batter, a corporal named Hassolt, lashed at the pitch—the ball skipped like a dirty white pebble into right field, where

Mason fielded it and threw in to second to hold the runner. There was a stir in the little knots of soldiers clustered along the foul lines and Sergeant Merrick, captain of the Company B team, coaching at third, began to holler: "Old Jumbo's fading, he's blowing sky-high . . ."

Far away on the horizon there were mountains like great beasts: mountains a hundred miles away. But around them there were only plains. The post was a dreary little huddle of huts and barracks on a tiny rise beyond the ballfield. Turning his head, Sam Damon gazed at it, the lumpy adobe buildings, the flag snapping out straight from its staff, the drifting plume of dust made by a solitary horseman coming from Valverde. He still felt mildly astonished at the chain of events that had flung him down here at Fort Early, in this vast desertland on the edge of Mexico . . .

He had gone back to Lincoln again a few weeks later and taken the entrance exams for West Point. He felt certain he'd passed; and when he'd come in from haying for Fritz Clausen and his mother had handed him the long envelope his heart had given the high, taut leap reserved for such momentous occasions. He had lowered his eyes.

"It's a very important-looking letter," Kitty Damon ventured shrewdly.

"Yeah," Uncle Billy said. "I couldn't help noticing the return address."

"That's bad manners, Billy."

"Do you think so? Maybe. Matt Bullen must be running scared if he's out recruiting suckling babes. Ever since Wilson's got in they're terrified the bloody revolution's on the way."

Sam sat down and opened the letter, ran his eye quickly along the lines. It was straight and to the point. He had passed the examinations with flying colors. The principal appointee had also passed, but he, Bullen, was pleased to inform Sam that he would definitely be named as principal appointee for the following year. He sent his warm regards.

The following year. Sam folded the letter with care. After the interview with Bullen, the exams, the soaring sense of possibilities, of destiny unfurling, the delay was like a defeat; cruel, not to be borne. A full year to wait. But he let no trace of consternation or chagrin cross his face. If that was how it was, that was how it was. They were all watching him.

"It's nothing," he said calmly, and slipped the letter back into the envelope. "Just a little idea I had."

Uncle Billy laughed once. "Black Matt trying to turn you into one of his grubby ward heelers, is he? That why you've been running to Lincoln all the time?"

That was the trouble with small towns: everybody knew everything about you; they knew when you used the privy and what for. Well, they wouldn't find out if *he* could help it.

"Oh no," he said easily. "No, it was a different matter entirely." He smiled. "It just didn't pan, that's all."

"Jesus, I hope not," Billy Hanlon said. "It'd be a sin and a shame to see you get mixed up with that bunch of tinhorn crooks, and so young in life at that." He scratched his chin with a thumbnail. "It isn't like the Hanlons to be secretive about such matters, I'll say that much."

"Leave him alone, Billy," Kitty Damon said. "He's old enough to know what he wants, and that's more than you can say."

"At eighteen? At eighteen you're the prize gull at the carnival."

"Well, you're not looking at any gull," Sam answered tartly; he rose to his feet holding the letter.

"It's all part of his secret scheme to set the world on fire," Peg put in slyly, grinning at him. "Honestly, I've never seen such a sneak . . ."

"Leave him alone, Peg," his mother repeated. Her sharp blue eyes rested on him a moment, dropped again to her sewing; he knew she had read his bitter disappointment. Quietly he went upstairs to his room . . .

Now, back of third base, Traprock Merrick clapped his hands. He was a squat block of a man with little button eyes and a mouth that made a huge black square when he shouted. He was pugnacious, harsh, given to much taunting of subordinates, and he was riding Kintzelman hard, shouting that he was all through, his arm had turned to blue glass, they were going to beat him right now, the way they always had. Jumbo stared at him a moment doggedly, then turned back to the plate. The batter, a lanky, round-shouldered Kentuckian named Cloren, drove the next pitch down the third-base line. Devlin darted to his right, leaped headlong, hit rolling in the dust and came up with the liner held high. The A Company crowd yelled and Sam whistled shrilly between his teeth. Old Dev. What a save.

The next hitter was already standing in, waving his bat. Kintzelman turned and waved Sam farther toward right field. Sam drifted over a few steps until Jumbo appeared satisfied, then spat in the base of his glove and worked it in with two fingers of his throwing hand, his feet spread, waiting.

. . . The following year. He had sat at Mr. Thornton's desk, weary from his day's work in the fields, listening absently to the shrill of katydids in the swamp, opening and closing his hands. It was impossible to keep his mind on the battle of Austerlitz. A full year. Matt Bullen might change his mind or forget about him entirely, he could even be defeated in November; Uncle Bill might succumb to wanderlust again— run off gold mining in the Yukon or hunting for sunken treasure in the Caribbean—and Sam would find himself carrying most of the load again. Anything could happen in a year. One day his father had been a healthy, vigorous man: a few weeks later he was minus a leg and wasted away to a shadow, his face the color of dirty flannel; a dying man. If you didn't force the issue, snatch at life when you could, it would turn on you like a snake. Sitting at the head of the stairs listening to the drone of voices down in the bar, impatience would catch him up and shake him like violent hands. You had to act, to act—

So he did what he had always done since he'd been a little boy: he acted quickly and without reservation. He took the Union Pacific train to Lincoln still again, and enlisted in the United States Army. Ability would tell: he would work his way up through the ranks, he would make a name for himself even before the year was up. Every soldier carried a field marshal's baton in his knapsack: hadn't the greatest self-made soldier of them all said so?

The recruiting sergeant, a tall Texan with a low forehead and a broad, engaging smile, was delighted with him. He'd make a first-rate soldier, he could promise him that. Advancement was rapid, it was a slick army, an expanding army—they were going to war with Mexico any day now, and then you'd see the fur fly. And he'd passed the West Point exams, had he? Keen, that was keen—his colonel would rush that through in no time at all . . .

His family's reaction to the news had not been quite so enthusiastic. It surprised him a good deal. His mother looked alarmed, then angry; her eyes began to fill with tears. Mr. Verney turned grave and tugged nervously at his beard. Uncle Bill became apoplectic.

"Why, you simple fool—you poor, ignorant, misbegotten idiot!" He began waving his arms; the tattooed eagles on his forearms shivered and writhed. "What did he offer you?"

"Who?"

"That stinking, conniving recruiting sergeant, that's who! What did he promise you? a dozen dusky maidens in a nipa hut and a bag of gold?"

"He didn't promise me anything."

"The hell he didn't—he painted a life of riotous pleasures, island girls and tuba by the flowing gallon, lolling under the palm fronds all day and all night too—and you fell for it! You ignorant sod, they'll wipe out the latrines with you for reveille! They'll have you holystoning the range and currying every bloody officer's horse in Fort Riley . . ."

Sam stared at him in dismay. Uncle Bill was shouting and swearing, and his mother was too distraught to say a word; even Mr. Verney was nodding in grim agreement.

"But Uncle Bill, you went to Tientsin and Samar, you told me yourself you—"

"I told you nothing! nothing at all! You'll wish you were dead . . ."

"I'll make my way up in the ranks. The sergeant told me there would be lots of advancement—"

"You'll *what*? Oh, you poor sod. You'll be sorry you ever were born! Why in Christ's sweet name didn't you listen to me—!"

"But I *did*, Uncle Bill—"

Wild Bill Hanlon smote his forehead. "God forgive me. I should never take a drop nor open my mouth for anything but victuals . . ."

"It's no good upbraiding the boy," Mr. Verney concluded with hollow resignation. "He's taken the action, and he must pay the price of it." He turned his sharp old eyes on Sam. "But how in Tophet a fine, promising lad like you could throw away his life in so foolish a manner is beyond me."

"But Mr. Verney, how can you say that? You were at Shiloh and Missionary Ridge, you marched to the sea with the Army of the Tennessee, the greatest hiking army the world has ever seen . . ."

"And so we were," the old man cried softly, "we swung along thirty miles to the day, a blanket and a canteen full of molasses, and before old Johnston knew it we were snapping at his flanks, burning ties and twisting iron—and when we took Atlanta even Jeff Davis knew the game was up . . . But that was *war*, boy!" Sam had never seen him so agitated. "You don't join the army in *peacetime*, to consort with thieves and drunkards, ignorant moonshiners and the riff-raff of the cities of the East . . ." Sam glanced at Uncle Bill, expecting him to flare with anger, but the old sergeant was only wagging his head unhappily and scratching his chin. "Outlaws, and men without names—that's what the Army's filled with now, boy . . ."

"Did you *sign?*" Billy Hanlon demanded wildly. "Did you sign a paper in his presence—?" Sam nodded. "Then there's no hope. You ringtailed, horn-headed prince of fools. You'll be sorry you ever took that train to Lincoln. You'll wonder why there ever was a human race—"

Wilgus, a tall, quiet ex-cavalryman, swung from the heels and lashed a tremendous liner to right that landed not three feet foul and skipped and bounded on down to the stables with Mason chasing it. Merrick danced up and down on his stovepipe legs with joy, roaring, "Here we go! *Everybody* hits! *Everybody* hits away . . ."

Uncle Bill had been solidly, mountainously right. He had been drilled until he staggered, he'd been kept at attention under a merciless sun and swarms of gnats, he had dug great square holes in the ground; he had done KP duty for a bunk that looked as far as he could see just like all the others, he had scrubbed mess tables and dug out latrines. Sadistic and horny-handed sergeants rode him, he did more manual labor in less time than he would have believed possible. He was woefully disconcerted. He kept his rifle spotless, he mastered the intricacies of close-order drill and the care of his personal equipment—and it all led to nothing. It was even as Uncle Bill had said: he was a rookie and he was made to feel it. There was no field marshal's baton anywhere in this dusty world of incessant guard duty and drill and fatigue details, let alone in his private's pack. As for the colonel, he had laid eyes on him just twice in the first three weeks. There were only sergeants and they were as omnipotent as God.

Jumbo had just thrown what was nearly a wild pitch, Thomas making a fine stop on his knees. Hassolt, quick as a cat and twice as bold, danced off first, chirping and hollering. The Company B bench with its supporters was all alive now. Sam moved back a step or two and pumped his glove.

What had rescued him—partly—were his marksmanship and his athletic prowess. On his first day at the range, wild with release from the dreary, interminable sighting and aiming drills, he had fired a possible at five hundred yards—nothing exceptional for the noncoms but impressive enough for a raw rookie, and Lieutenant Westfall had begun to keep an eye on him. Keen eyesight is a prerequisite for good shooting; he had always been an excellent hunter, and he didn't need to have the sergeants tell him that in the Springfield he had the finest infantry rifle in the world. He qualified as expert on his first record day.

The other avenue of escape was the company ball team. He could throw and hit a baseball harder and farther than most men, and he knew it. Captain Parrish had been delighted at the rare good fortune that had sent him this tall, rawboned Nebraskan with the quick hands and feet. The company commander was a lean, leathery man with bright blue eyes and fine silver mustachios, and he was a rabid baseball fan. He had played constantly in his younger days, but a Spanish bullet at El Caney had put an end to that. He could get around all right, he could ride superbly and walk the line like a clockwork soldier, but he couldn't field ground balls or run the bases anymore. All his passion was centered around a ball team that could whip those arrogant, invincible sons in Company B, and when he watched Sam convert two of Kintzelman's best curves into savage line drives that first practice evening, his joy was unconfined. Captain Parrish and Ted Barlow were as different as two American males could be, but they would have understood each other perfectly. There was suddenly, magically, far less KP duty for Private Damon.

Wilgus swung now, the ball lifted nicely, high, hanging in the dry Texas air off to Sam's left. He loped back easily and got under it, set himself, gathered it in. Slattery was right where he knew he'd be, a step or two up from the bag, crouched, his hands low, waiting, and he threw to him smartly to hold Hassolt, though there was no need for it—Company B already had a very healthy respect for his arm. Thomas came out toward the mound with his mask off, the little and forefingers of his right hand waving above his head in the traditional sign. Two out. Maybe they'd beat them after all, this time. The infield chatter started up again and Sam joined it, that crackling litany he loved. The dust churned around him fiercely again, and subsided; he rubbed his eyes and pulled his visor lower.

Davis was standing in: a spray hitter, crowding the plate, waving his bat back and forth like an angry cat switching its tail. Kintzelman, staring at him, took off his cap and wiped his forehead with his forearm. Sam knew what the big man was thinking: if he didn't get Davis he would have to face Corporal Hansen, the big blond Swede who had hit him all afternoon, who could always hit him—who would drive in the two runs and the game would be over. Company B would have won still again, in the late innings. Merrick was dancing up and down again, taunting him; he called something to Hansen, who was flailing three bats around his head and grinning. Sam glanced at Parrish; the Captain was standing now in front of the bench beside the water bucket, his arms folded. His face was expressionless.

Thomas gave Kintzelman a sign; he shook it off, shook off another. Sam scowled at his burly back. Jumbo was a good sergeant as sergeants went, but he thought too slowly, and along only one line. Couldn't he see Thomas wanted him to throw something different? Jumbo wouldn't. Two fast balls and a curve, two fast balls and a curve. He never varied the pattern no matter what Thomas or anyone else tried to tell him. Wisconsin Dutchman. And now he was tired, and worried; his mind was on Hansen more than the batter. But Captain Parrish would never take him out: Jumbo had once played with the Pittsburgh Pirates and Jumbo could therefore do no wrong.

The nervous tension of waiting in the outfield while Kintzelman fiddled around, the sense of powerlessness in a crucial situation, was irksome. He kicked at the withered stalks of buffalo grass about his ankles, swung his arm round and round to loosen it, and crept back another step. Captain Parrish had not moved. He could go in there and get Davis on curves if Parrish would only give the word; but he was a rookie and Jumbo was a sergeant and had played with the Pirates. Inflexibility—it was the worst human failing: you could learn to check impetuosity, you could overcome fear through confidence and laziness through discipline, but rigidity of mind allowed for no antidote. It carried the seeds of its own destruction.

The first pitch was in the dirt, Thomas making another fine stop and keeping Hassolt from breaking for second. The Company B crowd were all roaring and yelping now, riding Jumbo for all they were worth. Now he'll groove this one, to try to stay even, Sam thought; he'll put it right down the pipe, and Davis will know it's going to be a fast ball, a Fiji Islander would know it's going to be a fast ball, and he'll belt it. He crept back one more step and came to the set position as Jumbo reared back and threw. Davis' bat licked around like a yellow wagon tongue. Blue darter. It was coming toward him on a line, over Slattery's outstretched glove—then all at once it began to curve, bending down and away from him toward left center, coming very fast, bounced once flatly and kept on. He just had room to cut it off. Just barely. He was vaguely aware of everyone roaring, a shrill cry from Devlin at third, the streaking figures—and then, racing to his right, bending, in the most luminous and evanescent of flashes the thought: Merrick will hold Hassolt at third, they're afraid of my arm, he won't gamble on tying it up now, he'll hold Hassolt at third and Hansen will come up and knock them both in; and here I am, running through this particularly heavy patch of scraggly old buffalo grass—

Without any conscious thought he dipped down, trapped the ball deftly; then spun around in the wilted yellow grass as though bewildered, took a step back. There was an outcry and he could hear Merrick distinctly now, shouting, "*Go on, go on!*" He wheeled and threw with all his might. The ball went in low, just to the right of the mound, skipped once—and everything took on a perfect clarity: Thomas, his mask off, standing like a bulldog, waiting, Hassolt racing down the line from third, the ball taking a nice hop into the big black mitt and Hassolt falling into his slide early, much too early, and Thomas reaching down to him, the cloud of ocher dust that hid everything for a second, and then Sergeant Major Jolliffe's arm shooting into the air. Out. Out a mile. The game was over. He came running in with the others to the milling knot of players and spectators halfway between third and home. Merrick was protesting violently, square black mouth spread wide, his brows drawn down. He began to push his way toward Damon.

"Why you sneaky little rookie—what kind of a play is that?"

Devlin was capering with glee. "Go on," he crowed, "he gave you the decoy and you fell for it!"

Hassolt put a restraining arm on Merrick, who flung him off. He was livid with rage. "—a cheating trick! That's a cowardly, underhand farmer's trick . . ."

Sam stopped grinning. "You can take that back, Merrick," he said evenly. "You aren't in uniform now."

"Why, you insolent hayseed recruit," Merrick shouted. He lunged at the outfielder, swinging both hands. Sam took the blow on his shoulder, ducked the right and drove his own left hand into the Sergeant's side and felt the heavy man grunt with pain. Then there were arms pulling them both apart, holding them, everyone was shouting something—all of it silenced by Captain Parrish's thin, metallic voice:

"Men! Men! *Come to attention!*" Everyone became rigid. "I won't have this! On a field of sport. Disgraceful! Any more of this and I'll have you up for company punishment, each and every one of you. . . ." Severe and precise in his tight khaki uniform, wasp-waisted, the waxed points of his mustaches gleaming, he paced back and forth in front of them as if on a wound-up spring, while they stood there at attention, panting.

"Now. We strive to the utmost in contests of skill and strength—that is the way games were meant to be played. But we are sportsmen. Good sportsmen at all times. We do not cease acting like gentlemen and good Americans even in the heat of endeavor. Now . . ." He stopped pacing back and forth; and for all the priggish punctilio in his manner there was a steely force about him that destroyed any thought of laughter. Captain Parrish had come out of West Point to fight the Sioux at Wounded Knee Creek, he had assumed command of the remains of a company at

Santiago de Cuba while shaking with dysentery and Yellow Jack, and he looked as if he was ready to do it all over again if he had to. He fixed Merrick with his cold blue eyes and raised thumb and forefinger.

"Item one: Private Damon's maneuver—if it was that—was a perfectly permissible one, in the same category as a batter feigning a bunt, or a base runner bluffing a steal of base. You were perfectly at liberty to hold your man at third, Sergeant Merrick: you elected to commit him. Item two: you therefore had no just cause to assault Private Damon in any manner. Is that correct?"

"Yes, sir," Merrick said.

"Item three." The icy blue eyes rolled around to Damon and the Nebraska boy knew it was his turn. "Private Damon—even though in some measure provoked, you are guilty of striking a noncommissioned officer. A grave offense in itself. Very grave. I trust you are aware of that. Are you?"

"Yes, sir."

"Very well." Captain Parrish dropped his hand and resumed his pacing, and Sam saw that there was a method in the officer's madness. This ostentatious display of analysis and army regulations was artfully designed to allow time for tempers to cool. "Item four: however, you were both under stress, the incident was not in line of duty. And the occasion"—and Sam thought he saw the trace of a frosty smile quiver the company commander's mustaches—"we might all agree, was a highly unusual one." He struck his yellow leather riding crop against his breeches. "The incident will therefore be closed. Is that clear to everyone concerned?"

There was a low chorus of respectful assent.

"Very good. Sergeant Merrick, Private Damon: I want you to shake hands."

Sam stepped forward, his hand extended. They shook hands, but the Sergeant's eyes glinted in anger.

"Well met," Captain Parrish concluded. He glanced at the group again and brushed at one end of his mustache. "There may be those among you who feel the gesture superfluous. But it is ceremony that ennobles our everyday lives. We salute as a ceremony of respect, not to the man, but the rank which he wears and of which he aspires to make himself worthy; at colors we salute, not the flag itself, but that fluttering symbol of this great nation, one and indivisible . . ." Captain Parrish caught himself up, barked a cough, and slapped his thigh viciously with the riding crop. "We are a family," he pronounced. "A select and honorable family. We work hard and play hard, but at all times we practice good fellowship, personal honor, and fair play. We are the vanguard of the nation. We must be worthy of it." He brought himself to attention in a fierce little quiver, as a sign that the scene was to be concluded. "Very well. We will consider the incident formally closed. At ease, men. As you were and carry on."

The groups broke into talk again, a little subdued but still jubilant. Company B left the field dejectedly. Devlin was again capering for joy, his eyes dancing, his red hair gleaming in the afternoon light.

"Did you see old Sam give him the decoy?" he asked Thomas. "Did you see it? Ah, what a jewel of a play! Did you see it, Sarge?"

Jumbo Kintzelman nodded. As they started back toward the barracks the big man slapped Sam on the shoulder and murmured: "Nice going, younker."

"Damon . . ."

Sam turned, recognizing the voice. "Yes, sir?"

"*Was* that intentional?"

"Yes, sir."

Captain Parrish's gaze was bright and piercing. "I played a good deal in my palmy days. Sometimes a fielder is unaware that he's trapped a ball in his glove."

"No, sir. I knew I had it."

"I see. That's interesting. You thought it out, then, as you were playing the ball?"

"No, sir—it was more like a picture: Sergeant Merrick would hold Hassolt at third, and Hansen would hit safely again. And then the grass around my feet."

"I see. Remarkable." Captain Parrish ran one fingernail to each side of his mustache. "Of course if you had thrown wildly—"

"I didn't intend to throw wildly, sir."

"No, of course not." Captain Parrish's face broke into one of its rare smiles, a tight grimace involving scores of seams and wrinkles. "First rate. Let me congratulate you."

"Thank you, sir."

The Captain frowned faintly at this reply—a rookie was not supposed to thank an officer for commendation; Sergeant Kintzelman among other noncommissioned officers had impressed this fact on Sam, and he realized his error the moment he'd made it—but this was a moment of celebration, the realization of a dream, and Parrish merely nodded and smiled his bizarre smile as he walked away, murmuring: "Remarkable . . ."

Sam found himself staring after the officer. Devlin was tugging at his sleeve, saying something about the look on old Traprock Merrick's face, but he only half heard him. Was it remarkable? He didn't know. It had happened: it had worked. That was all he could for the life of him say.

The land was endless. Flat plains, and then arroyos whose channels were littered with boulders big as grain sacks. They slid or half-fell down one sheer water-cut side and crawled up the other, hauling each other up laboriously. There were mesas like huge rose-and-ocher hills sliced flat by giants, and more arroyos, and again more plains that stretched out and away until their eyeballs ached trying to stare to the end of them. There were hills, and thickets, and here and there enormous cactus trees with arms like signposts to nowhere erected by idiots. And over and under and through everything was the heat, and the wind, and the dust it bore, that coated them as they walked until they looked like a horde of tramps made out of dough.

They had started out from the post merrily enough, with the regimental band arrayed just outside the gate playing "The Girl I Left Behind Me." Captain Parrish had given them "eyes right" as they swung past the colonel, a short, red-faced man with white walrus mustaches, who saluted them smartly. They were marching to battle, they were going to catch up with a mean old Mexican bandit named Camargas who had invaded United States territory and robbed a United States post office. They were going to track him down and defeat him in open battle. Three columns flanked by cavalry were going to converge on Montemorelos, where Camargas' base of operations was—or at least that was what the sergeants said. It was going to be Buena Vista and Chapultepec all over again. Outnumbered five to one, twenty to one, it would make no difference—they were going to rout the infamous Greasers, avenge the insult to the flag, and plunge on to glory. It had been a still, clear morning and they'd been able to hear the strains of the regimental band for a long while. The sergeants had kept them at a smart column of fours, their packs were light and riding easy, and their veins pumped with the wine of adventure.

But that had been six days ago, and in the meantime the country had begun to tell on them. Their feet were sore, they had slung their rifles, and their shirts were stiff with dust and dried sweat; there was very little joking, and no singing at all.

"When we going to run into this Camargas joker?" Devlin queried aloud. "My feet hurt." He had a blue handkerchief drawn tight over his nose and mouth, and his campaign hat was pulled down over his eyes: he looked like a cowboy bandit on a drunk. "Tell you what, Sam."

"What?"

"I'm going to put that Pancho C. in a cage and take him back with me to Chicopee Falls and exhibit him at twenty-five cents a head. Then I'll retire on the profits. What are you going to do?"

"I'm going to lie in a pool for three days and nights." He was dying of thirst; he saw water everywhere—in still mountain lakes, in rivers, in thunderous waterfalls. His head throbbed and his throat was like scraped leather. His tongue felt like a bag of resin. It was dry country, a cruel country. A country without water. Only fools and outlaws would choose to live in a country like this.

"Well sure, but after that."

"Drink the pool dry." He would rather die than tell Devlin—even his bunkie Devlin—the truth. He was going to lead a charge, like Captain

Howard of the voltigeurs on the walls of Chapultepec, he was going to drag a mountain howitzer up to the belfry of the Church of San Cosmé and open fire on the gates of the city, like General Grant. The high places, take the high places. He was going to distinguish himself, right here in Mexico.

"I'm going to get me one of those jackets embroidered in silver," Devlin offered. "And one of those combs Mexican women wear standing straight up at the back of their heads." He heaved a sigh. "But I wish to hell I'd joined the cavalry."

"Yep, the cavalry gets the glory and the infantry eats the dust," Corporal Thomas told them. "Should have thought of that when you signed up."

Sam Damon wasn't so sure. He could not rid himself, even now, of the feeling that the infantry was where his destiny lay—that all his trials and triumphs were welded to foot-soldiering. It was hard to hold that idea in this baking heat, traipsing over this measureless land filled with dust and vicious little stones, each of which had at least three sharp points—

He heard Pensimer give an exclamation. Off to their right there rose a little plume of dust. Mesmerized, they watched it as it grew, slipped behind some thickets, reappeared—a horseman now, but a cumbersome horseman, growing larger, a top-heavy burden; and Sam saw there were two riders, one wobbling badly, swaying from side to side. Captain Parrish and Lieutenant Westfall cantered toward them and the strangers slowed to a trot, the overburdened horse wheezing, its flanks soapy with sweat. There was a little commotion among the horses, and they saw the swaying figure half-slide, half-fall to the ground. Captain Parrish turned and waved to Kintzelman, who said:

"Damon, Broda, Devlin! Get over there and lend a hand . . ."

They broke out of the column and ran over to the little group. One of the cavalrymen was talking to Captain Parrish, the other was sitting on the ground awkwardly, one of his feet bent under him, a hand gripping his thigh. As they reached him he raised his eyes to them and said, "I'm hit, boys. I'm hit . . ."

"Why, it's Gurney," Broda said in great surprise. Damon looked at Broda and then at the wounded man; he could not recall ever seeing him before. His belt was gone, his shirt was wringing wet, and blood was all over his breeches. Damon heard the other cavalryman, who was still mounted, say tensely: "Yes, in force, Captain. I'd say a hundred, hundred and twenty."

"A hundred and twenty?"

"Yes, sir. With lots of extra mounts. They must have come through the notch at Aldapán."

"Where is Hollander? Lieutenant Hollander?"

"I don't know, sir. The last I saw he was riding south."

"All right." Captain Parrish dismounted and knelt beside Gurney, who stared at him fearfully. "Take your hand away, son," he said.

"Won't cure it, I can tell you." Gurney took his hand away from his hip very slowly, as though the consequences of such a move would be fatal; the Captain peered at the wound, and grunted. "Give me your bayonet," he said to Damon. Sam slipped it out of its scabbard and Captain Parrish took it and ripped the man's breeches open, wiping at the blackened oval hole from which blood flowed in a slow, greasy stream. Gurney, who had watched the bayonet with apprehension, groaned now and then.

"Doc Haber'll have to dig that out," Captain Parrish said. He began to bind it swiftly and deftly, keeping the yellow gauze tight in his left hand. The blood kept seeping up through the cloth.

Gurney moaned again. "It hurts," he offered.

"Of course it hurts. Did you think it'd feel *good?*" Captain Parrish stood up, wiping the smears of blood from his hands with a kerchief. "All right. Get him over to one of the wagons."

Damon bent over and started to take the wounded man by the shoulders.

"No—don't pick me up, don't pick me up," he begged.

"Come on, Walt, it's only a minute," Broda said soothingly; then, in an eager tone: "Did you get one, Walt? Did you get one of 'em?"

"Give me some water, mate. A little water—"

Damon handed him his canteen, and the wounded man drank with feverish greed, clumsily, water trickling over his chin and shirt front, while the other three watched him in silence.

"Did you hit one of 'em, Walt?" Broda pursued. "Before they got you?"

". . . I feel sick," Gurney said. He had no interest in talking about the Mexicans or the skirmish, if that was what it had been, or the campaign.

"He'll be all right," Broda said to the other two apologetically. "Once he's in out of this sun." But still they squatted around him, watching his narrowed eyes, the perspiration streaking his face and throat, the way his hand kept hovering over the wound, pressing the thigh above it delicately. It was as if in the next second—the very next second—they would learn something of incalculable value from this bloody, groaning voyager from a terribly distant country.

"What are you men waiting for?" Captain Parrish called to them sharply. "Get him into that wagon and be smart about it . . ."

They leaped into action, then—picked him up, muttering and protesting, and bore him over to the wagon. It stopped, and they lifted Gurney over the tailboard and eased him onto a pile of tarpaulins.

"There you go, Walt," Broda said. "You'll be all right in here."

"Wait—" Gurney panted. "Wait—a minute—"

They paused. It was stifling under the taut canvas; the tarps smelled of creosote and damp rot. Damon hung on the edge of the tailboard, feeling the jolt and joggle as the wagon started up again.

"I want to tell you, mate," Gurney cried softly, "I want to tell you, there's a whole . . ." Then he stopped, gazing at Damon, shaking his head in slow confusion, his eyes wide.

"Come on, Sam!" Devlin called.

They had to run to catch up with their place in the column. Damon was furious with himself for letting the trooper drink from his canteen. Now he had even less than anyone else, and God knew when they'd get any more. He'd always been a water drinker—at home he was always pumping a dipper full whenever he passed through the kitchen, loving the cool, silken rush of water against his throat—and maintaining water discipline on the march was a continual torture. Why the devil had he done it? The fellow had spilled more than he'd drunk, anyway . . .

As they caught up with their squad Sergeant Kintzelman said, "What'd he do, stop one?"

"Yes," Damon said. He felt irritable and sullen.

"Where'd he get it?"

"In the leg, Sarge," Devlin answered. "The upper leg."

"Oh, then it's nothing much."

The two privates glanced at each other. Damon didn't see how a hole like that in your body, a hole that could have you groaning and bleeding like that, was nothing much; but he put it out of his mind. They were going to be in it now, for sure. The thing was to be alert, keep your wits about you and not get rattled no matter what might happen. He'd know what to do when the time came . . . But the moment in the wagon with Gurney still bothered him.

They marched on, more rapidly now, passed through a bone-dry riverbed covered with dense thickets, began to ascend a long slope to where a ridge ran back in the shape of a horseshoe. Great clouds came up, all black and silver like some mighty artist's painting of storm clouds, and the wind blew harder, whipping dust in their faces until it stung.

"Christ, it isn't going to rain, is it?" Devlin exclaimed.

Corporal Thomas laughed. "Rain like you'll never hope to see again, if it does. And then gumbo! Boy . . ."

The bugles were blowing now—sweet, sharp, windblown sounds. They were on a little table of ground, with the ridge on their left, the stony creekbed down and away to the right. The wagons were pulling into a tight clump, the mules tossing their heads and neighing. Captain Parrish was riding hard at the head of the column, gesticulating; his campaign-hat brim flipped up and down with the gusts of wind. Damon felt almost dizzy with impatience.

"What do they want us to do?" he demanded. "What do they *want?*"

Big Kintzelman grinned at him. "Take it easy, younker. The Old Man'll let us know."

They moved past the wagons, curving back on them—then all at once a nearby bugle blew, a new call: insistent, piercing notes. Form hollow square. They broke out of column. This was better. He knew just what to do, they all knew just what to do. He ran forward to where Kintzelman was gesturing, and knelt. Devlin, Broda, Chandler were kneeling beside him; the rank behind stood, their rifles across their chests. It was going to be like the Peach Orchard. He thought fleetingly, remotely, of Mr. Verney, of Uncle Bill and the lamplit porch with the June bugs bumping and sizzling against the screens.

"Load and lock!" Sergeant Kintzelman shouted. He pulled a singleton cartridge from his shirt pocket and inserted it in the chamber, plucked a clip out of his belt, ticked the noses smartly against his rifle stock and pressed it into the magazine, closed the bolt.

"Fix bayonets . . ."

He did this just as easily, was pleased to see that he was ready earlier than some of the older men. He felt no fear, only a kind of curiosity that brightened at the edges like heat lightning.

"All right, men . . ." Captain Parrish was sitting his horse behind them, and they turned to watch him. His yellow crop dangled from his right wrist. "You will hold your fire until the command is given, and then you will fire by volleys. No one is to open fire until the express command is given. I want that understood." His voice carried clearly in the wind. He rode off down the line.

The wait was interminable. The rain clouds rolling and melting on themselves dipped lower, filling the air with darkness. Light seemed to glow on bayonets and buckles, all the points of metal, as though to offset the sky's metallic gloom. The air was no cooler. From far off came a booming; guns or thunder, Damon couldn't tell. The earth was hot against his knee, dust stung his eyes, sweat ran in his eyes and mouth. Why fire by volleys with six rounds in chamber and magazine? Was that what you did repelling cavalry? assuming this *was* cavalry? And what if they broke through?

Then, like children at some distant, engrossing play there came a cry, or a series of cries, a medley of cheers and catcalls, whoops and whistles, and on the plain beyond the riverbed dust rose in massive yellow smoke. Sergeant Kintzelman behind him said something, but Damon could only watch in fascination as the slanting pillar of cloud, the high, lost cries, grew and grew—and then there they were, slipping out from under the canopy of dust, white-shirted figures with huge dark baskets of sombreros, fanning out and out until it seemed as if they must swallow the horizon, the limitless desert earth. What would stop them? Why didn't they fire? He was conscious of the fact that he was pressing the Springfield against his chest, that he was scarcely breathing.

They were nearer now—four hundred yards, three fifty, uttering their shrill, yelping cries, waving rifles and machetes and sabers, the horses plunging and dipping. He was aware of brief calls and exclamations in the ranks around him—but he himself was silent. There was a sudden thrust of panic at this violent, implacable onrush of horsemen— then it vanished. But still there was no command to fire.

They swept into the creekbed, and now he could see faces, huge brush mustachios under the hats, the teeth of the horses. Now. They must fire now, or they would be overrun and cut to pieces. Sure, *now*—

And all at once the horsemen broke to the right—went sweeping on down the streambed in wild parade, off to the left. Immediately above their heads—so low it seemed just above their hats—there was a tearing crash of thunder, flat as artillery fire, and rain fell, swept over them in pelting mad torrents, obliterating sight and sound.

"Cover your pieces!" Sergeant Kintzelman was shouting at them. But everything was soaked through, everything was drowned in silvered sheets. Beside him Devlin was whooping like a banshee, his head back, mouth open, catching the rain. Corporal Thomas was wrapping his neckerchief around his rifle bolt. Damon looked at them all in astonishment: the sense of outrage was so great it nearly choked him. What was the matter with them all? Didn't they care? Didn't they . . . ? A few feet away Kintzelman was grinning at him through the downpour.

"What happened?" he shouted.

The Sergeant shrugged. "Pulled foot."

"Why didn't we open fire? At three hundred yards—what if they hadn't broken away like that?"

Jumbo laughed good-naturedly; the water was streaming from his hat brim. "Take it easy, younker. They didn't want any." Bugles blew; they began to straggle back into the column of march. Around their feet the dusty baked earth was already turning into a rich, soft slime.

"Yes, but to let them get that close—" Damon protested.

"The Old Man's got his orders, too, you know." Kintzelman winked at him once. "The thing was to face them out, that's all: call their bluff." He had his rifle slung, butt downward, the bolt under his elbow. "There's more to this game than shooting . . ."

Damon stared at him. "You mean—that's it?"

"That's it, younker."

They were marching again. Everyone was talking animated now— even Corporal Thomas was whistling through his teeth.

"Did you see the hombre with the two swords?" Devlin was saying. "The gaffer in the black and gold jacket? He had a sword in each hand and he was banging them together like the cymbal man in the parade, back home . . ."

Damon made no reply. He felt bewildered, and cheated beyond measure. Looking back he could see nothing beyond the boulder-strewn riverbed and the spiny thickets of mesquite and chaparral. The rain had soaked through his woolen shirt and he shivered. It was over. Nothing had happened at all.

WHEAT

(II)

"What's the name of this place?" Ferguson asked.

"The Anvil Leads," Raebyrne replied. He was tall and gangling, with a freckled face and large, round, bright blue eyes.

"What kind of name is that? Leads where?"

"To the anvil, of course. Where'd you think?"

"Say, can we go see the sights, Sarge?" Turner said. "After the parade?"

"Maybe," Sam Damon answered.

"How long are they going to make us stand here? in the sun?"

"As long as it takes." Damon ran his eyes over the front rank. "Now, you've been given a signal honor. You're the first American troops to parade before the people of Paris. Now I want to see you march like soldiers, and not like a bunch of farmers or acrobats. Keep your elbows in and your faces front. And I don't want to see any goggling around at the girls. We're going to be parading down the most famous avenue in the world, and I want to see you act in a manner worthy of it."

"Then what, Sarge?" Raebyrne asked him. "What are we going to do then?"

"Then we're going to pay our respects to the tomb of Marie Joseph Paul Yves Roch Gilbert du Motier Marquis de Lafayette."

"Hot damn! He must have got writer's cramp just signing the hotel register . . ."

"Hey, Sarge," Ferguson said, "is it true we're all going to get three days' leave in Paree?"

"No, it's not. Now cut out your horsing around."

"Don't seem eccable we've got to be waiting on *them*," Raebyrne observed. "They ought to be waiting on us. We've come all the way hell-and-gone over here to bail 'em out, ain't we?"

The battalion was drawn up in the Court of Honor of the Invalides in Paris, standing at ease, which ostensibly meant one foot in place but didn't always. Damon ran his eyes over them warily and thought with weary indulgence, Jesus, these kids. They were nearly his age, a few of them were older, but he'd drilled them and inspected them and taught them how to clean their rifles and wind their puttees, and he felt like the father of a bunch of heedless, obstreperous children. Catching the eye of Devlin, now corporal of the second squad, he winked solemnly. Well, they were good stuff, but there had simply been no time to train them adequately. They'd come into camp straight from the enlistment offices, had been formed into regiments and divisions and shipped over to Saint Nazaire before they'd learned which end of a rifle went off or how to run through a decent manual of arms. Now they'd been picked ahead of the other American units for a demonstration in Paris—a morale booster for the French, Major Caldwell had said; the French were eager for a look at the Americans—and God knew how they'd carry it off . . .

"Raebyrne," he said, "hook up your collar."

"It scritches on my Adam's apple, Sarge. I'll get it hooked up in time."

"You'll hook it up now," Damon told him sharply. "Same for you, Turner."

He came alert. From the Seine the French contingent was coming: a steady, almost stately tread, their arms swinging in nice unison. Their horizon-blue coats swept back from the baggy breeches, their blue helmets had an antique grace, like the helmets of Napoleonic cuirassiers, only without the plumed crest. Their fixed bayonets were long, a spidery blue in the sunlight. Their faces were seamed and leathery and bearded; on their swinging left sleeves were rows of short horizontal stripes. A hush descended over the waiting battalion; the hobnailed boots of the French rang hard on the broad gray paving stones.

Major Caldwell, the battalion commander, cried: " 'talion . . ." and Damon saw Captain Crowder about-face and call: "Companee . . ." followed by Lieutenant Harris singing: "Pla-toooon. . ." and the ranks went through that quick little premonitory shiver.

"Ha—ten . . . *hut!*"

The files came together with a swift, quivering shock. It wasn't too bad. Raebyrne was a little late, Brewster was wobbling. The French came abreast, halted, swung to face them. They looked barbaric in their fierce black beards, like swamp rats and lumbermen pressed into uniform; but the weapons swung down and away like one man.

Major Caldwell cried: "*Pree-*zen. . ." and again the captains and lieutenants repeated the word in varying echoes that rang in the solemn courtyard: "*pree-*zen . . . *pree-*zen . . ."

"*Arms!*" The rifles rose and clashed in long vertical rows. This time it was terrible. Starkie didn't cut away his hand smartly, Raebyrne's piece went up in the air like a balloon, it looked for a horrifying instant as if Turner were actually going to drop his rifle on the cobbles. God, they were ragged.

Their band was playing now, the "Marseillaise." The poilus came to present arms, and their bayonets looked like a perfectly even ribbon of blue steel. There were ruffles and flourishes by the French bugle and drum corps, the drumsticks crossing over and back in looping folds and rhythms. There was an exchange of colors and then the high brass were walking the line, moving along the files at a smart pace. There was a portly French marshal with a pointed nose and rows of gold oakleaves on his kepi, and a French general with a ruddy, tanned face and a walrus mustache Damon supposed was Foch, and then General Pershing, looking fit and very stern with his cap visor down low over the bridge of his nose and his lips in a severe white line under his cropped mustache; then came General Harcourt, his expression weary and disgruntled, and after him some other French officers and Major Caldwell, very slender and erect, his fine features suffused with an expression both expectant and firm.

Then they were gone. While the party moved across the court to inspect the French battalion, Damon studied the poilus. Their faces were massive and grave behind their beards, but their eyes held a sharp, metallic glint that was unmistakable. One man in particular, a squat, bull-necked corporal, had drawn his lips down in a sneer of derision. They don't think very much of us, he thought; they don't think anything of us at all, they feel we're a joke—and the realization made him hot with resentment. Well, we'll see, he answered them with his eyes, smarting, restive. We may not look like so much right now, Froggies, but just you wait a little while; just you wait . . .

"Order . . . arms!" the command came, and was obeyed with alacrity if not precision. And then, "On right by squads!" and the echoing cries of the sergeants: "Squads right . . ." And they were marching now, under the gray-blue, smoky Paris sky and he was pacing his squads on the right of the column, chanting to them *wanh*, *hup*, *reep*, *fay-a-lo*, *reep fay-a-lo*, as Jumbo Kintzelman, now first sergeant with E Company, had sung it out for his ber.efit when he'd been a rookie in the white Texas dust. "Dress it up, now," he called sternly. "Bring your elbow in, Raebyrne. Straighten your piece, you look like a hodcarrier . . ."

They were on a bridge, a lordly marble bridge adorned with gods and goddesses and prancing horses in blackened bronze. Over the soft, pewter plate of the Seine, column half-left onto the Champs Elysées—the Champs Elysées!—more grand than he could ever have imagined it; and to his surprise he saw the sidewalks on both sides were jammed with people. They seemed to be women and children and old men—there were no young men anywhere—calling to them and waving. On up the great boulevard, past the rose and cream buildings with their slate roofs, the band blaring out "On the Mall," a tune he loved, the platoon marching fairly well, all things considered; and now the crowds were pressing toward them, girls here and there calling out to them in high, wild voices, words he couldn't understand. Everywhere were little French or American flags, and flowers; they all had flowers in their hands, flowers in garlands and bouquets, they were cheering in a high frenzy, drifting along with the inexorable movement of the troops; they pressed in thicker and thicker, they were smothering the platoon—

"Dress it up, there . . . Turner, the guide is *right!*" he thundered. They couldn't hear him. Nobody could hear anything now, the Parisians had swarmed against them, gesticulating, jostling; their voices were

like shrill surf. A young girl with bright blond hair had thrown a garland of flowers around Ferguson's neck, another was kissing Raebyrne
on the cheek, on the lips, had pushed his campaign hat wildly askew, he
was struggling to hold it on with his left hand while the girl, a pretty
little brunette, kept laughing and shrieking. Then Damon saw that she
was crying, laughing and crying at the same time.

There was no semblance of military order now; they were engulfed
in a tumult of women. A girl had flung a garland on Krazewski's hat,
roses and poppies pelted them in a storm, bouncing on their faces,
rifles, hats. He felt excited, vaguely embarrassed. It doesn't seem fair, he
remembered thinking, while all their men are away, at the front—then
forgot this concern as he saw up ahead the Arc de Triomphe looming
like the apotheosis of all victory—the thunderous testament of the le-
gionaries and Frankish lances and dazzling chasseurs à cheval—that had
gone here before him . . .

A girl was kissing Devlin who was responding amorously, while keeping his rifle nevertheless perfectly aligned; another girl had her arm
around Raebyrne, and was keeping pace with him; Ferguson was tossing
roses back into the bedlam on both sides. The band was playing again,
but all he could hear was the thump of the bass drum. Rifle barrels were
pointing every which way, like a pack of jackstraws. "Raebyrne!" he
roared—and Raebyrne, hearing him somehow through the din, shrugged
and threw him a roguish, apologetic glance. Lipstick was all over his
face. They swung around the arch slowly, ponderously, moving more
by impetus than by order, and the crowd was still thicker. More and
more flowers descended on them; the platoon looked like a floating
garden in the hot, filmy light.

"Ah, vous êtes si chic, Sergent!" a girl sang out; her lips brushed his
face, she was gone. Ferguson had given Turner and Brewster the elbow
to call it to their attention. Damon felt his face flush, then grinned in
spite of himself. What had she said—that he was a sheik? At the top of
the steps of some public building a one-legged man in a beret and a tight
blue suit was resting on his crutches and watching in amusement, nodding gently; two little boys, twins, were waving flags over their heads; a
woman all in black stood utterly motionless, her hands clasped at her
waist . . . All at once Damon was conscious of more and more of
them—women in black were everywhere in the churning mob.

The column pressed on, rapidly, absurdly, not really marching anymore; they seemed to float instead on a sea of women's hands and lips
and flowers, a drifting floral benediction. There were gardens laid out in
immaculate order and then the soft, brooding pile of the Louvre. At
Boulevard Sebastopol an elderly lady came up to Sam, reaching toward
him, saying something he couldn't begin to understand, and with a
gesture infinitely deft and tender wiped the sweat from his forehead
with a handkerchief redolent of lavender. He thought all at once of Mrs.
Verney with her tiny, lined face and mild eyes. He had known her only

as a little boy, but here she was again, with her lavender sachet, murmuring to him in incomprehensible French. *Feess*, it sounded like; something to do with *feess* . . .

We're the white hopes, all right, he thought. All he seemed to see now were wounded men, cripples, large-eyed little boys, and the widows in their black weeds. If we mean all *this* much to them—just a handful of rookies traipsing along; if they can get this excited about *us* . . .

Off to the right were the black spike cupolas of the Hotel de Ville, and the twin towers of Notre Dame; and dead ahead—they were entering it now—the Place de la Bastille, where a resolute National Guard had smashed the world's most terrible symbol of tyranny. All around him he could feel the beat of history; it hovered behind the wrought-iron gates and mottled plane trees and stern oak doors, it quivered above him in the still air. And the promise they bespoke, marching through Paris on the very Fourth of July, swept over him in a violent surge of pride, vainglorious and holy. History was moving with him now, had caught him up in its great iron arms, was thrusting him amid floral garlands toward he knew not what. But he was ready enough: he was eager for the journey . . .

And there finally was the cemetery, green and sacred under the chestnut trees. They were halted, and the French detachment drew up again facing them. Beyond the gates the crowd, deprived of movement, swelled against the mounted police who recoiled, muttering to their horses. The group of officers were moving up to the stone slab surrounded by its neat low iron railing. There was a gentle confusion: the big fat Marshal—was it Joffre?—was asking Pershing something. Black Jack shook his head, demurring, smiled, turned to a young officer on his staff, a captain Damon had never seen, who after a short consultation advanced to the tomb. As he started to speak his voice was drowned out in a mounting, shuddering roar—planes shot low overhead in diamond patterns, the red-white-and-blue cockades on their wings flashing; then they were gone. The captain had stopped. He saluted smartly, and cried:

"Nous voilà, Lafayette!"

There was a thunderous outburst of cheering; straw boaters and derbies soared in the air, the crowd surged against the gates in a wave of enthusiasm. General Foch was speaking again to Pershing who nodded, walked forward with his short, brisk stride and spoke briefly; but no one could hear a word he said, and no one cared. An orderly was bringing forward a large wreath of flowers. He laid it on the low railing and stepped back. Pershing shook his head—on an impulse picked up the wreath and leaning over the railing set it on the broad stone slab of the grave itself, came to attention and saluted. And now the crowd broke into complete pandemonium. A slender woman dressed in black broke through the police barrier and ran to Pershing, fell on her knees in front of him, her hands clasped to her face, which was streaked with tears. Damon saw the General's lips moving as he bent down to her, lifting her up. *Please, Madam,* Pershing was saying, *you must get to your feet, Madam. Please.* All around them was chaos, a delirium of joy and release, an excitement dangerously near hysteria. Damon could feel it in the soles of his feet. The platoon sensed it inchoately; a ripple of uneasiness passed over them, like a breeze through standing corn. An aide had hold of the woman now, who was sobbing uncontrollably, one hand to her face. All around them the crowd was still screaming. Damon exchanged glances with Platoon Sergeant Thomas, who pursed his lips. We got here just in time, Damon thought, watching the tears and clenched hands and the ponderous, swaying mob, the horses starting, sidling, giving way. We've got here just in the nick of time to save their wagon . . .

And at the same moment, watching these faces animate with hope, with grief and despair and terrible pride, it was as if he'd been given a vision of France: the gold-and-iron days of Charlemagne, the grim Dark Ages and Charles Martel, the steady consolidation of the kingdom with its intrigues and violence; the arrogant days of the Louis and then the Revolution and the Terror, the tumbrils shuddering through the narrow streets, and the Conqueror and all of Europe at their feet—and in so short a time the disasters of the Berezina and Leipzig and Waterloo, and Uhlans quartering their horses in the Tuileries—and again in 1871; all this bloody, tumultuous pageant long before there had ever been a town of Walt Whitman on the Platte River, before there was any sovereign state of Nebraska at all . . . and here they were, the inheritors of all this pageantry, weeping and laughing at a bunch of gangling, sloppy Americans; their backs to the wall. Lafayette, we were here . . .

His lips quivered in spite of himself. He was making history, standing in the cool shade of Picpus Cemetery; he was launched upon his destiny. It was a fierce and heady feeling. He had to bite his lips to suppress the smile.

"Mail-o!" Damon called. "All right now, mail-o!" Standing inside the doorway he began pulling envelopes out of the bag. He knew Captain Crowder would accuse him of spoiling the platoon if he should find out about this; but it was cold outside with a bone-chilling rain, and Damon didn't see that anything would be solved by falling them out in the company street just for a mail call.

"Turner!" he said.

The little West Virginian leaped off his sack and bounced up to him. "Yippee!" he crowed. "It's from my mama . . ."

"Raebyrne!"

"Yee-ho!" Raebyrne answered, and waved an arm.

"I'll take it to him, Sarge," Turner offered.

"No, you won't.—If you people can't come up here to get your own mail, you won't get it at all. Connolly! Davis! Hoffenstedt! I won't tell you twice . . ."

They came on the run, took their letters and drifted back to the straw pallets that served for beds. The room was huge and bare, a barnlike affair that had been converted into a barracks for French infantry three years before. Cold sank through its walls, welled up from the stone floor.

"Read 'em and weep," Damon said when he'd emptied the sack. "You will fall out in field gear in half an hour."

Ferguson gave an exclamation. "In all that rain, Sarge?"

"In all that rain. Advance by skirmish lines. Just think how soft that ground will be when you flop on it.—At least you'll be running around. Would you rather have close-order drill?"

"Drill, drill, drill," Raebyrne moaned. "I joined this man's army to fight Pee-roossians, I didn't sign up to stomp around holding a rifle a whole lot of fancy ways."

"First you drill, then you fight," Corporal Devlin told him. "That's how it is in the army. Don't be an agitator, now."

"None for me, Sarge?" Brewster said to Damon. He was a slender, delicate boy with sharp girlish features and a lock of hair that was continually falling over his forehead. "Are you certain?"

Damon nodded. "I'm certain."

"I can't for the life of me understand it." Brewster came from a wealthy New York family. Damon remembered his parents at the pier at Hoboken. His father had been wearing a Homburg and pince-nez and was talking earnestly to Captain Crowder, who was pleasant enough but wildly eager to get away from him; Mrs. Brewster was a frail woman in a blue satin dress and a large hat, who kept gazing up at the ship's side out of large, watery eyes. "Three months now and not a word from them . . ."

"Cheer up, kid," Devlin consoled him. "Maybe your mail was all on that transport that got torpedoed."

"What transport?"

"The old *Brahmaputra*, there. The *Eldorado*."

Brewster flushed, and flung his lock of hair back. "You're ragging me, Dev."

"How'd you guess?"

Brewster sank down on his sacking. "It's so cold in here." He pointed to the enormous hearth, now swept clear of ashes and andirons, and immaculately clean. "I don't see why we can't have a fire, with the fireplace right there. Why can't we have a fire, Sarge?"

Damon looked up from his letter, which was from his sister Peg and was bristling with gossip about the impending nuptials between Fred

Shurtleff and Celia Harrodsen, and had already irritated him severely. "Because Captain Crowder, Major Caldwell, Colonel Stainforth and General Pershing all say we can't. That's why."

"Well, it seems ridiculous to me." Brewster pulled his blanket up over his head and shoulders and rubbed his shins, looking frail and mournful. "I'm not accustomed to living this way . . ."

This sentiment provoked a hoot from Raebyrne, who had finished his letter and taken his rifle across his knees, and now was cleaning it with a pair of blue flannel bloomers he'd lifted from a window ledge in the town. "Why, this is nothing, nothing 't all. Why, back home you don't think of lighting a fire till your water freezes in a gold column just three inches from your nozzle."

Brewster stared at him. "Is that the truth, Reb?"

"Flaming gospel. Why, my Uncle Alpha froze so solid one night we had to lay him between two boar hogs—that's for body heat—and stick his feet in a tub of sour mash."

"Why was that?"

"Why, to get the cirkew-lee-ation going again! You could hear his brains snapping as they thawed out."

Brewster sighed, and blew his nose. "You're ragging me."

"Wouldn't call it that. Just conversation.—This is a good weapon," Raebyrne proclaimed to the room, and hefted the rifle. "It ain't as light as a Ballard, it ain't as handy as my Daddy's Sharps. But it'll do."

"It's the best infantry rifle in the world," Damon told him. "You take good care of it and it'll take good care of you."

"I aim to take good care of it. Only trouble is, it's got too danged many tricky parts."

"Is it true you fired a possible at a thousand yards, Sarge?" Ferguson asked.

"That's right."

"Thought I was stringing you, did you?" Devlin laughed at Ferguson. "I was lying right alongside him when he did it, too. You better learn to believe what your old NCOs tell you."

"Lot of good marksmanship is going to do us," Poletti said. He was a nervous, somber boy from Newark, left-handed and a poor shot. "Sneaking up and down in trenches, can't see a blessed thing fifty feet away anyhow."

"Remember that Frog officer they had over there to show us how to cut wire?" Turner asked them. "He just about laughed his head off watching us playing at skirmishers. 'Zees ees not zee bockskeen backwoods,'" he mimicked, holding his nose. "Zees is our war . . ."

Damon, who had been listening to this exchange, said: "Well, we're not going to be in trenches all the time."

"How come? That's what these poor jokers been doing for years, isn't it?"

"We're going to go through those German trenches and break out into the open. We're going to force them to fight our way."

"Hot damn! When we going to do that, Sarge?" Raebyrne crowed, and Damon noticed that now everybody in the room was watching him.

"Sooner than you think," he said meaningfully, although he hadn't the faintest idea what that meant. "Major Caldwell said that's what the strategy is. And if you haven't learned what you need to when we break out, you're the ones that'll pay."

"Then what do we have to learn all the trench warfare for?" Ferguson pursued.

"Because you've got to learn both. Trench warfare until we break out, and extended order afterward. Flanking tactics, what you've been doing. Can't you follow that?"

"Sure, I can follow that, Sarge."

"What I don't understand is why we have to do that close-order drill all the time," Brewster began earnestly. With the blanket over his head and shoulders he looked like a troubled young acolyte. "I can understand having to learn how to shoot and throw grenades, the bayonet practice. But why should we have to spend hours and hours learning right-front-into-line and on-right-by-squads and all that? and the manual of arms?"

Damon sighed, and laced his fingers together. Three beds down, Devlin was watching him and grinning. He remembered Major Caldwell smiling indulgently at First Sergeant Hassolt's angry chronicle of incessant rookie questions. "The American soldier has always wanted to know *why*, Sergeant. Baron von Steuben remarked on it at Valley Forge. Don't discourage it—it's a good thing. It's what distinguishes him from any other private soldier the world over—this feeling that it's his *right* to know why he's doing something. And why shouldn't he know? It's his life he's risking, isn't it?"

"Because that's what being a soldier is," he replied patiently now.

"But I don't see the *reason* for it."

"The *reason* is to learn to obey commands, to move quickly in unison."

"But if the object—"

"Let me finish. It's all part and parcel of being a good soldier. Because there's going to come a time—and it's not too far away, either—when you're going to be where all hell's breaking loose. Where you won't be able to hear yourself think, and where the temptation will be to do nothing and care less . . . and if you've learned to obey commands, to move without having to think about it, it'll make all the difference in the world."

There was a little pause. Brewster had dropped his eyes and was looking down at his slender white hands. Now somebody'll ask you how do you know what combat is like, and then what'll you say? Damon thought. You don't know any more about it than they do . . . He'd heard Jumbo and Hassolt and some of the older men talking about battle—the confusion and fear and the mounting desire to cower, hide, lie still; but that was all he knew himself.

"Well, sure, Sarge, I can take a holt of that," Raebyrne said after a moment. He made a violent grimace and scratched the top of his head. "Only thing, it leads me to a little ponder."

"Go ahead," Damon said wearily.

"Well now, supposing—I mean just supposing now, this here's what old Brewster would call one of them hypothical questions—supposing the hoosier giving the commands is giving the wrong ones?"

The barracks room was completely quiet now. Rain dripped flatly from the eaves, and in the next building somebody sneezed and broke into a fit of coughing. Even Devlin had stopped smiling and was watching Sam somberly, like the others.

"Well, that's one thing you don't have to worry about," he said slowly. "You don't even need to give it a thought. We've got the best there is in the whole U.S. Army, right here. Black Jack Pershing said so himself, if you need proof. Don't you worry, when we go over there's going to be no mistakes made by anybody."

"But, Sarge . . . just *supposing* all hell's broke loose, as you say, and the officer forgets the command, or he goes loose in the lid?"

Damon let his eyes rove slowly around the room. Very solemnly and distinctly he said: "Why, then obviously the thing to do is tell that officer he's a God damn incompetent fool and that you want to go back and do it all over again."

The long room broke into laughter.

"Old Sarge!" Raebyrne cackled, and slapped his skinny thigh. "That's a good one, damn if it isn't. You ever think of going into vaudee-ville?"

"I'd rather entertain you boys all day."

"I'm still not entirely convinced," Brewster observed. "Your original argument, I mean, not Reb's."

Damon got to his feet. "Well," he said, "you wait and see." That was the phrase that checked them every time: *you wait and see*. Yes, and he would have to wait and see, too. They all would.

A whistle shrilled out in the street; again.

"All right," he said in a different tone, and buckled on his pistol belt. "Let's go, you deep thinkers: rifles, belts, helmets, combat packs. Fall out. On the double . . ."

(2)

"Ugly frigging thing," Krazewski said. Crouching over the Chauchat automatic rifle, he yanked at the stock, twisting it on its bipod. "Look at it."

It *was* ugly. The bolt recoil section thrust back over the stock awkwardly, the left-hand grip looked as if it had been stripped from an eggbeater, the pistol grip felt angular and unpleasant to the hand. The whole contrivance might have been put together by a very imaginative and warlike nine-year-old boy. After the Springfield's clean, efficient lines it was ridiculous.

Raebyrne whistled. "What did the Froggies make it out of—salmon tins and baling wire?"

"It's ugly," Krazewski repeated sullenly.

"What do you care?" Damon said to him. "You going to enter a beauty contest with it?" He tapped the half-moon magazine. "That carries fifteen rounds. Your Springfield carries five. It's got a screen to hide muzzle flash and you can reload in less time than it takes to tell." He paused. "Anyway, we're wasting time. This is the automatic weapon they've given us and this is what we're going to use."

Krazewski rocked back on his heels and picked it up. "It's heavy."

Damon looked at the big private carefully. "It weighs eighteen pounds. The Lewis gun the Limeys use weighs twenty-six. Would you rather carry that instead?"

Krazewski swung it back and forth against his hip. "Ain't worth a frig," he rumbled. "Let somebody else take the damn thing." He stared at Damon in sullen defiance.

"For Christ sake, Kraz," Ferguson said, and Devlin began: "Now look here, Krazewski—" but Damon stopped him with a gesture. There was a silence in the two squads. He studied Krazewski a moment, his tongue in his cheek. This had been coming for some time, and now it was right here in front of him. Krazewski had been all right when they first got over. He was a huge man, not tall but mountainous in his bulk, with the slow humor of the Slav. He had been conscientious and steady, and Damon had thought of him as good NCO material; but the confinement and monotony of the training schedule, the long, chill months of drill and guard duty and police details had turned him morose and rebellious. He had been up for drunkenness twice, once for a fight with an engineer from the 17th, a man he'd beaten senseless and robbed into the bargain. Damon had read him off twice in the past week for slovenly appearance. It was too bad: if they'd gone right into combat he'd have probably done all right—but if they'd gone right into combat the battalion would have been slaughtered; and the battalion was a good deal more important than Private Stephen Krazewski of Gary, Indiana.

The Pole was still staring at Damon, his little eyes holding just a trace of crafty amusement. He was waiting to see what the Sergeant would do. Well. You stopped this kind of thing at once, or you didn't stop it at all.

"Look, Krazewski," he said. "You're the biggest man in the platoon, and you've got the makings of a reasonably fair marksman, and that's why I picked you. I still think I'm right. Now you're the Chauchat gunner for the second squad and that's all there is to it."

For answer Krazewski put the gun down and slapped his big hands against his breeches. His breath came quickly on the dry, cold air. "And suppose I say the hell with it."

The others were rigid, watching the antagonists with amazement and alarm. Sergeant Thomas' voice came clearly from another group near them on the parade ground.

Very quietly Damon said: "Krazewski, *pick up that gun.*"

Krazewski gazed back at him, motionless. Just when Sam was about to leap at him he bent slowly down and picked up the Chauchat, the very casualness of the gesture an insult. "You got the stripes on your arm, Damon."

"That's right. I do." He paused. "What's the matter—aren't you man enough to carry it?"

Krazewski's eyes narrowed to points of light. "I'm man enough to do more than that, Damon."

"All right," Sam snapped, "I'll see *you* behind the latrines after we secure. And I won't have the stripes on my arm." The Pole's eyes widened again: he hadn't foreseen this. He had sought the battle, Damon saw, but when it came in this manner it surprised him. That was good. He went on: "For now, you'll do as I say, and when I say it. Now give me that," and he deftly plucked the automatic rifle out of Krazewski's hands and turned to the others.

"All right. Now, I'm going to strip this weapon once, then you'll all do it; and then I'll do it once more." His voice was perfectly even. Raebyrne was wearing his broad grin, Devlin looked worried, Ferguson and Brewster were gazing at him in astonishment. "It is carried on the hip, for assault fire. It is most effective fired semiautomatically. The loader will keep close to the gunner at all times: it is his duty to reload—insert the clip, like this—and to take over the gun if the gunner is hit.

"Now: this is a long-recoil weapon, which means that the barrel-mount movement is over four inches. This necessitates a tube around the barrel mount—this sleeve—which retains heat excessively." They were crowded around him closely now, listening, watching him with something like awe. "Two springs are necessary for a brake system for this long barrel movement: the barrel recoil spring"—his hands were moving very quickly now, sliding and turning, setting the plates and

WHEAT (63)

coils and cylinders of metal deftly on a piece of tarpaulin—"and the bolt recoil spring. This one. Now, your key pieces are these: the extractor and extractor pin and spring—here—and the ejector—here—the firing pin, and bolt stem pin. Now, they've had a little trouble with the extractor, and the instructors' advice is for the gunner to carry a spare with him at all times." He paused. "This gun that Krazewski thinks is so ugly is what is going to give you the volume of fire on your flanks, to enable you to get in close to enemy positions." He had not once glanced at Krazewski—he knew instinctively that to ignore him completely would unsettle him more than anything else, now that the issue was joined.

"Tsonka," he said to a solidly built towheaded boy from Wyoming, "you're his loader. You will position yourself on Krazewski's right side, and feed the clips from this musette bag, as needed—like this." He paused again. "All right. Krazewski as gunner will strip the weapon first. Then Tsonka, then Raebyrne, then Turner." The silence was still impressive. He turned and looked at Brewster's thin, white, anxious face. "And the reason all of you are going to learn how to fire and operate the Chauchat automatic rifle is because if everybody in the squad gets killed but one man, I want that one man to be firing a Chauchat."

He handed the reassembled gun to Krazewski. "Okay. Go ahead." The Gary man glanced at him uncertainly, looked down. Damon shoved his hands in his pockets and watched Krazewski begin to field-strip the weapon.

"What are you going to do with him, Sam? Call in a barrage of seventy-fives on him, hit him with a log when he isn't looking?" Damon made no reply and Devlin went on, "Hell, you should have run him up. Let Crowder iron him out."

They walked quickly across the drill field toward barracks. The wind was icy cold, snow still lay on the ground in faint, powdery trails, like strewn salt; the ground crackled under their boots.

"Would you?" Sam said after a moment.

Devlin grinned and shook his head. "I don't know what the hell I'd have done."

"Well, I do." They entered the long cold room which was already empty. The Sergeant took off his overcoat, web belt and pistol and hung them up on one of the pegs at the head of his straw mattress. "Company punishment will ruin him, Dev. It'll just feed his gripe—he'll become a stockade rebel and be fit for nothing. This is between him and me: let's keep it that way. If I can't take care of him I'm not fit to wear three stripes."

Devlin watched him a moment. "You set yourself too many rules."

"Maybe."

"What if it was Jess Willard?"

Damon grinned. "Then I'd challenge him to a grenade-throwing match."

"With live grenades, I suppose. Sam, you can't always make everyone behave the way you want."

"Think so?" He handed Devlin his watch and his wallet and jack-knife. "Let's go."

"For Christ sake, keep away from him, now."

"I will."

"Don't let him get hold of you. They say he can twist horseshoes."

The latrines were set up in a muddy little field behind the stables for the officers' mounts and the remains of some old building, whose solitary wall was pocked and mossy with age. The word had spread fast; half the company was milling around the large enclosure, laughing and joking and slapping their arms against their sides to keep warm. Krazewski was standing with a blanket around his shoulders, surrounded by three or four others, among them Tukela, who also came from Gary, and who was talking to him earnestly, making short, quick little feints with his hands. Krazewski was paying no attention to the advice. Surrounded by all these well-wishers, he'd got his assurance back; catching sight of Damon he gave a thick, rumbling laugh, and called:

"Well . . . I thought for a minute there you weren't going to show up."

"When I say I'm going to do something, Krazewski, you can bet three months' pay on it."

"I thought you said there weren't going to be no stripes on your arms."

"Hold your water," Damon answered shortly. He took off his tunic and handed it to Devlin. The cold wind stung his shoulders and back. Well: he'd be warm enough in a minute or two. "All right, now," he said, raising his voice. "Give us a little room."

The chatter of talk fell away and the crowd gave back, Devlin push-ing them into a rough oval in front of the wall. Krazewski snapped the blanket from his shoulders and Tukela folded it over his arm. Damon set himself, studying the barrel chest and massive biceps. Someone called something but he was conscious only of the voice, not the words. Kra-zewski was strong as a bull, but he was not quick. He was holding his hands low, more like a wrestler than a boxer, and he was circling cau-tiously, his eyes barely visible in the thick slab of his face. You must make him lead, Damon thought. Make him come to you.

"What you waiting for, Polack?" he taunted suddenly. "More help?"

Krazewski swore and rushed at him then, his right hand drawn back like a club. Damon danced to the right and snapped a left into his face, felt the cartilage give. He ducked the right hand, drove his own right into the face again and moved away quickly. There were muttered exclamations from the crowd. Krazewski's nose was bleeding now, run-ning red into his mouth, and his eyes were wide with surprise and rage.

He came on again in a still wilder rush, swinging both hands. Damon caught the right on his arm and hit him in the eye, once more in the face, and ducked away—leaped in and belted him three more times as fast as he could move his hands. The body was no good, it was like trying to hurt a tree trunk; he would have to blind him, stun him, make him vulnerable.

Moving away from Krazewski's next rush he slipped in the mud, fell forward on his hands, thrust himself up again. The Gunner's knee caught him full in the chest. Straightening he caught a glimpse of Krazewski's face streaming blood, immensely close—and then felt a blow on the side of his head which spun him almost completely around. He moved to the left instinctively. His head was ringing. He slipped again— the ground was like wet glass now—took another blow on the cheek, and his neck cracked like a snapped stick. He got his feet under him, caught the Pole in the eye and full on the jaw. Then Krazewski was on him and had him around the body with both arms, his hands locked, and was bending him backward. He heard Devlin shout, "Let go, you stupid Polack son of a bitch!" and other voices calling: "No! No! Leave 'em alone . . ."

His lungs were burning, his head felt as though it were detached and floating in a foggy painful haze somewhere above his body. The man was strong. Terribly strong. Above him the scaly yellow wall wobbled and wavered, and Raebyrne was saying in a clear, calm voice: "I don't care if he *is* a sergeant, that's a low-down Yankee trick . . ."

He had to do something, and quickly. He drove his fists into the man's sides and it was like hitting a washboard. They swayed back and forth in the mud. He kept fighting for leverage, now gripping, now spreading his feet, wrenching and writhing against the massive arms that doubled and redoubled their viselike power. Everyone was shouting now. He heard Tukela yell, "Now, Steve!" Krazewski brought his head up sharply, and Damon felt his cheek open. Someone said, "Butting— *that's* rough enough"—a high, thin voice. The son of a bitch! All right. Anything goes, then. Anything goes. He hooked a leg behind one of Krazewski's and cocking his elbows drove his fingers into the strong man's eyes. Krazewski gave a roar of pain and bent away. Damon kicked his heel in behind Krazewski's leg and wrenched sidewise with all his might. They fell bouncing on the slick ground. He felt Krazewski's arms let go and rolled away, was up in a flash, saw the Pole scrambling to his feet, his face a comic mask of blood and yellow mud. But he was faster, he knew; he darted in, hit him once, twice, then swung his right like a ball bat. Krazewski, leaning into the blow, went down on his hands and knees, blood spattering on his powerful arms. He was shaking his head, slowly and doggedly, trying to clear it. He was dazed, Damon knew; he was halfway out. He had him.

"All right," he gasped through the bedlam of voices. "You—had enough, Krazewski?"

The Pole looked up at him, swaying like a stunned animal on all fours, slack-jawed; his eyes were filmy. Tukela was shouting, "Get up, Steve!" but Krazewski didn't hear him.

"You had enough?" Damon repeated in as calm a tone as he could manage.

Krazewski, still staring up at him, at last nodded dumbly.

"All right." Sam walked up to him and bent over. "Now, if you're not man enough to carry a Chauchat you come to me and tell me all about it and I'll give it to somebody else. You got that?"

Devlin handed him his tunic and he started to put it on, then held it in his hand; he didn't want to draw it on over all the blood and gumbo that slimed him. His ribs hurt, and his shoulder where he'd fallen on it. His cheek was slit; he could feel it stinging in the sudden cold. The circle had broken back. The rows of faces watched him, curiously silent now; it was as if they were ashamed of their bloodthirsty, feverish hilarity of a few minutes ago. He felt that cold, peculiar scorn the combatant feels for the onlooker. Only Raebyrne was grinning his broad-lipped, infectious Tarheel grin. Near him Krazewski had got heavily to one knee.

"Let's go get chow," Damon said. He'd got his wind back now, and his head had stopped slamming. "Come on, Dev. I want to wash some of this off."

He walked off through the raw dusk and the silence followed him, broken by Raebyrne's drawl: "Want to tell you, boys, we got us a stomp down, fire-eating sergeant. Kind that just loves to sort wildcats before breakfast." There was laughter then. "He hands *me* one of them catafalks I'm going to learn to shoot it if all it takes is glass aggies in a hopper . . ."

It was no kind of country at all. A few stripped and stunted trees, the shattered stone wall of a farmhouse in the shape of a camel's hump, and hundreds of crazily canted posts bearing tangles of rusty barbed wire. As far as a man could see, which wasn't very far at all. Everything lay bleak and cold in the night, and to Raebyrne it was the most stupid and pointless of official whimsies that had plucked them up out of Drouamont and dropped them in this stretch of ancient trenches where, for week after chill, sodden week, nothing happened. There had been the first nights in the line when bushes had stirred and posts had moved forward stealthily, and the night air had quivered with gunshots and alarms, and then with recriminations and stern rebukes from officers and noncoms. There had been that trench raid on the Second Battalion's sector where two men had been killed; and Johnson of B Company had been wounded when a patrol coming back in had been fired on by one of their own automatic riflemen. But that was all. The bushes and posts had returned to their inanimate status, the days and nights dragged along with work details, and out ahead and on both sides of them the front slept like a great dirty battered beast, exhausted by its blood drenchings of two years gone by; malevolent, half-stunned by cold.

"Piece of God damn foolishness," Raebyrne muttered aloud. He was lying in a shell hole about thirty feet in front of the trench, wearing hip boots and overcoat, and after two hours of this he was about as miserable as a man could feel. The hole was more than half full of icy water. By clinging to its leading edge with his elbows and drawing up his feet he could hold himself clear of the water; but as soon as he relaxed his grip his body would slowly work down in the slime and slide into the water again. His legs felt as if they were encased in iron pipes, he had a bad cold, and his head ached savagely.

"Now I didn't join up to lie in a mudhole like a worthless boar hog and peer out at a lot of barbed wire all night long," he went on. "Now damned if I did." On the early nights his own voice had frightened him, but now it helped pass the time to talk to himself and he did, gazing out at this battered, ghostly land where all those Frogs and Fritzies had shot each other up by the bushel basketful. Veer-dunn, Lieutenant Harris had called the place. Greatest battle ever fought known to man. Well, it didn't look very much like it now. Now all the fighting was in Flanders, Sergeant Damon had told them the other day. Up north. "Then why in thunder don't we sashay up there and *fight?*" Raebyrne had wanted to know. "Because you've got to learn how to be killed first," Damon had answered, "then you can go." And the platoon had laughed nervously, eyeing one another. Raebyrne snorted. He didn't hold with that kind of talk, and never would. "Those Heinies had better study up on how to get theirselves killed, it ain't going to be old Raebyrne. Not one time . . ."

Out ahead of him and to the right a rocket rose, a lazy climbing parabola of yellow, and below it a machine gun, like a deadly, persistent knocking; then darkness returned, and the silence. "Plain bedcord *fact* is, there ain't one cotton-ass Fritzie over there at all . . ."

His voice sounded puny, ineffectual, lost in this dreary eternity of cold and waiting, and he sighed. "Shoot, I could stand up and sling my old rifle and mosey all the way right into Berlin." The idea pleased him; he thought of himself creeping through the ghostly, abandoned trenches of the enemy, littered with spiked helmets and Meerschaum pipes and sea-green bottles of beer, on past woods and sleeping fields and moldering castles, across the Rhine and right on into Germany. There wasn't anybody could move through woods like old Reb. On past the barracks and hotels until he'd crept up on the palace where the Kaiser was sitting with his generals, the whole slew of them, studying up a campaign. He had slipped past a couple of stupid-looking sentries, he was in a hall as big as that train station in New York City, he'd raised his rifle as they turned toward him with the monocles popping out of their old lizard eyes. "Now you all can just sit tight where you are until I figure out how to take care of you, hear?" On the polished desk stood a phone on its cradle, a slender gold-and-silver phone, and he picked it up as casual as could be. "Just put me through to General Pershing . . . That's what I said. You want me to spell it out for you? . . . Why yes, you might call it urgent if it takes your fancy . . ."

His eyes were closed. He snapped them open and glanced around furtively. "Dark as the inside of a hairy dog," he murmured. His feet and legs were down in the water again and he drew them out groaning, and wiggled his toes unhappily. There was no feeling at all from his ankles down. "Man can get gan-garee living like this. Spasmosis." This was no kind of a war, no kind at all. He felt insufferably weary, dizzy with cold; there was a funny floating sensation at the back of his head and his eyes stung and smarted. Yesterday they'd drawn a wiring party, and the day before that they'd hauled ammunition, and now he'd been hooked for this miserable outpost duty. It was all right for Terry and Brewster and Starkie, those dauncy city folks, but it was no way for a mountain boy to waste his talents. He ought to be storming the enemy lines, picking off Fritzies like acorns on a post, or like his Grandaddy Joe at Chancellorsville, rising up all covered with Yankee blood and waving the Stars and Bars and roaring, "Come on back here—you going to leave a Tarheel to die all by his lonesome?" And the regiment had got hold of theirselves and come on back a-howling and whipped hell out of the Yankees and drove them halfway to Washington before they were through . . .

Another rocket rose, farther along, and again the short, hollow rapping of the machine gun. He snorted and cursed. There weren't any Germans over there. What there *was* was one stupid old sailor with no knot in his thread, like Noddy Fred Haislip back home, only instead of coming around cleaning out the privies and collecting slops for the tannery down at Boyne's Lick, this one padded back and forth along the trench all night with a wheelbarrow load of rockets and an oil drum and an old ramrod. Every few hundred yards or so the silly hoosier would stop and set down the barrow and pick a rocket and shoot it off and rap the oil drum a couple of times with the ramrod, and then move along again. Damn fool performance, and just what a German would do. If this was what they called fighting over here, no wonder that shorty-George Napoleon had done so well for himself.

He sneezed so violently he banged his nose against his knuckles. The fierce itching started again in the center of his chest, right under his gas mask, where he couldn't get at it, then shifted to his left armpit. "Damn old coots . . ." Of all the sad excuses for a war this one took the pitcher. That recruiting sergeant down in Boone with his great big smile—the smile of a land-office sharper, but he hadn't had the sense to see it then. "Well now, I'm looking to you boys for the straight skinnaymarinks: who's the best shot in the crowd?" Someone—Andy Ensor, probably—had pointed and said, "Orville, here." "That true, Slim?" "Sure it's true," he'd answered, before he'd thought. "Well, Slim, you look like just about what the doctor ordered." The sergeant had a hand on his shoulder now: a big, friendly hand, not too heavy, not too light. "That's what we want: men that can hit a flying squirrel in the eye in the dark of night, and fight like a barrel of wildcats into the bargain. Men that aren't afraid of the devil with horns. What do you say, Slim? Are you game?" And just what the hell could you say to that except "*Hell yes*"? And there he was, before he knew it, out front with the sergeant's arm around his shoulders, grinning like a loony at the county fair. And they hadn't even taken Andy because there was something wrong with his lungs . . .

He groaned and wiped his nose on his overcoat sleeve. All that talk about shooting up whole battalions of Fritzies and winning the craw dee jeery, and instead all he'd done was slave like a nigger toting damn fool things from one Godforsaken place to another. And now lying here in a sump hole of icy water gazing out at this pitiful country not fit for raising hogs, with the rest of the outfit snug back in the dugout sleeping away the hours. It was enough to make a man lie right down and cry like a natural child . . . Self-pity, drowsiness swept over him like golden dust; he dropped his head on his hands. Hadn't even had a chance at one of those wild Frog women. Black Jack had put them all off limits, MPs standing guard over them as if they were a bunch of society queens—if that wasn't the most sheerly *contrary* thing to find yourself in France and discover they'd turned it into a high-button camp meeting. French women knew all kinds of doozy ways of rutting, old Devlin who was half-Frog himself had told him about them one night back at Droua-mont. Worth a man's education laying out with one of them, the extraordinary things they'd do . . . His thoughts began to swirl in a slow riot of lust, finally fell back in sheer exhaustion to Maybelle on the Darbees' porch stoop, her eyes like great dark flowers, so close to his. "Orville, you know we've got to be continent. In all things." "What the Sam Hill's that?" "You know full well, Orville. Not until we're preachered up, that's what." He'd groaned in torment, their bodies straining and heavy in the summer heat, and the katydids in a wild scissors-clamor all around them. "Orville—*no!*"—and she had wrenched away despite all he could do and fled into the house, left him clutching befuddled at the trothless dark . . .

Alvina Maddow did not believe in continence, however. She herself had lain out with Andy Ensor and four of the others, he knew, but that other night it had made no difference to him, no difference at all on a voyage as mighty as that. "Did you like it, Orville?" "*Like* it," he'd breathed. "Alvina, it's the most—it's beyond—" Words nearly failed him. "It beats flying on a golden rug!" The hay was dusty against his sweaty face and neck; he heard again the sizzle chant of the katydids, the faraway moan of an owl . . .

He came awake in a dart of panic. He was pinned, a powerful figure had flung him on his back and pinned him, a hand had him by the throat, he saw the flash of a knife blade. This was not possible, not possible at all. He gave a faint, thin gasp. He wanted to be spared now, at this final instant of his life here on this lovely earth—he could not die, he wanted to surrender, yell whatever it was you yelled and he had forgotten the word. He had forgotten everything. *Trench raid* was the only clear point in the loom of terror. He was going to die: it wasn't fair! A long, relentless eternity of an instant whose sheer outrageous impossibility shocked him. The knife swept down, the fist struck him full in the chest, and with the blow air and voice came back to him.

"Oh—oh—oh!" he cried. And then: "*Kafferhaz!*" There was no pain. Then in the next instant he saw against the night sky the flat helmet, the crumpled gas mask carrier at the man's throat—and knew who it was.

"—Sarge," he gasped.

"Kamerad." Damon's voice was mocking. "You want to surrender, Raebyrne?" He raised his knife in the air. "That it?"

"Sarge, you scared me—"

"Is that right." Damon·lowered the brutal trench knife and Raebyrne felt the other hand leave his throat. "You're dead," the Sergeant said. "You know that? Dead and rotten. And they're free to walk right in there and butcher the lot of us. In our sacks. Doesn't that make you feel good, Raebyrne? knowing that?" He said softly and savagely: "You no-good son of a bitch."

"Sarge . . ." Damon had released him but he felt a complete inability to move. He was awash with a welter of conflicting emotions: he felt relief, guilt, fear, anger, resentment, he was hysterical with delight. "Sarge, I was cold—"

"Were you," Damon said. He could hear the knife going back into its scabbard, the *zlllt* of steel chafing steel, and shivered uncontrollably. "Of course that'll make all the difference in the world to them, all you've got to do is tell them that you were cold."

"Who's that, Sarge?"

"The Germans, you ninnyhammered idiot! Who did you think?" The Sergeant cursed under his breath, and Raebyrne heard him spit in disgust. Vaguely he rubbed his cheek: it was like another man's, some other man's far away. His chest hurt where Damon's fist had struck him. He felt nauseated.

"Now what kind of a trick is that?" he demanded, but his voice had no force. "Kind of way to wake up a fellow. . . ?"

Damon jabbed his collarbone with a rigid finger. "You know what you've done, don't you? You've fallen asleep on watch, on the line. You know what that means?"

"Sarge, the hours are too long . . ."

"Is that a fact. We'll have to adjust them for you."

"It's all the *water*. When my feet get cold—" Raebyrne broke off; he was seized with an almost irrepressible surge of laughter—succeeded in

less than a second by abject dread. Asleep on outpost duty. Asleep
on—

"You know what you could get. Don't you."

"I—guess so, Sarge."

"You guess so. Jesus, they're just dying to make an example of somebody like you, back there. They'll burn you at the stake."

"Yes, Sarge." He felt contrite, assailed by vague fears of courts-
martial, banks of scowling, implacable faces behind a battery of desks,
the sweating gray walls of prisons, even the black stake before the firing
squad. But nothing stayed in his head for very long; his thoughts rolled
around like marbles loose in a can. The swollen terror of that instant of
waking still held him with his teeth chattering, half-dizzy, sick at his
stomach.

"You God damned fool . . . What am I going to *do* with you?"
Damon struck his thigh, waved one arm—the arm that had held the
trench knife—wildly north and east. "They want to *kill* you, over
there! Cut your throat and leave you for the rats. Kill. *You.* Can't you
get that through your stupid Tarheel head?"

Raebyrne nodded, miserable. He had gone to sleep on watch. When
his buddies depended on him for their safety. Their lives. Even now he
could hardly comprehend what had happened. He could go to prison
for years. Years and years behind stone walls, in the dark.

"Sarge," he mumbled. "It won't happen again . . ."

"No. It won't. It sure as hell won't." There was a thick sucking sound
as Damon pulled his boots out of the water. He was staring at no man's
land. His face was visible now; for a fleeting instant the Sergeant's expression was troubled and uncertain, almost fearful—as though he could
see out in that swollen desert of muck and débris something infinitely
destructive and menacing to them all. Watching him Raebyrne was
filled with a nameless, all-pervasive affection for the Nebraskan—and an
urgent concern he could not possibly have explained. Old Sarge, he
thought awkwardly.

But when Damon looked at him again the Sergeant's face might have
been carved from flint. In a very quiet voice he said: "All right. I'm
going to give you one more chance, Raebyrne. I'm going to let you
off."

"Sarge, I—"

"Shut up. I'll do the talking. You're out and away the best marksman
among the rookies, and I think you've got the makings of a halfway
decent soldier. Maybe I'm wrong." He paused. "No man deserves another chance after an exhibition as disgraceful as this. But I'm going to
give you one. I'm going to leave this between you and me and God
Almighty . . ." All at once his hand shot out and gripped the private
between neck and shoulder, so hard he winced. "But if I ever catch you
on watch with one eye closed again, Raebyrne—if I ever see you even

blink!—I'm going to personally run your sorry ass all the way up to Black Jack Pershing and see to it they give you the Bastille for the remainder of your unnatural life. Now have you got that?"

"Yes, Sarge."

"Now get back to your post, Soldier. You *will* stay alert and observant until relieved."

"Right, Sarge."

"Right." Damon moved away in a sliding, slithering crouch, his hobnailed boots sucking and gurgling in the mud.

". . . The Bass Steel," Raebyrne mumbled. His mind was whirling in a disordered skein of images and sensations. His chest still hurt where Damon had struck him and he rubbed it tenderly, imagining instead of the Sergeant's fist a knife, the blade going down through his ribs into his vitals, his liver and lights. A rocket went up, far to his left, and he followed its tremulous course like a mole. "The Bass Steel." He was shaken all at once with a fit of laughter and doubled over helplessly against the mud, giggling and shaking.

"Old Reb," he murmured. "You almost packed it in. You almost left this kindly old world, without a flask for the journey . . ." The sweat was clammy on his forehead, his whole body was sweat-drenched now, clutched in one mountainous, trembling chill. For several moments he could not tell whether he was laughing, crying or hiccuping, or caught by all three.

"—Rugged old Sarge," he gasped finally, squinting at the charred and terrible landscape, no longer lighted by flares. The tomnoddy sailor had finally turned in. "Damn. Old Sarge really clapperclawed me, didn't he now? Treated me like something out of the midden. Now, I mean." Sniffling and hawking, watching the darkness gently lift, he felt his face slip once more into its easy grin. "Old Reb. Bouncing in the catbird seat. Let a smile be your umbrella . . ."

3

The road was jammed with refugees. Away to the north, artillery rumbled and shuddered, and the crowds surged toward the column as though blown ahead of the gusty mutter of the guns. The platoon peered at them as they streamed past—gnarled old men in berets and baggy trousers, women hooded in black shawls, bony horses pulling wagons that held chests and quilts and iron kettles and the dark, carved posts of bedsteads. All were walking except the sick and the very old. There were carriages Damon would never have imagined still existed: stylish cabriolets with cracked leather calash hoods, ancient tumbrils

with massive iron-bound wheels that could have borne nobles to the
guillotine, sulky-bodied phaëtons from the days of the Second Empire,
from whose windows elderly faces wreathed in black lace gazed fearfully. There were painted carts pulled by dogs, and wheelbarrows
pushed by little boys in sabots with grimy, tear-stained faces; there was
even a post coach listing drunkenly on a broken spring. They were all
piled high with the treasures of ten thousand abandoned homes: Limoges pitchers and rosewood clocks and chased hourglass cages where
parakeets clung and screamed. Women and children and old men, coming like the ocher froth on the leading edge of a flood tide, well-to-do
and poor commingled, indistinguishable in the endless, pitiful processional. A world is on the edge of falling, Damon thought, and his belly
felt hot with anger. But it will not fall, because we are here.

Now and then a farmer would wave to the column—a brief, half-
hearted gesture abandoned almost as soon as begun; occasionally a
woman would try to smile, but this was rare. The horde of faces were
gray with terror and fatigue. They had been turned out of their homes
the day before, and now the Germans were in them, looting and smashing. They knew. After four years the war had reached out without
warning and caught them in its iron fist, and nothing would ever be the
same for them. Walking in laced leather shoes or wooden sabots or bare-
foot they came on, clutching to their bosoms rabbits or pullets or shiny
copper pots. Now and then a mirror piled high in a carriage among
feather mattresses and armoires would flash like a shield in the hot sun,
dazzling the eyes of the platoon marching along the right-hand side of
the road.

"Look at 'em all—"

"Hightailing it ahead of the God dayamn Pee-roossians."

"Yes, and so would you, Reb. My God, half the country must be
running away . . ."

Farther on, in a little village square, hundreds of people were lying on
the dirty cobbles. They stared at the column dully, too weary now for
hope or wonder. A little girl in a pink pinafore dress was standing in her
grandfather's arms and wailing softly, her mouth drawn down in the age-
old expression of a child's anguish, deep and boundless. Turner muttered
something wrathfully, and Raebyrne called: "Don't you fret none,
honey girl, we'll get you back home. Those Fritzies ain't seen *us* in
action yet . . ."

"All right," Damon said. "Dress it up, now."

Yet it was sobering. Earlier in the day the platoon had been in high
spirits, calling out greetings and encouragement; but the steady onrush
of these frightened, despairing multitudes, coupled with thirst and heat
and the strain of the forced march from Drouamont, had begun to tell
on them. Gradually they became irritable, then sullen and unsure. There
was no end to this hot, dusty, undulating country, these powdery roads
lined with the gaunt black silhouettes of poplars.

"What kind of trees are those?" Tsonka wanted to know.

"Well, they're skirmisher trees," Raebyrne answered.

"Why skirmisher trees?"

"Because they keep advancing by line of skirmishers no matter where you find them. They never bunch up and they never go to prone position. They're just good, steady skirmishers."

"Well, they're not very damn much for shade . . ."

The guns were louder now, a steady, billowing rumble; drums beaten by malicious children. To their right were little rolling hills, and sloping fields furry with grain, and patches of dense woodland. They swung along, thirty-two inches to the stride, rolling their shoulders and flexing their arms against the numbing grip of the packs. They passed a farmhouse, barren and ghostly in the late afternoon light. In the next field a French battery was firing, the gunners pulling the lanyards as fast as the loaders could slam the breeches: a mesmeric frenzy. Damon watched them as they moved past; they were tired, unshaven, they stumbled when they tried to avoid each other, passing shells. Beyond those hills, then, were the Germans, divisions and divisions of them, coming like doom under a gray helmet. They had broken through at Cambrai, they had broken through at St. Quentin and the Chemin des Dames, they had all at once taken more ground than either side in four terrible years. They were going to try to wind it up now, cross the Marne, swing west and envelop Paris, but from the south this time . . . He felt it in his very bones: this was the moment, there would be no other.

"What I'd like to know is, where are we?" Brewster said.

"What difference does it make?" Devlin answered him. "You go where they point you."

"Yes, but I'd still like to know. It gives me a sense of—it gives me a sense of orientation."

"I saw a sign that said Poux," Turner volunteered.

"Poo yourself. I didn't see any sign that said Poo . . ."

"We're heading for Briny Deep," Raebyrne proclaimed. "Spotted it on that red-capped gravestone down the road a piece."

"Who in hell ever heard of a town called Briny Deep?"

Raebyrne thrust out his lower lip and spat. "That's where we're heading, all the same."

The room was narrow and had no ceiling. Most of the officers and sergeants of the battalion were packed into it; huddled around Major Caldwell, who was talking clearly and rapidly. A French one-to-twenty-thousand map—the only map of the area the battalion had—was resting on a shattered armoire; the Major's shoulder now and then moved as his finger traveled over its surface.

". . . and B Company will deploy along the high ground about a hundred yards beyond the railroad embankment—here. The French Two fifty-ninth is already dug in in the woods to the east of Brigny-le-Thiep, here. It will be B Company's responsibility to maintain contact with the French. It is expected that the main weight of the enemy attack will come from Cherseulles, with Brigny as its main objective . . ."

By rising on his toes and peering down between two heads Damon could see most of the map. There was what looked like a very broad meadow curving southwest toward Nantseche, where they now were. To the east were dense woods in a long, scarflike crescent, to the west patches of woodland surrounding a cluster of buildings—Raebyrne's Briny Deep. South and east of the town, beyond the railroad and nearly centered between the wooded areas were what looked like two isolated buildings, probably a farm.

"General Benoît-Guesclin has issued express orders that our positions are to be held at all costs. If dislodged from our original positions, unit commanders will counterattack vigorously to recover them." The Major paused. "Are there any questions?"

Captain Hillebrand of C Company said: "Is the enemy strength at Cherseulles known, sir?"

"No. It is not even certain that the Germans hold it. All we know is that the French have taken a terrible pounding and are falling back rapidly. Elements of the Fifth Prussian Guards Division and the Fifteenth Grenadiers have been definitely identified."

"Sir," Captain Crowder said, "my company still hasn't any grenades."

Major Caldwell looked back at him impassively. "There are no grenades. They haven't come up and they probably won't."

There was a silence in the room. The booming of the guns was heavier now. Lieutenant Jamison, the Yale boy, said: "Artillery is in a bad way, Major—Captain Henchey says the one fifty-fives are certain to be delayed for several hours. What are we to do if we don't receive any counterbattery support?"

Caldwell raised his head. "We must go it without them." There was another pause. A flock of shells shrilled overhead, a high whistling sibilance, and crashed a hundred yards away, and the room's occupants gave a little restless stir. Damon, his eyes on Caldwell, noticed that the Major had not moved a muscle.

"I'm sure I don't have to remind you gentlemen that the situation is grave, to put it mildly. We are entering the line at a crucial moment, a desperate moment. A great deal—a very great deal—will hinge on the quality of our efforts here." His gaze passed over the massed faces in front of him. "All eyes are upon us. We are a part of the first participation of American arms in this long and cruel war. There are those who are convinced that we Americans are lacking in audacity, in élan, in fortitude. That we will not and cannot fight. There are even those—and they are not simply the Germans"—his eyes flashed in the dim light—"who will rejoice if we should fail. I am counting on each and every one of you to give the lie to those foolish conjectures . . ." Another flight of

shells arched overhead and exploded close by; the Major put his hands
on the map. "There is no time to lose. Make your troop dispositions as
rapidly as possible. Make your orders brief ones, and above all encourage the greatest possible use of individual initiative by the men of your
commands." He gave a brief, mournful smile. "Good luck to all of you.
Dismiss."

The platoon was sprawled in the courtyard of a house, slumped
against the stone, when Damon and Lieutenant Harris came up. As
the men fell in, two others came straggling across the street—Ferguson
carrying an iron pot, Raebyrne with a bottle of wine and what looked
like a great pink corset adorned with ribbons and bows.

"Where the hell have you two been?" Damon demanded.

"Just a little happy foraging, Sarge."

Damon suppressed a smile. "You damn fools. All right, fall in . . ."

They stepped off in two files, moving gently uphill; and darkness
came like a breath of wind. There was a heavy low mass on the right,
woods, and later a row of poplars on the skyline. The pace was rapid;
hills and valleys came and went, their feet began to hurt, the pack straps
cut more deeply into their shoulders. They entered a patch of woods, a
pathway gray and ghostly in the dark, came out at the edge of a vast
wheatfield damp with dew. Shells came over again with their high, taut
sigh, and burst deep in the woods they had left. Walking on, they came
over the crest of a hill, and suddenly they heard it: the sound of a
machine gun. Dod dod dod. Dod dod dod dod dod. Then another—a
lighter, flatter sound, and after that the whine and crack of rifle fire.
Damon could feel the column tremble like an animal.

"Close it up," he said, his voice lower. "Close it up, now."

"Going to be rougher than a cob trying to get a little shut-eye around
here," Raebyrne observed genially. "That's the trouble with war,
you—"

Out ahead of them there rose the swift rush of vertical light, and
Damon called out: "*Stand fast!*" The column went rigid. There was a
flat crack and the flare started its slow descent, drifting softly, swaying
in the summer night like an indescribably beautiful, lustrous flower
sinking through water, and around them hills and woods and walled
ruins leaped into view starkly, without depth: a fairy stage set. The
column was still as death, their faces white and childlike under the dish
rim of their helmets, and to Damon it was as if he were seeing them all
for the first time: brash, uncertain, voluble, happy-go-lucky, resentful—
and as vulnerable as flesh alone can be. Going toward battle. The men
he'd trained and threatened and cajoled, who were now standing fast, as
he'd bidden them, without a ripple or a flutter. For the briefest of
instants, gazing at their bright, eager faces he was swept with the most

fierce and exultant pride—and then with the deepest, darkest sadness he had ever felt in all his life.

Then the flare went out, and darkness rushed back over them all like a cool hand. "All right," Damon called flatly. "Move out, now . . ."

"You'd think they could have got us grenades," Lieutenant Harris said. "My God, when you think of all the dumps cram-jam full of ammunition we passed coming from Charmevillers . . . What time is it?"

"Quarter to eleven," Damon answered.

"Quarter to eleven. Do you think we'll get a counterbarrage?"

"Yes, sir. I do." Actually he wasn't at all sure. There had been a haste about the whole two days, an atmosphere of confusion and improvisation that disturbed him; but it seemed better to show confidence now.

"I wish we knew where the front line was," Harris went on. He was a volunteer officer from Plattsburg and he was trying very hard not to show his fear, which was making him garrulous. "I'd feel a lot better if we knew for certain whether the Germans were in Cherseulles . . ."

Damon made no reply. He knew that what Harris meant was that he was unhappy about their position; he was himself. Why were they placed here out in front of the railroad embankment, facing rising ground? It felt all wrong; they ought to be dug in on the leading edge of the embankment itself, and at the edge of the woods . . . But you obeyed orders; and the orders of the French command had been to dig in here.

"What's that—over there?" Harris muttered. "If you could only *see* . . ."

There was movement on their right. Men were coming out of the woods, hurrying through the wheat, and in the dim light Damon made out the curved and crested helmets, heard the liquid patter of their talk.

"French," he said.

"What are they doing?" Harris asked.

"Dev," Damon said, raising his voice, "ask them what's up, will you?"

The group came through them, hurrying. One man was limping, giving a quick, tight groan every time his wounded foot touched the earth. Two others were lugging an assembled Hotchkiss gun, stumbling and panting over the uneven ground.

"Qu'est-ce qui se passe?" Devlin called. The men struggling with the Hotchkiss gun glanced in his direction, said nothing. Several more Frenchmen streamed by, and now Damon could see that their uniforms were filthy and torn to ribbons; some had abandoned or lost most of their equipment. "Les Boches sont là-bas?" Devlin called again, pointing over the hill, the bristling palisade of woods to their right.

A tall man, helmetless, with a dark-stained bandage around his head, swung toward them and said: "Oui, Boches, Boches, bien sûr—qu'est-ce que tu pense? des Esquimaux?"

"Then what you Froggies cutting and running for?" Raebyrne asked him.

The wounded Frenchman stopped momentarily, arrested by the tone rather than the words; his teeth flashed once in a savage grin. "Aaah— attendez un peu, hein? A vous le dé . . ." He nodded fiercely, glaring at them. "On verra, alors—vous sautillerez comme des lapins, vous! Petites soeurs . . ."

Devlin started to climb out of his hole. Damon, guessing at the epithet, said sharply: "Dev! Stay where you are. Reb, you button up your lip. They've had a hard time of it . . ."

Another clump of French straggled by, gasping and muttering, and vanished in the darkness. The place seemed infinitely lonely, bound in the thunder and crash of guns. Damon thought of the tough veterans facing them across the Court of Honor of the Invalides that hot, still morning almost a year ago, their faintly amused contempt, and thought: It must be bad, up there. Very bad. To make them come all apart like this—

He heard the taut sigh of approaching shells, a leisured trajectory that all at once began to accelerate, grew deeper in tone, hoarser, thicker, bending down—struck with a violent flash of orange light full in their midst. The ground under them lifted and shook, a quick, murderous jarring, and bits of steel spattered in the wheat.

Damon jumped to his feet and called, "Anybody hit?"

"Stretcher-bearer," a voice on his left cried tensely. "Stretcher-bearer . . . !"

He moved quickly along the line of foxholes. More shells swept overhead and crashed thunderously in the rear of the woods. He heard voices, came upon two figures fussing with a third, which was inert. "Who is it?" he said crisply.

"It's Van Gelder," came a voice which Damon recognized as Brewster's. "He's been hurt . . ."

Van Gelder, a stout, pleasant boy from Michigan, was lying perfectly still, breathing in short, swift pants. Damon put his hands on him.

"It's his back," Brewster said.

"How do you know?" This was Poletti.

"I heard it. It hit him in the back. It sounded as if someone had slapped him. I could hear it."

"All right," Damon said. He passed his hands down Van Gelder's back—his fingers plunged all at once into a deep, slick groove in the boy's shirt. There was an instant's hot repugnance, then an icy calm flooded with the need for action.

"One minute he was all right," Brewster was going on rapidly, "he

was just starting to say something to me—and the next there was this
slap and he let out a cry—"

"All right," Damon cut him off. "Take it easy, now." He faced rear
and shouted, "Stretcher-bearer!"—his voice nearly drowned in the roar
of shelling. Several shadows rose out of the gloom. "Over here," Damon
called.

The medics gathered around Van Gelder. "He hurt bad?" one of
them asked.

"No," Damon said, although he wasn't at all sure of this; he knew
Brewster and Poletti were listening intently, and he felt that Van Gelder
was still conscious, in spite of his silence. "But he'd better go back, all
right."

They lifted Van Gelder on to the stretcher, which went taut with his
weight. He gave a sharp cry, and then the thick panting began again.

"It's all right," Damon said, bending down. "They'll take care of you.
Just relax, now."

"—I was looking right at him," Brewster was saying hurriedly. "He
was just starting to dig his hole a little deeper, he was bent over—"

Damon looked up. Several of them were milling around, talking, listening to Brewster, asking questions. "Get back in your holes," he said
roughly. "What's the matter with you people—you want to get pep-
pered? Get back in your holes and check your weapons . . ."

He watched the medics move off toward the black screen of the
woods. First casualty, he thought; first man down. Who'll be the last?

His watch said 11:42; the hands, the numerals, looked green and
ghostly. Twelve o'clock, midnight—the barrage would open at midnight, and the attack would follow at 12:30 or so. It would be just like
the Germans to open up on the dot of twelve. He crept from hole to
hole, checking his squads. Ferguson, rat-faced and debonaire; Poletti,
nervous and very silent; little Turner, irate with impatience.

"Well, are the bastards coming or aren't they?"

"They're coming all right. Hold your water."

Krazewski, his big face flat and solid, fixing a clip to that ugly, long-
snouted beast of a Chauchat. "Keep that thing firing, now," Sam said.

"Damon."

"Yes?"

Krazewski snorted wetly through his nose. Since that afternoon behind the latrines he had consistently displayed the cleanest weapon and
become a marvel at field-stripping. Damon had praised him twice,
briefly, but the big man had made no response. Now he was grinning,
his face like a flat, sweaty moon. "I—just wanted to tell you. You're all
right."

Damon slapped the gunner on the shoulder for answer, crept on to

Tsonka, who had the stump of an unlighted cigar sticking straight out between his teeth. He would gradually chew it up entire; he was rarely known to spit. "Stick with him now, Tsonka. If Kraz is hit, it's your gun."

"Right, Sarge."

Raebyrne's skinny profile, the broad grin. "Sarge!" This uttered in a heavy stage whisper. "What am I going to do with these?" He held up what looked like a cloth sack.

"What's that?"

"Four honest-to-God hen's eggs, Sarge. Scrowged them out of that farm down the road a piece. I got time to cook 'em up a little?"

"*Cook* 'em! I *told* you no fires—" Damon had an urge to roar with laughter. "What the hell do you think this is, a church supper?"

"Jesus, Sarge, I can't eat 'em *raw! . . .*"

"Well, you can't eat them any *other* way, I'll tell you that. Knock the tops off with your knife and suck 'em clean. That's what the rich do," he added.

"The rich?"

"Sure—rich folks in town houses in Chicago. Boat-club swells." He had a swift vision of his Uncle Bill sitting by the table on the screen porch, his face flushed with beer, one arm gesticulating. "It's all the rage." He moved along to Brewster and said: "All set?"

The boy nodded, then shook his head. "Cold," he murmured.

"*Cold!*" Damon exclaimed. His own face and neck were slick with sweat.

Brewster nodded rapidly; he made a sharp little sound low in his throat, and licked his lips.

The Sergeant reached out and gripped Brewster's arm. "You'll do all right . . . Don't *think* so much! Just do what you have to do . . ." And with a final shake: "Be hard!"

And then Devlin, looking Irish and tough, his chin jutting out against the helmet's tight leather strap. "All set, Dev?"

"All set, Sam."

"Keep your eye on the Chauchat teams, won't you."

"Right you are."

He paused; Devlin was still watching him, he knew. "Good luck, Dev."

"Good luck, Sam."

The night was terrible. There were these tremulous sighs that mounted to a shriek, swooped in awful descent like some enormous blade scoring the vast black vault of the sky, and struck in mountainous crashes that lifted Brewster in all his frailty and flung him to and fro in his hole. At first he had wanted to get up and run, to flee into the woods from this place of darkness and terrors—once he'd started to climb out of his hole and Devlin had roared at him: "Get—down!" and he'd obeyed. Now the very thought of leaving this little place of safety was as unendurable as staying in it had been before. Shriek mounted upon arching shriek—and then vast jarring concussions that battered and buffeted him, turned him into a gasping, cringing rag doll. Where was he? Where was anybody? at all? A huge weight drove straight down upon him, smashed all his senses awry and fluttering. There, he thought, *there*, all right—but there was no end to the squeals and hammer blows. He could hear nothing, see nothing. He crouched lower and lower, clawing at the damp earth with his fingers in an agony of need, while the old soft world spat and heaved in an orgy of shattering, and train-loads of iron were hurled into factories of glass. No more, he thought, please no more, now—finally became aware that he was screaming the words like a child: "*No—more—please please—no more!*"

There was a little lull then; and his ears ringing, his sight marred by brilliant, darting rings and blotches, he remembered a football game back at St. Andrew's, a scrimmage with the varsity—he had been too small even to dream of playing on the varsity—a moment of feverish apprehension and then bodies far bigger and harder than his had come at him weaving and diving, had struck him down and rolled over him, leaving him trampled, ignominious, and thundered on; the torn earth of the football field had smelled and tasted like this earth. His nose had bled. Now they were doing it again. All over again. He discovered he was biting hard on the back of his hand. Never should have got into this, he moaned, or thought he moaned. Never should have come here. To this place . . .

There was a flat crash near him, another. He looked up, and around him the world burst into light—but light like some kingdom of the mad: an eerie, blue-white field struck with dark shadow, day without depth. An evil dream of light in which nothing looked the way it should, nothing at all. There was the embankment, the screen of trees to the left, but smashed and stripped now like mammoth cornstalks rent and dangling . . . He was facing backward. Was he? Jesus! He turned and saw in the crazy, subterranean shimmer a low black lump like an animal crawling, or rolling—a furry mass that split apart in clumps and piles, in figures swelling, jostling up and down. He saw the swept-down helmets glinting under the flare's evil glow, and was filled with dread so great it choked him. Those were—those were Germans. And they were coming to kill him. Thousands of them. To kill him—

The flare went out and darkness swooped in over him and blinded him. He heard firing close by, a Chauchat's dry, hiccuping rhythm, and someone was shouting in a clear, hard voice; but he could not understand one word. The tone reached him though, its threatful urgency, and he pushed his rifle out ahead of him and began to fire into the sparks and chains of light that hurt his eyes—kept firing, flinching with the recoil each time, heard nothing, realized his rifle was empty.

He gazed around him in a panic, could make out nothing in the awful, flash-shot din. Someone was screaming in a high, shrill voice, like a dog yelping. In pain. Someone in terrible pain. He clawed a clip out of his cartridge belt, a reflex action, hearing the thump and clatter of running men, their onrushing proximity; dropped the clip and ducked down and scrabbled for it in the dark, could not find it anywhere, conscious now of screams and hoarse cries, the dense roar of explosions all around him. Something slammed against the top of his helmet and his face struck the earth with an impact that momentarily stunned him. I'm dying, he thought with quaking awful protest, oh dear God, I'm dying now, God help me, it's all over, all the things I—

Something drove down on his back, dirt showered over his neck and arms. A boot, a man's boot. He cried out in pain. It was gone. Explosions swept him, drove him lower. *Stop this*, he was crying frankly now, *oh stop this awful, awful thing!* He had no sight, no sense, no functions—lay crushed like a potato sack and wanted only for it all to be over, just be over, forever and for good . . .

When he stirred again he was amazed at the stillness. He was here. In this hole. He was alive. He started to move, felt the pain in his back, stopped and reached around gingerly; there was nothing. His other hand encountered an object, a hard, round object. He pushed at it, picked it up and hefted it curiously. It was a German grenade. Potato masher. He let it drop in a slow wave of fear. That had been lying there. Beside him. For how long? With tremendous revulsion he reached out and picked it up again and tossed it out of his hole, heard it hit with a soft thud a few feet away. Then he felt consternation: suppose it should still go off—it could hurt someone else nearby. He raised his head. Far behind him he could hear the snare drum rattle of small-arms fire.

"Starkie?" he called softly. "Starkie? Corporal Devlin?" There was no answer. He was alone. He was here all alone, they had all run off and left him here in the open, to face everything all by himself. He felt a longing for the close presence of someone, anyone, so great he could have wept. He glared about wildly, but could see nothing but blobs and chains of gray streaming on blackness. This was terrible: if he could only *see*—!

He rose to his feet. Over to his left he heard voices. He had opened his mouth to call when one of them said: "Nein, nein, ist nicht schwer. Fleischwunde . . ."

Brewster sank back into his hole. All the fear he'd felt before was nothing to the boundless dread that gripped him now. Surrounded. He was alone, and surrounded by the enemy. In the dark.

"Wo ist Schroeder?" the wounded man asked. Firing to the south swelled up again, and Brewster couldn't hear the answer. The two men talked in low voices for a moment.

"Dieser Stacheldraht—er ist bösartig . . ."

"Kannst du weiterziehen?"

"Ja, sicher—bin erschöpft, weiter nichts . . . Halts fern von der Walde, he? Rechts, immer rechts, durch die Wiesen . . . Du sollst drängen."

"Richtig. Hals und Bein bruch."

"Hals und Bein bruch . . ."

Their voices faded, were lost in the distant roar of gunfire. Brewster strained to hear the rest of what they said. He was too afraid even to call out to them to surrender. Off to the right he heard horses, and the faint jingle of harness, the thin squeak of axles. Away. He had to get away from here. But where in God's name could he go?

Time went by. It seemed darker than ever, if anything. I'll wait till daylight and then give myself up, he told himself flatly, struggling to maintain a semblance of calm. There's no hope for me anymore—stuck out here like this. That grenade didn't go off and that's why I'm alive. They can't expect any more from me. I'll wait till daybreak and then surrender. That's the thing to do.

He heard movement close by, and froze. A man crawling, very near. Now he had stopped. Behind him and to the left. He lifted his rifle from the bottom of the hole, remembered it was empty and crouched there holding it, put it down again. "—Don't shoot," he started to say, but no words came out. Slowly he raised his hands above his head.

The figure moved again, a voice said, very softly: "B Company? First platoon?" A tone perfectly calm. "Starkie? Turner?" All at once Brewster recognized the voice—Sergeant Damon—and shivered with relief.

"No," he murmured, and lowered his arms. "Brewster."

"You all right?"

"I think—yes. I am." He was trembling violently and clenched his hands together. "Where is everybody?" He heard Damon off to his right and whispered loudly, "Sarge—wait . . ."

"Shut up," Damon murmured. Brewster could hear him pulling at something.

"What's the matter?"

There was a little pause. Then Damon muttered, "It's Starkie."

"Right over there?"

"Yes. He's dead."

Starkie was dead. Starkie, who had slept in the cot right next to his at Drouamont, who had that way of opening his mouth in silent laughter —Starkie who was collecting picture postcards of all the bridges in the world, was dead. Had been there in that hole, dead, all this time . . .

"Why didn't you pull out?" Damon had crawled near him again.

"What?" he stammered.

"If you're all right, why didn't you pull back?"

"I— couldn't . . ." He heard the tight, dry chink of metal on metal. "What are you doing?"

"Taking Starkie's clips. I was almost out of ammunition . . ."

Ammunition. How in the name of God could he think of *ammunition*—

"Come on. We've got to get out of here." Brewster was silent, shivering. Damon crept up to him, resting with his face so close Brewster could feel the Sergeant's breath against his eyelids. "Come on, now. We've got to make a break for it."

"Wait," Brewster whispered. The thought of leaving his hole was unbearable. "To go where?"

"Where the hell do you think? Back to our lines."

"Oh." He said suddenly: "There are Germans. Over there."

"I know. I heard them."

"They said to keep clear of the woods."

"They said that?"

"Yes. One told the other. To keep to the right and go through the meadow."

Damon paused. "Good. That's all right, Brewster. Good going. Come on, now."

"Wait—"

"You got your rifle?"

"Yes." He nodded dumbly. "But—it's not loaded."

"*Load* it, then . . ."

Damon was irritated with him, he could tell from his voice. He got a clip out of his belt and inserted it, wincing at the noise it made. The firing had died away to a sporadic rattle and pop, and still farther off the short stammer of a machine gun.

"We're going to crawl over that way," the Sergeant was saying. "Toward those woods."

Brewster said: "Where *is* everybody?"

"I don't know. Come on. Keep close to me. To my right leg."

"You mean we're all there *is?*" The thought of their being just the two of them was frightening, in spite of Damon's presence; a part of his mind was still clinging to the idea that the rest of the platoon was somewhere nearby, right behind the embankment or in the woods.

"Come on, now," Damon ordered him.

"—Don't you think we'd better wait?" Brewster whispered suddenly.

"What for?" The Sergeant had thrust his face close again. "Now listen here, Brewster. You're hauling your ass out of that hole and coming with me and that's all there is to it. Now, come on!"

He heard Damon start crawling away. He nearly screamed out, "*Wait!*" wriggled out of his hole then and began to creep along behind the Sergeant. The wheat was trampled now in long swatches, as if enormous animals had wrestled and rolled in it; the broken stalks pricked his cheeks and hands. Ahead of him Damon paused, shifted to the left. Moving on, Brewster felt cloth, an outflung hand: rough fabric, slick leather, a stench of body odor so strong it was sickening—and then the sweet, dense smell of blood. A German. Dead German. He wiped his hand on his shirtfront and clenched his teeth. He could see things better now, a little better: shadows of woods, of packs and bodies in the lighter gray shadows of the wheat. Firing rose, a swift, rattling crescendo far beyond them. His heart was thumping in an even rhythm; he felt helpless and exposed, crawling through this murderous, open field. He had to cough, he had to sneeze even more, he made a thick, gulping sound trying to suppress them. The noise they were making—the steady rustle and scrape—moving through the field was horrifying. When he heard voices again, ahead of them and to their right, he knew even before he'd made out a single word that they were German. It sounded like several men; their talk grew louder and more distinct with each second.

Damon's hand was on his neck. "We've got to run for it. Now. Get up and run for the woods."

"Run?" he echoed weakly. "Stand up and *run?*"

"Yes. It's the only way. Come on. Get set."

"I— can't, Sarge . . ."

"You can," Damon hissed at him. "You've got to!" The hand gripped him with fierce insistence. "Brewster. Come on."

"Don't leave me, Sarge. Don't leave me here—"

"*Do* as I say!—do you hear?"

"No, Sarge. I—"

Hands plucked at him, yanked him to his feet. He stood there swaying, his teeth chattering uncontrollably, started to mouth a protest— heard Damon's rifle right beside him, an absurdly loud crashing roar that half-deafened him, and saw the bright cone of flame from the muzzle. The shot released him. There was a scream and then a chorus of shouts, but he paid no attention to them now: he was running with all his might through the wheat, racing toward the woods with a speed he didn't know he possessed. He flew over the ground, ran right past Damon, who was singing for air. Tracers burned out into the night sky like red-hot wires, crisscrossing. Someone howled with pain, and a deep voice roared: "—Unterlassen Sie das, Ihr verrückten Bastarden!"

"Crazy bastards," he breathed. Running toward the dense mass of the woods under the seesawing tracers he was invaded by a wild, teeth-clenched mood of hilarity. Something droned past his right ear, like the plucking of a taut string, and he gasped in glee. Then he was in the woods, and an absolute dark washed over him. He leaned against a tree trunk, his mouth so dry it hurt him, his head pounding as though it would burst. But now he was safe.

Damon's hand shook him. The big man could hardly speak. "Now. We move—out. Follow me."

"But which—*way?*" he panted.

"Tree to tree. Pick one out and move to it. Then another."

"I can't *see* . . ."

"Like cowboys—and Indians. All right?"

Like cowboys and Indians. He started to giggle, choked it off. If Mother could see me, he thought. Here. Now. In these woods. Then fear of losing Damon absorbed him, right to his fingers and toes. He could see nothing, groped warily ahead until his hand struck the bark of a tree, then crept on, listening for the Sergeant's movements. Suddenly he could see a little: the trunks of the pines were a little blacker than the dark of the woods. The difficulty was in moving without making any noise. He kept stumbling, hooking his feet on roots, on dead limbs. Branches whipped him in the face and drove him frantic; when he stepped on some dead leaves it sounded like kicking bags of broken glass. What in God's name were they trying to do? How did Damon know what direction to *take?* Everyone was gone and here they were wandering around in pitch-dark woods—

There was a sound of movement. To their right. Not where Sergeant Damon was. He froze by a tree, his mouth opened wide to silence his own breathing. Someone was moving straight toward Damon, then he had stopped. Brewster tried to raise his rifle, found he could not. His whole body was shaking with every heartbeat, and his hands had no sensation. For an instant he wanted to scream something, anything, and crash off through the woods; then that passed and he felt suddenly very alert, completely aware of all that was going on around him.

The man took two or three more steps: he should be almost exactly where Damon was. "Konrad?" the man said once, tentatively; his voice was unbearably loud in the close dark of the woods. Why, he's afraid, Brewster thought in amazement; he's more afraid than I am. He raised his rifle calmly.

"—Konrad?" the man repeated. "Wo sind—"

Before he could fire there was a thick, meaty sound, a grunt; the slow, even rustle of leaves, and then stillness. Brewster went carefully toward this tiny commotion, holding his rifle at his shoulder.

"Brewster?" Damon's voice came.

"Yes."

"Let's go."

"What happened, Sarge?"

"I slugged him."

"Jesus." The man lay slumped by the trunk of the tree, a part of it now in the darkness.

"He's either a stray, or lost from a patrol. Let's get going."

For a time it was quite still; even the distant firing had faded. After the monstrous uproar of the bombardment, the collapsing walls of shock and the fury of the German attack, the silence seemed like a precious and tangible thing. Brewster could hear a frog croaking in some marshy place nearby. The pine needles here and there muffled their footsteps perfectly. He felt more confidence as his vision grew keener. As a child he had always been afraid of the dark; his most fearsome memory was a night when his parents had gone to the opera and the power had gone off while he was upstairs in his bedroom reading Conan Doyle—an onrush of sheer blackness without warning so sudden he had only gasped once, then lain rigid with the big book across his belly, while the darkness, swollen with terrors, descended on him pitilessly. After a very long time he had crept out of bed and lighted a candle—and his own shadow guttering and leaping along the wall had frightened him even more. But he *had* got out of bed and lighted the candle . . .

"Sarge," he whispered hoarsely when he caught up with him again. "It must be almost dawn . . ."

Damon nodded; his face was gray, with a web of tiny lines under his eyes. "We've got to be more careful. Don't fire at anything unless your life depends on it. If you do you'll alert the whole German army."

They worked their way along to the south and west, following a little ridge above a wood road. Twice more they heard men talking in German, and once they sank out of sight just as an artillery team trotted back along the road, heading toward the German rear. The riders were slumped over their saddles, their heads rocking, nearly asleep.

The ridge ended abruptly at the edge of a little ravine. The path ran down it for a way, between rock outcroppings covered with vines and old leaves. For some reason Brewster could not explain, the little gully filled him with dread. It looked exposed—so sunk in its depression, so bare of cover. To stop Damon he touched him on the shoulder and said: "Where are we going?"

Damon's brows rose. "Back to our own lines. Where'd you think?"

"—We'll never make it back, Sarge."

"Sure we will. Of course we will. I'll bet you my next month's pay against yours."

The Sergeant was grinning at him. "Hang on, Brewster. You're doing fine."

It was much lighter now; through the breaks in the foliage overhead the sky was pearl and lavender behind the clouds. Moisture dripped from the branches. They started down the gully, crossed it, and entered the woods again. A horseman was riding hard through the field at the edge of the woods to their right—an officer in an immaculate gray uniform, the bill of his cap drawn low over his eyes. His saber and the horse's bridle made a loud jingling in the dawn stillness.

"Hurrying back with the good news," Damon muttered, and spat. "Sons of bitches"—and Brewster was surprised at the anger in the Sergeant's voice.

The land ran downhill now; the trees thinned and the path wandered through dense banks of shrubs. They followed it in cautious little advances of twenty to thirty feet, pausing and peering ahead through the trees. Brewster had just come up to Damon and was about to say something to him when he saw the Sergeant stiffen. Below them, coming across the field, they could see a file of men walking.

"Prisoners," Damon murmured.

Peering down Brewster counted six of them, three struggling with a wounded man carried on a stretcher, and two others. They were guarded by two Germans, one at the front and one in the rear of the little column. They kept passing and repassing behind the screen of trees. The Americans looked awkward and weary, particularly the three struggling with the improvised stretcher, which was made out of two rifles and a poncho; the wounded man lay inert, his bare head lolling against the chest of the man at the rear. They're coming this way, Brewster thought in a flash of panic, they're going to come up this path. Right past us. But he couldn't avert his gaze. One of the men carrying the stretcher stumbled, and the guard at the rear shoved at him roughly. The American threw up his head in protest, snarled something. His face caught the light: an angular, bony face, a broad mouth—

"Sarge," he whispered, "—it's Reb! that's Reb! And that's Poletti with him . . ."

"You're right."

"And there's Corporal Devlin—"

Damon grunted. "Where?"

"In front. Walking alone. With that rag around his head. See him?"

They were easily recognizable now. They came along the path slowly, stumbling and slipping on the slope, the bushes swinging wildly as they passed. Their faces looked dejected and whipped. Only two of them still had their helmets. Corporal Devlin, then someone Brewster didn't know, then Raebyrne and Poletti and a stranger carrying the wounded man, who looked vaguely familiar. The guard at the rear called something and pushed Raebyrne, who glared back at him, in silence this time.

He started. Sergeant Damon was pulling him back up the path. "Come on, come on . . ."

"Where?" He followed, glancing back fearfully. They recrossed the ravine to the ridge. Back in the dense woods again Damon turned and said:

"We're going to jump them. Right here."

"Jump them?"

"I'm going to hit the one in the rear first, and when the man in front turns, you nail him. Got that?"

"I—"

"Don't move till I do. I want to jump the rear man first. We've got to take them before they can fire a shot."

"—how, Sarge?"

"Didn't you hear me? Didn't I tell you not to fire except as a last resort?"

Brewster stared at him. The Sergeant's face looked wrathful and stern, the way it did when he was reading off someone after inspection; only worse. He was serious about this. Completely serious. They were going—they were going to attack these Germans, he was expected to—

". . . Couldn't we—couldn't we just—cover them?"

Damon's eyes widened with exasperation. "And have them fire on you, or dive for cover and holler for help? There are Germans *right—over—there*," he hissed, pointing off through the heavy shadows of the woods.

"But—" he stammered. Fear rolled around inside him like dirty water. "But—I can't, Sarge . . ."

"You can. You've got to!"

"But—there's only two of us—"

"There's only two of them, too. And that's where they made *their* mistake, the sons of bitches . ." He pulled Brewster off the path with him. "Quick, now. Right here. Behind this tree. Remember: don't show yourself until you've heard me make my rush. I'm going to be right there—see? that pine with the burl low on its trunk? You must not *fire*—"

"But Sarge, I'm not—"

"Kill the bastard. Kill him! It's him or you!—and all the rest of us . . ." Damon was shaking him fiercely, glaring at him. "Brewster, if you let me down now . . . *stick him!* Run him through!" He gave the Private one final shake, then vanished through the bushes without a sound.

"Oh God," Brewster breathed. Crouched behind the broad base of the pine he checked his bayonet studs automatically. His face was soaked with sweat; it dripped from his nose and chin, kept streaming into his eyes and made them sting. His stomach growled and whined. From down in the ravine he heard the German guard's voice again, and pressed his hand against his stomach to make it stop growling. Drops of pitch on the black flakes of bark before his eyes were like globules of milky amber; he touched one, and his fingers came away furred and sticky. "We've come to a little conclusion about you, Brewster." Sohier's voice, lazy and mocking, the ring of faces watching him flatly from cots and desk corners. "It's the consensus of the group that your liver is just a mite on the pale side. In short, that you've got a saffron streak in you a mile wide, which keeps getting in your way. Ours, too. So this is just to let you know we'd appreciate it if you'd go your own erring way from now on and not intrude your company on us. Do we make ourselves clear, Brewster?" Markham, Bullert, Himes, all the others. A coward, they'd told him they wanted no part of him and they'd branded him a coward all the way through school because of that scrimmage, their faces smooth and smug and their eyes glinting with the amused contempt that had filled him with such sick shame—

They were coming up the path: he heard the muffled clinking of equipment, the thud of boots on the hard-baked earth. He saw movement, then the gray uniform, the face broad and square-jawed, well tanned under the flaring black helmet rim. His heart swelled up into his throat and wedged itself there; he had a terrible desire to flee, throw

down his rifle and race away through the woods and hide forever—who
would know? who would care?—replaced on the instant by Sergeant
Damon's wrathful, importunate eyes, the memory of that moment in the
common room at St. Andrew's. A flood of sheer rage coursed through
him, and a swift tensing of his muscles over which he had no control.

There was a thump like a batten struck against a blanketed log, and a
low, tremulous cry. He leaped out from behind the tree. The German—
not six feet away—had turned back toward the brief commotion; Brewster paused, staring at his back. Beyond the German the other faces
gazed back at him in a blurred frieze of amazement: white blank faces.
The man's back was broad, with sweat stains in large green loops above
the wide black-leather belt. He started to lunge and could not—stood
there staring, frozen, indecisive, at the shiny black bullet pouch, the
cylindrical gas-mask holder, a tear in the tunic pleat for one endless,
horrible instant and then the German spun back again, his eyes wide and
very clear, his lips in a thin, cruel line, and his bayoneted rifle described
a long, high arc through the level sunlight. Brewster had the swift
thought, *He's trying to hurt me*—and lunged down and in, the movement automatic and defined, a deep thrust, as Damon had taught him.
There was a shock and the bayonet went into the man's body just above
the metal belt buckle, which looked like the head of a snarling jaguar.
The man stiffened, his body arching toward his assailant, as though
trying to push the blade in still farther. Something struck Brewster a
blinding blow on the bridge of the nose; his sight darkened, blurred, he
saw as if through streaming glass the man's eyes rolling whitely. A hand
danced in the air, clawing and clawing at his face. They were bound
together by the bayonet, conjoined for an eternity of clawing, gasping,
writhing intimacy. Then all at once Devlin had snapped his arm around
the German's neck from behind and snatched his trench knife out of its
scabbard, was driving it into his back, once, twice, the blows like fists
pounding sand bags. The man sank to the path without a sound. Brewster kept wrenching at the blade, which would not come loose; then
without warning it did, and a greasy tongue of blood leaped after the
bright steel, gliding back along the blood channel. Lowering the
weapon, he looked up—at Devlin, at Raebyrne and Poletti and the
others, who watched him as if he were possessed of some magical and
terrible powers. It was over. He had done it. He had done what Sergeant Damon had ordered him to do.

Then he was bent over retching dryly, foolishly, brushing the
branches away in sudden petulance. He felt ashamed, then he didn't
care. Someone had a hand around his shoulders, was saying something to
him quietly; but the words meant nothing.

"I'm all right," he heard his voice say. He passed his hand over his
face, noticed with faint surprise that his palm was smeared with blood.
His nose felt astonishingly thick and furry. "I just need a minute. Or
two . . ."

But no one was listening to him, they were all doing something now: stealthy, quick movements in the dense ripples of light and shadow. Damon had signaled to the others that the enemy was not a hundred yards away, on their right; Raebyrne and Devlin were stripping the dead Germans of their cartridge belts. Everyone seemed to have something to do, and only he stood there, musing, dazed, bound in timelessness.

"What took you so long, Sam?" Corporal Devlin was saying to Damon, his eyes bright and beady. "I've had that call in for five hours now."

The Sergeant slowly grinned. "You know these French telephone operators, they never get the numbers right." He was still peering calmly toward the woods beyond the ridge. "Planning a little trip to Germany, Dev?"

"Why sure—it's just the time to lay in a stock of Bernkasteler Riesling before it's all gone—" Then he gave it up, his jaw dropped. "I guess so," he muttered. "Jesus, I guess so."

"What happened?"

"Hell, I don't know. Lieutenant yelled to fall back, I didn't think we were supposed to but it seemed like a hell of a good idea right then. I got back over the embankment with several of the boys, and the Heinies were swarming all over us, I didn't know who was what. I'd just drilled one who was all set to skewer Turner and was taking aim at another one, and something got me on the side of the head. And when I came to I was lying flat on my back with a head like New Year's morning and these two heroes and no weapons, and a thousand and one Heinies all around, pointing bayonets at my belly."

"All right, Corp," Raebyrne rejoined, "I know I ain't no hell-fire hero, all *I* know is I'd a been five counties away by now if I hadn't stopped to try and pick you up . . ."

"Lot of good that did you," Devlin murmured, though he grinned wearily.

Raebyrne shrugged. "Well, it come out all right in the end . . ."

Brewster watched them all strangely. His eyes strayed to the dead German, the square, tanned face and heavy body—then he looked away quickly. He had done it. They had called him a coward and wouldn't let him eat at their table or use the common room, but he wasn't a coward; he wasn't any more of a coward or a hero than anyone else. And he had made his body do what it had to . . . It was odd: he could not feel his hands, or his feet, or his nose, even when he put his fingers to it and pressed it gently. It looked huge, his sight was curiously affected. Damon's face seemed to come at him over a thick purple promontory.

"You all right, kid?"

"I can't seem to see too well," he mumbled.

"He must have caught you with the trigger guard, or maybe his fist. He broke your nose."

"Broke my nose?"

"Yep. It'll improve your looks. Give you more character."

"Everybody's nose has got to be broken once before he's a grown man," Devlin said. "Didn't you know that, Brewster? And then it's got to be rebroke."

"Shoot, all he needs is to slap a pulse of suet and ashes in a red flannel sock and hold it on for two days and two nights to draw the poison, and it'll cure it right smart . . ."

He smiled sheepishly. They were ragging him again, but it was different now. They were crowding around him almost eagerly, they all wanted to say something to him. He had come up to it; that was all he knew. Through tearing, blurry eyes he sought out Damon. "We did it," he said.

"You see?" The Sergeant was grinning at him. "You see what two men can do, Tim? You see? Now there's eight of us . . ."

He nodded. They were going to be all right; he knew it with a hard, fierce certainty alien to him till this moment. They were going to make it back to their own lines and nobody, not even the whole German Seventh Army lined up shoulder to shoulder, was going to stop them.

"I still say they're in there."

"Sure they're in there. Wouldn't you be?"

"I don't know what I'd be."

"Well. There's only one way to find out . . ."

The woods had ended in a little crescent-shaped horn, snipped off neatly at the edge of the wheatfield. The land, rolling south like some exquisite golden fur in the sunlight, rose to a little hill they couldn't see over. And in the middle of the long field, about a hundred yards from where they lay, in a cluster of fruit trees, stood the farm.

Damon studied it calmly, wishing he had field glasses. There were two buildings of gray stone with fine slate roofs. The main structure, which was nearer them, had a large open doorway for wagons and was capped with a curious sort of cupola with louvered shutters; it would be a fair-sized room, and it would command the entire stretch of fields between the two strips of woods—it could probably see over the rise to the south. Brigny Farm. He remembered the two little dots on the Major's map. There was no sound, no movement, but he was certain the Germans were in there. Not many, but some. A machine gun, up in that tower room. That's what it would be. It was too important for them to have left it unoccupied, even if it was well behind the lines now. What would he do if he were directing this drive to Barrecourt and the river? He would drop off a machine-gun team to cover a possible counter-attack, and move on. Well, he would also detach a squad or two to dig in around the well among the fruit trees, and man the other building. Of course, if he needed every available rifleman—

"Come on, Sarge," Poletti was saying in a thin, troubled voice.

Damon looked at him. "Come on where?"

"I don't know—out of here, somewhere out of here, anyway . . ."

"If they've got a gun up in that tower you wouldn't make it halfway to that crest."

"I don't know . . ."

"Well, I do." He jerked his head toward Jason, the wounded man, who was from C Company and had somehow got rounded up with the others. "And how you going to take care of *him?*" Poletti dropped his eyes. Yes, sure, you'd leave him here and take off, Damon thought; but he kept it to himself. "Am I right or not, Dev?" he asked.

Devlin nodded. Blood had caked on the side of his head behind his ear, and matted in his tousled red hair. "Not a chance. They'd squash us like flies against a window pane."

Jason, who had been hit in the groin, twisted his head and said feebly: "You got to get me to a doctor, fellas, you just got to. I'm going to bleed to death, I can feel it . . ."

"You're not going to bleed to death," Damon told him.

No one else said anything. It had been a bad morning. They had progressed slowly southward, with Damon and Devlin alternating as point, working their way through the forest. After an hour of this they had run onto two privates from A Company hiding under a fallen tree; one was badly wounded in the foot and the other almost incoherent with fear, but miraculously they both had their rifles and cartridge belts. Damon cut saplings for a full-length stretcher for Jason, which released two more Springfields, and he made crutches for the other wounded man; but this slowed their progress still further. It was hard to move quietly. Devlin and Raebyrne were fine, but Poletti and Brewster and Lujak, one of the new men, were city boys; and it was impossible to carry a man on a stretcher without a certain amount of stumbling and slithering. They had been very nearly surprised by a mounted German machine-gun section hurrying south behind them on a narrow road that paralleled the path, and they had had to hide twice from runners. They were hungry, and even more thirsty, and their nerves were on edge from this creeping, furtive procession.

"Maybe nobody's in there," Brewster said after a silence.

"Maybe." It just might be unoccupied, of course. Even the Germans made mistakes once in a while.

"Let me mosey on over there, Sarge," Raebyrne offered. "A little old scouting and patrolling. I'm a curly wolf on the prowl. How about it?"

Damon made no reply. He couldn't say why, but it felt wrong; it felt all wrong. Still, they had to do something. "All right." He drew his .45 out of its holster. "Leave your rifle and take this. It'll be handier. Now if the place is empty—"

He stopped. As though awaiting a cue a figure stepped out of the broad, dark aperture into the sunlight, then another, and moved to the corner of the building. They were both big men, bareheaded and without their weapons. For a long moment they gazed around them at the fields of wheat. The taller of the two pointed to one of the apple trees and said something and his companion laughed and nodded; then together they relieved themselves, turned and vanished into the shadowed doorway. And the little group of fugitives in the woods relaxed and glanced at one another uneasily.

"Well, now we know," Damon said quietly.

"That's for sure," Devlin muttered, and sighed.

Damon chewed at the inside of his cheek, watching the farm. The sight of the two Germans standing there by the wall, so blithely unconcerned, had made him angry all over again. The events of the past night seethed in him, reawakened. With the staggering discovery, just after midnight, that there was to be no counterbarrage, that there *were* no French on their right flank, that there were nothing but Germans over there streaming past them or pouring down on them like doom itself, that they would be swept away without even the bitter satisfaction of having delayed the enemy assault, he had moved from shock to dismay and finally to choking rage. He had fought well. Unable to reach Lieutenant Harris after the first onset he had obeyed orders, had covered Johansen and Turner and Krazewski, pausing and firing and running again—and finally had found himself all alone and gasping for wind in a thicket where the railroad embankment entered the woods.

His rage and his sense of responsibility had driven him back. It was all wrong: they had been deployed badly; the French had packed up and run; artillery had failed them; the battalion was clearly a sacrificial lamb offered up on the altar of desperation—and Harris probably had disobeyed orders in calling for a withdrawal; but he, Damon, owed a debt to the men he had lived with and trained for battle. He mastered his fear and made himself go back, still unable to believe two hundred and fifty men could have melted away before his eyes. Creeping from shell hole to shell hole, some of them littered with splinters of iron still hot from the bombardment, playing dead under the flares, his heart pounding so mightily that he felt it must be visible to any casual eye, he worked his way back. Twice he was almost stepped on by little bands of German infantry.

But when he had got to the line he knew it was all over. He found Davis and Hoffenstedt—or what he believed to be Davis and Hoffenstedt—as well as Starkie, though he hadn't told Brewster; the kid was obviously shaky enough. Where all the rest of them were he had no

idea. Some must have made it back to the reserve lines. The others—
killed or captured, or hiding in thickets and bits of woodland. Like
animals. His eyes had filled with rage. Oh, the bastards, the bastards!

Well: there had been Brewster. You worked with what you had.
And the little guy knew German: why hadn't he found that out before—
why hadn't anyone in the company found it out?

"I'm going to take off and look for water," Lujak was saying. A
stocky man with beady black eyes and overlong arms, he appeared to be
looking for an easy chance to run off and give himself up—or perhaps
hide out in some thicket for the duration. "My buddy here needs some
water, okay?"

"Stick around," Damon said briefly.

"Well, if we ain't going to do anything—"

"We've got something to do."

"Yes? What? I've got to have some water, I ain't kidding."

"There's water," Damon said, pointing his index finger like a miniature howitzer toward the open maw of the barn. "Right there." Several
of them turned and stared at him. "What do you say we go get it?"

There was a little silence, prolonged by the distant rumble and thump
of guns. Damon glared at the farm—he felt he could pierce its ocher
stone walls if he looked hard enough. He thought of the German soldiers standing by the wall so casually, pointing at the trees and laughing.

"Look at them," he said aloud, holding down his rage, his voice thick
with contempt. "Didn't even have their weapons with them, think
they're back in Munich drinking beer . . ." Then, cursing softly, gazing
up at the squat-roofed tower, listening to the martellato thunder of
divisional artillery, he had it: he saw what they had to do.

He put down his rifle and studied the men around him quietly. Poletti
was still terrified, half-stunned from his capture. Brewster's nose had
swollen to the size of a turnip—he could barely see around it. One of
the men from A Company, Henderson, was dangerously morose and
spoke only when spoken to; the other, a squat little Pennsylvania German named Schilz, responded quickly but looked unstable. Of the two
refugees from C Company they had picked up last, Burgess was groaning softly from his leg wound, and Lujak had meant nothing but trouble. Raebyrne looked ready for anything; and of course there was
Dev—he knew he could count on Dev right down to the wire.

Ten men. Eight effectives—two of them mighty reluctant—one walking wounded, one stretcher case. Six Springfields, two Mausers, one Colt
.45. Roughly twenty rounds per man. No food, no water. He thought of
Major Caldwell in the narrow room without a ceiling, the clear, unhurried voice. "Above all encourage the greatest possible use of individual
initiative." He smiled humorlessly. They'd be a trifle lean on initiative.

And yet he knew he was right. He felt it deep in his bones—with the
same harsh intensity he'd felt when his eyes had lighted on those two
small black squares on the Major's map the evening before. Even as he

squatted there crouched on his hams the first shells began to fall in the far woods to the west of the farm; branches and bits of débris boiled up and subsided. The slowly ranging shellfire, the long, curving meadow of wheat between its islands of wood, those two Germans who had left their weapons to step outside, all added up to something important. These two massive old buildings could be the key to the whole pattern —if only because they were where they were, and because the Germans did not value them enough . . .

"Well, I don't know about the rest of you, but I've had about enough of this," he said with terse finality. "It's about time *they* bought themselves a little trouble." He leaned forward and said quietly: "We're going to go over and take that farm."

They gazed at him in slow amazement.

"What for, Sarge?" Raebyrne said after a moment.

"Because we've got to. That's what for. We're going to take it and hold it until the outfit counterattacks and comes up and relieves us."

They all looked at the farm again. Devlin said: "How many of them do you think are in there, Sam?"

"Not many. And they won't be looking for us, if we work it right." Damon studied the farm again, measuring himself against it. There was a little trench, possibly for drainage, possibly a wintertime brook, that ran diagonally through the field to within twenty yards of the main building. The wheat continued right up to the edge of a stone-and-plaster wall, crumbling in several places. Then it looked like twenty feet to the broad loading doorway facing them. It was possible. They could do it.

"Look," he said sharply, "we'll never make it back across that field. They've got a perfect field of fire from that tower. They'll kill every last one of us." They stared at him in silence. "Now the regiment is going to counterattack—that's the preliminary bombardment you're watching right now—and it's going to come right through here, right over that rise."

"Well, why can't we just wait right here?" Poletti asked. "Especially if the regiment is going to counterattack . . ."

"Because the machine gun up in that tower is going to cut them down by the platoon before they ever get here, that's why. And that's what we're not going to let happen."

"How in hell do you know all this?" Lujak demanded.

"Because I was at the battalion briefing last night, that's how. And I saw the map."

"I still don't see why we can't just sit tight here," Poletti went on.

Damon whirled on him. "And get picked up all over again as soon as a Jerry patrol comes through, cleaning house? I'd think you'd have had enough of that for a while . . . We've got no choice. We get in there, dig in, and hold it for the regiment when they come through."

"Well, *I* got a choice," Lujak retorted.

"Not only that," Damon ignored him, "but there's water in there. Food and water. And a real place to crap out."

Their eyes flickered at this. All right. Whatever inducements worked. Besides, he believed it himself; he believed it utterly. They would be killed if they tried to crawl south through that field, they would be killed or captured if they stayed where they were. To go back through the woods was unthinkable. And there *was* safety inside those walls. If they could get to them.

"Sarge, you've brought me into camp," Raebyrne proclaimed. "I'm hungry enough to eat a sick snake."

Damon grinned at him. "Didn't you put those eggs away?"

Raebyrne cast his eyes dolefully heavenward. "Sarge, they was all rotten, every one."

The high, thin whistle came again; there was a bright flash and roar, a geyser of earth beyond the farm, then another still farther off. The shelling ranged back and forth fitfully, most of it falling far back in the direction of the embankment. When it let up again the sound of small-arms fire rose crisply.

"Come on," he said tersely, and got to his feet. "Come on, now. Are you going to lie around on your asses and get rounded up all over again?"

"Not me," Henderson said with sudden violence. "They're not going to capture *me* again."

The others were silent, but their faces were harder now. He had to get their assent for this: he knew it. "I know you're beat, but I want to tell you something." He pointed slowly toward the gray buildings. "They think we're yellow—they think we're only good for running away and giving up. Yellow Americans, no guts. Well, the bastards have got something to learn. It's about time somebody gave them the frigging word . . ."

"Right, Sam," Devlin said, "let's go get them." He got to his feet, and so did Brewster.

"Wait a minute," Lujak cried. "What the hell is this—do you idiots do everything this guy tells you? Look, he's dreamed this up, he's going to get you killed for nothing at all . . ."

Damon leaned toward him savagely. "Yes. Maybe you'll get killed. Well, isn't that just too God damn bad! Maybe you'll fall in the latrine tomorrow and suffocate to death anyway. But you're better than all those other guys lying around the embankment railroad tracks—aren't you? I want to stay alive just as much as you do, Lujak—and this is the way I see it and this is the way it's going to be!"

"You're a bastard, you know that?—a bastard—" Lujak began, but Henderson cut him off with a fierce, "Button your lip if you know what's good for you!" and Damon knew he had won.

"All right—now we're going to split up. Dev, take your detail right out to that point of woods down there, and—see that little hump there, that little shelf?—get in behind that and work your way as far as you can along it. If you draw fire, stay where you are and return it. If you hear *me* draw fire, get up and rush the place. All right?" Devlin nodded. "I'm going to go around to the right and up that drainage ditch or whatever it is, and in through that triangular break in the wall between those apple trees. See it? Give me about five minutes before you start out of the woods. I want to be just as close as I can get."

"Suppose they spot you first, Sam?"

"I don't think they will. They're looking for trouble to the south and southeast, they'll have set up facing that way." He looked at the ring of faces. "Reb? You want to come with me?"

"That's what I signed up for."

Brewster said. "Let me come, Sarge . . ."

Damon smiled. "I'm afraid not, Tim. Your nose has got in the way of your eyes. And I need a woodsman for this one."

"I can use cover," Henderson said.

Damon studied him a moment; the man looked steadier than before. He had large, capable hands and carried himself well. "Where you from?"

"Aroostook County. Maine woods."

"Can you track deer?" Henderson nodded. "All right. That's it." He turned. "Dev, the rest are all yours. Will you take the two Mausers?"

"Only three of you, Sam?" Their eyes locked for a moment. "What if they've got a detail sitting around downstairs?"

"They won't. That's what I've just figured out. You know why those two came out without their weapons? Because they came down from the tower. If they'd been just inside that door, one of them at least would have had his rifle and helmet."

"It's a gamble . . ." Schilz murmured.

"Sure, it's a gamble. But it's a gamble we're going to win." He turned to Lujak with soft ferocity. "And *you* are going to do what Corporal Devlin says—and no questions asked. Is that clear?"

Lujak paled and swallowed. "Yes," he muttered. "It's clear."

"What about us?" Burgess said, indicating Jason. "Me and this other fellow here?"

"You both stay here and keep quiet. You're no worse off than if we'd tried to get you south across that field. When we secure the place we'll come get you. That's a promise. And it won't be long."

He moved with infinite patience, his rifle held easily in the crooks of his elbows. The wheat was high, and darker than the wheat back home; their molasses-colored tassels bobbed gently above his head, bending down to him. He reached the ditch, waited for Raebyrne and Henderson, and then moved more rapidly, pausing every ten feet or so and listening. He encountered a German knapsack with broken straps, abandoned or blown from the back of some attacker, and a holed canteen. Insects hummed overhead, and far off, over the edge of the woods, an observation balloon hung like a fat silvery earthworm. He felt no fear at all. There was only the ditch and the blunt, dark tower of the farmhouse gliding along above the wheat halms. Twice he stopped and studied the tower, but could see nothing moving behind the louvers. Behind him he could hear Raebyrne crawling, a faint, slithering rustle.

He reached the edge of the wheat and raised his head cautiously. The view from the woods had foreshortened the distance: it was a good forty feet to the wall. A cart lay on its side, shattered, one wheel high in the air, its steel rim glinting in the sun. The apple trees, laden with small golden fruit, drooped in the still heat. He felt a tremendous thirst, and swallowed noisily. His watch said 11:48. Nine and a half minutes since they'd started. A lark danced high overhead, threw out a liquid burst of melody and fell away downwind, and with the sight of the bird he felt all at once immeasurably tired, assailed by fears. What if Devlin couldn't make it to that hummock-like ledge? what if a German was watching him right now through those slanted shutters? If there were a gun or a few riflemen down on that vast ground floor of the barn they would all be dead in minutes—

Don't think of that. The thing was to get in there, get over behind the wall. Eleven minutes. Time enough. He rose to one knee, lifted himself soundlessly and ran to the overturned cart and crouched there, breathing through his open mouth. He crept to the break in the wall, one hand on the dusty yellow mortar. So far so good. He turned back to signal Raebyrne—froze as he heard a short burst of machine gun fire. *Tak-a-tak-a-tak-a.* Maxim gun. They were up there. A rifle cracked, then another; he thought he heard a cry.

He put his head around the broken edge of wall, withdrew it. There was the cavernous opening. A wagon stood inside, a caisson—he could see the square green chest in the gloom. Nothing had moved.

It was at that moment that he heard the second machine gun, its clamor riding in over the first—and now beyond all doubt a series of high, yelping cries. Hit. Someone was hit. Oh, the bastards! He ducked through the break in the wall. A strand of barbed wire almost tore his helmet off, another snagged his right leg, crazy looping strands; he wrenched free in a series of frantic, tottering hops, hurdled over more wire and raced across the little courtyard under the clattering noise of the guns. The stone well with its little iron windlass, a scythe lying on the packed dirt with its broad scimitar blade and wooden cradle, half a dozen sacks full of grain, or dirt—his eyes found them all with a singular clarity, riveted on them; left them behind. He leaped over a high stone lintel, half-blinded by the sudden gloom, tripped on something and sprawled into a crate, banging his helmet against the wood, his breath singing in his lungs. He raised his head and looked right into a young, wild face, a shock of bright blond hair. A German, sitting propped up on a little platform. His tunic was open and his chest was heavily bandaged, and his right arm. Near him a body lay facedown, half-covered by a tarpaulin. Immediately above his head Damon heard the Maxim firing in long, even runs, muffled through the heavily timbered ceiling. For a brief, terrible moment he and the wounded German stared at each other. Then the machine gun stopped, the German opened his mouth to cry out in warning, and Damon bayoneted him through the throat. The boy fell over on his side. Blood spurted in swift dark jets over the white gauze.

No one. There was no one else. The caisson was loaded with some packs and boxes and that was all. He glanced back toward the doorway. He was alone. Ahead of him was a stairway of heavy timbers that turned twice on itself as it rose to the tower room. There might be a man on guard posted on the stairs, at one of the turns. No. There would be no one. Hurry. He had to hurry. If he only had grenades! He searched the two dead Germans in furious haste, found none on them, and straightened.

All right, then.

He snapped his rifle off safety, drew his pistol and ran a round into the chamber, hooked his little finger through the trigger guard. He crossed the room, went up ten steps and peered around the corner, swiftly ducking his head back in. No one. Good. The Maxim paused and started again, a long, yammering burst, and he went up the next flight two at a time, around the next turn, the next, and there they were—a vivid, quick tableau in the dim light coming in through the slits of the louvers: the gunner, bareheaded, hunched forward over his spade grips; his belt feeder easing the glittering belt of cartridges into the guides; the helper on his knees prying the cover from a box of belts; behind them an officer standing immaculate and erect, his field glasses to his eyes, on his face a squinting half-smile, like some count inspecting a rare and beautiful collection of lepidoptera—and on the far side of the gun, staring straight at him, a grenadier sitting on his hams with his back against the wall. But this man was unwounded and he had a Mauser rifle lying across his thighs.

Then everything happened at once. The grenadier raised his rifle, the helper too saw Damon and cried out, reaching for his Mauser. Damon, his knee on the third step from the top of the flight, fired; the grenadier doubled over himself without a sound; he shifted to the helper, who leaped up and then flopped out and down, slapping his hand against the floor. The officer swung toward Damon—in one motion flung the glasses at him and clutched at his pistol holster; the glasses struck Damon's helmet, drove it down over his eyes. He flipped it back with his left hand, his head ringing, in time to see the belt feeder drop the belt and duck behind the gun while the gunner wrenched at the mount, trying desperately to swing the gun around—a frantic series of actions that seemed to contain whole eternities of dreamy nightmare possibility as Damon, still without shifting position, fired at the belt feeder and missed, then at the officer, whose pistol flew back out of his hand and hit the far wall with a sharp crack as he fell, then at the bareheaded gunner, who had realized his error and let go the gun, was grappling for his pistol: he gave a brief, choked cry and slumped over the barrel of the Maxim. Damon snapped the Colt into his hand. The belt feeder rose up suddenly, his arm shot up over his shoulder and a black truncheon floated over Damon's head, struck the wall and clattered on down the stairs. Damon fired the Colt and the belt feeder slammed back into the wall, his helmet bouncing away; he snatched at another grenade and Damon hit him again and he went down. The first grenade burst beyond the bend in the stairs, a roar that shook the building. Then there was silence in the little room, broken only by the sound of the belt feeder's helmet rolling around on the timbered floor.

Never taking his eyes off the five figures Damon clawed a fresh clip out of his belt, tapped the steel noses once against the stock of his rifle, and thumbed it into the Springfield's magazine by feel. Not one of them had moved. He came up the last three steps cautiously, conscious of the other Maxim still firing. He glanced behind him down the stairway, where dust rose in a blinding white cloud. Crouching he checked the bodies; he had hit every man squarely between the eyes except the belt feeder, who was shot over the heart and in the belly, and who was plainly dying. He rolled the man over again, picked up his Springfield and moved to the louvers on the west side. One of them had been removed, and through the enlarged aperture he could look down on the other gun crew on the roof of the adjoining building, about fifty yards away. The roof had been hit by shellfire, and they were lying flat under the rough timber frame, protected by a few dozen sandbags. A grenadier was firing his rifle below Damon's right, behind the building. They had spotted Raebyrne or Henderson, then. For a second or two he studied the prone group, then, keeping his rifle barrel inside the louvers, fired from right to left: first the sergeant, then the grenadier, then the helper; moving toward the gun. The belt feeder, who saw the helper fall and must have realized what had happened, struck the gunner on the arm—then fell against him as Damon fired. The gunner leaped to his feet with astonishing speed, did a funny little dance in the center of the roof, catlike, bewildered—all at once threw up his hands and shouted something.

"All right," Damon called back. "You—stay—there! *Stay!*" He reloaded his rifle and looked around. The silence was suddenly almost overpowering. He was breathing heavily and his mouth was dry; aside from that he felt perfectly calm. He went over and picked up the German officer's field glasses and found to his surprise they weren't even scratched. He flipped the strap over his neck and swept the fields to the east and north, along the edge of the trees. He could see no movement anywhere. He might have been in a tower on the Gobi desert.

He heard the clump of boots on the stairs then, swung his rifle around. Raebyrne's face popped into sight and out again.

"Come on, Reb," he said.

They came up in a rush: Raebyrne, followed closely by Henderson and Devlin; then Brewster and Schilz. Once inside the room they stopped and stared at him and then at the dead Germans, the pools of blood seeping into the rough planks at their feet. Someone whistled softly.

"—You shot 'em all up, Sarge," Raebyrne exclaimed, "—like a hawk in an old hen coop!"

Devlin said, "You all right, Sam?"

"Sure I'm all right. How'd you make out?"

"Not bad. We made it about twenty yards or so down that draw before they spotted us."

"You got you a bleeding high orficer," Raebyrne crowed, bending over. "Look at his shiny go-to-meeting boots!"

Devlin went on: "Poletti got up and ran at the first burst."

"Jesus Christ."

"I know. I couldn't hold him. He was pretty jumpy, Sam. And it looked an awful long way to that wall. I didn't think myself we'd—" He broke off, said: "That Lujak stopped one in the arm."

Damon scowled. Down to six effectives now. "Where is he?"

"Lying behind the wall," Brewster volunteered. "He's not feeling too well."

Raebyrne cackled. "I imagine he's feeling right dauncy, is Mister Lujak." He wagged his head in wonder. "Old Sarge! He said he'd do it and he did it. The whole Pee-roossian army! Hot diggerty damn . . ."

Devlin was saying: "Sam, there's another gun—"

"I know. I took care of it."

They all fell silent again. Devlin blinked at him. "You mean you got *them* all, too?"

"All but one. They didn't know I was up here. Now, look . . ." He took Devlin's arm and drew him over to the east louvers. "You see those sand—"

Except for the four dead, the roof was empty. "Son of a bitch! He's decided to run for it—we can't let that happen. He mustn't get back. Dev, take two men—"

He stopped with a grunt; there he was, under the apple trees, running hard toward the distant patch of woods. He fired almost without aiming: the gunner staggered, stumbled and fell into a little pile of hay beside a tree. Damon put another round into him to make sure, heard Devlin's rifle right beside him; the body jerked with the impact and was still.

"God damn fool," he muttered. That was bad, a real lapse. He should have kept his eyes on him until they had him tied up—the whole plan could have been jeopardized . . . He shook his head as if to clear it, turned around again. They were all staring at him; they looked like drunks in the early stages—all eagerness and confusion. Get them going, the inner monitor said crisply. All of them. You're wasting time. You may not have much of it.

"All right," he said, "now let's get going. We're in here, and we're going to stay here. Dev, go on over and check out that Maxim gun. Set it up facing the other way. Toward the embankment."

"The other way?"

"Yes. Pile your sandbags at that end and pull out some planks at the gable. I'm going to turn this one around, too."

"Why, Sam?"

"Just a hunch. I think they're going to run up some reserves. I'll send you Henderson and Schilz as soon as I can. On the double, now."

"Check."

"One more thing. Don't fire until I do, no matter what."

"Right, Sam."

It was as if someone else were issuing orders—someone with a marvelously clear head, an eye for all contingencies. He sent Raebyrne with Henderson to get Jason and Burgess, he sent Brewster to fill all their canteens from the well in the courtyard, he had Schilz bring up ammunition from the floor below; he himself lifted out a couple of the louvered slats on the north face, and dragged the gun around so it commanded the long field behind them. Raebyrne found some black bread and sausage and a bucket of cold coffee that tasted like burned chestnuts; they bandaged Lujak, who had what appeared to be a flesh wound just above the elbow and who was by now thoroughly cowed; they carried the dead Germans downstairs and covered them all with the tarpaulin. Within twenty minutes Damon was sitting calmly in the tower room with Raebyrne and Brewster, chewing the dense black bread and sweeping the horizon with his new-found field glasses.

"High on the hog," Raebyrne proclaimed. He had stuck the dead Leutnant's Luger into the waistband of his trousers and was pouring from hand to hand some of the buttons he'd cut from the officer's tunic. "You know what they say, Sarge."

"What's that?"

"When times cain't get worse, they got to get better." He squinted shrewdly at the ceiling. "I knew all along you were making the correct move."

"You didn't sound very much like it back there in the woods," Brewster rejoined.

"Well, that's because I need time to come to a decision. I was just weighing the prodes and corns."

"The what?"

"The prodes and corns. I knew we could do it all the while."

"Did you," Damon said. "What took you so long getting up here, by the way?"

Raebyrne made a quick, woeful grimace. "Little bit of bad luck, Sarge. I made it over to the wall in fine form, and saw you duck inside. So I took off through the wall like a catamount in rut—and I got myself hung up on that bantangled wire and down I went, ass over appetite. And when I got up I was like a puppy on a leash, pulling and hauling and not getting anywhere. And finally, just as I was about to give it all up as a bad job, I come loose and went helling on in. Trouble is, it was plumb mass dark after all that direct sunshine, and I couldn't make out thing-one. By the time I found the stairs that grand old fusillade broke out up above. I said, 'That's old Sarge up there, doing battle,' and away I went. And *boom!*—off went that hand bomb, and smoke and steel shavings all over creation, and back down I went again." He grinned happily, and licked his lips. "So you can see, Sarge, it was bad luck that turned good. Because if I'd have been just a touch earlier, you'd have had to scratch old Reb. And there'd go your war . . ." He went off into his high-pitched cackle. "You get the two downstairs on the way by?"

Bent over the Maxim, studying it, Damon shook his head. "No."

Raebyrne blinked. "But Sarge, one of 'em was bayoneted in the—"

"Shut up, Raebyrne," the Sergeant said crossly. He had forgotten about the wounded man on the platform. Pumping the cocking handle he felt himself begin to tremble. The other two were silent, and he knew they were watching him. What the hell, he told himself fiercely, I had no choice. One yip out of him and we'd all be dead. But the tremor remained, and he rocked the gun up and down on its elevation bar. There is a price for everything, the thought came to him; a bleak solace. There are no free tickets to any land, and it doesn't matter if—

"Sarge!" Raebyrne hissed from the slits. "Two of 'em—coming this way . . ."

Two soldiers were coming directly toward them across the field; slender, awkward figures wearing the little round gray fatigue caps with the red piping around the band. Each was carrying two rectangular green metal boxes, just like the boxes on the floor by his foot. They had their rifles slung over their shoulders.

"Ammunition," he said briefly. "We can use it. Reb, you and Brewster go downstairs and keep out of sight. Let them come in and then cover them. Let them come in. No shooting, now."

They left. Damon kept moving from side to side, studying the woods, the distant skyline with his glasses. It was hard to say. Maybe he'd guessed wrong. If he had, they were done for, and he had sacrificed ten men to not much purpose. Why was it so quiet? Only a distant muttering, like summer thunder; no rifle fire anywhere. Where had everybody gone? And yet the Germans apparently intended to support these guns . . .

They came up the stairs, after a few minutes—two rawboned kids, looking ludicrous in the heavy square-toed boots. They were surly with fear. Brewster said something to them in German, and the taller one smiled a quick, frightened smile and bowed.

"What'd you tell him?" Damon demanded.

Brewster looked at him steadily out of his blackened, swollen eyes. "Sarge, I told them they were prisoners of war and would not be harmed."

He nodded. "Ask them if they are sending reinforcements to these buildings."

Brewster questioned them for a while without much success. They were Army Service Corps kids, they had just had the surprise of their young lives, and they obviously knew nothing beyond the specific orders they'd been given.

"Tie them up," he said.

"With what, Sarge?" Raebyrne asked.

"*I* don't know—find some rope, use your belts—just tie them up," he said irritably. He felt all at once unutterably tired; there seemed to be no end to this day of stealth and worry and decisions. He watched Raebyrne and Brewster fussing with the prisoners, glanced over at the roof of the other building, where Devlin and Henderson were shifting sandbags. He was weary from carrying the weight of their apathy, their fear, their unfocused resentment.

"Sergeant," Lujak's voice said behind him, tentative and querulous. "Sergeant, we don't have to stay, now."

"What?"

"Now the machine guns—now the Germans aren't here anymore. We could go back across the field to our lines. You remember, you said—"

He whirled around. "*Will* you shut your mouth!" he said with such vehemence that the wounded man gasped in fright. "I'm running this outfit, and until I'm wounded or killed, what I say goes . . ." The thought had been in his own mind, and Lujak's giving voice to it had enraged him. "What the hell's the matter with you—you're acting like a bunch of old women!" Brewster was watching him curiously and he turned away—saw Devlin was crouched behind his gun, signaling him frantically with his hands and pointing toward the north. He raised the glasses.

In the woods out of which they had come an hour before, shadows moved back and forth against the light; he had an impression of animation, a stirring, like a snake's coils in deep foliage. And then all at once there they were—a column of men, marching in perfect order diagonally across their field of vision toward the western patch of forest; their rifles slung, their free arms swinging ponderously. An officer was moving beside them, waving a crumpled piece of paper in one hand. He heard Brewster give a muffled exclamation.

"All right," he said between his teeth. He felt perfectly calm again, completely in control. "All right."

"Je-sus, Sarge," Raebyrne whispered, "there's a hundred crawling thousand of them . . . !"

"No, there isn't," he answered calmly, passing his glasses over the nicely aligned ranks, the blank, broad faces. "They're in company strength. That's all." He went back and crouched behind the Maxim. "All right. Brewster, you're going to be belt feeder. Take it like this, see?—and run it up out of the box."

"Right."

"Reb, take Brewster's rifle and stand there—right there. Lujak, here's my Springfield. You will load for Raebyrne."

"Sergeant, my arm—"

"You've got two of them, haven't you? I said: *you will load for him.*" He settled himself, adjusted the sight slotted in its vertical guides. "All right now, not till I give the word," he said to Raebyrne. "You will not fire until I give the word."

They were three hundred and fifty yards away, coming with surprising speed. The ditch that he had used for cover on the east flank of the farm took a sharp turn about a hundred yards or so from where they were sitting, deepened, and ran off toward the northwest. They would have to cross it if they kept on.

"Range three hundred," Raebyrne said, and released his safety.

"Easy, now." They were nearer. Their present course, if they held to it, would take them about fifty yards from Devlin's building. Going up to support Brigny-le-Thiep, then. They came on confidently, in silence; some NCO was counting cadence—and gazing at the column, so smart and fresh and vulnerable, Damon felt a sharp twinge of regret. In a few seconds he was going to kill, or try to kill, all of them. Damn fools. They should have sent out a patrol or two. No—someone had reported in: *We hold Brigny Farm,* and so of course they'd never thought to question it. Thank God they had incompetents on their side, too.

"Hell's fire, Sarge, they're going to be eating out of our mess kits . . ."

"Relax," he said. "The nearer the better." Up to a point. He rose and glanced at the roof across the yard. They were crouched behind their sandbag barricade; Devlin was behind the gun, Schilz at the belt, Henderson holding his rifle. While he watched, Devlin slowly turned his head and stared up at the tower; his eyes were shining with tension.

"Range one fifty," Raebyrne said.

"Sarge—"

"Hang on now." The officer had paused, was consulting the paper, obviously a map. The sergeant's cadence came sharply across the wheat now. Oh, the God damned fools! A rage mounted in the back of his head, but cold. He threw one last glance back toward the south. Nothing. Where in Christ's name were they all—had the whole lousy AEF vanished off the face of the earth?

They had reached the ditch. The first ranks dipped into it and clambered up the near side, slowly and in poor formation. It was deep, then, and fairly wide. Good. All the better.

"Range a *hundred*," Raebyrne breathed.

He knew they were all gazing at him now, even Raebyrne. The blood was driving against his temples and throat; his knuckles were white on the grips.

"—Sarge," Brewster was whispering hoarsely, "Sarge, I can see the fellow's mustache, that fellow—"

As the second detachment went into the ditch he called: "Open fire!" and thumbed the gun.

The sudden hammering roar was deafening. The ranks broke in all directions, the leaders pressing back toward the ditch, others standing in spraddle-legged confusion. He could see their belts, their chin straps, their mouths gaping in black soundless ovals. The officer was frantically waving both arms. The gun jumped and jittered, his forearms trembled with the vibration. He was conscious of the cartridges glittering like a snake's back, vanishing magically into the guide lips, the empty shells raining in bright little bronze jewels against the wall. When he paused he could hear Devlin's gun, and the high whining bark of the Springfields.

Now there were none left standing in the first contingent—only isolated figures that groped and quivered in the wheat. The officer was down, the piece of paper lying on his chest like a dirty white leaf. Damon shifted to the rear detachment, watched them flutter and wilt away. The gun went silent. Brewster was gazing at him in consternation, holding the belt. Stoppage. He yanked at the cocking handle. No luck. He reached in his shirt pocket for the little clawlike tool he'd picked up from one of the dead Germans and jerked out the crushed casing. It ran on.

The Germans in the center were deployed now, along the edge of the ditch. The rear contingent had gone to pieces, milling around and shouting. They were all in trouble, they were confused. But fire was coming from the trench: he could see the torch flashes from the rifle barrels winking here and there. They'd recovered quickly, doped it out. But they were pinned and they knew that, too: they had no place to go. His mind seemed to move along independent of his tensed, sweating body, analyzing, anticipating with a steady, hard objectivity. Then . . . then they would seek safety in attack—they would rush the farm as the least of three evils. An officer was kneeling at the near edge of the ditch, making long sweeping gestures with his arm—then suddenly his head dropped doll-like on his chest and he fell back out of sight. Raebyrne let out a whoop.

"Yaaaaa-hoo! That's for old Starkie . . ."

There was a shocking series of smashes right in front of him: the louvers shattered in a rain of chips and splinters, and light poured in on his face. He cringed, rose up again, his thumbs still jammed against the trips. Spandau, they had a Spandau. "Get—that—gun!" he roared, scarcely aware he was shouting at all. "Get him! . . ." Another burst ripped the shutters, there was the furious climbing whine of ricochets and someone behind him screamed. He ducked again, this time by design, was up again a second later to see Raebyrne still clinging to the right-hand corner of the shutter, blazing away, his slender body jerking with the recoil. The Spandau or whatever it was went silent, started, stopped again, and now he could hear Raebyrne talking steadily as he fired:

"—busted without a pack, you Borsch sons of bitches . . . *get* away from there! . . ."

They were all yelling now, hollering at the top of their lungs. The belt ran out: he and Brewster inserted a new one and raced on. Men were there, he reached them, they fell as if cuffed flat, or they leaped up, or spun away and down like faulty man-made toys. It was a deafening dream, a badly rehearsed tableau without rhyme or reason. He could feel nothing; his hands were numb, his eyes kept tearing from the jolting, jumping sight.

"Ya-hoo! there they go! Yaaaaa-hoo!"

They were breaking; they were running away across the field, back toward the woods, and now he could hear cries like children on some windy plain beside a river. He pursued them, the Springfields snapped and crackled. They were going to get away, some of them were going to make it, there were so many, so very many—

They were gone, had slipped off through the distant trees. They'd got away. He fired on and on, in a paroxysm of need, until the gun stopped firing, the belt had run out, and Brewster was screaming at him, his face pleading and wild:

"Stop it, Sarge! That's enough, *enough* . . . !"

He took his hands from the grips and wiped his face with his sleeve; it came away blued with dirt and grease and sweat. Out of it. They were out of it. They were all right. In the center of the ditch someone was waving a piece of white rag slowly, back and forth, back and forth . . .

He got up. Raebyrne, his face red as a beet, was capering with glee. "Did you see the sons of bitches! Did you see them run? A hundred to one! Old Sarge . . ." He grabbed Damon in an exultant rush and almost spun him around. "We could lick the world and ask for more! It's better than the Alamo . . ." Brewster was staring at them both, his face dead white, his mouth a thin, even, bloodless line.

Behind them someone was uttering short, broken screams. They all turned in surprise: Lujak, holding one knee with his good hand and rocking to and fro.

"What happened to him?" Raebyrne said.

"Ricochet," Damon answered. "I thought he'd be out of the way, over there." He leaped to the east side and leaned out. Devlin was sprawled wearily, with his arm hanging over the Maxim's breech.

"You all right?" he called.

"Yeah. We're all right . . . You?"

"Lujak. Hit again by a ricochet."

"That Lujak is unlucky."

"Isn't he?" He laughed, he couldn't help it, it was as necessary as breathing. Devlin watched him with a tired smile.

"Think we can stand 'em off again?"

"I don't see why not. How you fixed for ammo?"

"We're down pretty fine." Devlin paused. "They'll be back, Sam."

"I know. How many you think got away?"

"I don't know—ten or a dozen. What do you want to do about those people in the ditch?"

"Let's get them back here and tie 'em up." He moved to the north face. The big white rag, now tied to a bayoneted rifle, was still swinging back and forth. He raised his glasses. There seemed to be about fifteen of them; some were bandaging the wounded. "All right," he shouted. "Come on with your hands way up over your heads. Drop your belts and your weapons . . . Tim," he turned to Brewster, "tell these people what I just said, will you?"

He sent Raebyrne out to ride herd on the prisoners, went back and sat down on a cartridge box; he had a splitting headache and his eyes hurt. Think. He had to think. They'd been lucky. The next time they wouldn't be—the next time the Germans would come in three carefully spaced assault waves. And there'd be artillery preparation; mortars at the very least. They would be shelled. What had he better do? Go down to the courtyard and dig in? and then run back upstairs when they assaulted? But suppose they called down a creeping barrage on the position? They were perfectly capable of it. There wouldn't be a man left to fire the guns. Would he even have time to dig in? All the quick assurance of the morning had fled him; he felt burdened and unsure, prey to a thousand and one fearsome conjectures. Brewster had just finished binding up Lujak, who was saying in a faint, petulant voice: "—why can't we get *out* of this horrible place, oh God, why can't we get *away* from here!—"

"Shut up, Lujak," he ordered absently. Of course they could pull out now, abandon the place and take their chances. It was foolish to take a stand in a position you couldn't adequately defend; wasn't it?

But suppose they didn't attack for a while—suppose the word didn't get back to *their* regimental headquarters, and from there to division and corps and army; and then the conferences and recommendations, and finally the orders going back to division, to regiment, to division artillery . . . Both sides were terribly confused in war, he'd learned that much; and whoever acted with speed and resolution, made the correct response, got the advantage.

But what was the correct response?

He didn't know. He just plain didn't know. He'd better dig in outside. Dig in, and get Henderson and Schilz to go out and get that Spandau and as much Mauser ammunition as they could. He ought to send a runner, but who? With six effectives, who could he spare? Wouldn't he just be sacrificing a man, and needlessly? Everything seemed impossible, complicated beyond all unraveling—he felt himself adrift in the frailest of vessels, bobbing and sinking in a watery universe of menace.

He heard Raebyrne's voice in the courtyard below, high-pitched, peremptory, and the scrape and scuffle of boots. Wearily he got to his feet and went to the shutters, gazed out over the field, where hundreds of gray forms lay in windrows, in disordered clumps and splotches, as if flung down by the most powerful and careless of hands. A company of men. He had done that. He had wiped out a company of men. Like God. He had flung them down there like God sowing some noisome grain—

He began to tremble again: a stealthy tremor that began in his hands and then spread rapidly over the surface of his body in a hideous, demonic rash, until he was shaking like a whipped dog. He gripped the splintered wood with all his might, trying to force back the palsy as a man might shut a lid on a wild animal trapped. But he could not control it. He clapped his hands together tightly and peered down into the little courtyard, where Raebyrne and Henderson were carefully frisking the prisoners. Bareheaded, without belts or helmets, they looked frail and solemn and ashamed; they looked exactly the way Dev and Raebyrne and Poletti had a few hours before . . .

"Poor devils." Brewster was staring out at the field, blinking, his fingers to his mouth. "We slaughtered them like sheep. The poor devils . . ."

Damon threw him a glance. "You think they wouldn't have done the same thing to you?" he demanded. "You forgotten last night so soon?"

"No, Sarge. I haven't forgotten last night." Brewster's voice was surprisingly steady; it seemed incongruous, issuing from his swollen, misshapen face. "I know. It's war. But . . ."

"But nothing. The object of war is to kill, right? Destroy the enemy—by the use of mass, economy of force, movement, surprise. That's the aim of the game. We used surprise, right?"

"Sure, Sarge."

"All right."

"But"—Brewster waved a slender hand toward the courtyard below them—"a lot of them are wounded. Badly. It seems to me we ought to—"

"So are Jason and Lujak and Burgess wounded. That's the chances we all take. They took them, too. War is not a God damned strawberry social."

"Yes, I've learned that, all right."

"All right, then . . ."

The tremor—buck fever, palsy, visitation, whatever it was—had passed; with the brief exchange with Brewster all his resolution had returned, and his obstinacy. He remembered the disgrace of the night's disaster, the consternation, the dishonor; and his heart hardened. They were here, at Brigny Farm; and they were going to stay here. He had succeeded in capturing what could quite easily have been converted into an enemy strongpoint, and from it had inflicted substantial losses on that enemy. If they didn't accomplish anything beyond this they'd done a good deal. But they weren't through yet, not by a long shot. They would stay here, and fire at targets of opportunity until they were killed or captured or reinforced. They owed that much to Starkie and Davis and all the others, come what may.

He plunged into a fever of activity. He got the prisoners assembled and seated on the big barn floor, with two German stretcher bearers tending the wounded and Burgess sitting on the platform guarding them. He sent Schilz and Henderson after the Spandau and the Mauser ammunition, and set up a roster on digging foxholes in the area between the two buildings so that two men were working all the time; he dug the first hole himself, using a German spade. And half an hour later, again in the tower sweeping the horizon with his glasses, he heard the brisk popping of small-arms fire, coming from the south and west. He alerted Devlin, they manned their posts, and a few minutes later saw little clumps of men hurrying toward them over the hill. Germans, withdrawing in not very good order. This part of the big Friedensturm, at least, was not panning out. He let two small groups get as close as he dared, and opened fire. They thought at first they were being fired on by their own people by mistake, and tried frantically to signal the farm; then they realized their error and fled, those that were left. By now the enemy was streaming fitfully northward through the woods, some of them running; Damon could see the glint of metal behind the green leaves. He and Brewster dragged the Maxim gun to the east face and began to set it up for harrassing fire, and then Raebyrne yelled, "Here comes the cavalry!" and raising his head he saw coming over the distant rise the long wavering lines of men in khaki, the dishpan helmets, long rifles aslant in the afternoon sun; and he sighed with relief.

"I never thought I'd see it," Brewster was saying. "I never thought I'd see a sight so wonderful . . ."

"What the hell," Raebyrne scoffed, "it's only that contrary Second Battalion, running up to swallow all the glory. Bunch of—"

A torrent of bullets spattered the wall beside their heads and the three of them ducked.

"Why, the clodderpolls!" Raebyrne cried, "—the zany, jobberknowl- ing—"

Damon snatched up his rifle and flung himself at the shutters, drove the butt with all his might against the wood; it gave, splintered, sagged—then all at once the whole frame gave way and fell to the court-yard. He was flooded with sunlight; he had a glimpse of the wobbling khaki lines, now much nearer, and heard the stuttering cough of a Chau-chat. Tracers burned orange wires through the still summer air.

"Cut that out!" he roared. "Stop that God damned firing! . . ." They either couldn't see him or didn't care. Someone was pulling insistently at his shoulder. He whipped off his helmet and scaled it out of the win-dow; it hung in the air, an inverted brown saucepan, bounced once in the wheat. Another burst smashed against the stone, just below him. He looked around in a fury of need, saw the blanket Lujak was lying on and yanked it out from under him. Lujak shrieked with pain. Brewster was clutching at him, calling, "Sarge, get *down—!*" He shook off Brewster's hands, lurched to the open rectangle of light again and flapped the dirty, bloodstained blanket up and down, shouting: "No, no, *no* . . . !"

The gun stopped; and now the Yanks were running down the long slope through the wheat, their weapons held high, their gear clinking, a strangely festive sound against the clatter of rifle fire off toward Brigny-le-Thiep He stepped back from the window and rubbed his face, listen-ing now to the hollow thunder of hobnailed boots on the cobbles, the clamor of voices. And Raebyrne, leaning far out of the shattered aper-ture, waved one arm and hollered:

"Come on, you coon-assed gladigators—all aboard for the frigging Alamo!"

Damon knelt beside Lujak, who was holding on to his knee and moan-ing. "It's all right," he said. "They'll be up here for you in no time, now . . ."

"—Yes, but him!—what about *him?*" Lujak cried, pointing.

He looked. Jason was lying on his side, his body queerly twisted; one hand flopped back and forth on the floor. Damon reached over—recoiled with the slow rush of blood that had soaked the man's collar. Jason's eyes had rolled up under the lids. He was quivering all over, and his face was an awful bluish white. "What happened?" he muttered.

"I don't know, I don't know!" Lujak stammered. "It was when you were at the window, after you'd grabbed my blanket . . . You butcher!" Lujak shrieked all at once, "you filthy bastard butcher—you'll kill us all! *You* don't care . . ."

He got up. "All right," he said quietly, and the wounded man sub-sided in moans and shivers. "Take it easy, Lujak."

There were voices down below, the thump and rumble of steps on the oak stairs, and there was Major Caldwell, followed by the battalion adjutant, a lieutenant Damon didn't know, and two enlisted men. The Major's thin, almost fragile face was lined and tense; the front of his uniform was covered with dirt, and he had a rifle in his hand.

Damon rose to his feet and saluted and said: "Sir, B Company, Second Platoon reporting for duty with six effectives."

"Good morning, Damon." The Major returned the salute. "So this is where you've been keeping yourself." He pointed to the Maxim gun. "How'd you get that?"

"Took it, sir."

"I see. With these six effectives of yours?"

"Hell's fire, Major, he took it all by himself," Raebyrne broke in, "—busted in here all by his lonesome and shot it out with a whole passel of Pee-roossians, just like a hang-town draw fighter . . ."

"Be quiet, Reb," Damon told him.

The officers laughed and Major Caldwell smiled and said, "No, let him go on. What happened then, Raebyrne?"

"Why, *then* he spotted the other gun on that roof over yonder, so he touched off that crowd, just for good measure."

The Major's eyes gleamed. "Is that a fact?"

"I'll be dogged if it ain't, Major. You ask Tim here, or Corporal Devlin or any of the others. We come larruping up the stairs and there he was, inspecting the south forty with the Borsch officer's biraculors, standing up there proud as a frog eating fire. With his back to 'em! A tolerable hollowcast . . ."

"All right, Reb," Damon said. "All right.—Who got back, Major? who got back from the second platoon?"

"Well, some of them. Krazewski, Wallis, Tsonka, Turner—about a dozen others. They're still drifting in."

"Did Lieutenant Harris get back?"

"Not to my knowledge." The Major was standing at the eastern shutter, scratching his chin. "Well, well . . . Who's that over there?"

"Devlin, sir. Corporal of the second squad. And two men from C Company we picked up this morning in the woods."

Caldwell turned and glanced at him quickly. "You sent them over there to man that gun after you killed its crew?"

"Yes, sir."

"—And that ain't all, either, Major," Raebyrne broke in again. "Old Sarge seen 'em coming out of the woods yonder, half the tear-ass Pee-roossian army stomping in lockstep over to Briny-Deep, and he made us hold our fire till you could smell their feet inside their boots—and then we stood 'em off like Antietam Creek. I want to tell you, they was a might fitified! That old Fritzie officer looked like a coon hound shitting Bowie knives . . ."

"Thank you, Raebyrne," the Major said. "That's wonderfully graphic." He turned to Damon with his crisp, alert manner. "Now let me hear it from you, Damon." He listened intently as Sam gave him a short résumé, now and then nodding. When the Sergeant concluded he said: "Why did you decide to stay here? in this room up here?"

"I don't know, Major. It just—felt right. The height and everything." He paused, and for the first time he smiled. "I used to be a night clerk in a hotel back home."

The Major burst into laughter. "Did you? A night clerk . . ." He shook his head, still laughing. "I must confess I can't see you as a night clerk, Damon."

"I was, though, sir. A good one."

"I don't doubt it. I don't doubt it at all." Caldwell seemed to find the whole idea infinitely amusing. "*Night clerk*," he murmured, and stroked his mustache with his forefinger. "Well, well . . . Why did you hold your fire for so long on the support group?"

"I was certain they didn't know we were in here, Major. I wanted the main body in that ditch—I figured they'd take cover there instead of rushing the farm. And then it was such a long way back to the woods—I was hoping for a clean sweep."

"And I'd just as soon or a little never go through *that* again," Raebyrne declared fervently. "Major, it was worse than being tied to a tobacco rack hand and foot, with a nest of white-faced hornets crawling all over your ass . . ."

The Adjutant said, "How long were you planning to keep the hotel open, Damon?"

"Just as long as we had any transients, sir."

"Weren't you worried about being shelled?" Caldwell asked him. "It seems a little—exposed, up here . . ."

"We were digging trenches out there in relays. The only thing I was worried about was a rolling barrage—if they were planning an assault in force behind a rolling barrage, I didn't see how we could get back up here in time."

"Yes, that is a problem, isn't it? But what about food and ammunition—how'd you plan to cope with all that?"

Damon grinned faintly. "There's plenty of water in the well. We were going to eat their food and fire their ammunition as long as they'd keep giving it to us." That sounded rather puffy; he shrugged his shoulders and said: "Hell, Major, we were lucky—bull lucky. I guess I was hoping to press my luck a little more."

Caldwell thrust out his lower lip. "Yes, well, you've got to have a little luck in this business. It's like any other." He gazed out at the long north field with its windrows and heaps of mutilated figures in field gray, and nodded grimly. "Very impressive, Damon. Very impressive indeed." He put his knuckles on the sill. "There are a lot of doughboys down there right now who would be dead and dying if you hadn't pulled off this astonishing little exploit of yours." He turned and faced Sam with a boyish grin. "Maybe I'm one of them." Then his expression changed to the alert, expectant one. "You gambled on our coming back through here, didn't you?"

"Yes, sir."

"Why here?"

"I remembered from the map yesterday. I figured you would avoid the woods east of Brigny and drive back to the embankment, trying to envelop them; and this was the way you'd do it—following the curve of the field."

"I see." Caldwell nodded again. "You're a lieutenant, Damon. As of this moment."

"Yes, sir . . . Thank you, sir."

"Don't thank me. We're indebted to you. Devlin is promoted to sergeant. You can give him your stripes." The Major grinned. "I want General Hemley to hear about this." Several more soldiers had crowded into the room, among them Devlin and Henderson, looking resolute and dirty. Caldwell turned to them. "Boys, I'm downright proud of you. Now we took a beating yesterday. But we're back, and we're going to keep right on going. The next time we do this the troop dispositions will be better, and you will be equipped with grenades. Among other things. I can promise you that." He looked at the roomful of weary men, his eyes darting quickly. "They've been making mistakes in this war since the fourth day of August, 1914, and they're going to keep on making them from time to time. And we must take what we get and make the most of it. That's what you boys have done here. It'll be an inspiration to us all." He paused. "Well, let's get going. Staff tells us the Germans are planning to counterattack in force, using elements of the Ninth Prussian Guards."

"They're going to regret it, Major," Raebyrne said.

"You bet they are." Caldwell thrust out his lower lip again. "A whole lot of people are going to change their minds about the AEF before the next week is out." He shook Damon's hand. "Good work, Lieutenant. Report to me at fifteen hundred hours. We'll be reforming B Company."

"Yes, sir. Do you have—any immediate orders for me?"

The Major stared at him, and then laughed. "Why, stay right here, by all means. It's your hotel." He vanished quickly down the stairs.

Damon sat down on a German helmet and leaned against the cool stone wall. Devlin was standing by the open shutter and the two men stared at each other for a long moment.

"Well, Sam," Devlin said after a pause.

"Well, Dev." He handed Devlin one of the cigarettes the Adjutant had given him. "We're promoted."

Downstairs he heard the clink of shovels, and someone laughed hoarsely and cleared his throat. He dropped his hands in his lap. The elation he had dreamed of would not come. He thought of the German boy he'd bayoneted downstairs, the terrified scampering of the gunner on the other roof, the shrill, faint cries in the long field; and a cold remorse sifted through him like the breath of death itself. He had done what he'd promised himself—what he'd known in all wild ignorance he would; and yet none of it was what he had known it would be. It was not like it at all.

They left their clothes in sodden little dun piles and ran leaping and yelping into the river, and the water washed over them gently, silken cool against their naked bodies. The sky was clear and high, like summer skies back home, and swallows dipped and danced above the trees. The air was full of the smell of fresh-cut hay, and poppies, and little blue-and-yellow flowers they didn't know; but it didn't matter, the world was here under their hands, quivering with wonder and release. They hooted and hollered and splashed water on one another, they scraped mud from their necks and forearms and feet, they swam savagely for a few yards, whipping their arms back and forth, and then raced along the shore flapping rags of underwear. They chased one another up the bank and in again, pelted each other with apples or floated dreamily, their arms extended, gazing up at that achingly pure blue summer sky. They were free.

Turner stood on his hands underwater, his feet straight and white and thin, his genitals hanging absurdly from a forest of blond hair—collapsed sidewise to reappear red-faced and panting. Damon was lying beside Devlin on the bank and Raebyrne lobbed an apple at him and hit him on the belly and cried: "Got you, Sarge . . ."

Sam cocked an eye at him. "You're pretty salty, Reb."

"Pure quill fact. I do believe I'll light out for little old Paree."

"I don't advise it."

"Just for a spell. I won't disadvantage you none. Sign up for one of them sinful rooms with a Louise Cans bedstead and lots of purple hangings over the windows and a nice frisky little gin-feel and a demijohn of that handy-brandy, and I'll be tolerable satisfied."

"You would?"

"Shoot, yes. My wants are simple." There was a rope dangling from the branch of a massive plane tree; Raebyrne took a running leap, gripped the rope and swung out over the river; letting go he clutched his nose in a gesture of mock terror and landed with a thunderous splash, inundating the others near him, and reappeared, shouting: "Be damned to the lot of you—who got the jug?" He promptly got into a water fight with three of the others and raced away up the bank again.

Tsonka, winding a puttee with care, squinted up at him. "You're pretty cranked up, Rebel."

Raebyrne danced about on one foot, batting at the water in his head. "Well, I don't rightly know, Mike. But if I had feather in hand I'd call it flying." He began to dry himself with his underwear. "Yep. I been most everywhere God got land, and Paree is where I want to be."

"I wouldn't try it," Krazewski said, coming up out of the water. "Muleskinner told me that town is crawling with MPs. Said they got a hoosegow there so deep you'll never see the light of day again."

"Can't help that. What I need is, I need to get my ashes hauled, and that's the red-hot gospel. How about you, Tim?" he said with a wink at Brewster. "Ain't you on the incline for some of this Froggy round-the-world loving?"

Brewster blushed a fiery red to his collar bones. "Well, I'm not sure, Orville . . ."

"What do you mean, you're not *sure?* How can you even be in doubt?"

Brewster drew a deep breath and put his hands on his naked hips. "Well, the fact is—I've never been with a girl. That way, I mean."

"Oh, my battered tintype," Tsonka groaned.

"Well, I'm fair downcast to hear that," Raebyrne went on. "Hell's fire, son, don't you know that's what makes the world go round?"

"I think," Brewster said, a trifle self-consciously, "a person ought to save himself for the girl he's going to marry."

This sentiment was greeted by hoots and roars from the platoon.

"You think that's going to matter to *her*, Brewster?"

"What you think she's been doing while you're gone?"

"Hell, what *she* don't know won't hurt her none at all."

"Get wise to yourself! . . ."

"I can't believe you fellows mean that," Brewster protested, troubled. Damon raised his head and watched the boy, who looked white and fragile, standing half-naked against the dense green of the bushes. The swelling had gone down during the past two days, but his nose still had a high, thick ridge at the base. Damon remembered the look in his eyes over the glittering, shuttling cartridge belt up in the tower.

"Don't you know you'll get sick without your poontang?" Raebyrne said.

"Go on . . ."

"Just a question of time. You know when a horse gets the heaves?"

"No."

"Well, same thing. Pandication of the gonads. Ain't you never had *that?*"

Brewster tossed his head and turned away to finish dressing. "Aw. You're ragging me."

"Smoking hot gospel."

They milled around on the bank, trying to decide what to do.

"Well, I'll tell you boys. I'm going to latch on to a little of that tickly vang-rougee," Raebyrne announced. "Just for a starter. Now who's going to help this Tarheel to shoulder the load?"

"You guys keep out of trouble, now," Damon said, his eyes closed.

They gave him vigorous assurances and moved away along the river path, their voices growing fainter. Lying naked in the hot sun with

Devlin, Damon knew he should have given them the word, put the fear of God and the MPs into them, but he couldn't stir a finger. He felt inundated by a complete lassitude that lapped out into his eyelids, his fingertips, the roots of his hair. The sun lay on him like the warm breath of a goddess, birds called in the shrubs behind his head; and he didn't care—not for a single thing in all the world. Let them get drunk if they had a mind to, he'd get them out of it. God knew they'd earned it. They'd taken over Cherseulles from the Second Battalion; had dug in there and withstood two savage counterattacks and eighteen hours of nearly incessant shelling. Yesterday, famished and dizzy with lack of sleep, they had marched back to billets in the town of Charmevillers and slept the sleep of the exhausted. Moving along the column wearing Lieutenant Harris' gold bars, Damon had felt a slow, deep pride. His men. They were his now, to care for—the indomitable remnants of B Company who had avoided death and captivity. Tramping in the evening dust they had talked very little. They were subdued, but steady. They knew what they had done . . .

"Remember that parade in Paris?" Devlin murmured indolently; his voice seemed to hover in the still air above them. "I keep thinking of that girl that kissed me. The first one. She was a strawberry roan and she had great, deep, round eyes."

"It was quite a parade."

"It seems a long way back now, you know?"

"By God, I'm going to learn French," Damon said suddenly.

"Why bother? What the hell, Sam, there's only one language in wartime . . ."

"Sure."

They fell silent again, drugged with sun and languor. Damon thought all at once, with a slow throb of loss, of home. His sister Peg's last letter had been full of news. Ted Barlow had got a job with the Mac-Cormack people in Lincoln; Uncle Bill had joined up again and was raging away in Georgia, instructing recruits in the manual of arms and close-order drill; he had been infuriated at learning Sam had been made a sergeant. Mr. Verney had again been down with pneumonia. And Celia—Peg had saved her bombshell for last—had got married to Fred Shurtleff in the biggest, grandest wedding Walt Whitman had ever seen, with formal clothes and a reception on the lawn under a pink-and-white striped tent, with champagne and a five-piece orchestra that played waltzes and fox-trots, and after that a parade of limousines all the way down to the Union Pacific station. Peg had spared him none of the details. He smiled ruefully. Dear, lively, willful Celia. Well: he missed her, he missed them all—but the savageries and affections of the past week had turned them all to shadows. That part of his life was over; and now, lying on the dense mat of grass, he knew in one sense it always had been. But it was fun remembering . . .

The sun poured over his flesh like a gauze mantle, cloaking it in heat.

He was falling away through time, rolling with the roll of the earth's turning . . . He was lying at the edge of the big field near Hart's Island and the river was the Platte, steel gray under the long, white sky; the trees were cottonwoods and willows, and Celia was standing in her petticoats, dancing a funny little jig and laughing at him; laughing and laughing, mocking him. He moved toward her but she was far too fast for him—she spun away shrieking with laughter, now and then taunting him with words he couldn't understand; she was joined by his sister Peg now—a situation that embarrassed him subtly. In his sternest voice he ordered Peg to leave but she only laughed, and the two girls began to indulge in some kind of girls' confidences, all giggles and secrets and confusion; and he listened to them, half-irritated, half-amused, remembering, hidden back under the shade of the trees, a stoneware pitcher full of cold milk and a quarter of a black currant pie . . .

He started, hearing voices near them, women's voices, realized he had been asleep and dreaming—shot up in a sitting position in time to see through the thickets two girls gazing at him in great merriment. He whipped his shirt from under his head and flung it over him and hissed: "Dev!"

"What's the matter?" Devlin muttered groggily. Damon gave him a shove and he too sat up, saw the girls and snatched at Damon's shirt, pulled it over his middle and rolled away with it, leaving the Nebraskan exposed. Damon grabbed at his trousers. The girls had moved off behind some bushes; he could hear them talking, laughing softly. Damon grinned—then glanced in surprise at Devlin, who had leaped to his feet and was hurriedly dressing.

"Come on, Sam," he said. "Dépêche, now . . ."

"Daypesh *what?*"

"Don't let 'em get away. I mean it."

"What are you going to do?"

"Charm the pants off them, that's what. Hurry up, now."

"You're kidding."

"You watch. Come on, it's in the stars."

They dressed in madcap haste and ran to the thickets. The girls were some distance off now, heading toward a group of buildings near the shattered stone bridge. They hurried after them, walking fast, setting their caps aslant.

"Now let me handle this," Devlin commanded. "You'll see—there's nothing to it. Your first French lesson."

They caught up with the girls, who didn't seem averse to being overtaken, under a grove of chestnut trees.

"Mademoiselles," Devlin called, "—comment allez-vous aujourd'hui?"

They turned now, still laughing but wary. One was plump, with a smooth, round, pretty face like a china doll. The other was dark and slender; her eyes flashed in the sunlight like steel. Devlin made a funny

little bow, smiling at them. "Nous—sommes Américains," he declared
proudly.

"Oui, oui, sans doute, Américains!" They burst out laughing together.

"Nous aimons la France, d'ailleurs," Devlin pursued. "Elle est char-
mante, vive, généreuse—comme vous vous-mêmes . . ."

"Ah, vous parlez français assez bien, Sergent," the slim, dark one
said—and then she unleashed a burst of French Damon couldn't begin to
follow. Watching Devlin's face he could see he didn't have too good an
idea, either.

"Well, we've been swimming," he said in English, in some confusion.
"Nager, c'est vrai? dans la rivière . . ."

"Oui, nager, bien sûr," they echoed, and their laughter was like birds
singing.

"Maintenant, nous sommes très fatigués," Devlin went on. "Beaucoup
de blessés, beaucoup de mortes. Nos camarades. Une grande bataille."

"Ah." They got that all right. Their eyes—even the china doll's—
were all at once full of sorrow, anger, wonder, fear, regret. They had
such *expressive* eyes!

Devlin was talking to the slender, vivacious one. The plump girl with
the smooth, delicate skin turned to Damon: "You—officier?"

"Oh. Yes. Lieutenant." He gave it the French pronunciation.

"Mais votre ami"—she pointed one finger—"est sergent." And her
pretty little round face showed confusion.

He got that and felt absurdly pleased with himself. What the hell,
French wasn't so difficult. "Oui. Sergent. I"—he tapped his chest—"was
sergent, he was corporal. Until a few days ago. *I*—gave *him*—my
stripes. See?" He showed the pale shadows of the chevrons on his
sleeves. "Voilà! He is my—best ami. Bon ami."

"They just made him one," Devlin broke in on them. "Promu sur la
champ d'honneur. Il est un grand héro . . ."

"Vraiment, un héro?" Their eyes flickered up at him doubtfully.

"Sans blague. Son chef—ah, I can't say it. The blasted *verbs!* The
Major's putting him up for the medal of honor. Médaille d'honneur,
vous comprenez?"

"For Pete sake, Dev."

"Don't be bashful. A little artful bragging never hurt, especially when
it's true. For the love of Saint Denis, don't queer the pitch, now . . ."

They began to walk along the riverbank. Devlin was talking in animated conversation with the dark girl with the flashing eyes, whom he
had apparently appropriated by virtue of his French Canadian mother.
The chubby, fair one was prattling along beside Damon; her eyes darted
up at his, the blond lashes falling away languidly. He kept watching
them, fascinated. He understood more of her conversation than he
would have imagined: it was like glimpsing trout in a mountain stream.
Her name was Denise Renaudin. The war was terrible, everyone had

suffered. They had been afraid the Americans would never come. The past year had in some ways been worst of all. Her father was a prisoner of war in Germany, her brother (though Damon wasn't sure of this) was in a hospital at Angers, recovering from a bad wound. Life was hard.

At the edge of the town, Devlin turned. "Michele wants to know if we can help them out. The door to their place is broken. Don't you think we ought to give them a hand?"

"Absolutely," Damon answered. "Lead on, mister linguist."

They retraced their steps, followed the river to a second bridge, this one intact, and turned right up a tiny street filled with narrow houses jammed against each other like an old man's teeth. A church steeple dark as ancient armor glided along above the tile roofs. They turned onto a still narrower lane where the front doors—massive oak doors with carved lion's heads and flowered iron knockers—opened right onto the cobbles. Nearby Damon could hear the high rhythmic clank of a forge, and saw across the way the angry red glow, and showers of blue-white sparks like tiny stars. Michele turned and swung open one of the great doors, and they climbed the stairs to a gloomy landing.

"Voilà," she was saying, "c'est affreux, hein?"

It was *affrur*, all right—if *affrur* meant a complete wreck. The door to the apartment had apparently been forced, then smashed off its hinges; a funny-looking upholstered couch with a wavy, off-centered back had lost one of its claw legs, an oak table was lying on its side, its top split right down the middle. Michele was talking to Devlin rather nervously. Damon couldn't get very much of it. It had something to do with American soldiers at a café nearby who had got drunk and followed the girls home and forced their way in, thrown the furniture around and generally ransacked the place before they left.

"Did they steal?" Devlin demanded sharply. "Est-ce qu'ils ont volé des choses? monnaie? argenterie? choses comme ça?" They shook their heads. Had they reported the affair to the provost marshal, the military police?

The girls exchanged glances, shook their heads again rapidly. It was impossible: they didn't know the soldiers' names. They fell into an odd little silence; they seemed to be at a loss for anything to say. Damon watched the two women reflectively. There was something he didn't quite understand—and then all at once he did. He knelt down and examined the broken leg of the couch.

"Beautiful carving, Dev."

"Sons of bitches," Devlin was saying savagely. "Taking advantage of a couple of helpless young girls! Christ, I'd like to get my hooks on them . . ."

"Well. You won't."

"Probably some of that lousy Third Battalion—a bunch of counter-jumpers and plug-uglies if I ever saw any . . ." He was waving his arms; he had worked himself up into a fine French-Irish rage. "I'm going to raise hell, Sam. I'm going to see Caldwell—"

"Look, Dev—"

"—no bunch of tinhorn baboons is going to get away with a thing like this!"

"Dev, for Christ sake . . ." Damon got to his feet and stood close in front of him, tapping him on the chest with his forefinger until he stopped shouting. "Dev, they don't *want* to go to the MPs. Can't you see that?"

Devlin's eyes went blank. "They don't?"

"No. They don't. They—can't . . ." He gave the Sergeant a long, hard look. "Can't you see how it is?"

Devlin stared carefully back at him, then at the girls. "Sure," he said in a different tone. "Yeah. Sure. I can see how it is."

"Okay. Now the thing to do is fix the place up for them. That's what they want."

"Right." Devlin held a long, complicated colloquy with Michele, after which the two men descended to the ground floor and went out back through a little yard where three or four scrawny chickens scratched listlessly or bathed in the hot dust, fluffing their feathers. At the end of the yard was a sort of stone dungeon without a door. Devlin hallooed and a figure came out of the dungeon, a small, hunched-over man with white hair and mustaches and a narrow, leathery face that twisted into a mask of hostility on recognizing the uniforms. Devlin greeted him with a lot of Gallic frills and salutations; the gnome stared back at them implacably. The young ladies had sent them down to ask for some tools, Devlin went on in the friendliest manner. "Peut-être vous avez des outils, monsieur? marteau? scie à main? rabot?"

The old man gazed at them a moment longer, then turned away and led them inside to an ancient narrow chest with great brass handles at each end. He lifted the lid and crouched over it in a proprietary way, watching them.

"Oui, très très bon." Devlin picked up a wooden jack plane, spun the cylinder deftly and lifted out the iron, running his thumb along the cutting edge. "Look at that, Sam. That's great steel."

The grognard edged closer, his bright old eyes glinting in the damp gloom. "Vous êtes menuisier, vous?" he croaked, pointing a crabbed finger.

Devlin smiled. "Non, non—aide de charpentier, seulement. Mais mon oncle, il est maître.—De bon acier, hein?"

The old man smiled a wintry smile. "Regardez, monsieur," he said, and turned the block to the light. Burned in the wood was the legend *P. Grimaud, 1837.*

My God, Damon thought, that's thirty years before Nebraska was admitted into the Union—that's ten before the first permanent settlement. He watched the old man, who was drawing one of his gnarled hands back and forth beneath his mustaches and explaining something to Devlin about the plane, whose base was a rich, deep wood, smooth as satin with oiling and use. They cared for things here; it was an attitude he'd learned to respect in the Army. But war didn't respect any thing, or place, or person. It crushed everything that happened to stand in its way . . .

Devlin had shouldered the chest. They both shook hands with the old man and climbed the stairs again; the girls were sitting side by side, mending the upholstery on the couch.

"Bon. Au travail, hein?" Flexing his muscles, Devlin struck a pose in the doorway, full of prowess, noble resolve, the afternoon sun blazing on his face; the girls laughed, watching him.

They removed their blouses, took the door off and set in a wooden key where it was badly damaged, reset the lock and rehung it. They repaired the foot on the funny-looking divan, which Michele called a shays-long, and then began on the table. They had a great time. They hammered and sawed and chiseled and called back and forth to each other and the girls. It was very peaceful in the long, high-ceilinged room. Damon worked slowly and carefully; the old, worn tools came to his grip naturally, the shavings curled away from his hands and littered the floor around him, the sun poured through the casement windows; the girls chattered along, talking of things he only dimly understood— and it didn't matter. He felt as though some parts of him had been restored. Only the thunder-mutter of artillery off to the northwest recalled the war.

Later they built a fire in the hearth with the wood ends and shavings, sat at the repaired table and ate the thick green soup and drank two bottles of pinot noir; they tore huge pieces of bread from a long loaf and wiped their plates clean, the way the girls did. Devlin was talking a blue streak now, his thin, handsome face flushed with wine, pouring out French and English in a headlong potpourri. He told them of days in Chicopee Falls, his hometown, of coming off work from the mill in the early fall mornings with the sun burnished gold behind the trees and the ground crackling white with frost; and Michele and Denise talked about the war, the terrible days in '14, with the Germans at Charleroi, at Cambrai, at Soissons, and the Uhlans sweeping the country everywhere like a plague. They had left their homes and sat in the woods all night for two nights, hungry and miserable, not knowing what to do. And then the miracle, when General Maud'huy had captured the heights above Montmirail, and the sales Boches had fallen back . . . But that had been only the beginning, not the end. After that, year after year of war and no end in sight. Less and less food, clothes, implements—less and less of everything. And every family in Charmevillers in mourning. And only the year before the great mutiny . . .

Damon pricked up his ears at this—he had caught the word. A mutiny? in the French army? Well no, not really, Michele answered; it was simply a warning to the officers. The poilus refused to attack in the face of certain death; they would hold the line, but they would not advance, not anymore. They had suffered too much.

"Well, *we're* going to advance," Devlin declared. "And then this old guerre's going to be over toot sweet."

"You—croyez ça?" They were all talking in eerie mixtures of pidgin English and French, divining one another's replies more than understanding them explicitly.

"Of course! The Irlandais and the French can lick la monde. Didn't you know that?"

"C'est entendu! Mais—Sam . . ." and Denise pointed at Damon with an amused, quizzical look.

"Quoi? Sam's half-Irish. Same as me. We're going to run those Heinies all the way to Siberia on a sled, and bring back the Kaiser with an apple in his mouth. You watch our smoke." Picking up an apple from a blue earthenware bowl he popped it in his mouth and pantomimed the Emperor Wilhelm II with his head on a platter, mustaches drooping, eyes goggling—jumped to his feet, snatched up his soup plate and a gnarled walking stick he'd spied in a corner of the room, and fluttering the plate like a boater went into a strutting song and dance, his eyes rolling, his voice high and clear in the early evening stillness:

"*I'm gonna make a pickelhaube outa Kaiser Bill*
And then I'll sashay all over Paree!
Turn on my maximum power,
Light up the Eiffel Tower,
With Madame Pompadour to keep me compan-ee . . .
I'm gonna take the iron hinges off that Brandenburg Gate
And then I'll paint up the town of Paree!
Get me beaucoup de cuties
Who all know their duty's
To make a Turkish sultan outa me!"

The girls broke into applause, shrieking with laughter, and Devlin paused, pleased with the results. "Encore?" he called, his hand cupped behind his ear. "Do I hear an encore? Yeah, you're looking at Jolly Jack Devlin, the terror of the AEF . . ."

"Ah, Dev," Michele cried, laughing, wiping at her eyes. "You are si éveillé!"

"That's me."

"Et si—si débonnaire . . ."

"What's that mean? en anglais?"

She shook her head happily. Her eyes were half-closed, her hair fell away from her forehead in little dark waves, her lips were curved in the gentlest of smiles; and watching her Damon started. With a quiet little shock he saw that she was attracted to Devlin—not as a wild knight errant in khaki or an easy mark, but as a man. His vitality, his joie de vivre, his heedless generosity had reached her. He said in an undertone: "Dev . . ."

But Devlin didn't hear him. He came up to Michele with mincing, arch entreaty, bowed and said: "Est-ce que Mademoiselle me fera l'honneur de cette danse?"

Staring up at him, his blouse open, his puttees unwound, his red hair tousled from the swim in the Marne, she laughed—then her face became all at once very grave, almost pained. She rose to her feet and put her arm on his shoulder. He lifted her to him light as a feather, and began to sing softly:

> "Standing by the river, lights all aglow,
> Thinking of an evening out of lost long ago;
> Lord, all I can do is pray
> Let it be somewhere, someday . . .
> —Why did I ever let you out of my sight?"

They moved slowly, dreamily, around the little room. Michele's head was on his shoulder now; she seemed enervated, almost drugged, without will or constraint. And sitting at the table with his glass in his hand, watching the two figures clinging to each other, swaying, Damon felt brushed with dread, he did not know why. He looked away. Outside the windows the sun was sinking behind a graceful row of Raebyrne's skirmisher trees. The sky dipped into coral and lemon hues, a pale rose on the undersides of the little snatches of cloud; and the river looked not so much like water as metal cooling with the advent of dusk. Far away the big guns rumbled and bumped their slow avalanche of war. He shivered and crossed his arms. They must go. Now. If they didn't—if they didn't something terrible would happen.

"Dev," he said quietly. "Dev, we've got to go . . ."

"No." Michele turned and stared at him. "No—pourquoi? You go," she said to him; and to Devlin, pleading, "Qu'il part, alors—mais vous restez ici, un peu . . . Attendez!" she cried; running over to a large oak cabinet she lifted out a massive Gramophone with a fluted, four-sided trumpet. "Music! Pour la danse . . ."

Denise frowned and called something to her sharply, in warning; Michele replied placatingly, pumping the the crank with a kind of desperation. There was the high sea roar of the needle, and then a waltz spilled out of the speaker, tinny and tremulous. Devlin dropped his arms.

"I can't waltz."

"Alors, je vous instruirai," Michele said softly; and she swung lightly with him, chanting, "Un, deux, trois, un, deux, trois," until he'd caught the lifting, swooping rush of it, and they whirled together silently in the long room above the Marne, their shadow gliding along the ivory walls.

Sam picked up his wineglass and set it down again, and clasped his hands together on the table. He had the sense of spying on some fragile personal intimacy, and it turned him uneasy: he did not want to feel what he was feeling, and listened intently again to Denise. She came, she said, from a town called Pontoise, which was on the other side of Paris; she was only visiting Michele, who was her dearest friend. There was something about a Citroën munitions plant—they had worked in it together, Damon thought—and then Michele's mother had become gravely ill and Michele had come home here to be with her; and then she had died and Michele had been left alone in the world. What about her father? he asked. Oh, he had been killed in the first days of the war. Had there been a man? Denise nodded. Her fiancé had been killed at Madriant, the year before. Now there was no one to look after her except an aunt in Lyon whom she detested. Denise had been pleading with her to go to Lyon but she would not. She was so violent! so violent and headstrong (he felt Denise was saying this): she seized on some-thing—an idea, a hope, a person—and nothing else mattered. And now she persisted in staying on in this place alone, a prey to her loneliness, her despair . . .

He nodded sympathetically. "Triste," he said. "Very triste."

She heaved a sigh and gazed out at the river, now barely discernible through the filigree of branches. "La vie—ne se déroule point comme oh l'espère—quand on est jeune," she said with a kind of hard, sad finality.

He struggled with that, apprehending more from her face and intona-tion than from this elusive, liquid language; he reasoned it out—and was filled with consternation. "But *you're* young—and pretty—you've got your whole life ahead of you," he cried softly.

She gave him a slow sad smile. "All the same," she said; and repeated, "All the same . . . "

He was amazed; he could hardly bear the look in her steady blue eyes. It was crazy—she wasn't twenty, with everything right there ahead of her, on a platter . . . He reached out and took her small white hand in his; she smiled at him nervously, but that grave shadow lay in her gaze. I ought to comfort her, he thought. Earlier, he had wanted her as a woman; now he felt confused. There was something here he didn't understand. The waltz—Michele had put another record on the Gramophone— swooped in his head, flooding it. Drowsy with wine and sun, near sleep, he had nonetheless an awesome sense of alien, venerable worlds far beyond his grasp. He had rushed at life with boundless confidence and open hands; but this was another world entirely—and perhaps a much wiser one. Maybe there was more to life than energy and simple valor— more to it all than could be embraced by a willing heart and a sense of destiny—

The record had ended. He looked at Michele and Dev. They had stopped dancing and were talking now, holding each other. Michele's face was animate, impassioned; her eyes clung to the Sergeant's with a fiercely importunate intensity—she looked frail and wild and rather beautiful. Damon lowered his eyes. Denise was singing a plaintive little melody he'd never heard before and he joined in, humming along, not knowing the words and not caring, while the night breeze soughed in the open casements and somewhere nearby, perhaps from the belfry of the slate-dark church steeple, a bell tolled like the most delicate of chimes. Night. The world had relented for a time, had turned soft and pliant and full of deeps. What the hell, he thought. Let everyone catch at what little part of it he could, before the shriek and slam and dry-mouthed fear began again . . .

There was the click of a latch and he looked up. The wine in the bottom of his glass was black as ink; the empty soup plates on the table loomed like dazed faces. The room was empty except for Denise, who was sitting perfectly still, her tiny hand still resting in his.

"I'm sorry," he said. "Excusez moi, Denise. I was nodding off, I guess. We haven't had all the sleep in the world the past few days . . ." He leaned forward; in the sinking dusk he thought she was smiling in re-ply—then to his great surprise he saw that tears were running down her face. He touched her cheek.

"What is it?" he asked softly. "Don't be afraid. What is the mat-ter?"

She shook her head, still mute, still motionless: a lovely little round-faced Dresden china doll. She had not made a sound. Very gently he got to his feet and came around the table to her. As his hand reached her head she rose and threw herself against him and clung to him, trembling; and he felt her tears on his throat. But still she hadn't made a sound.

⟪ 6 ⟫

The camion swayed and jolted and jarred, roaring in the darkness, and around them the dust rose in clouds. There was a moon that looked immensely flat and old, riding along above the treetops; below it the far horizon glowed now, quaking like ruddy, malignant northern lights. Damon, sitting in the cab with the Annamese driver, asked him their destination in French, and drew a torrent of utterly indecipherable sounds. He grinned. The Annamese, hunched over the wheel like a squat, round-faced idol, returned an inscrutable oriental gaze.

"Okay," Damon said in English. "Suit yourself, buster, and go to hell."

The Annamese shook his head, his teeth flashed once. "No—you," he said, and pointed ahead to the quaking hearth of the horizon. "*You* . . ."

"I get it. Cheerful little monster, aren't you?"

They were running north now, almost due north. They were swinging out around the rim of the salient, toward the left-hand corner of the great sack the Germans held from Soissons to Reims. They were going to Soissons. Caldwell—now promoted to lieutenant colonel—had been talking to several of them about it the night before last, after mess.

"Mr. Ludendorff has made a fatal mistake. You do not abandon a sound strategical concept for minor tactical gains. It's like pawn-grabbing in chess: the results are usually disastrous. Ludendorff has allowed Von Boehn's initial success in the Marne Salient to cause him to give up his crucial plan for driving the British into the sea—the Flanders plan." The Colonel's eyes had twinkled in the lamplight. "The old squarehead doesn't know it yet, but he's lost his chance to win the war. More than that, their advance has destroyed the big stalemate once and for all: they have turned it into a war of movement, which is the way it began and the way it should have been waged. Now the doors are all open. We can thrust and envelop and thrust again, until we have Metz and Thionville, and the road into Germany."

There had been a little pause, and Damon had asked: "But Colonel, what if the Germans simply withdraw to prepared positions, the way they did in '17? Won't we be committed to trench warfare then?"

Caldwell nodded. "We would, that's true. But they won't be able to give up all that real estate this time. This isn't '17. And furthermore"—and he smiled his quick, alert smile—"they won't be able to because we won't give them time."

Captain MacDowell of A Company said: "Where are we going to attack, Colonel?"

"That's up to Grand Quartier Général. Foch and his people." Caldwell permitted himself a wry little grimace. "But, if I were going to hazard a guess—I'd say: Soissons . . ."

The truck dropped into a pothole with a bone-jarring jolt, careened on, swaying and rocking; and behind him Damon could hear Turner's voice, metallic with anger: "Jesus! That little Chink can hit *every* hole in the highway. He's a bleeding genius!"

"If they'd just file the corners off the frigging wheels, I'd settle."

A replacement named Mecklar moaned, "Night before last they shell the bejesus out of us, last night we get standby, and now penned in like a bunch of stockyard cattle . . ."

"Sing 'em, laddy-boy."

". . . what *I* want to know is, when are we going to get some shut-eye?"

"Sleep," Devlin answered him, "he's worried about sleep. You want to worry about where the next meal is coming from, if you want to worry . . ."

"Ah, don't bring that up, Sarge."

"Maybe we're going to Paris after all." This sad hope from another replacement, a scrawny kid from San Mateo named Dickey, brought forth an avalanche of hoots and curses.

"In full combat gear? You Simple Simon. Who let you out?"

"Don't be any stupider than you can help . . ."

"When I get home," Mecklar persevered, "I'm going to sleep for seven days running."

"When you get home!" Damon heard Krazewski's booming laugh. "Don't you know you'll be dead tomorrow night? Starched like a shirt. That's what we want you draftees for—machine-gun fodder and nothing else . . ."

There was another silence while the replacements digested this fragment of comfort. Damon resisted the temptation to lean out of the cab and roar at Kraz to keep his mouth shut for a while. Then in the next instant he was glad he had, for Raebyrne was saying, "Don't you worry, son. Just keep your head down, and your tin hat over your ass. And stick close to the Loot and do what he does."

"Every time *I'm* close to the Lieutenant he gives me something to do," Dickey retorted, and the older men laughed.

"No sirree," Raebyrne proclaimed, "this is different, Frisco."

"Don't call me Frisco."

"We got the best platoon leader in the whole Ass End First. Shoot, you drop him into a turpentine vat of wildcats and he'll clamber out with a fine fur coat for that little old froggy gal he's laying out with . . ."

"That's enough of that," Devlin ordered him.

"Why, no offense meant, Sarge. This Tarheel's full of nothing but admee-o-ration. You know that. Old Sam's going to get him another bunch of medals, and craw dee guerries for the lot of us, like last time, and he's going to run right on up to seven-star general. And I'm going to stick right along with him."

"What the hell is he?" asked Clay, one of the replacements from the cannibalized 41st Division; he was a round-faced, handsome boy with ash blond hair, who had rapidly gained a reputation for being a wise guy. "He's just a lousy officer, like all the rest of them."

"I'll remember that," Devlin snarled. "If there was any room here, I'd lay you out right now . . ."

"You'll find out," Raebyrne taunted Clay. "You ain't run against the elephant yet. You weren't down at Briny Deep, standing off a Borsch regiment—six of us, mind you!" His voice rang over the muffled roar of the engine. "Hell's fire, we'd have won the cotton-picking war right then and there if they'd sent the rest of their army at us, and could have all gone home. And old Loot, he did everything just perfect . . . It's the hand of the Almighty, it's resting on his shoulders. He is going to prosper in all he undertempts, and triumph over his enemies. And he is going to be saved."

"You hadn't ought to say that," Devlin muttered.

"I cain't help that none, Dev. It's the word of God, and you cain't tamper with that. And I ain't going to." There was a pause while he apparently reached around in the crowded, jostling mass of bodies. "Now I want you to cover him, Tim. Stick right behind him and give him cover. That's what I'm going to do—"

"Thought you said God was looking out for him, Rebel," Clay broke in mockingly.

"Well, that's all right. Even the Almighty can use a little help where we're going. Just you wait and see . . ."

"Where *are* we going?" Dickey asked plaintively.

"I'll tell you, Frisco." And Raebyrne changed his tone again. "We're going near about all the way, this time. I got the smoking-hot gospel, straight from Chaumont. We're going to tool all the way to Switzer-land—"

"For Christ sake, Switzerland's *neutral*—"

"Don't waylay me. And sail down the Rhine and ambush the lot of them, taking possession of the Yungfrowze and drinking Rhine wine as we go, till we run against the English Channel."

"Then what, Raebyrne?"

"Why, then we're going to have us a big celee-o-bration on the beach, and sail around to the Danderdells and whip the tar out of the Turks and civilize 'em with the bastaraydo . . ."

"Give 'em hell, Reb!"

"Don't you hatless Harrys realize Turkish women wear *pants?*"

Damon smiled somberly in the dark, listening to the laughter. He was a symbol, then: a talisman. Of course that had its good points—if they believed that as his platoon they were invincible, or destined to win, or just plain lucky, they would be better soldiers. Successful armies were built on esprit, on conviction in the face of those clouds of great uncertainty in which Clausewitz said three-quarters of all military endeavor was hidden—

Impulsively he slipped his hand in his breeches pocket, felt for and found the one-franc piece, ran his thumbnail around the broad ridge at the rim, chafed the lettering, the twinned cornucopias. He had seen it lying between two of the great scarred paving stones just outside Picpus Cemetery and picked it up with a curious sense of excitement. It seemed like such a propitious omen . . .

Luck. He rubbed his forehead with his hand, and sighed. He missed bunking with the platoon, living with them, more than he would have believed. But that was what change meant—there was no sense regretting it: you moved on to something else, and relationships changed. They liked him enough, though—and more importantly they respected him utterly: he could tell from the way they responded to his orders, joked with him off duty, asked his advice on personal matters or his opinion on things he knew nothing whatever about, and hung on his answers.

The officers were a different story. Some of them accepted him readily enough: he was a regular, one of the old men, and he was known. His exploit at Brigny Farm had gone through the division like the wind— he was known as "Night Clerk" in the messes; Caldwell had put him up for the Medal of Honor and General Hemley had concurred, and personally congratulated him. But there were others who were less enthusiastic: they resented his suddenly being on equal terms with them, or they felt he was too familiar with his recent associates. His commanding officer, Captain Crowder, was cool toward him, and Traprock Merrick, the old Baker Company sergeant from the days at Early, now a first lieutenant in the expanding line, had made some remarks about Sears Roebuck officers who weren't even dry behind the ears; but Sam continued to go his own way. Let them talk if they wanted to talk. He intended to field the best platoon in the AEF, and he would do it the way he wanted.

French villages slid by, their stone houses ghostly and remote in the moonlight; the fields ran off into the mist like some pale snow. The trucks swung out, overhauling French infantry in column of march, the moon glinting on their pretty casques of helmets. The Annamese driver was humming some fantastic tune that soared off into creepy nasal whines and dissonances. Behind him, the men had fallen silent. They were going up again, up to meet Raebyrne's elephant. Damon ran through the platoon in his mind, ticking off names, remembering aptitudes, weaknesses, worrying about some of the new men. After a time he stopped thinking, closed his eyes and dozed off—snapped awake, his head bouncing on his shoulder, to find it was dawn; and in the fields on both sides of the road were clumps of French, huddled around fires with blankets over their shoulders, like medieval men-at-arms camping in some desolate march of empire . . .

The camions rolled off into a field already trampled flat, and stopped; the platoon got down like old men, groaning and flexing their legs.

"All right," the cry came down the line, "fall in, fall in! . . ."

"Where are we, Sam?" Devlin was asking him.

"Beats me."

They formed up rapidly and were marching before they were fully awake, uphill and down. Up ahead the Colonel was setting a terrific pace. He can't hold this, Damon thought, nobody can, the whole outfit is going to be flopping around like catfish out of water. *How far have we got to go? How far?* He could see the question in the faces of the platoon, none of whom were joking or skylarking now. The road was hard and smooth, its great paving stones worn smooth as glass. One hill, and then another. The sun rose higher and bent its weight on them like bars of hot iron. Damon could hear the snapping of the metal catches on the canteen covers, the scrape of tops being unscrewed, and called:

"All right, now put those canteens away! You'll drink water when I tell you to, and not before . . ."

Someone cursed him in protest and he let it ride; better to have them mad than panicky. There was no end to this march. They plodded into a forest, out of it and on toward still another rise, and another; a shower passed overhead and drenched them, and then again the pitiless sun, and their shirts steamed. When the whistle finally blew they practically fell into the ditches beside the wheatfields.

"Five-minute break," the word came down the column. "Five minutes . . ."

"*Five* minutes!" Krazewski muttered. "Not even ten. Lousy forced march."

"You want to get there, don't you, Kraz?" Turner said.

"It can wait."

From far up the road the whistles blew again, shrill and insistent. Damon got to his feet and called, "All right. Let's go, let's go . . ."

The heat was worse now. His feet burned with every step and he could feel on the inside of his left heel the exquisite needle laceration of a blister starting. Dust coated their faces with its fine white powder and the sweat ran through it in little rivulets, giving them all a clownish, drunken look. They began to straggle; stumbling, falling back.

"Close it up," he shouted, "close it up, now . . ."

By noon they had reached a broad paved highway, gutted with men and matériel, all heading north by east. The world was moving north by east, big guns and poilus and carts of ammunition. Under a grove of trees a detail of MPs were sprawled, eating out of cans.

"Why, you look hungry, boys," a big, black-haired man called to them, waving his arm with its black brassard. "You look as though you ain't getting your three hots per. How about a nice bite of chow?"

Little Turner cursed him savagely, but Raebyrne threw them his broadest grin and hollered, "Couldn't chamber a morsel, Blackie, I'm full to here . . ."

"You look it, Slim!"

"Why, we been eating so heavy it keeps us skinny just carrying it around . . ."

They pressed on, at that same driving pace, outstripped the artillery, the supply wagons; at one point Devlin dropped back and asked him anxiously: "Have they broken through again, Sam? The Germans?"

"I don't know," he answered. "I doubt it." He didn't think they had—there would have been other, more ominous signs if that were the case. But then why such haste? Why were they being lashed along like this, day and night?

The afternoon wore away in fitful exhaustion; the sun hung above their heads, sank behind them; and on they went. They marched doggedly now, like robots, with set faces and glazed eyes, limping on their blisters. Their canteens had been empty for hours. They no longer wondered *How far?*—they were too exhausted even to curse. But they kept on going, en masse, overtaking here and there supine figures from other platoons. They were even too weary to taunt anybody, but a few labored comments ran through the files; and Damon smiled, remembering their raging protest at the forced hikes in full marching order he'd put them through on the roads around Charmevillers. Twenty minutes later he pulled abreast of the second squad, and blinked in amazement: Dickey was wobbling perceptibly, his head rolling like a doll's; Tsonka and Raebyrne had him under the arms, Turner had slung his rifle, Curtis was carrying his pack. Linked together they swayed and labored along, their heads sunk in their shoulders, striding in unison although there was no cadence. And Damon, trudging wearily beside them, felt the same hot rush of affection he'd known that night going up to the line above Brigny, under the flare—but now it was fused with a fierce, possessive pride: they knew the platoon was more than the mere sum of their numbers—they had imbued themselves with this knowledge and made it theirs. They were great, they were magnificent; he was proud to be their leader . . .

They entered another wood now, a wilder, more somber forest; and finally, miraculously the word came down for a two-hour break. They broke ranks, stumbled off the road and sprawled under the fine old trees. Half of them fell asleep beside their rifles. Devlin located a pump near a shattered farmhouse and went with a detail to fill canteens. Damon moved among the drugged, recumbent figures.

"Lieutenant, I can't walk any further, I just *know* I can't . . ."

"Why's that, Mecklar?"

"Look at that." The boy raised his bare foot, where a blister the size of a half-dollar had swollen, the dead-white skin inflamed like some slick, loathsome growth around a moon of raw red flesh. "I can't go on walking with *that* . . ."

"My, that's a fine one. Just like one I've got."

"You *do?*"

"Hell, yes. Everybody's got one. Let's take a look at it." Deftly he lanced it with his penknife, removed the dead skin and bandaged it with slow care, while Mecklar peered at him with frightened absorption. "There you go. Hang your socks from a tree branch for a little while before you put them back on, hear?"

"You'd think they could have driven the trucks up a little farther than they did, wouldn't you?" Brewster asked him.

"Yes, you would, wouldn't you?" He grinned. "But that's the way they do things in the army, Tim. We know all about that, don't we?"

"I'm beginning to learn."

"That's the pitch." He exchanged a few words with Krazewski, turned back to say something to Brewster; but the boy was already asleep, his face on the back of his hand, his long dark lashes curled against his cheeks.

*   *   *

It was dark when the word came to move out again, at the same frantic pace they'd kept up all day long. The right side and center of the road were choked with gun limbers and machine-gun teams, the mules' heads bobbing with their loads. The platoon, crowded to single file on the left-hand side, plodded heavily on, their heads hanging, their bodies bent forward at that awkward, ducklike tilt a man falls into when he is burdened with a pack and half a hundred pounds of iron and steel and is weary unto death.

The air became still and dense, like the air in a hothouse, and the outlines to all objects faded. To Devlin, marching at the rear of the column, they seemed to be walking off into some omnivorous and terrible void. *Going toward the end*, his mind kept repeating in a witless refrain of three strides. Going toward the end, the end, the end . . . Clay tried to drop out and he tongue-lashed him back into ranks. He hated Clay with a vengeance—the boy's natural build and conventional good looks, his free-and-easy manner. Smart little rich boy, father owned half of Cleveland; wait till they went over . . . Then in the next instant he regretted that, pushed the thought away. His mind, disoriented by the onrushing darkness, the stifling heat, danced about capriciously among a patchwork of discordant images: the dawn sunlight streaming in the high windows of the mill back home, glinting on the stack calendars, the feed rolls, the belt housing, turning them all to burnished bronze and gold; little Turner at bayonet practice, stabbing at the dummies with comic savagery, cursing; Michele leaning down over him, her face very full, her eyes, framed by her straight dark hair, immensely large and tender. "I will pray for you, Jack," she had murmured, her beautiful thin lips scarcely moving. "I do not believe in God anymore, I cannot, not after the hideous mockery of these four years— but I will pray for you nevertheless—" and her hair had streamed down around his face like the most delicate of curtains. "When He thinks of you even God should relent, a little . . ."

There came a deep booming, a mountainous rumbling shudder that was poised directly above them, and involuntarily his shoulders contracted. Guns? Aerial bombardment? Then there was a taut, whiplike crack, and the column seemed to ripple throughout its length with apprehension, resolved an instant later when a great slash of lightning shot across the sky above them—a gnarled tree, inverted, darting crooked limbs of light—and the rain began, tapping on helmets and rifle stocks, then lashing down in seething waves; utter darkness swooped in around them. It was impossible, under the high, flailing canopy of branches, to see anything at all. He heard curses, a cry, and the sounds of men sliding and slipping in mud.

"What's the matter?" he shouted.

There was a break in the file. Below him he heard the mutter of voices. There was a six-foot-deep ditch beside the road and someone had floundered down into it, followed by several others. "Come up!" he roared. He could hardly hear his own voice in the tumult of the storm. "Come on up here!" He reached down, caught hold of hands and rifles, hauled up a number of gasping, swearing shadows, got them moving again. "Close up, close up!" He moved close beside them, cupping his hand to his mouth to be heard. "Take hold of the pack of the man in front of you!" The rain lashed his face, shockingly cold. "Muzzles down! Your rifles muzzle-down!"

They staggered on, slithering and floundering in the muck. The rain came in torrents, in streaming, sweeping waves and they bowed their heads to it. In the lightning bursts he could see them vividly—linked hand to shoulder, bent over absurdly, tramping along in a lunatic lock step, their helmets pushed forward over their eyes. The rain had meant a temporary relief from the intolerable heat, but it was short-lived; now, in place of roasting, they shivered and shook, their teeth chattering, soaked to the bone. The road had dissolved in an oozy slick that was worse than ice. At one point Turner led six of the file right off into the ditch again, in a cursing tangle of arms and legs and rifles. When Devlin got there they were groping their way up to the road, clutching at the grass with their fingers. One figure was still lying at the bottom, and Damon was bending over him.

He called, "Who is it?"

"Clay again," Sam said flatly.

"—I can't make it, Lieutenant," Clay was protesting. "I just can't go any further. . ."

"Of course you can."

"No, I can't, I just can't . . ."

"God damn it, you can! If a hothouse kid like Brewster can make it, you can."

"Lieutenant, my leg—"

"I'll give you a hot-water bottle. You going to let the rest of them down? You're no worse off than anyone else." With a swift, impulsive motion Sam snatched up the other man's rifle and slung it over his left shoulder. "Come on, now. Let's go."

Clay said: "That's my rifle—"

"What do *you* want with it? You're flaking out. And I thought you Buckeyes had guts . . ."

Clay got to his feet and stood in front of the Lieutenant, swaying, his hands on his hips; his face, in the glow of Sam's torch, was flat with hatred. "Give me my rifle," he said tightly.

"What makes you think—"

"Give me my rifle!" In a lower voice he said, "I'll walk anywhere you will and a mile farther, Damon."

Sam handed him back his rifle. "We'll see about that. Now, let's go." He scrambled up the embankment and started off at what was almost a run. With an effort Devlin caught up to him and put his hand on his arm. "Sam—"

Damon turned. "Yeah?"

He paused. "Sam . . . this rain's pretty bad . . ."

"Best thing that could have happened."

Devlin gaped at him. "*What?*"

"This storm. Couldn't be better. They'll never look for us tomorrow morning after this."

"Christ sake, it *is* tomorrow morning . . ."

"That's right. So it is."

There was no end to it. Rain beat into their eyes and mouths, soaked their packs and blankets, adding its weight to an already intolerable burden. Caissons slewed into them, mules plunged into them in the flash-shot dark, braying and snorting. They drove themselves forward, each man's hands on the pack ahead, like a procession of arthritic old men bent over in dumb anguish, their knees bent to a tottering shuffle. In the lightning flashes Devlin caught glimpses here and there of gigantic dumps of ammunition, piles of shells stacked like cord wood, the lumpy outlines of tanks, streaked with their crazy, angular camouflage of browns and blacks and grays. Everything shrank to the next hundred paces, the next twenty, the next five. At one point he became aware of a terrific clanging, clattering roar, and looked around in surprise to see a tank bulking beside him in a stench of gas and burning grease. He decided he must have been dozing off. This shook him and he redoubled his efforts to keep his attention on the column, but weariness overtook him again in a slow, sure billow. He was no longer conscious of suffering in his feet or back or shoulders; these separate pains had all merged in one vast, all-absorbing torment as proximate as the beating of one's heart. His mind lost sequence again. Somewhere there was a field gun on the far side of the road, with a roan horse down and screaming; somewhere after that—or was it before?—there was a fallen tree, a great oak whose spiked leaves whipped his face as he swung by; and beyond it three soldiers from another company were clustered in the ditch around a man with a broken leg . . .

The rain faded to a sodden, intermittent dripping, then stopped; and looking up he saw clouds—darker than dark—sliding away beyond them, leaving a few stars that faded off to infinity. To the east, ahead of them, the sky was slate with dawn. He gazed at his watch, began stolidly to wind it. Almost four. Almost four o'clock. But the thing that struck him was the silence. They had outstripped the tanks, the artillery, they were out ahead of everything, and around them the stillness was astonishing. Could they get away with it? a surprise assault on the tough old professionals who had all the answers, who never were surprised by anything? Oh God, if only they don't know we're coming, he breathed; if only they haven't got wind of it . . .

There was a fork in the road and Lieutenant Landry, the battalion adjutant, was standing there with a couple of runners, motioning them off to the side with his walking stick. "Five minutes to make up combat packs. You have five minutes. And hurry. There is not a minute to lose."

The platoon sprawled on their knees in the wet grass. They were fumbling like sleep-drugged children at clasps and slings, and watching them, Devlin's heart misgave him. "Every man take his shovel or pick," he told them. "Whatever else you forget, remember that." He moved through them, repeating the order, and came on Damon, who had removed his Sam Browne belt and was buckling in its place a cartridge belt and extra bandoleers, like any infantryman. "I'll wear it in camp because it's regulations, but I'm damned if I'll wear it in combat." He dropped the shiny leather belt on the grass. "The boys know me by now—or if they don't they'd better."

Devlin moved up close to him and said hesitantly, "Sam . . ."

"Yes?"

"Sam . . . I'm not sure of them." He opened his hand. "They're awfully tired. They're half out on their feet."

Damon stared at him. In the rushing dawn light the lines in his face looked like hard metal furrows; his eyes had bright little yellow points in them. "They'll do it. We've got to do it."

"Sure, but without chow or even an hour's sleep—"

"I know. It can't be helped. We must do it anyway." He clapped the Sergeant on the shoulder once, lightly. "We'll catch 'em with their pants down. You'll see."

"Right, Sam."

The five minutes were gone. As though they'd never been. He heard whistles, and blew his own without thinking. The day was coming quickly now, hurrying toward them from the east, a sky flawless and irreproachable. They were slogging along again, bound in this strange stillness. Moisture dripped from the trees and plopped on packs and helmets. Now the ground was ripped and cratered with shell holes, the trees bore long saffron scars and splintered limbs; green branches were strewn across their path. Off to the left was a dense cluster of rubble, all that remained of some sleepy farm. They encountered tangles of barbed wire, and a shallow trench whose sides, reinforced by wattling, had broken down. It was half full of water. Beyond it stood a little group of officers, French and American. As they came up, Colonel Caldwell turned toward them.

"Over that way," Devlin heard him tell Sam. The Colonel's eyes were swollen, his face was white with fatigue. "By the edge of those woods, see? Keep on to the right until you see the Moroccans. Keep going forward, and hug that barrage. Hug it! And good luck to you, all of you."

There was a murmured, indecipherable reply. They swung out in line of skirmishers, in good order. Devlin looked at his watch. 4:23. He turned and gazed at the platoon. They were wobbling and wavering as they walked. Their faces were ash gray and wan; they looked like sickly older brothers of the men he had trained.

"All right," Damon said. He had turned to face them, holding his Springfield across his thighs. His voice sounded harsh in the silence. "I'm not a great hand at speeches. You new men, remember your three-yard interval. If anybody gets hit, let him lie. You automatic riflemen, keep wide on the flanks wherever you can; and pour it on. That's what you're there for, to let us get in close. Dev, I'm counting on you to make contact with the Senegalese as early as possible."

"Right, Sam," he answered. His voice felt metallic, with none of the edges filed off. Sweat was working down through his eyebrows into his eyes.

"Now, we're going to go through," Sam went on; his face looked hard, almost angry. "Don't any of you make any mistake about that. What we go after, we get. Any man doesn't do his duty here today has got a hell of a lot more than me to answer to. But I know you'll do your duty, all of you. Because you're good men. The best."

The ranks stood there doggedly, watching him. The silence was like great plates of glass bending.

"Fix bayonets," he ordered sharply. Their hands went smartly to their left thighs, the blades flashed in the light; and the click of the studs on the locking ring rippled along the line, dry and deadly in the stillness.

"All right, let's go," Damon said, and swung on his heel.

4:33. They were moving forward through the shattered wood. Turner seemed to jerk up and down with every step, as though his shoes had little wire coils. Ferguson was bent almost double and holding his rifle absurdly high, as if he were wading through a stream. Krazewski's face was contorted in a snarl, his huge white teeth bared. No one spoke. This was going to take hours. Hours and hours, walking in this crazy silence. Devlin was conscious of the pressure of the helmet strap against his chin, the sweat stinging his eyes, and the stark, solid quaking of blood in his temples. His mind, a captive bird, shot away from the moment, saw Michele standing on the little balcony, her hands on the iron grillwork; she was laughing, her head back, her dark eyes dancing with delight. "Ah, to think I'd stopped believing in anyone like you. Wasn't that foolish of me?" That quick, roguish look, her lovely lips quivering with mirth. "To turn so cynical? When there on the river bank, lying in all your naked glory, like a wild Irish king—"

It came: a crash like the collision of a thousand locomotives, and the high-vaulted whisper and shriek of their arching—and then ahead of them, near, very near, the ragged, monstrous detonations of their fall. Smoke boiled upward and more and more shells passed over, the air above their heads singing with their terrible passage, and geysers of fiery red danced and darted through the screen of trees. He kept waiting for the answering barrage, but none came.

Sam was shouting at them, his mouth wide, inaudible; his arm was pumping up and down, and making long, sweeping motions. He ran obediently, inclining toward his right. The earth lurched and tilted, flames flared, smoke rose in foul, belching towers. He could make out nothing ahead of him. There was wire now, everywhere, in sprawling, spidery strands and tangles. He vaulted over some, tripped, righted himself, climbed over a log—checked at a narrow little pit and a man in a horizon-blue helmet. French. Spotter, or advance post. He crouched, panting, the point of his bayonet a few inches from the face of the man, who eyed it wildly.

"Combien?" he screamed. "Combien de kilomètres aux Boches?"

The Frenchman's narrow, leathery face cracked in amazement. "*Kilomètres*—! Je m'en fou, cinquante mètres, *mètres! . . .*"

He raced on through the boiling, hellish roar, conscious of only one purpose; waves of concussion smote him in the face, dragged at him, bent him double. Bits of trees, leafy branches floated gently by.

Two helmets. Round and deep. He was on them before either they or he could react; he leaped the pit and dashed on. There came a descending, deepening shriek, like a giant knife blade drawn down an endless metal plate, and then the explosion. He was knocked off his feet; his head was ringing, his eyes hurt. All right. He was all right. He was up like a cat, mindful of nothing but Sam's stern injunction, bending still farther to the right. He glanced back furtively once, saw no one, fell sprawling into a rusty tangle of wire that slashed at him like an animate thing. God damn filthy stuff! He wrenched upward in a staggering, capering hop and got clear again.

He could hear the machine guns now, their flat, metallic, shuttling *pang-pang-pang*, in series, in chorus. He thought with a throb of dread of the embankment at Brigny, and gritted his teeth. There was a fearful slapping sound in a tree trunk near his head and he plunged out and down into a tangle of branches and torn green leaves, his head hammering; his sight turned blue, then red, then bright green—cleared at last. Someone sprawled down beside him, looked up. Turner, his eyes wide, his mouth open.

He nodded, as though Turner's gawping, strained face were exactly what he had expected all along, and started crawling off toward the right of the gun, which hadn't once stopped. Its hail swept over him, and bits of bark and leaves sifted down around his head. He waited: it swung off to the left and he snaked his way forward in a rush, across an open patch and into a slight depression, lay cringing again while bullets spanked into the earth a foot beyond his head and dirt stung his face and neck.

"—Jesus," he gasped. "No room. No *room* . . ."

Behind him now he heard the coughing, hiccuping burst of a Chauchat: a short sequence, then a longer one. The Maxim stopped, started again, and another Chauchat, back and to the left, began firing.

Lying in against the damp earth, his mouth dry, he nodded tensely: they were moving right now, automatic fire working scissors from the flanks, just as he and Sam had taught them. The Maxim stopped again. He leaped to his feet, saw the German bent over, struggling frantically to get the dead gunner off the weapon. He fired: the man threw both arms to the sky and fell backward out of sight. He shouted something, he did not know what, conscious of people running on his left now; he crashed through a network of brush—and all at once saw through the trees a clump of lean men in mustard uniforms and blue casques, running hard, their bayonets flickering like needles, uttering high, yapping cries. Senegalese. He crouched at the base of a tree, faced left again, raised his right arm and clenched his fist. Then he dropped to the ground.

The machine guns were everywhere—a snarling chatter that seemed to press against the inside of his skull. He saw Turner behind a log, firing, ran forward and sprawled beside him. Someone was shouting from a thicket on their left. He looked around him, watched Ferguson coming up in an ungainly, shambling rush, holding his rifle tight against his chest. There was the whine of a ricochet and Ferguson was gone. No, he had stepped behind a tree and now was peering out; his narrow, heavy-jawed face looked curiously guilty. He had started forward again when Devlin saw the grenade—a fat, round billy club spinning in the air. "Ferg-get-*down!*" he screamed. Ferguson turned toward his voice, his face pinched with perplexity. Devlin buried his head in his arm. There was a deafening, shocking crash, and things of terrible menace whined and sizzled and showered around him. He looked up to see Ferguson clutching at his face, soundlessly screaming; blood rushed forward over his eyes and mouth. Like paint, a huge bucket of scarlet paint thrown. *Ferg.* He was filled with rage—a black, seething fury that had no thought but vengeance. He felt nothing, no fear or weariness, no sensation in his arms and feet. He rose up cold as a shaft of marble, already aiming. The grenadier too came up with his arm back to throw again, and he shot him cleanly, effortlessly, fired again. The grenade went off in the thicket with a muffled boom.

"Come on!" he roared, and started forward, aware of Turner and several others moving with him. A gang of kids in a playground mob game, yelling and screeching. He leaped over a dense mat of twigs and branches and there they were. He was conscious of a flurry of field-gray figures fearfully close, whirling, reaching—then the place dissolved in a feria of violence. A man pointed a rifle at his chest. He bayoneted him once, withdrew. There was another, a huge man with a trench knife, an amazingly broad blade like a trowel. He swung around with the butt and the man went down in a sitting position. He pivoted to use the bayonet—and felt a tremendous blow on his helmet and shoulder that drove him to his knees. He clutched at his rifle, could not raise it; his arm was numb to the shoulder. He gazed upward to see the German raise the clubbed rifle again. All his soul protested, Oh no! Not again—

not to me! He drove forward into the man's legs, felt him give—and then something hit him in the small of the back and he was flung to one side. In an evil dream of confusion he got to his knees and drew his pistol fumblingly with both hands, heard a thick, choking cry, and saw his tormentor lurch backward against the emplacement, blood pouring from his neck.

It was all over. All at once. Raebyrne, his face tense and white, was cleaning his bayonet blade methodically on the uniform of a dead German. Sam was standing behind him wiping sweat from his face with a shaking hand. Little Turner was shouting, "Sons of bitches, sons of bitches—!" and kicking in a frenzy at a body in the corner of the pit. Devlin got to his feet, rubbing his shoulder, and the two Mexican veterans looked at each other, panting.

"You all right, Dev?"

He nodded. His rifle was buried under a body; he rolled the man away and picked it up. His arm was still numb and he flexed the fingers slowly.

"Yes," he said, for no reason he could see. "I made contact. With the Moroccans."

"I saw you. Good going."

There seemed nothing on earth to say. Blood was dripping from Sam's left wrist. "You—you're hit, Sam . . ."

Damon shook his head. "Wire."

"Oh," he answered numbly. It was like a kind of drunken brawl, endless and benumbing. What was next? What were they—

"All right, come on out of there, you bastards, come out—!"

He turned in mild surprise to see four or five Germans hurry out of a connecting pit, their hands high over their heads. Turner was pointing his rifle at them. The last man had a heavy mustache with upturned points, and was smiling apprehensively. Two of them began to gibber in German.

"Shut up!" Turner screamed. "You no-good murdering bastards—shut your faces!" The Germans gazed at him in alarm; the one with the mustache shuffled backward, crying something. Turner watched them coldly, his eyes slitted. "Yes, now crawl! Oh Jesus, yes . . ." and Devlin watched in dulled amazement as he very deliberately raised his rifle to his cheek.

"None of that!" Sam had stepped past him and pushed Turner's weapon up and away. "Take them back . . ."

"Shit to that! They let Ferg go back, I suppose—!"

"Terry, *take them on back*. That's an order!"

Turner gave Sam a surly, savage glance, then turned and kicked the nearest German, who almost fell. They went back through the trees, their hands stiff above their heads, the prisoner with the mustache still babbling in a high, strained voice.

"Come on, now. Let's go, let's go," Sam was saying to them tersely.

There was no rhythm, no ordered movement; there was no sense to anything. It was a treadmill—a jittering, bedlam treadmill of shattered trees and mangled corpses, of heaps of discarded equipment that kept flowing by like some foul river, laced by the spanking hammer of machine guns. There was a woodman's hut, which apparently had been used as a dressing station and was now abandoned, where there were stretchers and several medical chests and an improvised table covered with blood-soaked blankets, and a man whose head and chest were swathed in crimson rags held one hand to his eyes and kept reaching out to everyone with his free arm, moaning something in German over and over. There was a massive beech-tree at whose base two Americans lay side by side, their hands almost touching, like lost children asleep in a wood—except that one of them was half-naked, with his back laid open from neck to thigh, and the other, shot through the head, was Captain Crowder. Somewhere there was a Senegalese platoon sergeant who grinned at him, a vile and merry grin, and tapped at a curious collection of leaves, or mushrooms, or apple slices strung on a piece of wire around his neck—only they were not leaves or mushrooms or apple slices but human ears. "Cochon," Devlin heard himself say, his gorge rising, "sale bête d'un boucher. Crapule . . ." But the Senegalese had vanished. Farther on, a beautiful black-and-brown German shepherd dog yanked in terrible silent fury at the rope tying him to a tree, its eyes rolling; and still farther on, a machine gun cleverly hidden behind a log cribbing got Mecklar through the throat before they even knew it was there. The Chauchats tied it down, and led by Sam they went in and killed the crew, and swept on. And after that, some strange time after that, he had paused, his hand to his head, sick with raging, weak with slaughter. A wounded man was watching him, a wounded man sitting propped against a root bole behind an emplacement; his eyes still on Devlin he reached stealthily inside his tunic. Devlin fired from the hip; the German shook with the impact, struggled to withdraw his hand, then fell over weakly. The blood in his lungs and throat made a rattling, gurgling sound. His eye still followed Devlin, who started on by—on an impulse stepped back and reached down and lifted the man's hand out of his tunic. A stiff, small piece of paper fell to the ground. The Sergeant picked it up. A snapshot, a young girl with fine chestnut hair holding a baby in her hands and smiling, squinting a little in the sunlight. Behind her was a bridge with bronze horses prancing.

He put the photograph back in the man's hand; his breathing no longer made any sound. Devlin wiped his own hand on his breeches and hurried on, whipped by fear, regret, a scalding mortification that made him pant. "What the hell—it might have been a pistol; it could have been . . ." But there was no comfort in that. There was no comfort in anything at all.

Then all at once there was light, up ahead—oh Jesus, light!—and the giddy, sick treadmill slowed; they burst out of the woods and onto a high plateau all fair and golden with the wheatfields stretching off into the morning sun; and there, far over on their right they could see infantry in deep black helmets running back, carrying things. Running bent over, like tired old men.

"Hauling ass!" someone was yelling. "Look at them go!"

"*Get* them! *Get* the bastards . . ."

They were all firing now, furiously, offhand, kneeling or crouching, shouting to one another in a gleeful, savage rage. And remembering Brigny, Devlin heard himself mutter between his teeth, "All right, run like rats, *you* run this time, see how it feels . . ." He stopped to insert another clip and saw Turner kneeling beside him, firing in a frenzy at the distant scurrying figures.

"Terry," he said. "What are you doing here?"

"What?"

"Those prisoners you had . . ."

Turner's eyes narrowed, his pointed chin thrust against the helmet strap. "They made a break for it."

Devlin looked down, finished reloading. Of course. Because of Ferg. Well. But a kid like Turner—a kid who hadn't even really shaved yet . . .

Sam was waving them on now, shouting to them to spread out, spread out more, extend to the right. He gazed at Sam gesticulating, the monstrous naked sweep of wheat. Oh no, he murmured. His whole spirit recoiled, fled wildly from the field, the woods, the soil of France. No: they can't expect us to cross that field, walk on across that endless open place. For several seconds he was incapable of movement. I've been a good soldier, he told himself, I've done what I could, time after time. But they can't expect that of Jesus Christ himself—

Then his will took over, his training and his pride, and he was in the wheat, putting one leg in front of the other. There came the relentless spank of the Maxims, and shrill, forlorn cries, and he was crawling forward, with the hot, burned beeswax odor of the grass and the stench of cordite deep in his nostrils. The snapshot of the young wife splashed against the face of his mind like acid: the soft, round face, so proud and shy, under the prancing horses; and below his knee the bloody, tremulous hand. All the ardent fury of the attack had deserted him. His chin was trembling now, his head, his hands. You could go just so far on Irish temper, and then you ran down. It was true: he remembered once back at Fort Early, Sam saying: "Oh come on, Dev, you know you can't stay mad for more than five minutes, anyway . . ." What had he been hot about? He couldn't for the life of him remember.

His head ached brutally, he was shaky from the effects of the night march and no food for hours and hours; there were too many machine guns, too many Germans and they were all too deadly and implacable . . . He was swept with a desire as entrancing as the very gates of heaven to give up, to lie here prone and unobserved in the hot, gentle wheat and let it all thunder on beyond him, all the slashing and butchering, the curses and the moans; give it up, and go back to Charmevillers, to the still, high-ceilinged room and Michele . . . Yet he found himself crawling along, working his way forward with all the craft he possessed, cringing and gasping when the bullets sang their threatful way close above him, sizzling in the heavy heads of wheat; cursing himself for being such an insane fool, such a bloody automaton as to go on with this but constrained nonetheless, creeping and crawling, a filthy, hungry, frightened animal, toward what he knew could only, finally be his death . . .

A figure was coming toward him from the right. Sam, cradling his Springfield in his forearms, his face a powdery mask of urgency. "Dev. We've got to get this gun . . ."

Which one? he thought with bitter fury. Just which one of the frigging anvil chorus do you suggest? Aloud he said, "Yes."

"See those two trees over there? those two big chestnuts?"

He raised his head, dropped it instantly after a flash impression of two sturdy shade trees with powerful branches, and what looked like a little clump of stones at their base. He nodded.

"We're going over there. I've sent Kraz over on the left for some covering fire." Damon swallowed painfully. "If we get behind those two trees and stand up, we can spot them. You take one tree, I take the other. First I fire, then you fire while I reload. Got it?"

He nodded mutely. It was a fine plan: it was clever, impossible, brilliant, suicidal. He had no idea. Get behind those trees *and stand up*—! Only there lay Sam with his face only inches away; his sad, steady, deadly serious gaze. No! he wanted to shout. No! No more of this God damned madness! Don't you know there's hardly any of us left *now*—? What the hell's the matter with you—do you by some lunatic chance think you're immune—that a bullet won't starch you just as quick as—as Crowder or Mecklar or any of the others . . . ?

But he said nothing; he could refuse Sam Damon nothing.

"We've got to get them going," Sam was saying, "we can't stay here . . ."

He nodded still again. Only you, he thought, following his old friend off to the right, keeping his heels in view, creeping and pausing, his teeth chattering with fear, remembering the ambush on the path beside the ravine near Brigny Farm—only for you, and only this once, Sam—

Damon had paused and he moved up abreast of him. There was a shell hole and then a last little clump of wheat, followed by a barren place where wagons had gone, making a hard, narrow path. The grain lay white and broken in the ruts. Thirty feet. About thirty feet. In the open. Sam was looking at him. His face had that hard, heightened expression he remembered from Brigny Farm: a peculiar rigidity, and yet it was at the same time oddly expectant, and *aware*—as though he had seen all that might happen, and had made for it some fantastic provision. And suddenly he knew: he was afraid of Sam. He loved him, he owed him his freedom and perhaps his life, he respected him as all that a man and a soldier might be—but he was afraid of what he now saw in Sam's face. He felt his legs start to tremble.

"All set?"

He ducked his head in confirmation—he did not trust himself to answer; sweat was soaking his eyebrows and running salt into the corners of his mouth. He opened all the flaps on the right side of his belt. Fire passed around them droning, moved off to the left again. Sam was up and running hard; he looked hulking and enormous and utterly vulnerable. A geyser line of spurting dust skipped along the ruts behind him. He was down.

"Sam—!" he called—a barely audible sound. No: he could see him now, moving like a great brown lizard behind the field stones. He gathered himself together and hiked up his right leg, his weight on his elbows. You'll never make it, a voice told him with cold authority; they're waiting for you now. He shook with dread, a black certainty of death and maiming, kept glaring toward the trees. He couldn't see Sam anymore.

Then he heard the sound he wanted—the rolling cough of a Chauchat over on the left. Without a second's pause he flung himself up and ran. His feet seemed to churn through waves of hot, gelatinous resistance, an air heavy as water that turned his progress into some silly parody of speed. Jesus! It was so *far* . . . The trees, the boulders nevertheless swam nearer. The air around his head grew dark and burdensome with the rush and flutter of deadly birds: something plucked at his pack, something gave a shrill, short whistle behind his head. Then he was there, was lying behind a stone, gripping its hard, warm face with all his might, sobbing with exhaustion, while bullets seeking his very heart sang off the rock with catlike howls and shrieks. Sam—old Sam—was facing him with a look of calmest inquiry, as though they'd just finished a meal in a restaurant. He looked at the tree. It was like gazing up, crippled, at a church steeple. He thought, This is ridiculous, completely ridiculous. But now Sam was on his feet, calm as a diver at the edge of a carnival tower, the Springfield kicking with each round. The gun stopped. He rose up behind his tree just as Sam stopped to reload, and leaned out. He saw the freshly thrown-up earth, the gleaming stovepipe jacket of the gun, two helmets in a tight little cluster. He fired; the lead helmet sank down and away; he fired again, there was a series of smashing shocks right beside his head, and bits of bark and splinters flew past his eye and rained on his helmet. Another gun. He cringed, trying to draw his head and shoulders in under his helmet's rim. The Chauchat started again, its comical hiccuping rattling burst, and the gun swung away. He leaned out with wild urgency, heard a cry as the Chauchat went silent. Kraz. That meant Kraz. He found the other emplacement, better concealed than the first in some low brush, and emptied the rest of his clip into it. Sam was firing beside him now. He popped another clip home, leaned out, saw a German lunging forward at the grips and at the same moment several figures running through the wheat toward the gun pit. Now he felt nothing but the rifle's recoil, a harsh security that held him there, while another slug smashed into the tree. He felt no fear at all. In the right-hand gun—the gun that had nearly got him—a burly man leaped up with a grenade. He shot him, and the grenade fell in front of the emplacement. Four men rose out of the wheat and rushed forward; he saw the sun glitter on their bayonets—a swift and terrible dance of raised rifles and grotesque dartings and gesticulations, like the antics of marionettes. The gun chattered again, and one of the figures dropped his rifle and clutched at his belly; screaming in high animal cries—"*ah*-ha, *ah*-ha, aaaah-*aaah*"—he began running about in little staggering circles. Devlin fired at the gunner, fired again and again, saw a puff of dust as the slug went into the man's chest, another as Sam hit him, and still the gunner continued to fire, massive, indestructible, his teeth bared. Then Sam hit him in the head and the gun stopped; and a moment later a slender figure—was it Raebyrne? Johansen?—was standing in the nest, waggling his rifle over his head.

"That did it," Sam was saying. "There's more than one way to skin a cat."

"Some cat," he murmured. He put his hand on the smooth, chalky bark, felt the rasp of splinters, peered at the shocked and shredded places where sap was already oozing darkly down. He felt weak as water again, and the men in the field up ahead wobbled and wavered, half out of focus. Enough, enough . . .

"Let's go, Dev," Sam was saying. "Let's get on up there."

He shook his head, as if to clear it of fear and revulsion and dread—of all the treasonous things that pulled at his heart—and followed his lieutenant up through the field.

They reached Frossy Ravine by eleven o'clock and stormed the ridge. A lonely place of chalky earth and stunted trees, made more lonely by the dead and dying. There were no flanks that Damon could see. There was no anything.

"According to the map we're on it. Second objective line." He stared at the handful of men straggling up to him; they sprawled on the ground here and there, filthy, sweat-soaked, their uniforms torn by wire. He counted them. Twenty-one.

"Is this all?" he said wildly. "All of us?" No one answered him. Tsonka was carrying Kraz's Chauchat, Morrissey was carrying his clips.

Turner was there, Raebyrne, Brewster, Dev. "Where's Sergeant Hassolt?" he demanded.

"Legs got half shot off," Tsonka said.

"You know that?"

"I was lying there beside him when he got it, Lieutenant."

He saw two faces he didn't recognize. "Who are you?"

"Tyndall, sir, fourth platoon."

"And you?"

"Korettke—Company C. First platoon."

That meant—nineteen. He felt a raging despair that sank through him like stone. "All right," he said, "let's dig in, now. Along this line, running to there . . ." They stared at him apathetically, too benumbed by exertion and slaughter to move. They were near the end of things, he could see it in their faces. They were slack-jawed, their eyes were glazed with exhaustion. "All right," he repeated, more gently. "They'll be along in support soon. We'll hold here. Come on, boys. We've got to dig in . . ."

Three of them got to their feet and started to dig feebly at the hard, chalky ground. He turned away, nagged by worry. Company A should be on that line, over there, between that clump of trees and the crest of the ridge. And the Moroccans: where in the hell were the Moroccans?

"Guillette," he said. He pulled a pad out of his pocket and started writing in it. *Second objective reached at 1123. Losses very heavy. Will hold but must be reinforced. Damon.* "Here," he said to Guillette, who had come up to him, "take this back to battalion. Do you think you can—no. Wait a minute."

A line of men were coming out of the woods from their right rear, walking rapidly. They watched them approach in silence. Colonel Caldwell, his trench coat gone, his handsome uniform dirty and sweatsoaked, carrying a knobbly black walking stick, at the head of what looked like the better part of a platoon.

"Hello, Sam." His voice was crisp and cheerful.

"Good morning, sir." Damon waved the piece of paper. "I was just going to send this off to you. We're on second objective."

"So I see." He extended his free hand. "I'll read it right now." He ran his eyes over the message. "Very succinct. Very expressive." He folded the paper and slipped it in a pocket of his blouse. "I'm mighty glad to see you. I've just made contact with the Senegalese. I believe." He smiled faintly; the left side of his face was smeared with dirt and grease, and there was a long, bloody scratch—probably made by wire—running along his neck just below his ear.

"Sir, where is A Company, do you know?"

The Colonel raised his stick and pointed it casually over his shoulder. "This is A Company."

"That's all?" he muttered, aghast. "All that's left?"

"That's all, Sam."

"—But you came from down *there* . . ."

"Yes. Well, they were a bit off the track. We've just got things straightened out. Sam, we'll have to sideslip right as we go forward."

Damon stared at him. "Sir, I have only twenty-one effectives . . ."

"So I see. Well. We must keep pegging along. We can't quit now." He pointed toward a little patch of red-tiled roofs, a road, an apple orchard leading up to the skyline, hazy in the dense July sunlight. "Chauzy Ravine, Saubricourt, Saubricourt Ridge. And right over that ridge is dear old Augusta Suessionum, known to the uninitiates as Soissons." He raised his voice. "And we're going to take it. Right now. Let's go, boys . . ."

"You leading platoon assaults, Colonel?"

"Faute de mieux." Again that calm, steady smile. Damon was filled with consternation. Jesus! How could he be so calm?

Aloud he said: "Isn't Major Williams assault battalion commander?"

"Major Williams is dead. Captains Crowder and Hirschfeld are dead. Major Brill is down and so is Captain Pierce. No one knows anything about Captain Merrick. Colonel Stainforth is leading what is left of C Company."

"Jesus," Devlin muttered. "Oh—my—Jesus . . ."

"Well, how do we stand, Colonel?" Raebyrne asked him. "Are they whipping us or are we whipping them?"

"I can answer that one, Raebyrne," Caldwell answered; he raised his voice again. "We are whipping *them*. For a fare-thee-well. We've busted them wide open. Right over that hill"—he pointed the stick—"is Soissons. All their supplies and reinforcements must come through that town. We're going to take that town, and bag all those Germans out there, you hear me? Now let's go, let's go get 'em . . ."

They got up and went on, to a heavily wooded ravine where more enemy guns were hidden, and they lost Korettke and Farrell. In the apple orchard a French tank was stalled and German infantry were swarming over it like gray leeches. They shot them all off its iron sides, but the driver and gunner were both dead in a pool of oil and gas. Saubricourt was a mass of rubble, and for the first time Damon couldn't get them going; but some detachments of Moroccans came up, and the Germans in the mairie and two of the main buildings had had enough. Twenty-seven of them surrendered en masse, and Raebyrne and Tsonka found sausage and honey and bread and half a bottle of Cognac. Then Colonel Caldwell was calling to him, urging them on again, waving that crazy crab-apple walking stick and his pistol, and they were running, all of them that were left were running through bushes and the stumps of felled trees, up, up and over the ridge; and there they were at last on the forward slope, lying on their bellies, and Caldwell was saying: "Do you see it? Do you?" and looking through the glasses he'd taken from the German lieutenant at Brigny Farm, Damon saw the towers and roofs of Soissons, wreathed in smoke and dust. He made out the staccato plume of a locomotive getting up steam, and as he watched it, dirty black puff balls began sprouting on the tracks, the switchyards, in tight little configurations.

"—They'll do it, Sam," the Colonel was shouting in his ear. "CQC. They won't miss a chance like this. Two divisions, three divisions will do it. Press right on, leapfrog us, on over to Bazoches, to Mont Notre Dame, to Fismes, and cut the road up from Fère-en-Tardenois . . . Do you realize the whole damn German Seventh Army is there?—half a million Germans in that bag at the Marne!" He clutched at the younger man's arm, his eyes shining; Damon had never seen him so excited. "Do you see it? The chance we've been praying for—the classic pattern: attack from here, from Reims, and pinch off both flanks. It could cripple them beyond recovery. With a little luck it could end the war . . ."

"Do you mean it?" Damon murmured. The tempest of confusion and carnage and losses he'd been tossed in all day bore no relation he could see to anything so majestic as the end of a war.

"Sure, I mean it. Sam, those wires are hot from Fère all the way back to Coblenz! Old Ludendorff is telling Von Boehn to pull out, right this minute . . . But Boehn *can't* pull out that easily, you see—he's committed at the Marne, and the Bois de Condé, and Coullonges. *Time* . . ." Abruptly he said: "We've done a great day's work, Sam."

Damon slowly lowered his glasses. "I hope so, sir," he said. "We haven't got much of any battalion left."

The Colonel turned toward him, his face all at once resolute and grim. "They ordered us to do it. And we did what they ordered. It will be worth it—*if* Foch sends the power in now. Right *now* . . . Victory is a matter of opportunities clearly seen and swiftly exploited." He tapped his lieutenant smartly on the wrist with two fingers. "You mark my words, Sam. The German will never again take a step forward anywhere in France. And he could be beaten to his knees in two weeks, three at most. The war is over, if Foch and Pétain and Benoît play the end game correctly."

Damon ran his eyes down the line. Tsonka, black with grease and dirt, was cleaning Krazewski's Chauchat—but it was his now, Kraz was dead or dying in the long field—his hands moving with sure dexterity; Turner lay sound asleep, his thin, ratlike face washed of all vindictive rage and looking rather cherubic now, pressed against his rifle stock; Clay too was asleep—for all Damon's misgivings he had remembered his training and had fought creditably on several occasions—his helmet gone, the breeze ruffling his handsome blond hair; Brewster—fragile Timmy Brewster who doubted so deeply his valor in the world of men, but who nonetheless sat here, at the end of this terrible day, his head in his hands; Raebyrne was chewing at a leathery chunk of Kriegsbrot, his Adam's apple jumping outrageously; Dev—old Dev—was gazing with wild despair at the shrouded towers of Soissons, his hands gripping his knees.

. . . Oh God in heaven, let them exploit this, he found himself praying; and his eyes all at once stung with tears. He reached for his canteen,
remembered it was empty, and shrugged irritably. They had done what
they had been told to do: two days without food, three nights without
sleep, after twenty hours of the most punishing forced march of all
forced marches, they had thrown themselves with eager hearts at the
wire, the enemy rifle pits, the murderous, clattering Maxims, the
grenades. A green desire . . . Sitting there watching the festive little
pinpricks of shell bursts in Soissons he felt elation, sorrow, rage, a
tenuous hope; he did not know what he felt.

The Colonel was writing in his notebook now—that swift, concise
hand he secretly admired; he looked like the school valedictorian who
had somehow got lured into a playground roughhouse. Damon followed
the pencil across the page, then looked down the line. He had survived
again, as he had known he would; but there was no consolation whatever in the thought.

He started. Raebyrne, biting hugely into what looked like a glazed
black football, had just given him a slow, ponderous wink.

They plodded on, and the shells followed them in their lazy, baleful,
whispering course and swooped down in smoke and flame and terrors
unimaginable. They walked erratically, stumbling and sinking in the
spongy, lacerated earth, bent over, with slung rifles. In a nearby field
two trucks were burned-out wrecks, still smoking, and several bodies
lay sprawled near the cab of one. It was like a treadmill again, but a slow-
motion treadmill this time; the route was the old one of their advance,
but this was like a retreat. A junkyard world: waste and desolation had
proliferated until there was nothing left on every side but things broken
or disintegrated or abandoned. There were packs and helmets, field
pieces overturned and smashed, shattered machine guns and sheets of
filthy tarpaulin and corrugated iron and rusted rolls of wire on great
spiked spindles; there were bodies whole or rent or eviscerated, swollen
or shrunken, and the stench of death was like an unspeakably sweet, foul
mantle bound over one's nose and mouth. With the traverse of every
shell Sorenson gave a short, quavering cry that trailed off into a series of
moans.

"Cut that out!" Devlin shouted at him. "Jesus, Reb, can't you make
him keep quiet?"

"He won't pay me no mind," Raebyrne replied. "He's come down
with the grand megrims."

"—I'm sorry, Sergeant—I just can't help it, I can't . . ." Sorenson said pleadingly. The shell that had killed Morrissey the night before
had landed five feet from his hole. He had lost his helmet and his rifle
and was walking with a jerky, lurching stride. One of his puttees had

become unwound and trailed after him in the mud, and mucus was running out of his nostrils into his mouth. Another shell came over and he cried out again, went off into a confused, muted sobbing. "You don't know, Sergeant, you just don't know what I've been through . . ."

"Don't you bloody think so—!" Devlin said wrathfully. "—Christ, no, I've been in a big feather bed in Chicopee Falls the past five days . . ."

Dropping back beside him Damon murmured, "Take it easy, Dev," but the Sergeant only threw him a quick, wild glance and made no reply.

They went on, past a shattered tank, its gaudy camouflage designs charred and blistered by fire; past French Colonials huddled around cooking fires, past remnants of smashed wagons and heaps of empty shells. Damon plodded on, aware that he was setting too smart a pace but incapable of walking any more slowly. This random shelling was utterly unendurable now, leaving the line, going back. "Kill the lot of us," he muttered fretfully—flinched at a ripping detonation in the woods to their right. "Filthy, murdering bastards . . ." He felt furious and fearful and utterly discouraged. The French high brass had not exploited the Soissons attack, they had not even attempted a drive on Bazoches to pinch off the salient. The scarecrow platoons had been held on the ridge for two days, while Brüchmuller's artillery had worked them over with a disc harrow; and later Colonel Caldwell had told him glumly that no reserve divisions had been sent to the Forêt de Retz to exploit it, that the decision was apparently to push back the salient frontally; simply to push the Germans ahead of them, back to Ronchères, to Fère-en-Tardenois, to Mareuil . . .

Damon had stared at his commanding officer in wrathful incredulity. *"Frontally* . . . but that's—there's no point in it! That's pure and simple butchery—they'll get away, all of them . . ."

"I'm afraid that's true. Every bit of it." The Colonel's lips came together very firmly, his eyes were like flakes of jade. "Opportunity once forsaken is opportunity lost forever." He slapped the walking stick angrily against his breeches. "We will not have a chance like that again."

Another shell landed in the woods off to their right. There was an outcry, and then a series of unearthly, mounting screams that made Damon's blood run cold. He had halted without realizing it—saw all at once the horse burst out of the grove, trailing traces and a piece of the side rail of a caisson and an odd tangle of sacking. It fell, rose scrambling again, uttering its terrible, hoarse neighs—and Damon saw it was not sacking but intestines flailing in lumpy blue chains as the animal careened wildly about, its head swinging, blood pouring from its nostrils in a spray of foam. He stared at it in slow horror. There was a shot then, directly behind him, and the horse plunged forward into the field and lay still, quivering, its long head extended.

He swung around. "Who fired that shot?" he demanded hotly.

"I did," Devlin answered. He was still holding his rifle high against his chest.

"Dev, there's *people* in those woods . . ."

"—I don't give a shit if the population of the world is in those woods!" Devlin shouted at him. "Maybe Foch is in there—ever thought of that?—or that blood-sucking butcher Benoît . . ." He stopped then, and lowering his rifle rubbed his face with the back of his hand.

Damon opened his mouth, closed it again. There was something he ought to be saying at this moment; but he could not for the life of him think what it could be. He put his head down and went on walking quickly, flinching at the shell bursts and trying not to listen to Sorenson.

They were steaks, dipped in flour and pan-fried. Steaks for fifty men, and sixteen here to eat them. At the first bite Damon's jaws ached so fiercely he could hardly chew. The catch on his canteen cup slipped, as it always did, and the hot coffee slopped over his knuckles, but he didn't care; he sucked at the back of his hand absently. Food. Their first hot food in five days, their first honest-to-God meal in seven and a half. Peering at the oval mess gear in his lap piled high with other men's meat he was swept with a mountainous surge of anger at a system that would snatch men up and lash them forward to such massive butchery on empty bellies, decimate them and starve them—and then fail to execute the simplest, most rudimentary principles of war. For a moment he was on the verge of hurling his mess kit into the bushes . . . Then that subsided and he went on eating, his eyes half-closed, thinking of nothing but the taste of the food, the swelling warmth in his belly from the coffee.

"What took you so all-fired long, Fudge?" Raebyrne was taunting the mess sergeant, a swarthy little man with powerful arms and no forehead. "Been doing a little horse trading with the Frogs along the way? selling company stores?"

Fucciano waved his arms wrathfully. "What you mean, selling company stores? I run an honest mess—"

"Oh, sure."

"We been under *fire!* How could I move up? They been shelling us—oh Jesus-Mary-and-*Joseph* the shelling!"

Raebyrne guffawed at this and nudged Tsonka, who said in a flat, dry voice: "Jesus, Fudge, if we'd known *that* we'd have come over and bailed you out. We been having it easy . . ."

"Okay, you make fun, make jokes!" Fucciano put fingers and thumb together and shook his hand at them threateningly from the wrist. "We see who has last laugh, ah?"

"I declare," Raebyrne said conversationally, "that Fudge is so down-

right contrary if you throwed him in the Marne River he'd float upstream . . ." He turned in surprise to La Brache, one of the new men,
who was lying with his hand over his eyes; his helmet had plastered his
hair against his forehead so that it looked like a shiny black wig.
"Frenchy, better latch on to this baby beef. It's licking good, son."

"No. I can't eat."

"Why all not?"

"I—just can't, that's all."

"Well, as the Cooper's hawk said to the Leghorn: It's your funeral."

"—I told you not to use that word!" Devlin snapped at him.

"Don't take on, Sarge," Raebyrne said, aggrieved. "It's only a turn of
faze."

"Well, cut it out . . ." Devlin looked down at his mess gear, muttering, eating with taut ferocity; and watching him, Damon's worry grew.
The Sergeant's features seemed sharper, more pinched and drawn, as
though the past three days had burned and filed away the protective
skin, leaving only bare nerve and sinew open to the air; his eyelids
quivered.

"What the hell, Dev," he said softly so that the others, who were
arguing among themselves, couldn't hear. "What the hell—we made it
again."

Devlin raised his head, and Damon was astonished at the savage grief
in his eyes. "Sure. Isn't that great? And then they'll give us three days'
rest out of the goodness of their hearts, or maybe a week if they're
feeling particularly generous—or they haven't got the training schedule
set up yet—and we'll get a mob of stupid, silly, fire-eating replacements
who don't know shit from Shinola about any of it at all—and then we
can go up there and do it all over again. Won't that be fun?" His voice
rose. "Over and over again. Until we break, Sam. Until we wind up like
Sorenson, there . . ."

Damon felt a thick, boundless despair and looked away. Brewster was
listening to them now, so was Clay. "Don't talk rot," he muttered.

"It's not rot. It's the flat, black truth," Devlin went on, "and you
know it yourself. Isn't it the truth—*isn't it?*"

"Keep your voice down."

"Sure."

They heard it then—a wire-born humming that swelled to a deep
drone off to the east.

"That's the way to fight this cotton-ass old war," Raebyrne observed.
"Come, Josephine, in my flying machine. Clean shucks and a batman and
three hots a day, up in the blue all morning long . . ."

"I wouldn't want that duty," Brewster said.

"Why not?"

"I can't stand heights."

"Tim, you got more grabofrobias than my Grand Aunt Tirzah."

The droning was louder now—broke off into a series of muttering snarls behind the woods, and they could hear the sound of machine guns; a faraway, toylike popping.

"Shoot each other up, you good-time Barney Googles," Turner swore at them. "You're getting paid for it. Fill each other full of holes."

"There he goes—see him?" Raebyrne shouted. "Right behind that clump of sycamores, cutting up didos . . ."

The plane, it looked like a Spad—they had a glimpse of the red-white-and-blue roundel on the fuselage—dipped down behind the trees, curving and twisting. The faint popping came again, there was a crash, and another plane soared up over the fringe of woods, indistinguishable against the late morning sun.

"Ain't he the acree-o-bat, though? Will wonders never cease!"

"Come on, Reb, you know they'll never replace the turkey buzzard," Tsonka said, his mouth full of food.

"Yah-hoo! And here comes the happy cavalry—"

The droning increased, faded, rushed to a full-throated roar—and all at once there they were—three planes coming low over the screen of woods, their wings rocking and dipping.

"No, wait—"

"They're Boche—!" Damon screamed into the roar, "—Boche! *Take cover!*" He lurched to his feet, still holding his mess kit, and threw himself behind a bush. He had one last, fevered image of a narrow, angular, blood-red nacelle and the floating shimmer of the propeller— and then bullets were raining through the branches, ripping into the tree trunks and hitting the ground with quick, flat thuds. Something jarred his hand. He looked stupidly at his mess gear, which was suddenly three feet away and overturned, a great hole blown through the smooth, shiny tin. The hellish hailstorm ceased; above them there was a flat knocking snarl, and looking up he saw the black formée crosses. a leather helmet from which a chartreuse scarf streamed gaily. Then they were gone, climbing fast toward a group of gentle little clouds, and he heard the stuttering blast of a Chauchat as Tsonka led one of them up and away, his shoulders shaking with the recoil.

Damon got up. "All right? Is everybody—"

He stopped. La Brache was staring in amazement at his hand, from which blood streamed in thick, uneven spurts. "I'm wounded," he cried, stunned by the discovery. "Oh, I'm wounded!"

"All right," Damon said. "We'll get somebody, don't you—" And then, turning, he saw little Turner lying flat on his back with his arms clasped over his belly, staring at him fearfully. "*Hit?*" He mouthed the word. "Hit?" Turner nodded once, his eyes wide and unblinking, glazed with dread. Sam bent over and tried to lift his hands away.

"No, no," Turner breathed in a plaintive tone, like a child about to be deprived of a favorite plaything. "No, no, no . . ."

"—Oh, no," Brewster was saying, his face working queerly, "not— *Terry*—"

Damon stood up and roared "Stretch-er bear-er!" until his voice cracked. "Ellison!" he thundered at a runner hurrying by them two hundred feet away. "Get some of those people over here! We've got trouble . . ."

The planes were far away now, climbing high under the clouds like little red toys. If they can do that, he thought with alarm, if they can just swoop down and do that, and then be gone—

Two men were running from the bivouac in the woods. He saw the brassards on their arms and sighed with relief. Most of the group were gathered around Turner, who still hadn't moved a muscle; but blood was seeping out above and below his cartridge belt and creeping up the back of his blouse. Devlin was bent over him, talking to him urgently, his face contorted with anguish; Turner didn't seem to hear a word.

The planes were gone; Damon couldn't hear the faintest murmur of their engines. Out of nothing. A clear sky, out of the line, eating their first hot meal, sitting around eating—

"You bastards," he said with cold hatred. "God help any one of you if I ever get my hands on you . . ." His hands were shaking badly and he thrust them into his pockets. He was hollow with impotence and rage. Standing there watching the two medics come running up he knew, beyond the shadow of a doubt, all it was to be an infantryman: defenseless, pitiable, and alone; armed with nothing but one's own flesh and blood.

Everyone was moving back. It had been a victory—even the French said it was a victory—but the scenes they met were those of disaster and defeat. The enemy artillery still searched for them; gas shells dropped nearby with their soft, gurgling, plopping sounds, and their contents spread in a dense evil mist, staining the grass a hideous yellow. Dickey cried out and put his gas mask on, but the rest were too wretched to care: they hurried on, longing only for a place where they could sleep undisturbed for half a dozen hours . . .

There was a shout, and a gaunt, dejected group came toward them out of the woods with Traprock Merrick at their head. His face was flushed, and there were two Lugers jammed in his web belt. One arm was in a rag sling and he was twirling a shiny spiked helmet by its strap with his good hand. When he caught sight of Damon he threw back his head.

"Christ, if we haven't still got the Medal of Honor . . ."

Damon said, "Hello, Merrick."

"I thought they knocked you off long ago."

"No, I'm still around."

"Shame." Merrick slipped the German dress helmet back on his wrist, pulled a Cognac bottle out of a bulging musette bag and took a long drink. "Where have you been? Embuskaying it back at Cotterets?"

"That your company?" Damon asked.

"That's it." The Captain's mouth drooped in a mirthless sneer. "Chicken-livered bastards—I had to kick their asses every step of the way to Paulnay Ridge. Jesus, if they had any guts at all, *any* of them, we'd be dipping our peckers in the Rhine right now." He replaced the cork with finger and thumb and shoved the bottle away out of sight, grinning contemptuously at the remains of Damon's platoon, who watched him apathetically. "That's a gutty little crew you've got, buster. And with a couple of prisoners. How dainty . . ." His eyes had begun to glitter. "Know what I do with prisoners, Damon? I line them up in little stacks of three, like dominoes, and then zip-zip-zip!—and they're paying their respects to Valhalla . . ." He walked with leisurely menace toward the two German prisoners, who drew together, stiff with fear. "Look at them" he muttered, nodding. "Big tough hombres. Full of piss, aren't you? Ah? Let's see you dance." He pointed at their heavy boots, making little circling motions with his forefinger. "That's right. Tanz."

"Leave them alone," Damon said sharply.

Traprock turned in amused surprise. "Anything you say, Medal. They don't mean a thing to me—plenty more where they came from." For a moment he scratched at his belly through his open shirt. "When we going up again? You hear anything from the Old Man? You've been brown-nosing with him long enough . . ."

Sam gazed at him—the flat, ruddy face with its slack mouth and black bristle of beard, the little brown eyes glinting with what could only be the most blissful anticipation. He was barely recognizable as the sergeant Damon had played against in Texas.

" . . . I'd think even you've had enough for a while, Merrick."

"Me?" The Captain laughed thickly. "Not on your tintype. I'm having the time of my life. Why didn't we get over here sooner? Shit, man, I hope they keep it going for fifty fucking years, and then some . . ." He patted the swollen musette bag protectively. "High on the hog. Don't tell me you haven't been making out, Damon. Getting your rocks well rolled down there at Charme—"

"Shut your filthy mouth!"

Damon turned; Devlin was glaring at the Captain, one arm extended. Merrick's presence seemed to have roused him from the mute despair that had gripped him since Turner's death. "Just shut your face, you hear?"

Traprock grinned. "Well, if it isn't the crummy little Mick jailbird, still hanging a—"

Devlin started for him. Sam called, "Dev!" but the warning was unnecessary. Merrick's good hand flowed back to his belt, reappeared with a trench knife—a fearfully quick gesture. Devlin stopped, his eyes on the blade.

"Threatening an officer, ah?" Merrick taunted him, his eyes alight with the feverish glitter. "Three months' confinement and reduction to

next inferior rank, forfeiture of all pay and allowances—but I'll waive that. Come on, Mick." Devlin made no reply. "Want to play, Mick? Do you? Come on, then . . ."

Devlin looked at him, his mouth working—unslung his rifle with a snap of his arm and elbow. Damon lunged out and gripped him around the shoulders, pinning the weapon to his body. Devlin struggled against him in silence.

"—Dev," he said, "cut this out, now! I mean it!"

"Let him go," Merrick was saying, "let him try it—I'll blow a hole in him you could put your fist through . . ."

"—You bastard," Devlin shouted all at once at Merrick, "—go ahead, kill me, kill every frigging living thing on earth!—that's what you want, isn't it?"

"Dev—"

"Then you'd be happy, wouldn't you—you rotten no-good blood-drinking son of a bitch!—"

Sam had his rifle and was pushing him back now, murmuring, "Dev, *Dev* . . ."

The Sergeant dropped his arms. "Ah, the bastards," he moaned; he was shivering and tears were running down his dirty cheeks. "The no-good, butchering bastards . . ." And looking past his anguished, bony face, Damon saw four old men in baggy blue blouses, moving steadily across the long field, around the black lumps of bodies, their scythes rising and falling in an even rhythm. The field where they had left Krazewski and Moore and Saunders. Watching the mowers, he felt his own eyes fill with tears. He turned away and called, "All right! Let's move out . . ."

"Ah, you milksops," Merrick shouted hoarsely. "You timid old women—you want sugar-titty to suck . . . ?"

His laughter followed them across the long field.

The rain kept falling, as though there were a hidden purpose in it, some clever strategic plan to inundate all of Western Europe, perhaps wash it clean again. When they reached the bridge Damon told the driver to pull off under the trees, and got out.

"I won't be more than twenty minutes. Don't leave this wagon for any reason, will you?" He slapped the door of the big army Dodge.

"No, sir. I won't."

It was the same bridge, the same promenade under the chestnut trees, the same narrow, upturning streets without curbs or sidewalk. It was the

same, and yet somehow strangely altered—as though the past several weeks, the coming of autumn had laid it under some spell. A pretty little town, as French towns on the rim of the war zone went these days. He turned up the collar of his trench coat and buttoned it. The big guns couldn't be heard anymore; the leaves were ocher and yellow and hung limply, waiting for death. The stone towers at the ends of the bridge looked curiously worn and insubstantial, like sugar towers dissolving in the cold rain.

He walked past the railroad station, turned left and went uphill, past the bakery, the confectioner's shop, still closed—when would it open again?—the forge, where he could hear the dry sizzle of steel being ground against stone. Without pausing, he swung open the great oak door and went in, climbed the stairs in silence and paused. Inside he could hear someone moving, the clink of a plate. He knocked twice, briskly. The movement stopped, there was a swift subdued murmur; then footsteps came to the door and Michele's voice said: "Qui est là?" A wary, guarded tone.

"Courier, Madame," he said in a hoarse sing-song, and stood motionless. After nearly twenty seconds the bolt was shot back and the door swung open a crack.

"Oh, Sam," Michele said. "What a surprise!—You make a joke with me . . ." She still had not opened the door any farther. "Denise is in Pontoise, she has been there for three weeks now, I thought you knew—"

"I've come to see Dev," he said.

Her face gave an almost imperceptible little quiver. "Jack?" she queried. "Jack is not here, Sam, I am sorry, why should he be here?"

"That's what I don't know," he answered.

She must have sensed something from his tone, for she said: "I am sorry, Sam, but I cannot visit with you now. Perhaps tomorrow, all right?"—and she tried to close the door; but he had eased the toe of his right boot into the crack while they'd been talking, and now blocked it. Slowly he forced the door open with his hand.

"Sam, I have already said—"

"I just want to talk to him, Michele. Nothing more than that. I know he's here." He moved into the room and sat down in the high-backed wooden chair near the table.

"I tell you, he is not here . . ." Her slim, pretty face was pinched with fear and anger. "I ask you to go."

"Michele, I've been riding half the day." He opened his coat but did not take it off. The door into the bedroom was closed. All at once he felt weak with fatigue: his head was floating and his belly burned. "Dev," he said in a low voice, without moving.

"If you do not go," Michele warned, "I call the police . . ."

"Dev," he repeated. "It's me. Sam."

Michele came up to him swiftly and said: "Go. Please go. I will tell you where you can see him tomorrow, only *please go—!*"

He made no reply. He was too tired to argue with her, and beyond that he had really nothing to say. He was here. Dev was here. That was all there was to it. There was a heavy silence, invaded subtly by the forge across the street—a long-drawn metallic whine, broken off sharply by several measured blows of iron on iron. The hammering stopped, there was another interval of silence—and then the bedroom door was flung open and Devlin stood there, staring at him. He was wearing a faded blue shirt and a pair of baggy trousers gathered in at the waist with a narrow yellow leather belt.

"—Jack," Michele said sharply.

"Oh Christ. I told you this wasn't any good." He stood there doggedly in the doorway, watching Damon. His face looked gaunt and very pale. "Hello, Sam."

"Hello, Dev."

"You—get leave?"

"No. I took off for a day."

"Did you? What the hell for?"

"To see you."

Devlin took a pack of Gauloises out of his shirt pocket, put one in his mouth and offered the pack to Damon, who shook his head. After a moment Devlin lit his cigarette; he still had not looked at Michele, who was standing perfectly motionless by the long windows. "Why, I haven't got a whole hell of a lot to say to you, Sam."

"I suppose not."

For the first time he noticed the new insignia on Damon's shoulders. "I see you made captain."

"Yeah."

"Congratulations . . . You look kind of tired, Sam."

"Yes. The burden of command, and all that rag."

"And all that rag. How's the outfit?"

"Rocking along."

"What's left of it."

"What's left of it."

"How's old Jumbo—he a little upset about my taking a powder?"

"Jumbo's dead."

"No . . ." Devlin's glance darted to the wall, to Michele, back to Damon. "Why Christ, it was only a—it was only a slug in the arm, Sam—"

"Well, it—he got gangrene."

"Jesus . . . who's sergeant major now?"

"Right now there isn't any. Nobody wants the job. A new man named Taylor's coming in, a transfer."

"Well. That's charming. C'est drôle, hein? très drôle." Devlin laughed

once, became sober again; sauntered up to the table and swinging a chair around straddled it, his arms over the back. The two men looked at each other in silence.

Finally Damon said: "You haven't been out for a while."

"No—I've been taking it easy. Getting rested up, for a change." His face was white and drawn in the dull light. "Getting ready to go up again, aren't you?" he demanded suddenly. The Captain nodded. "Sure. Why not? Nothing better to do . . . Well, this was real nice of you to drop in. Right out of the blue . . ." He grinned mirthlessly. "Getting a touch lonesome, eh? Misery wants company. That it?"

"They miss you, Dev," Damon answered in a low voice. "The whole bunch. Raebyrne was talking about you only yesterday. He said all sergeants were ornery and stampageous, but if God made him choose—"

"The hell with that," Devlin broke in flatly.

"What?"

"I'm not going back, Sam. I'm through."

"I see. For good?"

"For ever and a day. There's no point in it, Sam. No point in it . . . All that slaughter. At Brigny and Soissons. And for what? So the frigging brass could foul it up all over again. You and I could have done better than that stupid bastard Benoît. A five-year-old kid could have done better—you know that . . ."

"I guess you're right. The only trouble is, the five-year-old kids aren't running it."

"No, they aren't—they certainly aren't." He leaned forward, his eyes infuriate. "I'll tell you who's running it though, Sam, because I've seen them. The fat little porkers in their Prince Albert coats and their black limousines, with their fat little poules on their arms. You think they want Foch to end it—you think they want *anybody* to wind it up? Jesus Christ, they're having the time of their lives, turning out the shells, hoarding all the butter and bacon and stashing it away . . ." He waved one arm. "I heard one of them. Right down there in the square. Dressed to kill, with a droopy mustache and eyes that would turn you to stone. His dirty sidekick asked him something, and he said, 'Il faut faire des concessions mutuelles, mon gars'—and then he turned to me and told me to polish up the headlights on his chariot. Handed me a five-franc piece, and walked off. Just like that . . . Concessions mutuelles, all right. And we've got to creep across a thousand fields for that? So that they can go on making a fortune on hand grenades and uniforms?"

"Maybe you're right."

"You know I'm right. It's a dirty, filthy game—there's no *sense* in it, Sam . . ."

Damon nodded. "You figure on lying low till it's over."

"That's right."

"And then—what'll you do then?"

Devlin shrugged once. "Get me a job. Carpenter, cabinet maker—I used to do carpentry back home, you remember . . ."

"I see. Sure. And then, after that?"

"After what? What do you mean, after that?"

"After a few years have gone by, and you want to go back to the States, back home, see your family—"

"The hell with that." Devlin scowled. "I won't ever go back."

"Or you want to go for a little trip. To London or Luxembourg. A vacation to get out of the rut." Devlin made no reply. "Out into the country. Take the train: Brigny-le-Thiep, Verneuil, Soissons . . ."

"Look, Sam—"

"Verdun, Metz, Saint Avold . . . And then they come to the border, and the customs inspector wants to see your papers—"

"No!" Michele came up to the table and leaned over it. "He is not going back to your filthy war. He is staying here. No more killing. No! Go on back—leave us and go back there and blow each other to bits, until no one is left in this endless madness . . ." Damon watched her in silence, while she struck her breast with her fist. "He will stay here and live, with me. In love. Yes, love! . . . You think I don't know?—you think I am a fool, a weak woman and a fool?" She whirled around, darted to the huge oak chest, wrenched open one of the doors and began pulling out an armful of framed photographs, spilling them on the table in front of Damon, striking the glass with her nails. He saw a handsome officer with a graceful dark mustache seated on an upholstered chair, a heavy-set older man, a farmer or perhaps a mechanic, wearing a helmet, two young boys in tight-fitting tunics, hatless, their arms around each other's shoulders, smiling in a sunlit courtyard. "My father, at Le Cateau, my uncle, at Verdun. My brothers, l'un mort, l'autre grand mutilé de guerre—" she was abandoning her English in her rage "—et mon cousin Guy, et là, là, mon fiancé Edmonde, aussi à Verdun . . . Et pour quoi, donc? Dites moi, Capitaine! Dites moi, je vous en prie."

She stopped, panting a little. "You think he is a coward to stay with me, hein? Ah, of course—because you are all so heroic, so noble, so brave . . . Well, he is worth ten of you, a hundred, a thousand! Un homme plein de sensibilité, plein d'émotion . . . You find that strange, do you?" she cried, though Damon had not changed expression. "That a man wants to live in peace and dignity, in 1918? Why couldn't you leave him alone—since you knew he had come here . . . But no—you could not, could you?" She leaned forward, her arms at her sides, her large, dark eyes glittering. "You, Captain. You have killed, have you not?" Damon nodded, almost imperceptibly. "Ah yes, of course—all those medals . . . How many, Captain," she pursued savagely. "How many?"

"Mitch—" Devlin began.

"Be still!—How many, Captain? Make me an estimate."

". . . Too many," he said softly.

"Ah oui, assurement." She laughed, a brittle, silvery laugh. "And it pleased you, hein? When you did it. It gave you a deep, secret pleasure in your soul—"

"No," he muttered. "No."

"Oh yes, I say yes!" she hissed. "You found it a secret, and sweet."

"Mitch, no," Devlin protested, "he was only obeying orders, like any other poor son of a bitch . . ."

"Ah—*orders!*—"

"No more of that," he shouted at her. "You don't know anything about that! You can't judge him that way—"

She whirled on him. "What are you all—some glorious freemasonry of death?" she cried. "Some privileged élite guard of disaster? with secret countersigns? You are the only ones who can speak of suffering? And the other part, too—the dirty, secret pleasure . . ." She turned back to Damon again. "You have decided in all your wisdom he is a coward to stay here." She leaned forward again, her breasts rising and falling passionately, her face flushed, her lovely dark hair disheveled. Her anger beat in her cheeks, her eyes; she looked breathtaking and terrible, and Damon thought with a pang of that afternoon after Brigny, a hundred thousand years ago, and two figures in close embrace, swaying in the twilight, with the curtains stirring in the soft breeze off the river. "No! I say he is brave to stay, the bravest of the brave—and you, all the rest of you, are the cowards, the cattle, the craven, drunken fools . . ."

She stopped and turned away. For a moment no one said anything. Across the street they could hear the thin, sibilant whine of the scythe blade being ground again.

"Yes," Damon said after a moment. "Maybe it *is* more courageous, Michele. I don't know for sure. Maybe you're right . . . But that isn't all of it." He glanced at Devlin, who was gazing at him imploringly—as though the force of Michele's appeal had stripped away his harsh defiance layer by layer, leaving only a raw, naked anguish. "Think of your life, Dev. The whole rest of your life. What will you do? What will you think about? When it's over, and some old doughboy comes through here, looking for landmarks, for graves. When she has a boy of yours, who begins to ask a thousand and one questions. When you're lying in bed late at night and you can't sleep . . . You'll get to hate yourself, Dev. You will. You'll even get to wish you were with Starkie and Kraz and Turner and the rest of them."

"—Yes and I God damn near did end up with them, too. All the good guys . . . and what for?—so the slackers and profiteers can feed on our carcasses? I say fuck it!" he cried. "I say fuck this filthy war . . ."

"So do I," Damon answered quietly. "With all my soul. But that's no answer now. You're *in* it, Dev."

"The hell I am—"

"Yes, you are. You signed up for it when I did . . . Sure, I know—it's

rotten; and fools and sons of bitches are running the show. But you're in
it, and so am I; and the only hope is to get it over with—and then make
sure nothing remotely like it ever happens again."

"—And just how do you plan to manage *that*?"

"I don't know. But I'm damned well going to try . . . Dev," he said
urgently, "you can't live this way. You care too much. Maybe some
men can, but you can't. You'll dry up and fade away to nothing, you
know it. You'll hate your own guts more and more each day . . ."

There was a long silence. Devlin looked down at his hands and shook
his head slowly. "What the hell," he muttered, "I couldn't go back now
if I wanted to."

"Jack!" Michele cried.

He gazed at her desperately. "I can talk with him, can't I? It's just
talking . . ." She gave a muffled groan and put her hand to her mouth.

"You can come back," Damon said.

Devlin laughed harshly. "Oh, sure—I can come back: under guard and
in irons . . . if you think for one minute I'm going to rot in some
stockade—one of Black Jack's fancy little labor battalions—"

"You won't have to." For the first time Damon leaned forward and
put his hand on the Sergeant's arm. "It's all fixed up. The Old Man's full
colonel now. He's got the regiment."

"Caldwell?"

Damon nodded. "You can come back with me tonight and there'll be
no questions asked. I'm the only one who knows where you are. The
company thinks you're in the gas ward at Nanteuil."

"What do they think that for?"

"Because I told them so. Look, I've got the regimental Dodge waiting
down by the bridge."

Devlin stared at him; after a moment he whispered: "You mean you
got the limousine? . . . Jesus."

"I've been covering for you on the roster, and so has the Old Man.
You won't get the stockade if you come back with me tonight. I give
you my word."

"And suppose we get picked up going back. What then?"

Damon put his hands on his knees. "Then I'll go up with you for
harboring a deserter, and they can bust me and lock me up, too."

"You'd do that for me?"

"Of course I would."

Devlin looked down again, ran his hand along his jaw. Michele gave a
cry—a wild, abandoned cry that was half a gasp, and ran to the table.

"Non, non, Chéri," she pleaded, "ne te laisse pas faire—Jack!" He got
to his feet and she flung herself on him, gripping him around the neck in
a violent, animal way, as if she were mortally afraid of falling. For a
moment they swayed by the table, locked together, while the rain
drummed on the long windows.

"Mitch, honey," Devlin murmured. Slowly, with infinite reluctance he pulled her hands away from his neck and held them in his own. "He's right, Mitch."

He turned away and went into the bedroom and closed the door behind him. Michele stood for a moment, staring at it; then she walked up to where Damon was standing.

"Bête," she said. "You hurt everyone you touch. You are hateful." She was weeping now, steadily and quietly, staring at him. "You are so certain. So certain! And also afraid. Yes. To leave him here. Outside your carnival of horror . . ." Very clearly and slowly she said: "I hope you are killed, Captain. I pray that you will be wounded horribly, grotesquely, most painfully—and that you will have a great deal of time to suffer, and think about it, and suffer some more . . . Je prie pour ça de tout mon coeur." Then she struck him in the face with all her might.

He swayed backward. He felt all at once cold and hollow; her imprecation had shaken him, filled him with fear such as he had never felt before.

". . . That's not true," he heard himself whisper. "I am not like that . . ."

She made no reply, merely went on staring at him, her large eyes stony with hate, her lovely, gaunt face streaked with tears. They stood like that, nearly toe to toe, looking at each other, until the bedroom door opened and Devlin came out. He was wearing his uniform. Half the buttons were gone, and his breeches were torn at the knees. He had cut off his chevrons; the cloth where they had been made dark, triangular shadows below his shoulders. He was carrying Lieutenant Gillespie's musette bag in one hand. He stood looking at the other two for a moment; then slung the bag over his shoulder and pulled down hard on his blouse.

"Okay, Sam," he said.

As soon as he spoke Michele turned and walked to the window.

"Mitch," Devlin said.

She made no answer.

"Mitch . . ."

Without turning she raised a hand swiftly and dropped it; and this brief movement seemed more desolate than anything she might have said.

"Ah, honey . . ." He went up to her and put his arms on her shoulders; she gave a groan then and fell against him, seized him with all her might, and wept and wept. "Ah, Jesus," he said. "Ah God, Mitch, I can't help it, I've got to. I've got to, Mitch—"

An instant longer she clutched him to her—then all at once wrenched out of his arms and ran into the bedroom and slammed the door. The two men stood staring at it as if it possessed some hard and irrefutable answer it was desperately important for them to fathom.

"Go on in," Damon said after a minute, "talk to her if you want."

"No. Wouldn't do any good. Nothing will do any good." Devlin rubbed his face with his sleeve. "Let's go."

They went down the long flight and out into the street. It was still raining. Across the street the fire of the forge flared and sank, flared and sank as a young boy in baggy trousers pumped at the bellows; and a baldheaded man with short, powerful arms brought a cherry-red bar of iron to the anvil and began to beat it, the hammer rising and falling with implacable persistence. Catching sight of Devlin the blacksmith paused, his face blank with inquiry; then he looked down at his work again. The iron flattened, the orange sank to wine red, to ruddy purple . . .

Damon found he had stopped at the entrance to the forge, his hand on the wood.

"Come on, Sam." Devlin pulled once at his sleeve; his voice was toneless and hard. "What are you waiting for? Let's get on back to the lovely frigging abattoir . . ."

"All right." But still Damon went on gazing at the iron, half-mesmerized, unable to avert his gaze.

The sniper's rifle cracked, a thin, remote sound; the bullet struck a shell casing or some piece of metal and whined away like a snapped guitar string. Raebyrne said: "Try again, you cross-eyed ornery Pee-roossian." Reaching out of his hole he offered the blue tin of Argentine beef to Pelletier, who waved it away, muttering: "Keep it. I can't get it down. Tastes rotten to me."

"Well now, it does appear a mite swively."

Tsonka watched Raebyrne with distaste. "How you can put that crap away is beyond me."

"Mike, I'll eat anything around this swamp I can find. Excepting love apples, of course."

"Except *what?*"

"Love apples. They're a poisoned fruit."

"*I* never heard of them . . ."

"He means tomatoes," Damon said; the sniper was getting on his nerves and he found himself anxious to talk. "Isn't that what you mean, Reb? Tomatoes?"

"Bright red fruit on a furry green vine about two foot high, full of juice, bearing around August," Raebyrne explained patiently. "You don't want to touch those. Fruit of the devil. Give you strangles." The sniper fired again, the slug slapping into dirt, and Raebyrne shook his fist over his head and called angrily, "Just keep it up, you contrary son of a bitch, and I'll starch you like a go-to-meeting collar . . ."

It was a terrible place they'd found themselves—a land so desolate and battered its very existence seemed to assault credulity. There was nothing the eye could recognize: a swollen, heaving terrain churned into an immense pudding of ridges and shell holes littered with big gun shells like bloated stovepipe sections, barbed wire in rusty, tangled snarls, abandoned helmets and bits of weapons—all of it like some growth spawned by a race of giant toads. There was no sun. It reminded Damon of the gale-whipped North Atlantic three days out of Hoboken—but a sea hideously frozen into clay-and-water immobility, and spiked with the scarred stumps of trees. The moon might look like this, perhaps; but the moon in all its hard, boundless aridity could never fill the heart with such despair as this—for the moon held no frantic, blasted arms of trees, the mangled remains of what had once been orchards and tilled fields and the homes of men; the moon did not give off incessantly the sweet, foul odor of death . . .

He heard it, then—that, thin shearing sound, like the ripping of the most delicate silk. He shouted, "Get your heads down—!" He had just time enough to be seized by dread, and then the dry, tearing noise swelled into a colossal indrawn breath, hung suspended above their heads, deepened to a threnody of rapidly descending shrieks—and the wasteland around them shook and jolted. 77s again. He forced himself to raise his head, saw nothing but churned earth and the blue-white flashes of the bursts. Nothing else. There was no movement on the crest of the hill a quarter of a mile ahead of them. Glancing back to where the old mill had been he saw, or thought he saw, a figure dive into a shell hole; and wondered if it was Blake, one of the battalion runners. If it *was* Blake—

There was a deeper note now in the bending roof of sound: a bubbling rumble that mounted to an all-consuming roar, then broke apart in a thunderclap of unbelievable magnitude. Another, behind them. Bracketed, they were bracketed. Nine-inchers. That God damn filthy mountain! The air grew dark, then red, then filled with dancing flashes; the ground rocked and heaved. Damon found himself doubled up like a foetus, gripping the Chauchat handles in a maniac's clutch and gasping for breath. The very air had been caught in a set of malignant thumbscrews, was being crushed into something solid—a mailed fist that buffeted and battered and crushed the helpless flesh beneath it. Jesus. This was worse than the embankment at Brigny, this was worse than Saubricourt Ridge. He felt rather than heard a brief lull and tried to raise his head, could not. What was it?—bombardment preliminary to counterattack? Where in Christ's name was our own artillery? What were they doing—playing pinochle back there? Where was anybody at all?

The burdensome freight-train rumble came again; there was a detonation that seemed to take place just beyond his left shoulder, and the great mailed fist had hold of his brain, was squeezing it calmly into pulp. He bit his helmet strap in a paroxysm. Shrapnel sang through the air like bandsaws run by a brace of madmen; something struck his helmet with a sharp, bright clank—and at that instant the fear gripped him firmly and completely. He had awakened around four thirty that morning after a two-hour catnap, clutched with dread. *Today*, the thought had lain on his soul; *today you will get it: you will be killed: and when you least expect it.* For the next few hours, under the pressure of work and defensive measures, he had thrust the evil dart of premonition aside; but now it returned. Cringing, contorted, he tried to beat off the fear. This barrage—was it moving? was it rolling? he could not tell. He could not feel anything but the monstrous, stunning pain of the pressure waves, the incessant slam of high explosive and the whine of splinters. Think! he commanded. But his mind had no intention of obeying—it wandered away derelict and craven, it cared about nothing but repeating with dogged, importunate insistence, No, no, not today, I've gone this far, not today, oh God I'll do anything but not right now, let up, please, I've had enough of this, let up, enough—! . . . and then as the bombardment redoubled its fury it abandoned even this plea and began to prattle in feverish panic: *How much wood would a woodchuck chuck, if a woodchuck could chuck wood? Why, he'd chuck as much wood as a woodchuck would if a woodchuck could chuck wood . . .*

He was lifted and dropped as if thrown. Someone very near was talking rapidly. *He* was. He was talking. Aloud. Nothing could survive this, nothing. No creeping thing or the waters under the earth, our Father Who Jesus *God—!* A terrible crepitation that was like the exploding of his very own soul, his head was slammed against the barrel of the Chauchat, his ears rang and rang. *Why he'd chuck as much wood as a woodchuck could chuck woodchuck would—*

. . . It had stopped. Had it? Sight and sound returned in sliding, faltering rainbow panels, wobbling strips of sensation. His eyes were streaming from cordite fumes. He felt sick, and when he wiped his face and eyes his hand shook wildly; but he was alive. Just the same. He was all right. Smoke lay overhead in dirty, rolling clouds. A few shells were coming over, but far to their right now, toward the 39th. It was over, for a while.

Then he heard the cries. He straightened, peered anxiously to his left, saw Raebyrne talking to Tsonka, and Devlin crawling out of his hole; and was flooded with relief. He called in a clear, calm voice: "Who's hit?"

"Me, me—!" It was Ellis, one of the replacements. A long tear in the upper arm, blood soaking the sweat-blackened wool.

"Conger!" he shouted. He climbed out of his hole and began crawling from pit to pit, checking the line. Walsh had a tiny fragment in the neck. Pelletier lay at the bottom of his hole. Below the hairline was a huge slick cavity of bone and gristle and tissue from which blood was pulsing, soaking the wet clay. No face at all. No Pelletier. Farther on he saw a hand move and called "Clay?" There was no answer. He wriggled through the muck and slid into Clay's hole, and grunted. The boy's body had been blown almost in two and his face, pressed against the mud, was gasping for air; his eyes were rolling crazily and his lips were drawn back from his teeth in a tight snarl, hideous and feral; his mouth kept opening and closing with a dry sucking sound. Blood lay in a pink froth around his lips.

"Oh, Jesus," he muttered. He heard movement and turned to see Brewster crawling toward him. "No," he said. "Go back . . ."

Brewster stared at him, his thin face tense with fear. "Bill?" he whispered; and then: "No, I've got to see him, I've got—"

"Tim, go back to your hole!" He pushed at Brewster's shoulder. "Don't look at him."

"No—not *Bill* . . ." Over the past month he and Clay had drawn together, the brash cockiness of the Ohioan forming a strange complement to Brewster's shy diffidence. It was hard to believe they could be friends; but after Krazewski's and Ferguson's deaths, Raebyrne and Tsonka had teamed up, and Brewster had turned to Clay. It was part of the ceaseless, pathetic reshuffling of friendships among the old men after battle, when the replacements came in. Now Brewster was gazing at Damon, his mouth slack with fright, shaking his head and murmuring, "Not Bill, not Bill—he's not hurt, is he?"

"—He's in bad shape," Damon answered roughly. "Now go back to your hole!"

Brewster turned away and dragged himself off like a beaten animal through the slime; and at that moment the awful gasping of Clay's mouth stopped. He gave a long, trembling shudder, his fingers clutched the clods of earth convulsively, and his life ran out. Damon tried to turn him over and the boy's body started to come apart in his hands. He swallowed two, three times, fighting off nausea, left Clay's hole and wriggled his way over to Ellis, who was being bandaged by Conger.

"What do I do, Captain?" Ellis kept saying. "What do I *do*?" After staring at the wound for several minutes he now had his eyes resolutely averted, like a child waiting for the needle.

"Nothing for now. Just take it easy." The sniper fired then and he ducked. Clay's blood was all over his hands, and his hands were shaking badly. He felt sick and weary and overborne—unequal to anything, no matter how trivial, that might come up. There was so much *blood*. Ellis was watching him with large, fearful eyes and he wiped his hands on his mud-caked breeches. "Just sit tight and take it easy," he said with a desperate semblance of calm. "We'll get you out of here any time now . . ."

They had entered this fog-shrouded nightmare landscape of the Argonne nine days before, in a morning assault in concert with the 39th and 17th Divisions. After a perilous reconnaissance the afternoon before, Damon had sent them forward in echelons as fire teams rather than in the murderous platoon front; they'd got through the wire, had lost contact with both flanks, regained it, had taken the German trenches and pushed beyond them through lacerated woods to the remains of a village called Miravalles. The Germans had counterattacked that night in a driving rain, without success, and later had shelled them incessantly with 77s and toxic shells. The next day the Company again started well, but in this flooded, boggy landscape it was hard to move and almost impossible to see, and once more they lost contact with both flanks. Damon went forward the day following, picked up Manion's Chauchat and got them going again, fighting savagely from rifle pit to rifle pit, from gun to gun. After terrible losses they reached the second phase line from Chabert Mill to the St. Aubry Woods; and there—or what once had *been* the Chabert Mill and the St. Aubry Woods—facing a series of steadily ascending ridges crowned with the ruins of farm buildings, where the Germans were entrenched in force, they'd been stopped for good. The Third Battalion had come to grief in an evil marshy place called for some perfectly inexplicable reason Les Festons, A Company had been cut to pieces by shelling, the whole advance had bogged down in mud and rain and uncertainty and the hateful chatter of the Maxims. Next morning the fog and rain had lifted—and it was then they saw the mountain looming on their right, with twin peaks like misshapen little horns, sheathed in oak and fir and laced with great blunt outcroppings of blue-black stone.

"Mother of God, what is that?" a replacement named Santos muttered.

"The Mont de Malsainterre," Damon told him.

"Are we going to have to take *that?*"

Their faces were scored with dread. He told them no, that was for the Thirty-ninth, the Grizzly Bears; but for the rest of the afternoon they kept glancing at it with increasing apprehension. Early that evening on its gaunt stone flanks flashes came and went like fierce little pinpricks of light; and soon after that their desolate, muddy world was swallowed up in a maelstrom of shrieks and detonations. They were ordered to advance again the following noon and they did, and after a thousand private agonies took another patch of this tortured moonscape. But there was no getting away from the mountain; the shelling increased, and Damon, raging, watched his half-company shrink to a platoon. Again. All over again. It couldn't happen still again: but it had. He had two captured Spandaus set up on their flank at the base of the Mill and deployed his people as skillfully as he could; but they had other worries now. The kitchens couldn't be brought up under the mountain's interdicting fire; he sent Johansen and Hughes back on a canteen-filling detail and both of them were hit. Devlin had successfully led a little group back for tinned beef and salmon and that was what they had been living on for three days; for the past eighteen hours they had been drinking water out of the shell holes. And continually rasping him, like a needle pressing on a nerve, was his fear of a German counterattack. If they took it into their heads to come down from those smashed-up buildings on the ridge the Company could never stop them; he knew it in the pit of his stomach, and it combined with the recent bombardment and the nerve-wracking presence of the sniper, to add to his fear. He had to get hold of himself: he had to!

"Sam?" He looked up; Devlin was sprawled at the edge of his hole. "Peters wants me to take over one of the Spandaus. All right?"

He shook his head. "No. I'd rather—would you take a water detail back in an hour or two?"

"Sure." Devlin's face was perfectly expressionless; but his eyes flashed once at Damon—a swift, outraged glance; fell away. He had taken hold well since his return to the Company. He had been competent and resourceful, and in the initial assault on Miravalles he had fought superbly; but in place of his old emotional force, the extremes of levity and exasperation that had made him the bellwether of the outfit, he now moved with a mute, dogged stoicism. Formerly gregarious, he was now a loner; only his eyes occasionally—just as now—glowed with a fiery, rebellious light, scornful and raging and full of peril. "Whatever you say, Sam," he concluded; and added tonelessly, "That means we don't get relieved today, then?"

"I'm afraid not, Dev." He watched the Sergeant swing away, and a pang went through him. "Dev—" he began.

"Yeah?"

"If anything should—" but he couldn't say it: "happen to me"; he refused to say it aloud "—go wrong today, send Reb back to Battalion: he's got the best chance of getting through. You know what I mean?"

"Sure, Sam . . ." Devlin's face was shaded with concern. He started to say something, then his lips came together and he crawled off toward Lieutenant Peters' foxhole. And with his departure came the high-arching shriek of a flight of 77s. They struck far in their rear, behind the Mill.

"Why in God's name don't we get out of this place . . . !"

The tenor of the voice alerted him. He turned. Brewster, bareheaded, his hands fluttering in front of his face, was climbing out of his hole.

"Tim!" he shouted. "You stay put, now . . ."

"—ridiculous! I tell you—stay here in this wretched place until we're all killed, every last—"

"*Brewster—!*"

The New York boy was on his feet now, walking quickly toward the rear, gesticulating. He had left his rifle. Damon leaped out of his pit. Brewster crouched, and drew his bayonet with startling dexterity. "No!" he cried. "I'm going home, you hear?—I'm going *home!*—"

"Tim, look—"

"Don't you try and stop me, Damon! I know you! Just don't come near me, that's all . . ."

There was a quick, low whistle in the air near them and then the crack of the sniper's rifle. And then Brewster was running—stumbling and sliding in the mud, his eyes wild. Damon made a sudden rush and dove at him, pinioning his arms; they fell into a shell hole in a clumsy tangle. Brewster had lost the bayonet but he was wrestling with surprising strength; he squirmed and flailed like a netted fish, struck Damon on the side of the head and in the throat.

"Let me go, you monster!" he screamed. "Let—me—*go!*" Just when the Captain didn't think he could hold him any longer, all the strength went out of him; he stopped struggling and lay panting on his side, his hair in his eyes.

"All right, Tim," Sam said quietly. "Take it easy, now."

"—ridiculous—mice in their holes until the cat stamps on them, yes!—until every one of us is crushed to pudding . . . Don't you *see—!*" His face, gray as old ash, was convulsed, his mouth slack. He began to weep, then; great dry sobs that were nearly like laughter.

Damon held him gently, felt the boy shivering. "Take it easy, Tim," he murmured. "Try and hold on, now. You don't want the new men to see you—"

"—I can't help it, Captain, I've done everything you've told me, everything they've wanted for months and months, but *I can't stay here any more—!*" He coughed thickly, and tried to break away again. Damon gripped him in a bear hug and he subsided.

"—leave us here day after day and nobody cares . . . it's all right for *you*, you haven't any nerves at all, you don't know—but I won't stand for it!—no more of this, ah God, no more, no more . . . !" And again he dissolved in shuddering, gasping sobs, his hands over his face.

". . . It's all right, Timmy." Holding the frail, slender body in his big arms he rocked him to and fro, speaking in a low, even, crooning voice. "It's all right, now. You won't have to do any more, Timmy. You'll be all right, now . . ."

The sniper fired again, and he heard the low drone of the bullet overhead. Holding Brewster, comforting him with a soft, meaningless litany, he felt a fearful anguish sweep over his soul. Was that how they really saw him? under the web of griping and jocosity, the awe? as a flint-hearted, blood-drinking killer with twin silver bars on his shoulders who lashed them on from hell to ever lowering hell, laughing at their torments? A Traprock Merrick? . . . He didn't believe it.

But he could not raise his eyes to the others at that moment.

"How do you stand, Captain?" Lieutenant Colonel Weyburn said.

"Sixty-three effectives, sir."

"I see. How would you estimate their fighting capabilities?"

Damon paused and looked down. They were sitting in piles of rubble in the cellar of the Chabert Mill, a gloomy vault damp with seepage from the incessant rain. Over the lintel hung a large, beautifully lettered sign, now split, that read *Kommandoposten Dambacher XLVII*, under which some wag had scrawled in chalk: *Welcome to Valley Forge. Bring your own monkey meat.* But that had been four days ago . . .

Colonel Weyburn was staring at him expectantly. He was a broad-shouldered man with a quiet voice and clear brown eyes; he'd been sent out from a stateside garrison post to take command of the battalion after Major Williams had been killed. He was a good officer, a good administrator—but now, watching the solid, ruddy face, the small mouth pinched with just a touch of annoyance, Damon felt beleaguered and resentful. What the hell did Weyburn know about it? He hadn't been up here . . . He shot a glance at Caldwell, but the Colonel was scraping mud off his boots with a piece of shingle.

But *estimate their fighting capabilities—*

"They're good men, Colonel," he answered Weyburn in a level tone. "What's left of them. I—Lieutenant Peters and I—have their full confidence." He paused. "This is a very different outfit from four days ago. We have been under heavy and almost incessant shell fire from the Mountain. I'm worried about them if we should be attacked." He paused, and glanced at Caldwell again. "I have participated in three major campaigns and seven engagements and I have never made this request before. The Colonel will bear me out." He took a deep breath and said: "I think my company needs to be relieved."

Colonel Weyburn grunted, and rubbed his hands back and forth along his thighs. Three shells struck in the ravine behind the Mill and the room shook slightly; the candle stuck in a salmon tin guttered, righted itself again. "It's not a question of relief," he said after a moment. "It's a matter of going forward. Regaining momentum."

Damon's mouth fell open. "*Attack?*"

Weyburn nodded. "The Grizzlies jump off at fourteen hundred hours. We are to coordinate our attack with theirs, so as not to expose their left flank."

Damon shut his eyes and clenched his hands to still their trembling. The idea that sixty-odd men, out of an original two hundred and fifty, after nine days in the line and four of interminable shelling, without rest or hot food, should be ordered to advance still again up a slope nearly destitute of cover and swept by machine-gun fire, seemed such madness that he could only roar with laughter. But no laughter came.

"May I see the orders," he said.

Weyburn's eyes dilated. "Now look here, Damon—"

"Let him see them, Archie," Colonel Caldwell said quietly. "He's going to be risking his neck carrying them out, isn't he?"

The battalion commander drew a crumpled sheet of paper out of his trench-coat pocket and handed it to him. Yes, there it was, all right. All so nicely planned, chock full of those high-flown Latinate words staff members loved to use. The last paragraph read:

Every effort must be made to convince the enemy that he is being threatened by continuous attack, thus compelling him to commit his reserve elements to battle. It is essential that our forces preserve the offensive attitude which has been adopted since September 26th.

Preserve the offensive attitude. He stared out of the cellar entrance at a frieze of mud and splintered branches. Preserve the offensive attitude.

"—On whose authority?" he heard himself say. "Who ordered this?"

Weyburn frowned at him and wrenched his neck inside his collar. "Now, just a minute, Captain—"

"No! What sick, misguided son of a bitch dreamed up this piece of lunacy—?"

"Do you refuse to carry out these orders, Damon?" Weyburn demanded hotly.

"No—what do you take me for?"

"Gentlemen," Caldwell murmured.

"Of course I'll carry it out," Damon went on, lowering his voice. "I've been ordered to attack and by God, I'll attack. But right now, right at this particular moment, I would merely like to say what I think of a staff that would send men out into this muck, leave them for days on end in positions commanded by an enemy-held mountain—and then coolly expect the survivors to attack once more!"

His voice rang in the room. Lieutenant Peters stirred nervously; Weyburn was staring crossly at the candle, his lips pursed.

"Sam . . ." Colonel Caldwell looked haggard and worn. He had suffered from gas at the Bois des Lions, and his skin had a greenish pallor; but his eyes still held that balance of alertness and compassion. "Sam, we've been promised relief. The New Yorkers are going to pass through us at seventeen hundred this evening. We've been asked to make just this one more effort . . . I know you've had a bad time out here," he went on quietly. "Very bad. The Thirty-ninth will be carrying the brunt of it. Divisional artillery has promised us a twenty-minute barrage of all calibers. Look, we'll give you everybody we can scrape up—cooks, clerks, orderlies, everybody. That's a solemn promise. We'll beef you up all we can. Just one more effort, Sam. That's all they're asking."

Damon handed the orders back to the battalion commander and nodded in silence. It was what he had said to the ten at Brigny, what he had said to Dev on the night march to Soissons: we've got to: we must do it anyway. Now it was only being said to him. Still again. Why did it always come down to this, why were they always faced with this draconian law of desperate choices, harsh alternatives that were no alternatives at all? Back at Chaumont men in spanking-fresh uniforms went smartly from room to room, passed their pencils over situation maps and scratched their clean, dry foreheads and toyed with alternatives; but here, in the mud and rain and thunderous hell of high explosive, there were no alternatives at all.

Colonel Caldwell was regarding him: that small, sad smile that understood so much, forgave so much, and went on hoping. This is the last time you'll see him, the thought darted. You might have known.

"Yes, sir," he said, and got to his feet. "We'll do it. But I'd like to meet the gentleman who wrote that." He indicated the orders Weyburn still held in his hand. "If I could have just five *minutes* with him it would make my day."

"Sorry, Sam." The Colonel's eyes glinted once. "Rank Hath Its Privileges, you know. You may hold my blouse, however." He turned with his most stern, attentive air to Weyburn, who was blinking at him in amazement. "It's quite all right, Archie, you'll get used to this sort of thing out here. What you don't yet see is that you're in a very strange land."

"Yes, Colonel," Weyburn said.

He crouched kneeling against a wall, panting, sick to death, half-dizzy with exhilaration, not knowing whether he was retching or coughing or laughing, or all three. Bright yellow leaves lay all around him like festive curly ornaments. He was so tired his thigh muscles jerked in spasms and his eyes would hardly focus—even now, here on the ridge, he was inclined to regard the whole thing as a wild hallucination.

He had no idea why they deserved such good fortune, after so many bitter tribulations. At 1410, right on the heels of the barrage, he had slung the Chauchat around his neck and blown his whistle and his sixty-some scarecrows, beefed up by all the woebegone culls of the regiment, had scrambled out of their holes and gone forward stiffly, waiting for the hail of steel. None came. They went on up the hill, past abandoned rifle pits and emplacements, empty ammunition boxes and rolls of wire, unable to believe their eyes. Then shells started falling around them from the Mont de Malsainterre and they faltered. Damon hollered at them, waving his arms, calling some of them by name and got them running, and they went the rest of the way in a rush, up and over the crest and into the fringe of woods beside the ruins of the Cavagnole Farm, whose shattered stone walls looked gaunt and forlorn against the beeches.

It was unbelievable. They were there. They had made it. He looked up gleefully, watching the line move up with him, taking cover smartly, fanning out along the ruins of some ancient trench. Then he heard the roar of small-arms fire on the ridge to his right, across the swamp, and he knew what had happened: the Grizzly Bears had broken through, and the Germans had got out while the getting was good. But it didn't matter. They'd made it up to the line, the shelling had let up completely;

the black stone of dread that had lain in his heart all day, that implacable premonition that he would not survive it, was false. He knew it now. They would dig in and sit tight, and the New Yorkers would come up and relieve them. And that, praise God and Allah and Thor and Zeus the Thunder Darter, would be that . . .

"What'd you do, Cap—get 'em on the party line and tell 'em the barn was on fire?" Raebyrne, with his helmet low over his eyes—a bright, solicitous hound's gaze—was standing beside him.

"Why no—I told 'em I was calling in every mortgage in the county by sundown." He jumped to his feet and threw his arm around the Carolina boy and hugged him. "God damn you, Reb, you old coon hunter—how's that for sheer generalship?"

"Plain frazzle-ass luck, you ask me."

"*Luck!* Why, I knew we were home free all along . . ."

"Didn't look much like it down the road a piece, Skipper."

"Oh, that—that was just to keep you in line. Discipline, Reb—for Christ sake, discipline!" He was shaking so it was all he could do to keep from running in circles, wrestling Raebyrne to the ground. "All right," he called, "we'll use this piece of trench here and tie in with that clump of trees. Tsonka, take the gun over—"

He was pointing at the end of the trench when he heard the shot. The unmistakable report of a Mauser, thin as a plate of glass snapping. His head whipped around. Not twenty feet away Devlin had clutched his belly in both hands. He gazed at the Captain—a terribly bright, terribly intense gaze; then sank to his knees, still holding his belt. The rifle fired again and Damon screamed "Cover!" The company scattered, diving into the sections of trench, shell holes, behind piles of rubble. Devlin was on his face now, his hands under his body.

"Cover!" Lieutenant Peters was shouting. "Spread out—"

Damon found himself crouching against the wall. Oh, Dev. The Mauser cracked again, the bullet whined away in a shrill nasal ricochet. It came from the building beside him. Somewhere in the building, in the ruins. Oh Dev. He whirled around and ducked through a gap in the wall of the house. There was no upper story, only a piece of masonry that rose up to where the roof had been, near the peak, and had refused to fall. He swung the Chauchat on its sling so he had it on his hip ready to fire, and picked his way over the débris of fallen timbers and heaps of rubble. On the floor pulverized glass lay in white trails, like salt. An inner wall was intact. He eased up to the doorway—ducked in and away again, caught a glimpse of movement in a far corner behind a chest. He ran forward, firing from the hip. The gun got off one round and jammed. Still racing forward he clutched at his pistol, couldn't get it free. The figure rose up: slight body, long rifle held high. He snatched at the Mauser, tore it out of the German's hands in one savage wrench. The figure moved backward, crouching; Damon saw a round face, snub nose, dark blue eyes wide with fear, a wrinkled uniform buttoned to the collar, the sleeves hanging over his hands. A boy. A young boy. Not fifteen, he couldn't be fifteen—

"Ah!" he gasped. He struck the boy on the side of the head, a back-handed blow. The absurdly large coal-scuttle helmet fell off the sniper's head and crashed on the broken crockery and plaster; the boy tumbled backward and hit the wall. Wordless, Damon followed him, cuffed him as a harsh father might a rebellious child, once, again— whirled away. "Oh shit!" he cried with all his heart. He had never felt such anguish in his life. He gripped the Mauser by the barrel, raised it over his head and brought it down in a fury on the piles of stone and mortar, again and again, until the stock split and shattered and his hands stung.

Someone had hold of him, was shouting something at him over and over. Someone else was trying to pinion his arms to his sides. Why should they want to do that? The German boy was still facing him defiantly, but his lips were trembling; he was trying hard not to cry. Blood was running in a dark thread from the edge of his cheek.

"Captain!" Tsonka was shouting in his ear. "Captain, *Captain—!*"

He dropped the ruined rifle, wrenched out of Tsonka's iron grip, pushed his way past Santos and Miller and went outside. Conger and Monteleone were bandaging Devlin; they had put him on his back with a blanket under him. His eyes opened and closed very slowly, as though he couldn't manipulate them; one hand kept sliding back and forth in the mud.

"Hello, Sam." A faint, weary voice that seemed to come from behind a mountain, kingdoms away. "I . . . thought . . . too good be true . . ."

"Dev, we'll get you down right away, don't you worry—" He said to Conger: "Pick anyone you want and take him down. Right now."

Conger frowned. "Captain, I thought you said we—"

"*Do as I say!—*"

He walked away, afraid to stay near Devlin any longer; he felt as if his entrails were on fire. "All right, you people," he shouted at them. "Let's get dug in, now! What are you waiting for, a God damn en-graved dance card?" They hurried away from him, their eyes slanting back toward him fearfully. He went up to one of the Spandaus and wrestled it over to the far edge of the trench, set it up on its ungainly rocking-horse mount, cleaned it of mud and fed in a belt. Then he sat down on the fire step and went to work on the Chauchat stoppage. He dug out the shell casing and checked it; it was neither cracked nor sprung, which meant it was either the firing pin or the extractor. Prob-ably the extractor. He had spares for both in his musette bag. He took off his trench coat and spread it on his knees and began to strip the weapon. Behind him he heard the murmur of voices as Conger and three others left with the stretcher, but he did not turn around.

"Captain?" Santos' voice: melodious and tentative.

"What is it?"

"Captain, Sergeant Tsonka wants to know what you want done with the—with the prisoner . . ."

He looked up in a spasm of grief and rage. "Shoot him. Spank him. Give him an Iron Cross First Class and send him home—*I* don't give a damn . . . only keep him the hell out of my sight!"

"Yes, Captain."

The four figures were descending the hill now, joined by their burden; they made an animal, some sort of new, war-created animal with a low-slung, lumpy belly and eight legs . . .

The stretcher-bearers slipped into a tremulous bubble, and he shut his eyes, bent over the Chauchat again.

Oh Dev. I thought neither of us would ever be hit. I thought if we stuck together, right close together—

No more of that.

It was the extractor, as he'd thought. Broken cleanly right at the neck. He threw the defective pieces into the bottom of the trench, rummaged in his musette bag and found the replacement and oiled it heavily, then wiped it dry. He was conscious of the absence of talk around him; even Reb was silent. Very slowly and deliberately he began to reassemble the automatic rifle, inserting the sleeves and cylinders of metal, warm in the gray October air.

The café was jammed with khaki. Men crowded in shoulder to shoulder at the little bar, or milled aimlessly at the door, or wandered through the press, bending over tables and shouting greetings to one another. Two homely, perspiring girls hurried through the dim light serving drinks, and in the far corner of the room a soldier was pumping away furiously at the pedals of a player piano, while five or six others, arms wound one another's shoulders, roared out the chorus:

> *"She can get herself malade from a lousy Home Guard,*
> *She can Sam Browne all over Paree;*
> *She can spread her dimpled knees for the hairy-assed MP's—*
> *But she'll never make a sucker out of me—*
> *(I've been taken!)*
> *No, she'll never make a sucker out of me . . ."*

Damon emptied his drink again and set it carefully in front of him, staring at the ripples in the glass. A tall, redheaded corporal named Dalrymple was saying: "When I get back home I'm going to go into politics. I'm going to become mayor of San Francisco and I'm going to take every God damn bribe they hand me."

"No—wireless is the coming thing," Miller answered. He was short and fat, wore glasses, and his expression was genial and very attentive, as though he were talking to some rich, crotchety old aunt. "Think of it—a wireless set in every home in America! Do you realize what that will mean?"

"Won't work," Raebyrne declared.

"What? Of course it will—it *does* work. Just because you—"

"If I can't see it and feel it and pick it up, it isn't there. And if it isn't there it won't work. Don't argue with a mountain man." Raebyrne reached into a sack by his feet and pulled up a deep red, long-necked bottle. "Now this here is Leapfrogmilk, I believe. Compliments of the Eighty-'leventh Braveerian Infantry." Someone jostled his arm and wine spilled on the zinc. "Damn. Give me room. How about a pull at the jug, Skipper?"

"No," Damon muttered. "No more for me."

"Aw, come on. It's the pure quill. You can taste the feet of the Pee-roossian maidkins that stomped the grapes . . ." One of the French girls came by, her hands full of empty glasses, and Raebyrne reached out with his free hand and called, "Hey now, cutie. Let's us go spooning, all right? A little hoochy-kooching, all by our lonesome?" The girl gave a sharp, exasperated laugh and twisted away and he called, "What's wrong —ain't I upstanding enough?"

"With *that?*" Tsonka demanded. "Reb, you're cock-eyed drunk."

"I ain't going to put her in the rotarygruel . . ."

Damon drank the sweet, thin German wine, rubbing his face with his knuckles. Drinking never made any difference: he only became steadily more clearheaded and cold, until his mind's eye became a jeweler's glass, burning down into a pinpoint of diamond light. What Uncle Bill called the German discipline. But his cheeks were numb. Somewhere a glass smashed, there were angry shouts and after a while gentler, more conciliatory voices prevailed. He thought of the bar back at the Grand Western, imagined it choked with foreign soldiery, Pop Ainslie serving them, his sister Peg carrying drinks, dodging the outstretched hands, trying to smile, trying not to hate these sweaty, drunken strangers . . . He sighed, and emptied his glass again. They profaned everything they touched, shattered and wasted, and the most pitiful part of it was they didn't mean to, most of them: they only wanted to—Jesus Christ, they only wanted to shove certain things away out of sight, they only wanted to remind themselves that they were *here*, breathing, feeling . . .

"Look at that." Raebyrne was pointing to a narrow space between their table and another where a body lay facedown, now and then twitching as some soldier bumped it or stepped on it. "You know, that Pulver's pretty drunk."

"Yeah." Tsonka crushed out his cigarette in the palm of his hand. "Dumb draftee bastard."

"I'm a draftee," Santos said huffily.

"Yeah. Well. You're a Dago."

"I am like hell a Dago."

"Well, what are you, then?"

"I'm Portuguese."

"Portagoose!" Raebyrne crowed. "Well, I'll be dog! I don't believe I ever met up with one before . . ."

The group at the piano was larger now, and for a moment the singing drowned out everything else.

> *"They say Napoleon's mad*
> *About this jazz-crazy fad,*
> *He's teaching Josie the Grizzly Bear;*
> *And even Aphrodite*
> *Wriggled out of her nightie*
> *To be the hit of the Follies Bergère! . . ."*

"Damn all, I never did get to Paris yet," Raebyrne moaned. "I promised Brewster a tolerable stomp-down time in that villy . . ." His face fell, he shoved his hair out of his eyes. "Men, I feel like hell is one country mile away and every fence is down. God, it's the only time I feel low, now—sitting around waiting for the horn to blow again. I wish old Brewzie was here. You know that, Mike? He was a finicklish little guy but he was one of the best. You know that, Stonk?"

"He was. One of the best."

"Or old Clay," Dalrymple said. "He was full of laughs. Remember the time he filled his canteen with van blonk on the night march to Soissons and puked all over Ferguson's pack? That was some comical . . ."

"Well actually," Miller offered in his genial, eager manner, "I know I haven't been with the company very long, but I'd have to say of all the fellows I miss most I'd have to say Sergeant Devlin—"

There was a thump. Damon raised his head to see Miller bent over the table gripping his leg, his eyes fearful behind his glasses. Tsonka was glaring at him and Reb was saying loudly: "Who's cutting out with me to fetch up some devilment? How about you, Skipper—we going to dig up some of this fancy-ass poontang they all talk about?"

He had to get out of here. Now. He thrust himself to his feet and snatched up his trench coat; his chair went over backward. He had planted a foot on poor old Pulver. Miller was looking up at him, frightened, one pudgy hand at his collar.

"—But he's not going to die, is he?" Miller stammered. "I mean, I thought—"

Tsonka said: "Shut up, you stupid four-eyed son of a bitch."

Damon paused, watching Miller. For a piece of an instant he wanted to smash that fat white anxious face; then the impulse vanished. He jerked his overseas cap out of his belt.

"Pay him no heed, Cap," Raebyrne said. "Look, where you going?"

"Never mind." He turned away.

"What's the matter, Skipper?" they called after him. "Hey, what's the matter? Don't go, now . . ."

He thrust his way through the press, jostling the men in his path. Someone cursed him and he whirled around, ready to fight; but no one was looking at him.

Outside, the day was sliding swiftly toward dusk—a plum-colored light that softened the trees, the edges of the warped, narrow houses. It had stopped raining and the air was cool; the leading edge of autumn. He walked quickly, slamming his heels into the great gray paving stones. Once clear of the town itself he fell into a dogtrot, and finally ran hard across the fields, slipping and stumbling in the wet earth. On his right he saw an orchard and stopped. They were thin, scraggly trees, their few remaining leaves wet and drooping. The smell of rotting apples rose around him densely. He threw himself down on a mound of damp hay and lay there spread-eagled, his head pounding, and stared upward, trying to think of nothing but the Champagne sky, the tortured skein of clouds streaming west. Behind him, toward Mont Noir, he could hear the choked mutter of the big guns. He had a stitch in his side, and his belly was churning. Sitting up he gagged himself with two fingers, but nothing came up. The odot of rotten apples was almost suffocating.

All at once he found himself crying—the hurried, hiccuping sobs of a ten-year-old, his shoulders shaking. "Oh Dev," he muttered. "Oh Dev, forgive me . . ." Then it passed, and he wiped his eyes and face with his handkerchief and lay down again, watching the first stars glow their way into being.

He was not up to it. He wasn't hard enough. He ought to be like Weyburn, or the Old Man. Maybe it was even better to be like Merrick, carrying on mocking conversations with the corpses of his command as they were borne past him, roaring with mirth as he slaughtered his prisoners. It was better than this—anything was better than this. He was not a real soldier. He was good only in combat, and that would not last: he was full of fear now. At times like this he felt every death, every loss, as if chunks of his flesh were being flayed away. They kept drifting toward him in their agony, flung up in the clarity of surf: Van Gelder panting in the hot dusk, the slow roll of Jason's eyes under their lids, Krazewski's shattered chest, Ferguson, Turner, Clay, Pelletier, Dev—

He squeezed shut his eyes. Listening to George Verney and Uncle Bill he had dreamed of a fellowship of danger and high sacrifice, a soaring affection that laughed at all adversity . . . and in its place he had found only squalor and bereavement. He had found out about the elephant. Turning his head he could see flaring on the horizon the dulled sheet lightning of the front.

Two poilus came around a corner ahead of him. Walking slowly now, his body chilled from the damp hay, oppressed by his thoughts, he watched them absently, frowning. They'd had several more than they could handle, which was odd because one rarely saw French infantry drunk in the streets. Then the poilus brought up short; the stocky one pulled at the tall one's blouse in a brief, swaying argument. Damon kept walking toward them. The short one started to run, the other held onto him—then both lurched off down the street in confusion.

They were up to something. Something fishy. He broke into a run, caught up with them and said: "Soldats: attention! Qu'est-ce qui passe, hein?"

They stopped, resigned, and came to a tottering attention. The shorter one went into a ridiculous sidewinder salute, swayed backward until he bumped against the wall, and said: "Franzay soldatch. Mwah."

It was Tsonka. Drunk as a hoot owl. Beside him, blinking, Raebyrne broke into his sheepish, hound-dog grin. "Howdy, Skipper." He touched the high-horned French garrison cap, which was on his head askew. His arms stuck out of the blue tunic sleeves like long white pipes.

"For—Christ—sake," Damon murmured.

Tsonka relaxed then, and threw Raebyrne a look of intense disgust. "You and your hillbilly schemes. Fifty frigging streets in this lousy burg and you have to take this one . . ."

"Just what in hell do you think you're doing?" Damon demanded.

"Go ahead, bright boy," Tsonka said wearily. "Go ahead and tell him. Maybe you'll get another craw de gayre out of it."

Raebyrne swallowed and grinned again. "Well, Skipper, fact is we swapped uniforms with a couple of these here poyloos. They didn't mind none at all."

"I've got that far," Damon replied. "Now let's go back into *why* you did it."

"Well, it was a ruse, Cap. To get on the inside of one of those Frog bee-rothals. Some of that red plush and Gramophones and naked cuties."

". . . You damn fools. Do you realize what they could do to you? out of uniform?"

"Why, we ain't exactly *out* of—"

"Don't argue with me. You realize what you'd get if the MPs picked you up?"

"Seemed like a lewdling idea at the time, Skipper."

"Oh Jesus, yes," Tsonka echoed sourly. "Name of the game."

"They'd spot this silly dodge in a minute. Before you even opened your mouths. Two American NCOs—all right: where are the poilus?"

"The what, Cap?"

"The Frog doughboys, you ninny! The other two chumps . . . Where are *they*, by now?"

"I suppose back in the staminay."

"Back in the *what?*"

"The gin mill," Tsonka appended sourly. "Place with the blue shutters, back of the station."

"Tell you what, Skipper," Raebyrne said, "I'll hustle on back and get 'em for you, and we'll—"

"Oh, no you won't. We're going back there and find them together. If you think you can still walk, that is."

Reb looked hurt. "That's a misling word for an old campaigner, Cap."

"What'd you try to do—drink the whole sackful empty?"

"Well—no sense saving the stuff."

"What do you mean by that?"

"Hell, we're going back up to the line in seventy-two hours," Tsonka replied calmly.

"Where'd you hear that?"

"Sanderson got it from Jonesy, who got it from Tillman over at the message center. Swore it was the straight skinnay. Isn't it?"

"Beats me," Damon muttered. "It probably is."

"Well, then. No sense leaving it for the fucking casuals."

They were walking quickly toward the station. Raebyrne was holding himself exaggeratedly erect, his big feet slithering on the wet cobbles. "I don't have the luck of a sick snake," he observed mournfully. "Trying to get next to a little sin in this man's army is like scratching a poor man's ass."

"You chumps," Damon taunted them. He didn't know whether he was angry or amused. "Thought you could saunter past a couple of gimlet-faced MPs in that rig and run on upstairs and pick yourselves up a nice fat dose."

"Not me, Skipper." Raebyrne reached in his pocket and drew out a small misshapen knob, indecipherable in the darkness. "I got my Grandaddy Clete's horse chestnut."

"What do you do with that," Tsonka demanded, "—rub it against her muff?"

"Hell no, Mike. It's got bacteractic qualities. Like fever root. See, there's a spot on it that's—" The chestnut fell through his fingers and rolled among the cobbles. Raebyrne got down on his hands and knees. "See, Cap? It's trying to find its way back to the soil."

"Come on, Reb."

"I *cain't* leave my Grandaddy Clete's tamulook—"

"God damn it, Raebyrne!"

"Skipper, I've been carrying it next to my heart ever since Briny . . ."

Damon groaned, yanked his flashlight out of his pocket and began to play it over the stones, which looked like hundreds of slick little wizened loaves of bread. "All right, there it is. For God's sake, pick it up and let's go!"

The café, like the one he had left earlier, was crowded, tawdry, wreathed in smoke. Soldiers slumped around the little tables, singing, arguing, staring at nothing through narrowed lids. The woman behind the caisse looked dark and monumental and forbidding.

"There's a side door," Tsonka said. "Whyn't we use that, Captain?"

The poilus were in one of the two rooms in back, drinking wine from a bottle. Damon recognized them at once. They were obviously ill at ease in the American uniforms, which hung on them like tentage. When they caught sight of Damon entering with their two benefactors their eyes rolled. They jumped to their feet.

"All right," Damon said, closing the door with his foot. "Let's change back, and fast."

Raebyrne's eye fell on the bottle of wine. "You mean right away, Skipper?"

"No—next April. The man who takes more than three minutes for the entire change gets two days' company punishment." He offered a free translation of this warning to the Frenchmen, looked at his watch and said: "Go!"

The four went into a paroxysm of disrobing, snatching at bits of discarded clothing, hopping about eerily. Climbing out of the strange breeches Raebyrne sprawled off balance and sat down hard on the floor, jerking the shirt off over his head. Tsonka was sitting in one of the chairs, tugging frantically at the awkward French leggings. Leaning against the door Damon began to laugh. Jesus. Of all the crazy stunts. Of all the ridiculous, asinine schemes . . .

"Thirty francs and two perfectly good bottles of Heinie rotgut," Tsonka muttered, plunging his powerful legs into his own breeches. "Why in hell do I ever listen to you?"

"You didn't find nothing wrong with the idea a while back," Reb retorted in an injured tone.

"Shut up, both of you, and get dressed," Damon commanded. And then, watching Raebyrne swaying naked in the small, meanly lit room, he thought all at once of the afternoon on the bank of the Marne; those slim white bodies gamboling in the shallow water, so soon to be shattered, drained of life and grace, dumped into trenches, bloated, putrescent, crawling with flies . . . His eyes filled with tears.

Raebyrne was staring at him with maudlin solicitude. "Anything wrong, Skipper?"

He shook his head and turned away. When he spoke again his voice was harsh. "Jesus, do I have to ride herd on you jokers *every* minute of the day to keep you out of trouble? Haven't you got more sense than to pull a silly stunt like this?" he demanded savagely. "Haven't you got any *pride?*" He shook his fist at them, glaring beneath his brows—aware that he was acting like a damned fool and not caring, while they stared up at him, worried and rueful. "They need you, those kids—who have they got to look to but you older men? What else is going to glue them together if you're not there? Answer me! I can't show them every-thing . . ." He checked himself and lowered his voice. "If I ever catch you in foreign uniform again I'm going to run you up to the Colonel myself, and ask him to throw the whole book at you, chapter and verse. You got that?"

"Yes, sir," they sang in soft chorus.

"All right. Now get out of here and go back and sack in and sleep it off before you dream up any more trouble. You've had a real good day of it as it is."

"Yes, sir!"

"All right. Good night."

"Good night, Cap."

He swung the door behind him with his shoulder and went out quickly through the smoky hubbub of the café. He could not have trusted himself to say one more word.

〔10〕

The front of the church had vanished in a great pyramid of rubble but the altar end, the transept and ambulatory, were relatively intact; and the wounded lay in two long, curving lines below the leaded windows, whose remaining bits of glass glowed like subterranean treasure against the clouded gray light of day. Damon walked along the rows, past mummy-swathed faces, bandaged arms and bodies swaddled in blankets. Here and there medical orderlies and doctors paused and bent over, or stood in little groups talking, like warehousemen waiting for a work call to ready freight for shipment.

Devlin was two from the end of the left-hand row, lying perfectly still. His face was white and smooth, waxen, lightly sweating, although the October air was cool. His eyes watched Damon steadily as he approached.

"Hello, Dev."

"Hello, Sam . . ." His voice was hoarse, and very faint, as though he feared if he spoke too loudly it would jar something irreparably.

"Well, I see they finally got you in church."

"Yeah. About time, I suppose. How's it going?"

"Worse than ever. The New Yorkers have bogged down completely at Aillettes. We've got to go up the line again, day after tomorrow."

"No rest for the wicked."

"That's the pitch."

"How's the outfit?" Devlin asked; but he was only feigning an interest, Damon knew; he didn't really care.

"All fouled up. Same as usual. We've got some new men. Kids. Most of them haven't even fired a rifle . . ."

He clenched his hands softly and looked down between his knees. Why was it he could think of nothing to say? People kept milling around in the aisle behind him where he squatted, talking matter-of-factly of knee resections and draining and the next ambulance train leaving for No. 1 at Neuilly, and he couldn't seem to keep his thoughts on anything. It was inevitable, he told himself tersely, the way things were going. It was pure blind chance, that kid could see all of us coming up over the rise: luck of the crazy draw.

It wasn't my fault—

His eyes darted from the shattered windows to Devlin's face and back again. He ought to be full of distraction, amusement, something—for Christ sake *something*. He'd come all the way back here to see his oldest, only friend, comfort him, pass some time . . . And yet the part he couldn't get around was the way he'd shaken in his boots all that day, so sure it was *he* who was going to stop one, be lying here in—

"—Reb's still feuding with Fucciano," he heard himself saying, a bit too rapidly. "Told him if he tried to palm that lousy goldfish off on them one more time he was going to retire him to Blooie. Said Fudge had no guts as a forager, and he was going to talk up a general chowline strike until Fudge gave them all an honest-to-God stomp-down bedcord meal."

"Old Reb," Devlin murmured with the ghost of a smile.

"They were at it hot and heavy. Fudge said he'd fry in hell before he gave Reb another lick of slum or dunderfunk or monkey meat or goldfish or anything else. And Reb said that was fine by him, he was challenging Fudge to a contest of culinary science in three hours. So Reb and Tsonka took off foraging and scrounged two tough old laying hens, all bone and gristle. They started a fire in a Boche helmet right next to Fudge's field kitchen, and Reb laid his mess gear over that for a frying pan. They'd stolen salt and pepper and a bottle of capers, probably from under Fucciano's nose, and they went into a big business about cooking the birds. By this time half the battalion had gathered around—which was just what Reb had been waiting for. He reaches down into his breeches leg and hauls out a bottle of Rhine wine he's been carrying around ever since we stumbled into that crazy Lotus Pavilion, and while the crowd looks on in horror pours some of it over the chicken, sprinkling it with some beet sugar he's promoted from somewhere. And then the clincher: he gropes around in his overcoat pocket and whips out one of those red-and-white checkered tablecloths and spreads it out on the ground, hauls out still another bottle and invites half the platoon to partake. He'd set himself upwind of the field kitchen and Fudge just about went crazy . . ."

He had run down, in spite of himself; he'd stopped. Devlin's face looked so white it was almost transparent; the smile had left his lips, he was rocking his head back and forth on his gas mask—a fevered, tremulous motion that seemed obscurely fearsome.

"I'm telling you, Dev," he hurried on, "you're going to have your hands full with this new bunch. There's a kid from Kenosha named Tuckerbee who won't wear a helmet, he says the metal causes a short circuit in his—"

"Forget it, Sam."

"What?"

"Never—kid an Irishman." He raised one hand, dropped it again. "I'm not going back to the outfit. I'm not going anywhere."

"Sure you are. Of course you are, I've got—"

"I've bought the whole wad. I know." He looked squarely at Damon. "I'm going to check out, Sam."

"The hell you are," Damon said sharply. "Who gave you that crap?"

"I know, Sam. You think I don't know what peritonitis means? Don't —let's not horse around, Sam. I . . . can't afford it."

Damon bit his lip. Anybody would say it was just chance, we were in line of skirmishers, milling around, I'd just grabbed Reb around the middle, I was telling him it was only a question of—

"Sam . . ."

"Yes?"

"Sam, write to my ma, will you? Tell her I was the one hit the till at Natupski's. That's why I joined up when I did. Tell her I told you. But I was drunk, I didn't know half what I was doing, it was on a dare and I was drunk. Sober I'd have known better; I would. Will you tell her that?"

"Sure, Dev." He paused, said in a low voice, "You want me to—to go to Charmevillers?"

The two men gazed at each other for a long moment. Devlin shook his head once, slowly. "No. No point. It'd only be—hard for her, hard for you. That game's over. She knew."

Damon looked away wildly. His hands were slick with sweat and his mouth was dry. In the ambulatory window above him a frieze of mounted knights charged valorously, their lances quick black splinters in a medley of plangent blues and reds and golds. One figure lay beneath the hooves, however, its body collapsed in ugly postures. Oh, shit, he thought weakly. Oh, shit. In another medallion nearby a boy in a blue tunic sat by a silver stream and stroked a lyre—

He leaned forward, aware of perspiration crawling down through his scalp. "Dev." He could not say it. He couldn't. Then he could. "Dev. I wouldn't have had this happen for the whole world. Dev . . . I swear it."

The dying man gazed at him unsmiling. "You did what you thought was right, Sam. You're that kind of guy, you see a thing and that's the only way it can be, and you drive right on. You pull people with you, Sam. Nobody can say no to you. Because you're so sure. And so far you've always made it work. You did what you felt was right . . . But you're wrong, Sam." And now there were tears in Dev's eyes, huge glinting drops that hung on his lower lids, then broke over and down each side of his nose. "What good was it? Sure, I went back and did what you wanted.—Am I better off now? Is anybody in this whole sad fucking world going to be one notch better off for my being rolled in a poncho and shoveled under? I think not, Sam. Not any way that I can see . . ."

He raised one hand and wiped his eyes and nose; his eyes looked enormous in the thin waxen cast of his face. "Sam. Remember the march to Montemorelos? the trooper, the wounded trooper we carried over to the wagon?"

"—Gurney," Damon said, with a croak.

"Remember how he kept wanting to tell us something, how he kept trying to say something and then he couldn't? Remember? . . . I know what he felt, now—it's funny: it's something you *hear*, something you've been told, when this happens—something terribly important about life, all of life and yourself and the future, and it's all so *clear!*— but you can't for the life of you explain it to a God damned living soul . . ." He smiled then—a faint upward curving of his lips that was more desolate than his brief tears. "You don't understand either . . . I know that sounds foolish. I know."

"No. It doesn't . . . I think you need to get some sleep, Dev."

He made a little movement to rise and Devlin reached out and clutched his wrist—a faint, tremulous pressure. It was so faint! "No. That's just what I don't want . . . Oh, this is a bad way to go, Sam. A sorry way. If it'd been like Ferg or Starkie—or even Kraz or Turner. But lying here like this, with the thing breaking you down brick by brick. It's no way . . . Sam, remember the ball games at Early?"

"Dev—"

"Remember old Parrish, the time he made you and Merrick shake hands, that afternoon we beat them? Pulling away at his waxed mustache. 'We are a family. A select and honorable family.' He was a good man. What happened to him?"

"Lost a leg at Vaux."

"Well. He's out of it . . . Remember the Paris parade, with the girls all winging roses at us? Remember all the—Sam, don't leave me here, just a little, you can't leave me here right *now*—!"

Damon eased himself down on the edge of the field cot, which creaked with his weight; he could hardly see. "I won't leave you," he murmured. "I won't leave you, Dev."

"Good. Good. I knew you wouldn't run out on a buddy. Your oldest buddy . . . Sam, remember Jumbo Kintzelman and the rattler, back at Early?" he begged; his eyes were terrible. "When Colonel Hobart's wife went after it with a hoe and old Jumbo standing there silly as a crane?"

"Dev. Try to rest. Try to get some sleep."

"No. No . . . Stay with me, Sam. Stay here with me—ah, please . . ."

Damon put his fist against his mouth. "I'll stay with you, Dev. I swear it. Try and sleep. Try and sleep."

The room was spacious and high-ceilinged. Heavy velour draperies of wine red hung at the windows. There was a walnut writing table where the Colonel was seated, and a massive armoire against one wall, and a ponderous couch with lions' claw feet and lions' heads on the arms where Damon was. There were chairs and cabinets and hassocks. On the interior wall between the windows was a flamboyant painting in blacks and reds and blues, of a German officer in riotous embrace with a naked woman who wore a devil's horns and tail and had cloven hoofs, while assorted beasts and angels—were they angels?—looked on with avid interest. Damon found himself staring at it numbly.

"Yes, quite a riddle, isn't it?" Colonel Caldwell said. "Queer people, the Boches. I've left it on the wall—I keep imagining if I study it carefully enough I'll learn something profound about the German character. I assume my opposite number commissioned it. Do you suppose I could get Raebyrne to work up something for me?"

Damon turned to him, startled. "Sir?"

Caldwell smiled. "Nothing. I'm becoming fatuous as I grow older. Tell me: what's your strength?"

"One hundred seventy-two, with the new replacements."

"What are they like?"

"All right, I guess. They're brighter than the old breed, but they're softer. Better at close-order drill, worse at skirmishing. Poor marksmen, on the whole."

"I hear you're hiking them pretty hard."

"Yes, sir, I am. I believe it's the best conditioner."

"So do I." The Colonel smiled. "How about your new officers?"

"Shaw is good. Zimmerman I'm not so sure about: have to see how he works in. Their spirit is excellent."

"How's Wilgus working out as first sergeant?"

"Very well, sir. He's just what they need. Solid old-timer with no nonsense about him."

"He was in Mexico, wasn't he?"

"Yes, sir. He was."

"Did you know him down there?"

"What, sir?—yes, I did. Slightly. A great stickler for detail. Not quick, but thorough. There was—it's a . . ." He stopped; he had lost the thread of his thought. His mind was empty; he felt suddenly afraid. Colonel Caldwell was looking at him with that alert, on-point expression. "I'm sorry, sir," he said simply. "I forgot what I was going to say."

"What's the trouble, Sam?"

"I don't know, Colonel." He paused. "Devlin."

Caldwell said gently: "Is he dead?"

"He's—in a coma. They tell me he won't last the night."

The Colonel sighed and pinched the bridge of his nose. "Yes. Peritonitis. Very good friend of mine died of a bullet in the belly at Macloban. Not very joyful. One of these days they'll find a way to seal up the peritoneum without infection. Of course by *then* they'll have invented a projectile that will infect *every* internal organ on entrance, I suppose." He got up and going over to a musette bag hanging on an ornate brass hook lifted a bottle out of it, crossed to the armoire and poured some of its contents into two painted stem goblets and brought them over. "Here. Join me in a drink. Not the proper service for it, I dare say. To tell the truth you look as though you could do with one."

"Thank you, Colonel. I could. I could do with one."

It was Cognac, a very good Cognac: dry and fiery, it flamed its way down his throat and lodged in his belly, cauterizing, burning away thoughts of betrayal and death. Death and betrayal. He sat still on the imposing Empire couch, his head lowered, tears stinging his eyes.

"Sam, it's not your fault, you know."

He looked up. "I'm afraid this time it is, sir. Quite definitely."

Caldwell shook his head. "If he had wanted to stay with her—had really and truly wanted to desert for good—there would have been nothing on this earth that would have pulled him back. Least of all you. No, he wouldn't have lasted two years at that game, and something inside him knew it. He is too proud. Some of them can. They're doing it—some of them are hiding in Paris now, there's a whole bunch in the Montmartre area, the MPs are hunting them down: the rebellious, the craven, the sensitive. The ones that war always destroys, good and bad . . ." He got up and began to pace slowly back and forth in front of the tall windows, where the rain fell without letup. "Don't torture yourself. When Grant wanted to bow out after Shiloh, they say Sherman talked him into staying on. Uncle Billy used some very clever arguments, but don't be fooled: Grant stayed on because he knew in his heart, all the backstairs politicking and preferment and calumny to the contrary, it was the only proper course for him." He stopped by the obscene picture, his back to Damon. "Devlin is a good soldier. Something shook him at Soissons. Do you know what it was?"

"No, sir. Maybe it was just—Soissons . . ."

"Yes. That's possible. Anything could have done it, I suppose. Perhaps he was simply sick of slaughter. God knows I am; God knows when I look at—"

The Colonel checked himself and folded his arms. "War is a—serious—business," he said with great deliberation. "Yes. Serious. That's why I've relieved Merrick."

Damon started. "Relieved him, sir? Sent him down?"

"Back to Blois. Do you feel that's too harsh?"

"Why, I don't know . . ." He looked at Caldwell uncertainly. "I've never liked him myself, I've never approved of certain things he does. But he's good in combat. He's utterly fearless—"

"That's just it." The Colonel paused, staring again at the mural. "He has no fear. None at all." He pointed at Sam, nodding. "*I will have no man in my boat who is not afraid of a whale.* That's the crux of it. There's something very wrong with Merrick: he's not a *man*. I wasn't aware of it at first; but battle always brings this out. That action at Paulnay Ridge—to expose his people that way, and for nothing! It's perfectly all right with me if he wants to hurry toward his own destruction. Though I shouldn't even say that, he doesn't have that right any more than the rest of us. But he has no right whatsoever to sacrifice good men to this crazy lust or whatever it is. I won't have it." He scratched his scalp at the hairline. "There are only a few like him, thank God—the Cadmus soldiers—and they're more of a menace than a help: if you can't measure danger, how on earth can you evade it? For the Merricks war is not a serious business . . .

"Ultima ratio regem," he murmured, musing; and his handsome face looked all at once unbelievably stern. "Yes. But let's make sure it *is* the last argument. Because once the eminent heads of state in all their infinite wisdom decide that it must be, once the drums begin to beat—there is nothing ahead but fear and waste and misery and desolation. Nothing else. Once the engine has started it must shudder and rumble to the very end of its hellish course, come what may. And you and I and a few million others are the ones who must cling to the machine as it grinds along."

Abruptly he turned to the map on the long side wall. "This is what we ought to do. Break in this way." His fingers traced a quick arc on the heavy paper. "Etain—Briey—Thionville, outflank Metz, knife in to Trier. Do you see it? But we won't. We'll be flung at the Meuse— here—in a long, stupid, costly line. The concept of pierce-and-encircle is not in the French lexicon. And these are the descendants of Napoleon! God damn fools," he muttered.

"Then why are we doing it?" Damon asked quietly. "Why do we agree to this folly?"

Caldwell turned from the map. "Because we have no choice. To falter now is to breed worse evils than we have. We are saddled with leaders whose concept of strategy and tactics has been destroyed by four years of unparalleled numbers, mountainous losses. It is like asking blind men to run an obstacle course. They are no longer capable of *thought* . . ."

"But General Liggett—"

"Ah, Liggett, Connor, Marshall—of course. But we lack the power to make our desires prevail. They needed us desperately, we came in our tens of thousands and spilled our blood quite generously from Cantigny to Montfaucon. But now times have changed: now they know they will win, and they are prepared to go their own way."

"Maybe we should have insisted on certain strategic concessions as part of the price of our entry into the war."

"A trenchant observation." Caldwell grinned. "Go straight to the head of the class. Well, it was complicated. We only had four divisions of assault caliber as late as last April, and it was touch and go on the Marne—a poor time to make strategic requests, I imagine." He slapped his thigh once. "But it's not that: we seem to be incapable of insisting, that's the meat of it. We are a race of headlong altruists. We rush to a foreign land in a deluge of embattled sympathy, we give away clothing, cigarettes, our rations. We even on occasion"—and his eyes sparkled— "repair the battered living quarters of certain comely French civilians. We do everything in our power to proclaim our good intentions, our nobility of purpose, our loftiness of soul . . . and all because we think we're too good for the rest of the world."

"Is that the reason?"

"Yes, more or less. We can't be bothered with the sordid details, the actualities of human motivation. We stubbornly, sublimely refuse to see man as he is, Sam—we're so damned certain about how he *ought* to be. *We* know how he ought to be—he ought to be American . . ." There was a sullen mutter of guns off toward Brieulles, and the Colonel paused, his nose up, as though trying to scent their scope and direction; he shook his head. "No, that hasn't got it. We know what man is, all right, but we insist on overlaying that knowledge with a mass of sticky sentimentality . . . We know how man treats man. You've only to read the reports of hard-bitten post commanders on the frontier, complaining of the vicious debauchery of entire Indian tribes by Astor's people, the cycles of boom and panic engineered by ruthless stock operators that impoverished hundreds of thousands; the way children were treated in scores of New England mills. Yes, and a fairly general attitude toward the black-skinned man in this great democracy of ours . . ."

A great rumble surged toward them, broke into the rhythmic grinding roar of trucks passing, shifting gears, straining in the mud; the room shook.

"The Blue Ridgers," the Colonel said. "Moving up to have another go at Malsainterre. From the south, this time. —We know," he went on, his voice pitched flat against the noise of the camions, "we know, but we avert our eyes—it's so much more fun to prate of man as a noble creature, a semidivine being bursting with goodness and mercy and all kinds of generous thoughts. It—takes our minds off ourselves . . . Well, he *isn't* a noble creature, as well we know by now: he's a remarkably clever animal whose talents have outstripped his powers of reason. And his deepest instincts seem to be greed and vanity and self-interest."

"But the idea of helping your neighbor," Damon protested, "of sharing what you have—"

Caldwell nodded. "Yes, the nation was founded on a dream—but look at the reality. The men who fought in the War for Independence were promised the western lands as payment for their service—they certainly didn't get any other remuneration. But when the war was over the vested interests pulled every trick in the book to grab it all for themselves; and it took federal creation of the Northwest Territory to secure the veterans their forty acres . . ."

Muttering and fuming he peered out of the window, where the procession of trucks and artillery ground their way past, slewing and snorting in the sullen rain. "Look at them," he murmured. "Going up there again, full of fire and hope and high resolve . . . Day after tomorrow it's our turn again.

"I can never get over the incongruities," he observed softly, as though carrying on a private dialogue with some inner antagonist. "The essential absurdity of the soldier's life: look at us, standing here well groomed and housed and fed, all at our ease—while up there a few miles men are living and fighting and hiding and dying like some particularly odious species of ferret. A few miles away . . . I shouldn't trouble myself over such thoughts; a good soldier wouldn't, I suppose. But I can't help it. I can harden my heart, but I cannot alter it. What an awfully *lonely* calling it is!—you continually find yourself alone with your speculations, your afterthoughts, your fears. I should never have been a soldier; but Father was determined I should go to the Point, and so the Point it was. And here I am, and there they are, out there, in their thousands; and we must get on with the bloody business. Get on with it and get it behind us."

He sipped at his brandy. Damon found himself studying covertly the slender, delicate face, drawn now and yellowed from illness and strain; the high forehead and fine straight nose, the eyes whose bemused, undeviating gaze seemed to behold the world in all its folly, all its avarice and violence and self-deception, and still go forward resolute and undismayed . . . Feeling a soft little wave of affection, Damon looked down. Dev had told him he could always pull people with him, that no one could say no to him. Was that true? It was terrible if it was: he didn't want to have that kind of hold over people. But here beside him stood a man who could exercise far more than will—who inspired others by the force of his intellect: by his wit, his compassion, his imagination, by his early and all-embracing wisdom . . . If I could have a father again, this is the kind of man I'd want, he thought.

The Colonel sighed and dropped his hand from the heavy drapery beside the window. "I suppose I'm becoming a misanthrope," he said gloomily, staring. "A Diogenes who doesn't even need to take up his lantern and start combing the town. I've always hated the breed: it's easy enough to mock life. Tommy says I'm getting to be a morbid old man—and she's only been reading my letters. She says I don't know what trouble is—she's working in the fracture ward at Savenay and I daresay she's right. It can't be the jolliest kind of duty for a high-strung, willful girl. She's so emotional! I can't imagine where she got it. My parents always had themselves in hand, and the Sawtells were dull as dishwater. Even Cora was sort of subdued; very sweet, very dear, but— well, subdued . . ." He sighed again, and Damon shifted his feet respect- fully. He knew the Colonel had lost his wife some years before, that he had an only child, a daughter named—incongruously—Thomas; that was all he knew.

"God knows, she's had a hard time of it," Caldwell went on. "Cora's death was a fearful blow to her—she was so little: it must have seemed as though the sky were really falling, like Chicken Little. I know it did for me. And then I didn't know what to do with her. My sister took her for a time, and Cora's sister Marilyn, and she didn't like that much better. And all that time I was trudging around from Schofield to Leaven- worth to Tientsin to Monroe . . . I should have made a home for her: a real, honest-to-goodness home, full of nine-to-five regularity and salary raises and neighborhood children she'd have grown up with, found a boy she could have married . . ." Abruptly he snorted. "Forgive me, Sam. It's the kind of afternoon when all your sins come back and perch on your soul like vultures, picking and tearing . . ." He turned and gave the Captain a swift, quizzical look. "Two hours ago General Liggett asked me if I wanted the post of assistant divisional commander."

Damon's jaw dropped in spite of himself; the idea that a man who had just been given the post of ADC in one of the three finest divisions in the AEF could be standing there by a window pondering over parent- hood and human destiny and the American zeitgeist, filled him with amazement. "Why—congratulations, sir!" he stammered. "You're going to take it, of course . . ."

The Colonel nodded. "Yes: I'm going to take it. I imagine I'll do as good a job as the next man, maybe a little bit better."

"And it'll mean a star for you—maybe two of them."

Caldwell smiled. "Yes. I suppose so. I'll become a crabbed, unap- proachable old fool, eating like an epicurean and wrangling with the French brass every afternoon. The prerequisites of power." Outside, the trucks had ceased, and there came now the ponderous wooden sound of boots on cobblestones, men marching in cadence, and now and then a high, sharp cry of command. The Colonel turned again to the window and watched the infantry moving past: a muffled, shapeless frieze in the rainswept dusk. "Yes. Every old soldier dreams of that day when he will put a star on his shoulder: it would be dishonest not to admit it. And it usually occurs—when it does—as the result of a war. And yet"—and he squared around to Damon suddenly, pointing back down toward the street, his face stamped with a terse, almost wrathful concern—"I swear to you I would give it all over and gladly, without one second's hesita- tion, if those men out there were heading the other way, toward St. Nazaire and Marseille . . ."

"I know you would, sir," Damon said; but the Colonel was staring out into the rain again.

"Deliver us from sentimentality!" he exclaimed softly. "When we win this war—and we're going to win it now, in six weeks or less—do you know what old Foch, that master strategist, has in mind? He plans to use us all as labor battalions, to rebuild the villages in Champagne, Picardy."

Damon's head went up. "*They wouldn't dare . . .*"

"Don't bet on that. I had it from no one less than General Connor himself. Yes. Coolies. Because things are getting back to normal, you see. It's no longer *Save us! Our backs are to the wall.* The Boche aren't at the Marne anymore." He set a fist firmly in his cupped hand. "They don't respect us. And they don't respect us because we don't properly value ourselves—and *that* is because we refuse to accept the bloody world as it is . . ." He walked up to Damon and stood in front of him in an attitude of affectionate menace. "Don't *freeze* on things, Sam. Like those muffinheads over at Bombon. Promise me you won't let your mind atrophy. Self-righteousness. It's the occupational disease of the soldier, and it's the worst sin in all the world. Yes! Because it spawns arrogance, selfishness, indifference. We may not be seeing so much of each other for a time now, what with one thing and another . . . Don't let the weight of things numb you. Read, think, disagree with everything, if you like—but force your mind outward. Promise me that."

"Yes, sir, I will." Damon nodded slowly. "I will, Colonel."

Both buildings—they had together formed a country inn—had been demolished, but the fountain and well miraculously remained intact. Raebyrne and Tsonka were lowering the bucket while the others crowded around them, their canteens in their hands. The rain had stopped. Clouds kept streaming overhead, shouldering each other powerfully off to the west; rifts appeared here and there—and then, low on the horizon the sun broke through, a whirling red disc like the eye of a madman, and flooded everything in the courtyard with a fierce crimson hue. To Damon, sitting on the stone steps in front of the nonexistent inn, studying the map with Lieutenant Zimmerman, the men looked stained with blood: their faces, their hands and weapons and canteens were bathed in it, indelibly. He watched Genthner recoil a step and heard him mutter: "Jesus . . ."

"What's eating you, boy," Raebyrne demanded, "you of the opinion it's full of tadpoles? Damn good chance."

"Look at it—look at the color of it . . ."

"You poor ignorant city boy—that's sunshine!"

"It's bad," Santos muttered. "A Jonah."

"A what?"

"A sign—an evil sign."

"Look," Tsonka declared, "if there's one with your name on it, it'll find you if it has to turn the latch and open the door."

The light increased, grew still more violent under the bank of clouds. The wind was cold. A big gray car was coming along the road from Apremont, rocking powerfully on its springs as it eased its way in and out of the holes. Its windshield held a placard with three white stars on a red field. At the edge of the courtyard the car slowed and finally stopped.

"Man, just look at that wagon," Tsonka said. "That's the way to fight this frigging war: from the backseat of a staff limousine."

Raebyrne gave a long, low whistle. "When I get back home I'm going to get me one of those chariots. Hood so long I'll have to back up two, three times to turn a corner. Just cavort around, proud as Lucifras. I guess you know it's going to be the vee-hicular wonder of the world."

"What's it going to look like, Reb?"

"Why, it's going to be a Clee-o-patra's barge on diamond wheels. Going to have a pull-out bar stocked with sour-mash bourbon, and a double-size foldaway bed, and a flush toilet that plays 'Good Morning, Mister Zip-Zip-Zip' every time you pull the solid-gold chain handle. And a wireless connection to the old homestead out at Flat Lick."

"Where in hell is Flat Lick?" a replacement named Wilts wanted to know.

"Son, you don't want to have to ask that question of your old squad leader. It's spang in the heart of Swain County, in the shadow of Big Smoky. And that's nothing less than God's country in the morning . . ."

An officer had got out of the car and now was walking briskly toward them: a tall man with a white, handsome face, a captain, wearing an immaculate uniform and riding boots, and carrying a swagger stick capped with thirty- and fifty-caliber shells that sparkled as he moved. The eerie light fell on him until his face and body glowed ruddily; he seemed to materialize out of its scarlet aura, take shape from it. He stepped inside the wrecked iron gate and encountered the company runner, a boy named Nugent, who had just come into the courtyard and was yanking his canteen out of his belt.

"Where is your commanding officer?" the captain asked him.

Nugent was having trouble unscrewing his canteen top; all his desires were focused on the bucket Tsonka was holding. "I don't know," he answered carelessly.

The officer's eyes flashed. "What do you mean, you don't know?" he said sharply. "You don't know *what?* Is that the way you reply to an officer?"

"No, sir!" Nugent was stunned by this immaculate apparition that had appeared out of nowhere and was now so furious with him. He started to salute with his right hand, which was still holding the can- teen—recognized the impropriety of that and tried to shift it surrepti- tiously to his left hand and in his confusion dropped it. It clattered on the worn stones. He bent over to retrieve it.

"Stand at attention when I'm speaking to you!"

The command froze Nugent erect again; he stood there rigidly, too paralyzed to salute, his eyes wide and bulging. Some of the men around the well had turned apprehensively.

"Now"—the Captain slapped his swagger stick against his pressed breeches—"where is your commanding officer?" But Nugent had been struck dumb. "Are you a complete imbecile?—answer me!"

"He's right over there, Captain," Tsonka called to him from the well, where he was still filling canteens. "Near the front stoop."

The tall man turned slowly and stared at Tsonka; there seemed to be no expression on his face. Then very deliberately he walked toward the men at the well. Tsonka, watching him approach, paused, and the rest of the group gave way. There was something unsettling in this officer's manner, his long white imperious face now a deep crimson from the unnatural light, his cold amber eyes; the replacements fluttered nervously.

"You people come-to-attention!"

The group around the well stiffened one by one, with varying degrees of reluctance, until finally Tsonka lowered the bucket and dropped his arms to his sides. In the stillness Raebyrne's voice came very clearly, drawling: "Fer Chrahst sake . . ."

"That's enough! You people had better learn some military courtesy," the Captain said. "Discipline is entirely too lax up here. When an officer asks a question he expects to be answered in a smart and respectful manner." And he passed his eyes over them one by one—a gaze neither spiteful nor indulgent, only severe.

It's his voice, Damon thought, watching; his voice. It was incisive enough, it was pitched neither too high nor too low—but something about it was wrong; it lacked—it lacked human vibrance. Faintly metallic, disembodied, it was like a field order translated into sound; it had no flaws. Damon got to his feet, holding the map in one hand, and said: "May I help you, Captain?"

The officer swung around with that same deliberate, imperious air; nodded, and moved briskly up to him. "Are you in command here?"

"Yes."

The officer nodded again. "Massengale, First Corps staff. I must see your regimental commander at once."

"You passed him," Damon answered. "Colonel Weyburn's CP is in Dammartin, about half a mile along the Thièvremont road."

"I see." Massengale's eyes were running distastefully over the line officer's filthy, torn trench coat, the Chauchat slung around his neck, the cartridge belt and enlisted man's haversack. "You *are* an officer . . ." Damon nodded. "Where are your insignia of rank?"

Without taking his eyes from him Sam carefully removed his helmet, reversed it and held it so that the Captain could see, nearly effaced by mud and a maze of scratches, a large yellow lozenge. "Here."

Massengale's lips parted in a frosty smile. "I believe that's contrary to regulations, isn't it?"

"I suppose it is," Damon answered quietly, "but to tell you the truth I don't give too much of a damn." He leaned around Massengale and called, "All right, boys, as you were"—and before the staff officer could say anything he went on: "Is it your custom to keep weary troops standing needlessly at attention, Captain? That's contrary to regulations, too—as well as being downright bad manners . . ."

Massengale's face became very smooth and long; his gold eyes glinted. "I find discipline in your command very lax, sir. Very lax indeed. You must remember that discipline is one of the cornerstones of morale. And morale is to all other factors as four is to one."

Damon bit his lower lip. Beside him Lieutenant Zimmerman was standing worriedly, now and then sniffling; the gang around the well were listening openly to the exchange. He rubbed one hand against his thigh. He felt a towering, raging disgust for this person before him— this immaculate, well-fed prig from staff with his cold, forbidding manner, who quoted Napoleon and could be the emissary only of more bad tidings, of carping disparagement and impossible demands. Holding his voice very level, he said: "Captain, my men have just come from seventy-two hours in the line and forty more in close reserve, during which time they have been under almost constant shell fire. They are tired and hungry and thirsty and they deserve a good rest. Aside from that, their morale is as good as that of any outfit in the American Expeditionary Forces, and perhaps a little bit better. Now if you will kindly take both yourself and that disgusting Packard out of my sight I'll try to go on with my map reading."

The bucket had stopped in midair; he heard Zimmerman draw in his breath. Massengale's lips came together, and two faint white crescents leaped into place at the corners of his mouth. He snapped his swagger stick under his arm and produced a leather-bound notebook and a slim gold pen from his blouse pocket—a gesture so automatic it had become effortless. "I was willing to overlook the utter absence of military courtesy in the troops of your command, and your own unpardonable appearance, as the unfortunate products of conditions in the field. But I cannot brook any such insolence as this." He pointed the heel of the pen toward Damon. "Not to me, you understand, but to that authority I represent. Is that clear?"

"Perfectly."

"Your name, rank and organization, please."

"With pleasure. Samuel A. Damon, Captain, Baker Company, Second Battalion. Serial number 03012."

Massengale started, the pen stopped writing. "You're Damon? Night Clerk Damon?"

"That's right."

The staff officer's face underwent a swift little quiver of transformation—broke all at once into a frank, utterly charming smile. "I stand corrected, Captain. The error is mine. Completely." He replaced the notebook and pen. "Why didn't you tell me who you were?"

"Does it matter?"

"Of course. Of course it does." Drawing off his glove he offered his hand to Sam who took it, puzzled. "Anyone with a record like yours would have no disciplinary problem. That's axiomatic." He lowered his voice perceptibly. "It's just that since the German peace overtures General Bannerman has become concerned about a letdown in the morale of the front-line troops. Their will to fight. He has specifically directed that unrelenting pressure be kept on the enemy forces in the field."

"Unrelenting pressure."

"Those are his words.—Well, I've got to be getting on. It's been a pleasure to run into you, Damon, even under circumstances as—irregular as these. No hard feelings, I trust?" The Nebraskan shook his head. "These are days of tumult, I know. Days of tumult and tension. I've been missing out on a good deal of sleep myself." He smiled again—that lively, charming smile that made him look like a much younger man, and slapped his breeches with his swagger stick. "*Somebody's* got to be the monster from Staff, you know—drive around with changes of orders in a disgusting Packard . . ." With an airy wave of his gloved hand he turned to go.

He wants it to go on, Damon thought; he gripped the handle of the Chauchat. He doesn't want it ever to be over. He loves it.

"—Wait," he said suddenly. "What change of orders do you have for us?"

"Oh." The lean, handsome white face was smooth and remote again. "You are to pass through the Seventy-second and attack on the Delambre-Sylvette Farm line. Oh-ten-hundred hours tomorrow."

". . . the Mont Noir?"

"That's it. Good luck, Damon—I know *you'll* have it! I'll look forward to seeing you again."

"Sure." Somberly he watched Massengale stride briskly back to the staff car and get in; the big limousine pulled away, swaying in the slick mud of the road. The company gazed after it like a horde of ragamuffins on the fringe of a society wedding.

"Well, it's a drôle war," Sam murmured to Zimmerman. "The word is drôle."

"Yes it is, Captain."

"See what a help a Medal of Honor can be?" Zimmerman was looking at him uncertainly, not knowing whether to laugh or not, and he chuckled wryly. "That's all right, everybody'll get one if it goes on long enough . . ."

The sun had vanished behind the layers of sullen dark cloud; it was

going to rain again soon, he could smell it in the wind. The map was
fluttering ponderously in his hand.

It was a long slope, reaching away to an escarpment of pines. Another
long slope to cross, but this time there was no cover. There were shell
holes, a few bits of trench that had been dug in an effort to connect
some of them and then abandoned; there were some sickly, stunted
bushes and a few ragged tufts of grass. That was all. And all around and
ahead of Damon men were walking quickly, jerkily, like comical sticks
of puppets on wires.

His feet and legs were soaked through, his whole body ached from
lying in the rain and muck under a bent piece of tin, waiting for the
jump-off time; his stomach alternately griped and heaved. He squinted
through the fine drizzle, studying the line of fire at the top of the slope.
Bois des Douze Hirondelles. A pretty name. There were no swallows
there now. A thousand yards. More—twelve hundred perhaps. And no
artillery support. Last night on the phone back to regiment he had raged
and pleaded—had finally fallen into a stony acquiescence. Not possible.
Very well. Just not possible. But to send men up this mile-long billiard
table without artillery—

Morehouse and Warniesz and several others were drifting in toward
him and he said, "More interval—keep your interval." Morehouse glared
at him—a look of popeyed outrage, as if he'd just cast the most vicious
aspersions on his mother's chastity. "Spread out—to your left," he said
irritably, waving his arm, and reluctantly they drifted back. "Don't
bunch up now, boys . . ."

They always did that, the new men. Misery loved company, fear
sought the shelter of kindred flesh. Why not? There was damned little
comfort anywhere else. Up ahead Lieutenant Zimmerman was leading
the first wave, the tails of his trench coat flapping whitely as he walked.
Quiet clung to them. Far off to the left, in the woods below Mont Noir,
the rolling patter of machine-gun and automatic-rifle fire, dry as dust,
drifted toward them, and in the long valley to their right there was the
insistent drumming of battle; but they themselves moved in a cone of
silence, broken only by the cry of an officer or noncom. The lines
wavered and rippled like a flight of wild geese. But slowly, so slowly.
They were no nearer, for all their efforts, they were tramping a treadmill that cunningly slipped them back and back to their jump-off line,
and still they plodded forward, the replacements fighting the urge to
bunch up, bobbing up and down, up and down.

Why was it so quiet? For the tenth part of an instant he thought of
Malsainterre Farm, the silence and then the empty trenches, and his
heart flowered with a sickly, frantic hope—then he struck the thought
down. The Germans had no intention of pulling out of a ridge line that

anchored the entire position: they would stay, and stay . . . He felt no fear, only a seeping, oppressive dread that chilled him more than the fine end-of-October rain. It didn't get easier: it got harder and harder with each immersion, each trial, until—

Wheeeeeeeeeet—

That thin, demonic rending of earth and heaven, a mounting scream— and then a hideous yellow ball exploded over their heads, followed by the deep snarl of steel; all around him heads ducked in unison. Shrapnel. Morehouse was staring up at it, transfixed.

"All right, come *on*, now!—" he shouted. Another blossomed to their right, and he heard the bright cry of pain. He had time to think, This is going to be pretty bad—and then the whiplash cracks came in furious succession, a celestial rafale that glowed an evil orange against the dirty roof of the sky, and showered down death and mutilation. A storm of iron; it spattered around them, moaning. A line of soot-black geysers rose up ahead, a putteed leg came sailing at him, struck and rolled beneath his feet. All he could hear now were cries.

—They were down, half the first wave, in a shell hole. He could see the helmets. Lieutenant Zimmerman was kneeling at the edge of the hole, screaming at them, gesticulating. No good. They could not stay there. He ran forward easily, his feet seemed to bounce over the soft, wet earth. He grabbed Zimmerman's shoulder and shouted, "No! Not that way. You must lead!"

"They won't follow me—!"

"Easy, now. Easy. Yes, they will. You must be—" A giant fingernail raced down the blackboard of the heavens and snapped off above them. Zimmerman was staring at him eagerly. He was all right. He'd be all right. "The new men need some visible symbol of authority," he said as calmly as he could manage. "You must provide it."

"But if they won't even—"

"They will. They must! I'll show you." He walked quickly around to the front of the hole and waggled the snout of his Chauchat in long, looping gestures; their eyes followed him. "Hobbs! Welcker! Get up— come on, now. You can't stay there. Up you go, now. Just up to that row of pines, that's all." There was another burst overhead and iron spattered on the ground around the shell hole. "Boyce, you can get hit down there just as easy as up here—now God dammit let's *go*, we're holding up the whole crowd. Hobbs, come on now, just up to that line of pine trees—just up there, that's all I'm asking . . ."

Hobbs drew his feet up under him all at once and got up, scrambling; Boyce followed him, then the rest. "That's it," he shouted, "now we're rolling . . ." Down the line to his right he saw Tsonka routing out some others. He walked on, watching Zimmerman out of the tail of his eye. Beside him a man went down screaming shrilly, clutching at his leg, ahead of him someone else—was it Miller?—faltered, hung poised in the air like a man tumbling backward off a roof, and then fell, his throat and chest a bloody, crawling mass. Now he could hear the machine guns, the death drone of bullets. It was like a sleet storm, a sleet storm engineered by the devil. A Chauchat team went past him, the rifle racketing away— and then a terrible orange sun burst full in their faces and they were there no longer, only a wormlike disheveled pile of rags and viscera and blood from which one naked arm jerked violently, back and forth. They were falling all around him, falling like leaves, like blocks, like worn-out sacking. Oh, the bastards! The old rage seized him; he saw ahead now the harsh, webbed gloom of the pines, the fresh dirt of the pits. Too late. The Boche had waited too late to open fire—they were going to get in there, they were going to take them, he knew it absolutely.

"Come on, *come on*," he roared. Dead ahead he saw the deep round helmets with their flaring rims, the gray-green uniforms, the flash-flash-flash of a gun muzzle. Walking forward he fired, watched as if in a murky dream the gunner sink away, another swing into place, fired again and again, aware that he was now shouting something indecipherable at the top of his lungs, over and over—

Something struck him a violent blow on the thigh. He was down. He was lying on his side, his left leg numb and burning. He got to his feet and fell down again. His leg. His leg wouldn't hold him. He was hit. At long last. After the. After all the.

He felt his thigh gingerly—then savagely. Yes, he was hit. Blood—his own blood this time—smeared his fingers in thick, warm skeins.

This wouldn't do. This simply would not do, he had to *get up and get in there*. So near! He gritted his teeth, drove all the grim determination of a lifetime into the command *You will* and rose to his feet—groaned aloud at the sickly hollow grating, a great pulsing globe of pain that swallowed up everything but its own fiery presence. *You will*. He lurched forward for several agonizing strides. Ahead of him the earth heaved and tilted giddily, in a goblin's carnival of bayonets and clubbed rifles, men grappling with one another like clumsy shaggy animals, a final babble of shrieks and hoarse cries—and the guns were silent.

They had got in. They'd done it. Now the—now the company was to wheel left, pivoting on the ridge line. A halt of. Halt of forty minutes, and then drive north-northwest through the woods—

Someone was tugging at his shoulder. Why were they always yanking at him? He was down again, on his knees, propping himself erect with the rifle. Raebyrne was crouched beside him. Old Reb, his face white and masklike against the bright orange stubble of beard, his eyes wild.

"Skipper! Skipper—you're hit . . ."

"—Go on," he cried, a garbled croak he could hardly hear in the racket and crash of gunfire and grenades. He gestured. "Go on, now . . ."

"I won't leave you, Cap—I won't leave you now!—"

"Get on in, Reb. That's an order. An order. Deploy your people—get

into those pits before their batteries start working us over . . ." But
Raebyrne was paying no attention. What was the matter with him?
Didn't he know what to do by now, for God's sake? Raebyrne, the
fresh wet dirt of the emplacements, the feathery black somnolence of
the pines glowed and faded like a forge fanned by bellows. He'd better
say it again. If they didn't find some cover—

He looked up. He was lying on his side now and Raebyrne was trying
to bandage him, fumbling absurdly with a packet of white gauze. "Reb,
you clumsy Tarheel," he said, or thought he said. "Can't you do any
better than that?" Then he caught sight of the blood moving in a silken
scarlet sheen over Raebyrne's hand and forearm, and grunted. Well.
They'd all had it. They'd all had it, then. "Help me up," he demanded.

"Skipper, you can't—your leg's shot half off . . ."

"The hell it is," he muttered, but fright gripped him. He tried to get
up: the hollow grating soared into a terrific electric bolt of pure pain
that made him cry out. He subsided, then. Nothing. There was nothing
left.

"—get you back, I *swear* I'll get you back, Skipper, take it easy,
now . . ."

"Sure.—Bandage yourself," he said. His head had cleared again, but
there was still this unpleasant glowing and fading sensation.

"Captain, the position is secured."

He looked up in surprise. Zimmerman. Breathing hard, and without
his helmet, but his voice perfectly steady. The pistol in his hand was
smoking gently at the barrel. Like me, he thought. Like me, after
Brigny Farm. "I've organized the company sector to repel counterattack. Our strength is forty-seven."

"Forty-seven?" he murmured. "Forty-seven?"

"That's it."

"Where's Lieutenant Shaw?"

"Badly wounded, sir. He's not conscious."

"How are they doing over on the left? You'd better get in touch with
Ballard."

"Captain Ballard's dead, sir."

"Well, Russo then, Russo's got the—"

"I don't know where Russo is, Captain. Nobody knows. We seem to
be pretty much on our own up here."

He nodded dumbly. Forty-seven. He felt all at once very infirm and
fragile. Monteleone and another medic had come up, and Raebyrne was
talking to them; figures moved here and there around him in mysterious
patterns. Why didn't they keep still! He had to find out whether Weyburn still wanted them to jump off for Second Objective as planned, if
Ballard and Russo were held up. But Ballard was dead—

"Help me up," he said to Zimmerman.

"You'd better go back, Captain. That's a pretty bad wound."

"Nonsense," he said. "I'm staying. Where's Guillette?"

"He's dead, sir."

"Jesus. Genthner, then. I want to get word back to Battalion as soon as possible. And let's try to make contact with Able right away."

"Captain—"

"I tell you, I'm staying. As long as there's one God damn one of us left, I'm—"

But the world had betrayed him now: the world was a disc that began to swim in violent circular oscillations, spinning faster and faster, faded and brightened, faded again. He was lying on his back now, feeling quite cold. Zimmerman was crouched over talking to him but he understood not a word. He smiled and nodded and patted the boy on the shoulder. "You're all right, Harry," he said. "You're going to be a good officer, the best. The company's yours now. Take good care of it, there was never one better. You just make contact with the boys in Able. The Old Man will get support up to you in no time, you can bet on it . . ." Had he said all that? But Caldwell was gone now, Caldwell was a general back at Division, far away . . . Zimmerman's face looked oddly worn— thousands of little lines stroked in with some ingenious engraving tool around his eyes. Well. He'd be a lot more weary than this, he'd find. But the company was in good hands, and that was something.

The sky was heavy with rain clouds and the air was suddenly, unbearably cold. People were still moving around above him: they seemed as powerful, as graceful as gods, free to live and move and have their being far beyond his chilled infirmity. The swirling circle of the disc increased. He knew he could not get up now under any circumstances whatever. He was through, finally; and that was all there was to it. Anyway, the company was in good hands, he would bet his last franc on it: his lucky one-franc piece. If Harry would just hurry up and tie in with Able now, they'd—

It was shining. Shining on his face, a curious silver flickering. He was looking straight above him, but oddly all he could see were billowing, sweeping shoulders, silver and black like burnished armor. Then it broke, and there was sky of the purest, rarest blue. He gazed at it, absorbed. It had a clarity, an *importance* it was quite necessary to decipher—or perhaps not decipher but merely accept, open one's heart to, allow to reveal itself in all its truth and clarity. To acquiesce to that, yield to it! In all the world there was nothing so profound, so blessed and remote as this sweep of azure sky beyond the ragged bits of cloud. Late afternoon sunlight fell on his face again, the slant October sun that pressed pale orange against his eyelids; then that too yielded, became part of this discreet and glorious serenity . . .

Behind him Raebyrne's voice said tersely: "All right, Nugent. Git a holt, now."

He closed his eyes. He was swinging, swinging basket-free, a weightless suspended jolting. Pain soared in a high red cone into his brain and burst there, like a rocket, in stabbing wire tendrils. Jesus. Ah, Jesus. He knew he was groaning out loud, and tried to choke it back. An interminable jolting slithering journey. How far? How many burning everlasting hours before they would set him down?

"It's all right, Skipper . . ." Reb's voice above him, panting, thin with urgency. "Just a mite further. Just a mite further on, now . . ."

A cobbled yard. A worn ocher wall over which the gnarled branches of an apple tree reached torturously. It was so *cold*. He had never been so cold in all his life. Someone was bent over him asking him something but he couldn't catch it, started to ask the man to repeat his question. But the man was gone. Slowly he turned his head to the right. A broad, tough face was squinting upward fiercely—an expression so ecstatic it was fearful to watch. Great, trembling groans issued from the parted lips. But now there was no sun, no truth-sustaining arch of sky.

They had picked him up again. Pain leaped up into his groin, his guts, drove down into his feet and lay burning in the very marrow of his bones: it blurred and darkened everything around him queerly. He bit his lip. Farmhouse, a long white wall seamed with a million cracks, and a harsh, clinging odor like raw gas and alcohol and burned iodine and lime. The smell of pain. Faces peered down at him. One of them, very lined, very tired, broke into a frosty grin:

"Bless my soul. Sam Damon. Don't tell me they finally put *you* down."

Gimlet Gardinier. Crusty old Yankee sawbones, with a white stubble of beard and puffy, narrowed eyes.

"Not for long," he answered; but he knew that wasn't true. His voice sounded tremulous and furry, and it distressed him.

"Well, let's have us a look-see."

There was a flowering throb of pure agony that ran its roots into his brain, his heart, his vitals. Oh Christ! He cried out again, he couldn't help it, gnawed at the back of his hand until he tasted salt. Then it receded to dark, slow pain, waiting.

"Doc . . ." He tried to raise himself on one elbow. Hands restrained him. "Is it—bad?" he gasped.

The Gimlet's face shot back into view. "Well. Needs work, I'll say that. You won't be doing the Turkey Trot for a while."

"I'm not—" He couldn't help it: he tried to bite it off and he couldn't. "I'm not going to lose it—am I? the leg?"

"What? Of course not," Gardinier snapped. His voice sounded extremely cross. "What in Tophet gave you that idea? You simmer down, now."

He closed his eyes, then; he was ready to weep with relief. What the hell. Let it go, now. Let it all go.

Hands were slapping vaseline on his face, roughly gentle; he could feel the long wooden battens pressed against his arms. Someone was saying, "All right, Captain. Let's breathe in, now. Breathe deeply, while I count to ten," and the ether cone came down over his nose and cheeks. There was a swift leap of revulsion at the cold, raw stench of the sulphur, instantly suppressed. The voice was counting softly, beguilingly toward ten. Soft, sinking tones. The universe swelled, narrowed to an endless vault of the deepest Arctic blue—and then the healing, lordly dark.

Miss Pomeroy came down the aisle, swaying, looking more radiant than ever, her blond hair in a fine gold crown around her starched cap. "Oh, I've such good news!" she cried in her soft, husky voice. "Such good news, and I don't want a grumpy word out of any of you all day long. It's over, the war's almost over! They've signed the armistice. At eleven o'clock just"—she examined her watch, turning her wrist outward—"ten minutes away. Think of it!" She tossed a copy of *France Soir* to Warrenton, and clasped her hands. "Eleven o'clock. The eleventh hour of the eleventh day of the eleventh month. Isn't that thrilling?"

"They should have made it the eleventh year while they were about it," MacCullough said dourly. "Then we'd all have been too young to go to the ball." But this witticism was drowned out in the general hilarity.

"Will you marry me now?" asked Hancock, who was handsome and a Harvard man. Miss Pomeroy smiled at him and shook her head prettily. "You promised me you would, you know."

"You promised *me* you'd stop all this nonsense and get back on your feet," she retorted.

"How about me, then?" a burly, balding captain with a broken nose named Weyermacher called to her. "I'm in better shape than he is . . ."

"—I won't marry any of you unless I can marry you all," she cried. This evoked a roar of protest and approbation, and several schemes for a mass wedding were bandied about. Tom Stillman, the ward orderly, would be best man; that lousy YMCA slacker Peckenbough could conduct the service, and Doc Marcus would give the bride away; they would emerge, one by one, under an arch of crossed crutches and Balkan frames; and the bridal bed—the bridal bed would be—

"Now, that's enough," Miss Pomeroy chided them; she blushed more prettily than anything else she did.

"Get this, Damon," Warrenton said; he was holding the French paper directly over his head with his good arm. "Oh my God, it's priceless.

*Herr Erzberger then replied that they had come to receive the proposals
of the Allied Powers toward the conclusion of an Armistice. To which
Marshal Foch replied tersely: 'What proposals, indeed? I have no proposals to make—no proposals whatever.' A silence ensued, the German
delegation appearing confused and rather despondent.* Can't you just
see it?"

"Stupid old fools," MacCullough muttered.

"Don't interrupt him," Damon said. Secretly he envied Warrenton,
whose father had been with the embassy in Paris for years, and who
spoke four languages fluently. "Let's have some more of it, Don."

"*A silence ensued.* Oh yes, I read that. *At length Count Oberndorff
queried: 'How do you wish us to express ourselves, Herr Feldmarschall?'
'That is for you to decide,' the Marshal retorted crisply. 'Do you wish
to ask for an Armistice?' 'Yes,' murmured Erzberger. 'Good. Then if
that is so, say so—and formally.' 'Yes, Herr Marschall,' answered Count
Oberndorff. 'That is what we are formally asking.' 'Good,' repeated
Foch, and he picked up the document. 'Then I will read to you those
conditions—and only those conditions—upon which it may be ob-
tained.'* "

Herberger let out a whoop. "That's belting 'em, Ferd!"

"I'm glad the pompous ass is good for something," MacCullough
growled.

"Don't say that—he's a great man, a great general." Herberger was
indignant. "He's going to go down in history."

"Lucky bloody history."

Then, floating across the carefully tended formal gardens from the
town of Angers they could hear bells pealing—a silvery, jostling caril-
lon; and what sounded like faraway shouts and cries. Damon, turning his
head to the right, encountered Major Borgstad's pale, gaunt face and
mild brown eyes. The Major had a sequestrum and was scheduled for
further surgery later in the day.

"So it's over," he observed quietly; his face was bubbling with sweat.

"It's over," Damon answered.

"What was our furthest line of advance, do you know?"

"Gièvres, Stenay, a few crossings of the Meuse. Near Sedan."

"Still in France."

"Still in France."

In the town the bells were clashing gaily in three octaves. Hancock
was telling the ward, "We're *all* wasting our time. Hélène is going to
marry only one bird in this whole dreary charnelhouse." He grinned
maliciously; he had been a pilot in the 94th Aero Squadron with Ricken-
backer, and was the only officer in the ward who could get away with
calling Miss Pomeroy by her first name. "She's going to marry none
other than Lieutenant Percy Arthur Fernishall, and we'd all better face
up to it like little men."

There were a few feeble cheers, and a murmur of felicitations, which shook Fernishall, a shy, slender boy from Duluth who was completely and hopelessly in love with Miss Pomeroy and couldn't bear to joke this way about her. He glowered at the flier from under a loose lock of chestnut hair. "You're just cynical, Hancock," he declared darkly. "And unfeeling. Nothing is sacred to you . . ."

Hancock was incredulous. "Me?—Reverent Rick Hancock, unfeeling? What calumny, Perc my lad." He laughed, watching the boy's face. Several nights before he had bribed Stillman into sneaking him an outsize trench coat and contrived to make his way, festooned with bandages and carrying his dakin's tubes in his hands, out of the hospital and had then talked an old farmer into pushing him in a handcart all the way to La Reine Fière. The ward had been in an uproar when he'd returned hours later, singing lustily, his pockets full of bottles and a webbed sack over his shoulder crammed with presents which he distributed up and down the ward—a soccer ball, a pair of skates, two fat Chinese dolls, a pack of Tarot cards, ivory knitting needles and a little blue porcelain cow for pouring cream. Miss Carmody, the head nurse, and a stern disciplinarian, had ordered him back to bed in a voice for guard mount—whereupon he had kissed her on the cheek while the ward gasped, and bounded back in bed, trench coat and all.

"Why, everything is sacred to me," he went on. "I am—for instance, I'm unalterably opposed to the practice of sodomy. You ask Weyermacher if I'm not—"

"That will do, Lieutenant," Miss Pomeroy said primly, and the way she looked when she said that was charming, too. "Honestly, you're the limit."

Damon looked out at the sky over the Loire, gray and distant above the naked trees. So it was over—this vast adventure into which he had flung himself with all his youthful ardor and unquenchable pride. There had been whole worlds to conquer—and now he occupied a ward bed and dreamed of a bottle of Bourgueil, which Tom Stillman might or might not bring him tonight . . . He had been wrong about the world. He had gone forth believing he was indestructible in the fury, the lordliness of his ambition, and he was not indestructible; he was like all the others. Vulnerable flesh, old mortality.

The chill trembling began—subtly this time, like a spring wind, and his stomach knotted in a series of spastic clutches. There was the instinctive, inexorable tug to call Miss Carmody and ask her for "some medicine"—which after the manner of hospital form meant a quarter-grain of morphine sulphate—then he beat it back down, and with shaking fingers lighted a cigarette and puffed at it deliberately. He was coming off the drug, and he was coming off it all the way. Others had and he would. Borgstad was watching him, his square flat face drenched in sweat, and he smiled at him over clenched teeth. Down in Angers the bells were still ringing but more faintly now, as though they were tiring of their headlong hilarity.

The ward was quieter suddenly. Doctor Marcus had entered, was talking to Miss Carmody in a low voice. Behind him Miss Bishop, a heavy girl with powerful arms and a stolid face, was pushing the white-enameled agony wagon, which emitted its falsely festive little tinkle; Damon saw Marcus drawing on a pair of rubber gloves with finicky care, and he felt the old tensing high in his chest.

"Rather thought we might get away with it today," Warrenton murmured tonelessly.

"Yes. I'd hoped so, too."

Down the ward Marcus began to work on Grossman, an artillery captain whose feet were a maze of shattered bone; Miss Bishop had just handed the Doctor a shiny, long-necked probe. Damon looked away. It was ward etiquette to busy one's self when another man's wound was being dressed.

He studied the hard dull weight of the November sky. It was over, and out there they were throwing their helmets in the air, firing off celebratory rounds, and crowding into the estaminets, trading their coats and shirts for vin rouge . . . Were they? How many were left from his old company? Who had survived?

From the road that ran behind the hospital there came the blare of brass, underlain by the somber thump of drums, as some doughfoot—it would be Captain Kebhart and perhaps an enlisted man or two from across the courtyard—went west. Damon could picture the procession— the big Dodge truck with its broken spring and the three flag-draped coffins easing along behind the band, flanked by a firing squad of surly medical orderlies, their rifles pointing wearily in every direction but the right one, their feet shuffling in rhythm to Chopin's "Marche Funèbre"; and later the brief, blunt ceremony by the open graves, the chaplain's voice insubstantial under the lowering November sky, and then the ragged crash of the volleys . . .

"Ten—thousand—dollars for the folks—back—home," Hancock sang sonorously to the band. Damon glared at him, and Weyermacher rose on one elbow and said fiercely:

"Rick, that's Kebhart going by. If you don't shut your stupid face this once I'm going to climb out of this bed and beat your teeth in."

There was a little silence and then Hancock said, "Sorry, Bert . . . I forgot."

This was where it ended, then—the bugles, the cheering, the flags and sashes and bright swords: here in long, bleak rooms, in sweating chambers redolent of blood and vomit, of gangrenous flesh and shattered bone; or in the long, bleak battlefield pits. So far from home.

He went on smoking, his fingers now and then scratching at his chest, his eyes averted from the north end of the ward, where Grossman was groaning thickly under the probe, and thought again of the old platoon, of that slow parade of the dead and disfigured, of whom he was now indissolubly a part: Van Gelder and Starkie and Kraz and little Turner and Johansen and Brewster and all the others; and Dev. Most especially Dev. And all he could think of now was the thin pathos of their going, their piteous mortality. They had come with all their hope and eager bravery and fire, and been cut down, and others had come to take their places and been cut down in turn. They had their moment, their brief, imperiled time of laughter, of fear and wonder and spendthrift valor, a sweet and indispensable nobility—and then they were gone, shoveled under the alien French soil, and there was nothing left of them to keep them alive. Their wives—if they had been lucky enough to have them— would tire of loneliness and celibacy and turn to other men; to their families they would become shadows, frozen in some beloved act, perhaps, some hallowed little moment of childhood or youth, held in a chipped gilt frame; growing fainter with each indifferent year, until finally they were not even shadows . . .

But he had known them, and loved them; and he would remember.

The spastic trembling had passed; he felt better. One bell was still ringing in the town—a deep cathedral boom that seemed to sink into the farthest recesses of his soul . . . He had done all he could and a little more, and none of it had been any good to anyone. He had driven himself to absurd extremes of savagery and daring, and all it had meant was that the men whose lives and welfare he had worried himself sick over day in and day out had been killed or wounded almost to a man. What kind of man had he become? His sense of moral obligation, of duty and sacrifice, had led him to kill with cold ferocity, to drag his best friend back to death, to draw upon himself the fear and abhorrence of the more sensitive souls under his authority. And now the great butchery was over, the documents had been signed; no one had lost and no one had won, and here he lay with a great hole in his thigh and tried not to think about Ducky Marcus, who had now reached Herberger's bed and had just taken a small, silvery instrument from Miss Bishop's fair right hand.

He saw Caldwell coming down the ward in the falling light, moving with that quick, purposeful stride, and his heart leaped. He raised his hand, Caldwell's head ticked with a barely perceptible nod; he drew nearer, and now Damon saw on his shoulders the single star.

"Good evening, sir. Congratulations."

Caldwell appeared faintly embarrassed. "Yes. The gratifications of command: before, men only suspected you were a heartless monster; now, you have dispelled all doubt." He raised his right hand then and Damon saw it was held in an anterior splint.

"What happened to you, sir?"

"Ridiculous, isn't it?" Caldwell peered at it as if it were an article he'd purchased and was disappointed in. "Well, it saves me the trouble of returning salutes. Shell fragment," he added crisply. "Broke two metacarpals. Two days after you were hit. We carried Mont Noir that afternoon, broke into the clear. I—didn't tend to it properly; and it became infected. Nuisance really." He looked back down the ward. "How are they treating you?"

"Wonderfully, General." It seemed odd to be calling the Old Man "General." But there he was, the same old vigorous incisiveness that had always made Sam want to rise to the occasion, stretch his faculties to the limit. "It's been luxurious. The beds are soft, the nurses are either beautiful or efficient—and sometimes they're both. We've been deluged with fudge and other goodies at odd hours."

"Yes, well, tell me about yourself. I mean, how are you—" He broke off as Miss Pomeroy came up to him, smiling her fresh, buoyant, intoxicating smile, and carrying a folding camp stool.

"Won't you sit down, General?"

"Why yes, thank you." He and Miss Pomeroy chatted a few moments, before she sailed away down the aisle again. It was the first time Damon had seen Caldwell in the presence of women; his manner became even more courtly and gracious.

"Yes, I see what you mean," he murmured. "Burn my clothes, Doctor —I don't want to go home." With his good hand he rummaged around in his overcoat pocket, drew out a long cylinder wrapped incongruously in a piece of green toweling and reaching under the head of the bed slipped it into Damon's musette bag. "There. Think we got away with that? It's a very good Scotch."

"Thank you, sir."

"Don't give it a thought. To the victors, you know." He gazed at Damon for a moment. "Strange, isn't it? Hard to believe it isn't all still grinding on and on, that we've got to go back up there in a day or so . . ."

"Yes," Damon said.

"We're not, though. And thank God for that. How are you coming along?"

"The bone's knitting fairly fast. I'll be walking soon. How's the outfit?"

"Griping and groaning. We're billeted along the Rhine. Among a populace both servile and defiant. Curious people, the Germans. I will never understand them. I've said that before, I know."

"How's the company?"

"In excellent spirits—as why wouldn't they be? Zimmerman is good material, as you said. No Night Clerk, you understand; but he'll do very nicely. Which reminds me: your promotion to major went through just before the curtain came down."

"Oh," Damon said. He was astonished at himself; it was so remote from the train of his thoughts these past weeks that he felt nothing at all. He gave himself a little shake and said, "Why, thank you, sir—I'm sorry, I had no idea—"

"Don't thank me. Or anyone else. You would have had the Battalion if the dear old war had gone on a bit and you hadn't had to try to take the Ridge all by yourself."

"Zim couldn't get them up, General. I didn't think I was going to be able to for a while, there. That shrapnel was the worst I ever saw."

"Yes. Gouraud has cited the regiment for that engagement. You're to get another French croix, and so are Russo and Zimmerman, a few others. And now the hue and cry is: Home before the snow falls. Jim Harbord won't quite do that, but he'll bust a gut trying . . ." Watching Hancock joking with Miss Pomeroy at the other end of the ward, he hummed softly:

> *"Say, no more Bois de Boulogne,*
> *I want a girl of my own—*
> *Hey, no more fine or champagne,*
> *Give me the sun and the rain*
> *Of my—home—town . . ."*

Damon said: "Are you heading back for the States, sir?"

"Oh, no." The General shook his head. "No, I'm merely exercising the privileges of my exalted rank. They didn't need me at Division—they don't need *anybody* at Division, or anywhere else, it seems. So I gave myself a seventy-two-hour pass and raced over to Savenay to see Tommy—only to find she's been transferred to Neuilly. Little Minx never even wrote me about it." He shrugged. "The Spartans were right: only have sons. Put all girl babies to death as rapidly as possible." He got a package of Lucky Strikes out of his pocket, offered one to Damon, and fumbled one-handed with a box of matches until Damon gave him a light. "Thanks. This is the most maddening affliction: the simplest, most primeval acts become impossible. Have you ever tried buttoning your fly left-handed? It's a great reminder of human frailty." He watched Breckner hobble slowly down the aisle; when his eyes narrowed they were laced with dozens of fine lines. "Well, they won't all get home by Christmas, but there'll be a mighty exodus for the next three months or so.—What do you think you'll do when they let you out of here, Sam?"

"I don't know. I'm scheduled for a convalescent leave in Cannes . . . I haven't given it an awful lot of thought, sir."

"Of course not."

"I suppose I'll go back home . . . I have a good chance at a job in the bank in my hometown."

"I see." Caldwell's eyes roamed around the room. "I thought perhaps you might consider staying on."

Damon stared at him, the cigarette halfway to his mouth. "Stay on? In the *Army?*"

"Why, yes. It's a possibility. You could go a long way, Sam. You've made a fine record for yourself, and your majority has come through . . . Though there are reasons a lot more telling than those."

The Captain looked away, at Warrenton sleeping softly in his great plaster cuirass and gorget, at Suskin with his long legs rigged to a web of lines and pulleys. "But—that's ridiculous," he cried softly.

"Is it?"

"I mean, what for? What's the point in it? There can't *be* another war . . ."

"Perhaps not."

"There can't be . . ." Caldwell was watching him, a quizzical gaze brushed with amusement, and it nettled him. "No, this has got to be the last one," he declared, "and no kidding. For good and forever. The world can't go *through* another one like this."

The General's face became serious and intent. "No. It can't. That's true." He said in an even, musing tone: "It will have to go through one of a different kind."

There was a little silence between them. Across the aisle Herberger and Morse were flipping coins at drinking glasses at the feet of their beds. At the end of each series Herberger would call out to Breckner, who would hobble over and collect the coins with his good arm and hand them back to the players.

Damon raised himself on his elbows and said: "Do you honestly believe that? That there will be another war?"

Caldwell looked at him calmly and nodded. "I'm afraid so."

"—But that's impossible! After all the slaughter—after all *this* . . ." He waved his hand down the bleak white corridor, to include the supine figures, the limbs in traction, the amputations and drainage tubes and frames and sandbags, and beyond that the cemeteries, the barracks and dugouts and tents, and beyond them the vast gray wreckage of France. "No!" he said hotly. "After this things will be different. These gay little international disputes will have to be settled by—compromise, adjudication, something . . . It's got to be!"

"I wish you could be right about that."

"It's got to be! There's no other answer, no other way."

The General paused a moment. "It's a time to think that, to believe that with all one's heart; I know . . ." He leaned forward on the creaking camp stool, holding his wounded hand in the good one. "Sam: do you honestly believe people are going to stop being greedy and resentful and full of pride and prejudice? Do you think they will quit hating and fearing—do you think the lordly heads of government are going to abandon their methods of seizing and holding power, of gaining advantages over their neighbors? Why should they change? What should cause them to abhor the only rules to the game they know? And even if they were to do so, do you believe for one minute their own citizens would let them get away with it?"

He paused, his lips curved in that mournful smile. Damon, lying back again, watched his quick, perceptive eyes and felt the force of that high intelligence, that purposeful equanimity of view that saw so clearly the limits of hope and wisdom; and beyond that the possibility—no, it was more than that, it was a hard obligation—for a man to be all he could be within those implacable limitations . . . He knew Caldwell was right and for a moment it filled him with the blackest terror. He closed his eyes.

"To think," he murmured, "to think that a vicious bastard like that Benoît would again have the chance—a chance to . . ."

"Yes: he's a butcher and an incompetent, and you are right to hate him. But for all that he was doing the best he could. Same with Foch: blindness, awful failure of imagination . . . But what about our auto makers back in Detroit, who couldn't be bothered with the war, who couldn't interrupt their profits long enough to produce the tanks we needed so desperately at Soissons, at Malsainterre? What about them? Stupid old Benoît doesn't look so bad alongside that . . ."

Damon clasped his hands together. Then what's the sense in it? he wanted to shout. What the hell are we all hanging on for? Why face any kind of future at all? But he said nothing. He was bleak with desolation, his mind in a turmoil; he did not know what he thought.

"The thing is, so much of it has been handled incorrectly," Caldwell went on in his even, thoughtful voice. "General Pershing was talking to several of us the other day. He's a hard man, he's too dogmatic, too arbitrary in some ways, I know. The spit and polish in the billets, this silly Sam Browne belt business. But he has that faculty for cutting through to the essential thing, the kernel . . . He's convinced it was all handled badly: the surrender. Which ought to come as no surprise, I suppose—the war was abysmally conducted so I guess there's no reason to expect the peace to be very different. Foch should never have negotiated with the civilian leaders at Compiègne; it should have been Ludendorff, Hindenburg, von der Marwitz: the army. The *army* should have surrendered—or else we should have gone on across the Rhine to Berlin and taken those iron hinges off the Brandenburg Gate. As the song says. Maybe that's a little extreme, but in the main he's right. Because the army is saying now they weren't beaten in the field—that the home front, awash with defeatists and Reds, betrayed them." He paused again, musing. "It gives rise to some hard thoughts. Especially hard to contemplate this winter. General Pershing believes it will have to be done all over again one day."

Damon was stunned. He looked wildly around the ward, dropped his eyes. All over again. Done all over again . . .

Caldwell had leaned forward and put his hand on Damon's shoulder. "And if that day comes—and God help us, it will come—the country will have need of people like you, Sam. Immediate and deadly need. Because it'll be the same thing all over again. I saw it in Tampa in '98: three hundred freight cars without a single bill of lading. Winter uniforms—for a jungle war with Spain!—worthless canteens, tons of beef already putrefied. At Siboney they dumped the horses overboard—and expected the terrified creatures to swim three miles to shore. You saw a little of it at Hoboken and St. Nazaire. It seems to be our history: we are indifferent, unprepared—then all of a sudden we're shocked, roaring with righteous wrath, ready to rush off into battle with our pants down . . ." He paused. "Only the next time will be worse. Planes will fly faster, tanks will travel farther, guns will shoot faster and more accurately than they have this time. The surprise attack on the unready nation will be the hallmark of the next war. And if there aren't men of your caliber ready and able to take charge of things when that day comes, it will go very hard with us. Very hard indeed."

Caldwell bit his lip and chafed the gauze paw with his fingertips to warm it. "I'm no good at speeches. George Marshall says I'm too verbose, too overintellectual, my expressions aren't forceful enough." He smiled. "Perhaps I ought to take lessons from Raebyrne."

Damon looked up eagerly. "How is old Reb?"

"Raising several kinds of hell. Zimmerman made him a sergeant. I think it'll be a disaster, but it's his decision, not mine. Raebyrne's becoming a kind of doughboy legend in a whacky, incorrigible sort of way. I got him and Tsonka DSCs for their work in the Ridge action and pinned them on them both in a full-dress divisional review. Shook hands with Reb and asked him what he was going to do when he got home." The General grinned ruefully. "I shouldn't have asked him that. He looked me right in the eye and said loudly: 'Major, first off I'm going to stand this little old rifle under the downspout at the weather corner of the old homestead. And every morning I'm going to step outside and watch the rust close over the bore.' "

"Old Reb," Damon murmured.

"Yes. Pungent. My entourage had considerable difficulty maintaining the proper gravity during the rest of the awards and decorations. And of course that isn't all. Reb seems to be imbued with the idea"—Caldwell shot a precautionary eye in the direction of Miss Carmody, who had entered the ward—"that availing himself of prophylaxis is a sign of effeminacy. I believe I've disabused him of it."

"How'd you do that?"

"Quite simple, really. I borrowed some photos from Hugh Young of syphilis victims in various stages of disintegration, and let him study them for a while. They make the leper colony on Molokai look like an Atlantic City beauty contest. Hugh omits no details. Then I followed that up by telling him that if he got it every child he sired back home in Flat Lick would have two heads and he would have to cut one of them off himself, immediately after parturition. That apparently did it. Another two weeks and I'll have him delivering continence lectures to the regiment. In any event, I'm told the Beloved Tarheel now goes forth well sheathed." He lowered his voice discreetly, and Damon saw Miss Pomeroy coming toward them, bearing a large platter of fudge.

"General, won't you have some?" she entreated him radiantly. "It's still warm."

"Gladly, thank you." He made a courtly little bow and took a piece. "Sweets from the sweet. Couldn't I stay on here until I'm fully recovered?"

"I don't see why not," said Warrenton, who had awakened, "—maybe the heartless creature will spend more time up here and less with the poor, downtrodden enlisted men."

"But I'm always available!" Miss Pomeroy protested—and then blushed enchantingly as half the room roared. "Still, it would be delightful to have a general in the ward," she reflected. "We've never had one."

"I can imagine," Caldwell answered drily. He popped the piece of gooey brown stuff into his mouth and winked at Damon. "Does outclass beet sugar over hardtack fried in bacon grease, Sam. Pretty cushy." He watched Miss Pomeroy's progress through the ward, licking his fingers. "Well, we're a grand and glorious nation, but it strikes me we're all a little naïve—we think if we pick the other fellow up and dust him off and shake hands, we can all wander into the corner saloon and tell one another what swell guys we are. A pleasant view of the world, but a touch sentimental. Now you take Wilson: he's an intelligent man, a cultured man—there aren't many of them left around these days—but look at these Fourteen Points. Does he really think the heirs of Talleyrand and Bismarck and Palmerston are going to turn overnight into a bunch of Tibetan lamas oozing mystic brotherhood at every pore? . . ."

He brushed the front of his blouse with one hand and sighed. "*Wonders are many, and none is more wonderful than man . . . speech, and wind-swift thought, and all the moods that mould a state, hath he taught himself . . . Without resource he meets nothing that must come; only against Death shall he call for aid in vain* . . . Beautiful isn't it? I used to know it all, once, the whole passage. God, it'll be nice to get back to some of the important things in this world, and stop worrying about the dark forebodings of G-2 and the whereabouts of ammunition dumps and misfiring on one's boundaries." Rising, he shrugged into his overcoat and buttoned it clumsily, staring down into the courtyard, where three nurses were pushing patients in wheel chairs. "It's over . . . Now everybody wants to race back home and make a million dollars. And there'll be precious little talk of the war or the army until the big, hot holidays, when they'll suck in their bellies and get into their uniforms and strut down Main Street behind the band. And stand perspiring in front of the bandstand beside the town hall and listen to some red-faced fool rant on for three-quarters of an hour about that last full measure of devotion and valorous sacrifices on the field of honor. And that'll be all they'll remember. Until the next time . . ."

He turned away, turned back again. He seemed loath to go and yet ill at ease, uncertain; Damon had never seen him this way. Then he slapped his gloves against his thigh. "Well, I've got to head for Neuilly and try to track down that headstrong, tempestuous girl of mine." He stepped forward and took Damon's hand in his left. "Good luck, Sam."

"Thank you, sir. Good luck to you. And thank you for going to all the trouble of coming by."

"Don't mention it." Caldwell turned away, turned back again, caught in this strange indecision. He placed himself so that his body blocked Warrenton's view of them and said in a low voice: "Sam . . ."

"Yes, General?"

"Sam, our paths may diverge now, perhaps for good. I shall be sorry, if they do . . . I want you to know I'm proud of you. You're all I could have wanted in a son, if I'd been privileged to have one."

"Thank you, sir. I wanted to say something a good deal like that, myself . . . I can't tell you how much it's meant to me to have served with you. To have known you."

Caldwell cleared his throat. In a different voice he said, "Sam— think about it, will you? Don't do anything hasty. Think about what I said just now. You'll never make a banker, you know. Why go through life suspecting everybody's motives? That's what you'll be—a spider sitting in a web, accumulating capital: a prudent soul . . . Sam, you'll make a terrible banker."

Damon grinned. "You're probably right."

"Think about it, Sam. You were made for better things . . . There are far more ignoble ways to pass one's days than in the service, believe me. Promise me you'll give it some thought."

"I will, sir."

"Good." The General moved off down the ward with his quick, vigorous stride, nodding now and then to a recumbent figure and finally to Miss Pomeroy, who gave him her most refulgent smile. Then he was gone.

From the facing bed Herberger said: "Who's the big brass, Damon?"

The Captain put out his cigarette. "The best officer in the entire Anus End Forward, that's all."

"So *that's* how you picked up all those shiny medals."

"That's how."

"Some guys just can't resist playing drop-the-soap with the higher echelons . . ." Herberger gave a sleepy wink. "Say, how's about a nip from that bottle?"

"Damn it, Herberger, don't you ever miss anything?"

"Not when it comes to booze. When it comes to booze I'm a walking Marconi set. What do you say?"

Damon grinned at him. "Come and get it."

"Aw, now don't be a dog in a manger."

"What's this, what's this?" Warrenton said brightly, swiveling his head in the hard white plaster collar. "Unlawful possession of grain neutral spirits in the wards? Calls for an investigation."

"All right, all right," Damon said with resignation, scratching at his chest. "I'll get Breckner to peddle it around."

Well, it was true: there were far more ignoble ways to pass your days than the way George T. Caldwell had. Down in the courtyard a boy sat in a wheelchair—a young, guileless face like Brewster's, or Morehead's or Dickey's; the winter light played along his throat, the curve of his cheek.

It was impossible it could come again!

But if it were to come again there would always be the Dickeys and Brewsters—fearful, trusting, uncertain, looking for the glance, listening for the calm, easy word of reassurance . . .

12

Cannes was another world he could never have imagined. A clear cameo world with the great blue dream mountains of the Esterel across the water, and a liner lying at anchor in La Napoule like a pretty little vanilla-frosting decoration. The sun was bright, the air was cool and clear, like spun glass, and on La Croisette everyone was out strolling. There were Englishmen with round red faces and cloth caps, and Russian noblemen who had been gambling all night, with waxen faces and tight pearl-gray jackets and silk cravats; there were American aviators in wasp-waisted tailored uniforms, their overseas caps worn at perilous angles, there were British color sergeants limping ponderously, with cold, white eyes, there were one-armed French staff officers with monocles and the faces of overbred greyhounds . . . and everywhere, surrounded by the men, were women wearing fur pieces that hung luxuriantly from their arms and shoulders: women with complexions like marble and dark, mysterious eyes, and a golden assurance in their incomparable beauty that bore them along like mist. The world of dreams was strolling along La Croisette in 1919 . . .

Damon would walk one hundred paces and then stop and sit down on one of the settees facing the sea and rest the leg; wait ten minutes and then get up and go on again, fighting the twinges, the pins-and-needles burning and the thick, massive ache that sank into the hollow of his groin. He could walk almost all the first hundred yards without using the cane now; which was a distinct improvement. Farther along, on the little trampled stretch of beach some fishermen were playing boule and he paused, watching. An old man with heavy white mustaches made a beautiful soft throw: the stone ball, rolling leisurely, curled out around two others and came to rest four inches from the cochonet, and players and onlookers murmured in admiration as the grognard turned away. His big, dark fingers were curled as though they still held the ball.

There was a brief consultation among the players and a young fellow with wild black hair and long sideburns ran forward several steps and threw—a hard throw that hit the old man's ball and drove it ten feet away. There was a burst of excitement and the young fisherman flung back his head and laughed, and spat on the sand. The old man's face was perfectly expressionless.

Damon walked on, along the Quai St. Pierre, resting more frankly on the cane now, riding up over it, his elbow locked. Out on the seawall two men in faded blue jackets were fishing with bamboo poles from the rocks, and a French sailor was strolling with his girl, their arms clasped around each other, their heads just touching. The pompom of his cap was like a bright red carnation. The girl laughed once, and turned, flinging her hair back—a slender face and large, mischievous eyes; and Damon, reminded of Michele, started and then looked away.

Michele.

At the end of the wall he sat down again and watched the water. It was fretted with a feathery, iridescent quality that ceaselessly shifted: now it was like metal, now like dust, now like a strangely pulsing oil. Below the surface seaweed swayed in long, dreamy scarves against the stone.

Michele . . . well, she had got her wish—part of it anyway: he'd had plenty of time to suffer, and think about it, and suffer some more. Lying in the long, still ward reading or staring upward, sleepless in the small hours, struggling against the need for morphine, watching the slow garnet arcs of cigarettes of fellow vigilants, he had reflected on all that had happened to him and to ten million others . . . and hadn't got very far; though he'd tried. Experience was valuable only if one imbued it with meaning, drew from it purposeful conclusions. The fact of the matter was he had never *thought*—he had acted, swiftly, intuitively; now he must school himself to think, think soberly and well. What conclusions, then, was he to draw?

War: war was not an oriflamme-adventure filled with noble deeds and tilts with destiny, as he had believed, but a vast, uncaring universe of butchery and attrition, in which the imaginative, the sensitive were crippled and corrupted, the vulgar and tough-fibered were augmented— and the lucky were lucky and survived, and they alone . . . And was that all? Was there no truth behind this—didn't the just cause triumph, the good deed resound to heaven?

He raised his eyes to the gay little forest of masts of the sloops and yawls in the marina, the dancing movement of blue and yellow figures on their white decks. No: there was no such truth. The mightiest battalions, the most lavish and efficient supply trains won the day, and Roland in the rocky wilderness of Roncevalles could wind his horn until his eyes popped out of his head . . .

The sailor and his girl passed behind him. "Non, non," he heard her say, laughing, "c'était un malentendu, mon ange—je le prenait pour toi. C'est vrai!"

He did not turn around. What was the truth of things, then? Here he sat, on the warm, worn stone. He had been spared: had it been for a reason? A year ago he would have said *yes* without hesitation—but now, brushed by the descent of those uncaring wings, he no longer believed it. Dev, Krazewski, Crowder had died, and he had been spared—because he had been spared. They had not won because their cause was just, or because God was on their side. They had won because they had more men and more equipment, because they were valorous in their fresh, foolhardy ignorance, while the Germans were stunned and weary from four years of hell and losses. He would have been killed too, in four years of it; he knew that now beyond any doubt. He would have gone limping back to the line, and the next decoration would have gone to his mother. There was no celestial ordering of events that he could see. Men set them in motion; men failed or succeeded according to their abilities, their skill and fortitude and resources, and the luck of the draw. Ludendorff had almost won in the Chemin des Dames drive because he had planned it with meticulous care and his troops had executed it with skill and discipline; he had lost because his men, worn by hunger and privation, had stopped to loot and drink, because they were more weary than anyone—even Ludendorff—had thought, and because Americans like himself had been flung headlong into the crucial breaches, and had stemmed the rush. If there was a destiny that shaped our ends it was a very capricious one: the Allies had invoked God's aid, so had the Central Powers, each side had felt its cause was just and true, and had committed crimes innumerable for the greater, the all-important end. It was all part of the "sacrifices" required for victory. But for his own opposite number, the German Major limping arduously through the bitter, wintry streets of Kassel or Leipzig, all those sacrifices had been in vain, a mockery—and so, if a fair and lasting peace were not effected by the Big Four, would be his own "sacrifices" as well . . .

He sighed, got to his feet and walked back along the Quai, and on an impulse stopped at a café terrasse on the little park facing the Port. Dropping into a spidery iron chair he hooked his cane over the table's edge, ordered a vermouth cassis and let himself sink into the clop of horses' hoofs, the creak and jangle of produce wagons, the tin hoot of taxicabs. He saw an artillery officer from the 329th he recognized vaguely, his neck in a yellow leather brace, an aviator riding in an open fiacre with two Red Cross girls, their skirts fluttering in the light breeze. They were laughing at something the flier had said, bending forward, their pretty white throats extended. Celia had looked at him like that; a summer evening long ago. He'd had a letter from her during the Argonne offensive that even then had made him smile.

Everyone back home here is so thrilled about you, Sam. Your tre-
mendous bravery, and all your medals. Father and Mr. Clausen want to
name the plot in front of the town hall Damon Square. *Think of that!*
You'll be immortal!!! Peg says Mr. Verney can't talk about anything
but you, he keeps saying to everybody, "I knew that boy had the stuff
of heroism in him, I knew it." He has a map of Flanders on the wall of
his room with colored pins in it, and he insists on reading the news aloud
every day, word for word. Peg says he's driving them all crazy. Well,
she doesn't mean it, of course, because they're all proud of you, too.
It's wonderful, and I feel like saying to everyone, too: "I knew it all
the time." I keep remembering that time on the lawn at your mother's,
when I ragged you so about your knowledge of your future destiny,
and everything. But it was true, after all. How did you know!!! I guess I
should have believed you then, shouldn't I? Everybody should have.
Fred is at Camp Shelby, he says it won't be long before his unit is going
overseas, too. I'm thrilled and at the same time I'm scared. I mean it
seems so terrible this war has to go on like this. Those Huns are such
horrible beasts. The old hometown is so deserted now, but it's nice
being back here with Mummy and of course Father. I imagine now
you're a Captain and a war hero you don't have much free time, but if
you should have any I'd be thrilled to hear from you, I really would . . .

He smiled, sipping his aperitif. A part of her had regretted not waiting for him; moping around the house, waiting for the baby to come.
After all, a Medal of Honor winner was a more engaging asset than a
lieutenant in the coast artillery. Damon Square. That rectangle of withered grass and mud where Walt Kearney and Jake Linstrom used to sit
in the shade of the elms, straw hats down over their noses, half-asleep . . .
General Pershing had personally decorated him, back at Debremont. He
had felt the brief tug at his blouse as the pin was thrust through it—and
then the Iron Commander had shaken hands with him and that stern face
had given a grim, frosty smile. "Congratulations, Damon. I'd swap the
stars on my shoulders for this medal. I mean it." He probably would have,
too. But now it was peacetime once again, the colors would fade, the
armies shrink, Fred Shurtleff would go back into business in Chicago
and his young, vivacious wife would bring up her babies and give lavish
dinner parties in a town house fronting the Lake . . .

"Captain Damon?" a voice said. "Oh—Major, I'm sorry. Say—
congratulations!"

He glanced up. A first lieutenant was standing beside him: a stocky
man with a homely, bony face and a beaklike nose and quick, lively
eyes. A face he remembered at once but couldn't place. Then he could.
"Hello. Krisler, isn't it?"

"Yes, sir. Please don't get up. I just saw you sitting there—"

"Oh, yes. Russell's Battalion." He got to his feet anyway, taking his weight on the good leg. "That lovely briefing on the way up to Malsain-terre. I don't remember seeing you afterward—did you get it there?"

Krisler nodded, touched his chest with a quick little motion of his thumb. "Shell fragments. I was lucky, though. Just above the lung. What about you, sir?"

"Smote me hip and thigh. Mont Noir. Sit down, Krisler. It's on me."

"If I'm not disturbing you any . . ."

"God, no. I've only been sitting here brooding. I'm sorry not to recognize you right away."

"No reason you should, sir—I'm surprised you remember me at all." Krisler gave a quick, warm grin. "I was in a very subdued mood that evening."

"Yes. I was, myself. What's your first name, Krisler?"

"Ben, sir."

"Good. Let's make it Ben and Sam." He smiled at the Lieutenant. "As a matter of fact this leaf is sort of superfluous. I won it at Base Twenty-seven, Angers."

They sipped the cool, tart wine and talked idly, watching the strollers. Krisler was from Menomonie, Wisconsin, where his father owned real estate and ran the town paper. He had gone to West Point, graduating in the class of 1919 a year early, and when Damon had seen him he'd been with the Regiment only two hours.

"I didn't have the faintest idea what was going on—all I knew was my assignment and that was it. To tell you the truth, I was scared. Nothing was at all the way I thought it would be."

"It has a way of acting like that," Damon murmured. "That's a tough way to start out with troops. How'd you make out?"

"I haven't any idea. I picked up the fastest wound stripe in history." When Krisler grinned his homely face looked boyish and mischievous. "Morey and I got them all through the wire, and we took out the first two guns with grenades. We were going great in spite of the rain and mud and everything, and I thought, Hell, we'll be in Berlin by six P.M. And the next thing I knew I was lying flat on my back and my wishbone felt as if a mule had kicked it. And my noble command roaring by me without so much as a glance." He scrubbed his close-cropped black hair with his knuckles. "I wasn't planning to launch a six-year Peninsula Campaign, like old Dick Wellesley, but I sure as hell thought I'd last more than four hours . . . All that spit and polish on the Plain gone to waste. What class were you?"

Damon said: "I never had the advantages of West Point."

Krisler glanced at him a moment—then grinned his gleeful, face-cracking grin. "Yeah! Isn't that the truth. But the worst part of the place was the stony-dungeon humorlessness. Not one West Pointer in fifty has a real sense of humor. Jesus, they all think a joke is a long story that has a dog in it with a man's name."

Damon laughed; he decided he liked Krisler a good deal. "You must have had a bumpy time of it there."

"The upperclassmen considered me unsound. Frivolous, they called it. 'No plebe can afford to be frivolous here, Krisler. We are taking it upon ourselves to see that you rid yourself of that odious characteristic.' Why in hell do they always think they have to talk like Dr. Johnson? I made the mistake of telling one of them that, once."

"You lasted four years up there with that attitude?"

"Three. Our academic careers were cut short so as to fit us into the grand conflict. I was just as happy, to tell you the truth." His jet black eyes glinted, his jaw flexed; and Damon saw there was a lot of steel under the headlong bravura. "It became a game after a while—a grim, methodical kind of game. They threw it all at me—I eagled and dipped and braced and walked my punishment tours hour by lonely hour . . . but every evening I looked in the mirror at my ugly phiz and told myself: 'You have not lost your sense of humor.' And it worked." He watched a pretty French girl at a nearby table for a moment with eager interest. "Well—I take that back about all Pointers. Colonel Caldwell's got a sense of humor, all right. Nothing seemed to be happening that night, and I couldn't find anybody that knew anything, and when I saw Caldwell I ran up to him and said: 'Colonel, my orders are to take command of the Third Platoon, C Company, First Battalion.' He gave me a really marvelous look and said, 'Thank you, Lieutenant—I shall return to my duties with a lighter heart.' "

Laughing, Sam said, "He's a BG now, you know. He's coming down here himself—I'll be seeing him in a day or so."

"Are you going to rejoin the Regiment at Hexenkirche?"

Damon stopped smiling. "I don't know. Are you?"

"Absolutely. I already know German: why waste it?—Come on over to the Casino," he urged. "Let's watch the world at play."

"You're pretty fired up for an invalid, Ben."

"You're looking at the most frivolous man in the Anal Enema Flatulent. Come on . . ."

They finished their drinks and walked through the little park. The leg felt better again—whether it was the relentless exercise or the vermouth cassis Damon wasn't sure. He could tell Krisler was having his own troubles; his breath came unevenly and his face was blotched and strained.

In silence they climbed the steps and entered the cool, hard light of the foyer, stood for a few moments at the edge of the salon where groups of people sat drinking and laughing; the long room was all aquiver with the bright, powdery chatter of French. Refracted light from the Port played across the ceiling in shimmering scales; the women's dresses glowed.

"Damn, I wish I knew the langue du pays," Krisler observed. "Not just classroom garble, but enough to really function. Do you?"

"A little."

"A sleeping dictionary's the best way, I'm told. A feel for the patois."

"What? Oh, sure." Damon was watching a man with straight dark hair and a fine mustache who was standing in front of a small group—they looked English, though perhaps they weren't—regaling them with some hunting exploit: there was a rapid pantomime of consternation with the beast charging, all horns and hoofs and malice, followed by panic and a heroism born of desperation; the principal fired, a perfect shot, and stood with his foot on the jungle monster, heroically, posing for congratulatory pictures. The group around him—the men were all in civilian clothes—rocked with laughter and begged for more; and Damon felt a swift tremor of resentment, and then bleak indifference. This was one of the playgrounds of the rich: the world was going back to normal and the rich were back here, playing. It was all natural enough. For all he knew the man was Boy Bradford, V.C., D.S.O., M.C., and a brigadier in the BEF at twenty-four . . . Beyond the group he could hear the spidery, running click of the roulette balls and the bored monotone of the croupiers: "Faites vos jeux, sieurs-et-dames, faites vos jeux . . ."

"Let's go in and watch the play," he said.

Krisler shook his head. "I think I'll sit me down for a spell. All this big-time excitement. The proximity of beautiful women leaves me breath-less." Damon noticed he was perspiring lightly; he looked still paler, the skin drawn tight over his beaked nose. It might be better if he left him by himself for a bit.

"All right. I'll make a lightning tour of the premises and tell you which games are rigged."

He started toward the gaming room, then on a sudden impulse veered right and moved out along the colonnade, gripping his cane tightly, glancing at the couples standing here and there. Meeting Krisler had thrust the problem of his future into the forefront of his mind again; he lighted a cigarette and stood beside one of the columns, gazing out at the yacht basin, the graceful sweep of the blue and white and mahogany hulls, the glitter of their brass appointments. The stern of one vessel said *L'Aiglette, Cannes.* Two men were stowing crates of provisions in her hold. They were free now, free to sail to Halmahera, Timor, Pala-mangao: the exotic isles . . .

He had done all right, in a certain sense. He had carried in his pack, if not a field marshal's baton, at least a battalion executive officer's walking stick. He could lead men, inspire their confidence and respect, he had that tactical feel the Old Man talked about—that seventh sense that had nothing to do with book learning or map reading or training manuals or educated guesses, either. He had found his niche. Had he? Or was this all a delusion, won at the expense of other talents the iron demands of battle had stifled? No man knew what was in him, deeply and irrevoca-bly his: we were all of us strange creatures under our skins—poets and seers, captains and pioneers—what man could say what was finally his destiny? Resting one arm against the cool ivory plaster he arched his back and frowned. *Farewell the*—how did it go? *Farewell the plumed troop and the big wars that make ambition virtue! Farewell the neighing steed and the shrill trump, the spirit-stirring drum, the something something something; and oh you mortal engines*—that was good, mortal engines—*whose rude throats the something Jove's dread clamors counterfeit, farewell! Othello's occupation's gone!* Was that at the heart of his confusion after all?

He sighed, shifted his weight again and glanced around him, almost guiltily; there, framed between two pillars like some classical embodiment of woman, a girl was standing, talking to a French cavalry captain and an older man, a civilian wearing a rosette. She was facing the sea, her face aglow in the afternoon sun. She was stunning; beneath her copper-colored hair her face displayed an exciting balance of fragility and force, like some exquisitely tempered steel. Damon was certain she was the most beautiful girl he had ever seen. The two men were telling her something amusing· and her lips broke into laughter, her eyes danced, she stirred and shifted like a pretty little sailboat moored to some ponderous barge, longing for the open water . . . He found that he was simply standing there staring at her, his cigarette burning his knuckles, content just to watch this lovely creature, bask in her exuberance and charm. The somber fury of the Argonne, its losses and terrors and foul redolence, slid from his soul like evil scales.

The girl was speaking French rapidly; he could hear an occasional phrase. "Oh!—mais c'est trop drôle, ça!" she exclaimed once. "Il fait la bête . . ." What did that mean? Her laughter was deep and rich, a delightful change from the strident soprano clatter of most Frenchwomen. He knew he was being rude, unpardonably rude, staring like that, but he could not bring himself to stop: it was like a medal—the rarest sort of medal, rarer even by far than the baby-blue ribbon with its five white stars he'd won at Brigny Farm—bestowed on him for the dangers he had passed. Why shouldn't he feast his eyes on beauty? A cat could look at a king, as his mother said. Besides, there was something else: he had seen her before somewhere—or no, she reminded him of someone, someone he'd known well . . .

The trio was joined by two others, a French lieutenant of artillery, a handsome, slender man, and a voluptuous, full-faced girl in a flaming orange dress; and the group burst into animated greetings and explosive little bursts of laughter. The girl with the copper-colored hair now appeared a bit constrained: her face seemed graver, more intent; she didn't like the newcomers. Her eyes flashed out toward Damon once, irritably, returned to the group. Abruptly he turned away, went off to the far end of the colonnade and smoked another cigarette. As had happened several times before in his life he had the sensation that everything was arrested, held in sweet stasis—waiting for some episode, some event thunderous or trivial, to tilt it and impel it forward again. He was caught in a time bubble, as he'd been that afternoon with Celia on the lawn, or lying on the bank of the Marne with Dev—

Near him at the end of the promenade an old man in a wheelchair, a proud old man with a monocle and a jade cigarette holder, a count or baron from his manner, was arguing with a fat young man in tweeds, pointing one trembling finger at him as he talked. The baron was furious; his swollen dark jowls were quivering with rage.

"—No pride!" he barked in impeccably enunciated English, "you have simply and horribly not one particle of pride!" The angrier he got the more amused and indifferent the fat young man became.

"But Uncle Alexis—" he began.

"You are heading for perdition—that special perdition of indolent, of uncaring souls!" The nephew laughed and shook his head indulgently, disbelieving, intent on dissipation, on folly, and turned away. "You mark what I say, you young devil!" the old man called after him hoarsely, pointing the shaking white finger. The young man turned and made a series of vague, propitiary gestures with his plump hands, then went off with alacrity toward the grand salon. Damon's eyes, returning, encountered the baron's; the old man glared at him and nodded—as if Sam were the author of all this brainless perversity—gave a swift, wild gesture of exasperation, whipped out a handkerchief and spinning his wheelchair around began to cough into it rackingly, his shoulders hunched . . . Damon started. The girl was walking toward him, alone, in another few seconds she would pass by the column where he stood; she was moving with a firm, easy stride, her slim little figure very erect; feminine yet assertive. He felt his heart leap. Before he had thought he took a step toward her and said: "Pardon me, Miss . . ."

"*Pardon?*" The word was French. Her eyes had shot up to his— sharply, a trifle forbidding.

"Mes homages, Madame." He saluted, the way he had seen French officers do on greeting ladies. "J'ai pensé que vous—que vous étiez—"

"Ah, you speak French, Commandant," she replied in English, with a charming French accent; and she smiled—that devastating, electric smile that sparkled like sunlight spilled over water.

"I'm sorry," he said. "It's only that I thought—I could have sworn you were American."

"Really? What a remarkable thought! Why?" She seemed intrigued by this, her charming little head held on one side.

"Oh, I don't know—just the way you were laughing over there, with those other people." She was quite young—eighteen, nineteen; the whites of her eyes were so clear they were almost blue. "I must apologize for staring . . ."

"Yes, you *were* staring. Is that the custom in America?"

"I guess our manners aren't all they could be, compared with Europe . . . It's just that you reminded me of—people back home . . ." His instincts had received a severe jolt, but he persisted. "You're sure you're not *part* American?"

She laughed her low, musical laugh again. "As sure as one can be in this world, Commandant." Her eyes moved away from him now. "No, my mother is Spanish and my father is Count Edmonde de Besançon." She paused, then said softly: "I am the Countess de Vezelay."

"Mes Homages," he repeated gallantly, though his heart had sunk out of sight. Married. And to a bloody count. Yet he couldn't bear to end the conversation. "Really? Where is Vezelay? I've seen only a very small part of France. A very sad part."

"Of course, that goes without saying.—Oh, it is a hill town in Burgundy. Very romantic, very historic, very imposing. We feel it is quite beautiful in its own insufferably austere way. The castle is so gloomy and cold after October—anything that gloomy and cold *must* be imposing." She smiled at him merrily. "That's why I am down here. For the sun!"

"Of course."

"And to see old friends. Now that this wretched war is finally over."

"Of course," he echoed. "It must be a great relief to you."

"—How charming that you thought I was an American!" she pealed. "That is delicious. I must tell Ramon, it will delight him . . ."

She'll leave now, he thought. But she didn't; from her purse she removed a cigarette case and selected a gray, gold-tipped cigarette. Damon offered her a light, took out a Camel and said: "Will you permit me?"

"Mais certainement, certainement . . . What extraordinary manners you have, Commandant."

"Do I?"

"For an American, that is. Tell me about yourself. Where is your home in America?"

"Oh, it's a very little town. You've never heard of it. In Nebraska."

"Goodness! Where is that?"

"Well, it's out in the Midwest. On the edge of the West, actually . . ." It didn't matter what they talked about, just as long as they could go on talking and he could stand here braced on his cane, his leg a throbbing hot cone, and bask in the delicate beauty of this vivid, copper-haired girl. Who in God's name was it she reminded him of? "It's a—sort of a transitional state," he went on.

"What do you mean—transitional?"

"Well, you see it extends from the Missouri—that's a major tributary of the Mississippi—"

"Oh yes, the river of our Père Marquette and De la Salle . . ."

"—yes, that's right. And it runs west across the Great Plains, almost to the edge of the Rocky Mountains."

She frowned. "They are tedious, are they not? the Great Plains?"

"Well—they certainly can't compete with *this* . . ." He laughed and

gestured toward the yachts, the sails of boats like swollen peppermint
and scarlet shells against the vibrant blue of the gulf, the dreamy cobalt
ridge of the Esterel. "But there's—I don't know, a magical quality about
them, a kind of simplicity. Especially in the spring, in early May, when
the willows and cottonwoods along the river turn that rich yellow-
green. It's sort of the color of life itself, in a way; like starting in all over
again . . ."

He broke off, embarrassed. She was watching him intently—and more
than that too, he saw: a little more than that. He could almost swear
there was more. A trace of softening in her eyes, a swift little shadow
of wonder and sorrow. Was there? He grinned and gave a short shrug.
"I guess I'm just homesick," he said. "I haven't been home in three years
now. I'm getting sentimental."

"You have a sentimental streak then, Commandant?" she asked softly.
"And you a soldier?"

"Yep. Purple and pink and a mile wide." They laughed together. She
evinced no desire to go although her cigarette was nearly burned out. "I
keep having this feeling I've seen you somewhere before," he offered,
watching her carefully. "I hope you don't mind."

"Not at all. I really doubt it very much, however." She glanced at his
cane. "You have been wounded?" he nodded. "But you are wearing
no—what my husband calls his kitchen battery . . ." She brushed her
fingers lightly above her left breast.

"Oh. I'm not overly fond of wearing ribbons."

"Really? Why is that?"

He stared at her a moment. "Because I think it's out of place. There
aren't enough medals struck since the beginning of time to reward the
bravery and suffering of the past four years. Many men have done
courageous things that have never been rewarded, and bushel baskets
full of medals have been handed out to staff officers for no reason other
than favoritism or propinquity."

"That is an interesting theory, I have never heard it advanced before.
But surely courage under fire—"

"How can you assess courage precisely? Every man has something
he's mortally afraid of, and there is no man living who won't finally
break under pressure if it's cruel enough and incessant enough . . . So
how can anybody but God decide who is worthy of a medal and who
isn't?" He stopped and lowered his gaze, aware that his voice had risen.

"Well!" she exclaimed. "You are so—so—"

"So prejudiced about this," he finished for her flatly. "Yes, I am. I've
had some experience along these lines."

She glanced at him out of the corner of her eye. "You *were* wounded,
though? severely?"

"Severely enough for me."

"Some of them cut their fingers opening a tin of corned beef and they need months to recuperate. And others smear their faces with vaseline and pretend they—"

He smiled grimly. "Not in my outfit, they don't."

"Ah. You are very stern, then?"

He studied her again. It was hard to tell which way she would jump, this beautiful little countess. He could swear at certain moments she was kidding the very socks off him; yet her face remained attentive, congenial, brushed with that trace of sadness. Her voice held a soft, low vibrance that stirred him. If it were possible for a man to fall irretrievably in love inside of five minutes, he thought in blank amazement, I've done it. I've done exactly that . . .

"Oh, just average, I guess," he said aloud. "No," he amended, "I'm strict. In certain things. I don't care too much about what my boys do on their own, that's none of my business. But there are certain areas where you can't allow any fooling around." He realized he was sounding pompous and stopped. Christ Almighty, he was prattling along like old George Verney! "I guess I should have introduced myself," he said. "My name is Damon. Sam Damon."

She started visibly at this: her eyes seemed to cloud over and then brighten curiously. "—Damon," she stammered, "Damon—why, you're— you're one of the most decorated men in the whole American army . . ."

Now it was his turn to stare. "What makes you say that?"

"Well, why—" she floundered "—well you see my father is, that is he was attached to your division, as liaison officer . . ."

"But that would be Colonel Hénissart," Damon began, "or Lefebvre, Captain—"

"No, it was early, my father was with the Americans earlier, then he was transferred. Before he was wounded. He was returned to his regiment." She was gazing at him almost fearfully, her eyes darting. "I should not have kept you standing, Commandant," she said. "Forgive me . . ."

"It's nothing, I need to exercise it—"

"And now I must go, I have an engagement, you must excuse me."

"May I escort you—"

"No. That will not be necessary. It has been pleasant speaking with you, very pleasant."

"I hope I may see you again," he ventured.

"That is possible," she breathed. She was consumed with impatience. "Au revoir, Commandant . . ."

"Au revoir, Madame."

He watched her hurry away along the colonnade, the sunlight flashing in her lovely hair. Just his luck. And it had seemed so possible. So completely and naturally *inevitable*—the whole encounter. His mind riotous with romantic liaisons in gloomy chateaux, on gleaming yachts, at thés dansants on red-tiled terraces overlooking La Napoule, he saun-

tered back to the salon, where Krisler was sipping at a canary yellow
drink as if it were nitroglycerine. He sat down beside him and motioned
to a waiter. "What you got there, Ben?"

"They call it Pernod. *I* call it licorice."

"That's for me."

"You look as if you've netted yourself a thirty-pound bass. What's
up?"

"I just had a strange little adventure. The funniest kind." All of a
sudden he felt quite exuberant, filled with mirth. "I ran into a French
countess who's scared of me. What do you think of that?"

"I'd say she was using damned good sense."

"Yes. So would I. The only trouble with that is she's afraid of me for
the wrong reasons." He leaned forward and tapped Krisler significantly
on the wrist with two fingers. "What would be your reaction to an
absolutely stunning highborn French chicken who knew all about the
personnel of the old Wagon Wheel?"

"I'd say she was a sneaky Hun spy who hasn't found out the game's
over."

"So would I, buddy." He sat back and sipped at the drink, which
tasted like caraway seeds soaked in licorice, and slid fur over his front
teeth. He was surprised to find that his leg had stopped throbbing completely. Why was that? The salon, the stuttering click of the roulette
wheels, the silver laughter of the women, held him bemused. He had
fallen asleep in a world of gray mud and convulsive horrors, and had
wakened in a land of dreamy opulence and beauty, pierced with love . . .
For he was in love: he never doubted it for an instant. It was the
happiest moment he had ever known.

"Now why do you suppose," he said aloud, "a beautiful French
countess would sit up nights boning up on the TO of the old Wagon
Wheel—and then run away from a nice, clean, innocent kid like me?"

"You have trench mouth," Krisler said.

The two soldiers looked at each other and laughed uproariously.

And then two days later—a cool, windy day with the waves beating
in lustily from Isle Ste. Marguerite—he was pounding out his two-
mile walk along La Croisette and saw ahead of him General Caldwell
and two other officers—and the girl. There was that same quick, pleasurable pang under the heart: he increased his pace, though it hurt.
Caldwell noticed him and the girl turned at the same moment, her face a
quick flash of fright. He saw the strong resemblance in feature, the
delicacy, the alert intelligence and grace, and said to himself, "Idiot!"
He was shaking with inner laughter. He saluted the officers and said,
"Good afternoon, General. Gentlemen."

Caldwell broke off and shook hands left-handed. "Sam! God, it's good to see you on your feet again. I tried to call you last night but I can't for the life of me get anywhere over the phone in France. The minute you pick up the receiver they shift from French to rapid-fire Basque. Have you met my daughter Thomas?"

Damon brought forth his gravest smile. "No, I don't believe I have."

"Tommy," the General was saying, "this is Major Damon. You've heard me speak of him."

"Of course. How do you do, Major," she said sweetly.

"How do you do, Miss Caldwell." Conscious of her eyes on him he turned to greet the other two officers—Lieutenant Colonel Forsythe of Division Artillery whom he knew, and a British full colonel named Evringham with a square, brick-red face and a heavy gray walrus mustache that looked as if it were pasted on.

"Sam's here on convalescent leave," the General was saying to Evringham. "He was nothing less than my right arm when I had the Regiment."

"Where were you wounded, Damon?" Evringham asked.

"At Mont Noir, Colonel."

"Ah. Quite." Evringham grimaced under the walrus mustache. "Good show."

"Damon's real show was that amazing rear-guard exploit at Brigny," Colonel Forsythe appended. "That was his big day."

"Ah. Quite."

"Oh, of course, you're the famous hero!" Tommy Caldwell cried. Her eyes were shining, and Damon knew she was going to pay him back. "You're the man with all the incredible medals. Why don't you wear them, Major? Poppa"—she turned to her father quickly—"why doesn't Major Damon wear all his incredible medals? Isn't he supposed to?"

"Yes," Forsythe chimed in, "why aren't you wearing them, Damon? This is certainly the place to be wearing them."

Damon smiled. "It's—more or less an oversight, sir."

"I know why," Tommy pursued brightly, "—he doesn't want to embarrass all the rest of you. Isn't that it? Or perhaps he feels self-conscious with them. Do you feel self-conscious about them, Major?"

"Now, Tommy," General Caldwell said in a diffident, almost mournful tone.

Her eyes fluttered. "Have I said something wrong? something untoward?"

"Not at all, Miss Caldwell," Damon heard himself say. "The fact is I've found them just too much of a burden to carry around: all that silver and bronze—it throws me off balance. Wouldn't you find it too much of a burden?"

"*I* wouldn't have had anything to do with them in the first place," she declared. "I think it's a lot of silly tin-soldier nonsense."

"Now, Tommy—"

"It's like those silly silver wigs the British judges and lawyers wear. Perfectly ridiculous."

Colonel Evringham's cheeks shook with dismay; his eyes went a little out of focus. "Oh, I say," he murmured.

Tommy Caldwell laughed merrily. "Ego bolsterers, pure and simple. What would you all do without your headdresses and shell necklaces? You know perfectly well you hand these trinkets around to each other like children at a marshmallow roast . . ."

"Oh, we all collect trophies, Miss Caldwell," Damon broke in on her, smiling. "Wouldn't you say? But it's only our essential innocence that's at the bottom of it. We're just what we profess to be, no more and no less—you can read everything we are on our shoulders and over our hearts. What could be more artless than that? Whereas with ladies"— and he smiled at her meaningfully—"how is Machiavelli himself to read them? You encounter some utterly charming creature en promenade, say, she is dressed ravishingly and glittering with jewels, she makes the most entrancing allusions to ancestral chateaux and royal yachts and embassy receptions for three hundred eminent souls—but what is *she?* Echo answers. Is she a countess or a common adventurer?—or even worse? No, Miss Caldwell, you malign us poor soldiers . . ." He paused, shaking his head; she was gazing up at him, speechless, her lovely clear eyes wide with consternation. "How did one of Colonel Evringham's noblest monarchs woo his future bride in France? *Take me, take a soldier; take a soldier, take a king: and what say'st thou, then, to my love?*"

"Bless my soul," murmured Evringham. "Who's that?"

"Well, well," George Caldwell said. "Well, well, well . . ." He was staring at Damon in delighted amazement. "Sam, that was trenchantly put, if I do say."

"Oh, you *would,*" Tommy retorted, "you boys always stick to-gether."

"I wouldn't say Sam needed any help." He eyed his daughter a moment, mischievously, then consulted his watch. "Sam," he said abruptly, "I wonder if I could impose on you for a bit. Tommy has a few errands in the town and I wonder if you'd mind going along with her."

"Poppa, Major Damon has no interest in tagging along—"

"I'm sure he wouldn't mind." Over his daughter's head the General threw Damon one of his most significant glances. "Would you, Sam?"

"Not at all, sir. I'd be delighted."

"Poppa, really—"

"Colonel Evringham's time here is limited and there are some things we need very much to talk about. Tell you what. We'll all meet at the Blue Bar at—four fifteen. Agreed?"

"It'll be my pleasure, sir," Damon answered.

"And Tommy—"

"Yes, General?" she said with fearfully precise enunciation.

"Try and show Sam your sunny side." He beamed at her slyly. "You do have one, you know . . ."

Damon took her arm and they moved off under the rusty green of the umbrella pines. He could feel her body stiffen when he touched her, and it delighted him. He wanted to roar with laughter, dance a jig on the seawall, tweak the nose of a frosty French grande dame with a lavender neckband and silver hair piled high. He hadn't felt like this in a long time, a terribly long time—perhaps never quite like this in all his young life. And most delicious of all was the fun of holding it all inside him where it trembled and flashed like mercury.

Idly he asked: "How long have you been in France, Miss Caldwell?"

"—All right," she retorted. "All right. You're noble. You're Sir Percival in khaki and all the blinder-fluking rest of it."

"I don't know what you mean."

"Of course not. Soul of honor. God! You should have been an Eton boy."

"Why's that?"

"You know perfectly well I've been changing bedpans for two years. You're impossible!" She seemed nearly ready to burst into tears. All at once she brightened and said: "Well. I fooled *you*." She stopped short and glared at him hard. "Didn't I? Didn't I fool you?"

"Yes. You did. Almost completely."

"What do you mean, *almost—!*"

Sententiously, as though reading from a regional guide, he declaimed: "The ancient abbey at Vezelay was the seat of the Knights Hospitallers since 1482. The façade was admirably restored by Viollet-le-Duc in 1887 and is one of the finest examples of Romanesque art in Burgundy. It may be visited weekdays from—"

"You didn't know that then!" she challenged.

"No. I didn't."

"Suspicious sneak. Are you one of these people who can't admit it when they're beaten? I detest them."

"No, I'm not. You had me: you did. Only"—he watched the other couples drifting by—he was part of a couple now, delightfully, miraculously—"there was something I couldn't quite put together. My instinct told me—"

"Oh, you run on instinct, do you?"

"Yes, indeed." They had reached the Port, and stopped to watch the boats. "This is like a fairy tale," he mused, "this whole town. Built of dreams. It's hard to believe that this little fairyland and—all that mess up north are the same country."

"Yes, and—" she began; stopped herself abruptly.

"And what?"

"Nothing." Frowning she looked away at the water.

". . . Are they tedious?" he said solicitously.

"What?"

"The Great Plains?"

"Oh, stop it," she said, and then laughed. They both laughed now, looking at each other.

"Do you do things like that often? impersonations?"

"As often as I can."

"I see. Why?"

"Because I don't like the world the way it is—that's why. So I change it." Her face became bright and animate again. "See how much more exciting it was? I was a countess, with castles and villas galore . . . Don't tell me you weren't thrilled, because you were."

"Yes, I was."

"You see?"

"But not because of that . . . I like it much better this way."

"That's because you're so pedestrian."

"I suppose so.—Let's go up to Le Suquet," he proposed. "I've wanted to go up ever since I got here. Are you game?"

"Fortress." Her lovely lip curled. "You Martians: you're all in your blasted glory, aren't you?" Again she stopped and faced him, hands on her hips. "You're not West Point, are you? I can tell you right now I won't even *promenade* with a West Point product. Are you?"

"No. I'm not."

"Thank God for that, anyway."

"But I guess I'd better tell you I was accepted for the Point before the war."

"Why didn't you go, then?"

He shrugged simply and grinned. "Glory."

But she did not laugh. "Paths of glory lead but to the grave," she said.

He nodded. "Who said it?"

"I don't know."

Le Suquet was directly above them now, like a proud little mauve toy of a fort, a child's creation. They went up through the old city, past the markets: garlands of oranges still on their bright, leaved branches, lettuce in crazy hottentot heads, a fish stall with rouget still jumping about flailing their tails, octopi in a milk-colored slimy ooze of flesh and tentacles; on up through sweating dark passages with skulking dogs picking at garbage and crabbed old women bowed low over their loads, worn and toiling . . . and then they were on the battlements, the wind blowing fresh and fair in their faces, and far to the west Nice lay in a low ivory crescent below the mountains. On the parapet, her hair blowing back from her cheeks, Tommy seemed more at ease, and talked about herself.

She'd been working at Field Hospital Number One at Neuilly and had just been released; most of the patients had been evacuated and there was no further need for her. She'd had a bellyful of things military, if anyone should ask her. Her mother had died when she was six, and she'd been brought up on army posts in Texas, in Georgia and Washington

State and the Philippines. There had been aunts who had come to help
out, there had been vast, crooning Negresses and chattering Filipinas
and Mexican women like squat Buddhist idols; she had eaten frijoles and
hominy and water buffalo and God knew what else. She had ridden
practically since she was able to talk; she'd had a dog she'd loved, a
hammerheaded brute named Aguinaldo who had died of snakebite at
Folsom, and she had cried for five days and nights and nothing could
console her; she had cut her teeth on a bugle and stood to colors from
time out of mind, she'd worn some sort of uniform half her life—and
now there was no one, *no one* in the Western World who was as
thoroughly sick of it as she was.

"I'm going to become a courtesan," she declared. "A celebrated, competent, high-class courtesan, and take up with a White Russian millionaire; or an Egyptian prince. With one of those lovely white yachts
right—down—there . . ."

"Sounds like fun," he admitted.

"Doesn't it? And sail round and round, from Cannes to Cyprus to
Aden to Tahiti and back again by way of the Seychelles—isn't that a
lovely name? Seychelles—getting more blowzy and sinful and dreamy
all the while. Now and then of course I'll write poetry, and sip absinthe
through a glass straw."

He watched her out of the corner of his eye. "What about your poor
old father?"

"Oh, he can take care of himself. He's a *general* now, for heaven's
sake . . . I can remember when he was a first lieutenant: a thousand years
old and a first looie. Acting company commander. Now he's down there
in the Blue Bar with the rest of the brass, arguing about who exposed
whose flank at Sleazy, and why the Ninety-ninth Dragoons weren't
deployed on the Noodle-Wombat-Dodder line, as planned. Boy, you
pirates have made a good thing out of this war."

"Oh yes, we've had a royal time of it," he said levelly. He knew she
was baiting him, and yet there was a wild, tempestuous note he couldn't
take hold of—as though she had caught the contagion of the mistral
gusting across from the Esterel.

"Haven't you, though. More fun than a barrel of scorpions. 'Men!' "
she chanted in a pompous basso, 'men, we've got to take that hill. Now
I've got to go back to my mess and see if the wine's been properly
chilled for dinner, and I want it captured when I come back.' But of
course the wine *hasn't* been properly chilled, the orderly has been
working his fingers to the bone shining Colonel Bubbleguts' boots and
pressing his uniform for that evening's amorous conquest. And so of
course Bubbleguts slaps the orderly in the guardhouse. By then"—she
was staring at him defiantly, laughing—"by then the chauffeur has come
by with the Rolls-Royce, all spic and span, and Bubbleguts has to make
up some excuse as to where he's going, so he picks the battalion billeted

near an old chateau he's had his eye on for some while and sends word to them to prepare for inspection. They've just come out of the line—what's left of them—they're filthy and exhausted and their equipment and clothing is a wreck. But orders are orders, any tom fool knows that, and the poor beggars drag themselves to their feet and clean their weapons as best they can and fall out for inspection, standing in the rain . . ."

"You've left out the delousing station," Damon said.

"I'll get to that. But Bubbleguts has no intention of inspecting them, his mind is set on that vacant chateau. He has himself driven there and is delighted to find it has a wine cellar, a buxom, cooperative femme de chambre, and a nice soft bed, not to mention a gorgeous view of the surrounding country, including *that hill*. It's all just too providential . . ."

Her voice was higher now, and tense; her eyes flashed like crossed swords. Damon had stopped smiling. "Suppose we drop this," he suggested.

"No, but wait! The best is yet to come. Old Bubbleguts—trust him!—is on the phone to Chaumont about the possibilities of promotion. Nothing doing. General Sackful-Paunch is adamant: 'My dear boy, *I* can't recommend you for BG—your casualty figures are far too low. Get 'em up where they belong and I'll see what I can do.' Bubbleguts is cast down about this, but not for long. Decision, decision! And what should he see but the battalion—they've finally realized they're not going to be inspected after all and they're plodding wearily back to the delousing station. The only trouble is, Bubbleguts is a trifle fuzzy, what with all the larded quail and bottles of Chateau Pomerol and chasing the cooperative femme de chambre around from room to room, and he's lost his orientation. 'They're attacking,' he cries. 'Good boys!' In a flash he's on the line to artillery. 'Give me a barrage at K42,' he orders. 'But Colonel B, that's *behind* us, that's back at the—' 'Are you telling me how to run my command?' Bubbleguts roars. 'I *said* K42 and I *mean* K42—I want everything you've got! . . .' Of course he's got it confused with a football play back at the Point—on, dear old Army team—but the artillery officer can't know that, orders are orders, old bean, and he pulls the lanyard. And yep, you guessed it—the first salvo lands smack in the middle of the column: and up they go! Oh my God, it's just too hilarious for words, all those arms and legs flying through the air, and the medics running around trying to find enough to—"

"That's enough!" He was on his feet; he had seized her by the arms, was shaking her. "Enough! *Stop it*, now . . ."

"Oh you've had enough of it, have you—!"

He felt dizzy with anger. "Now you listen to me—a lot of God damned good men got blown all to hell-and-gone in this dirty business, and you're not to mock them, you understand?"

"—I suppose—"

"You can think anything you like, but you don't mock them to me . . ."

"—You think I don't know that?" she raged at him, "—you think I haven't had plenty of this idiot game of stinking dressings, the bottles of pus and filth—listening to them groaning hour after hour . . . ?" And now suddenly she was weeping, her face stained with tears, making no effort to brush them away. He stood there, confronting her, not knowing what to do; then because he was still holding her shoulders he put his arms around her very gently; sobbing she fell against him.

"—Damn you all," she moaned. "All you foolish, noble sons of bitches . . ."

"All right," he said in a low voice. "Who was he?"

She flung her head back as if he'd struck her. "—An aviator, that's who he was, and a far finer person than you'll ever be, a wonderful person . . . No, excuse me," she broke down again, "—I don't know if he was finer at all, maybe he wasn't. Excuse me, Major. I don't know. But he was so sweet. His smile . . . His plane was hit and he tried to land it and his spine was broken all to pieces. He tried to land the plane because he didn't have a parachute. Why didn't they give them parachutes?" she cried thickly. "Why didn't they? The Germans had them. Why didn't we?"

"I don't know," Damon said.

"It was so hopeless. And he never gave up. He would still give that smile. Ah, God," she sobbed as if her heart were broken past all mending. "It's so rotten . . ."

"I'm sorry," he whispered. "God knows I am."

Two American sailors came around a corner of the battlements and began to watch the scene with a certain sly avidity. Damon turned on them his most forbidding glare and gave a quick, peremptory jerk of his head; the sailors withdrew in alarm. Tommy Caldwell had felt the movement though, and raised her head in time to see them scurry out of sight behind the stone.

"Company," she said; embarrassed now she turned away, wiping her eyes. "Stupid. I don't know what's the matter with me. I haven't cried over Jim in—a long while. Really. I'm all wrought up down here, I shouldn't have come." She shook her hair back. "Now my face will look like a redflannel washcloth for hours and hours. Jane said it would change my whole life to come down here. Jane was my superior, a nurse at Neuilly. She came down here on leave and met a captain in the Guards who owns half of Australia." Sniffling, she blew her nose. "Wasn't that lucky?"

"Yes, it was."

"She's going to be a Melbourne heiress." She looked at him with a droll, plaintive expression. "You're not by any chance a millionaire, are you?"

He shook his head. "No. I'm just a poor dumb farm boy."

"Who went after glory," she said.

"That's right," he said. "That was me."

But this time, her pretty little nose and cheeks flushed from weeping, she smiled.

"I have swum in every ocean in the world," Elise Lilienkron declared. She was a tall blond girl with a hard, handsome face and eyes like wood smoke. Her father had once been a diamond merchant and on the Riviera she was known as the Empress. "I have swum in the Atlantic and Pacific, and of course the Mediterranean, I have swum in the Indian Ocean at Puri, and in the Sea of Japan at Wakatsu."

"How about the Black Sea?" Ben Krisler asked.

"Yes. In the Black Sea. At Trabizond."

"Oh come on, sweetheart," Lieutenant Poindexter said. "You're not going to tell us you've swum in the Arctic Ocean . . ."

"I did." She nodded portentously. "At Bodö, in Norway."

"Empress baby, that's not the *Arctic* . . ."

"It is north of the Arctic Circle."

Poindexter turned to Tommy incredulously; his thumb lay along the line of his jaw, which made him look very handsome. "Is it? You've been all over the place."

She shrugged happily, watching his eyes. "I pass. Ask Sam—he knows all those impossible things."

"Okay, Major," Poindexter said with a sign. "Is it?"

Sam smiled. "If she's swum at Bodö, she's swum in the Arctic Ocean. The Arctic Circle runs from Traenen over to Kuzomen in Finland. And Bodö's north of that."

"Oh-my-God," Poindexter groaned, and Elise smiled at them all archly and murmured: "You see? He knows."

"I instinctively distrust a man who knows something like that," Poindexter proclaimed.

Tommy said, "Now Sterling, don't be rude."

"Sam knows all kinds of things," Ben Krisler said, and rubbed his hair with his knuckles. "He's got a memory like a deadfall. He's going to be chief of staff by 1939."

Arlene Hanchett, a Red Cross girl Tommy had got for Ben for the evening, leaned forward at this, her mouth open. "Is he really going to be chief of staff?"

"I don't know why not. *I'll* vote for him."

"1939?" Poindexter said, coming back into the conversation. "What's all this idle talk about 1939?"

The six of them were holding down a table at Le Jongleur Ivre, a stylish little cabaret off the Rue d'Antibes where dancers jostled one another pleasantly under a murk of cigarette smoke to music from a tumultuous six-piece Negro band. The bass drum said in red circular lettering *Long Tom Jethro and His Delta Serenaders*. Tommy Caldwell, humming the tune—it was "After You've Gone"—held her glass to her lips and watched the dancers shuffle and collide, and the great blue panel on the wall above the bandstand where a red giant with a hat whose brim made the shape of an infinity sign tossed in the air around him a poniard, drinking goblets, a walking stick and showers of golden coins. Someone she didn't recognize waved to her from the floor and she waved back happily. On the table were several bottles of Moët-Chandon —Poindexter had insisted on ordering it, he said there was no champagne like Moët-Chandon, no matter what anybody said—and their party had by now become sublimely convivial.

"What about the *Caspian* Sea, Empress baby?" Poindexter was saying with an air of sly triumph.

Elise nodded seriously. "Yes. At Balakhany. That is near Baku."

"God, *that's* helpful. I never heard of *either* place . . ."

"That is because you are so provincial," she answered in her faint, untraceable accent, and gave him a dreamy smile.

"I don't know about that. I've had my moments." Sterling Poindexter was a tall young man with dark, wavy hair and fine shoulders, and he moved with the easy grace of the world's favored. His uniform had been custom made at Selfridge's and his Sam Browne belt was of Russian calf worked soft as doeskin and polished like horn. He had been wounded in the foot at the Bois des Rappes and he would never forgive the Germans for ruining an excellent pair of Peel's boots. Tommy thought he was the most attractive man she had ever laid eyes on. As though conscious of her regard he filled her glass with champagne again, his wrist turning the bottle subtly as he poured, and she smiled at him, liking him, the party, the Jongleur Ivre, the various soldiers and girls who stopped by their table every now and then to say hello and then move on. A perfect evening, she thought, and Dex brought it into being. He does everything right.

To defend him she said to Elise: "Dex sailed the old *Feng-huang* all the way from New York City to Tahiti with a crew of five. At the age of nineteen."

Poindexter snorted. "Kid stuff." He looked at Sam, who was sitting on Tommy's left. "Ever done any sailing, Damon?"

Sam shook his head and grinned. "First boat I ever was on in my life was the *Tom Jefferson*, coming over here."

Tommy smiled. That was Sam all over: simple, no-bones-about-it direct. Poindexter looked disconcerted. "You're joking."

"Red-hot gospel."

"You'd like it, sailing. Great sport." His fine blue eyes measured the

Major. "By the by, what are you going to do with yourself when you get demobbed?"

"I don't know. I haven't made up my mind yet."

"Poppa's been at him," Tommy put in. "Poppa's been trying to talk him into a career in the blindy-freaking Army."

Poindexter rolled his eyes to the ceiling. "Oh-my-God. What for, sport? We've made the world safe for plutocracy . . ."

"Maybe."

"No, but I mean what'll you play for an encore? You've got all the trinkets in the store, now."

"Why shouldn't he stay in? He's got a great career ahead of him," Ben challenged. He was gripping his nose between his first two fingers, the way he always did when he was aroused.

Poindexter waved a hand at him. "I can't argue with you—you're already corrupted." He turned to Sam again. "No, but you can't go on in this idiot's paradise, shining your puttees and saluting the flag. Can you? I know I'm being insubordinate and all that hoopla—but it's no *future.* They'll start pulling down the building in a few months and you'll be back to lance corporal before you can sneeze."

"That's what I keep telling him," Tommy added.

"You mark my words, nobody back home is even going to want to *hear* about the Army. My old gentleman knows some very influential people. Senators and people like that. All they want to do is call the game and box the deck. They think the guard of honor at Arlington is a threat to the peace and stability of the old U S and A."

"United States senators?" Sam asked him. "They think that?"

"Hell, yes—United States senators. Who did you think? Look, we made our mistakes, we came over here and helped fill up the cemeteries and added another glorious page and all that. Now let's go home and write it off. Only a sucker stays in a game when it's clear the cards have gone against him. You know that. You write off your losses."

"Just write them off."

"Why do you want to rot away in some two-bit post out in the Badlands? There aren't even any Indians to skirmish with, anymore . . ." Dex's eyes twinkled gaily. "Come on back and the old gentleman will give you a job down at the shop."

Sam grinned. "What would I do?"

"Do? That's off the topic, baby. It isn't what you do, it's how you do it. Oh, you have a whole slew of telephones and you keep calling people up and telling them to coil with Anaconda and stand fast with Standard Oil. It doesn't matter, everything is going to go right on up, anyway. What you do *really* is play polo and tennis and go sailing up and down the Sound. That's what it's all for . . ."

"Sounds great," Sam said. "Just wrap it up and forget it and go home."

"Now you're talking."

"Until it happens all over again."

"What?" Poindexter demanded—and even Elise and Ben looked shocked. "What in hell are you talking about? Jesus, what a prophet of doom. There isn't going to be another conflagration. We've all been to it, remember?"

"There could be," Sam replied calmly.

"What an un-American attitude," Elise declared, frowning.

"Your friend is laboring under an idée fixe," Dex said to Tommy. Ben had engaged Sam in conversation and he listened for a moment, then produced a beautiful little gold cigarette case and offered it to Tommy.

"I love that case," she said, taking a cigarette. "It's so—it's so extravagant."

"Baby, it's yours." He placed it in her palm and closed his hand over hers.

"Oh Dex, no," she protested. "I can't accept this . . ."

"I don't see why not. Provided you take the inscription to heart."

She turned it over. In lovely spencerian script it said: *I could fall big for you. Signed, Icarus.* She smiled in spite of herself, then stared at him. The day before he had sent two dozen roses to her room, and the day before that a terrifyingly huge bottle of Arpège perfume in the shape of a heart.

"Would your old gentleman get me a job down at the shop?" she asked him teasingly; but he didn't smile.

"Don't be stubborn," he murmured; his head was very near hers, and she could see the little golden lights at the centers of his pupils. He had rowed number seven at New Haven, he was famed for the reckless, headlong brand of polo he played—and here he sat, so near her, very persuasive and very determined. "Why fight against the inevitable? Here I am and here you are. What could be more logical?"

"I thought you hated army brats," she faltered.

"A callow prejudice I've just abandoned. You simply don't know what you're hesitating over. They'll love you in Oyster Bay, darling-girl. And you'll love them."

"What about Oyster Bay?" Sam broke in on them vigorously.

"Major"—Dex's brow knotted in a pained expression—"we'll go into that later, okay?"

"No, where is it?" Sam pursued genially. "On Long Island, isn't it? Between Glen Cove and Huntington, isn't it?"

"Yes. That's right."

"What's it like there? Tell us."

Poindexter straightened wearily. "You wouldn't like it, Damon. You really wouldn't."

"Why's that?"

"It's too sedentary, too raffiné for you. You're a big, sinewy, rock-ribbed farm boy with a heart of gold. Whereas on Long Island everybody's got a skin of gold and a sinewy, rock-ribbed heart . . ."

Tommy laughed. It was fun sitting here between two handsome men who both wanted her—yet at the same time it brushed her with dread, with the sense of being hunted by harsh, implacable forces. She did not want to become involved, as these two immensely dissimilar men each wanted her to be; her spirit was still raw. At times it seemed to her that everything she had loved had been destroyed. Her mother had vanished in a flurry of medical officers and hushed nocturnal consultations; Aguinaldo had been killed by a snake while she had looked on in terror; she'd had a crush on a boy named Arthur Brell the year she was fourteen—and all that winter he'd been ill with pneumonia, emerging at last from bed a tearful, six-foot wraith who wavered as he walked; and then there was Jim—

"Shall we dance?" Sam was saying to her now, smiling.

"I'd love to," she replied.

"Oh Damon," Dex scoffed. "Come off it. You know you can't dance . . ."

"Just watch me."

She got to her feet with a shiver of relief, and they moved out into the press on the floor. They had seen a lot of each other during the past week. They had motored up to the eagle's roost of Gourdon-la-Saracène, high above the tiny white thread of the Loup River, awesome with its turrets and sheer rock walls; they had descended into the pink-and-jade caves of St. Cézaire, they had stood on the spot of beach at Fréjus where Napoleon had landed from Elba for his final, cataclysmic tilt with destiny. They had walked and talked and argued, and kissed lingeringly on the rocks at Golfe Juan, borne on a flood tide of sentiment, watching the sun sink below the flaming winter Riviera sky. She had found him attentive, forceful, a little fearsome. He had done all these audacious and terrible things, had advanced through all the fires of hell while everyone around him had blanched and faltered—and here he stood, simple and unassuming, telling her about the execution of Marshal Ney, asking her about Palamangao and Luzon. He sat up half the night reading, dreaming—there was so much he wanted to know about the world. Half-jealous of her father's affection for him she tried to dissuade him from staying on in the Army; she painted the blackest pictures she could remember or imagine. He listened, smiling, and kept his own counsel; she had no idea what he was thinking.

"Sorry," he murmured now.

"It's nothing. You're doing wonderfully." He wasn't a good dancer. He might have been, he had a good sense of rhythm; but with his bad leg it was impossible to tell. He kept lurching off onto his right foot and then checking abruptly to compensate; but she'd learned to follow his lead. The little lights flashed over her head and bathed them all in magic saffron and indigo hues; she saw Ben dancing with the Hanchett girl, their shoulders bouncing up and down as if they were stamping on a bed of stiff wire coils. She could feel the music entering her spirit like thunder, pounding in her blood.

"I've had too much champagne," she said, "and I don't care. It's wonderful . . ."

On the bandstand above her Long Tom Jethro was singing, his eyes closed, the trumpet dangling from his fingertips, a silver bauble:

> "Down in Voodooland
> Where the monkey-girls swing
> They do the buck-and-wing
> It's so ecstatic
> To go acrobatic
> In hop-hazy, palm-lazy, jazz-crazy Voodooland—!"

And then, his eyes still tightly shut, he raised the trumpet to his lips, and the melody showered around them like silver rain. Someone near shouted, "Hey!" and now the horn's bell dipped and swayed, blasting its clarion call over the thump and rumble of drums. She was reminded of parades, reviews, of bugles piercing the still dry air of morning.

"He means it, you know," she said aloud.

"Who's that?"

"Dex. He does. He'll get you that job, if you want."

He looked down at her—an expression that troubled her subtly. "You've got only one tiny little flaw."

"And that is?"

"You pay entirely too much attention to Lieutenant Poindexter."

"—How can I help it?" she cried. The nervousness swept back—an alien trembling somehow lodged in the marrow of her bones. "He's so attractive. You're all attractive, of course, but Dex is most of all."

"That isn't everything—"

"He wants me to share his fortunes. Fortune is correct, I suppose. How do you think I'd look as an Oyster Bay matron? Riding to hounds and our own sloop out in the Sound, and lovely, lush, lawn parties under the elms? It sounds so grand . . ."

"It wouldn't last," he said.

"Oh, really? And why wouldn't it?"

"He'd tire of you." She stared at him in angry amazement. "He would," he continued. "That kind of man is never content with one woman—you'll be barely settled in and he'll start looking around—"

"Well, I like that!" she exclaimed. She was furious; she was so mad she stopped dancing. Someone stepped on her foot and she cried, "Ouch!" and swore. "Of all the nerve—who do you think you are, telling me I can't hold a husband? You're insufferable!—and smug—just because you've been ordering troops around you think you can say anything you want. Now you can take that back, Sam Damon!"

"Wait, I didn't mean—"

"I know just what you meant! And you can take it back—right now . . ."

Up on the stand the Negro bandleader chanted:

> "It's so entrancing
> To keep on dancing
> In toe-tappy, skip-scrappy, jazz-happy Voodooland—!"

"I meant you—you'd be unhappy . . ."

They swung past the stand, the drummer caught her eye and winked, rapped out a thumping, shattering *rat-a-pa-kan, pa-kan!* and she laughed, dancing again; all the fury had gone out of her.

"Don't be mad," Sam was saying in her ear. "I take it all back. The whole thing. I didn't mean it that way."

"Oh, I can't stay angry at anybody for five minutes," she cried. "it's my Huguenot blood." She saw his face change, stiffen into a much older man's; remote and very hard. "What's the matter?"

"Nothing." His eyes were so sad! She had never seen such sadness in a person's eyes. "An—old friend of mine once said that. That same thing."

". . . I'm sorry." She looked off over his shoulder—at the drummer, at Ben, his beaked, bony face cracked open in its huge grin; at the red giant on the great blue wall. That was how life was—a tipsy juggler who caught some of the glittering objects and dropped others . . .

He had lurched against her badly; his face was taut and strained.

"You're ill," she said.

"No."

"It's your leg—it's hurting you." He nodded. "But this is absurd, Sam! You're such a bingo-bongo old masochist. Why on earth didn't you *say* so?"

He looked rueful. "Because then we'd have to go back to the table and listen to Poindexter."

"Dex is all right."

"Sure he is. But I want you all to myself."

"You can't always have everything you want. Even if you are one of the three most decorated men in the AEF.—This is silly," she said, after another minute. "Come on, let's go back to the table. Dex is such fun! I want to hear more about his—"

"—Don't marry him, Tommy," he said; the words seemed to burst out of him, as if he had been holding his breath for hours. "Don't marry him."

"Why not?"

"Marry me instead."

"You!" she cried mischievously over the band. "Why on earth you?"

"Because I love you, Tommy." They had stopped dancing again; he was holding her so hard it hurt. "A good heart, Tommy: a good heart is the sun and the moon . . . I want you to be my wife. Please say you'll marry me."

She made a swift little sound of distress—part gasp, part groan—and tossed her head. "Oh, damn!" she said.

"What's the matter?"

"I didn't want this to happen. I didn't, I didn't—"

"Why?"

"This shouldn't have happened—it's just cheap sympathy . . ."

His eyes were filled with alarm. He said, so quietly she could hardly hear him, "It can't be just that . . . you feel something for me, don't you? Don't you feel something?"

"—No," she stammered, "—for *me!* I meant for me!" She was in a turmoil; she realized she'd misunderstood him, that he'd meant himself, because of his wound—she could sense his relief in the changed pressure of his hand. At that instant she didn't know what she felt, beyond the weight of his insistence. He was so compelling! She was aware of nothing but his nearness, the pressure of his arm around her, the steady, importunate force behind him. She could feel herself sway toward him, body and soul, like some marine plant in a mighty tide . . .

"You're very sweet," she murmured, her eyes held to his. "A sweet, good man . . . A girl could fall in love with you, Sam."

His face became animate with joy. "Marry me, Tommy," he repeated. "Say you will. Marry me."

"Sam, I—"

There was a burst of applause behind them, doubled, redoubled—a pattering wave of handclapping. With a violent start she saw they were alone on the floor, the bandstand was empty, everyone was watching them . . .

"Come on back, children, all is forgiven," Poindexter called out.

"Sam," she whispered, "they're *looking*—"

He held her tightly. "Will you?" he breathed tensely, triumphantly. "Will you?"

"Oh God, you're trying to ruin my life," she wailed.

"What? No—"

"You'll stay on in the Army and become a fat, pompous idiot gushing regulations and pawing the lieutenants' wives at the Saturday night hops. I can just see you . . . oh, damn!"

They were suddenly bathed in amber light—it hurt her eyes. She tried to break away, and at the same moment a slight man in tails with a leathery face and pale golden eyes had tapped them both on the shoulder, was saying in French, a confidential stage whisper that carried into the far reaches of the room: "If I could just borrow a bit of the floor for a moment or two—you don't *mind* . . . ?" Laughter rang out, the piano was playing a strident little cabaret tune; all at once Tommy remembered the affiches on La Croisette and near the station. It was Claude Guétary. He still hadn't smiled.

"I'm sorry," Sam was saying in some confusion, "I didn't realize the—"

"Not at all. I know they'd far rather watch *you*. Don't go. Here—" he produced from nowhere at all a high, four-legged stool and perched on it, his legs crossed in rapt attention. "Go on with the scene and I'll coach. Fine. Go on. He's imploring you, begging you to give him one, just one more chance. Isn't he? But you've had enough, of course you have, life is too short to go on putting up with his infidelities and amours. Still, there he stands, looking so trusting, so noble, eh?—and you can't help but wonder, 'What is he made of, this fine, upstanding Yank officer? What are his dreams, what is his private life—what is he *really* like?' " Claude Guétary made her a deep bow. "And *that* is precisely why I am here, Mademoiselle—to show you what your man is made of. Alors, on verra, hein?"

And now he was moving around the bemused Sam, his hands darting, flowing, fluttering with a deceptive casualness, his dead-pan voice commenting on each discovery. From Sam's tunic pocket he drew a pair of black silk lace panties ("Now we're approaching the truth of the matter"), from an ear a dirty, battered piece of what looked like a military map of Africa, across whose face was scrawled in black crayon the single word *MERDE* ("No wonder it took you four years!"), from his blouse a blacksnake whip ("So that's how you treat your men, eh?—or is it your women?"), from his mouth a rubber hand grenade which he tossed to a nearby table amid shrieks and howls, from the other ear a marshal's baton festooned like a party favor with pink and blue ribbons ("You can dream, can't you?"). The club was in an uproar. Laughing, blinking in the yellow spotlight glare, Tommy could see Sam had adopted the role of straight man: he grinned, shrugged, gaped in amazement—and finally threw out his hands in a fleeting Charlie Chaplin plea . . . At that moment she knew she loved him. While the audience roared and squealed and Guétary produced in bewildering succession a brassière, a pistol, a baby chicken and a half-empty flask of Cognac, she reached up on tiptoe and kissed Sam on the cheek.

"I will," she said. "I'll marry you."

He gazed at her enraptured; he seemed scarcely aware of the litter of objects at his feet, the howling audience around him. "You will?" he said. "You will? You mean it?" She nodded. Sam bent over and whispered in Guétary's ear—a pantomimed message behind his hand. The magician's eyes glinted, he laughed soundlessly, reached deep into Sam's breeches pocket, twisting and squirming, while Sam twisted and squirmed back; drew forth a large ring on a white silk ribbon, slipped the ring through Sam's nose and handed the ribbon to Tommy, made some indecipherable signal to the pianist—and to the thunderous strains of a jazzed-up wedding march of Mendelssohn Claude Guétary bowed and handed the baton to Sam. "A consolation prize." And then to the crowd: "Ladies and gentlemen, an American hero and a good sport, Commandant Dai-mone—and his bride to be!"

They were borne back to their table on waves of congratulation and hilarity. Everyone was talking at once. Ben had grabbed Sam's hand and was pumping it up and down. "I knew it. I knew it!" he crowed. It had to happen, it just had to, didn't I tell you that? It's wonderful."

"You might congratulate *me*," she chided him. "After all, I'm the one who said yes . . ."

"When did all this happen?" Poindexter demanded.

"Just now."

"Just now—he proposed? *He* proposed to *you*—and *you* accepted?" She nodded at him happily. "Well, of all the suicidal moves—"

"Do I get to kiss her now, Sam?" Ben was saying. "Do I get to kiss the bride now?"

"Keep your shirt on, buddy." Sam had left the ring clamped to his nose, which gave him a barbaric, vaguely threatening air.

"Well—on account."

"On account of what?"

"On account of I'm so beaucoup zeegzag."

Poindexter was still looking at her reproachfully, shaking his head. "Felicitations," he said hollowly. "I hope you'll remember, when you're scrubbing his shirts in a tin tub at the bottom end of Agony Row, you had the world at your feet . . ."

"*I'm* placing the world at her feet," Sam retorted.

"You are so sentimental, Dex," Elise said with imperious ennui. "And so dishearteningly naïve. Why did you tell him you would make him a millionaire if you didn't want him to propose to her?"

"That offer is withdrawn," Poindexter barked, and drained his glass. "You can have the girl or the job, but not both."

"Too late!" Ben chortled.

"Don't be a bad loser," Sam said broadly. "Isn't that what they teach you at New Haven—to lose gracefully?"

"I flunked that course. And while drinking my champagne, too. Haven't you two *any* sense of propriety at all?"

"Dex," Tommy pleaded, "you wouldn't want me to ignore the calling of my heart, would you?"

"Calling of your heart—it's just all that damned tinsel and bric-à-brac. Tommy, I'm—I'm actually disappointed in you."

"I think it's delicious," Elise said in her indefinable accent. "Every woman should yield to every mood, every adventure—psychological, sexual, geographic—"

"—oceanic," Ben put in.

"Why not? I have lived with nine different men, and each experience was more exciting than the one that preceded it."

"Have you really, Elise?" Arlene Hanchett said eagerly. "Nine different men?"

The Empress sighed wearily. "You Americans. You are so circumscribed. Does one choose to eat boiled potatoes every day of one's life?"

"How about the Red Sea, baby?" Dex said.

"Yes." She turned her dense, smoky eyes on him and nodded. "Briefly. At Aqaba."

"Oh, well—if it was only briefly . . ."

Later they left the others and took an open carriage through the sleeping town, along La Croisette and out to Golfe Juan, where the pines made a crouching canopy, hissing in the sea wind. The air was fresh and cold in their faces and full of salt, and to Tommy the thop-clop of the horse's hoofs was indescribably merry. The stars too seemed very near. It was curious: a moment caught you up and you did something, took some action—and all the constellations of sensation and desire shifted. She had been lonely for so long; now, cast adrift at the end of this pitiless war she wanted with all her heart to be a part of someone, bound to someone indissolubly. Beyond the point they were night-fishing, the lights playing over the inky purple water, turning it, like one of Claude Guétary's sleights, into dazzling little patches of topaz and emerald. She huddled against the rough cloth of Sam's overcoat and turned her face up to his.

"Are you happy?"

"I've never been happier," he answered. "Truthfully. Never in my life . . . I feel I can lick the world with one hand." He squeezed her powerfully. "Oh, we're going to have a wonderful life, Tommy," he exulted. "Full of—oh, I don't know. Love, and all kinds of adventures. Castles and sultans and coral lagoons . . ."

"You've had too much champagne."

"Yes. But it isn't that. It's you. All I want is you."

She felt a stealthy fear—what if I should fail him?—followed swiftly by delight, and a passionate need to be loved, to be taken, invaded, and made complete.

"Oh kiss me," she murmured. "Kiss me. Now."

His lips were rough and warm, his arm forced the breath up into her throat; the world rocked and hummed around her, stars rained in white tumult down the Mediterranean sky. She was filled with a glad terror—she thought her heart would burst out of its shell.

"Oh Sam," she said, laughing at the thought even as she uttered it, "promise me it'll always be like this."

"I promise."

"Never any quarrels or misunderstandings . . ."

"Never a one."

"Good.—Poppa will be pleased," she said after a moment.

"I hope so."

"He will. He thinks the world of you."

"He's the finest American soldier in France. And you're the loveliest girl."

His lips were moving above her eyebrow, along the line of her cheek; she shivered in a tender agony of happiness and pressed against him.

"Are you cold?" he asked.

"No. No, I'm not cold."

Over at Nice across the water the lights glowed like a sprawled necklace of blue diamond brilliants, trivial below the stars; the waves washed timidly against the shore.

When she put her hand in his overcoat pocket to warm it she felt the little papier-mâché baton.

(III)
CHAPARRAL

{ 1 }

"We're a close-knit little community, you'll find," Edna Bowers said. With a blued, arthritic hand she smoothed the front of her print dress. "We have to be. Living out here on the Plains."

Desert is the word, Tommy Damon said to herself. Gobi Desert without end, amen. Carefully she poured tea from the cracked pot whose top was chipped so that the lid sat on it drunkenly, tilted toward the snout.

"Of course, ma'am," she said aloud. "I'd offer you lemon but I'm sorry to say we haven't any."

"Don't mention it, dear. If you haven't any you haven't any, and that's all there is to it." Edna Bowers was the wife of the regimental quartermaster. She was a thin, bony woman in her late forties, with pale gray-green eyes that were continually narrowing into a fierce squint; it was said she was very nearsighted and refused to be fitted for glasses. Originally she came from Idaho; but that had been a long time ago. Now she sipped at the tea, and her mouth quivered. "That's the strangest tea I ever tasted. Where'd you get it?"

"It's Darjeeling. A British officer in ordnance, a friend of my father's, gave some to us in Cannes. Sam's very fond of it."

"Oh. *Indian* tea. I might have known." She sipped at it again and her lips puckered, as if to burn this evil taste indelibly into her tongue. "Well"—she brightened, and set the cup down with a clack—"I know how it is on your first post. We started out at Sill. That was long before the New Post, of course. And the conditions were trying at times."

"Yes," Tommy murmured. "I can imagine." She pulled her blouse together—the buttons were too small for the buttonholes and it kept popping apart—and tried surreptitiously to tuck it into her skirt at the back. She had been gluing down the cracked and curling linoleum in the bathroom floor when the Major's wife had stopped by for what was obviously a friendly and prolonged little chat. She straightened her spine in the rickety rattan chair and tried to suppress her annoyance. "Yes, I remember, ma'am," she responded. "We were at Sill when I was nine."

"Were you?" Mrs. Major Bowers said. "Then you must recall some of it. We knew your father and mother at Kearney. You were just a baby then. Mrs. Caldwell." The faded eyes narrowed. "What was her first name?"

"Cora."

"Cora. Poor thing." The Major's wife sipped bitterly at the tea. "She

(251)

was always poorly. Tubercular, you know. They never last. She wasn't built for service life. She *tried* hard, of course. But George had his hands full, I can tell you."

"Yes, I know."

"The things that man put up with! Why, I remember Liza Courtiss told me when she was at Oglethorpe . . ."

Tommy inclined her head, an expression of pleasant inquiry frozen on her face. With the wives of rank you spoke softly, you smiled in agreement, you listened, and listened, and listened; and agreed. Even if what you were hearing happened to be a morass of lies and prejudices and misinformation. Mrs. Bowers was a busybody, and a gossip. There were even those who called her—privately—a mean old bitch; but she was the wife of a major. She—Tommy Damon—had been the wife of a major, too—not long ago: now he was only a first lieutenant, though very senior in grade. Whatever that proved. Her father had been a brigadier and was now a lieutenant colonel—though very *junior* in grade. She bit down on her lower lip. In civilian life you were demoted—fired or let go or transferred to the boondocks or put down in one way or another— if you were obviously incompetent, if you drank or were insubordinate or made grave mistakes, jeopardized the function of the firm. In the Army you were demoted for being ardent and competent and loyal: in short, for being a good soldier. Being a certain kind of good soldier was out of style now.

After Cannes, after Paris and New York and Trenton, Fort Hardee had been a rude shock. Following a confused three-day visit with Sam's family they had driven south from Nebraska across the endless, blowing prairies, the second-hand LaSalle Sam had insisted on buying in New Jersey, thus depleting their already meager savings ("We'll save money in the long run, honey—we'll beat train fare, and it'll give us mobility, you'll see"), jolting and shuddering in the corduroy ruts, mile after dusty mile. She remembered the country—she'd seen enough of it as a little girl—but even so she was unprepared for Fort Hardee. It lay in a sea of withered grass, its baked, barren parade ground flanked by ancient faded frame structures and the even more dilapidated enlisted men's barracks. A detail—it looked like two or three forlorn squads—was doing close-order drill in the middle of the field; their figures shimmered and wobbled. When they stopped at the main gate the heat closed around them like the breath from a brick kiln. Gasping she glanced at Sam, who was looking at her inquiringly.

"Are they tedious, your Great Plains?"

She made herself smile. Mustering a trace of her French accent she murmured, "But how enchanting to escape those cold, draughty salles at Vezelay! . . ."

"Good girl." He slapped her knee lightly in approval and put the car in gear. She sat very still in the heat, pulling her satin blouse away from her skin and fanning her face with a section of the Omaha *Herald*, while he reported in. He was gone a long time. Compose your soul in patience: her father's line. Had her mother gone through this? Probably. Undoubtedly. She got out of the car, but the early afternoon sun made her giddy, faintly sick to her stomach; rings began to form in front of her eyes, coiling out in red-and-black distending bands. She got back in the car again. The metal sill was too hot to touch. Four dejected figures in floppy hats and fatigues, with the big white P stenciled on their backs and trouser legs, staggered along carrying two huge cans, followed by an MP whose shirt was soaked through between the shoulder blades. She watched them sadly, filled with the old, remembered sympathy: punishment in the Army was so harsh, so final. Why should a man who had done wrong be made such an outcast? Well, presumably they knew what they were doing. Presumably. From far away there came the hollow, drawn out *whoooom* of something exploding, a sound premonitory and disquieting; she shifted in the seat and passed her wringing-wet handkerchief over her face. What in God's name was taking him so long?

When he did finally come out, however, he was smiling. "Twentyeight C," he said, elated. "I told you they'd have quarters. A real break. Fellow just transferred out."

". . . Before the war," she permitted herself to say, "the commanding officer used to come out and escort a newly arrived officer and his bride to their quarters on the post. Or if he was otherwise occupied the post adjutant did the honors."

"Oh, that—that was the *ooooold* Army," he chided her. He seemed positively gleeful and it filled her whole sweltering, suffering soul with resentment. "You'd ordered the band alerted, a regimental march past? Dreadfully sorry, old cock." He went into the British intonation he had picked up in Cannes. "CO has decided on a coronation ceremony instead. Westminster Ca—"

"Oh, shut up!" He glanced at her, startled. "I've been cooking out here in this *car*," she protested, "for hours and hours . . ."

"I'm sorry." He squeezed her arm. "Didn't mean no harm. It wasn't exactly empyrean in there, either; twiddling my thumbs. They weren't all that overjoyed to see me. Trouble is, they don't know what to do with me. They don't know what to do with everybody. There's too many of us, all of a sudden."

"Charming."

"Adjutant seems to feel the fields of glory have passed him by."

"And no wonder. The whole place looks right out of *Beau Geste*. You're quite sure we haven't got the wrong desert? You're sure this isn't the Sahara, and we only wanted the Painted one?"

"I guess it's no prize." Sweat had formed in a little bubble under his chin—he seemed oblivious of it and it irritated her. "Maybe it isn't as rugged as it looks. Let's go see what we drew."

They crept down the row, past the handsome old fieldstone building that undoubtedly was the commandant's, past the yellow homes of the field grades with their porches and brick walks; on down the row, the houses becoming progressively older and shabbier. She looked down at her fingernails and told herself, I will not be upset; I will not, no matter how disappointing it is, he needs the cheerful support of a loving wife and I am a loving wife; he needs—

"I guess this is it, honey."

She got out of the car without looking and followed him up the parched earth and into the building.

The sills were rotting. The walls were a hideous dirty caramel and the paint had been laid on too thick and carelessly, so that it had run down in buttery rivulets and built up on the molding in long shiny lumps and blotches. The floor had been shellacked a wild oak shade long ago, but now it had peeled; it was scuffed and scarred, and there were large brown water stains. In a far corner of the room stood a pair of officer's riding boots, their leather cracked; one boot had toppled over, and was split at the heel. In another corner there was a little cairn of beer bottles, old newspapers and stationery and discarded odds and ends of clothing.

"You're sure, Sam," she said. "You're quite sure these are our quarters?"

"Yep. Twenty-eight C," he repeated. "That's what the man said. Besides," and he gestured vaguely, "the place is—pretty empty."

She made no answer, merely hurried from room to room in growing consternation, her heels snapping on the worn bare floors. The bedroom was tiny and airless and was painted a violent shade of green. Everywhere paint was curling off the ceilings like lichen. The toilet had an overhead tank of blond oak, from which water dripped sullenly on the brown linoleum. The kitchen had a wood stove like a wounded black battleship; the sink was fearfully chipped, and leaning out from the wall uncertainly. One of the faucets was covered with a great dirty fist of adhesive tape and twine and it too was dripping. Two of the windows had broken panes. There was virtually no furniture: a chest of drawers, a chair with a broken back, a deal table in the kitchen, and that was all. Débris was everywhere—old clothes and playing cards and children's toys and magazines and shiny black bits of phonograph record; in a corner stood a ukulele with its neck broken and only one string.

"You'd think they could have hoed the place out," Sam was saying. "It certainly is in poor shape."

"Poor shape—!" she burst out. "It's a wreck! A shambles . . ." She glared at him. "Do they honestly expect two human beings to live in *this—*?"

"Well, if the—"

"Where's the furniture? the wherewithal?"

"Honey, look, you know they don't—"

"I don't mean Tabriz carpets or Louis Quinze escritoires, for God's sake, I mean the damn rudiments of existence!" Her voice was pitched too high, she knew it; she was ranting. Damn. Not three minutes in their first post together and she was shouting like a fishwife; but she couldn't help it. After the wedding in Paris, the months in Coblenz and the turbulent weeks in New York and Trenton, after all the festivities and hopes and bright resolves, this was too much, too much. "What kind of a lash-up *is* this, anyway?" she cried. "Is anyone really supposed to live here? or is it just a joke in rotten taste?"

"Sweet, they're converting . . ."

"Converting from what—from nomads to cave dwellers? I never saw such a filthy, battered pigsty in all my life! What did they *do* in here— drag anvils around? Look at the floors!" She caught her foot in a man's service shirt, a smelly mass of khaki rags—kicked it into a corner in petulant rage. "They specialize in demolitions here, do they? Well, they ought to start off by jamming a satchel charge under this pitiful piece of junk . . . !"

A screen door slammed nearby. She stopped, exasperated, outraged, maddened by the heat, the interminable drive across this drowsy, sweltering country, and now this abject wreck of a house that looked like a stage set for the last days of some drunken derelict, and not their first home together.

"Honey."

Sam was looking at her—that steady, affectionate, indomitable gaze, a touch rueful and apologetic. As though *he* were to blame! And she'd acted as though he were, too—what a fool. All of her melted with contrition. What a solace that gaze was: what an infinite solace and joy!

She walked over to him and put her head against the broad, solid swell of his chest. "I'm sorry, darling," she murmured. "I just got—sort of carried away . . ."

He held her comfortingly. "Sure, sweet. You're all tired out from the drive today. In the heat."

"Forgive me?" She turned her face up and closed her eyes. His cheek was damp and pleasant in its pressure.

"It's not too bad, you'll see," he went on. "I'll hop over to the QM right away and see what I can promote in the way of GI cots. And ammo boxes—they make great seats and tables, everything."

"Do they, darling?"

"Absolutely. I'll find out how soon they can get them over here. Then we'll get to work, see what needs fixing first. I've got some tools in the luggage rack, you know. We'll make out. It's not so bad."

He brought in the bags they'd been living out of on the drive west and stacked them in a relatively free corner, then left with the car. Tommy changed into jeans and shirt, found two cartons under the sink and began to dump the various mounds of refuse into them. Then she started in on the bedroom, sweeping and scrubbing in a mounting, self-generating little frenzy—an exertion that was only a prelude to what she would accomplish with Sam's help, over the next three weeks. So this was what they were allotted, was it? Very well, then. She narrowed her eyes and set her jaw. She would not lose control like that again. She thought of her father, and a moment when she had said, "I know one thing—if we once find a place to settle down and stay put I'll never complain again!" He had smiled at her gently and answered: "Can I depend on that?"

That had been during the wedding dinner—a horrifyingly sumptuous affair at Foyot's for the whole party George Caldwell had insisted on giving. He'd suggested a military wedding at the Regiment but she had put her foot down on that: she and Sam had met outside the orbit of Mars and they would be married that way. The dinner however was fun. Ben Krisler was there, and so were Harry Zimmerman and Walt Peters from Sam's old company, and Liz Mayhew and two other girls from the hospital at Neuilly. Ben read aloud a dreadful poem of his own composition bristling with fantastic predictions and warnings, Harry presented her with a silver bowl in behalf of the Battalion, Liz got quite sweet on Walt, and everyone drank lots of wine and became very merry. The haut monde French diners at the adjoining tables grew cold and disapproving—which made them still more irreverent. As Ben proclaimed, this was a historic occasion and they were going to celebrate it for all they were worth. And afterward they had got aboard one of the lovely old excursion barges and slipped down the Seine in the deep lemon light of early spring . . .

But now they were at Fort Hardee, where life was certainly real if it wasn't earnest. Sam got three cots that first day, two for the bedroom and one for the living room, and she made couch covers out of muslin she dyed a deep blue in the washtub. She dyed some condemned target cloth and made curtains of that. Sam got his ammunition boxes and in time she covered those; he repaired the sink and the stove and the front steps. She drove in to Hazlett and bought two chairs in a second-hand store, three Indian rugs and a brass floor lamp in the shape of a flamingo. They painted and mended and glued and sewed; they surprised each other with their skills, evoked each other's praise. The little backyard with its sunflowers drooping in the baked earth was hopeless, but she didn't care about that; for the time the interior was all that mattered. They made their courtesy calls and were called on in turn, and she could hold her head up; she had her feet under her now. The quarters were at least decent and fit to live in, even if they were worn and battered.

"—Most of them don't care a hoot or a holler," Mrs. Bowers was saying now, her lips tight with displeasure. "The Major was talking about it only the other day. They've been over in France, away from post discipline and living the life of Riley, and they all want to give themselves airs. It's a pity. There simply isn't the old esprit there was before the war."

"I suppose not, ma'am," Tommy said vaguely.

"*Suppose* not! My dear, you can take my word for it. Teach their grandmothers to suck eggs, some of them . . . Where've they assigned the Lieutenant, by the way?"

"The Lieutenant—oh, Sam," she answered, startled. "Oh, he's in C Company."

"Mmmmh." Edna Bowers paused. "Not the Point, is he?"

"No, he's not."

"Enlisted man, wasn't he?"

She looked directly at the gaunt, muscular face, the gray-green eyes. "Yes he was. He was awarded a battlefield commission, in France. The same day he won the Medal of Honor."

"Yes, the Major said he was a mustang," Mrs. Bowers went on as though Tommy had made no answer at all. "But myself, I didn't believe it. I said, 'Hiram, you must be in error. No girl of George Caldwell's would marry anyone who'd been in the ranks.' But I guess he was right, after all." She took another noisy, displeased sip of tea. "Well, it's a new Army and no mistake. They're taking all kinds now. The Major says it's impossible to keep to the old standards of excellence. It's a new world, now—an awfully funny one in some ways . . ." For an instant her eyes clouded with what might have been the merest flicker of fear; then it passed. "Well," she set down her cup, "we'll just have to make the most of it all, I guess." She gave a mirthless, brittle laugh. "This New Army!"

Tommy looked at the wall opposite her, the field where two children were running after a little white ball. God, she thought; why is it the mean ones who always go visiting—and why do they always pick *me?*

". . . I guess you're right, ma'am," she tried with her brightest smile. "Although actually, being an army brat myself—and Sam was in the Mexican Expedition with General Pershing in '16 . . . so I hope you'll forgive me if I feel we're more or less Old Army, in a sense, ourselves."

The Major's wife shot her a sharp, forbidding glance—rather startling in those faded, uncertain eyes—and again gave vent to that high little bark of a laugh. "Well you're not, my dear, and I can tell you that right off plain. Whatever gave you that idea?"

"Well, as I say—"

"Your father, yes. But not you two." A long, bony finger rose and fell in front of her like a siege gun being cranked. "You've got a lot to learn, Miss, and don't you forget it."

Tommy lowered her eyes and bit her lip. It was going to be more difficult than she'd thought. She'd tried to walk warily, put her best foot forward, enter into the vacuous ritual of food and clothes and the comparison of various posts at home and overseas—talk she found footless and depressing after the thunder of the past three years. But here she was, the wife of a junior officer on a hidebound army post in the heart of the Great Plains—and here was this odious gossip and martinet watching her with unconcealed disfavor. I rub people's fur the wrong way, she thought unhappily—it's the way I smile or phrase things.

"I'm sorry, Mrs. Bowers," she said. "I certainly didn't mean to say anything out of line . . ." She had got the words out, and surprised herself; and having said that, she was able to go on to say more. She could school herself to this: it would be hard, it would be unpleasant but she could do it. Anyone could do it. It only needed—well, a kind of discipline . . .

To divert the course of the conversation she rose and said, "May I show you our quarters? They're not very grand, but Sam and I can't help but feel pleased with all we've done with it—it was really in fearful condition when we reported in. The previous tenants must have been—" She suppressed the upsurging witticism—for all she knew the Jukes who'd defiled the place were bosom friends of the Bowers. She finished, "—a bit lax about things." Relieved to be on her feet and moving about, she led the older woman through the meager rooms, proudly showing her the curtains and pillows and rugs, the various repairs in ceilings and floors, the new work table and—her pride and joy—the kitchen cabinets Sam had made.

"Ummmh. Carpenter, was he? on the outside?"

"What? Oh no, ma'am, he's just very handy with tools."

Mrs. Bowers turned and faced her; she had the habit of certain spinsters of using her body rather than her hands when she moved, as though she wanted to push at people with her flat, hard breasts. "Well," she considered, and her tongue roamed in her cheek, "I can't for the life of me understand why you went to all this trouble with quarters, when you're going to be ranked out of them by the end of the week."

Tommy found she was gripping a chair back; she did not know what her face looked like. "Oh no!" she cried. "They wouldn't dare—!"

The Major's wife gave her little dry crow. "Wouldn't they! Just you wait, my girl."

"But it was a wreck—a complete wreck! We brought it back from nothing . . ."

But Edna Bowers was already clumping back through the living room to the front door. "That's the Army, my dear. I told you you had a lot to learn."

Tommy started to say something and bit it off; she was visited by a mountainous urge to lash out at this rawboned, vindictive figure, roaring threats and imprecations—an impulse that must have been revealed in her face, for the older woman's eyes shone with an irrepressible gleam of triumph; she laughed once more, wheeled and was gone.

"Mean old bitch," Tommy muttered savagely. She wiped the perspiration from her upper lip. A gust of air came in through the open windows, rattling the drawn shades, and that smell swam in her nostrils: an odor of brass and dried dung and parched grasses and burning.

By the time Sam came in she was half-wild with apprehension and thoughts of vengeance. "Is it true? Sam? Is it?"

He sighed and sat down on an ammunition box that passed for a bench, an end table, or a footstool, depending on one's needs of the moment. His face was burned red from the sun and wind and his eyes were narrowed with fatigue. He nodded simply. "She's right. Captain's coming in Friday. He rates it."

"Oh, no . . ."

"I wasn't going to tell you for a couple days more. We'll have to move out."

"After all this work . . . We've just fixed it up for someone else! Of all the cheap maneuvers . . ." Then, standing in the center of the room, it struck her like a dart—the next quarters they would move to would be still meaner and more disheveled than these had been, because it was further down the scale. If these were quarters a *captain* rated—

"Oh, my God," she groaned; the thought was almost more than she could bear. "Oh my good God." She clenched her fists and blinked to stop the tears of rage she could feel stinging her eyes. "Oh, it's so unfair!"

He shrugged unhappily. "That's the system."

"Which makes it all just fine, I suppose. What do we do now?"

"I'll hit the adjutant, see what's available. Something'll turn up."

"Yes, and I can just picture what it'll be, too—a cave in the side of a hill with a stone for a table and two smaller stones for matching chairs . . ." Her head went up. "Look, Sam. You rank all the lieutenants on this post, don't you?"

"I'm senior to all but one, I think."

"Well, let's rank one of them out." He shook his head. "Why not? This miserable captain's booting *you* out . . ."

"That's his privilege."

"All right—and it's your privilege to kick someone else out, the same way."

He took off his campaign hat and set it over his knee; right below the hairline his forehead was white along the sharp line of the hat, which gave him a ludicrous, surprised expression. "You want me to throw out the MacDonoughs with their three kids?"

"Well, why should it be us?"

"Because we're stuck with the detail, that's why."

"For heaven's sake, Sam!" There were times when his stubbornness exasperated her beyond measure. "That's no answer—give me five good reasons why we shouldn't do it."

"I just don't believe in doing things that way."

"I remember once at Tarleton when I was a kid a full colonel came in and everybody had to move out, all the way down the row, like dominoes . . ."

"My, *he* must have felt good."

"What difference does it make how he felt? It was his privilege . . .
You yourself just said it was the system."

He got up and faced her, his hands hanging at his sides. On his shirt
were half a dozen wavery lines, like tide marks, where the sweat had
dried; his breeches had a small tear at the knee. "I'm not defending
everything in the system," he said.

"I certainly hope not."

"There's plenty wrong with it. Plenty. If I'm ordered to abide by
some regulation I'll do it; but if I'm given any latitude I'm going to go
my own way. Go by what I think is right." Looking at her then, his face
softened. "Honey. I'm sorry. God knows I am. After all the work
you've done—the trouble you've gone to around here. But I can't see
the sense in adding to what I regard as a basically stupid, toplofty
practice."

"Toplofty—it's downright sadistic—"

"I know. I can't say I'm any happier about a lot of it than you are.
And maybe someday they'll work out a better one, but right now the only
thing to do is go along with it."

"All right. But I'll tell you one thing—we're going to take every stick
out of here, Sam. All the curtains and cabinets and furniture you built,
all the stuff we've got together."

He smiled grimly and stood up. "You bet your life," he said.

She nodded, watching the fine long slope of his shoulders, his slim
waist and legs; his limp was very slight now—he did exercises religiously
every morning and evening to build up the thigh and calf. She felt that
instinctive sway toward him—his needs, his moods, the stern, vigorous
cast of his mind; but hard on that came the swift little thrust of her own
ego.

"Sam," she said; and when he turned, "you're not *always* right, you
know . . ."

"I'm not?" He wiggled his eyebrows in disbelief. "Where did you get
that ridiculous, insubordinate idea? Drive it out of your head this
minute."

"All right," she laughed. And then more faintly: "All right . . ."

She stood in the middle of the room—that all at once, because someone had said three words, was no longer theirs. Across the parade
ground a bugle blew, its notes as sharp as if cut out of the bronze plate
of the afternoon sky. She felt she'd failed Sam obscurely, this afternoon
with the Major's wife. She could have found some way to charm her,
couldn't she? some way to have avoided that malignant bark of
triumph? No, it was probably impossible—nothing she could have done
would have made the slightest particle of difference. Sam was in the
bathroom now; she could hear the thin, dry roar of the shower on the
section of condemned tentage she had made into a curtain. He was
humming sonorously, a tune from the war:

"—no more van blonk or champagne,
I want the sun and the rain
Of my—home—town . . ."

He was singing: at a moment like this he could stand in that decrepit, antique tub with the rust-laden water slamming against the back of his neck, and sing. It was wonderful; it was horrible. Chafing her arm rapidly, staring at the drab yellow enlisted men's barracks across the parade ground she felt her eyes fill with tears, and she didn't know whether it was from love or anger or despondency. She just didn't know.

They worked quickly, setting the copper-jacketed half-pound blocks of TNT into place against the steel. The wind coming down the dry riverbed blew hot in their faces. When they were all in position Damon held a piece of board against them, and Corporal Campbell began passing the wooden chocks and wedges to Sergeant Torrey, who fitted them into place against the board and the flanges of the I-beam. Damon watched him, counting, thinking 12 inches times .35 inches equals 4.20 square inches, trying not to forget anything. He disliked demolition work. An army's job was to conserve, to maintain, not to destroy. Every time he worked on a problem like this one it seemed like such a loss, such a defeat. But it had to be learned.

Campbell had dropped one of the wooden blocks; he lunged for it, almost losing his balance, and cursed. Sergeant Torrey was glaring at him, and he glanced apprehensively at Damon. He was a tall, wiry man with good hands who had been a mechanic in France.

"Sorry—" he muttered.

"Take it easy," Damon said to him mildly. "Plenty of wood. And all the time in the world." This was not true, especially today, and they all knew it; but it sounded vaguely breezy and reassuring. While Torrey went on inserting the wedges he looked around. Corporal Wallace and his squad were strung out on the far side of the mock-up bridge—the side facing the mythically advancing enemy—prone over their rifles. Peering down through the girders he could see Howland sprawled by his Browning Automatic Rifle, his left arm locked over the stock right behind the rear sight, his chin pressed against his knuckles. What an ingenious idea, using that gas port to drive the piston, and then fitting the recoil spring in a tube in the stock. If they'd only had them in France, instead of that ugly, cranky, flimsy old Chauchat; if they'd only had them for the Meuse-Argonne drive—

He shut the thought out of his mind and checked the second squad on the near bank. It was going all right. By the book. Everyone was where he should be. Off in the shade of a thicket Captain Townsend was sitting on a rock, watching them through his binoculars. His mustaches looked like black streaks of paint against his cheeks; a bizarre continuation of the glasses.

Sergeant Torrey had finished with the wedges. Campbell passed the rope around the beam in a double strand, and Damon picked up the rack stick and tightened the rope until it vibrated and the chocks ground softly against the copper jackets. Compression. Compression was what made for blasting efficiency.

Torrey was cutting the end of the time fuse now. Damon took a detonating cap out of the box and shook it gently, blowing on it to clear any dust out of the open end. Torrey rolled the tip of the fuse between thumb and forefinger to make it neat and round, and Damon slipped the cap carefully over the end of the fuse, picked up the crimper and crimped the tetryl cap close to the open end. Campbell was watching them with an agonized absorption, his hazel eyes crinkled up, sweat streaking his face. Catching the Corporal's eye Damon winked once and grinned; Campbell swallowed and smiled palely. He is seeing it going off, Damon thought; the vivid yellow flash in our faces, the blinding, the burns. It was a mistake putting him on this detail; nobody with an unbridled imagination should do demolition work, no matter how capable he is manually. Some kind of psychological fitness exam ought to be given first. Was that possible? Sergeant Torrey on the other hand was fine for the job; the ex-miner from Denver was perfectly calm and unruffled, seeing nothing but what was before their eyes—an excellent initiator of detonation for other less sensitive explosives: 13.5 grains of tetryl and 7 grains of a mixture of 90 per cent fulminate of mercury and 10 per cent potassium chlorate, contained in a neat, shiny little cylinder. Nothing more.

"Let's hook her up," Damon said.

Torrey removed the cork from the center of one of the TNT blocks and inserted the cap into the hole. Campbell tied a piece of string around the fuse just above the cap, leaving enough play between the knot and the cap to protect it from any pull, and made it fast around the block.

"All right, boys," Damon murmured.

Campbell, with a look of wild gratitude, was already yanking himself up, his shoulders hunched like a monkey, to the shaky catwalk of the mock-up. Sergeant Torrey left more deliberately; slinging the field chest over his shoulders he swung himself up hand over hand, and set off at an easy, sure-footed walk. Damon waved to Wallace, a sweeping motion of his arm back to the near bank, and Wallace's men started back at ten-second intervals, their feet ringing on the slender iron, and began to drop into the ditch beside the second squad. Damon swiftly checked the tension in the rope, the set of the wedges and the priming of the center block, and looked around again—made a brief, peremptory gesture to Howland. The BAR man started back, running and then turning, simulating a covering fire of five rounds, then running again.

All right. Charge properly sited and primed, all men under cover, covering fire from friendly bank. Now the part he didn't like. Why in hell did they have to do it this way instead of with a blasting machine and electric caps? Because presumably there could one day be a rearguard action, a bridge to be blown where there would be no plunger or caps. *Ideally, the competent soldier seeks to prepare himself for every possible contingency* . . . He smiled, thinking of his father-in-law, the alert, twinkling eyes. But Colonel Caldwell was half a world away now, at Tientsin with the élite 15th Regiment, keeping watch on the marauding columns of Feng Yu-hsiang . . .

He picked up the fuse. He had cut it at two feet, and Torrey had snipped off about two inches in case of dampness and for a clean insertion. At a burning rate of 32 to 40 seconds to the foot that left a maximum of 76 seconds, a minimum of 59. You could get anywhere in one minute's time—you could make it halfway to Tientsin if you had enough TNT at your tail. With his penknife he split and opened the end of the fuse, took a kitchen match from his pocket and twisting away from the wind struck it and held it to the fuse. There was a dull glow, then a quick stuttering hiss as the flame started off along the wrapped cord. He glanced at his watch, straightened, swung himself up through the girders and ran back along the trembling catwalk, trying not to limp, trotted up the hard, rocky earth of the road, leaped into the culvert and crouched there. Some of the men in Wallace's squad were staring at him as if he'd just descended from heaven. He grinned at them, shook his head in the time-honored gesture and studied his watch, tensed mildly for the explosion. Forty seconds, fifty, sixty. The spindly little black hand swung on. Seventy, seventy-five . . .

He looked up. Sergeant Torrey was watching him questioningly. Minute and a half, now.

"What's the matter?" Campbell was saying. "Why didn't she go?"

"Misfire," he answered shortly. He raised his head and peered at the silly black-iron skeleton across the gulch, wondering what the trouble was. The fuse had been cut square, he'd inserted it well, they'd done—

"What seems to be the trouble, Lieutenant?" Captain Townsend appeared at the edge of the culvert. His right hand was held cupped in front of his belt; the glasses swung from their strap around his neck.

Damon bit his lip. He had that hilarious, defiant surge of reaction a man always feels on occasions of great preparation that come to nothing at all: the Christmas tree that fails to light up, the champagne cork that refuses to pop, the festive moment of departure, with the hosts lining the verandah, when the car won't start . . . What the hell did you expect, buddy—a flag salute? or a brass band? he wanted to shout. That deadpan old Claude Guétary would have had a field day with a moment like this.

"Apparently a misfire, Captain," he answered aloud.

"Apparently . . ." Captain Townsend was still staring down at him. He had a flat, broad face and his eyes were placed very close together, which gave him an irate, imperious expression. "Don't you *know?*"

Damon shook his head slowly. The Captain grunted; he still held his watch in his hand, a flat gold timepiece with Roman numerals for the hours. "Right—on—schedule," he pronounced. "And no blast. Very nice. Very edifying." He swung his arm up and down the ditch. "Enemy cavalry have by now cut every last one of you to pieces, of course." He had returned from the war with a British accent—why, no one knew, for he had been assigned to the railroad station at Bourges for the duration—and it became more pronounced now as he studied the bare black steel girders, chewing at his lower lip. "What did you use to light the fuse, Damon?" he asked idly.

Damon stared up at him. He knows perfectly well what I used, he thought irritably, he could see my back teeth with those glasses. "I used a match, Captain."

"Did you? And why did you use a match instead of a fuse lighter?"

"Because a match is surer."

Captain Townsend smiled. "Yes. I can see that." The smile faded. "You realize of course that the fuse lighter is an article of issue."

"Yes, sir. But it is one—"

"That's all, Damon. When I want further information from you I'll ask for it. Is that clear?"

"Yes, sir."

The fuse lighter was a paper tube whose open end was crimped to the time fuse. It had a ring fastened to a wire that extended down into some friction powder inside the tube. You were supposed to give the ring a quick tug, which would ignite the friction powder and so ignite the fuse. The only trouble with this complicated arrangement was that it didn't work very well or very often. On all time-fuse problems everyone used kitchen matches, which were a good deal more reliable, and everyone knew it.

This charge had failed to go off, however.

"Who cut the fuse?" the Captain asked.

"Sergeant Torrey, sir."

"Did you examine it?"

"Yes, I did. It was cut properly."

"I see. And who inserted it in the block?"

"Sergeant Torrey, Captain."

"And did you examine it?"

"Yes, sir. It was inserted correctly."

"And who crimped the fuse?"

"I did, Captain."

"Did you. And Sergeant Torrey examined *your* work, I suppose." Damon, growing angry, made no reply to this. The two squads were sprawled along the edge of the ditch, watching in silence. "You *feel—*"

Captain Townsend said slowly, the pause in itself an insult, "—that you crimped the fuse properly, Damon?"

"Yes, sir."

"Sir," Sergeant Torrey said, "would the Captain permit me to make a statement?"

Townsend shifted the close-set, irate gaze. "What is it, Sergeant?"

"Sir, Schoentag over in Number Three said those blocks hadn't been turned in a hell of a long while . . ."

"And of course you believed him."

"Well, sir, I . . ." Torrey trailed off, eyeing Damon furtively. A combat engineer in France with the Rainbow Division, he felt the Captain's displeasure—and something beyond that too, some heightened antipathy he did not understand.

"That remains to be seen." Townsend was standing a little apart from the men in the ditch. He had pocketed the gold watch and taken his swagger stick from under his left arm and was slapping it against his breeches, a rapid drumming: one-two-three-four, one-two-three-four. "Well, that's that," he observed. "Remove the charge," he ordered, and turned away.

Damon felt his jaw drop; he watched the Captain's broad back, the swagger stick drumming against the whipcord. It sounded like someone beating a rug a long distance away. Sergeant Torrey's face held the same cold amazement he imagined his own must be showing. No one in the culvert had moved.

Captain Townsend stopped and turned around. "*Did* you hear what I said, Lieutenant?" he demanded.

"Yes, sir," Damon answered.

"Very well: what are you waiting for?" The two men stared hard at each other for a moment; then, "Remove the primer, Sergeant," Townsend said crisply to Torrey. "Lieutenant Damon seems incapable of action for the moment."

Damon clamped his mouth shut. This was impossible. Clearly and thoroughly impossible—and yet here it was: happening. Sergeant Torrey's eyes rolled around to Damon's—a smoldering disgust touched with that wary uncertainty. Then with enormous reluctance he climbed out of the ditch and started down toward the bridge. His heels struck little bursts of dust in the road.

Damon jumped to the top of the culvert. It was incredible how far away Torrey had got in those few seconds. "Sergeant!" he called.

Torrey turned with alacrity. "Lieutenant?"

"Disregard that order. Come back here . . ." Townsend had stopped again and was watching him. "On the double!" Damon shouted.

"Yes sir!" Torrey came back up the little rise at a dogtrot. Damon motioned him back into the ditch with a nod of his head and turned to face Townsend, whose approach seemed as dilatory as the Sergeant's movement toward the bridge had been brief. There was a kind of reluctance in the man's walk, as though he wanted to prolong this moment as much as possible, not out of fear but its opposite—some furtive, extraordinary pleasure it gave him. Damon closed his hand and opened it again; his heart was beating solidly, rather thickly, and it irritated him. Watching the Captain draw nearer, his bootheels scraping on the stones, it seemed to him he'd been granted some strange prevision of this moment: he and Townsend facing each other in silence under a vast white sky. From the first morning he had reported for duty he'd had the sense that a line had been drawn. Townsend had studied him from the chair behind his desk: the thin, rather dreamy smile and those closely spaced blue eyes that fastened on him almost eagerly, alight with some unfathomable pleasure. There had been some small talk and then Townsend had said, "Did you enjoy yourself on the Riviera, Damon?"

Just the question in that odd British accent; and the faint smile that disconcerting gaze belied. Damon had glanced at him, and then grinned—perhaps the man was awkward socially, perhaps it was a nervous affliction, perhaps he himself was imagining things—and said: "Yes, sir—hugely. As a matter of fact I met my wife there."

"Did you? I rather thought it had been earlier."

"No, sir—Tommy wouldn't have looked at me earlier!" But Townsend did not smile at all, much less chuckle, and his heart sank. The man had no sense of humor: it was going to be a long tour.

"I guess it must have been quite a lark," Townsend was saying; it was the first time Damon had seen that irate, incredulous glare. He thought with a rude little shock: Why, the man doesn't like me! He doesn't like me at all . . .

He said quietly: "I was sent to Cannes on convalescent leave, Captain."

But Townsend had got to his feet and was glaring at a section drawing on the wall of a steel truss bridge wired for demolition. "I'm afraid you won't find it much like the Riviera here, Damon." His voice was level, but there was a curious little current of tension running along its under edge. "No tales of glory around the glowing fireside, no singing of grand old refrains, no ceremonies and awards on Thursday afternoons . . ." Ah, that's it, Sam thought. He said nothing. "We are concerned with the practical things, the bread-and-butter side of warfare. The things that, ultimately, turn out to be the most important ones." He turned and faced Damon again, and now there wasn't even the trace of a smile on the flat, heavy-jawed face; the British intonation, too, had faded. "Explosives and demolitions are an exact science, to be computed exactly and rapidly. There is a great deal to learn, and it must be mastered in its entirety. I shall expect attention to the most minute detail, and immediate responses. Not quick, not prompt—immediate. Do I make myself clear?"

Now the Captain had reached him. His eyes were wide and baleful;

they looked almost white in the flat, dusty light. In a thin, hoarse voice he said: "Lieutenant, I gave that man an order."

"I am in charge of this detail, Captain."

Townsend's body gave a curious little tremor. He raised the swagger stick as though to salute with it, then began drumming on his breeches leg with it again. The rest of the detail were staring at them like men in a trance. Damon thought, If through some immense mistake on the part of fate I ever become Chief of Staff I personally am going to break every God damned swagger stick in the American Army over the head of every God damned officer carrying one.

"Damon," Townsend said tensely, "—I order you to remove that charge!"

"Sir, I refuse to carry out that order."

Townsend took out his watch and studied its face. A muscle in his fleshy cheek flickered once above the wing of the mustache. "I will give you that order once more, and you will have one hundred and twenty seconds to carry it out. Exactly—"

Lowering his voice, Damon said as rapidly as he could: "Captain, you know very well in the event of a misfire a blasting detail should wait a minimum of thirty minutes before even—"

"That's enough!" Townsend shouted. His head shook and he jerked at the brim of his hat. "Now let me get this straight, Damon. For the record. I have given you a direct order in connection with a blasting problem and you have refused to execute that order—repeatedly refused. Is that correct?"

"Captain, a misfire such—"

"*Is that correct!*" Townsend screamed.

Damon gripped his belt with both hands. It was fantastic. Stupid and murderous and fantastic. What sense was there in staying up till all hours with a wet towel wrapped around one's head studying the Vertical Radius of Rupture and overcharged craters and the combustible properties of trinitrotoluene, committing to memory $N = R^3KC + 10$ for breaching charges and $N = \dfrac{D^2}{20}$ for shattering charges for timber— what good was all that arduous and unpleasant effort if some Anglophiliac idiot with a swagger stick and an untraceable thirst for vengeance couldn't even remember the primary precaution for a time-fuse misfire?

But Townsend knew: of course he knew. His lips were working under the flaring cavalryman's mustache, and his features were marked with an almost desperate eagerness. The rest of the detail were watching in awed fascination, all except Sergeant Torrey, who had turned his back to this pleasant little scene.

But to read a man off in front of troops—!

"Yes, sir," he said evenly. "That is correct."

"Good." Townsend's lips closed neatly; yet he seemed at the same time curiously disappointed. "Good. We understand each other. You admit, then, to direct disobedience of orders in the execution of an important training exercise."

"Captain, it's not—"

"*Do* you? Answer me!"

"Yes, sir."

A figure jumped up and scrambled out of the ditch: Conte, a young soldier on his first hitch, with silky black hair and a gypsy face. "I'll go unhook the thing, Lieutenant." He waved a hand. "What the hell—I don't mind." He started off down the road.

"Conte, stay where you are," Damon called.

"It's all right. Won't take a minute. I ain't scared to tackle it—"

"I said come back here!" Damon roared; the boy stopped in the middle of the road, his rifle hanging across his thighs, uncertain. Damon cursed; he realized the boy had offered out of some half-formed idea of absolving him, removing the obstacle to this ugly impasse. Glancing at Townsend he saw the Captain had already realized the boy's motive and decided to misinterpret it for his own purposes. Townsend's eyes were glittering now with malignant delight.

"You see?—even that boy's willing to do it, Damon."

"It's not a question of whether he's willing or not."

"Isn't it?"

"No. It's a matter of common sense."

Townsend smiled the slow, almost dreamy smile. "I do believe you're a bit windy, Damon," he said in his crispest British intonation. "Can it be that you're a bit windy?"

"Sure, I'm afraid. Any man with any brains would be."

Townsend nodded several times slowly, as if this confirmed everything he had known. "And they said you were such a tough hombre. A killer."

"I refuse to risk anybody's ass for no reason at all, I'll tell you that . . ."

"Interesting." The swagger stick went rat-a-pa-*kan*, rat-a-pa-*kan* against the flare of his breeches. "Do you know what I think, Damon?" the Captain asked, in a husky whisper. "I think you're a four-flusher. A great, big, enormous fraud."

Damon brought his teeth together. After Soissons and Malsainterre and Mont Noir and all those months lying on his back at Angers, after all the graves among the newly mown wheat, the ardor and remorse and desolation of spirit—after all that to have to stand here on the edge of a dusty ditch and take this kind of abuse from a criminally irresponsible, vindictive son of a bitch like Townsend was hard to bear. Very hard to bear. Sergeant Torrey had walked twenty feet down the culvert and was standing with his back to the officers. On the road near the bridge young Conte was swinging his rifle idly and digging a hole in the packed dirt with the toe of his shoe.

"A fraud," Captain Townsend repeated with soft, implacable tones. "You're not fooling anybody, Damon. Not a blessed soul. All those medals—and with a mail-order brigadier for a father-in-law. What could be easier?"

Sam gripped his hands together and gave back a step. He wants that, the thought pierced his rage. He wants you to tell him off, hit him, lay him out—he wants that more than anything else in this world: then he'll have you where he wants you. Yes, and then he'll send Torrey—whom he doesn't like, either—to defuse the charge . . .

"Well, Damon. Haven't you got anything to say? Eh?"

You son of a bitch: you gutless, pitiful, homicidal son of a bitch. He shifted his feet and looked steadily at Townsend. "Perhaps the Captain is right," he answered in his most toneless voice.

It was as if he had released a spring. Townsend reared back and thrashed the swagger stick against his legs. "All right!" he shouted, gesticulating. "You're in arrest! I'm placing you in arrest for direct disobedience of orders. You are confined to quarters until further notice. Is that clear?"

"Yes, sir."

"Good! Now, take off." Damon made no move to go. "Did you hear what I said—! I told you to move out . . ."

"Very good, sir." He faced the culvert and called: "Dee-taillll . . . fall in!"

Townsend cried, "You have no authority—"

"I'm taking my men back to camp," Damon cut him off hotly. "That charge should not be touched for thirty minutes to three hours, and you know it and I know it and so does everybody else . . ."

Townsend's face was white. "Stay where you are, you people!" They paused, then came on up out of the ditch in groups of two and three at Torrey's urging. "Damon, I'm warning you!" Townsend shouted hoarsely. "If you march these men back from here—if you try to take—"

The explosion seemed to leap into being from inside Damon's head, so unprepared was he—an absurdly vast crepitation like the end of all worlds, that echoed and reechoed along the rocky bed of the ravine. Damon had just time to think with astonishing lucidity *open-hearth steel tears and may throw fragments in any direction*—then he had screamed *"Take-cover!"*—gripped the man nearest him around the shoulders and dragged him to earth beside him. In the next instant the concussion rolled up in a hot, tight wave and shook them like a great dog, and the earth quivered; and there came the whir and whine of steel fragments pattering down in a ragged shower. He raised his head. Voisselle, the boy he had pulled down, was gazing at him round-eyed.

"You all right?" he asked.

"Yes, sir," Voisselle said, a little breathless. "I guess so."

Damon jumped to his feet. Half of Wallace's squad, led by Sergeant

Torrey, had dived back into the ditch; they were getting up now in a clumsy tangle, like the survivors of some wild, drunken brawl. "All right?" he called. "Everybody all right?"

Someone was shouting. He turned. Conte, sitting in the middle of the road like a child, his feet out straight, both hands clamped to his neck. "*Ow—ow—ow!*" he yelled. Damon ran down the road. As he got near the boy stopped crying and squinted up at him fearfully. He knelt down and said, "Take your hands away."

"I can't," Conte said.

"Of course you can. You want them to grow that way? Come on." He pulled away his fingers: the old sight of torn flesh, milk-white around the lips of the wound, blood oozing down in a rich silky pattern. "Not bad," he said. "Easy one."

"What happened?" Conte said. He was panting as if he'd run a hard hundred yards, and his voice was dry and shrill. "What—happened?"

"Charge went off. A little behind schedule." He plucked open the snaps on Conte's medical pouch—pulled out a pack of cigarettes, two packs of gum, and several gumdrops congealed into a sticky little mass. "For Christ sake, Conte," he said irritably. "What kind of a soldier are you, anyway?"

Conte said, "*I* don't know," in a faint yet querulous tone that made him want to laugh. Damon got a compress out of his own packet and tied the tapes around the boy's neck. Suddenly he felt light-headed, almost frivolous; the savage anger had vanished with the blast.

"Why didn't you throw yourself on the ground and cover your head and neck with your arms, the way you've been taught?" he asked.

"I . . . forgot."

"You were lucky."

"*Lucky*—!"

"Sure you were. Look at that son of a bitch over there." He pointed to a jagged splinter the size of a table knife lying six or seven feet away. "That one could have got you here"—he pressed the rich black hair at the base of the boy's skull—"or here." He touched the shoulder blade just over the lung.

Conte shivered and said: "I never saw it."

"Of course not. You never do."

"Jesus . . ." The boy turned with the slow, fearsome care of an invalid and looked at the bridge, where girders curled back from a void in warped and blackened ribbons. "I didn't know *that* would happen," he protested, pointing at the splinter.

"What did you think would happen?"

"Well—I thought it would all just—disappear . . ."

"Nothing disappears. Or very little, anyway. Things turn into other things, but they go somewhere, they have to go somewhere . . ." Damon realized he was talking too much and took a deep breath. "There. This'll fix you up till we get back."

"It—hurts," Conte said.

"I imagine so." The others had come up and were standing around, pleased at this diversion.

Sergeant Torrey said, "He all right, Lieutenant?"

"Sure. It's light. Come on, Conte. Get up."

Conte looked at them all doubtfully. "I don't know as I should."

"What? Don't be stupid," Torrey said. "Get up, Conte."

Everyone was talking at once, milling around.

"Did you see it blow?" Campbell said nervously. "All that stuff flying every which way—it's a wonder we weren't all killed . . ."

"What happened?"

"Hangfire."

"Hangfire . . ."

"Jesus, Sarge, and you'd have been right up there trying to pull that fuse!" Campbell went on, his thin face a mask of apprehension. "You'd have been straddling that frigging I-beam, right about then . . ."

"Miss is as good as a mile," the Sergeant answered, and shrugged; but he threw Damon a long, enigmatic glance.

"What about me?" Conte protested. "Where do you think I'd be?"

"Oh-oh," Torrey muttered. "Here comes old Hangfire," and the talk died away.

Captain Townsend came up to them. His hat had been knocked off his head and he was carrying it in one hand. Something had bumped him in the nose—probably his field glasses, when he fell or threw himself flat—and one nostril was bleeding lightly, the blood soaking into his mustache. "Lieutenant Damon," he said, and cleared his throat.

"Yes?"

"We—the exercise is concluded." He gazed at the wrecked bridge, dabbing at the nostril with his little finger. "You may march the detail back to barracks."

"Whatever you say." He hadn't felt such loathing for a man since he'd seen Benoît-Guesclin at the review at Bombon.

"Damon . . . you are not to consider yourself in arrest. You are not confined to quarters."

The Lieutenant took a cigarette out of his pocket and lighted it, watching Townsend narrowly. "May I ask why, Captain?"

"Because I have rescinded that order, that is why." And the thin, distant smile crept back into the Captain's face.

"Many thanks, Captain, but I'd prefer it to ride as it stands."

Townsend made no answer; he turned to the group. "Men!" he said sharply. "This has been an exercise, a problem in demolitions like any other, and you will so regard it." He ran his eyes over the detail; he could see the hatred and contempt in their massed gaze, and perhaps a few minutes ago, shaken by the blast, he would have been vulnerable to it. But he had armed himself again in his supercilious British manner and his animosity, and he was determined to have his way. "You are advised

to overlook what you may or may not have overheard here this afternoon. The problem is completed, and the incident is closed. That is all."
He walked away quickly, patting a clean white handkerchief to his
nose.

"The son of a bitch," Sergeant Torrey muttered. "The sneaky, un-
derhanded, chicken-shit son of a bitch."

"Don't let me hear you using language like that about a commissioned
officer," Damon said; he smiled. "I can't hear you."

"The bastard didn't even apologize . . ."

"Why should he? No future in that."

He ordered the detail to fall in and they started back to the South
Gate. Torrey gave them route step and dropped back to Damon.

"What the hell, Lieutenant," he muttered. "Maybe it's all for the
best."

"Maybe." He smiled wearily, following the Sergeant's thought. "But
what about Conte? Why should I take the rap for not having my men
properly under cover?—especially when it isn't even true? Should a
murdering son of a bitch like Hangfire"—he knew Torrey's sobriquet
would stick now, no matter what came of it—"feel free to pull something like this any afternoon he feels the urge?"

"Sure, Lieutenant—but if you insist on standing charges and demand a
court there'll be a stink that'll blow all the way to the AG's office in DC.
And where'll it get you? They'll back each other up and all you'll have
is a lot of trouble in your 201 file." He was silent for a moment. "I hope
I'm not sticking my neck out too far, sir."

Damon shook his head. "No, that's the way my mind was running."
He felt sore and defeated; the garrulous release following the blast had
receded, leaving him beached on the shoals of despondency. Torrey was
right: after the hangfire Townsend had realized that his plan to provoke
him had failed; now he wanted it all dropped and forgotten. If he,
Damon, were to force it to a court-martial it would set the post in an
uproar—and it wouldn't stop there, either. And the rank would probably look out for their own, and he would pick himself up a fistful of
trouble; he'd be known as a trouble maker, an agitator . . .

But did you let something like this roll on by? What about the next
officer Townsend took a savage dislike to, and the next? In France he
would have laid the son of a bitch out, and welcomed the consequences;
had his wound, the reduction in rank, the months here at Hardee sapped
his capacity for acting clearly and vigorously, doing what he thought
was right? or was acquiescence the wiser course? Of course, nothing
much *had* happened, Conte's injury was slight—maybe Townsend's
hatred for him was a unique and isolated thing . . . He sighed, and
watched the detail stomping along in the dust.

"Lieutenant," Torrey said.

"Yes?"

"Whatever you decide to do, I want you to know I'll go right down the line for you. All the way. And so will every man here."

He glanced at the Sergeant gratefully. "Thanks, Torrey," he said. "I'll remember that." He sighed again, kicking at a clod of earth. "Maybe it's just as well to let the whole lousy business blow over."

Torrey grinned his slow, contained grin. "For the good of the service."

"Yeah. For the good of the service."

The dust blew away from their feet in a sun-drenched ocher cloud.

(2)

She heard his steps on the back stoop, the thump of the screen door, then silence. Another day, another dollar. She lay motionless, unsmiling, on the narrow issue cot; her body felt thick and alien and vaguely repellent. The heat pressed against her like a hand; the army blankets she'd hung up sopping wet in the windows at noon were already dry, their corners flicking idly.

Usually he would call out something jocular, like "Hello, countess!" or "View halloo, sugar-doll!" and then the door of the icebox would bump somberly as he got himself a bottle of root beer, which he loved. But today she heard none of these sounds, and it disturbed her: it mingled with the peeling paint, the gaunt, bleak absurdity of the ammunition boxes and crates and issue chairs. They had moved down the row, to a dwelling as dilapidated as the first: this one had been policed and the floors were better, but the plumbing was worse and there was something wrong with the wiring—the naked overhead bulbs would flicker, or go out abruptly and come on again with a sickly apricot glow. Sam fiddled endlessly with the wall switches, without success; it was somewhere in the walls, a faulty connection or crossed wire, maybe; something was wrong. This time there was no wild dismay, but neither was there the angry determination that had carried her through the weeks of scraping and mending. They moved in the curtains and furniture they had made, and for a while she tried fitfully to repair and restore; but the fire had gone out of her. Where was the incentive, when any moment that crocodile of a post adjutant could say three words and they'd be ranked out again? Sam assured her it wouldn't happen, but she was never certain. The weeks crawled their dreary way into months, the winter slipped bleakly by, and in the spring she'd become pregnant.

There were still none of the familiar sounds. He was probably sitting in the living room on a serape-draped ammo box, hunched over, elbows on his knees: a pose she'd once told him was distressingly proletarian. He'd grinned at her and adopted a simpering, effeminate attitude, one knee over the other, elbow in palm, fingers curled delicately—"This more what you had in mind? Oscar Wilde?"—but he hadn't changed his way of sitting, except when they were paying or receiving calls . . . He was sitting there, his brow creased, now and then rubbing his jaw with his knuckles. Something had gone wrong: the thought sank into her soul like a bar of iron descending through water, fathoms on fathoms down. I must be a good wife to him, a dutiful wife, she told herself with virtuous rigor; give him the affection and support he needs . . . But the thought lay on the surface of her mind, oil on glass. Now, in this second sweltering summer at Fort Hardee, she could only put her hands on her swelling belly and knead it gently, this sack that had been grafted on her by some malicious sorcery; lie there sweating in her slip, feeling gross and unattractive and slightly sick, bereft of energy . . .

She closed her eyes, in derelict fancy dreamed of soft green river-banks, of sheltered coves bordered with stands of cedar, of a large white house, gabled and porticoed, that gave on smooth flagstone terraces under the shaded rustle of the maple trees, and sweeping green lawns, and the carefree laughter of old friends. She was swimming in the cove, she was rolling indolently in the damp, furry grass, she was talking animatedly to three handsome men in blazers and white flannels who had just returned from Taormina, Damascus and Algiers (she was going there herself in a few months or so), they were all of them sipping at Tom Collinses, tart and ice cold under the shimmering celadon canopy of the leaves; and later there would be—

Sam came into the bedroom: that quick, lively stride, without even the trace of a limp now. He had overcome it completely, performing the exercises Doc Terwilliger had given him, doubling and redoubling them with a conscientious rigor she'd found she resented almost as much as she admired. Of all the wounded men he was the Tweaker's star pupil, a glowing object lesson to the wayward and dilatory saddled with adhesions and cramps and poor articulation . . . the way I'd have been, she thought, if I'd been wounded: lazy—full of self-pity.

"Hello," she murmured, to let him know she was awake.

"Hello, sugar."

She raised her head and opened her eyes and smiled at him, thinking, I wish we hadn't quarreled last night, that was silly, it was my fault as much as his—probably more. But his back was turned toward her now; he was taking off his shirt, which looked black with sweat in the olive gloom cast by the blankets. The tan line ran along his collar cleanly; then there was another one, even sharper, a meniscus above his shoulder blades made by his undershirt. He hung his belt up on one of the hooks

C H A P A R R A L (275)

on the side of the closet. You could read his life from the clothes and equipment on the hooks and pegs: the inspections, the close-order drill, the field problems and OD duty, the practice with the company ball team after hours, the infrequent post hops. And yet it was hard to imagine, too—that curious, blunt, inarticulated language of men.

Guiltily, a little defiantly, she watched him remove his leather puttees. He absolutely refused to wear riding boots, and once when she'd remarked on it she'd been surprised at the vehemence of his answer.

"Because it's a rotten symbol of caste, that's why. Like this damn Sam Browne belt. They're as obsolete and silly as a halberd. Their only function is to set the officers and enlisted men still farther apart."

She'd grinned mischievously. "Poppa wears them."

But he refused to joke about it. "He didn't in the line, I can tell you that. Besides, your father's an inveterate rider. He's seen cavalry duty, and he was brought up in the old school."

"Oh, you're so stubborn, Sam," she'd protested. "Can't you see?— boots look so much more—so much more comme il faut."

"Dashing, you mean."

"All right then, dashing! What's wrong with that? What's wrong with trying to enliven the old penal colony a bit? Should I wear a blanky-fluking Mother Hubbard because poor Mrs. Schooner wears one over on Soapsuds Row?"

"When they become articles of issue to the enlisted men I'll wear them," he'd replied firmly. "And not until." They'd had two subsequent discussions on the subject but he would not give in; he kept his good pair shined to a terrifying luster; but they were still puttees buckled over shoes . . .

He was standing on his head, his feet braced against the wall; while she watched, thrilled and irritated, he lowered himself onto his neck, his legs flexed—then with a sudden, powerful thrust snapped himself up onto his feet.

"—God, you're so *energetic*," she groaned.

"No, I'm not." He was doing bicycles now, chin doubled against his chest, legs in the air churning soundlessly. "I'm tired as all get-out."

"Then what do you *do* it all for, then?"

"Only way to keep in shape. Eternal diligence—is the price—of agility . . ."

She sighed crossly, and flopped over on her side. There were times when his eternal diligence was enough to drive her out of her mind. He made her chafe with remorse. She ought to be up and about, demure and enticing in a blouse and skirt, offering a cooling drink, a motor trip, her love—what on earth was the matter with her? She was bound here, a lump of swollen flesh, on this sagging, dreary cot. Why couldn't the Army give its married couples a double bed? was that too damned much to ask?

He was watching her with concern now; he came over and sat on the edge of her cot. "How are you feeling, honey?"

"Oh—thick and greasy and thoroughly unappealing." She smiled wryly. "I can't bear the sight of food, I guess it's the heat. And then I'm swept with visions of coquilles St. Jacques—remember the coquilles St. Jacques at Chez Félix?—or water chestnuts or truite aux amandes or caviar or God knows what loony delicacies I have or haven't eaten. And then next minute I feel revolted at the very thought of it. I ought to have been born a satrap or a padishah or something, and then I could have a horde of little Nubians offering me things and I could kick them or kiss them, depending on my mood . . ." She broke off; she sounded like a hysterical spinster—one of those fierce, narrow women, popeyed and with corded throats, she had feared all through her childhood. She'd better get herself in hand. "I'm sorry about last night," she murmured. "I really am, darling."

"So am I," he said. "I ought to have had more sense."

"No, it was my fault, I know it was. I can't seem to get *caught up* with myself . . ."

"What do you mean?"

"I don't know." She chafed her neck. "I keep feeling if I could have two weeks—just two weeks in which nothing at all was going to happen—I could get rested up and ahead of the house and feeling chipper again. But instead it's the other way round, time's going faster than I am—and pretty soon I'll be a month behind, and then two . . . Silly, isn't it?"

"Poor honey-lamb." His rough hand passed over her forehead and back through her hair. "It's no fun at all, is it?"

"No. It's no fun . . . I guess I thought it would be. You know—the way they put it in the soupy junk impressionable romantic young girls always read: *and with the magic passage of the months her tread grew heavier, her eyes soft with the tender thrill of promise.* Baloney. You want to yerk all morning long and your feet hurt and you feel like a damn penguin."

"I know . . . I wish I could get you away somewhere."

"Wouldn't that be nice? Waikiki, or Como, or maybe I could swim in the Arctic Circle, like that sexy Elise dame. God, I'd like to *shiver* for about ten minutes steady. You know what I did this afternoon?"

"What?"

"I put on that cotton dressing gown of yours and took a cold shower and lay down here wringing wet."

He looked alarmed and took her hand in both of his. "Honey, you shouldn't have done that—it's dangerous . . ."

"Nonsense. I was completely dry in twelve minutes. By my watch. Anyway, it amused me for a while." She took a deep breath and said: "Well. And what kind of a day did *you* have?"

"So-so." He put his hands together and began to pick at the edge of his thumb, another habit she felt was proletarian although she hadn't told him so. "Actually, we got some unpleasant news."

"Oh?" She felt bound in a kind of soft panic. What now? she wailed inwardly. What new indignity, imposition, betrayal—what new sacrifice have they decided to ask of us? She forced herself to lie perfectly still.

"There's been another reduction."

"What do you mean?"

"Congress. They've cut the authorized strength again." He put a cigarette between his lips and left it there unlighted. "By one hundred twenty thousand men, five hundred officers. All promotions stopped."

She stared at him. For the merest second she didn't know what to feel—elation or wrath or despair. She studied his face, which didn't seem to tell her anything. "What are you going to do?" she asked after a pause.

"Nothing much I *can* do, sweet. That's what the country wants, I guess: no more foreign entanglements, no more armies, no more taxes— no more nothing but rumble seats and bootleg gin and business as usual."

"—But you can't *stay in*," she burst out.

His expression was merely inquiring, mildly surprised. "Why not?"

"Because what's the *sense* in it if there's no future for you here . . ." She heaved herself to her feet—she had never been able to think clearly lying down—and began tramping around the airless little room, her hands at her belly. "You'll be dropped, won't you?"

"Not unless I resign. Pete Lovewell's going to—he's so mad he won't even talk about it."

"I should think so. What about the Age-in-Grade bill?"

"I don't know. CO says they'll never pass it."

"They'll demote you again," she declared.

"No, they won't."

"Move you down another thousand files on the list, that's just what they—"

"No, look, honey . . ."

"No—*you* look!" All at once she was wild with rage. She had promised herself she wouldn't blow off, after last night especially she had sworn she'd hold herself in line. But the heat, the wind and dust and this wretched wooden shack with its low ceilings and ridiculous plumbing and silly sticks of furniture, the seven-foot-high sunflowers along the back line with their swaying idiot eyes, all gripped her like a vise. She was lonely, she was pregnant and helpless and now this latest decision of the elected representatives of the nation struck her as the final, supreme insult. The whole thing was impossible, impossible!

"What has to happen to you, Sam?" she cried. "How much do you have to take? Really? Do they have to bust you to PFC and maroon you for life on Easter Island before you'll see the light?" She clenched her hands at her sides. "They don't *want* us, they don't *care* about us, we simply don't exist for them. Why do you go on beating your head against a wall? The wall's a lot harder, I can tell you that . . . What are you trying to do—!"

He was gazing at her, troubled, frowning. What in God's name was the matter with him? How could he sit there looking so calm and unmoved and insanely indomitable? Couldn't he see what was in the wind—?

"Tommy," he was saying quietly, "your Dad wouldn't let—"

"Never mind Poppa—stop invoking Poppa all the time! Do you think he has any more brains than you do? letting them bust him down, and deep-six him with China duty?"

"The Fifteenth—"

"I know all about the Fifteenth—their esprit and their discipline and the beauty of their wives and everything else. What has that got to do with the price of tea? Bitter tea, too. You think I don't know about Army politics just because I'm always knocking the system? It was a sop and a butt detail all in one. What Poppa *ought* to be is a Deputy Chief of Staff, or in Plans—at the very least he ought to be teaching at the War College. But no—those creeps in the Munitions Building hate him because he's got more guts and intelligence, more sheer ability than they'll ever have if they live to be a thousand . . ."

He was nodding at her grimly. "Yes, I'll sign that," he muttered.

"You bet. And it's the same thing with you. Look at Marden, look at that sniveling phony Townsend. They hate you because you're too good for them, because you're better than any of them could ever be, and they can't forgive you for that and they never will! Their hands are against you, Sam—"

He gave a somber smile. "My record's got in my way."

"That's a miserable way to have to put it. What kind of mystical order do you all think you belong to, anyway? My God!" She flung an arm at the cracked ceiling, the flaking walls, aware that the gesture was hysterical, melodramatic and pointless—and not caring. "Look at us! Look at us! It's indecent. It's degrading! . . ."

That was all she had to say. It seemed. No terms she knew could improve on them. There was a brief silence while with trembling fingers she lighted a cigarette, contrary to Dr. Terwilliger's orders, and puffed at it savagely while Sam sat on the bed and looked at her.

"What do you want me to do, Tommy?"

"I don't know. Get out, get out of this—!" She bent toward him. "There are any number of ways to live like a human being, just any number, like running a freak show at a carny, or raising chinchilla, or eating cocktail glasses—anything *sane* . . ."

"Tommy," he said in a patient, weary tone that set her teeth on edge, "if we're going to sit down and talk about this—"

"—then let's be serious. Swell. Great. All right—let's. What's so silly about admitting one's mistakes, giving up this monkey-suit, monkey-shines existence as a bad job and going on to something else?"

"Such as."

"Well . . ." The idea had been stirring in the back of her mind for some months, off and on, but she wanted to present it as if it had just occurred to her. "Well . . . what about Dex?"

"Who?"

It infuriated her that he didn't recall the name instantly. "Sterling Poindexter, from Cannes, *you* remember. He offered you a job in his father's brokerage firm . . ."

Sam grinned. "And then retracted the offer."

"Oh, that didn't mean anything—that was only his kind of sophistication. I'll bet he'd give you one in a minute."

"The world of business." His upper lip curled.

"What's so terrible about that? That's what the world's doing, isn't it?—the sane, intelligent world, I mean: the one that's getting something out of life . . ."

"Honey, I couldn't do that. Sitting in an office with a lot of telephones, talking about stocks and bonds—that's no kind of life for a man. Hell, they aren't even real—they're just a lot of gilt-edged paper, they don't even stand for anything—"

"They stand for *money*," she cried shrilly, "—that's what they stand for! . . ."

"Please try to keep your voice down. Skip came home the same time I did.—Tommy, I'm no sweet talker, I couldn't con a bunch of people into handing over their dough."

"It isn't *conning* them, it's convincing them. Of course you could, your beloved troops believe you, don't they?—when you tell them what they ought to do . . ."

He smiled wryly. "They haven't got a whole lot of choice."

"Don't be silly, they idolize you, I've heard them. 'He's rough but he's square, he's straight, he'll go to bat for you any day of the week if you've got a solid beef.' I've heard them, they think the absolute heaven-sent, shining-glory *world* of you—!"

And to her surprise and anger she was weeping. She gave up then and sat down on the cot with a bump. The hell with it: the completely bloody hell with it anyway. She couldn't even argue a point satisfactorily anymore. His arms were around her now, he had pressed his face against her hair and was talking to her, murmuring gently, and she slumped against his protective strength like an exhausted child, not really listening to what he was saying, feeling spent and soothed.

"Honey," he was saying, "honey-girl, you're all worn out from the heat and carrying the baby and you're all worked up and distraught, and you've got everything blown up out of all proportion."

She rubbed her forehead against his neck and wondered if she had.

Maybe it *was* all nerves. She didn't think so, she didn't think that at all: but it was possible, of course.

"Honey, I know this is bleak duty right now, but it won't last, you'll see, I'll get a change of post soon, I'm sure I will. And things will be better. Sweet, maybe this isn't the sun and moon and all the stars, this life, and there's a lot of ritual and repetition in it, I know that too, but there's ritual and repetition in everything, it's always there. Here it's out in the open more, that's all." His hand held her easily: it felt so big. "The thing is, I believe in what I'm doing. This outfit of mine, they look to me for—well, for help and advice, how to be better soldiers, better men in general. Tommy, they *count* on me, is what I mean . . . If I went into business it would be just to fill in time, go through the motions: I wouldn't believe in what I was doing. And pretty soon I wouldn't be any kind of man at all. I'd begin to despise myself for it, and then you'd begin to despise me too, and you'd be right; because there wouldn't be anything there to respect. Don't you see, Tommy, a man has to do what he can think well of himself for doing, or he's nothing. It might be all right for some of them to go into business, but it wouldn't be for me—if only because I was at Soissons and the Argonne. And alongside everything I saw there, nothing in the business world is very real. Do you see what I mean? The businessman goes for his profits and most of the time he doesn't see where it's leading; and things go from bad to worse, you remember how it was, and he pulls the country along with him, the politicians and the churches and the newspapers and everyone else, and finally somebody says the word, the terrible word there's no going back from—and the businessmen go right on piling up their profits, and the politicians rant on and on about that last full measure of devotion . . . but it's the little guy—the clerk and the farm boy and the carpenter— who's left hanging on the wire with his guts all over his knees. And I'm the one, Tommy. I'm the one who has to lead him into that filthy, endless horror and try to bring him out of it again. I know I'm the one."

She turned her head. His face looked older and sadder than she'd ever seen it, even on the dove battlements of Le Suquet: the lines around his nose and mouth etched deep, his eyes dark with a steady, angry sorrow. Sad Sam Damon, she'd heard a few of the soldiers call him: Sad Sam. Because of his initials, but it was more than that—it was because of this unspoken, constant tenor of concern that underlay even his humor, his skepticism—and which she'd scarcely guessed at. He was always siding with the enlisted men, fighting for them; he'd been on the carpet over them twice already. He was always saying they ought to have a club of their own on the post, and a canteen that sold beer, and a better-looking fatigue uniform; one night at the club he advanced the idea that the enlisted man would never have complete faith in Army justice until he was allowed to serve on courts-martial—a thought greeted by an embarrassed and impervious silence and a rather tart rebuke from Colonel Lomprey. She would wake at night to see him hunched up under the dented gooseneck lamp, his baseball cap tilted forward to shield his eyes, studying French, or ballistics, or reading Jomini or Clausewitz, or even Trevelyan and Gibbon and Thucydides.

"Darling," she would call softly, "It's late—you'll ruin your eyes . . ."

"Just a few minutes more."

He read like a starving man in a granary, and he retained what he read. He said he had to catch up, he'd missed out on so much that the Pointers and the older men already knew, there were so many fields he had to master; and always, studying late or sitting calmly attentive during the courtesy calls or singing at the piano with the others at the post hops after the rank had left, there was that persistent little current of preoccupation, like voltage moving along a cable—a sense of preparation, of holding himself in readiness for a day of sudden exigency and trial. But he didn't look like that now: now the anguish, the naked appeal in his eyes seemed boundless.

. . . He's suffered, the thought came to her with a rude, small shock; he's suffered terribly, more than I could ever have realized. It was hard to think of Sam as having suffered deeply—it was like so many aspects of him she could not put together. She could never believe he could have done the fierce and terrible things he had—storming machine guns, holding out against waves of Germans, carrying men forward on the force of his own ardor and tenacity—somehow she could never reconcile all that with the gentle, unassuming man who was her husband. But he *had* done those things, and he had paid the price of them; and that had made him what he was . . . Shocked, humbled, she put her arms around his neck.

"—I want to be a good wife, Sam," she said softly. "I want to be everything a woman can be to a man. I mean it. I just got—down in the dumps. All this excess weight I'm lugging around." She hugged him hard. "Just a momentary lapse, darling. I'm going to take a brace, as of right now. That's a promise."

He was murmuring some reply, some demurral but she hardly heard him. He was right, she saw: bound fast in death, in violence he had come upon a hard and anguished truth about this world, and it had brought him to the edge of complete despair—and then he had come back from that, and resolutely built his life around that most unwelcome truth . . . And if it had served him this well, it ought to be good enough for her.

"Disregard these hysterical nothings," she said aloud. "It's just a legacy from the years with Ramon at Vezelay." She smiled, and dried her eyes and blew her nose on the huge red handkerchief he always wore in his hip pocket when he was in the field. "Disregard them. I'm all right now." She shook her hair back. Now remember, she told herself fiercely. This moment now: remember it, and don't let him down. "What would you like for supper? Lamb stew, lamb goulash, or cold lamb?"

He smiled, then. "Cold lamb would be fine, honey."

He leaped from the running board of the truck before it had stopped and ran up the short rise toward the post infirmary, his holstered pistol flopping at his thigh. Squatting in the gray, pitiless dawn light the old building, with its mustard-colored clapboards and tall narrow windows, looked like anything but a hospital. He went in on the dead run, flinging the door wide ahead of him. There was no one at the desk. He hesitated, started down the corridor—then saw Dr. Terwilliger coming toward him.

"There you are, my bucko." Captain Terwilliger—known as the Tweaker to his intimates—was a short, wiry man in his early thirties with a soft, plump face and bushy, taffy-colored eyebrows that turned up unexpectedly at the ends, giving him an air of mock ferocity. Beaming, bristling, he advanced on Damon; with his surgical gown billowing above his putteed calves, his turquoise eyes sparkling, he looked like a jovial little satyr. Catching the look on the Lieutenant's face he threw back his head. "Fie, Damon! A soldier, and afear'd?"

"Doc, Colonel Lomprey let me ride a truck in early—"

"That was noble of him. Noble. Even so, you're too late."

"What—"

"Look at you! A sight. Out playing hide-and-seek amid the heliotrope—or is it prisoners' base this time? Ah, you happy children of Mars." Eying Damon in amusement, he laughed. "Composure, composure, my dear Angst-laden Leutnant! Where is the bearing that terrified both furious Frank and fiery Hun?"

Damon blinked at him. Dirty, unshaven, his uniform blanched with dust and dried sweat after three days and nights of maneuvers, he was too weary to respond to Terwilliger's sallies. He licked his lips stupidly and said: "How is she?"

The Tweaker clapped him on the shoulder and bowed. "Let me end the suspense, the hideous tortures of nescience. Let me be the first, the very first to congratulate you on the arrival of a son and heir. That's speaking in purely euphuistic terms, of course. Right now he looks like neither son *nor* heir."

"A boy?" Damon stammered, "—a baby boy?"

"What did you expect:—an arachnid? a cephalopod? Medical science can work wonders, it's true—but certain metamorphoses still escape us." He clapped his hands and proclaimed: "Weight seven pounds nine ounces, length twenty-two and five-eighths inches . . ."

"How is she? Tommy?"

Terwilliger glared at him. "Your wife! We don't care about the *wives*, Damon. This is the New-Old Army: what we're after is cannon fodder: *bring forth men-children only; for thy undaunted mettle should compose* . . . ever read any Shakespeare? No, you wouldn't have. Oh, the military parts, sure—Othello's agony, and Harry at Harfleur . . ."

"*Doctor—*"

The Tweaker relented then, and jammed his hands in his breeches pockets. "She's fine. Racked and battered, but she's fine. I don't mind telling you, it was a struggle. Our Tommy is a very brave girl, and an obedient one, but her pelvic girdle is not an obstetrician's dream. For a while it looked as though I'd have to resurrect my ancient skill with the forceps."

"Doc, how about letting me see her . . ."

"Anon, anon. The girl needs rest. Do you wish me to curtail my saga of trial and triumph, torn as I was between conflicting loyalties? Who will write my citation if I do not? At three eighteen I was summoned down the hall to the side of Columbine Crawford, consort of our revered Second-in-Command, who was writhing and tearing at the bed-clothes. 'I don't care *who's* in labor, I'm a desperately sick woman!' 'Where does it hurt?' I queried. You'd have thought I had just at-tempted her chastity. 'Here—and *here!*' Clutching with beringed fingers at her lineae albae, her recti abdominis, her pubic crest. 'If you haven't the brains to know what it is then I can tell you—I happen to be suffering from eclampsia!' " The Tweaker smote his forehead. "*Eclamp-sia!* Where did she come by that word? None of the symptoms what-ever. But it sounds ferocious, you see—it smacks of cramps and iron pincers and Greek classical horrors, and that's all she needed." He shook his head, his eyebrows flaring. "Pure fiction. Menopausal jimjams. *And* some sort of psychic competition with your beloved I won't attempt to diagnose without a witches' cauldron."

"You mean you left Tommy and went—"

"Rank Hath Its Pressures, oh prince of Night Clerks. You will be familiar. In any event I gave La Crawford a sedative and patted her fanny—figuratively speaking—and hastened back to your helpmeet, who was now nearing her moment of truth. Ever take up bullfighting?"

"Doc, look—"

"Hush. At four forty-seven, while Mrs. D and I were grappling with the very mystery of life itself, came a high old ruckus from Number Seven and I was informed Queen Columbine absolutely commanded my presence, under threat of court-martial. I returned word I was quite willing to stand trial before a kangaroo court armed with knouts and bamboo rods the following day—but not until; and I told Mitchell, who's a good sort even if she is a touch deferential—to keep her pinned down." He drew his lips back from his teeth in a ferocious snarl. "No—dice. In a matter of minutes Her Majesty was screaming that the pain was driving her mad—and before you could whisper Krafft-Ebing she'd begun to trip the light fantastic up and down the hall, fulminating with threats and vituperation. 'The Surgeon General!' she hollered. 'The Surgeon General will be notified of a medical officer who is unable to distinguish between a routine matter and a genuine, critical illness!— who can't even show a decent respect for rank, the common courtesies of the service—'

" 'Go back!' I roared at her. '*I* am in command here! Go back to your bed!' Her face went blank with fright—an expression I must confess I've never seen there before. It felt so good I said it all again. Before she could recover, Mitchell and I bundled her into bed, where I socked her with an injection of sodium pentobarbital, enough to knock out a Percheron in its prime—and then returned to the Grand Struggle. And after a series of gyres and ululations there's no point in going into here, your better half gave forth a shriek that rent the welkin, I bore up and she bore down and voilà!—a lusty babe with the eyes of a poet and the body of a raw worm, roaring with rage at this great stage of fools . . ."

He glanced at his watch, gazing mildly at Damon's impatience. "There. My song is ended. You can go in and see her." He sighed, and Damon saw that he was very tired. "She was a good girl. A very good girl."

"She's all right, then, Doctor? really all right?"

Terwilliger nodded. "But it was a difficult business, I'll tell you that much."

Damon took his hand. "Thanks," he said. "I can't thank you enough, Doctor."

"Of course you can. Everyone can. Go ahead in . . . No more than ten minutes," he said, his voice suddenly sharp with authority. "You got that?"

"Yes, sir."

"I don't want you hanging around in there for hours, the way some of them do. She's a very tired young woman; she needs all the rest she can get." The Tweaker pulled at his eyebrows, whose ends stood up still more fiercely. "Now I've got to wait until Dame Columbine comes around." His face beamed like a satanic cherub's. "Maybe the old bat'll get a one-in-a-million reaction—maybe she'll be in a suspended state for decades. Think what a blessing that'd be!"

Damon went down the hall, feeling dizzy and nerveless. Tommy was lying perfectly still, one arm behind her head; her whole body had that peculiar inertness of the spent—as if it wanted to be part of the bed, the olive-drab coverlet. He was on the point of going back to ask Mitchell if it was all right to disturb her when he saw that she was looking at him. Her face was white, with deep fatigue lines like bruises under her eyes; she looked like a thin little invalid sister of Tommy Damon.

Hesitantly he moved up to the bed, her eyes following him, and said: "Hello."

"Hello, darling." Her voice was faint, a little tremulous.

"Honey, I got back as quick as I could. I'm sorry I wasn't here when—when it was going on." He bent over and kissed her—then saw all at once the baby crooked inside her right arm. He started, fascinated, watched the gnomelike face, eyes squeezed shut, contort in displeasure, the arms and legs slowly pumping, little barrel body straining in a mighty, writhing effort, as if it sought to change its very state. Then the face turned placid, the eyes opened: they were Tommy's, green and piercing. Tommy's boy. He reached down and touched the tiny hand; it closed on his forefinger with minute ferocity, gripped and gripped. His son, too. His own son. The solemn magic of the moment filled him with gratitude and wonder, made him tremble.

". . . I'm sorry you had a bad time of it."

"No," she said. "I wouldn't have missed it for worlds. Not for worlds." There was a ring of assertive calm in her voice he'd never heard before. "I mean it. I did something. On my own." She smiled then—a wan, triumphant smile. "Look at him. Isn't he tremendous?"

"All there and a yard wide," Damon said. He felt foolish standing there beside the bed: clumsy and inconsequential.

"What a time you gave me." She rubbed the point of her chin softly against his pink round head. "What a time . . . I'm going to name him Donny," she declared.

"Donny? Why?"

"I like the name."

"But—after whom?"

"Nobody. He just looks as if he ought to be named Donny."

"Donald Damon." Thoughtfully he considered the name; he couldn't say he really liked it. "All right. If you want to. I'd sort of hoped—"

"No," she said firmly. "We're not naming him for Poppa. We've been through that, remember? He's not going to have things hanging over his head. Things to have to measure up to all the time. No more of that."

"Well . . ." He could not keep his eyes off the baby: he wanted to pick him up, crush him in his arms, run all over the post with him, shouting like some crazy kid. "Well, could we call him Donald *Caldwell* Damon?"

She smiled. "You're incorrigible. All right." She straightened in the bed. "Ooh, I hurt."

"Where?" he murmured anxiously.

"Everywhere." She gestured. "Down there, mostly. Old Columbia made a scene of it. I could hear her ranting up and down the hall outside. I remember, at the worst part—it was like being in a barrel of pain, a revolving barrel, you know?—I remember I saw the whole thing, clear as day. I wanted to yell, 'Oh shut up, you mean old bitch! You're just jealous!' Maybe I did. I was actually laughing. The things that go through your mind at such times. You know what I thought of, Sam?"

"What?"

"That young viscount or whatever he was on the promenade of the Casino at Cannes. With the crippled old man. Remember? The way the boy made fun of him. How amused he was!—and indifferent. The old man had all that wisdom and no strength; and the boy . . ." She brushed back her hair with her hand, a gesture insuperably weary. "What a long journey. So long—I never had anything *last* so long . . . For a while there I thought I was going to die—tear all apart and die. And I thought, What a mistake life is: you're never ready for each thing that happens to you. And then I thought, No, that's the marvel of it—if you *were* ready there'd be nothing to it at all, it would be like frogs in a pool, eating and propagating and swimming around endlessly, nothing more than that . . . Pain makes you think, doesn't it?"

"Yes. For a while."

"I know. And then it gets worse and you can't think anymore, you only *know* something. Like a very bright tiny light. You aren't even afraid anymore, there's no place for it . . . And then I went whirling along out of that part of it, too, there was just this thing I wanted to do more than anything else, no matter what. No matter what. And I did. It almost killed me but I did it."

She looked up at him, her eyes glowing softly. "I even wanted to laugh at the Tweaker, because he didn't think I could. He'd begun to get panicky, I could tell—he'd stopped glaring and hunching his shoulders the way he usually does: he was talking nervously to Mitchell, I couldn't get anything he was saying, but I could tell by his voice . . . And then I did it—I won!" She gave a quick, gusty sigh. "All that—all that *struggle*. That's what life is, isn't it? Struggle. Struggle to breathe, to grow, to learn, to be good. Look at him! . . ." Her voice was faint but sharp with triumph: she looked fragile and powerful, full of pride. At that instant he wanted her so badly his legs trembled. The baby twisted toward her blindly and she cradled him with an almost automatic gesture; a lioness enfolding one of her cubs with a protective paw. She was so *altered*—like boys after their first battle, in their shy hilarity reaffirming their glorious corporeality, offering thanks the only way they knew for being spared. Gazing at his son he thought of that afternoon on the bank beside the Marne, the still, silver water, of Reb and Tsonka and big Kraz and Brewster and Dev—ah God, Dev—and all the others, and his eyes filled with tears. This was for them, this boy: for their dreams, their passion, their tremulous mortality. They were not dead, they still lived on in memory, and in the promise of this boy—

"What's the matter?" Her face was searching, troubled.

"Nothing," he answered. "Just thinking." He bent over and kissed her tenderly. "You're a very lovely girl, Tommy. To give us a son like this."

"Sweet.—How are the maneuvers going?"

"Oh—so-so. We did some things well, some not so well."

"You look like the wreck of the Hesperus."

"Yes. Well, it's pretty dusty out there." He paused. "I had to get tough with a couple of them—they wouldn't take it seriously. They don't want to behave as though it's the real thing." He smiled faintly. "Which of course it isn't."

"Sam." Her eyes shot up at him, very bright and hard.

"Yes?"

"You've got to promise me something. Right now."

"All right. What's that?"

"You've got to promise me you won't let him go into the Army. Donny."

He grinned, looking at his dirty, sweat-laced uniform. "You picked the perfect morning to bring that up."

"No. I'm serious." She raised her free hand as if to warn him. "He's got to do something—more meaningful; more rich and vital and reward-ing, somehow. Don't you see? Not so lonely and barren . . . Don't you see?" Soberly he nodded; they watched each other a moment in silence, thinking their own thoughts. "Promise me that, Sam. Please."

He hesitated. "But if the boy shows an aptitude—"

"No!" She struck the coverlet with her fist. "That's just what I mean. You know how kids are influenced, even if nothing is said. They don't know anything about themselves, and you're such a strong personality. You can make anyone do what you want—all of us . . ."

"—Don't say that," he protested fearfully. He had the eerie sense that she'd been following his thoughts for the past few minutes.

"But it's true, darling. You know it is. Any boy would want to do what you're doing. No—you've got to promise me you'll do everything in your power to steer him away from the service. From all—*that* . . ."

A bugle had just broken in on her, playing mess call—that most inane of all summonses in its staccato reiteration, the call he knew she hated so she could hardly stand it; there came the sound of voices, running feet, hoots and cries, and a distant clash of pans. Soupy-soupy-soup. He looked around him at the mean little room with its cheap wooden parti-tions greasy with shellac, the stains in the ceiling wallboard, the facing cot—mercifully empty this morning—with its chipped white frame and frayed sheets, the bedside lamps with their dented shades . . . this whole straitened world caught in a web of duty and national neglect and self-denial. What a dungeon to immure one's love in! He felt all at once unpardonably guilty—as though he had jilted Tommy, or married her under false pretenses, or callously philandered. She hated this world, she'd known it ever since childhood and hated it with all her might; she had gone back into it for his sake, because she loved him. He passed the back of his hand across his forehead. And everybody wants a better life for his child, he told himself, a better, fuller life than he's had, it's natural enough . . .

Her eyes had not left him. She seemed to be prepared to wait for a lifetime for this reply; and he was ready enough to give it. He thought of Sherman running into Grant on the streets of St. Louis that dismal autumn of 1857, one old soldier bankrupt and jobless, the other almost a drunk, eking out an existence selling cordwood. What had Sherman written his wife about the service? "It is too full of blind chances to be worthy of a first rank among callings." Well, it looked a good deal like that, all right.

And yet Vicksburg had been only six years away . . .

"Of course," he said aloud, aware that the silence between them had grown too long. He reached out and took her hand in both of his. "Of course I promise, honey. I'll do anything reasonable in my power to dissuade him from a military career."

"No matter what the circumstances?"

He nodded. "No matter what the circumstances. I give you my word."

"Thank God," she breathed, as if a tremendous burden had been pushed away from her heart. He smiled at the soft fervor in her voice; and catching it, she laughed once. "Well, it's true. I was more afraid of that than anything else. You don't know what that bugle can do to a kid. Colors and retreat . . . Maybe only an army brat can."

He kissed her lightly. "The Tweaker told me ten minutes: I don't want to outstay my welcome around here. You ought to get some sleep, honey."

"Yes. I could sleep for three days and three nights. What are you going to do?"

"Right now I'm going to send a cable to your dad."

She laughed and shook her head. "Poor Poppa. The boy he always wanted. Well, at least we won't have to give him a *girl's* name . . ."

He walked down the steps and out into the cool, flat air, feeling light-headed from lack of sleep. The post looked curiously deserted; he had that stealthy, footless delight that comes from having legitimately evaded a duty one's companions are still saddled with. He considered walking to mess, realized he couldn't show up looking the way he did. He didn't want to go back to their quarters and start coffee and eggs all by himself. He paused a moment, then turned toward the enlisted men's mess hall. Sergeant Swicka, who caught for the company ball team, would give him an unofficial handout; and he had to tell somebody. He was a father, for God sake! The father of a seven-pound, nine-ounce boy. They'd have a party when Tommy came home—Skip and Liza and the MacDonoughs and Tom and Meg Warren, just a few friends, he'd rustle up some booze from that shady character in Hazlett with the scar at the edge of his mouth; he'd get Moose Schultz to bring his accordion and they'd have a sing; and Tommy could wear that lovely lemon-yellow dress again, and she and Skip would stand on the ammo boxes doing imitations and they'd all try to guess who they were . . .

He had just reached the back steps of the mess hall when the reaction hit him. She could have died. A few hours ago. Before I got back. She might have died . . .

The fear pierced his vitals like a steel splinter. He found he had sunk onto the bottom step, was gripping the worn wood with both hands. The very idea of losing her loomed before him like a gale of endless night. Thank God, he muttered inaudibly. Oh thank God—

There was a step on the porch. He turned. Sergeant Swicka's square, blunt face was leaning out around the screen door. "You all right, Lieutenant?"

"Hello, Steve. Yes, I'm all right . . ."

"You don't look so good right now."

"No," he said. "No, no, I'm fine." Swicka's solicitous expression, his bristling black hair like a porcupine's quills made him want to laugh, but he couldn't. Oh, thank God, he cried to himself in a sick ecstasy of relief, nothing matters as long as nothing happened to her. Nothing else matters at all.

"The Rivayra!—gee, it must have been keen," Mae Lee Cleghorne said, and her flat Oklahoma voice throbbed with emotion. "What was it like? Tell me."

"Oh, it's very sunny, and gay," Tommy Damon answered. "With grand hotels along the waterfront—in Cannes it's called La Croisette—all white and black with turrets and things . . . I wasn't there very long, you know. A little less than a month."

"A month in a place like that—that's forever!" Mae Lee cried. "Gosh, I'd give anything if we could get to Europe." She was a thin, nervous girl with straw-colored hair combed back from her forehead and fastened in a sort of tousled topknot. At the moment she was seven months pregnant, and the long, tight swell of her belly gave her a pitiful, anemic look. "Jack put in for Tientsin—you know, the Fifteenth. Jack says in Tientsin you rate a number one and a number two boy and a coolie and an amah. Imagine! But they say nobody draws China except a few favored people . . . Rusty!" she shouted, and a little towheaded boy playing near the edge of the buffalo grass turned and called, "What?"

"Come here to Mama."

Rusty stared at her resentfully. "I'm playing tractor . . ."

"All right. Don't you go any further than that, now.—Look at him," she said to Tommy. "He looks like he's just come in off the reservation. I've got to get his hair cut." She sighed. "Boy, I wouldn't mind having one of those amahs around the old plantation. I'm so sick of washing and mending I could spit." Eagerly, a little deferentially she asked: "Do you think we've got any chance for China?"

"Sure, you do. Half of it is the luck of the draw, anyway . . ."

"How is it your daddy hasn't asked for Sam, honey? Doesn't he want to go out there?"

Tommy frowned, her eyes on her sewing. "I don't imagine the AG's office would take a very happy view of that," she said, a little more tartly than she'd meant to. "Besides, Sam would never ask it of Poppa. You know Sam: he'd never ask favors of anyone."

"I know . . . He's so proud. Only trouble, there's such a thing as being too high-crested in this world. I mean, what's the good of it if it lands you out in a place like this?"

"You've got a point," Tommy said. "You've certainly got a point, Mae Lee."

The two women were sitting on the Damons' cramped porch—it was too narrow for four to sit on it except in a row, like the inmates of some old folks' home—sewing and keeping an eye on their offspring. Donny was perched on a blanket waving his arms and crowing at Rusty, who was pushing a little iron fire engine through the dust and rubble, making harsh barking noises. Beyond them the land swept out and out—a faintly uptilting expanse furred with grass and dotted with squat black clumps of mesquite and chaparral. Tommy gazed out at it, her eyes narrowed from the glare, hating its pitiless, arid force. Fort Hardee had been by almost any standards a hardship tour, but Fort Dormer was worse. It lay a hundred and fifty miles southeast of El Paso, sunk deep in desert. Their quarters were two tiny rooms with concrete floors and adobe walls, this tiny porch and a sort of lean-to tacked onto the back of the structure which served as the kitchen. The wind blew for days, a thin, high moan like the keening of dead souls, and the sagebrush and wild indigo tumbled endlessly over the desert floor; red dust sifted in and over and through everything—food and clothing and the scraps of furniture they'd brought down from Hardee. Lizards raced along the woodwork uttering their chittering war cries, snakes crawled up the icebox drainpipes, scorpions dropped from the ceilings and writhed about on the cold, damp floor, whipping their terrible curled tails. The land drifted away toward Mexico and the end of time—a sink of desert harboring an infinity of loneliness and despair. It was not quite America—and it certainly was not overseas. A limbo. Another limbo in the great American wasteland, only worse; for while Fort Dormer could boast a vivid past abounding in crafty Indian attacks and the tenacious, indomitable figure of General George Crook, it was able to offer very little in the way of a future: it had no post movies, the commissary was poorly run, and the commandant, a dour little Presbyterian minister's son named Howden, took a dark view of the frivolities attendant on the Saturday night hops. Sam had been elated when he'd first been informed of the change of station—he was told he would command a company; but in two months a captain was assigned to the battalion, and Sam had had to give way . . .

Only half listening to Mae Lee, Tommy watched Donny crawling about on the blanket, his head bobbing up and down. It was nine o'clock, and the sun hadn't yet begun to burn oppressively, but already the desert shimmered and rippled in the heat waves. Cruel country: country without water was cruel country. Men weren't meant to live there—she'd noticed that only hard-bitten, implacable natures, true solitaries, responded to it. Lieutenant Colonel Pownall's wife, who was brought up in the Big Bend, had said to her at one of the post teas: "There's only two kinds moved in down here: good tough and bad tough: but whichever, they're all tough!" She'd laughed softly, and her dusty slate eyes had rested for a moment on Tommy. "This country's hard on people: it runs through them, in a manner of speaking . . ."

"I keep feeling if we could just get away," Mae Lee was saying to her now. "Some place totally different—foreign and, you know, exotic. Jack wouldn't be so restless: he might become more—satisfied with things. More attentive, the way he used to be. He's so touchy!" She laughed, too volubly, and her eyes darted around the porch. "He's been acting so different lately, I don't know what to make of him. Mama always told me it's human nature for men to lose interest, but I never believed her . . ."

Tommy frowned. One of the things she disliked about post life was the incessant intimacy among army wives: the confidences, the unburdenings, the gossip—and the inexorable division of this narrow, isolated world into hostile forts of trapped, put-upon women and carefree, self-indulgent men. You could tell by the changed tone when one of these sessions was beginning. Yet here was this waif of a girl, obviously troubled by her husband's increasing lack of interest; it was a genuine fear, she was seeking help, reassurance. Was there any? Tommy had watched it happen in the year they'd been at Dormer. Jack had enlisted in that last rush of hometown fervor before the war had ended; they had met at a dance that fall—Mae Lee had told her the story half a dozen times. They were married in a military wedding asparkle with all the fairy-tale panoply of crossed swords and a white tower of a cake and soft shadows under the magnolia trees, and the punctilious babble of an officers' club reception . . . and in the middle of it all stood Mae Lee, starry-eyed at her rare good fortune. She could leave that grim little Oklahoma town and her mother's soured litany of disparagement and denial, and dwell in a clarion land of receptions and dances and parades. A new life . . .

Now, five years later, under the hard, shadowless sky of west Texas, the sea change had come. Jack Cleghorne, fresh out of Arkansas, had seen still another world—one in which Mae Lee was no longer the sum and substance of his dreams. He had met women from the subtler, more sophisticated cities of the North and East; and they filled him with a restless hunger. He danced with them, brought them coffee or punch, his romantic eyes sharp with longing. They had seen so much, they possessed graces so far beyond anything he had ever known; and here he was, marooned in a border station, tramping a somber treadmill of marches, inspections, drill. Ambition, hot reveries consumed him. He had missed the war to end war through no fault of his own, he was still a second lieutenant pinned far behind the promotion hump—and nothing reminded him of all that so much as Mae Lee's fearful deference, her flat Oklahoma gaucherie.

Yet he was a good man, Tommy knew; he was neither small nor vicious. He would not leave Mae Lee; he would not philander—at least not yet. Now he took his nagging restlessness out in field problems, in the company ball team Sam ran, where he played an aggressive third base. He was through with Mae Lee really, that was the trouble; he had outstripped her in a few short years. All that was needed was an Irene Keller to break it open. There was one on every post—vivid, high-strung, a superb rider and dancer, drawing the junior officers around her like flies, her eyes glittering with that peculiar inward glare . . . Mae Lee had sensed all of this in a dumb, intuitive way; recoiling from its terrifying implications she had sought solace elsewhere. Now she was pregnant again—an event she publicly deplored, knowing the additional drain on Jack's meager pay another child would be. It had been instinctual: Jack had been attentive and affectionate to her before, when she was carrying Rusty; why shouldn't he be again? But he wasn't; this time he was moody and irascible.

Tommy glanced at the girl. Her cheeks looked white and drawn; there were great strokes of fatigue under her eyes. Oh God, she'll begin to weep now, she thought crossly; if there's anything I can't stand it's weepy women: can't they get a grip on themselves? Then in the next instant she felt an overpowering rush of affection.

"Oh well, men," she said aloud finally; her voice was flatter, more callous than she'd intended. "They've got their own world, they go their own way. The plain truth of the matter is we were biologically mousetrapped. From the start . . . Men don't ever stick with anything, for the simple reason they don't have to. There aren't any consequences. *We've* got the consequences, all of them, and they know it and it makes them feel guilty, so they go running off and fire rifles or blow up old tar-paper shacks or throw a baseball at each other as hard as they can. It gives them the illusion they're doing something grand . . ."

She trailed off, fuming; she felt she was being disloyal to Sam with this headlong tirade, but at the moment she couldn't help it; it seemed true enough. What *were* they doing, right now? Sitting around in the company office probably, telling each other raunchy jokes or reminiscing about dear old Corned Willy Hill, while their devoted spouses were mending and washing clothes and watching over their precious offspring. "The whole system is rigged," she ranted on. "They doll themselves up in all those stars and bars to make themselves feel important—it's ego building pure and simple. It gives them a sense of accomplishment and good fellowship and all that drivel—"

She broke off in distress. Mae Lee was crying now, great shiny tears that dripped on to the apple green pongee dress she'd let out and let out until it looked like a shiny old tent.

"—Tommy, he doesn't care about me anymore at all . . ."

"Of course he does."

"It's Major Keller's wife. He's—he's attracted to her." The girl's eyes were large and hollow with fear; hanging on her with desperate hope. "What am I going to do?"

"It's nothing," she heard herself say, "she's always making a play for every man in sight."

"At the hop two weeks ago. She was dancing with him."

"Sweetie, he's got to dance with her—so does Sam. It's a duty dance."

"Not that way. And Jack was—responding . . ."

"Irene Keller is a—well, we know what she is."

"He's fallen in love with her. Just head over heels . . ."

"No he hasn't, honey." Tommy was out of her chair and had her arm around the girl now, rocking her gently. "Now, you're just worn down from carrying the baby and you've got everything all out of proportion. Jack's a fine boy—he's just wound up over the change in battalion COs. Sam's the same way, they've got these things on their minds. Just the other evening Jack was telling me what a wonderful help you've been to him this past year . . ." Gently she soothed her, thinking: God forgive me, what the hell, they're lies in a good cause. "Go on in and take a nap and you'll feel better. I'll watch Rusty."

"No. It's not fair."

"Sure it is. Of course it is. I'll wake you at eleven thirty. Okay?"

"Thanks, Tommy. I didn't mean to come all apart like this." Mae Lee heaved herself up and waddled off around the porch to the Cleghornes' quarters next door.

The important thing was to keep busy. Occupy your mind—and if you couldn't do that, occupy your hands. She went out into the yard and changed Donny and put his sun hat back on his head; he promptly pulled it off. The fire engine Rusty was playing with kept losing its rear wheels, the cotter pin that held the axle was gone; she took a hairpin and put it through the hole and bent it back on itself so it would hold, at least until Jack could fix it properly. She finished her mending, went back out on the porch and started working on the new couch cover. The heat was solider now; the wind out of Mexico had a dry, relentless pressure. Time floated by. A bugle blew, a detail of men was drilling on the parade ground; she could hear the voices, muffled by distance, the hesitation and pounce of the commands: "Col'm-layff . . . *harrrr!* col'm-layff . . . *harrr!*"

She found herself staring at the tremendous sweep of desert with a kind of humorous amazement. Why was she doing this? What on earth had caused her to fall back into the identical world she had grown up in? Why couldn't she have married an archaeologist, a rajah, a business-

man like her Uncle Edgar? Well yes, love: you fell in love with a man
and you followed him on into life. But why had she chosen to fall in
love with Sad Sam Damon? Was there some higher law we all obeyed
unwittingly? Doc Terwilliger, back at Hardee, said it was nothing more
or less than the destiny of the human animal: we sought unerringly the
familiar trail, repeated our patterns, good and bad, with all the witless
absorption of our hairy-faced, bare-buttocked ancestors: we chose our
own poison. Was life nothing more than a lazy, elliptical traverse back
upon our own origins—were we only flying a great circle? Had the
cadences of drum and bugle burned their way into her soul so deeply
she could never erase them?

Passing the needle rapidly, evenly along the hem she thought about
her mother. One scene she remembered clearly: there was a bright, hot
space framed by the greenish yellow scarves and wings of jungle. A man
in a gay blue skirt and vest and a bright yellow headcloth had come
forward with a slow, undulating walk, like a man dancing in a dream.
His skin was a coppery gold and his slanted eyes glittered. Two men
behind him were bare-chested, with massive gold bracelets on their
arms; they carried curved knives that flashed in the sun. One of them
was holding a tasseled purple parasol over the first man's head as they
moved. And then there was Poppa, looking very thin and straight in his
tight-fitting khaki uniform; he walked right up to the man in yellow; he
bowed, and they shook hands, and the wall of men at the edge of the
jungle roared and shook their spears and swords. "That's the Sultan,
dear," her mother was saying. "The Sultan of Palamangao." Out on the
oily water red-and-blue boats slid by with copper-colored pirate sails,
and deep in the jungle a gong struck once, again—a thin, quavering
sound that made her neck prickle. The Sultan of Palamangao. Her
mother was holding her up so she could see. And then, filled with
delight at the dancing, pirouetting figures, the bright silk robes and
parasols and swords, she felt her mother's arms trembling; and twisting
around quickly saw she was afraid . . .

She peered out into the glare of the yard. Donny had been talking
to himself—a chortling recitative that grew into crowing excitement.
She expected to see Rusty teasing him, but the Cleghorne boy was
crouched several feet away near the edge of the grass pushing his engine
along. Donny was sitting bent forward on his blue-and-white patch of
blanket, clapping his hands at a speckled section of hose whose end
seemed to be hanging from the clothesline. But the clothesline was five
feet away. And then all at once the piece of hose moved and her eyes
focused on the flat, square-snouted head.

She gave a quick, taut gasp.

The snake shifted his head to the right, to the left again, uncertain,
puzzled by the small, chuckling creature, the waving hands.

"Oh," she said. "*Donny—*"

He paid no attention; he was absorbed in this gliding, beguiling pattern of brown-and-white diamonds that moved without moving. He laughed, his bare round head waggling. She had come to her feet. She started forward in a lurch, checked herself. The snake was too near, she was too far away. To run to the blanket would be bad: it would coil and strike before she could get to Donny and pick him up, and there would be nothing she could do. Again she started to move, and stopped. Donny was quieter now. The snake's sudden immobility had bored him; he was gazing up at the sky. She felt cold and hollow and filled with a sickly, foaming substance that had caught in her throat. She looked around wildly once. Rusty was moving away from the snake, unaware of it. There was no one to call. Anywhere around. She must do it alone. Herself.

To turn her back on the scene at the edge of the blanket was actually painful. With the soundless alacrity of a dream she moved into the bedroom, up to the bedside table Sam had made from a weapons chest, opened the drawer and took the holstered automatic and unsnapping the catch drew out the weapon and darted back to the porch. The snake was gone. No—it was coiling. It was coiled. The .45 was loaded but Sam never kept a round in the chamber; she knew that. She gripped the receiver with her left hand; it was all she could do to throw it back. It shot forward again with its clashing metallic sound. She went down the steps sideways, conscious of the screen door slamming hard behind her. Rusty had turned toward her now—in the scan of her eye she saw him freeze with alarm, then start to scramble to his feet.

"Stay where you are," she said. "Rusty. Stay right there. Don't move."

The boy remained motionless, his eyes white and round. Donny had seen her too but all her concentration was fixed on the snake, who had finished coiling. Its head drew back with mesmeric deliberation, the tail a vertical blur; the rattle made a dry, whirring sound, like a bad mechanical toy. She pushed the safety catch off by feel and gripped the big pistol in both hands, her left locked over her right, as her father had taught her at Schofield Barracks years ago. The end of the barrel wobbled up and down past the snake's head. It looked enormous—gross and fearsome, a glittering spring all coiled for death. Donny was talking to her, and she heard Rusty call something, his voice thin with fear.

"That's a good boy," she said. Her voice was a reedy croak, an old hag's false, forbidding tones. The baby moved suddenly then and she gasped, swung the gun to the right. The barrel kept wavering. The buck. That was what she had, she'd heard them say it: somewhere. "Hold—*steady*," she said, half-aloud, and gritted her teeth. You idiot. Steady. She brought the nose of the weapon down until it rested just below the lidded agate eye, holding fiercely with her left hand, and squeezed.

There was a stunning roar. Her hands had been flung up in the air and struck her in the forehead; her wrist hurt. The snake was coiled still tighter, writhing and looping. She brought the gun down and fired again, into the scaled tangle. When the smoke cleared the snake was stretched out, its terrible jaws gaping, its head making short, feeble lurches. The thick body was torn in half a dozen places; blood lay bright and slick on the scales.

She darted forward and snatched Donny up on her hip, moved over to Rusty, who started to cry, a high, agonized wail. "It's all right, Russ." She put the arm holding the gun around him. "It's all right, now." Another screen door bumped and she saw Elaine Kneeland running toward her from two houses up the line.

"What happened?"

"Rattler," she called back. She felt perfectly calm now; as if all her blood had turned to spring water and jelled. "Be careful, Ellie."

"You shot it—!"

"Be careful, now. They go around in pairs. Usually." She remembered Sam's telling her that. "The other one is probably a little way out in the grass. Take Donny, will you?"

"What? No, wait—"

She felt no fear at all. She advanced into the buffalo grass, moving softly, putting her feet down toe first, curving a little to the right—saw the flickering pattern in the sere yellow stalks. She fired twice more. The second snake doubled up in wild contortions, writhing and flailing, as though trying to divest itself of its skin. She stood calmly watching its death throes while Mae Lee clumped down the back stoop of the Cleghornes' quarters, gripping the railing, her face pinched with apprehension.

"It's all right," she called. "I got them both." The powder fumes caught in her sinuses and she coughed. She thought of the rifle ranges at Schofield and Benning, and smiled. Her wrist still hurt, but not severely. From across the parade ground she saw two men in fatigues running toward her.

"Seventh Cavalry to the rescue," she remarked. She walked back and bent over Rusty, who was roaring with surprise and fear. "There, there," she murmured. "Everything turned out all right, you see?"

"It was right there—that close to the blanket?" Mae Lee breathed. "My God—with the kids that near . . . You saved them!"

"Nonsense."

"You did . . ." She gazed at the pistol. "I couldn't have done that."

"Sure you could." It now seemed like the most commonplace thing in the world. You see a rattler, you shoot it: that's what you do.

"No, I couldn't," Mae Lee insisted. "I'd have died of fright. I'd have died."

The soldiers came running up; they were carrying shovels. The first one, a rangy, redheaded man with a broken nose and bushy eyebrows, called: "What's the trouble, lady?"

"No trouble," she said calmly. "Rattler." She pointed. "Two of them. I got them both."

They went over and peered at the corpses. "Don't get up too close to 'em, Dinny," the redheaded man said. "They can sting you after they're dead . . . What a monster!" He gave a long, low whistle. "*Nine—frig-ging—rattles . . .*" He whirled around. "Beg pardon, ma'am!"

"That's quite all right."

"Where'd you learn to use a gun like that?"

Tommy looked hard at him; this was lèse majesté, and he knew it. "Several places," she replied shortly. "I see you've got shovels with you. Will you bury them for me, please?"

"Why—sure, ma'am." He stared at her, awed. "Right away."

Juliana Bentik had come up from four sets down the row and every-one was clustered around her now, chattering like a flock of magpies. She took Donny back on her hip. He gazed at her a moment—then all at once threw back his head in that doll-like way, and laughed without a sound. With his two stubs of front teeth he looked like a jovial little old man. She heard a short, imperious voice, and turned. Amanda Pownall, the Second-in-Command's wife, was coming toward them quickly down the back line. She was wearing a plain gray cotton frock and carrying a wicked-looking lever-action cavalry carbine in her right hand, her seamed face composed, intent. She took in the whole situation at one glance. "Thought that's what it was," she said. "Good girl."

"Thank you, ma'am." Tommy felt absurdly pleased at the com-mendation, and then angry with herself for being pleased.

"She got one of the varmints right though the head, ma'am." The redheaded soldier raised one of the snakes on the shovel blade.

"So I see." Mrs. Pownall examined the swollen, drooping body with interest. "Nine rattles. A regular granddaddy. Thank the Lord some of you girls know how to use firearms decently. If there's anything I can't abide it's helpless females."

There was a little silence. To fill it Tommy said: "I'd better go in and clean this pistol before Sam gets home, or I'll never hear the end of it."

"You know how to *clean a pistol?*" Mae Lee whispered in amaze-ment.

"Course she does," Amanda Pownall snapped. "Every Army wife should know how to field-strip and clean small arms, at least. What we ought to do is run a short course, evenings. I'll speak to Harry." Her lined face cracked into its tough, wintry smile. "My mother shot a redskin right off his pony during the Sioux wars," she said to Mae Lee with relish, and transferred the carbine to her left hand with almost careless professional competence. "Well, that's that." Her eyes glinted warmly at Tommy. "Your papa"—she accented the second syllable—"would be proud of you, Thomas."

She walked off, her skirts fluttering, the carbine's curved brass butt plate glinting in the sun. Now, after the flurry of excitement, there was a reaction: everyone was apathetic, no one knew quite what to do. The rattlesnakes were buried without honors, and the soldiers sauntered back to their detail. Elaine went in with Mae Lee to calm her down, and Tommy took Donny inside and put him down in his crib.

"Dango," he muttered. "Heh dow lub a gan." He waggled his head, scowling at her crossly, and she realized he disliked the gunpowder smell. "Good," she said aloud. "Remember it. Hate it all your life." With a tremulous rush of affection she caught him up and pressed him against her heart. "My baby," she murmured. "My own baby boy." And her eyelids stung with tears.

In the bedroom the drawer to the bedside cabinet was still open; the holster lay on her pillow. She had no recollection of dropping it there. She got out the brush and thong and the little bottle of Hoppe's Number 9 solvent out of the cabinet and sitting on her cot began to clean the barrel. She knew she ought to field-strip the weapon but she'd forgotten how to disengage the receiver. She drew the cleaning pads through the barrel, watched them emerge as greasy black wads.

I did it, she thought, inhaling the pungent banana-oil–and–ether smell of the solvent. I actually did it. I saved my baby. The one time I met a crisis and Sam wasn't here to see. Of course if he'd been here he'd have done it—better and quicker; and I'd have never known whether I could have met it or not . . . Now he would never know what she'd felt those—what? minutes? seconds? It now seemed like hours and hours. Nobody would ever know but she. That was how life was, perhaps: you fought your bravest battles unapplauded and alone.

She had poured some oil on a rag and was cleaning the chamber when her bowels clutched in a spasm that made her gasp; she jumped to her feet and half-ran to the toilet. Sitting there, streaming, she began to laugh. "What every Army wife should know," she breathed. Shivering, gripping her knees, she began to sob tightly. Laughing and sobbing she pressed her head against the cool, rough adobe wall.

The couples moved up the steps; the uniforms were somber against the bright splashes of the women's gowns, pasteled now in the dark. All the lights were covered with Japanese paper lanterns, a burnt orange hue; the club looked curiously spacious and festive, freed of the usual overhead glare. On the stand, draped with black and gold, the band was playing a waltz. Tommy, talking with Elaine Kneeland, recognized Sergeant Kinch playing inaudibily in a mute, his thick fingers fluttering over the valves, and the drummer, little Private Ostrowsky, hunched over, his head cocked, listening to the dry patter of the snare. The walls were filled with placards and banners. One was a replica of a battle

streamer, but larger, and said: CAMBRAI—ST. MIHIEL—MEUSE-AR-
GONNE and another, the largest of all, centered above the bandstand, proclaimed: WELCOME GENERAL PERSHING.

"To think he's actually *here!*" Elaine Kneeland exclaimed; she was a
plain, heavy woman with fair hair and a placid smile. She plucked nervously at the front of her gown, like a staff sergeant getting ready to
stand inspection. "That he came all the way down *here*, I mean . . ."

"Yes," Tommy answered dryly. "Just think of it."

Then Colonel Howden's aide, Lieutenant Geyger, was standing in
front of them, his body faintly inclined, giving them that distant, official
smile. Sam murmured, "Lieutenant and Mrs. Samuel A. Damon," for all
the world as though they hadn't seen each other three hours before, and
Lieutenant Geyger repeated their names to Captain Tyson, the post
adjutant, who relayed this precious information to Lieutenant Colonel
Pownall, the Second-in-Command, who passed it on to the CO. "For
that is the way it is done in the Army," Tommy murmured to herself,
smiling, moving along the reception line. But tonight was different, for
tonight Colonel Howden, instead of being his frosty, paternal self, was
looking fiercely alert, almost pugnacious; he turned to his right, murmuring their names still again—and there was General Pershing, looking
exactly as he had in France, tall and stern and with a twinkle in his eye,
iron and old leather, everybody's dream of a grandfather-hero. His face
broke into its quick, martial smile, deep lines outside the mustache, and
he was saying, "George Caldwell's girl, of course, of course, how are
you, my dear?" and to Sam: "Yes, the Night Clerk—Brigny, wasn't it?
What a pleasure to see you again, my boy, a distinct pleasure!" He had
taken Sam's hand in that grip that could make a man wince, his eyes
sparkling, and she was glad she'd insisted on Sam's wearing his ribbons
that one evening, even though it had brought them very close to a
quarrel. "Howden," General Pershing was saying, "you didn't tell me
you had young Damon down here with you!"

"Why—I didn't think of it, General," the Colonel said, glancing fearfully at them all. "I didn't realize you knew him . . ."

"Know him!" The Iron Commander's eyes glinted with displeasure.
"I pinned that Medal of Honor on him myself. He's one of nine names
in my own private Pantheon of heroes, Howden. One of *nine*."

"Yes, sir," Colonel Howden said, and gave Sam a startled look.

There were other officers who had come to Fort Dormer with the
General of the Armies; they were standing to one side in a little group,
as though not to dull the luster of the General's presence. They had the
urbane, casual assurance of all staff officers, and she began greeting them
perfunctorily—all at once she stopped. A tall captain with a long,
straight nose and high cheekbones and cool amber eyes was bowing
toward her and saying, "I had the honor of serving with your father
briefly, Mrs. Damon." She smiled in confusion. What was his name?

Her heart still dancing from the encounter with Pershing, the sheer force in the man, the avalanche of memories he had released in her, she'd missed it.

"You probably don't remember me," he was saying to Sam. "We met in France—"

"I remember it perfectly, Captain Massengale. A courtyard near St. Durance."

"Ah, you *do* remember!" Massengale laughed easily, and she saw he was quite handsome; his face looked younger and less cold when he laughed. "I was afraid our meeting might have been swallowed up in the pressure of circumstances."

" 'Days of tumult and tension,' you called them," Sam answered; he was smiling, but there was a trace of iron in his voice Tommy had learned to recognize.

Captain Massengale watched him with faint amusement. "Did I, Damon?"

"Your very words, sir."

"How remarkable you remembered them! Perhaps it was the alliteration." He smiled, his lips curving broadly without affecting the expression in his eyes. "Well, they're over and gone now. *When the hurly-burly's done, when the battle's lost and won—*"

"*That will be ere the set of sun,*" Sam went on quietly.

Massengale's eyebrows rose. "How apt! No one thinks of that line. Danielsson here tells me you've become quite a military history buff. Is that true?"

Tommy watched the two men, not concentrating on what they were saying, listening only to the intonations of their voices, their changes in expression—a habit she had fallen into as a girl at post functions; you could learn more about people that way than by following the words. She was conscious of a current between the two men; they were cordial enough, they exchanged views and welcomed each other's opinions . . . but there was something—the merest shade of punctiliousness on Massengale's part, the faintest suggestion of overcorrectness on Sam's. They've had a quarrel, she decided abruptly, and the thought gave her a strange thrill of excitement. That time in France.

They were calling for the grand march now. General Pershing had taken the hand of Mrs. Howden, rank followed rank, and the column, smoothly assembled, wound back and forth through the long room to the strains of "Sabers and Spurs." Tommy moved along with Sam near the end of the procession, disliking its formalized severity but constrained nevertheless to admire the mesmeric flow of polished leather, glinting buttons and insignia in the soft orange-gold light.

Then the band broke into "Rose of the Rio Grande" in honor of Colonel Howden, who was a native Texan, and the slow, glittering serpent broke up into couples. Tommy danced with a bachelor officer named Breslyn, and then Jack Cleghorne cut in, looking moody and roguish.

"Jack, you're a born fool," she said, laughing. "You know you ought to be performing your duty dances."

He shrugged. "Time enough for that. I want to talk to you."

"No, you don't."

"That's right. I don't. I want to bask in your reflected glory."

"You'll pay for it, Mr. Madcap."

"Everybody pays for everything."

Everyone was dancing now; she saw General Pershing go by with Mrs. Howden, forcing her robust bulk along manfully, his face set in a hard, glassy smile. Sam was dancing with Major Kostmyer's wife; he winked at her once—the flick of one eyelid, his face grave—swung away again. The band was playing "Avalon," a tune she loved, Jack was watching Irene Keller over her head and talking about nothing in particular, and then he stiffened and stopped, and looking up she saw it was Captain Massengale. Jack gave her an arch, significant glance from under his brows, and bowed out. Massengale swept her off and away with astonishing ease; he was a superb dancer.

"—You can't be a Pointer," she protested.

He laughed. "Why not—has it gone out of fashion?"

"You don't dance like an Academy product. There's a marked absence of by-the-numbers marching and countermarching."

"Oh, we're not as bad as all that, are we? . . . Of course"—he threw her the quick, utterly charming smile—"I forgot—you're a renegade. A very engaging one, however."

"Thank you, sir."

"No, I learned at a dancing class in Albany called Monsieur Charbet's. He was a very correct Frenchman with black satin pumps and a pince-nez with a lovely long blue ribbon. He used to call in a flat, despotic voice he never had to raise: 'Gardez les bienféances, mes jeunes gens! Bienféances et élégance. You do not pump, you do not prance, you are neither British guardsmen nor Apache tribesmen—grace and decorum!'" He laughed pleasantly. "I dislike acquired skills. What I value are the natural ones, the miraculous endowments—those attributes the Greek gods and goddesses sprayed their favorites with, like perfume. Those are the delightful talents. Don't you agree?"

Surprised, off-balance—this man apparently never said what you expected he would—she laughed. "I don't know—I've never thought much about it, I guess . . ."

"A daughter of the Army, without a violent opinion? I'm surprised at you . . . Take yourself, for instance. Your beauty, your élan, that quality of expectation—all that is nothing you acquired: it fell around you like a mantle and you wore it without thinking."

She threw her head back. "You've never met me before . . . !"

"That doesn't matter. It's apparent in a moment—you have such a rich sense of enthusiasm, of life's windy mornings—you've no idea how thoroughly I envy that: you just *know* people are going to be good all day, and that the next garden is going to contain all the golden apples . . ."

"I'd better get out of the desert, then!" She started to laugh, and stopped. When he was serious the high, Indian-like cheekbones gave his long face great force. She lowered her gaze and contented herself with dancing for a few moments, careful to keep her fingers from touching his shoulder bars and tarnishing them. She didn't know what to make of him. It was officers' club chatter, gallant and gay, running along the edge of impertinence—and yet there was a powerful current flowing underneath it: he was reaching toward her, in a way she couldn't quite fathom. Abruptly she said: "Are you married, Captain?"

His smile was easy and remote again. "Why do you ask?"

"I was thinking what an extraordinarily lively time of it a wife of yours would have."

That pleased him immensely. "That's grand—I must tell that to Emily the next time she finds fault with me . . . I won't have to wait long!"

The number ended then and they drew apart and applauded. He made no move to leave her, which was surprising. The orchestra began to play "After You've Gone," and the memories of France rolled back over her again. She thought of rainy nights at Savenay, with the sea wind swirling the leaves in drenched little tempests and the casements rattling, and the lonely, sepulchral murmur of the wards . . .

She blinked. General Pershing was dancing with Irene Keller; her fleshy, handsome face was glowing, her eyes rested on his in adoration, she was talking to him with rapid insistence. Tommy could imagine the pattern of plea and cajolery, self-deprecation and eye-fluttering adulation, all of it nicely calculated to display Bart Keller's desires and capabilities in the most attractive light. The bitch, she muttered under her breath. Well, there was always one on every post—and there she was, doing her damnedest in the three or four minutes she had. She would do it, too—she'd nail down Schofield or the Presidio or Monroe before she was through. General Pershing was entranced with her.

To turn the subject from herself Tommy said: "It was nice of the General to come down here into the wilds to visit us poor beggars in red."

Massengale's expression changed—he was again dispassionate, reflective, astute. "The Chief likes to break precedent now and then," he said evenly, watching Pershing and the Keller woman for a moment. "He feels it keeps people on their toes. We've covered a lot of ground on this trip. No post is less important to him than any other. We can't all sit on the right hand of the throne—but they also serve who only crawl through the cactus and the thistles."

She cocked her head; his long, pale face wore a mournful smile. "Still, you'll admit there are more exciting places to serve, Captain."

"Yes indeed. I don't believe in bromides when the facts are quite the reverse. However, the Chief holds that the good officer goes where he is assigned, and gives the best of which he's capable. But of course you know that as well as anyone here, don't you?"

She started to make a rather sharp retort—references to her Army upbringing had begun to irritate her increasingly—but his expression was friendly, sympathetic, quite guileless. She moved easily in his arms, following his lead, conscious of this undercurrent of excitement he had struck off in her. Being in his company, listening to him, you thought of power, of the rush of great events: barricades, and cabinets falling, and proclamations to cheering crowds from somber marble balconies . . . He will go far, she thought, watching the proud, ascetic discipline in his face, the strange amber eyes. He will become Chief of Staff, if events follow a logical course; or even if they don't. Yet—her eyes rested for the briefest second on his ribbons—he had no combat decorations; the French, Belgian and Italian ribbons were what a competent—a very competent—staff officer would get, if somebody in a position of influence was there to get them for him . . .

"Yes, I believe in serving where I'm assigned, too," he was saying. Quick as her glance had been, he had intercepted it. "I've always thought the post of military attaché to our London embassy would be just about the sweetest cream puff of them all. However, there's a rumor that the man *in* that most delicious spot would prefer to be back in Washington . . . Life is a curious thing, isn't it? When I was seven—"

He broke off, disengaging himself so dexterously she started; looking up she saw General Pershing's squared, solid face, flushed now with dancing and the warmth of the club.

"You can't have all the young, beautiful ones to yourself, you know, Massengale," the General said.

Tommy stared at him. He was going to dance with her: the General of the Armies, guest of honor at a formal dance-reception, had decided to dance with the wife of a lowly first lieutenant. She was conscious of a frieze of astonished, delighted, outraged faces at the edges of her vision. This simply wasn't done. But Black Jack Pershing was going to do it.

"It was merely a reconnaissance, sir," Massengale was saying without a trace of surprise. "I was about ready to report in."

The General laughed quietly, and stepped off with her. "Decided to dispense with protocol," he informed her. "No reason the young fellows should have all the fun.—I can't *stand* women who have no sense of rhythm," he said sternly. "No excuse for it."

"You've certainly surrounded yourself with some exceptional officers, General." It was the first thought that had come into her head. Everyone in the place seemed to be watching them. Colonel Pownall had stopped dancing entirely and was staring at them, his mouth open.

"What? Massengale? Yes, he's first rate. I'm very pleased with him. Wonderful balance of forcefulness and tact. Just what I needed on that damned Peruvian mission . . ." His face turned rock hard at some recollection, then brightened again. "Tell me about your father, my dear." They chatted for a while; the orchestra was playing "Chérie," and Pershing now and then hummed a phrase of the refrain. Tommy felt like shrieking with laughter. She had the General all to herself now until he left her: no one in the armed forces of the Western World would dare to cut in on him.

"And what about that mustang of yours? How's he getting along?"

"Oh, splendidly, sir! He's so enthusiastic . . ." She heard the trill in her voice, and was irritated by it. She hated women who fluttered and gushed around general officers—she remembered what her father had once said about Army wives always acting as though a general were going to exercise some eerie droit de seigneur at any moment. "It's just his whole life, and you can't say any more than that."

"A fine lad. Fine. A fighter! The very spirit of the AEF. What a feel for troops! To lead, to *lead*, not to drive—there's the essence of command, my dear."

"Yes, that's so true . . . The only trouble is, he keeps neglecting me." And she smiled mischievously, to give him a clue.

"No! I'll have him on the carpet at oh-eight-hundred hours tomorrow. What are the charges and specifications?"

"He's forever studying on his own, nights and Sundays, when he hasn't got the duty. It's incredible—military history and ballistics, and do you know, he's taught himself French and Spanish all by himself? so he can read it and speak it?"

"Has he really?" The General beamed. "I worked nights to get my law degree when I was training cadets at Lincoln . . . Gad, I hope his French is better than mine. I remember at Bombon I tried to have a conversation with General DuMaurasque's little girl—she was six or seven—and I got off what I thought was a splendid sentence. She stared back at me without one glimmer of response. I bent down and said, 'Comprenez vous, mademoiselle?' She shook her head and told me: 'Non.' "

Tommy laughed: she could understand why women thought Black Jack Pershing attractive. But "Chérie" wasn't going to last forever. "No. Sam's steady as a rock, General. I'm the one that's worried, actually. I'm afraid I'm hurting his career." This time she did not smile mischievously.

"Why's that, my dear?"

"Because of Poppa, sir. I'm afraid there's a lot of talk about Sam marrying me to further himself, and so on. Of course it's utter rot, but it can't help him any."

The Iron Commander's eyes glinted. "I know. They said the same things when I married Helen. Let them talk. It keeps them busy when they get tired of pushing papers around. There's only one thing that matters anyway, and that's when the country is threatened."

"I know, sir, if only it doesn't prejudice people against him. He deserves so much . . ." And then she decided to risk it. "He feels he's missed out on so much, General, not getting to the Point. He was accepted, you know, for the following year, but he was so anxious to get into the Army he enlisted, that was in '16—he was with you in Mexico, I guess you know that. But he feels he's missed so much in terms of schooling, the balance of theory and practice—the kind of thing that Benning would give him, the company commanders' course . . ." .

The General's eyes seemed to veil slightly—for a second she was afraid she'd gone too far; then he nodded, his mouth firm under the neatly trimmed mustache. "He ought to go to Benning. He certainly ought to go."

"He'd really respond to it, sir. Not that he'd ever mention it himself, he's happy to be serving anywhere he's sent . . ."

The number was drawing to a close. Sergeant Kinch's horn was nicely weaving the plaintive little melody.

"Well," Pershing said. "We'll have to give it some thought.—What's this I hear about you shooting a dozen rampaging diamondbacks with a forty-five?"

"Oh, that—that was strictly in line of duty, sir!"

The number ended. The First of the Doughboys stepped back and bowed and moved off in the direction of Harriet Jamieson; a member of his staff, a captain named Coleman, asked her for the next dance. She felt thrilled and overwarm and nervous drifting about under the orange petals of the lanterns—she was talking much too rapidly. I danced to "Chérie" with General Pershing, she thought; if nothing else ever comes of it, I can tell my grandchildren that.

Hours later, back in their quarters, undressing, she said: "That fellow Massengale—he's extraordinary, isn't he?"

Sam was drawing off his puttees. "Yes, he's pretty impressive."

"We danced two numbers. What's his background, do you know?"

"I'm not sure. Amherst, I think, or Williams—one of those exclusive rich men's colleges. Then the Point. Class of '17. Marv Hansen says he comes from a wealthy family in New York State."

"How'd you meet him?"

He rubbed his eyes and yawned. "Oh, he was coming up with some changes in orders and he got lost. We were just coming out of the line."

She watched him. "That was all?"

"Well, no." He grinned at her. "Some of the boys were a little casual with him—or he thought they were, anyway, the staff often thinks the line doesn't show enough snap-to deference; and he got pretty fierce with them. I had to straighten him out a bit. When men have been in the line for days you don't talk to them that way. We were both captains then, fortunately."

Her mind perched on this thought for a moment unhappily, then swooped on. "That's what you ought to be. An aide to General Pershing."

"Me?" He smiled his slow, sad smile. "Honey, I'm a troop commander. I'm not a fancy dan, full of drawing-room charm and classical references and the right word at the right time and all that."

"You could learn . . ."

"Maybe. I doubt it." He chafed his naked shoulder with a thumbnail. "I'll tell you: I think you're either born with it or you're not. Like curly hair."

Tommy started faintly—she'd just remembered Massengale's opening confession. Was that *his* divinely bestowed attribute? "You don't think he's learned it, then."

"Oh, some of it, maybe. But not the charm, not the instinctive move toward the politic reply." He paused. "Massengale will never make an enemy and he'll never have a friend."

"Oh, he has lots of friends—"

"Not the kind I mean. Not the kind that'll stick by you in the clutch."

"That's ridiculous." She fought the deep pull of his mind. "How can you possibly know anything like that?"

"It's just a guess. An uneducated guess." He grinned again. "A lot of the Chaumont crowd were like that. They sat back there and fiddled with their mosaics and gave the orders—they didn't have to be around when they got carried out."

"You've said yourself General Pershing was a soldier's soldier . . ."

"He is."

"Well, he ran things at Chaumont, didn't he?"

"Honey, every man in power finds himself surrounded by a coterie. That's in the nature of things. A few are unselfish and devoted, some are brilliant and ambitious in a broad sort of way, most of them are self-serving and ambitious in a narrow sort of way. You can't blame Pershing. His job was to get on with the business, using what material he had at hand."

"You excuse anybody you want to," she fretted; she felt rebellious, vindictive, full of disorder, she didn't know why. "He's going to go a long, long way," she declared, pointing her finger. "Massengale. You wait and see."

He studied her evenly. "You're absolutely right. He will."

"He's got all the qualities needed."

"All but one." Sam tapped his heart with two fingers. "He doesn't care enough. About people. There's something lacking there, some funny little—lack."

"How do you know *that?*"

He got up and went to the window, where the desert wind puffed the blue target-cloth curtains, faded now on their weather side to a pale azure. "He doesn't think people are important. Not desperately important, I mean. More important than thrones and symphonies and triumphal arches."

"My God, Sam. You just said you only met him once before this . . ."

"That's all a man needs, most of the time."

"Snap judgments." She dropped the hairbrush on the bedside chest. "Old Mr. Dead-eye. Well, this time you're wrong. He has a fine sense of humor, a real natural warmth—I could feel it. You're wrong."

He made no reply, and this upset her more than if he'd produced some sudden, annihilating refutation. She passed her hands over her hair, raised the mosquito net and slid into bed, tucking the net down around her tightly, pulling it taut against the T-bar at her head. "I had the strangest feeling," she could not help saying aloud; she felt all at once light-headed and irresponsible in the sultry heat, the late hour, the slow, humming silence after all the fanfare and exhilaration expelled on the breath of power's passing. "I had the feeling you and he are tied together, somehow—that you're going to meet years from now in a tremendous crisis."

Sam chuckled. "He'll be far beyond the likes of me."

"Don't say that . . ."

"I don't begrudge him that. If that's what he wants."

"Well anyway: you're going to. In some desperate emergency."

"Lord, I hope not." He was lying on the floor, naked except for his underdrawers, doing leg exercises; his body was lean and hard, with the ridges of muscle bright in the lamp's frail glow. "He'd be a formidable adversary, I know that much."

"Yes, he would." She lay perfectly still, watching his exertions. "But he's afraid of you."

He stopped and looked toward her. "What makes you say that?"

"Nothing." She laughed, and pumped her feet up and down in the bed like a little girl; she felt bound in excitement. "Two can play that psychic game of yours, you know."

"You're pretty cranked up for a weary wife and mother. Singled out by old Black Jack himself for a turn around the floor. I hope it doesn't go to your head." He rolled over on his stomach and began doing push-ups. "What did you talk about with him all that while?"

"Oh—several things: we discussed Poppa, and my resourcefulness, courage and marksmanship; and what a superb dancer the General is."

"Nothing more than that?"

"Oh, yes—you. We discussed you at length: your predilection for snap judgments, your stubbornness, above all your pigheaded, bone-headed recalcitrance about wearing your—"

He leaped to his feet, pulled the mosquito net out from under the mattress and reached in and kissed her; she gasped with surprise. She felt a swift shiver of dereliction mingled with covert glee. It was the first time in their marriage she'd lied to him in an important matter—it was the first time she'd schemed and maneuvered, tried to arrange something behind his back. Did he suspect something of it? She remembered Reeny Keller's face when she'd been dancing with the General: avid, almost imbecilic with guile . . . Had she herself looked like that, for all the world to see? Was she turning into a campaigner, then?—scheming, snatching at the propitious moment, one with that company of hard-jawed, ferret-eyed women she'd watched with such loathing all these years?

Sam was making love to her; her thoughts tossed themselves upward in dreamy fountains, dissolved in rainbow bands of pure sensation. It was fair enough, she thought falteringly, Sam deserves it if any soldier in the American Army does—and nothing may come of it, anyway, and I don't care—

She drew him to her, her blood thick with desire, her fingertips burning; it mingled hotly with the excitement of the dance, her moment, her daring, her folly. For one last moment she looked backward coolly. But I won't do it again, the thought stirred, and stopped. It will be my one wifely indiscretion: and there it will remain . . .

"It was genius," Ben Krisler said. He scrubbed his cropped black hair with his knuckles feverishly, his eyes snapping. "A moment of pure genius. Wasn't it, Sam?"

"What? What was genius?" Marge demanded.

"You tell it, Sam."

Damon smiled at him; it was obvious Ben was dying to tell the story himself. "No, go ahead."

"Well, all right." Ben drained his glass and turned to his wife and Tommy. "Swanson started it all—you know Swanny, he taught half a semester at Alligator Bend Aggies or some place and he's never got over it—every time he opens his mouth it sounds as if he's revising a bloody dictionary—"

"He's a divine dancer," Tommy broke in, "—which is a good deal more than you two clodhoppers can say."

Ben blinked at her, suddenly crestfallen. "I wouldn't say we're all that bad . . ."

The girls looked at each other and laughed, and Tommy said, "Of course not, you're both Vernon Castles on wheels. Carry on gaily."

"Well, Swanson gets on his feet and hems and haws around for a quarter of an hour, and then finally he pulls a long face and says, 'If the Colonel will permit me to say so, it is my contention that the subject is too complex to be covered adequately in the time allotted.' Or some such dunderfunk. And Colonel Marshall's eyes got that curious pale gleam in them—you know that look, Sam—and he says: 'You genuinely feel that, do you, Swanson?' 'Yes, sir,' Swanny says, 'in point of fact I do.' 'Captain,' old Marshall says in his crisp way, 'there is no military subject that cannot be covered adequately in *five* minutes, let alone twenty. It's simply a matter of compression—and a knowledge of what is important and what is extraneous.'

"Well, Swanson's mouth gave that funny smirking twitch, and a couple of muffinheads at the back of the room shifted their feet. And the Colonel, who doesn't miss one hell of a lot, gets a little twinkle in his eye and says: 'I see we have some skeptics in our midst. All right. I will now demonstrate that any topic, of no matter what scope, can be successfully outlined in five minutes. Give me a subject, Captain.' Old Swanny blinks at him. 'Any subject at all, Colonel?' 'Any one at all.' There is a pause, and then Swanny says, 'The Civil War,' and the whole class roars with laughter. 'Very well,' says the Old Man with a grin. He nods at Sam and says, 'Time me, Damon, if you will, please.' And Sam looks at his watch as if we're getting ready to jump off at Montfaucon and says: 'Go.' "

Ben slapped his hands on his breeches. "And he did it! The whole works—early southern victories, inadequacies of command and discipline in the Army of the Potomac, then Shiloh and the Mississippi strategy of Grant and Sherman, the turning points at Vicksburg and Gettysburg, the breakthrough into Georgia and the Carolinas and the threatened encirclement of Lee's Army of Virginia. I've forgotten half of it. And he stops and turns to Sam and says, 'Time?' and Sam says: 'Four minutes, fifty-two seconds, Colonel.' "

"I think that's wonderful." Marge Krisler sighed and wrinkled her nose. She was a plump, pretty blonde from Krisler's hometown of Menominee, Wisconsin who had married Ben on his graduation from West Point in the spring of 1918. Essentially a farm girl, simple and good-hearted, she had an almost mystic reverence for things of the mind. "I think it's marvelous, being able to hold all those facts and—and philosophies in your head like that . . ."

"They call him a stuffed shirt, some of them," Ben said. "Well, if he is, that's exactly the kind of stuffed shirt I want to be. And he doesn't give a damn what anybody happens to think, either."

"He gives more of a damn than you do, Benjy," his wife replied mildly, "or he wouldn't have got to be colonel."

"He's a great man," Damon said, and sipped at his drink. "He's going to rebuild the Army."

"If they don't bury him in Outer Mongolia first," Tommy observed.

"Bury him?" Marge looked concerned. "Why should they do that?"

"Politics, politics, Margie my love. How did you think little soldier boys get to be Chief of Staff? It's the same old war between Peyton March and Pershing, only we're getting down to the second generation." Tommy pressed out her cigarette in a big, ugly, green-glass ashtray. "MacArthur will get it. MacArthur hates him with a passion."

"How do you know all that, Tommy?"

"A big bird told me. There's a power struggle going on in Washington right this minute. And MacArthur is in on the ground floor with that God damned permanent star of his. Wherever have you been, all these years?"

"Canal Zone," Marge answered mournfully, and they all laughed.

The four of them were sitting in the Krislers' quarters, which were painfully adjacent to the Damons'—only the thickness of one-inch siding separated their sleeping offspring—after a forbidden meal of scrambled eggs and toast, cooked on a hot plate Tommy kept in a commode under a ragged serape. They had been to the post dance that evening and had observed all the amenities, drunk the innocuous punch and chatted pleasantly with the other officers and their wives. The rank had—mercifully—left early and they had spiked their drinks and danced furiously and long; and now they were back in their own two-family set for what Tommy called The Hour of Truth and No Consequences. The men had shed their blouses and the girls kicked off their heels. Ben had produced a label-less bottle filled with a cloudy fluid that tasted like burned pine needles but which he swore was topflight gin; and they were sipping at it and talking in an affectionate, desultory way of the things they'd wanted to talk about all evening. For Sam it was the nicest moment of the week—he loved these Saturday nights, listening to the lively exchanges between Tommy and Ben, and thinking of nothing in particular.

"Poppa knew Marshall on Palamangao when they were both shave-tails," Tommy was saying. "I remember he told a wonderful story about him. He was leading a patrol out in the jungle and they were wading across this river. There was a splash near them and someone yelled, 'Look out for the bandy-flaking crocodiles!' and the whole bunch panicked and ran right over him and stomped him into the mud. He picked himself up and climbed the bank, called the detail to attention, gave them right-shoulder arms and marched them all right back down into the stream and then back out again. Then he inspected their weapons and carried on. And he never said another word to them about it."

"I can just see him," Ben chortled. "Perfectly impassive, all over gumbo and vines. Command presence." He grabbed his big nose between thumb and fingers. "That's an interesting problem. How would you have handled that, Sam?"

"I'd have been out of that water fifty feet ahead of the nearest trooper. No crocodile is going to nibble *my* toes."

"They say they go for the genitals every time."

"Ben!" Marge said.

"Cold fact. Sort of an antipasto before the main course. Comes from the Sanskrit *krakalooloo*, meaning: 'to castrate with one swift bite.' "

"That's enough," Marge threatened him. To Tommy she said, "Honestly, it's embarrassing—he's always got his mind on his private parts."

"That's right," Tommy rejoined, "—and if it's not on his it's on yours."

"What's more important?" Ben demanded in the general laughter. "You have five seconds to think up a happier alternative, all of you . . ."

"It's odd, isn't it?" Marge narrowed her large hazel eyes. "I mean thinking of Colonel Marshall as a young second lieutenant, all covered with mud."

"You see?—there's hope for us yet, gal," Damon offered. "One of these days Ben and I'll be leaf colonels running the Infantry School, imparting words of wisdom in all directions."

"Fat chance," Ben said, suddenly gloomy. "Sitting out in a rain forest in Mindoro, more likely."

"Oh, no more tropics," Marge protested, "—can't we keep out of the jungles for a while? Honestly," she said to Tommy, "you should have seen the shape our set was in at Gaillard—all tangled in vines and thorns, the porch falling in and lizards running around the walls . . ."

"I've seen them," Tommy said with feeling.

"Jesus, I'll tell you camp followers what *I'm* waiting for," Ben declared, and his homely face contorted in a glare of comic outrage. "It's for that golden day when Joey grows up and graduates from the Point— and we can both be lieutenants in the *same company together!* Won't that scrape at your old heartstrings, though?"

"Cheer up, son," Sam told him. "Just think—I may never live long enough to reach the rank I had in the spring of '19."

"You both love it," Tommy accused them. "You're both morbid, masochistic romantics and you love every minute of it, or you wouldn't put up with the whole idiot game . . ."

Ben scratched his scalp furiously. "Maybe she's right, you know? Why *do* we put up with it?"

Damon set down his glass and grinned at Ben, liking him. The first student officer he and Tommy had laid eyes on after reporting in at the Infantry School had been Ben, crouched on his hands and knees in the red dirt and swearing at a yellow wicker baby carriage he was trying to repair. The two men greeted each other with wild enthusiasm. It had seemed like the greatest good fortune; and when they found they'd been assigned to the same set, it struck Damon as the hand of destiny.

Tommy had ridiculed the notion. "You mean because you had that drink together, the day I bamboozled you all over the place in Cannes? Don't be silly. The Army's like Times Square—everybody's always running into everybody else sooner or later. There's a diabolical little termite sitting in the AG's office gleefully moving the pegs around, just to fox credulous souls like you . . ."

All the same she'd been pleased, he could tell; she remembered Ben with affection, and she became fond of Marge. It was a happy arrangement: the two men ran together in the early morning to keep in shape, and now and then played a game of chess; the girls went shopping in the Damons' car or took the children—the Damons now had two, the Krislers four—to the pool. And Damon continued to regard it—surreptitiously—as the hand of destiny.

Ben was holding the bottle toward him again. "Have another snort and wash all your troubles away."

"No more for me." He shook his head. "I've got to get up early tomorrow."

"What in hell for? On the seventh day even the Lord collapsed in the sack."

"He's teaching himself German." Tommy made a face. "Twenty-five words and one irregular verb a day. Zuvereingeschmashen haben worden sein. God, what a language."

"You're learning *German?*" Ben gaped at them. "In addition to everything else?"

"Well you see, he wants to be ready for any contingency. For instance, if he's sent as military attaché to Berlin."

Krisler shook his head. "By God, when I break out of this place I'm going where they've never heard of the printed word. I'm going to put in for Tahiti, and paddle around with armfuls of dusky maidens. And become the oldest, meanest lieutenant in the dogface Army." For an instant he glowered at the little room with its meager furnishings—the motheaten sofa whose back was covered with a violent orange rebozo; the scarred oak chairs; the teakwood taboret surmounted by a cloisonné lamp—acquired, both of them, in the Chinese shops of duty-free Panama City—looking wildly incongruous in this rough company. "Consider this domicile. As a marble hall, I mean. As a real, five-alarm, ring-tailed wreck." The girls both pounced on him for this, and he gave a quick, rueful grin. "I know, honey. Just shooting off my foolish mouth." Humming, "Oh, we'll hoist Old Glory to the top of the pole," he poured himself another drink.

"You're going to feel terrible tomorrow," Marge warned him.

"Then let's live tonight. Right? Besides, tomorrow never comes."

Ben was delightfully, distressingly mercurial. One moment he would be filled with soaring enthusiasm, the next with dour forebodings and violent imprecations against the powers that be. Actually he had—as Damon quickly saw—a lively imagination and a powerful sense of justice, which he tried to obscure through a harsh, peppery pugnacity. His name was synonymous with defiance. He had got in trouble down at Gaillard with his battalion commander over the inadequate medical facilities for the Puerto Rican enlisted men, and at the officers' club at Bragg he'd got into a row with a captain over the status of Negroes in the Army, and had asked him outside—an affair climaxed by replies-by-endorsement, office hours, and a demand for an apology Ben had refused to give.

"You're a born rebel and a troublemaker," Marge would tell him with a strange mixture of rebuke and awe. "Whatever they've got, you're against."

"Only ninety per cent of it, honey," he'd answer with his crusty grin. "The remaining ten per cent I'm a solid conformist."

For all that, he was a good soldier. In the tactical problems, where the instructors leaned toward vigorous and unorthodox solutions, he excelled; he was good with troops, and he knew weapons inside and out. His real failing was a deep dislike for bookwork—he had graduated from the Point as the class goat—and Damon had taken him under his wing, tutoring him now and then, calming him, steadying him down.

"Too much deadwood around," he was saying now, his heels cocked on the table. "That's the good thing about Central America, Sam—every couple of years they throw themselves a real, bang-up revolution, and they line up all those superannuated bastards and bump them off and start over again with company grade types like you and me. It's good for a country to turn everything upside down, smash all the crockery and start fresh: prevents hardening of the brain pan."

There was a faint, brief rap at the door. It opened tentatively, and a figure was standing in the shadow. "Anybody home?" a hoarse voice queried. Damon, turning, heard his wife sigh and Ben mutter something. The door swung open farther then and admitted Major Batchelder, their instructor in logistics and supply. He was a pudgy, balding man with a very broad, flabby nose that looked as though it had been made of rubber and painted by some whimsical child.

"No, we've just taken off for the Greek Islands," Ben's voice came flatly. "Little pleasure cruise, to get away from all the chicken."

For a moment Major Batchelder gazed at them uncertainly, teetering a little—all at once winked, his large mouth hiking up hugely at the corners. "My students," he declared. "My happy, carefree students. Mind if I come in?"

"You're already in, Butch," Krisler answered. The junior officers had got to their feet, the women were wearing their shoes again. "Well: how are things among the nabobs?"

"Fluid. In the extreme." Batchelder produced a silver flask whose bottom half was of leather sewn tightly around the metal, gave it a quick little shake and slipped it back into his hip pocket. "Muriel's angry at me," he said truculently, eyeing them.

"Damned if I can see why," Ben said.

"No, it's worse. She hates me."

"They all do, Butch," Ben answered. He had sat down again and picked up his glass. "That's the woman's mission. Our job is to beat up on subordinates and do everything in as stupid a way as possible. And *their* job is to hate our guts for it."

"Ben," Marge pleaded, "you know you don't mean that . . ."

"Of course I mean it. Why shouldn't I?" His anger at this capricious intrusion had turned him savage. He couldn't throw one of his instructors out on his ear—which was what he dearly wanted to do—and so he glared at Damon and his wife. "I'm at my most meaningful early Sunday morning . . ."

"Oh, she doesn't," Marge said consolingly to Batchelder. "I'm sure she doesn't hate you, Major."

"Call me Clarence."

There was a brief silence. "Come in and sit down, sir," Marge went on. "Would you like a drink? I'm afraid there's only this funny old bottle of Ben's—"

"That'd do very nicely," the Major said with alacrity. "Fact is, I'm just a trifle low on the oh-be-joyful at present." Picking up the bottle he poured three fingers of gin into the glass Marge had brought him and drank off half of it. "Now where else could this happen?" he mused genially, wiping at his mustache with a forefinger. "Where else but in this small happy family? This band of brothers . . . ?"

"Nowhere else," Ben answered dryly, leaning forward, his eyes snapping. "A thing like this couldn't happen anywhere else in the whole wide world. Can you imagine what that *means*, pal?"

"Ben," Damon said quietly, but the Major's thoughts had wandered back to Muriel, a tall, stern woman who was a Daughter of the American Revolution and owned a silver tea service worth, it was said, two thousand dollars. ". . . Perhaps if we'd had children," he murmured.

"I'm sure they would have taken after *you*, Clarence," Tommy offered.

Batchelder's face changed: with the lightning perceptiveness of the alcoholic he had caught the note of sarcasm, although Tommy was smiling at him winningly. His eyes dropped, he coughed into his hand. "I know. I lack ambition. Muriel says I don't see life as the obstacle race it is—she says I try to run around the barriers instead of—putting myself *at* them properly. Her father was cavalry, you know. If I hadn't been assigned to that course at Riley I would never have met her at all . . ." He gazed at the stained fiberboard ceiling with a kind of fearful wonder, as though this thought had never occurred to him before.

"I just know you'd have made a good father," Marge said impulsively.

His face gave a little quiver, and he pointed at her. "You're the girl I should have married," he declared.

"You should have thought of that sooner, Clarence," Tommy said sweetly.

"It's just like old General Forrest said." Ben's lips drew back from his teeth. "Just a case of gettin' thar fustest with the mostest. Get me?"

Batchelder frowned in distaste. "That's very crudely put, Krisler."

"You're looking at a crude character."

Damon sat with his hands in his pockets, listening uneasily to the exchanges. It was no secret that Batchelder had been sweet on Marge for some time—they'd kidded her about it now and then. But this was the second time in as many weeks he'd dropped in late and sat drinking their liquor and gazing with wistful adoration at Lieutenant Krisler's wife. Borne on befuddled dreams of congeniality and rapport, he would stay on and on, and keep them up till dawn if they let him. Pathetic old bore. Military courtesy demanded they play the gracious hosts; but this hardly fell into one of the prescribed categories. He'd better break this up and forestall Ben's mounting irascibility. From behind the partitions one of the Krisler children—it sounded like Joey—muttered in his sleep. Damon got laboriously to his feet, yawned and said: "I think Donny just called, honey."

"Oh, really?" Tommy caught his glance and rose quickly. "I hope you'll excuse us, Major, but I've got to check on the children."

"Of course." A good West Pointer, mindful of his manners, Batchelder stood up and made an odd little bow. "I daresay it's getting on a bit."

"Hell no, pal," Ben drawled. "Only about quarter to two."

Damon said quickly: "May I offer you a lift back to quarters, Major?"

"Well, no." Batchelder coughed. "Fact is, I'm in a bit of a jam—I wonder if you boys could give me a hand."

"What's the problem?"

"It's the old chariot. She won't budge. Happened right out there on the back line—I was taking a little turn before retiring. Why I stopped in, matter of fact."

"Fan belt go?"

"I don't know what it is, actually. There was this grating noise, and she sank down on one side and quit."

Ben threw Damon a quick, exasperated glance but he ignored it. "Let's take a look."

The night was overcast, without a moon; the air was cool and moist. The three of them walked uncertainly along the back line, following the beam of Sam's flashlight.

"Let's see now," Batchelder said. "It was right about—ah, there she is."

In the soft yellow cone of light appeared what looked like an old-fashioned shay bonnet—suddenly identified as a car top violently canted. About fifteen feet beyond the back line was a drainage ditch, and the Major's Hupmobile had its two left wheels in it.

"How'd you get down there?" Ben demanded.

"Well . . . I figured I'd made a wrong turn."

"I guess so."

Damon got down on hands and knees and looked under the car. The gear box was resting on a half-submerged boulder. "She's hung up," he said to Ben. "We'll have to rock her off. She'll slide down another couple of feet, but that won't make any difference. Once she's clear of that rock we can pull her out with the LaSalle."

"She's at one hell of an angle, Sam."

"Yes. But she won't go over."

"—I can't go home without that car," Batchelder confided to them in a stage whisper, swaying close to their faces. "They never let you forget it, you know. Once they've got the upper hand. It's hell."

Damon pressed the flashlight into his palm. "Just hold on to that, will you, Major? Just hang on to it good and tight." He and Ben took hold of the front bumper and began bouncing the car while the instructor hovered around them, calling encouragement and advice. On the second try Damon felt the chassis move—and saw to his horror that Batchelder was lying prone halfway under the car. He shouted something, the car began to slide—it was impossible to hold it now—eased off the stone and checked at the bottom of the ditch with a bump and a quiver. Damon leaped around to the low side and called: "Major!—" There was no answer. "Christ," he muttered. "Oh—my—Christ . . ." Light from the torch shone up fitfully through the wheels. "*Major—*"

"She's clear, boys," Batchelder's voice came cheerfully. "She's clear . . ."

"You all right?"

"Can't seem to move my arm."

Damon snatched up the flashlight. The instructor's sleeve was pinned under the wheel at the wrist.

" . . . Stupid son of a bitch," Ben was saying hotly, "—don't you know enough to get in out of the *rain?*"

They lifted the wheel enough to free the Major, who scrambled to his feet, bumping his head on the fender. "Hot work, what?"

"Why don't you go someplace and sleep it off?" Ben demanded.

"My boy, that's hardly fair . . ."

"Major." Damon took a deep breath. "Would you go back and get us another flashlight? We're going to need two for this. Ask Mrs. Damon to give you the battle lantern."

"Right." Batchelder turned like a wound-up tin soldier and stomped off toward the house, humming "Three O'Clock in the Morning."

"Jesus, that was close," Damon muttered.

"Dry your eyes. Why couldn't it have been his head?"

Damon went over and started the LaSalle; it turned over on the third try and he backed over to the ditch, nursing the choke with care. He got a length of tow rope out of the trunk and made it fast to the frames of both cars, while Ben started the Hupmobile. The racket was deafening.

"Now when you feel her start to move, open her up easy and cramp your wheel as little as possible. Okay?"

"On to Berlin."

With both engines roaring full blast the Hupmobile rocked, shuddered, and then came up out of the ditch with ease. Damon backed up to put slack in the rope and reparked the LaSalle. Sweating, tired, he felt curiously exhilarated by the little crisis, the old car's performance.

"Man, that buggy's got power to burn.—What happened to Barney Oldfield?"

"Probably went to the latrine and fell in."

"Nope—God protects all fools, drunks and field-grade brass." Leaving Ben to disengage the tow rope he went back to the set. As he stepped on the back porch he heard Batchelder's voice and then Marge's; something bumped heavily, and there was a sound of scuffling. He went in through the kitchen of the Krislers' quarters—and stopped in amazement. The Major had Marge wedged into a corner of the couch; his arms were around her, he was bent forward trying to kiss her and Marge was struggling lamely and saying, "Clarence, please, Major—"

"Margie, dear—I'm a *lonely* man," Batchelder was murmuring with passion, pressing her back on the couch. "A *lonely* man: don't you see?"

"No, now Clarence please, you've—"

"All these months—I've dreamed about you from afar . . ." The Major's head moved like a drugged chicken's as he tried to kiss her throat. Marge's eyes encountered Damon's—a glance he could see was neither terror nor desire but simply distress. She had changed into a housecoat after the men had left and it was hiked up around her hips; one of her slip straps was broken. A strand of hair was hanging low over her forehead, and her cheeks were flushed from exertion; she looked disheveled and provocative, and the Major was plainly aroused.

Damon stepped up and tapped him briskly on the shoulder; he gave a little jump and turned. "Everything's ready, Major," he announced in his most official voice. "All ready to go."

"What? Look here, Damon—"

"Time to go home, sir. *Home.* Car's ready and waiting."

Batchelder squeezed his eyes shut in distaste. "Good heavens, man, can't you see I'm—engaged? Where's your—your sense of the *fitness* of things? the proprieties? . . . What car?" he shouted angrily.

"Muriel's car," Sam said portentously, nodding at him. "You remember: Muriel's car. It's up out of the ditch now."

The Major's eyes clouded. With reluctance he got to his feet and pulled at the front of his blouse. "Quite. Right with you." He turned to Marge in an effort to summon up the tender-eyed ardor of a moment ago—without success. "Well," he said. "Perhaps—another time, my dear."

Marge pulled her housecoat together, laughed nervously and brushed back her hair. "It's all right," she breathed, "—but you'd better go, now . . ."

Damon steered the Major out the front door and around to the back line where the Hupmobile was standing, its motor running smoothly. Ben was nowhere to be seen.

"There she is," Batchelder cried softly. He clapped Sam on the shoulder. "I can't tell you what this means to me, my boy. All in the family, aren't we, Damon? All one loyal, good-hearted little family, tried and true . . ."

Sam watched him depart, grinning, shaking his head. The fatuous, addlepated old fool. He'd make it back to his quarters and cringe before the icy wrath of Muriel, draw off his boots and tumble into bed; and Monday morning he'd hold forth with admirable precision and some wit on the advantages and drawbacks of combat loading for amphibious assault on a hostile shore . . .

He turned. Ben Krisler leaped down the back steps and rushed up to him, his face white and wild.

"Where is he?" he cried. "Where is the son of a bitch?"

"Ben, what the hell—"

"He's gone! You let him go—!" he raged. "And you're my friend . . ."

"What's the matter?"

"The sneaky, sniveling bastard—I'll kill him! I'll break every bone he owns!"

Damon grabbed him by the shoulder. "Ben, for Christ sake—"

"The hell with you—get out of my way!"

He flung Damon to one side and started off down the row. Sam leaped after him and caught him around the waist and they went down, rolling in the dirt road of the back line. He was astonished at Ben's strength; though short, he was agile and in superb condition; and now he was filled with rage.

"Sam—let—me go," he panted.

"No."

"Warning you—*son* of a bitch!"

All at once he shook free, kicking and flailing, and leaped to his feet. Damon caught hold of an ankle and brought him down again and they crashed into the wooden platform that held the GI cans. After nearly a minute of clumsy grappling and floundering Sam got a half-nelson on him and held him pinned against the platform. Ben went on struggling furiously. A light flashed on, and Sam heard Marge's voice above them:

"Stop it, Ben, please stop! Please stop, now . . ."

"—Let me up," Ben said.

"No."

"Sam, I'm warning you—"

"Ben, don't be a God damn fool," he panted. "He's drunk, he didn't know what he was doing . . ."

"The hell he didn't!"

"—he won't even remember it tomorrow . . ."

"By Jesus, *I* will—!" And he began struggling again, got an arm loose and clipped Damon in the face and neck before he subsided.

"All right, you go ahead and beat him up, he's too loaded to defend himself anyway, even if he could, and you'll get a court—*listen* to me! At the very least. You'll ruin your career for good. And for nothing at all . . . Is that what you want? A general court? Is it?"

"It's true, he's right," Marge was saying, right above them. The flash-light—she must have snatched it up from the kitchen table where Damon had left it when he'd come in to find Batchelder—kept playing over them and the garbage cans, the dead wisps of grass. "Listen to him, Ben, you've got to listen to him . . ."

Krisler relaxed again; there was a pause and then he said: "All right. Okay. Let me go, Sam."

"Promise you won't take off after him?"

". . . I promise."

"No fooling?"

"No fooling."

Damon released him and both men got to their feet and stood without looking at each other, a little shamefaced, like schoolboys caught in some truant act.

"Please, Ben," Marge murmured, "come in now, come inside . . ."

He glowered at her, his face gnomelike and harsh in the fitful light of the torch; his cheek was skinned and bleeding. "How could you let him *do* it?" he groaned.

"Ben, it was nothing, I—"

"What do you mean, *nothing!*"

"Ben, he grabbed me! I was in looking at Susan and the baby and I came back into the living room to get the glasses and there he was, right there—and he grabbed me and started ranting . . ."

"He had your clothes half *off*, for Christ sake—you didn't have to just stand there and take it!"

"Ben, honey"—she was starting to cry, her hand to her mouth—"I didn't know what to *do*—he's one of your instructors . . ."

"You think I give a swift shit about that?" he stormed at her. "What I care about is *us*, you and me—they can take their stupid service schools and jam them up their nickel-plated ass, for all I care—"

"*Very pretty!*"

The three of them turned. It was Tommy, now in bathrobe and slippers, standing on the little back porch they shared. "What do you want—a medal or a cough drop? Well, you listen to me, Ben Krisler: you can take your lunatic heroics and jam them up *your* ass! You hear?"

Startled, Damon gazed up at her. She was furious, her breast rising and falling, her hair whipping around her face; she looked barbaric and embattled and utterly beautiful. He hadn't seen her like this since that afternoon on the parapet at Le Suquet, when he'd fallen in love with her. Ten years ago. He remembered that day all at once with a sad, tender pang. Ten years ago. Now she towered over them, her eyes glittering, incontrovertible in her beauty, her wrath.

"What did you think you were going to do?" she demanded. "Kick him in the groin and put him on report—is that it? Why don't you grow up! Do you think they're going to drum him out of service and make you a brigadier? You idiot!—they'll stick you in a nipa hut on Cebu until your toes rot off . . ." Marge was crying softly now, and Tommy came down the steps and put her arm around her. "Come on, honey," she said tenderly, "come on in and I'll give you something so you'll sleep. Come on in, and let these wounded heroes go and avenge their tarnished bloody honor . . ."

They trooped into the Krislers' quarters one by one. Marge sat down at the kitchen table. Tommy gave her a handkerchief and put the coffeepot on the hot plate coil. The two men stood together awkwardly just inside the screen door.

"You ought to be *glad* somebody's willing to make a pass at your wife!" Tommy lashed out at Ben, who gazed back at her guiltily, rubbing dirt and sweat from his neck. "You ought to draw a tour spliced to dear old Muriel, or Nina Swanson, and see how you like that. Yes— some sweet, deadly, willful bitch who'd hound you morning and night, about a set of silver service or your bill at the post tailor's or why in hell you aren't pulling duty at Fort Myer. It's a wonder there's anything left of us to make a pass *at*, truth to tell. You don't know how well off you are, that's half *your* trouble . . . For God's sake, go over and *say* something to her!" she commanded. "Can't you see how she feels?"

Ben looked penitent and cowed. He went over to Marge and kneeling by her chair put an arm around her. "I'm sorry, baby," he said in a low voice. "I—jumped to conclusions."

"It's all right," Marge said; she caressed his cropped head vaguely. Her little button nose was red and her eyes were swollen. "It doesn't matter."

"I'm sorry."

"Honey, I was just trying to . . . to let it pass over. He's such a sad old dope of a man."

"He's a dirty sneak."

"No—he's sad. I can't dislike him—even after that . . ." All at once she looked at Damon. "Only what are we going to do now?"

That was what they all said at such times. Sergeant Torrey after the hangfire row with Townsend at Hardee; Spofford during that stupid court-martial at Fort Halleck, when it was perfectly obvious the hanky-panky involving post-exchange funds went a good deal higher than Demarest; Corporal Taylor in that ruckus over the Indian girl at Dormer. *What are we going to do now?*

"Do?" Tommy said. She swung around, holding the dented tin percolator in her hand. This was presumably a woman's province, the violation of the defenseless wives of subalterns by drunken and irresponsible brass; he could tell she resented Marge's appeal to him. "Do? Why, be just as sweet as apple cider, that's what to do. Honey wouldn't melt in your mouth. And then let him know—just as sweet as apple cider—that if he ever tries anything like that again, you'll remove one slipper and give him a swift crack right across his flabby purple old nose . . ."

"Oh, I couldn't do that," Marge responded anxiously.

"Why in hell not?"

"Tommy," Damon broke in, "he was pie-eyed—he won't remember any of it at all."

"He drove home, didn't he?"

"That's a reflex action. He won't recall a thing." He came up to the table. "Look, Marge, he's infatuated with you, he has been for some time and he forgot himself. That's all. It was a momentary—aberration, and now it's over and done with. What's important is the school—"

He stopped: something he'd said had caused her to break down again and he didn't know what it was. "No," she was saying, "no . . ."

"Marge, it's true. Let's admit it and set it aside and go on from—"

"No," she said, weeping disconsolately. "I know I'm not attractive. I know. They're only interested in me for one thing . . ." All three of them murmured in protest at this but she remained adamant. "No, it's always been that way. Ever since high school. You can't fool yourself about things like that."

"That's not true, Margie, you mustn't think that. Many men find you attractive, for a lot of reasons," Damon heard himself saying, astonished at his own vehemence. "You're witty, and intelligent, and—and lots of fun . . ." He groped his way along, feeling her gaze fastened on him in a kind of hopeless last appeal. He glanced at Ben, who now looked simply confused. Why in hell was he always the one expected to hold the fort? Well he was, he was stuck with it, and that was all there was to it. He went on, elaborating and inventing; and, surprisingly, it worked. The adolescent hobgoblins retreated, Marge's anguish dissolved; she became soothed, sipping at her coffee. And finally she said in a faint voice, "Oh Sam, you're so good to us all. What would we do without you?"

In time Tommy gave her a bromide and put her to bed while Sam talked with Ben, minimizing the whole incident, calming him down, and still later they went back into their half of the quarters and checked the children. Donny was sleeping restlessly, as he always did—convulsed like a climber clinging to a rock face, his forehead sweaty, his eyelids twitching, the bedclothes wound around his wiry body; but Peggy lay as placid as a fairy princess, her cheek in a lovely little curve, her braids pressed against her throat. When Damon kissed her forehead she did not even murmur to herself. How different we all were: how bewilderingly different! The rebels, the acquiescent, the driven and the serene—and everyone toiling along with his full marching order of dreams and fears; some straggling, some falling by the wayside, a few turning off into the jungle or even firing into the column with the savagery of the desperate and lost. But for all that, the procession still wound its laborious, errant way . . .

Tommy was brushing her hair at the little vanity when he came into the bedroom. Yawning he sat down on his cot and said: "Well, it's nice old Butch doesn't go for your type."

"Isn't it?" she said. "Isn't it just?" She gazed at her own image severely, her neck arched. "Well," she said, "you patched things together again. Old Mr. Bromide. But it's no solution."

"What do you mean, honey?"

"All that." She tossed her head toward the partition. "Nothing's solved, you know."

"Honey, nothing's ever solved for good."

"Some other rummy or self-appointed post stallion will start climbing Marge, and Ben'll blow his stack and lay him out and then the fat will be in the fire."

"Maybe so," he answered.

"Maybe? Inevitably. You've only bought him some time, that's all."

He watched her a moment. It was almost 3 A.M., his eyes were burning and his shoulder ached where he'd piled into the wooden frame; but she seemed to want to talk this out, and he was willing to indulge her. "That's what it's all about, isn't it?" he asked. "Buying time? It's like the kids, and mumps and measles: you get over one crisis, and move on to the next."

"But this is totally different—the precipitating factors are different, don't you see?" She set down her brush and turned to face him. "Why do you do it, Sam?"

"Do what?"

"All that—bucking her up, bailing him out . . . Why go to so much time and effort with him?"

He lighted a cigarette, and said: "There are times when nothing is as important as loyalty."

"But if he's only going to get in trouble sooner or later—"

"He's a good officer, Tommy. And a good man. He's terrific with troops—you've never seen him. He'll make a fine commander."

"If he ever gets the chance." She looked down at her hands. "You take too much on yourself, darling. You really do. You can't keep people from being what they are."

"I'm not trying to do that."

"Haven't you ever wondered *why* he's running along the edge of insubordination all the time?"

Probably for the same reason I have to be always helping everybody out and you break out in tantrums, he wanted to say—because of something that happened to us when we were seven, or twelve; and what the hell would *that* prove? But he stilled the impulse. "That's just the way he is, I suppose," he said aloud.

"It's because he hates the Army," she declared. "That's why."

"What makes you say that?"

"He hates the whole system, from muzzle to butt plate—and yet he's stuck with it. He can't stand it, and he can't leave it. And maybe he's not so far off base, either." She looked at him from under her brows, her eyes very deep and intense. "Sam, has it occurred to you that the wrong things are on trial here? that it's not a question of Margie's sexy body or Ben's violent temper, but the whole impossible, myopic lunacy of the Army? Has it?"

Watching her without expression he nodded. "Yes. It's occurred to me."

"I've been giving it a lot of thought. Between letting Bubbles De Grace Charleston all over my toes and smiling winningly at Peavey and passing the canapés around like a good dutiful junior officer's wife, that is." She got up and stood straight as a sentry on post, hands at her sides. "You know something, Sam? It's all a pretty little fraud. This whole band-playing, spit-and-polish system you're wound up in. It is simply insane. The *system* says you're all noble knights in modern armor, holding the wall against the shaggy barbarian invaders. The *fact* of the matter is that there aren't any invaders anywhere around—and if there *were* the American public wouldn't give a hoot in a gale. The *system* says Batchelder is a fine, upstanding old soldier and Peavey is a brilliant tactician and Votaw is a wizard with weapons, and that they're all officers and consummate gentlemen. The *fact*—the *truth* which nobody can mention inside this myth-laden booby hatch—is that Votaw is a pompous ass and Peavey is a power-drunk sadist, and dear old Batchelder is a miserable, wretched, skirt-chasing rummy! . . ."

The last sentence, spoken in a low voice but with great intensity, rang in the little room. Damon said quietly: "He drinks more than he should."

"Oh, Jesus. You sound like Poppa.—He's a disgrace to the uniform eighty-five per cent of the time."

"Not quite . . . He was badly gassed at Vauquois."

"All right, and you were badly wounded at Mont Noir and Ben was badly wounded at Malsainterre. What does that prove? That your luck ran out—that's what you used to say, anyway. Why should he be able to barge in on the four of us at any hour that pleases him? Why should he be *honored* so?"

He sighed, and rubbed his face with one hand. "You don't have to worship at his feet. The theory is that you respect the rank he holds."

"But I don't respect *him*—!"

"Look, Tommy, we don't any of us come up to all we might in this world . . ."

"That's no answer—"

"Ideally he would act in such a way as to command the respect of the lesser grades."

"The fact is that Batchelder can't command the respect of a frog, and that they busted you down from major without a qualm. The *fact* is Courtney Massengale remained a captain, and now he's made major, and he's just been assigned to the War Monuments Commission."

He felt himself start in surprise. "Where'd you hear that?"

"Jeannette North told me. Yes—per diem and a fancy apartment in Paris and a private car to go tooting around to all the battlefields—the ones *you* crawled all over and left your friends on—taking notes for a cute little guidebook." Her face was hard now with scorn. "And he hasn't any combat record at all. Who has a better right to be there, doing that—Massengale or you?"

Well, it was a blow: more than he would have believed. A man who had never been in the line, never cringed under the shriek and slam of high explosive, never stepped out into the terrible chatter of the Maxims—that he should walk through the cemeteries where—

He dismissed the thought; took a deep breath. "Honey, every profession has its own preferments and favoritism."

"And how!"

"All right—people are people. Why do you expect the Army to be immune? It's full of people, too. And some are like George Caldwell and some are like Clarence Batchelder; and most of us are somewhere in between. Do you think I'd have got to be a major without your father's influence?"

Her eyes flashed up at him. "You did it on sheer ability—sheer courage and personal example! He told me so . . ."

"Not quite. Plenty of people did as much as I did, or more, and they didn't get to command a company of infantry." He smiled at her. "*I* think I earned my way, but look at it from the point of view of somebody like Batchelder: Caldwell takes this brash young sergeant—an enlisted man, mind you, next thing to a recruit, he wouldn't even have been a corporal if it hadn't been for our entering the war; he writes him up for every decoration under the sun, pushes him up to a majority— and the conniving little bootlicker not only grabs everything within reach but marries Caldwell's daughter into the bargain, to advance himself some more . . ."

Tommy's mouth drew down wryly. "Well: at least nobody can accuse you of that."

"Of course they can. Anybody can accuse anybody of anything. There's no action on earth, from Adam on down, that can't be misconstrued, if the beholder has the inclination." He paused. "You know all this, honey. You've known it longer than I have."

"No. I didn't know it at all." Standing by the window now she gripped her arms together as if she were cold. "I just accepted it. And then I rebelled against it, without really knowing, either . . . I got a letter from Marie Lovewell today," she said.

"Really?" Pete had resigned from the service when they were at Hardee. "Why didn't you tell me?"

"I wanted to think about it awhile first. I wanted to talk with you about it." She studied the toes of her slippers. "Pete's been making a lot of money building houses in and around Chicago—there's a big building boom, apparently. They've got a lovely place out in Evanston and the kids are in private school. Marie was asking me about places to stay in France. They're going over to Europe in a month or two. A vacation."

He found he was looking at the two parallel grooves in the floor that had probably been made by some heavy piece of furniture. The round nickel alarm clock on the bed table kept up its dry, furious ticking— when you listened to it closely you were almost certain its rhythm varied, that it picked up and then fell away again, every twenty seconds or so.

"Where are we going, Sam?"

He glanced at her uncertainly. "What do you mean?"

"I mean where are we headed? really? You'll finish up here and you'll stand high in your class, maybe at the top, and it'll go into your 201 file—and where will they send you then? Luzon, Wyoming, back to Texas, Nicaragua maybe—another school, another post sunk deep in the plains. And we'll go on showing up at the Saturday night hops, and you'll go on drilling people and studying the campaigns of Artaxerxes or learning Finno-Ugrian on your own . . . and then in ten more years, or twenty, you'll be back to major, if you're lucky, and ready to be put out to pasture, and the kids will have the glorious possibility of other army brats to choose their mates from . . ." She ran her hand through her smoothly brushed hair, disheveling it abruptly. "What's it all for, Sam? Really and truly. You know something? Life's going by, *our* lives, the only ones we have—and we haven't got a whole awful lot to show for it, either. Our lives, Sam . . ."

To his surprise she was not on the edge of weeping; she had not raised her voice. But there was something in the flat, controlled tone and the set of her face that frightened him more than tears.

"I don't know what to say," he murmured. "I can't tell you anything I haven't already. I just feel my place is here, that's all."

"But why?" she cried softly. "It's against all reason—"

"*War* is against all reason."

"And so you're going to sit here, like Votaw, waiting for another war, hoping for another blood-letting that will give—"

"*No*," he said tightly; he was angry all at once. "You know better than that." He raised his hand. "If God came into this room right now and told me there'd never be another war—anywhere, any size—even for just my lifetime, I'd dance for joy. Don't say that, because it isn't true."

She bit her lip, came over to him and pressed his head against her breast. "I'm sorry, Sam. I had no right to say that. I'm sorry."

"I know there are Votaws around. Maybe there's more of them than there should be."

"Maybe we ought to leave the Army to the ones that want killing, that love it and pray for it—maybe we ought to leave it to the butchers and the sadists."

He shook his head. "There are enough of them anyway. Let's make sure there are a few of the other kind."

"Sam . . ."

"Uh-huh?"

"Sam"—she leaned back and looked at him—"you're not scared, are you?"

He smiled at her slowly. "I'm scared of a lot of things. Scared of what in particular?"

"Of the outside . . . You're not afraid you couldn't make a go of it?—the way Pete Lovewell has?"

"No," he answered. "I could get a job in civilian life and a good one. Why couldn't I?" He paused, searching her face. "Don't you think I could?"

"I don't know. It's—everything seems to move so fast out there. This is such poor training for the world. So many of them seem to be just floating along, passing time. Look at Howie Searles, playing piano at the parties and telling funny stories. Or Walt Marburger with his card tricks and home brew. The funny thing is, after awhile it *does* begin to look complicated and demanding, out there beyond the main gate . . . You're too good for this, Sam!" she cried softly. "These Batchelders and Votaws and Searleses. Can't you see that?"

"You're always saying that."

"But it's true . . ."

"I'm too good for what was good enough for Grant and Lee and Wood and Pershing and Colonel Marshall and your dad?"

"Yes," she nodded. "You could do better. You could do such tremendous things, I'm sure of it. But it's impossible, the way the cards are stacked. And every time you have to temporize with a jughead like Batchelder it makes you that much less a person. It's a war of attrition, Sam: you have to give up more than you can ever get back . . ."

"Maybe so." He released her, then drew her to him gently and took her onto his lap and kissed her on the cheek. The early morning breeze stirred in the tall pines at the far end of the row and then subsided, like a night animal changing position in its lair. "I love you, honey," he murmured in her ear. "You're just this whole world to me, you and the kids. I know I haven't got a bushel of money and a string of horses and connections in the AG's office, and I can't blow my own horn the way some of them can. But I *care*, honey. I care about this world and this country and what's happening to it."

He paused. We don't talk enough, he thought; we talk a lot but not about the really crucial things. Maybe it's a good thing this crazy wing-ding came off tonight. Suddenly it seemed terribly important that she see and understand what he felt about this—more important than anything else they'd ever had between them.

"I've been detailed for this, honey. That's what it is. Like a soldier who's drawn outpost duty beyond the front lines. He's just drawn the detail, that's all. He didn't ask for it, it was laid on him—maybe because his platoon leader thought he was more alert or competent or careful than the others, or maybe the sergeant had it in for him and stuck him with it, or maybe it was just the luck of the draw. But that doesn't matter—there he is: he's drawn the obligation, he's out there, and what he does during those hours will mean the lives of all the rest. And so he's got to do everything in his power to prepare himself for that moment. I'm like that man. Don't you see?"

She gazed at him for a moment with terrible intensity—and then she smiled the saddest smile he'd ever seen on a woman's face. "All right, Sam."

"Do you see? Do you really?"

"Yes," she said. "I see."

He felt all at once overjoyed; he would never have believed ten short years ago he'd have been so lucky as to have married a girl as wonderful as this. "Tell you what, honey," he said. "I'll have two months' accumulated leave when school's over here, and I'll put in for it. We'll go anywhere you like—mountains, seashore, north or south. For as long as you like, anywhere you say. How'd you like that? You name it, we'll do it."

She laughed then—a laugh that was like a gasp, and kissed him. "All right, Sam. If you can stand the gaff I guess I can."

"It's a deal, then?"

"It's a deal." She nodded slowly. "You know something? You're a good man, Sam Damon. You're a good man but I'm afraid you're an awful fool."

He pressed his face against her breasts. "Maybe so," he murmured. "Maybe so."

In the summer of 1929 they went north for accumulated leave. Damon took the back seat out of the LaSalle and built a frame on which he laid two cut-down mattress pads, where the children were to play and sleep during the long, hot afternoons, in a welter of toys and cookie crumbs and discarded clothing. Their camping gear he stored under the frame— a light tent with a fly, bedding rolls and cooking utensils. Tools went into boxes clamped to the running boards, the spare tires were lashed to the radiator. Tommy made fun of him. "Darling, you'd think we were crossing the Gobi Desert." He'd laughed, hammering and sawing and fitting, but he'd persevered: the trip was a symbol, and like all symbols it must be flawless, executed with perfection.

It was a voyage of discoveries. Tommy was like a new person: she laughed and sang, told stories to the kids or played games with them. They rambled over the rutted, washboard roads, Tommy reading from the "Routings for Motor Car Tourists—Central United States" a disillusioned captain named Whelpey had given them. "Thirty-eight point two. *At Triola, jog right. DO NOT CROSS railroad tracks. Grandview Hotel on left. Veer right with main wires, keep Catawba River on left, jog left four point six miles to Hermes Perps' Blacksmith Shop. Right at huge elm tree.* Oh honestly!" She doubled up, convulsed with laughter. "What if the tree's blown down in the meantime?"

"Or Hermes Perps. Maybe he's sold the place."

"He *does* sound flighty . . . The names!" she cried. "Listen to this: *Ask condition of bridge at Whoopingarner's Feed Store, center town.*"

"You'll never find him. They've incarcerated him by now."

"What's incarcerated?" Donny wanted to know. He had turned into a wiry, intense little boy dominated by an insatiable curiosity.

"That's when they sick the law on you," Damon answered him, "and throw you in the calaboose."

Singing a song about the calaboose they rolled on, running west by north, through pine forests and savannah. In the early morning meadowlarks shot down the sky in wild abandon and deer danced away through the woods, their scuts swaying like tasseled white plumes. The country seemed to swell before them, fanning out beyond the tarnished Indian on the radiator cap, in wave on wave of wonders. Sometimes, driving into the setting sun, or lying in his bedding roll with Tommy and the children fast asleep and the stars pouring like luminous dust across the heavens, he felt as if they were the last family traversing the virgin earth and he their sole and vigilant protector. When they reached the Platte, its feathered fringe of willows and cottonwoods crouched against its sandy banks, the sienna-and-blue strip of water under a cloudless sky, he felt his heart leap with recognition.

The family was still further dispersed. Uncle Bill had given up farm work and opened up a hardware store, which was doing fairly well; Ty was clerking for him. George Verney had died of pneumonia and been buried in his Grand Army uniform, as he'd requested. His mother looked thinner, but her manner was as crisp and vivacious as ever. Peg had married; she came over with her brood, and everyone sat around eating too much food and drinking lemonade or Uncle Bill's homemade beer, and talked about crops and the heat.

"Ah, the money's all in the hands of the eastern banks," Bill Hanlon declared. "Bloodsucking monsters. *They* don't care . . ." After a year of venting his spleen on quaking recruits from Oregon and California he had finally shipped overseas—only to arrive at St. Nazaire on the fourteenth of November, 1918—a defection from paths of glory Mr. Verney hadn't failed to remind him about when he got home. Now, his Philippine exploits eclipsed by this newer, greater war, and George Verney dead, he railed at the government. "A pack of tinhorns and thimbleriggers. And that Coolidge!—dried-up husk. Run a pin into him anywhere and you know what you'd get? Liquid ice, colder than Greenland's icy mountains. You know what we called his kind in the Old Army?"

"Billy," Damon's mother said.

"It's the truth! And this Hoover—a sweet-talker, a pussyfooter with the face of a baby . . . What we need is a soldier, a fighter—another TR to bust 'em up, the conniving, slippery, pork-barreling grifters . . ."

"Maybe Sam ought to run," Peg offered slyly. "He's a soldier-hero—and a man of destiny." She made a face at Sam who smiled at her, pleased that his favorite sister had kept her spirit. She'd lost her first child in the big flu epidemic, and her husband was a gaunt, colorless farmer named Jellison.

"Sam!" Bill Hanlon crowed with amazement. "They'd eat him alive! They'd serve him up on a platter, garnished with mortgages and their cheating, nefarious stock certificates. What does Sam know about farms and farming? No, what we need is someone tough as rawhide, wily as a lynx on the prowl, and with the courage of a regiment of lions . . ."

Damon laughed with the others; but he was ill at ease. It was pleasant enough sitting here in the ladder-back rocker sipping beer, but he couldn't escape the sense that they all felt he was evading the issues of life, which were palpably farming and putting in gas ranges and refrigerators; that he had chosen to slip away into a remote and unnecessary world. On Main Street Fritz Clausen called out to him, "Not still playing soldier, are you?" His tone was congenial enough, but that seemed to epitomize the town's attitude. *Sam Damon? Oh sure, a regular fire-*

*eater with the AEF in France—they named the plot in front of the town
hall for him. Used to be smart as a button, too. What in hell is he doing
roaming around army camps for, now it's over? About time he stopped
fooling around and settled down to business, isn't it? Can't bear to take
off that uniform, I suppose. Well: no accounting for some folks . . .*

He became restless, without knowing exactly why. He took the children to a ball game—Ted Barlow was still coaching the Warriors—and
then swimming at Hart's Island. He passed a weary, commiserating hour
with Mr. Thornton, who was bedridden with dropsy. Pop Ainslie, now
demoted by prohibition to caretaker of the Grand Western, pressed
on him a bottle of genuine Canadian scotch for old-times' sake. Big Tim
Riley had been killed in a lumbering accident up in Minnesota right
after the war. He did not see Celia Shurtleff; she was now a grand lady
in the upper echelons of Chicago society—Peg showed him a clipping in
the Rotogravure . . .

Sitting on the old porch, rocking idly, he watched the great apple tree
where the children were playing. That was his daughter swinging up
and away, shrieking, her dress in a feathery billow above her fat little
knees: his daughter . . . Tommy was telling about Donny's birth at
Hardee and Tweaker Terwilliger, and he watched the others' eyes on
her. They didn't know how to take her—she was too volatile, too high-
strung and sophisticated for them. A woman who had been brought up
in the Army, of all places . . . He thought with a little shock: And they
don't know how to take me, either. It was true. He had run off to
Mexico and France and won all those tin medals, there was the picture
of Black Jack Pershing decorating him for valor cut from the Omaha
Herald and framed, hanging above the chiffonier in the parlor; and here
he was, silent and preoccupied, in slacks and a faded old shirt, an emissary from this unfathomable world of violence and punctilio. Time
changed people; time and experience estranged them irrevocably. The
realization was like a chill wind. He wasn't needed anymore . . . He was
glad when they left two days later for Lake Erie, where Tommy's uncle
had offered them the use of the untenanted gardener's cottage for six
weeks.

They rolled east along the Platte, across the fierce green seas of Iowa
cornfield, the red earth. They crossed the Mississippi on the new bridge
at Davenport, where they caught sight of a riverboat downstream, its
stovepipe stack pouring black smoke, side-wheels churning silver water;
they woke up the children who bounced up and down, their eyes wide
with excitement. In Kentucky they camped in lush meadows where
slick brown horses grazed and nickered at them, cut back across Ohio
and ran up along the French-blue sweep of the lake, and reached Erie
late on a blazing hot afternoon, after radiator trouble and two punc-
tures.

The Downings' house looked unbelievably splendid. It was set back from the road behind a majestic sweep of lawn—a stone pile three stories high, with two cupolas and slender white columns flanking the big front door. The verandah was cool and deep, framed with wisteria and morning glories. A brand-new green Packard stood on the neat graveled drive.

"Momma, are we going to live in that?" Donny inquired.

"No, dear. We're going to be in the gardener's cottage. I told you."

"That's bigger than General Murrow's quarters—that's bigger than anything!"

"Yes, dear. It's a very spacious house."

"They must be rich!" Donny had his head between theirs, peering forward through the windshield as they approached. "Are they rich, Momma? Aunt Marilyn and Uncle Edgar?"

"They're quite well-to-do, yes. And see?—there's the lake. It's lovely! All so cool and green." She put her hands to her hair, pressing at it.

"Will we have a sailboat?" Donny asked.

"I don't know, dear," Tommy said. "We'll have to see."

Marilyn Downing came out to meet them. She was a tall, capable woman with iron gray hair and a quick, pleasant smile.

"What courage!" she called. "To drive all the way from Nebraska. In this heat!"

Inside it was cool and still, the reflected light from the lake muted by the heavy curtains. There were carved mahogany chairs upholstered in petit point, marquetry tables resting on an oriental rug of the softest indigo and magenta hues. A grand piano, its wing up, stood at the far end of the living room, a silk shawl thrown across one end; there were glass cabinets with coil cloisonné vases and figurines and in the dining room a handsome rosewood sideboard where serving silver lay gleaming against a blue velour cover.

"Marilyn, it's lovely," Tommy exclaimed. "It's what you just dream about . . ."

Carrying Peggy on his hip Damon watched Tommy's eyes as they roamed over these hundred and one appurtenances, these things of wood and cloth and metal that bespoke wealth, permanence, grace—the good life. She would have had all this if she'd married another man: someone like Poindexter. She would have a stable full of horses, and a home of her own crammed with Renaissance furniture and a yacht out on the Sound; just as he'd said. She could be living more elegantly than this, and not chained to an infantry subaltern of twelve years' service who didn't have a pot to piss in—

"Ed couldn't get away early," Marilyn was saying. "There was a meeting he couldn't leave. He'll be home in an hour or so—we're having some friends in for dinner. I imagine you'd like to get cleaned up and settle in."

The caretaker's cottage was built like a Swiss chalet, with a high-peaked roof and fieldstone fireplace. It was modest enough, but compared to what they'd lived in over the past ten years it was palatial. There was a little flower garden and a porch, the kitchen was fully equipped and there were porcelain set tubs in the cellar, part of which was decorated as a playroom, with a hobby horse and dart board and a jungle gym painted in red and yellow. The children were ecstatic. They unpacked and took turns bathing—there was a huge built-in tub in the bathroom surrounded by blue tile—and later they went over to the main house and sat on the wide flagstone terrace sipping Tom Collinses and gazing at the broad plate of the lake, glaucous and remote now in the late summer evening haze.

It was still another world—as strange as Walt Whitman had been, but in a different way. Here the atmosphere was nervous, exciting, crammed with wealth and appetite. Everyone kept interrupting everyone else. Damon was anxious to hear their opinions on Briand's treaty draft or the three-power naval conference at Geneva, but nobody seemed to be interested in any of these things. They were in the market. Everybody in America was in the market. The men talked casually of brokers' loans and market pools and automotive shares and eight per cent income on ten percent margin. He understood very little of it. They spoke of someone named Bruce Barton, and someone named Raskob; they laughed uproariously about a little old cleaning woman in Teaneck, New Jersey who had invested fifteen dollars a week and ridden it into a cool million.

"You ought to come up here and settle down, Sam," Edgar Downing told him. He was a pudgy man with reddish gold hair; when he talked he moved his hands in quick, short, chopping motions. "You're missing out on a barrel of fun."

"Not to mention the happy wampum," a man named Headley said.

"Why don't you take yourself a leave of absence? six months or so, see how it works out?"

"I'm afraid I can't do that, Mr. Downing."

"What's the matter, can't they spare you down there?"

"It'd mean resigning from the service," Tommy explained.

"Is that a disaster?" Headley inquired innocently, and there was general laughter.

Dinner was vivid with old silver and Burgundy in slender stem glasses and the still glow of tapers. Downing was still excited about Lindbergh's flight. "The nerve that took! The raw, unbridled daring . . . it's what's made this country the greatest place on earth." His eyes were snapping with enthusiasm; he looked like a man who ran on impulse, on momentary excitements, and stopped to think afterward. "Why didn't you take up flying, Sam? That's where the future is."

"You may be right, there. I certainly plan to learn how to fly if I get the chance."

"What branch are you in, Damon?" a man named Nickerson asked him; he had served with the field artillery during the war, and they talked for a few moments about some wet, weary villages in the Argonne.

"Sam received the country's highest decoration," Marilyn informed her guests. "The Medal of Honor. And several others, I believe."

"Is that right?" Headley inquired. "What did you get it for? Invent a new filing system for the seventh and eighth carbon copies?"

Damon watched the shiny round face, the broad, thin smile. "Nothing as intellectual as that," he said quietly.

Headley's face sobered; apparently he realized he'd gone too far. "No, really? What was it for?"

"An action near the Marne."

"Oh, blow your own horn a little, Sam," Tommy protested. Her face was flushed with holiday gaiety and the wine; she was wearing the sky blue dress she'd bought in Columbus before they'd left Benning, and she looked slender and young and vivacious beside the other women. "You're so *reticent!*" To the others she said, "He rescued some of his men that had been captured by the Germans, and attacked two machine-gun positions and took them single-handed; and then he repulsed a counterattack by a whole company of German infantry and held the position until the regiment came up and recovered the lost ground."

The women gave exclamations of uneasiness and wonder. Headley said: "That fellow York captured a whole battalion, didn't he?"

"Sam's unit was fighting a crack Prussian regiment," Tommy said, and her eyes glinted in the candlelight. "Sergeant York's exploit was carried out against reserve troops."

There was a little silence. Damon smiled to himself: well, there was old Butch Batchelder's loyalty from the bottom up, all right. Aloud he said, "Anyway, it was long ago and far away."

"Amen to that," Nickerson agreed; there was laughter and the conversation ran along again. Damon saw Tommy's eyes flash at him once in rebuke, but it was true: what difference did it make? This Headley was a fatuous clown, that was all.

"George—that's my sister's husband, Tommy's father—told us Sam was the ablest officer ever to serve under him," Marilyn offered.

"What else could he say?" Tommy retorted gaily; she'd recovered herself in a trice. "He couldn't very well admit I'd made a mistake, could he?"

"Is that so?" Edgar was looking at Damon with sudden interest. "But you're a lieutenant, aren't you?"

"First lieutenant," Tommy said. "And very senior."

"That doesn't seem right—you'd think the Army would brush off some of the barnacles and reward individual initiative, the way business does. Look at Hank Farwell—he was a clerk at Macomber fourteen years ago. Now he's a vice president, making better than twelve thousand. It beats me how you can put up with it—the sheer waste of talent, of ability . . ."

Presently the women rose and went into the living room. Edgar got out the brandy and a box of cigars and the talk turned again to business, but this time their own. The factory Downing owned made containers of all kinds, for food and toys and utensils; there was much discussion about the merits of a new machine that had recently been installed.

"I want you to come down to the plant and see it, Sam," Downing told him. "Does everything in one operation—surfacing, cutting, folding, gluing. One continuous process. It's a dandy."

"I'd like to see it, Mr. Downing."

Downing waved one of his chunky hands above his head. "Oh come on, call me Ed. Let's not have any of that Army formality." He grinned. "There's no rank around here, you know."

Damon smiled back, but made no reply. No, they didn't wear bars or leaves on their collars, they didn't rise at mess or stand to for officers' call; but there was certainly rank here. He kept out of the conversation, listening, intent, studying the four men. Forst was fat and voluble and eager to please; Headley was waspish and shrewd—a clown with a purpose, relying on charm. Nickerson was the interesting one: a tall, bony man, silent, a bit dour, given to pessimistic reflections. Tommy had told him a little about Nickerson; his father had been wealthy, with his own firm, then had lost it in the panic of 1907—which might account for the scornful reticence of the son, his faintly injured air. But he was solid; he would gripe and drag his feet on the little things, but in the pinches he would be the best of the four. Freer of self-deception than the other three, he would see the important thing and battle for it. Damon bit at his thumb, amused at the course of his thoughts—that compulsive Army habit of reading men as though you were about to lead them in battle . . .

"I still say the problem lies with shipping," Nickerson was saying now.

"Oh, I wouldn't want to stir up Karl over nothing, Bill," Headley replied.

"It isn't over nothing."

"Besides, what would you find out if you did? My God, that place is a labyrinth. One of my kids was fooling around down there Saturday and got lost, and I had to practically call out the fire department."

They talked on, and Damon listened. A decade of training manuals and classes and the brusque tutelage of men like Marshall and Stilwell and Bradley had taught him to cut through extraneous detail to the heart of a thing; and surfeited with food and drink and the long day's drive he watched the night sky beyond the long windows and entertained himself by trying to analyze the problem.

Part of the trouble was that they had only one eye on the plant. The other was on the stock market, where the big money was being made, in an atmosphere of risk and excitement and vanity he could only guess at. They were constantly taking trains east, they were on the phone to their New York brokers; their minds were on Wall Street, and Erie was running a very poor second. The talk was desultory, and at cross-purposes. Nickerson harped on the loss of customers' firms, Downing on the expense entailed in reshipments; Headley and Forst defended the yard and talked of rail foul-ups and confusion in the office. Sam gathered it was a question of organization, of timing; but there was something else the matter, something he couldn't quite put his finger on . . .

"This must be pretty damned dull for you, Sam," Downing said all at once. "Having to sit and listen to all this."

"Not at all. It's very interesting."

Nickerson snorted, and Edgar laughed and said, "Your father-in-law would say we haven't gone to the heart of the problem. I can just hear him. Simply a matter of studying all the factors involved and taking the most effective course. Or—what's that other phrase he likes?"

"Bringing the proper point of leverage to bear," Headley supplied with his thin smile. Forst laughed, and even Nickerson gave a sardonic grin. This made Damon angry. George Caldwell wouldn't fumble around for half an hour talking about everything but the point at issue, he thought; where do you get off, making fun of him? But he held his temper.

Downing must have seen something in his eyes, however, for he leaned forward over his elbows. "All kidding aside, Sam, how would you handle something like this in the Army?"

Damon set down his glass. "Well, I'm probably talking out of turn— God knows I don't know anything about business methods and problems. But we once had a situation pretty much like this in France in terms of priorities—which I gather are the main issue here. Why not treat it like a combat loading problem? work up a set of stencils with priority symbols—a yellow triangle for top priority, say; then a red diamond for second, and a blue shield for third. With line numbers above and number of parcels for that particular shipment below. And the railway people would treat them accordingly."

"You don't know the lot crew, Sam," Headley interposed. "You'd never get Karl Preis to adopt any newfangled scheme involving colored cartoon pictures, even if it would solve the problem. I can tell you that."

"I'm not so sure," Downing said. "Why shouldn't he go for it?" The others were silent but Damon could feel their disapproval. A peacetime soldier telling *them* what to do with their plant? *Nerve* of the guy. But there was also something else—that sense he'd had earlier that there was a missing piece to the puzzle.

"Why couldn't we do that?" Edgar demanded. "I like it. Sweet and simple. Just what we need—cut through some of the fuzz around the place."

"Karl won't like it, Ed," Nickerson said.

"Maybe he won't." Downing puffed hard at his cigar. "Maybe it's time everybody stopped worrying so everlastingly about Karl Preis." He hitched himself around in his chair. "Say, how'd you like to come to work for us, Sam? Tomorrow morning. I mean it. Be a hell of a lot more fun than sitting on your fanny at the beach all day long." He pulled at his cigar again, his eyes glinting. "I don't image a young fellow like you would want to lie around like a drone for the better part of two months."

Damon finished lighting a cigarette. Edgar's face was genial, ruddy from all the alcohol, but his eyes held that bright measured gleam he remembered from Mr. Thornton, from Congressman Bullen, Colonel Weyburn, Colonel Howden. It was the look that meant: *All of life is a series of bargains; I am power—and my wishes, my suggestions and speculations are not without their own aura of authority.* Oh yes; there was rank here, all right. It was the way the world was; he had learned that early and well. Watching Downing's eyes, the impatient, restless hands, he understood. It was a deal; this was in return for the use of the caretaker's cottage.

And there was something else that pressed for recognition. He remembered the night of the fracas with Batchelder at Benning, and later in their bedroom Tommy's question: *Are you afraid, Sam?* A born competitor, constitutionally unable to resist a direct challenge from any quarter, he wanted to do this—he wanted to show her he could make a go of it in a civilian job, no matter how difficult or thorny it might be. Then too, the extra money, whatever it came to, would be handy. It would give them a little leeway.

"Why, I'd be glad to go to work for you," he said. "If you feel I can be of any help."

"Good," Downing said, and slapped the table. "That's what I like—a man who can make up his mind fast. Who knows what he wants." He glared at Nickerson. "There's too damn many milksops and mollycoddles around these days."

They talked a while longer, and then Marilyn came in and broke it up. Back at the cottage Tommy threw herself on the wide double bed and flung both arms out. "Now this is more like it, Sam." She crowed softly. "Now why can't the blessed Army match this?"

"It will—when I'm post commandant," he said. "Uncle Edgar is post commandant here."

Looking up she made a face at him. "This is—not—a—post," she declared. "It's heaven on Lake Erie, and we're here! No demands, no obligations. Sam, kiss me thunderously." He complied. "Oh, this is going to be ambrosial!" She rolled over on top of him, her hands locked around his neck. "I feel as if school's out. Reform school, that is . . . Sam, tomorrow let's go down to the lake and picnic. Just lie around all day and swim and eat. Marilyn says there's a lovely little point that's all grassy and secluded."

Damon drew a breath. "Afraid I can't do that, honey. You take the kids down and I'll join you later on."

"Why not?"

"I've got to get up early. I'm going to work at the plant."

She let go his neck and bounced to a sitting position. "You're kidding!"

"Not at all. Starting tomorrow I'm employed as troubleshooter in the logistics section, which appears to be in a bit of a snarl." Briefly he told her about it.

"But Sam—that's ridiculous!" she exclaimed. "We're here on *vacation* . . . what's he paying you?"

"I don't know."

"You don't know—!" A curious look came into her eyes. "Why did you take it?"

"A lot of reasons. We can use the money. And we're their guests, you know. He suggested it."

She waved one hand in distress. "But this isn't the Army—a suggestion doesn't constitute a *command* . . ."

He smiled at her. "Well. It does and it doesn't. We do owe the Downings something for all this lakeside luxury. And he asked for my help. Besides," he went on, "it won't have to cramp our vacation much. You and the kids will have the lake and the tennis court. I'll be home every evening; and we'll have the weekends together."

She dropped her eyes, and he knew what she was thinking: If he did well, if the salary he got was a good one—and it probably would be—he might be tempted to resign from the service and stay on here, to move up in this heady world of business; the children could go to private school, and soon they'd have a house like this on the Lake, with gardens and smoothly cropped lawns and a new Packard standing on the drive. All the comforts. Hanging his trousers neatly on a hanger he bit his lips. Was he being fair to her? He didn't know. He honestly didn't. All he knew was that he had to do it.

The men came out of the sheds casually, watching him—the quick, covert, faintly defiant glance men give when they've been corking off. Damon knew it well enough—he'd done it himself on occasion. There would be a coffeepot on a hot plate in a cleared space among the crates and cartons, and a few tins of doughnuts or pastry, and some battered magazines. But this was 8:30 in the morning.

The last man out was big, and run to fat, with a round, chinless face and shrewd little brown eyes that crinkled jovially as he smiled. He called: "Hi there, Art. What's on your mind this fine morning?"

"Hello, Karl," Headley said. "You're looking very chipper."

"It's my bouncing personality, Art—that's what you're seeing." He laughed, eying Damon. "Who's your friend here?"

"Karl, I'd like you to meet Sam Damon. Sam, Karl Preis." They shook hands. "Karl's been running the lot here for more years than most of us care to remember."

"More years than most of you *can* remember," Preis answered, and some of the lot crew laughed softly.

"That's right." Headley paused. He was hoping to get over the next hurdle with one of his witticisms, and it wouldn't come. "Well." He cleared his throat. "Boys, this is Sam Damon—he's an officer in the Army, and he's an expert on shipping. Mr. Downing has sent him down to see if there's anything he can do to help us straighten things out a little bit here, during his leave. Now, he's outlined a couple of schemes concerning priority shipments that sound pretty good to us. Mr. Downing wants you to give him a hand in any way you can, while he takes a look at things."

There was no response to this, and Headley went on rapidly, to cover the silence. Preis was staring at Damon with his bemused, crinkly smile. A show-off, Sam thought quickly. A blusterer, a bully; and Headley is afraid of him. He had been mildly surprised when Downing had sent Headley down to the lot with him instead of coming down here with him himself. The best way to delegate authority—assuming that was what you wanted to do—was to delegate it directly.

"Well, I guess that's about all," Headley concluded. "I know you'll all of you do a great job." He turned to Sam. "I'll see you in the office at four thirty." He walked away quickly.

There was a short silence and then Karl Preis strolled up to him. "Well, Mr. Damon. What's on your mind?"

"First, I'd like to check against these." He held out the sheaf of manifests in his right hand.

Preis laughed genially. "That's a tall order. Those sheds are crammed to bursting. Besides, we got a loading detail around eleven."

"Well, let's work on it till then."

They went into the first shed and Damon started checking against the office manifests. There was a solid wall of cartons reaching all the way to the roof. St. Dizier, he thought: the same thing. Everything dumped in helter-skelter, no order or plan. They don't know what they've got, or where it is.

"How is it you didn't leave more alleys?" he asked.

Preis gave his indulgent laugh. "Space, Mr. Damon. The way things have been going, space is at a premium."

"Then couldn't some of it be stacked on skids outside, under tarps?"

"There's no need for that. I've got it all in my head."

Damon nodded; he would have to make his first move right now. He said, "Well. Let's take a look, anyway."

The fat man was incredulous. "You mean *move* all that stuff?"

Damon smiled at him and took off his jacket. "Looks like the only way, doesn't it?"

"Aw, now look—"

But Sam cut him off flatly. "Mr. Downing told me expressly he wanted a complete and accurate inventory of the lot. And that's what we're going to do. Now let's get on it, all right?"

Preis's shrewd little eyes narrowed. "Where you going to put it all?"

"Right outside there. It's a nice day."

"Okay. It's your funeral." He turned to the lot crew and called off several names. "Mr. Damon's planning to empty out the sheds this morning." There was some laughter and a wiry man in a pale blue shirt called, "What in hell for?"

"He's going to check against the office lists," Preis went on with his jovial smile, and there was more laughter. "All right. Some of you give him a hand."

They began moving cartons outside and stacking them on pallets. The summer heat had gathered high up under the tin roofs, and before long Damon's shirt was soaked through. Preis watched them from the doorway, his hands in his over-all pockets. It wasn't long before Sam found what he imagined he would—a number of containers with markings different from those listed on the sheets.

"These are three-ninety-threes," he said to Preis.

"What? Yeah, that's right."

"But according to the manifest they ought to be in Number Seven. What are they doing in here?"

"Oh, that." Preis shrugged. "It was nearer the siding. I've got it all in my head."

That told him all he needed to know. If this was how it was in the first shed he'd tackled, this was how it would probably be in all the others. He thought of Tommy taunting him once when he'd drawn duty as mess officer down at Dormer. "You want everything all to be so *organized*—what binkle-bankle difference does it make?"

"We'll have to move them," he said aloud. "To Number Seven."

"What?" Preis cried. "What's the sense in that? Number Seven's full up, anyway."

"Then we'll have to make room there, too."

The lot superintendent muttered under his breath. "Damon, I'm telling you, you're just making work for yourself." As though explaining something to a child, he said: "Number Seven was full, so I had these run in here."

"Is that why they didn't go out on the twenty-third?"

Preis blinked, and then his face began to turn red. "Look, the office— some dame types up a list and they think they've solved it all. There's no *need* for it, I can tell you . . ."

Damon smiled to himself. It was marvelous: it was fantastic. All those fancy cocktails and liqueurs, and Radio stock soaring to 400, and flying trips to New York and Chicago—and they couldn't cope with one barrel-bellied bully who was blocking all the traffic.

"Preis," he said quietly, "these three-ninety-threes are going to be moved over to Number Seven."

The big man swore. "You don't know what you're talking about, Damon."

"No? I'll make a little bet with you. Just a friendly little bet of twenty dollars. I'll bet there are some more three-ninety-threes back in here. And part of at least three other lines. All tangled up."

Preis opened his mouth to shout, then stopped. The sweat lay in the folds of his neck. Very slowly, he grinned. "Damon," he said, "suppose you and I have a little talk about how things are around this lot."

The lot gang had stopped and were listening avidly now. Sam set down the sheaf of manifests on a carton. "All right, you tell me. How are they?"

"This lot is running fine just the way it is."

"Is it?"

"And that's the way it's going to remain. Just like it is."

"Preis," Damon said, "you'll do as I say, and you'll do it at once."

The lot foreman swore violently, and then laughed. "Is that right? On whose authority, Damon?"

"Mr. Downing's."

"You want to go running to Ed Downing, is that it? get me fired?"

"No, I'm not going to go running to Mr. Downing."

Preis gave the quick, ugly laugh again. "You bet you aren't! My old man owned half this factory—"

"I'm not impressed by your old man."

"—and I got a hefty interest in it right now . . . Go ahead," he shouted, "you go ahead and run up to Ed Downing and see what he tells you . . ."

Several of the work gang laughed, and the wiry man in the blue shirt said, "That's telling him, Karl!"

This had happened before, then. Periodically some sacrificial lamb had been sent down here to "straighten things out"; and each time the magnitude of the chaos and Preis's bullying had sent him back with his tail between his legs, and the lot had gone from bad to worse.

But this time it wasn't going to turn out that way.

"Preis," he said softly, setting himself, "I'm not going to go running to anybody at all. I'm going to tell you one more time to empty this shed. And if you give me any more talk—any more at all!—we're going to step outside this shed and I'm going to beat some sense into your stupid head."

The fat man's jaw dropped, his eyes bugged out. "—I got a bad back," he said loudly.

"Is that right."

"Yes, that's right—you don't believe me? Look here, then . . ." and he slipped the straps of his over-alls and wrenched up his shirt, revealing a broad white girdle bristling with bone and straps and buckles. "Every-body knows that . . ."

Damon grinned at him. "Well you see, I didn't. I thought it was *all* beer."

Someone in the lot crew snorted, and Preis, his face purple, began to shout. "You lay a hand on me and my boys'll take care of you fast enough, you'll see!"

Sam smiled at the gang, watching them; they were still enjoying the fun, though in a slightly different way: he could sense the change now. "Well, I certainly don't want to take on the whole crowd," he said easily. "I thought this was just between you and me, Preis."

"This isn't the Army, you know, Damon—you're not ordering buck privates around here—"

"Right as rain, chief."

"Why don't you get the hell on back to your polo ponies and riding britches and officers' clubs and let us run this lot our way, okay?" Preis waved one arm toward the factory. "What do you know about any of this? Hell's bells, you couldn't even *make* it on the outside—or why else did you stay in? Tell me that, ah?"

". . . The food," Damon said in an easy, drawling voice. "I stayed in for the food, Preis."

The man in the blue shirt laughed wildly at this, and several of the others were grinning. It was going to be all right from here on. The foreman must have sensed it, too—he was waving his arms again and shouting: "All right, we're going up to Ed Downing right now, Damon, we're going to settle this right away—"

Now was the moment. Right now. He walked up to Preis until his face was only inches from the super's. "Preis, you've been goldbrick-ing on this lot for years and you know it. And everybody else knows it, too. Now you're going to stay right here and help straighten out this mess because the whole business depends on it." He could see the uncer-tainty in the other man's eyes. Preis wanted to run away, but his pride wouldn't let him. He looked baffled and angry and frightened: he didn't know what was going to happen next—and he, Damon, did know. And that made the difference. "This firm is losing customers because the shipments are fouled up, and only because of that. If it loses too many the firm will go under and there will be no jobs in the plant or out here in the lot, either. Have you ever thought of that? Because that's what will happen."

The foreman had dropped his eyes, and he talked on quietly and smoothly, making sure the crew heard every word. It was going to go through, because his will was harder than Preis's; because—because peo-ple couldn't say no to him. Well, if that was how it was, then let it work for him. It was so simple! A simple matter of enforcing obedience, of checking a destructive and foolish defiance, and those moguls and big-time operators up there in the company offices didn't know how to cope with it. But he did, and he was going to make it work. They would not have understood what made him stand there in the heat, calmly, implacably facing down this petty tyrant: it was not money or advancement or fear or vainglory, but a sense of the fitness of the thing—the essential rightness in doing a job conscientiously and well, bringing order out of chaos.

"But the firm isn't going to go under," he went on, pitching his voice so it was clearly audible over the distant whine and drum roll of the plant. "You're going to stick with it and give me a hand here because it's for the good of the firm. Because it's a time of prosperity and this factory is going to grow, get bigger and better in every way, and have its share of that prosperity. It means hard work—a lot of hard work—but once it's done the whole business will flow like a river, without a hitch or a foul-up."

Abruptly he broke away from Preis and faced the group directly. "All right," he said crisply, "let's turn to. We're going to load outside, under tarps, and see what we've got—and then we're going to whip this lot into shape. And then we're going to keep it that way." He ran his eyes along the crew. They met his gaze, most of them; three of them were smiling faintly, which was a good sign.

"All right," he said. "Let's go."

That was step one. Step two took a little longer. He worked hard. He got to the lot before seven in the morning and he worked until after six at night. It took three weeks but he did what no one had done since the plant had started—he accomplished a total and precise inventory. He reorganized all the sheds according to type and function of container, he initiated a coherent and legible system of symbols that were swiftly intelligible to the lot, the plant, and the office; he got the priorities plan in effect for all shipping. It was exhausting but he did it. He got caught up in the problem; he was bursting with ideas, he could think of nothing else. He even changed the boundaries of the lot to facilitate freight-car loading. Then at Downing's insistence he attacked the raw materials warehouses and set them in order. There was no further trouble with Preis, who pitched in with a vengeance. When Damon heard him bragging to Nickerson one afternoon about the efficiency of the shipping section he knew the campaign was over. Downing was astonished beyond measure; he raised Sam's salary to two hundred a week, then two fifty.

The lush, late summer days slipped by. Weekends they went for picnics on the lake shore or sailing in the Downings' boat; and one evening Peggy tapped the living-room wall with the flat of her little hand and said, "This is our *other* house, isn't it, Daddy?" and he took her in his arms and kissed her. Tommy was radiant and relaxed. It was an idyll—a lovely summer idyll, for all the hard work at the lot, and he was content to let it go at that. They lay in bed late on Sundays, and swam and fished and had a few couples from the firm to dinner. There were no bugles, no parades.

Tommy said nothing more after that first evening, but he could sense her eyes on him now and then. The days swept away, and finally there were two weeks, and then one; the air turned cool and clear with fall, and the first aspen leaves began to skip through the light air, swirling golden shadows.

Downing called him in one afternoon and told Miss Rainey they were not to be disturbed. "There's a future for you here, Sam—you must know that by now. I'll be frank with you. I didn't think you could do it. The Army—well, you know as well as I do, lots of them are just drifting along, letting Uncle Sam foot the bill." He chopped at the air with his blunt hands. "You're different, you've got what it takes. Stay on here with us and I can promise you sixteen-five in two years. Why stay on in the Army?—there's nothing there for your kind of man. Sure, I know you made a great record in the war—but it's over, Sam. There aren't going to be any more wars—and if there are we aren't going to get into them, I can tell you that. Hell, *here's* where the challenge is, the opportunity . . ."

After dinner he sat on the porch, listening to the katydids sizzling like a thousand mechanical buzzers, while the children played in the field and Tommy moved about in the kitchen; and thought about it. It was harder to decide than it had been in '19. He could make his way as a businessman. Tommy would be happier, unquestionably, out of the world of the Army; there would be money for the good things of life they'd been denied; he might even strike out on his own in time, be his own master—there would be no more Townsends or Batchelders to serve under.

And yet . . . he was afraid of this world. He feared it; not as an arena where he could not prove himself—he had dispelled that qualm effectively enough—but as a good seaman must fear a recklessly piloted ship. It was too ungoverned, too avaricious, too headlong: in a world where such dizzying profits could be piled one upon another so heedlessly, where bootblacks could make a killing in Allegheny or Union Carbide, he did not want to enlist his services. It was—it was demeaning; his love of the tangible, of concrete and demonstrable values and materials, was assaulted. Erie Container made boxes and boxes were needed, it was true—but that was not what was dominating the mercantile world; what was running it was this roaring Bull Market, this careening skyscraper of brokers' loans and ten per cent margin, of credit capital. It was like a war predicated on incessant advance and continual victory—what would happen at the first setback, the first rush of doubt? It would be an engagement without any power of maneuver, with no reserves—it would be a disaster; and then what would happen to all the banks and factories?

Across the field at the edge of the woods Donny was running, carrying Peggy piggyback. He tripped and fell. There was a commotion and then Damon saw their heads above the tall grass. Peggy was crying and Donny was bent over her solicitously.

"I'm sorry, Peg," Sam could hear him say. "I didn't *mean* to fall down, for heaven's sake . . . I told you I'm *sorry*. You can't blame a person if they can't help it . . ."

Damon rubbed his jaw with his thumb. There was more to it than that, he knew; a lot more. He had chosen to spend his days in the world of men. *Life* was what mattered, its slow, priceless pulse, its burning fragility; his debt lay with those importunate Flanders echoes that had never really left him. The private could aspire to be a general because both general and private, at their best, recognized the dire importance of strategy, fortitude, the value of their imperiled existence; but when the machinist became the executive he left the world of tangibles and human conjugacy and entered a shadow world of credits and consols—a world that seemed to reward nothing so much as irresponsibility and boundless greed. And when the thunder rolled down upon them—as he knew it would—how would he feel, playing with paper, striving to outwit his fellows, drinking imported Scotch evenings and listening to the brittle parade of comedians on the radio . . . ?

Abruptly he got up and went into the kitchen. Tommy was putting the dishes back in the overhead cabinet. She was humming—a tune he all at once recognized:

> *It's so entrancing*
> *To keep on dancing*
> *In toe-tappy, skip-scrappy, jazz-happy Voodooland—!*

The song that band had played at the Jongleur Ivre, at Cannes. Long Tom Jethro and His Delta Serenaders. He smiled, remembering. Her figure was as fine as the day he'd met her—that lithe, leaping quality he loved. She reached high above her head with the pitcher, up on her toes. When she puts that pitcher on that shelf our life will change, he thought absurdly.

"Honey," he began, and stopped. "Honey, I can't take it. The job. I just don't think it's right."

Turning she nodded. "I knew you'd want to stay in."

"I'm sorry. I just can't see it any other way."

"It's all right. It ought to be what you want, Sam." Her teeth lay on her lower lip. She looked rested and calm and very beautiful; but there was that shadow behind her eyes that always ran a quick tongue of fear through his vitals.

He went up to her and kissed her softly. "You look very lovely," he said. "You've got to admit I've got an eye for beauty. Even if I can't see the woods for the trees."

She smiled then—a slow, sweet smile. "Oh well. We'll manage. It's been lovely. A real vacation. Just like Cannes."

"Yes. I was thinking of it, too." He took the little package out of his pocket and gave it to her.

She blinked up at him. "But—what's the occasion?"

"No occasion. It's just for you."

She opened the wrapping like a little girl, pressed back the cushioned top, gazed in silence at the pearl earrings, faintly blue against the black velvet. "Oh, they're lovely," she exclaimed softly; she touched one with her forefinger. "They're—oh, Sam . . ." And her eyes all at once filled with tears.

"Never mind the money," he said.

"—It's not the money . . ."

"I wanted to buy you these. For years and years. And now I could."

Her arms went under his and around his waist; her face bore the strangest expression he'd ever seen—a look compounded of love and apprehension and gratitude and boundless dismay; the tears rolled whitely along her lower lids and she shook her head, blinking, to clear them.

"Oh Sam," she whispered, "you're such a *good* old curmudgeon. What's a woman to do with you?"

He wished he could hold her like this forever—here in this still room with the evening shadows flowing across the field and the katydids a soft roar and the children's voices like sea birds crying.

"Just stick around," he murmured; he pressed his mouth to her hair. He felt weak with loving her. "Just stick around."

(6)

The military policeman said: "Good evening, Captain." He stepped aside, the big gate swung open and Damon passed through, conscious of a sinking sensation as he moved inside the crazily laced strands of wire; inconceivable as it was, at times like this he could never entirely rid himself of the idea that he wouldn't get out again. Following the MP, his eyes roamed professionally around the little street. The stockade was spotless and bare: there were no washlines, no pets, no soldiers playing catch—there weren't even tufts of grass at the edges of the buildings or around the tent pegs. Everything was invested with that fierce immaculacy of the penal institution; there was no place for evidences of human frailty, human warmth. The cascao had been pounded into a flat, white causeway that hurt the eyes, edged by the faded dun pyramids of tents; all of it motionless, caught in silence, cooking in the tropic sun.

Inside the guard hut the sergeant rose and said, "Sir?"

"Are you holding a man from E Company named Brand?"

"Yes, we are, Captain."

A hoarse, high-pitched voice called from the office: "Who's that, Hurley?"

The sergeant went toward the office door with a cautious, bent-kneed gait. "It's Captain Damon, sir."

"Well, now . . ." There was a short pause. "Ask him to come in."

Damon walked into the office and said, "Hello, Jarreyl."

First Lieutenant Jarreyl thrust a dog-eared magazine away with his elbow and heaved himself back in the swivel chair, which squeaked shrilly under his weight. "Well, Damon . . ." He made no effort to get to his feet, salute or shake hands. "Down to give a few words of encouragement to one of your boys?"

"None of my boys are in here right now, Jarreyl."

"That's a shame. I always look forward to having one of them down here. You know?"

"Yes, I know."

Lieutenant Jarreyl grinned up at him, nodding slowly. He was a barrel-chested man with long arms and a short, thick neck in which his head sat like a pumpkin in a tub of tallow. He had been an intercollegiate light-heavyweight champion at a Texas college, then had turned professional for a year or two before enlisting in the Army. In addition to running the prisoners' stockade he captained the regimental boxing team at Fort Garfield.

"Just a little social call?"

"Something like that." Damon went over and sat down in one of the two canvas chairs. "As a matter of fact I'd like to talk to Private Brand."

Jarreyl's brows rose. "The Indian? What do you want with him?"

"That's my business."

"It's mine, too." The stockade officer scowled. "I can tell you right now you're wasting your time. Crazy son-of-a-bitching redskin—he's gone right off his rocker."

"That so?"

"Tried to break away from a work detail at Taligán. He was damned lucky Andersen didn't blow his head off—I can tell you *I* would have. Then he tried to take on two of my MPs last night. Had to have a short pacification session with him. Tough little monkey. But just not quite tough enough." He smacked his hands together lightly, fist against paw. "Ah, they all come to me, Damon," he said in his high, gravelly voice. "All of them—the hellions and the wise guys and the misfits. All the characters that think they're something special. You know?" His small black pupils glinted under the rolls of gristle; two gold teeth gleamed softly. "They all come to papa."

"And you iron them out so nicely," Damon answered, "there's nothing special about them at all."

"I make good boys out of them. I get them to see the light. You know?"

"If you're such an evangelist, how come you have so many repeaters?"

Jarreyl's mouth made a deep little O. "Well, I guess some of them are just harder to teach than others."

"And this Brand is hardest to teach of them all."

"Nothing like that. He's reverted to type, that's all. He'll come round in time."

"Maybe." Damon watched the thick, square face, the little ignorant eyes, bright now with suspicion. What was it that made them all so insolent, so ruthless? Proximity to personal degradation? the occupational hazards of the trade? He hated MPs. He knew they were necessary, a necessary evil, men being what they were, the system being what it was—lonely, rootless soldiers marooned at the jungle's edge, ten thousand miles from home; but he hated them nonetheless.

Jarreyl was gazing up at the ceiling with false indifference. "Tell you what, Damon. If you've got a message for him, I'll be glad to deliver it for you."

"I'd rather do it myself, thanks."

The stockade officer leaned forward, his blocklike chest straining against the cut-down shirt, which was damp with sweat. "You know something, Damon?" he inquired softly. "You seem to have got the idea somewhere that you're pretty special yourself."

"That's right." He smiled for the first time since he'd entered the stockade. "Just special enough." He turned his face toward the six-bladed fan that was revolving listlessly on a windowsill. He had heard what went on here nights, when Jarreyl rolled in drunk or savage, and decided to have some fun with the inmates; he knew what the "pacification sessions" usually were—he knew the kind of men Jarreyl had surrounded himself with: the brutish, the wily, the dulled. Everyone on the post, who cared at all about finding out, knew. But Jarreyl was the privileged protégé of Colonel Fahrquahrson; his teams usually won the interisland championships, and he could do no wrong.

Damon had seen him fight a few times: a crowding, butting, gouging attack, full of low blows and elbows and heeling, the referee's angry warnings and the forfeiture of rounds; Jarreyl always had the crowd on its feet, roaring with approval or imprecation. The Colonel was delighted with him. "How that boy can maul 'em!" Damon had heard him cry once, wagging his head. "How he can *maul* 'em!" Only the native troops were silent: they hated Jarreyl, and with reason. Damon had heard him on the subject of the Filipino. "He's a gook, ain't he?

And a gook is second cousin to a nigger." And then the false, glittering grin. "Maybe even *first* cousin. You know?"

"What's a Texan, Jarreyl?" he'd asked in the silence. "First cousin to a Mexican?"

That was the way things had started between them. Ten months earlier Damon had taken over a company whose commanding officer, he'd been tersely informed, had been sent home on a medical survey—which he soon found out was a pleasant euphemism for acute alcoholism. The outfit was slack. The noncoms were good enough but they'd gone stale; they were merely coasting, running out the string. The topkick was a phlegmatic, morose man named Huber who was interested in nothing more than rounding out his fifth hitch and playing cribbage in the company office. The food was catastrophic.

Damon had changed all that in short order. He'd busted Huber and replaced him; heads rolled among the cooks until the food was up to what it should have been. He drilled the company hard, hiked them back into shape, worked on their quarters and their personal appearance. He overhauled the ball team and got it rolling again. He demanded a full, hard day, but he was generous with passes. The company got the word quickly enough; and when they found he was willing to listen to their troubles after retreat and would go to bat for them, they began to respond. At the end of four months they were calling themselves Damon's Demons, were known throughout Luzon as the Hiking Fools, and were easily the smartest company in the regiment.

As a reward he organized a dance for them in the mess hall. It was a modest enough affair, with a pick-up seven-piece band culled from the battalion, banana leaves and sampaguita and tree orchids for floral decoration, and a fruit punch that tasted like a perfumed soap dipped in licorice. The affair started awkwardly, with the Filipino girls fluttering in a tight knot at one end of the hall and the boys milling uncertainly at the other. Tommy, sensing the situation, improvised a grand march and then danced with First Sergeant Wilberson, whose face wore the expression of a man ordered to carry a priceless tray full of china across a frozen river. After that, though, the men who knew girls began introducing them to some of their friends; the band shook down and started to play together, and the floor began to move, the island girls in their full-sleeved ternos and piña-cloth skirts and high-necked panatelas swirling like rose and saffron birds against the khaki. When a lively corporal named Torgan got up on the stacked mess tables and called for three cheers for Captain Damon and the hall echoed with their roar, Sam felt oddly moved.

The trouble came when it was all but over. He and Tommy had left with his junior officers, and most of the celebrants had gone home when some men from E Company had decided to crash the party. Even then nothing would probably have happened if two members of Fox Company hadn't been spiking their fruit punch with tuba, and if one of the interlopers hadn't made what one of the tuba drinkers considered a derogatory remark about one of the girls. A small but violent melée had ensued; and before Wilberson and another NCO could break it up, Jarreyl's MPs had locked up nine men from Fox Company on drunk and disorderly charges. Enraged, Damon had gone to Jarreyl, who laughed at him.

"Some of your sweet little demons in trouble, Damon? Just raising hell when *I* found 'em."

"You've got nine of my men down here and you've thrown the book at them—"

"That's right."

"There were only two of them who'd been drinking—Ahearn and Klepich . . ."

"How do you plan to prove that?"

"And what about the jokers from Easy—the ones that started it all?"

Jarreyl had squinted his little black eyes into slits. "Damon, I'm afraid I just don't know what you're talking about."

"I get it," he muttered. "I get it now."

"I thought you would."

Still raging he had gone to Fahrquahrson. The Colonel heard him out with an air of patient irritation; he was a slight man with small, sharp features and curiously pointed ears whose lobes he kept fingering as he talked. He had made a fine record as a battalion commander in France.

"You claim your men were *not* drunk or disorderly, Captain?"

"No, sir—not nine of them. Two had been drinking, I realize that . . ."

"Now, Captain, at an affair such as you've described . . . Couldn't you be mistaken?"

"No, sir! I have just interviewed sixty-three members of my company. My men would not lie to me."

"Yes. Well . . ." Fahrquahrson smiled indulgently, gazing at the wall on his right, where in a framed photograph a group of high officers were inspecting a color guard. "Well now, of course I appreciate such partisan devotion to your command . . ."

"Sir, if you will permit me, it's not blind partisanship but a question of simple justice. Only two of my men could be construed as being guilty of the charges listed. And the members of E Company—who had no right even to be at the function—were not even taken into custody."

The Colonel glanced at him sharply. "What conclusion do you draw, therefore?"

"That my men have been discriminated against unfairly and deliberately."

"By whom?"

"By Lieutenant Jarreyl, sir."

"Why on earth would he do that?"

Damon took a deep breath. "On grounds of personal animus, sir. Lieutenant Jarreyl and I—do not see eye to eye on many things . . ."

"And therefore he is taking it out on your command?"

"Yes, sir."

Fahrquahrson scowled at him. "That's a very grave charge to bring against a fellow officer. Are you prepared to substantiate it?"

"Sir, I am."

There was a short silence. "Well, it's a very unfortunate episode," the Colonel said after a pause. "Very unfortunate indeed." He eased himself back from his desk and got out his pipe and tobacco pouch. "Sit down, Damon." He began to stuff pinches of tobacco into the pipe bowl. "This is your first tour of duty in the Islands, isn't it?"

"Yes, sir."

"You've had nothing but stateside duty prior to this: is that correct?"

"Yes, Colonel. Ever since France."

"Yes. Well. Now, this dance. You say it was your idea."

"Yes, sir. A few of the men approached me about the possibility of holding one as hosts to some of the Filipino girls, and I approved it. I am ready to assume full responsibility—"

"I see." Fahrquahrson gazed off at the photograph again, his eyes narrowed. "It's a good idea to feel your way into things here, the way you would in any new post. It's a good idea not to stick your neck out until you've had a chance to observe what's accepted practice. Do you follow me?"

"Yes sir, I believe I do. It was my understanding that my action was in line with the directive to maintain cordial relations between the Filipinos and the service."

The Colonel pressed the pipe's bowl with his thumb. "It's a matter of judgment, Damon. Judgment and restraint. There are problems in terms of our forces here that don't apply anywhere else. Problems of face, prestige, the fitness of things." Carefully he held the match to the bowl, and the flame leaped in slow, even spurts, brightening his leathery cheeks. "Now I've served at Tientsin, and three tours here—one of them before the war—and at Shafter: I think I can say I know the Pacific and its people as well as the next man; maybe a little bit better. I've made good friends among the Filipinos, and the Chinese, too. Lots of friends. We greet each other when we meet, we exchange cards or presents every year . . ."

He stroked the lobe of one ear. "But these things don't mix, Damon. East is east and west is west, you know? And never the twain shall meet. As the bard puts it." Colonel Fahrquahrson smiled a pale, avuncular smile. "The Filipinos are fine people—they're lively and good-hearted, they're always ready with a smile or a song . . . But they're *Asiatics*, Damon. You mustn't forget that. They're simple, uneducated farmers or shopkeepers or fishermen or whatever, with strong ideas about caste, and face, and the white man—nine out of ten of them are waiting to see us fall on our faces, do you realize that? See us lose our poise, our essential dignity here." He leaned forward and his steady, light brown eyes came to rest on Sam's. "Oil and water, son. Oil and water. It just won't mix. That's why you won't see them at the club, and why we don't go to their functions, except the official ones at the palace. Separate is better." He paused. "I appreciate your gesture, but in the future I suggest you avoid this kind of social intermingling. Do I make myself clear?"

"Yes, sir."

"Good. I guess that's all, then."

"Sir, about my men . . ."

The Colonel gave a little quiver of irritation. "Yes, yes, all right. I'll have a talk with—with the individuals involved. A matter like this is best put out of the way as quickly and quietly as possible . . ."

Outside, in the compound, there was a quick, dry bark of command; then silence again. Jarreyl was still staring at the ceiling and whistling through his teeth, off-key. Damon got to his feet. "We're wasting time, Jarreyl. I want to see Brand and have a talk with him. In private."

"I've decided I don't think it's such a good idea. What with one thing and another."

Sam walked up to the desk and placed both hands on it. "Lieutenant," he said evenly, "I want to see Brand and I want to see him right away. Now do you want to go down the line on this or do I see him?"

There was a short silence while Jarreyl stared at him—a covert, measuring look. "You'll go around on anything, won't you?" he muttered. "Just anything . . ."

"No. Only certain things."

Then the stockade commander relaxed and grinned his sly, ugly grin. "It's your funeral. Don't say I didn't warn you.—Hurley," he called, "get the crazy Indian and take him down the line."

"Yes, sir."

"Good-bye and good luck, pal," Jarreyl said in his high, craking voice.

Damon went outside and paced up and down in the white glare, frowning at the tent rows, the drooping acacia trees outside the compound—heard the dry jingle of steel chain and turned. Brand came toward him with that mincing, arduous shuffle, the leg irons clashing; his eye rolled wildly toward Damon. His face was cut and bruised, blood had matted in his hair and stained his fatigue jacket. Then he had passed on by, the chaser gliding soundlessly behind him. Their shadows were black on the cascao. Damon turned and followed them down the row until they stopped; Brand went to rigid attention. The Captain preceded him into the tent, which was empty except for two wooden chests stacked one above the other and a field cot without a pad. He turned and motioned Brand to the chests and said to the MP, "Wait outside there, will you?" Sitting on the cot he offered a pack of cigarettes. Brand shook his head. Damon shrugged and put the pack back in his pocket.

"My name's Damon," he said.

Brand made no reply. His hair was black and smooth but he did not have the flat, stolid face of the Plains Indian. Even now, with his lips cut, his nose swollen and one eye nearly closed, it was evident that he was a good-looking boy; his eyes were onyx against the warm bronze of his skin. Damon had played against him in baseball and had watched him competing in the regimental gymkhanas. Now all his whiplike grace was gone. The knuckles of one hand were badly swollen, and from the way he sat, hunched over himself, the Captain knew he had been hurt in the belly or groin.

"José's cousin Luis asked me to stop by and see you," Damon offered. He paused. "Luis Funzal. He says you're a friend of his." Still the Indian stared back at him sullenly. "I'm not here in any official capacity. He says you've been given a rough shuffle."

"—He does," Brand said in a quick, fierce whisper, his eyes full of scorn.

Damon glanced at him. "Why, yes. He told me you've got—"

"—and you want to play the big officer, come down to do me a favor," Brand went on savagely, in the same hoarse whisper. "That makes you feel big, makes you feel good, ah?"

"Now look here, Brand—"

"Well, fuck you!—I don't need you! Or anybody else. No favors from *anybody*—you got that? . . ."

Damon lighted his cigarette, watching the dark, burning eyes. It was hard to tell. There was hatred in the boy's face, and a reckless, headlong fury, but there was also pride and resilience. A rebel, a maverick, the kind that always, sooner or later, got into trouble. He thought, with the sharp ache of memory, of Dev, and Raebyrne, and Clay. The ones with pride and fury . . . It would take—it would take a special kind of gambit.

Or maybe nothing would work at all.

"I'd have thought you had more pride than this," he said quietly.

Brand glared at him hotly. "*Pride*—that's all I've got!—I've got enough of that to burn this rock to the water's edge! . . ."

Damon shook his head. "You're digging yourself a grave six feet deep, and you know it. Next thing it'll be solitary, and after that—" He broke off. "You've got me baffled, Brand. And I don't like to be baffled. I like to think I'm a reasonably intelligent soldier. But I guess I haven't learned very much in twenty years' service if I can't figure out why a sharp little trooper like you has decided to give up. All of a sudden." The boy's eyes flickered then and he knew he'd scored. "I had you down for a tough cookie, a dogface who wouldn't ever take shit from anyone else . . . Why am I so wrong, Brand?"

There was a silence in the tent. The Indian thrust his hand across the base of his nose. "I got my own reasons," he muttered.

"Fair enough. But why let them destroy you, to no purpose? Why not make a good fight out of it, at least?"

"I'm making a fight—"

"Sure. But the wrong people, and the wrong way. What about Mc-Clain?"

Another silence. Brand eased his ankles in their dull iron collars and eyed Damon distrustfully. "What's your angle, Captain?"

Damon grinned. "I told you. I don't like to be wrong about a man. And if I am wrong, I want to know why. That's *my* pride . . . Now, what's your angle, Brand?"

The boy dropped his eyes again, fidgeting. Damon smoked quietly, looking out through the tent flaps. The heat was draining from the day now; the breeze had begun in the tops of the acacias, a gentle, liquid seething, like magic rain. He could feel the sweat drying at the sides of his neck. In the scan of his eye he saw that Brand still looked sullen, but it was the effect of confusion now, not animosity. He decided to wait a while. Maybe I was wrong, he thought; maybe I guessed wrong completely.

He had been in the bedroom three days before, changing his sweat-soaked uniform for a fresh one, when he'd heard the sound of men's voices in a clamor of argument. A year ago he would have hurried through the house to investigate, but now he was familiar with the Filipino's excitability and love of drama, and he went on dressing. He was pinning the double bars to his collar tab when he saw the thin, mobile face of José, their houseboy, reflected in the mirror.

"Capitàn, deve venir para hablar a Luis. Ahora mismo!"

Damon smiled. The affectionate effrontery of the Filipino had been one of the pleasantest surprises of the Islands. Loyal, hard-working, warm-hearted, they nonetheless regarded you as their property from the moment you took them on.

"Who is Luis, and why must I talk to him," he inquired.

"My cousin. From Camiling." José pulled into the bedroom a short, stocky boy wearing the uniform of the Philippine Constabulary. "Here is Luis."

"Sir!" Luis saluted powerfully; Damon returned it. José brusquely ordered: "Tell the Captain your story."

Both the children of course caught most of the recital, and the topic was vigorously pursued during lunch.

"Sergeant McClain's got a broken wrist and lacerations," Peggy said. "What are lacerations?"

"Cuts and bruises," Donny, who was home on vacation from the Bishop Brent School in Baguio, told her knowingly. "Brand must have really klonked him."

"*Klonk*," Tommy said. "What kind of a word is that?"

"It's just—you know: a slang term." He had turned into a slender, rather awkward boy with his mother's piercing glance, her rapid shifts in mood. "The fellows use it all the time."

"But what were they fighting *about*?" Peggy wanted to know.

"God alone knows," her mother answered, "and He won't tell. Money, or liquor, or some poor little feebleminded Igorot girl."

"Now, Tommy," Damon said.

"Well, it's true; isn't it? Cherchez la femme." She was smiling, but her voice was a bit shrill. She was thinner than she'd been back at Oglethorpe or Beyliss; there were rings under her fine green eyes and she was perspiring through her powder, although it wasn't a particularly hot day. She hated the Islands, he knew. After the grim years at Beyliss, with the country in the black slough of the Depression and the shock of the fifteen per cent military pay cut, she had looked forward to the Luzon tour with high anticipation; but it hadn't turned out that way. She tried to bear up under it well enough, she ran the household efficiently and well and involved herself with half a dozen charitable post activities, shopping expeditions to Las Tiendas on Quiapo and an occasional drive to Lake Taal with some other Army wives; but she was only—and quite literally—sweating it out until his tour was over and they could leave this land of thick, damp heat and pelting monsoon rains, where anything leather could grow a three-inch beard of mildew overnight, and the talk at the club revolved increasingly around Japan . . .

"It's enough to make a pacifist out of anybody," she was going on. "If they're not swiping a parasol from some Chinatown shop they're tearing one of the Pinpin Street barrooms all apart, beating each other's brains out or pulling some scrawny girl limb from limb. Why don't they just put *up* with it?" she demanded. "The way the rest of us do . . . ?"

"Maybe they haven't got your fine, firm fortitude," he answered.

"Very funny. Well, it's true: they live like animals, most of them, from payday to payday—and then all they can think of is racing off the post and getting themselves a lot of booze and a lot more of you-know-what."

"What's you-know-what?" Peggy demanded.

"Girls, silly," Donny rebuked her. "My God."

"What do you expect them to do?" Damon said to Tommy, "—take up ballet? write odes to the tropic moon? What chance have they got to meet any decent women? They can serve as orderlies in the CO's house, but they can't go out with the CO's daughter . . ."

"How true," Tommy answered, and rolled her eyes.

"—I don't believe it," Peggy said suddenly. She had her lower lip stuck out, her brown eyes snapping—for a second she reminded Damon so forcibly of his sister that he smiled.

"Don't believe what, honey?"

"That he did it. Brand."

"Of course he did it, stupid," Donny broke in, "—he admits it, a whole lot of people saw it! He struck a noncommissioned officer with a piece of lead pipe . . ."

"He drove us over to Cavite once," Peggy persisted. "He was nice—he was so quiet and neat."

"They're just the ones," her mother replied, passing the bread. "The nice, quiet ones. They draw trouble like flies."

"He shouldn't have picked up the piece of pipe, should he, Dad?" Donny asked.

"No. He shouldn't have. He was probably trying to defend himself. That's what it sounds like, anyway. Anybody would be afraid of a knife."

"Anybody, Dad?" Donny's face was very solemn. "You wouldn't be, would you?"

"Sure I would." He smiled at his son's consternation. "There's nothing wrong with being afraid. Every man's afraid at one time or another."

"Isn't there anyone who isn't afraid of anything?"

Sam glanced at Tommy who was eating industriously, her eyes averted. "I knew one man who wasn't afraid of anything."

"Who was he?"

"A man named Merrick, a company commander. In France. Your granddad relieved him and sent him to Blois."

"Why did he do that?"

"Because he was needlessly risking other men's lives along with his own. Your granddad's contention was that any man who had no fear at all was so far removed from the human race that he was a permanent menace to all concerned."

"The first great myth," Tommy said to the boy with sudden, still vehemence. "That every soldier is always, eternally brave. Myth Number One, you could call it.—Peggy, don't play with your food, now. You're too big a girl for that."

"Dad," Donny said, "if the sergeant tried to stab him with a knife, wasn't he justified in picking up something to defend himself?"

"I'd think so, yes. Of course you'd have to know the circumstances."

"Well, that's what I don't understand. I'd tell them *I* wasn't guilty," Donny declared, and put down his fork. "Why won't he do it?"

"That's just what bothers me, Don," Damon answered. "That's exactly what I can't figure out, either."

"Sam." Tommy was staring at him; that vertical line had appeared in the center of her forehead. "Are you getting yourself involved again?"

"What makes you say that, dear?"

"You've got that moony, loony, *earnest* look on your face, that's what makes me say that. Look—he isn't even in your company. You just *purchase* trouble . . . Now, why—?"

"Addicted, I guess." He winked at Peggy, who giggled and squirmed in her chair. Donny was watching him gravely. "With some gentlemen rankers it's cards, with some it's women, with others it's brown-nosing—"

"Sam! Is it absolutely necessary to use phrases like that in front of the children?"

"I'm not a child," Donny answered, "I'm fourteen and a half."

"Sycophancy," Damon amended. He felt a sudden, sourceless hilarity. "Meant to say that. Toadyism. Obsequiousness. Favor currying. My— we have a lot of words for it, don't we? Tufthunting: ever hear that one?"

"Sam, that's obscene!"

"Isn't it? Or lickspittling—"

"That's worse . . ."

"You can't get around it—the occupation begs the terminology. To each his vice. With me, it's the dogface soljer and his misadventures."

Tommy stopped laughing. "The only thing wrong with that is, the dogface soljer hasn't got an awful lot of influence on the promotion board."

"My God, that's right." He smote his forehead. "I'd almost forgotten."

Tommy shied a hand at him. "You're incorrigible."

"But if Brand's not guilty—" Donny began again.

"Stop up your ears," Tommy commanded him. "Your father's fallen prey to the lure of the Islands. They've turned him inside out and rotted away his good sense. If he ever had any."

Sam stared at her, laughing, mildly surprised—aware she was right. It was true: he'd been turned inside out. As they'd slipped up the channel past Corregidor in the old *Thomas* the first morning, the land breeze had reached him—an odor of orchids and wood smoke and cinnamon and a thousand other things he couldn't place. Bancas dipped through the green water, their lateen sails like exotic copper-colored seashells. Off the starboard bow lay Manila, flat and gray-green, with here and there the pink and white cubes of buildings gleaming in the hot, hard light. The Pearl of the Orient. After the dull years of stateside garrison, the close-order drill and classes and OD duty, he'd felt something stirring in him, straining, bursting out of its husk. It was a world full of wonders. In the markets the women held huge fish high above their heads, swaying rhythmically, crying songs in Tagalog; men in woven hats and loincloths padded along in a tireless dogtrot, the great loads at the ends of their shoulder poles rising and falling as if lifted on invisible wires; turbaned Arabs went by as majestic as the heads of state, ferocious-looking Moros drew up to him entreatingly, unfolding little squares of rag to reveal fantastic solitary jewels. "Sir, for you this magic pearl, for you this perfect gem! The only one of its kind in all the Islands—perhaps the world! Sir, for you, only two hundred pesos." Turning it now, deftly, between thumb and finger, while the dull nacre came alive in a little rain of colored light. "Think of it, noble sir—a personal gift to my father from the Sultan of Palamangao! But for you, only one hundred *eighty* pesos . . ."

Up in the valley the pace was gentler. Women moved through the rice fields, their long skirts tucked up around their thighs, bending, rising, planting the bright green sickle shoots, and deep in a wallow a ponderous carabao bull, immersed to his broad black snout and swept-back horns, languidly chewed his cud. In the evenings smoke rose from the barrios in pale blue spirals, and there was the light rubato of songs and laughter. The Filipino was always singing or laughing or gesticulating—his appetite for adventure, for wit, acquisition, exchange of views, was boundless. Sauntering along, barefooted, straw hat thrust to the back of his head, razor-sharp bolo swinging unsheathed by his naked calf, he looked ready for anything the world might offer. And there was more than that, too, Damon saw—there was a sturdy, unwavering sense of his individuality, his unique force and future as a man. If the Filipino was not perhaps all that he hoped for, he at least knew what he wanted to be.

Confronted by all this gaiety and strangeness and expectant ardor, Damon melted. He purchased cat's-eyes and bunches of bananas, he picked up a Moro barong with a horn handle for Donny—one day he even bought for Tommy a great prickly bomb of a *durian* fruit from a wizened old crone who assured him that any woman who ate of it would remain forever beautiful and young. Tommy told him the insides smelled like horse manure dipped in sulphur, said she preferred to grow old gracefully, and begged him to stop lugging home produce at odd hours. He acceded, but this fascinating, tempestuous end of the world had caught at his heart. Here, among these churning millions, lay the hurrying course of the future; he could feel it beating in the air around him. It was out of Asia that the new series of shock waves would come. He dropped everything else in his nocturnal reading and studied Forbes on the Philippines, Hughes and Anderson on the exploitation of China by the Western World, Rewi Alley's terrible accounts of brutality and death in the silk mills and match factories of Shanghai, where a million sickly children worked in the terrific heat until they fell exhausted among the machinery, and were thrown out to die; he read Sun Yat-sen's stirring *San Min Chu I* and Latourette and Abend and Du Halde, he read Kawakami and Young on the rise of Japanese militarism, and Lea's ominous prognoses of a Japanese conquest of the Philippines from Lingayen Gulf. The West had rushed into a vacuum and exerted its force; and now the reaction was coming. The dumb, shackled giant had begun to stir, and look around him—for good, for bad. Here was where the great clash of swords would come, not just for the next war but for the next century. Asiatic man was no longer asleep, no longer power-less . . .

Up the line, swollen in the silence, he heard Jarreyl's high, hoarse voice, and then laughter. Calmly he looked at Brand. A man would be destroyed: this man. The blind, vengeful grinding of Army justice, the wanton fury of one outraged heart—spiraling down, each feeding on the other, to end at death or maiming. Another good man gone. The waste. The long, murderous waste . . . The only thing he remembered clearly about the boy was the afternoon Jack Folland, who was notori-

ously wild, had sent Brand flat on his face with an inside fast ball that
would have taken his head off. Brand got up, dusted himself off, and
promptly ripped the next pitch into right center field for two bases. He
had scored later, too, on a close play at the plate. Yes, he was a fighter,
all right.

"You think every man's hand is against you, Brand," he said in a low,
unhurried voice. "But you're wrong. Only every other man's. There's
always a minority of silly bastards who, for various reasons, enjoy
swimming against the current. Believe it or not, I'm one of them. And
believe it or not, I believe in justice."

"—*Justice*," Brand said with savage scorn, "—I can tell you about
justice, I can tell you things about the law that would shake you up
good! . . ."

"That's right. But that won't prove that justice doesn't exist, or that it
can't sometimes be reached."

Brand's lip curled. "Talk."

"Sure—talk. What have you got that's better? Taunting these stockade baboons into killing you? They'll do it, friend, in their own time
and in their own way. They haven't anything better to do."

He paused. "You say you're a fighter. All right. Let's give them one
good battle over this. Why let them always have it their way? The next
time McClain will be even rougher on someone—because of you. Because you didn't try to stop him now. Why not, Brand? But I can't give
you a hand—nobody can—unless you tell me the story: all of it."

The Indian gave him a quick, dark glance, started to say something—
then stopped himself and pressed his fingers against his split cheek.
Damon took out the pack of cigarettes again and offered it silently. It
was touch and go for a moment, while several kinds of pride and defiance mingled and swayed. Damon watched him, liking him instinctively,
emotionally, against the dry pull of reason, keeping his face perfectly
impassive. It had to be up to the boy now.

"All right," Brand said. He took the cigarette and put it carefully
between his cut and swollen lips. "I'll tell you. All of it. In confidence."

"In confidence," Damon answered.

Your whole life was chance. They could say anything they liked,
they could tell you it was hard work or brute strength or being sharper
than the next man or getting to know the right people, but all that was
small potatoes. What ruled a man's life was lucky accident, and the
power to read signs clearly, as his grandmother had told him. Some were
false, some true, and it required the greatest wisdom to read them
purely. Like the morning he'd been assigned as driver for Estelle
Melburhazy. He had been out behind the maintenance shed, stuffing
some rags into the waste bin, when he saw the thirty-caliber bullet lying

in the dirt, nearly buried; he'd picked it up quickly. The shell had been drilled, the powder leeched out: it looked deadly but it was powerless. He was still puzzling over it when he swung by the big villa on Rizal Avenue.

She came out of the house and smiled at him as if she'd known him for ten years. Her eyes were wide and candid, flecked with amber; her skin had a dusty delicacy that fascinated him. He guessed she was about thirty-one or -two.

"What's your name?" she asked, after he had closed her door and started off.

"Private Brand, ma'am."

"Brand. What a curious name. Have you been branded?"

"Not yet, ma'am."

She smiled at that. "Are you of Mexican extraction?"

"No—I'm Indian."

"Really? Full-blooded Indian?"

He nodded and said with some pride: "I am descended from Chief Joseph."

"Oh yes. The Trail of Sorrows."

He made no reply to this and they moved along the chaotic, crowded streets; she told him where to stop and wait for her. She shopped with an assertive indifference that astounded him—as though all these objects had been brought into being with such exertion and craft for her amusement alone. Thai tribesmen had wrenched the tusks from the mouths of dying elephants, naked men wearing bone plates over their nostrils and ears had plummeted down the murky ocean depths off Ceylon, women had squatted before huge looms hour on tedious hour, in order that Estelle Melburhazy might point a fine, immaculate finger and nod genially to the tradesmen. She bought silk scarves from China, a bolt of Madras cloth, a jade pendant, a tribal fetish of ebony from the Malay states, two copper pots, a little yellow rice bird in a bamboo cage. Whatever she liked she bought quickly, without debate or palaver, and moved on, to the consternation of the shopkeepers.

"They expect you to bargain with them," he offered once.

"I know." Her face looked much younger and prettier when she smiled. "But I don't want to."

"And you only do what you want to do."

"Of course!" She laughed; she had a way of tossing her hair back and raising her chin as if she were dismissing a topic, that intrigued him. "Isn't that what life's all about?"

"I suppose so."

He had never seen anyone like her. She had just spent in two hours more money than he'd ever seen, and here she was asking him what kind of food he liked best, what his home was like, whether he planned to stay on in the Army after his hitch was up; or, suddenly dreamy and preoccupied, watching the turbulent wash of people in the streets, her fine blond hair close against her throat. There was in her movements the faintly amused indolence of the wealthy and experienced. Her father was connected in some way Brand didn't understand with both the import-export business and the Army; he was now in Mindanao. Her mother had divorced him and remarried someone in the movie industry. Estelle herself had been recently in Paris, and was going back there in a year or so, perhaps sooner. It was a pleasant pinnacle from which to view life . . .

The following afternoon she asked him to drive her up to Tagaytay Ridge. They wound their way up past the barrios, weaving around the carabao carts filled with nipa or coconuts or bamboo. On the flat rocks by the edges of streams women were beating their washing, calling to one another over the flat slap of the paddles, while the children played under the trees.

"What a way to live," Estelle murmured.

He turned and looked at her. "They live very well. They are a proud people."

"*Well*," she answered, and raised her brows. "I'm being rebuked, it seems. Do you know any Filipinos?"

"Of course. I know several." He told her of evenings with Luis's family, the nipa hut crowded and smoky, the big iron wok full of pork adobo and rice, the glasses and gourds of calamansi juice or pale, emerald tuba, and the kids squatting in the corners crunching on sugar-cane sections; the stories exchanged by sign language and fitful transla-tion, the laughter.

"I wish I knew some Filipinos," she said wistfully. "Besides the maids and houseboys, I mean."

"Why don't you?" He threw out his hand. "There they are . . ."

"I couldn't do that," she protested.

"Why not?"

"Well—it just isn't done, Joe."

"Look," he told her, "if you can buy out half the Quiapo markets in one morning you can go out to the barrios and make some friends . . ."

She found this amusing. "You're remarkable, Joe. You really are."

"What's so remarkable about that?"

"You're so naïve. It's captivating." A few minutes later they reached the summit and she told him to pull off into a grove, where the papaya trees threw down fierce, broad patterns of shadow. It was the most tremendous view he had ever seen. He was used to mountains, heights and awesome vistas, but this made you feel a little like a god. Far below them Lake Taal swept out and out toward the great purple mountains; bancas glided over its deep blue surface, their gold and scarlet sails like magic wings, and on the grass green, terraced slopes figures moved among the rice paddies, rising and stooping. The breeze blew strong in their faces.

"They're like toys," Estelle breathed, "—tiny little toys of people . . ."

He passed his eyes down the giant emerald steps of terracing to the water's edge. "Imagine spending your whole life there," he said. "Working that one plot, there. All your life."

"That's all they're good for . . ."

He swung around, angry, and saw she was having fun with him. He smiled and tossed his head, watching her. One moment she was gazing at him, her lips parted, with that silky, amused expression—and the next she was in his arms, kissing him with desperate eagerness, her body trembling as if she had fever.

Nothing like this had ever happened to him. He had gone to the whore houses on Pinpin Street once or twice with some of the members of his company, usually when he was drunk, and hating the whole episode—the raw, bare rooms, the callous inspection of his genitals, the brief, heartless coupling and release followed by the chipped basin and small frayed towels; the incessant chatter among the girls. And—what repelled him most of all—the casual post mortems over beer. Lying with a woman ought to be a proud and secret thing, like prayer or maybe a duel; not the stuff of ball games and parades. And now, here, wonder of wonders, it lay before him in the person of this languid, wealthy girl who gripped him so urgently and moaned her need and her delight . . . Later, her head back against the car seat, dreamy-eyed, she told him about playing Vingt-et-un at Monte Carlo casinos, or riding a camel toward the Great Sphinx at Giza, or slipping into the harbor at Rio with the buildings rising like salt towers up the green slopes beyond the beach.

He spent every free minute he had with her. They strolled through the crowds on Dasmarinas Street, they went swimming at the beach at Ponbal, they wandered along the Luneta and gazed off toward Cavite where the hulls of Admiral Montojo's ill-fated warships lay like great black-ribbed serpents in the ruddy orange light of the setting sun, and the thunderheads boiled up out of Mindoro in baleful, churning black towers. And then they would drive back to the house on Rizal; he would let her off at the front door, run the car into the garage and slip in the back entrance, to find her already sprawled on the bed, half-undressed, waiting for him, her arms extended.

"Hurry now, Joe, you—oh, I want you!"

His mind was caught in a tumult of sensation. This pale-blond woman with her small hands and feet, her immaculate bra and step-ins, was clamoring for him. For Private Joseph Brand of E Company. Her very greediness flattered him. She was a torrent of invention, of rapture, and he was equal to it: what she desired he could fulfill with ease. And when, rocking her tousled head on the pillows she cried, "Oh, you're delicious—oh, you're *burning* me!"—he knew a tight, swollen triumph that turned him giddy.

"Do you love me?" he would demand, almost harshly, withdrawing a little, holding her still. "Do you?"

"Oh yes, oh God, yes, anything—oh don't stop *now!* . . ."

She bought him things—a watch with a luminous dial, a pigskin wallet, a balisong knife with a carved haft—and he accepted them with grace. If it gave her pleasure. The objects meant little to him. But at inspection, during close-order drill or fatigues he would hold the knowledge of this affair of loving to himself with the prideful secrecy that had sustained him for so long in the white man's world, parading this new dance of emotions before his mind's eye like a bazaar vendor exhibiting the rarest of jewels to a privileged friend. He took even more pride in his appearance, withdrew still further from the few men in his company that he traveled with.

In three weeks it was all over. Her mother, now living in Santa Monica, was seriously ill. She would have to fly back to the States.

"When will I see you, Estelle?"

She looked at him with the vacant, languid smile. "I don't know, Joe. Have to see." She packed hurriedly and made arrangements. He kept clear of her, contented himself with watching from a distance as she left in a calesa for Cavite. That night he tossed in his cot, seeing her sliding high over the long, westerly roll of the Pacific, hurrying toward the sun. In no time at all she would be half a world away. The next morning the reaction set in; he felt irritable and confused—he wondered what he had done up to now with himself; how he'd got through the days.

The day after that McClain began riding him. McClain was a sergeant, a heavy man with a handsome, fleshy face and wide-set, pale green eyes that dilated strangely when he smiled. He found fault with Brand's work on a truck and gave him extra police duty; when Brand remonstrated, he smiled a slow, sly smile and said, "What's the matter, Brand?—you got that tired, overtaxed feeling? You missing out on something good lately?" and the other men standing nearby laughed. They knew, then; they'd found out. He felt a quick flash of anger, and suppressed it doggedly. Filthy pigs—nothing was sacred to them, particularly where a woman was concerned. They fouled everything they touched.

When Ives the dispatcher put him on report for being fifteen minutes late on a run, he knew he was getting the treatment. Grimly he made sure that his shop work was impeccable, his appearance flawless. But the harassment continued, and the attitude of even some of his friends changed. The treatment. He had stepped out of line, he was to pay for it. And every day there was the sly, jowled face of McClain, the booming voice.

"Think you're too good for anything else, eh, Indian? Jazzing some nice white pussy. Made you feel pretty big, didn't it? Best you ever did for yourself . . ."

And finally, stung by the interminable riding, the memory of those royal hours he retorted: "What's the matter, McClain—you jealous?"

The Sergeant laughed. "Jealous!—you poor sod. Jesus, that's a hot one. I gave up on that before you even shipped out here. Half the regiment's been banging that bag for years. Why hell, she's known as the Manila Pegboard . . ."

The others had turned from their benches, watching him and grinning. He felt sick with rage and mortification. McClain was shaking with helpless laughter.

"That's a filthy lie," he said thickly.

"What do you want me to do—describe her room to you? You want me to draw you a diagram?"

The whole shop was laughing at him now. His grandfather had been right: the white man was faithless, and wily, and boundlessly cruel. There was no limit to his hatred and his greed. None whatever.

But that she had let this insolent fat-faced bastard actually undress her, climb into that bed and enter her body—

"—Still doesn't believe me," McClain was saying, wagging his head. "Hell, she'd lay anything in pants, animal-vegetable-or-mineral. And she finally got around to you—and you think that makes *you* so special! . . . Brand, you're the last man in. You want me to tell you the way she likes to do it? —you want me to describe the way she puts her—"

He had no sense of decision, of willed movement. McClain's face swept nearer strangely, its expression shifting from mirth to blank surprise as he lunged in and swung, and felt the shock high in his shoulder. Someone whispered something in an awestricken voice, but he didn't hear the words. There was only the frieze of faces and he followed in quickly, riding his fury, swinging as hard and as fast as he could. He reeled from a blow on his cheek he never felt, pressed in again. McClain fell hard then, bumping against a fender, gripping it awkwardly as he went down, dragged himself up again. Brand started in—all at once brought up short by the long, narrow blade.

"All right," McClain said in a low snarl. Blood was streaming from his mouth and the corner of his eye. "I'm going to carve you good—"

Even then he felt no fear; only hatred, and the need to arm himself with something better than his bare fists. Someone had seized him by the arm and shoulder but he spun away, raced between two vehicles, darted along the green metal machinist's bench, the press drills and vises—saw the length of pipe and snatched it up and whirled around. McClain was on him, a heavy shadow against the light. He danced to one side and swung the pipe. The knife clattered on the concrete and McClain grabbed his arm with a short, fretful cry. Now Brand heard Ives shouting: "Break that *up* now!" But he didn't care. They were all enemy, all of them. To the end, then. He dropped the pipe and hit the Sergeant again and again, felt the blood spatter in his face and throat; then slamming him against the side of a truck he seized McClain's throat in both hands and squeezed with all his might. The fat face swelled, congested, flushed a deep red. Voices clamored in his ears, hands pulled at him and struck him but nothing could reach him through the churning red froth of his rage. This monster was going to die. Now.

Then something struck him on the back of the head—a sharp, cold dart of pain, and darkness rushed in over him like the wings of a great bird.

He stabbed out his cigarette and crossed his arms on his knees. His legs ached from the drag of the irons and his head burned and throbbed. The Captain was watching him in silence; a slow, sad smile that was not malice or contempt—a smile that distressed him. There had been a man like him back at Gray Forks: Mr. Canby, a thin, gaunt man with thick wrists who headed the Bureau for Indian Affairs, who had told him he ought to try to get an education, finish high school—or at least go to work in the moccasin factory at Gant Creek: there was steady pay there. He had looked out of the window at the high red flank of the mesa. Hand-made moccasins, turned out by machine. What he wanted to be was a mechanic—but there was no job for a mechanic at Gray Forks; the few Indians who had cars kept them running themselves. And there in town was Charlie Mantowari, back from Hawaii, with his pressed uniform and ribbons and the four chevrons and the little gold ladder of hashmarks, playing cards with Big Foot and Johnny Owl and the others, talking of long ago battles in France, and Diamond Head, and the Islands . . .

"So then you gave up," Damon was saying.

He shook his head angrily. "They gave up on *me*. And I'll die before I give them an inch of ground."

"Same thing."

"What?"

"Same thing," the Captain repeated. "A rebellion like yours is just as bad as lying down and letting them walk all over you. Worse. You're telling them to break you in little pieces. You're asking for it."

"I don't see it that way," he answered.

"What other way is there to see it? You sit here, refusing to defend yourself, fighting Jarreyl and the whole stockade—and McClain is on pass in Manila, stripes and all, laughing at you still. It doesn't make sense . . ."

He set his jaw. "I've got my reasons." He had said all he was going to, even for as straight a guy as this Damon looked to be. There were things a man had to keep to himself, no matter what.

Damon had taken his penknife out of his pocket and begun to clean his fingernails. "She doesn't need your protection, you know," he said. "Miss Melburhazy. She can take care of herself, she's been around." Brand could not hide his surprise, but the Captain's eyes were still fixed on his nails. "You're playing McClain's game, Brand—you're doing just what he wants you to do: saying nothing, wiping yourself out . . . so he can even get back in with her again."

This angered him and he started to speak, but Damon held up his hand, watching him now with that mournful, unsettling gaze. "All right, maybe she's a nympho, maybe she's sick, maybe she's just a rich gal out for thrills. I don't know and I don't want to. It's none of my business, anyway." He pointed one finger bluntly. "I'll tell you one thing—she wouldn't be worrying about *your* good name if the shoe was on the other foot . . . Let it come out at the court, if it does." He smiled wryly. "Don't worry—the rich very rarely suffer in a situation like this. It's people like you and me who get stuck with the check."

Listening, he fidgeted on the boxes. This Damon was sharp, no doubt about it—he'd spotted the whole thing in a flash, he knew more than he'd been aware of himself. The penknife had a horn handle, like Mr. Canby's. A sign. Like the deactivated cartridge. That had been a sign he'd read incorrectly, though.

Damon snapped the blade shut and turned to him directly. "How many people saw the fight?"

"I don't know—seven, eight guys."

"Then they saw him draw the knife on you."

"Yeah. But that doesn't prove anything—they're all scared of Mc-Clain."

"We'll see about that. Maybe I can make them a little bit more scared of me. —He definitely pursued you with the knife?"

"Hell, yes—he almost had me when I turned around . . ."

There was a little pause, while the breeze plucked at the tent flaps and sent the cascao dust spinning in fine white eddies.

"It's up to you," Damon said quietly. "All in your own hands. We can beat this—most of it, anyway, with a little luck. I think we can. But you've got to want to battle, yourself. And in the right way, not this private war you're waging with the stockade." He leaned forward, fist on his thigh. "You've been a good soldier, Brand, with a clean record right up to now. You could make something of yourself if you want. Now, how do you want it?"

It was hard to change when you'd made up your mind; hard to back away on a resolve. But now, looking at the lined face, the steady, unabashed gaze, he knew the Captain was right and he was wrong: he would destroy himself this way, and nothing would be solved one way or the other. He'd been wrong about Estelle, too—and now his pride was causing him to beat his head against a wall. Here was one white man—and an *officer* at that, for Christ sake—who felt he was something more than a sneaky no-good redskin son of a bitch; who read him like a book and wasn't afraid to sit there and tell him so.

"All right, Captain," he said. "It's worth a try."

"Oh, we're going to have another one of those Sistine Chapel sunsets!" Tommy Damon exclaimed. Her eyes turned like a little girl's toward the balcony where the evening sky, streaked with feathery bits of cloud, burst into a torrent of vermilions and golds, fiery against an azure that paled to infinity. "They're just incredible, aren't they?"

"Yes, they are," Emily said in her soft, remote voice. "They almost make it all worth it, sometimes . . ."

Massengale glanced at her, but her expression was quite serene. "Darling," he chided her lightly, "you're so sere and Bostonian this evening."

"Well, it *is* the least they can do, Court," Tommy said, "after frying our brains to a crisp all day long."

"Rewards and punishments, eh?"

"Oh, no! I only believe in rewards . . ."

The four of them laughed, and Massengale leaned forward and patted Tommy's hand; she was one of the few people he permitted to call him Court. He had never called anyone by his nickname—he'd made it a kind of minor trademark of his—and he firmly discouraged the use of his own. If Damon had ever done it he'd have crawled all over him. But Damon had never called him anything but Captain, and now Major.

"That's the spirit," he commended her. "Still, there's no evading the effects of climate on the human animal. Have you ever noticed that the plastic arts stem from the tropical and semitropical lands? and the interior, mystic ones from the north? For instance, can you imagine a really first-rate Scandinavian painter? or a Sibelius from the Mediterranean basin?"

"Scarlatti came from Naples, I believe," Emily said quietly.

"An isolate exception. The point is that we associate music, the most mystic of the arts, with the north—Wagner, Bach, Mozart. And the descriptive, the pictorial media with the south: Leonardo, Titian, El Greco and so on."

"What about literature?" Damon asked him.

"—I haven't got that worked out yet," Massengale answered, and they all laughed again. "It's true, though—sometimes I think life is nothing more than a series of rewards and punishments levied on us like furloughs and fatigues. It's Emily's ferocious New England Calvinism rubbing off on me, I suppose. That's why I always pray to Huracán and Quetzalcoatl every evening as the sun sets. It's how we got this little eyrie here, you know."

"Don't kid me, Court," Tommy taunted him. "I know how you got this little eyrie—you twisted Luis Martegaray's arm in the most charming manner!"

Blinking, he feigned shock. "My dear! A lowly career officer on the far-flung battle line—I only bow my head and serve."

"Yes—but you do it so much more *graciously* than the rest of us . . ."

He smiled, running his eyes over the light, high-ceilinged room. There were latticed windows made of scores of squares of translucent mother-of-pearl shell, which slid into wall recesses after dark. The floors were mahogany, and gleamed like ruddy glass. The Spanish chest on one wall was two hundred years old and had belonged to Don Basilio Augustín Davila, the Captain-General of Manila, who had surrendered to Dewey. There were low rosewood chow-chow benches, nested ifilwood tables, porcelain lamps adorned with dragons and exotic fish, dark now against the gleaming white walls. Above their heads the huge-bladed fans turned softly, like blunt protective wings. An impeccable taste, if he did say so. He had assembled it slowly, with care, in this spacious apartment high over Manila, had staffed it with the most competent and deferential servants, and the Massengales' dinners were the talk and envy of the post. It was exactly the impression he wanted to convey—a dignified, almost somber elegance, tempered by his own wit and catholicity of view. Tonight was the kind of evening he liked most, though—a simple dinner à quatre, free of the other pressures, the unremitting effort involved in impressing superiors whose minds were painfully, pathetically limited and slow. Like Fahrquahrson. That fatuous idiot, living some kind of pukka sahib India garrison dream laced with California calisthenics—couldn't he see the world had changed beyond recognition in barely the last *twenty* years? No, he obviously couldn't. But to have to serve with such mental basket cases . . .

"Emily," Tommy was saying, "this sauce is delicious!"

His wife smiled softly. "Don't praise me. That's Courtney's doing— he supervises all the sauces and salads. It drives Asunta wild, but she puts up with it."

"She does well to," he murmured.

"Ha! the steel hand in the velvet glove," Tommy teased him. "But what'll you do when they get their independence and we all have to go home?"

He shook his head at her, his eyes narrowed. "Not a chance."

"But isn't that what President Quezon has flown stateside for?"

"It can't possibly work. Have you gone over and watched them? the legislature?" He took a sip of wine. "It's a Breughel—a jungle Breughel. A gentlemen in a fancy barong-tagalog gets up and makes a maundering speech for *Independence Now;* a representative from Bontoc—he is still wearing his straw hat—wants dominion status, an Igorot in a polo shirt interrupts him to shout about the price of sugar, a great fat hulk from Davao offers a gurgling testimonial to the greatness of the Moro peoples.

The Manila gentleman attacks him savagely, the Moro insults both him *and* the farmer from Bontoc. The chair bangs and thumps away—it ought to be a bolo, not a gavel—and by now everyone is roaring at his neighbor with no one listening to anyone else. A barrio cockfight is a good deal more dignified."

"What do you think we ought to do with the Islands, Major?" Damon asked.

"Outright annexation."

The Captain's brows rose, and Tommy cried: "Oh, but we can't do that, can we?"

"Why not? We are still responsible for their defense, according to this cockeyed constitution of theirs. Why not treat it like the Northwest Territory, earmarked for eventual statehood? Everybody thinks we're at the end of our national expansion—as though the Pacific Ocean were some sacred blue barrier. Why? We're not going to give up the territory of Hawaii, are we? Then why all this pussyfooting about the Philippines? See how they're situated—like a compact little necklace slung right across the throat of Asia . . ." He talked on, developing his theme as the ideas came to him, watching their faces: his wife, benign and veiled; Damon respectful, attentive and very steady; Tommy frankly captivated and alive—her eyes sparkling in the candlelight, her lips just parted in that charming way that made her look even more lovely and disturbing than ever.

"Look at the geographical logic of the situation: 225 miles due north of Mayraira Point is Formosa, 400 miles north by east Japan's island chain, 750 miles due west the Indo-China Coast, 120 due south the Celebes and Halmahera. We have a dozen points of contact with Southeast Asia . . ."

"From another point of view you could say we were well inside the jaws of Southeast Asia, couldn't you?" Damon asked him.

"Only if you hold the thesis that all salients are untenable, which I don't think you do. An adequately supported salient is a source of anxiety to one's opponent, and an ever ready base for taking the offensive against him. Beyond that, you're flying in the face of the inherent thrust of history. The basic terrestrial movement is westward." Recent studies revealed that infants first start to walk in a westerly direction. Europe had moved west across the Atlantic for a thousand years, the Mayans had peopled Oceania, following the trades—anthropologists had noted the recurrent elliptic eye motif in Yucatán, Tonga, the Sepik River cultures. "We trekked west because we had to. The Louisiana Purchase, the War with Mexico, Seward's Alaska venture—they were all in a certain sense perfectly necessary, as natural as breathing."

"Except for the poor old Indian, that is," Emily said quietly.

"Oh my God, don't bring up Indians!" Tommy exclaimed, "—if I hear anything more about Indians I'll shriek . . ."

"Oh, yes," Emily said. "The court-martial. I think you did a noble deed, Sam."

"Thank you, ma'am," Damon answered with a wry, mournful smile.

"He drove us all crazy with it, I can tell you that," Tommy told them. "Sat up till all hours preparing the case. Reading tomes that would choke a carabao. Ridiculous! You'd think he was defending Emile Zola . . . They said he had tears in the eyes of half the court when he got through. I don't believe it, though. Do you, Court?"

Massengale laughed, watching her lips. "Lo, the poor Indian! whose untutored mind/ Sees God in clouds, and hears him in the wind . . ." The trial of Brand had become a cause célèbre on the post for the last month—a source of mirth, irritation and violent argument in the messes. Everybody had an opinion. The fault was McClain's for not keeping a private in hand; the fault was Jarreyl's for running such a stupid, bloody Andersonville; the stockade was a trifle severe perhaps, but there was no help for it, it was simply necessary to keep the EM in line: if you started making exceptions where would you stop? Damon's heart was in the right place, but his enthusiasms were unfortunate; he was quixotic, he wasn't sound—trouble with him was he'd never got over being an EM himself; he was a God damned fool who ought to run his company and keep his nose out of things that didn't concern him—injecting the racial issue into a fuss of this sort was bad medicine out here in the Department, where we had a position to maintain; the whole affair was prejudicial to the best interests of the service . . .

The wrangles, the cautious, muffled arguments had gone on and on; Massengale had listened in amusement. The question of the Melburhazy girl was dynamite, of course—if her involvement became a matter of record it could have some serious consequences. Colonel Fahrquahrson was furious with Damon, and it was rumored that General Whitley was displeased by all the notice the affair was getting throughout the Islands. But the Captain had skirted the girl's implication neatly. When he'd been able to establish the fact that McClain had been drinking the morning of the episode and had pursued Brand with the knife, the anti-Damon faction went into fits; and his summation on the duties and responsibilities of noncommissioned officers was a little masterpiece. The court's deliberation had been brief: Brand was acquitted, the case was closed, and everyone heaved a sigh of relief.

Massengale watched the author of all this acrimony seated at the other end of the table—shortened now for the four of them—eating with deliberate care and listening to his wife. Damon was a disappointment to him. Taking the case had been stupid, essentially: stupid because it alienated those in power without accomplishing anything commensurate. He'd handled it superbly, but what good was that? Now Fahrquahrson and half the rank out here had him down for a Bolshevik, a guardhouse lawyer. That was the trouble with Samuel: for all his competence he was really like most career officers—he had never got over being a boy, stamped with a boy's enthusiasms. True, he wasn't a poker addict (though he did play occasionally), he didn't philander or turn into a rummy the way a lot of them did; and he did continually struggle to expand his mind to meet military and political problems— which was what had attracted Massengale to him in the first place. But it was all wasted if he let sentimental impulses like this business with Brand ruin his chances for advancement . . .

"How is the noble red man?" he asked, his eyes twinkling. "Is he properly grateful?"

The Captain's face became very still and somber. "Yes," he said. "He's grateful."

"Oh, Court," Tommy cried, "—how can you *ask* such a question? He's wild with worship, he says he'll follow Sam wherever he goes—he wants to be Sam's orderly."

"He could do worse," Massengale observed.

"But Sam won't do it. He says Brand is NCO material and it might stand in the way of his getting ahead. But Brand says he doesn't care." She tossed her head, and her hair swung delicately against her throat. "He's so devoted! They're all like that. Loyalty from the bottom up, I believe it's called."

"That's what it's called," Damon said. "Don't let this digression of Tommy's interrupt you, Major. Go on with your westward theory, will you?"

"Oh. Yes—I'm sorry, Court." Tommy looked charmingly rueful. "I get up here in this palace and everything goes to my head. But honestly, do you think we ought to just—take them over? the Philippines?"

Soberly he nodded. "We were moving correctly—Hawaii, Commodore Perry's trip to Japan were in the right line. But then we turned sentimental. We allowed a simple geographical obstacle to prevent us from pursuing our destiny. The Pacific. We shrank from it: it was perfectly silly. We should have gone on to Manila *then*—not as a result of the accidents of battle—and established our hegemony in Borneo, New Guinea, possibly even New Zealand and Australia. Don't be shocked— we're talking of the vast movements of peoples here, not a romanticized concept of representative democracy. An ocean empire, sustained by small, efficient, professional garrisons and a vast fleet based at Salamaua, Brunei, Soerabaja—even Bangkok . . ."

"Court," Tommy chided him, "you're not an army man at all—you should have gone into the navy."

He smiled, pleased with her. "You know, you might be quite right about that. There's a finality, a sense of clean strategic force about naval operations that the land service can't match. Don't tell old Fahrquahrson, though—he'll start huffing and puffing and slashing at the desk with his crop. It's bad enough to have him mad at Samuel without his getting down on me."

"Wouldn't we have run into the Dutch and British interests if we'd followed that course?" Damon asked.

"Of course. The turn of the century was full of clashes: the British and French almost went to war over Siam, the Dutch and Portuguese wrangled over Timor—even the United States got into the row over Samoa with the Germans and the British. It was the great heyday of Western ascendancy, the imperialist apotheosis; and we should have led it, not dragged our feet the way we did. Can't you see it?—a huge oceanic salient from New Guinea to the Ryukyus, oriented toward that vast, swollen belly of the China coast. That was the true line. But we got all muggled up in murky ideas of international brotherhood, universal self-determination."

"What about the Drang nach Osten?"

"A counterwave, an anomaly. Doomed to defeat from its inception. It never really succeeded, Samuel. Such German elements as tried to establish themselves only became Slavicized. The East Prussians are more Asiatic than West European—look at their mystic fervor, their incredible fatalism. They paid the penalty of swimming against the tide. That's why our AEF excursion in '17 was doomed to disaster—we could no more impose our doctrines on Europe than the sun could reverse its course."

He watched the Damons as he talked, catching up threads of history, geography, political science, weaving them into the fabric of his design. The part you transformed in people was the part you possessed, and only that: all the rest was a walled-off area as remote as Tashkent, a land you never penetrated. Tommy was leaning forward, her hands folded beneath her chin—he could almost feel her spirit swaying toward him in the soft dusk, entranced and suppliant. But it was Damon he wanted, not the woman. Many officers fell under his influence in a rush—became, like Ryetower or Burckhardt, devout supporters, "Massengale men" who recognized his ultimate ascendancy to power; or they broke away in confusion or fear and stayed outside the orbit of his concerns, as poor Storey had. But Samuel had done neither. He had been attentive, respectful, even on occasion deferential (though some of that was probably the matter of rank); but there was never that sway of acknowledgment, that final surge of acquiescence that let you know you'd left your mark.

Abruptly he broke off. "That's enough hindsight theorizing," he declared.

"Oh, don't stop," Tommy protested. "It makes me feel like Bismarck—or Clemenceau. Remaking the map of the world . . ."

He laughed, eying her through half-closed lids. She felt it, too—this hunger to transform, control, possess. If only she were a man . . .

"Tell me, how's your father?"

"Oh, he's fine. Happy as can be. He loves teaching—he says the new generation is brighter than anyone would think. What do you suppose he meant by that?"

"Miles Draper wrote me he did a monograph on the First Marne that was masterful. Miles has nothing but praise for him." Of course old Caldwell should have been teaching at the War College long before this; he'd been held back all during the time MacArthur was Chief of Staff. The old feud. Now the Chaumont crowd were getting in their innings, and the realignments and reshufflings were starting again, the gears grinding—you could almost hear them way out here. And yet MacArthur was the ranking general officer of his age group; he would command the armies when war came . . .

"Wonderful man, your father," he said aloud. "That great intellect, that *manner*. Has he ever had political ambitions?"

She blinked in surprise. "No—not that I know of."

"It's a pity. Couldn't you see him as Secretary of State? that combination of force and tact?"

"Oh yes—he'd be in his element!" Her eyes shone. "Things to—well, to mold, to fashion . . ."

"That's it."

"But he'd never put himself forward in any way—he's almost as bad as Sam. He's always felt the army officer should be unpolitical."

"Yes: the old tradition. But these things are changing. Perhaps you should pray to Quetzalcoatl and Huracán."

She laughed, her eyes very wide and clear, and for an instant Massengale had the sensation that he was being drawn into them, as into a still, deep pool . . . Sitting erectly in the high-backed Spanish chair with the candlelight playing over her, she was uncommonly beautiful. She was vivacious and lithe and she had that exciting delicacy of feature, her father's legacy. Gazing at her, half-obsessed, he saw her all at once sprawled indecently on a couch, her lovely face puffed and sodden with drink, her hair in wild disarray, her dress torn from her body and her exposed thighs smeared with dirt, blood, offal—and his heart leaped tightly. Then the vision vanished and the old fear returned; he looked down.

She was saying: "Sam's the one that ought to go into politics, after that court-martial triumph. But he'd never do it, either. Why are people all so perverse?"

"The fatal flaw." He lighted her cigarette, watching her lashes droop softly toward her cheeks. "You wouldn't want us to be without our fatal flaws, would you?"

"Oh, it isn't everybody," she said. "You haven't got one at all. . . ."

The familiar disquietude began to seep into the edges of his heart. He picked up his butter knife and bent it rhythmically between his fingers. "Perhaps," he said lightly, "you just don't know me well enough."

The dinner party broke up then; the two women vanished into the living room and he and Damon went into his study, which looked north toward the governor's palace. For a time they talked desultorily of one thing and another. Everything seemed to be in a state of flux. Craig's appointment as Chief of Staff had surprised Massengale. He had been certain Drum would get it—but of course Craig had been on Pershing's staff, too, as well as an old favorite of Hunter Liggett's. His moment had come, he'd seized it; but what had been the precise confluence of obligation and influence that had led to it? Hugh Johnson had the President's ear now, he knew that much; and Johnson had been a lieutenant in Craig's first cavalry troop. He sighed. In any event the balance was shifting. The Pacific was where the power lay now: Drum in Hawaii, MacArthur here putting the Philippine army together, Hazlitt down in Palamangao . . .

"How about a game?" he asked. "Feel up to it?"

"Fine, Major, if you do."

Ramon brought in the chess set and a bottle of Grand Marnier and glasses and they began to play as darkness fell, and the cries of Manila drifted up to them faintly. You could tell so much from a game of chess. If a man was rash, if he was smug or laggard or unimaginative or timid—there it all lay before you, revealed in the space of an hour, as surely as if you had put your hand on his inviolate soul. Massengale liked to launch an overwhelming attack out of the traditional Ruy Lopez, sending up his knights and bishops in unorthodox ways, pressing unusual variations that would open up vast areas of assault; or to lie back behind the dense intricacies of the Sicilian or the Dutch Defense and then explode with devastating effect on either flank, watching his adversary's mounting consternation through half-closed lids.

Damon usually denied him these pleasures; he never panicked, he never succumbed to easy pawn grabbing or wildly speculative diversions. He took his risks, but soberly, and when he forced exchanges it was with a judicious care—decision tempered with reluctance, as though he were always conscious of the worth of the pieces he had sacrificed. Above all he was imaginative, and tenacious beyond belief; he never lost sight of the main objective.

Their games followed a fairly consistent pattern: an early onslaught by Massengale which resulted in a minute positional advantage; resourceful defenses by Damon, and then a fierce, attritional struggle that ended in a close victory eked out by one or the other—or, more commonly, a draw. Tonight the same pattern emerged, but the exchange with Tommy had unsettled Massengale, filling his mind with conflicting speculations. *You haven't got one at all*, she'd said, her eyes full of wonder, the reflected light from the candles glinting in them; tiny saffron points. Little she—or anyone else—knew. Well, that was *his* Tashkent; everyone had one. Even Hugh Drum. Schuyler had written him that there was great opposition to Drum in high places, that he'd never get it; they were looking elsewhere, among the younger men. "In any event the solution is political, not military." Schuyler liked to salt down his letters with rather pompous generalizations. Pershing was no longer listened to as he had been—there were those who said he was becoming a senile, tiresome old man. Massengale smiled faintly. They could accuse the Old Man of a lot of things, but senility was not one of them: what he thought he had good reasons for thinking. But perhaps his day was done. The rumor was he'd given Drum his blessing, and now Drum was on Oahu, raging and scheming . . .

In any event the solution is political, not military.

Damon had moved again. He bent forward over the board, pursuing the possibilities, his mind running on two levels at once. As a result of the exchange of knights Samuel had succeeded in advancing a knight's pawn to the fifth, and had supported it deftly.

He translated a bishop and sat back again, relaxing his mind—watched beyond the screens the lights in the palace flaring through the dense stands of acacia. He loved Manila: Manila was bold and wild, a barbaric white citadel all tangled up in pagan and Christian attitudes, a torrid arena where Malay and Igorot and Chinese and Moro swarmed, vying with one another. On nights like these, with the stars sweeping near in great silver globes and rowels, he could feel his senses dilate as if under the influence of some potent drug. There was so much that could be done—so very much. Long vistas swung open into the future—he could almost put his finger on the boundary stones of his future achievements, triumphs, glories. In a sense his life had started here, in these islands: it would find its culmination here as well. All the tumultuous dreams of years trailed through his mind, burgeoning, demanding solution . . .

He had been raised in a huge Federal stone house with white pillars, overlooking the Hudson. The front parlor—no one ever went in it except for serious occasions—was sedate and still, cool under the drawn shades; there was an Empire sofa of horsehair with a carved back, and slender marquetry chairs and a rosewood organ with porcelain stops. On the center wall was a full-length portrait of his father in dress uniform, holding a sword; and in a glass case on the lowboy was the medal he'd won at Bamolos in '98, in those very hills out there beyond the palace. "A glorious victory, Courtney. Captain Pershing himself told me it was the most valiant action of the entire campaign." His mother's voice: high, like the upper register on a cello, but more insistent; she had been slender and pretty, with her hair in loose, brown waves over her temples, and her eyes rested on his with a soft, implacable ardor. "You must live up to him, Courtney. In every way. So that he would be proud of you."

The sword was in another case; it had been brought back by a brother officer a few years later. He had taken it out one afternoon, secretly, and drawn it from the scabbard. A slender, blued blade adorned with the most delicate leafy scrolls, still bluer; the tassel on the hilt had tickled his wrist as he'd raised it to the salute. His father's eyes watched him from the wall, animate and commanding.

In every way.

There were ponies he rode, and the great downward sweep of dun fields to the river where he swam in the lazy July afternoons, when the elms drooped in the sultry heat, and even the birds were still; there were lawn parties where people came in carriages and automobiles and stood around holding tea cups and chatting, the great hat brims of the ladies bobbing gently as they moved. His mother and his Aunt Harriet took him to the stiff French Renaissance palais of the Capitol at Albany, and looking down he listened to the voices of the legislature thundering like the voices of gods; and later his Uncle Schuyler, who was a state senator, had smiled at him and shaken his hand and asked him if he wanted to go into politics when he grew up. The men talked politely with the ladies, and stroked their mustaches; their watch chains bristled with little gold charms. He had said nothing, but standing there holding his mother's hand he knew that one day he would rise and speak in that great hall.

In a year it was gone. All gone. He was only nine but he remembered the hushed, feverish consultations, the cries of consternation, the huddled conferences and hasty departures. And then his mother had come to him, her face distraught and dark with fatigue. "Courtney. A dreadful thing has happened, Courtney. You must listen carefully to Mother." It had something to do with investments, with things that had defaulted, papers that had once been valuable but were valuable no longer. (Later he understood it all too clearly.) It was very serious. That winter Grandpa Massengale died: he remembered moving up to the long, dark coffin—and then the shock of his grandfather's face, looking little and pinched and mean; not his grandfather at all. He had burst into tears and his mother had taken him outside, into the white, stinging cold.

They were poor. Well, they were not exactly poor, like the Briards or the Lauchmans in that dilapidated farm on the edge of the river; but their lives were different. They still lived in the old house—the parlor and several of the upstairs rooms were closed now, permanently—but all the land down to the river was not theirs anymore; there were no more lawn parties, or trips to Newport or Boston. They were "in straitened circumstances," his mother said. As the years went by he was to find out it was worse than that: to be without means among the wealthy is a very special kind of poverty.

Aunt Harriet, his mother's sister, had come to live with them. In the winter nights, up in his father's study with a blanket around his knees doing his algebra or history, he would watch the snow flung like rice against the window and listen to the murmur of their voices by the fireplace in the kitchen. They were planning for him; he knew it. Now and then, overcome by curiosity, he had crept partway down the stairs and heard snatches. He was to go to West Point: Uncle Schuyler had the connections to get him the appointment, the education itself would cost nothing; then he would choose the Corps of Engineers and go forth to do great deeds in the service of his country, like that wonderful Colonel Goethals down in Panama.

"It's on your shoulders, Courtney," Aunt Harriet would say; she was smaller than his mother, pale and rather homely, with buck teeth and a prominent nose. "You're all we have in the world—if you don't succeed God knows *what* we'll do! . . ."

"Now, Hatty," his mother would answer, but it was not reproof; her gaze was full of supplication. It was all on his shoulders now—everything: he knew. Huddled in bed, the old timbers snapping in the dense cold, remembering their smothering embraces, the portrait in the front parlor, he would clench his fists in nameless anger and resolve to do better, still better. He *must* . . .

The Point had been a shock. He had been prepared for the drill, the long hours of study, the severity of classroom regimen; he had not been prepared for the casual, calculated humiliation, the nocturnal barbarities. But he was strong, he was disciplined, he had learned early to conceal his emotions and mask his real thoughts. He endured it; there was nothing else to do. At night, dizzy with sleeplessness, his arms and legs twitching uncontrollably from the hazing exercises, raging silently at the lunatic prattle of responses he'd been forced to commit to memory and prattle on demand, about the number of lights in Cullum Hall or the number of gallons of water in Lusk Reservoir, all of them swathed in their preposterous, florid verbiage—lying there biting on his blanket to keep from moaning with fury and despair, he would think of those two women in the long, dimly lit kitchen by the fire, and hate them with all his might. They had got him into this! *They knew,* and they had done it. It was unspeakable . . . With time he realized they did not know: how could they? He would never tell them—and who else would have? But his heart hardened like green wood in fire.

He had survived, however. It was a triumph of will. In a paroxysm of inverted pride and self-denial he had suppressed every heretical thought, every tendency toward rebellion or dejection or idle dreaming. A poor boy caught in the world of the rich, this was the only way to success. He was going to succeed, no matter what it cost: no matter what. He went out for track because being a letterman was good politics—and then discovered he liked it. He ran with a vengeance; he liked the throat-searing, head-quaking exhaustion of the quarter-mile, the cruel punishment of the race, the preposterous fact that it was a sprint—a sprint that lasted one whole incredible circuit of the track. In his senior year he was unbeaten.

And he studied, he drove himself. It was the best way to banish the ache of loneliness, the bovine, extrovert simplicity of his classmates, most of whom bored him to tears. He read voraciously; he had a quick mind, a retentive memory, and an iron will. And he had charm; he could make himself liked when he chose. What he did not feel he could simulate admirably. Very few people were ever aware of the difference. He graduated Cadet Captain and second in scholarship. There had been a short tour of duty at Fort Eustis, and then the war had come . . .

Damon had just moved, and he leaned forward again, concentrating on the game. There was still that damned knight's pawn. Like a rock. He could not dislodge it. He feigned an attack on the queen's wing, he assaulted with twinned rooks in the center, but Damon parried each stratagem, each shift in pressure—it was almost as though the Captain were anticipating his moves. He became irritated, half-angry—it was uncanny!

In the living room Tommy laughed once—a short, two-note laugh, and the women's voices ran along again in an inaudible murmur. He shrugged, and looked at his watch. This was silly: it was late. Besides, he had other plans for the evening.

Abruptly he said: "Samuel, I've had enough. Let's call it a draw: that all right with you?"

"Sure." Damon smiled. "I'll gladly settle for a draw."

"Good." He poured another finger of liqueur into their glasses, and for a few moments they talked about the assassination of Viscount Saito during the recent army revolt in Tokyo, and the Seven Demands presented to Nanking by Japan.

"What do you think about that, Samuel?"

"I think Chiang Kai-shek is making a great mistake. The Ho-Umezu Agreement was bad enough. It's a dangerous policy to call in foreigners to help solve your domestic troubles; the Japanese won't stop with that."

"Probably not. You know what MacArthur said when Quezon asked him if he thought the Islands could be defended? 'I don't think so, I *know* they can.' He's just what we need out here." He stretched his legs and threw an arm over his eyes. "It's curious, isn't it? This whole idea of the man of the hour, the hero coming forth in a moment of stress—the Greek myth, the Barbarossa legend, Carlyle's theory of the hero born out of the needs of the situation. It's been carried too far, of course, but the fact is that the 'great' man, the individual of superior intellect and will, does come forward more often than not. Chaos is the condition of man—chaos and uncertainty. The person who can act with force and decision at such a moment, turns the consciousness of his time. What is the epic but poetic celebration of this assertion? Whether it's Jason or Achilles or Napoleon . . ."

"But aren't we more or less persuaded that their great arrogance rendered them vulnerable, brought them to grief?"

Massengale took his arm away from his eyes; this was why conversations with Damon were so much fun. "Ah, but that's the limitation of art. The search for form. Art is only a facet of life, a tightly ordered facet, and therefore it's inferior to it. Life—flesh-and-blood actuality—is the material realization. Look at Alexander, Frederick, Caesar: they seized the chaotic elements around them and forged them into instruments of their will—melted them all down and recast them in new and exciting forms . . ."

"Alexander died of fever, wounds and drunken excesses at thirty-two," the Captain answered slowly. "And his empire fell apart in months."

"A matter of luck. Frederick died full of honors. And Bonaparte had his ten fabulous years as Emperor of the French. It's not a question of duration, necessarily. The point is they changed the essential chemistry of the world . . ."

He sat watching Damon, who was silent. The excitement of the moment had him now, fully—that tingling sensation, half-exultation, half-defiance, that nothing else could ever match. The immanent *force* of it! The long regality of will . . . He remembered an afternoon when he was twelve, when a group of them were camping in the woods. He had told Henry Schneider, a neighbor and the son of the local butcher, to take the potatoes out of the fire. The boy had refused, and when he'd pressed him had called him a coward. He could still summon up that moment with hot clarity—the little circle of faces, eager and pitiless, the thick hiss of the embers, Henry Schneider's round face red with anger. He knew he could not fight him: he would be beaten and humiliated. Slowly, very slowly, with all of them watching, he had put his arm into the fire, felt the incredible icy searing thrill race over his flesh. He had not cried out, he had not even gasped, though the pain had blurred his vision; their faces had all gone tight with fear. Someone had uttered a short, muffled exclamation. He had even managed a tight, crooked smile, though his eyes were stinging, and repeated the order . . . He had cried that night in bed (he'd told his mother he had slipped and fallen in the fire); but no one had heard him. After that his authority was unquestioned: they did what he wanted or kept out of his company. None of them wanted to fight him. They were afraid . . .

"Samuel," he said suddenly, "what would be your reaction if I were to tell you you're wasting your time?"

"In what way, sir?"

"In all kinds of ways." He swung around so he faced the Captain directly. "Look, Gleason's going to be transferred soon. For reasons you may or may not know about. How'd you like to come over to MacArthur's staff?"

The Captain grinned. "I doubt very much if I'm wanted on *anybody's* staff right about now."

"Not necessarily. I've talked to the General about you. If you were interested, I think I could arrange it. Of course I don't have to tell you there must be no more affaires Brand . . ."

Damon nodded and pursed his lips. "Well, it's—I certainly appreciate it, Major . . . It's only that I'd have to say I feel my place is with troops."

"Nonsense. Your place is where you're most valuable, where your talents are recognized. You worry too much about your command, Samuel. It's all noble enough, but there's no purpose to it. Most men have simple appetites, limited horizons. They develop a craving for drink, like McClain, or they lose their heads over women, like Brand there, or they want to smash things, or they simply waste their substance in vague and incurable daydreaming. After all, what distinguishes the leader—the hero, if you like—from the common run? He needs food, he grows weary, he has to empty his bowels as faithfully—and as ignominiously—as the meanest clod. What raises him above the ruck is intellect, training, flexibility of view—but above all an unswerving will, the unshakable desire to forge that will on events, his fellowmen. And most men simply aren't capable of it."

"A very good commander said, 'Each of you is a leader,'" the Nebraskan answered softly, almost as though it were an appeal.

"Oh, sure—an admirable way of handling troops in a desperate situation. Trapped in hostile country, fighting rear-guard actions, fear of mutiny, all the rest of it. A little masterpiece of morale building. But do you think for a minute he really meant it?" Damon nodded. "But Samuel, be reasonable—the average soldier can't begin to comprehend the simplest command problems."

"No, he can't. Because he hasn't been given the opportunity."

Massengale tapped his front teeth with his thumbnail. "Lord, oh lord: when are we going to cure you of that roaring mustang background of yours?" Damon was smiling, but he knew the Captain was angry, and it pleased him obscurely. It was the right move; it was, in a nutshell, the measure of his superiority over the Nebraskan. And yet there was this other thing—this slow, stubborn assertion of something—what was it?— that he could not touch, could not mold: it was irritating.

"You're an anomaly, Samuel," he said after a little pause. "You're a wild anachronism—you've completely failed to identify yourself with the interests of your class."

"My class?"

"Yes—you're a Regular Army officer, you're not a thirty-year NCO mothering your brood, kissing some and kicking others. You were one once, briefly. But you're not now. Look, it's all right to be a maverick if you want to be, a bit of an eccentric—maybe all great leaders have had a little of that, from Joshua on down. But you shouldn't be *known* for one. That's just sentimental—and destructive. This business with Brand—what has it got you but trouble? All that dissipation of your energies—he's just one man, and a private at that . . ."

"That's right, Major." And Damon's face while he watched it grew solemn and very hard—for the thinnest fraction of time Massengale felt a stark thrill of fright, such as when a gecko fell from the ceiling at night and landed on his bare skin. "He's just one man."

"But your job is to deal with man in the mass—it's on how you cope with *that* problem that your ultimate success as a commander will rest." Damon was silent again, but he knew the Captain had something to say. He ran on, "Look at yourself honestly: no frills, no evasions, no sentimentalities. You have ambition, drive, a thirst for knowledge—which is power—a need to enforce the momentum of your will on the inertia of circumstances. Yet you are completely out of rhythm with your age; you are failing to move with it."

"Am I?"

"Yes, frankly." He leaned forward a little. "What's happening is that we're moving into an era of centralization, of authoritarian control. It's part of the long oscillation of history: authority to anarchy and back again. In the late Renaissance every individual sought to act, fulfill his own destiny, express his individuality, his unalterable will—in art, violence, moneymaking, religious defiance, what you will. That was the apogee of anarchistic tendency for the millennium; now the pendulum is swinging back the other way. Read Spengler, read Ortega—you're a reflective man. Look at Italy, Germany, Russia. People seek authority, they need it: they *want* to be told what to do, how to act: it's become instinctual. And in an authoritarian era the army is always the sharpest instrument of policy."

He sat back and waited for some marked response—an ejaculation, an argument, even a grunt. But Damon made no reply; he sat immobile in the split-bamboo chair, with that curiously attractive grace of the good athlete in repose. He looked dulled, half-asleep—but Massengale knew if a grenade were to come crashing through the screen beside them the Captain would be on his feet in a flash, doing something: the right thing, too. For a moment the thought filled him with a consternation that was almost despair; then it passed. Every man had his price, his weaknesses, his temptations; every man sought the approval of someone living or dead, worshiped at some fleshed-out image of his heart's own fancy . . . And what a team they would make! This was the vision he had often teased himself with, over the past year: he, Massengale, as the master strategist, the planner, the diplomat, threading his way through the labyrinths of interdepartmental intrigue and high policy (aided and abetted by Uncle Schuyler, who was now, Quetzalcoatl be praised, a senior member of the all-powerful House Armed Services Committee), while Damon devoted his energies to field command. An unbeatable combination. But it had to be understood that he was to lead, determine their courses of action; and Samuel must give unmistakable evidence of his own intentions, his own allegiance. There was the rub . . .

"I'm going to say something *you'll* call highly heretical," he offered aloud; he touched the tips of his fingers below his chin. "Do you know something? The problem of morale is so much drivel. Oh, you can find

isolate instances such as your Xenophon. But I mean really: in an ultimate sense." Damon smiled slowly and it irritated him. "What's funny
about that?"

"I was just remembering the first time we met, Major. In the courtyard near St. Durance. You felt some of the boys were pretty disre-
spectful—they were trying to get their canteens filled, remember?—and
you quoted me that old adage of Napoleon's about morale being to all
other factors as four is to one."

That memory of Damon's: that incredible memory! Had he said that?
Yes, he probably had. He didn't remember the incident; what he did
remember was the solid, blocklike indomitability of the figure in front
of him, the weary, hard defiance; and then he had taken out his notebook and pencil and—

"Did I?" he queried lightly. "Yes, I probably did . . . Sure, we must all
of us pay lip service to it—even the Little Corporal. It has its value in
effecting given ends, filtered down through the ranks. But you know as
well as I do that it's command that makes the difference. All the fire-
eating esprit in the world is useless without a commander's craft and
inventiveness. Look at military history: the invincible Macedonian
phalanx sends out its massive hammerblow at Pydna, and the three
Roman lines bend and bend and bend with the impact, and contain it
like a web, and chew it up. Did the Romans have a higher morale? I
doubt it. Pakenham's valorous grenadiers march resolutely into the
withering fire from behind the cotton bales at New Orleans, the knights
at Crécy ride into that gray storm of cloth-yard arrows, and are no
more. It's been the same in every age. The irrefutable triumph of strategy, of command disciplines! Look at Hannibal's brilliant victories—he
won them with mercenaries: Goths, Asturians, Nubians—elephants, for
God's sake. After Cannae every single family in Rome went into mourning. *Every single family!* Did you know that?"

"But Rome won the war," Damon said quietly.

It was this curious stubbornness that was intriguing. He could run
rings around the Nebraskan, marshal a perfect wilderness of facts and
deploy them in perfect order, he could push him off balance, run him
ragged—but always there was this strange little point of resistance he
couldn't quite overpower, like a rock in the middle of a riptide . . .

Damon's reference to their first meeting had made him think of the
war, and he remembered the day he had gone up to the line with General
Bannerman and Colonel Mulhouse, the morning of the Malsainterre
offensive. A gray, evil morning, but it was dry in the captured German
dugout on the crest of the hill. The regimental commander was on one
phone, an artillery spotter was on another, and out ahead, in the gray-
brown murk the crashing patterns of fire and black smoke crept forward and back, forward and back. The noise was terrible, like a sack
resting on one's head and shoulders—he had never realized it could be so
burdensome; and yet there was at the same time a curious sense of

release, almost inebriation . . . Someone in the dugout was shouting; he put the field glasses to his eyes and there they were, going forward, lumpy and drab in the mud and rain, like men searching for something they do not want to find, their rifles all aslant; stumbling toward that distant tree line on the far slope; and falling now, floating down dreamily or dropping as if tripped, and then groping feebly in the wire and bits of shrubs and shattered trunks of trees. General Bannerman was shouting, everyone around him was shouting and cursing now, Colonel Mulhouse was talking furiously into the phone . . .

And then, watching another company deploy, and then another, gazing hypnotized through the long slit between the logs, an astonishing thing had happened: those men out there ceased to be men and turned into spots, or rather configurations of spots; without any meaning at all. They rose and fell, slipped and struggled but they, like the bushes and the wraithlike trunks of trees, were nothing more than patterns of light and shadow. And over everything—the lumpy corpses, the mud, the snarled strands of wire—a silence fell, a silence as sheathed and impervious as the first, still snow of winter. He turned and looked at Bannerman, and the General's face had vanished too, into a configuration of pink and silver spots. He shut his eyes; but no one seemed to have noticed. It was the only time in his career he'd ever fouled up an order. The General had shouted something at him—a recommendation, a reminder, something—and he'd got out his notebook and pencil, but he'd written nothing there at all.

He had recoiled from the vision, fixation, visitation, whatever it was—in real terror. That night he'd got deliberately drunk (he did not drink to excess ordinarily, he hated the loss of mental control it brought on) and had fallen fast asleep. The next day had been a busy one, what with the changes in orders and the necessity of committing reserve units to overcome the German resistance, and the insistence of the spots was fainter. Three days later they had worn away almost entirely. And the following week, on the way to Vieux Moulins, watching the artillery and machine-gun companies hurrying forward, he had smiled at the antics of the mules, the waved greetings and curses and shouts, as the mighty procession pushed on, like some vast bristling serpent, all horns and scales, through the ooze: an entire world in motion, bound in one consuming idea. Glancing at General Bannerman's red, flushed face, his snapping blue eyes, Massengale had felt a surge of exultation so great he had trembled inside his trench coat. To set this all in motion—with one word! It was—it was as near to godhood as man would ever reach . . .

"Samuel," he said with quick intensity, "we're going to be at war: very soon. Do you realize that?"

"Yes, sir. I do."

"A great, swarming, devastating war—desert and jungle and ice cap. And this time we will suffer immense casualties, along with the others."

"I'm afraid you're right. And it'll be so unnecessary—"

"No war is unnecessary. Wars come because men want them—they satisfy a very deep urge in human nature. They're every bit as inevitable as eating or rutting."

"A biological necessity of the first importance," Damon said slowly.

Massengale glanced at him, but the Captain was not smiling. "Yes: that's the way a German would put it, of course . . ." Twisting in his chair he pointed a finger at the other man. "Samuel," he demanded, "can you honestly assure me that Brand won't get into trouble over some other hot little skirt? or go off on a bust and tear half of Pasay apart?"

"No. I can't."

"You see? You can't reform men—you can't save them from what they are. Men—most men—are a passive element. They let themselves be acted upon; they crave it, without it they'd probably go mad. You worry too much about your people, Samuel. You can't do everything—you're merely spreading yourself too thin. And what's the sense in it? War is coming—on seven-league boots now. You know it and I know it. The problem is to be in the most advantageous spot when it comes, the place exerting the greatest possible leverage."

Damon shifted his feet, frowning; Massengale could sense his disapproval. It was the wrong line to take with a man like this, it would accomplish nothing; he shifted to flattery as a transition.

"You've done a great job with Fox. You're a perfect miracle worker with troops—I wouldn't have believed it possible. Kemperer says you've remade the company."

"They're good material."

"Oh, stuff and nonsense. *You* did it, all by yourself. But look, you have talents above and beyond that. You'll never be satisfied with a company, or even a battalion. You're too good for that . . . Why bury yourself out there in troop-and-stomp?"

Damon said: "I serve where I'm ordered to, I go where I'm sent."

"Oh, hell, that's no answer." He felt a surge of exasperation, and let a little of it bleed through in his voice. "If you can serve your country more effectively in a more authoritative, more meaningful position, you have an obligation to do so. You're shirking your responsibilities every bit as much as the officer who turns into a drunk or a wastrel. You're guilty of pride, man."

"Pride?"

"Yes, of course—what did you think it was? It's your private vice—the egalitarian fallacy." He snorted crossly. "That damn fool Acton. There's nothing essentially corrupting about power if it's used wisely, for the objective in view." He raised one hand. "Come on, now—all the libertarian nonsense aside: wouldn't you give your eyeteeth to command a division?"

"Yes," Damon answered after a moment. "I'd like to lead a division."

"Well, then. What's that but power—your company multiplied by seventy? Think it over now, give me an answer."

Damon was sitting hunched forward, his forearms over his knees. "It's true," he said after a pause. "If that's power, I guess I'd enjoy it, all right." His eyes came up and met Massengale's. "And I certainly appreciate your offer. I know it's an extraordinary opportunity you're presenting me. But I've got to say—I think I'd better stay with my boys."

There was a silence. Massengale put a fresh cigarette in the long jade holder and lighted it, listening to a houseboy singing down in the garden behind the house—a high, clear voice in the night air. They were always singing. To his surprise his belly was tense with anger. *I was wrong about him,* he thought with terse implacability; *he has no ambition, no real caliber—he's just another of the Army's perpetual adolescents, bemused by sentiment and dreams . . .*

Well: it was too bad. But that was life. You made your choices and followed them, and they determined your career. Every man had his limitations, reached a certain point he couldn't surmount, and there he stopped; and this was Damon's, obviously. If this incorrigible, self-immolating fool wanted to vegetate grandly in company offices and banana posts for the rest of his days that was his affair. It was disappointing—he'd hoped for more from this man, he'd believed he could shake him out of this futile, destructive pattern—but *people* were disappointing: it was the one rude, unalterable hallmark of the human condition. People let you down, continually and lamentably; and there was nothing to be done about it.

He got up and began to put the chess pieces back in the velvet-lined box, pleased by the cool, silky texture of the ivory, feeling his anger ebb. "Well, we'll talk about it again," he said. "Let's go in and join our long-suffering spouses, shall we?"

"Certainly, sir. Fine."

But leading the way into the living room he knew he would never bring it up again. He had already discarded Damon—in the maneuvers and campaigns to come the Nebraskan was not the kind of confederate he wanted: he would never be able to depend on him. He'd look up this young fellow Fowler at Clark Field; feel him out, see what he had to say for himself.

8

The mountains looked as if they had been flaked from a vast piece of flint: jagged rock outcroppings black in the late winter light. There were no trees. Far below, the valley stretched away in miles on miles of barren earth, a soft dun shadow. Ancient. So ancient and so barren. The wind blew without haste, calmly and surely, as though it knew it would

eventually penetrate everything, erode everything and sweep it away—
men and habitations and soil, and finally the black flaked flint of the
mountains. Until nothing was left. A wind that blew from Siberia, with
nothing to stop its bitter progress.

Damon eased himself away from the oblong aperture in the wall and
sat down. His feet were numb with cold and his back and thighs quivered from the incessant climbing. A little knot of men were squatted in
the corner of the bare, narrow room—it was really a cave with two
walls of stone erected on the downhill side—bent over a battered piece
of paper laced with rice-grain characters and symbols and soft, meandering lines. Damon smiled wearily, watching them and listening. There
was no other sound in the hut. No matter where or at what moment in
time you found yourself, at Arbela or Agincourt or Antietam Creek,
war always resolved itself into a group of men hunched over a map in a
squalid place, talking in low voices. He thought of the farmhouse before
Brigny, the desultory shelling and the heat. But these men around him
had made a forced march of forty-odd miles through the cruelest country he had ever seen, to reach this mean small room in the bitter cold;
they had not had a hot meal in more than twenty-four hours. He was
the most warmly clad man in the room, and he was chilled to the
bone.

Lin Tso-han was talking, with steady, soft insistence. He had a thin,
worn face, a large, mobile mouth and heavy black brows, like Groucho
Marx, that moved eerily up and down when he spoke; his eyes were
quick and nervous. He was wearing the plain blue uniform of the private soldier, stripped of all insignia of rank. F'eng Po-chou was listening
to him, crouched on his big thighs, as squat and imperturbable as a
Buddhist figurine. At one point he asked a question. Lin's finger traced a
quick, erratic course over the map. F'eng nodded, and the old man
with the gnomelike face they called Lao Kou—old dog—muttered
something hoarsely; the scar that ran across his nose and cheek looked
blue in the cold. Listening hard, his head aching with the effort, Damon
began to get it, or thought he did. F'eng's detachment was to simulate an
attack in force on Wu T'ai from the east, draw fire, break off and lure
the Japanese garrison out of the town up the Yen Teh valley in a long
arc. At a certain predetermined moment Lin was to assault the village
with the main body from the northwest, wipe out the weakened garrison,
cross the Sian Railroad four li below the town, and hike northwest to
Tung Yen T'o. Something like that. But the fly in the ointment seemed
to be a Japanese column moving toward Wu T'ai from the south . . .

"K'un nan," F'eng said tersely, and Damon found himself nodding. It
was difficult all right, there was no doubt about that. It sounded fantastic, with one hundred and twenty men and no heavy weapons. But they
were certainly acting as if they were going to try it.

Lin became still more persuasive: he did not raise his voice but there
was no mistaking the urgent note that had crept into it now. Damon

caught the nouns: medical supplies, drugs, ammunition. It was a tre-mendous opportunity, a rare opportunity, before the enemy column got there and made it all impossible. F'eng said nothing, spat on the hard, gritty clay floor. It was obvious that he was unhappy about his role, and Damon knew exactly what he was worrying about: that moment when he must break contact and start up one of those terrible exposed slopes on the double, with only two automatic weapons—and highly unreliable ones at that—to cover his people. F'eng's glance fell on Damon, who looked away. Nothing ever changed in war. It was always, monotonously, cruelly, the same: one man telling another that a mission was important, that his chances were good, more than good really, they were excellent, and so forth and so on; and the subordinate listening stolidly, realizing that it was going to be done, that perhaps it had to be done, but hoping nevertheless against all faint, fond hope that the whole operation could be postponed, avoided, forgotten. An avalanche, say, or an earthquake or flood or even a tidal wave. But there would be no tidal wave deep in Shansi Province, four hundred miles from the Yellow Sea, on the edge of the roof of the world . . .

Taking off his boots he massaged his feet, changed his socks from left foot to right, and put his boots on again. Well. Plans and operations. Battle. Nothing ever came for free in this world, nothing; and nobody knew it better than these Chinese guerrillas, squatting in a perfectly hyperborean cave in the Black Tiger Mountains. He had marched with them for twelve days, stopping at the bleak, battered villages, eating millet out of the communal four-foot iron pan, sleeping huddled on the hard clay k'angs where they had to change position every two hours so that the men farthest from the fire wouldn't freeze; he had found out what kind of men they were.

But to have to go into battle, not for the destruction of the enemy's field force or the capture of strong points, but for the seizure of medical supplies . . .

He chafed his hands briskly; his mind wandered, he no longer caught even individual words in the soft, unhurried musical lilt and dip of Mandarin. Sitting against the wall beside him a young soldier called P'ei Hsien, a thin boy with a smooth round face, was writing in the dirt with a cartridge; his lips moved soundlessly, like a young child's. Damon followed the point of the bullet as it stroked in the characters. *Man. Rice. Earth. Sky. Woman.* And then, falteringly: *Give us back our rivers and our mountains.*

Damon swung his head to the right, encountered the gaze of a man with high cheekbones and narrow, liquid eyes; he was heavy for a Chinese, and looked like an Aleut hunter. Damon had forgotten his name. The man grinned and bobbed his head once, and Damon grinned back. The Eskimo was carrying a French Lebel rifle of World War vintage; the stock had split and was fastened tightly with strands of hemp woven with incredible care. The original sling had worn out or been lost and its new owner had substituted a Japanese sling of bright yellow leather. How in God's name had it ended up here, in the possession of a guerrilla way up in Shansi? Had it come from Tonkin? from the French legation at Tientsin? from the Japanese? What a story it could tell . . .

The Eskimo, following his gaze, patted the long, narrow bolt and grinned again. There was no ammunition Damon could see, nothing on the man's belt or hanging from his shoulders.

"How many?" he asked slowly in Chinese. "How many rounds do you have?"

"Twelve," the Eskimo said. Proudly he tapped his trouser pocket and Damon heard the soft chink of shells. They were loose in his pocket. He had no clips, then. That meant he had to feed the Lebel like a single shot. Back to Civil War days, to Shiloh. And when those twelve rounds were gone—

F'eng had got to his feet. He had a Japanese wristwatch of which he was very proud; he wore it British style with the face on the underside of his wrist and he extended his forearm now, checking the time with Lin Tso-han. All the arrangements were made, apparently. There were two more exchanges, and then F'eng drew himself up smartly—an incongruous action in the frayed, dirty quilted jacket and visored cap that was like a railroad engineer's—and said: "Tsui ho sheng li." Damon got that. *For the final victory.* Lin repeated it, but neither man smiled. They shook hands and F'eng went out into the wind; a moment later they heard the sounds of the detachment moving out.

Lin glanced at Damon, and his eyebrows went up and down; then he began talking to Lao Kou and two younger men. Damon forced himself to listen intently, struggling to catch this terribly elusive language where each syllable sounded like five or six others, and the lifts and drops of pitch were still more bewildering. He'd prepared himself as best he could in the short time he'd had, and he'd sought conversation with everyone—merchants, coolies, soldiers; but he could barely make himself understood, and it annoyed him. But this boy P'ei beside him— he was easily twenty-one or -two—was just learning to write his own language; and the Eskimo could neither read nor write. He looked at them both again. The Eskimo offered him half of a hsiao ping; he took the piece of hard, round biscuit and began to gnaw at it methodically. A bullet for a pencil and a beat-up Lebel rifle, he thought; and a piece of Chinese hardtack. Damon, you're a long, long way from home.

It was an odd sensation being a military observer: rather unpleasant. It was like being lifted off the ground, floating and kicking, unable to use your feet—or as though you'd been dropped stark naked into a huge garden party of strangers; very polite, very gracious and well-mannered strangers, it was true, but who were nonetheless quite conscious of your astounding nudity. Now, on the verge of observing his first action against the Japanese he felt ill at ease, extraneous, without the sustaining force of purpose, the fierce absorption of duties and responsibilities. He wasn't cut out for this kind of work. Massengale could do it, he'd be superb at it—this was just his meat, sitting by and watching the events unfold, crisis and countermove, making trenchant observations and witty analogies . . . Only Massengale wouldn't have taken the detail in the first place.

He'd been astonished when old Metcalfe had called him in and put it up to him. He'd been filled with confusion—but his heart had leaped. China! All the old dreams of his youth reared up like thunder. The far-flung adventures amid sandstorms, jade palaces, shrouded figures swaying to great brass gongs—

"Why yes, sir," he'd said. "I'd like to go very much. Only I don't know if I'm qualified. I don't have any Chinese—I've never drawn Legation duty. And I've never done any intelligence work. Captain MacLure, over in G-3, has a—"

"No," Colonel Metcalfe said flatly. "I want you."

"Yes, sir."

Metcalfe threw himself back in his chair, his hands behind his head. He was a big man with a great broken nose and bristling red hair that rose in two tufts above his ears. "I want a line man.—They say you're tough," he went on in his dry, sardonic voice. "A boondocker. They say you pace your own marches and walk 'em all into the ground, and next day you're ready for more. Is that true?"

"Well—" Damon paused for only an instant, "—as a matter of fact it is, Colonel."

"Good. That's what I want. Somebody who can eat it up and then come around for seconds. As far as I'm concerned they can take these fancy-nancy double-domed linguists and file 'em under Extraneous."

Monk Metcalfe had a reputation for being an eccentric. A Harvard Phi Beta Kappa man, he had made a brilliant record in France on Bullard's staff; then he had amazed and disgusted all the Old Army brass by requesting intelligence work—at a time when that section was looked on as nothing more than a general dumping ground for the incompetent or unstable. But the Monk went into it with a difference. He had covered Abd-el-Krim's war against the French and Spanish in Morocco, he had watched the Greco-Turkish conflict, he'd been in Shanghai when Chiang Kai-shek had crushed the Worker's Army in 1927. He was fluent in eight languages and could get around in eleven more, his essays and analyses in the *Infantry Journal* were the pride and despair of the service, he played the oboe, he knew more about Asia than any three men living, and he was forever in hot water with Washington.

"I want you to go up north," he said through his teeth, which were fastened on a dead cigar butt. "See what they're doing up there."

"You mean the Tupei Army, Colonel, the Manchurians . . ."

"No. Farther than that."

Damon blinked at him. "You mean—the guerrillas?"

"Yeah." The Monk's eyes took on a bright, ferocious gleam. "What's wrong with the guerrillas?"

Damon grinned in spite of himself. "Why, nothing that I know of, sir. It's only that I—"

"They're fighting the Nipponese, aren't they?" And before the Captain could reply: "You bet your old Aunt Tillie they are. That's more than the lordly Kuomintang is doing, I'll tell you that much." He heaved himself up out of his chair and began to stomp up and down behind his desk, his big hands dug deep into his hip pockets. "In face a lion but in heart a deer," he chanted in rhythm. "In face—a lion—but in heart—a deer . . . Who said that, Damon?"

"I don't know, sir."

"Good! If you'd told me I'd have thrown you out of here. I'm sick of savants, I'm weary unto *death* of scholiasts who can transpose Chaucer into Urdu but who can't trot down to the latrine without palpitations. Give me an officer who can do anything a PFC can, and do it double. And then do it again. For Christ sake, give me an officer *who thinks like a private soldier!*"

Damon decided the Monk did not want any reply to this, and he was right. "They *say* you've got an open mind," he went on, and shot the Captain a baleful, suspicious glance. "I won't ask you if you have—any dumb son of a bitch says he's got an open mind. Calvin Coolidge would tell you he had one. So would Savonarola." He pulled fiercely at one of the tufts of wiry red hair. "But you've been in plenty of trouble—enough to lead me to think you've got one. Would I be right?"

"I've been in plenty of trouble, Colonel."

Metcalfe laughed, a flat, sneering cackle, and ran a knuckle back and forth under his big nose. "You're on everybody's excremental roster in the Department. I know." Again he paced back and forth, humming snatches of what sounded to Damon like the *Scheherazade Suite.* "Except the doughfeet," he murmured after a moment, squinting up at the chipped and flaking ceiling. "Except the poor sons of bitches who fight the dirty old wars . . ."

He bent double and crouched behind his desk so fast that Damon started, flung open a drawer and hauling out a bulging manila folder and two pamphlets dumped them on his desk. "Here: memorize everything in those. I mean *commit to memory.*"

"Yes, sir."

"You haven't got all the time in the world. Oh, wait—you better have one of these. Fenn Five Thousand." He pulled a fat little blue-bound dictionary from the shelf behind him and tossed that on the rest of the heap. Collapsing in his chair he watched the Captain gather up the books and folders and fit them under his arm. "Damon."

"Yes, Colonel?"

The Monk's face was all at once somber and homely. "Damon, they're fighting a very new and very different kind of war up there. And they're winning . . ." He yanked at the tuft of hair. "They haven't got a pot to piss in—and they're winning! Not everywhere. But here and there. They've got five Japanese divisions tied up out there. If what I hear—if I can believe only *half* of what I hear, it's one of the most important things that has happened in the conduct of war in this century." He grinned then, his jaw extended like a shark's, and came up out of his chair again, slamming his hands on the desk. "The how and the why, Damon! The *how* and the *why* . . ."

So he had drawn two pairs of field shoes, broken them in and dubbed them, dug up the lightest-weight sleeping bag he could find and a sheepskin-lined coat; he'd bought a tough little copper teakettle to boil his water, got out his old mess gear and a folding canvas washbasin; he'd gone over to the dispensary and drawn iodine, quinine, bismuth, paregoric, aspirin and a roll of adhesive tape. He'd sat up till all hours, reading and rereading, memorizing place names, peoples, customs, and the hen-scratch avalanche of characters, writing them over and over until they were etched into the walls of his brain. He was going to China. He was going to the far end of the world, and he was going to be prepared . . .

He had reckoned without Tommy.

"But, Sam—" She had stared at him for a moment, her mouth working; then she shook her head rapidly. "You're joking," she faltered. "No—you're really joking . . ."

"No," he answered, "it's the truth."

"*China!*—but you're due for a change of station in six months—we can *leave* this filthy, miserable steam bath. We can go *home!* . . ."

He shifted his feet. "Well . . . you can go stateside if you want."

"Don't use that term!" she cried. "It's vulgar and hateful . . ." She had just returned from a shopping expedition to the Quiapo markets, and her blouse—a delicate teal—was stuck in places to her shoulders and breasts. "Did you put in for this?" she demanded.

"No. No—he asked for me. Metcalfe."

"That *idiot* . . ."

"He's not an idiot."

She laughed harshly, an indrawn gasping. "Oh no no, of course not—he's another misunderstood Galahad. Like you."

"Tommy, look—"

"You agreed. You told him you'd go." He nodded. "Just like that. Without a thought for me, or the children, or anything else . . . *China*," she hissed between her teeth. "As if the Philippines weren't insane enough . . . What about Donny now?"

"Donny?"

"Yes, Donny—we've been over it enough. Or have you only pretended to be listening? That school up at Baguio is a farce, it isn't going to prepare him for college. He needs a year or two in a decent preparatory school back home—you know that just as well as I do . . ."

"Well, you could take him back—"

"Oh, that's ridiculous!" All at once she whirled around, hands on her hips, and faced him. "It's just that you *want* to go—for the adventure of it. Isn't it? Well, isn't it?"

"—No," he said, after the briefest of pauses, "of course not—look, it isn't going to be exactly a picnic, you know . . ."

But that hesitation had betrayed him. Her eyes flared, she came toward him with a kind of threatful intensity, her head lowered, looking sweaty and gaunt and unlovely; and for an instant he thought, She's not herself, she's sick; it's all this heat—

"—We've got a new song," she was saying tightly, her eyes blank and glaring. "A new song, did you know? It's called 'How About Me.' Yes. Me. *You* may find it the essence of delight to go traipsing footloose and fancy-free through the pagodas and joss houses while I'm stuck here on this baking hot rock—no!" she shouted. "No! Enough—I've had enough . . ."

"Honey," he remonstrated, "Josefina's in the—"

"Good! Let her hear! Let her hear about the American Army man on vacation—"

"It's not a va—"

"—vagabonding around that miserable, stinking country while the whole rest of the world—the dull, dumb, sensible part, I mean—goes on making something of itself . . . No!" she cried in a voice abandoned to grief and rage. "All—I've had all of this stupid, willful, selfish lunacy I'm going to take—all of it! I'm through!"

He had seized her by the shoulders, was shaking her with slow, rhythmic purpose. "It just so happens this is not a lark," he was saying tightly, "and I don't expect it to be one—as a matter of fact I'm going where hardly anybody's gone before . . . I'm going because it may—just possibly may—be the most important thing I'll ever do in my whole life. Because somebody's got to do it, and I'm stupid enough to flatter myself I'll do a better job than most . . . Now you get hold of yourself, Tommy."

She was gazing up at him, her eyes wide with fear. ". . . *Where* are you going?" she breathed.

"The North. Shansi."

"But—that's the *Reds* . . . they're cutthroats and bandits, they're just rabble—Joe Cullen said they've slaughtered whole—"

"Joe Cullen never went a mile north of Hankow."

"They'll kill you," she cried softly. "They'll kill you just for your clothes and papers . . ."

"Maybe they will . . . But I don't think so."

She stared at him a moment longer, raised one arm and flung it down in a gesture of angry despair. "Oh, Sam! Oh, I just can't stand it! I just can't stand it—!"

"Tommy, listen—"

"No!"

"Listen to me—"

"No—oh, I can't bear it, what you've let them do to you!" And she broke out of his arms and ran into the bedroom.

He stood there, sweating lightly, hands at his sides, gazing after her. In the kitchen Josefina was dicing something on the cutting board, the knife rapping sharply on the hard wood, while she sang "La Paloma."

They had made it up—at least partly. At Cavite with the Metcalfes and the rest of the little party there to see him off, she was lighthearted and steady, the good army wife; but the smile she gave him as he kissed her and started down the ramp to the clipper was the saddest he'd ever seen. He was selfish, he. was betraying her and the kids; was he? He didn't think so; but he knew with a soft sinking in his heart that things would never be quite the same between them.

The journey had taken weeks—there were times he thought he would never get there, inching his way across China, curving west and north in a slow arc around the Japanese advance. He was nearly crushed to death in a train ride to Chinkiang; a dilapidated, perilously listing steamer choked with more refugees carried him to Hwaining; he chipped in with a Persian sales representative and a free-lance pilot from Ashtabula, Ohio in an ancient Chandler whose top was gone, and whose driver, a nervous little Chinese who said he was a correspondent for a Nanking paper but who acted suspiciously like a deserter, was dangerously un-mechanical and almost suicidally nearsighted. At Kweichow he secured transportation on a cart, then on a hammerheaded pony that would buck like a goat for no discernible reason; and finally wound up on foot. He'd felt as though he were slipping backward through time, gliding back along the chain of man's painful mechanical progress, returning to ele-mentals. When he had reached Liuhsien at last in the company of his guide and two students from Hankow, and saw a man coming toward him in the horizon blue uniform of the private soldier, he had felt it was only fitting that he arrive on foot. An infantryman was what he was . . .

It was quiet in the cave-room now. Lin Tso-han was sitting on the ruined, fireless k'ang, studying the map and rocking gently back and forth, humming. Catching Damon's eye he smiled quickly. "Well, we shall see," he said in excellent French. "What do you think of my plan of battle, Ts'an Tsan?"

Damon went over and sat down beside him and they talked for a few minutes. Yes, he'd got it correctly: it was to seize the medical supplies that had been brought in several days before. A raid. He pointed to the defile two or three li below Wu T'ai. "Why not ambush the supporting column here?"

Lin smiled. "Oh, they are too strong for that."

"But"—he chose his words carefully—"it's the most effective way to win a war: the destruction of the enemy forces in the field."

"Clausewitz," Lin said, and his eyebrows went up and down. "It is one way—a very good way. I wish we could do it. But in this particular case, you see, it is more important to have those supplies. You have no idea how much they are needed."

Damon said nothing; over the past six weeks, moving through the camps and makeshift hospitals and shattered towns, he had come to have a very good idea indeed. He pointed to the map again. "What if the column arrives sooner than you think?"

"Then the attack is abandoned. But the reports we have are very reassuring."

"What if the garrison in Wu T'ai is stronger than you think?"

"That is unlikely, too."

"But what if that farmer was wrong?"

Lin shrugged. "Then someone else would have come to us with a different report. No one has." He paused. "The people are our eyes and ears, Ts'an Tsan. Our intelligence corps, our quartermaster, our communications network, our medical-aid men. And on occasion they even form our mobile reserve."

"They must have to be able to run like hell, then," Damon murmured in English. Lin did not know English, but he must have divined the retort because he grinned suddenly and his eyebrows went up and down twice.

"What if Captain F'eng Po-chou fails to lure the Japanese out?" Damon persisted.

"Then we abandon the entire operation. We only attack if we are certain of superiority." With a trace of pedantry he stated: "Never fight a losing battle, Ts'an Tsan: that is guerrilla warfare."

"But—what if it just sort of turns *into* a losing battle, Colonel?"

"Then we disperse."

"*Disperse?*"

Lin spread his thin, bony fingers. "Break up, melt away. No force exists. Then we reassemble at T'eng-shi. That is all planned for. A detailed plan of retreat, all possible alternatives—that is the most necessary part."

Of all the crazy ways to fight a war, Damon thought; of all the zany, ass-backward strategies. But it seemed to be working . . . He put his finger on the map again. "What if that relieving column has cavalry, and they get here before you have completed the operation?"

"Then we break off and disperse."

"I see." Damon paused, watching the other man. "But suppose—just suppose the Japanese commander down there is very, very clever. Suppose he sorties all right—but the detachment is under orders to pursue Captain F'eng only as far as the pass, here, and then circle back on the double, just as you're making your assault here?"

Lin said slowly, "That would be very clever of him, very clever indeed."

"Yes, and then the column coming up from Chang-hsien fools all your scouts and patrols and reaches here at the same time?"

Lin's face became very smooth and homely and hard. "Then we will sell ourselves dearly, and die like men." His eyes fell on the boy who was still diligently writing on the smooth earth floor. "You must understand, Ts'an Tsan. Our tactics are the tactics of the weak. The Japanese have artillery, they have planes and tanks and endless ammunition. We have nothing but some old weapons and our legs. And the people." His eyes glinted all at once. "But in the end that is everything. You have read *War and Peace*, of course?" Damon nodded. "Do you remember when Kutuzov learns that the French are continuing to advance on Moscow—do you remember how he falls on his knees and thanks God? That is it, precisely," he repeated, in his oddly tuneful French. "Let them come on, all of them. Let them wade in deeper and deeper, into the still, dark ocean of Shansi, Honan, Hupeh. And soon they will sink beneath the surface where they cannot breathe . . . But we can, Ts'an Tsan. The people are our hope and our mainstay, the water through which we guerrillas swim—and where the foreigner drowns."

A soldier came in and spoke rapidly to Lin, who nodded. "Now we wait," he said to Damon, and began to fold the tattered map with meticulous care. Sitting back against the wall with his feet drawn up and his arms locked around his knees, he smiled at the American, and sighed. "The hardest part. Waiting . . . It would be nice to have a fire, wouldn't it?"

"Yes," Damon answered. Nice—it would be heaven on a breakfast tray. He passed his eyes over the men crowded into the cave-room; two were asleep, several were cleaning their weapons, some were conversing in low voices; a few looked back at him with that bright, interested glance he'd come to associate with the Chinese. There seemed to be no bitching or despondency that he could see—there was certainly nothing insubordinate about them at all. He shivered, an uncontrollable spasm, forced himself to relax; rolled his shoulders and chafed his hands and neck. He had a sense of foreboding about the coming action: it seemed unnecessary, hazardous, full of pitfalls and absurd, childish stratagems. Down there in that village was a detachment of superbly equipped soldiers, the well-disciplined members of a tough, aggressive army that had never been defeated, that was able to move at will through this vast, desolate landscape. When General K'ung Chun-sho back at Chengteh had asked him what he wanted to see, he'd answered readily enough that he wanted to observe guerrilla operations at close hand—specifically examples of the short-attack, extreme mobility. But now, six weeks and four hundred miles later, he didn't feel like such a fire-eater. He wasn't twenty-two anymore, he was thirty-nine; he was tired and hungry, he hadn't entirely recovered from a bout of dysentery, and worst of all was this relentless cold, which seemed to seep into his vitals deeper each day, sapping his will, his clarity.

Lin Tso-han was looking at him—a calm, measuring glance, not unkind. To cover his irritation he said: "How is it you know French so well, Colonel?"

Lin smiled. "And living with these untutored peasants?"

Damon grinned back, but he said: "I was a farm boy, Colonel. It just seemed to me unusual."

Lin laughed at this. "Oh, it is unusual—oh yes, very unusual!" He leaned back and closed his eyes. "No—I was one of the privileged ones. The favored. Born to rule." His wide, mobile lips curved faintly. "I had scores of amahs, tutors, instructors, I had the handsomest of educations. My father was a wealthy and a violent man. Yes," he nodded; he seemed almost asleep. "A wealthy and a violent man. And I was even more of one. I was tuchün of a large district, a general at twenty-six. Through no ability of my own. I had twelve thousand men under my command, and hundreds of thousands who feared me like the plague. A heady feeling, when people come running and fling themselves on their hands and knees, their foreheads thumping against the earth, as you pass. You feel like a god on earth . . ." He paused, as though deciding how to phrase his thoughts. "And the opportunities! I became a lover of pleasure. There are so many pleasures in this world, and I saw no reason why I shouldn't have all of them. I took from the treasury of the province whatever I needed—and I needed a great deal, Ts'an Tsan. Why not? When it is all there for the taking you would be surprised at how very much you need.

"First of all I loved pomp and show. I had more than the average man's love of vanity. I had twenty-four uniforms of different hues, blue and plum-colored and white and forest green—with elaborate shoulder-boards and belts and buckles, and banks of decorations that flashed like celestial bodies. I was really decked out, you understand. I had my own personal bodyguards and *they* all had a change of uniforms, too. Very snappy—incorporating the best features of the Prussian and British lines. I could utter one word and that élite detachment snapped like clockwork.

"From there I went on to women. I had a splendid harem. You know, I suspect, the intoxication of commanding men, Ts'an Tsan, but have you ever felt that far keener, far more inebriating excitement of possessing a courtesan, an immensely skilled and sophisticated woman who is yours alone, who exists on this earth purely and simply to minister to your every whim, to anticipate each desire almost before it has arisen? or when the senses tire of that, the still more entrancing delight of taking a young girl, a fresh young virgin who lies terrified and quivering beneath your hand? It is a kind of fearful drunkenness, compounded of greed and shame and brutality—one can bathe in it, as in a vast muddy pool. I could not stop wanting them. I had—oh, let's call them emissaries, whose duty it was to scour the province for me and select the fairest, the youngest, the most timid of girls; purchase them if possible, or simply carry them off if that should be necessary . . . And my hunger became greater and greater, I would rise from despoiling one weeping, desperate little creature with a choking, infuriated desire for another, and another, and still another. Lust became a lust for lust, feeding on itself like the Cambodian serpent devouring its own tail."

Lin sighed, and stroked the side of his face. "Of course I tried now and then to busy myself with other things. For example, I became interested in statecraft. Statecraft. That's the word we love to use to describe the conniving for political power. I had power: I wanted more. Who does not, in such a situation? I was rich and young and proud and ambitious. What more could anyone ask? I began to intrigue—everyone was doing it, those were the days when the big warlords were running affairs with a high hand. Even the European powers and your own government, Ts'an Tsan, were not above dabbling in this most fascinating of games; and I knew I would be better at it than most. For instance, I made an alliance with Tsao Fan-t'ing against Chen Hsi-teh, and then at just the right moment I deserted Tsao and joined forces with another petty potentate, K'ang Shi-mao, a kindred spirit who liked wine and young girls; and together we intrigued and raped and plundered to our hearts' content. It was like being licensed to commit any crime you chose, in any order and to any end . . .

"Well: I made mistakes. What impetuous, headstrong young man would not, given no wisdom and a fine, lordly indifference to suffering and death—particularly the suffering and death of the soldiers I commanded? I had no real knowledge of strategy and tactics. I only thought I did. I was brave, yes, I rode at the head of my spanking Prussian garde du corps, I took risks: but it was the bravery of a man who does not really value life—either his own or anyone else's . . . Have you thought much about yourself, Ts'an Tsan? as a military man, I mean?"

Damon hesitated. "Probably not as much as I should have."

Lin smiled quickly. "That means you have, then. Yes. You are a very unusual American officer. Not like the types in Shanghai, or with the foreign legations in Peking. Which of course accounts for your being out here among the heathen. Even so, you are a professional soldier . . ." He brought himself up sharply. "There is a part of us—of you and me—that wants to die. Yes, it's true. Perhaps that's why we are excited by the military life. It furnishes so many excellent, so many vivid opportunities . . . And then there is the other part that wants to be better, that wants to love, to pardon, to grow into nobility, into tranquillity of soul. That part was almost dead in me in those days. Almost. Oh, once in a while I would be visited by a quick, stealthy nudge of uncertainty, of fear, of outright despair. But I overrode it. Why not? There was always a way out. Something to fall back on, for divertissement. If I sacrificed too many of my soldiers needlessly in a frontal assault on a fortified place, it was no great matter. What the devil—they were only farm boys, weren't they? Like yourself, Ts'an Tsan. There were always more. What did it matter if they tried to hide or escape, if many of them had to be delivered to my officers bound hand and foot?" He gave Damon a sharp, sidelong glance. "I imagine you have seen some detachments of the Kuomintang's volunteers, Ts'an Tsan."

The observer nodded; near Hanyang a detail of young men had shuffled past him in chains, herded by armed guards, toward some barracks. What were they, he'd haltingly asked the officer in charge, criminals or deserters? "Recruits," the officer had answered with a stiff smile. He had watched the detail move away.

" 'As you would not use good iron to make a nail, so you would not use a good man to make a soldier,' " Lin Tso-han murmured. "Old Chinese proverb. We have thousands of them. The only difficulty is, those lowly nails keep the roof from falling on your own proud and inviolate head . . . But I never thought of that. I was enjoying myself hugely. There is a tremendous delight in this, too: You give a crisp, harsh command, from the throat, from the belly, and this mass of armed men—your property, no, more than that, the very extension of your soul—starts forward like a great, bristling animal. Bent to your will. I suppose you have felt something of that, Ts'an Tsan."

Damon was silent a moment. "Yes," he said, "I've felt that."

"Well, I reveled in it. It made my blood beat faster, my breath quicken. Man en bloc, an echo of my will. What a glorious feeling! At my command the bugles would shrill and they would surge to the attack, and I would watch through my fine German field glasses as the little figures scurried and scampered. When one fell I would swing my glasses on to the others. And then at the crucial moment, after the wall was breached and the batteries silenced, I would ride in with my bodyguard and harry the poor devils of defenders running before us in panic. I averted my eyes from the groans of the wounded and dying as I rode in. What were they to me? I was victorious, wasn't I? This was what *I* wanted, and that was sufficient. The town would be taken, and then would come that supreme intoxication—the entering of a captured citadel. Like all those plump, terrified little virgins, but magnified a thousand thousand times."

He picked up his weapon, a Thompson submachine gun, ejected the twenty-round box magazine with an almost contemptuous deftness, took a piece of rag out of his pocket and began to run it over the forward assembly, as though he needed to busy his hands. The gun certainly did not need cleaning.

"Gift of the American government," he said. "Through the good

offices of the Kuomintang." He smiled wryly. "When I run out of
ammunition for it I will be very sorry. I've never once had a stoppage."
For a moment he gazed out of the hut's entrance toward the valley, the
flint-dark shoulder of the mountain. "But then came winter, and snows,
and times of no campaigning. I fell into spells of lassitude and dissatisfac-
tion, I picked quarrels with subalterns and servants, quarreled needlessly
and disastrously. Disastrously for *them*, you understand. Not for me. I
meted out punishment like the Khan. I—began exploring other vices. I
had so much time on my hands, so much wealth, such a terrible hunger . . ."

He paused and sighed—a long, slow sigh that was a more eloquent
admission than the words that followed. "I took to the poppy." His
fingers moved nervously over the gun's receiver, and his voice sank
lower. "I entered that sinking, melancholy world where you are, finally
and irretrievably, god—god of all gods, drifting on a rainbow cloud of
light and wisdom . . ."

Lin cleared his throat and put down the weapon. "But then the cloud
dissolves. You find yourself slipping below the sweet rainbow stream,
sinking faster and faster—until finally you plummet cold and forsaken
through the darkest of terrors and smash against a pavement of naked,
trembling anguish. You stagger to your feet and hurry back—but now it
is flight, not search. Terrified flight." He pursed his lips. "For every vice
there is a corresponding price, and opium extracts the most exorbitant
remittance of them all. I lost weight, I became listless and dull—or when
the terrible, frosty pangs reached out for me, savage and feverish. I
went along like this for quite some time, alternating between nirvana-
sloth and raging activity. At the mercy of my appetites. The wheel
had swung its full circle: *I* was the captive now, the farmer boy delivered bound hand and foot to death. But I would not face that . . .

"And then a curious thing happened, a very curious thing, and to this
day I do not know exactly why I reacted as I did. A moment—it is still
as clear as crystal. I was at the theater one evening; and during an
intermission a servant came to tell me that my mother was dying. I left
immediately and hurried to her. She had been ill for some time—it was
cancer—but when I went in to see her now I was shocked by her
appearance. She had been a great beauty, celebrated for her wit and
refinement—and here she was a haggard scarecrow, the shadow of her
skull thrusting out through her wasted flesh. I tried, you know, to talk
of various things, little things—in my distress I even began to speak of
her recovery and a trip we would take together. She stopped me with a
gesture. 'Oh my son,' she said, 'if I could continue this life by raising my
hand, I would not raise it.' I was horrified: it was the most terrible thing
I had ever heard one human being say to another—and this was my
mother! I begged her not to say that, I pleaded with her, I fell into a fit
of weeping; and she merely lay there and smiled at me, the saddest,

weariest smile, and murmured: 'Pu p'a, hsiao Lin, pu p'a.' Don't be afraid. The way she had when I was little . . .

"Just before dawn she died. I got up and went out to my car and ordered my driver to take me home. I had stopped weeping, but I was neither stunned nor sleepy. I felt unnaturally alert, my senses quickened to the pearl gray dawn streaked with rose above the mountains, the fierce green shoots of rice thrusting out of the mirror plate of the paddies. It was a little like the moment before battle—that sacred, profane vividness that burns to the very pit of your consciousness; you have felt it yourself . . ."

He caught himself up again, brusquely. "Well; there I was, returning to my great house in my car, a tumult of acute, almost painful sensations, aware of the ominous stirring of the opiate beast deep in my vitals, when I noticed a girl child, a baby lying naked on a dung heap. It is not an uncommon sight. You have undoubtedly seen something very similar here and there in this vast, pitiless, tortured land of ours, Ts'an Tsan— the girl baby abandoned by the poorest of the poor, tossed in the dead of night upon the manure piles to die; for there is no place for her kind, no hope in such interminable, mountainous poverty, she is merely another mouth to feed, come to rob those other already desperately hungry bellies—"

He stopped. Damon glanced at him, and saw that the guerrilla leader's face was very hard.

"There was no reason it should have affected me," he went on after a moment. "I had seen such sights by the thousands. Only this infant was still moving, feebly, stretching her tiny hands and feet, twisting her head in a tremulous little agony—to hold on, to clutch at that spark of life. A tiny white form, immaculate and lovely, moving on that pyre of filth. It burned into my consciousness like molten iron . . . And then— and this is what is so singular—not twenty seconds later I had this sudden fierce pain in my heart: a stab as though someone had driven a sharpened stake right through my chest and held it there, probing and twisting. I doubled up, gasping, I struggled and struggled for air, I tried to cry out for help—and I could not make a sound audible over the smooth, liquid crooning of the motor. A heart attack, a savage and fatal seizure. I was going to die. In minutes. No more intrigues of state, no more battles, no more concubines or virgins or opium, no more riot of indolence and luxury and power over men. It was terrible. In a few moments, a few racing moments, I would be no more. I was going to die in my prime."

There came a boom, another, flat and distant, bowling up the valley in troubled reverberation; there was a stir in the room, and several heads were raised.

"Seventy-five," Damon said.

"Yes. Krupp. That is their favorite method of reconnaissance." Lin

Tso-han smiled grimly. "Reconnaissance by fire. Singularly wasteful, but it bolsters their confidence. I imagine we should permit them to continue." Calmly he went on: "My aide and chauffeur in the front seat, beyond the glass partition, saw none of this; they never thought of turning around. My retinue riding behind me saw nothing amiss, either: they merely thought I'd bent forward to pick up something, or perhaps had dropped off to sleep. And I was paralyzed, panting, each breath a rending thrust of the iron bar; I was sliding into a black whirlpool of pain, sliding and skittering round and round—a whirlpool whose center held this curious, hard stillness, and the thought: *You are one. You and that abandoned baby of the lao pai hsing, the common people—you are one and the same. You thought you were a race apart, but that is a lie, and now you will face it. Now. It—that baby—has been discarded like a piece of rubbish before it could even taste of life, and you have been so favored—if you choose to call it that—that you have tasted all the fruits of this world a thousand thousand times over; until in fact you have grown weary of them. And yet for all your wealth and cunning and expensive tastes, you are the same: she is dying and you are dying. So you are the same: in death and in life.* Round and round the thought went, bright as a polished shield, and I kept turning from it in agony. I wanted to cry out, scream aloud and summon help—and all I could do was gasp and grunt and feebly wave my hands; like that abandoned baby girl . . ."

Lin chuckled softly, and his eyebrows went up and down. "Of course it was not a fatal heart attack at all. Not even a heart attack. I found out later it was a hiatus hernia and no more—though that trivial ailment can make you believe for a time you are on the edge of the grave. So I was not dying, I was relatively young and healthy again. But everything was altered. I could never again shake off that moment in the car. Why that little girl and not I? why I and not that baby? It went on and on in my head like the crooning of an imbecile: perfectly inane and perfectly irrefutable. I could not keep it out, I could not think of anything else. I was—obsessed. I put up my sword and forsook my pavilion of women and began to read. I had been well educated—that is to say I'd been superbly tutored by German Doktoren and Russian governesses, I was at home in four tongues—and I shut myself up in my beautiful study that looked out over the Yü-tze Valley and read. Everything! Not as one reads customarily, for pleasure or diversion, but to learn. Plutarch, Rousseau, Adam Smith, Descartes, Marx, Thoreau—there was no end to what I wanted to know. Have you ever felt that, Ts'an Tsan?—a hunger for knowledge so desperate you begrudge food and sleep, you cannot wait for another dawn to get on to more and more?" Damon nodded. "Yes. Well, I had that fever. I had to know: it was more important than life."

From far down the valley there came the bark of a 75 again, rhythmic and desultory, as if for a ceremonial.

"So I read and read, and at the end of six months I was exhausted; but

I had come to some conclusions. If a system could produce me—an arrogant, selfish, debauched young murderer and brigand—as an ideal, as something to aspire to, that system was wrong: a world of greed, corruption, favoritism, crushing taxes, the most blatant and ruinous disregard for the rights of man. It was quite simple, really—there was no need to have read all *that* much: I was rotten. And I was the direct product of my society; and so were the slaves I ordered about so grandly, and so was the abandoned girl child."

He sighed and puffed out his lips drolly. "Then came the difficult part. Everything up to then had been vivid, exciting, the opening up of worlds. Now it became very hard. I had to remake my life, act on all this new-found wisdom and enlightenment—I had to decide on a course of action and hold to it. And I did. I divested myself of my immaculate garde du corps, I gave the women pensions and provided for them one way or another as best I could, I put an end to my military forays and political intrigues." He sighed again, and rubbed his face with his thin, tapering fingers. "But all of that was relatively easy. The opium was something else . . . But I did that, too. I broke myself of the craving. I booked passage for Melbourne on a British vessel—and when I returned I was cured." He turned and gazed at the American, his eyes dark with memory. "You have no idea what that means. No idea."

"I came off morphine without any help at Angers in 1918," Damon said quietly.

Lin smiled. "Ah. Then you do have an idea. A good idea. Yes." He nodded. "Well, then I went abroad. To France and Germany. But not for pleasure. I studied and read, I attended the Sorbonne, I talked with professors and military men and politicians and farmers. And everything I saw I related to China. For, foolish as I was, headstrong and self-indulgent and arrogant as I was, I loved China even then—more than I knew. And slowly, inexorably, I came to this conclusion: the Kuomintang has failed us. It's as though your Washington had died in 1781, and Hamilton—a very selfish Hamilton with a large and greedy family—had seized control of the government, put to death all your Paines and Jeffersons and reinstated the British taxes and military occupation that had brought on your War of Independence. Chiang has turned back, not forward: immense corruption and the oppression of the lao pai hsing are the order of the day. You have seen it for yourself. And so for me the choice was clear . . .

"But it was difficult!" He laughed once, his teeth short and even in his broad mouth. "That Bible of yours! You have no idea how strange it sounds to an Oriental. And yet parts of it are so moving. There is one place in particular I often think of: the place where the young man comes running to Jesus and asks him what he should do to inherit eternal life, and Jesus answers, 'Sell whatsoever thou hast, and give to the poor, and come and follow me.' And then it says of the young man: 'And he was sad at that saying, and went away grieved: for he had great possessions.' Well, I had them, too—greater perhaps than Jesus' sad young man. But I sold them all, and gave to the poor." He opened his hands. "And here I am." He laughed again, softly. "But I must confess I expect no treasure in heaven."

The mountain loomed above them, blue-black, its spines and ravines softened in the late afternoon light. The wind was bitter. Lying on his belly behind a low ridge Damon chafed his hands and blinked repeatedly; his eyes kept tearing in the cold, and the drab, lonely village wobbled and wavered as though under water. He thought somberly, I'd give a hundred dollars for a cup of steaming hot coffee right now. A hundred dollars cash. He felt an overpowering need to urinate, although he'd relieved himself less than half an hour ago, and his jaws trembled as if he had palsy. For the past two hours they had been working their way down toward the village, and were now deployed in a wide arc less than a hundred and fifty yards away. A soldier ten feet from Damon had a huge broadsword slung across his back; the blade looked silver in the dull light.

Wu T'ai. Eight or nine battered dwellings huddled around a large building with a horned roof of blue tiles, where the remainder of the Japanese garrison was. Damon looked at his watch: less than three minutes now. If everything went according to plan. How could anything go according to plan with this scarecrow outfit, weapons from the dark ages and no hot food for two days and this wind? God, it might be possible without the *wind*—

A soldier came around the corner of the nearest building: flat, toadstool helmet and mustard-colored overcoat, tightly buttoned, moving with the deliberate, languid gait of a sentry. He was short and stocky and was carrying his rifle at sling, with the long bayonet fixed. Damon felt his head contract tautly into his shoulders, but the sentry's eyes passed indifferently over the hillside; yawning, he clapped his hands together, and then leaning against the wall of the house began methodically to pick his nose. The enemy. A cold, unhappy young man very far from home, who would soon be dead. Damon thought of the two German boys outside the farmhouse at Brigny that hot July morning so long ago. Now here he was again hiding and watching, at the other end of the earth. He glanced at Lin Tso-han, who was crouching behind a great boulder twenty feet away; but the guerrilla leader's expression was completely unreadable.

Beside him the Eskimo stiffened; and following his gaze Damon saw two figures coming along the road from the south. Two old women bent nearly double under huge loads of twigs. The Japanese sentry, watching them, pushed himself away from the wall and called something, waving one arm as though to hurry them. The two figures hobbled nearer; one of them answered something in a thin, croaking voice.

The soldier shouted again and uttered a harsh burst of laughter, shocking in the cold air. They were very near him now. Then the sentry must have seen or suspected something, because his left hand snapped the sling off his shoulder, but he was too late. There was the flash of a knife, a short, sharp cry. The soldier stiffened, then slumped, and for an instant the three figures drew together in what looked like a swift and violent embrace. Then the Japanese was lying in the road. One guerrilla had his rifle, the other was buckling on his cartridge belt; they darted away between two houses to the right of the post.

At that moment Lin raised his arm and a dozen men leaped to their feet and ran down the slope in perfect silence; and from the opposite hillside another group came hurrying, flowing down over the rocks, fanning out to each side of the blue-tiled building. There was a shout, two rifle shots—and then the flat snapping of a Nambu: quicker, higher pitched than a Browning. Damon looked again at Lin; the desire to go down there was almost overwhelming. The Nambu stopped, started again, and the firing rose to a sudden roar, like grease in a pan. Lin raised his arm and he and the rest of the group ran down the slope, spreading out to the right of the building; he thought he saw Lin vanish down the alley between two hovels that the guerrillas had used. Damon glanced at the Eskimo and P'ei Hsien, who had been detailed as his bodyguards; neither was paying any attention to him—their eyes were riveted on the long, blue-tiled building, which seemed larger now in the falling light; figures came and went like shadows. There was a stuttering flash from the window on the side facing him, and he could hear the Nambu chattering away, a slithering, slapping sound. They'd shifted it, then. If there was only one. If there were two—

A figure was crawling along the base of the wall, below the winking light of the Nambu. Lying very still, like an old bundle of rags right under the barrel. Then suddenly, magically, an arm went up; there was a flash of pure orange light as the grenade exploded inside, and the Nambu was silent. There was the hollow crash of another grenade, then another. The figure vaulted into the room, followed by two more; and gradually the rifle fire died away in a desultory, trivial popping.

Got it. They'd got it. Just as Lin said they would. Principle of Surprise, Principle of Economy of Force, Principle of Simplicity. Of course Lin would not put it that way. "Tactical superiority is the answer," he had said the day before, in his precise, musical French. "The problem is to achieve tactical superiority. It is always possible."

"What do you mean—it's *always possible?*" Damon had demanded.

Lin had smiled, his eyebrows had lifted and fallen. "Careful planning, patience, distraction, decoy, diversion, feint, any ruse that will work—"

"Any at all?"

"Any at all. But above all the feint. We call it: The Principle of Pretending to Attack the East While Attacking the West. And once the attack is launched, unwavering decision. If you do these things, if you select the most vulnerable spot in the enemy's anatomy, isolate that particular element—you will have achieved tactical superiority over him at that moment in time, even though he may have an over-all strategic advantage . . ."

Beside Damon P'ei had scrambled to his feet. "Ting hao, Ts'an Tsan," he said in his high, clear voice. "Pao huai-la, tao-la—"

All at once the boy spun around and pitched forward on his face, slithering on the stones; and Damon heard the snap of the rifle shot. Something stung his cheek, bits of stone: the ricochet sang away like a band saw. He turned his head, and his heart misgave him. Six or seven Japanese, helmeted, their rifles long and bright in the dusk, running toward them, high on the mountainside. Where had they come from? Another shot droned through the air. He struck the Eskimo on the shoulder and shouted: "Ch'iang tai!" and in English, "There! Over there! . . ."

The Eskimo, who had started to go to the aid of P'ei, turned, raised the Lebel with calm deliberation and fired. One of the Japanese stumbled and fell. The rest kept coming in a lumpy, bandy-legged run, swelling out of twilight like squat giants. Damon started to reach for P'ei's rifle; a bullet sang by his head and he ducked. The Eskimo, his face completely expressionless, fitted another round in the chamber, plucked back the bolt and fired again. Damon raised his head. No one. They'd taken cover. Damn fools—they could have had them in a rush. Another slug struck a rock nearby, showering them with chips of stone and dust. The Eskimo fired again, and started to hunt for another bullet in his pocket. Damon thought of all the clips for Lebel rifles he had seen in '18, the crates of small-arms ammunition and Springfields and grenades, the mountainous dumps from Bar-le-Duc to Sancerre, and groaned. The Japanese would rush them in a minute, another minute. He pulled his pistol out of its holster and ran back the receiver in a shivering spasm—looked around him wildly, thinking, Did I have to do this? really do anything like this? I could learn their God damn goofy tactics without getting into this kind of a stupid, crazy—

The Eskimo fired again and clawed another cartridge out of his pocket. No cover. There was no cover all the way over to that houselike clump of rock. Fifty yards, sixty. In a moment the patrol would get up and rush them, and they would take no prisoners. That was for sure. He poised near the edge of the shallow depression, estimating his chances. It was nearly dark, the edges of rock melted into one another softly. But now, looking back, it seemed bright as midday in a desert. The Eskimo was probably down to five or six rounds, maybe less. In another few minutes he'd run out, and this patrol or whatever it was would be in their laps. He'd give it just—

The Japanese were up, on a command; up and running toward them, their rifles swinging like scythe handles. He raised his pistol and fired—

heard at the same instant a deep, blasting roar. Tommy gun. One of the
Japanese lurched into a silly pirouetting skittering dance and fell, then
another; the remainder broke and ran and the gun followed them, struck
them down.

Looking back he saw Lin Tso-han crouched with several others, firing
in short, clean bursts. He jumped to his feet and ran forward; the
nearest of the Japanese was not twenty-five feet away. He bent over and
unhooked the soldier's belt with its boxlike brown leather cartridge
pouches and buckled it on above his own, then picked up the Arisaka
rifle.

"Ts'an Tsan, are you unhurt?"

He nodded. "Where did they come from?"

Lin shrugged. "They must have sent out a patrol on this side at the
same time the main body set out after F'eng. The unexpected. War is
full of the unexpected."

"Yeah," Damon muttered. He was shaking now, and out of wind. He
slung the long-barreled rifle.

Lin was watching him, frowning. "Ts'an Tsan—"

"You'll want it, won't you?" he answered defiantly. "Another weapon.
Isn't that what you're after? I'm taking it with me."

Lin scuffed one foot, then grinned his comical Groucho Marx grin.
"That is inconsistent with your status as military observer."

"How true."

They walked quickly over to P'ei. The boy was dead; the bullet had
passed through his skull above the ears. Damon gazed at the smooth,
round face; with his eyes closed, the lips faintly curled, the boy seemed
to be smiling slyly—as though in quiet glee at having escaped the bitter
cold, the meager rations, this interminable war that had never been
declared. "He's so young," Damon murmured half-aloud, and the
thought chilled him: he had never thought that of any soldier he'd seen
killed in combat.

Down at the Japanese command post everyone was moving with
haste, lashing boxes of medical supplies to packboards or rigging lines
around them. Two men came out carrying the Nambu, which looked
wicked enough with its heavy corrugated barrel and the curious tilted
boxlike hopper fixed on one side of the breech. Six-point-five millimeter;
and no problems about belts or faulty linkage—just keep dropping five-
shot rifle clips into the hopper. Darned clever, these Japanese. Still
sweating from the close call he watched them hurrying. And now they
were going to carry these medical supplies and captured weapons away
with them, in addition to their meager personal gear; up one mountain
and down another . . .

He stepped into the command post: a welter of smashed furniture and
strewn papers, dead bodies sprawled under tables and chairs. In one
corner there was a little commotion; he moved up to the knot of men,
and stopped. The hardbitten old officer they called Lao Kou was lying

very still, his face slick with sweat. What looked like a series of shadows
was gliding out from under his back and buttocks.

Damon turned away and went outside again, into the cold night. The
sense of alienation, of sheer uselessness was immense; he kept opening
and closing his hands. A man he hadn't seen before, a farmer in a
sheepskin vest and cloth trousers, was talking to Lin Tso-han, who was
listening, his face stern. He spoke rapidly to two of his officers, then gave
the command: "Tsou pa!" and here and there other voices took up the
cry softly:

"Tsou pa! . . . *Tsou pa!* . . ."

"What is it, Colonel?" Damon said.

Lin looked at him as if he'd forgotten his existence. "Japanese. Only
five li from here. We must move quickly." He went into the post and
gave an order, and the soldiers who had been inside came tumbling out
and started forming up with their loads. Damon followed Lin inside.
The Commander had knelt over Lao Kou and was asking him something.

"Mei yu pan fa," the old man muttered, his lips barely moving. "Mei
yu fa-tzu . . ."

The Observer caught the phrase. "What's impossible?"

Lin looked at him, his face flat and utterly remote. "Nothing."

"*What* can't be done? Can't you rig a stretcher for him?" Lin looked
at him without answer; outside there was the clink and rustle of the
column moving out. Damon stared at the Colonel. "—You're not going
to leave him here, are you?"

"Go out and take your place in the column, Ts'an Tsan," Lin said.

"What? Look, for Christ sake—"

Lin came to his feet. "*Fu tsung ming ling!*" he said tightly; then, in
French: "You will obey orders. Now, go!"

He got it, then. He drew himself up and saluted smartly and said:
"Yes, sir," and turned and went out. The end of the column was already
passing swiftly; he saw the Eskimo, nodded and stepped out behind him,
fell into the quick, driving rhythm of the march. As they swung west
across the railroad tracks he heard the shot—a muffled pop that sounded
like a crushed paper bag, a child's game. "Jesus," he muttered. "Oh—my
—Jesus. What a dirty, filthy war . . ."

They were walking at a speed that astonished him, half-running
up a slope that cut back and forth between rock shoulders. His face
broke out in sweat, he lost his wind, he had a stitch in his side. Then he
caught his second wind, and held it. They were moving up Wu T'ai
mountain, a narrow ascending trail that led past boulders big as cattle;
below them the village had already vanished in the darkness, like a toy
that has sunk to the bottom of a pool.

"How far," someone just ahead of him said. "How far to Pa-hsüeh?"
and another voice answered: "Forty-seven li."

He did some painful calculating, then. His mind, slowed by hunger and cold and the physical effort he was making, worked haltingly, like a gun whose grease has congealed. A li was one-third of a mile. So, 47 divided by three was 15⅔. Sixteen miles, nearly. But they had already done 53 li the day before, and 14 getting into position that afternoon. Which made 114 li, or—divided by three—34—no, 38 miles . . . But that was only Pa-hsüeh, and they had to get to Tung Yen T'o before they were out of danger. All of this at 3⅓ miles to the hour, up one mountain and down the next.

They reached the ridge, followed it for half a mile and then descended, along a twisting path strewn with stones that rolled and skittered underfoot like large malicious marbles. Once he fell, sliding on one hip, felt the hot, dry burn on his thigh. He got to one knee. Someone's arms were under his, hauling him to his feet; he glared at the Samaritan—but it was a face he didn't recognize. He muttered, "Thank you, comrade," and struck out again, cursing savagely under his breath. The Japanese rifle bore down on his right shoulder, the lumpy cartridge pouches jostled at his hips, chafing the bone with every step. What in God's name had he picked it up for? The sling, even in this biting air, smelled queerly—of mildew and old brass and fish. Why of fish?

He was falling back. One by one they were passing him, these ragged figures in their quilted uniforms and cotton-cloth shoes, burdened with their packboards, their breath coming in quick, dry gasps. He gaped at them. It was impossible—he was a martinet about physical fitness, he'd earned the reputation of a hiker among hikers at Beyliss and on Luzon; and here he was almost at the end of the march, in danger of becoming a straggler. He, Sam Damon, a straggler . . .

They crossed a dry riverbed, and the dust rose in choking clouds; he could feel it on his teeth, in his throat. They climbed again, reached a flat little knoll where there had once been a dwelling or a shrine. Someone gave a command, and they sank to their knees or sprawled against the stone. Damon stretched his legs out slowly; his thighs were quivering, and the old wound throbbed. He took a sip from his canteen and it was worse than no water at all. Surely now they were safe: surely now they could rest for a time. Just sit on the flintlike stone and rest.

Lin came up, the snout of the Thompson silhouetted behind his ear, and crouched down beside two of his officers, talking low and rapidly.

"Ai-la!" one exclaimed. "Erh-pen kwei—t'a ma-ti . . ." and Damon smiled through his weariness. Men cursed the same way in any language. The Japanese were certainly mother defilers, any way you looked at them . . .

The hurried colloquy broke up, the officers rose to their feet, and the dread command came again: "Tsou pa!"

He couldn't believe it: they'd been resting three minutes, perhaps four. Trying to hold his voice even, he said, "What is it?"

Lin stopped in front of him. "Bad news, Ts'an Tsan. Japanese cavalry, coming from Hung-chou. We must really hurry now . . ."

Damon watched him posting a light rear guard, and then fell in again. The march ground on, at an even faster pace. He gulped down two aspirins and offered some to the Eskimo, who politely but firmly refused. They crossed another mountain, and another. He lost all track of the sequence of events, of images. Somewhere there was a narrow pass where the wind froze the sweat on his face; somewhere there was an uneven, twisting track above a gorge where a river roared densely and the spray stung his hands and cheeks; somewhere—and the sight of it had shocked him into a little transport of raging effort—a soldier had passed him, his feet making a curiously slapping noise, and looking down he had seen the man was wearing composition sandals.

He was beyond the sharp edge of anguish now. He had lost all sensation in his legs. They swung on and on, lifted and fell, someone else's legs entirely, his own ended in a vast area of suffering surrounding his right thigh; his kidneys ached, his head swam with fatigue; he had fallen into a stooped, slouching walk, his hands pressed against his hips and his eyes staring dully at the ground—he dreamed of water, water in rivulets and fountains and green-banked streams and still pools, of sandy beaches where he would lie for hours, sprawled under towering, lazily leaning palms . . . then he would become aware that he was in danger of straggling again; he would fling such treasonous thoughts out of his mind, concentrating with the fervor of an acolyte on holding this savage, impossible pace through the night cold, climbing, climbing, step on step on step in a hard fury of will . . .

There was a ledge that sloped out trickily, a configuration of stone like an abstracted deposition, and they were on the highest ridge of all, the wind on their left cheeks. A thread of moon lay low in the east, and the mountains rose around them—a stately, indigo sea tipped with silver. The top of the world: they were gliding along the very top of the world, far above the sordid pains and foibles of mankind, among these mountains older than time, older than passions or fears, older than the gods . . . He glanced behind him. Only the Eskimo, who had dropped back—out of courtesy, he knew—and Lin, and two scouts. No one had fallen behind him; no one had straggled. Sixty-eight men had marched 38 miles and fought a battle in 16 hours, and not one had fallen by the wayside. Not one. He thought of the terrible day-and-night march to Soissons in the wind and rain—he had carried someone's rifle that night, too, hadn't he? Ferguson's? No, Clay's. But men had straggled, they had fallen by the wayside. Not many, but a few. But this was farther, and harder, and performed by men in pitifully inadequate clothing and with empty bellies. Weaving on his feet, half-stupefied with exhaustion, he gazed up at the dancing wilderness of stars, the sickle of moon, seized with an exultation he hadn't felt in years. How had they done it? How had they *done* it!—every last man of them . . . It was fantastic. They were underfed, underclothed, underarmed—but they had something no other troops he'd ever known had, that was for sure. They had it to burn . . .

Later, at Tung Yen T'o, beyond weariness and quite sleepless, he was writing furiously in his journal by lamplight when Lin came in. The little man's eyebrows rose and fell.

"Still up, Ts'an Tsan?" he said softly. He tossed his head in the direction of the heated k'ang where four men were huddled together, asleep. "Was there no room at the inn?"

"No, I—" Damon still felt a bit ill at ease with the Commander after the episode at Wu T'ai; he gestured vaguely. "I wanted to get it all down, as fully as I could . . ."

Lin stretched his arms. "Ah, the literary life." He sat down opposite the Captain. "Perhaps you'll immortalize us in Alexandrines."

"You ought to be . . ." The fervor in his voice surprised him, and he grinned to hide it. "Do you realize what you've done, your unit? Do you realize not a man dropped out of the line of march? not one? I've just been logging it. Do you realize how fantastically unique that is, after a march like this one?"

Lin nodded simply. "I have been a soldier ever since my early manhood. But this is a new army. A new world."

"How can they do it, Colonel? What has given them such endurance, such—such sheer force . . . ?"

"Hope." The guerrilla leader smiled gently. "Hope, and dignity. Hope for a new China, a China free of foreign armies, foreign concessions, free of famine and ignorance and misery; and the dignity of equality." He looked directly at Damon. "Many have said it—many lands, many leaders. But we live it." He tossed his head toward the exhausted forms on the k'ang. "That's what they know—that some must lead and others must follow, but that leadership is an obligation and not a mark of caste. We are the only army where the officers live like the men. Where leadership is based on respect, on proved competence and only that."

Slowly Damon nodded, thinking of Jarreyl, and Townsend back at Hardee, and Merrick, and Benoît-Guesclin. Yes, an army without caste or privilege, free of that terrible gulf of hatred, of resentment or contempt—an army without stockades. What an impossible vision . . .

"When you ask men to die, to endure great hardship, they have the right to know the purpose that demands that sacrifice," Lin said softly. "They have the right to be treated like men—with all honor due them— all honor due their inextinguishable souls . . ." He broke off, his face all at once fearfully stern and forbidding; but his eyes glistened in the smoky orange light from the crude little oil lamp. There was a short silence while the two men looked at each other.

"—Colonel, I want to apologize," Damon murmured, "for my—for questioning your orders at Wu T'ai."

Lin looked down. "It's I who should apologize. For my anger." He sighed and rubbed his nose. "If we had tried to take him with us the Japanese would have caught us at Chunsho Valley. And in any event he would probably have died. He knew." He peered at his hand, chafing his fingers delicately against his thumb, and now tears hung in his eyes, wetting the long lashes. "A good friend. The best of my officers. A good friend." He sighed again, and now his face fell into a series of blocklike planes. "Do you know how he came to us?" Damon shook his head. "He lived near Tamingfu, in Hopeh. A simple sheepherder, content to pass his days in peace and poverty. He had even worn the queue. And then the Japanese came. They slaughtered his sheep, they killed his son, they raped his daughter. What he did not see, he heard. For two weeks he walked around like a dead man, without hope or fear. And then one night he came in, to find four Japanese asleep in his house, with no one on guard. He told me: 'All of a sudden I came awake. I was a man. What was I doing, standing there? I was a man.' He paused there in the dark, watching the Japanese, listening to his daughter moaning in the next room. Then he went and got the knife he used for butchering sheep, and killed them, one by one. The fourth soldier woke up and fought, but he killed him before he could cry out.

"Now he had four rifles. He went to his relatives and told them what he had done. Two were afraid, but he convinced the others. They knew what would happen to them all, in time. He armed them with the rifles, and they assaulted the small Japanese garrison in a merchant's house in the town. He overpowered the sentry with a ruse, and they took the post. Now he had twenty-seven rifles and a pistol. He persuaded neighbors to join his band and left for the hills. In time he had two companies with four automatic weapons. All from standing in the dark with a butcher knife."

Damon said: "What happened to the people of the town when the Japanese came back?"

Lin's eyes narrowed. "It went very hard with them."

"I would think so."

"That is guerrilla warfare, Ts'an Tsan."

"But the people," Damon protested, "the women and children, the innocent bystanders—you're involving them in this war of yours. It's like putting them in the front line without weapons . . ."

"Yes," Lin nodded, "that's it, exactly: the front line. But not without weapons."

"But what do you call—"

Lin raised a hand. "Ts'an Tsan, you have seen Hangkow, you have heard about Nanking—do you think those planes make a neat distinction between the soldier and the little child? Japanese artillery has shelled defenseless towns, their soldiery have raped and slaughtered without scruple. I have seen it. No—it is they, in their arrogance and greed who have said, 'You are all the enemy, a lesser race, to be enslaved.' And every boy who cuts a Japanese telephone wire in the night, every farmer who comes running to us with information of enemy movements, every woman who hides half a tan of millet in the earth—all of them know this in their innermost hearts. *And they will not be despised* . . .

"No! It is the Japanese who have made this a people's war. That is the great irony—they planned to bring China to her knees; instead, they have brought her to her feet. She will never be the same again . . ."

The lamp sent a long spiral of black smoke toward the ceiling and Lin frowned at it. "It is curious, how the world sees us. The inscrutable Chinese, remote, impassive; a horde of coolies, China's swarming millions—as though we were a race of lemmings incapable of grief or laughter, without idiosyncracies . . . The fact is, the Chinese is the most individualistic of people—he cannot help seeing himself as monumentally unique, sacred and inviolate. More so than the American perhaps, Ts'an Tsan. And the Japanese hates this in us—and in you, as well. He will turn and attack you, of course; in his own good time. But for vastly other reasons."

Damon said: "Can you hold out until that day comes?"

"We will hold out until the end of time itself. The Japanese will never conquer us: we will drain them of every soldier, every rifle, every tank and lorry they send here, until they give it up as a bad job and go home . . . provided *you* do not give them the victory, Ts'an Tsan." He smiled at the Observer's incredulous stare. "Yes. The United States has furnished Tai Nippon with more than half of all war matériel she purchases abroad."

"That's not true!" Damon exclaimed in English. Lin made a soft, importunate gesture. "Where did you hear that?"

"In one of your own papers, Ts'an Tsan."

"Which one? When? I don't believe it . . ."

Almost reluctantly Lin took a worn, bent notebook out of an inner pocket, slipped a grayed, much-folded, sweat-soaked clipping out of the back pages and handed it over. It was a UP dispatch from what looked like *The New York Times*. There it was, in chapter and verse: it was true. Damon could feel his face burning as he read. When he finished he folded it up and handed it back. He felt a terrible rage compounded of shame and confusion; then it passed, leaving in its wake only a hard implacable stoicism. He rubbed his hands on his trousers.

"I'm sorry, Colonel Lin," he said quietly. "I should not have doubted you. I am out of touch with my own country. With events in my own country. It seems.—And I had to come out here to learn this," he muttered. "All the way out here . . ."

"Among the heathen Chinese?" Lin asked, and wiggled his black eyebrows.

He smiled back. "Among the heathen Chinese . . ."

"Well, heaven will not delay a traveler."

"Is that an old Chinese proverb?"

"Oh yes, Ts'an Tsan."

"I like old Chinese proverbs. Is there one for every occasion?"

"Very nearly." Lin rose with a grunt, stretching his arms and arching his back painfully. "And now I suggest we try to sleep a little. Before another day is upon us."

Damon got to his feet; his legs were so stiff and sore he thought for a moment he would fall, and gripped the rough wood table with both hands. "What will you do after the war, Lin?" he asked, to cover his dismay. "Sit in a room overlooking your Yü-tze Valley and write your memoirs? Read *The Romance of the Three Kingdoms?* Or will you travel?"

"Oh, I will not survive this war, Ts'an Tsan."

Damon stared at him; the little man was smiling—a slow, infinitely sad smile. "All my old comrades are dead except Tsai Huan-tung, and he is faraway now, in Chahar." He shook his head. "I have been lucky, very lucky, so far. Once in the arm, once in the leg. But the third time will be fatal. After this war . . . I never think of it. That's a luxury for others, not for me." He opened his hands, to include the bare, neat room, the men sleeping in a huddled group behind him. "This is my life, the end of my life. For a new China—where the girl child is not left to die on the manure pile. For a China where the Sons of Han can live as they were meant to live. Like men."

Watching that thin, furrowed, indomitable face with its roguish eyebrows, Damon felt a wave of hot sorrow wash through him. Yes, he thought, gripping his hands together, let them win; let them hang on and win through to their victory. Yes, he thought, and by God, land to those who till it—and honor and dignity to those who have suffered so much and so long in its name; and his eyes stung with tears.

He reached out and gripped Lin Tso-han's arm. "Tsui ho sheng li," he said.

Lin's eyes glistened again. He nodded. "Yes!" he cried softly. "To—fina' vic-t'ree . . ." It was the only English Damon had heard him speak. And then in French: "You are learning Chinese, Ts'an Tsan. What a curious thing for an American to do." All at once he grinned. "Ah, if only all Americans were like you, and all Chinese like me, eh? What a glorious world it would be . . ." He chuckled, as though it were the funniest thing he'd ever thought of. "And now we must get some sleep, before we both fall down in a stupor."

Outside, the first light was breaking over the mountains.

(9)

In the club on Dewey Boulevard the orchestra was playing "Thanks for the Memory." The rooms were decorated with flags and bits of bunting; there were battle streamers, crossed sabers, and piles of cannonballs made of papier-mâché, and couples drifted through the discs of blue and scarlet and amber light in sharp, gaudy patterns. There were infantrymen from the Army of the Continental Congress in blue-and-buff coats and tricorns, there were volunteers from the War of 1812 in gray tunic and busby—an impersonation affected by slight modifications on the West Point uniform; there were doughboys and Confederate cavalrymen—there was even a Fire Zouave of 1861, in red pantaloons and fez, and sporting a scimitar. Several participants were decked out in curious combinations of turn-of-the-century Spanish uniforms, the product of ransacking Manila shops or the homes of Filipino acquaintances. There was an Arab, a Moro, a Prussian Oberst with a monocle and Kaiser Wilhelms—there was even the inevitable wag sweating profusely in a helmet of cardboard and chain-mail skirt made of hemp and painted silver, but Emily Massengale couldn't tell who he was because everyone was wearing a mask. Colonel Semmes, who had set the theme of the ball—"The Soldier in History"—had insisted that everyone come masked and remain that way until midnight.

The women had more latitude, though most of them tried to conform to the theme, and there were several Molly Pitchers and Molly Starks in crinolines and bustles and gathered bonnets; but there were also southern belles, buckskin lasses and medieval ladies in horned hats and long velour trains, gathered up now for dancing. A Salvation Army girl in a drab Mother Hubbard smock had a placard around her neck that read "Doughnut & Choc. 75¢." There was also a camp follower in the full and original sense of the term—Emily Massengale, sitting in the row of chairs near the verandah, suspected it was Kay Harting—fitted out in a yellow silk dress slit above both knees, ostrich plumes, a giddily plunging bodice and two beauty marks, one above the other.

"Look at *him!*" Susan Gantrell, sitting beside her, cried. She was dutifully wearing her mask but nothing could disguise the Georgia accent or the quick, birdlike inclination of her head. "Genghis Khan . . . This is such fun, isn't it?"

"Yes," Emily said absently. The mask bothered her if she shifted her gaze quickly so she kept her eyes front and let the dancers slide across her field of vision.

"Oh look, look at that!"

"What?"

"The tall one—the tall one in the gorgeous uniform! . . ." And there, gliding into Emily's line of sight, was a man in the dazzling uniform of a Napoleonic marshal, the short sea green tunic with gold epaulets and red facings, tight white breeches, ermine-trimmed hussar's jacket worn off the shoulder. "Where ever did he get it?"

That would be telling, Emily thought. Courtney—it was he—was dancing with a stout little woman dressed as a Chinese empress, all brocade. Millicent Lange, that would be, with a costume picked up from the Tientsin tour. Courtney moved out of her vision, moved into it again, circling slowly; he was smiling, his lips curving under the mustache. He'd had the costume made for a ball in Washington when he'd been one of Pershing's aides, and had insisted on including it in their personal gear wherever they went. Our dreams betray us, she thought somberly, and sipped at her drink; we can offer a mask to the world, but our dreams betray us all the same. She herself was wearing the Phrygian cap and short skirt and boots of a Jacobin woman of the French Revolution, she hadn't really known why. Now, watching Courtney gracefully swirling and gliding in his gorgeous uniform, she did know. "Liberté, égalité, fraternité," she murmured, and smiled to herself.

A giant dressed as a Confederate cavalryman, with slouch hat and a massive black handlebar mustache, came up to them and bowed from the waist. "Ladies, is it your intention to deprive a gentleman of your terpsichorean talents on this memorable evening?"

Emily recognized Jack Cleghorne instantly. She said, "Well, you can't very well dance with us both, Joe Wheeler."

"Hampton, ma'am. Wade Hampton, CSA. Yours to command." But now he faltered. "I must confess myself faced with an impossible dilemma—*two* such charming ladies . . ." Susan giggled and he turned to her, offering his arm. "Would you care to do me the honor, ma'am?"

"Why, Gen'l, Ah'd be delaaaghted," Susan cried in her broadest Georgia drawl, and rose.

Emily watched them go off across the floor, which the Filipino boys had coconuted to a rich, ruddy gloss. The orchestra was playing that Cole Porter tune "Anything Goes," and she hummed along with it. Sitting there she felt curiously secure behind the mask. What a joy it would be to wear one always—all day and all night. Slip through life incognito and carefree . . . She sipped at her drink, a pink gin, replaced it on the little red Chinese table beside her with slow, fastidious ease. Her fourth. Yes, fourth. The trick was to exercise care: the utmost tactical care in sustaining that fine, reassuring stasis, where everything rocked in a soft luminosity and all threatful, demanding things were far away. She sighed. Her feet, which had begun to swell abominably out here in the islands, already hurt her, but the tight, dry burning high in her belly had receded, like a well-banked fire. Gastric ulcer. Was it? She had a gastric ulcer, then—but no one was going to know about it, not even Courtney. Especially Courtney. Because that would mean—

The band had shifted to "All of Me"; a raggedy-pants private of '76 was dancing with the Manchu empress now, the Zouave was pirouetting with one of the Molly Pitchers, the Napoleonic marshal was with a slender woman in an Empire gown caught tightly under the breasts, a gold coronet and an upslanted blue mask adorned with brilliants: the Empress Josephine, obviously. Our dreams betray us. The woman's head was back, she was laughing, her throat fine and white. Who was that? The constant dipping and swirling of the couples dizzied her and she closed her eyes. It was odd: she'd been married to Courtney for eighteen years—and yet when she thought of him she never saw him full face but always in profile: the long, very straight nose, the thin lips curved in faintly mournful, almost deprecatory amusement, the eye—it was always the right profile—narrowed and speculative, as though searching for something. Eighteen years in March . . .

They had met at a picnic at Bar Harbor the second summer after the war. Courtney had been staying with the Holways. She would always remember the moment she had first seen him with a quick little catch at her heart, half-attraction, half-fear: standing tall and slender against the pines, in a sweater and flannel trousers. He always looked taller than anyone else—he liked to say it was a matter of bearing. Eliot Holway was saying something about the French, what a Godawful mess their government was in, that traitor Caillaux, and Courtney had replied, "Yes, but you'll have to admit they've done brilliantly with what they've had, for over a thousand years."

"Oh yes," she'd said flippantly. "You're that army officer, aren't you?"

He had smiled—a faintly disdainful smile that irritated her. "The very culprit, Miss Pawlfrey."

"No, but I mean you're sort of a perennial."

"Unregenerate is the word." The others on the porch had laughed.

She had disliked him violently at first: his quick, calm assurance, his wit, the almost casual ease with which he could turn his mind to any subject offended her Boston sobriety, her conviction that all rewards must be earned. But later she found herself attracted to him. At the picnic the following afternoon he swam farther and longer in the bitter, icy water than any of the others, even her brother Forbes. He didn't know how to sail, coming as he did from New York State, but he caught on fast enough. Around the booming campfire later he sang a very funny London music hall song, and told stories about General Pershing, reviews and audiences with crotchety, lizard-faced French duchesses in draughty drawing rooms at Rambouillet or Saumur. His smooth dark hair was disheveled, his face ruddy in the firelight. He was such a change from the stalwart, straightforward manner of Forbes, or Eliot Holway or George Wainwright. Walking along the shore together, climbing over the furrowed granite, he had wanted to know what she was thinking.

"You're not supposed to ask a girl that," she'd retorted.

"Oh come now—if you want equal rights with men you've got to expect to be treated like them."

She laughed. "That's true, isn't it? That's what Father says: no authority without responsibility."

"Yes. I've heard him."

They both laughed, watching each other a moment. Then she said: "I was thinking how odd it is you're not married."

"Odd?"

"Well, a man of your—your experience . . ."

"My creaking old age, you mean."

"Oh, heavens, no—but all you've seen and done."

He moved a bit ahead of her, climbing a long, rough shoulder of rock. Spray from the surf blew over them. "No excuse, sir. As we used to say back at the Point. The fact is, there just wasn't time for it."

"No O-A-O?" She had picked up some of the slang from Ruth Holway, who had gone to dances at West Point.

"No One-And-Only. Life was real and life was earnest. I went right out to a platoon in the South. And then we entered the war. Isn't it curious, though?" he mused, as though the idea had only just occurred to him. "I never once thought of it then. Romance and marriage."

"That's a tall one!"

"No, I mean it." He reached down to her, took her hand and drew her up to him—a sudden proximity that made her heart leap; his eyes were sparkling. "The fact is, I simply haven't met a girl who's taken my fancy. Until now, anyway . . ."

He visited the Pawlfreys in Boston a month later, and she took him to teas around the Hill or out on Beacon Street, or kept him all to herself. She was enchanted with him; she couldn't think of anything else. Here he was—this handsome, brilliant officer with a glittering future (people said just that—*glittering*—it was one of the words that never failed to cluster around Courtney Massengale, all the extravagant words: brilliant, arresting, astonishing—he drew epithets the way a polished steel magnet picks up filings; even staid, crusty old Boston used some of them), and he was hers to display. Nothing like this had ever happened to her before.

He loved Boston, which surprised her: he liked to walk the narrow, crabbed streets in the raw east wind, looking up tablets and mementoes. Crossing the Common under the lordly elms, he asked her where Clinton's troops had been quartered during the British occupation. Laughing, she said she didn't have the faintest idea.

"But that's terrible," he rebuked her. "Here you are, surrounded by history—the very foundations of the country's traditions—and you don't know something like that?"

He was smiling, but he was serious: she'd learned to tell. He took her education in hand. They stood where the crowd had been behind the

Old State House when poor Crispus Attucks fell under the British bayonets, they walked along the grassy ridge on Breed's Hill (the battle had
not been fought on Bunker Hill, he warned her, that was a myth unsupported by all historical evidence) where Prescott had slapped his trembling riflemen on their behinds with his stick, calling tightly, "*Show* the
bastards, now! You show them!" He even dragged her up to a desolate
clump of buildings near an abandoned football field in Dorchester which
Washington's troops had seized, and where they'd mounted the guns
that had forced the hated Redcoats to evacuate the city.

"Do you know, my great grandfather Charles Massengale came all the
way from Selkirk to fight here? And then went back in '77 and commanded a regiment at Bemis Heights."

"Where's that?" she wanted to know.

He threw back his head in mock outrage. "My dear young girl, they
obviously teach you nothing in the Hub. Nothing . . . *Saratoga!*" he
cried. A woman passing by stared at him and he bowed and gave her his
most charming smile before turning back to Emily. "The great turning
point! The supreme, triumphant moment after which nothing could
ever be the same. Your father says you had an ancestor here at Dorchester Heights—so you could say our forebears fought shoulder to shoulder . . ." His eyes flashed, tawny against the gray northeast sky; his long
white face looked eager and proud. She had never loved him more than
at that moment.

Her brother Forbes was less enthusiastic. "Well—been out wandering
down memory lane?" he inquired when they came in one afternoon.

"A harmless pastime." Courtney regarded him tolerantly. "The trouble with you people is you've got so many traditions you don't half
value them anymore."

"We don't wave the gaudy flag over them, if that's what you mean."

"Oh Forbes, don't talk rot," Emily said. "You're just jealous. Because
you were too young to go to France."

He started to laugh, and then his face set in that stolid, quizzical way
that meant he was getting angry. "Well, now," he said.

"Come on, Emily," Courtney broke in. He never called her Em, or
Emmy, the way the others did. "That's hardly fair. We couldn't *all* of
us be heroes. Why weren't *you* turning out doughnuts under a tent
fly near St. Durance?"

"Because *I* was marching down Tremont Street in the suffragette
parades," she retorted gaily, and stuck out her tongue.

"Em!" Forbes protested, but Courtney threw back his head and
laughed.

"Women's rights! What makes you think you deserve any?"

"Any woman is as good as any man."

"Demonstrably false." His eyes were still twinkling. "The Periclean
Athenians never let them out of the house."

"No, of course not—they didn't dare!"

"Possibly you're right." His smile was devastating; she had never in all her life met such a compelling man—she'd never known such a man existed. "I'll bet I can learn to make a sauce Hollandaise before you learn how to drive an automobile." His face seemed incredibly, dangerously close to hers. "You see?" he murmured. "And you said any woman is as good as any man . . ."

She was seized with a twinge of vertigo. The backs of her hands, her eyelids were tingling, and she laughed to conceal it—a laugh that was like a catch of breath. "Oh," she cried softly, "but you're not *any* man! . . ."

Her parents had been rather constrained when she'd told them. A hesitant conference in the long, silent room, somber with the tasseled cloth lamp shades and the curved interior shutters drawn; the birch fire hissed and snapped behind the grate.

"We don't know an awful lot about him, dear."

"Momma, he comes from a very good family, the Camberlins know them . . ."

"It's not that." Her mother's face, usually so square and placid, looked troubled. "You're rather young for this, Emmy."

"I'm twenty."

"You're sure you're not getting carried away?" her father asked. He was smiling but his eyes were quick and piercing over his bifocals. "The war's over, you know."

"Gracious goodness, I know *that!*"

"It'll mean long stretches in out-of-the-way places. Army posts aren't the most festive abodes on earth."

"Yes, but there'll be . . ." She faltered, but not for long; this was something she wanted very much. "I mean there'll be money, won't there? I'll have some of my own . . . ?"

Her parents exchanged a glance, and her father nodded and said, "Yes. Of course. I've told you that. But that isn't everything, you know."

"Anyway, that won't be forever," she said proudly. "It'll be different with Courtney. He's no run-of-the-mill Army product, you know—he's a permanent captain, at twenty-four." Their massed reluctance distressed her; this was her chance, the chance of her life, and she wasn't going to fluff it: she couldn't! "He's been picked by General Pershing to serve on his personal staff. You'll see—Courtney's going to be a military attaché, and a general before anyone else in his class."

"Maybe so." Her father smiled at her again, fondly. "Just try to be sure about it, Emmy, that's all."

"It's been such a short time," her mother persisted. "Are you sure it's what you really want?"

"Oh yes," she said, "it is, I know it is! . . ."

She knew she was right: she knew it. Courtney would accomplish great deeds. He was going out into the world where things were happening—away from Boston, the tortuous little streets and Sunday afternoons, the dances at Mr. Papanti's, the parochial encounters in book-shops, at Symphony, in the swept dirt walks of the Public Garden. He was getting away from all this! and so was she . . .

The tune—a dreamy ballad called "Deep Purple"—was over. She reached for her glass and saw it was empty; restrained the movement of her hand. The atmosphere in the club seemed warmer, caught in a humming rhythm. Out of it came the French marshal, his sideburns luxuriant and full, his collar adorned with golden acanthus leaves; a sleeve of the hussar's jacket swung gently. With care she rose to her feet, bound in that slow surge of excitement and despair she'd known for years.

"May I have the pleasure?" he was saying.

"Certainly, noble sir.—Why me?" she protested as they moved over the ruddy mirror of the floor.

"Why not?"

"But—then everyone'll know . . ."

"That's just my strategy. To throw them off. Not a single man has danced with his wife tonight, to my knowledge."

"How can you tell?"

"Oh, it's easier than you think. I've made a little game of it—I've identified every man here but two or three."

"And the women?"

"Ah, that's even easier!" She missed a step, lurched a little; his hand at the small of her back stiffened. In the guarded tone she hated he asked: "How are you feeling?"

"All right. A little tired."

"I wish you'd go over and see this new man, Dowe. He was trained at Johns Hopkins."

"Perhaps I will."

"I wish you would. Have you danced with old Pilchard yet? or Fahrquahrson?"

"Good grief, Courtney," she exclaimed, "I don't even know who they are . . ."

"I'll point them out for you, then." His voice was flat with sarcasm. While they danced he went on talking, about the importance of the dinner party they were giving Thursday, something she must remember to say to Colonel Swayzee; every now and then she murmured, but she had stopped listening. The band was playing "Yesterdays," a tune that could stir her to tears, and her mind drifted away, thinking of the apartment in Paris overlooking the lovely little Parc Monceau, the still, green tidelands of Chesapeake Bay, San Francisco with its brisk white salt cubes of houses running down the hills in the smoky dawn light, and beyond them the vast blue sweep of the Pacific. Yesterdays. So many lovely places; so little hope, so little joy.

She had been excited by it all at first: the new quarters, the recep-tions, the new acquaintances, the courtly formalities—like Boston graced with a southern warmth—the paternal affection of the senior officers. He did not make love to her for several evenings, and this disturbed her vaguely; when he did she was shocked by the tempestuous force of it, the mounting flood of words, hoarse cries, the frenzy that frightened even as it inflamed, the pressure of this alien flesh that burned her own, the two hands that gripped her throat, squeezing and squeezing at her life until she thought her heart would burst. What was wrong? Had he gone mad? His hands had left her throat. He was weeping now, a dry, husky groaning. Was this what men did? It couldn't be—! What was wrong?

"What's the matter?" she whispered, caught in dread. "What is it, darling?" For a time he made no reply, merely went on sobbing like a weary, frightened child, while she absently stroked his head.

". . . It's been this way," he murmured after a long silence. "I don't know why . . ."

"But what *is* it, dear? Are you in pain?" She was trembling badly herself now; she had assumed he would lead in this, as he had in everything else, and the growing silence frightened her more than the abortive lovemaking. "Are you in pain?"

"No"—he gave a tight, exasperated laugh that was like a sob—"I'm not in pain . . ."

"What is it, then? Is there anything—" she hesitated—". . . I can do?"

He shook his head wildly. "No. Nothing . . ."

Ejaculatio praecox. She had looked it up—later, much, much later—in a medical journal. A hateful, ugly phrase. She did her best; she tried to help him all she could, lent herself to all kinds of schemes—pathetic, shocking, bizarre: she forced herself to do them. For she did love him, with all her heart. She let him dress her in wild, provocative ways: she was an Indian princess, an Arab dancing girl, a Chinese courtesan. Occasionally they would succeed—such as the night he dressed her as a prostitute—but such moments were rare; she could never know. It went on and on, after the teas, the dinners, the pleasant, proper etiquette of receptions: a tense, humiliating ritual that left her whirling, dry-mouthed, quivering with a frustration that sapped her strength. Finally, one night, when she had given herself to a desperate expedient that revolted her utterly—still another occasion for failure, lying bound in mortification, strained beyond all endurance, listening to his taut, harsh sobbing, she cried: "God—think about *me! Me!* Can't you—?"

He raised his head and gazed at her with cold, implacable reproach; got up and left the room. Weeping she ran to his study. The door was shut. She asked him if she could come in. There was no answer. She tried the door; he had locked it. Softly she called to him that she was sorry, she hadn't meant it—only couldn't he see, couldn't he see what this did to *her*—? Waiting she shivered. There was only silence, an automobile horn bleating over on Pennsylvania Avenue, and the brisk, martial ticking of the clock in the living room.

After that there was much less between them. He read late, he busied himself with his work until all hours; often he didn't come in until two or three. He never needed much sleep. He was considered the best-informed junior officer on Pershing's staff, a man to watch. They entertained with lavish care—there was plenty of money for it: her money. Courtney took over more and more of the culinary specialties—he became renowned in Army circles for his salads and sauces; though he deprecated praise.

She thought: if we had a child, that would heal the breach; some of it. At first Courtney resisted the idea, then gradually relented. Early in the third year of their marriage Jinny was born—the issue of numerous patterns of revulsion, acts of coupling in which she scarcely participated. But Courtney seemed to be delighted with the baby, who was beautiful. Jinny was always a beautiful child. People never stopped remarking over it—that bright, intense, pear-shaped face with its deep amber eyes, which had so early manifested such willfulness. Where had she got it?

"No," she'd said to Jinny one day when she was three, "we don't say things like that."

The lovely little mouth had set. "I will."

"No. You won't. You are not to say it again, or I'll punish you."

Jinny had looked up at her, then, her eyes dark with that merry, defiant glare. "But I will *think* it," she said. And watching her Emily had felt a slow, cold thrill of fear. She was afraid: afraid of her own child. Inevitably she thought of *The Scarlet Letter* and Hester Prynne's daughter Pearl—also extraordinarily beautiful—whose mischievous, wanton sensuality reflected the circumstances of her birth. Was it a punishment, then? the sins of the fathers? But she, Emily, lacked the Salem woman's indomitable fortitude . . .

Gradually it was borne in on her, beyond a doubt: Courtney did not love her. He had married her for her money, her position, the Boston tradition he admired. He did not love her; he did not love anyone. Watching him with the child she saw he was incapable of love: what he offered in its place was only a voracious absorption of the object, a manipulation of responses, the involvement of the other in the circle of his own concerns. What he sought had nothing to do with love, the baring of hearts or the sharing of a particular, fragile view of this discordant world. She saw it, and despair sank inside her like a weighted corpse consigned to burial at sea.

But she could not leave him: her pride alone would not let her. To go back to Boston, the tyranny of those Sunday afternoons, the silent, musty rooms where the motes turned slowly; to pace out the frozen sarabande of Symphony, church, bookshops, the Esplanade and feel the weight of pity on every hand—no: she could not do it. And she was a

Yankee: she had chosen this life and she would stick it out; to the bitter end. Only once did she revolt—during the Battle Monuments Commission tour in Paris; a dinner party. Not a particularly important one. She didn't know why she'd forsaken it—only that the weather was so beautiful, the chestnut trees were all in blossom, the couples leaning toward each other over the café tables seemed to promise something very rare; she walked on and on, through lordly squares and gloomy battered tenements and fragrant parks until she reached a great bustling outdoor market where there were stalls filled with goblets, suits of armor, trays of medals, buttons, and old coins . . . Later she had an apéritif at a sidewalk café, watched a painter blocking in the Pont du Carrousel and a corner of the Louvre; and then for a time she just sat, footsore and still, watching the lights tremble and dance in the impenetrable slick of the river.

Courtney was waiting for her in a stark rage. "What happened? What *happened* to you—?"

"Nothing," she replied. "Nothing happened to me."

"You mean you—there was no *reason?* . . ."

"No. None."

He had seized her by the shoulder. "Don't ever do that again. Do you hear? Ever!"

She looked up at him dully. "Oh, it's not as serious as all that, is it?"

"—Listen." He was holding her against the wall with one hand; his face was white and very hard. She began to feel alarmed. "I'm going to tell you something. For your own good. Do you understand? For your own good." He was panting; the words came in short, sharp exhalations, as though he were out of wind. "When I was twelve I had a pet squirrel. I caught him in a box trap and kept him in the cellar. He was the only real friend I ever had. I taught him to come and perch on my shoulder— right here—and take a walnut out of my hand. He even let me stroke his fur. I loved that squirrel like nothing else in this world . . . And then one day he bit me. Do you understand? This squirrel—my real friend—bit me! In the hand . . . I couldn't believe it, I cried and cried—and he just looked back at me, snapping his tail . . ." His eyes narrowed until she could barely see the pupils; he gripped her coat at the throat and shook it with slow emphasis. "I'll tell you what I did. I'll tell you. I put his head in the vise on my workbench and I filed his front teeth down to the gums. And every day after school I went down to the cellar—and I watched that squirrel starve to death, surrounded by walnuts . . . Now do you understand? *Do you—?*"

She didn't know whether she did or not. She didn't know what she felt. She shut her eyes, opened them again.

"Now I want you to promise me," he was saying very slowly between his teeth. "Here and now. Right here and now. I want you to promise me—on your word of honor—that you will never do a thing like that again."

She lowered her hands. On her word of honor. She could not take her eyes from his. Down on Avenue Wagram the taxi horns sounded festive and remote . . .

An Indian Scout in a buckskin jacket and crow feathers swung by, clutching a heavy woman in a turban and pantaloons—a Nautch girl, perhaps. Courtney was talking about an argument between colonels Fahrquahrson and Metcalfe over the meaning of the Japanese blockade of the British concession at Tientsin, and she let his voice slip along the edge of her consciousness. She saw Kay Harting again, laughing wildly, dancing with a Moro juramentado naked except for a pair of loose silk trousers gathered at the ankles, his massive chest and arms laced tight with strips of bamboo. Lieutenant Jarreyl—she knew. Of course, that was what he would love to be, a Moro running amok, shrieking hate and vengeance, hashing and slashing with his bolo in an orgy of blood and destruction. His mouth was pressed against the Harting woman's throat now; she was still laughing fiercely. Watching them, Emily thought for an instant of Sam Damon—gone now, deep in the mountains of Shansi or the loess hills of Chahar or God knew where, trudging along through the stones, the blued dust. So far away . . .

Back at Leavenworth, while Courtney was enrolled at the Command and General Staff School, she had become ill. It had started innocuously enough, with migraine headaches and pains in her chest; then she began to experience difficulty in breathing, palpitations, and a recurrent vertigo that left her weak and nauseated for days. Doctor St. John treated her for Ménière's disease and the dizziness left with time, but now her arms and legs were convulsed with sudden spasms, and violent shooting pains in her head made her cry out. Doctor Silvia diagnosed it as the onset of relapsing fever; old Doctor Stannard disagreed with both of them and gave her the codeine prescription.

Then the world changed—from jagged splinters of sound caught on the tips of her nerves, the unbearable rasp of commands, the shriek of bugles that seared her flesh—changed to a soft, wool-wrapped world of gentle languor. She gave thanks, and took it regularly whenever her nerves got bad again, which was often. Time altered, slowed in dulcet, lapped meanderings; time and distance, held in a Bellini stillness. It didn't matter where she was—a bridge afternoon or a benefit or working in the garden: time held her in its arms and nothing mattered—neither Courtney's icy silences nor Jinny's devilish pranks, nor even the savage duels of will between father and daughter. In time's long domain nothing could reach her. It mattered not at all that a Democrat, and a Democratic Roosevelt at that, was in the White House, that a strutting little pouter pigeon had brought a rearmed Germany to the Rhineland, that Japan had started a bloody war of conquest in China; they happened, they were "events," but with the remote substance of a newsreel seen years later.

It was deliverance, a reprieve, and she guarded it like the most precious of jewels; she became extremely clever at walking that quivering, treacherous razor's edge between torment and withdrawal. On the occasions when she had trouble, others—like Elaine Kneeland or Tommy Damon or Mimi Metcalfe—supported her, protected her. She played the game; she got through the days, got through the still longer nights. There were no more children, no more nocturnal grapplings and shamed silences. Courtney made—as everyone had known he would—a brilliant record at the Command and General Staff School; his 201 file bore the magic legend *Recommended for High Command;* and he went out to the Islands in an atmosphere of high anticipation.

But here things had gone wrong. MacArthur had received a directive from the Chief of Staff transferring him to the States; furious, he had requested retirement—and Washington had accepted with ominous alacrity. Marshall, that quiet, plodding G-3 from the First Division and Infantry School, had been made Assistant Chief of Staff over the heads of a score of senior officers, and Courtney's Uncle Schuyler said in his last letter it was in the cards that Marshall would be Chief. MacArthur's arch rival from France! It seemed impossible.

"It can't be!" Courtney had fumed on reading the letter. "What does he mean—*in the cards?* Why, Drum has it in his hand—all he has to do is go down to Washington and take it. Or De Witt, or Rowell . . ."

Everything had gone wrong. MacArthur, his chief patron, was out of the Army, fussing around with his Philippine Reserve Army and feuding with Washington; Europe was getting ready to go to war again; everyone was lining up choice regimental commands or staff positions in the most advantageous places—and here he was, stuck at the jungle end of the world: a sitting duck if the Japanese took it into their fanatical yellow heads to attack. In a flurry of design he requested transfer to Washington, put in for the War College, wrote Pershing, Drum, Connor, Bannerman; he pumped Uncle Schuyler for news out of the Munitions Building; he had wires out in all directions. His whole career was slipping through his fingers. But who would have believed it? That dull, sour, solemn Marshall—*Chief of Staff* . . . It defied all logic, all sense!

Finally, one evening, weary of his interminable speculations and schemes, she had said: "Oh, why don't you give it up, Courtney."

His eyes had flashed at her sharply. "Give what up?"

"All this—finagling. What difference does it make? If they want you they'll call for you."

"Don't be absurd."

"Either the war will finally come along and you'll make two stars, or three, or thirty-three; or it won't, and you'll be put out to pasture."

"That's a perfectly fatuous remark. Why should I hide my light under a bushel? waiting for some mythically omniscient, divine call? That's a silly, romantic notion."

"Maybe."

"The squeaking wheel gets the grease. That's the Third Law of Thermodynamics." He smiled thinly. "Isn't it also an old New England adage?"

She said, "It doesn't seem to have helped General Hugh Drum a great deal."

"He'll get it. You'll see. He's got to get it . . . though he's going about it in the wrong way. He's pushing too hard: he's built up a climate of resentment. I don't intend to make any mistakes like that."

"Only the really big ones, Courtney."

His face became very white and long and hard. "What do you mean by that?"

"Why should it matter to you?"

"*I want to know*," he almost shouted. "Tell me!"

She put down her embroidery and folded her hands. "Like dropping Sam Damon. For one thing."

"Damon? He's ruined his career twenty times in the last fifteen years. And now crawling around in the mountains with the Reds, playing cowboys and Indians . . . he's a fool."

"Maybe."

"No maybes about it. He's going to be the oldest captain in the history of the United States Army." He snorted, watching her in amusement. "If the Age-in-Grade Bill had ever gone through they'd have had to throw him out years ago."

"Then why did you spend so much time with him last year?"

"Because I thought there might be something worth salvaging. But there isn't. He's a sentimental fool—the dangerous sort that never profits from experience. There's nobody in a position of influence who would touch him with a twenty-foot lance. Even his father-in-law's given up on him."

"How do you know that?"

"It's obvious, isn't it? If old Caldwell thought he was any good he'd have asked for him, in some capacity or other. He knows Damon's a washout, just as everyone else does."

She was angry, for no reason she could see. "You're wrong, all the same. Even though I know you're never wrong about anything." She leaned forward and said softly: "There'll come a day when you'll get down on your knees and pray for him to bail you out."

His eyebrows rose, he smiled at her. "My—that'll be a sorry day indeed."

"Yes," she said. "It will. But it will happen."

"And will he be there to save me?"

She paused. "I don't know . . ."

He had stopped smiling then, and got to his feet. "An unprofitable conversation, if ever there was one. He'll probably never come back, anyway—there's another rumor floating around that he was wounded watching an ambush of a Jap supply column; and if you get wounded in *that* neck of the woods, believe me, it's good-bye, boys, just break the news to mother."

"Does Tommy know about it?"

"No. I don't imagine so. I got it through the grapevine, from Folsom. What's the good of telling her? It would only make her more frantic."

Gazing up at him then—the handsome, lean face, faintly hawklike with its high-bridged nose and high cheekbones, his hair turning silver at the temples—her heart misgave her. She still loved him; she loved him, she feared him, she pitied and revered him—and all this mélange of feelings, balanced so precariously on the hopes and despondencies of eighteen years, brought her close to tears. She felt her chin begin to tremble; she wanted to rush to him and clasp him to her breast, crying softly that nothing mattered, nothing but the fragile affection of two lonely people who touched each other, heart to naked heart . . . but he had already turned away, was walking swiftly back along the corridor to his study. There was no way: no way to get back to anything. Bending over, blinking rapidly, she went on with her piece of embroidery, which was an old Chinese design of a dragon and a crested bird . . .

The music had stopped again, without warning.

"You might try to keep your mind on the subject for a moment or two," he was saying tersely. "Or are you too far gone for that?"

"I have had exactly three drinks since arriving at this bear garden," she answered.

"You know what I mean."

The band started again, blaring into "The Carioca," and the dancers began to leap and bounce about. Jitterbugging, they called it. She started to say something and stopped. All at once the teeming blue serge and taffeta and gold epaulets made her eyes swim. She felt dizzy, quivering, on edge.

"I've got to sit down," she said. "I feel a little tired. You go and dance."

"All right . . . You'll be careful now: won't you?"

She nodded, watched him move off into the press. A refugee from Valley Forge, with rag-wrapped feet and a scarf stained with mercurochrome wound around his forehead, came up to her. She shook her head; he turned away crestfallen, and passing by one of the long mirrors she saw that she looked very attractive in the upcurving red satin mask. Hateful, hateful! Trembling badly now, nauseated, her stomach burning again, she hurried toward the ladies' room.

"I'm telling you," Bob Mayberry said, swaying in front of the table. "If Guam isn't properly fortified and reinforced, I—I don't know what I'll do."

"Tell it to the crummy Navy," someone answered.

"No no no," Jack Cleghorne broke in, "—what we need is a standing army of two million men . . ."

"A peacetime draft!" Mayberry, who was very drunk, looked shocked. He had lost his Indian headdress during the course of the evening, and his blond hair kept falling into his eyes. "You're off your chump, buddy."

"It's going to come to that, anyway . . ."

Tommy Damon, sitting at a table in one of the adjoining rooms with the Cleghornes and Major Thompson and Courtney Massengale, listened to the argument indifferently. It was late. The unmasking had taken place at midnight to a chorus of shrieks and hoots of surprise, the prizes had been awarded, and the high rank had gone home; and the party, like all service parties, had noticeably relaxed. Biff Lanier and a short, stocky engineer lieutenant from Fort Caceres were Indian wrestling. Bill Styles, known to Fort Garfield as Mandrake, was doing magic tricks at a nearby table. The band had quit for a while and a group was gathered around the piano, singing softly in harmony.

"—gonna land at Lingayen Gulf," Mayberry was saying doggedly, one hand extended in front of him; he kept staring at it as though it might turn on him. "Three divisions, reinforced. Come straight down the valley—"

"No, they won't. That'll be a feint. The real landing will take place at Lamon Bay, and Legaspi—"

"All right, boys," Alec Thompson said mildly. "That's enough."

"True, isn't it?"

"Not necessarily. We'll stop them on the beaches if they try it."

"With what?" Mayberry demanded. "Banana *fronds—?*"

"A big air corps," an adenoidal man from Clark Field named Klaus said. "Planes, what we need. Clouds of planes. They'd never try it if we had two fighter-interceptor wings at Clark . . ."

Tommy finished her drink. Mae Lee was saying, "Honestly, I get so sick of all this strategy talk."

"Boys will be boys." Jack Cleghorne was looking at her and she made a face at him. With his slouch hat and cavalry mustaches he looked fearsome, much more masculine. Curiously, most of the women looked less imposing with their masks removed. Mae Lee, dressed as a Confederate belle, had looked mildly seductive; now, unmasked, she had reverted to her confused, ineffectual self. She was thinner and bonier, if anything, than she'd been back at Fort Dormer—she was like a child playing in cast-off grownups' clothes.

In spite of Alec Thompson's admonition the men went on talking of war, of invasion. On the brink: the world was hanging on the brink. Italy had invaded Ethiopia, Germany had invaded Czechoslovakia, Japan had invaded China, everyone under the sun had invaded Spain. It was the new international game, invasion. And here they sat, laughing and singing and playing games and talking about the CMTC as a viable cadre for a citizen army, the inadequacy of the Canal Zone defenses, the devilish intricacies of the Maginot Line, and what the Japanese were or were not going to do—

"You haven't been listening to a solitary word I've been saying," Jack Cleghorne's voice came, sonorous and plaintive, "but I don't care. Long as I can just sit here and gaze into the stagnant pools of your eyes . . ."

"You're just saying that to flatter me off my feet," she replied. "I heard every golden word."

"What'd I say, then?"

"You said . . ." She gave it up with a giggle. "Sweetie, be my hero and get me a drink."

Jack went off toward the bar. Young Tom Wilcher, fresh out of VMI, came by their table and began to argue with Mayberry. Courtney, sitting on her left side, was staring moodily out at the night, where the palms and mango trees now and then flared into shaggy, swaying masses in the distant blued dance of lightning. Wilcher was laughing, his head thrown back, his throat looking white and vulnerable. They were going to be sacrificed: all of them sitting here, drinking and chortling in their outlandish costumes. War was coming, and they would be overrun by the little yellow men with the exquisite manners and brutal, suicidal impulses. All of them. She thought with a fierce little tremor of Donny, in school up at Baguio—thrust the image away. Why in God's name had she stayed on here? She could be in San Francisco right now, or in Washington, or at Oglethorpe with Poppa if she'd chosen. What was the matter with her—did she have suicidal impulses, too?

Jack came back with her drink and she downed half of it in a gulp. The hell with it. All these years of wretched living quarters and scrimping and saving, of poor pay and no promotions—and what had he done but take it into his idiotic head to go traipsing off through the wilds of China, dodging Japanese patrols and eating rice out of the communal bowl (and doubtless picking up all kinds of nefarious diseases in the process), playing Halliburton and Lord Byron and T. E. Lawrence and Christ alone knew who else, while she sat here in the heat, waiting for it to rain cats and dogs; waiting to be captured and raped by the Japanese. Jesus God. He'd already been reported killed once and kidnaped twice. And his letters, that firm, concise hand on disheveled bits of paper, were hardly what one could call reassuring . . .

And as though the mission weren't enough, the sheer outlandish absurdity of wandering off into a perfectly barbaric land where almost no observers civilian or military had ever gone at all, to stay on for month after interminable month; in addition to being tabbed as a post Bolshevik, a guardhouse lawyer and the self-appointed messiah of the EM— in addition to all that he was going to be dubbed an eccentric, a crank, an Oriental screwball. "Poor old Damon." She could hear them in the clubs, in the regimental offices, in the bivouacs, showering down after a day in the field. "Poor old Sam. Gone off the deep end now for sure." The idiot, the idiot! She felt a hot rush of anger against him. The night air was heavy as water, still as smoke; for a long, tense moment she wanted to put her head in her arms and weep.

The band was playing again: "It's Been So Long." Jack Cleghorne told a funny story and she laughed, shaking her head. She'd had too much to drink and she didn't care. She was abandoned here on this rock, in the arms of this Great Big Happy Family, close quote—all right, then: that was all there was to it. Jack asked her to dance with him and she did, slowly, sensuously, putting her body into the beat, gliding and swaying, her eyes closed, enjoying herself; enjoying the moan and thump of the music, the bright clink of glasses and the shivery, empty laughter of girls, and under it all the sullen barrel-rumble of the approaching storm. She would let the night roll open like a play revealed, she would give herself to it, and let come what may. She danced with Court after that, then with a pilot from Clark named Prentiss, watching over his shoulder the few remaining dancers, the die-hards, the noblest of them all, who dipped and capered in the soft light. La Garde meurt, mais ne se rend pas. At the Grand Ball at the Duchess of Richmond's in Brussels they danced like this, two days before Waterloo, swirling in their gaudy circles . . .

The band had gone away again. She was at the piano, gathered around Chink Hammerstrom, singing with the others: Meadowlark Walters, with his soulful beagle eyes, who sang tenor, and Mayberry's wife Jean, and Mae Lee; and Ben Krisler, dear Ben, dressed outrageously as one of Sherman's bummers, with a torn blue uniform blouse, trousers chopped off above the knees, and a crushed top hat that had slid forward on to the bridge of his nose. He had one arm around her and one around Mae Lee, and was carrying the tune lustily.

> "Never knew the night could be so lonely and long,
> Never knew the blues would be my favorite song,
> Now I know—
> Wish I could tell you so—
> All I hear is your good-bye . . ."

When they had finished they all applauded one another.

"Oh doggone," Ben was saying sadly, "that's Sam's song. Damn it all, Sam ought to be here tonight."

"Yes, he should," Mae Lee cried. "Tommy, what would he have worn?"

"God alone knows."

"If Sam was here he'd be dressed as a Lexington farm boy with his powder horn and ramrod," Ben said.

"His ramrod!"

"Sure, his ramrod—you don't expect him to be without his ramrod, do you?"

"You've got ramrods on the brain," Meadowlark told him. His beagle's eyes opened and closed as if a child were manipulating some lever behind the lids.

"Damn right," Ben proclaimed. "I'm *never* without my ramrod. *Or my powder horn.*"

"Yes, well, you keep your powder dry," Mae Lee retorted.

"You're inebriated," Meadowlark rebuked him. "D'you know that?"

"True. But that's a lot better than being drunk."

This set them all off into gales of laughter; they swayed back and forth, their arms interlocked, paralyzed with mirth. Below them Chink kept playing blues chords, like sea bells, like horns, like lonesome prairie trains.

"I love a night like this," Ben was saying to her, his face animate and intense. "It breaks it up, shuffles all the cards. You know?"

She nodded, smiling. If I had a brother I'd want him to be Ben, she thought; and after that: And then Poppa would have had his son and I wouldn't have been named Tommy and—what else wouldn't have happened?

"If only old Sam were here," Ben was saying lugubriously. "That'd make it perfect."

"Well, he isn't," she retorted, "and it's a damned good thing."

"What?" They were looking at her, startled. "Oh, don't say that . . ."

"I will! If I want . . ." She felt all at once furious with Sam; bereft and bitter and raging.

"Don't say that, Tommy."

She laughed savagely. "Is that a direct order? or an indirect one?"

"What? No, look. No, Sam's the finest guy that ever wore the uniform of the old U S and A." Ben turned to the other men belligerently. "And I'll fight any son of a bitch here that says he isn't."

"Oh, shut up, Ben," Tommy cried. "You sound like Tom Swift!"

"—But sweetie . . ." He looked at her, blinking in consternation. Gazing angrily at his homely, bony face, the deepset, passionate eyes clouded now with hurt and confusion, she thought: He's going to die. Violently. She knew it beyond a doubt. His body shattered and eviscerated in a welter of smashed weapons and tentage and papers . . . The vision sickened her, made her still more savage; she wrenched away from him.

"Loyalty from the bottom up," she hissed at him. "I despise it, you hear?—I'm sick to death of it!" And while they watched her, goggle-eyed, she brought her hand sharply to her pelvis and cut it away, the obscene parody of a salute she remembered from her childhood at Fort Sam. "Give me—give me treachery from the *top down!*" She walked off in a fury.

"Come back," they called, pleading. "Tommy, please don't be sore . . . Tommy—hey, we'll sing 'Liza' again, just for you!"—and that almost stopped her; but she went on from room to room, bound in the perverse, black pounding of her heart. She let Mandrake, still playing magician, skillfully draw a jack of diamonds from her bodice; someone handed her a pair of dice and crouching, shaking them high over her head, talking to them softly as she knew you should, she threw; the dice rolled up against the dark, burnished baseboard and galloped back. She had another drink and got into an argument with Marge Krisler about a novel she hadn't read—and found herself without any perceptible transition engaged in a low, intense conversation with Courtney Massengale.

"Self-delusion," he was saying. "That's the leitmotif of our era. Look at our advertising, our manners, our popular songs." His face was very near hers; his eyes seemed to shift from amber to gray and back again in the splashes of scarlet and saffron light. "We have no capacity for seeing ourselves with any perspective."

"Yes," she declared. "We're a joke, all of us. And nobody sees it. Absurd—a herd of forked animals shuffling around in a maze, bumping into one another. And yet we condemn ourselves to pretending it's all one fine, long regimental review . . ."

His eyes had darkened again, he was watching her in surprise. "You see that, then," he murmured. "You really see it . . ." There was a heavier drum roll of thunder, as though the storm had just brought its biggest guns into position, and the corners of the tablecloths flipped stiffly in the gusts of wind. "That's what's unique about you—you want to plunge beneath the surface, get into the murky substance of things . . ."

"Yes," she said. "I'm sick of living on parade."

He nodded. "You want grandeur. The real grandeur, not the ruffles and flourishes that content most women. You want dimension—to measure yourself against. Don't you?"

She nodded silently. Yes, that was it: she wanted with all her heart to move—if only once!—across the greatest stage. She felt that old pull toward him, the dense surge of her blood. "A sense of windy mornings"—he'd told her she had that quality about her, long ago, the night she'd danced with Black Jack Pershing; and now here he was talking to her with an almost violent intensity about petty, undisciplined minds who succumbed to the emotional trappings of a world besotted with its own sentimentality . . .

That was fun, and strange; but nothing was quite so entrancing now as dancing with Jack Cleghorne in the dim deserted room behind the long verandah to the tune Chink Hammerstrom was playing, hunched there over the piano like a consumptive barrelhouse entertainer, a cigarette drooping from his lips, his fingers flicking darkly over the keys.

> "I wander for hours on the docks in the rain,
> Then find myself headed for France in a plane;
> My eyes fill with tears at a split of champagne—
> That's the awful trouble with love . . ."

"You're ravishing," Jack was saying in his fine, deep baritone.

"I *am*," she answered. "I *am* ravishing, aren't I?"

"Come away with me."

"All right. Where to?"

They went into a dip, he bent her back, back, the mahogany paneled walls reeled. "To Cebu. To Palamangao."

"Been there. Years ago. Centuries ago."

"Iloilo, then. I'll get rooms at the Princesa."

"Fine," she answered, "just give me time to pack an overnight bag."

"Will you, Tommy? Will you? You can take the steamer—I'll meet you there, I'll be off weekend after next."

She raised her face then and saw he was serious: completely serious. She stopped dancing. "Jack," she said. "Jack . . ."

"Oh, hell," he said. "Listen—"

"Jack, this isn't the way it's supposed to be."

"You're wonderful, Tommy, you are . . ."

"I'm not. I'm a dull, dumb bunny."

"Ever since Dormer," he murmured; his hand was broad and insistent on the small of her back. "Ever since Dormer I've dreamed of us, just the two of us, someplace off by ourselves—"

"Jack," she pleaded; she'd begun to tremble a little. "Jack, for one thing there's Mae Lee—"

"The hell with Mae Lee."

"You don't mean that. You know you don't. We'd better forget this. Jack. All right?"

"Oh, hell," he said, and dropped his hands. "God damn the bloody service—why can't we live like human beings?"

"We are: we're living like human beings. All kinds. Let's forget this, Jack. Please?"

"Sure," he muttered. "I know. All the lovely people we don't want to let down."

"Well . . ." she said lamely. "Well . . ."

"Sure. Hell, yes."

He was gone, stalking off through the long room like a scene out of John DeForest. Outside, the approaching storm muttered and rumbled; the room flared into bright daylight and vanished again, and a door bumped twice. "Not within ten miles of the post flagpole," she murmured, and laughed shakily. It was war, the threat of war that was making everyone act like this. Wasn't it? Or was it she herself, floating free and unattached through this cloistered little world? A disruptive influence—

She hurried into the next room like a freezing man moving toward a fire—stopped in the doorway to hear Klaus saying:

"Where does he think it'll get him?"

Ben turned and faced him with deliberate menace. "Oh, I'm sure he'd be a lot better off pulling wires for himself back in D.C."

They're talking about Sam, she thought with a rush of despair, of rage.

"For God's sake, Krisler," Courtney said sharply. "Think it out, will you? What concrete objective will it accomplish?"

"I don't know what it'll accomplish—the point is he's had the guts to go out there and see for himself."

"It's a matter of relative values."

"Relative values," Krisler echoed sarcastically.

"Yes. Precisely. Any idiot can figure that out for himself."

"Well, this idiot—"

"The problem is force: patterns of force. That's what determines the course of events—not hole-and-corner Jacqueries at the bleak ends of the earth. When war comes it's the grand dispositions that matter, not the picturesque little sideshows."

Ben walked up to the table where most of the others were sitting and put his fists on the edge. "When war comes," he said tightly, "Sam and I will be on our picturesque little bellies in the boondocks, that's where we'll be—and *you'll* be on the first available Clipper to Alameda . . ."

There was a sharp, stunned silence. Someone gasped; Tommy heard Marge cry, "Ben!" and then Alec Thompson's voice cutting through everything:

"Lieutenant, that is an entirely offensive remark. Insubordinate and offensive. You will withdraw it instantly."

"Is that right," Ben said. "How about—"

"Instantly!" Thompson cried in his parade voice. "You will withdraw that remark and offer apology in full to Major Massengale—or you can reply by endorsement tomorrow at oh-eight-hundred hours! Do you hear?"

Ben came slowly to attention—a fantastic scarecrow figure in the battered opera hat and sawed-off breeches: his eyes glittered in the dulled saffron light. The only sounds were a harsh burst of laughter in the bar, and the treble patter of the piano. Tommy realized she was holding her breath.

"Is that a direct order, sir?"

"Lieutenant, it is!"

"Very good, sir." Ben was standing at perfect attention now, but his eyes were blazing. "If that is a direct order—" The rest of his words were lost in an ear-splitting crash of thunder that seemed poised directly above their heads, as though the entire island had been detonated. At the same instant Court was on his feet.

"It's all right, Alexander," he said to Thompson, his voice carrying clearly on the void left by the thunderclap. "My courage has never been called in question, and I don't think it is now." Taut with dread, Tommy couldn't believe her eyes. Court was smiling!—a smile neither patronizing nor vindictive but simply benign, at ease with things. "These are days of tension. Tempers are bound to run high." He ran his eyes along the ring of silent, watchful faces. "I think we're all of us in the habit of making too hard and fast a distinction between the staff and the line. It's an outmoded position, and inadvisable. Our finest leaders have served in both capacities. Let's not forget that essentially we are one arm, all of us—and it's the strong right arm of a great nation." He paused briefly, and the smile broadened a bit more. "We've all made quite an evening of it. Let's more or less forget this, shall we?" Moving up to Ben he gave him a soft clap on the shoulder, and walked off into one of the adjoining rooms.

The group broke up then, in a flurry of release. Marge Krisler had hold of the ragged collar of Ben's GAR tunic and was saying tearfully: "Oh Ben—what's the matter with you? What kind of a thing to say is that?"

"Nothing less than the truth," he muttered.

"Now you stop! No more for you tonight. You're going home . . . Why do you have to fight with the whole blasted world?"

He looked at her somberly. "Habit, I guess . . ."

Out on the verandah the wind whistled shrilly against the screens; the bamboo awnings clashed and clattered like warriors beating their swords against their shields. Tommy leaned into the wind, breathing deeply. Sad Sam Damon. He had bewitched them all: he was a cause of friction and division even when he was two thousand miles away . . . Before her the bay lay in a deep, black void below the lights on Cavite neck and Sangley Point, which sparkled and danced like pinpoints of fire. There were no stars. Above her the acacias swept their great feathered branches up and down, and the odor of the Islands—dense in the warm, damp air—assailed her senses. She spun around in revulsion. What were they doing here, these members of the strong right arm?

"Damn you, Dewey," she muttered, "why didn't you run aground out there in Boca Grande? Why couldn't you have lost the battle of Manila Bay?" Then her father would never have had to meet the Sultan of Palamangao, and she wouldn't be wandering forlornly now along this endless verandah, the unattached female in this Great Big Happy Family; for that matter, she probably wouldn't have been walking along the colonnade at the Casino in Cannes, watching that AEF officer come toward her and say, "Pardon, Madame, mais—"

There was another titanic crash, and the gardens below the verandah leaped into visibility—a shutter-flash, jittering and silvered. The lights in the club went out. There was a murmur of surprise from the salon and then a woman's shriek of laughter. Tommy hurried back into the club, bumped into something, almost fell—she had the sensation, moving in the pitch darkness, of falling forward through space. She laughed soundlessly, her arms extended before her like a child. The lights came on and promptly went out again. The wind raged against the shutters and something fell to the floor in a shivery tinkle of glass. A voice called, and there were several answering shouts. One of the Filipino boys came running from the kitchen carrying a hurricane lamp, its flame flaring red against his white jacket, and shadows darted against the walls like savage dancers. It was really very funny. She paused in the returning rush of darkness, swaying on her feet. She was drunk, there was no doubt about that. She was drunk, it was late and she couldn't find her way back to the others. Or didn't want to. Yes. The murky substance of things; what Court had said. Why was that? She would have difficulty getting home now if she wasn't careful. Or maybe even if she was. Yes: especially if she was. There was no knowing. With this storm. A door swung shut with a crash. The rainy season was coming, with a clap of doom. Good, good! To hell with being careful. Or circumspect. Where did it get you? or anybody? The Japanese were coming ashore at Lingayen Gulf; or they weren't. Somewhere Chink was playing a frantic boogie-woogie tune and she leaped into a frenzied little dance all by herself, humming, staring wide-eyed in the dark.

> *"Head like a 'gator, nose like a yam*
> *But when she wants to boog-it, ooh! ooh! hot damn!*
> *Hey, boogie! Wiggle-waggle all the time . . ."*

A door bumped behind her; there was the sound of a step, another. She turned, saw nothing. "Who goes there?" she demanded. "Advance! —and give the boogie-woogie countersign . . ." There was no answer. She felt the flesh crawl on her shoulders and skull—and then heard herself laughing. So much the better, so much the worse. She went on dancing. She would—she would do something outrageous, something unthinkable: she decided she was going to shock the pants off that odious stuffed shirt Thompson. For talking to dear, crazy, cantankerous old Benjy that way. What would it be? Something fitting and proper for this asinine collection of toy soldiers on pa—

She gasped. A hand had seized her, then another. A huge body pressed against her. There was the sudden stench of sweat and oil and liquor— her hands encountered vast areas of flesh, slithered in an expanse of greasy muscle. Jarreyl. His face pressed against her cheek, her neck, his hands pulled at her gown, yanking and tearing.

"Come on, baby. Let's you me play. Right here, right now."

"—Oh!" she groaned. "Let me—go!"

"Sure, baby . . ."

She writhed in a spasm of revulsion. His arms were like iron; he had one hand between her legs now, the fingers pinching and grinding.

"You—beast," she panted. "Drunken—dirty—beast! I'll *kill* you . . ."

"Sure you will." He was grinning, she could tell. She jabbed her fingers into his eyes; he grunted, gripped one of her breasts so hard it hurt. In a paroxysm she drove her knee into his groin, scratching and slashing at his eyes with her nails. A chair went over in a crash: it seemed hundreds of feet away, like something falling in a tunnel. But

she was alive now, filled with energy and inventive rage—she was quite
ready to die fighting this vicious monster. How I hate him! she thought;
how I hate and despise him! It's good to hate, good to fight with hate . . .

He reached down between her legs again and she raked him twice
more across the eyes, broke away and staggered into a table, hurting her
hip. He was on her again, had seized her by the hair this time. There was
a high, flat tearing of fabric, and she thought with boundless rage: My
costume, that I slaved over for five whole days—and hit him across the
bridge of the nose with the edge of her hand. Her head snapped back
with a crack that felt as though her neck were broken; he had pinned
one of her arms against her side and was muttering, "All right, you've
had your fun, now let's go—"

"—Swine!" she shouted; but it was only a whisper. He had caught her
free arm now, was twisting it behind her. She tried to knee him again;
her arm was driven out and down with a wrench so violent she gasped
with pain—but now her left arm was freed, and she kept raking and
scratching at his eyes.

All at once he was gone—flung away violently: no hands were hurting her. She realized her eyes had been tightly shut. She opened them.
The club lights were flickering dully, a burned orange. She saw Jarreyl
go stumbling backward in a staggering fall across the room, his slick
yellow body tumbling through the tables and chairs. Courtney Massengale was standing in front of her saying:

"All right now, that's enough!"

The lights dimmed still more, rose again, flickering. Jarreyl came up
through the collapsed bridge tables and chairs, his hands slapping against
the wood, got to his feet and started toward them in a crouching rush.
She heard a click—a neat, metallic sound over the roar of wind and rain;
Jarreyl stopped, blinking. Court had a long, thin knife in his hand; he
was holding it easily, at the level of his belt, his palm up, the point
toward Jarreyl.

"All right," he repeated. "Now get out of here."

For a second she thought the stockade officer was going to fight.
Then he straightened, swaying slightly, wiping his face with the back of
one hand. Blood was streaking his nose and cheeks where she'd
scratched him. I gave him a bloody nose, she thought. Good. If I could
only have put out an eye—just one of his eyes—

"Maybe you'd like to put that knife away, Massengale," Jarreyl was
saying thickly.

Court smiled. "For a fair fight?" His voice was full of sarcasm. "Don't
be a God damn fool."

Jarreyl looked around him quickly in the gloom. "All right," he
snarled, "assault with a deadly weapon—mandatory paragraph for
courts-martial—"

"That's right." Court laughed softly. "And drunk and disorderly, felonious assault on the wife of a superior officer? What paragraph do you think *that* is?"

Jarreyl watched him sullenly, dabbing at his bleeding nose and eyelid.

"Maybe I should have worn that bolo after all."

"Maybe you should." All at once Court said with cold savagery: "Now get out of here, you filthy rummy!"

The rain was lashing the verandah behind them with a high roar. Jarreyl paused a moment longer, uncertainly; pointed to the knife. "I'll remember that," he muttered.

"So will I. Now make yourself scarce."

Jarreyl moved out of the room, padding on his bare feet, his shoulders rolling.

"Thomas?" Court was saying. "Are you all right?"

She had sunk back against a table. Her gown was torn open nearly to her knees; her neck hurt, and her arm. The lights flared up, and then went out again, but now from various rooms there was a soft yellow glow from the lamps.

"Thanks, Court," she breathed. "Oh, thank you. He crept up on me—"

"He's an animal. He ought to be put in a cage and sent to Zamboanga to scare the natives. Are you really all right?"

"Yes. No. I don't know—I'm all undone . . ."

His arm was around her, steadying her, holding her erect. "Come on. Let's get out of this. Do you have a wrap?"

"A what? No. No, I don't."

"All right." He unsnapped the catch around his throat and handed her the hussar's jacket. "Here. Put this over your head."

"My head?"

"Yes. It's raining guns."

She went out on the verandah and down the steps in a turmoil. She felt headless and stunned; her body was like a riptide in a channel, rushing back and forth, seeking outlet. She was conscious of shockingly cold air, of rain beating on her face and arms in stinging needle waves, and the plunging branches of the acacias. Then they were in his car, with the gale thundering on the roof, and sliding through the teeming spikes of rain, the wipers were going, and across the boulevard lightning flashes revealed the bay as a slate platter now, scored with a thousand silver scrolls. She realized that he was breathing heavily; his face looked harsh and agitated. Catching her eye he said sharply, "There's blood over your left eyebrow."

Numbly she wet her handkerchief with her tongue and rubbed at it, felt the faint sting of the cut. "Court?"

"Yes."

"Where's—your wife?"

"She went home," he said in a suddenly shaking voice. "You know perfectly well she went home a light-year ago . . ."

"Yes."

Then he was looking at her directly, his face white and magisterial and wild in the flashes. "My wife is no wife at all. To me. *As* you know."

She stared at him. "—I didn't," she stammered.

"*What?*"

"That is, I suspected--"

"Of course you did—why *shouldn't* you—!" he almost shouted.

"Look out," she warned, "—you're driving too fast . . ."

He glared at her again. "Do you care? Do you, really?"

"—No," she answered, "no, I don't in the least. Drive just as fast as you like." His morose, contained fury excited her. All her senses aroused from the battle with Jarreyl, the naked sexual force of it, and the taut, strange duel between him and Court, she thought, All right: I'm ready now. I'm ready for anything at all. The lashing rain, the straining featherheaded palms and booming wind had sealed them off together, gliding through the tropic darkness. When he stopped in the little grove behind her quarters and shut off the motor she thought, Maybe he'll beat me now; maybe he'll—

"Poor little grand little girl," he was saying. "Poor Andromeda. Chained to all the sad, hopeless, romantic dreams." His face was very near hers, as it had been in the club, but his expression was different—it was stamped with a fervor that shook her. "It has nothing to do with you. Nothing at all. You don't want *this* . . ." He flicked the hand resting on the wheel's rim toward the massed bougainvillea, the palms, the naked, storm-whipped bay. "All this obeisance and servitude . . . You want to change the shape of things, have them at your feet. A world at your feet."

"Yes," she said tensely, "that's what I want . . ."

"I *knew* it!" His voice was exultant and fierce. "Oh, we two, together—do you realize what we could have accomplished? Why, we could have swept the stars into a basket . . ."

"It's true." She came against him, then. She wanted it—she wanted to be possessed by him, dominated and devoured and overwhelmed. She knew she desired it with all her might. She could no more stop herself now than a man falling from a cliff into the sea.

"—not only that," he was saying, "but you have fire, and delicacy, and balance . . . Let's make a pact, you and I. A pact of—"

"Take me," she breathed. "Please. Take me now."

"What?"

"Now. I don't care. Right now." She reached up for him, curving toward him, adrift on a sea of yielding.

"No—wait," he said. His eyes were white with anxiety: he looked like a man faced all at once with an unexpected and fearsome choice.

She gazed at him in wordless consternation. He had withdrawn a little, stiffly—he was saying: "You don't understand—it's not that at all, that's no answer—" The corner of his mouth twitched faintly once. "You don't understand at all . . ."

Staring at him, watching his eyes, she began to understand. She was flooded with rage, with mortification and disgust.

"—You bastard!" she cried.

"No, now wait—" He raised the hand resting on the wheel, as though to ward off her anger. His eyes were full of fear now; she could see it clear as day. "You've misconstrued what I've been saying . . ."

"—I've misconstrued nothing! Not a damned thing! . . ." If she'd had a weapon in her hands at that instant she would have tried to kill him. "I understand—all too well!" She was still trembling; her eyes filled in spite of herself. "Oh yes, I understand—don't you think I don't!" It was all clear to her now, what no one—not Fahrquahrson or MacArthur or the AG's office or the Chief of Staff—knew about Courtney Massengale. She knew: but the cost, the *cost* of knowing—!

She pushed open the door, and her right arm and shoulder were immediately drenched. He reached toward her, saying, "Thomas, look, you don't—"

"No!"

"*Tommy*—"

"No! I said *no!* No more!" She yanked the hussar's jacket off her head and shoulders and flung it in his face. "You dirty—oh God, oh God, you—*coward!* . . ." His hand caught at her shoulder now, but she twisted away from him and leaped out into the rain, caught her heel on the running board and felt it snap off. She turned, frantic with confusion and despair. Rain was streaming in her eyes, pelting her—a chill, aqueous burden. He was staring out at her, motionless, his face drawn and hard, his eyes narrowed to slits. His mouth curved down at one corner, she could see it in the faint emerald glow from the dashboard. To do this to someone!—someone you'd known and liked, seen from day to day—

She whirled around. Holding her torn gown together, coolly sobbing, limping on the heelless shoe, she ran through the rain.

The cargo net rippled and swayed, the forty-foot launch far below lifted and yawed away, straining against its lines. The men descended gingerly, crablike, their rifle butts now and then catching in the rope strands. Someone below him swore and looking down, Damon saw Tellerman gripping a fist and glaring upward.

"*Vertical* strands," he called, "grip the verticals. You know better than that." Well, cargo nets were not the answer—their six-sided weave was no good for this. What they needed was a perfectly square webbing, so no one would be tempted to grab the cross strands and get a boot on his fingers. Below him, nearer now, the launch lifted and sank rhythmically, and he watched it through his knees, timing the surge. He caught up to Millis, who, his head craned, was looking nervously down.

"Your belt, Millis," he said.

"What?"

"Your belt should be open."

"Oh—I forgot, Major."

"So I see." The boy glanced at him in distress, not wanting to let go with either hand, and Damon said crisply: "Never mind it now. You're holding up the show. Come on and get in the boat."

He timed the launch, caught it on the top of the rise and jumped; the fall made his feet sting. Lieutenant Feltner was saying, "Come on, you people, move up now, give 'em room," and Damon followed the general movement toward the bows. The lift and fall of the launch against the ship's iron side was mesmeric. It certainly looked like more than a three-foot rise. Down here, low over the water, the breeze was fresher; clear and cold.

"Just *breathe* that ocean air," a voice crowed beside him. Jackson, thin as a rail, his handsome, lantern-jawed face creased in delight.

"All set, Jackson?" Damon asked him.

"Just straining at the barrier, Major."

"That's the pitch."

Boretz was watching both of them distastefully. His face was rigid and the knuckles of his hand clutching the gunwale were white. This was stupid: every man ought to know how to swim and swim well. The marines insisted on it and they were right. If you fell overboard you still might drown before you got rid of your pack and rifle, but you might not; and at least you'd have some confidence about saving yourself.

They cast off, easing away from the bulging gray wall of the ship's side, and the swells caught them unfairly, rocking the boat like a big, ungainly cradle. Millis, three men behind him, was swallowing, the tip of his tongue protruding from his mouth. Off to the east a row of oil tanks squatted like totems to a new mechanical race of gods, and beyond them the dunes, where they were to land, rolled and broke in low saffron hillocks. Damon looked at his watch. Eight seventeen. Men were still creeping down the nets and dropping into the boats; clumsy, shaggy birds falling out of a tipped nest. The white cloth bands on their helmets made them look bizarre, like some medical detachment.

"We going to reach the line of departure on schedule, sir?" Lieutenant Feltner asked; he was a slight man with the face of a harassed clerk, and the complexities surrounding this enterprise overawed him.

"Not a chance in a million, Ray," Damon answered cheerfully.

Sergeant Bowcher, overhearing them, snorted. An old regular who had served nearly everywhere, he turned his flat, brick-red face toward the ship in disapproval. "Ought to be wider nets. Then the launches could come alongside in series—five, six of 'em."

"Ought to be a lot of things," Damon said.

Bowcher snorted again. "Think we'll fool 'em any?"

"Wouldn't be surprised. If they're as fouled up as we are, we can't miss."

Bowcher grinned and shook his head; Lieutenant Feltner looked shoreward anxiously. They were part of the first joint amphibious maneuvers ever held in divisional strength—an operation already marked by confusion, mountainous paperwork, and interminable wrangling with the Navy, who had stonily insisted they had neither the ships nor assault facilities. As executive officer of Third Battalion, 477th Regiment, Damon was taking a company and supporting units ashore in a diversionary feint to draw defenders away from the main landing on Monterey Beach, east of the commercial pier. They'd had eighteen days' training but it was not enough—not nearly enough. A Marine Corps colonel named Buckman had told them amphibious assault was the most difficult of all operations—except amphibious withdrawal, which was even worse—and it was easy to see why. There were a hundred thousand problems: combat loading of the vessels, debarkation of troops to the landing craft, the weather, hitting strange beaches without fixed positions—

"How long are we going to be at this?" Millis asked no one. "All this rolling around?"

"That's what she said," Jackson retorted, "when the bed broke." There was a chorus of laughter, and someone said:

"Join the Navy, and be a frog . . ."

They hung in the swells, wallowing and sinking. Millis was sick all over his jacket and the pack of De Luca the radio operator, who swore at him.

"—Sorry, Vinnie," Millis croaked feebly, wiping his lips. "Real sorry."

"You stupid bastard. How'm I going to get that off?"

"Didn't know—it was going to happen."

"Next time put your head over the God damn side . . ."

They had trained for several days on the float at Lake Hadley, using wooden pontoon boats. But the lake had been calm; the reflections of the tall pines had hung in the water like green glass. Here the wind was biting cold—now and then the spray lashed them lightly; the raw, greasy fumes from the boat's engines made them all cough. Three planes went over, Navy fighters in a tight, fat clump, heading toward Point Piños.

"What the hell are we waiting for?" Dougherty demanded.

"For you to start puking!" Jackson yelled at him, laughing.

The coxswain, a tall man in a pea jacket standing at the raised platform at the stern in front of a canvas screen, called something, and the motors roared; Damon saw him shove his hip against the snakelike pipe of the tiller. The assault waves had formed now, raggedly. Eight forty-two. Not too bad. The launch, moving with the wind and waves, had fallen into a tight, slewing motion that was exhilarating at the same time it made him feel queasy. Starker, a sergeant and ex-merchant seaman, was watching him slyly to see if he was going to be sick. What a boot for the Battalion that would be—old Sad Sam, the Night Clerk, the hiking fool, flashing his hash all over the command! He took several slow, deep breaths, gritted his teeth and grinned back at Starker, who all at once looked rather green around the gills himself.

"Hoo-eeeee!" Jackson yelled. "Ya-hoooeeeee!"—a piercing, racketing rebel yell that had half a dozen of the men grinning.

"All right, Jackson," Lieutenant Feltner called, but without force.

They swept on, the sunlight dazzling on the water, the winter air fresh and bitter, smelling of salt and old iron. To the west the pine hills behind Monterey lay in a dense feathery green, and off to their left Mount Toro rose up gray and gaunt and sere, like the hide of a wolf. The beach, far away, looked pure white. Here and there the morning sun flashed in the windows of houses along Alvarado Street like mirrors tilted. Idyllic. An idyllic place to hold a landing exercise. Japanese infantry might be looking at it from this vantage point, someday. Would they? It was possible; just possible . . .

Little black puffs bloomed from back of Del Monte Heights, and Sergeant Bowcher pointed and said: "Spotted us." Damon nodded. Simulated artillery. While he watched, a TBF came low along the shore, smoke belching from its tail in a pretty white rolling plume that spread and thinned, churning on itself. They were swinging off to the east now, running at an angle to the shore, racing on the blue water, pitching and rolling. His arm was tired holding to the gunwale. Millis was sick again, bent over, retching between his knees. My God, he thought, that boy must have eaten five breakfasts this morning. Now Boretz beside him was sick, and Martinez; it was catching. Ahead of them the smoke was breaking into rifts and snatches, torn by the wind, and through it he could catch glimpses of the oil tanks. They were nearer now, much nearer; he could make out the scaling ladders running up their sides. Here and there stands of eucalyptus were visible, looking ragged and yellow against the pines.

There was a shout; he looked aft. The Navy chief in the well below the tiller platform held up three fingers. Three hundred yards. Sergeant Bowcher raised his head and roared: "All right. Load and lock! Load and lock!" Damon watched the platoon fumble with the clips of blank cartridges, their rifles clashing against each other as the boat dipped and swayed. This would need rehearsing, too.

Now he could see the surf. It looked heavy—wide, frothy fans sweeping up the beach and sliding away again; a ponderous, looping motion, hidden by the next grainy, emerald shoulder of breaker. They clearly hadn't been expecting anything like this in the operations room at six this morning. Feltner was shouting some instructions to Sergeant Bowcher and he gripped Boretz's arm and called: "Keep a good grip on that lifeline when you go over the side. Along the gunwale. Here!" Boretz and Millis both nodded; they were looking at him as though he'd just asked them to jump into a cauldron of flaming oil. "And your rifle *high*—over your head!"

The launch lifted more steeply now, pitching, the slick combers sliding past at the gunwale's edge and dropping astern. The coxswain shouted something, and the sailor in the bow leaped up on the stem, a mooring line coiled in one hand. They lifted wildly, set down with a thud that jarred their spines, lifted again. The seaman was gone. Damon glanced aft once more, saw the chief's arm shoot up. Sergeant Bowcher was roaring over the dense thunder of the surf, "Over—you—*go!*"

Damon flung himself up and over, pivoting on his left arm. The water took him like a million fiery needles and he gasped—he had no idea it would be this cold. His feet hit solidly, then went out from under him the next instant as a wall of water swept over his head. Damn. This was more than they'd bargained for. Gripping the rope he let the surge carry him toward the bow, remembering with an almost giddy gratitude Colonel Pearson's insistence on the installation of lifelines on all launches, much to the disgust of the Navy. Something struck his thigh; he turned, saw a hand with a rifle moving abreast of him, not five feet away, then nothing, then a legginged foot spin into view. He lunged out, hanging onto the line, reached into the swirling white froth and clutched something—an intrenching tool, then an arm; hauled the figure up by main strength. Millis, his mouth gaped wide, eyes rolling frantically. They slammed back upon the bow; the boy came against him with a rush that banged their helmets together like dulled cymbals. Millis was gripping his neck and shoulder in a paroxysm. Damon laughed in spite of himself. "Stay with it now! Keep your mouth closed! . . . Get a drink?"

Millis went into a fit of coughing, wagging his head. "—*Terrible!*"

Damon laughed again. "Hang on to that rope!" He grabbed another man named Reidy and pulled him back to the boat's side. The power of the surf was astonishing: it had the ponderous, irresistible force of earth moving, of a landslide. He caught hold of the mooring on the next surge, struggled forward—went to his knees in the undertow, got up and ran out on the flat beach. The sailor on shore, minus his white hat, was pulling with all his might on the painter. Looking back he saw a dozen men in the water, clinging to the lifeline, not moving; with their tin hats and glaring eyes they looked like a row of kids hiding under some basins.

"Come on!" he roared; he couldn't keep from grinning. "Get going now, come on! It won't get any easier . . ."

Two other boats were ashore. Another had broached and was rolling dangerously, its whalelike underside looking raw and vulnerable. Once out of the water it was easy: the sand was a light tawny color, hard as clay baked in the sun—nothing like the Atlantic beaches. The platoon was coming ashore now, sinking and swaying in the surf, bunched on the mooring line or floundering in the water like drunks trying to find their way home; the launch rocked and banged cruelly, the helmsman fighting the tiller, trying to keep her from broaching. There was a better way to do this; there had to be. If there were enemy infantry in those dunes—if there were only two machine guns—they would all of them be dead or drowned by now . . .

He ran up the beach, shivering, glad of the exercise, the delicious freedom from the massive dragging weight of the water. Up ahead he could see four, five men running swiftly. There was no sound of firing. Good. Or possibly it was a trap. To his right he could see Cavallon and DiMaestri and several others milling around and talking to one another excitedly: they had just braved the terrors of the deep, and now they wanted to exchange tales of comfort and glory.

"Starker!" he shouted, catching sight of the Sergeant. "Get those men going! What are they waiting for—champagne?" Making a fist he pumped his arm rapidly up and down. Jesus: what would they do in the real thing?

He loped through a gap in the dunes, where pebbles winked like onyx jewels in the sunlight. His teeth were chattering but his body was warming up and he ran hard, feeling in high spirits after all the paper work and delays. Millis was scampering along beside him, and Braun, the runner, and two others; and he winked at them solemnly.

Emerging from the cut, he paused. The ruined granary, or warehouse or whatever it was supposed to be, was nowhere in sight. They'd been put ashore too far east. Up ahead he could see Lieutenant Feltner and two other men lying prone in a manzanita thicket at the top of a dune; their fatigues were slick and black with sea water. While he watched, Feltner gave the hand signal for *take cover*, and one of the others rolled over on his back and gingerly raised his rifle above his head with both hands. *Enemy in sight*. Damon frowned. Too bad. Well, it was probably to be expected. He remembered old Joe Stilwell at Benning, the lean, ascetic face, tart and professorial, the shrewd little eyes behind the steel-rimmed spectacles: "Strategical surprise in an opposed landing, gentlemen, is extremely difficult to accomplish, as air and surface scouting can be carried out a long distance to seaward, and may very well result in the premature discovery of an approaching expeditionary force. *Tactical* surprise, however—as regards the commencement of operations against a particular beach on a particular time—is often possible. And every effort—repeat, *every effort*, gentlemen—should be made to effect it."

Now they'd lost it. Well, at least they might be able to siphon off some of Atkins' people opposing the main landing.

But the curious thing was there was still no firing.

He worked his way up to the top of the dune, dropped down beside Feltner, pulled out his map, wiped his field glasses against his shirt and peered through the tortured black stems of the manzanita. Yes, there were the railroad tracks, the eucalyptus grove, the two buildings marked on the map, the broken wall, and just beyond the tracks the old road from Seaside. He could see no movement—he was about to turn impatiently to Feltner when a man stepped out of the shadows of the grove, an officer, raised a cigarette to his lips. For a moment he peered west, toward the main landing, where small-arms fire now crackled briskly; then he turned and Damon saw the wide red band on his left arm. Behind him, half-hidden in a clump of scrub oak, stood a motorcycle and sidecar; the flag orderly squatted beside it, waiting. He sighed with relief.

"Umpire," he said to Feltner, who peered through his own glasses with a harried, drawn expression.

"Oh yes. I'm sorry, Major. I didn't see it—I just saw him moving. Jackson here spotted him."

"That's all right. Better to be safe than ruled out." He turned to Jackson. "See anybody else, Hawkeye?"

The Kentucky boy studied the buildings, the grove, the rise beyond it. Damon followed his glance, saw it pause on a ground squirrel, move on again. "Nary a soul," he murmured. "Except for the feller with the scooter."

"Good." Damon got to his feet. "We're wasting time. Let's go on down there." Turning to Sergeant Bowcher he said: "Wave them all on up, on the double."

"Yes, sir."

He hurried down the slope to the clump of deserted buildings. The eucalyptus trees smelled of smoke and urine and beeswax, an alien but not unpleasant odor. As the men came up he deployed them. He had two squads fill the breaks in the old wall with dead brush and placed the BAR teams there, set up his machine guns in the bushes on each flank, and sent out scouts in both directions along the edge of the road. The umpire, a lieutenant colonel with a tired, lined face and a taffy-colored mustache, watched him silently. He nodded once, went on giving orders.

"Now if anything comes along that road I don't want any firing or rebel-yelling or anything else," he told Bowcher and Starker and several other NCOs. "No one will fire except on command. Pass the word.—Where's De Luca?"

"Right here, Major."

"Get on that box of yours, Dee. Get me HATCHET. Quick as you can." The boy bent over the black bulk of the portable radio, fiddling with it. There was no sound. "What's the matter?"

"Can't get them. Can't get anything . . ." De Luca looked up angrily. "It got wet when we came in. These lousy 131s, I tell you, Major—"

"All right," Damon cut him off. "Keep at it. —Braun!"

"Yes, sir."

"Get back to the main landing. Your best bet is double back to the beach. Find Colonel Wilhelm or Colonel Westerfeldt and tell them I have reached the old Seaside Road unopposed and am dug in, interdicting all White movement. I am also in a position to exploit the left flank of Del Monte Heights through Torre Canyon and Hill 83."

"Yes, sir." Braun turned to go.

"Wait a minute. Repeat that back."

Braun stared at him. He was a quick, eager boy, with a good eye and fine stamina, but he was shivering from the Pacific and visibly nervous. "What, sir?"

"I said: repeat back to me what I've just told you."

Braun got the first part right, the second part wrong. The usual pattern.

"No," Damon said patiently. "I'll say it once more and then I want you to give it back exactly." He repeated the message while Braun hung on his words, his mouth open. This time the boy got it right and Damon smiled.

"That's the pitch. Take off, now. Speed is important."

He made some other dispositions. The radio sputtered and roared for a moment, then went out again, while De Luca cursed at it. He studied the map with Feltner and Captain Booth. The sound of firing drifted up to them from the main landing, punctuated with the thump of artillery from the White forces. It was going to take too long. Far too long, with a runner. It was a difficult decision. He could leave a token force here—a machine-gun squad, say—and push on inland; he could bend south and west to hook up with the regiment; he could stay where he was. Part of him wanted to push off for Del Monte; but if the Whites were to take it into their heads to come up that road in force . . .

The umpire was gazing at him—a steady, piercing gaze that held just the faintest suspicion of a smile at the corners of his mouth. He felt a rush of irritation, thrust it aside. He looked at his watch. Nine twenty. Was that all? They'd hardly got ashore. No: it would jeopardize too much to leave the road lightly held. The beachhead had to take priority. It was a great chance, a tremendous chance; but he would have to pass it up. The umpire had opened his notebook and was making some notations, biting on his mustache. Damon wondered what he was writing, then forgot about it, looking around. All eyes were on him. One word from him—one word!—and this supine, cleverly concealed configuration would leap to its feet and dispose itself in columns, in ranks, in skirmish lines . . . He sighed. The sun felt warm in the grove. This would be a lovely spot to live if it was this sunny and warm in January. A place to retire, maybe; when the hurly-burly's done, when the battle's lost and—

He started. Jackson, on the slope to his right, was pumping his rifle frantically up and down. He signaled back. "All right," he said, his voice loud in the quiet. "Enemy in force, coming up the road. You will fire only on command."

Horses. Cavalry, coming up the road at a fast trot. A full troop. He ran his eyes over his command: they were perfectly quiet, staring ahead over their weapons. A maneuver, an exercise, but there was nevertheless a faint swelling in the throat, that old, thick pulsing of the blood. Rodriguez at the machine gun near him was grinning, his eyes slitted. Damon wondered where he'd seen that look before, couldn't remember. He watched the troop approaching, bobbing along. Damn fools. Walking right into it. He waited until they were within a hundred yards or so and said crisply:

"Open fire."

The sudden uproar of blanks was deafening. The lead riders reined up, milling; then one of them raised his pistol and all at once they were charging, coming straight down the lane of disintegrating macadam and weeds. Damon heard himself exclaim: "For Christ sake—" The machine guns clattered away, the loaders feeding the belts smoothly. The cavalry was rushing nearer, as if borne on the cool wind—fifty yards, thirty, at full gallop, a fearsome onslaught: they looked enormous, full of might; the pistols winked brightly here and there against their mass. Two men jumped up from their places by the wall. "Halsman! Brien!" he roared at them, "—get down!"

And then they were on them—a thundering, howling legion. Damon had one last glimpse of the flag orderly wildly waving a huge white flag and Rodriguez still grinning, intent, rocking the gun's muzzle upward—and then men and horses were everywhere, leaping over the wall, wheeling and dancing, spraying sand in their faces. Damon jumped up, shouting angrily, heard a whistle shrill in sharp bursts: three, four times. The umpire was standing upright in his sidecar, pointing at several horsemen.

"No, you don't! Halt your command," he shouted. "Halt your command!"

There were now several fights going on inside the wall. Two infantry men had pulled a trooper from his horse and all three were rolling in the dirt; another soldier was sitting down holding his shoulder.

"All right," Damon called, going over to the combatants. "Break it up, now!" Sergeant Bowcher was pulling them apart. Another infantryman was crawling away through a perfect forest of horses' legs.

The troop's captain, a tall, wasp-waisted man with black mustaches and a thin hooked nose, shouted some commands, danced up to the umpire and saluted. "Murdoch, Troop C. I shall accept their surrender."

"You will not," the umpire retorted. "I'd say it's very much the other way around."

The Captain stared down at him. "What's that you say?" Horses were still milling all around the buildings. Bowcher had broke up the fist fight, and the dismounted trooper was looking for his horse. "These people," the cavalryman demanded, "—what the hell are they doing here, anyway? Way out here?"

"Let me read you something, Captain." The umpire took a piece of paper out of his blouse pocket and unfolded it. "Quote. The Orange Forces will execute a diversionary feint in conjunction with the main landing at oh-eight-thirty hours in the vicinity of the Oliveira Farm, with the end in view to securing their left flank and interdicting the superseded Monterey-Seaside Highway." He replaced the paper. "This force has been deployed here for nine minutes."

The troop commander scowled. "Very well. We've overrun them."

"I think not. In point of fact, Captain, you've been all but wiped out." He opened his notebook. "I am ruling that you have just sustained eighty per cent casualties."

"*Eighty!*" The troop commander struck his thigh. "That's preposterous . . ."

"Is it? Where was your route security? You came up that road at a fast trot without outposts or point. Why, Captain? Look at Orange's field of fire, look at his automatic weapons." He pointed to the gun positions, the gunners, dappled in the sparse shade of the eucalyptus trees. "I am forced to rule that your troop is eliminated as an effective fighting force."

The Captain swore, glaring at the umpire, then at Damon. "It wouldn't have happened like this in a real combat situation, I can tell you that . . ."

"No," the umpire said quietly, watching him. "You'd have just murdered one hundred and fifty good men."

The Captain swung his horse around in a fury. "All right," he snapped, "—what do you want with us now? What do I do?"

Damon stepped up to him. "One moment, Captain. Your mount, please."

"Eh?" Murdoch looked as if Damon had asked him for his breeches.

"Dismount your troop, please. We want your horses."

"*What?* That's insane—what do you want with them?"

"We're going to ride them."

"You're going to—?"

"That's right. Ride them."

The Colonel sat down on the sidecar and began to laugh, bent over, his hands on his knees.

"Sir," Damon said. "They're ours. I need them."

"That's rot!" Murdoch shouted. "I appeal this—Colonel, I appeal this!"

The Colonel finally stopped laughing and looked up at the cavalry-man. "The Orange commander is within his rights. Dismount your troop. They're his—if he wants them."

"Now, wait!" Murdoch protested. "That's out!—if we're dead so are our mounts . . ."

"Not necessarily. I rule"—the umpire made a quick little notation—"that forty-five horses are unwounded and recoverable by the Orange forces."

"All right," Damon called. "Who can ride? Who's ever been on a horse? All who can ride step forward."

There was a great commotion. Soldiers climbed into the saddles, laughing and calling to one another, while the dismounted troopers glared at them.

"This is more like it, Major," Jackson said. "Riding in style . . . Where to?"

A powerfully built private named Stankula was lying half across a saddle, his legs flailing in the air; Bowcher and Chip Booth were laughing at him wildly.

"Stankula," Damon said, "you're from Brooklyn—you've never been on a horse in your life."

Stankula grinned, still struggling ineffectually. "Ain't anything to it, is there? Just climb on and stay on."

Damon laughed. "All right. Someone show him how. If he falls off, he stays off.—Hines, I want you to hold here, with the machine guns. Set up a two-way block in case of any retreating White forces."

"Right, Major."

He swung into the saddle of Murdoch's mount. The umpire called to him: "Major, I am ruling that you have sustained two per cent casualties. Your orders, please."

"Oh. Yes. I am detaching my weapons platoon to hold a block on the road. With the remainder of my command I propose to advance, mounted and on foot, via Torre Canyon and Pilarcitos Ridge to Hill 83, flanking Del Monte Heights."

"I see." The Colonel jotted something down in his notebook. "Very well. De l'audace, toujours de l'audace . . ." Laughing he went over to his umpire-circuit field jack. "Good luck, Major."

"Our team is red—hot," Colonel Westerfeldt chanted. Standing in the center of the tent he did a shuffling two-step, slapped his belly lightly and repeated: "Our team is red—hot!" He was a big man with a heavy, bearlike body and a full, genial face and was easily the most popular officer in the division. "Collins!" he shouted.

A thin, dark-haired soldier stepped inside the tent flap and said: "Sir?"

"You found Colonel Wilhelm yet?"

"No, sir."

"Well, keep at it. He's got to be around here somewhere. Doubt if even Dutch took off before we secured the problem." Turning back to Damon and Lieutenant Colonel MacFarlane he struck a sententious, martial pose. "Now I called you gentlemen over here for a very important conference. Yessir." Bending over a chest at the foot of his cot he took out a handsome leather case, unfastened half a dozen straps and extracted a bottle and four nested brass cups. "The time has come, the walrus said, to talk of many things: of flanks and mounts and landing boats, and looping double wings . . ." He cocked an eye at Damon, who grinned.

"Pretty damn clever, Westy," MacFarlane said; he was short and powerfully built, with a low forehead and square, bulldog face. "Is that a Westerfeldt original?"

"It is. Thought it up only this noon. I think it's pretty good myself." He rose with a grunt. "Alice says I'm getting fat. That's insulting, by God. Sam, am I getting fat?"

"I've never seen you looking thinner, sir."

They all laughed and Westerfeldt cried: "Ah-ha! That's a two-edged thrust, I perceive." His fine blue eyes twinkled with amusement. "After all, look at old Hunter Liggett—he went all the way up to army command on two hundred and forty pounds. By God, his luncheons! They were the talk of the First Corps. Remember?"

A young second lieutenant named Chase entered the tent, and paused.

"Yes?" Westerfeldt said. "What is it, Hank?"

Chase saluted. "It was that report you wanted on those poison-oak cases, sir." His eye fell on the bottle and cups. "I'm sorry, sir. I'm intruding—"

"Nonsense! Come on in and sit down. You're in luck. We're just about to pour a libation to the god of army landing exercises." Standing at the folding table he filled the cups with care, and handed them to the other three. "Hank, you can have one, too."

"Thank you, Colonel."

"I believe in coincidence and timing. If Colonel Wilhelm comes in though, you've got to give yours to him." He raised his cup. "Here's love and luck," he said; he drank and licked his lips. "I want to tell you: General Bonham was by here a little while ago. He's very pleased, very pleased indeed." He rubbed his broad, fleshy nose, chuckling. "Couldn't get over that escapade of yours, Sam. He's an old Redleg, you know—tickled him pink and purple to see the horse arm discomfited."

"That was certainly a stroke, Sam," MacFarlane said.

"You made the God damn maneuvers," the Colonel went on, "that's all you did. Watch 'em change the rules about the capture and use of enemy mounts . . . You never were with cavalry, were you?"

Damon grinned. "The closest I ever got to a horse in line of duty was currying mounts at Early in '16."

"That's what I thought. How'd you ever get the idea?"

"I don't know, Colonel. It just popped into my mind." He took another sip of his drink. Was that true? Yes, substantially—there had been his anger at Murdoch's stupidly and vindictively leading that charge, knowing he was rushing blank ammunition, and all that milling around inside the wall—and out of it the idea had come . . . Half an hour later they'd taken Hill 83 from a somnolent, astonished battery; and the fat had been in the fire. Atkins, terrified at this sudden hole in his right flank, had panicked, committed his reserve in two futile assaults on the hill, suffering immense losses. After that he'd steadied down and fought a skillful delaying action out toward the Reservation; but by then he'd had nothing left. Only the umpires' decision to conclude the problem had saved the Whites from an annihilating double envelopment. And all for the want of a horseshoe nail . . .

"—I wish it was still going on," Chase was saying to Westerfeldt in his high, clear voice. "The problem, I mean."

"Why's that, my bucko?"

"Well, you learn so much from carrying things out. It stops being theoretical."

"All right." The Colonel heaved himself to his feet and going over to the map board pulled the piece of cheesecloth from it. "Tell you what: the problem's still going on. It's fourteen hundred hours and you're in command. What do you do?"

The boy went up to the map. "Well, I'd send Third Battalion along the road there, behind the beach—"

"Wrong!" Westerfeldt picked up his cup and drained it. "White's artillery still commands that stretch and there is virtually no concealment for two hundred-odd yards. Right, gentlemen?" The two battalion commanders nodded assent. "Persist in that course, my bucko, and you'll collect an ass full of arrows."

"Oh no, wait—Major Damon's force," Lieutenant Chase said.

"Now you're talking. What do you want to do with them?"

"Well, I'd send them wide around Hill 107, here, and then wheel left through this stand of oaks."

"Splendid!" The Colonel beamed at him. "Only thing—these little wavy lines, here. See 'em? That's a steep climb, hand-over-hand, uphill. You wouldn't get very far . . . Aside from that, your plan is masterful."

There was a deep, sustained groan from under the table and Westerfeldt leaned down and began to scratch an enormous dog under its loose jowls. "Hello old Pompey boy," he said. "Hey is that old Pompey boy is

he hey old rough-and-rugged trooper boy. Ready for anything. Is he
now." Grinning down he scratched its scruff. "He's all footsore and
weary from all the heavy campaigning. Yessir." The animal dropped his
shaggy head on his front paws and sighed. "By the way, gentlemen,
General Bonham requests the pleasure of our company—and stuffed
wallets—for poker this evening. Not you, Hankus," he said to young
Chase. "Your face, I regret to say, lacks the necessary guile for the deed.
That comes, however, with age." He chuckled richly, and poured them
all another drink. His full, genial face with its Roman nose and rounded
jaw made him resemble one of the last of the Bourbons, chaffing a
young courtier in the privacy of his own chambers. "Look at Major
Damon: the devil himself doesn't know what's going through *his*
mind . . ."

"It's the truth," MacFarlane said with his quick, blunt laugh. "Sad
Sam. He looks asleep half the time."

"Yes—and all the while he's scheming up a way to beat you. Slats
Hatcher down at Gaillard told me you had the spittingest, raunchiest
company he ever saw on Luzon. Said they'd have flapped their arms and
jumped off the barracks roof if you'd asked them. How'd you do it?"

"They were a good outfit," Damon answered.

"Oh hell, don't kid a kidder, Sam. There's more to it than that."

Damon grinned. "Well—God knows I had enough practice at the
company level."

The others laughed and Westerfeldt said, "By gar, that's the truth.
How'd you feel giving up all that time-in-grade just to become the
youngest major in the whole game?"

"I was willing to make the exchange, sir."

"I'll bet you were. I've been around this man's army for a long, long
time—and I've yet to see a man turn down either a promotion or a
decoration. Yessir. *Four things greater than all things are—Women and
Horses and Power and War.* Who said that, Chase?"

The Lieutenant blinked at him—said quickly: "Tennyson, sir?"

"*Wrong!* One more mistake today and we'll have to make you
laundry officer. You won't like that very much, will you?"

"No sir, I won't."

"Tennyson! Is that what they teach you kids these days?—Kipling,
Henry my boy, *Kipling*— he knew more about soldiering than all the rest
of them combined. More about a lot of other things, too . . ." The
Colonel got to his feet and stretched arduously. "Well, I don't know
about you gentlemen, but I for one am going to shower down and get
spruced up, and then I'm going over to pay my respects to Wee Willie
Atkins and see if I can cheer him up a little. He must be mighty cast
down right about now. It'll be Canton Island for Wee Willie for sure.
Or maybe Ascension." He finished his drink. "And then how's for some
golf, Mac?"

"Raring to go," MacFarlane answered.

"All right. Soon as I get back we'll go over. Sam, how come you never learned to play golf?"

"I guess I just never seemed to find the time for it, Colonel."

"You should have. Why with your baseball swing, you'd be a natural. They've got a course over there at Pebble Beach that's a thing of beauty and a joy forever.—You won't forget tonight now, will you, Sam?"

"I'll be there, Colonel."

His own tent was empty. Standing at its entrance he watched through his glasses the confused bustle at the pier, where they were still unloading the trucks and supplies. To the right, a thousand yards down the beach, where the main landing had been, a group of sailors and engineers were gingerly trying to ease a bulldozer down the ramp from boat-rig A perched on the bow of a fifty-foot launch.

Abruptly he went over to his cot, pulled a pad out of his dispatch case and started writing without pause.

Dear Dad:

Well, we got through it—more or less. That is to say we got the troops ashore, and some of the artillery, and a few of the tanks. But we had four near drownings, and ½ doz minor injuries. The surf, while heavy, was not prohibitive: I can imagine occasions when it would be substantially worse. And I'd hate to imagine what would have happened if a few of von Boehn's machine gunners had been dug in there along the dunes, behind a lot of wire. In fact, I don't need to imagine. Simulated conditions, they say. Sure, of course—but the trouble is that too much of it is simulated: the whole damned operation is so far removed from hard-and-fast actualities it borders on the fantastic.

To begin with, soldiers ought to know how to swim. There are a dozen things an able-bodied young American of 1940 should know how to do: drive and make minor repairs on a car, shoot a rifle and pistol, ride a horse or a bicycle, speak and read two foreign languages, send and receive with signal flags, Morse, etc. etc. (You've heard me on this, I know—Tommy loves to kid me mercilessly on this point, adding wonderfully esoteric talents such as riding camels, entrechat, poison blow gun, and so forth and so on.) Anyway, a man on the water who can't swim is only half a man. All troops should be required *to swim a distance of 100 yards in full clothing, and wade 300 yards through hip-deep water with full combat pack.*

Our training schedule was ridiculous. As you can imagine. My guess would be that a minimum of 6–8 wks is necessary for the training of troops for amphib assault. Cargo nets are no good. What we need is a broad, square-meshed landing net, and LONG HOURS of practice in climbing and descending—particularly dropping into the craft. What happens is: the launch rises and falls; everyone gets scared and stops, and everything jams up.

The SCR-131 is inadequate for amphib ops, to put it mildly. (In point

*of fact we could have lost the entire maneuvers because of their faulty
performance—and almost did so. We had NO radio communication for
4 hrs.) We ought to have the 171s, at least—or preferably something
still lighter—and they ought to be thoroughly waterproofed. These
were not.*

*But the most pitiful inadequacy of all is in the ldg craft itself. Motor
whaleboats and launches are simply not the answer: they won't beach or
retract well, it's impossible to get out of them in any order or dispatch,
they offer no protection or covering fire. What we need is a shallow-
draft boat built like a lighter, almost a sea-sled, with an armored bow
and two machine gun tubs forward, that would skid right up on the
beach and hold there, and drop two ramps. Or maybe a bow that became its own ramp, like that experimental craft you wrote about that
Higgins is building . . . Of course what we could really use is a squat,
broad, open-cockpit tank with lots of armor, a 37-millimeter gun and
two mgs up fwd, that could run screw-driven through the water and
then waddle right up the beach on its engines, like a big, tough turtle. Is
anything like that being considered back there, where all the great decisions are being decided?*

He broke off, set the pad aside and took off his shoes. From down the
row there was a shout, and then a lot of boisterous laughter. There
was more talk he couldn't hear, and after that several voices rose in
song, off-key:

> *"Hey, we'll hang Old Glory from the top of the pole,
> And we'll all sign over—in a pig's ass hole! . . ."*

Listening he smiled, remembering the days at Early. The war had come,
at least to Europe: a funny war of threats and elaborate casemates where
the combatants lived like firemen, or sailors, reading the papers and
drinking vin rouge or Schnapps. But that wouldn't last long . . .

He picked up the pad again and went on writing rapidly:

*Anyway, we won the game—or so the umpires decided—and old
Westy's in fine fettle (he told us Gen. Bonham was very pleased with
the way things went). And now there'll be a lot of bourbon and golf
and poker and all-around good fellowship at odd hours. Which is all
well and good. But what's being lost sight of here is that we are woefully unprepared for any kind of amphibious operation anywhere at
all.*

*We had a lively Christmas up at Beyliss—wish you could have been
with us. Your grandson, you'll be delighted to hear, now smokes a
Kalmia briar pipe, quotes W. H. Auden, and was never up before
eleven, to my knowledge. (He's also something of a lady killer, to hear*

Peggy.) He finally condescended to a chat with me between social obligations—he went to some pains to explain to me that the current European conflict is nothing more than the logical ascension to power of mass man, and that our best course, as a nation of clear-thinking individualists, was to pass by on the other side and let them beat one another's brains out. This was a bit disconcerting, but it was such a welcome change from LAST Xmas when poor old Europe was in the grip of colonial imperialism's last gasp, that I listened to him gratefully. (Growth is change, but is change growth?) I do hope to CHRIST he isn't going to turn into an Ivy League esthete: sherry flips and white shoes and oxford button-down; too good for this world.

Well, that's a bit too harsh, I guess. I'm tired. (What was it old Ely used to say? A tired officer is a pessimistic one.) I know the boy's got good stuff in him (how could he help but have that!) and it'll shake down with time. Peggy is growing up with a rush: boys are no longer hateful gangling beasts, a Magnavox portable phonograph is the key to all the kingdoms of heaven, and Gene Krupa is groovy. (WHO is Gene Krupa???) Tommy has recovered from that miserable siege of eczema and is carrying on like the wonderful, valiant girl she is

He put the pad down again and went to the front of the tent and looked out. The bay, in close, was a deep blue, shading off to metallic cerulean grays out beyond Point Piños, taking its color from the full silver clouds slipping low over the horizon. Nearby, across from his tent, a piñon jay was darting around in an oak, shaking the sharp holly-like leaves. The wind had dropped. Staring at the bay he rubbed his eyes slowly.

He had come back from China to find that everything had changed. Monk Metcalfe had been killed in a plane crash on Cebu, and in his place was a dapper, testy little man who scarcely listened to him and shoved his report into a desk drawer with a finality that was all too apparent. They were not, he was informed, overly concerned about the antics of a crowd of unwashed guerrillas; the focus of interest was the Republic of China and the Japanese drive on Changsha. He had saluted and left.

Everything was in upheaval. Pampanga Province seethed with a farmers' revolt against the big landlords; the trial of Benigno Ramos, with its disclosures of Japanese offers of aid for his projected insurrection, held ominous overtones. Courtney Massengale had sailed for home, assigned to the War College. Colonel Fahrquahrson had been transferred to First Corps Area. And Europe had gone to war again . . .

The most disquieting change, though, had been in Tommy: she seemed both more despondent and irascible—her moods swung from a dulled preoccupation to quick outbursts of temper, as though all her wry humor and equilibrium of past years had been worn away, leaving the exposed nerve, quivering and inflamed. "It's just habit," she'd said one evening, apropos what he couldn't recall—some trivial matter. "It's all just a matter of going through the motions. We're in the habit of loving each other so we go on doing that, too; that's all."

"Don't say that," he protested. The flat finality in her voice had filled him with a peculiar fright. "It isn't true, honey. It's no habit with me . . ." He took her in his arms then, but she only smiled sadly up at him.

"Isn't it? Maybe it isn't."

Or she would flare into sudden, unpredictable rages, accusations, bits of recrimination. "Oh, stop it, Sam! Honestly, you sound like Mahatma Gandhi in a boy scout suit. Nobody *cares* about the Baltic States, nobody *cares* about the people's war in China—Jesus God, don't be such a roaring, crashing, never-ending bore!"

Even getting back to the States, to Beyliss, hadn't made the difference he'd hoped it would. Donny had been accepted for Princeton—but this triumphant realization of her dreams, instead of delighting her, had made her gloomy and apprehensive. Then, a month or so after that, she'd been afflicted with this curious rash on her arms and thighs, that swelled and cracked and suppurated, and burned like fire. Even her father's promotion to brigadier and his own to major hadn't assuaged her. Finally she'd gone east to Erie to stay with Ed and Marilyn Downing for a few weeks, and had come back feeling more her old self. But it was a surface attitude: she had never forgiven him for China, he knew. He had gone because it had struck him as important, and because of the adventure of it—and it had turned out to be one of the most cataclysmic things that had ever happened to him; but in the doing, something equally important had been lost between them. Perhaps that was simply how life was—part of the grim, inexorable equation: you never got anything without paying for it, in kind and in full . . .

The clouds had drifted majestically off toward Santa Cruz now; the sea was an achingly deep blue, almost unreal. The air was crisp and clear. A country like perpetual early fall, day after day. This is where we ought to live when it's all over, he thought. Right here, somewhere in among these pines, looking east toward old Toro and west to the sea. Sit in the broad gold bands of sunlight, and read, and fool around in the garden, and do a little cabinet making, get a lathe and tool shop and build some things . . .

They were singing another song, far down the hill, their voices swelling and falling in the puffs of breeze:

> *"The coffee in the service, it's really mighty fine,*
> *It's good for cuts and bruises, and tastes like iodine—*
> *Oh! I don't want any more of this aaaarmy life!*
> *Man, I just want to go home! . . ."*

He turned and went back into the tent and sat down on his cot.

Damon swung. The mallet head met the blue-striped wooden ball with a soft, clean *clack*, the ball rolled smoothly ten, fifteen, twenty feet over the fresh green lawn and hit the yellow ball, and MacConnadin said:

"God damn. You Army people are shot with luck."

"I wouldn't call it that," Damon said, grinning.

"Hell, no. I'll bet you practice secretly."

"Of course we do, Bert," General Caldwell said; he cupped his hands over the bowl of his pipe, his face grave and intent. "Didn't you know that? We've just converted all the parade grounds into croquet fields. War Department Order two-two-dash-four-one-three. Every Friday to be known officially as Croquet Day. Why, we've even got company cups, crossed mallets on a wicket sinister. They're of silver—the regimental cups are solid gold, of course."

"What a charming idea!" Laszlo Perenyi exclaimed. His handsome, roguish face crinkled up with glee. "So much more sensible than poking pins in maps or slapping recruits in the backside with a swagger stick."

"Yes, isn't it?" Caldwell's eyes twinkled. "Every profession to its perversions."

Laszlo went into a fit of laughter. "Yes, that's it, that's it exactly! How to live comfortably with one's vices."

"Look," MacConnadin said. "Are we playing croquet or aren't we?"

"Right, right!" Laszlo cried: he darted across the lawn in his beautifully pressed flannel slacks. "A vos ordres, Bert. Zu Befehl. I would like to win one of those gold ones," he said in his charming Hungarian accent; he was on his knees examining the lie of his ball. "Discomfit the military in all their arrogance. Wouldn't you, Bert?"

"Yeah," MacConnadin growled good-humoredly. He was a big, balding man with a red face and a powerful square jaw that thrust forward when he grinned. "I wouldn't mind getting some of it back—I knew all the taxpayers' money was going *some* God damn place . . ."

"Bert!" Hélène MacConnadin called from the poolside terrace that overlooked the croquet field.

"What?" he answered.

"That's the fourth."

"Fourth what?"

"Fourth God damn!"

"Cheer up, baby. The day's young yet."

"Your men are a bad influence on him," she said to Tommy. "Every time he's with the Army he thinks he has to swear more."

"—Oh, he'd swear anyway," Tommy replied. "He's the swearing kind. Aren't you, Bert?"

"You said it, sister," MacConnadin said, and grinned at her happily.

They were at the MacConnadins' home high in the hills behind Woodside for the regular Sunday morning croquet game, where George Caldwell, now Deputy Commander, Western Defense Command, based at the Presidio in San Francisco, was a frequent guest. The Damons, who were spending the last half of Sam's thirty-day leave with the General, had been invited, along with Laszlo Perenyi, the portrait painter, for the weekend. The MacConnadins kept a perennial open house, and on almost any occasion the bemused guest could find himself in the company of touring pianists, Zen teachers, biophysicists from Berkeley, actors from little theater groups in North Beach, or a bunch of big-boned, heavily tanned, amiable college kids from Mills College or Stanford, where two of the MacConnadin children were enrolled. "Hélène collects house guests the way Francie collects phono-graph records," MacConnadin was fond of saying, "—or the way I collect board memberships." And then he would wink his slow, com-plicit wink and drain his glass.

Laszlo made his wicket with a crow of delight and then looked appeal-ingly at MacConnadin, who said with brusque humor: "Come on, shoot, you frazzle-headed Bulgarian." It was a rule at Bert MacConnadin's that there could be no consultations between partners on strategy or tactics, and ferocious penalties were exacted for any violations.

"Hungarian, please." Laszlo held up his hand. "The last of a noble tribe of Magyars."

Damon took his club in both hands and brought it smoothly up over his head and behind his back, the way he'd used to do with a baseball bat to loosen up his shoulders, and filled his lungs with air. A starkly clear morning, with the moisture on the great oaks glinting like translucent pearls. Far out, the Pacific swept away clear and level, a gray-blue universe of ocean, and to the south half a dozen headlands rode out into it like shaggy green beasts crouching. A strange, vibrant peace, bound in fine Indian summer weather, though it was already December.

On the terrace Tommy and Hélène were sprawled in deck chairs, sipping at their coffee and talking in low voices, idly. Beyond them Peggy, standing at the base of the diving board, made a face at a young boy with bright red hair who was bouncing a slick blue-and-yellow beach ball at his feet. The boy laughed and shied the ball at her twice, then threw it. She put out her arm and the ball caromed off her little fist and bounced away across the lawn. Catching Damon's eye now she waved at him. He waved back, watching his daughter advance in that proud, decisive stride, one, two, three, arms pumping, and stamp and lift off the board in a lovely, soaring arch, curving down through the still California sky like a slim, beautiful naiad in her powder blue swimsuit and cap. *Schloop.* She was gone: his daughter. She had been there, stamped against the sky like the quintessence and culmination of all female grace, half-child, half-woman—and then she had vanished. It all seemed part of the faintly baffling stillness of the day; a glorious, fragile instant that caught at his heart. Peggy had climbed out of the pool now and was walking toward the boy, her cap in her hand, shaking out her hair with proud little darts of her head. *"Beautiful!"* he wanted to call out to her—checked the impulse. She would think he was an old square. His daughter. Seventeen, nearly. What did she think of all this carefree opulence and splendor around her—swimming pool and stables and immaculate bent-grass lawns and terraces and servants? Was she resentful, adulatory, amazed—or did she simply take all this dazzle for granted? Was this a way of life she would want to make her own? His daughter.

Laszlo had just overshot his wicket and MacConnadin cried, "For Christ sake, Perenyi! A five-year-old kid could do better than that."

"But I am not a five-year-old kid," Laszlo answered drolly. "I am a weary, tortured, tormented, sensitive genius with only the *soul* of a five-year-old kid . . ."

"That cost us two shots."

"The Army won't catch us, Bert. Never fear. They are too wrapped up in plans to defend this hemisphere, plans to crush all our potential enemies: Slavonia, Paragonia, Dementia. That's why they are two wickets behind. You can bet the German General Staff is not playing croquet this fine, glorious morning," he went on, needling Caldwell, who was studying his lie. "They are coming to grips with the important things. They are issuing orders, drinking vodka, shooting prisoners, raping women . . ."

"They're going to be drinking Uncle Joe's private stock in the Kremlin by Christmas," MacConnadin said.

The General made his shot cleanly, and straightened. "I think not," he said.

"Oh, come on, George. They're in the suburbs now. They're riding the streetcars, for Christ sake."

Caldwell smiled. "They may surround the city; they may even get into it. But they won't be in the Kremlin."

MacConnadin scratched at his belly and his eyes began to gleam. "How'd you like to make a little wager on that?"

"All right."

"George, I got five hundred says the Germans will dictate peace terms from inside the Kremlin on Christmas Day."

Caldwell smiled again, a different smile. "That's a little steep for me. Let's make it twenty-five dollars."

"You're on." MacConnadin laughed, wiping his mouth with his hand. "And I gave you Army boys credit for being sharp. Why hell, George, the Germans are unbeatable."

"No military organization is unbeatable."

"He's counting on the snow," Laszlo interpolated. "The cold. Am I right, General?"

Caldwell shook his head. "Not entirely. It's something else." He looked at the balls near his feet and Damon could see his eyes moving in quick, darting passages, the way they did whenever he was studying a problem. "They lack something," he said after a moment.

"They do?" Bert retorted. "Well, I'm damned if I know what it is."

"They lack the ultimate audacity." Caldwell nodded, frowning. "They possess a certain inventiveness, they plan superbly, they execute with ferocity and care. But then there comes that moment." He glanced at his son-in-law with a quick, fond smile. "That terribly lonely moment when you must make a further decision—a huge one. One that has nothing to do with everything you've anticipated. With the whole future in doubt, with hopelessly inadequate information and exhausted from the strain of the battles already fought, you have to summon up all your energies and decide, quickly and clearly; and act." He took his pipe from his mouth. "That's where they break down."

MacConnadin chuckled heavily. "They don't look very broken down to me."

"No, they're in excellent shape—right now. But they've already missed their great chances."

"You mean the invasion of Britain?"

"Before that. When they failed to take Gibraltar. Their armor was in the Pyrenees and on the loose. They could have run across Spain and seized the Rock and sealed off the Mediterranean for good."

Laszlo said: "But Spain is already part of the Axis, George."

"Not entirely. Spain is benevolent to their cause, but she is a neutral; and she is worn out from her civil war. Spain will blow with the wind."

"You're crazy, George," MacConnadin broke in. "It's as clear as a bell. The Germans are going to take over all of Europe."

The General shook his slim, white head. "They will fail to make the last, most dangerous move. They will guess wrong. And they'll be beaten again."

"And who's going to do that?"

Caldwell looked at him calmly. "We and the British."

"Oh, go on!" MacConnadin shouted. "There you go again—when are you soldier boys going to wise up to the facts of life? This country doesn't want war—you're the only ones who're always talking about it. You can't get it out of your systems . . ." He slapped his mallet against his trousers. "Look, you can do business with Hitler, I don't care what you say. It's just a question of going about it right. Look at the Swedes, they're making a hatful of dough with those weapons contracts. Coal, steel . . . Hell, I was talking to Joe Kennedy only a couple months ago—"

"Mr. Kennedy," the General said crisply, "has a rather meager historical sense."

"He was ambassador over there, wasn't he?—until that stupid bastard Roosevelt kicked him out . . ."

"Bert!" Hélène's voice carried down from the terrace. "For heaven's sake!—"

"All right, all right . . . Look," MacConnadin went on, "I'll tell you what's going to happen. The Germans are going to conquer Russia, and then the Limeys will get wise to how things are. And then Germany will be the center of Europe. Isn't that what Napoleon did?"

Laszlo stuck his hand in the front of his sport shirt. "Uh, yes—with a few insignificant differences."

"Well, I mean for a while, there . . . Let's face it, the Germans speak our language. The industrial complex, a higher standard of living. If you look at it at all objectively, the Germans *deserve* Europe. Look at the way France fell apart, there. The Germans are smart, they're aggressive. They're out after markets, they want to expand, that's all. They're going to overhaul the whole structure over there—more power to 'em . . ." He shied a hand at the General, who was looking at him quizzically. "You people act as if Goering's going to drop a bomb on Washington any day."

For the first time in some minutes Damon spoke, pointing seaward. "Our trouble, when it comes, is going to come from out there."

"Who?" MacConnadin stared at him. "Japan? They've got their hands full in China."

Damon looked down. All at once the curious serenity of the day, the laughter and horseplay of the young people around the pool, MacConnadin's brash and breezy assertions, angered him. I wish I was out there, he thought, looking seaward; on Luzon, or on Wu T'ai mountain, on the ridge. I certainly don't belong here.

The General was saying, "Sam spent the better part of two years in China, Bert."

MacConnadin, however, bent over and made his shot, a good one. "Hell, they're smart businessmen, too. The Japs. Don't think they aren't. What do they want war with us for? They know what they're doing. They know what they want and they're willing to pay for it, too."

"Yes, I know," Caldwell answered dryly. "I've sat there on the hill and watched freighter after freighter steam out through the Golden Gate, loaded to their Plimsoll marks with scrap iron. For the Rising Sun to go on rising with."

For a moment the two men stared at each other. Then MacConnadin scratched at his shirtfront and said: "All right. Why in hell not? They pay for it, George. Cash on the barrelhead. Is their money any worse than anybody else's?"

"No—I'm sure it's every bit as good. The only thing is it's quite possible it's all going to come back to us in a very pointed form—with all the points heading our way."

"Stuff and nonsense." Bert MacConnadin swung his mallet back and forth between his legs. "You know what? You fellows have a—you've got a war psychosis mentality."

Laszlo drew himself up proudly, all five feet six inches of him, and cried: "La Garde meurt—mais ne se rend pas!"

"What the hell does *that* mean?" Bert demanded.

"It means—" Laszlo's lined face assumed its sly, roguish look, his eyes bulged. "It means: As long as war is regarded as wicked it will always have its fascinations."

"Hey, that's pretty good." MacConnadin laughed; he had recovered his bluff, hard jocosity. "You worrywarts!" he jibed the officers. "The way to swing it is study the angles and then act accordingly. The Japs have got no more idea of going to war with us than they have of flying to the moon. In the first place they haven't got the stuff to take on an outfit like the U.S.A.—"

"Yes, they have," Damon heard himself say all at once, "—and you're one of the people who've been giving it to them."

There was a sudden little silence. Laszlo was staring out to sea, his lips pursed, whistling inaudibly. MacConnadin was glaring at Damon, red-necked and uncertain, hands on his hips. The General had glanced at him once, not sharply, and turned to study the lie of the balls. Well, the hell with it. Damon put out his cigarette on the sole of his shoe, scattered the tobacco and rolled the tiny wad of paper in the tips of his fingers. He'd been discreet, amenable, deferential at gatherings such as this for twenty years—Jesus! was it *twenty years?*—and now all at once he was sick of it. He didn't give a damn. He'd say what he thought, once in a while; and the chips could fall where they might. Conscious of the silence, of Hélène's and Tommy's voices coming clearly down to them from the terrace, he walked over to where his ball was lying in the rich, soft grass, thinking of Lin Tso-han in the peasant's hut at Tung Yen T'o.

"All right, Sam." MacConnadin was twisting his neck inside his open collar. "Now let me get this straight. You're predicting we're going to war with Japan. Is that right?" The Nebraskan nodded. "Okay. Suppose you're right. Just suppose, now. When's it going to happen?"

Damon paused. The General was watching him now, his fine, alert face perfectly expressionless. "Soon," he said. "Sooner than you think."

"Like when?"

"Three weeks," he said briskly; thinking, They'll wait to see whether the Germans can take Moscow, and if Rommel can contain the new British counteroffensive against Tobruk and Benghasi. "Six at the most."

"And what's your opinion, George?"

Caldwell pursed his lips, squinting. "I'd say that's a trifle pessimistic. I'd say three to six months. Maybe eight."

"Uh huh." MacConnadin nodded. "Well, that's the future. When you're running a corporation all by your lonesome, six or eight months can be a long time. The fact is, I'm not a hell of a lot interested in a war coming half a year from now." He sipped at his drink, replaced it on the iron filigree table at the edge of the lawn. "I've never been to Europe or China or all these God damn National Geographic places. I've just stayed at home here and tended to business." His eyes glinted in the morning light. "It's easy for you guys to say. You've always had security. You weren't sweating it out, back there in '31, trying to keep your head above water. You've never had to meet a payroll and nothing in the till, the house mortgaged to the attic, fifty creditors bearing down . . . I built Bay City Car and Foundry up from a motheaten old shop over in Oakland, and now I've got a payroll of forty-two hundred, and four plants and a fleet of six ships . . . and what *I'm* interested in is a return on my investment. Now. Today. Get what I mean?"

"Somebody's got to worry about these things," Laszlo remarked, "—and who is going to if you don't, Bert?"

"You said it." MacConnadin grinned at him; he had caught the note of sarcasm and chosen to indulge it. He bent over and stroked the ball—a fine shot; picked up two wickets, using the General's ball, drove him back within three feet of Laszlo and positioned himself superbly. Damon watched him with an inflamed sense of admiration and contempt. He was so sure of himself: so sure! He knew what he knew—and he understood so little. It was terrifying. For a moment, standing casually on that broad, immaculate lawn beneath California's perpetual springtime, Sam wanted to snatch the industrialist up by the hair of his head and drag him out over the limitless watery leagues of the Pacific and the purple hills of Shansi to a crumbling stone building where men—even as he and MacConnadin—were dying of gangrene because there were no adequate medications or operating facilities; spirit him on across deserts and lonely, inland seas to where hostages picked at random in a village square—even as he and MacConnadin—were crumpling in windrows before the Spandaus and Schmeissers; still further to a country of narrow tiled roofs and crooked little chimney pots, where children wailed in the smoking ruins far below the fading drone of bombers . . .

Then the impulse passed. He'd already said enough: more than enough. It was his turn again. The General was dead on him, and out of position as well. He would have to take the wicket cleanly and roll at least thirty feet beyond it in order to reach MacConnadin with one shot. It was the only hope. He took a deep, slow breath and bent over, all his concentration focused on the blue-striped ball at his feet.

Reclining on the padded deck chair, smiling vaguely at Hélène's indolent chatter, Tommy had been listening to the argument down on the croquet lawn with increasing resentment. Ever since he'd come back from China Sam had been like this—silent and contained, and then all of a sudden he'd say something that made everybody furious. He was—he was like a man with a murder on his conscience; and every now and then, in spite of himself, it would burst out and turn the atmosphere all tense and unpleasant. Ridiculous. At one point she was on the verge of calling out, even going down there to break it up, but then she thought better of it. If Bert won the game he'd be in a good mood; if he didn't she could probably jolly him out of it at lunch, smooth things over a bit. But if Sam thought people would take an unlimited amount of this kind of carping—

"—I mean really insufferable," Hélène MacConnadin was saying in her rich, husky voice. "One of the founding families here—you know, like the Kearneys and the McAllisters, and how she loves to give herself airs, hoity-toity, my God! Wanted to know if I'd be interested in serving with her—get that, *serving* with her—on this new Golden Gate Performing Arts Council. By which of course she meant would I give her a check for a thousand dollars—"

Making sounds of agreement Tommy watched Sam bent over his ball in that attitude of easy grace and taut concentration he brought to anything he did. Janice, the younger of the MacConnadin girls, had come out on the terrace, calling something excitedly, and Bert, still looking a bit vexed, told her to keep her voice down, but Sam heard nothing. Perfectly rapt, he swung. The ball went through the wicket and rolled on and on, curving faintly, and just knicked the yellow ball.

"Bull luck!" MacConnadin hollered. "Just shot with it . . ."

Sam was grinning at him, wiping his palm on his trousers. Irritated, Tommy glanced at her father. But the General had no interest in the game; he was staring up at Janice, who was saying to them all: "I don't care what kind of a gag it sounds like, it's true—they're dropping *bombs* . . ."

She turned her head in sudden fright.

"Now sweetie," Hélène was saying, "you mustn't play games with these neurotic old Army people, you know how gullible they are—"

"Mother," the girl said, shaking her head violently, "it's not a joke, I mean it!"

She came erect in her chair. But the General was already running across the lawn, was bounding up the steps to the terrace, taking them two at a time, Sam right behind him; their faces looked smooth and alien—the faces of younger, harder men. Their eyes passed over hers, moved on. There was a commotion at the long glass door to the living room. Margaret, the colored maid, was standing at the edge of the breezeway gripping a towel in her hands calling, "Some of you better hear this . . ."

She was on her feet without knowing it. The children skylarking around the diving board were staring at them; Hélène's face was tilted up toward her in amused outrage, saying: "What's the matter with everyone—have they all gone crazy?"

Tommy looked at her an instant, wordless and fearful, then half-ran across the shaded terrace, through the breezeway and into the long, cool living room with its two grand pianos placed back to back at the far wall, its built-in bookcases littered with Kachina dolls and Inca figurines, the bright orange sectional couches grouped around the Italian marble coffee table; hurrying toward the group clustered around the radio, which was innocently playing dance music, and now a girl with a lovely deep contralto was singing, "—when you held me tight, it all seemed so right, but it was only a summer dream . . ." The music went on, dreamy and sad, and they all stood there staring at one another like imbeciles while the others trooped in from the terrace and Janice was saying defiantly:

"Well it *was*, he *was* saying all that about bombing. At Pearl Harbor."

Her father reached down then and turned the dial and there was the voice—the old, crisp, authoritative tone overlaid with a new tension, a little unsure. Listening, she felt her nails cutting into her palms. This was bad. As bad as it could be. The voice chattered and clattered, filled the room with its terrible news; then there was music again, Percy Granger's "Country Gardens," and Bert MacConnadin was saying:

"What's the matter with them—weren't they on guard or whatever the hell they're supposed to be doing?—"

The radio was of teak, with ebony dials; an ebony panther was crouched on its surface: a wonderfully smooth, powerful panther, snarling at nothing in particular. She felt sick; physically sick, as if her belly had been poisoned by bad food. It was over. Again. A line had drawn through their lives again, through all their lives, that could never be recrossed. Gazing out into the bright light of the patio she saw Peggy drying her hair; she was talking to the Elkins boy, smiling up at him and drying her hair absently with a towel, fluffing it, her head tilted charmingly. Donny, she thought with a pang of pure terror. *Donny—*

"Why, the bastards," MacConnadin was saying hotly. "Those little yellow monkeys—why for Christ sake, they can't even *see* straight!" He gazed at them all, his face choleric and red. "And they got away with it! What's the matter with those people out there—don't they even know their business? Probably boozed up and sleeping late, with a—"

"There's no sense knocking the Navy," her father said sharply; he looked the way he did when he was very angry and trying to suppress it. "We're all at fault here . . ."

"*Somebody's* at fault, that's for sure!"

"Bert—" Hélène said, but wagging his head balefully he ignored her.

"By Jesus, if something like this happened over at the plant there'd be hell to pay, I can tell you that!"

The General looked at him. "Oh, heads will roll—if that's what's bothering you."

"Well, isn't it bothering *you?* I should think it ought to . . . Jesus, you even called it!" he exclaimed, pointing to Sam. "You knew it was coming, all of you! Why in hell didn't you do something about it, take some measures, if you knew—?"

"*—We wanted you to have a good return on your investment,* Mr. MacConnadin," Sam's voice broke in the room. He was shaking with wrath, and his face was terrible. Tommy had never seen him look like that: it frightened her into silence. "Now. Today. Just part of the return."

MacConnadin, taken aback, for all his angry bluster, by the sheer, obdurate menace in Sam's face, muttered: "What do you mean by that—?"

"Exactly what I said."

"All right," George Caldwell said pleasantly; in the pause he smiled at his son-in-law—a sad, worn, weary, indomitable smile. "Let's get moving, Sam."

"Yes, sir."

Hélène said, "Oh, you're not leaving . . ."

"I'm afraid we must, yes," the General answered, turning toward her. "And at once. I hope you'll forgive our hurrying off—"

Everyone was talking at once now. The children had come in from the pool and were arguing excitedly near the couch; their wet feet made crazy, barbaric footprints on the bright tan carpeting and Tommy stared down at them, thinking again of Donny, walking now under the elms or sitting in his room in slacks and a pullover, his long legs extended, reading—maybe listening to these same bulletins. She shivered. The hot, tight nausea was gone, but in its place was a worse sensation— of boundless fear, no solid earth beneath one's feet. How bad was it? If Hawaii were under attack—

Her father and her husband were talking to each other in low, even voices. The radio kept repeating the same announcement over and over again. Hélène was shouting at the kids to stop dripping water all over the rug.

"Bert," Laszlo Perenyi was saying, "about the portrait—do you want to set a time for tomorrow?"

"*Portrait—!*" MacConnadin glared at him, wide-eyed with outrage. "For Christ sake—with *this?*" He jabbed one fat finger in the direction of the radio. "Don't be an ass!—"

Laszlo faltered. "I see—I only thought—"

"It's out! Forget it. I may be sleeping at the plant tomorrow, for all I know. Portraits! Jesus, man—haven't you got any sense of *proportion?*"

"Of course, Bert." Perenyi's head went up. All his roguish levity was gone; his face was all at once very smooth and impassive. "Of course."

"Tommy," Sam was saying to her; he had hold of her arm. "Come on, now. Let's go."

"All right." She nodded, called: "Peggy, we're going . . ."

The girl's face brightened in consternation. "Gee, Mother—I'll have to pack!"

"There's no time for that," her father told her. "You come along later. Or your mother will come get you."

They said their good-byes with haste. MacConnadin kept his hands in his pockets with Sam, then took one out for the General. Tommy went up to Hélène and said, "I'm so sorry—I hope you'll excuse us . . ."

"Of course. We'll see you again soon."

They went down the terraced steps. Sam pulled the car in close to the edge of the lawn and she swung herself into the front seat. She didn't know what she felt—her thoughts were swirling in a vat of resentment, worry, naked dread. Her father got in beside her and they pulled rapidly away down the drive. Hélène and several of the kids were standing at the top of the steps, waving, and she waved back absently. MacConnadin was nowhere to be seen.

Her forehead was hot and she took a handkerchief out of her bag and wiped her temples and neck. They drove down the winding road through the big oaks, the smoky sunlight falling in racing needlepoint patterns over the car's hood, the tires shrieking softly on the curves. The radio boiled with static. The two officers were staring straight ahead, talking as though she were not sitting there between them. As though she were not there at all.

"What'll you do?"

"Pack my bedding roll and drive straight down to Ord. Ought to make it by two-thirty if I move out."

"I'd think so."

"What's the disposition?"

"Probably Rainbow Five."

"Think they'll invade?"

Her father paused. "My guess is no. Not for several days, anyway. Air raids on the major cities in a week, probably; maybe less. Of course you never know, with the sons of Nippon: they may have an invasion in force all planned. It *seems* impossible . . . but you never know."

"What about evacuation?"

"With five million people?" Caldwell shrugged bleakly. "Where are you going to put them? run them east—over desert down south, mountains up here? There's snow in the Sierra now . . ."

"*Invade!*" Tommy cried suddenly; the import of all this talk, delivered in such terse, remote tones, had finally penetrated the turmoil of her mind. "The Japanese?—invade *us?* this country?"

"Yes," her father answered calmly. "It's distinctly possible. Why— did you think there was some kind of house rule against it?" He sighed.

"And if they do decide to land, God help us all. We haven't got enough thirty-caliber stuff to stop a sick cat. Few million rounds. We can run through that, and then get ourselves slaughtered. I don't know what Joe Stilwell's got down at Ord, but he can't be much better off."

The car swooped left violently, flung Tommy forward and toward the wheel. She put her hand against the dashboard and cried, "For God's sake, Sam! What's the matter with you?"

Sam looked at her. "I'm driving too fast for your taste?"

"You're driving like a crazy drunk . . ."

"Would you prefer to walk it?"

"If you don't slow down and act your age—"

"Now, Tommy," her father said, "this is a time for haste. Be reasonable."

"*Reasonable—!*" she shouted. Everything had happened so fast, so crazily, with no warning at all—everything was altered and there had been no preparation. She felt enraged, overborne—it all had seemed to spring from that row during the croquet game . . .

"You could at least have been civil," she declared. "Lashing out at your host that way—how do you think Hélène feels?"

"Hélène has my profound sympathy," Sam replied.

"You just blew off at him, said the first thing that came into your head . . ." A delivery wagon shot out of a side street and Sam swerved wildly, the tires wailing, swung around it and raced on. "God *damn* it, Sam!" He made no answer, just kept driving faster and faster, the car lurching on the winding, descending road, and it stung her to fury. "Cheap self-indulgence," she said hotly; she couldn't stop herself. "Now you're going to be heroes all over again, and you think you can hurt anyone's feelings you want to. All he was doing was expressing an opinion, a point of view—but no, now you've got your fine little war and you—"

Sam stamped on the brake. The car skidded to a stop with a shriek and a lurch that flung her against the dashboard again. "Sam, if you—" she began. He had turned from the wheel and gripped her shoulders with both hands.

"Jack and Mae Lee Cleghorne are on Luzon, so are the Dehners and Pink Whitehead. Ben and Margie are at Schofield. They're maybe dead right now. Have you got that? Has it penetrated?" She stared at him, hypnotized: that look was in his eyes again—the same expression she had seen in front of the radio with Bert MacConnadin. His face looked like iron being beaten in a forge.

"Oh, sure," he said tightly, holding her. "Sure, everyone knows—the army officer's just a playboy with a one-track mind, everybody *knows* he's just dying to stir up wars so he can get himself promoted and decorated and get every mother's son butchered like cattle at the first opportunity. Everybody knows he's nothing more than the product of the Prussian staff system—a born killer with no education, no savoir faire, no appreciation at all of all the finer things of life. Like pools and patios and stock options and foreign markets and a good return on investments. All the real, good, true, noble things . . ."

"There, there," her father murmured.

"Now it's started again—the frightened kids, the dirty decisions and stink and misery and broken bodies and all the rest of it . . . and *he* sold them the iron for years! Good men have been dying for four years in China and now it's our turn—because he wanted to rack up a pile, play the big shot in his lousy hillside castle . . ." His eyes were suddenly wet with tears. "Can't you put *any* of it together? Can't you?"

"All right, Sam," her father was saying gently. "All right, now. Let's go along."

Sam released her then, and threw the car in gear. The radio ran on, the voices crisp and feverish over the static. Guam was under attack, and Wake Island. Shaken, silenced, she watched the sere, burned hills, the sienna basin of the lower bay slip past them. Could it really happen? could Japanese troops be running along this road, shouting, firing into the little stucco bungalows—could such an impossible thing as that really happen?

"But he's got two boys—the older one will be drafted," she faltered, thinking: Donny, *Donny*. And her heart tightened. "Doesn't that matter to him?"

Sam made no reply.

"Yes, it matters," her father answered after a moment. "It matters. But apparently it doesn't quite matter enough."

From far behind them came the soaring and descending wail of a siren; Sam pulled over sharply and a red fire-chief's car went by, its roof light flashing with trivial gaiety in the sun. She fell silent, then, and the men went on talking brusquely, in monosyllables, while they ran along the Bay shore, with the city rising up ahead of them like a lovely sliding cubist pyramid. At Market and Van Ness they cut through Golden Gate Park, which looked lush and green after the dry grass of the San Mateo hills; and now all at once there were other cars, hurrying along with them, and here and there someone they recognized. The faces all looked the same: they were all stony with tension and dread. They passed Tim and Mildred Haigler chugging along in their old Plymouth; Mildred's lips parted in a sudden flash of surprise, Tim nodded grimly. They started up the hill.

. . . It isn't fair, she thought. All these years of doing without, of skimping along, cut off from the country, all the just deserts and easy times. And then, just when Sam's made his light colonelcy and you've begun to get enough rank to live halfway decently, a miserable, hideous war comes and they have to go to it: go out and try to hold the line against the countries that have been preparing for it for years . . .

She put her hand on Sam's shoulder. "Darling," she said, "I'm sorry." She knew he disliked any expressions of affection in front of a third party, even her own father; but she couldn't help it. Now, here, frightened and confused, before he kissed her good-bye and hurried south to his new command, she wanted to apologize, she wanted to be forgiven. "Darling, I didn't mean to speak like that. It was stupid."

"It's all right." He had taken her hand, was threading his way through the crowd. Officers and men were running across the parade ground in slacks, in shorts, in sweaters; one was still carrying a golf club in his hand. "I shouldn't have blown off at you myself."

"No, it was my fault, darling . . ."

"It was both your faults," her father said amiably. "And mine for knowing Bert. Now let's go on to fresh woods and pastures new."

Her eyes were full of tears; she looked down at her hands. No family, now: they all would be scattered to the winds. This little time together, and then these two men of hers would be flung half a world away—and this time she could not follow. I've got to see Donny, she thought, swallowing, blinking, trying not to cry, knowing they'd both be cross with her if she gave way to tears right in the middle of this violent confusion; I've got to go east and see Donny soon . . .

"—if there's an air raid tonight," Sam was saying, "if they should come over in force . . ."

"They won't come tonight." Her father shook his head. "Maybe in two, three days. But not tonight."

The car had stopped. She looked up, saw the headquarters building. An officer was running up the steps. Two soldiers were pushing an ammunition cart down the street, an awkward, galloping run, their arms flexed, and a dog was sitting in a patch of grass watching them, its ears cocked. I won't cry, she told herself, I won't—

"Good-bye, Tommy," her father said. He kissed her on the cheek. "Good luck, Sam." They shook hands across her body, and Caldwell opened the door. "Keep in touch with me, now."

"I will.—Sir?" Sam leaned across her.

"Yes?"

"Sir, I've never requested a favor or a change of duty before in my life . . . But when you're given a field command, I want to serve with you again; if you'll have me."

The General smiled at him fondly. "Thank you, Sam," he said. He shook his head. "I won't be given one. This is going to be a young man's war, this one: they won't want me. Perhaps it's better that way." He pointed a quick, slender forefinger. "You'll have the field command: not I."

"I can't believe that, General . . ."

"Well: we'll see." Caldwell's lips curved in the wry, mournful little smile. "But right now let's plunge our fingers into the dike."

He hurried up the walk with his brisk, erect stride.

IV
LIANA

(1)

The big plane tipped, tipped again, the frame gave a flat, cracking sound, a steel ship's timbers; and peering down through the opposite windows Damon saw the dense green mat, like a lush, terribly expensive rug against the turquoise plate of the Solomon Sea. There was a thin white scarf curving lazily south-southwest, a small boat's wake, and some pieces of island like a broken pot. All the rest was ocean.

"Looks peaceful enough." Ben Krisler, sitting beside him on some grenade cases, wrinkled his forehead, staring down. "Nice and pleasant from up here. Caribbean playground sort of thing."

Damon nodded. It was a neat picture from seven thousand feet: the way the world looked to gods and goddesses, swooping around, sleeping with each other and sipping ichor—it was probably how it looked to Congress or the General Staff, far away in Foggy Bottom. The long view, the smooth view, with the boundaries nicely delineated and the gaily colored little symbols for airfields and harbor facilities and the road nets bright, spidery lines, and the rectangular boxes for military organizations deployed along the boundaries . . .

From one of the open compartments up forward the radio operator's voice sang out: "Roger-roger-roger, Dad. Approach pattern Charlie Thuh-ree, I read you . . ."

The wing went up, tilting them still harder. On their right were mountains, purple under churning towers of rain cloud; on their left was the sea. They were held in a bowl of light, with the New Guinea coast sprawled in shadow below them. Sunlight slipped over the stenciled crates and boxes lashed to the cabin floor, and the plane's occupants, perched on the crates and folded tarpaulins—there were no bucket seats—began to stir restlessly and glance at one another. There was a surgeon assigned to the 477th, a captain of engineers named Hertz, and a detail of seven kids in the care of a sergeant, destined for the airfield. One of them, a towheaded boy with a soft, round face said something and several of the others laughed; but the sergeant frowned at them and they ducked their heads and began to check their equipment.

The radio operator was coming toward them. "Take hold of the straps when we set down," he called through the pulsing roar of the motors. "Liable to be a little rough coming in."

Ben wrapped his hands around the web straps as though they were cesti. "Well, Sam—here we go again."

"They say it's easier the second time around," he answered.

"Ought to be. Look at all the practice we've had."

He grinned at Krisler tightly. The past ten months had been frustrating and bitter. The Sunday night of Pearl Harbor the regiment had marched out of Fort Ord and bivouacked among the madrone and manzanita in the hills behind Los Laureles. The next day there was a report—confirmed—that the Japanese fleet had left Pearl Harbor and was heading for California; he'd been assigned a sector of coast from Bixby Canyon to Lucia—a preposterous stretch for one battalion to defend: all at once the wide, grassy flats at Point Sur, the hazy blue expanse of the Pacific began to look treacherous and terrible. But the Japanese—if they had actually entertained thoughts of an invasion—had lost their nerve and turned west again; nothing beyond two sporadic shelling incidents by submarines had occurred.

After that everything had been alarums and excursions, as Spider Spofford put it. The world was toppling like a hill of glass. Manila fell, the Celebes, Rabaul, New Ireland, the Solomons, Singapore. MacArthur obeyed the Presidential directive and flew to Australia; and Skinny Wainwright, left holding the bag, surrendered the starved and exhausted remnants of the Bataan force. Jack Cleghorne had been killed, Mandrake Styles was missing, Bob Mayberry was believed to have died on the death march. Borneo went down, then Java, and the Japanese started down the New Guinea coast. Were they actually going to invade Australia? A terrible spring—a spring of bewilderment and grief and helplessness. Vinegar Joe Stilwell staggered out of the jungle beyond Homalin, haggard and tight-lipped, at the head of a weary little party of technicians and British infantrymen and Burmese nurses, and informed the world in no uncertain terms that they'd got their teeth kicked in. Burma was gone, the Wehrmacht opened its great summer offensive toward the Ukraine, Rommel had virtually wiped out the British armor and was rolling unimpeded toward Cairo and Suez. And here at home congressmen rose to decry the absurdity of gas rationing, and dollar-a-year men blandly assured the public there was plenty of rubber, plenty of aluminum and copper and steel—and then other dollar-a-year men said there *wasn't* plenty, there wasn't nearly enough of anything at all . . .

There was chaos and confusion everywhere you turned, and no time to do anything. In one period of eight days Damon had received three contradictory sets of orders, each one superseding its predecessor—and when the dust had cleared found himself back at Fort Ord, training infantry. They were cadred to death: they would just about get the regiment up to strength and functioning well when word would come down from some higher headquarters ordering them to detach all their best officers and NCOs to form a new regiment somewhere else; and they'd have to start all over again. It was no consolation whatever that old Caldwell, now a major general with Army Ground Forces in the nation's capital, wrote him one of his masterful letters predicting the turning point of the war in the final week of July, with Hitler's decision to split his Army Group A in a drive on both Stalingrad and the Baku oil fields, and the Auk's stand at El Alamein. "God knows I don't want to sound euphoric about this: the road back is going to be long and grim and bloody—a lot longer and grimmer and bloodier than some of the breezy gentry from Detroit and New York City seem to think. But I honestly feel it's the low-water mark. From now on the initiative should rest with us."

Meanwhile he, Sam Damon, was standing in the yellow dust, teaching awkward, eager kids how to fall on the dead run, rifle butt down first so as not to foul their pieces; how to make up a combat pack; how to dig a foxhole, how to crawl rapidly without sticking their tails up in the air—and the months went by. When General Westerfeldt, bogged down at Moapora with a reinforced brigade, had wired asking him to take command of the old regiment from Beyliss, he had leaped at the chance; he'd phoned Ben, who was fuming and fussing as range officer at Tarleton; did he want to come out as Damon's exec? Did he! Give him six hours. And here they were, scant weeks later, the bitter waiting over, dropping down to Kokogela Airstrip on the Papuan coast, at the sad, bad, ragtag end of a war . . .

The plane was still turning; with the wheels down it seemed to lurch awkwardly, stumbling on itself through the waves of air. Now there were scars in the green mat, the snake scars of truck tracks, and here and there a hut, its nipa thatching dead and silvered against the jungle. What looked like disjointed sections of warped planking stuck out into the little bay, and beyond it the stern of a ship rose orange and scabrous out of the sea. But there was still no movement anywhere.

"Looks sort of deserted," Ben observed. "Think everybody's gone home?"

"Wouldn't blame them if they did, Colonel," Hertz answered.

Now the runway swung up toward them, pocked with dark round spots like stains where the bomb craters had been filled. The feathery heads of rain forest rushed toward them. The runway swung forward and out of their vision, leveling off; the wheels touched, lifted, the plane bounced jarringly, rocking and swaying, the ammunition boxes strained against their lashings. And now, pouring by on both sides, Damon saw the parade of wreckage.

"Jesus, it looks like the city dump," someone said.

It did. There was a Kittyhawk with its wings sheared off, a P-39 with its tail assembly gone and its propeller bent like bright silver ribbon, the fire-blackened fuselage of a Marauder, a C-46 crushed like tin foil, two more wrecks burned out and unidentifiable. His eyes followed them bleakly. The airstrip was being worked over—the Japanese apparently could bomb it at will.

They were bumping along now, clumsily. A jeep with a sign that said "FOLLOW ME" was racing ahead of them, leading them past more smashed aircraft into a revetment.

"All out for Pango Pango," the towheaded boy said.

"Shut up, Morrison," the sergeant told him.

The crew chief knocked up the catch and swung the cargo door out—and the air hit them, heavy and foul, an efflation of pestilence and decay, overpowering in the swift, damp heat. Damon felt sweat break out on his face and neck.

"The sewage disposal problem here is terrible," the towheaded kid said.

Damon slung his '03 rifle while the privates watched him curiously, and stepped down into the hot, foul air. His eyes met Ben's; they winked at each other at the same instant without expression.

"That your gear, Colonel?" A skinny corporal with red hair and a wide mouth was looking at him. "Those two barracks bags. That all?"

"That's the pitch."

"I read you." The corporal slung them into the back of a battered weapons carrier, then Ben's two bags. "Travel light and you can shag ass if the situation turns fluid. You know? Jesus, I don't mind telling you, I've seen them come out here with more junk than six men and a boy can handle. Valpacks and numbered footlockers and boxes. One character had a whole library and a refrigerator. Yeah!" The corporal laughed and swung in behind the wheel. "One of them little gray Norges, all crated up. I don't know what the fuck he thought he was going to plug it into."

"Maybe his asshole," Ben said pleasantly.

The corporal cackled once, his mouth halfway to his earlobes. "Hey! That's a daisy-cutter. Yeah. He didn't last long, that one. I ain't naming no names, but he went out of here like a singed flamingo, feeling real sorry for himself. I don't know *where* the reefer went." He turned to the group milling around the plane. "Anybody else heading for the Double Seven?"

"Yes, I am." It was Stackpole, the surgeon, a sallow-faced man with a quick, irascible manner. He had two footlockers and a barracks bag and a medical chest with reinforced metal corners, and the corporal, still sitting behind the wheel, supervised the loading, which was done by two airfield personnel. Stackpole got up in back with Ben, and Damon swung in beside the driver, who stared at his rifle with interest.

"Going hunting, Colonel?"

Damon looked back at him impassively. "No—I figured I'd trade it for some souvenirs."

The corporal cackled again and slapped his knee. "God damn. That's a good one. I want to remember that." Wagging his head he proclaimed: "If there's anything that gets my rocks off it's an officer with a sense of humor. You know?"

"Anything to oblige."

Stackpole pointed to the corporal's neck, where there was a large raw sore, oozing yellow mucus. "That's a jungle ulcer."

The corporal's eye rolled around to the surgeon. "You wouldn't jazz me, would you, Doc?"

"Why don't you get it treated?"

The corporal threw the little truck in gear and they started off. "A beaut," he muttered between his teeth. "Oh boy. A beaut."

There were two more smashed planes, a burned-out six-by-six and a corrugated iron shack collapsed in a tangle of twisted metal, from which smoke was rising in faint little blue whorls.

"You had a raid recently?" Damon asked.

The corporal squinted at the road. "We have a raid every afternoon, Colonel. Just like going out to the frigging ball park. Every time we see one of ours it's like finding a long-lost friend, I'm telling you."

"But what about our air cover?" Stackpole demanded.

"Well, it's kind of uncovered, right now."

On their right in a little clearing was a welter of crates and bales and dunnage, heaped indiscriminately, half-sunk in nearly a foot of water. Nobody seemed to be doing anything about it; no one even seemed to be guarding it. Damon stole a glance back at Ben, who was studying this morass of rotting supplies, his lips pursed. No; things definitely did not look good out here; not too enterprising, from all appearances. He started to query the driver, thought better of it. It was all here, to be seen.

The track swung into dense jungle, deep in shade, then broke out in ghostly fields of ten-foot-high kunai grass. Twice the road was under water and the weapons carrier slithered and slewed, its wheels spinning. Once they pulled over to let a hospital jeep go by; both stretcher racks were full and more wounded and medics were hanging on the frame and fenders. Farther on there was a broad slash that ran off to the southwest, covered here and there with low vegetation—perhaps some attempt by the Japanese at an airfield—and after that a mangrove swamp, an oily, treacherous slick, with the roots of the trees arching down into the water like spiders' legs. The stench was terrific.

"I do believe you get a little precipitation out here," Ben said. The corporal shot him a glance of wild outrage—then laughed uproariously.

"Je-sus, Colonel: I guess so! You want to see a mudhole turn into a roaring creek in ten minutes you've come to the right place. I mean . . ."

They had left the age behind—the age of planes and faucets and slab sidewalks; they were moving back through time, held in the stink of the swamps, the damp, terrific heat. There was something infinitely oppressive about it—it was like an implacable weight on one's back. It made Luzon seem balmy . . .

The trail turned a corner, the harsh wall of jungle thinned a little and then off to the right, toward the sea, they heard three spaced gunshots—

the unmistakable crash of an M1 rifle: the final round echoed and re-echoed over the noise of the engine.

"What was that?" Stackpole said. Nobody answered him and he said, "That's pretty close, isn't it?"

"Some donkey blasting at a crocodile," the corporal said disgustedly. "Or seeing things. You know?"

Ahead stood a grove of coconut trees and what must have once been a copra shed, its roof collapsed, rotting quietly in the jungle; and back under the trees a row of sagging pyramidal tents, black under the fierce celadon canopy. Two soldiers stripped to the waist were dejectedly digging foxholes behind the tents, the muck clinging in lumps to their entrenching shovels.

"End of the line, gents," the corporal informed them. Putting his little fingers to his teeth he gave two sharp blasts. The diggers straightened and dropped their shovels, and climbing out of the holes began walking slowly toward them. "Brigade Headquarters—that tent at the end, Colonel," he said to Damon; then swung his arm back across the clearing toward the long green hood of a hospital tent, barely discernible in the forest, and said to Stackpole: "And over there's Agony Hall, Doc.—And right up there"—he cocked one bony finger westward up the trail where now they could hear a muffled popping and bumping, dry and dusty and far away—"is Never-Never Land. With bells."

"When's the floor show coming on?" Ben asked him.

The corporal doubled up in mirth. "Hey, that's a daisy-cutter. I got to remember that one."

His laughter followed them through the mud to the end tent where a guard stood picking his nose with a thumbnail; seeing the two officers approaching he came listlessly to attention and saluted. And all at once there was General Westerfeldt coming out to them; he was wearing khaki and leggings, his sleeves turned up.

"Sam! Say, it's good to see you, boy . . ."

"It's good to be serving with you again, General." He saluted, but Westy ignored it and seized his hand in both of his own. He had aged a dozen years since the Monterey landings two years ago; his face was deeply lined, the flesh hung from his jowls in blued folds. All the old jovial assurance had gone out of it. He's sick, Damon thought—and then: No, it's more than that.

To hide his astonishment he turned to Ben. "Lieutenant Colonel Krisler, sir."

"Glad to have you with us, Krisler." The General returned Ben's salute and shook hands. "I don't know you, but Sam was keen on having you with us—and I don't kind telling you that's more than good enough for me." He smiled wryly. "Not everybody's exactly wild to come out here to Poverty Row.—Come on in and sit down." He led the way back inside the tent and lowered himself heavily into the canvas chair behind his field desk. The sides of the tent were rolled but the air was

stifling; there was not the faintest puff of breeze. "Sit down, sit down."
He shoved a pile of papers away from him and rubbed his eyes slowly.
There were deep ovals of sweat under his arms and around his collar.
Scowling he pulled the wet cloth away from his body. "This damn
prickly heat, it can drive you crazy." He picked up a pencil and gripped
it in both hands. "It's been rough, Sam," he said after a moment. "I don't
have to tell you how rough it's been."

"Yes, sir. I know."

Westerfeldt shot him a glance. "What are they saying down in Brisbane?"

"I didn't hear much, General," he lied. "We were only there overnight, really. Well, they're disappointed the operation's been slowed
down . . ."

The Brigade Commander grunted. "Are they. The sons of bitches. Sit
around in their fancy suites at Lennon's, drinking gin-and-limes and
shooting directives—" The field phone strapped to the side of his desk
rang and he broke off and picked it up. "BULL MOOSE. Yes. They
didn't. I see . . . Now, look—well no, I don't think so. What? . . . Well,
I'll have to think about it, Frenchy, I don't know. Yes. I'll call you back
in a while." He thrust the phone back in its leather jacket and lifted the
cloth of his shirt away from his skin again. "Oh, it's easy for *them* to
holler. They aren't sitting here in this lousy swamp with the Japs staring
down their throats. Getting bombed and strafed almost every afternoon.
Wondering when the next planeload of supplies is coming in. If ever . . .
Do you know what I've got for artillery?" he demanded, leaning forward. "One one-oh-five. One! With sixty-seven rounds. And half a
dozen one-pounders and some thirty-sevens. I haven't got anything to
work with. The Japs have got all the stuff—they're getting reinforced
from the sea, the trail down from Bowari . . ."

Damon listened to him with what he hoped was a reasonably sympathetic, attentive expression. It was very bad, then; much worse than
anyone had intimated. When the General bent down to pick up a sheet
of paper that had fallen from his desk he stole a glance at Ben, who
rolled his eyes.

The General straightened heavily, scuffing his feet on the tent floor.
"Old Pompey," he said with a slow, sad grin. "I keep thinking the old
fellow is right there, by my foot. He knew he wasn't going to make the
boat . . ."

"How's the old regiment, General?" Damon asked.

Westy had hunched forward again, gripping the pencil. "Yes. Well,
that's it, Sam. They've had a hard time. They're good boys, I don't have
to tell you that—but they've had a hard time. That long march up from
Kokogela. They've had no training for this kind of thing, no really
adequate training, there wasn't *time!* Christ, I never thought anything
like *this—*"

He broke off and snorted. His mouth looked slack and worn, an old man's mouth. Is he too old? Damon wondered with a pang. Too old? He thought of George Caldwell standing beside the car at the Presidio headquarters building that Sunday morning of Pearl Harbor. Westy was almost his father-in-law's age.

To pull him back he said: "Who was running the outfit, General?"

"Mac. MacFarlane. You remember him."

"What happened?"

"He got sick. Scrub typhus. The diseases here, Sam—the bugs! They're in the kunai grass, the water, everything, mosquitoes, mites, you've got to be careful—"

He snapped the pencil away and clasped his big hands, staring down at them. "Three weeks ago was the worst. I guess. Some of the boys broke and ran. I tell you it's uncanny, you can't *see* anything! They're in the trees, in holes in the ground, they're everywhere . . . But the bastards—they've been *training* for this kind of thing for years! Living in the jungle, getting along on a handful of rice and a mouthful of water . . . You've got no idea what we've been up against, Sam. I had to relieve Chuck Leffingwell. Relieve him! My best friend, from the old Tientsin days—do you think I liked doing *that?*" He glared at the two men a moment, his mouth working; snatched up a piece of paper and shoved it at Damon. "Read that. Go ahead—read it."

Dear Westy:

It should be abundantly clear to you by now that time is of the very essence. It is immaterial that our troops are largely untried, that the Japanese are experienced jungle fighters, that the supply situation is not all that it might be—all that is of no consequence whatever. You must work with what you have. Your mission is to seize the Japanese field fortifications at Moapora by 12 November, and nothing else matters. No necromancy or legerdemain is going to effect your purpose. Battle is your solution—and your only solution. Strike skillfully and resolutely— for, as I have often admonished, fate is long and time is fleeting.

Cordially,
MacArthur

"Yes, that's the kind of thing I've been getting. Do you know what he said to me? At Moresby? He said: 'If you fail to take Moapora, do not bother to come back.' Yes!" He leaned forward again, his eyes all at once glistening with tears. "Have I ever failed to do my duty?—what was expected of me as a troop commander? Have I?"

"Certainly not, General." Watching Westerfeldt's face, harassed and suppliant and sweating in the thick, still air, Damon began to feel troubled. Maybe it wasn't as grim as all this. Nothing was ever as grim as it *could* be. Aloud he said: "Could you brief us a little on the situation?"

"What? Sure. Sure." The General heaved himself to his feet and went over to the situation map, which was tacked to a board with a transparent overlay. Damon saw what looked like two irregular bulges running inland from the sea and then curving along parallel to a river and trailing off to the northwest. "We've got from here—this grove—to here where the line is now, in nineteen days. And that's where she stands. We just can't grind it out anymore. The Japs have got all the high ground—from the Mission, here, over across Watubu Creek to the copra plantation, here. Coconut log bunkers, they've had months to prepare them—the God damnedest defenses . . . My boys are in the swamps, wading in water to their hips, all day and all night. The only way forward is on the trails, and the Japs have got them all covered. Perfect fields of fire . . ." He turned away from the map. "I've asked for air strikes, I've asked for pack howitzers, I've even put in for a diversionary landing up here at Luala, using the Four eighty-fourth."

"They're not here?"

"No, that's half the trouble. The Aussies got them for the Timobele operation right after Milne Bay and then they wouldn't let them go. And then finally they did—the idea was to send them overland from Timobele; and they got stuck in the swamps down there. You don't know what this country is like, Sam. You just can't imagine . . ." Westy went into a long harangue involving area commands and jurisdictional wrangles, the gist of which seemed to be that Westy's outfit was a provisional brigade, assembled hastily for the Moapora campaign from two unattached regiments that had been doing garrison duty on Malekula and Efate in the New Hebrides. At the conclusion of the Moapora campaign—or perhaps during the campaign, Westy wasn't very clear about this—the 484th, which had been hung up for some strange reason over at Port Darwin, was to join them, and the 55th Division was to be officially formed.

Damon went over to the situation map. "What about the flank here? beyond the river?"

"It's all swamp, Sam. Mangrove swamps for miles—nobody can get through them. A crocodile couldn't make it . . ." All at once he gripped the Colonel's arm. "Sam, I'm counting on you. Don't let me down."

"I won't, General."

"Sam, they're sick. They're out on their feet. The kids. Half of them are down with fever. Go on up there and fire them up."

"Yes, sir."

"If anybody can do it, you can . . ." Westerfeldt went to the tent's entrance and called: "Miller? Take Colonel Damon and Colonel Krisler up to the Four seventy-seventh.—Sam, I'm holding a conference for all regimental and battalion commanders at nineteen hundred."

"We'll be here, sir."

"And Sam?"

"Yes, General?" Damon turned.

"Don't—take any chances, will you? Take care . . ." That distressed, pleading look was back in his face again. It was more than solicitude; it was an old man's trembling fear. It was the wrong look to send a man—any man—up to the line with.

"I won't, General," he said.

They went out into the still, damp heat and looked at each other.

"Well," Ben murmured, "I'm beginning to see why they hollered for the fire brigade."

Damon grinned at him. "Meaning you and me?"

"Hell, yes. We're all they've *got* . . . Makes you kind of tingly all over, to be spearheading the Allied advance in the Pacific, now doesn't it?"

The jeep swung up beside them and they climbed aboard.

14 Oct 42.   Charming scene at CP. Everybody hanging around, passing time of day, drinking coffee: old home week. Leaf colonel named Caylor ensconced on the throne. Natty type, hair neatly plastered back from center part, shrewd little eyes, nicely cared-for fingernails. Westy sent him over from his staff when Mac succumbed. I said, "Where's the line?" "You mean the front? It's right—about—here." His little pinkie following the tracing on the overlay. "I'll have a jeep ready for you." I looked at him. "Can't we walk it?" "Well—" his eyes falling off "—it's quite a way, Colonel." Turned out it was four and a half miles. FOUR AND A HALF MILES. Jesus Christ. I said: "What's opposing you?" "Well, there are extensive fortifications along this general area here, at the edge of the Grove." "What do you mean—extensive?" "Well . . ." little pinkie wavering around on the celluloid ". . . that is, there are a number of log bunkers, reinforced by—" "Have you seen them?" Surprised now, his eyes sliding up at me. "Me? No. Of course not. These are reports, we have a full file of reports . . ." Hadn't even once been up there. I thought his uniform looked wonderfully impeccable. Another one of the pukka fucking sahibs. And men up front lying in the muck waiting on him.

Told him I wanted him to take out a patrol and verify some of these reports. "A patrol?" Tapping his shiny little nails on the desk. Switchboard operator and runners gaping at me in amazement. "Yes, a patrol. What are you—too good for it? *They're* doing it out there, aren't they?" Was in a cold fury. Oh, these holier-than-thous! His face full of bewilderment and disapproval: too stupid, too pompous even to be scared. "That's not a part of my duties. My duties are—" "You're relieved," I said. "As of this instant. Get your gear together and clear out." "Now, Colonel—" "Take off!" I said. "Very good, sir." Happy to be out of it. Good riddance to bad rubbish, as Peg used to say.

Wandered league on weary league along trail toward the front. People crapped out every which way, huddled under shelter halves and ponchos. Pleasant surprise at 3rd Batt CP. Little Feltner, looking more clerical and harrowed than ever. Holding the fort. Thought for a moment he was going to burst into tears. "I heard you were coming, Colonel—I spread the word." Now it was only about TWO miles to the line. Everybody's got an air corps complex: bemused by communications networks, victory at long range. Don't fire till you see the white of the next continent. Found an abandoned Jap dugout behind B Co CP and told Ross and Beasley to hoe it out and move in. This enraged Ross but he complied. This is the end of the pukka sahib trail.

The old crowd in the line. Deep in the swamp, perched on exposed tree roots like scrawny pelicans. Rather resentful at seeing me: that crooked, narrow, glance. ("What the fuck is HE doing here—coming up to see how the other half lives?") But some of them pleased. Bowcher now sgt major, Stankula buck sgt, Rodriguez buck sgt, Braun and Millis cpls. The expanding line. Wanted to talk about Monterey Bay and the horses. Jackson still a PFC. Kidded him about it. "Well, I had a big career going, and then I got busted down for a little fo-ray in Melbourne." That grin that nothing can subdue.

But they're in pitiful shape. Pitiful. Twenty-two days in the line without relief. Shoes coming apart, beards, fatigues hanging on them in rags, indescribably filthy and haggard. Running ulcers, malaria, dengue, dysentery, Christ knows what else: 1/3 of the command down with something or other. Westy wasn't kidding. All look half-starved. "What are you getting to eat?" "Well—Ks, Colonel. When we can get them." "How about hot chow?" "Well, they say no cooking, it draws Jap fire." "That's a roaring crock—if you wiggle your *ass* it draws fire!" This from Jackson. Intermittent sniping, just enough to keep you on edge. Decided to get them a hot meal by noon tomorrow if they give me the bastinado for it.

Worst country in the world. Bar none. Raining again. Waded in knee-to-hip-deep water for over a mile around perimeter. Fired on twice. No damage. Got the word from Feltner. Japs attacked in force on 30th, several platoons skeedaddled, dropped their weapons and ran. Lost all they'd gained. Still happening sporadically. Asked Osterhaut at Able about estimated enemy strength in the Grove. "Gee, I don't know, Colonel." They are afraid to patrol. Jungle has them licked, more than the Japs.

Their morale is very, very low. Have got to jack them up, any way possible. Chow, shoes (but WHERE?), relief (ditto). But mostly Dad's Force of Personal Example: they feel they've been left here to rot—uncomfortably near the truth. Going to have to carry them on my back next two weeks. There are going to be some changes made around this place: everyone pulls his weight or over the side he goes. There are not going to be any reinforcements: either we do it or we go under. Told Ben he'd have to hump, too: get everywhere, lead patrols, assaults, anything. He said, "Jesus, don't I know it, Sam. Don't you worry: I'll be right there." He will, too. Good old Ben. If this war is going to be won—and it does not look like a breeze tonight—the old fuck-ups and troublemakers are going to win it.

Big pow-wow back at Westy's less than sensational. Dutch Wilhelm full of ponderous Germanic phlegm and pomposity, but steady; only tired. Dickinson shifted over from G-3 to CofS: well, Westy had to give it to somebody, I suppose. Tart, tenacious Yankee, maybe a little over-awed by "burden of command"; maybe not. Frenchy Beaupré irascible and tense, staring up at the tent roof, dirty crusty compress sticking up above his collar; only one of them that's been near enough to the front to get creased. Prince Hal Haley over from Moresby, cap jammed over one ear, tilted back in his chair, ankle on knee, exuding that good old Air Corps charm: no skin off *his* ass. Specs Cruse droning on and on, scholarly and meticulous and utterly maddening. "The majority of enemy works linked by communications trenches." (Who hath measured the ground? to quote the bard.) "Recent activity reveals an increase in anti-tank ditches being constructed along southwest boundary of airstrip and east of Grove. Triangular patch of jungle between Watubu Creek and Mission dense enough to furnish excellent concealment for both attacker and defender." (*There's* a clever thought.) "Enemy strength estimated at seven to eight hundred." Even Dutch's eyes wide with disbelief at that one. Why does G-2 ALWAYS underestimate enemy strength? do they pick them for their boundless optimism—or is it simply a way of bolstering their own courage?

Plan is for Dutch's people to jump off at 0630, preceded by 8 light tanks (all we've got from what I can gather) along old cart track toward airstrip. We're to jump off at 0640, along no cart track old or new. Attack order received without huzzahs. These are apparently the tactics that produced no results three days ago. Frenchy protested that the cart track simply will not hold up armor, and I suspect he's right. This is not what Georgie P would call tank country. Confab went badly. Westy kept wandering off subject, falling into petty wrangles about the use of two captured Jap barges for transporting elements of the 484th up from Kokogela. They can't get here in time for the operation, so why squabble about it?

Dutch convinced we won't make it: could see it in his eyes. Short dissertation by Herb Hodl over shortages in mortar shells, followed by listless debate on artillery preparation, which will not be lavish. Frenchy again staring at ceiling, looking as if he wanted to throw us all into a pit of coral snakes. Westy turned to Haley about air support. "You want it, Wes, you can have it." That glittering professional smile. "We'll give you a strike at 0600, tree-top level. Really work them over." Frenchy all at once exploded. "Oh Jesus, yes, by all means come over and lay it on my crowd again! Maybe you can do even better this time— maybe you can wipe out EVERYBODY in the forward positions!—" Prince Hal no longer smiling (a certain relief). "Now just a minute,

Beaupré—" "Sure, bombs away, mission accomplished—just spare us, will you, Haley? Spare us the heroics. I'd rather let the fucking Japs do it!" Westy calling, "Boys, boys! This isn't getting us anywhere . . ."

True enough. A short silence. Debated whether to say anything. Could use two days—even one—badly: reorganize, straighten out some of Caylor's mess. But as junior member of the firm determined on silence. To request postponement would only sink them all lower. Some of them resent my soaring in out of the blue like this, anyway: Hodl, Dickinson, Frenchy. And Westy has his heart set on attack. What the hell. Maybe it'll go through.

More walla-walla and paper passing, followed by a short fight talk by Westy. He is frightened, and weary unto death. Stuck out here at the ass end of the line, no support, every man's hand against him, MacArthur breathing down his neck. Pretty rough, all right. Wound up pleading with us. "I know we can do it, boys. Just one more effort and we'll be out of this . . ." Worse than if he'd said nothing. Filed out like a team after a fearful first two periods, taking field for even more disastrous second half. Frenchy turned to me violently. "Hear you fired Caylor and sent him home. Big mistake." "Is that right?" I demanded crossly. "Yeah—you should have put the son of a bitch to work hauling ammo till he dropped and then shot him in the balls." And he walked away without another word.

These conferences are stupid. Brass should go to forward units— assuming they ARE forward, that is—not other way round. This just wastes time, pulls commanders away from their outfits, where they ought to be 100% of the time.

Had a twinge of panic coming back to the CP in the dark. There is simply not a breath of air: like hot, thick blanket dropped over you, strangling you gently. Wild fusillade at Baker—had terrified visions of large-scale attack, breakthrough, massacre in the swamps. Turned out to be trigger-happy outbursts. Gave them hell. Mosquitoes beyond belief— makes Luzon look like that God damned Everglades Club.

What the hell: maybe it'll go through. But I don't know.

The night was perfectly still: the thick, ominous silence before disaster. Damon shook off the thought. Accustomed to the darkness now, he saw Bowcher's hand move, and inched his way forward, conscious of the preposterously loud slithering rasp of his clothing on the crushed and matted growth, trying to minimize it. To his right the jungle hung in a high, bristling, malevolent mass—trees and creepers and fronds so tangled and interwoven you could feel their solidity. He worked his way up beside the Sergeant, felt the lips against his ear:

"Bunker. There. See it?"

Staring hard he shook his head: relaxed then and swung his head slowly back and forth, and did see it—a narrow horizontal bar, blacker than black, broken by foliage. Then he saw another behind it and to the right, and what he thought was still another, stepped back to the left.

There was death. Well echeloned. Watching him calmly, perhaps. Perhaps not. He nodded, studying the emplacements, the lay of the land. The oppression and fatigue that had burdened him back at the CP, after the conference with Westy, was gone; he felt alert, all his senses alive, ready for anything that might arise. The immediate area—the relatively open approach, the slight rise toward the bunkers, was beautifully covered. But there was a declivity, a sort of trench that ran across the front of the nearest one and then curved back at an angle between it and the one to the right. Could a squad get in there? Would a solid volume of covering fire enable them to work their way between the two and flank them? It looked possible. And what would be behind them? two more? twenty-two? An M1 opened up—*slam, slam, slam*: shocking detonations that racketed and reechoed through the jungle. Then silence again. Some triggery bastard. Didn't they know better than to give away their positions with rifle fire like that? Shapes shifted and rearranged themselves. He conferred briefly with Bowcher and they worked their way along the little draw, which was filled with detritus and the spines of creepers. He was conscious of the presence of the nearest bunker, immediately to his right now, like a thumb on the nape of his neck. Mosquitoes whined savagely against his face and eyes; he resisted the desire to slap at them, rubbed his cheek against his shoulder. A huge mango tree loomed ahead of them, an all-arching black mass, as if holding up the harsh wall of the forest. Something—an insect, a tiny lizard— raced over his wrist and pattered on the leaves. Sweat was streaming down his cheeks and behind his ears. Moving forward now required a conscious effort of will. Bowcher's pauses were becoming longer: he too was feeling the pressure of moving in unknown land, to the rear of one of the bunkers. But his whisper was perfectly calm:

"Want to go on?"

Damon debated. The incessant, unanswerable, maddening dilemma— whether to quit with what you knew or risk it to gain still more. He raised his head, moving his eyes through the savage gloom—and heard, immediately ahead of them, the rhythmic *tchnk* of an entrenching tool: a thick, dull sound, methodical. He let it decide him, put his lips to Bowcher's ear.

"No. Seen enough. Let's go."

With infinite care he turned and started back. He felt curiously depressed now, weary and inadequate. Sweat soaked his face and stung his eyes. The air, this close to the earth, was weighty and foul, like some descending gas. He was seized with impatience to get back to the CP, find out what Ben had encountered, if anything else had come in, and fought against the tendency to hurry. There was so much to do, and no time to do it. Something scurried minutely in the brush ahead of him, and he waited and then moved on, taking his weight on his hands and elbows and knees. Far off, in Wilhelm's sector, he heard a mortar shell explode, followed by two more.

He reached the edge of the draw, worked his way past the two stumps, the oval bush, and waited for Bowcher to come up beside him. He felt unutterably tired—he wanted the Sergeant to lead going back to the outpost. The prospect of creeping back down into the stinking water of that swamp, gripping the slimy black tentacles of the roots, filled him with revulsion. He waited, thinking of nothing, while Bowcher moved up on his left side; wiped the mosquitoes and the sweat from his forehead and cheeks with his hand.

When he opened his eyes again there was a man. Standing in front of him, not eight feet away, an earthen gray against the darkness. He almost gasped. Bowcher's fingers, resting on his thigh, had gripped him in a convulsion. He could not move. While he stared at this apparition, transfixed, his throat swollen unbearably, the man raised his arms and stretched, arching his back like a cat, and released a deep, low sigh; then began to flex his legs, raising them against his chest and then lowering them, his footfalls scarcely audible. And now, mingled with the stench of the swamp, was the acrid odor of sweat and urine and something denser, like sour wine and woodsmoke. Damon gazed at him stupidly, filled with alarm. Where had he come from? There had been no sound of cloth brushing against bushes or bark, or the crisp rhythm of footsteps. It was as though he had dropped from the sky . . .

The Japanese stretched again, a kind of luxuriant indolence in the simple movement. He was stretching because he'd been confined. Perched in a tree? He was bareheaded, a solidly built boy with short, thick arms—Damon could all at once see him more clearly; he had no weapon in his hands. Damon started to reach back for his pistol, put his hand on the hilt of his knife instead. He would have to kill him— quietly. If not, all hell would break loose. They might make it by running back, they might not. Probably not. Or they could wait here and see what the sniper did. It seemed impossible that he wouldn't see Damon in another second. He eased the knife out of its stiff new sheath and brought it up beside his face. Bowcher's hand had relaxed and gone away—probably to his own knife or pistol; but the Sergeant was waiting to see what he would do. What would he do? It was crazy to crouch here like this, waiting for him to turn, spot them, scream an alarm—

Something tapped the visor of his utility cap, then his knuckles. Tensed for the act he started—realized in the very next instant what it was. Rain again. Spattering now on his hands, his back, the great damp pliant leaves above and around him. Rain. Within five seconds it had swollen to a slashing downpour, sweeping over him in chill washing waves that cut off sight and sound in its burdensome roaring, smashing on the dense vegetation like the blows from a thousand flails. He was soaked to the skin, and wildly shivering. He wiped his face against his sleeve and looked up. The Japanese was gone. He had vanished, just as quickly. He could not have run, could not have climbed. Then—then he had gone down. Spider hole. He lived all day in a spider trap near this oval bush, and came out at night to stretch. What a war . . .

He could have laughed with relief. When you gonna come again, rain? Shot with luck. So far.

He swung his head near Bowcher's. "He's gone. Let's move out. You lead." They crept swiftly away through the seething thunder of the rain.

The dugout had that intolerable stink the Japanese always seemed to impregnate everything with: like rotting fish and roasted chestnuts and ether and untended urinals. They would never get it out of the place no matter what they did. Feltner put his head down, trying not to breathe. He felt light-headed, a trifle dizzy, and wondered idly if he was getting malaria. Nearly everyone else had. People came and went, Colonel Damon kept cranking the field phone and talking to various people and Feltner tried to hold his mind on the operation but it kept skittering away, taking refuge in snatches of reverie or reminiscence. The worst of it was they were all tired now, worn down; it was nothing like the early days when they'd first got here. God, it seemed like twenty years . . .

Watts was gazing at him again—that adenoidal stare, mouth open; and Feltner looked away, scowling. It was awful, waiting like this for things to get going. But when they got going it was worse. It was a choice of perfectly insufferable evils. Of all the places he could be right now, he had to be in the hottest, filthiest, most dangerous place in the whole lousy globe. Well, one of the most dangerous. Russia was worse, probably; or some parts of China—if you were a Chinese. But that was all. Was it chance, the plain luck of the draw, as Ross said—or was there some grand design that had brought him here from California, from Georgia, from Philadelphia; from the somber, hushed offices of Llanfear and Watrous? He could still be there—it seemed impossible this morning, but he could—adding up the long, neat columns of figures, taking masses of unrelated data and translating them into the precise tabulation of a corporate entity, in black and white: balanced, functioning, present-and-accounted-for. The Army had appealed to him originally for this very reason; his marriage had foundered, he was weary of Philadelphia, and there was an uncle in the Inspector General's department whom he saw infrequently, and whose life and manner gave forceful evidence of the service as a world of order and precision, of strict accountability. It took him two months to discover he'd mistaken symbol for actuality: he was appalled by the waste and inefficiency of the peacetime Army.

But war! War overturned all the counters. In war you took a relatively organized, relatively precise and accountable instrument and watched it disintegrate into a hash of disastrous fragments before your

very eyes. It was hideous. Equipment—valuable, expensive equipment—
was lost or thrown away, supplies never arrived as planned, men melted
away—on stretchers or under ponchos or, worst of all, were reported
missing in action. Units lost contact with one another, supply dumps
went up in roaring infernos or rotted in the muck and tropic sun, nobody
knew half the time where anything *was;* and the more one struggled to
cope with this avalanche of spendthrift heedlessness and chaos the
worse it got . . .

"—yes, along the creek," Colonel Damon was speaking into the
phone, his eyes roving idly around the dugout. "Just get as far down
there as you can. That little knoll, what we talked about. Flank it if you
can, get in behind it and take it out of there—it's key. Yes, I know.
Keep right on top of them, now, Benjy. Right. Right. Good luck,
boy."

Feltner watched him as he rang up Third Battalion, issuing orders, his
voice perfectly casual. Once Damon caught his eye, and winked; sweat
hung in a greasy gob at the point of his chin, dripping on his trousers,
and his fatigue jacket was darkly stained across the shoulders. He'd
come in from that patrol at quarter of three, soaked to the bone and
shivering; then he and Krisler had been in a huddle for half an hour or
more, then he'd been on the phone to Colonel Wilhelm and then he'd
gone up to the line companies. At five thirty he'd come back into the
CP and said: "I'm going to take ten. Wake me if anything comes up,"
and had lain down on Caylor's field cot and gone sound asleep, had
waked in ten minutes to the dot and swung his feet to the floor, wanting
to know if the grenades had got up yet.

Feltner sighed, waiting, clasping and unclasping his hands and watching the regimental commander. He could never be like that. Never.
MacFarlane had been quick, tearing around and shouting at people; but
Damon acted as if it were an exercise back at Beyliss. Which it wasn't. It
damned well wasn't. Less than a minute now. He could hear men moving past the dugout—the rustle and chink of armed men walking. There
was no talk, no laughter.

"What's on your mind, Ray?" Damon was watching him—a funny
glance: faintly mournful, faintly amused.

"Nothing, sir. Just—waiting."

"Yes, there's always plenty of that, isn't there? Well, your troubles
will be over in a few seconds." At that moment off toward the airstrip
there was a clatter like faulty engines without mufflers, and firing began,
rising to a martellato fury, punctuated with deep, even detonations like
the bass drum in a percussion section, and the Colonel said: "Didn't I tell
you? Here we go." Standing up he buckled on his cartridge belt, picked
up his '03 and went out of the dugout.

Feltner followed him outside into the glare; the ground was spongy
and slick from the rain. The Colonel was standing easily, his arm against
the trunk of a tree, watching the green figures move forward through

the bush, their helmets smooth and dark against the verdure. Damon said something to him and he tried to listen, hating the intrusive force of the gunfire, which had increased. He had learned to identify them—the taut bark of the M1's, the higher whine of the Arisaka rifle, the heavy *dod-dod-dod* of the machine guns, the dense cough of grenades—he could pick them out: it was the aggregate that overwhelmed him. It was impossible to think with any clarity while something like this was going on. Firing rose to a rolling bellow of sound, and now the Japanese machine guns began, the Nambus—a hysterical shuttling clamor that pressed at his eardrums. Against his will he saw Boretz on the ground the first day, writhing and rolling, his hands to his head, uttering sharp, yelping screams—drove the image away with a tremor of impatience, his eyes narrowed against the uproar. He must keep his mind clear, he must—

"They're not moving," the Colonel was saying.

It was true: they'd all hit the dirt. There wasn't a helmet to be seen. It was going to be like the other times, then. The weight of the past six weeks settled over him. The Japanese had everything—an unlimited amount of ammunition, the higher ground, hundreds of bombproof fortifications, you could never *see* them—

"Let's go," Damon was saying.

He looked around, startled. "Sir?"

"You don't think we're going to hang around here, do you?" The Colonel's face looked all at once very hard and blocklike: a younger, tougher man. "Come on, let's go up and earn our pay for a while." And he started walking forward briskly, his rifle held loosely in his right hand, his head down. For a moment Feltner thought of his father, walking ahead of him through the stubble, hunting, out in the Poconos. Unslinging his submachine gun he called to Watts and Everill, and hurried after him, toward the Nambus, which sounded much louder. Grasses, leaves slapped wetly against his leggings, the dizziness seemed worse, and his eyes hurt—shifting them caused quick little flashes of pain. How far was Damon going? What were they going to do? If the troops were pinned down—

A soldier was running toward them, bareheaded, wild-eyed, one hand in the air. Feltner remembered him vaguely, couldn't recall his name. Oh Christ, he thought. Of all the moments. Of all the times! The Old Man'll ream him out, and then me and everybody else in sight. At least he'd hung onto his rifle; that was something.

But instead the Colonel smiled. "What's the matter, son?" he asked cheerily.

The soldier—*Phillips!* That was his name, Phillips: good—had stopped in dismay, panting. He swung his free arm backward wildly. "The Japs—!" he cried, over the guns' clamor. "There's thousands of 'em . . ."

"You're sure of that?" Damon had come up to Phillips and now paused briefly, confronting him.

"—they're charging—all over the place! We got to have reinforcements, we can't stop 'em—"

"Aw, I don't believe it . . ."

The Colonel's tone was so relaxed, so deft a balance between sarcasm and casual, matter-of-fact rejoinder that Phillips gaped at him, then began to grin foolishly. For the first time he seemed aware of Damon's rank.

"—For Christ sake," he laughed shakily. With the ebbing of his panic he felt empty, a bit resentful. "I tell you, there's a million of 'em out there, Colonel . . ."

"Well, let's go see," Damon said, his voice now just a shade peremptory. "Come on, now." He pushed on by. Phillips started to say something more; then he caught sight of Feltner and his mouth came together.

"Phillips," Feltner told him sharply, "you get hold of yourself now. Cut that out."

"Yes, sir." Phillips wheeled around all at once and fell in beside him, even got in step, which irritated Feltner beyond all bounds. He had a fierce desire to roar at the private, threaten him with all manner of dire punishment—then an equally intense impulse to laugh. His face felt tight and smarting, as though he had poison ivy, and it was hard to breathe. This was going to be difficult—to keep walking like this toward the dry, frenetic hammering, the snap and drone in the foliage above their heads.

"Colonel—" he said sharply.

Damon turned. "Yes?"

"Hadn't you better take those eagles off?"

The Colonel shook his head. "Boys don't know me yet, most of them."

"General Westerfeldt has issued strict orders—"

"I know. Better this way."

Jesus Christ, Feltner thought; he stumbled on a root and almost went to his knees. The Nambus were firing in short bursts now, like hundreds of vindictive old women in a terrible quarrel. Bits of leaf kept falling here and there around them. It was like a dream, strolling along this way—but an evil one. This was going to be bad. End badly. If they kept walking forward like this, through the still, oily water, if they just kept *walking*—

They were among the assault platoons now—he was aware of men crouching under shrubs, behind fallen trees, in water-filled holes. It frightened him more looking down at them; he felt guilty and angry and foolish all at once. One winter afternoon when he'd been nine or ten he'd been walking carefully along the top of a brick wall and several schoolmates had started throwing snowballs at him and laughing; now, here, he felt the same burgeoning fear and sense of betrayal, the desperate need to lie down, get away, make it be over.

"Come on, boys," the Colonel was saying in that calm, invocatory, obdurate tone that seemed to make walking along upright like this both a trivial whim and the gravest obligation of man to man. How could he talk like that—! "Just over that little hump, there. We've got to get over there, they're counting on us today. All of us. *Let's* go, now . . ."

Their eyes rolled up at him under their helmet rims—a concert of resentment, amazement, distrust. A clear, boyish voice said, "Who's *that?*" But the Colonel paid no attention, talked on, moving through them, the chin strap of his helmet swinging against his jaw. "Come on now, boys, we can't stay here and let them down, *you* know that . . ."

A machine gun opened up suddenly, savagely near, and tracers burned like thick orange wires into the bushes ten feet away. Feltner found himself on the ground, gripping it, breathing through his teeth; he had no recollection of leaving his feet. Just above his head there was a ricochet like a fiddle string snapped. He looked up to see the Colonel still walking back and forth, talking in that impossible conversational tone. A piece of bark chipped away from the ridged elephant hide of a palm not three feet from his face, and the Colonel grinned and cocked his head in that brief little gesture Feltner remembered his father using with other workmen in the packing plant back in Trenton. "Look at that," he was saying out loud. "Pitiful. Couldn't shoot in China, couldn't shoot on Luzon, still can't hit a God damn thing, here in New Guinea . . ." He put his hands on his hips and faced two men directly. "Come on now, boys. What do you say? Just up to that little rise. Who's coming with me?"

And as though that near-miss had released him, a thin, sallow-faced soldier got to his feet, then two more, one of them a sergeant named Prince, who turned and started shouting at them, waving them up; and then there were a dozen or more, hurrying, pumping their rifles across their bodies. They were up. They were moving.

"*That's* it," the Colonel was calling now, swinging his arm like a track coach waving his runners along, "*that's* it, *now* you've got it, let's roll, now . . ." and then, fiercely: "*Let's take 'em!*—" A man went down with a sharp cry but the rest paid no attention; they were all running and throwing themselves down and getting up again, going toward the machine guns, which now formed a solid bar of sound.

The Colonel had turned to the left, was making his way through vines and plants like octopi, like banana trees gone crazy, threading his way. "I ought to check on Kraus's gang next. How far are we off the trail, Ray? I wonder if we could come out right next to the—"

There was the snapping whine of a rifle and a slap like a hand against a thigh, and Archimbeau, the Colonel's orderly, grunted and started down, sinking in almost dreamy reluctance to his knees. Someone shouted, "Cover! *Cover!*" The ping-crack came again, and then a ragged burst of firing. Feltner was on his belly under a small bush with great drooping oval leaves. He had no idea where Damon was; he couldn't see Archimbeau anymore, or Watts. The rifle fired again and there was a *whunnnk!* right beside his head. He gasped, and jerked his hand back as if it had been burned. Down. The bullets were all going down. Into the ground.

He looked up, through dizzying layers on overlapping layers of vegetation, squinting with frantic eagerness. There was nothing to see. His heart was pounding unbearably—his whole body quaked with its beating. Behind him somewhere Archimbeau was saying something, or groaning. It was impossible to *see—!* Still he stared upward, painfully, riding down on his fear with all his might. The nasal slap came again, and he saw—or thought he saw—the most delicately perceptible flicker of movement in the dense canopy of green. He jerked himself to one knee, raised the Tommy gun and fired a burst. The gun's pneumatic yammer almost stunned him—but at the same time it sponged away his fear. He felt angry, exhilarated, in some crazy way a part of the deafening, racketing weapon, its servant rather than its master: bound in its brutal, shocking, liberating force. He jumped to his feet, darted a few yards to the right, crouched behind a tree and fired again. Then there was silence. Nothing. He wanted to look around, to find Damon, but he didn't dare shift his gaze.

. . . He was conscious of a pacing sound, like the softest of feet advancing through the air—the air!—toward him. The sound went on, no louder, but his fear was gone. He raised the gun calmly, waiting, but the pacing continued, dulcet, oblique, slowing now. A pacing.

A dripping.

A branch ahead of him bobbed. Splotches of bright red on the broad spatulate leaves, which danced under the impact. The blood fell in long, glutinous arcs and globules. He gazed at it numbly. It was so incredibly scarlet and slick, lying on the leaves, sliding down in long skeins. It was so *red*. And now, far up, obscured, a branch rocked with a slow, faltering motion.

He lowered his eyes. The Colonel, looking at him, gave that quick, crisp nod of his. "Nice work, Ray."

Was it? Maybe it was. He didn't know. He lowered the gun. He had killed a man; unquestionably. Yet he felt none of the things he might have expected to feel—there was neither remorse nor exultancy nor terror; he was conscious only of a weary anger, as though he'd been tried beyond his patience. A savage fusillade came from the left now, and tracers ripped scissoring through the vines. The waste, he thought, the incredible waste of material in this war. Of bullets alone. Then the ludicrous aspect of the thought struck him. He got to his feet. The Colonel was already crouched over Archimbeau, had turned him over. "In the chest," he said. "We've got to round up a litter party."

"Yes," he said numbly; he watched Archimbeau's eyes opening and closing like a sleepy baby's. His frown, too, was like a baby's: he seemed neither terrified nor in pain. His lips were moving slowly; Feltner bent down.

". . . You get him, Captain?"

"Yes—I got him, Archie," he said tersely. "I got him good. Now take it easy. We'll get you out of here."

They rounded up a minimum stretcher party for Archimbeau, and then went over to First Battalion. Things were no better there. They waded through an evil place where the swamp was black with rot and stagnation, and several bodies, facedown, rocked gently in the little waves they made as they went by. There was a low rise where they lay on their bellies and watched Tom Hurd and a sergeant work their way up within ten feet of a bunker before they both were hit. They were killed instantly, but the Japanese gunners kept hosing them down, and the two bodies quivered and twitched as the torrent of bullets pounded into them. "Oh, the bastards," he heard himself saying, raging, on the edge of tears, hating all Japanese forever with a hate blacker than the swamp they'd crossed. "Oh, the dirty, butchering bastards . . ."

Back at the CP all the news was bad. Colonel Krisler, who had jumped off with Third Battalion, had got down to the Knoll but had been stopped there. The 468th had made it to the edge of the airstrip, and was now under heavy counterattack. Second Battalion was out of communication with How Company. And later, sitting in the foul-smelling dugout eating a K ration tin of pork and egg yolk, Feltner had glanced at his watch in dulled surprise to see that it was nearly two thirty. All those hours. His head ached, and his belly heaved thickly; he felt desolate, fearful, overcome by the malignant power and craft of this enemy who held all the cards, and who knew so well how to play them, one by one.

"It looks grim, Colonel," he said.

"It's not over."

"If we don't make it, if we can't break through to the beach with this one—"

"Then we'll try something else."

"—We're not even *killing* any of them . . ."

"That's what they want you to think." Damon ran his tongue around the edge of his cheek. "They're dragging back their dead. Didn't you see the blood on the rifles?"

"Yes, but our losses—if they get any worse—"

"Take it easy." The Colonel's eyes flickered around the dugout, though they were out of hearing of everyone except Everill, a lineman who was working on the field phone in the corner near them. "Calm," Damon went on; he smiled his slow, mournful smile, chewing on the K ration. "The higher your rank the calmer you must be. You must instill confidence." The smile came again. "Even if you don't always feel it yourself. I've seen things in China so bad I didn't think any of us would get through the next hour. But we did; and they're still going strong over there." He wiped his mouth with a big red handkerchief. "Every man—well, almost every man—is afraid. And fear makes for worry, and worry for pessimism. That's where you come in. You must check it at the source. It's your job to bespeak confidence, calmness, optimism."

Feltner looked at him for a moment. "Then—it's sort of living a lie, isn't it?"

"Yes. If you want to put it that way. But so is all of life. You don't make the world a present of your innermost thoughts, do you? I'd guess you never told your wife every single thought or emotion or temptation that passed through your mind during a single Sunday afternoon at home. I know I didn't . . . Of course it's absurd, if that's what you're thinking. But *war* is absurd, Ray: war is dishonest, and cruel, and vicious in all its forms. And here we are, sitting at the ass-end of the world, with decisions to make, and a couple thousand kids looking to us for help—for some plan, some move, some miracle that will get them out of this hideous hell and send them home again . . ."

There came a series of deep, dull explosions from over on the left, beyond the Knoll.

"Mortars," the Colonel said. "A battle's like a forest fire, Ray. A big, bad, raging forest fire, out of control. And you're trying to stop it, you're in charge. So you get people working here, in this place, get them to face the heat and sparks and battle it—then you move around to check somewhere else and fire some other people up; you try to keep in touch everywhere you can, you encourage, instruct, plead—yes, and threaten if necessary. And at the same time you try to be more vigilant than the fire. And above all you never let anyone see you're every bit as full of doubts and fears as the lowliest private in the rear rank. That's your job." Damon smiled again. "That's all they're asking of you."

Everill called, "Colonel! WOLVERINE to you . . ."

The Colonel was on his feet before Feltner had set down the little green ration tin. "Ben? Sam. They are. In force? All right. All right . . ." and Feltner, peering over Damon's shoulder, could see his fingernail scoring a short arc at the edge of the Knoll below the copra plantation. "All right. Hang on tight, Ben boy. I'll get you something. Christ knows where or how, but I'll get you something . . ."

17 Oct 42. Worst day yet. 2 tanks knocked out, remaining 3 bogged down in that excuse for a road. And that-a is that-a. Dutch's crowd got across west end of the airstrip, then Japs counterattacked in force and he pulled everybody back. Lost nearly everything he'd gained. Why? Was on dry ground (Jesus: DRY GROUND), could have supported them. He is too prudent. There is a time for withdrawing and a time for hanging on to what you can grab: this is time for hanging on. Westy's pessimism has infected him—they are all succumbing to apprehensions.

Air strike awful. Really awful. Flight of A-20s came in at treetop level, blasted and strafed How and King. Two BAR men fired back at planes: could not blame them. Six dead, seventeen wounded. So much for Prince Hal and his dead-eye dicks. Granted this terrain is fierce: but there's Larotai Point and the cove and that sunken maru, not to mention the Grove and the roof of the Mission. There are enough points for reference. Can't they SEE? or don't the bastards give a shit?

One break. One tiny, nervous break. Bowcher got to the sea, on that spit of land between the river and the copra plant or whatever it is. 23 effectives and 1 mg. Got to him at 1530 with LaRocca's platoon and 2 mgs—best I could do, way things are going. Asked him what he thought. "Hell yes, I'm staying. Feel that frigging ocean breeze!" I said: "Suppose they hit you from both flanks at the same time?" "They won't: they can't coordinate their attacks, anyway—their communications are more fouled up than ours." "I doubt it," I said. He grinned: his face black as a minstrel show end-man's. He'll hold it, all right. He had them dug in in a long horseshoe, with a connecting trench for switching guns. He is TERRIFIC. Told him he was a captain as of right then— thought of Dad and Brigny Farm. He said: "Let's see how we make out." He is one cool cookie.

I asked them: "What do you need?" and drew a chorus of great replies: "Well—they use like a bed for it." "Nothing you can bring me on a platter, Chief!" They are really up. Kid named Frohman did a crazy striptease shimmy right there, with the Japs not a hundred yards away on both flanks, turned toward me a great ragged hole where the seat of his trousers used to be. "How about some riding britches, Colonel? or a cast-iron jock?" All of them looking like scarecrows, half-starved, most of them shaking with fever. Thought of Dev, and Raebyrne. *All aboard for the frigging Alamo.* Put the thought down hard. Told them if they held I'd give them all bronze stars and personally throw them a party they'd never forget. I will, too.

Hated to leave them out there on that lonely strip of sand.

Rocky time coming back. Sniper opened up, then bunker nobody had seen before, hit Smith and Watts. Already burdened with two of Bowcher's wounded. Again Feltner did well: little CPA is going to be all right. Westy never liked him because he wasn't W's kind of man. Of course not, he's his own kind. He just needed a little time to get his feet under him. When bunker opened up I hit the dirt in a panic, thought I was hit. Got up all over mud, couldn't find my rifle, started floundering around for it. Feltner looked at me, perfectly serious, Tommy gun smoking. "Confidence, calmness, optimism." Had to laugh.

Later found holes through medical pouch, left sleeve. Lucky as hell. Japs do not fire unless directly attacked, consequently we are bypassing strong points, never know they are there. And manned. Is this intentional or part of old Nip rigidity? They have no capacity for improvisation, apparently; what they decide on they stick to. Thank God for that—if Westy's opposite number had brains-one he'd have launched a combined flanking movement from the Bowari Trail and the Watubu Creek, gone out around the swamp and cut us to pieces. I'd give ten thousand dollars (which I haven't got) for old man Shiraga's tactical possibilities. Just *one* of them.

Zipped over to Brig Hq with my morsel of good news. Westy just back from Timobele. Rowing with the Aussies over the 484th. Almost came to blows with Lawlor, from what I can gather. He's sick, won't admit it: has lost over thirty pounds, eyes flickering around. Barely hanging on. MacArthur's directives stinging him, press riding him now too, snapping at his heels. Bunch of them outside the tent. "Would you say then, General, the attack *was* adequately prepared and executed?" Curtin, little bantam rooster in blue Navy fatigues (where'd he get those?). Westy turning on him: "I don't know what the hell you mean by *adequately*—I have complete confidence in my staff. We're doing all we can with what we've got. What do you want? If we had one tenth the stuff they're sending SouPac every day in the week . . ." Moross cutting in deftly, "May we quote you on that, General?" "No, you may not—! For Christ sake, man—what do you take me for? If you had any idea at all what conditions are like up there, in the line . . ." Last man he should have said that to. A lot of them have been hanging around Brig Hq and the hospital, picking up yarns 9th hand, but Moross was up there for both attacks. Could see him getting mad. "I've been up there far enough to see three perfectly good M3 light tanks up over their bogies in mud and water—do you plan to use them as floating batteries?"

Went from bad to worse. Dickinson trying to pour oil on the raging waters. "Harry, you know perfectly well losses must be expected in operations of this kind—our intelligence and supply problems out here are almost insurmountable." Half-hauling Westy away before he blew up completely and ordered them all in irons and brought World Opinion down on his weary, sweating head.

Thought he'd be elated by Bowcher's big bust-through: seemed only to make him more gloomy. "I don't like it, Sam. They'll hit him on both flanks, won't they? They'll be wiped out. I don't like it at all." Seeing disaster in every situation: perils, losses, drawbacks, negative side of things. Told him I was virtually certain the Japs didn't have communications to coordinate assault on both flanks, that morale in Bowcher's crowd was excellent. Tried to tell him it was thin edge of the wedge, could enable us to roll up Atainu Point area in 2 days. "It's a gamble, Sam." "Yes it is, General. But I'm confident we can make it pay off."

"Maybe so." Sitting hunched over, dejected, eyes puffy with lack of sleep, face bruised and slack, only his lips moving; sweat standing out on his forehead in great gobs. "Maybe so. I don't know. That's a diversionary business, anyway: it's the airstrip we've got to nail down. That God damn airstrip." I refrained from pointing out that possession of the strip will mean nothing if the Nips can douse it in mortar fire from the Knoll and the Mission. He doesn't see the possibilities here: too weary, too worn down.

He said, "I'm sending in Koch's people with Frenchy day after tomorrow." The last reserves. Could not keep the surprise out of my face. "Well, what do you want me to do? I've *got* to take Moapora—I've got to! In *five days* . . ." Gazing out at the boondocks, blinking, hands hanging between his legs. "It's no fun being a general, Sam. I can tell you that. Nobody comes around anymore. There you are, all by your lonesome, grappling with the whole sad damn mess, trying to get out from under. It's like a God damn tent collapsing on you in the dark . . ."

Talked with Dick afterward, then Specs. They are beginning to come apart, too. Afraid we'll be left to death and capture and all the attendant horrors. Like Bataan. Another sacrifice to the national optimism and indifference, while the Congress dances and Nelson and Knudsen squabble over which plants get the contracts. Well, it isn't very reassuring. No Navy, no supplies getting in except dribbles from Prince Hal's celestial charioteers. (Air drop of clothing scattered over half of Papua yesterday afternoon early: would take a three-division sweep to find a tenth of it. Whose bright idea was that?) Could feel fear in the tent, like odor of sweat. Or worse. Everyone very near the edge, one eye on where to light out for. If the situation turns fluid, as that whacky redheaded driver from Kokogela airport said.

Monterey seems very far away tonight.

The rain fell in smashing waves, incessant, torrential, as if it wanted to wash the world away, obliterate all blood and detritus and mire, return it to the omnipotent and cleansing ocean. Gradually the mud floor of the tent began to glisten with the passage of water—slender trickles and rivulets that joined, swelled into a larger stream; and objects like helmet liners and discarded ration containers began to float, drifting sluggishly toward a far corner. Sitting at his field desk with his feet up on a box, Damon released the plunger on the Coleman lantern and pumped it smartly for several seconds, adjusted the mantles; then again picked up the Japanese diary, its cover stiff with dried blood, and began making his way laboriously down the delicate rice-grain characters.

The enemy act like children who have lost their parents. They make jerky movements in the jungle, they look around them fearfully, exposing their bodies. They even call to each other now and then. They do not run away anymore; but they are afraid. They fire wildly at nothing. At night they are even worse. At the slightest sound they work the cocking handles of their guns, reveal their positions and fire with reckless abandon into the jungle. Are they paid for the amount of ammunition they use up each night? It is possible. They are lacking in patience, in discipline. Their grenades are good but they release them too early: they fear their own grenades.

Damon nodded grimly. Some truth in that: though possibly Lieutenant Niizuma would want to revise that part about the grenades—if he were still among the living. Rasmussen, the brigade intelligence officer, now down with malaria, had told him there was nothing of any tactical value in the diary; but that depended entirely on what one was looking for.

Where are the reinforcements we were promised from Wokai? If we could only attack! Now, while the Yanks are afraid . . . But Colonel Eguchi says that we are to hold our fortress. And we will. We are the warriors of Yamamoto. Great Japan has never lost a fortress to the enemy.

Quite true. He got up and splashed through the water to the map board, which was hanging on a frame braced against the tent pole, unhooked it, and propping it up against his desk studied it for the hundredth time, moving with slow tenacity over the patches of jungle, the trails and enemy strongpoints—and especially the Watubu Creek, which wound its way circuitously to the sea just beyond Larotai Point, secured now by the reduction of the Japanese force on the east bank of Bowcher's Bastion. They were at the river and there they sat helplessly, while Westy frantically mounted still another attack on the terrific defenses guarding the airstrip. Tomorrow at 0700 Koch and Frenchy were going to try it again. Another frontal assault.

He sighed and rubbed his eyes. The air in the blackout tent was close and foul in spite of the lashing rain outside; mosquitoes made a treble moan around him, bumping against his forehead and neck. It was no good. The key was the Mission—there on the high ground, dominating the airfield and the beach. And the key to the Mission was the Watubu. Deep, tidal, sliding toward the sea in a slick brown plate, only forty to fifty feet wide. If they could force that, they could wheel on down the left bank to the sea and drive across behind the Mission; and the strip, pinched on two flanks, would fall in a day. But there were only two landing craft, captured Japanese boats from the Kokogela battle. For lack of a nail the kingdom was lost. For a while he toyed with the idea of building rafts out of coconut logs, dismissed the idea. Too cumbersome, too unwieldy and slow, too defenseless—their occupants would be swept overboard by a hail of fire from the far side. It would have to be quick, deadly, done in a rush: or not at all. But it was the only way he could see.

The Coleman lantern flared and dimmed like a faulty circuit, making him blink. The water in the mud floor of the tent was several inches deep; the legs of his and Ben's field cots were nearly obscured. He had to think! Tomorrow's assault would fail—there was no reason on God's earth to see why it should succeed—and two days after that Westy, in desperation, would pull the 477th out of the river line and send it in against the strip; and after that the Brigade would be finished as an effective fighting force. They would disintegrate. Dickinson had already made a veiled reference to the possibilities of withdrawal to Kokogela. But it would not be a withdrawal—it would be a panic-stricken, disorderly rout, marked by insubordination and collapse, harried by Japanese air and patrols . . .

He'd better get some sleep: he wasn't doing himself or anyone else any good sitting here like this staring goggle-eyed at the yellowed, dying mantles of the Coleman. But instead he picked up another diary whose final entry was stroked in with a nervous, erratic hand:

Ah, this is a cruel, wretched land, this black, airless jungle. Are we to be left here, sick and hungry and forgotten? Can it be here that I will meet my fate? I will fight to the last drop of my blood, as a loyal son of Hyogo. But it is a bitter thing. I hold the symbol of the clan deity close to my beating heart. Oh, to see once more the high, green terraces of home!

A hand pressed against his shoulder, a voice said: "Sam . . ."

He opened his eyes. Ben, in fatigues and patrol cap, soaked to the skin, his eyes red with exhaustion; the three days' growth of beard made his face look even more bony and lopsided. "What you doing, feeding the mosquitoes?"

"I guess so. What's up?"

"Sam, we've got something, I think. Goethals' patrol found four native boats hidden along the bank. On our side, about a mile upstream."

Damon sat up; his feet went into the water with a dull splash. "Are they in good shape? Will they float?"

Ben nodded. "I've just been up there with him. One's a little leaky."

"How big are they?"

"Thirty feet or so. You could get a dozen guys into each one of them."

The two men looked at each other for a moment. Damon rubbed his jaw. "It's a long shot."

"Yeah, it's a long shot."

"If there were only a dozen of them . . ."

Ben sat down on the ammunition crate; with the cap's sodden visor shading his eyes he looked like a tough, dirty kid planning some piece of

deviltry. "I've been thinking about it, Sam. I've had a thought. Suppose
we rig lines on them, fore and aft. We rush the far bank, then detail
people to stand by the lines. Meanwhile we haul the boats back empty
from this side, load them up, and the guys on the far side haul them
back. Then we keep doing it." He raised one hand, fingers extended.
"It's got a lot of advantages: it'll be twice as fast as paddling, nobody has
to make the ride back to this side, and the lines will avoid any foul-ups
in landing."

Damon nodded. "But the tow-men will have to stand up there, on
both banks . . ."

"I know. But if we can just get a toehold over there . . . Christ, I can
swim the God damn thing!"

"Not with eighty pounds of gear you can't. Or anybody else."
Damon stared hard at the map board. "They'd be sitting ducks . . .
unless we made a night crossing."

Ben's face went slack with consternation. "A night crossing! Jesus, I
don't know, Sam—they're pretty weary. I don't know if they're up to
it."

"They've got to be. It's the only way." He could see it now, quite
clearly: the four lakatois in the center, the two Japanese barges on the
outside. Pin the far bank down with mortars and machine guns until the
last possible second. Use Ben's lines idea until they'd ferried two companies over, then swing the boats around and rig a pontoon bridge
with them for heavy weapons. It was possible: it was distinctly possible.

"Only thing—that first wave is going to be rough," Ben was saying.
"Japs at the Narrows are loaded for bear."

"We won't cross there. We'll cross farther down, where it's wider.
We'll give them a heavy preparation up there, too—maybe it'll siphon
some of them off. Then I'll block left, and you and Stan Bowcher go for
the water behind the Mission."

Ben gazed at him silently for a moment. Then he said, "It's worth a
try."

Damon looked at his watch. Quarter to three. Too late for anything
tonight. What they ought to do was tie it in with the assault on the
strip. He took the receiver out of its box, cranked the field phone and
said: "BULL MOOSE."

"BULL MOOSE," a voice answered, after a pause; he knew it was
Albee, the General's aide.

"This is BOBCAT," he said briskly. "I need to talk to the General."

"Sir, he's asleep."

"I imagine that's true, since it's three A.M." He threw a baleful glance
at Ben, who had blown out his sallow cheeks. "Would you wake him,
please. This is urgent."

"Very good, sir. I'll—just a moment, Colonel. Will you hold on?"

"Naturally." Albee ought to be a laundry officer. Damon could see
him standing in the silent tent, frowning with indecision, he could sense

the working of the man's mind: it was three in the morning; the General never liked to be disturbed; was it really important? The line buzzed and crackled faintly. Could a Japanese patrol have tapped it? Almost impossible—it was constantly checked, and the Japs were not probing. Why should they? All they had to do was sit back with their hands on the triggers and let the stupid Yanks come to them . . .

"Sam?" a tart, thin voice said. "This is Dick. The General isn't feeling well, and I'd rather not wake him unless it's awfully crucial. Has anything come up?"

He shrugged at Ben, who was picking at his nails. "Yes, there has. We've found a way to do that Christopher thing, and it would be good if we could tie it in with the SHAMROCK assault. But we'll need a minimum of eighteen hours. Is there any possibility of postponing tomorrow's—today's—attack?"

"I'm sorry, Sam. The General left word about that expressly. No changes. Categorically no changes, no postponements. Koch's battalion's already staging, you know."

"I know."

"I'll go over and rout him out if you insist. But I can tell you now he'll never consent to scratching it." Dickinson sounded apologetic and troubled. "He's determined that we get through there with this one."

"I see." Well. It probably wouldn't accomplish anything to get Westy up: he'd come to the phone angry and befuddled—and a request like this would sound like the very reluctance and defeatism he believed he was combating. It wouldn't do any good. "Okay, Dick," he answered. "You're probably right. Sorry I woke you up." And to the switchboard man: "Break it down."

Ben waded over to his cot and rolled in under the folded mosquito net, fully clothed. Lying on his back he unbuckled his web belt and slid it out from under his hips with a grunt. He looked utterly done in.

"Well," he said sonorously, "ours not to reason why. Ours but to dry an eye."

They came back along the trail toward the field hospital, sliding and staggering in the muck, the stretcher bearers cursing, panting under their loads, the walking wounded wavering like pathetic drunks. One man was holding to the side of his face a sopping red rag, the blood running down through his fingers and over his wristwatch; his good eye rolled wildly at Damon as he passed. Another boy, helmetless, his face dark with strain as if from carrying too great a weight, clinging to his belly, his buddy helping him, half-carrying him, saying in a soft, fearful tone, "Take it easy, Danny, take it easy," over and over. Another litter, its occupant belted to the frame, his arm snatching feebly at the air above his head; one leg ended at the knee in a thick knot of blood and gristle and blued slivers of bone. Someone had tourniqueted it crudely with a bayonet scabbard. After that an ambulance jeep, skidding and slewing in the black ooze, full to capacity, with a corpsman perched precariously at the top of the rack, holding a bottle of plasma high in one hand, the tube curving down to one of the recumbent bodies. Then two walking wounded, one boy gripping his arm close to his body as though holding some infinitely precious jewel, fearful of deprivation. A short, swarthy man, his head thrown back, teeth bared in pain, swinging along on one leg between two friends. Another stretcher figure, on its belly, one arm dragging loosely in the muck; the bandage had slipped with his bearers' exertions and in the center of his bared back a great red hole was visible with blood bubbling out thickly: a rich crimson soup. Behind them, up the trail, the great and little guns bumped and clattered like some beast whose fiery breath had singed them all, was still reaching out for them.

A two-man stretcher team staggered by; their patient, whose arm and shoulder were clothed in a scarlet sponge of rags and gauze, cried: "Jesus, oh Jesus, can't you put me down for a *minute*, let me rest?—just for a *minute* . . ." and the medics both sank to one knee, gasping for breath. One of his crowd; Damon recognized the rear bearer—a thin, beak-nosed man whose eyes shot out to his with quick murderous intensity, slid away. Damon knew that look: it was the look of a man so crazed with exhaustion and despair he no longer cared what he did, or why. Now there was a boy staggering badly, trembling and shaking his head, shouting now and then in a shrill, clear voice. Then another stretcher case with cratered head wounds from which Damon averted his eyes. Jesus. In the head. He dreaded that more than any other, more than belly or face or testicles. To stop one in your *brain* . . . Standing there at the junction of the two trails, weary and harassed, listening to Dickinson, watching this procession of boundless agony, hearing the groans, the pleas and imprecations, he thought: I shouldn't be here; I've got no business here. But still they came on, ragged or feverish or comatose, each of them dominated by one thought. He could feel the alarm grow inside him. Half the rifle companies were down to sixty, seventy, eighty effectives *now*. What would be left?

Dickinson was saying: "I've just had word from Pryce-Sealey at Timobele. He says they've got hold of a coastal transport."

"What size?" he asked absently.

"Eleven tons. We should be able to load several companies, a full battalion perhaps."

Damon watched the narrow, lined face, the cautious gray eyes. Eleven tons. One day to load, two more—or would it be three?—to creep up the coast at night under the Japanese bombers . . . and here, right here, was a prize package of disaster staring them full in the face. Eleven tons.

It began to rain again, the flat, washing roar advancing like surf through the forest—sweeping over them, drenching and pervasive, walling each man off in his own shabby world of fear and misery and anger. And still the wounded came past, lurching, falling to their knees and getting up again, their faces white against their beards; drifting, beaten shadows. Dickinson, whose back was to the proceesion, was still talking on in that brassy Maine accent about ammunition levels and tonnage tables and the possibility of the loan of two Bren gun carriers from the Aussies.

"Ah, there he is," the Chief of Staff said with sudden relief. They stepped across to the north trail, where weeks ago some wag from Chicago had placed a sign that read: 47TH AND STATE. The rain faded, then let up abruptly, and the jeep came out of the jungle gloom, rocking and sliding. General Westerfeldt got out, followed by Haley, his raunchy garrison cap cocked back on his head, and Hodl, who was staring dully at the ground. As Damon and Dickinson came up Haley was saying, "If the Gap opens up tomorrow we can run everything we've got. Angels can't do more."

Westerfeldt turned to Hodl. "How do we stand right now?"

The G-4 said tonelessly, "My inventories show two days' supplies."

"Two *days* . . ." Westy stared at him as if the Major had struck him in the face. "Hal," he turned to Haley, "you've got to get through tomorrow—you've *got to* . . ."

"If it can be done, we'll be there. With cap and bells." He threw them all his glittering Air Force smile, tossed out one hand. "What the hell, fellers—things are never as rough as they seem. Love'll find a way."

How the hell would you know, you slaphappy fly-boy? Damon wanted to shout at him. He hated Haley with all his heart: too much rank too fast, coupled with that delightful insouciance only flying above the blood and mud and swamp stink at nine thousand feet can give you . . . But the General said nothing. His eyes rolled white at Haley, his mouth worked once, but no sound came. Then Haley was in the jeep and skidding and swooping along past the stretchers, the wavering, pitiful processional.

Damon said quickly: "General, I'd like to outline a plan for your consideration."

"What? All right—come on back with me. Dick, what have you heard from Koch?—how's he going?"

"The situation's relatively unchanged since fourteen hundred, sir.—I just got word from TOPGALLANT," he went on earnestly. "They say they definitely can give us those two carriers. If we could use them conjointly with the Third Battalion of the Four sixty-eighth at the east end of the strip . . ."

Westerfeldt nodded absently. His eyes had encountered the column of wounded; watching them he rubbed his lips with his hand. His shoulders sagged, his forty-five hung halfway down his trouser leg; the barrel end of the holster was filthy with mud. "Yes, yes, I guess so. We'll have to see . . ."

It began to rain again, less heavily. Near them a blond boy was sitting on a log, his hands wrapped around his knees; at every cannon or mortar explosion he flinched; his eyes were closed, his mouth was drawn down in anguish and he was weeping, rocking back and forth and weeping. "Ah, no," he moaned softly, rocking, "no, no, no—it's not my fault, ah they can't, they can't . . ."

Westerfeldt stopped, his eyes transfixed on the boy. "What's the matter with him?" he demanded suddenly. He went up to the log. "Now look here, soldier . . ."

The blond boy's eyes opened, full of fear. "Ah, no, no, no," he repeated, wagging his head. "I tried, I swear to God—but it wasn't my fault . . ."

Westerfeldt shouted: "Look, soldier: you stand up when an officer speaks to you!"

The boy sprang to his feet with astonishing alacrity. "—Shut up!" he screamed all at once. "Shut your face, you rotten bloody butcher. Kill us all—what you care . . . nobody! And I tried and tried . . ." Tears were running crookedly through the mud and stubble on his face; pale, clownish streaks. There were deep blue hollows under his eyes. "You hear me?" he cried wildly. "Fuck you to hell! . . ." He tensed, as though to make a lunge at the General, then before either Damon or the Chief of Staff could intervene he collapsed on the log again, sobbing. "Ah I couldn't help it, ah God, it *wasn't—my—fault!* . . ."

Westerfeldt was staring down at him, his face white and sweating, his eyes vacant. "Now, son," he muttered. "Now, son—"

Dickinson had bent over and seized the boy by the arm. "Soldier, you return to your unit. You hear me? You go back to your unit!"

"Never mind, Dick . . ." The General had started off again. Damon caught up with him near the operations tent, and Westerfeldt turned to him with a tense, distraught expression. "What was it—what was I—"

"General," Damon repeated, "I've a plan I'd like to outline for you, if I may. A plan for crossing the Watubu."

Westerfeldt stared at him, mopping at his face. "Can't be forded."

"I know that, sir—"

"There are no boats, no boats anywhere, Sam, I tried to get some from Corps, I've been trying the Aussies—"

"We've found four native canoes, in good condition," Damon broke in on him. He developed the idea as rapidly and clearly as he could, watching Westerfeldt's face. The General was still staring slackly down the trail. "Their defenses are weaker there, just because the stream *is* so deep. We've scouted it thoroughly. They're not looking for us to hit them there . . . He took a breath and said: "We could do it tonight."

Westy's eyes came back to him in alarm. "A *night* crossing? Sam, that's the toughest operation in the book—"

"I know, but—"

"—you can't ask boys as—as weary as these, to try anything like that . . ."

—They'd one hell of a lot rather try that than go up against the airstrip bunkers frontally, time after time, Damon almost said—bit it off. "They'll do it," he said urgently. "If we get across there we can cave in the position—go through to the beach and come in behind the Mission and the strip defenses. We can crack the whole front wide open."

Westerfeldt was still gazing at the trail; his face looked like old candle wax; all the blood had drained out of it. His cheeks and throat were slick with sweat. He shook his head. "I don't know, Sam. It's risky. Awfully risky. Four native boats—"

"General, I know we can do it. It's the chance of a lifetime."

Westy closed his eyes, made a brusque little gesture with his hand. "All right, all right, Sam," he answered testily. "Let me think about it. Let me think about it a bit . . ." He turned and called to Dickinson, who was still talking with Hodl: "Dick—contact Bart Koch, will you?—and see what he says about Ostrow's people . . . Christ, I don't know," he remarked to no one in particular; he pulled off his helmet and mopped his face. "This miserable, stinking country—"

His voice was drowned out in a series of shrieks; they both turned. Down on the trail a stretcher-borne soldier was screaming terribly—a series of yelping, animal cries, his hands clutching at his head.

"You—you people there!" Westerfeldt shouted. "Can't you give that man something, quiet him down . . . ?"

The medics looked back at them, and one of them cried, "Christ, Mac, I've given him two syrettes already . . ."

Damon looked down at his feet, listening to the General, who was running on about the report of a counterattack on Frenchy Beaupré's battalion from the Grove, his eyes darting here and there. He wasn't going to agree to it, Sam knew; he would wait and wait until it was too late. He was taking longer and longer to make up his mind—which was now following this slow parade of the sick and mangled streaming toward the long green tents in the grove beyond the clearing. Damon hooked his thumbs in his belt, thinking. He had to convince the General of this, he had to, even if he got sore at him. Another day like today—

"—telling me he wouldn't accept the responsibility!" Westy was saying angrily, wagging his head. "Where does he get off with that—I've known Frenchy since he was a hell-raising shavetail at Bailey. How much does he think a man will take? I'm telling you, *one more word* and he's on his way to Australia . . ."

A man was walking toward them from the field hospital: a slight figure, bareheaded, stoop-shouldered with weariness, wearing red scarves on his forearms—scarves that turned out to be layers on layers of blood; his khaki shirt, his trousers were spattered and smeared with it. Major Weintraub, his beard blue in the hot light, looking like a brilliant scholar who has just been unfairly graded by a pack of academic incompetents.

"General—"

Westerfeldt faced him. "Yes? What's on your mind, Nate?"

"General, would you come across the road and talk to the badly wounded? Just for a few minutes?"

"What's that?" Westy's eyes darted at the doctor and away again. He looked cornered.

"Just for a moment, sir. It would buck them up. They need it badly, most of them. They're pretty low . . ."

"I . . . Well, I—no." The big man shook his head doggedly. "No."

Weintraub's eyes flashed at him. "But General, they *need* some—"

"Did you hear me—I told you no!" Westerfeldt shouted. His hands were clenched in tight white balls. In a lower tone he added, "The answer is *no*, Major. I can't spare the time . . ." He threw a desperate, fearful gaze at the somber tents, the rain clouds boiling on themselves like a deadly gray broth, the barbaric wall of jungle. "Sam," he said in a tremulous mixture of mandate and supplication, "go over and see them, will you? Talk to them?"

"All right, General." He watched Westy walk away unsteadily toward the headquarters tent.

"The bastard," Weintraub was saying in a cold fury. "The one-way, cold-blooded bastard."

"He's not cold-blooded," Damon answered, walking toward the long tents.

"No? What is he, then?"

"He's—he's sick." But he knew that was not the reason.

Weintraub grinned mirthlessly. "Well, isn't that just too fucking bad," he said in a savage voice. "How unique. I'll tell you something. I took the temperature of every man in one company two days ago. What was left of them. For my own edification and amusement. Every single man was running a temperature. Every—single—man. You can't expect sick men to fight . . ."

"We have no choice."

"Is that right." Weintraub threw him a look white with hate. "That's easy for you to say. You can smash up the crockery; we have to try to paste it back together again."

Damon made no answer. It's not my detail, he thought resentfully, it's not up to me, most of the troops don't know me anyway. I don't mean anything to them. Walking in step with Weintraub, now stiff with anger, into the olive gloom of the tent, along the rows of field cots where medical corpsmen bent over bottles of plasma hung from mosquito racks like stained garnet wine bottles. Wine of life. The men, drugged with morphine, stirred like blind puppies or lay as still as death, in a stench of alcohol and ether and blood and vomit and excrement. The return on the investment. Oh Jesus—to have Bert MacConnadin here in this cave of agony, for twenty minutes! for just *five*. Or Ed Downing. *All the merchants and the kings . . .*

"Don't let me keep you, Doctor," he said quietly. "I know how busy you are." Weintraub walked quickly off through the ward.

The faces turned to Damon—angry, indifferent, smiling dreamily. A medic was just drawing a mustard-colored pad cover over the head of one patient, exposing the blue tubes of ankles. Three cots down Damon saw a face he recognized.

"Millis," he said, approaching the painfully thin face with its over-large, suppliant eyes, the bandaged legs. "How you doing, son? Anything I can bring you?"

It was several seconds before he realized Millis couldn't understand anything he had said.

In the thick, velvet darkness the opposite shore looked far away. On the surface of the river there was not a flicker or a ripple; it might have been a void, an impassable gulf that sank to the center of the earth. Lying flat on his belly Damon swung his head to the right, passed his eyes over the dulled mounds of helmets, like clay bowls under the spikes and palps and scrolls of vegetation. The moist, rich earth beneath him seemed to be shifting, tilting him over on his back, the helmets shifted subtly. Dizzy. He was dizzy, and sick, his head felt as if it were about to burst into flame. He had the bug: some bug. Beside him Captain Bowcher brought his arm up in front of his face, as though to read his watch. Damon stared at him dully. In a few minutes some of them would be dead, perhaps all of them. In three hours it would all be over: he himself would be dead or wounded, he would be successful, he would be a failure—incompetent, insubordinate, to be court-martialed, sent home in disgrace. What right did he have to do this?

They'd made elaborate preparations for the crossing that afternoon; and at dusk he had gone back to Brigade, leaving Ben in charge. Westy was sitting on the edge of his cot, a sheaf of reports in one hand. Sweat was pouring into his eyes; he looked ready to collapse.

"Hello, Sam." His eyes were watery and wide. "How are your boys? Tell me the truth."

"Why, they're all right, General. They're—"

"I just heard from Dick, he's over at BADGER." His lower lip trembled and he put his hand to his mouth. "Dutch says his people are incapable of advance . . ."

Damon took a deep breath. "General, if I could explain this crossing once more. I'm convinced we can bring it off." He launched into the plan again, going into more detail—broke off when Westerfeldt swayed backward, gripped the mosquito bar to steady himself.

"General—you all right?"

Westerfeldt kneaded his belly slowly with one hand. "I feel pretty rocky. Little fever. I'll be all right in a while. Go ahead." He peered out under the tent flap, furtively. "I don't know, Sam. I still don't like it."

"General, it's our only hope." He leaned forward, gesturing. "If you can just give me enough mortar shells to get us over there, we can swing it."

"We can't stand any more losses. We just can't stand it, Sam . . ."

"We've got to try it. We can't go along like this—we have no reserves, the companies are down to sixty and seventy, most of the men are ill. We've got to take a few risks now."

"I don't know. I don't know . . ."

Damon rose to his feet. "It'll go—we'll make it go. You've got to let me do this!"

"I—"

All at once Westy broke down, rocking back and forth, his head in his hands, his shoulders shaking. "Oh God, I can't look at them. My boys. I can't look at them anymore! Ah God help me, I don't know . . ."

Damon paused there above him, glanced around wildly. There was no one else in the tent or within earshot. He reached down and gripped the General by the shoulder. "Let me do it, Westy. Now. Give me the word!"

The phone rang. Westy lurched to his feet; his face looked green. "That'll be Dick." Damon stepped back. The General leaned over his field desk, swaying, hanging on to the side of it with one hand. "I'll contact you later, Sam. Better wait on it. I'll see—I want to talk to Dick . . ."

He went back to the CP in a tumult of rage and frustration. Ben and Feltner and the others were waiting for him in the dugout. They could tell from his face apparently but still Ben said: "How do we stand?"

"Couldn't talk him into it. He's sick. Afraid to try anything now."

"How did Koch and Frenchy make out?"

"No dice. Ran out of gas after gains of thirty to forty yards."

"Oh, Jesus."

"Oh Jesus is right."

"But the stupid bastard—doesn't he see what the score is?" Ben chipped dried mud from the back of his hand with his thumbnail. "Well God damn it, I know what I'd do if I were you . . ."

"Well, you're not me," he answered curtly.

"Check." Ben handed him a K ration container. "Here—have some of this vitamin-packed dinosaur turd. Keep your strength up."

Feltner was listening to this exchange with distress: clearly one did not address a regimental commander in this manner—nor did a regimental commander reply in this manner, either. Damon winked at him, tore open the end of the flat dun carton and shook out the little olive drab tin. Ben was fingering his own carton reflectively. "How many of these you suppose are kicking around in the supply depots? Probably a hundred million of 'em."

"Yes, and Tommy's uncle's been making most of them, too."

"No kidding."

"Yep. Erie Container. He's making millions at it. Millions."

"I'm so glad for him."

"Yeah. He'll be a God damn dollar-a-year man next." There was a certain grisly satisfaction, crouched here spooning this cold, gelatinous hash in a rotting, sweltering, water-logged dugout on the Papuan coast, thinking of Uncle Edgar sitting in his clean, well-lighted office, joking with Headley (Wells Nickerson had died in '38 of a heart attack), gazing out at the long, windowed façade of the plant, getting on the phone to Somervell, on the phone to Donald Nelson. Back there life was good—full of contracts, and raises, and glowing, limitless horizons . . .

Sergeant Chambers came in with a patrol and made a report to Ben, and he watched their faces. They were coming all apart. He knew the signs: the dulled, vacant gaze, the memory lapses, the incoherence, the flashes of unfocused rage; the alarming rise in combat fatigue cases, like the blond kid this afternoon. Cowardice, Traprock Merrick had called it. But too much battle made any man a coward, in time: any man alive. Where did you draw the line? Exhaustion, despair, disintegration of resolve—what difference did it make?

The phone rang then and Meigs called: "It's BULL MOOSE, Colonel."

He sprang to his feet and picked up the receiver with an exasperated little tremor and said, "BOBCAT here."

"Hello, Sam? Dick. You'd better get over here right away. The General's sick."

"What's the matter?"

"He's delirious. Nate Weintraub's over here with him now. He's running a fever over a hundred and four, he's completely out of his head. Nate says he's got both malaria *and* dengue." Dickinson's tart New England voice was hoarse with worry. "I don't like the look of it, Sam. I want to call a meeting—all regimental and battalion commanders and execs. I think we'd better."

Oh Jesus. Another conference! More walla-walla, and confusion, with fear spreading like an oil slick through the whole command. Ben and Feltner and the others were all watching him—a mute, tense expectation that clutched at his bowels. Dickinson was going on about a mortar attack on Frenchy's lines and he ignored him, gazing back at the faces in the dugout, thinking *delirious, fever of a hundred and four*—

"Why Dick, we can't," he heard himself saying firmly. "It's out of the question. We've got this crossing to execute. You know all about it, don't you?"

"Why, no—what crossing?"

"The Watubu, here. The General gave it his final okay at fifteen hundred. This afternoon. We jump off at twenty-two thirty. He was going to call me right about now over fire support."

"—a night attack?—"

"That's right. He said he was going to issue an attack order to BADGER for the same time, and a diversionary feint by Koch. Didn't he talk to you?" Feltner was staring at him in horrified amazement; Ben was grinning tightly, his eyes glittering. "Didn't he talk to you about it, Dick?" he pursued.

"No—as I say, I got back from seeing Dutch, and Albee came running out and there he was, in a coma. On his cot. I don't know—there's some notes on his desk but I can't—"

"Don't worry, Dick," he broke in. "Hold on tight, now. Look, just take some of this down." He ran through an attack order, improvising, putting the pieces together, his eyes closed.

"I don't think Dutch's people can do much of anything, Sam," Dickinson answered worriedly. "And a night attack—"

"That's all right. Just tell 'em to make some noise, give 'em the old decoy. If they suck some people over there from the river that'll help."

"But twenty-two thirty . . . can you be ready by then?"

"Sure can," he said briskly. "Been ready for hours. I'm sure we're going to make it, Dick. Just hold on tight. And you'll get that sixty ammunition up to us by twenty-one thirty or so, won't you? I know we're going to bust it wide open."

He handed the phone back to Meigs. All right. Direct disobedience of orders. No, it wasn't that, actually—it was worse: he was inventing orders, he was arrogating command to himself. Perjury, insubordination —mutiny, for all he knew. All right then. Enough, enough! This pattern of unnecessary butchery had to stop, before they were all dead or down. He'd been a good soldier, the dutiful and obedient subaltern for years and years, and now he was through. With bells. If these kids all around him—bearded, filthy, sick, frightened—could drag themselves forward against the Nambus day on hideous day, he could put his highly checkered career on the line in their behalf. It was little enough.

"All right," he said. "You heard the orders. We execute as planned. England expects every man to do his duty."

Feltner was speechless. Ben was scrubbing his cropped head furiously with his knuckles. "Jesus Christ, Sam. You went in with both feet, didn't you?" He nodded. "They'll brush your ass back to Frisco so fast it'll smoke all the way."

"Probably."

His exec laughed soundlessly. "Shoot! You're just as bad as I am. You like to think you're a sound, steady, by-the-book type, but you're not. You're just another crazy bastard."

"Yes," he said.

"Think we'll get away with it?"

"We will if Westy stays off his rocker. And if we make it over there."

"Uh-huh. Well, that sort of defines the issue, doesn't it?" Ben stood up, clapped his helmet on his head and shoved it forward over his eyes. "Well: all set for Operation Styx."

"—Don't call it that, Colonel," Feltner protested.

Ben winked at him solemnly. "Just whistling my way through the graveyard, kid."

The jungle crouched in its threatful silence. Not long now. Ten minutes more. Men would die, soon, because of what he had decided. The hell with that: he wouldn't think of that. Think of—other things. It ought to work. It was hanging on a shoestring, but it ought to work. It had to. Earlier, he had hooked two grenades through the rings of his pack suspenders and slung his Springfield, called in all available officers and NCOs—there wasn't time for anything else—and handed it to them straight. "This is not going to be easy. I don't believe in cheap bromides. But it is our only chance. The fate of every man in the Brigade lies with what we do tonight. That's why we must make it over there. And we will. That's all."

Firing burst out upstream, at the Narrows, and the sky paled with the glow of a distant flare beyond the forest. He peered forward anxiously. It would alert the posts facing them here, but it was worth the gamble if it drew some support away. He felt as if his head were lifting off: his dizziness, lying out here in the damp dark, was worse. He was coming down with malaria. Yes. His hands were trembling, and his whole body was laved in sweat. He had to stay on his feet. He had to!

Time was so elastic: it had raced all day, while they rigged the boats with lines, and Pioneer and Demolition brought up logs and planking with slow care. Now it crept with wretched dalliance. The men in the machine-gun emplacement just behind him stirred softly. If the Japanese suspected anything they gave no sign. The reeling, dipping vertigo was worse now, and the nausea. Lights seemed to burst up and down in front of his eyes, and he felt weak as water. He gritted his teeth, locking his hands under his chin. He had asked for this, he'd set this assault in motion, for better or worse—and now he'd better carry it out.

For no reason at all he thought of Donny. Donny in a school play about Columbus. There had been a scene involving the mutineers, and then Jinny Massengale, who as Queen Isabella was accompanying the mariners through some wild dramatic license, had just told him that he must persevere in his quest, that she believed in him. Left alone on the stage, Donny wrestled with himself—a Hamletesque soliloquy involving much eye-rolling and gesticulation. At this point—it was just before the curtain—Perry Blissman, offstage, shouted, "*Land ho! . . .*" And Donny, distraught—Perry in his enthusiasm had hollered his line exactly one scene too early—started violently, then dropped his head in his hands and moved unhappily offstage, to thunderous applause as the curtain fell. All wrong, of course, and the discovery of America, when it did come, was a touch anticlimactic—yet there had been something singularly effective about that moment . . .

He looked at his watch. The second hand had begun its darting movement up the left side of the face. Snipping off the seconds, which now began to race again. Five four three two one zero. Behind him he heard the metallic *thunk* of the mortar shells and a second later, deafening, the machine guns. Their tracers swarmed in violent crossing skeins, festive and terrible, answered by the blue-white flashes from gun muzzles on the far bank. He was on his feet, had seized hold of the rough wood of the banca's side. They ran it forward into the river: the water went to his waist, his shoulders. He groped his way back, holding on to the outrigger. Men were piling aboard in haste, cursing, bumping one another. But they were getting in. He heard someone call in a clear, even voice, "Roll 'em," and the craft slipped away from him into the stream, its occupants bent low, paddling furiously.

"The line," he shouted, "—who's got the line?"

"I've got it," a shadow beside him answered.

He was seized with a rush of vertigo like fainting, went to one knee.

"You all right?" a voice said, and then went on quaking in fierce reverberant echoes in the painful core of his brain. —*all right? all right? all right?* This was bad: he must not let down. The mortars were lashing the other bank in a series of flat, coughing explosions. A flare burst high overhead, a blinding yellow light that made him gasp—and there they were, all six boats, at midstream, water swirling white around the paddles. Machine-gun tracers from the other shore burned into one of the lakatois. He was screaming, "Get him! *Get him!*" at the top of his lungs.

Then the flare went out and the distant bank erupted in a madcap roar of gunfire. A flashlight blinked—two and two—and they were pulling on the line with all their might, the lakatoi gliding swiftly back toward them. The roll and crash of firing was like a wall, shutting out sight and sound. A man beside him grunted and fell away, rolling in the brush and mud. The banca bumped against the muck. His turn now. He climbed over the outrigger, gripped the supporting ribs and swung himself aboard, while the others piled in behind him. He leaned forward in the bow, felt the line—taut and dripping.

"All set," someone shouted.

He yanked the light out of a cargo pocket and flashed it. Tracers swam like tiny orange comets near his head and he ducked, steadying himself as the canoe began to move. But slowly. So slowly. Behind him he heard a dull splashing, saw two men lying halfway out of the boat, paddling wildly. Must have found them in the bottom of the boat. He laughed, a feverish cackle—reached forward and seizing the bow line began to haul up on it with all his might. A geyser rose to his left, a faint gray plume, subsided. Knee mortar. Ahead of him he could hear grenades, martellato and deep under the crackle of rifles. They were getting in. Good. Good. He realized he had been holding his breath for a long time—exhaled with a gasp. There was the bank, dead ahead, the little knot of figures pulling. They were there. He leaped out of the banca, fell full length in the mud, got up shakily. The craft was empty, was vanishing again. The other boats were landing for the second time. Mortar shells were dropping in the water now, and on the far bank. He swung to his left, fighting his way through waist-high brush—all at once fell into a hole. His knee hurt, his groin. He was lying on top of a body—a vile, sticky body. Up. He had to get on his feet. He climbed painfully out of the hole and moved along. They had to get the line set up here—the Japanese would be coming downriver soon, they had to hold them or it was all a failure. He turned, but they were moving all around him, ghostly and resolute. He felt a rush of pride so great he thought his heart would burst. They were going to do it. They were going to be all right: he could tell. Someone was shouting commands in a flat, even voice. Who was that? Words. He could hear words like dew falling from high leaves, like pebbles dropping down the deepest well, falling distantly with that soft, slow, ringing *plop*, and then vanishing. In the ice walls all around. Jesus, what ice walls! He was shaking and murmuring words he couldn't understand.

He had collapsed against a tree trunk, his hand on the wrinkled hide of the bark, he was vomiting, gagging and vomiting, and the ground kept tilting and lurching like bristling, greasy surf. He had never in all his life felt so sick. Not even at Malsainterre. Not even at Wu T'ai. Ah God, Wu T'ai. He had to keep going. God, don't let me crap out, he muttered soundlessly, his teeth chattering. Just that. All I ask.

With a groan he rose on reedlike stems of legs and went on, retched again, gripping his head in both hands. Lights swelled and faded, faces swept up to him and away, caught inside a curious bubble that was his own body streaming water, boiling, dissolving before his eyes. The next step was Ben. Ben was to lead Baker and Charlie of First Battalion down the meadow. Below Hart's Island. No. *Ben.* Too late, the Japanese were waiting just outside the blackout flaps, grinning: *they* weren't afraid of their own grenades. Fallen overboard, he was drowning, there wasn't time—! Lying outside himself this way, a court-martial offense at least and what did they care?—they weren't going to forgive him for this. Think! The gauze was over his nose, his mouth, he was drowning in his own bodily juices while they held a colloquy over him, the plan. *The plan.* Was to dismember him, pour his rotting body into several containers of unequal—

"Colonel. Colonel—"

A broad, heavy-jawed face, wide-set eyes, black with grime and sweat. A face he knew. Or thought he knew. The eyes glinted brightly. Christ, would it never be day?

"Colonel, are you hit?"

"He's burning up, Wally. *Colonel*—"

He had hold of the voice. The voice he knew. The face. He never forgot a name. The dizziness was worse, the sick hot febrile debilitation, but clinging to the voice made a difference. If he could hold on—

A deadly burst of firing. Nambu. Very close. He was down. Flung down. Lying in a pulpy wet matting that stank of rot and oil and nutmeg. Someone's arm was over his shoulders. A grenade—a fiery orange flare of light, wild with shadows. Another. And with the thunderous crash of the grenades the hideous bubbling veil began to clear. He was cold, now, entombed in icy conduits that were his bones, but the world was distilling slowly, hesitantly, distant and stark, like coming up out of ether. A fresh world, the edges hard and even. A tangle of fronds and creepers, and Feltner looking at him with alarm. Thank God.

"Colonel—"

"The line," he said. "Are they digging in—?"

"You all right, Colonel?"

"Of course I'm all right," he snapped. His teeth were chattering so badly he couldn't hold his jaws together, but his mind was clear. Thank God for that: that was all he asked. "Is King digging in along that support line?"

"Yes. They're right on the button. Everything's going great."

"Good. Come on."

Downstream now the racket was terrific—a rush of small-arms fire that swelled into one vast clamor. "Go on, Ben," he thought, "tear 'em apart"—realized he must have said it aloud. Feltner was grinning at him, a funny little grimace of relief.

"We're going to make it, Colonel! We're going to do it . . ."

"You bet."

Their own perimeter was the key. He hurried up to the line, watched figures bending and recoiling in the dark, their shovels lifting; near him a machine gun squad was setting up, the gunner adjusting the tripod so the traversing dial was level, clamping the legs and stamping the trail shoe into the soft earth, the assistant crouched above him deftly seating the gun's pintle into its housing, the loader sliding the deep-green ammunition box into line with the feed opening, the brass tag of the belt snapped through swiftly; no fumbling, no mistakes. They've learned, he thought with a throb of prideful affection; they've learned their trade, they're soldiers.

Around them the dark was undergoing a curious change—a subtle, silvery distillation that sifted like powder through the forest. Moonrise. But now it would work for them. He dropped to one knee and put his arm against the trunk of a tree. The land fell away gently, and the trail—the nice, dry Japanese trail they now lay astride—opened into a grove, ghostly gray in the changing dark, with the palms like lazy, graceful feather dusters. Tom Keyes, the King Company captain, swung his arm wide, palm down. The machine guns began firing in short, flat bursts; and now, as moonlight began to tip its way into the grove, Damon could see the silhouettes darting and hear a high, wild cry like an animal in great pain.

The whole line erupted in gunfire. He raised his rifle and aimed at the scurrying, dancing, moon-shot figures, felt the old, harsh, comforting kick of the stock against his shoulder. Tracers looped high around him, a liana vine fell in a sodden serpentine through the moonlight. But he could hear no sound. The Japanese came on, stumbling, waving their weapons, their mouths wide—but he heard nothing. He was moving in that cone of quiet, of indelible calm that slipped over him in battle like a hood. He emptied his clip, inserted a new one, cut down two Japanese who were scuttling unscathed through a forest of tracers, shifted to an officer who was standing spraddle-legged between two trees, firing a pistol in each hand—a rather tall, slender man who ducked his head as though under a whiplash, then rolled out of sight behind some bushes.

Then the grove was empty of movement. The machine guns had stopped, and sound rushed into his consciousness again—a mélange of screams and isolate gunshots and imprecations and threatful commands. He crawled back to where Keyes was standing in a hole, talking urgently to a runner.

"How you doing?"

"Okay, I guess. Phelan's platoon's had a bad time. If they try it again—"

"They'll try it again. But now we've got them coming to us. Better this way, right?"

"I'll tell the frigging world. If they only haven't got tanks."

"Don't worry. If they'd had any they'd have used them long before this."

The moon rose higher now, bathing the trail and grove in a vibrant, milky light. Pioneer and Demolition platoon got the pontoon bridge laid across the Watubu and ammunition parties came up, stretcher bearers went back with their enormous burdens; the signal party brought the lines over. The Japanese attacked again, a poorly coordinated rush in something like company strength, and the perimeter cut them down; the survivors melted back into the forest. There had been no word from BULL MOOSE. Damon ate half a K ration cheese tin, and kept it down. The chill ebbed but the boiling debility stole back upon him, and he walked up and down outside the foxhole CP mopping his face and blinking, fighting the twinges of vertigo. He had to hang on. Just another—another three to four hours. A gamble. An awful gamble. The crossing was good; the left flank was secure—they could beat off a dozen more counterattacks, especially if they were all as piecemeal and disorganized as the last one. But dead ahead, behind and beside Ben's thrust was one long exposed flank. What if the Japanese threw a couple of companies down the slot between the airstrip and the Mission before

Ben could come in behind it and seize that high ground . . . ? They wouldn't: they were off-balance. They could . . .

No: he knew it was right. He could feel it in his bones. Mortar shells began crashing into the grove and he jumped into the hole beside Keyes, who was on the phone, asking for more belted ammunition for his thirties. He sat in a corner of the hole, listening to the dusty sounds of battle from down river: they sounded sporadic, unsure—as though one of the participants was breaking contact; but there was no knowing. The moonlight fell in slick silver scars and blossoms around him. If you could only *know*. It was like trying to play chess blindfolded, or that goofy game the Aussies played, called "Are You There, Moriarty?"—in which two contestants, blindfolded and prone, clasped left hands, and one asked the question—and on receiving a muffled answer, let fly with a furled magazine, hoping to clobber his unseen assailant over the head . . .

A figure loomed up out of the zebra-quilt of moonlight and shadow, a tall, slender man gasping for breath. "This—CP? Where's Damon?"

He got up. "Right here, son."

It was Jackson, his eyes glittering white under his helmet; he knelt down at the edge of the hole, panting. "We're down there. At—the beach. We got to the jetty—" He broke off, gave a laugh that was like a sob. "Colonel, they're shagging ass!"

"What do you mean?"

"Trying to take off in a couple of barges. All their brass. We got 'em all, right by the jetty . . . I shot me a frigging general!"

They were all crowding around him now. "A general?" Damon demanded. "You sure of that, Jackson?"

"Sure, I'm sure! Any joker with a gut that big has *got* to be a general . . . Christ sakes alive, look at his toad stabber!" He extended an arm: Damon saw the jewels glittering on the long curved phallus of the sword hilt like serpents' eyes. "Bowcher's got all their papers and crap." He pushed the samurai sword into Damon's hands. "For you, Colonel. Souvenir—straight from the top. Caught 'em asleep at the switch, the rotten slope-head bastards!" He laughed the tight, indrawn laugh again. "Yeah! One for Millis, and one for Braun and one for Gantner—oh *Jesus*, didn't we clean house! They're cracking, and it ain't from shacking, I want to tell *you* . . ."

"That's great, Jackson," he broke in. "Now what about the pivot?"

"What? Oh, yeah: Colonel Krisler says to tell you we're wheeling west on the Mission. Meeting only light resistance."

"Great. Tell him: let her rip."

"Right, Colonel." He got up, glaring happily at the faces around him, reluctant to leave this small, rapt audience. "Oh, didn't we nail the sons of bitches!" he cried softly. "After all these months—taking it off 'em all these months . . ."

Damon sat down again in the mud, the samurai sword across his knees; his legs would hardly hold him up. Watching Jackson move off down the trail he felt all at once close to tears: a watery-eyed old man.

He had violated all the rules. Arrogating command to himself, night crossing of an unfordable river without artillery preparation or adequate assault craft, and now advance against a fortified position in the dead of night. But there were times when you had to throw the book away. Maybe you could do something like this only once in a war: maybe you shouldn't ever do it. But they hadn't had much choice.

And there had been those diaries he'd pored over night after swelter-ing night—those tortuous rice-grain columns tinged with mounting exhaustion and despair. He'd been right, he'd read them right: the Japanese had been at the end of their rope, too . . .

God, he was weak. So weak he was afraid to try to get up from this foul, wet muck. But he could think, now. The thing to do was—the thing to do was compound the felony.

He took the speaker out of its jacket and cranked the mechanism briskly. "BOBCAT here. Put me through to BULL MOOSE."

There was that high, crackling hum and then Dickinson's voice, nerv-ous and tart. "BULL MOOSE. What have you got?"

"How's Westy doing?"

"Well, he's still pretty badly off, Sam. This malaria's pretty serious, you know."

Damon felt himself grinning wearily. "Yeah, I know. Dick, we've shot the moon. Position is secure. Our friends are coming apart at the seams. WOLVERINE has taken a bath and turned the corner, and is about to genuflect—if you get what I mean."

"Really?" Dickinson's voice broke with astonishment. "You mean he's made it to—"

"That's the pitch. Dick, they've assumed the angle. Ben caught a slew of their brass taking off for points west in landing barges, shot 'em all up. The attacks on our left flank have been disorganized and feeble. They're all shot. Now, have you alerted PORCUPINE for that tea tango we talked about?"

"But Sam," Dickinson paused. "They're dead on their feet . . ."

"So are we. And we made it. Look, this is the time. Right now. We'll never get another chance like this."

"All right, if you say so, but—"

"I tell you, we've got 'em on the ropes—I can feel it! Shoot the works. Those last two tanks, the Brens, everything. Knock heads, pull anything in the book—but *get them moving* . . ."

"Right, Sam. Right." Dickinson's voice seemed firmer. "I'll do every-thing in my power. That's a promise."

"Fair enough." Damon grinned softly in the dark; he was on the verge of retching and his head was aching so he could hardly see. "Angels can't do more."

* * *

The late afternoon sun had dipped behind the mountains, and the Grove lay in shadow; the breeze off the water stirred fitfully among the palms. On three sides of the cemetery the massed ranks stood stiffly, somberly, staring at nothing, and Ben Krisler, posted out front of the Regiment, passed his eyes over them and then looked across the Grove to the Mission, its old white walls battered and blackened by fire and demolition, looking forlorn and hollow. To Krisler it seemed to symbolize the whole battle—its desperate hope, its losses, its astonishing unreality.

He brought his gaze back to the platform made of planking laid across upended fifty-five-gallon drums where Chaplain Unterecker, a roly-poly man with a round, genial face, was reading from the Scriptures, his voice fading and rising as he looked from the text to the troops.

". . . . *Praise ye the Lord for the avenging of Israel, when the people willingly offered themselves . . .*"

Well, they'd done that all right.

". . . *when thou marchedst out of the field of Edom, the earth trembled, and the heavens dropped, the clouds also dropped water . . .*"

Amen to that, Reverend. The War Song of Deborah. Pretty apt, all things considered. What had caused Unty to choose it? He frowned. Hearing the Old Testament always aroused a certain confusion inside him. He saw his mother's fine, proud face, her faintly oriental eyes, dark above the tablecloth, heard her deep, vigorous voice. "The Jews were the first people to honor the law. The law and the prophets." And his father setting aside his paper, watching her mildly. "Ruth, what's the sense in filling his head with all that? This is America—there's no distinction here. Every man is like another." "Of course, dear. Only he ought to know, that's all. And remember." "Well . . ." and his father had raised the paper again.

Every man is like another. In the rough, open-handed Wisconsin of his boyhood there had been few shadows. His father was a Wisconsin Squarehead who liked to go to the ball games down in the Hollow and wasn't averse to throwing his energies into a Sunday barn raising, where the long, impromptu plank table sagged with cakes and gherkins and meat pies, and the kids played shrieking tag until their fathers roared at them to get out from under foot. His mother sat and sewed and laughed and gossiped with the other women. They went to the Lutheran church —his father's church—they celebrated Thanksgiving and Christmas and Easter Sunday and the Fourth of July with a lot of noise and gastronomic excess, like their friends and neighbors.

It had been the Point that had shocked him awake. His father had been wrong. Jews were not Americans: they were vulgar, offensive, grasping, unpatriotic; they did not succeed to high command. Not that anyone really said it in so many words—or rarely: it was borne in on him the way tarnish spreads on steel. We were all Americans, we all had come from Europe, sooner or later, richer or poorer—but there were those who were not as worthy, who were inferior. His father hadn't known this; his mother had. Was that why she had given way to his father's Christian world . . . ?

"*. . . then was war in the gates: was there a shield or spear seen among forty thousand in Israel? . . .*"

He was no coward; no one could ever accuse him of having run from a fight. But he made his decision during those spartan, tormented days on the Plain: he wanted to be praised or damned—it was usually destined to be the latter, he reflected wryly—for what he was, for his own dreams and convictions; not for the acceptability of his father's race, or the inacceptability of his mother's. And beyond that, Cadet Krisler had perceived a sharper truth: that his mother's "inferior" origins could negate completely his father's "superior" ones. The purblind contempt behind this attitude had aroused him. All right: if the world was prepared, in its senseless bias, to damn him out of hand, he would meet it with reticence. He would not lie, but he would not disclose. He had gone off to France steeped in the defiant bitterness from which all his insubordinate wrath had stemmed. To this day there weren't three men in the whole United States Army who knew his mother was Jewish.

"*. . . They fought from heaven; the stars in their courses fought against Sisera. The river of Kishon swept them away, that ancient river, the river Kishon. O my soul, thou hast trodden down strength . . .*"

Now, standing here in the afternoon stillness, the spanking new eagle and cross of the Distinguished Service Cross hanging from his left shirt pocket, the jungle ulcer burning his buttock, he felt stirred by the somber, stately verses, their slow, majestic fervor. It was as though he had been found derelict in some profound and irreparable way. Yes, and I'm part of that, he wanted to shout, my mother's people—all the hopeless and impossible battles, like this one: Jericho, and little David, and the sword of the Lord, and of Gideon . . .

Chaplain Unterecker had concluded. The flag slipped wearily down to half-mast, and the bugle threw its long, piercing notes through the tropic air.

Let them sleep, Lord. Krisler followed the rows of crosses that marched back and back, fiercely white against the jungle fringe. There they lay, the ones that had no luck. Svelland, who had single-handed cleaned out two bunkers full of raging, shrieking Japanese before they got him; and Petschek, who had been shot by a treetop sniper; and Marshall and DiMaestri, killed by a mortar burst crossing the river, and Wells who had been hit and had drowned in the swamp in the first day's attack; and all the others he'd never known, who had perished before he'd landed here at Moapora . . . It was odd, and a bit cruel. There they lay, far from the fields of home, two crossed sticks and a dogtag, killed in a moment of heroism or cowardice or ignorance or ignominy, but all of them killed in the fragile splendor of their young manhood; and to some heart ten thousand miles away their present moldering was a source of immeasurable grief. And to others—even to many standing here in the still, heavy air—it was nothing at all. Only here, before his eyes, were there no distinctions of race or breeding. Here they slept together, not berthed separately under the neat serration of the crosses but rolled together into one long trench—Christian and Negro and Jew, patrician and laborer: all of them were good enough to die, to sink to mortality and lie together.

Only in time of peace were they unworthy.

The bugle's somber notes went on pealing sadly. His eyes kept roaming about—he could not help it—saw off to his right, drawn up on the other side, Colonel Wilhelm, looking unutterably weary and grim; behind him and to his left Frenchy Beaupré standing stiff and defiant, tears streaming slick and bright against his cheeks. Many men were weeping now, their mouths working, throats swelling as they swallowed painfully and squeezed shut their eyes. But his own eyes were dry; the old mordant anger stirred inside him. They were dead. They had been shipped out here to this pestilential mangrove swamp far beyond the confines of the safe, sane world for ends they were not to share, and ordered to seize a patch of that swamp or be killed: and they had been killed. It was stupid, it was vicious, it was monstrous and flint-hearted and disgusting; but there was nothing to be done about it, beyond what they were doing now . . .

The dirty, bloody hell with it.

It was over. Chaplain Unterecker had descended. There was a short pause and then Sam, whom General Eichelberger had designated Acting Divisional Commander after Westy's hospitalization and departure, climbed up on the oil drums and called: "At ease," and the ranks relaxed in a faint, sonorous murmur. There was a little commotion and then two officers—it looked like Feltner and Chase—handed up a sheet of plywood which Sam turned face outward, holding it with one hand. And Krisler heard behind him the drone of surprise. Sam stood there silently a moment, as though he didn't know quite what to say.

"This is the first time you have ever been assembled as a division," he began, the words clipped and clear. "You are the Fifty-fifth Division. And for your shoulder flash I have chosen a salamander. Not because the gecko is our constant little friend here in the tropics where we have been ordered to serve. But because from ancient days the salamander was believed invulnerable to fire. So he is crouching here between two flames, with his right foot stamping on a broken samurai sword. You have come through the fire, and you have had your victory."

He paused, looking out at them as though he sought to meet the eyes of every man in the massed battalions. His face was drawn, his shirt hung on him in loose, damp folds; the knuckles of the hand holding the plywood piece were bony and white. Old Sad Sam, Krisler thought

softly; you crazy, rawhide old son of a bitch. Walked out a malaria attack that would have felled a carabao in its prime—*walked it out!*—hung
on and hung on and were there on your feet when the last bunker behind the airstrip went down. We're here, standing right here, what's
left of us, because of you and nobody else. And anybody that doesn't
know it ought to have his head examined. And you could be down in
Brisbane right now, confined to quarters and waiting to stand trial for
a general court, just as a starter . . .

"This division—our division—has no long and illustrious history,
glowing with great traditions. Neither do its regiments. No American
unit had any history of great traditions in 1775. They were built up over
the next hundred and fifty years. This division—the Salamander—has
just begun. It is going to make its proud traditions from this day on."

He looked down; when he raised his head again his face was resolute
and grim. "This will be a long and cruel war. We have just set out, all of
us, on a very thorny, bloody road—and no men know it better than
you soldiers standing here. Some hard things have been said about you—
some of you have heard them. What is important—what is memorable—
is that you have put behind you the bad days of panic and despair and
done what no other soldiers have ever done in the history of the world:
in spite of faint support and under the worst conditions imaginable, you
have taken a fortified position from the Empire of the Rising Sun. It is
an honor to serve with you all."

There was an instant's dead silence, and then from the adjacent battalions, from behind Krisler, the cheer began—a cry that swept through
the grove in a wild treble roar. Krisler about-faced. Jimmy Hoyt was
cheering, so were Chip Booth and Mac Klementis and the rest of his
officers. He tried to call the regiment to attention and gave it up,
watched them all—gaunt and ragged and hollow-eyed, dressed in fatigues or khaki they'd scrounged from God knew where—their barracks bags were still lying somewhere in the muck at Milne Bay—while
they waved their rifles and pounded one another on the back and shoulders. There wasn't a man there who didn't weigh at least twenty pounds
less than when he came to this evil place; there was not a man who
hadn't seen sights and done deeds he never wanted to see or do again.
Yet there they stood, in all their tatterdemalion nobility: wobbly,
raggedy-ass, indomitable. The solemn Johns and the hellions, the comics
and the squares. All that were left on their feet over thirty-seven terrible days and nights. No one back home would ever know what this had
meant, in blood and agony and terror and iron determination: no one.
There had been only the communiqué issued by MacArthur's headquarters eight days ago—"Allied Ground Forces succeeded in capturing
Moapora Mission, clearing the Kokogela area of enemy forces"—and
that had been all. Nobody would ever know what they had endured.

And now, staring at them hard, laughing, at Bowcher with his Silver
Star and Jackson and Rodriguez and De Luca and the others who had

gone all that weary way with him, down the river through the flash-shot dark—to his great surprise he found himself weeping, wildly and unashamed.

The air in the Statler Bar was vibrant with talk and the rattle of glasses and the easy laughter of women; it quivered with power. Admiral Rolfe Haymes, head of Southern Sea Frontier, and a mixed party of six or seven were chatting quietly at a large table. In one of the far corners Packy Vinzent, his broad, florid face grim, his eyes popping, was giving a group of officers his version of the tank battle at Sidi Bou Noura, and the chicanery and toadying that had led to his relief. Courtney Massengale, moving calmly through the tables, smiled to himself. Tough break for Packy; but that was how the old flag wagged. It was a hard world, the air near the summit was rarefied. The clock was still ticking very fast, as the Chief said; and those who couldn't think on their feet, be right the first time and no second guesses, had to go.

Everyone was here—at this fleeting, fashionable hour between the office pressures and the official Washington evening. Colonel Frénart, head of the Vichy mission, looking gloomy and supercilious, was listening to a woman with a hard, beautiful face and high-piled blond hair. Catching Massengale's eye he nodded with a gloomy smile; Massengale nodded back. Poor old Vichy: caught now between the American eagle and the German condor. Their day was waning. To his right, Kjelsen, the junior senator from Nebraska, was talking earnestly with Jim Wiggen, one of Nelson's bright boys on WPB, and beyond them Van der Sluys, the Air Inspector, and a group of young women were laughing uproariously at a story a colonel in procurement was telling. Power. It rose from the tables, hovered over the little orchestra, the smartly uniformed waitresses, it mingled with the cigarette smoke and perfume and alcohol and rose with a faint, pleasurable giddiness to the brain. The world's farthest reaches reverberated to what was said and done here in Washington in the early spring of 1943. A delectable sensation. Massengale nodded to a man on the Priorities Board he disliked; there was a noisy quartet of Navy fliers, a fat British brigadier all by himself, with an untouched martini sitting before him—and there on his right was Lieutenant General Caldwell, with a little group; a group that held Tommy Damon.

"Massengale . . ." Caldwell had risen with alacrity, although there was certainly no need for him to do so, and they shook hands. "How are you?"

"Bemused, General. Bemused."

Caldwell laughed, one arm extended toward the table. "You know everyone here, I daresay. Margie Krisler, Tommy, my grandson Donny —oh, no you don't, do you? This is his fiancée, Marion Shifkin. General Massengale."

He greeted them in turn. The boy came to his feet. He was in uniform, an enlisted man; sergeant. Curious. He was taller than Massengale remembered him, with a steady, calm manner, Tommy's flashing dark eyes. The girl was small and mouselike, not pretty, with a Slavic jaw and a candid, rather vulnerable glance.

Caldwell was saying, "What are you doing in this den of arrogant iniquity?"

"Just passing through, General. I just got young Tanner off for— well, for foreign parts; and I was playing hooky on my way back to the salt mines."

"How are Emily and Jinny?" Marge asked.

"In fine fettle. Emily's up in Boston visiting for a week or so. Jinny is undermining the foundations of higher education."

They laughed, and Caldwell said: "Come sit with us, won't you?"

Tommy was gazing up at him, her face flushed and agitated, her lips parted in a fearful plea. Please go, her eyes said; please. She had never looked as attractive to him as she did at that moment.

"I'd be delighted," he answered Caldwell. He smiled his most charming smile. "I'm not intruding on a strictly family affair?"

"Goodness, no!" Marge Krisler uttered her full, shivery laugh. She had put on weight in the years since Luzon, but she still had that inviting warmth that certain men found appealing—which was one of the crosses poor old Krisler had to bear. "We're all sitting in the dumps, trying to be cheerful," she went on. "Cheer us up."

"Yes, cheer us up, Court," Tommy said. "Tell us all about Casablanca. How was Casablanca?"

"Oh—exotic, ebullient. The prevailing mood was optimism."

"Optimism!" the women exclaimed.

He nodded. "The President and the Prime Minister were in the best of spirits. Negotiations and planning went forward in an atmosphere of practical jokes and repartee, and the promise of good things to come."

"A touch premature, isn't it?" Caldwell said dryly.

"Yes, sir, I imagine so. But the African landings were a great tonic. Everybody felt we'd got momentum, we were going forward now; that kind of thing. The consensus is we've achieved a really excellent working relationship with the British."

"You mean they're extremely pleased that we're doing what they want us to."

Massengale laughed. "I suppose that's more or less it. Though they do have some enormously capable staff planners. And of course they've been through the mill."

"The Chief isn't entirely happy about it, is he?"

"Not altogether, no. He'd have preferred the other thing. Several others, in point of fact." The entire table was watching him now, a little warily, almost fearfully; it was amusing to toss out oblique references to high policy, conflicts and decisions most of the country knew nothing whatever about. Old Caldwell knew, however; his fine, courtly features were impassive but his eyes held a faint sardonic gleam. They always knew more over there in Ground Forces than you suspected. The Old Army grapevine.

"But the Chief's a great team man," he concluded. "He gets solidly behind whatever's decided."

"Oh Court, you're such a diplomat," Tommy teased him.

"That's true, isn't it? You should have heard me at Aïn Krorfa," he informed them seriously. "It fell to my lot to present Bus Barron in all his irascible glory to the inhabitants. Bus is from Alabama—southern Alabama at that—and the natives began to express a few reservations: putting their hands on their scimitar hilts, things like that. Well, it was going from bad to worse—you know how tricky these things can be, General—and I had visions of the whole Moroccan venture going up in the fire and sword of a Lucknow. Finally I threw open my hands and cried in my most flawless French: 'Gentlemen, fear not. I have brought you a blood brother in General Barron. His skin may be white—but his *heart*, gentlemen, is as black as your own! . . .' "

Caldwell and the women were laughing, the politely dutiful laughter that one employed when rank told some pleasantry, good, bad or indifferent. The Damon boy did not laugh, however; he was watching Massengale with a steady, distinctly non-adulatory gaze. A trifle miffed he said: "Where are you stationed, Donald?"

"Maxwell, sir."

"And your duty?"

"B-17s, sir. Waist gunner."

"I see. Leaving to join the Eighth soon?"

The boy's face turned flat and hostile. "I wouldn't know, sir."

Massengale laughed easily. "Good for you.—He's going to make a commendable soldier," he said to Caldwell.

"I'm certain of it," the General replied with some constraint.

Massengale glanced at Tommy; her eyes darted to her son, back to his—all at once she looked down, smoothing her gloves in her lap. She's afraid, he thought; she's nearly out of her mind with fear. Impulsive, devil-may-care Tommy Damon. He remembered when the boy had enlisted; they had met at a War Department reception in the fall—Tommy had accompanied her father, who was talking to someone else—and the eddies and flow of social pressures had beached them alone in a corner.

"How are things?" he'd asked her lightly.

"Things are—terrible," she'd answered; a fierce exhalation that astonished him. "Things are just as awful as they can be . . ." It seemed that Donny had left Princeton that afternoon, or the day before—she wasn't too clear about this—and had enlisted in the Air Corps. "After he'd promised me, too," she cried softly, "—his solemn promise." Her eyes had glittered as if she had fever, and her lip trembled. He had watched her in a curious little confusion of amusement and pity.

"But—aren't you proud of him?"

"No, I'm not proud of *any* part of this stupid, stupid idiot's delight!" She glanced around the room wildly; he could see that she was on the edge of bursting into tears. His amused curiosity became tinged with caution. For all he knew she might fly into one of her headlong rages, one of "Tommy's tantrums"—this would be an unappreciative setting.

"Perhaps it's not as bad as all that," he observed.

She stared at him as though he had just called her a coward. "Oh!" she said tensely. "Oh, God. What do you know? What the hell do you know about it, anyway? *Staff*," she sneered, and he saw that several drinks had preceded the one she held tightly in her hand. "You're all a pack of gold-braided, flunky, play-acting fools . . . *He* put him up to it—I know it, I know it!"

"Who?" he queried.

"Who do you *think*? He's been after the boy, that's what it is. Some of that lovely, divine *force of personal example* . . . What in holy hell are you laughing for?" she demanded hotly, though he could swear his expression had not changed. "God, I'd like to have two weeks to run this country. Just two weeks. That's all I'd need. What's the play where the women take over, where they refuse to wangle-dangle until the men stop hacking away at each other—what's the name of it?"

"*Lysistrata*," he murmured.

"Yes, well they went at it all wrong—they should have grabbed the household cash and some clothes and the kids and sailed away to a nice, quiet, palmy isle, and let the poor sods blow each other up until there's not one of them left."

"Isn't that rather shortsighted?"

"Why? Because it doesn't allow for propagating the precious race, you mean? Don't worry—there'll always be one or two males sitting in the bleachers, egging the other ones on. A few prudent souls dug in down in the good old Munitions Building . . ."

He smiled—though he knew it was a dangerous thing to do. "You can't have it both ways, sweetie," he told her evenly. "We're all of us either suicidal maniacs or self-sacrificing heroes."

"—Don't tell *me* what I can or can't have," she began in a low, fierce tone—but then, mercifully, her father and a colleague had come up to them; and after a few moments he'd beaten a decorous and grateful retreat . . .

"How's Samuel?" he asked her now, abruptly; though he knew.

Her eyes became flat and calm again. "Oh, he's fine."

"They're back in Australia now—he and Ben," Marge offered. "We think they are, anyway. Rest and Rehabilitation. They both got malaria."

"I shouldn't wonder. That was a splendid job they did at Moapora. We had a radio not long ago from Sutherland—he calls them the Gold Dust Twins."

"Sam just got his first star," Marge ran on happily, "and Ben's a chicken colonel. Isn't that terrific?"

"It certainly is. No two doughfeet deserve it more." So the Night Clerk had caught him again. The fortunes of war. Except that he was very senior in grade—he was in line for his second star soon.

"Remember, back at Benning," Marge was saying to Tommy, "when Ben used to rant and roar about him and Joey being lieutenants together in the same company?"

Tommy rolled her eyes. "What would we all have done without World War Two?"

"No, but you know what I mean, honey."

"I certainly do. There were even times when *I* thought our grander halves were going to wind up privates in the same squad . . ."

Massengale joined in the laughter, thinking of the night of the masked ball on Luzon and Ben standing there in that idiotic bummer's rig, with his hands on the edge of the table. Well, he hadn't grabbed the first Clipper back to Alameda; but here he was, moving through the palace, sitting on the right hand of one of the lordly sieges of power—and those two highly emotional gentlemen were out at the hot gates, sword in hand . . . No gods, no Parcae spilled our fortunes with the dice. We did for ourselves. It was all there for the seeing, that tumultuous evening: Ben's headlong self-immolating defiance, and Jarreyl—*Jarreyl*—with his destructive malice, and Tommy standing by the car, her hair wild in the rain, screaming at him—

He thrust the memory away as though it had never been. "From what I hear," he said to Caldwell, "they were lucky to bring it off. It sounds as though it was touch-and-go for a while, there."

The General nodded; his eyes flicked over to the others, who were now engaged in talk. "It was a lot closer than that. Hardly anybody has any idea how bad it was. If it hadn't been for Sam . . . They should have given him the division," he added grumpily.

"How is it he didn't get it?"

"MacArthur said he was too young. Apparently you've got to be a Methuselah to get a command out there." Caldwell smiled a wintry smile. "Over in Africa you're antediluvian if you've completed grammar school. The magic age seems to be fifty-two."

"Who got it?"

"MacArthur—or somebody in his bull pen—asked for Duke Pulleyne."

"The cavalryman?"

"None other. Christ, they ought to have had more sense . . . Curious man, MacArthur. Imaginative, austere, great showman, but—" The General broke off, bit on his pipestem. "Well: we all have our failings. God help the poor devils who have to pick up after me."

"Oh Poppa, you're just sour because they won't give you a field command," Tommy chided him. "Break down and admit it . . ."

Caldwell looked at his daughter placidly. "Joe Stilwell's sixty. Krueger's even older. I guess I'd have held up as well as Muggsy McComb. Or poor old Westy."

"He down in Australia?"

"No. They shipped him back. His heart was affected."

"Must have been pretty grim, all around."

"I guess *so.*"

Massengale sipped his drink. What a Godforsaken business. Stuck out there at the farthest end of Poverty Row. The men, the equipment and supplies were going to Africa, to Britain, to Pearl Harbor and Nouméa— they were going everywhere but Kokogela and Milne Bay. It was fantastic—MacArthur, the nearest thing to a military genius the country had, forced to eke it out with leftovers, handouts, the barrel scrapings. Well, it was the old feud: the Chief's hand was against him, and Halsey's. And just plain distance. Nobody wanted to go out there— who in hell would, in his right mind? With a few exceptions the only people being sent out there were the culls, the misfits, the hell-raisers, the clowns.

"—I hope they give them a real good long rest," Tommy said. "In Australia." She was watching him warily now, that shadow of entreaty still behind her eyes.

"I'm sure they will." His face was grave, he knew; grave and compassionate. But the dark interior laughter welled up again. That was the entrancing part about Operations: there was nothing you didn't know— or that you couldn't find out, if you were highly enough placed, or if you went about it correctly. There was so much he knew: that Sicily had won out over Sardinia, that that dull, colorless, plodding Bradley was going to be given a corps, that in June the division in which Damon and Krisler were serving would take part in an assault on Wokai, a tortuous peninsula running northwest from that ugly dragon's head of New Guinea—a vicious place abounding in cliffs and caves and impenetrable rain forest. Nobody at this table knew it, Damon and Krisler certainly didn't know it; but that was what was going to happen. The mills of the gods, grinding slowly and surely . . .

Listening to Caldwell he sighed, but not from ennui. At certain moments, going to the safe to draw out maps or secret documents, or attending conferences in the still, calm, nicely ordered rooms, he would be visited by a tremor not unlike those fugitive, precarious seconds before the onset of orgasm—but without the ensuing sense of loss, the depletion, the all-consuming chagrin. This endured. Dry-mouthed, exultant, he would draft an action radio and hand it in for dispatch, beholding in his mind's eye the parade of preparations, the signal flashes from a hundred bridges, the tense flurry in the operations rooms five thousand miles away, the issuing of weapons and clothing, the crating and strapping of field desks and rations and tentage, the interrogation of prisoners and refugees, the outpour of general orders, special orders, field orders, memoranda—the whole ponderous uprooting of tens of thousands of men toward some distant, furious rendezvous.

—Yet the originating force was not his. That was what rankled. He could advise, he could suggest, emend, implement—but he was not the *source* of action. He could not conceive and fashion this modern-day epic, like a Renaissance sculptor confronting his colossal block of marble . . .

"How about you, Massengale? Aren't you hankering for a field command?" Caldwell's eyes, friendly, alert—that astonishingly penetrant gaze. Almost as if he had been reading his thoughts . . . But that wasn't true, of course; the General had merely picked up the thread of the earlier conversation.

"Yes, General," he answered, "I am indeed. The Chief says not for a while yet. You know his phrase: 'When the right day comes.' " He smiled —just the right combination of ruefulness and acquiescence. "And believe me, when the Chief says something, that's it."

"Yes. I'm sure of that."

All of which was not quite true, but old Caldwell didn't know it. Rearden had asked for him as ADC during the early planning for Torch, and before that there'd been an opening as Chief of Staff for the 19th, training down at Bragg. He had decided against both moves. Of course he would need a field command to properly round out his career, equip him with the credentials to reach his goal. But it was better to wait: it was going to be a long war, this one. There would be Italy, and then the big cross-channel invasion—the British at their very suavest wouldn't be able to talk the Chief out of that—there might even be an Adriatic offensive, Churchill was very keen on it. And then there were the Philippines, Formosa, the China Coast—all before Honshu and the Grand Assault across the great Kwanto Plain. There was time. He'd get his second star soon, but he didn't want a division: he wanted a corps. It was the highest tactical post, an opportunity to give real scope to his talents, realize that high, hard dream of the perfect battle, the grand envelopment and annihilation that bespoke the pure science of command. A chance would come. There would be mighty battles in Flanders, the Po, the valley of the Loire, but he was not sure he wanted that. Eisenhower had disliked him ever since that row over the Philippine Army budget in Manila, and he'd crossed swords with Bradley when they were both assistant secretaries at the War Department. Clark was difficult to get along with, and Patton was impossible. Allen and Hodges were boy scouts, and so was Truscott—none of them would ever amount to anything. The Pacific war contained the ingredients he needed. An opportunity would present itself, an independent operation, perhaps an island where a corps commander would have a relatively free hand in the forging of a twentieth-century Cannae. Meanwhile he could wait, here at the taut, vibrant center of things, where the first words were spoken in thunder, and the earth trembled. Uncle Schuyler, now a senator, and on the Armed Services Committee, was the most powerful ally a general officer in his position could hope to have. Patience, and a watchful eye . . .

Caldwell's senior aide, a quiet, rather colorless man named Palmer, came up to the table and engaged the General in a whispered conversation; Caldwell excused himself and left with him. The women and Donny were talking about Styles and Mayberry and Finch and some of the others who had been caught on Bataan. Poor devils. Hanging on, praying for help that could never reach them, unaware they'd been written off with grim finality months before. The fortunes of war. He expressed a suitable concern, and turned to the girl, who was gazing off across the room.

"I suppose you're planning a wedding?"

She glanced at him quickly. "Oh no—no, we're not."

"No nuptials?"

"Don doesn't want to get married. He feels it isn't the right thing to do."

"Why's that? Afraid of the noose?"

She smiled—a slow, even smile. "Oh no. He just feels with his—with things the way they are, we ought to wait for a while."

"And you agree?"

"No, sir—I'd like to get married right away. But I'm willing to do what he wants."

A contained, placid girl. None of Jinny's nervous, volatile fire. He thought of his daughter with a slow, heavy throb of anxiety. She was so beautiful, so mercurial and willful—and he could not reach her. Whenever he thought of her he always saw her standing in a patch of brilliant sunlight, in the middle of the Tabriz carpet, her long, dark hair whirling about her head, her eyes filled with that merry, malicious glare—on the verge of some new piece of devilry. He had scolded her, he had spanked her—once he had completely lost his temper and whipped her with a fair leather belt—and still she defied him, mocked him, baffled him. She had come down from college for the Christmas holidays—and then after three days told them she was leaving, with some airy reference to staying with a classmate in Connecticut.

"—But you just got here, Virginia," he'd protested. "We've planned a party for Thursday . . ."

"Can't be helped!" She'd shrugged her thin shoulders and made a face at him. "That's what you get for having such an overwhelmingly popular, sought-after daughter."

"You should have let Mother and me know, if you had contracted for an obligation of this sort . . ."

"Oh, it's not an *obligation*—goodness! you turn everything into a formal guard mount—Nanny Darlington just asked me if I'd like to spend a few days up there with her and I said yes. Why under heaven do you make so much *out* of everything . . . ?"

Watching her he had felt the old anger, the old despair, stir him. "I don't think you should go," he heard himself say flatly, though he knew it was wrong. "You had better stay here at home."

Her eyes dilated with rage. "Why, that's ridiculous," she cried, "I've got to go—you've just told me yourself it's a social obligation!"

"Then you may phone them and tell them you cannot get away."

She tossed her hair back wildly. "I'm *not staying here* . . ."

"You will if I say so."

"Oh, let her go, Courtney," Emily had protested wearily, "—if she wants to go, let her. What good will be served keeping her here against her will?"

"Families gather together for the holidays," he declared.

Jinny laughed. "So you can parade me around as the sweet and dutiful daughter? the crowning achievement in a—"

"Will you be silent!" He lowered his voice. "It's little enough . . ."

"*Little—!* It's a lot too much!"

"Let her go, Courtney—"

He'd left the room, unable to contain himself any longer; had gone to his study and read for an hour or so, until calm had returned, until he had things well in hand again. He had let her go up to Connecticut: there had really been no choice. He could have held her, but she would have retaliated with some barbaric, unforeseen, ruinous stunt that would have been infinitely worse than explaining her absence from home Christmas week to Stegner and Blaine; infinitely worse than being deprived of her presence, wondering at odd moments what she was doing. At Shafter she had scalded their maid's little boy with water from a tea kettle; in Paris she had built a fire in the middle of her room and nearly precipitated an international crisis; at Leavenworth he had drawn a reprimand from old Embree when it had been discovered that she'd been phoning various officers' homes and impersonating the wife of the Commandant. Of all her capricious, destructive pranks that one had frightened him so badly he had merely sat on the couch gazing at her.

"Why did you do it, Virginia? When you know how important the school here is to me—when I've told you, Mother's told you, time and time again . . . *Why?*"

For the briefest moment her gamine's face had glowed—as if she couldn't resist telling him: and yet she *would* resist it, for to disclose the motive would have immensely diminished this perverse and beguiling pleasure.

"*I* don't know . . ." She shrugged, looking away—fully aware of the admissions implicit in this evasion, and aware that he, too, knew. "It just—struck me as such fun at the time! . . ."

Punishment had never cured it: she seemed to welcome punishment in the same way the dutiful child approaches the reward for good conduct. He could not touch her. Charming, malignant, devious, she had danced through life—fighting him, tormenting him, eluding him. He could never know what she was thinking . . .

"What does your father do?" he asked the Shifkin girl abruptly.

"My father?" Her eyes dropped, came up to his again. "He's a correspondent, a foreign correspondent. He's in Tunisia now."

Yes. New York City Jews. The pattern was clear now. How had young Damon run into her? "And you're in school, I suppose."

"Yes, I'm a sophomore at Barnard."

That followed. "My daughter is at Bryn Mawr."

"Yes I know—Don's talked about her."

"Of course. They've known each other since they were children." This reminded him of still another unpleasant episode involving a war memorial at Beyliss, and he frowned and said: "How do you feel about his going overseas?"

She paused, her eyes on his stars, his ribbons. "I don't think I should say."

"Why's that?"

"Well . . ."

"Are you afraid of hurting my feelings?"

She gave a shy smile. "It isn't that. It's only that I think the whole war is wrong."

"Really?" He expressed surprise. "I should think the Nazi racial theories in particular would afford a certain justification."

"Yes." She nodded soberly. "We haven't any choice, I suppose. But with war—things are lost."

"Things like what?"

"Well"—she was ill at ease now, a bit troubled—"certain rights, certain liberties. And then they're never recovered again. When war comes people get into a habit of mind, accept things they wouldn't otherwise."

"War impels people toward Fascist doctrines, then."

She shook her head, watching him curiously. She was quick; very quick. They always were. "I didn't mean anything as *final* as that. It seems to me more a kind of reliance on a whole series of attitudes—everybody comes to feel that they're solutions: things like violence and power, and making sacrifices . . ."

"You don't approve of the individual making sacrifices?"

"Oh, yes." Her large, oval eyes were very serious now. "Only it all depends on what the sacrifices are for . . ."

"Fine. What should they be for?"

"A world without prejudice, for one thing," young Damon said; he had been listening to the exchange for a few moments, and he entered it now with a kind of soft passion. "A world without color lines, without one-tenth of its people living like kings and the other nine-tenths like desperate animals . . . If we simply sink back into the same tired old world of spheres of influence and power politics and gunboat diplomacy, there isn't an awful lot of sense in it."

Massengale smiled at them tolerantly. "I don't think you need to worry about that this time. The world that emerges from this struggle is going to be a very, very different world indeed."

"I hope so," the boy said. "I hope so with all my heart."

"A new heaven and a new earth," he answered, and laughed; but they only watched him steadily, distantly. They were not charmed by him, they never would be. Poor little babes in jungleland. All those hifalutin history and government and economics courses and they understood nothing of what made the world hum: their tremulous youth refused to see that there would always be the avenues to power, and that men— being men—would always snatch at them; for no other facet of human endeavor could bestow such magical, seductive guerdons . . .

"Margie—bless my soul, it's old home week!" It was Meadowlark Walters, looking more puffy and soulful than ever with his basset hound's eyes and mashed-in, pulpy nose; a light colonel now—terrifyingly—over in Somervell's section. Perhaps they could still lose the war after all. There was some rather boisterous badinage and then Walters asked Marge over to his table to meet Iris and her sister. The men rose, and at the same time the Damon boy looked at his watch and said, "We ought to be moving along, sweet."

"Moving along where?" Tommy said quickly.

"I promised two of the guys we'd meet them at this place we know."

"Can't they come here?"

The boy smiled at her fondly. "Well, I think they'd feel more at home there—it's not quite so high-powered as this."

The Shifkin girl rose, then. Donny bent over to kiss his mother, who took his hand in both of hers. "Will I see you tomorrow, dear? Poppa thought we might—"

"Oh, sure."

"Why don't we have breakfast together? If you don't mind getting up."

"Fine." He laughed once, softly. He was wearing his hair as long as was consistent with regulations, and he looked suddenly very young and carefree. "I've changed my hours," he answered. "I get up early now."

They said good-bye to Massengale quickly and firmly, moved off through the forest of braid and brass, the Shifkin girl rather diffident, young Damon tall and assured and a bit defiant. Tommy's eyes were following her son as though he were about to enter a burning building. Then the couple passed out of sight and she turned back to the table; her face did a funny little quiver, and her eyes filled with tears.

"Well," she said, and clasped her hands demurely at the table's edge.

Her face was faintly flushed. She was dressed in a Paris blue suit that set off her deep copper hair and green eyes; a lemon silk scarf floated at her throat. She looked proud and lovely and utterly defenseless; and Massengale knew now why he had sat down and stayed on through the inconsequential talk, the arrivals and departures.

"Well," Tommy repeated. "I'm getting maudlin, it seems. A silly, maudlin old woman."

"That's the last thing you are," he murmured. "The very last."

"Oh, I don't care if I am. This damned, dirty war." Her eyes flashed around the room with a savagery that surprised him. "Look at them. With a little objectivity, I mean. Gulping down Scotch and bourbon like toads, grinning like toads . . ."

"It's their day in the sun," he answered.

"I know all about their day in the sun. *They* don't have to go overseas, face the bullets and shrapnel—oh no: *they're* all taken care of . . ."

"Some do. And some do not."

She nodded stubbornly, implacably. "Yes. Well, most of them don't." She took a sip from her glass, set it down again and looked at him—a direct, wanton gaze that unsettled him. What was she going to say now?

"I don't suppose you would, would you," she observed.

"I might. What?"

"See to it he doesn't get sent to England. To the Eighth."

His brows rose. "Sweet, we go where we're sent . . ."

"Some of you do," she echoed him. "And some do not. Most of you wangle the cushy jobs, the nice fat berths along the Potomac. So dignified . . ." The orchestra had begun to play "Poor Butterfly," in a much more dreamy, saccharine way than he remembered it, and she exclaimed: "That song!" Her expression changed all at once, her mouth quivered again. "Please, Court. Please. For old-times' sake. For any reason, or no reason at all. Will you twitch wires, pull strings, cut orders, whatever they do—Jesus God, will you do *something?* . . ."

She's going to weep now, he told himself; wild little tough little Tommy Damon is going to break down completely and we'll initiate a scene, right in the center of the Statler Lounge . . . But she didn't break down. Her voice remained steady, she controlled the trembling of her lips. "He's all I've got, Court. Really all. In my life. I swear to you, nothing else matters but that boy . . .

"I can't help it. I used to have such contempt for craven or scheming women. Irene Keller, Kay Harting, the Rutherford bitch. Remember them? The vamps, the menaces, the pleaders and connivers . . . Now I know—I'm just like them. I am. I'd do anything, commit any crime on earth—any!—to keep him stateside . . . You don't believe me?" she demanded softly, with a faint smile. "Just try me, then. Ask me anything. I'll do it without the slightest qualm. Do you see?

". . . I know," she went on after a little pause. "I'm a disgrace to the service. Conduct unbecoming a camp follower. I know."

"I won't put you on report," he said.

"Please, Court," she whispered. "Keep him here, at home . . ."

The importunate anguish in her voice, the naked pain that shadowed her eyes seemed actually to trouble the smoke-laden air between them. For an instant his mind rioted with images of the two of them at sea, in a hotel room overlooking some bay, moving through full-dress Washington receptions—then the extravagant congeries of vision subsided. Nothing could come of it. Nothing. Too many obstacles lay in their path, not the least of which was—

". . . But there's Samuel," he replied, not sure of exactly what he meant by that.

She made a frantic little gesture with one hand. "He's saving the world from the Yellow Peril. Or maybe it's only the Black Knights. Sir Modred or something. And now he's a general. Only Sears Roebuck rank but he made it, he always knew he was going to be one, and now he is. Oh Jesus . . ." She put a hand to her chin, and now her face, drained of irony and anger, looked simply defeated and sad. "I did what he wanted—and he wanted me. I can see that now. It's always the way. He gets everybody to do what he wants."

Not everybody, Massengale thought; oh, not everybody. He said nothing.

"That's what he did at Moapora. I know. He got them all to do what he wanted—no matter what *they* wanted to do. He probably told the nasty little Japanese to go and jump in the ocean and they all did. After all, he's only got their bandy-fluking emperor to compete with, there. Command presence. I'm sick of it, sick to holy death of it . . ." She raised her head again, her eyes glistening and savage. "I swear to God, if anything happens to that boy I—"

She broke off and looked away feverishly, and he inserted a cigarette in his long jade holder and then offered her one. He felt none of the dread that was consuming her. Watching her eyelids droop before the flame, he thought: my son. It could have been my son, our son, and we would not be sitting here like this. We would have a set out at Myer, and the boy would be at the Point or perhaps VMI; and she would know how to charm the Chief and Handy and McNair—she would even know how to handle Jinny, they're very much alike in certain ways . . . He gave way to the old, dry interior laughter. Her impact on him was so compelling she could, momentarily, make a romantic even out of him.

"Look, I'd do what I could—" he began; but her expression was so desolate and bereft he fell silent.

"This war will never be over," she said in a dull monotone. "It's still 1918 really: the same war. It never ended. We only thought it did. It's the same one, and it's going to go on for a hundred years. Oh, they'll change the uniforms and tanks and planes, they'll talk about different objectives, different war aims but it'll be the same broken, gasping bodies in the wards, the same forlorn little burial parties nobody knows or cares about. It'll go on and on because we can't let it alone. We've become more fond of war than of anything else . . . Look!" she commanded, sweeping the room with her eyes. "Look what it does to us—what a ducky injection in the adrenals, the sex glands! It's like alcohol or masturbation or drugs. Why should we give it up? It's so much *fun* . . .

"You know these idiots who are always saying, 'Gee, if only I had my life to live over'? Well, I'll join the club. I swear I wouldn't do a single solitary damn thing I've done. Not one. I'd marry a rich sportsman or a big-time publisher or an oil magnate—I'd get myself so wrapped up in money and family and privileges that nothing could reach me with a bangalore torpedo . . ."

You'd find that wouldn't do it, my girl, he almost told her; the world would still get at you. Besides, if you want to dream the great dreams you must be prepared to pay the price. You won't do it.

Aloud he said: "Yes, that'd be pleasant."

"—What do you want, Court?" The question startled him. She was staring at him frankly now, looking—if it were possible—even lovelier than before. "There you sit: so composed and debonaire. Is life that clear, that meaningful to you? Do you really hold it in your hand so firmly? Don't you ever wake at night, your palms moist and your heart wrung with terror—?" Her eyes hung on his, almost fearfully. "No, I guess you don't . . . I do. Oh God knows, I do.—Court, don't you ever have a desire to break all the windows, kick over the cart, bust your way out of the whole, silly, sickly pattern of play-the-game and row-the-galley? What's the use of all the striving and conniving, when it all turns to dust anyway, and we all depart in darkness, as the old Bible says—doesn't that ever make you want to throw it all over . . . ?"

It was very, very strange . . . Gazing into her glistening emerald eyes, held there, entangled, he felt for one slow heartbeat the rush of desire for a life free of sycophancy and manipulation and scheming; free of the worry, the tireless approaches, the disappointments, the strain of bringing timid or stupid or downright hostile people around to seeing things the way you saw them . . . Then it passed, as lightly as a cloud slipping across the sun, and he smiled and said: "But then who'd do the world's work, darling girl?"

She lowered her eyes; he knew she would not say anything more. In another moment he saw Caldwell coming toward them through the cocktail boom and chatter.

"Tommy, I'm going to have to go back to the office this evening. Gene tells me there are two things that just won't wait." Noting her agitation he frowned, glanced at Massengale, patted his daughter's wrist. "Now, honey," he said. "You mustn't get all wrought up over things.

It's natural the boy should want to see some of his own crowd, show off his girl . . ."

She nodded rapidly. "It's all right. I'll get over it."

"Look at Marge—she's got *three* boys . . ."

"—Yes, and Harry's a chemistry major, and Benjy's far too young to go, and Joey's safely stowed at West Point."

"Honey—"

"Isn't he? Well, isn't he?"

Caldwell regarded her a moment, mournfully. "Now honey, you know that's not true."

She looked down again; she was pulling her gloves all out of shape.

"I know," she muttered, "it's not. I know. That's a perfectly rotten thing to say." She looked up at the ceiling. "Margie's a wonderful gal and I'm a rotten bitch."

"You mustn't get so worked up about things . . ."

Listening to them idly, Massengale caught again the dry, distant interior mirth. What a farce it was—what a devastating occasion for comedy! All this apprehension and protectiveness when around them the very chemistry of the nation was being altered, the old counters were losing their currency. The old way was individual—the embattled farmer with his musket, the businessman personally responsible to his associates and clients, a government responsive to the will of the people. But none of that was true anymore. The core now was diffuse, technological, manipulative: now the counters were the tank and the heavy bomber and the radar screen, the corporation and the interlocking directorate; and the host of government agencies proliferating on all sides like some lunatic anagram game—OPD, WPB, OPM, OTD, OPA, OSRD, OWI—were concerned with exhorting or soothing or distracting the citizen, with engineering his responses rather than with handing him anything resembling the truth . . .

Here was old Caldwell, ostensibly such a wizard in the matter of training and equipping the new dogface soljer; a tireless, perceptive, reasonably imaginative soul, one of the organizers of victory—and yet he hadn't the remotest idea about what was happening. The Shifkin girl saw more than he did. The Shifkin girl was right in essence—she didn't understand it but she felt it in some slow, visceral way. Postwar America would bear no more similarity to prewar America than the Restoration Monarchy bore to Revolutionary France; what would emerge would be a vast, impersonal juggernaut of industrial cartels, a mountainous administrative bureaucracy and a prestigious military junta—and beneath these, far beneath, an emotional and highly subservient citizenry whose attitudes and actions would be created, aroused, manipulated, subverted by the roar of the mass media . . . it was so clear! Why couldn't the dunderheads see it? Whoever *could* see it—whoever rode this wave deftly, keeping just ahead of its boiling crest—would hold the future securely in his fine right hand . . .

They were still talking about Donny. That arrogant, ill-mannered boy! It was time to move along. The moment—a kind of moment, with its revelations and overtures—had passed. It was time to move out along the broad, stately avenues, seek the solace of the long, still rooms where the maps and charts and intelligence reports and appreciations and tables of organization and equipment cast their shadows far into the lives of men, transformed them irretrievably . . .

He rose and said: "I really have to be going. Thanks so much for including me, General." They shook hands. "Thomas, it was a distinct pleasure. As always."

Her gaze was remote and tired. "Good-bye, Court."

As he moved off through the lounge Caldwell was saying, "You'll have him all to yourself tomorrow morning. Why don't you go to a movie—there's a new show at the palace down from the Circle. I ought to be home around eleven or so . . ."

"What I like best is lemon meringue pie," Ben Krisler declared. "No—Washington cream pie. And not because I'm a flag-waving type, because I'm not. With that cool, runny yellow cream and the chocolate drooling down all over it. Christ, what a dessert! Doesn't it make your bleeding mouth water, Sam?"

"Oh, you Fitzroy Yanks," Hallie Burns protested. "All you think about is your tucker."

"Not at all." Ben squinted at her happily. "That's all I can think about right *now*. At other times I think of movies, I think of—oh, all kinds of things . . . for instance—"

"Never mind, I can guess," Hallie said. She was a slender, handsome girl with a beautiful clear complexion and saucy violet eyes. "If it isn't a beano it's the Sheilas."

"I'm rough and tough," Ben concurred. "I'm a ring-tailed bandicoot."

"You're a devil with horns."

"That's just because you're seeing him away from home," Joyce Tanahill told her. "American men are actually the most docile creatures in the world."

"There you go."

"They are! Anything their wives tell them they do. Their wives run them around with a ring through the nose."

"Nurse Tanahill, you're out of line," Ben said.

"Yes *sir*," she sang impertinently, and did a rapid two-handed parody of a salute.

"Not me," Ben proclaimed sonorously. "I've alway been the czar in my domain. What I say *goes*. Isn't that right, Sam?"

"Absolutely."

"Hear that? Sam never told a fast one in his life. He's seen me in my best moments and my worst."

"Well, all I've seen are your worst," Hallie retorted, and sifted sand through her large, graceful hands.

Damon smiled, his eyes closed again, letting the voices float around him, footless and playful. Not far away the little waves tumbled toward them lightly, innocently, *sho-wa, sho-waaaa*, and the sun breathed softly on his lids. In the field behind the strip of beach some of the more energetic members of the Division staff were playing a noisy game of softball, and two other couples were wading in the shallow water near the sand cliffs, hunting for shells. Australia. A green and lovely land. It was pleasant lying here in the sun, torpid as a lizard, sprawled on your back against the warm earth, drawing strength from its vastness. Like— who? The man Hercules defeated by gripping him around the body and lifting him off the ground until his strength had ebbed. What was his name? He couldn't remember. But it was true: the happiest moments of his life were times like this, lying in green fields, in hammocks, on the banks of rivers—

"What are those things on your heel?" Hallie Burns was asking Ben. "Those ugly raw red holes, there?"

"Those?" He bent over to examine them. "Those are chigger bites, ma'am. Or *Chegroes*, as we call 'em up no'th." The others laughed and Ben glanced around, pleased. "Oh, I want to tell you, girls, it was rough out there in the swamps. No sauce bigarade, no napery in the messes . . . why, do you know the floors of the officers' club weren't even *waxed—!*"

"Oh, you stager . . ."

"It's the truth! Only the brutes survived." He threw out his jaw, a violent military caricature. "It brings out the roaring beast in a cobber . . ." Leaning over suddenly he bit Hallie on the thigh.

"Ben! Stop it," she cried; she slapped him and rolled away. "You're half crackers . . ."

"You said it, sister."

"There are *people* around," she protested.

"Only Sam. Old Sam won't tell. He's still out of his head with dengue. Aren't you, Dad?"

"Yep."

Ben rolled over on his stomach; the leading edges of his shoulders were already pink. "Say how about going to the flicks tonight?"

"Beaut!" Hallie cried. She opened her violet eyes very wide, the way she did when she wanted to say something she felt was immensely perceptive or startling. "Do you know, somehow or other I just can't fancy you as a colonel."

"Why's that?"

She studied him narrowly. "You haven't enough side. All our colonels are wowsers."

"What's that mean?"

"Stuffed shirts," Joyce said. "Pompous types."

"That's because you've only seen me in my off-duty hours," Ben reminded them. "Relaxed and fancy-free. On duty I'm an unholy terror. Firing Squad Krisler, they call me in the Division. Why, only yesterday I found two men with tarnished shoelace eyelets and had 'em whipped and pickled."

"Whipped and pickled!" Hallie cried. "That sounds like a bonzer pudding . . ."

"It is, as a matter of fact. We make a kind of jelly out of the corpses later on."

"Benjy, stop it!"

"It's the dinkum oil."

"Listen to him," Hallie Burns laughed. "Sounds for all the world like a Collins Street Squatter . . . But all the same, you're no colonel. I'll bet you're a masquerader, like the bloke they caught in Adelaide going around three pips up. Soliciting funds, he was. And then he made the mistake of going out to the track, and some nark did for him . . ." She sighed and tossed back her rich red hair. "Short life and a merry one."

Ben retorted: "If you think *I'm* a phony, take a look at Sam—who'd ever take him for a cruddy general?"

"Oh, but Sam's different," Joyce Tanahill said.

"Why's that?"

"I don't know . . ." Her eyes rested on Damon a moment: deep brown eyes, whose irises were as clear as autumn skies back home. Her hair, worn close to her head, was a fine, dull gold. "He makes you want to do something noble."

"Oh my God," Ben scoffed. "Just because he looks like a beat-up imitation of Gary Cooper with a crew cut—"

"No, it's not that." Resting on one arm she looked at Damon again. She was a tall, quiet girl who had her own style of joking; but this time her gaze was acceptant and very grave, and Damon felt a slow, firm pressure under his heart. "He looks like somebody you could tell your troubles to."

"Nurse Tanahill, you're out of line again," Ben declared.

"Yes *sir!*"

"Would I cure them?" Damon asked her. "All those troubles?"

She gazed at him a moment longer—then shook her head quickly, and he couldn't tell whether it was denial or wonder. She looked away, and he studied the fine, high forehead and broad cheeks, the large brown eyes that found the world neither unduly complicated nor unduly harsh; what solace that steady gaze must have been to Millis and Boretz and the other stretcher cases flown in from Kokogela! What a deep, aching reassurance that there was a corner of earth free of muck and desperation and uncaring slaughter, a green little isle of gentleness and calm . . .

He rubbed his eyes and stared at the sea. A film of unreality still lay over everything; like the onset of fever, but benign. He could never get over it. There was always something outrageous, almost mad in such a swift violent passage from squalor and death and anguished decision to this equally strange land of beds and sheets and steak-and-eggs and bright, well-appointed rooms and pretty women. He should be used to such transitions, God knew; but he wasn't, he never would be. Ben was different. What Ben encountered *was*, and there was no more to be said about it. Battle, beach parties, bars—he moved from one to another with a free, zestful acquiescence. He himself never could accept it so easily— bemused, guilty, for days he would feel he had no right to be whisked up and away and dropped into such casual opulence and frivolity and ease. And this time, intensified by fever and all the furor attendant on the capture of Moapora, it had been worse than ever . . .

Lennon's Hotel was always full: a gaudy, meretricious parade of observers and correspondents and politicos. They wanted to visit Moapora or Buna or the Salamaua front, they wanted to be present at reviews and awards presentations and staff conferences, they all wanted to talk to Sad Sam Damon. They cared nothing about the price exacted—the base hospitals overflowing with fever cases and wounds, nor the pitifully inadequate means bequeathed to the theater; there had been—unexpectedly—a victory, a bright little stop on their pleasurable itineraries, and they flocked around demanding dinners, conferences, interviews. Damon bore with the first half-dozen genially enough; but when he saw they had no desire to air or correct problems, that they were interested not in the truth of a long war against a tough, resourceful enemy but in the illusion of a cheap and easy victory, that they cared nothing about the heroic achievement of some ill-prepared and decimated GIs but instead about himself as a kind of minor celebrity, he made himself as unavailable as possible.

On his third day in Brisbane MacArthur sent for him. He left an irate Ben in the bar of the hotel and rose in the private elevator to the suite of the Supreme Commander. In the gaily papered little L-shaped foyer he rang, feeling nervous, and cross with himself for feeling nervous.

MacArthur was waiting for him in his study, standing by one of the windows, reading some reports. He had changed greatly since Damon had last seen him on Luzon; the long, proud face was drawn, the high brow furrowed, the lips that Damon remembered as rather full and mobile were nearly effaced now—in a broad, harsh line that pulled down sharply at one corner. It was an irascible face, a tormented face—

He saluted and said: "Sir, Colonel Damon, Four seventy-seventh Regiment, reporting as ordered."

"Damon." MacArthur smiled briefly and shook hands; indicated a long leather couch. "Sit down, sit down."

Damon seated himself, though the General continued to stand. The quick, birdlike eyes were on him and he gazed back, trying to look interested and respectful and at his ease. He knew about the infinitely graded scale of greetings MacArthur used, which ranged from the carelessly returned salute and curt acknowledgment to a warm handclasp on both shoulders and the ringing exclamation: "Comrade-in-arms! . . ." Apparently he'd fallen somewhere in between—not a distrusted subordinate, and by no means a "MacArthur man." It's because of Dad, he thought; and because I refused Massengale's offer back at Garfield. That's part of it . . .

"Damon, I'm proud of you," the General was saying, moving back and forth above him. "You went up there and did your duty. Which is more than most of them did. I wish I'd had a chance to see you on your way out from the States, but there simply wasn't time for it. One can't do everything. Damon, you picked that brigade up and made them fight the way I knew they could all along. It was magnificent. It was in the great tradition of American arms."

"Sir," Damon answered, "I will be pleased to inform the men. They did it."

MacArthur glanced at him sharply, and began again. "I understand your name is on the next list of general officers. Is that true? Who recommended you? Eichelberger?"

"Yes, sir."

"Good." The General turned and stared at the huge map of the western Pacific on the wall, his hand to his chin. "A crucial operation. Crucial. I *had* to have Moapora. Seems absurd, doesn't it? All those thousands of miles, all that water . . ." He turned sharply, his eyes piercing. "You realize that, don't you?"

"Yes, General," he answered quietly.

"I know what you're thinking. Not much finesse to it, was there? Stupid, head-on slogging. Well, there wasn't any other way. No landing craft, inadequate air cover, and the *Navy* . . ." He chafed the back of his neck; his hair was long, rather shaggy at the neckline. "Well, there won't be any more Moaporas now. Now I can go back to artful dodging. I've got a few tricks up my sleeve. Yamashita and his friends are in for some surprises before this year is out." Abruptly he said: "Tell me about the Fifty-fifth."

"Sir, they're a fine outfit—they've found themselves, as you've just said. But they're very weary and worn down. Our medical records indicate a seventy percent latent or active malaria rate. They need a good, long spell of rest and recreation." He paused. "I estimate a minimum rehabilitation period of four months, possibly six."

MacArthur resumed his pacing. "I'm afraid that just isn't in the cards,

Damon. Just not in the cards. Well. I've been promised the Forty-first, and the Eighteenth—Swanson's division. Do you know him?"

"Yes, General. I served with him at Benning, and at Beyliss."

"They say it's a good division. Superior organization, adequate staff work. Well, we'll see. God knows I need them badly enough." Hands sunk deep in his hip pockets, his eyes narrowed, he began pacing again. "Three divisions, two more promised. Perhaps. Five divisions, to retake New Guinea and the Admiralties and the Philippines." He shook his head. "How do they expect me to operate on that? Five divisions. Now all I need is amphibious elements and air groups and transports and engineer battalions . . ." His mouth drew down tautly. "*They've* all got them—Nimitz has got them all right, Eisenhower's got them—they're stockpiling matériel at Norfolk and Plymouth and Oran and Pearl Harbor and everywhere else. Everywhere but Australia . . ."

He swung around, and Damon was astonished at the wrath in the seamed, drawn face. "Do you know what they *did* send out here? Huntzicker. Yes. The Parson. To read me a sermon on how the main effort is to be against *Germany*. To tell me that we are a secondary theater of operations. As though I were not already supremely aware of the fact. *I* had to stand here and listen to that hound-faced moron for twenty minutes! Oh God, for the days in France, Damon—when the country was *behind* us, when men of competence, men of *principle* were running things back there . . . I tell you, this is intolerable. Intolerable! Damon, am I always to be condemned to lead a forlorn hope? a lonely, lost cause?"

Sam started to say something and checked himself. MacArthur wanted no reply; he kept pacing up and down, up and down, raging softly, bitterly at the incompetents back in Washington, the fools and sycophants and petty, vindictive tyrants who would place personal spite and aggrandizement ahead of the welfare and safety of the greatest nation in the world. Yes, Damon thought, watching the lean, spare body, the proud, handsome profile, the blazing eyes, yes, but when *you* were Chief of Staff and a lieutenant colonel named George Catlett Marshall modestly requested duty with troops, you sent him to a one-battalion post at poor old Fort Screven to work with the CCC camps, and after that exiled him to Chicago as senior instructor with the Illinois National Guard . . . And who was *then* the gentleman?

MacArthur was pointing a finger at him accusingly. "Damon, we could still lose this war! . . ."

"I realize that, sir."

"Do you? Thank God you do. It doesn't seem to have occurred even remotely to anybody else . . . Listen to them back there—sitting around some conference table mewing at each other and Knudsen asking them, 'Who wants to make machine guns? Anybody here want to make machine guns?' " He raised one arm threateningly. "They can come down from Timor and Torres Strait and land out there on Moreton Island, but I will never surrender. Never! I will die first. If need be I will seek the end in some final charge . . ."

Damon watched him stalk off across the room. There was something wrong here; it was too threatful, too wild, too high-key. The Supreme Commander had wheeled around again. "I know what they're saying about me back there. Don't you think I know? *Dugout Doug*," he said softly, and his mouth drew down. "Do you think I haven't heard it whispered, seen it scrawled on fencing? . . . I came out as the result of an explicit Presidential directive and for no other reason!" His voice rang in the bright, airy room. "I obey orders. Don't you, Damon?"

"Yes, General."

MacArthur picked up the long-stemmed corn-cob pipe from his desk, fiddled with it, musing—pointed it like a pistol at Damon's chest. "Caldwell. Your father-in-law. What's his position on this matter?" Damon hesitated, staring at him. "Go on, speak freely."

"I wouldn't attempt to speak for General Caldwell, sir."

MacArthur ducked his head, and began to ream out the bowl of the pipe with quick, harsh little strokes. "How about you, Damon? What's your attitude?"

He wouldn't have believed it; he wouldn't have believed it if he hadn't been sitting here on this leather couch, watching the proud, drawn face, the omnivorous eyes. It was wrong to ask a subordinate a question like this—he could only guess at the immense inner torment that had provoked it. He knew what he ought to say, what tradition and deference and diplomacy and his career demanded—and yet he could not say it: he could not get it out.

". . . I believe it's a matter of individual conscience," he replied quietly.

"Do you. What would you have done, Damon?"

"I don't know, General. I have never been in that situation."

"Of course not. But what do you *think* you would do?"

Damon drew a breath. "I believe I would stay with my men, sir."

MacArthur swung around with abrupt violence and started pacing again. "Then you're a damned fool. A double-dyed romantic fool. Like all the rest of them." Damon made no reply. "There are contingencies considerably more important than the morale of a regiment, or even the fate of an army . . ." He bit on the pipestem, his jaw outthrust, as sharp as his nose. "Well, I guess that's all."

Damon got to his feet with alacrity and saluted. The General returned it casually. Sam walked across the room. As he reached the door MacArthur called his name.

He turned. "Yes, General."

"Whip them into shape, Damon. Drive them hard. Time is of the essence."

"Sir, I'd hoped they could be given a real rest, now that they—"

"It's out of the question. The schedule will not permit it."

"Very good, sir. If it has to be done."

"It does. Believe me, it does." MacArthur was still standing by the desk, staring at him intensely. "Whip them into shape . . . you're a good soldier, aren't you, Damon?" he added in a strange, admonitory voice.

He paused, looked back at the Supreme Commander. "I don't know, General," he said slowly. "I don't know whether I am or not."

MacArthur smiled then—a bitter, mirthless smile; dismissed him with a gesture. Damon descended to the lobby in a heavy turmoil of relief and resentment, rage and hilarity and gloom. Ben was in the cocktail lounge hunched over an empty glass.

"How's the situation?"

Damon blew out his cheeks. "Fluid. Very fluid."

"Not good enough. You're relieved."

"You know, I might be, at that."

"What'd you do—rip the scrambled eggs off his cap bill?"

Damon sank into the opposite chair and sighed. "I just told him he shouldn't have shagged-ass out of Bataan."

"Mother Machree. Now what did you want to do that for? I'm *associated* with you." They laughed, and Ben waved for a waitress. "You look as if you've seen a ghost."

"No. No ghost."

"What's in the wind?"

"Storm signals. Another operation."

Ben scrubbed his scalp with his knuckles, his eyes wide. "You're kidding."

"Afraid not."

"The outfit? The Division?"

"None other."

"Jesus. No rest for the wicked." The two men looked at each other— a long, hard, enigmatic glance. Then Ben said, "Well—let's live tonight. What're you drinking? The gin here is—well, it's escharotic."

"Wow. I better have some, then."

The bar, called the Victoria, was crowded with the uniforms of several nations. The wainscotting was so dark the room seemed to sink below a horizon line of smoked ebony, and the walls were painted with scenes of desert and jungle where kangaroos, furry koalas, rock wallabies, wombats, bandicoots and platypi peered out, through a labyrinth of leaves and tangled vines, at faces only a little less strange than their own.

"Dig all those marsupials," Ben observed. "Rough dodge, you know: teats jammed down in the pouch, no placenta at all."

"That's the woman's problem."

"Well, it's just as hard on the male. How'd *you* like to have your scrotum slung up ahead of your hammer?"

"Damned awkward."

"I'll tell the world."

"What happens when you get an erection?"

"Then you've got to do it standing on your head. Or hang by your toes." Ben leaned forward confidentially. "Tell you the truth, I'm only making an educated guess. I'll ask the next marsupe I run on to. That's a promise."

Their drinks came and they raised their glasses.

"To the Salamanders."

"Through the fire with clean attire."

"Ass—best—us . . ."

The world was strange. Up at Huon they were still fighting, slopping through the muck, peering frantically into the bristling, impenetrable viridescence and cursing all jungles forever; and upstairs the Supreme Commander sat alone in his study gazing at maps and charts, reflecting darkly on the incompetent and vindictive souls in Washington and—very probably—on the deplorable lack of loyalty on the part of subordinate commanders; and here and in other bars soldiers and women laughed and argued and drank more than was good for them . . .

He sighed. He was going to be a general. If MacArthur didn't send him home first. So odd. In '24, in '31, in '38 it had seemed impossible, beyond his wildest, most vainglorious dreams. And yet he felt no elation at all. He was happy, yes—to be sitting here with Ben, alive, unmaimed, all his senses alert and quivering and receptive; but above it, hanging over it, was the bitter expanse of the cemetery at Moapora, the long, sepulchral gloom of the hospital tents, the gear rotting in the marshy clearing at Kokogela; the division in rows on rows of pyramidal tents in the hills behind Devon Bay, laboriously filling up with replacements, kids from Brooklyn and Big Spring and Salinas and Fletcher's Landing, who couldn't crawl noiselessly for two hundred feet or strip a weapon in the dark . . . Sitting here, now, in this smoke-burdened, noisy room, listening to Ben telling him a story about Jackson's extraordinary ruses to bring the company mascot, a dog named Gogarty, ashore at Melbourne he felt the old, long-forgotten urgency gripe at his vitals— this vast, uncaring enterprise in waste and misery and destruction that was even now preparing to pick him up again and fling him into the flame-filled maw . . . He was here. Here. In this foolish, noisy, lovable Australian bar. His hand—there—was gripping the glass, which was slick and cold; his heart beat thickly, comfortingly, his arms and legs tingled with the gentlest of pleasurable sensations. He was alive, here, his flesh clamoring its silly, sacred immanence, and time was hurrying toward its end . . .

Ben had finished the anecdote: the dog—and Jackson, dressed as an Australian dock worker—had been apprehended. Damon became conscious of another voice nearby, a British voice languid with the authorities of two proud and pleasant centuries.

"Tradespeople, inventors, efficiency experts, expediters—I grant you that. No question. But in battle, confronted by the thousand-and-one strategic and tactical dilemmas—no. They simply haven't got it, that's all . . ."

He turned. A British colonel with a flat, ruddy face and a low neat dark hairline was leaning forward, talking to another officer and two women, an American Army nurse and a girl in a blue dress who looked startled and upset.

"Joyce here's a Yank, you know," she said in the pretty, faintly Cockney accents of Australia, indicating the nurse.

"Yes, I know. No offense." The British colonel's teeth were a bony white barrier below his mustache. "Matter of racial aptitude, don't you know. Quality, upbringing. Why dispute it? Eh? Only the truth. Lorries, supply dumps, traffic control, petrol and ammo levels—top-hole. American way. If the PM had any sense at all he'd simply insist on their running up supplies and let us take care of the fighting end of things, don't you know. Only correct solution . . ."

"Listen to that." Ben was glaring at the Englishman, his eyes snapping. "That character could get to be unpleasant after a while."

"Relax, Benbo. He's loaded."

"I don't care. Drunk or sober he's unsavory. I didn't come into this glorified taproom to listen to that."

"—After all," the Australian girl was saying, "the Yanks are here to help defend us—I don't see why you have to bite the hand that feeds you . . ."

"My point exactly. Hewers of wood and drawers of water. But as for the art of war—"

"But sir," the nurse protested, "our forces have been fighting up there in Papua and winning a—"

"Bless-my-soul *Papua*. Raw-ther! My point exactly. And they have the infernal cheek to offer it as a victory. *That* farce . . ."

"That did it," Ben said flatly.

"Look, Ben—" But the Wolverine was already on his feet and moving over to the offending table. Damon rose and followed him, wondering idly what would come of it. A fight, an apology, another round of drinks? Ben was always getting involved in situations like this—on trains, in roadhouses, on ferries: he seemed to require these confrontations, as though to purge the hot, contentious defiance that incessantly flayed him. What the hell, Damon thought; maybe we can both get sent home on the same slow boat to Frisco.

"Good evening, ladies," Ben said, and bowed. Their faces turned up to him, vacant with surprise. Ben looked at the British colonel calmly. "You know something, chum? You're just a trifle obnoxious."

The Englishman's eyes slid up at him. "Not entirely sure that it's any of your business."

"You just made it my business."

"Eavesdropping, were you?"

"As a matter of fact I've been trying to ignore you, but I've had no luck at it."

The other British officer, a major, said: "Ronnie—"

"No, no." The colonel waved a hand. "I want to pursue this a bit."

Ben said in a flat voice: "I understand you feel the Moapora operation was a farce. Is that correct?"

"Ah." The Englishman's teeth appeared again, huge and bare. "One of the heroes, I presume."

Some of the adjacent tables had fallen silent now, and Damon was conscious of the chorus of talk at the bar.

"That's right, chum," Ben answered. "One of the heroes."

The Britisher smiled a slow, derisive smile and looked at his companion and then at the girls. Still watching them he said to Ben, "In point of fact I don't believe we've been introduced."

Ben reached down and with a quick, fierce grip on the Britisher's tunic yanked him to his feet; his chair went over backward with a hollow thump. Standing, the Englishman was three inches taller and outweighed Ben by thirty pounds, but the American had acted so swiftly he could only gasp. Still holding him tightly, his face inches away from the other man's, Ben said in a voice that rang like a bugle in the room: "—And you come to your feet when a fellow officer addresses you! . . ."

The other officer had risen now and Damon moved toward him, girding himself for battle. But Ben's tormentor was still so shaken by this turn of events he could only bluster: "Take your infernal hands off me! How dare you lay hands on me this way!"

"I just did, pal."

"I am a personal friend of General Blamey and attached to the staff of—"

"I don't care if you're a personal friend of the Emperor Augustus— you can step outside right now, or you can stand here in this room and hear me call you a loud-mouth liar and a son of a bitch and a swine!—"

"For your information—"

"*Which is it?*"

The room was almost completely still. The Englishman's eyes flickered nervously about. Ben had released him a few seconds before, and he twisted his neck inside his collar. "Gentlemen and officers," he breathed, "do not make scenes of this sort . . ."

"This one does," Ben answered lightly; and Damon, watching his eyes, his suddenly relaxed stance, knew that Ben had realized the other man would not fight.

"Ronnie," the major said in pleading tones, "wouldn't it be a whole lot better if—"

"Be still!" The Englishman turned to Ben again. "We were sitting with these ladies, Colonel, and I'll thank you to—"

"Then why don't we let the ladies choose?" Ben pursued; smiling

again he made the same funny little bow. "How about it, girls?" he
asked them. "Two Limeys or two Yanks? Roughly equal in rank, in age,
in girth—but the heart, ladies: the *heart!* What do you say?"

Damon saw the nurse give a soft, radiant little smile, the girl in the
blue dress run her tongue along the edge of her teeth in a merry,
malicious grin, while the whole room, utterly quiet now, watched and
waited. Then all at once the Australian girl, looking at the British colonel from under her brows, still smiling, burst into song, slapping her
hand against the table top in rhythm.

> *"Fellas of Austryl-yeh,*
> *Cobbers, chaps, and mites,*
> *Hear the bloody enemy*
> *Kickin' at the gites . . ."*

The room swelled into singing, raucous and bellicose. The Englishman tried to speak to the girl but she only sang louder, laughing; he
turned to Ben, but the singing drowned his words. His companion
pulled at his blouse; they glanced at each other and then left quickly
through the press, to roars of laughter.

> *"Blow the bloody bugle,*
> *Beat the bloody drum,*
> *—Uppercut and out the cow*
> *To Kingdom-bloody-Come! . . ."*

The refrain was followed by a cheer, and a chorus of approval and
commendation from the Diggers in the room ("That's showing them
the way, Yank!" "I heard 'im slang you, I did—the dirty little
dingo . . ."). There were handshakes, introductions, and drinks all
around. Damon brought over their glasses and they sat down with the
girls.

"What a bonzer cove you are," Hallie said to Ben. "Did you hear
them barrack you? You're the dinkum oil."

Ben threw open his hands. "Whatever *that* is, that's me . . ."

"Sorry about all that," Damon said to the nurse. "Ben's the impetuous
type."

"Thank heaven someone shut him up. It was disgusting. Are there a
lot of Englishmen like that?"

"Let's hope there are only a few—for Eisenhower's sake."

"It's always the nasty ones who have the connections. He's a friend of
General Blamey, did you hear him?"

Damon nodded. "Not worried about repercussions, are you?"

"Oh, no," she laughed. "They can't put us in the stockade—they need
us all too badly!"

They had another drink there, and then went on to what Hallie Burns referred to as a sly grog shop, obviously some kind of speakeasy where the gin was even more escharotic and a three-piece band—fiddle, accordion and clarinet—wheezed along brightly, and the tiny dance floor shook to the thump and slide of boots. Hallie seemed to know everybody. She worked for the war office, but as a civilian secretary. "I will not put on a uniform," she informed them. "My pa said it's the beginning of servitude and the end of the private dream."

"But suppose everybody felt like you."

"If everybody felt like me, Benjy," she retorted, her violet eyes glowing, "it'd be a lot wilder world. When my pot-and-pan put on his uniform I told him: 'All well and good, chum, but you'll never get out of it again.' And do you know, it was true as your eyes. He never did."

"Why do you call him a pot-and-pan?" Ben wanted to know.

"*I* don't know." Hallie shrugged happily. "Rhymes with old man, do you see? Instead of a wife you have a trouble-and-strife. Instead of head you say lump-of-lead."

"Hey, I like that. Can we make up our own?"

"Can't see why not."

"Where's your pot-and-pan serving now?"

"He's not, love. He's dead and gone. Stopped one at Tobruk." They all expressed condolences, but she was having none of it. "What's over is over. No sad songs. That's what war's for, isn't it? to kill people. Anyway, it's all chance. Like dice in a hopper."

"Do you really see life that way?" Joyce asked her.

"Of course. What else is there? We're all just leaves floating down a river: the wind blows this way, the current pulls another, kids poke some with sticks, some come to rest on the riverbanks, some fill with water and sink to the bottom. But the stream keeps rolling along anyway."

This inaugurated a long, earnest, rambling discussion about free will versus necessity. Ben declared that we had oceans of choice. "When I make up my mind to do something, that's it."

"God stone the crows," Hallie said, and rolled her eyes. "You're just a piece of taffy in a taffy machine: you stretch any way they pull you."

"Oh, the Army, sure—but what about just now? I went over and laid into that insufferable Limey, didn't I? I decided to shut him up and I did."

"Taradiddle." She blinked at him impudently. "What you saw were two fine and tricksy Sheilas and over you came. He could have been talking in Maori."

Ben grinned at her. "Maybe so. But then why did I lay into *him?*"

"That's easy. He stands for what you've always hated."

Ben stared at her. "You could see that?"

"It could have been painted on a hoarding, love . . ."

Their argument ran on, amicable and aimless. Damon turned to Joyce. "What do you think?"

"I've changed my mind. I used to think we had all kinds of free will—now I'm not sure we have much at all. I think we're pushed along by a thousand things we don't even recognize, we don't even know are working on us."

"Slaves to passion?"

She smiled faintly, and nodded. "Yes—sort of. Passion and obligation."

"How about marriage?" he asked impulsively. "Do we choose, or are we chosen?"

"Don't ask me that." She laughed softly but her eyes were grave. "It was the mistake of my life."

"Your pot-and-pan?"

"Ex-pot." He was a physics instructor; she had met him at a party at Berkeley where she was a pre-med student. "I told myself I was making a noble choice—renouncing an illustrious career for the man I loved. It wasn't true at all. I was scared to death I was going to flunk out—I would have, too, I know it—I can see now I was looking for a way out all along; and Brad was the answer." Her hands were large and capable, the fingers long and nicely tapered; her large, clear eyes were shadowed with a humorous ruefulness; her voice was deep for a woman's, and a little husky. "It's funny—he seemed so much older than I, so much more wise and disciplined and reliable. It took me three years to discover that he would never grow up, that he didn't want to. And I did. Badly . . . I've got a theory about people."

"What's that?"

"We all stop at a certain age. Really stop. And everything after that is just a repetition of all the earlier attitudes, going through the motions. We freeze, sort of. At a crucial place."

"Traumatic catalyst?"

"Not necessarily. It can also be a time of your life when everything was most vivid, and you want that time to continue. Or when you became aware of things being terribly different from what you thought they were. For instance my sister Georgia stopped at fourteen. She's thirty-two now, but she's really still the willful little adolescent resentful of the adult world that betrayed her when Dad left home. There's no *reason* she should cling to that moment, but she does, somehow."

"How about you?"

"I stopped at twenty-two, I think. When Mother died of cancer. We'd never been very close but I was seized with a sense of obligation— that I must sacrifice myself for the good of mankind: medicine, social work—and now I'm out here. Not a very interesting syndrome, I'm afraid."

"How about me?" he felt constrained to ask. "Where did I stop?"

". . . I don't know you well enough." She smiled again: it was a lovely smile, a surprising smile—it transformed her broad-cheeked, placid, almost plain face into a younger, more attractive woman's. That sense of solace, of resilience and trust in her large, brown eyes reached out to him; he was all at once conscious of the heavy male voices and the clump of boots above and around him, and time's racing.

"Tell me more," he heard himself saying eagerly, gliding on the gin, the hard pressure—aware that he was guilty of a kind of dereliction and not caring, not caring at all. His hand held this glass which was cool and moist, his heart beat densely, this girl sat here beside him looking wistful and vulnerable and composed. Life. Warm flesh, animate flesh . . .

"—This Aussie patois is tremendous," Ben broke in on him. "It's full of surprises. You know what they say for money? Bees."

"Why's that?"

"Bees-and-honey. Get it? A bastard is a swell guy, and a cow is a bum, but you can't say bum—"

"No you can't, Benjy," Hallie sang.

"—and smooge means—what do you think smooge means?"

"To get soot all over you from cleaning the chimney flue."

"No—it means to neck with a girl . . . I'm going to settle down here. When this late incommodiousness is over and they toss me on the slag pile I'm going to come out here. It's my kind of subcontinent."

"And you're my style of Fitzroy Yank," Hallie concurred.

"Great. Let's dance."

"Beaut!"

The fun, the need—which was also the fun—was in talking. About all the things you could remember—the trivial things that swept back over you with the fine emerald clarity of time: the rich, faintly gritty taste of buckwheat cakes on a chill fall morning, with the pheasants moving hesitantly through the stubble, the cock like some exotic Eastern satrap; or May afternoons with the apple trees in blossom and the humming-birds dancing at the bells of the lilies; or desert evenings with the sky swept in vast skeins of mauve and orange cloud and the smell of sage dusty and pungent, like wildly scattered spices. The evening swam away; they danced and drank and told one another all their lives' histories, sympathized and made predictions, compared tastes in food in different parts of the country, parts of the world. Frenchy Beaupré, just out of hospital, came by, looking like a fierce little rooster with his red hair, which grew perversely in two directions, making that curious ridge through the center of his scalp; and later Jimmy Hoyt with a Red Cross girl named Alma Mergenthaler, who giggled at everything anyone said and announced that she wanted to settle in Australia, too . . . It was curious how things repeated themselves, slid around again until you felt you'd been here long before. Damon thought of Devlin and Michele dancing to the tinny Gramophone in the narrow, high-ceilinged room overlooking the Marne, and later Denise sitting there so still, the tears staining her pretty little china-doll face. So long ago. Was it *déjà vu* he had? No, that was something else. It was certainly a different war, a very different war—and yet these moments, these images rose up so poignantly the same . . .

And then all at once it was late, very late. They went out into the cool night air and piled into the jeep Damon had promoted from command headquarters that morning. When they reached the place where Hallie lived Ben got out, too.

"Old indomitable commander." He drew himself up solemnly and saluted. His face was pale, and slick with sweat. Damon thought of the open carriage, rolling east along La Croisette toward the rock-and-pine headland of Golfe Juan. Ben was still holding his salute rigidly. "Terrible he rode alone, With his yemen sword for aid," he declaimed. "Ornament it carried none, But the notches on the blade."

Damon grinned. "Take care now, Benbo. 'For the fever gets in as the liquor dies out,' you know."

"Kipling," Ben answered contemptuously. "You're relieved. If you can't get your command across that pitiful little excuse for a creek I'm going to find me someone who can."

"*Hush,*" Hallie hissed at him. "Come along, now."

"Victory follows me, and all things follow victory. Who said that?"

"Napoleon," Damon answered.

"You're relieved. If you can't manage to get across—"

"Hush, Benjy!"

"Check." They moved up the steps. At the door Ben turned once more, his arm raised. "This must be a peace of victors, not—" Hallie pulled him inside and the door bumped shut.

They drove slowly through the deserted streets, the soft, depthless glow of false dawn. Damon glanced at Joyce now and then; she was looking straight ahead, a little preoccupied. At the hospital entrance he let the jeep roll fifty feet and switched off the key, got out and walking around to her side helped her out.

"It was fun," he said.

"Yes, it was, wasn't it?"

"Have you figured out yet where I stopped?"

"Stopped? Oh . . ." She shook her head, her teeth on her lower lip. She was so tall her eyes were almost on a level with his. "Maybe you haven't stopped yet."

"Maybe people stop and then start up again."

"Maybe."

He picked at the skin at the edge of his thumb. Joyce was still standing there, her face attentive and serene, her eyes very large in the dark. Across the street the MP on duty was watching them with the callous avidity and suspicion common to all sentries on night duty.

"Are you on today?" he asked.

She nodded. "But I'll get a catnap this afternoon. I never need much sleep anyway."

"You don't?"

"Five or six hours. We all got a lot less than that during the Moapora operation."

"So did we."

They smiled at each other a moment. It would be easy to fall in love with this girl, the thought swept over him. After all these years, all the alarums and excursions; terribly, fatally easy . . .

But he was not Ben. He could not slip away somewhere and climb into bed with her, as Ben had with Hallie. There was Tommy, and the kids, and all the patterns of allegiance and obligation with which his life was invested. The fierce, unreckoning need to touch, to assert the importance of his imperiled self still thrust at his vitals; but he forced it back.

"—I'd like to see you again," he said awkwardly. "May I?" She nodded; she was absolutely motionless. A moment longer they hung there, bound in this curious air of expectancy, of suspenseful, unresolved colloquy that hummed between them in the Queensland night. Then he stepped forward and kissed her—a strange, solemn kiss, a ridiculous kiss like an older brother's—and released her.

She gave a little sigh, as though she'd been awakened in her sleep; then straightened and said, "Good night."

"Good night." He watched her move off toward the gate—the fine, easy carriage, her head high. Tall girl. He could see her all at once at fifteen, with that deep gold hair in braids and freckles over her nose and her ears too big, chewing gum and reading. The MP came to attention and saluted; she returned the salute smartly and moved out of sight. You God damned fool, he told himself; there was a strange constriction in his throat. The sentry was staring at him again, and he turned away and got in behind the wheel . . .

"I'm going in for a swim," Hallie Burns was telling them now. "What's the matter with you cows? All you ever want to do is lie around in a bloody torpor . . ."

"We're storing up strength," Ben replied. "For the ordeals to come."

"You can't store it up. It's like underground water: if you let it go by, it's gone forever. Come on in with me, Joyce."

"All right."

"Are they like all the other Americans, Joyce? these military blokes?"

"No—they're a race apart. They don't know what's going on in the rest of the country. They live like the Baltic barons—you know, their own preserves, their own codes."

"Blasted aristocrats."

"Worse. Much worse. Unnatural appetites."

"Nurse Tanahill, you're confined to quarters . . ."

"Yes *sir!*"

Damon smiled at the desultory ritual banter, studying Joyce with the almost merciless scrutiny one occasionally visits on a good friend. He found her more appealing outdoors, in the warm sunlight; her large-limbed, indolent grace seemed more suited to sea and sand and green upslanting fields. Behind them there was a sudden chorus of yells and cheering. He turned his head, saw the flying runner, the capering, gesticulating figures. Long drive. He picked up a small stone and tossed it loosely in his palm. The mantle of languor still hung over him. Another three days, or four, they would get the word and the laborious machinery would start up all over again—the preparation of attack plans and manifests and codes and troop dispositions, the pattern of arguments and rehearsals and post mortems that had only one end in view: the seizure of enemy-held territory and the destruction of the garrison force. So that the pins and arrows and black lines on the maps could move forward another stage . . .

"What are those fences doing out there?" Ben asked, pointing. "Those low wood and wire backstops, there?"

"Oh, it's an old shark net, I guess," Hallie answered.

"Sharks? You've got sharks swimming around here?"

"Bloody fine chance!" She laughed saucily. "Come on, Joyce. Let these lizards lie around on their backsides." She ran to the water, her feet lifting and falling on the sand. Joyce followed her more slowly, swaying as the water reached her thighs, then dropping forward out of sight, to reappear a few yards farther on, kicking a soft white froth. The two men watched them in silence.

In another tone Ben said: "What did Sutherland say?"

"Full training schedule. Range, conditioning hikes, field problems. The works."

"Jesus, I wish those sons of bitches in operations could be out there in the boondocks," Ben went on crossly. "Crawling through the muck and ducking mortar fire. Just for a week. I wish—" He subsided again. "Ours but to wawl and cry. What do you think we'll draw, Sam?"

"I don't know. I think Madang, or Ulingan."

"Jesus, I hope we don't draw New Britain. Dick says coast watcher estimates put a hundred and sixty thousand Japs at Rabaul." He scrubbed his scalp feverishly and said in slow, comic outrage: "A hundred and—*sixty—thousand* . . ."

"Come on in, Sam," Joyce was calling. "It's wonderful! You'll regret it . . ."

The girls were standing in the shallow water; they looked slim and glistening and vivid, like the first women at the birth of the world. Hallie pointed and they both looked off up the coast, shading their eyes. He would always remember this moment: the bright, lithe limbs against the blue sea, the pale, smoky Australian sky.

"Come on, you two! It's so warm and lovely . . ."

"What the hell, Sam. Let's go join them."

"Right."
The two men got to their feet and walked toward the water.

12 Jan 43.   Duke Pulleyne roared into camp yesterday. Face like a shingle hatchet, smooth silver hair, spots of fiery color high on his cheeks.
Cigar chewed half through, long-barreled .38 in an open holster. Dashing cavalryman. "Damon! Brilliant job, brilliant. How many of the little
slopehead bastards did you starch? Great stuff. What shape's the Division in?" Just like that. Full of piss and vinegar, one of those perpetually
wound-up types. Never heard a word I said. Well, Christ knows he'll
need all the p & v he's got up there on the old Guinea Hen, as Jackson
calls it. Tore around like a couple of drunken firemen, disrupted Hoyt's
batt working on bunker assaults, some of 484th later. Pulleyne not impressed. "What's the matter with them? They fart around like a bunch
of tired old men . . ." I said: "They *are* tired, Duke." "Well, they
better shake the lead and get cracking. They're soldiers—with a big,
dirty job to do." How true. He's picked up a crypto-British bush jacket
made of some shiny golden chino, with patch pockets: banks of ribbons,
oversize stars. Doesn't know quite how to take me—kept vacillating
between deferential queries about Moapora and profane directives on
How to Run a Lean and Mean Division. Never had combat command
before—went up to take over a company in the Wild Wests on Nov 10,
last war. Training divisions at Bragg and heartily sick of it. Can't say I
blame him. Only why did they send him OUT HERE?

Immediate clash of personalities today between him and Dick—could
see it building. Tart sober Yankee, flashy impulsive Virginian. "Any
man that needs more than three minutes to make up his mind about
anything hasn't got any God damn business leading men." Wants to
hold a review, says he wants Div to get to know him. Not much doubt
that they're going to do *that*. Maybe it's a good idea: I doubt it. There
isn't all the time in the world.

Div coming back, slowly. Nothing succeeds like success. To coin a
phrase. *Now* the supplies roll in, T/O&E swelling. Nobody would have
been caught dead with us three months ago.

Donny arrived in UK last week. Short ltr, full of forced casualness,
new worlds, etc. Suddenly felt afraid, reading it. Hope to God they give
them plenty of time to shake down. Wished we'd been closer than we
were. A soldier never gets to know his kids well enough: you should be
able to but you don't—military life is too unsettled, confused, full of
external artificialities to permit it. No word from Tommy now for five
weeks. She will always cling to the idea I influenced him—she'll never
believe I tried to dissuade him in all those ltrs last fall, once right in
middle of Moapora mess. Begged him at least to stay on until graduation. Wish I'd met the girl—she seems like a good sort. He's got his
mother's flair for violent extremes, impulsive action. What changes this

past year has made! All the agony, and ambition, and uprooting—and we've only just got started . . .

6 Feb 43.   Got word Tuesday from SWPC HQ: Wokai peninsula. Big surprise all around. Bypassing Madang, Aitape. Long pow-wow most of yesterday. High cliffs running along peninsula. We've drawn Red Beach, are to drive inland and take airfield; Swannie's Div to land on Green west of peninsula, and pinch it off, take it from land side. Lot of complicated verbiage which, boiled down, means: we will be under intense artillery fire all the way to the strip, until peninsula is reduced. Much walla-walla over whether there were or were not 2 trails from cove to airfield: not even God seems to know. Maps are fantastic—they seem to be based on some myopic missionary's abstract of a drunk's interpretation of a New Guinea headhunter's fancies. Aerial reconnaissance is even worse. Ben is right, the only *sane* place to fight is in that clean, well-charted rectangle Namur-Saarbrücken-Nancy-St. Quentin, where they've been slaughtering each other since Romans and Charlemagne, and every bloody hill and patch of woods has had a monograph written about it.

Pulleyne in a wrangle with Hodl. "450 tons—you people get too worked up about supply levels. The thing to do is get in there fast and nail down that airstrip." Glaring at us, wagging his handsome silver head. "I want to tell you, there's too much worrying going on in this lash-up. Worrying about supply and flanks and everything else." Ben and Frenchy exchanging disgusted glances. Well: Duke's good in some ways—he's shaking the outfit up. If only he didn't keep going off at half-cock. Read off a lieutenant yesterday for negligence—and then it turned out man wasn't even involved in the exercise. Wanted to put Div in field scarves "to sharpen their esprit." I told him he was OUT OF HIS MIND, they would mutiny and massacre us all, commandeer a boat and start for home. He muttered and rumbled and chewed on his cigar.

It finally came out this evening after chow. "Sam, whose Division is this, do you know?" Didn't know what he was driving at, and said so. "All I hear is Damon this and Damon that, and how-Sam-did-it." Looking at me like a fierce old turkey cock. "That's what I want to know: are you going to be running this lash-up or am I?" I said: "General, I intend to carry out your orders to the best of my ability. If I overstep my authority and try to run the Division, I hope you'll relieve me at once. On my part, if I feel you are in error about some matter, I will bring it to your attention directly and promptly, and to no one else." "Fair enough," he said, and muttered: "There's one hell of a lot of old-home-week and down-memory-lane in this command . . ." Well, there is: but what does he expect? And it's his problem, not mine. Been having my own battles to fight.

Did get one thing hammered through: two canteens for every GI. Hodl hit the roof. "I haven't that many in stock." "Requisition them, then." "Sam, they'll never carry that extra weight." "Wouldn't you?" He looked at me nervously. "I don't know." "Well, I do," I told him. "I've taken a little poll with most of the Double-7 and the project is running about 40 to 1 in favor. Let's do it." Still thinks it's unnecessary, a whim. Why are G-4s always so UNIMAGINATIVE???

Had a dream about Joyce last night toward morning. A beach like Monterey with heavy, slow surf and boats capsizing everywhere, terrible mortar fire. Got caught on wire, couldn't get free, filled with panic, sinking in ooze. Joyce gliding by in lovely outrigger with candy-striped sails, two men (couldn't recognize) hugging her, she laughing and having a great time. I cried out, they noticed me, one of the men queried her. She replied: "Well, I can't save him. He's stopping. It's too bad, but that's how it is." Woke up shaking. So much for dream life.

Fine letter from Dad: may be given combat command in Africa, where things are not going too well. To put it mildly. Old Man really elated, almost giddy. "For God's sake DON'T tell Tommy or she'll have forty fits. Brent said: 'Of course it'll mean a bust.' 'Suits me fine,' I told him, 'whenever you say.' But I don't think they'll want an old bat like me." By God, I wish he was out here running the Salamander. I'd feel a lot better about things.

16 Mar 43.   Ready as we'll ever be. I guess. Not enough TIME. Not nearly enough, especially for landings. Rehearsal off Castlereigh an unholy fiasco. Hoyt's people landed ½ mile down the coast, message centers hours behind, everyone yowling and howling and generally carrying on. Maybe a bad practice means a good game.

Ben wonderful with Rgt. Standing on jeep hood wearing that wrinkled patrol cap with the bill turned up like Donald Duck. "Now in case anybody's in any doubt about it, this is the outfit that took the first real estate from the Jap Empire that was ever taken by *anybody!* We took the first one, and we're going to take the last one." A murmur, tentative: not knowing quite how to take this. Ben watching them, hands on his hips. "All right, now let's hear it: who's going to win this war?" "We are . . ." "Wrong!" Glowering at them. "The buck-ass sad-sack privates are going to win it!" A roar. "With a little help from the NCOs . . ." Another roar, louder. Had them with him now. Waving my old '03 I gave him when he took over. "Now I'm going to be on that beach right along with you, and I'm going to be carrying this oh-three. I stole it from General Damon after they slapped so much rank on him he couldn't be seen around with it any longer. It's going to be noisy as all hell on that beach, and you know and I know those Nips are going to be trying for officers—and I want to look just like the rest of you . . ." A terrific roar now: would never know the battered old Double-Seven. Pounding each other on the back and throwing their helmets in the air.

Perfect speech: kind I could never make. Cornball and tough and raggedy-ass. Pulling the replacements and the veterans all together—or rather, formalizing it, they've been pulled together by the hikes and battle courses.

Ben lives direct: chow, drink, fistfight, girl. No shrinking, no doubts. The way I ought to be. I can't, ever. Those faces—so young, so eager and so trusting—if I got up there to joke with them like that I'd more than likely break down. I let things go too deep. I tell MacArthur I'd have stayed with my people on Bataan, and then I kiss Joyce T., and then I raise hell with Haley because of his lousy lack of participation in the assault plan—and then I worry about all three. Should not be like this. A good commander is like a man in a barroom brawl: belting one joker in the chin, picking up a chair in time to drop some hoodlum with a knife, throwing another one into the mirror behind the bar—and all the while maintaining a nice surface numbness, with one eye cocked on his two sidekicks, and the other open for every possible contingency. Ben is better with troops than I am.

Coming up to me later, full of eagerness under the trees. "How do you like 'em, Sam? Think they're ready to go?" Big square ITC stenciled on his helmet, all over the jeeps and trucks. I said: "ITC—what the hell's that?" "*In The Clutch*, Sam. What they needed was a visual motto. Gap between the newcomers and the old crowd was too great." "It also stands for *Idiot Trucking Company*," I retorted. Grinning at me. "Sam, they can say it stands for *I Take Cucumbers* if they want to—it's what they need." Pulleyne hit the ridgepole when he spotted this happy colophon. "Doesn't he know Hildebrandt's got a Corps order out about special markings? What the hell's he think he is, anyway—a privileged character? some kind of colorful five-alarm hot-shot?" "That's right, Duke," I said, "—just like you." He glared at me. "Jesus, you're salty." "General, he's done wonders with this regiment, you'll admit that." "But the Japs'll know just what outfit's facing them." "Duke, the Japs know when you took your atabrine last night." Finally talked him into letting it ride.

Worried about Tommy. Can't seem to reach her anymore. Her letter strange and disturbing—veering from drab, factual observations to wild emotional outbursts; as though her mind has been maimed. All her old hatred of service boiling out now, because of Donny. She needs a villain so *badly*—and here I am. Is that fair? Probably not.

23 Mar 43.   On the water. Plan is to loop north as if we're intending to hit New Hanover—then break off west for the Guinea coast again. Damn ruseful. Japs probably taken in about as badly as a Reno pit man. Something *final* about being at sea, moving through the dark, throbbing. Standing at the rail with Ben, watching the wake churning astern in slow, molten chains. Three nights to battle. Worry. The certainty—the cold, oppressive certainty that so many of those kids below us, all around us, will be dead. The dirty, diseased hand of waste. Waste of time and lives and hope and innocence.

"Sam." "Yes?" "Sam . . . I got the Joe Blakes." "I won't tell on you." Silence. "Sam—I've got a bad feeling about this beachhead. I don't know . . . the kids are all right. I mean, most of them took after me, they'll land on their feet. But Marge—she's sort of . . . well, you know. She can't take care of herself . . ." Silence. The thump and seethe of water against the cool iron. "If anything goes wrong, would you keep an eye on her? look out for her?" "Sure I will. That's a promise." "I know I haven't got any right to ask it." "If you haven't I don't know who has." "Yeah. Well. Thanks, Sam."

He's gone. The nights are so *long* at sea. The stars come and go behind invisible black snatches of cloud. So long and lonely. Waste again, waste and remorse now, flooding blackly. Why did I go to China? Did I need to quarrel with Tommy that time after the dance at Beyliss? Should I have refused to give the boy permission to enlist? I've been headstrong when I could have been wise, craven when I should have been bold. I haven't understood very much. Why did I go and get Dev and drag him back? Who in God's sweet name am I to judge *anybody* on this earth? Here we are in our thousands, rushing in gray shells toward the unknown. What is the end of all our fear and sacrifice?

Ah God. God, help me. Help me to be wise and full of courage and sound judgment. Harden my heart to the sights that I must see so soon again, grant me only the power to think clearly, boldly, resolutely, no matter how unnerving the peril.

Let me not fail them.

〔 5 〕

There was a draw, where a trail wandered beneath the palms, and beyond that a low hillock laced with branches and smashed fronds and bits of débris, the sunlight falling trickily across its face. And somewhere out beyond that was the airstrip. But where? Two figures, looking ridiculously clumsy and bedraggled, scuttled to the right of the hillock in a shambling run, dropped out of sight. A tiny yellow star deep in the crushed mat of vegetation winked merrily, and splinters and chips spurted from the loose earth above the pit. Cringing against the dry, dusty cascao, Joe Brand thought, I'm glad I'm not up there having to do that right now.

At the far edge of the pit Colonel Krisler was sawing one arm back and forth and shouting, "Keep it up, now! *Give* it to the sons of bitches—!" His face blackened with sweat and grease, he looked like a

gnome from some bewitched mine. The bright yellow scarf he always
wore around his neck in combat was wringing wet. A figure loomed up
at the edge of the pit, tripped and tumbled into the hole, spraying coral
dust over them all.

"Colonel," he panted, "—we can't—hang on . . . we got to have help
over there—"

"Who's we?"

"Charley—Captain March . . ."

"—*Look out!*—"

There came that soft, sighing shriek, thin as parting silk, and the
whole world flung up like surf; black smoke billowed down around
them, and shell fragments whined and hummed. A pillar of flame rose
up to the right, again. The earth tilted like a rough sandy table tipped
by giants. Brand found he had clamped both hands to the back of his
neck. The dead Japanese soldier who had been lying just beyond his
leg was gone, buried all but for one arm. The runner was lying on his
face in the bottom of the pit, his fatigue blouse blown off and blood
running in fine streaks from a long gouged curve in his back; his arms
kept moving as though he were trying to swim, little looping motions.
At the back of the smashed-in bunker Damon was huddled up in a
tight crouch with his head pressed to the radio, and Brand could see his
lips moving. Above the General, far above and beyond his helmeted
head, was the cliff face, a shadowed gray wall from which quicksilver
flashes came and went, and the puffs of exploding shells. Sitting ducks,
Brand thought savagely. Dirty yellow bastards will kill us all yet. His
hands, when he brought them away from his neck, were shaking
slightly, and his head ached from the pressure waves.

Lieutenant Chase, Damon's aide, was grinning at him and he winked
back without changing expression. Inscrutable redskin on the warpath.
Yeah, sure. Where did they all get the idea that the Indian was such a
fire-eating warrior?

A medic was in the bottom of the pit now, working on the runner.
Two more shells swooped down and crashed to the left, and the ground
under his belly shook in protest. A machine-gun team went by in a
heavy, labored run: Rodriguez, one hand wrapped in a bloody rag, carrying the tripod. Damon had handed the headset back to De Luca, the
radioman, and he and Krisler were bent over a map and talking intently.

"Well, where is he now?" he heard the General say. "Is he—" The
awful sighing came again, like the flutter of threatful wings. The blast
tore the very sky apart, turned it black and savage, a wall of fiery water
crashing over him, beating against his flesh. He found he was groaning,
gasping for air; he felt old, and feeble, and filled with tearful rage.
Nobody can live through this, nobody anywhere—oh-you-stupid Navy
hit that *cliff*—! Something slammed into his helmet and drove his face
against the bolt of his carbine. With great care he reached up and felt
the metal: a shallow groove, that was all. Damon was still talking to

Krisler, who was nodding in agreement. Jesus, how could they sit there like that, calmly talking? . . . It was easier in the line. You had things you had to do, the whole bunch of you were involved in the deal—you didn't have to sit on your ass like this, waiting for the Old Man to call to you and take off for some place else. They can call it a cushy job if they want, he thought crossly, Higgins and Goethals and the rest of them: it isn't so God damn cushy right about now . . .

Back in the operations room on board the *Sirius*, that morning, it had been cool under the moan of the blowers. Maps and charts lined the walls, sailors came and went with chits of paper, the radios crackled and hummed. Admiral Endicott, looking like a bony, irritated schoolteacher, kept picking up his white coffee mug and sipping at it and setting it down again. General Pulleyne kept passing his hand through his smooth, silvery hair and glaring at the situation map as though he could change the shape of the bay, the contours of the ridge. Damon was sitting very quietly, bent forward, his hands hanging limply between his knees.

A swabby passed a slip to Pulleyne, who glanced at it and handed it to Damon. Brand could read it from where he was standing, inside and to the right of the weather door. CROSSBOW TO CUTLASS X REQUEST ALL OUT NAVY 753513 X ALSO AIR MISSION URGENT

"What have they got—the whole God damned cliff fortified?" Pulleyne demanded.

"Must be pretty rough," Damon answered, "for Ben to send something like that."

Brand stood easy, listening to the short, terse arguments, the orders. It wasn't very reassuring. In the line, in combat, struggling to maintain contact with a dozen, two dozen men, sunk deep in the rank jungle gloom, you could comfort yourself sourly with the thought that back at Battalion, back at Regiment and Division, they could see what was going on—where everyone was, the threats and enemy dispositions, and take countermeasures. Now he could see that they didn't know much more than the squad leader—that in some ways it was worse, because there wasn't even the hot, raging satisfaction of trying to kill, of going forward, or the healing presence of one's friends: here in this cool, dry, magnificently equipped room they didn't know either—and they had to sit here and wonder, and worry, and pray they wouldn't guess wrong. CROSSBOW—Krisler's regiment—was clearly in trouble, and CLAYMORE hadn't come up with a report in half an hour or more. There on the wall was the map, with the beach designations and phase lines neatly stroked on the overlay in grease crayon, the probable enemy concentrations and the airstrip and the slender threads of trails—and it didn't mean anything: there was no correlation between this room and the beach a thousand yards away.

"You better go in, Sam," Pulleyne was saying. "Go get hold of Dutch, see what's the matter there—and then get over and check on

Krisler. Find out what's holding him up like that. We've got to get in there, grab that airstrip . . ."

Damon had come to his feet quickly. "Right away, Duke." He turned to Chase and Brand. "All right, boys. Let's get moving."

Pulleyne followed them outside on to the deck, still talking to the Old Man. "Don't take any fool chances, now. They're throwing a lot of crap around in there . . ."

"I won't, General."

They went quickly over the side, hand over hand. The LCVP looked boxlike and trivial far below, the upturned faces like bland white flowers. Then they were aboard, the boat swung out and away—and the world changed again. The morning sun slid a diamond shawl over the water, and dead ahead lay the beach, a faint dun patch hazy under the smoke. Gripping the warm iron of the gunwale, swaying with the boat's motion, he watched the Old Man talking to Lieutenant Chase. There was something fantastic about the three of them going ashore for the purpose of bringing order to a battle. He was conscious of that thick swelling high in his chest, right under his windpipe, that he remembered from Sendaiadere. The shore was clearer now; the ragged fringe of jungle was apparent here and there through the smoke, and the cliff on the peninsula was like a mesa, high and brooding in the sunlight. Their craft picked up speed, and the swaying grew worse. There was a towering white column of water near them that seethed and swayed and then subsided; the boat slewed left. Lieutenant Chase's face was slick with sweat, but he grinned and nodded when Damon said: "Miss as good as a mile . . ."

Life was a matter of luck. Luck and fate and chances—and reading the signs with wisdom, quickly. Anybody who said it wasn't was a dummy or a liar. There was that afternoon on old Sendai he'd been chopping with a machete at the jungle around his shelterhalf and thinking distantly of Estelle when Tompkins had cried, "Ten-*hut!*" and he'd swung around to see Damon standing there grinning at him. He was in khaki and there was a small neat star on his utility cap.

"Well—" he started, caught himself. He was a regular and the rest of his squad were staring at them. He came to attention and saluted and said impassively: "Good evening, sir."

"Hello, Brand." Damon had returned the salute and then shaken hands and asked him how he was feeling. "What you doing—clearing the west forty?"

"Yes." He gestured casually with the machete, which he'd transferred to his left hand. "Stuff grows while you look at it." Tompkins and the others were still gaping at him. Kids.

"Come along with me a minute," Damon was saying. "I want to talk to you." They moved slowly toward the end of the clearing. "How's it going?"

"Can't complain, sir." He felt a heady rush of excitement; *General*

Damon was walking along with him, asking his opinion! "They're shaking down. Draftees, city and town kids, most of them. They think if you lie down on your belly and look at each other it's scouting and patroling." Behind him he heard Tompkins whisper in awe and incredulity, "—a frigging *general!* . . ." He turned and glowered at them to shut them up, though he felt a deep, fugitive pride. "They've all been through high school, though. Every last one of them."

The General was smiling faintly. "Well: it takes all kinds."

". . . Congratulations, sir," he said awkwardly. "I heard you'd got a star. Are we going to be assigned to your command?"

"No. I came over to see you." He looked up; Damon was facing him, his hands sunk in his hip pockets. "I remember you once said you'd like to serve with me. Well, I need an orderly and I wonder if you'd be interested. It'll mean a lot of late hours, running around, a lot of headaches. And I'll be the biggest one of all. It'll mean another stripe for you, though not right away. But Captain Orr tells me he's pleased with your work; and maybe you could go farther if you stayed with your outfit. You'll have to decide about that yourself. Anyway, think it over and let me know tomorrow."

"I don't need to think it over, sir. Hell, I'd go right now. Only thing, I'll need to get cleared . . ."

Damon smiled. "That shouldn't be too difficult. If you're sure you want to do it."

"I'm sure, General." He was, beyond all doubt. It was a sign such as he'd never had before. "Whenever you say."

"No time like the present. I've got a jeep at the battalion office. Go ahead and pack your gear. I'll see about getting some orders cut for you."

It had been like that. One moment, and his whole life was changed again. Chance. Like the night long ago when he'd waked from a nightmare and smelled the smoke, dense and foul, clinging to his throat. Fire. Without a sound he had jumped to his feet and run into the main room through churning clouds of smoke, to the hearth, the old rug whose edge was alive with crawling maggots of glowing coals. Coughing he'd snatched up the rug and made for the door. The rug had burst into flame all at once, searing his face; in a paroxysm he'd dropped it, caught it up again and plunged outside and flung it on the hard clay where it burned furiously, the flames torn low to the earth by the plains wind. His forearm was burned, and his foot. And behind him then he heard a stirring and a cry. He would always remember that moment. Chance. But you had to seize it by the throat, as the Old Man said, or it was nothing—it would drift past you like a still river. And it was more than that, too: standing there in the clearing with the machete in his hand, watching those steady, sober eyes he knew he wanted nothing more than to follow this man who had taken such risks for him and given him back his dignity, his place among the white men—that he would will-ingly follow him as long as breath was in his lungs . . .

A man came running from the left, from the direction of First Bat-talion. Captain Lund, looking like a wild-eyed scarecrow, bathed in dust. He slid down into the hole. "Colonel—everybody's down! We've lost everybody . . ."

Krisler grinned at him brightly. "You've still got me, Swede."

"Hear it?" Travis was saying to Chase. "Do you?"

"Yes." Chase doubled down in the pit and grabbed the arm of Damon, who was on the radio to CLAYMORE. "*General*—"

And then, peering forward over the shattered, embedded logs and débris he heard it, under the groan and crash of mortars and the popping of rifle and machine-gun fire—a brash, dusty clatter, like a tractor work-ing in a distant field; then another. Oh no, he thought, watching Damon and Krisler scramble up to the leading edge of the pit, their faces rigid with tension; remembering Sendai all over again, that same coughing clatter and everyone running through the tangle of roots and vines, oh no, *no:* constrained to watch with the others now, all his senses alert and quaking—seeing then at the far end of the draw, bristling with fronds and branches, the squat black form.

"Tanks!" someone shouted. "They've got *tanks*—"

The machine gun on their right opened up, the gunner half-reclining on one hip, his helmet tipped back. From all points tracers curved in toward the tank and caromed away like sparks from an acetylene torch. It paused a moment, turned and came on again. Brand looked back. Damon was back on the radio again, talking rapidly now. "CARBINE to CUTLASS. CARBINE to CUTLASS . . . Duke? This is Sam. Look, I'm with CROSSBOW, we've got troubles . . . What? Let me talk to Pulleyne. Who is this? . . . He's what? You say he's what?" Damon's face was strained with the effort to hear. "*Gone ashore*—but what's the sense in that? How in Christ's name can I reach him? . . . All right, all right. Dick, look, we're under attack by tanks. Five or six, maybe more, I can't tell yet. Now what about Bailey's tank company: have they got ashore yet? . . . *Recalled* them! Then where in hell are they—just milling around out there somewhere? All right, never mind. What about artillery? . . . No, no naval fire—they're into us *now*. Get on Harkavy and tell him to divert any and all armor to Red Two. Yes, Red Two. When Pulleyne contacts you, tell him we're in serious trouble over here. To send Bailey in as soon as possible. And tell him CROSS-BOW will hold. Out." He handed the headset to De Luca and called, "Hank! Joe!" Brand crept back through the pit.

Colonel Krisler was staring at Damon, his head close to the Assistant Division Commander's. "We stuck with the lease?"

"Looks like it."

The tanks were nearer. There were four that Brand could see now, coming through the grass, beetling up and down in the rubbish heap of underbrush and cascao, their guns wavering like antennae.

"—we've got to do it the hard way," Krisler shouted. "All I've got are rifle grenades, Sam. Thirties won't stop the bastards . . ."

Damon had seized him by the arm. "Hang on here, Benjy. There's no place to go—"

"Do tell."

"I'll get you something. I will!" The General waved to Brand and Chase and they left the pit in a rush, jogging in and out of holes, crashing through the dense growth, the open spaces. Tracers passed over their heads; then they were over a rise and the jungle lightened toward the bay. Shells were falling in the shallow water inside the reef. Brand, hurrying after the General, felt an almost tearful relief at being out of sight of the tanks.

The beach was a maze of wreckage and confusion. There were no tanks ashore, or none that Brand could see. Two amphtracks lay out among the concrete obstacles, half submerged, LCVPs bobbed far out or drifted idly with the current; men were frantically passing ammunition cases and ration boxes from hand to hand. Off to their right, away from the ridge, men were still wading ashore, their rifles held high. Immersed to their thighs they seemed motionless, trapped in the oily water; then all at once they reached the shallows and broke into a nervous run, scampering up the beach toward the palms. Everywhere men were digging in, gesticulating, straining under loads—an incessant, haphazard parade of desperation and stealth under the shells, which flung up plumes of white water or black bile.

"MacRae," Damon was saying calmly. "Keep your eyes peeled for him . . ."

Lieutenant Chase said, "Right, General," and Brand nodded dumbly, threading his way through a swarm of shell craters, crouching or frantically working figures, smashed crates, twisted sheets of corrugated tin, logs, crushed water cans, abandoned packs and rifles and the frayed stumps of trees. How were they going to find anybody in this—let alone the Beachmaster? A corpsman was bent over a massive, torn body: the big knife moved once, twice, jerkily and came away running red. Brand turned away his eyes. Two planes swept in toward the cliff, their engines howling; their rockets sent cloudy, smoking fingers against the cliff face, which erupted in fountains of smoke and flame. Three wounded lay in a row, one man with an arm across his eyes. Beside him a bottle of plasma hung from a rifle butt, its tube gently swaying. The thin, burdensome shriek swept near and Brand threw himself into a hole, felt the concussion slam against his body. His head, his eyes and all his teeth ached in one vast throb of sensation. Another shell crashed savagely near, and fragments rained grossly against the cascao. Sendai was bad, the worst he could imagine, but this was terrible—there wasn't any end to it. That lousy *cliff*—!

He looked up to see Damon walking swiftly along the edge of the
water, and Chase hurrying to catch up with him. Angry with himself,
feeling shaky and harassed, he clambered to his feet and ran along the
hard sand. The General was talking to a worried-looking young lieutenant with a freckled face who was standing beside a jeep filled with
bedding rolls and cases of rations.

"—orders of the chief of staff," the boy was saying. "Colonel Bowsma.
He gave me—"

"I'm taking it," Damon answered. "Right now."

The lieutenant looked frightened. "No—you can't—"

"Oh, yes I can. You're on the wrong beach anyway. You should be on
Green One." The General motioned to Brand and Chase. "Come on,
boys, climb aboard."

"No, but I'm not to surrender this vehicle to anybody—"

"I'll give you a receipt, Doc," Damon shouted at him over the motor.
"Ask me tomorrow . . ."

They were creeping along through the wreckage, moving toward the
cliff, which was still raining shells on them in spite of the planes. The
young lieutenant was gazing after them, shouting something. Turning
back again, Brand spotted a figure he recognized, tapped Damon's shoulder and called, "Down there! MacRae . . ."

The General stopped the jeep with a lurch and swung out of it.
Major MacRae, the Beachmaster, was sitting propped up against an expeditionary can. He was stripped to the waist, streaming sweat, and
there were two bloody compresses on his chest and one on his upper
arm. He was wearing a bright blue baseball cap, and his great square
face was red and angry.

"Mac!" Damon called. "You seen Pulleyne?"

"No. He ashore? I thought he—"

"How about tanks?"

"No got, General."

"What's for artillery?"

"Nothing yet—at least not before I got hit . . . No, there were some
thirty-sevens, I think a couple of thirty-sevens down by the old pier,
before those Zeroes came over. That raid shook everything up . . ."

"All right." They went bucking and snorting along, now in the water,
now in behind the trees, past an aid station in a shattered pillbox, past
stretcher parties hurrying down with their burdens to a waiting amph-
track at the water's edge. The Old Man spun the wheel and they swung
around a wrecked Japanese landing barge, dipped into a hole and rocked
crazily up out of it. Behind them came a high, snarling hammer, swelling
unbearably, and twisting in the back seat Brand saw the plane coming
low, hanging fifty feet above them, the kicking pattern of bullets ripping their path down the beach. At the water's edge a soldier was standing, firing at it offhand, the spent shells spinning past his helmet like tiny
bright yellow toys—and a heart-beat after that the plane was past them,

rolling up and out over the ridge, the orange-red balls on its dun wings looking garish and absurd.

"Bastard," he muttered. His teeth were chattering, He crouched in the back of the vehicle among the bedding rolls and tentage. "I hope you burn . . ."

The jeep stopped so sharply he was flung into Chase. Damon was yelling, "Come on, come on," was already out and running, and he followed closely this time, in a spasm of relief. At the sea's edge, near a smashed LCVP, half-sunk, he saw the rubber wheel, the shiny, slender barrel. Thirty-seven. Lying on its side, the dirty brown water washing against the perforated plate of the shoulder guard.

"Come on, boys. Give me a hand . . ."

They crouched in the water, straining, rocked the gun upright. Damon worked the firing lever, daubed at the recoil cylinder with his big red pocket handkerchief. "Plenty of oil. Sight mount's okay. Breech block's okay. She'll serve."

Brand said, "Yeah, but Chief—"

"Don't worry, we're going to demount it." Reaching down he pulled the trail pin. "All right, come on. We're going to set her on the hood."

"On the hood of the *jeep*—?"

"That's the pitch. Come on."

Brand took the barrel, the other two the breech end; they lifted it clear of the mount, carried it laboriously over to the vehicle and manhandled it up on the hood, the folded-down windshield frame. The windshield itself shattered, and the glass slithered around on the metal. The barrel stuck out over the radiator like a wild snout.

Jesus H. Christ, Brand thought. Now I've seen everything. How in hell's he going to see to drive? Chase's expression was a study.

"Come on, come on," Damon was shouting over the roar of explosions and rifle fire. "Let's get *ammo*—"

They waded into the landing craft, whose deck plates were warped like barrel staves. A body was floating in the water, facedown, hands extended, rocking gently in the waves formed by their movement; close to the body the water was stained rust red. Brand stepped around it and picked up a box with a black stripe through the center that said SHOT, FIXED, AP, M51 WITH TRACER.

"Make sure it's AP," the General shouted at him, and he nodded. Chase had begun to throw some of the bedrolls out of the back of the jeep and Damon said, "No, forget it—there isn't time! Get in, get in! . . ."

He already had the vehicle in gear. Brand flung himself into the front seat and grabbed the breech of the gun. Pieces of the glass from the windshield kept sliding down onto the fenders. They were bucking their way back along the beach, Damon hanging far out in order to see around the gun shield.

"Hank!" the General roared. "Break out that ammo!"

Chase pulled out his fighting knife and began to pry at a corner of one of the crates. Brand remembered then and reached back and pulled the ax out of its bracket over the rear wheel.

A hand struck him on the shoulder. "No!" Damon was shouting at him. "Let *him* do that! Not you! Stand up and clear the track for me . . ."

He pulled himself to his feet, almost fell out of the jeep as it dropped forward into a gully and out of it again, bouncing crazily. *"Make way!"* he roared, waving his carbine back and forth, glaring at the maze of hurrying, laboring figures who ducked out of the way. Faces turned toward them in fear, in fury, in blank amazement: a master sergeant with a luxuriant black mustache pointed at them and roared with laughter.

"Will you dig the fucking tank destroyer—!"

Brand grinned; hanging onto the gun shield for dear life, waving his rifle and roaring, listening to the rending crash of wood as Chase smashed open the ammunition cases, he was taken all at once with a fit of mirth.

"—For Jesus sake," he hollered at the beach, the howling, astonished faces, the débris, the exploding shells. "For Jesus jumping *sake*—!"

"God damn right . . ." The General was grinning now, lying almost horizontally, driving with one hand, squinting ahead. "Hank," he called. "You got 'em open?"

"Check!"

"They all AP?"

"Right . . ."

"Hank, you ever fired one of these?"

"Christ, I never *saw* one before . . ."

"I did," Brand yelled. "At Harper! Thousand-inch range—"

"Good duty." Damon nodded. "You're first loader. Hank, you're second loader!"

"Check . . ."

To the right now, slewing on the shattered palm branches, back along the trail, the ammunition carriers and stretcher parties and walking wounded scattering in their path, yelling at them, cursing. The crackle and yammer of fire was a continuous, pulsing roar now. Off to the right again, and up the little hillock, through grass and lacy bushes like overgrown willows that whipped at their faces, stinging. Near them a machine gun team was firing furiously, huddled in a tight knot, their helmets almost touching each other. Someone was waving at them frantically from a hole twenty feet away. The jeep stopped with a jolt that threw him against the gun shield. For an instant Brand could see nothing ahead—then, in the harsh, tricky zebra-patterns of light and shadow under the trees, unbelievably near, a little forest of bushes and fronds stirred, swaying, and below it a caterpillar tread began its slithering, snakelike, rippling motion. All the hilarity went out of him. The tank looked huge and terrible, its deadly pinhead turret gleaming under the shrubs. Bullets sparkled on its shovel-like snout and danced away merrily, and its machine gun dipped down to the left, the bursts indistinguishable in the uproar. It was close, fearfully close, moving faster now. Standing there gripping the top of the gun shield Brand felt naked and utterly alone. *Tank.* But he could only stand there, conscious now of two others off to the left, mesmerized at their ponderous, lumbering malevolence. The lead tank had turned, was moving diagonally across their field of vision. A tiny orange pennant stood out stiffly from a slender, quivering mast. It was inside the CP where they'd been with Colonel Krisler. It was—

"Posts!" Damon sang out; he had come to his feet in a crouch, his hand on the elevating wheel, his eye to the scope. "Posts! AP, right front, zero range, commence firing . . ."

Zero range, Brand thought. Jesus, I guess so. But moving was better. He swung back on the operating handle with his right hand, and turning on his hips extended his left. Chase slapped the base of the shell into his palm. He slipped it deftly into the breech, pushing it home until the cartridge rim engaged the lips, withdrew his hand and swung the handle back into the latched position and called, "Up!" and reached back with his left for another shell.

The crash of the gun was deafening. He was pinned against the seat; the breech had slammed against his chest and arm. Jesus. Recoil. Unmounted gun. His arm hurt as if it were broken. He felt stunned, powerless.

"Come on!" the General shouted; he was bleeding over one eye. "Let's go, now . . ."

Brand struggled against the weight of the gun; they wrestled it forward onto the hood, and wedged the top carriage inside the windshield frame. He caught one swift, terrible image over the shield of an angular, mountainous hull, two rows of widely spaced rivets running up to a curious little binnacle lamp, and below it the rectangular towing ring flailing at the leading edge of the iron—then he had crouched and received another shell from Chase and slammed shut the breech, throwing his hands in front of his face. But this time the gun held its position. He heard Chase call, "*Got him!*"—a strangely thin, hilarious shout, and then he lost himself in the rhythm of loading, the shuttered glimpses over the shoulder guard of Damon's face perfectly impassive, his eyes slitted, looking into the sight, feeling now and then the gun move as the Old Man pressed his shoulder against the traversing bar.

"Chief!" Chase shouted. "He's turning! He's—"

The gun crashed. Brand had swung back for another round when there was a series of stunning shocks against the gun shield and a ripping crash of glass and metal. He cringed, reaching back—saw two black holes appear by terrible magic in Chase's fatigue blouse, another in his throat, and blood spurted in thick scarlet jets over his forearms. For a rapt eternity Chase stood there, his eyes fastened on Brand's with terrified accusation—then he sprawled into the tangle of shells and bedding, his face inverted now, mouth wide and gasping and filled with red froth.

"Chief!" Brand cried, "—Chief, he's hit! Chase . . . !"

"*Load the gun*," Damon answered. "Come on!"

Brand glanced at the General, who was peering intently through the scope, his big shoulder hunched against the traversing bar; let go the operating handle and groped behind him in a torment of admiration and despair thinking, Jesus God, it's like they say: the son of a bitch hasn't got any nerves at all. He snatched up a shell. The nose was slick with blood. Blood was everywhere now, soaking into the mattress pads and tentage, gliding over the brass casings. He dropped the shell, caught it up again in a tremor of haste and loaded it and locked the breech and cried, "Up!" in a falsetto croak, groped for another, and another, burying himself in the mesmeric fury of serving the gun, which crashed and crashed, and swallowed sound. *Get them, get the bastards*, he thought savagely—was mildly surprised to find he was speaking aloud. Cordite fumes stung his nose, and the acid-bright stench of raw gas. Gas tank. They'd hit the gas tank. Jesus, if she cooked off now—

He was swept by so many perils he felt nothing: he had moved beyond them, out of their orbit. Nothing could touch him, crouched here, snatching up cartridges, snapping the breech open smartly, lifting his hand away from the recoil. He was nothing, he was beyond everything: the gun was animate, he was the oiled and glistening machine, the servant serving. What the hell, he thought; go out this way as any other. But the thought did not penetrate beyond a certain point; it lay outside his rage, the desperate, sweating ritual he was performing.

The gun fired again. Damon cursed. There was a violent *clang!* against the gun shield, another—and then a searing rush of flame that boiled redly around him. On fire. All that raw gas. He jumped, caught his foot on something and fell in a heap, leaped to his feet again, saw the Old Man, inside the flames, reaching back struggling. Oh Jesus. Chase. He plunged back into the blast of heat, got his hands under the big man's arms and wrenched and tugged with all his might. His blouse, his sleeves were burning. Damon shouted something at him but he couldn't hear him. He gave one last terrible pull. Chase's body came loose and fell on top of him. He jerked free, rolling and writhing on a ragged mat of crushed bushes and leaves that scraped his face. Pain raced brightly along his arm. He unsnapped his belt, tore off his jacket and flung it away from him in a panic. Someone was hitting him. Damon. Beating at his legs—quick, smarting blows. Then the General was pulling him to his feet, shouting. He was on his feet, he was lurching through air like foul gray surf; they had fallen into a hole where a man with both hands clutched over his belly was staring at them numbly. He closed his eyes and opened them again. His right arm was charred and blackened and oozing like a great burst blister, and his neck burned. He was all right. He looked up, to see Damon peering at him. The Old Man's face was

black and oily, like a stoker's, and a thread of blood had run down
from his forehead, smearing the grease red.

"You all right, Joe?"

"Yeah." He nodded solemnly.

"Wanted to get away from those shells. Before they start to go
off."

Brand gazed back apathetically at the jeep, which was all aflame now;
the thirty-seven's barrel drooped ridiculously over the hood. My aching
ass, he thought; oh my aching ass. The Old Man would check the
frigging temperature gauge on the furnace they were shoveling him
into, in the dead center of hell. He looked back with slow amazement to
see Damon crouched at the edge of the hole with an M1 in his hands. He
crawled forward and raised his head.

There was a tank near them; one tread was gone and it kept shuttling
and beetling back and forth on the good one, its engines roaring. Another to the left was burning savagly, enveloped in flames, and two more
sat perfectly still, with smoke seeping out through the drivers' and
gunners' ports. Another one was crawling off into the jungle, its brush
camouflage quivering. Jesus, he thought—or said—or thought, staring.
They had done all that: he and the Old Man. And Chase. All that. While
he sat there stupidly watching, the hatch of the tank with the shattered
tread opened and a man hoisted himself out and hung there—a slender
figure with a brown sweatband around his forehead, looking wildly
down. Why doesn't he jump? Brand wondered; get the hell out of
there? In the next second he doubled over and his body hung down
from the tuna-can turret, his blood flowing in a smooth, silken skein
over the iron. A man leaped up on the side of the broken tread, between
the bogie wheels, up on the fender. A man with a bright yellow scarf
around his neck. Brand saw his hand go to his mouth. The handle spun
off into the air, glinting. Krisler stuffed the grenade into the aperture
and slammed the hatch down on the man's body and jumped to the
ground. There was a muffled thump, like a firecracker in a lard can.
From inside a hand pushed up the hatch a foot or so, and then slid
slowly back out of sight. The moving tank had vanished.

Holding his arm Brand gazed around him. Shells were still coming
down on the near edge of the strip and back toward the beaches. A
medic was kneeling out in the open, working on Chase. Damon was
talking to a machine gun sergeant. The jeep was still blazing merrily,
and so was the easternmost of the tanks. It was as though he had been
asleep—or no, not so much asleep as under a spell, and had only just
come out of it. His head ached fiercely, his ears were still ringing, his
arm hurt so he could hardly flex it. But what he needed most was a
drink of water. He reached back for one of his canteens, remembered
he'd got rid of his belt, looked toward the jeep; but the thought of
pulling himself erect and going over there was more than he could face.
His trousers were still smoking just above the knee and he slapped idly

at the scorched fabric and tried to moisten his cracked lips with his
tongue.

"Here you go." Damon was holding out a canteen. He nodded his
thanks, tilted the fat metal canister and felt the cool liquid sluice his
throat and mouth and slip in slow, even, pulsing bands to his stomach.
Navy water: they wouldn't be getting any more of that for a long time.
He handed the canteen back to the General, who took another few
swallows and said: "Pretty rough."

"You're telling me." He had never in all his life been so utterly
depleted. He felt as though all his fire and resolve had been bled out of
him, like that Japanese tanker whose blood was still sliding richly down
the side of the armored hull, obscuring the serial numbers.

"Jesus, Chief," he said numbly, "I don't want to go through another
day like this one."

"Neither do I, Joe," the Old Man answered; and Brand saw with
surprise that the General's hands were shaking so he could hardly screw
the top on the canteen.

Captain Bowcher signaled once—his left hand, extended, fanning the
air in little patting motions; and one of the soldiers crouched on the
ridge above the cliff face moved a few paces. Sergeant Jackson, his BAR
resting on the stone barrier, said something to Bowcher, but his voice
was pitched so low Pritchard couldn't hear him. He wiped his face with
his hand. The cliff swept around in a nice curve, so that the effect was
that of an outdoor theater, with the stage raised in a series of small
ridges. The stone was gray-white, blinding in the sun's glare, and the air
was close with dust. Here and there shrubs like stunted, starved thorn
trees struggled upward from the rock. The Salt Mines, they all called it.
Nearly everyone was crouched behind the ridges and knobs of stone
and staring intently up at the cliff, whose face was dotted with holes like
misshapen dark mouths. For a time the only sound was the rumble of the
fifty-five-gallon oil drums being rolled along the bed of the weapons
carrier in the center of the stage.

"Animals," a big man named Lubbock said. "All they are, animals.
Dig holes in the ground and hide in them all the time. Jesus, they must
love to swing a pickax."

"It's not very resistant," Bryce answered in his clear, precise voice.
"Calciferous limestone. You can score it with your thumbnail, you
know."

"Do tell, Bryce."

Pritchard squinted out into the glare of worn white rock laced with
crevices. Nobody had stirred except the engineer detail, which was now
manhandling the drums from the little truck's tailgate and easing them
carefully along over the stone.

"It's very porous," Bryce went on; sweat had gathered in a small greasy pendant at the point of his chin, which made his face look still thinner and more scholarly. "The whole area is probably honeycombed with elaborate vaults and passages."

Corrazzo, kneeling on the other side of Lubbock, said: "You wouldn't snow me now, would you, Bryce?"

"Certainly not. There are whole cultures who still live as troglodytes."

"As *what?*"

"Cave dwellers. Our ancestors all used to live in that way."

"Keep your eyes on the God damn caves," Sergeant Jackson told them.

Corrazzo regarded Bryce with tolerant amusement. "Well, I can tell you right now *my* ancestors didn't live in no caves."

"Sure they did. Unless they were lake dwellers. But that's much less likely."

Randall, a correspondent for the Associated Press, laughed pleasantly. "You're a kind of GI intellectual, aren't you, son?" He had a handsome chubby face and rimless glasses, and he craned his head past Pritchard's to watch Bryce a moment, his lips moving. "How'd you come by all that high-powered education?"

Bryce glanced at him once, coldly, then up at the cliff. "Yes, I made it all the way through grammar school," he replied dryly. "Does that amaze you?"

Lubbock snorted and wiped his cheeks with his sleeve. "That's telling him, Bryce. Hell, Bryce got so God damn much education if they knew about it back in D. C. he'd put Marshall out of a job . . ."

"I said let's knock off the grab-ass and watch the caves," Jackson said curtly, and they fell silent.

Pritchard turned and looked at Damon, but the General, standing behind a curious narrow alcove in the stone, was watching the working party beside the weapons carrier and talking to Lieutenant Hanida, asking him something. Hanida, a Nisei whose flat, bony face looked more Mexican than oriental, shrugged and squinted up at the caves. Far off beyond the ridge, near Dakmata Village, there came the *bump-ump-ump* of artillery, and somewhere out of sight a plane droned wearily. Sixteen men were killed here this morning, Pritchard thought, staring up at the cliffs, the ragged black maws of holes, the twisted, stunted bushes. My predecessor was killed on D-Day. He had never been a worrier. He'd done well enough on the beach the first two days; he'd straightened out some of the mess on Red Two after Major MacRae had been evacuated, and salvaged a lot of gear. To his surprise the interminable shelling from the ridge hadn't shaken him the way it had so many of the others; a dreamy, almost cheerful fatalism had taken hold of him: there was the job to do, supplies to be got ashore, an example to set before the men. But that had had nothing to do with this parched, silent place where enemy eyes—you could feel them on you—watched from some of those hundred caves. He wondered how many of them were directly below where they knelt—faces turned up toward the crevices, the matted fibers of roots, listening . . .

Captain Fulkes, in command of the engineer detail, a short block of a man with pure white hair, had walked up to where Damon was standing. "We're all set."

"All right." The General turned to Hanida. "Let's try it once more, Dan."

Lieutenant Hanida raised the bull horn and blew into it; there was a sharp, dry roar. He began to read from a mimeographed sheet of paper. The words, so alien to Pritchard they were like sounds from some extraplanetary race, echoed and reechoed from the walls.

"What's he saying?" a kid with an Arkansas accent asked.

"Who won the fifth race at Aqueduct," Corrazzo answered sharply. "How the hell should I know what he's saying? Ask Bryce—*he's* got all the five-alarm education . . ."

The giant voice crashed on and on, the sounds tumbling over one another in the rock-borne echoes. Pritchard kept one eye on the General. He longed with all his heart and soul for a drink from his canteen but he didn't want Damon to see him; besides, God knew when they'd get back to the CP and that great, white, blessed, obscene udder of a Lister bag. Sweat was streaming down his back and chest, stinging in his eyes. Wait and rush, wait and rush. Life in the Army. He glanced crossly at Damon, wondering what he was thinking, what he was going to do. The General's face was drawn, the eyes and lips puffy with heat and fatigue; the cut around his eye from the tank battle had got infected, and Stofer the medic had cleaned it out and put a compress over it, and now the compress was twisted and dirty. Pritchard had been surprised when the General had asked for him as aide—surprised and immensely pleased. He'd imagined himself arriving at staff meetings, contacting Corps, fending off importunate colonels, furnishing a deferential, sympathetic audience to the ADC in the small hours of the night; he hadn't pictured a time like this, here in the Salt Mines, waiting in a glaring eternity of heat and uncertainty—

Lieutenant Hanida had finished. Very slowly he set the bull horn in the jeep and began to fold the mimeographed sheet of paper into smaller and smaller pieces. Nothing stirred. The engineers crouched in the shade under the tailgate of the weapons carrier stared at him apathetically.

"I don't see why they shouldn't come out and surrender," Bryce said in his clear, cultured voice.

Sergeant Jackson, his eyes still riveted on the cliff, said: "Would you?"

"But after all, they must realize they—"

The shots were brutal in the white stillness. *Whack-ack!*—like the snapping of a colossal whip, and one of the engineers leaped up in a wild theatrical gesture, arms flung wide, and fell like a dropped sack. At almost the same instant there was the ripping blast from Jackson's BAR and bits of stone chipped away around one of the holes; then a chorus of gunfire. Pritchard realized he was gripping the rock in front of him with all his strength. He relaxed his hand and turned, encountered the somber, bronze face of Brand, the General's orderly. He grinned and rocked his head; Brand did not smile back, but he did wink—the slow, droll dropping of one eyelid. Pritchard was a little in awe of Brand. The Indian had been on that 37-millimeter gun with the General on the first day; his forearm had been badly burned and was still wrapped in gauze. Smoke was trailing blue from the barrel of his carbine. Pritchard wished he'd been there, with the gun, that day. But if he had been, he'd probably be dead. Hank Chase was dead . . .

"All right, cease firing!" Captain Bowcher shouted, and the shooting stopped. "You haven't got anything to shoot at, save it . . ." But his voice was not peremptory; there was a comfort simply in firing your weapon at such a time. To Jackson he said: "Think you got him?"

"No. But that's where the son of a bitch was. That hole just to the right of that off-side W, there . . ."

"Was is right."

"Hell, the Old Man's wasting his time. What's he waiting for—an engraved invite?"

There was a violent commotion behind the weapons carrier now. Two aid men had run over and knelt beside the wounded man.

"Captain," Randall said to Bowcher, "I can't for the life of me see why you don't use grenades on them. You've got plenty of grenades, haven't you?"

"Yes, we've got grenades."

"Then why don't you use them?"

Bowcher's gray eyes moved around to the correspondent. "Because in the first place most of them are too high to reach. And in the second place the tunnels run uphill, and when you lob a grenade in, it just rolls right on out again and blows your balls off. That's why."

"All right, Tom," Damon called to Fulkes in a steady, flat voice. "Go ahead."

"Right." Fulkes stood up and began giving commands. The working party bent over the drums, removing the plugs, and gas splashed out gurgling, shining like molten silver in the hot, flat light, running down into the fissures at half a dozen places. The men worked with a stealthy haste, in near-silence, like children engaged in some malicious prank, tossing the empties back in the truck bed. The air was raw with gas.

"All right, move out," Fulkes cried. The detail scrambled into the vehicle, flinging themselves on the tailgate, as it careened and bumped down the path toward the draw. The silence grew. Fulkes lifted a grenade from his belt, pulled the pin, looked around sharply, called, "Fire-in-a-hole!" and let the arm fly off and tossed it. It hung in the air briefly—a fat little green oval—and then fell rolling. There was an ex-

plosion and the center of the Salt Mine leaped in tearing orange clouds
of flame, followed by a seething low roar as it ignited below ground.
The waiting men leaned forward, their faces brightened in the torment
of flames, their eyes wide. And then, far below them, deep in the rock,
as if coming from another, darker world, rose sounds like girls singing,
animals squealing, dogs howling in boundless grief and pain. Pritchard
stared at the blackened stone, where smoke now rose in thin swirling
columns. Screams. Those were men screaming down there. Hundreds of
them, in a muted chorus. He found he was looking at the others near
him; he couldn't help it. Young Bryce was white and pale, his lips
trembling; Jackson's eyes were slitted but his knuckles were white on
the grips of the BAR. The screams went on, rising on one another, in
thirds, in fifths, in tremulous, fearful octaves—and now they no longer
sounded like human beings, not even like animals, but some outlandish
acoustical device turned up past all tolerance. Bowcher had his head
lowered, Randall was swallowing, his mouth slack; Damon was looking
at the cliff face, his face implacable and hard. Only Brand met Pritchard's eyes—a fierce, passionate gaze that seemed to say, *Yes, if it has to
be, so be it: I know and you do not.*

Pritchard shut his eyes. We are burning them. We are kneeling here
burning to death a hundred, a thousand, God alone knows or ever will
know how many human beings. One summer afternoon long ago he had
lain in his cot in the little tent he'd pitched in the field behind the house
and read a book called *At The Earth's Core*, a tale of swamps and eerie
lights and molten lava pits where hobgoblin automatons prowled and
butchered in the most fiendish ways . . . But that was fantasy. *This* was
the earth's core and they were crouched at the edge of it, unable to meet
one another's eyes. Bryce was sick suddenly, bent forward on one knee,
gripping his rifle, retching a dark yellow bile that hung in thick chains
from his lips and chin. Pritchard felt his own gorge rise, and a hard
pressure against his forehead. For a wild, fleeting instant he had the
certainty that he could summon up some word, utter some blessed
incantation and the barrels would be back in the weapons carrier, the
engineers sprawled casually in the shade under the tailgate, Bryce
would be explaining to them all, in his crisp Ivy League voice, the
nature and properties of calciferous limestone—

There was a shout, a child's cry, palpable and near. His head snapped
around, he saw a man running out of one of the easternmost caves in the
long, curving gallery, moving in faltering, lurching strides. His blouse
was on fire, and his hair—he floated, his back arched, shaking his head
back and forth as if to throw off this blazing burden; but his haste only
fanned the flames more briskly. There was a short, crashing fusillade and
the Japanese fell as if thrown and slid forward down the rock face and
lay quivering, tiny flames still burning crisply at the back of his skull
and his uniform.

The screams were fainter now, had fallen away to a low moaning,

scarcely audible; the very air around them seemed calefactive, teeming
with wild, mephitic odors. I don't want to be here, Pritchard thought;
there is no reason why I had to be here. He started to get to his feet.
There was a deep boom, and the ground beneath them shook like a
heavy branch in a gust of wind; then another, then a whole succession
of detonations. Fulkes called something to the General, who was nodding silently. An ammunition dump, that was what it was: the flames
had reached explosives and the great caves, their generators blasted to
fragments, were pitch-dark now and airless, glowing fitfully in the
rocket showers of bullets and mortar shells and grenades. But now there
was no living soul to fear them.

Then the explosions too died away, and the stillness was like a sudden
rain. They got to their feet slowly and looked at one another, survivors
of some bizarre disaster. Fulkes was bent over, hands on his knees,
peering down into one of the crevices, from which smoke was eddying
in faint black spirals. It was over. All over, here. Bryce was wiping his
mouth with a greasy black sleeve. One hundred, five hundred, a thousand men had died beneath their feet while they watched and listened.
At the earth's core . . .

Damon had called to him and Brand, and he hurried over, following
the General along the path that led down to the airfield. There was
something he wanted to say, something significant and very pressing;
but he could not for the life of him think what it was. Before he could
speak, the General had turned to him.

"Harry, contact Colonel Wilcher at the airstrip and tell him the Salt
Mine is secured. Then notify Regimental Headquarters."

"Yes sir," he answered.

"General . . ." It was the correspondent Randall, his eyes narrowed
behind his glasses, his mouth slack with intense distaste. "General
Damon . . ."

The ADC stopped. "What is it?"

"What was . . ." Randall seemed to be out of breath. "Was that—that
hideous business back there—was that necessary?"

"I thought so."

"You did," Randall said in a loud voice. "Well, let me tell you I for
one didn't find it very edifying . . ."

Damon turned and faced him heavily. "Randall, the men in this regiment have been fired on from this CP for days. We have taken over two
hundred casualties here in the past twenty-four hours. I have notified
General Toyada of my intentions, informing him that his campaign is
lost beyond salvage, and offering him every opportunity to surrender by
leaflet, radio and public address system, in his own language. We cannot
get at them, they will not surrender, they will not come out and engage
us in open warfare. We cannot use the airstrip until their base here is
destroyed. For reasons you cannot know I have been ordered to render
the strip operational by six hundred tomorrow. What do you suggest?"

Randall waved his hand distractedly. "But that was just—that was just butchery, wanton slaughter . . ."

"Was it. Well, now—what was it on D-Day when we were lying there under the ridge and *they* had hold of the handle?"

In an angry voice Randall cried: "Well, there must be some way— some better way than *this!*"

The General's eyes rested on the correspondent with bleak contempt. "Well: when you find it you come and let me know and I'll be more than happy to use it. Until then you leave me to my wanton butcheries and I'll leave you to yours."

He wheeled away, his face black with anger, and Pritchard had to hurry to catch up with him. Behind them two shots rang out as Captain Bowcher continued his duel with the uppermost caves.

(6)

Damon put down the pencil and rubbed his eyes. The rain kept thundering on the tent roof like drumfire, cutting off all other sound. No let up. Rainy season on Lolobiti. An island like a deflated, twisted football a hundred and forty miles beyond the interminable New Guinea coast, first step toward Halmahera and the Philippines. But the G-2 estimates had been wildly wrong again, the Japanese had fought stubbornly and resourcefully. Swanny's people had run into trouble and bogged down, the timetable had gone all to pieces and old Thiemann, under pressure from MacArthur, had sent the Salamanders up from rest camp on Wokai. For a week they'd made good headway along the coast. Then the rains had started, and that was that. They were already behind in supply. Tetlow was screaming that his guns were down to four hundred rounds. In his mind's eye Damon could see the trails, already soaked, disintegrating into quagmires, then sluggish streams over which burdened men struggled ankle-deep, knee-deep in gumbo.

He stared at the olive drab pigeonholes of the field desk in front of him—Westy's old field desk, then Duke Pulleyne's, now his by right of succession when Duke had been wounded by mortar fire on the next to last day of the Wokai operation. Interchangeable parts: he, Westy and Pulleyne were all interchangeable parts. If he were hit, he would recommend Ben, who was already on the list for BG, as Divisional Commander. They would come and they would go, each of them, but the Division—that great bristling Salamander, the corpus and weapon of their individual hopes and wills—would go on.

It would go on, that is, if it were victorious, if it accomplished its mission with dispatch and did not incur the wrath of the emperor . . .

He sighed, pumped up the Coleman lantern and went over to the situation map, stared at the knotty configuration of coastline and the strangely artificial bars outlining the amphibious envelopment just beyond Point Komfane, running his finger over the area although he knew every distance, every elevation, every troop disposition by heart. He and Dickinson had spent four days on the operation, laboring with slow care. It was a perfect situation: the beach was good, the coast was flat, the main Japanese supply trail paralleled the beach. Jimmy Hoyt's battalion was to make the amphibious assault, and when the Japanese diverted forces to contain it Ben's regiment was to pass through the 484th—now Frenchy Beaupré's—break through the Japanese MLR and drive northeast toward the coast road and make contact with Hoyt. They had checked and rechecked everything half a hundred times, argued over the timing, deliberately tried to pick flaws in the scheme; everybody had confidence that it would go through.

And yet, peering at the map in the flat, quaking light under the rain's thunder he was brushed by a stealthy tremor of disquietude. Maps were cruel. There was no substitute for going up front, for incessant reconnaissance. Staring at the pictures created by grease pencil on acetate overlays made for pessimism. That was part of what had sickened Westy, paralyzed him and pulled him all to pieces. Duke on the contrary had gone to the other extreme—had raced off to the front so often and impulsively his own subordinate commanders hadn't been able to locate him half the time; his staff work had suffered, he'd lost his grip on the tactical situation, trapped in the web of minutiae and confusion in which battle abounded.

The only trouble was the higher you got, the less you were able to get up front. You were drawn inexorably away from what was essential —until finally, like MacArthur, you sat in a lofty, immaculate tower three thousand miles from the war and gave yourself up to dreams and schemes, the symbols without the realities that bore them; until at last perhaps you even mistook symbol for flesh and blood . . .

He drifted back from the map and sat down at the desk again, holding in his mind the geographical configurations, the order of battle. It had to succeed: it had to. Preparation is the first essential for success, old Vinegar Joe had drummed into their heads back at Benning; therefore prepare, and prepare, and prepare again. But you couldn't prepare for everything. There was the recon report that didn't come in because the rubber raft carrying those six men had become wrecked on a coral head; the battalion of Imperial Marines some harassed Japanese commander had bivouacked by pure chance right behind the assault area; the four tanks G-2 knew nothing whatever about and that someone had accidentally sent forward from the airstrip through the kunai grass . . . What was out there, in that empty triangular area between the sea and the trail and the jungle? Was General Watanabe sitting in his funny little round circus tent of mustard and ocher, studying *his* map—was he deciding at this malignant midnight hour to move a detachment over to the area north of Point Komfane, just on the chance that the Yanks—? Were they digging in with the patient, dogged industriousness of their race, stringing wire and emplacing guns? Would they be sitting over their sights and mortar tubes, watching placidly for the ghostly white wakes of landing craft?

Too much imagination was the death of the commander. God knew you had to have *some*—unless you wanted to be a fatuous dunce like Packy Vinzent, or a cold-blooded, methodical machine like Slingerland. You had to pounce on possibilities, sustain flexibility, dare the unforeseen, conceive of fresh and unorthodox plans, improvise when those plans went awry, bounce back from dismay with confidence. But too much imagination—and even a little too much was worse than much too little—and you became prey to a thousand and one fears that ate at your will like acid. Worst of all. There they were, out there, in their thousands: sleeping fitfully or staring into the teeming dark, or playing cards or writing home, laughing or cursing or held in stony, fearful silence—and what happened to them tomorrow, whether they ate or went hungry, fought or rested, lived or died, was up to you . . .

He sighed again and picked up the clipboard. Ray Feltner had come in with a message he'd picked up from coast watchers of a Japanese convoy in the Molucca Sea, approximately thirty miles off Lembeh Point. Where were they headed? Air had nothing on it, nothing at all. Callison had a report of 120 enemy planes on Tajeng Airfield on Salawati, but Haley said he couldn't do anything about it because it was a purely jurisdictional problem with the Aussies. Jesus. Spheres of Command. How comforting to know that if the Japs took it into their heads to come over some evening early and plaster the daylights out of you, it was all because it was purely jurisdictional.

The whole business with air was extremely touchy. Prince Hal had come in yesterday snarling with rage, saying he'd made up his mind to establish a bomb support line two thousand yards in advance of all US ground forces, no missions whatever would be accepted inside of that line—and that was final. What this meant of course was no tactical air support at all. After a while Hal had calmed down a little and the story came out: he and Frenchy Beaupré had got in one unholy row over that last short drop at Suanggi and Frenchy had sent him by special courier a Japanese decoration they'd found on some dead officer. This was dangerous: he'd have to sit on Frenchy and go to work on the fly-boy as soon as possible, stressing how much air support had meant at Wokai, and so on and so forth.

Oom Paul Thiemann was flying in tomorrow from Wokai to hear all about the amphibious envelopment. He was a big, balding St. Louis German with an excellent tactical sense and he would see it was the way to break it open; but his chief of staff was a pompous little snipe who would poke holes in the plan just for the fun of inserting his own. The other problem was that Thiemann wanted to take Dutch Wilhelm back to Wokai with him as Corps Operations Officer. It was a good thing for Dutch; it would get him out of the line and give him a chance to get over his jaundice and jungle ulcers, and it would mean a star for him. He couldn't stand in his way, if Dutch wanted to go; but then who would he give the 468th to? He couldn't give it to Dickinson: Dick was a staff man and always would be. Winslow might work—he'd had a battalion at Wokai—and he was good with troops; but he was impetuous and breezy and Dutch was imperturbable and methodical. There would inevitably be friction—Dutch had run the regiment for so long, and his officers all thought the way he did and distrusted outsiders. And if he did give it to Winslow, what would he do for a G-3? Spellar was out of the question: he'd been under a lot of strain, and he was getting tired and jumpy; if a couple weeks' leave in Australia didn't put him back in shape he'd have to send him home.

The Division hospital had been hit by a solo Betty early that morning and Nate Weintraub wanted it to be either moved or dug in. They'd had a stormy session, everyone was getting ragged. He himself suspected it was an isolated instance—according to one report the bomber had been jettisoning its load under attack from two P-47s from Wokai—but you couldn't know. Was it by any weird chance connected with the Salawati group? or even that damned convoy? Major Calder and four nurses had been severely wounded and three patients killed and twelve hurt. Old MacChesney had been wild, her hair loose under her cap and a foot-long bomb splinter clutched in one shaking hand. "What *I* want to know, General Damon, is what you intend to do about this, and right now! It is *impossible* to function efficiently under these conditions . . ." Gazing at her angry, distraught face he had been filled with relief that Joyce was back at the base hospital at Désespoir—then had felt guilty at harboring the thought . . . The trouble was that if you dug the hospital in it would be under water. Maybe if they went down two feet, and then sandbagged with soil, that would raise the walls to four feet, which ought to protect them from anything but a direct hit, which you couldn't protect anything from anyway. He'd get the headquarters working parties on that first thing in the morning, all they could spare.

The rain let up again, to a soft murmur, and again he could hear the distant, ponderous thump of artillery. He stretched, and rubbed his eyes with his knuckles. The essence of leadership was an unerring ability to winnow the essential from the trivial or extraneous. Fine. But it wasn't that simple. In the terrible, impromptu colloquy that was war the essential could melt away, the trivial could translate itself into the desperately crucial with a rush. If Thiemann should disapprove the amphib

operation; if the hospital should be hit by a whole flight of Bettys; if
Prince Hal should repair to his tent and sulk for several days; if that
Japanese convoy should turn about in the night and race east-northeast
for Cape Sopi or slip through Morotai Strait and be standing off Cape
Gamtjaka tomorrow noon—what then?

Christ, he was tired. Two kids in Swede Lund's battalion had got
killed souvenir hunting in a cave on the Ridge. He'd have to get out a
good stern general order on that, threaten any violators with loss of pay
or some such. It wouldn't stop the incorrigible ones like Jackson (who
was said to possess three samurai swords, a hara-kiri knife, several battle
flags and a Belt of a Thousand Stitches, not to mention innumerable
pistols, bayonets and officers' caps his squad kept to barter for beer with
the amphibious engineers—or, if an opportunity presented itself, for
liquor with the pilots back at Wokai); but it might check some of the
feckless and unwary. This cave crawling had to stop, and pronto.

And he had to write that letter about young Phelps. Jimmy Hoyt had
already written the boy's parents, but he wanted to add a note. A thin,
willowy, rather flat-chested boy with horn-rimmed spectacles and a
diffident, mystified air: the last man he'd have believed could have led a
platoon well, let alone anything beyond that. Looking at him you
thought inexorably of Sunday afternoon concerts, or garden parties
where proud and gracious aunts in large hats sipped tea and turned
indulgently toward a pale, gangling boy in pinafore and knickers—and
your heart sank. Diedrich had told Hoyt that Phelps was capable, a good
leader, but that didn't necessarily mean anything: platoon sergeants
often had their own reasons for saying things like that—with a pliant,
unassertive officer a sergeant could run a platoon his own way. There
had been nothing whatever to indicate that Cecil B. Phelps, 2nd Lt. AUS,
at the critical moment of the fighting for Tobaloor Village, would order
covering fire and climb up on the roof of the commissioner's residence,
tear off a quantity of tiles and throw grenades down on the defending
Japanese garrison until he was wounded through the chest and shoulder;
that he would then rally his platoon and go forward, flushing the enemy
out of two pillboxes until killed by intense fire from a supporting
bunker. Like Tim, he thought quietly; another Timmy Brewster. Cecil
B. Phelps was one of the principal reasons they had taken Tobaloor; he
was one of the principal reasons Tojo wasn't going to get away with his
Greater East-Asia Co-Prosperity Sphere. Damon had recommended the
boy for a Congressional Medal; but the letter was more important.
Rolling the pencil between his hands he remembered old Jumbo Kintzelman on the range back at Early. "The good Lord made some men big
and He made some men small. And then He gave us gunpowder as the
big equalizer. Now don't any of you rookies forget that, hear?"

Well, it was an equalizer, all right . . .

There was the thick, sucking sound of field shoes slopping through the mud outside, and a low exchange of voices; and Damon felt a quick, anticipatory lightness at his heart, a stealthy guilt. God, I'd welcome a sick crocodile tonight, he thought. Just anybody at all.

There was a fumbling at the blackout curtain, and a voice said tentatively: "General?"

"Come in."

The inner flap was raised and dropped, and a figure slid inside and stood there. Ben, ponchoed, his helmet shoved forward over his eyes, streaming water from every fold.

"Benjy." He felt hugely, inordinately pleased. "Come on in and hunker down by the fire. How's everything?"

"Just bloody puddle-wonderful." The Colonel pulled off the poncho and dropped it with a wet *thwack* on the earth floor. He was wearing a .45 in a shoulder holster, and an indescribably dirty gas mask container was hanging on his left hip. "What the hell are you doing up at this hour?"

"Communing with myself."

"Dizzy bastard." Ben flopped into a chair. "Boy, I'm telling you I ever lash down a deal like you've got I'm going to flake out like old Shafter down at Siboney in '98. Sunk deep in a hammock with a mint julep in one hand and a palm-leaf fan in the other. And a couple of dusky maidens to tend to my every want."

"Sounds pretty fine." Damon watched the Regimental Commander a moment. *He's got something on his mind or he wouldn't have stopped by at this time of night,* he thought. All at once he felt vaguely depressed. "Only trouble is," he said aloud, "you're in the wrong war for that kind of fun and games, dad."

"Isn't it the truth? I ought to have been with Marlborough, or Charles XII of Sweden. The Boy King. Living off the fat of the land, with a great big long baggage train of booze and women and gold coins." His lean, bony face cracked in a ferocious grin. "Maybe I was. Georgie Patton says he was a legionary with Caesar and a Knight Hospitaller and one of Napoleon's marshals and God knows what else. Believes it implicitly."

"Yes, I remember."

"Know something curious about these preincarnations of Georgie's? He's always an officer. He's never some poor son of a bitch carrying a spear or sweating his left ventricle off at the wheel of a twenty-pounder cannon."

"Blood will tell."

"Sort of nice when you can pick your slots, isn't it? Jesus, can you see him now—tearing around the Sicilian countryside, all swaddled up in history? Syracuse, and Robert Guiscard, and Hannibal? *Soldiers! Forty centuries look down upon you* . . . Frenchy says Mac wrote him from Licata every day's a witches' Sabbath: Georgie's got a whole caravan of limousines and they go wheeling around, bells ringing, sirens wailing, lights flashing . . . Can you imagine when he gets to *Rome?* All that *gla-wahr* . . ." He glowered at the tent wall. "I know he's a tanker and a frigging tactical genius and all that—only now and then I just wish they'd shipped him out here among the snakes and fuzzy-wuzzies: he'd have gone right out of his medieval Miniver Cheevy mind."

He pulled off his helmet and set it beside his chair. He had picked up an undiagnosed tropical rash all over his scalp, and Weintraub had decided to treat it like impetigo, shaving off his hair and smearing his head with a deep blue dye; he looked weird and irascible, and ten years older than he had when they'd lifted up over San Francisco Bay that smoky morning twenty-two months ago. He's angry, Damon thought, he's really upset about something. It isn't like him to beat around the bush this way.

"What's on your mind, Ben?" he said. "Anything you want to look at again, go over?"

The Colonel's eyes shot up to his, shot away. "What? No. We're ready. There isn't all the room in the world down there for staging, but we've got it worked out. Gene was screaming about how we were all going to get knee-mortared to death but I got him simmered down. That lad has a positive obsession about knee mortars. Do you suppose there's anything Freudian there? I told Dutch we ought to come up with a penile rocket—you know, you fire from the hip, so to speak."

"How's he look?"

"Who?"

"Dutch."

"Well. Okay." That reticence again. "I don't know. He's pretty tired, I guess. Is it true Oom Paul wants him back at Corps?"

"Yes."

"You going to let him go?"

"Sure. I don't want to stand in his way. He'll get a star out of it."

"We're going to miss him."

"You're telling me."

"I guess he could use the rest. I guess we all could." Ben glanced warily at the Division Commander. "They're all over your ass, aren't they, Sam? Dauntless Doug wants us to be in Manila Bay by tomorrow night, I suppose."

Damon leaned forward, hands on his knees. "Ben, you can say it. This attack order: aren't you satisfied with it? Don't you feel it can go?"

"Yes, sir. I do." Then he turned facetious again. "Pierce and destroy, envelop one wing, cut the enemy's lines of communication. The grand tactics of the Corsican, all rolled into one. I'd have hollered if I didn't."

"How do the boys feel?"

"They're wet and they're weary. But they're up for it. I was talking to them earlier. They know they can break it open. We've got the momentum this time." He started to scrub his scalp with his knuckles, remembered just in time and dropped his hand. "If only Dutch's people

make a good push over on the left, tie down as many of the bastards as
they can . . ."

"They will. I'll have Winnie over there goosing them." He looked at
the map; the sense of disquietude, of untraceable anxiety licked at him
like the passage of a snake's scales. What was wrong? What the hell was
wrong with the plan? Ben's homely, blue-smeared head was a comfort;
he felt a warm little hum of affection for this cantankerous, irrepressible
man he'd known so long, endured so much with, who was dearer to him
than any man living—and then the affection too mingled with the fear,
became submerged by it.

"You'll—be careful now," he said suddenly. "With this one. Won't
you, Ben?" The Wolverine looked at bit startled and he dropped his
gaze and clapped his hands together. "I mean, don't try to win it all by
yourself . . ." I'm getting to sound like Westy, he thought hollowly. All
full of forebodings and solicitude.

There was a pause while the rain picked up again, thundering. Ben
fiddled with his belt buckle, picking at the mud caked around the brass.
"Listen to it rain, will you. There isn't this much water in the whole
world . . ." Abruptly he reached into the gas-mask container, rummaged
around among socks and K rations and tropical chocolate bars and bore
patches and drew out a bottle of Ballantine's. "How's about a drink,
Chief? It's on me."

Damon stared at him. This was as unlike Ben as he'd ever seen him.
Does he think I'm coming apart? he wondered with a start of panic—
thrust away the thought. "Where'd you get that?" he said, for the sake
of saying something.

"Been toting it around. One of Hallie's employers in the Ministry or
whatever it is. Going-away present. See? Seal's never been broken."

"God stone the crows," Damon said; but Ben did not smile. "Just
what are we celebrating?"

"Nothing. Everything. Georgie Patton's reincarnation as Hasdrubal
the Hairy." He pulled a tin cup out of the gas-mask container. "Come
on, Chief. Don't be a dingo."

He didn't know what to say. He reached up and took his own canteen
cup off the top of the desk and extended it. Ben poured freely, the
liquor a bright orange against the metal. "Hey, that's plenty," he protested. He lowered the cup and said in a kind of bantering defiance:
"You think I need it?"

Ben looked back at him steadily. "Everybody out here needs it . . .
You're tired, Sam," he said after a moment. "You're keyed up all the
time—you're wound up too tight. You need to relax."

"Yeah but look, Ben, I got a thousand—"

"Don't be such a plaster saint!" Krisler burst out sharply—then gave a
slow, deferential grin. "I'm telling you, I won't offer it twice."

Damon shrugged and grinned back. "It's your booze."

"You're a bricking-A. Here's to 'em."

The aluminum lips clicked dully. "To the Salamanders."

"To the Scrofulous Saurians."

It went down like dense smoke, very dry and bright; Damon shivered, then felt the slow warmth in his guts. All right: he was too keyed up. Maybe. Probably. Who in Christ's name wouldn't be? What alternative was there—except putting on your hat and climbing aboard the next B-25 back to Wokai? Well, at least it wasn't the operation Ben was concerned about; and it wasn't Hallie. What the hell. He sipped at the Scotch, glancing now and then at the situation map and listening indifferently to Ben, who was running on about a kid in Bowcher's company named Muldoon.

". . . they're learning. But Jesus, it can give you the jumps every now and then. He was guarding the CP just before dark down at the Taro Patch and all of a sudden this dogface comes out of the boondocks in spanking new fatigues singing 'Don't Get Around Much Any More.' Muldoon told me: 'I couldn't see his stupid face but I said to myself, "Buddy, you ain't getting around much anymore at all," and I pushed off the safety. He started hollering, "Don't shoot, buddy!"—well, I wasn't having any of *that* crap and I blasted him good.' Turned out it was a Nip loaded down with grenades like a Christmas tree. 'But Doon,' I asked him, '—if you couldn't see his face and he was speaking perfect English, how did you know it was a Jap?' He said, 'Colonel, anybody in this hell hole with a monkey suit *that* clean is either a Slopey or a rear-area commando. And not even a rear-area commando is going to be featuring split-toed shoes . . .'" A lizard dropped from the tent roof and fell on Ben's sleeve and crouched there, his tail a slender green whip. "Cute little bastards, aren't they? Except when they get in your coffee or your shoes. I put out a regimental special order: Any GI who injures a gecko draws three weeks' company punishment. They went for it big. Did I tell you what Jackson said to Bill Bowcher when we laid on that mortar barrage two nights ago?"

"Ben," Damon said gently. "Ben."

"Yeah?"

"Ben, what's on your mind?"

The Colonel gave him a sudden, very sharp glance and looked down. "Sam, you want to take a drink."

"Look, I just—"

"I mean a good stiff one. Right now."

The cup was polished smooth and bright from many scaldings, and had a little lump at the lip. He felt a cold hollow thrust under his heart. "What is it?" he asked.

"Sam, you want to hold on to yourself. A little. I've got some rough news . . . Rusty just got a TWX from Pearl. Relayed from DC. And— and to DC from the ETO, Sam . . ." His face held a fierce, pleading look. "Sam: it's kind of bad."

There was a heel print on the earth floor. With a raised ridge across its center. His heel print. That meant the heel of one of his shoes had been cut by something.

He said in a whisper, "—Donny?"

Ben nodded. "Over Pfalzmund. The big raid."

". . . It's confirmed."

"The plane caught fire, lost a wing. No chutes."

He set the cup down on the field desk; picked it up and took a long drink, set it down again. He nodded. "Okay."

". . . Jesus, Sam. I wouldn't have had it happen for the world."

"That's okay." Tommy, he thought; oh my God, Tommy. "Does she know?" he asked.

Ben shook his head. "Nobody but you. Fats Hebert sent it on from the Eighth . . . I'm sorry, Sam. Jesus, I'm sorry."

"That's all right. Thanks." He was standing up. He hadn't realized he had got to his feet.

Ben got up and splashed some more whiskey into Damon's cup, banged the cork into the bottle with the heel of his hand and jammed it back in the gas-mask carrier. For a moment he stood there awkwardly, hands at his sides. "Sam, I'd give everything I own not to have to tell you that." He bent over and struggled into his poncho, clapped his helmet on his head. "Sam . . ."

The lamp was flickering wildly, flaring and sinking: it needed to be pumped up. He felt numb, without breath or blood or feeling. He looked at Ben, whose face was twisted absurdly. "Oh Jesus," he breathed. "Oh, dear Jesus."

"Sam: you want me to hang around?"

He shook his head. "No. I'll be all right in a while. I'll see you at seven."

"Right." Ben gazed at him a moment longer—all at once grabbed him by the shoulders, a fierce, hard embrace; let go and ducked out of the tent. Damon heard him talking with the security detail. Then the voices died away altogether and the rain started to roar again.

He sat down. My boy is dead. There was no reality to the thought. He couldn't grasp it, take hold of it somehow. He was without a son. It would take some getting used to. After all these years.

Well: that was what war meant. Killing. The killing of men. If anyone should know, he should.

He went over to his cot and pulling an ammunition box out from under it took out a folder and began to run through Donny's letters until he got to the one he wanted, the one the boy had apparently written just before his first mission.

. . . I remember what you said about being afraid. Back at Garfield, the time Brand was in the stockade. Remember? I don't think I'll make a very good soldier myself. Not your kind of soldier, anyway. I know I think too much, worry too much about things. But I'll do the best I can,

and maybe it'll be good enough. It's got to be good enough, because we must win this war. We must and we're going to.

But I'm not going to war for the reasons you did. I'm going so that there will be an end to war, to militarism, to tyranny—so that there will never again be situations that will breed starved and diseased and desperate men—like those people we used to see on Luzon. You say it's impossible (I can see you sitting there saying it), there will always be wars for the reason that men are what they are—greedy and self-indulgent and power-hungry. I say it IS possible, that man can and must change, and that it must come now. And if we have to give up some of our sacred prides and prejudices, if we have to do with less in the way of material comforts, if we must live lives of real austerity and sacrifice in the world to come, so be it. So be it, I say. Let it come. The German pilot who will shoot at me believes in his country, right or wrong, too—else why would he be up there, risking his life? I believe his country is wrong: but what if one day the objective truth of the matter is that my *country is wrong? What then?*

No: it must come: a new heaven and a new earth—absurd and childish as it sounds; for unless it does come this will all be for nothing. All the blood and misery and destruction, all the sacrifice, for nothing at all. The dirtiest insult to the millions on millions of human beings who are suffering so much in the hope of a cleaner, nobler world.

There was more but he put the letter down. His boy was dead. The letters were all he had now. With a swift, grief-bound clarity he remembered an evening on Luzon when he'd come in late and found Donny wide awake, sitting up in bed, chewing at the inside of his cheek.

"Dad, I've been thinking and thinking about this—I can't get it out of my mind, I can't figure it out . . ."

"What's that?"

"Well, here I am—Donald C. Damon, an American, here in the Philippine Islands in 1936, lying here on this bed . . . but *why*, Dad? Why aren't I a Tagalog farmer, or an Italian stevedore, or a Negro sharecropper—of all the people I could have been, why am I this, here? Why am I *me?*"

Damon had sat down on the edge of the bed, suppressing a smile, amused at the boy's agitation but nonetheless respectful of the depth of the search that had provoked it. He knew his son had a finer, more ruthlessly inquiring mind than he, and there was something both pleasing and saddening in the thought. Donny would be one of those men who suffer more than others, who press for the ultimate truth, and the realization humbled him a little.

"I can't answer that, Don," he said after moment. "No man can. Life is a mystery, and the most profound philosophers in the world haven't been able to get beyond that."

"But then what, Dad?—why should anybody care about anything? If it's all just stupid *chance* . . ."

He leaned forward and put his hand on Donny's foot. Perhaps he'd answered a little too hastily. He'd just returned from an evening at the Massengales', where there had been a lot of epigrammatic wit and a good deal of brandy. But the boy was genuinely troubled.

"The best thing to do is accept it," he said. "Accept what you are and go on from there. You can't change the circumstances of your birth and condition—it's unprofitable to torture yourself with too much speculation as to why you've been placed in existence at a given point in time . . ." Then, touched by the need to pass on to his son and heir the doubtful legacy of his own strained and arrant experience, a sense of continuity of effort from father to son—or perhaps it was only the brandy—he'd added: "That's the whole challenge of life—to act with honor and hope and generosity, no matter what you've drawn. You can't help when or what you were born, you may not be able to help how you die; but you can—and you should—try to pass the days between as a good man . . ."

Now he chafed the stubble on his chin and sighed—a sigh that was half a sob. Words. What mattered, what remained was the iron fact that his only son was a charred mass of matter in a twisted, fire-blackened cage of steel and aluminum somewhere deep in Germany, among the firs, the bristling turnip fields.

". . . I can't write her," he murmured, half-aloud. I can't. I haven't got the guts. He gripped his chin in his hands. She would never forgive him now. Never. Why should she? He had stood all his life for armed force, for Flanders Fields and *pro patria mori*—and this was where it had led: a weary, apprehensive, sonless general who commanded nothing. He had spent half a hundred hours planning this amphibious envelopment, but once the landing craft turned toward the line of departure and the 477th jumped off for Komfane, he was as powerless as any Papuan native watching from a jungle peak a dozen miles away. He was a military broker in emotions—prodding Dickinson's excessive caution, slapping down Frenchy's explosive pugnacity, soothing Haley's wounded ego; exhorting, threatening, mollifying, praising, displaying competences he didn't own, feigning a confidence he could not feel . . .

He was a fraud. A fraud and a fool.

He sipped at his drink, though he knew it would afford no solace: liquor had never dulled his sensibilities. The gale increased again, in thunderous torrents of water that overflowed the foxholes and drainage ditch outside his tent and began to seep across the packed earth under his cot. Off to the left, toward Berabwe, there was the remote, hollow tapping of a machine gun; again, then the dull thud of mortars. His son was dead. And out there, a few hundred yards away, they were fighting: staring at the fitful dark, crouching hip-deep in water, shoulders hunched under their helmets, checking by feel for grenades, flare cartridges, alarm cords, power phones, struggling to hear sounds of human movement against the lashing fury of the rain. The focal point of what Washington was pleased to call The War Effort. The private in his concealed outpost, soaked to the very marrow of his bones, hungry, shaking with malaria, a jungle ulcer suppurating on his neck, his guts griping and burning with dysentery spasms, straining to hear, alone with his fear of the shadow darker-than-dark, the near flurry of move-ment, the knife, the cataclysmic flash of the grenade: held together by loyalty to his squad mates, pride in his company, grinding hatred of the enemy who had killed and mangled the bodies of his friends, fugitive dreams of that hometown whose inhabitants now worried about B-cards and points for roast beef and shoes and liquor, who cursed the ration boards and cheered and clapped at the newsreels between the feature films . . . There, in that outpost, on that three-square-feet of ground, was where the real war was being fought, no matter who denied it; and how that private did tonight—whether he had the hardihood and the craft to resist exhaustion and debility and slumber and kill the weary, sick, re-sourceful enemy who sought his life—would decide who would win this war, and nothing else.

His own son was dead, that boy out there on outpost was his son, they all were. Death was not an individual matter. We liked to think it was, but it was not. The death of one man touched us all, stripped us all. We were all one erring family, and nothing made us more conscious of this unalterable fact than loss. We were all one. On edge, stupid with weari-ness and grief he nonetheless felt he could reach out and touch them— George Caldwell peering through glasses at some gray stone Castello in Sicily, Jack Cleghorne rotting in the Bataan jungle, Westy training draftees in the red Georgia dust, Ed Mayberry hiding in the Mindanao rain forest, Meadowlark Walters in hospital at Algiers, Lin Tso-han huddled in some rude cave deep in the Wu T'ai Mountains—he felt he could reach out, giant-like, and embrace them all, the living and the dead, hold them to his breast, awestruck before this great wave of courage and sacrifice and hope that sought, however falteringly, how-ever imperfectly, to put an end to a peculiar day of tyranny, the harsh voice that shouted man was no more than the tool of man . . .

But he could not hold it. Before his gaze the fire ran out in spurting fanlike columns, in scrolls, raced across plains and streams and mountain ranges, and now all he could hear were the screams, rising muffled and animal, soaring into a howl of all man's perdurant inhumanity; the faces around him, white and shaken, turned away, their gaze would not meet his—

He wiped his eyes with his hand, picked up the pencil and clipboard and folded back to a fresh sheet of paper and wrote:

Dear Mrs. Phelps:
You have, I know, already had word from your son's battalion com-mander, Lt. Col. Hoyt. I know, too, how pitifully inadequate any words

are at a time of such immeasurable loss as you must feel; but I feel
impelled to write a few lines in any event.

Your son was a most courageous soldier, and his actions at Tobaloor
Village were in the finest tradition of the United States Army. I have
recommended him for the highest honor our country can bestow; and I
am proud to have known him. We shall all be the poorer for his loss.
When this vast and most cruel of wars is over and we have established
a more generous world than this, perhaps we can all of us take some
comfort in the thought that he is one of the men who made that world
possible.

> *Sincerely,*
> *Samuel A. Damon, Maj. Gen., USA*

It meant nothing. Nothing at all. Words. What did his mother care
for citations, or medals, or letters of condolence? Her boy was dead.

Well. Sometimes they were all we had—words. They had to serve,
flesh out the heart's soft cry . . .

He turned the page and wrote his wife's name; wiped his sleeve across
his eyes. The rain battered against the tent roof and crept in greasy
rivulets beneath his feet.

Life is a cheat, and time kills life. Future possibilities. The cheapest
cheat. How can we laugh, dream, couple when in the next moment,
the next black rush of time—

But there, there are always those who have an answer. Trying to solve
it. Lynx-eyed darlings, oh yes. American Century. Put all your eggs in
one basket and watch the basket. Four Freedoms, save-salvage-and-sur-
vive, do unto others, live in the strength of the Lord, what *filth*—*!*

The glass was short and broad-mouthed, last of a set bought in Cleveland in 1929; the gin swirled richly around the ice, white spirits. The
curtains lifted and fell in the hot September breeze. A car passed, its
tires a hiss of spun silk on glass. Behind the wall the Millmans' radio
gabbled on and on, bursting with news. Devouring life.

I can't stay here. I can't stay in here any longer.

Tommy Damon rose to her feet, but the sensation was worse—a
mountainside filled with great rock slabs falling, splitting off and falling
in an interminable soundless crush of rubble and dust, timed now and
then to the ebb and puff of the curtains.

"I've got to see Poppa," she said urgently, and put her hand to her
head. But he wasn't here. Any longer. He was—where? He had refused

to tell her when he left, the noble stoicism game, and of course she had known better than to ask. The game all must play.

But now it was different. Now she had to know.

She half-ran to the phone, misdialed once, then correctly. "I want to speak with Army Ground Forces." Her voice sounded curiously thick, as though she had a light cold, or had just wakened. "Colonel Hammerstrom, please."

"I'm sorry, Colonel Hammerstrom is engaged right now. Could you—"

"No, I can't." She rode in over the aide's cautious voice. "This is Mrs. Samuel Damon."

"Oh yes, Mrs. Damon. I'll—"

"Would you tell him it's urgent. Very urgent. I'll hold on."

"Very good, ma'am."

There was a long pause in which she heard voices, the halting tap of a typewriter, the rustling of papers—was it?—dreamlike and faraway, like the sway of surf. Then Chink Hammerstrom's voice, hesitant, wary, a touch somber: "Hello, Tommy. How are you?"

He knew then: he knew. They always knew before anybody else. Rage choked her, she nearly dropped the receiver.

"Chink," she said calmly. "I've always been a good girl. You know? Never asked any favors, never stepped out of line. Right?"

"Of course—"

"But now I've got to know. Where's Poppa?"

"The General? Why, he's in Britain. I thought you—"

"No, I mean really. *Really* where is he—?"

"In England, sweet. With a mission I really can't tell you about. You know I would if I could."

That shade of reserve, of distance. He knew and he wasn't telling. And this was Chink Hammerstrom, who used to play "The Bontoc Blues" and "Thanks for the Memory" at the parties on Luzon! But there, you see?—the future killed time, and time killed life . . .

"Then why haven't I had a letter in seventeen days?" she demanded.

"Why, I don't know, honey. The mails are a royal mess, I can tell you that. Look, if there's—"

"If he's in Sicily the Germans certainly know it," she cried hotly. "They know where he is and what he's doing a damn sight better than you do—don't you think I know *anything*? I was in France, last war—they know all about it when you go to the can . . ."

"Tommy please, honey, I can assure you he's in no danger whatever—"

"Oh Christ!" She struck her free hand against the telephone table. "Oh, stop it—tell me! Tell me! . . . Look, Chink," she said in a hard, flat voice, while the anger held her suspended, "I know. D'you understand? I've just been given the word. About—" But still she could not say the name aloud. "—that . . ."

"Honey, I'm so sorry, we all are. We didn't know whether word had reached you or not—"

"No—and you wouldn't run the risk of anything, would you? Christ, no . . ." Oh, this stupid, despicable men's club! Her eyes had filled again, her voice was hoarse; she cleared her throat wildly. "Well, you can make it up to me. Right now. You can tell me where Poppa is!—"

"Tommy, look. This is terrible for you, I know. You mustn't get to brooding about this. Let me call Sue—"

"Oh, *shut up!*"

She slammed the phone at its cradle: it fell off the table and began to swing by its cord, banging against the table legs. Chink's voice was squeaking, "Tommy? You there, honey? Tommy? . . ." She was crying again, helplessly, wagging her head from side to side. Insufferable brass-and-braid fraternity! The letter was lying open on the bed where she'd first read it, wretched, hateful letter. She snatched it up and tore it into bits and pieces and flung it away from her. Who did they think they were fooling—besides their idiot selves, that was? Oh God, she hated them, hated them with all her soul—if she could wipe them all off the face of the earth by saying one word she would shout it at the top of her lungs . . .

Then in the next moment she felt remorseful, frightened at the letter's destruction, as though she had willfully cut herself with a sharp instrument. Still crying stormily she got down on her hands and knees and began groping for the pieces, gripping them tightly in her hands.

There was a click above her head, then the hard whine of the dial tone. She put the phone back on its hook, thinking of Edgar, now with WPB. But he wouldn't know. All he knew was what had to do with him. The plant was making boxes for rations, waterproofed liners for crates, containers for survival kits. Survival kits. Marilyn had bought a place out in Rock Creek Park, a crazy Norman manor house with zigzag open beams and everything inside smoky and dim and a turret on the right-hand corner. It had formerly belonged to Tremayne, the steel man.

The sententious radio voice behind the wall had concluded. A band was playing now, a girl was singing in full, syrupy tones:

> "*Never knew the night could creep so lonely and long,*
> *Never thought the blues would be my favorite song—*"

She found a handkerchief and wiped her eyes and took another sip from the glass. He liked to sing, that time she took them both to see *The Mikado* in Tacoma he'd been enraptured, for months afterward he would wrap that ragged old patchwork quilt around him, one arm held gracefully in the air the way the actor had done. "A wandering minstrel I, a thing of shreds and patches, of tattered songs and snatches, and dree-eamy lu-ullaby . . ."

The phone was ringing: she sat looking at it stonily, glad of its insistent clamor. Once she reached out, dropped her hand again. No. Nobody. Let it ring. She counted for a time, forgot, lost count, tried to think of nothing at all: could not.

Finally it stopped.

Court would know. Court was cold and hard and selfish, Court saw through this sentimental noble-sacrifice-club game better than anyone, he laughed at it. He would tell her and put that part of her mind at rest. At least that. He knew it was all the king of frauds, he knew all along—why hadn't *she* ever seen it?—there was neither past nor future, there was only the sweating bubble of *now* that encased the feeble flesh. Without thought she phoned OPD and got his aide, a pleasant, extremely self-possessed boy who courteously told her the General had left the office but that he could be reached at his home at four.

But she could not stay in here any longer.

With numb tenacity she washed her face and combed her hair, found her purse and crammed the shreds of letter into it. She'd had too much to drink. Well. Then she had. She let herself out quietly. The foyer was deserted. Mr. Canaday smiled from behind his desk, that sly, fondly forbidding appraisal, his bifocals flashing once.

"Afternoon, Mrs. Damon. Lovely weather, isn't it? But warm."

"Yes. Very."

To him, to everyone she was the same woman they had seen yesterday, and the days before. But that wasn't true. She thought all at once of the day she'd first begun to menstruate, down at Fort Sam: the pain, deep and alien and burdensome, the faint, lonely fear—and after that a kind of timorous pride. Walking around in the post exchange later she had smiled at the service wives, thinking, No one knows about me, but I am a different person from yesterday, from what they know of me: I am a woman now, but none of them knows it . . . Now again she was altered, but in a different way.

The streets were very neat. Curious. Curious how wartime made people neater. Like children who have been promised a movie, a camping trip. If they're good. They all kept their yards tidied nicely, the sidewalks were clean, their victory gardens were contained in careful little plots. Rubber and tin foil and aluminum and old newspapers—so many drives. Of course the government didn't use any of it—Edgar had told her himself all that tin foil was useless, and the aircraft firms couldn't use old aluminum anyway. But it kept everybody happy, collecting things.

She stepped out smartly, feeling the heat now, the smoky, oppressive September air. The embassies stood sedate and proud behind their wrought-iron grillwork, their neat brass placards. Men in fine silk suits got out of shiny black limousines and hurried into offices, their faces tight with the exercise of power; at the corner the newspapers blared. PATTON AT MESSINA. SEVENTH ARMY ENTERS MESSINA. SICILY IS

Ours. Georgie Patton with his yacht and his polo ponies and his high, squeaky voice and prissy cruel mouth and his pistols and his avatars. The war was being won—with dash and fury. Victory. Factories were pouring out the tanks and planes and bullets, the armies swelled and swelled, Presidential advisers flew off to Cairo, London, Moscow; destiny, history, glory, victory, those words that rang in men's hearts, unfolded everywhere above them like a panoply of banners—of course it was of no consequence at all that one B-17 whirled to earth a flaming, cart-wheeling wreck, one solitary figure slumped against the shattered glass of the blister, groping feebly as the flames, sucked backward roaring, reached him and the electrically wired, sheepskin-lined suit began to—

She was panting in the heat, half-running. She must be calm. Calm, if nothing else. She counted the squares of concrete that rolled up toward her, chipped at the corners. It didn't matter. Figures glanced at her, figures on sticks of legs with plates for faces. Mechanical toys, they drew near and vanished behind her. There was no plan. Nothing mat-tered anymore but cruelty: cruelty and ambition, those were the fuels the world ran on, there were no others. The stronger ate the weaker, and increased. Why didn't everyone see it? It was *there*, for all to see—

A woman in a floppy flowered hat glanced at her sharply; she threw her a look of unutterable hatred and hurried on, reached Dupont Circle. Pigeons swirled in a tight, flickering pattern, rising, their wings a taut, dry whistling in the slant sunlight. At Benning he'd kept pigeons in a loft Sam had made by screening in part of the attic floor of the set, and the low, liquid crooning had driven them all half-crazy nights. He had cared for them religiously, feeding them, changing their water, scraping out the droppings and keeping entries on the broods. He'd known them all by name. On the title page of the notebook was the phrase: *All About Pigeons.* One morning he'd told her, "I dreamed I was flying, Mom. Really flying! Out over the roofs and pine trees, just soaring and soaring on and on. It was like being in heaven . . ."

A bar, on her left: blue grotto gloom with the icy, festal glint of glasses. The air was cool and raw. She shivered, slid on to a stool near the door and said: "Gin, please. Over ice."

The bartender's eyes slid up to hers mildly. "Just ice?"

"That's right."

She reached into her purse for money, saw the torn pieces of the letter and closed the purse again, looked around her blankly. When he was eleven he'd torn up a drawing he'd made of musketeers fencing on a parapet; he'd torn it up by mistake and had been inconsolable. While he'd been at school she had gone through the trash barrel on the back stoop until she'd found the drawing, smoothed it out and pasted it together for him. His eyes had gone wide with joy. "Oh Mom, that's wonderful—oh, that changes *everything!*" He'd flung his arms around her; his cheek had been warm against hers. So smooth and warm—

Count the bottles, read the labels. Teacher's Highland Cream, Four

Roses, Old Grand-Dad. The officious, admonitory radio voice had returned—the bartender was tuned to the same station the Millmans had
been. He brought her drink and she listened numbly. The Russians had
recaptured Karkov. Allied planes had bombed rail centers and airfields at
Naples, Foggia and Rome; Army ground forces were encountering
fierce Japanese resistance on Lolobiti, but had secured Sibolán on New
Lorraine.

Odd. How odd to be sitting here in this chilly air-cooled bar thinking
of Sam out there on Lolobiti. She could see him—conferring, giving
orders, moving around, watching everything with that steady, stolid,
maddeningly resolute gaze, kicking some and kissing others, getting on
with it. Yes. Getting on with it. He was a major general now, two stars,
he had his own division. It was monstrous. One of the solvers, he
couldn't help it. Solutions and systems. And of course this was his
chance—his chance to prove his worth, serve his country, put all the
years of maneuvers and range work and nocturnal study to use, he was
finally given rank and responsibility commensurate with his abilities—
and it was all dependent on battle, the killing of fathers and husbands
and lovers and sons—

The gin burned coldly, like medicine, like varnish, like new-cut pine
branches. He'd hated to take medicine, he would close his eyes and
wrinkle up his forehead, once he pretended he was well to get out of
taking any. That other time at Benning when he had a fever and said his
neck and the back of his head hurt and they'd been afraid it was polio—

Two sailors were at the end of the bar, hats shoved forward over their
eyes, their faces red and harsh, burned by wind. She watched them
idly. Big, powerful men. Gunner's mate second, she saw the sleeve of
the shorter of the two, who strolled back to the phone booth in the
rear of the room and sank inside; his bell-bottom trousers stuck out
whitely. The bigger man called something to him, a piece of advice. His
arms were folded: the biceps pressed against the smooth duck. She
looked away again at the ranks and rows of bottles. They did look
military; she'd never felt it before. An empty liquor bottle was called a
dead soldier. "*That* soldier's done his duty," Poppa used to say when he
threw out an empty.

Poppa, she thought, and her eyes filled with tears. Oh, nothing was
as cruel as this. Condemned to sit here at this bar while the radio went
on and on, adding up the ledger of battles, bombings, the count of dead
and captured. Man eats man. That was the only truth. Man eats man, on
a platter of steel.

My son. I saved my son once. Shot and killed a rattlesnake and saved
my son's life, so that he could be burned to death in a foreign war . . .
Closing her eyes she remembered the flat desert light, the hot, dry wind
in her face, the great dead weight of the automatic pistol and her quaking fear. Guns. Shep Thorndyke had shot himself at Beyliss, very late
one night. The short, hollow *crump* sound like a paper bag popping but

denser somehow, more sinister. Sam had been on his feet before she'd raised her head from the pillow. Sam had gone over, barefooted in his pajama trousers, and found him. Outside. He'd gone outside on the lawn, as though he hadn't wanted to soil the set. That had been Shep all over: quiet, unassuming, self-effacing. The best battery commander he'd ever seen, Sam said. Olive hadn't been there, Olive had been in Hadley with Prinz, that arrogant Prussified fascist son of a bitch who loved to bow over your hand and tell you Hitler had the right idea, that international Jewry were at the bottom of all the world's problems, that the Republican party were sentimental fools, putting up namby-pamby do-gooders like Hoover and Landon; what the country *needed* was a strong man who would really take over the reins, put an end to all the molly-coddling and clean out that pack of Bolsheviks and dreamers and wastrels who were turning the USA into a sinkhole of decadence. Insufferable. Everyone on the post had known but Shep. Old Maitland had actually called Prinz in and talked to him about it. Man to man, don't you know. But he hadn't reckoned with Olive. Why? When she had a wonderful, considerate man like Shep had she turned to that icy monster? And then Shep had found out somehow. She'd seen him that evening at some CMTC function, standing at the edge of a group; pleasant, diffident, self-effacing. Good old Shep. And the next time she'd laid eyes on him he was a corpse. Buried with full military honors and now Prinz was on the staff at COSSAC in London. Sexual infidelity. God, what a farce, what a supreme absurdity to do away with yourself over—the brief, wet straining of flesh—when there were a thousand thousand things that could rend the very—

"Where you from, sugar?"

The sailor was standing beside her, the big one. Foot on the rail, elbow on the bar, drink in his hand. His face looked less brutal when he smiled. She stared at him silently.

"You look just like a girl I used to know in Henderson," he said in his easy, soft drawl. "That's near Memphis. Ever been down there?"

A pickup. He wanted to pick her up. Right like this. She did not know what her face looked like. The radio talk had stopped, there was music again. She went on gazing at him, listening to the deep, lazy voice. Yesterday she would have been flattered, enraged, amused. Yesterday she—

It was too much. Too much. That she should be sitting here today, in this place, and a gunner's mate second class should actually be hanging over her with genial complicity—

"I—" she started to say. "Do you realize I'm—" But her voice failed her. All she could do was shake her head back and forth. Tears began to run down her cheeks; she could feel her face trembling.

"What's the matter, sugar?" His face was hard and flat again, indistinct.

"—No," she said. And again: "No. I'm—I've got trouble—"

"You have? What kind?"

"The worst," she said. "Oh, the worst there is. Believe me. In this world . . ."

The bartender was speaking, she didn't hear the words. The sailor was backing away, his eyes clouded and unsure. "Gee, I'm sorry, lady, I'm right sorry, now I *am* . . ." He walked back to his companion softly, rocking forward on the balls of his feet as though the floor were very slippery.

"Nothing." She pushed a bill across the dark, burn-scarred wood.

"Do you need help, ma'am?" The bartender was watching her, a stem glass and a neat white towel in his hand.

She shook her head. But she couldn't stop crying. "No. I'm all right. Thanks."

"You're sure, now . . ." His face was round and grave, his eyes were strangely piercing. "I could get you a cab in ten minutes."

"No, it's quite all right."

"You be—careful, now. Won't you?"

"Yes. I will."

Outside it was cooler. Or no, hotter, but the air had lifted, instead of weighing upon her throat and shoulders it now held aloof, licking at her gently, like the air at the edge of the sea. His room at Princeton had no pennants on the walls, that was considered juvenile and rah-rah, he'd explained; but in the corner of the mirror above the dresser there was a theater bill from the Martin Beck and on the dresser a champagne cork and a snapshot of several kids eating hamburgers and drinking beer and laughing in the hollow of a sand dune. "Cape Cod. Kid stuff. It was fun, though." Sprawled in a fashionably decrepit easy chair, wearing a cashmere pullover and flannel slacks and loafers, his hair flung forward over his brow in a loose brown lock. It was impossible that this relaxed, handsome, broad-shouldered young man could ever have been the excited little boy who came racing out of the pine woods at Benning calling, "A butterfly!—I saw a butterfly, so *blue* . . . !"

The cars. Count them. Buick, Chevrolet, Ford, another Ford, a roadster—convertibles, they called them now—the canvas torn and faded and full of stains. At Myrtle Beach he ran barefooted all the first day, in a breathless ecstasy, his first sight of the ocean, and that evening he sat on the cabin steps crying, furious at the pain of the sunburn while she patted cocoa butter on his insteps—

She had stopped, was leaning against a high iron gate that smelled of rust. Nobody could stand this. Could be expected to. Nobody. She could feel her heart turn on itself. High above the trees the Monument followed her like a harsh stone finger of God. She stopped and peered up at it. Shep Thorndyke had used his service pistol. In the bottom of Sam's footlocker was a German Luger wrapped in a white undershirt. A boy named Raebyrne had given it to him. Was it loaded? Probably not. Or perhaps it was, there was no knowing.

But she could not do that. Could she?

She walked on, feeling faintly sick and light-headed, blinking at the circling storm of pigeons, the parade of cars; forcing herself to look at people's faces, signs. At the street she knew she turned left and counted the doors, stopped before one and climbed the steps and rang. There was no answer. Why should there be? She rang again, feeling her soul thrust against the bell. But he had to be here: he *had* to be. If she didn't see Court, if she couldn't see someone she could talk to in another few minutes she did not know what she would do. She could not go along this way, remembering.

The bell rang hollowly through the still hallway. No one. She peered vaguely into the soft gray gloom behind the glass panels; then sat down on the low, wooden chest from China, black and ugly with its carving of vines and dragons, felt the thick ridges press against her buttocks. There was Peggy, she thought with curious detachment; she'd have to get in touch with her soon. Very soon.

. . . It was China, she told herself savagely, gripping the smooth, soapy wood with her nails. That was what had done it. When Sam had taken off and left her there alone in Manila to contend with the schools and the household and the heat. What the hell did *he* care? New worlds to conquer and away he went, looking like a kid with a secret bar of candy in his pocket . . .

She was shivering, overwarm and trembling in every limb. She needed a drink: but that was absurd—she'd had far too much to drink already and she knew it. She wanted to leap to her feet screaming obscenities, race off down this stately, shaded street smashing the glass in all the cars with a stick; then the impulse receded, leaving her dulled and weepy. No, it wasn't his fault, he'd made his choice and God knows he'd stuck to it. It was her own fault, she'd destroyed herself just as surely as if she'd lain down before a locomotive. Did everyone? At Benning—or no, before that, at Dormer when she knew it was all bitter tea and she'd done nothing—or even back at Hardee when she'd lain in the shrouded, stifling room and felt the first astonishing tug and thrust, deep in her body—

Someone on the steps. The outer door swung open. Emily Massengale, a bag of groceries in her arms; looking at her very steadily, without surprise. Tommy recoiled in a flash of fright. She realized she'd had no thought whatever of seeing Emily.

"Tommy! How nice to see you."

"Hello, Em. I thought you were in Boston."

"I was. Have you been waiting long?"

"I don't know. No. Not long."

Emily was groping sightlessly for her key. "Marion left—that's the

third girl since last fall—so I thought I'd try to do it myself for a while."
She thrust the door back with her knee. "Come on in. I've been over at
the library most of the afternoon."

"The *library* . . ."

"Yes." Emily glanced at her—that wintry Boston look. "There are
still a few books around. Not that anybody *reads* them, of course."
Holding the door open with her shoulder, she turned. "Come on up."

"Well no, Em—I was just passing by—"

"Oh, come on. You haven't anything better to do with your time.
Don't pretend you do."

"All right." She didn't know, then. Tommy moved down the long,
cool hall, her eyes fastened on Emily's back, hating her with all her
might. The house—the Massengales had bought it while Court was at
the War College—was stately and calm. The mélange of furnishings
from Paris and Manila and Tientsin disposed themselves in a kind of
outlandish ease with the teak couch and leather chairs, the marble cocktail table. The dining room held the great refectory table from the
Garfield days; in the living room were the lacquered end tables and the
Spanish chest and the incredible Han Dynasty vase Jinny had smashed
to pieces and which they'd had to have reconstructed, at terrific expense.

"Look," she said, "I'm sorry, Em—I shouldn't have come, really—"

"Why on earth not? I've hardly seen a soul since I've been back. I'll
put on some tea. Or would you rather have a drink?"

"No." She swayed toward the door. "I can't."

Emily was gazing at her earnestly. "You're ill, Tommy . . ."

"Yes. No. I'm not." She could not stay here. Or anywhere. Say au
revoir. But not good-bye. This elegant room, this pale-faced, middle-
aged woman standing there regarding her with slow alarm had no meaning—it was all, like the world outside, bars and cabs and shaded circles, a
dolorous stupid trance. A revolving screen and only one thing had truth.
A terrible truth. Only one event, one—

"Tommy . . . Tommy, what's the matter?—have you heard something?"

She really didn't know, then. No. She couldn't have known and be
that frightened. Watching crookedly the snub-nosed, wrinkled face, the
badly set hair, Tommy almost smiled in sympathy. She shook her head;
then again—still again, for the twentieth time that afternoon—tears
were pouring out of her eyes, turning her weak and defenseless. Treason
tears. But it wasn't any use: nothing was.

"Ah, Em," she said. Then she was in the other woman's arms, sobbing
hoarsely, maudlin and desolate. "Ah Emmy, I've lost him—I've lost him,
ah he's gone . . ."

Emily's face was ugly with dread. "—*Sam?*" she whispered.

She threw back her head, glaring at Emily wildly, flung her hand

away. "No—my Donny, my *Donny*—he's been killed! Ah, the worst . . ."
She tried to stop herself and couldn't. "The worst thing has happened
to me. The one thing I've feared, lain awake and feared more than
anything else—oh, if you knew how I feel! If you could only *know* . . ."

"Oh, I'm so sorry," Emily was saying gently, "I am. So very sorry,
dear . . . Come now, and sit down."

"No." But she was seated on the lovely teak couch she secretly envied; she had a glass in her hands. Pale roseate swirling. Emily knew she
always drank gin-and-bitters. "I'm drunk *now*," she muttered. "I guess."
She started to her feet in a burst of unfocused agitation. She couldn't sit
here. She couldn't sit anywhere. Oh Christ. Emily had hold of her by
the arms, was speaking to her softly; but she couldn't stay here, all the
same. "I've got to go, Em. Yes. I must."

"*Where* are you going?"

"I don't know, I don't know—! Jesus God, how should *I* know? Save,
salvage and survive—"

"Tommy, you've got to get hold of yourself . . ."

She threw back her head and laughed savagely. "Oh yes," she
shouted, hearing her voice crack and waver, "—oh Christ, that's rich!—
and feel time rotting in every flock of pigeons, soaked in fire—"

"Tommy—"

"—have you seen their *faces* while they play these games?—really
looked at them, I mean? Of course not, *you* wouldn't see the blades
clashing and slashing, scissor teeth swarming at you, they *love* it! What
shit! Don't tell me they don't, I *know!*—"

"Tommy!"

"—don't you understand—I can't *think!* Keeps crashing in. I can't
think about anything else. Absolutely any, anything else at all! Not for
fifteen seconds—" She had broken down again. No use. Sobbing she
raised her head and a hand. "Emily, I swear to God you don't know
what suffering is until you've lost your son in war. You haven't got any
idea . . . I'm going now," she declared, and wiped at her eyes.

"No, Tommy, look—"

"I can't stay. Can't stay here."

"Tommy, for heaven's sake *sit down*."

She sat down obediently; but it was only for a minute. ". . . What am
I going to do?" she heard herself whispering, "Emmy, what am I going
to do?—with all the days and months—? I can't do it, Em. I can't!"

"Yes, you can. Right now what we're going to do is play a game of
chess."

She glared through her tears at the other woman, who was setting
Court's inlaid board on the coffee table. "You're serious . . ."

"Of course I am." She had started to arrange the pieces on the
squares. "You can play, can't you?"

"What? No—"

"Of course you can. Come on, now. You've got the blacks." She advanced her queen's pawn. "Make a reply."

"Oh my God . . ." She couldn't tell now whether she was laughing or crying. "*Chess*—! You're crazy, you know, you're really crazy, the way they've always said . . ."

"No. I'm not. Not the way they've said, anyway. Come on and move."

Tommy gazed uncertainly at the mild gray eyes that seemed all at once so full of force. What had happened? She dropped her gaze to the board, but her constant weeping made the pieces wabble and shift. She murmured, "I can't . . ."

"Yes, you can."

"Em, I can't. You don't realize . . . I can't think of *anything* but that! . . ."

"You can. Force your mind to it. Queen's pawn four. *Here*. Force it!"

"You didn't have a son, a son—!"

"No. I didn't. I had something else."

"Oh that," she cried, incoherent, abandoned, "—as if sex is anything to this—as if his failure to get it up is anything com—"

She broke off in a flash of terror, half-sobered by the admission. Emily's expression was unchanged; only her eyes tightened a little, as though with pain. The two women gazed at each other a long moment, in silence.

"Oh Em," Tommy murmured finally, "forgive me. Shouldn't have said that. I've had too much to drink. Too much of everything. Forgive me, Em. Please. It wasn't anything, I swear—I mean, nothing came of it . . ."

Emily was smiling at her sadly. "I'm sure of that."

"I ought to keep my stupid mouth shut. Only I can't, it seems. It doesn't matter. Nothing happened."

"I believe it. I've had a certain familiarity with the problem, you might say." Emily pushed a bishop back and forth with two fingers, watching it. "Does Sam know?" she asked gently.

"*Know*—he wrote the wretched letter, I heard from *him!*"

Emily nodded. "Someone in the Eighth Air Force notified him early, then." She looked down. "How hard it must have been for him."

"*Hard*—the letter was cold enough, I can tell you that . . ."

"What do you expect him to do—break down and go all to pieces, the way you have?"

She looked fiercely at Massengale's wife. "Why should he? He doesn't feel anything . . ."

"Oh, doesn't he."

"Of course not, it was nothing to him—let Donny enlist, go overseas—No! I can't ever forgive him. Ever!"

"Sam loves you," Emily declared quietly.

"I don't care if he put both hands in fire for me, I can't ever forgive him for this. I can't! . . ."

Emily Massengale folded her hands in her lap. "I want to tell you, *you're* a damned fool, Tommy Damon."

"You tell me that *now*—!"

"Yes. Right now. This seems to be an occasion for frank talk. If I could have had one year with a man like Sam—just one year!—I'd thank my stars for all eternity. You're a damn fool and your own worst enemy: but then, you always were. Now take a good stiff drink and make a move."

Watching the worn face, the mild steady eyes, Tommy was filled with consternation. She saw all at once that Emily was stronger than she; tougher, more resolute. But how was that? When all these years Emily had been the pliant, vulnerable soul, the fugitive . . .

"Emmy, I'm plastered now," she murmured.

"Not too bad. Concentrate! I'm going to try to beat you. You're going to pay me ten dollars if I win, and I'll pay you thirty dollars if you do. Come on, now."

"All right."

She had never played much. Her father had taught her the game long ago, at Fort Sam, and in the long evenings at Dormer, early in their marriage, Sam had given her queen or rook odds; but she had never liked the game or taken it seriously. Now she was astonished at Emily's aggressiveness: she found herself in dire trouble at the end of eight moves. Angered over a mistake in posting she'd made she fought back, forcing herself to concentrate, looking ahead, grappling with the distending possibilities. The cries from the back courtyard died away. She avoided a checkmate, extricated her king, and got well into end game before she had to succumb.

"There," Emily said. "You see? An hour has passed. An hour and a quarter." She was watching Tommy gravely, speculatively. "You see what you can do? One whole hour. That's how you get through each day. Each hour of each day. Do you see?"

She looked down. The burdensome ache of loss had swept back into her consciousness again; but she had been free—partly free—for a time. Her glass lay untouched on the little lacquered table; she picked it up and sipped at it, set it down. "Is that how you got through?" she whispered.

Emily Massengale smiled a sad, wry smile. "You know how I got through. All of you did. For a while I kidded myself that nobody knew, and then that only a few close friends did—and then I didn't care anymore who knew and who didn't. But that's over. I'm over it, now." Crisply she said: "I wasn't in Boston visiting relatives. That was the official line, you might say. I was at a place in Connecticut, a very expensive place, where they treat people with my problem."

"You mean you got over it? the habit?" Emily nodded solemnly. "But why? What has changed?"

"Nothing's changed. Except me, apparently. And the world. Oh hell, I can't claim any credit for it. It was just that one day I sort of—waked up. Realized there was never going to be any love in return—that Courtney is incapable of love as I used to dream of it; and Jinny herself mistakes violence for affection. I know some of it is my fault, that I've failed where I should have succeeded; but that is how it is. I've got to straighten up my own attic. I can do something now, to help in the war; and I'm going to."

There was a little pause.

"Em," Tommy said in a low voice, "did you ever think of—putting an end to it?"

"Oh yes. Many times." She smiled faintly. "But that's not my style. I'm a Boston Yankee. The tendency is to stick it out." She watched Tommy for a few moments calmly. "Look: five million mothers will lose their sons before this war is over; ten million will lose their homes and possessions. What makes you so special? The *woods* are on fire, Tommy. You think about Sam. Keep your mind on what you have: Sam, your father—"

"That's easy to say," she burst out. "My God, I don't even know where Poppa *is*, they won't tell me! . . ."

"What difference does it make? He's where he's been sent—he wouldn't have it any other way. You *know* where Sam is. Tommy, the world isn't interested in your personal jimjams: a thousand men died in Russia this morning, three hundred in Sicily, five hundred in China, a hundred in New Guinea—the world's got well beyond particularities today. That's what it took me so long to see. But I see it now, all right. Your job is to get through the days, one by one; and get some purpose into them."

Tommy gripped the glass as hard as she could, half-hoping it would break and cut her hand. "Words," she said sullenly.

"Sure. The doing is harder. Don't think I don't know. But that's what you've got to do, just the same."

She put her head in her hands. She felt exhausted, chaotic and mindless, aware of a rough, hard affection for this cool woman who had freed herself of drugs and won through to such equilibrium. It was amazing . . . Yet life was a cheat all the same, time devoured life, past and future were shadows without grace or honor, and the thought of tomorrow was a great wet black culvert, a blind journey.

She said: "Em—I don't know how I'll last for a week. Even a week—"

"I've shown you. One way." Emily Massengale got to her feet and put the chess board away. "Now," she said briskly, "we'll go out in the garden and root around for a while. Horticulture. Come on—I've got a smock you can wear, and some shoes. Up with you, now . . ."

"Hallie was right," Joyce Tanahill said, sponging Ben Krisler's chest with deft, light strokes. "You're a devil with horns."

"Why, that's a dark canard," he protested. His entire right arm was swathed in bandages and his left ankle was locked in a white club of a cast. "I'm just a clean-cut American dogface with clean-cut, healthy instincts."

"Oh brother." She bent low over him, lowering her voice so that Colonels Rutherford and La Mott, across the room, couldn't hear her. "Tell me true, now: did you actually pinch Coulter on the fanny? She was furious."

"Aw, she loved it . . ."

"She did like hell. She was going to put you on report."

He grinned. "On report to who? My commanding officer?"

"No. General Kime. The Island Commander."

His lip curled. "Garrison commandos."

"I talked her out of it—just barely. I told her you had a history of satyriasis."

"What in hell's that?"

"Hot pants. Look, you can try to pinch Morandi or me or even Hutch—but you *can't* pinch Coulter. She'll fix your wagon."

He winked up at her. "More challenge with Coulter."

"You're incorrigible. You'll get yourself sent home . . ."

"Is that a disaster?"

Smiling indulgently she shook her head. He'd lost weight; his face looked more bony than ever, with his big curved nose. All his hair had turned gray and his skin was yellow from atabrine. The bandaged arm smelled of sweat and alcohol and disinfectant and that dense, overripe odor of torn and mending flesh.

"Nope," he proclaimed loudly, "they're not going to send *this* doggie home until he gets damned good and ready." He watched her slyly a moment, dropped his voice discreetly. "Bet you wish it was Sam flaked out right here, instead of me."

"—Oh no," she answered instinctively, before she'd thought—then grinned to hide her confusion. "No, he'd be more trouble than you are."

"He wouldn't slap old Coulter on the pistol pocket."

"No. He wouldn't. But he'd be more trouble."

"Kind of trouble you'd love to touch, though." She could feel his eyes resting on her as she moved around him, toweling him, straightening his sheets. She knew what he was thinking, and obscurely it pleased her. He was a simple, happy-go-lucky nature, but in some ways he was immensely shrewd. "Don't kid me," he murmured. "Takes a goof to spot a goof."

"I guess it does."

"Hey, aren't you off today?"

She nodded. "Hogan's way behind, and there's nothing else to do. It's easier to keep turning over." Actually the fun part of the day was seeing Ben; and as usual she prolonged the ritual, plumping up his pillows, arranging his cigarettes and putting fresh water beside his bed and reminiscing about Devon Bay, now far behind them. She'd been shaken when Ben had been flown in from Lolobiti. The wound looked terrible: a mortar fragment had plowed the length of his arm, laying open the flesh from wrist to shoulder; but actually it looked much worse than it was. The piece Weintraub had taken out of his ankle, no larger than a marble, had been far more trouble. Joints were the worst. But after the first three days his natural ebullience had reasserted itself, and for two weeks he'd kept the ward in a mild uproar, teasing nurses, baiting Stackpole and Tilletson, organizing money pools on the next Pacific D-Day, and sending out scatological communiqués on toilet paper sections.

She said teasingly, "Why don't you try and get some sleep, like Colonel La Mott?"

"*Sleep?*—when I can have a great big beautiful doll ministering to my every whim? Bernie can sack in if he wants—he's dead from the waist down anyway."

"You're just a menace." She winked at him and turned to go.

"I'm a —what's that word?"

"Satyriasis." She formed the term with her lips, extravagantly, so that Rutherford wouldn't hear.

"Great. You've made my day."

There was a thorax in recovery, and then an amputee whose dressing needed changing. After that she took the desk for a while and gazed out at the dazzling light on the hard-rolled cascao beyond the Quonset hut, the drooping feather-duster heads of the palms, their trunks all curving lazily to the right. For four months the base hospital had been situated on Isle Désespoir, a pleasant little kidney-shaped island on the edge of the Bismarck Sea which the GIs had promptly renamed Dizzy Spa. It was no spa—it was hot, and the rains were devastating, but there was a satisfaction in moving up. Everything was moving up now, creeping through the green web of islands to the north—but so slowly. It would be years. Any idiot could see that—you didn't have to be a general. While she made entries in the daily report her thoughts turned to Sam. Now that the Division had come back here from the Lolobiti operation she could not keep him out of her mind. Invariably she imagined him standing in front of a group of soldiers with his hands on his hips, his head thrust forward, talking quietly and forcefully. That was how she always saw him. His only son had just been killed over Germany: Ben had told her. He had a wife who was beautiful and slender, and a daughter who was college age. He had a family in Nebraska he sent money to, and his wife was the daughter of General Caldwell, whom Ben revered and told her had been kept from high field command because of a lot of asinine rules about age and the jealousy of incompetents and self-servers back in DC. Ben became very hot and profane whenever he got on this subject, and she had to calm him down; but when he was talking about Sam or his family she never interrupted him. She stored up information about Sam she gleaned from Ben or other Division officers and men, such as his heroism at Moapora or Wokai, his obstinate championing of the enlisted men, his inordinate love of root beer and strawberry ice cream—even unwelcome bits such as his wife's extraordinary good looks—as though in some indefinable way it brought him closer to her.

Her mind drifted back to Devon Bay and the moment by the jeep in the soft, false dawn; then—as so often now when she thought about Sam—into a simple, inane little fantasy. The scene was San Francisco: the war was over, the Japanese had surprised everyone by surrendering all of a sudden, Sam's wife had just died of a swift, incurable, painless disease; they had met quite by accident at a friend's house on Telegraph Hill and had gone from there to the St. Francis, a corner table, and he was sitting facing her, his hands clasped, his thumb against the point of his chin, he was saying—

She picked up the day sheet and began to read it, frowning. This daydreaming was silly. Silly and pointless. You made your own life, you were the victim of your own predilections. Life did not dispose itself conveniently before fantasy. She had met Sam, had a few brief moments in his company—she was lucky to have had that; and she ought to let it rest there. Most people in this world never met anyone who even approximated their ideal—or even anyone who was very sympatico; and it was nothing to weep over, either. Look at her marriage to Brad . . .

Marty Hutchens, her tentmate, had no patience with this dreamy oscillation between reverie and the acceptance of fate. She was a good-humored brunette from Lynbrook, Long Island who was terrific in surgery and very popular in the wards, and her credo was quick and simple.

"What the hell, you only live once," she'd told Joyce late one night when they were lying naked on their bunks and smoking. "I can tell you right now, you won't get a second chance. Make a play for him."

She had laughed softly. "He's a two-star *general*, Hutch."

"So he doesn't have urges? Don't be naïve." She pronounced it like the aisle in a church. "Listen, he's got the same chemical TO-and-E as a PFC."

"Besides, he's got a wife and family."

"Yeah, and from what I hear it isn't all it might be, either. Harry Rutherford says she doesn't even write him! Jesus, these stateside glamor-pants bitches—I'd like to have five minutes with some of them. I'd slap their snooty pusses so hard they'd be walking backward the rest of their crummy little lives. Harry says when their son got killed she wouldn't even—"

"That's enough, Hutch," she heard herself saying sharply. "Lay off it. You ought not to peddle everything you hear."

Hutch sat up and swung her feet to the floor, facing her, her thick black hair low in her eyes. "Hey—you're really gone on him . . ."

"Yes," she answered after a little pause. "I'm gone on him."

"Oh brother." Hutch put out her cigarette in the ashtray an amphibious engineer had made for her out of aluminum from a crashed Zero. "A torch. Well, go after him then. Look—you're here, he's here. What do you want, a citation for chastity? They're not stocking them these days . . ."

An aid man from the 55th came by now, a slender blond boy from Montana named Rowes, walking with that pins-and-needles uncertainty of the newly ambulatory, and she chatted with him for a moment. He had been hit in both buttocks and on the inside of his thigh, a scant inch below his genitals; and he still felt awkward about it. She could imagine the remarks that would greet him when he returned to his outfit—the flood of obscene banter designed to cover their own fears. She felt that men put too much emphasis on their genitals, worried too much about this particular kind of wound. Was it the worst of all? the very worst? Was it more insupportable than the loss of both legs or both arms, or eyesight, or the terrible head wounds that often left the victim only the dazed, paralyzed facsimile of a man? Yet they all continued to fear it most—clapped their helmets over their crotches or pulled pad covers or barracks bags over them during shelling or bombing raids. If they were hit in the groin or thighs it was the first question they asked the medics or the surgeon, in boundless fear—

Well, it was a terrible thing. How would she feel, for instance, if Sam . . . ?

She cleaned out the lab, and helped change dressings on a sergeant with second-degree burns on his legs; then she went down to the supply hut to draw linens for one of the wards. She came out into the hard, tropic sunshine, blinking—and there he was, a thumb hooked in his hip pocket, absently flipping a big yellow coin, peering down the row. His eyes fell on her; his mouth parted slightly and his fine dark eyes came all alight.

"Hello," he said.

"Hello."

He came up to her easily. He was thinner, and drawn with fatigue—

he looked so terribly tired, as though he could never in all the years of his life get slept out again. But his eyes rested on hers with a kind of peaceful wonder. The tight pressure under her heart eased all at once.

"I guess you came down to see Ben," she said quickly, and pointed. "He's up in sixteen—"

"I know. I was just talking with him."

"He's driving us all delightfully wild."

"I don't doubt it." He paused. "Who I really came over to see was you."

She smoothed the top sheet on her arm with care. It was odd: she had the sense that the fierce tropic glare subsided just beyond them, that the corpsmen and nurses and attendants were passing in a curious twilight. "Everybody says you saved the beachhead at Wokai."

"I had a lot of help."

She paused; she didn't know whether to speak of the boy or not. She felt she should—and yet she was afraid he would be hurt if she mentioned it quickly, casually, in this breath-drawn moment of their meeting. "It must have been terrible," she could not help saying.

"It was rough in spots."

"And now you're back. Another victory."

"Another victory." And for an instant his face looked so sad, so careworn and defeated she yearned to hold him, hold his head against her breast. She loved him more she would have believed possible: it made her unsteady. It must be apparent to everyone passing them—by the way her head was inclined, the set of her body, the position of her feet. Everyone must know—and she didn't care. Let them see. Let them.

"Thank God you're all right," she said.

His eyes kept coming back to hers. "Ben said you were off today."

"I am. I just"—she gestured with the linens—"well, keeping busy."

"—Come for a ride," he said impulsively. "Around the island. We'll go swimming. I've got a jeep."

"Of your very own?"

"Of my very own." This time he smiled. "Come on."

"Yes," she said simply. "I'll come."

The beach was small, a taut white crescent between miniature promontories of rock. The water inside the reef was a shifting skein of moods—yellow as gold dust, greener than emerald, with strips of the most lambent, heartbreaking turquoise. They swam in the still, warm water of the channel, picking their way around the coral heads that looked like sculpture roughed in by blind old masters, and then lay under the palms that ringed the beach; and the sun's rays fell on their bodies in a strident lattice of light and shadow, like some barbaric ceremonial. Farther down the cove two native women were wading in the shallows, naked to the waist, wearing long, bright calico skirts, hunting for cowries; one of them was carrying a baby, and a small boy with a stick raced in and out of the water, splashing quicksilver.

For most of the afternoon Sam had been silent; now suddenly he began to talk. Propped on his elbows, staring out to sea, he told her about a French village by the Marne with red tile roofs and narrow casement windows; the celebrant clamor of the shops in Manila; the harsh purple mountains of Wu T'ai, with the farmers in their pale blue shirts and straw hats. He talked about a captain who destroyed his own command in his contempt for life, and a brutal stockade officer who sought to turn men into animals, and an indomitable Chinese guerrilla leader who was forced to put to death his best friend; he told her about a stupid French general named Benoît, and his father-in-law, and General Westerfeldt, a good soldier who just hadn't had any luck. She lay still and listened. It was like some vast Achilles shield of battles lost and won, families sundered and reunited—an endless voyage of folly and exigency and hope and loss . . .

"You've seen so much!" she exclaimed softly. "So much of the world . . ."

"Pretty dreary way to see it," he answered after a moment. "Hell, all I've been is a soldier. A man of war."

She glanced at him, saw he was watching the native women across the cove. The sun had slipped westward, reaching in under the trees, and the sea glittered. The women had stopped looking for shells. One of them sank into the water, her skirts billowing, gently dousing the naked child who crowed with delight, waving his tiny arms.

"That's the only thing that matters. That right there."

She turned back to him again, and saw his eyes were filled with tears. His face was almost serene in its hard impassivity, but the tears kept coming, spilling over his lids. He made no effort to avert his face or close his eyes. She reached out and put a hand on his arm. "I'm so sorry," she whispered. "So very sorry, Sam. Ben told me."

He could not take his eyes off the baby, who kept squealing with delight, waggling its head in an ecstasy of sensation. He started to speak, stopped, his mouth working. After another moment he said: "I heard a kid on Wokai: 'No freaking nerves. What a flint-hearted, iron-bound son of a bitch.' Referring to me. No nerves, no feelings. Just a rugged boondocker, a driver, thinking in terms of units, percentages, risks, breaking it open." He gripped one hand in the other. "It isn't so. By God, it isn't so . . .

"Sure I'm tough," he said suddenly. "We're here, we're *in* it, there's nothing to do now but get it over with—the quickest, savagest way, dog-eat-dog . . . I've got fifteen thousand kids to worry about. Sure, I'm tough," he said, and looked at her for the first time since he'd begun to talk this way. "What the hell am I supposed to do—chant dirges and tear my clothes, pour ashes on my head? lock myself up in some stone tower, crying about what a heartless beast man can be?—wash my hands of it all? If I thought about them all the time, lying in the aid stations with the tubes in their arms, lying there in the muck, looking up at me with those terrible eyes—if I didn't shut that out of my mind . . ."

He licked his lips. The laughter of the women and children drifted over the amber water.

"The buck private lies there in the mud shaking all over and says, 'Oh God, what a frig-up. *Look* at that two-star son of a bitch—Jesus God, how can he be so *stupid?*' And there it is—it's your fault, you see. Your fault. Whatever's wrong, you're to blame. You and only you. Nobody else. And then when you have to write those letters home—"

He broke off. His face was stiff with anguish. She had never seen such naked, unabashed suffering in a man's eyes. "Sam," she said, but not to stop him. "Sam . . ."

"I didn't do it right," he went on. "I thought I'd foreseen every possible contingency. But I hadn't. And they paid for it . . ."

She understood only part of it. There had been an amphibious landing behind the lines—and by some freakish chance the Japanese had just brought in reinforcements earlier that very night on that same beach, and they were all dug in there and alerted. The assault battalion got ashore, but with heavy losses, and with their radios out of commission. Then for no apparent reason the enemy launched three attacks in force on the Division front just before Ben had attacked. The 477th had broken them up and cut their way through, but it had cost them another six hours, and by that time Jimmy Hoyt's battalion was decimated and virtually in the water.

"But," she said, "if you couldn't know about the reinforcements—"

"But I should, I should have made sure. Some way or other. I sent them in, didn't I?"

"Sam," she said in a pleading voice. "Look, you couldn't help it . . ."

"I could help it. It was my business to help it. And I didn't. Two hundred and thirty-seven dead," he said tonelessly, implacably. "Who maybe might not have died at all."

"But it ended the campaign . . ."

"Yeah," he said. "Sure." He closed his eyes then, bent forward and his shoulders heaved. "—Oh, the bastards," he cried softly. "The bastards that bring this on and don't care about a single thing beyond their oil deposits and rubber plantations and their filthy long-term capital gains . . ."

She put her arm around him. "Sam," she whispered. "Dear."

He seized her then—a desperate, half-blind clutch that made her gasp; his jaw was hard and wet against her cheek. Pressing her fingers against his shoulderblades, stirred by his stormy, terrible grief, she was conscious of the simple power of her love. She loved him, and she didn't care a fig for all the rest of the world—the native women or Base Hospital 212 or the Pacific Theater of War or his wife or the future of the free world. She held him in her arms, flooded with a wild, ardent joy.

The moonlight lay on the edge of the cot; the woven rush matting on the tent floor gleamed like braided silver. Twisting his head Damon looked at Joyce, who was lying with her head on his shoulder, her long-limbed body voluptuous and acquiescent and still, glowing like ivory. Her breasts were cool and smooth. Gently he sighed. The dark, irascible anguish that had rent him for weeks and turned him morose and exacting had receded with the past hours: he felt washed, shriven, somehow absurdly absolved. In response to his movement she stirred, and he felt a swift, faint tremor of sensation pass over his body like the wind over a field of wheat.

"Such a lovely girl," he murmured. He felt a mild astonishment at himself, lying here in the moonlight in his tent with this girl. After all the years of conjugal fidelity while the post wolves prowled and philandered, after all his strictures about simplicity and self-denial and the obligations of officers and commanders . . . Yet he felt neither guilt nor apprehension, and it amazed him. He had sought it, it had come, and he was glad. Their lovemaking had astonished him: it was as if they had known each other for years: an easy sarabande of overture and response that swung them, hammock-like, from pleasure to pleasure—and then a mounting, urgent felicity that was like the assuagement of raw wounds.

Her eyes were watching him: such a steady gaze! A shy, indomitable calm that—he realized with a little start of surprise—was greater than his own.

He said: "What are you thinking?"

"How very happy I am right now."

He nodded. She was not tormented, enslaved by the future, by consequences and contingencies. He respected that in her; it accounted for the sweet generosity that drew him. Inevitably, without rancor, he thought of Tommy. In her despair she had chosen to blame him for the boy's death—an accusation that at first had shaken him terribly . . . and then later granted him a curious absolution. If she wanted to feel that, it was her privilege; but he refused to accept the charge. He was guilty of a lot of things, God knew—but not Donny. If anything, his profession would have served as a barrier, not an inducement; the boy would have gone to war in any event, as twelve million of his contemporaries were doing. It was unfair, but that was Tommy's way: *Tommy* was unfair— her careening emotions craved a tangible object, a nameable source for her grief: and there he stood, booted, bristling . . . He chewed lightly at the inside of his cheek. He could see now he had always dreaded the day that headlong, vengeful destructiveness of hers would be turned against him. Now it had happened—and he was not shattered by it, as he'd feared.

Abruptly he looked at Joyce, who ran the tips of her fingers along his brow and nose and cheek. This was a different kind of emotional involvement—a little like the difference between quicksilver and old gold. There would never be the hot, fierce catch at his heart he'd known with Tommy—that darting, magnetic excitement that could make him feel like a pirate striking a chest of buried treasure. This was slower, deeper: a southern stream under the oleander and Spanish moss . . .

Down in the tents across the road where the Division was bivouacked, they were singing, drunk on beer, their voices hoarse and heavy:

> "Hey, we got the word, rolling out on the ship,
> They said they preferred that the boys didn't skip
> Just like a big bird: Jackson, this is the strip—
> Moa!—pora! Man—alive . . ."

A lugubrious, minor-key chant, heavily syncopated. Damon could see them—sitting on the ground, on cots, on ammunition boxes, sweating, their heads swaying, the tops of the beer cans glinting in the light of the pressure lamps like gross bronze coins. His boys.

> "They said to be brave while you're going ashore,
> 'Cause that's the ninth wave and there ain't any more,
> Just crawl in that cave, bud, you're covered with gore—
> Wokai! Lolo! Just—survive . . ."

Two of the supply clerks had written it after the operation. It had caught on like wildfire, and he had defended its use to the horror of Dickinson and Specs Cruse, who had argued that its sentiments were nothing less than a travesty of the fine old ballads of World War I. "This isn't World War I," he'd told them quietly. "This is World War II—and this is the way they see it." That expansive, cheery fervor of 1918 whose absence the Staff bemoaned was as dead as Nebuchadnezzar: these kids armed themselves with a grisly sardonicism, an inverted pride in their own terrible competence, the bitter sacrifices ten thousand watery miles from home. Maybe the song didn't compare very favorably with Berlin or George M. Cohan, but it said what they felt. It said what they knew. There would be another operation, and another, and sitting there swinging their beer cans and gazing at one another, they knew many among them would die, as surely as the rising of tomorrow's sun. They knew it, they accepted it—but they had their own wry protest to make as they moved resolutely toward death and maiming. Listening, staring up at the moonlight he felt a thrust of affection for them so great he nearly groaned aloud—a surging pride, but humble, before their trust, their simple clear-eyed courage.

> *"Press home the attack, pal, we're all under fire,*
> *Then find me a sack, 'cause it's time to retire,*
> *Hey, whip off that pack, Jack—you're hung on the wire—*
> *SALA!—MANDER! Double—five! . . ."*

Beside him Joyce stirred and said: "Cheery little song."

"Cheery little war. Wouldn't you say?" He smiled grimly. "They can sing it as long as I'm running things. I made it the official Division song."

She raised her head. "Sam—you didn't . . ."

"Hope to die. Got Boxley to do an arrangement and rehearse the band, and they played it at that traveling USO show two weeks ago. The kids went wild—drowned out the band. Gave me a standing ovation. I thought old Dick was going to lead a mutiny afterward. Staff came in a delegation to protest that it was detrimental to divisional morale."

"Yes, Colonel Rutherford—" She stopped.

"Go on. Ruthie said I'm a radical and a slave driver. And I have a line sergeant's mentality."

"Oh, you know everything. Well, a lot of them say you're both too easy and too hard on the men. You're overly lenient with things like the beer ration—and then you drive them till they drop." Her hand lay on his chest. "Some of the men's arches are broken down, Sam. And we've had several serious injuries from individual combat training." She searched his face. "Isn't that a mistake—to sustain injuries like that before they even get into battle?"

He frowned, and rubbed his eyes. "I hike them hard because it's the best conditioner there is. Also it's the only way to surprise and dislodge your enemy without having to fight him. Speed of movement. There are some GIs who can't stand the pace, and we try to reassign them. And the majority who do measure up own the confidence that they can outmarch any other outfit in the Army. I know it's unfashionable to think so in certain circles, but group esprit *can* mean the difference between getting up and running, and staying where you're supposed to.

"As for the combat training: what are you going to do? You can't take a boy off a nice, neat, tree-lined Ohio street and say to him, *Cut that man's throat from ear to ear.* He'll look at you as if you're crazy. He's incapable of the act. But in the line, on patrol, on outpost duty that is what he may very well have to do. Kill savagely and quickly and silently, like a beast of prey. He has to be trained to do it, Joyce. Man is not an instinctual killer, no matter what they say. Oh some, sure—a few men are the Cadmus soldiers, the dragon seed: but not many."

"Is that true?" she asked. "It seems to me there's a very deep human instinct to kill."

"There's a certain fitful desire to destroy in all of us—a delight in violence, in maiming, in killing, especially on provocation—even though remorse follows. But in cold blood, *without* provocation—if man is an instinctual killer, why is it so hard to get him to use the bayonet? So the capacity has to be instilled. Somehow or other." He paused. "Do you know there are many men who won't fire their rifles in combat? It's true. They will hold a position, they will dig in and endure shelling admirably, they will even advance under fire—but they won't shoot to kill the enemy. It took me a little while to discover that. And of course with the bayonet they're even more reluctant."

She shivered. "It's terrible, actually," she muttered. "When you lie here and think of it. Barbaric and awful . . ."

"Yes. It certainly is. But here I am. Commanding a division that must kill the enemy—a clever, resourceful, very brave enemy, make no mistake about that—or be destroyed. To be soft on them is to risk the death of all those people over there across the road; and ultimately the loss of the war . . . Yes, I'm hard on them. On my staff officers, too. Too hard, maybe. But I don't see any other way."

"No," she said after a little pause, "I don't suppose there's any other way."

She sat up in bed, her hands locked over her knees, and he watched her: the strong short nose, the firm chin and fine, high brow, silhouetted against the moonglow. He wanted her again—he was faintly amused at this sudden adolescent ardor. She had been largely silent during their love-making: her engagement was all interior, and deep. She had said so little, she had meant so much—she had restored him. Restored to duty. To equilibrium. He moved his hand slowly down the slope of her neck and the slope of her shoulder and over her breast and back. She turned and smiled at him, shyly pleased.

"I'm in love with you," he said.

She took his hand and pressed it to her. "Oh, darling."

"I'm afraid I'm in love with you," he repeated.

"I'm glad that you're afraid."

Down in the tents across the road voices were raised in argument, an increasing clamor, overborne finally by one voice, wild and declamatory, echoed by a distant cheering. Someone making a speech, he thought; running for emperor of Dizzy Spa. King of the Salamanders.

"I don't approve of this, you know," he said suddenly. She frowned, and he saw she misunderstood his words. "I mean it's only my rank that's brought this about." He gestured. "*They* can't meet girls here, take them back to their tents. Why should I?"

Her lips parted in the slow, indulgent smile. "Oh, Sam—you're such a chief justice . . . You should because for once you're lucky. Because we needed each other and wanted each other. Isn't that good enough for you? Everybody can't be equal in everything *all* the time. Some people seize a moment for life, for love—and some don't. Sam"—she raised her long, supple hand and clenched it until it quivered in the air between them—"you can't live like this—all tied up like this. Month after month. You'll go to pieces if you try."

He nodded. "I know. It's true . . . I only meant—I guess I meant I don't know where we can go: this thing between us."

She shook her hair back with an easy, indolent sweep of her head. "Let's just go along from here. Whatever you want it to be, it'll be. That's all right with me."

"You mean that?"

"Darling, I look on all the time between us as a wonderful present I never expected. I feel I'm lucky just to have laid eyes on you."

She was in love with him: utterly, irretrievably. He felt a surge of pure delight—and then a sharp twinge of apprehension. It's the way I fell in love with Tommy, he thought.

"I suppose you've found out by now," he said.

"Found out what?"

"Where I stopped. Your theory."

"Oh. Yes. I think I know."

"When was it?"

"Oh—when you were in France. Some cold rainy night in France."

He gazed at her in dismay. "But I never told you about—that . . ."

"I know you didn't. But that's when . . . But I like your theory better."

"Which one was that?"

"That people stop and start up again. That's what you've done—it's the hardest thing of all. You'll always do that."

Yes, he thought, and it'll always cost me. But I'd rather have it that way.

He drew her to him again. She lay back on the cot, which squeaked shrilly and then was still. The moonlight threw a long, milky quadrangle across the tent floor.

The door swung open violently. Major Prengle stepped inside and said in a high, clear voice pitched perfectly between presumption and deference: "Gentlemen, General Massengale."

Ben Krisler rose to his feet with the others, the chairs scraping on the polished teak floor. Lieutenant General Courtney Massengale, followed by the Corps staff, passed quickly along the outside wall to the head of the table and said, "At ease, gentlemen. Be seated, please."

Krisler sat down again, conscious of the tart twinge of pain in his ankle, narrow as a knifeblade. He stuck his leg out under the table and picked up his cigarette. Here on Walewa Heights the trade winds blew clean and cool, whistling softly through the screens. The walls of the Staff Conference Room were nicely plastered, a warm dove-gray, and the end wall was draped with heavy maroon cloth. A home away from home, he thought wryly. The building was the old Dutch governor's residence, which had been used by Takura and his staff some months before. American planes had demolished one wing and riddled the rest of the structure, but the base engineers had repaired it cleverly; and sitting here at the beautifully polished narrawood table with its faintly ovoid sides it was almost possible to believe that nothing had ever happened—no war, no Japanese occupation, no grinding island campaign. Beyond the long windows the Bismarck Sea lay like a smooth green mat under a flawless sky; and on the far horizon rose the two smoky mounds of Benapei and Tokun, twin stepping stones to the Philippines.

Staff Sergeant Hartje said, "No smoking. General's orders," and Krisler reluctantly tamped out his cigarette in the brass ash tray made from the base of a Japanese 79-millimeter shell. Massengale had paused to talk to Admiral Farnham. Krisler watched the white, handsome face with its high cheekbones, the smooth silver hair, a trifle long, that swept back from the widow's peak high on the forehead. The effect was incongruous—like an athlete stern and wise far beyond his years, or an aged man kept magically, supernally young. Krisler stared at him rudely, studying the three stars on the starched collar, the pale, faded look of the khaki shirt. Real salty. How had he managed that—soaked it in brine nights? Five would get you fifty he'd dyed his hair white to impress MacArthur.

Bucky Warren came in, late as usual, all full of piss and vinegar, with his pilot's cap looking as if he'd slept on it, and said: "Hello Ben, you sad-sack sourball son of a bitch. How they hanging?"

He grinned and answered, "Just the way you left them." The exchange made him all at once aware of his nervousness, and he glanced at Sam who was sitting on his left, penciling a letter order draft. The Divisional Commander threw him a somber look, and Krisler knew he was wondering the same thing: why hadn't Captious Court come in loaded down with maps?—if this *was* to be the big moment? It was just like Massengale—get everybody on edge and then stand around chewing the fat with Bliss Farnham as casual as all get-out. Dizzy sadistic bastard. He fretted with the pad and pencil in front of him, chafed his thumb and forefinger against the single star on his collar. Flag rank. Thanks to Sam. Here he was, in the inner sanctum, on the edges of that remote and awesome world where the thundering decisions were made . . . and he'd

one hell of a lot rather be back with the Regiment. It was confusing.
You wanted to move up if you could, the rewards were gratifying—
there was no change so great as the leap from colonel to BG—writing
Marge about it had been fun, and so was the booze party the gang had
given him. But the higher you went the farther away you were pushed
from the things that meant the most. He missed the moments with
Frenchy and Jimmy Hoyt and Stan Bowcher, the arguments at mess,
the bets, the needling and horsing around.

And now, of all the lousy breaks the poor old shat-upon Double Five
had to draw, they'd had to pull Captious Courtney for Corps Commander. After all these years. Ours but to sanctify . . .

"Well, Gentlemen." Massengale was at the head of the table now.
Ryetower, his chief of staff, had taken the vacant chair to his right.
Massengale himself remained standing, watching them all; that quick,
piercing glance that held the faintest glint of—what? malice? challenge?
amusement? Then he smiled, a swift upward movement of his lips. "I
trust you realize I haven't called you all here idly." Turning he said,
"All right, Edward," and Prengle and Sergeant Hartje stepped up to the
wall behind him and drew the heavy maroon curtains.

There it was, under its acetate overlay, incisive and bold; a ragged
parallelogram marked with bays and streams and a thin, faltering road
net. With its crested northern promontory flanked by a semicircular
bay and a long peninsula at the south studded with smaller off-shore
islets, it looked very much like a screaming cockatoo with stubby wings
flying frantically north-northeast, its long tail shedding bits of feather.
Staring at it Krisler thought, *I knew it.* Of all the stunts: of all the
cheap, phonied-up routines! He shot a glance at Sam again; but the
Nebraskan's face was expressionless.

"Gentlemen," Massengale was saying crisply, "we have drawn Palamangao, as you can see for yourselves. This is of course the first operation for the Twenty-ninth Corps, and it behooves us to make of it a
memorable occasion—one which our comrades-in-arms will honor and
our enemy abhor. Palamangao is, as you all know, the largest and most
important of the Visayan Group, and the vinculum between the Luzon
and Borneo operations which are to follow. Consequently I have given
our task the code name PALLADIUM, after the Trojan aegis, which
Ulysses and Diomedes had to carry away from Troy before that mighty
city could fall." He paused, picked up a pointer with a fine ivory tip,
and stepping up to the map tapped a long and relatively unbroken
section of coastline just above the cockatoo's tail. "The initial landing
will be here, at Babuyan. Designation, Blue Beaches 1 and 2. General
Damon's Division will land at oh-six-thirty on the twenty-second, driving inland to successive phase lines Green, Orange, Blue and Red, here.
Objectives are the villages of Ilig, Fotgon and Umatoc, the severing of
the Kalao-Dalomo highway, and principally the seizure of the airstrip at
Masavieng. At oh-eight-hundred on the twenty-third, General Swan-

son's division will assault here"—he pointed to a large oval bay above
the bird's left wing—"on White Beaches 1 and 2, with successive phase
lines as indicated, its objectives the occupation of Dalomo and the cutting of the Reina Blanca-Fotgon highway, and a link-up with the Fifty-
fifth Division near Masavieng and the airstrip. General Bannerman's
division will be in Corps floating reserve, to be deployed as circumstances dictate. The bulk of the Japanese forces, all reports indicate, are
concentrated here at Masavieng, and here, southwest of Reina Blanca."

For a moment he paused, studying their faces. "What we are going to
effect is a classic, a Cannae battle: a double envelopment between the
two assault forces. Once their union has been effected, the combined
force will wheel east and south around the mountain chain here, and
drive on to the east coast at Kalao, Apremanay, and Warminster. And
the campaign will be ended." He lowered the pointer. "Well, that's the
rough cut. Are there any questions of a general nature?"

"Sir?" Porky Bannerman asked.

"Yes, Paul?"

"How'd that name Warminster get in there?"

There were some chuckles here and there around the table and Massengale smiled. "Some renegade remittance man, I assume. I suggest we
put G-2 to work on that right away." He handed the pointer to Sergeant Hartje and sat down easily. "All right. Now to the maddening
specifics. Colonel Fowler has the definitive material on enemy troop
concentrations. I imagine it would be a good idea to hear that now, see
what we're facing."

Fowler, a slender, bespectacled man, arranged some papers in front of
him and began to read rapidly and intently: "The basic island garrison
consists of the Ninety-fourth Keibitai, elite naval units, Admiral Ochikubo commanding. Army units currently identified are the Eighteenth
Expeditionary Force, consisting of the Thirty-ninth and Ninety-second
divisions, General Murasse, sent in from Manchuria to reinforce the
basic island garrison, and more recently the Eighty-third Division, transferred from China, Lieutenant General Kolusai commanding. There are
also three independent regiments, the Forty-eighth, Seventy-first, and
One twenty-second. Estimated strength of all units is thirty-eight thousand. The naval forces—"

Oh my Christ, Krisler thought crossly—why not make it $39.95? a
real bargain. He stole another look at Sam, whose mouth was drawn
down faintly at the one corner he could see. Yes: not fooled either. Boy,
it took talent on the part of these G-2 types to be so infernally, eternally
wrong. It was a standard joke around the Division: of any intelligence
estimate, double it and add twenty per cent—which was invariably correct. He drew a cigarette out of his shirt pocket and rolled it back and
forth between his fingers. All this showmanship and theatrical window
dressing. What kind of a way to run an operation was this? Customarily
the field orders came down from Corps first, to allow time for study,

and then the conference was held. There was something unpleasant and disconcerting about the way Massengale had done this—the sly unveiling, the preamble, this goofy code name. What you *wanted* was a solid, slam-bang word like BOLERO or ANVIL or COUGAR, not some fancy monicker full of mythological connotations. He glowered at Fowler's pigeon lips and longed for the rude, phlegmatic honesty of Thiemann—now, alas, bumped up to command of the Hawaiian Department . . .

Fowler droned on and on. Benapei and Tokun seemed very far away, sunk in the ocean haze. Idly he watched the faces around the long table. Porky Bannerman, plump and cherubic and absorbed, just out from Bragg with his spanking new 49th Division, eager to show he was as tough as anybody on the beach. A general in every war since 1812. Massengale had been on old Bannerman's V Corps staff in France—and now Porky was a DC under Massengale. Turn about, of a sort. Had Massengale twitched all kinds of wires in Washington to bring that off? or had Porky requested it when he learned Massengale was being given a corps command out here? Anything could be swung if you had the right talent for playing drop the soap. Anyway, here he was—and it was no coincidence.

Swanny—deliberate, a little stuffy, nursing his ulcer, still resentful over the Lolobiti operation, when Thiemann had reamed him out for not taking Komfane when he had the chance. Pulling at his lower lip, already worrying about replacements, CP locations, supply areas, unable to see the great north woods for the superabundance of trees. But he was good with troops, and what else mattered? The staff could pass the God damn papers around.

Farther down the table the Navy brass, sitting shoulder to shoulder, with the air of rich men at a small town PTA social; secure in their gold-braided conviction that the Pacific war was their war, their theater for decisions—still convinced, despite the terrific bloodletting of Tarawa and Saipan and Guam that the golden road to Tokyo lay through the thousand atolls. None so blind . . . Tug Murtaugh, in charge of the Support Force, glowering like a toy mastiff under his wiry brows, looking as if he wanted to tear every Japanese carrier apart with his bare hands and eat it; beside him Bliss Farnham, who would be in command of the Expeditionary Force, examining his fingernails with that effete, supercilious manner: an almost ludicrously deceptive exterior that gave no hint at all of the iron nerve that had never faltered down at Soputa Point, with the transports half unloaded and the *Syracuse* going down by the stern and the Zeros coming in from every point of the compass and the air intelligence people wringing their hands. People could still fool you.

Across from him Bucky Warren, with his handsome, square-jawed face—why were all these fly-boy brass so eternally goodlooking?—with his crash bracelet hanging from one wrist and on the other a black-faced

chronometer that could probably do everything but send out press releases. Well, he *was* an improvement on Prince Hal, who'd gone back to
a desk job in Florida. They said he was slated for a B-29 command soon.
Good: the Navy could have him all to themselves to row with. Hell, the
whole air strategy was insane anyway. The Micronesia bases had bled
half a dozen divisions white, and what would it accomplish? They'd find
out they'd lose so many bombers in the Tokyo raids they'd have to
seize some of the Bonins in order to nail down fighter strips to escort the
monsters. And bombing wouldn't make the Japs give up any more than
it had the British in '40 or the Germans now. That old bromide. But it
was so convenient, so clean and final-sounding . . .

And then Sam, beside him, his face mournful and impassive, looking a
lot more rested after the months of training schedule. His boy was dead.
His only boy. And everything all gone to hell between him and
Tommy. God damn women, anyway—they only crudded everything all
up with sentimental notions of pedestals and undying devotion and incessant attentiveness and Christ knew what else. War did it, probably.
No, it cut deeper than that—they'd got it all mangled up with hussars
and crinolines and perfumed hankies and What Every Woman Knows.
Which wasn't very God damn much. "Honey," Marge had actually
written him once, "it buoys me up so to know you're thinking of me
out there every free moment of the day." My God—there were whole
days during an operation he never thought of her at all, and a damn
good thing, too. All you needed was that kind of horse's-ass distraction.

He sighed, and scratched his itching scalp. Well, that wasn't fair to
the old gal: she was worried about Joey now. Going out to Manton
Eddy's division, east of Paris. A shavetail fresh out of the Point, going
up to the line, just the way he had. What a long time ago that seemed.
But Joey was different, he was like Marge—easygoing, no sweat, roll
with it. He'd never carried any wild chip on his shoulder: he wouldn't
take any unnecessary chances, he'd make out all right . . .

Bryson was up now, doing his stuff, maundering on about ammunition
and rations estimates, and the 600 tons to be landed the first day, and the
absolute necessity for 30 days' supply; his furrowed brow shiny with
sweat, his chin vanishing into his collar. What the hell did he think—
that everybody was going to be sitting on the beach in a tight little
circle, cheering him on as he unloaded? God, it was stupid, sending
corps staffs out here, all wrapped up like Christmas goodies: stupid and
insulting. Here they sat in this bloody palace—Frenchy had nicknamed
it the Petty Trianon and the sobriquet had stuck—loaded down with all
the rank they could carry, overweight and overpaid, eager to be in on
The Big Moment. Meanwhile the hours slipped away, awash in papers
and walla-walla. Ours but to ossify.

He'd stepped out of line really, writing Tommy that way. He'd had
no business doing it except that they'd known each other so long, at
Benning and Garfield. He'd only started out to convey his condolences,

and then the more he'd scribbled the more worked up about it he'd got and the more it had turned into a kind of goofy appeal. Stupid. He should have kept his mouth shut, it probably only made her worse. Women were tricky creatures, tough to cope with on anything above what you might call the operational level. Sam hadn't made any mention of it though, so perhaps she hadn't told him; she certainly hadn't answered his own letter.

His arm felt stiff and crampy, and he thrust it down between his legs and kneaded the flesh above the elbow. Well, the Tanahill girl had been a good thing: Sam would have jumped out of his skin if that hadn't happened. His stomach had been giving him trouble—something that had never bothered him before—and he'd been awfully worn down and irascible after that amphibious flap . . .

Bryson had finished the Dead March from Saul. Massengale introduced the problem of air cover and Krisler raised his head now, listening intently.

"My reports indicate that there are four hundred and fifty to five hundred planes on Palamangao, and another probable two sixty in the Visayas," Murtaugh was saying in his high, hoarse voice. That's exclusive of what they can fly in from Formosa, of course."

"Oh come on, Tug," Bucky Warren protested. "You're getting Asiatic. They can't field half that many. Our last two raids we drew only forty-five interceptions and destroyed one twenty-five on the ground. Hell, all they've got is the flag and two guys to hold it up. Nip air is kaput."

Murtaugh stared at him ominously. "I wish I could share your optimism."

"You can. It's easy. The field at Masavieng is a wreck, Tug."

Farnham said: "On precisely what do you base that statement?"

"Personal inspection at two hundred feet." Bucky's smile could be even more glittering than Prince Hal's. "Confucius say: One bird's-eye view worth a thousand timid estimates. If you boys weren't sitting around in the wardroom all the time guzzling chocolate malteds you'd be a hell of a lot more optimistic about this jamboree. Whyn't you get on your bikes and ride down to the PX now and then?"

"Joyriding," Murtaugh muttered. He and Bucky had been at loggerheads ever since the Vunakanau hit-and-run when the Air Force had flown a covering strike and run into a hornet's nest, and Bucky had accused the Navy of letting the Nips read their mail. If there was anything the Navy was sensitive about it was security, and the marshmallow fluff had really hit the fan all the way back to Pearl. "I'll tell you why I haven't been buzzing Visayan dromes," Murtaugh went on balefully, his deep blue eyes lost under the hanging thickets of brows. "The reason, friend, is because for the past five days I've been folded into a slit trench on Tacloban while they worked over the beach in squadrons . . ."

"Hot damn!" Bucky Warren slapped the table; the gold ID bracelet jingled gaily. "I'd give six months' pay to have seen that! Did you get your shoulder boards crumpled, mate?"

Tug nodded, smiling grimly back. "Okay. Have your fun. We'll see how you make out when they start raiding from the Luzon fields."

"Gentlemen," Massengale broke in genially, "we seem to be wandering rather far afield, wouldn't you say?" He turned to the carrier admiral. "Would you proceed with your operational capabilities, Spencer."

Murtaugh blinked at him. Nobody had called him Spencer since he'd left home in Galveston, Texas thirty-six years ago. In some confusion he peered at a sheaf of notes before him, cleared his throat, and looked up again. "I am prepared to commence strikes on the seventeenth with seven carriers. Five full days, weather permitting."

"Can you guarantee air cover over both beachheads, Admiral?" Bryson asked him anxiously.

Murtaugh's face convulsed on itself until there seemed to be nothing but eyebrows and jaw. "Colonel, I'm guaranteeing nothing. We will take out the strips and intercept everything we can from the Visayan and Luzon fields. I have seven carriers and about four hundred planes operational, and this number, less losses, will be what I will have for PALLADIUM."

"Then what's your problem, Tug?" Bucky chided him. He was irritated because for the first time he would have to wait on the Navy until the strips were secured and he could fly his people in. The total flight distance from Benapei to Davao on Mindanao was 470 miles, and it was another 380 from Davao to Palamangao. "If I could get a couple of my groups up here and work over that rock for five full days the troops could go ashore with their rifles on their backs."

"Oh sure," Murtaugh snapped, "—the way they did at Wokai."

"What do you mean by that? Enemy air capability was practically nil on that beachhead. That cliff was your baby, not mine . . ."

"Gentlemen," Massengale said. "Surely there will be opportunities galore for all arms on PALLADIUM. I have complete confidence in Admiral Murtaugh's carriers to maintain air support until the Air Force can make the Masavieng and Reina Blanca airstrips operational. Let us go on to greener fields."

"We will do everything in our power," Murtaugh went on dourly. "But I must emphasize that we cannot stay beyond the afternoon of the third day following the landing."

"Now wait a minute, Tug," Bucky protested. "You'll have to stick around a while longer than that. If the Masavieng strip isn't operational with parking space for at least one fighter group, my hands are tied . . ."

Bliss Farnham examined his nails with care. "I'm afraid it's a bit more complicated than that, Bucky," he murmured. "Tug has commitments at Lingayen Gulf which he must meet. Admiral Kincaid has explicitly—"

"But look, you've got to hold that tiger until I can get my gang in place—that was the deal . . ."

The argument went back and forth, hung between Warren's over-weening recklessness and the Navy's excessive caution, with Ryetower now and then interjecting something, referring to his notes. He was a rather heavy man with a sharp nose and overlong hair. Massengale was sitting back, watching his Chief of Staff with faintly patronizing indul-gence—the look of a parent toward a child who is trying to enter an adult conversation. Ryetower was a plugger, methodical, cautious, a touch pessimistic—Krisler could see some of it in the narrow, com-pressed lips, the pinched expression around the eyes. But deferential, genial, and possessing to a marked degree that unique ability to dissolve his own personality in the desires and attitudes of a superior. He had been a Massengale man since the days with Pershing, right after the war. Krisler had known him at Bailey. What was abundantly clear was that Massengale was going to be his own Chief of Staff.

He looked hard at the map. He didn't like the assault plan: it was too complicated, too chancy. That secondary landing in Dalomo Bay—what was the sense in it? Amphibious landings were risky enough, desperate enough as it was, without compounding the perils with *two* of them, sixty-five miles apart by water. Where in Christ's name was Massengale getting all the AK's and landing craft from? He glanced suddenly at Farnham, but the Admiral was listening—or pretending to listen—to Ryetower, the fastidious cast of his face intensified by the arch of his eyebrows and the long, white lids. The whole deal was needlessly elabo-rate. The main landing at Babuyan astride the Kalahe River was good enough, or bad enough—there was room for two divisions to come in abreast there: the Double Five on the left, Swanny's crowd on the right. Secure the beachhead, drive in to Ilig and Umatoc and cut the road, and then pass Bannerman's green division through them for the assault on the airstrip, with Swanny throwing a block on the right flank toward Kalao. What was the purpose of all this seaborne Cannae envelopment talk? What did Massengale think—it was all going to be smooth, grassy plains with paved roads and lordly hills studded with historic old castles for comfortable OPs?

The air cover hassle had apparently been settled for the time being: Massengale was going to hit CINCPAC for three additional days' naval support, and Tug had agreed to leave four carriers in the area until D plus 7, contingent on Kincaid's approval. Burckhardt, Massengale's G-1, a powerfully built man Krisler had served with at Gaillard, was giving a report on the replacement depot at Isle Désespoir and the projected establishment of a forward depot on Wokai. Fussing, fidgeting, Krisler watched them in his mind's eye—the kids in their shiny fatigues policing between the tents, grab-assing in the chowlines, huddled in rows at the movies, their eyes glittering under their chamberpot helmet liners, rapt and still; sitting on their cots engaged in the interminable, stultifying games of 21 and hearts and pinochle or writing the letters that always began: "Dear Folks: I can't tell you where I am right now, but it's hotter than it ever gets in Gaines Corners, and there's a whole forest of palm trees right outside my tent . . ."

This was an operation conceived by a man who had never knelt in water up to his waist, who had never peered wildly through the wet murk of jungle, straining to see until the eyeballs ached, or sweated a five-gallon expeditionary can of water up a mud-slick trail, wincing at the raucous cries of birds and praying it wasn't Nip snipers signaling to each other. The fact of the matter was that Sam should have had the Corps command when Thiemann left. Or even Swanny for that matter, he had time in grade on everyone. A DC in the area should move up. But MacArthur thought Sam was too young. Hell, yes: if you weren't seventy-seven and ossified from the knees up you were too young. Boy, Lightning Joe Collins had got out of the Theater in the nick of time—he already had a Corps in France, he'd probably roar all the way up to Army command by the time they got into Germany. If three-star staff types like Massengale wanted combat commands they ought to be willing to step down and take a bust to get a division.

Sure: and the moon should make extremely edible green cheese . . .

The breeze was fair and fresh in his face; the sea glittered prettily beyond the broad lacy fan of the reef. Unreal. This room, the maps and typed lists and papers, the contests of personality, the feuds and assertions of will were a dream. What was *real* was First Sergeant Jackson passing back and forth in front of the replacements, lean and minatory, saying: "—he's out to kill you, any place, any time, any way he can. Now you've been lally-gagging around back in the States and they've filled you up with a lot of bullshit about the Nip being stupid and half-blind and chicken all the way through. Well, I'm here to tell you he ain't stupid, he ain't half-blind, he ain't the least little bit chicken—and he's never heard word-one about the Geneva Convention. So get *that* thought out of your feeble minds right away. You're out here for one thing and one thing only: to starch the fucking slopehead bastard before he starches you . . ."

Massengale was looking at him; slumped in the high-backed narrawood chair, his hands on the carved arms. It seemed to be a smile—that is, the lips were turned faintly in that direction; but the amber eyes held no hint of amusement. A contained, enigmatic stare, like the gaze of a cat crouched in long grass. What was this all about? Maybe it was the cigarette Krisler was holding by its ends, between thumb and middle finger: the Corps Commander considered the act insubordinate, even though he hadn't lighted it. Maybe that was it. In spite of himself Krisler felt constrained to return the gaze—a moment of naked confrontation that fused with his anger at this ominously elaborate tactical plan, his resentment at these visiting firemen in their clean new khaki with their talk of beach gradients and phase lines and cover plans . . . It was stupid, he knew, making a duel out of this—it was worse than stupid, it was dangerous; but he could not break his glance. He couldn't.

Just then Burckhardt dropped a sheet of paper, or the breeze took it out of his hands—a tiny commotion that enabled him to look away. To his surprise his heart was pounding thickly and sweat had broken out under his arms. The cigarette had snapped in two; tobacco crumbs were strewn on the dark, oily, brilliantly patterned surface. He put the pieces in the shell-butt ashtray with slow industry. What the hell was the matter with him? He was afraid, then: afraid. Not because Massengale had three stars, he didn't care a hoot in a gale for that. It was something else, something entirely different—the kind of alarm a man might feel on glimpsing the long gray ridge of a tidal wave offshore, or a high wall swaying, about to fall on an unsuspecting crowd. It was a fear he had never felt before. The cold-blooded son of a bitch, he thought almost frantically, sweeping the tobacco crumbs off the table's edge into his palm, he's going to kill every last mother's son of us. If it fits in with his plans.

His ankle throbbed dully, deep in the bone; he thrust his leg across the floor, encountered one of Bryson's feet and withdrew it. He felt a little ashamed of himself—staring back like some truculent schoolboy. Sam had warned him about this when Massengale had first come out six weeks ago. "Ben, I know your nose is out of joint because of that go-round in Manila. I'm not wild with delight myself. But the object of the game is still the same. And Massengale is our CO. I hope you'll bear that in mind."

"Yes sir," he'd said promptly. You didn't horse around with Sam at such moments. But the trouble with Sam was he was just too straight. A mean son of a bitch was never a mean son of a bitch to Sam: he was always digging up extenuating circumstances. Not that he couldn't be tough enough when he had to be—at Moapora he'd relieved that stupid, arrogant bastard Caylor so fast he never knew what hit him; and he'd sent Hodl home after that fiasco on the beach at Wokai. But sometimes he didn't see what was there, before his eyes.

Actually his own apprehensions about Massengale had turned out to be groundless. The Corps Commander had congratulated him on his star, had shaken hands with him and smiled and said, "How's everything up front?" This was in reference to a breezy query he'd made, on his way up to the line at Komfane, of a dirty, exhausted corporal who was filling his canteens at a water cart. He'd spoken more to pass the time of day than anything else. The corporal had looked at him narrowly and made no reply. Three hours later he was jolting his painful way back on a stretcher, lavishly soaked in his own blood—and as luck would have it, overtook the same outfit that contained the weary corporal, whose eyes now brightened with interest. "Well, Colonel," he'd called, "—how's everything up front?" "Fluid," he'd murmured, and managed a grin, though it had almost killed him. "Plenty fluid . . ."

Yet Massengale's use of the tale—which had become a stock line around the Division long before his arrival—had irritated him: he felt Massengale had appropriated it unfairly, for his own devices. It shouldn't have been offered so casually by someone who hadn't in a sense earned the right to say it. At the time, though, he'd been relieved. Massengale had made no reference then or later to the night of the masked ball in Manila. "Why, of course," he'd said to Thiemann, "I served with Benjamin on Luzon. In happier days." He had wondered if Massengale might even have put it behind him—but now, watching a little covertly those close-set amber eyes, he knew this wasn't so . . .

Burckhardt had finished; they were discussing the operation now. He came alert instantly.

"What's the road like," Swanson was saying, "from Dalomo to Fotgon?"

"Surfaced with about four inches of cascao, General," Fowler answered.

"All the way?"

"No—only as far as Menangas. From that point it's a simple country road."

Swanny looked at him. "You mean a buffalo trail. Unsurfaced."

"Yes, that's correct, General."

Krisler saw Swanson's eyes move southwest along the meandering red line that led to the airstrip, and rest on the heavily grease-penciled ovoid rectangle that symbolized a heavy enemy concentration below the airfield, astride the junction. "The old highway from Reina Blanca was paved, wasn't it?"

"Yes, it reaches to within four or five miles of Menangas."

"I wonder if the Japs have done anything more on it. They usually don't."

"There are no reports of any work on that highway, General."

"I see." Swanson's eyes moved over the map again. "Well, we'll just have to do the best we can with it."

Sam spoke for the first time that morning. "Yes, you'll have to make the time, Swanny. My crowd will have the rough going."

Slimy end of the stick, Krisler thought. The price of excellence. Ours but to crucify. He looked at Massengale, but the Corps Commander's face was unreadable; he was watching Sam, who was studying the mimeographed G-2 estimates on the Japanese troop dispositions.

Slowly Damon raised his head. "General . . ."

"What is it, Samuel?"

"You said that General Bannerman's division is to be held in Corps floating reserve."

"That's correct."

Sam paused a moment. "I assume, then, that it will be in support of the main landing on Blue."

Massengale pursed his lips; his eyes were almost colorless. "I want to hold them here, off Facpi Point, so that they can move either way, depending on conditions at the time."

"But since the main landings are at Blue, and the bulk of the enemy concentrations are south of the airstrip, Blue will be the beachhead in need of reinforcement."

The two men looked at each other for a moment. It had become very quiet in the conference room. Then Massengale smiled. "Don't worry, Samuel. We'll anticipate developments. I didn't realize the illustrious Double Five required additional support."

"We will be bearing the brunt of the assault, General."

"Which was precisely why I chose your division. I have unbounded confidence in its audacity and valor."

It was curious. From where he sat Krisler could see Sam at less than full profile—yet for an instant something flickered across the Nebraskan's face; the merest shadow. Then it was gone and Sam said in a dry, remote tone: "I will inform the men, sir."

There was more talk then about feints, and a cover plan for Negros; and after that a report from Corps G-5, Colonel Carruthers, on the Filipino population and the Mendarez guerrilla force. By then it was nearly noon and Massengale said:

"Well, gentlemen, I think we've made a splendid start. I suggest we adjourn for lunch. A pause will give the doubting Thomases a chance to resolve their doubts, and the implementers occasion to implement.—Spencer," he said to Murtaugh, who blinked at him again, "you'll check with Admiral Kincaid at your earliest convenience?"

"Yes I will, General."

"Good, then. Good morning, gentlemen."

Hollingford, Sam's driver, was waiting for them in the jeep. Krisler ducked in and Sam followed him, saying curtly, "Division mess."

"Yes, sir."

They moved away from the grand white building with its screened verandah: and their eyes met.

"What do you think, Benjy?"

"I don't like it. It—doesn't jell, Sam. First place, what's he want with a two-ring circus—isn't one landing enough? And then that business of the floating reserve—"

"Yes," Sam said with surprising vehemence. "That's it exactly. *Exactly . . .*"

Krisler was startled at this; was there even more to it that he hadn't seen? Sam's reaction was disconcerting; it turned him jocose.

"What the hell," he offered. "Ours but to flip and fry."

"*The son of a bitch.*"

Krisler turned, astonished, to see Sam glaring at him. Hollingford was staring straight ahead at the smooth, narrow ribbon of blacktop.

"You know what he wants, don't you?" Sam demanded, and his eyes bore a look of wrathful torment Krisler had never seen there before. "Don't you?"

"—Why no," Krisler answered after a moment. "Hell, no—beyond wanting to play Hannibal and Caesar and Napoleon all rolled into one . . ." Perplexity assailed him. "Why, what else is he after, Chief?"

"Figure it out for yourself." And Sam relapsed into sullen silence, staring woodenly ahead. Krisler knew better than to pursue the point: when Sam slipped—it was rare enough—into one of those morose silences, your only play was to let him strictly alone. Anyway, they had plenty to do now, with Palamangao—PALLADIUM! Jesus—a scant seven weeks away. They'd have to get the terrain tables set up, the scale models of Babuyan Beach, speed up the training schedules. Maybe they could run two assault exercises on Benapei before they had to pack up. They could use two of them.

Twice he rolled an eye over at Sam, but his expression hadn't changed. Old Sam, he thought with a rush of angry affection; old scrap-iron boondocker, old imperturbable. All the things we've been through: the riverbank at Moapora, and the tank assault on Wokai, and the ridge, and the dawn jump-off at Komfane. All the tight places. Old Sam—if they give you a bad time I'll boil them in oil and skin them alive. I will.

The jungle flowed by, dense and drowsy on either side of the new highway. Hollingford slowed, and ahead of them rose the gate, surmounted by a large, neatly lettered sign:

YOU ARE RECLINING ON THIS LUSH TROPICAL ISLE
COURTESY OF THE 55TH INFANTRY DIVISION
VICTORS OF MOAPORA—WOKAI—LOLOBITI—BENAPEI

Beside him Sam grunted, and gave a sad, wintry smile. On a tree trunk below the sign someone had written on a short plank in a loose, flowery hand:

But I'd one hell of a lot rather recline back in Sioux Falls.

29 Oct 44.   Went over to Petty Trianon yesterday to beard the lion in his fancy den. Am convinced beyond all doubt Pala assault plan is unnecessarily complicated and artful—and therefore unsound. Blue landings are sufficient: blast inland, cut highway, seize airstrip, seal off Tanag Penin if he wants to, block on right flank vs. Kalao, drive on north to Dalomo and ultimately Reina Blanca. Then push east to Kalao, secure the butts. Why all this split-second timing with 2ary landing, all this doubling of assault craft, LCIs, transports? burdening Tug with 2 unloading areas, 2 beachheads to furnish cover for? Hazards—and pressures—are not worth surprise which may or may not be achieved.

Massengale very affable, at ease. (He DOES seem supremely confident.) Ryetower there, made no move to leave, CM made no effort to shoo him along. Intentional? Was damned if I was going to ask to see him alone. Said I thought White landings weren't worth price of admission, urged him to reconsider. He gave me that hooded smile of his. "I believe we can cope with it adequately, Samuel. The tactical considerations alone dictate audacity." Old-Salt-at-Helm-Dept. Some rather desultory fencing and politesses, and finally I threw the meat on the floor.

"The reserve division, sir—it is definitely understood that it is to constitute my reserve on Blue." Ryetower scowling at me as though I'd been writing dirty words on the walls. Massengale got up and went over to the window to commune with himself. After a while: "Why do you ask?" "Because my G-2 has unequivocal reports that Murasse's division has moved into the area south of the strip, between Ilig and Fotgon, and that extensive work on fortifications is going on there." "Who's your G-2?" "Lt. Col. Feltner, sir. He's a very good man, very reliable. Aerial reconnaissance has checked out guerrilla reports." "Oh yes, the little fellow ..."

He came back and sat down. "You look daunted, Samuel. That isn't like you." His eyes measuring me—that look I remember from Luzon days. "Don't you have confidence in your command?" Refused to get sore at that. "Yes sir, great confidence. But I don't feel that any unit should be asked to accomplish a task beyond its capabilities." He looked down at his desk, fiddling with a key ring with a Phi Beta Kappa key on it. Odd: had never noticed it before. Maybe it's an honorary one he picked up during the Washington tour. Well, we all have our rituals, our lucky coins and mementoes. "I feel it's essential to the over-all success of the operation to keep things flexible, Samuel. If the enemy should take it into his head to make a determined stand at Dalomo, or the—the left flank of White, I want to be able to shift either way, as the situation develops. A mobile reserve is a pearl of great price, Samuel. If you are held up unduly on the Babuyan side, I want to be able to punch through from Dalomo. It's imperative that we secure that airstrip at the earliest possible moment."

Right then it hit me, all at once. *Left flank of White.* That little hesitation. And not mentioning the name. He intends to try to do both: Swanny can slug his way through to link up with me, and he will throw Porky's outfit in to swing north from Dalomo and take Reina Blanca. Of course. Hail the conquering hero. And I'm left there holding the bag, trying to press home an attack against two divisions and assorted independent units. Just peachy.

Felt very angry. Ryetower watching me with no expression at all. He knows, too. I said: "In that case, General, I feel I must insist upon tactical control of the Forty-ninth Division as part of my reserve." He went back in his chair. "Now look, Samuel—" "If not," I went on calmly, "in view of the intelligence reports on dispositions of enemy strength, I cannot accept the responsibility."

There it was. Dead silence. Ryetower staring at me in open-mouthed amazement. Even Massengale's eyes wide. Very long moment. I thought of the Double Five, all the kids and the old men, the afternoon at the cemetery at Moapora, the night at the river with everyone pushing and pulling me around like a helpless drunk, and the beach at Wokai and Sabotnak grinning at us and hollering, "Dig the frigging tank destroyer!—"

For a while I thought he was going to take me up on it, tell me to pack my bags and get on the boat. His face got very long and arch— what Joe Brand calls his Grand Sachem Look. All the blood seemed to have left it, even his lips. I could see that vein running bright blue up into his scalp under the widow's peak. Then all at once he laughed and got to his feet again. "Samuel, Samuel, what are you saying? One would think this was the meeting between Brutus and Cassius. [A similar thought had occurred to me, though not on quite so lit'r'y a level.] Let's not be at daggers drawn over this. PALLADIUM will furnish laurels enough for us all." I said, "I have very little interest in laurels, General." "An old war horse like you? Come on . . . I'll give you my word—if you're sufficiently pressed and call for the Forty-ninth you shall have it—is that what you want? Does that satisfy you?"

Felt foolish standing there, so grim and unbending in the face of such magnanimity. "Of course, General. I only felt—" "Now I don't want you to give it another thought. Of course you shall have it if circumstances warrant it. Surely you can't believe I would jeopardize the fate of the entire operation over such a matter . . . ?" "Of course not, sir. I didn't mean to imply anything like that." Ryetower glancing from CM to me like a baffled spectator at a tennis match. Why in hell should *he* look apprehensive? He'll be on the good ship *Fargo* sipping ice cream sodas and listening to the radio reports.

He sat down again. Sweating in my shirt, jungle crud under my arm burning. Very close call. Some desultory talk about the preliminary bombardment. He's very pleased that CINCPAC granted 8 days of cover. Ben is right—he's got the Navy in his pocket, he must have buttered Ernie King to a turn during that long, lush Washington tour with OPD. Well: them as has gits, as old Mr. Verney used to say.

Casually he picked up a handsome little model of a native banca sitting on his desk. "A gift from the headman at Walewa Village. Lovely thing, isn't it?" His fingers gliding along the oily dark wood of the hull. "I thought I might send it to the President. For his ship model collection." His eyes rising to mine. "Do you think he would like it?" Thought of the lakatois at the river, the tracers dancing on the black water, and Ben after the phone call with Dick. *All set for Operation Styx.* "I'm sure the President would appreciate it very much, General."

And then, without any preamble: "How long have you been out here,

Samuel? Since September of '42, isn't it?" "That's right, General."
"More than two years. That's a long time . . ." Musing, looking off
across that sweep of achingly vivid emerald and cerulean and indigo sea,
all ours now, with the mighty Jap garrison penned up in Rabaul, rusting like a plowshare in winter rain. Then, directly: "Do you think you
might need a rest?" Felt startled, off balance: his voice solicitous, but
there was more underneath it. That cool, flawless thing. Maybe he was
angry (in *his* way) after the horn locking of a few moments before. Or
testing me, perhaps. Loyalty from the bottom up. Sure: but how about
from the top down?

"Not at all, General, I feel fine—I've had a good long spell of rest and
relaxation since Benapei. Nate Weintraub gave me a clean bill a month
ago." Musing again, staring into space, biting on that pacifier of a jade
cigarette holder. "I worry about some of you Thermopylae people—out
here in the dark days when the clock was ticking so fast and no time to
do it all . . ." Ryetower's face infantile in admiration. Pearls of wisdom
from on high. Well, maybe that's too hard on him, maybe he means
it—some of it, anyway. Does he? Raising his eyes to mine. "Would a
week down in Brisbane be any help?" "No, sir, I don't think so. And
there's so much to do right now." Sure, a week of fun and games at
Lennon's—and wake up to find I'd been relieved. No thank you. Still
could not read his eyes. They are impossible! So light, with those tiny
points in the pupils, so curiously without depth or shine. That's it—they
don't shine any. "I'd fly you home for a spell if there was time for it."
Chewing on the jade holder. He thinks I've had it: war-weary, losing
my grip. Felt suddenly afraid: thin cold fear in my guts, like the start of
a chill. Nothing like the sensation of a moment before, when I called
his bluff on the 49th. Is he really contemplating relieving me—just like
that? He wants me out of the theater, clearly. Ben and me both. The
hoodlums, the radicals. The bad soldiers. "I really do wish you could get
home, even for a few days. It could be important in so many ways."

No: he is not going to relieve me. Not yet, anyway. He needs me too
much for Pala. The Division would go up like a rocket if he sacked me
now, and he knows it. They'd fight for Ben, all right—but Ben's a worse
headache than I am. Ryetower couldn't get them out of their sacks, and
neither could Burckhardt; and he knows that, too. Maybe after Pala is
over. Of course there'll still be Formosa, or China, and then the home
islands. He'll wait to see how we carry off the sacred PALLADIUM
from lofty Ilium.

But what the hell did he mean by that? *In so many ways.* Has he
found out about Joyce? is that some sort of threat? Ryetower would
have his own ways of finding out. The hell with him: the hell with all of
them.

"Have you heard from your father-in-law, Samuel?" "Not for some
weeks, General—not since he went ashore in France." "I see." That
solicitous, feline gaze. He knows something. About Dad, or Tommy.

Something or other. That old queasy feeling. That's the hell of service life—everybody knows all about it but you. That discreet murmur over highball glasses or porcelain mugs or canteen cups; the covert, distressed glance. "Suppose you heard about . . ." The Club of Noble Martyrs. Tommy's phrase. Can see her lip curling, that white flash in her eyes right now, here, clear as day.

But it's more than that: it's as though he knows about Tommy—really knows something. Knows and won't tell me. Power-and-Pleasure Department. God, it's easy to hate people sometimes. Well: he'll never tell me—and maybe it's better that way.

Great naval victory up north. Three-pronged Jap attack beaten off. Near disaster, apparently: Halsey fell for decoy, went tearing off after Ozawa's Northern Force and left beachhead wide open with Sprague holding satchel. There seems to be one hell of a lot of riding off into the wild blue yonder in this war. But then, when Kurita had cleared San Bernardino Strait and rounded Samar, a scant 2 hours from Leyte and the amphibious shipping, right when he had it all in his hand—he broke off and headed west again. Why? Fooled by the jeep carriers? communications break down? lose his nerve? Opportunity once forsaken is opportunity lost forever: Dad's line after Soissons. Halsey finally turned back in a panic, but too late to do any good in either direction. Well: all's well that ends well. I guess. (Tell that to the poor bastards on the jeeps and the tin cans.) Jap losses 4 carriers, 3 BBs, 10 cruisers, 11 destroyers 200-odd planes. They've lost the war right there—their fleet as a fighting arm has ceased to exist. Why don't they quit?

But they won't. Just the way Germany won't. Why be surprised at that? We wouldn't either. Not fashionable anymore. To the bitter end. So be it.

Jimmy Hoyt's injury very upsetting. Everybody drives too fast around this rock. All of them, they think it's a sign of testicular prowess to burn up the track. They're not proving a God damn thing except that their bodies are softer than drop-forged steel. By Christ, I'm going to crack down, fine the hell out of them. What Lucian did in Sicily: 50 bucks per infraction. Bad omen, all the same. Now who'll take over my beloved 477th? I could move Ray Feltner over, they all know him and like him, but then what'll I do for a G-2? Bowcher's what they need, rock 'em and sock 'em, but he's had no combat experience over company level, he shouldn't try to jump to a regiment. Put too many noses out of joint. See how he does with 3rd Bn this time out. Guess it'll have to be Johnny Ross. Check with Ben, he's had the outfit more recently, he may have some ideas.

How I railed for years at the old fogey brass and the way they came down on "you young officers"—and our foibles and inadequacies. Now I'm one of the old fogey brass. The way it OUGHT to be is, I ought to have Regiment with Ben as my exec. As at Moapora. Then I'd be out from under all this paper-passing and walla-walla and cross-purposes. But then of course I wouldn't have 2 stars AND a command car AND a pyramidal tent of my ownest own—and think how sad I'd feel not to have all THAT crap.

Great mail call today. Finally heard from Dad: furious at Montgomery over foul-up at Falaise, terrific chance missed not breaching Siegfried Line while Germans were reeling and joint was undefended. Still pleading for a field command, without success. At least he made it back to France again.

Funny lovely old letter from Peggy, saying her mother is furious with *her* for quitting school to take that farm job. Why? If that's what she wants to do. There's too much of everyone telling everyone else how to run his life these days. Felt oddly pleased. Back to the soil in one generation. I'd like some of that, right now: moving along the rows, shucking corn, ripping back and down, the lemon cob bursting out of its hairy pale green husk like some savage little birth; or working up a fallen oak, the saw pouring back and forth in its thin, rhythmic sing-song and the sawdust spurting red on my left boot with every lunge; or walking over the stripped fields, just about time now, the stubble crackling underfoot like glass, frosty in furry blue webs in the morning sun. Dear Diary. I'm homesick. And tired.

No word from Tommy.

I have such a black feeling about this op. Can't shake it. He's trying just too damn much. Audacity, downright gambling, sure—but in the right place, for the right reasons. We're out of the rainy season anyway, the island is big. So why all the fancy footwork?

But I suppose it'll look particularly good in an after-action report to GHQ SWPA, and Washington . . .

He hates my guts. There it is. He hates my very guts, and I despise him and fear him. Not HIM actually—more what he will do, what he is capable of: like those visitations of the gods as mortals in Homer. There is something terrible inside him, in his soul. He talks about the big picture and command problems and knowledge of terrain but all that has nothing to do with it—it's this other thing that slips along just under the surface.

I keep coming back to that moment in the wrecked courtyard near St. Durance. He doesn't feel—he doesn't LOVE MAN. Yes. Old homo mensura, with his prehensile claws and splayed feet, with his nobility and greed and hope and vanity and wonder, his immense possibilities. People. The guy bent over at the sink trying to work the sludge out of his knuckles with solvent, and his wife at the stove with her hair in curlers, shushing the kids over the booming racket of the radio. Her face catches the light in a certain way, or that tender, dreamy look comes over it as she watches the baby, and the guy at the sink straightens and moves up behind her and steals a kiss, and she laughs, fussing a little because he's still wet and soapy—and then turns and hugs him in the middle of the kitchen floor, with the kids squabbling over the toys and the radio yammering away . . . All the men and girls with their dreams and derelictions, their quarrels and reconciliations, wrenched away from those intimate things now, those naked things, snatched up and flung harshly into jungles, mountains, burning desert sands for the preservation of this way of life we believe in so passionately—and which has so many glorious things about it that the simple contemplation of it, late on a hot, still night like this one, between the jungle and the sea, 10,000 miles from home, can move you almost to tears . . . . Only it's not all glorious, it's not nearly all it could be; and after all the anguish and losses the guy at the sink is going to want some changes made. And by God, they had damn well better be made, too.

But Massengale doesn't see any of this. He can't love that guy at the sink, trying to work the grease out of his knuckles. And because he can't love him he himself is only half a man.

And one more thought at this late, dark, heavy hour: if I despise him and am afraid of him, how much of a man am I?

Sergeant Brand turned from the tent entrance and said: "Sir—Generals Massengale and Ryetower." His expression was perfectly impassive but his jet black eyes were glinting, and Feltner thought: Here comes trouble. The gods are loose again.

"Thank you, Joe," Damon answered; his face had stiffened. Feltner got to his feet and picked up the sheaf of reports, but the General said casually, "No—why don't you stick around, Ray? We may have to refer to some of the stuff you've got there."

"Very good, sir," he answered. But it wasn't very good at all: it would be a lot nicer to be back in his tent, or down at the beach. Or back on Lolo, or Désespoir, or Timbuktu. There was the clatter of a jeep engine outside, then it stopped abruptly. A brief premonitory silence ensued, and then Massengale stepped into the operations tent, followed by his Chief of Staff. He was wearing neatly pressed khaki and a garrison cap with the grommet removed from the brim, and paratrooper's boots that still held a high polish; he wore no sidearm, though Ryetower was carrying a .38 in a shoulder holster.

Feltner, Pritchard and Brand all came to attention and Damon rose and came forward saying, "Good morning, General. Lyal."

"At ease, gentlemen," Massengale said. "At ease, everyone. As you were. This is no time to stand on ceremony . . ." He peered back irritably through the tent entrance and Feltner thought, No, it certainly is not—but you'd have blown your stack if we *hadn't* all popped to in your august presence.

"Your security seems lax to me, Samuel." Massengale was still looking out of the entrance, frowning. "Haven't you a security guard around your headquarters here?"

"Yes, I do, sir. But I reduced it substantially yesterday."

Massengale turned. "Why is that?"

"Because they were needed up on the line."

The Corps Commander made no rejoinder to this. He walked up to the situation map, which was tacked to a drawing board mounted on a kind of easel. In his right hand he held a curious object, neither a swagger stick nor a wand, which he kept running back and forth through his fingers. Feltner finally, suddenly identified it as a large Japanese fan, a very ornate one with an ivory handle and extremely narrow rods. Massengale had picked it up in Dalomo, or more likely someone had given it to him, and Feltner found his eyes kept going back to it. Unhappily he shifted his feet.

Massengale was moving the tip of the fan over the troop dispositions, his eyes narrowed; the thin, almost pretty lips were pressed tight, a muscle in the cheek Feltner could see flexed repeatedly. He was not sweating—now that Feltner thought of it, he had never seen Massengale perspire, no matter how hot it got—but his features looked sharper, more feral and intent, as though sanded down by the abrasions and tensions of the past two weeks. At the right flank, where the Third Battalion of the 477th was positioned, the fan stopped, and tapped the acetate briskly twice. Damon, standing beside his superior officer, said nothing. Feltner encountered Pritchard's eyes, then Brand's; the orderly, like the rest of them, was still standing, though he had relaxed, and that look was back in his face—an intimation of angry, defiant amusement. Or was it contempt? Feltner had become fond of Brand after the Wokai beachhead and that incredible exploit against the tanks, for which Damon had got him the DSC: Brand had entered that small, select fraternity who had fought with Sad Sam closely, intimately, guarded his life from peril. And he'd liked the Indian's morose sarcasm, the fiery independence of manner, barely controlled. Now, constrained by Massengale's presence, Feltner found himself watching the orderly resentfully. What the hell—it was all right for the EM, they had more room for defiance, they could sit around and bitch and spin their interminable rumors and legends: they weren't placed so closely to the sun's scorching rays—

"You appear to have lost momentum, Samuel," the Corps Commander observed crisply.

"We're slowed down, yes."

"And after such scintillating successes on the first two days . . ."

"The Jap has changed his tactics, sir," Damon answered. "He's decided to relinquish the shore positions in order to hold more strongly farther back—and work over the beachhead with artillery."

As if in corroboration of this analysis the thin, dry whistling arched overhead, ending in two sharp crashes in the beachhead area, followed almost instantly by the roar and rushing passage of retaliatory batteries.

"I'm aware that the beachhead was not defended," Massengale retorted irritably. "You mean to say you don't think it was as the result of air and sea bombardment?"

"No, I don't. If they had wanted to stay, they would have stayed."

"I don't agree with you."

Damon made no reply. The roar and crash of the artillery duel grew in the brief silence. Feltner gripped the sheaf of reports and stared at the clutter on the bulletin board on the other side of the tent wall, in front of the field desks. There had been virtually no resistance on the beaches: the assault elements had splashed ashore and hurried, incredulous and elated, past abandoned pillboxes and communicating trenches and pushed on into the jungle, the first low hills. Was it somehow going to be a pushover? were the Nips through? It was uncanny. The succeeding waves came on in, the perimeter swelled rapidly, the supply parties landed and began to form their unloading lines . . . and then, with no warning at all, there came the murderous whipcrack of high-velocity 47s and 70s, drenching the beach in dirty smoke, smothering the shouts of alarm, the cries of the wounded and dying.

Two hours later the advance inland had run up against the old, terrible pattern of interlaced bunkers and sniper fire: a slow, bitter advance scored with the inevitable losses. The Old Man had called on all the tricks he'd learned in two years and four campaigns—carefully coordinated artillery barrages, short tank assaults with infantry in close support, flamethrower and BAR teams in tandem, feints and flanking movements—but the grease-penciled lines on the map crept with agonizing slowness toward the airfield. The 18th Division, which had had the same easy landing at Dalomo, had virtually ground to a halt six miles north of Menangas. By then it had become amply clear that the Corps G-2 estimates of enemy strength were wildly inaccurate: instead of 38,000 there were more than 55,000 Japanese on Palamangao, and they were tough, disciplined troops, ably led and determined to resist to the last man. Feltner, listening to the generals talking, watching their faces, felt worn down, exasperated by the oppressive cunning of the enemy, his stubborn hardihood and fanaticism, his swarming, illimitable profusion. It would never be over. Each island, each campaign—except for Moapora, nothing would ever be as awful as Moapora—was worse: more prolonged, more costly. And there were so terribly, bloody, aching many more to go . . .

"Samuel," Massengale was saying, "I'm not at all happy about our telephone conversation this morning."

"I realize that, General. I'm sorry."

"Frankly I'm chagrined at your attitude over an insignificant little pivoting movement like PYLON."

Damon compressed his lips. "Sir, I feel it is too hazardous at this time. To put the Regiment through a maneuver like that would expose its entire flank for the better part of a day." His voice was level, but tinged with entreaty. "I've just talked with a patrol leader who is convinced the Japanese are staging for a major attack on the axis Umatoc-Argíhan, possibly by tomorrow."

Massengale shrugged. "A spoiling attack, perhaps. They certainly won't commit themselves to an assault in force, with Swanson's people moving against their rear."

"But that's only one *part* of their rear. They have the mountains at their rear here, and the trail from Apremanay and Kalao, and plenty of room for maneuver on both sides of the mountains. A guerrilla report has two regiments moving up from Agusán."

"Filipinos," Massengale answered, and smiled. "Come now—how much credulity can you place in an emotional people like this, without training or education, who don't know an oxcart from a Rolls Royce?"

"They know a man with a rifle when they see him, General. They've been hiding out in the boondocks watching the Japanese for three long years."

There was the high, taut whistling, softer this time, and a detonation less than fifty yards away; then another. Everyone in the room stirred except Massengale, who was frowning at the map, the fan at his lips. If I get killed, Feltner thought in a quivering fury, if I get starched standing here like a dodo bird because that arrogant bastard has got to prove he's impervious to shellfire, I'll haunt him right into his grave . . .

"Let me pass Winnie through Mac's people, swing west toward the water and then break in on Menangas from the far side," Damon was saying eagerly. "I know we can open it up that way. We'll be looking down their throats from this J Ridge—they'll *have* to pull out, then."

"But that's heavy jungle, most of it—you can't move through that . . ."

"Yes, we can. The boys are good in jungle. And they'd far rather try that than this straight-ahead slogging."

"—But that's precisely why I'm asking you to execute PYLON," Massengale retorted irritably. "It's the perfect way to envelop the airstrip—swing east of Fotgon and we'll bag the lot. I don't know why I can't bring you to see this . . ."

"It's simply inviting trouble, General. Murasse is a resourceful and aggressive commander—he has already assembled forces here, above and below Umatoc, and here at Fogada. I don't believe he'll let us get away with it."

Massengale glanced at him sharply. "Murasse? What about Murasse?"

"He's a very experienced and competent officer. He distinguished himself as a regimental commander during the Yangtze Valley campaign in '38."

"How do you happen to know that? from your tour there?"

"No, General. My G-2, Colonel Feltner here, has assembled an excellent file on him."

He included Feltner with one hand, and the Corps Commander turned. "Oh yes. Feltner. Well—isn't that percipient of you." The amber eyes came to rest on him for a moment.

Only then did Feltner, striving for an expression that was neither servile nor hostile, notice that the Corps Commander was in a barely suppressed rage. His lips were almost white; a vein high on his forehead stood out in a fine blue ridge. Did the Old Man realize it? Probably— which accounted for his measured tones.

Massengale had turned back to the map again. Everyone was silent, waiting. God, how long was this stupid scene to prolong itself? Feltner was surprised to find he was rigid with tension, his legs trembling, the sweat slick on his face and neck. It was the moments: the interminable, burdensome moments such as this one, that dragged on and on, and burned their way into your very soul like molten lead. Over on the left, toward Fotgon, an automatic rifle uttered its dry, rolling bark, followed by the crack of a mortar shell—and, as though this had ignited some flammable substance, a brief, crackling eruption of firing. The silence in the headquarters tent grew.

"Why don't you wear khaki?" Massengale demanded with intense irritation.

Damon stared at him. His green fatigue jacket was soaked through across the back and at the waist, where he wore a web belt with a forty-five and two canteens and a medical pouch. "This will serve."

"You'd be immensely cooler, I can tell you that."

The Nebraskan shrugged, and nodded toward the line; he seemed perfectly at ease. "*They're* wearing them, out there . . ."

"You have different responsibilities. Vastly different."

Damon gave no answer to this. He looked a lifetime older than when Feltner had first seen him, in that rotted, sagging dugout at Moapora; but his eyes were still bright and steady. Listening to the tortuous, unequal struggle, Feltner felt a curious sadness. They were all changed, all of them. God, yes. And then some.

Massengale said: "Samuel, I have no hesitation in telling you that I want that pivoting movement to take place as ordered. It is the correct answer."

"I don't believe it is the correct answer, sir," Damon replied mildly. "But it's your decision."

"Thank you. It is indeed. You are dissatisfied with it, then?"

"Yes, I am. As I said this morning, I feel it entails too great a risk at this time, in terms of what might be gained."

"But I *must have that airstrip by tomorrow* . . ." Massengale took a deep breath. "Surely you realize the significance of Masavieng Airstrip for the Visayan campaign."

"The field has been neutralized for four days. And raids from Negros and Mindoro have been negligible."

"But for our use, *our use*, man! Can't you see the importance of land-based fighters for raids *against* Luzon, Mindoro, Negros?"

"Yes sir. But not at the risk of imperiling the beachhead and the operation."

Massengale stuck the fan under his arm and locked his fingers together. "All right. Let's imagine the worst. Suppose he does hit you in the flank, in force, times it perfectly. Can't you cope with that?"

"Certainly, General—by calling in two regiments of the Forty-ninth Division."

"For this? Oh come, now . . . You're not that badly positioned, are you? Where's your reserve?"

Damon tossed his head once. "Out there off Facpi. The battalions I've got in reserve are exhausted from nine days of continuous action." He paused, said: "I cannot guarantee that I can contain a major attack on my flank in the midst of a pivoting operation such as you propose."

He should leave now, Feltner decided. Right now: they weren't going to need him for any Intelligence data. He could get out of here. But he knew he would have to break in on them to excuse himself, and the circumstances did not encourage interruption in any form. His glance fell on Ryetower, who was listening to the exchange with a curiously intent, almost eager expression; and all at once—like a thunderclap—he realized what the presence of Ryetower, a brigadier general, meant at this conference. His heart began to beat in ponderous alarm.

At the same moment Massengale said tightly: "General Damon, are you taking it upon yourself to tell me how to run this Corps?"

"I am trying to advise you, sir. That is part of my duty."

"Is it . . . If your conscience precludes your conducting this operation, I trust you realize I am quite ready to relieve you and bring in someone else who *will* conduct it as it should be done!"

"General," Damon said, and his voice was flat and hard, "it is your privilege to relieve me whenever you want to do so."

Massengale's face gave a curious little tremor. Lowering his head he walked up to Damon with a slow, careful tread, at once delicate and full of menace; whipped the fan out from under his arm and tapped it gently against his knuckles. There was something trivial and yet oddly compelling in the gesture, like an actor who has forgotten his lines but has decided to hold his audience through sheer personal force. Finally he stopped tapping the fan; their eyes had met, not a foot apart.

"What's the trouble, Samuel?" he asked in a soft voice. "Are you afraid?"

There was absolute silence in the tent. In the far scan of his eye

Feltner saw Brand make a quick, impulsive movement, instantly checked; otherwise no one moved. Feltner could hear the blood washing against his ears; the two figures seemed to quiver in the dull ocher light under the canvas. Damon's face darkened slowly and steadily until it looked like old bronze.

"General," he said very quietly. "That's a rotten thing to say. It is untrue, and it is insulting." His eyes, which had never left Massengale's, were cold with contempt. "If you feel I cannot carry out your orders you are perfectly free to give the Division to anyone you please." He paused, and his glance flickered over to Ryetower with a kind of baleful amusement, went back to the Corps Commander. "If you order this movement I will execute it to the best of my ability. But I will tell you one thing—you won't find anybody in the Southwest Pacific Theater of War who can carry out orders he doesn't approve of as well as I can. And I think you know that, too."

A few seconds longer they stood in the center of the tent, their eyes locked on each other. Then without preamble Massengale turned away with a brief, airy gesture. "I imagine that is so," he said. There seemed to be no residual emotion in his voice—no anger or fear or gratification— and this absence seemed more fearsome to Feltner than all the threat and vituperation that had gone before. Massengale peered at the situation map still again—raised the fan and poked at the road junction beyond Fanegayan as though he wanted to punch a hole through overlay and map and drawing board, tent wall and jungle beyond. When he glanced at Damon again, Feltner was amazed to see that he was smiling. "I daresay you're right about that. Touché . . . Nevertheless, PYLON goes off as ordered."

"All right, General. If that's how you want it. But if I should be hit in the flank and find myself in trouble I am calling in elements of the Forty-ninth Division, as last agreed."

"Oh, let's not borrow trouble, Samuel . . ."

"I merely want that understood, sir."

Massengale gazed at him a last long moment, musing, tapping his lower lip with the geisha fan. "All right. But I can tell you right now you won't need it." Abruptly he turned. "Come along, Lyal."

He left the tent rapidly, followed by Ryetower; and a moment later the jeep motor roared. Feltner thought of a day in fifth grade when the superintendent of schools had come into the class and chosen him to write a motto on the blackboard. He still remembered the silence of the room behind his back, the dry, patronizing voice of the superintendent, the chafe of the chalk as it moved over the worn slate.

Bring me men to match my mountains.
Bring me men to match my plains,
Men with empires in their purpose,
And new eras in their brains . . .

He was surprised to find he was shaking with relief and rage and disgust.

"The filthy rotten son of a bitch!" he gasped; and at nearly the same instant Brand muttered, "No-good bastard . . ."

"That's enough of that," the General said. His eyes rested on them all severely, then glinted with angry mirth. "You can *think* it all you want to. But you can't say it out loud. I won't permit it in my command."

"That suits me," Feltner answered.

Brand was perfectly motionless. Pritchard looked scared and hollow, his eyes darting from one man to another.

"What's the matter, Harry," Damon asked him, "—did you figure you were on your way up to a line company?"

"No, sir," the aide said promptly, while Brand and Feltner grinned; then, because he felt himself the junior member of the firm, so to speak, the newcomer who had not carried the tattered standard at the Chief's side at Wokai and Moapora, he added hotly, "—but I'd made up my mind, if he relieved you I was going to tell him off! . . ."

Damon grinned at their laughter. "Well, it's a good thing you didn't." The shelling began again, down the line to the left. The Old Man stared out of the tent, his big shoulders sagging in the sweat-soaked green fabric.

"Jesus, you'd think a man—" He stopped, rubbed the side of his face with his hand, while they watched him in silence. "Well," he said briskly, "you all heard the gentleman. What is it General Krisler says? Ours but to pine and sigh."

"Yeah—ours but to college try," Brand said. "He's got a million of them. Ours but to shit and shy . . ."

Two more shells landed with a stunning crash at the far edge of the grove.

"I could see them, General," the pilot said. He was a slender, handsome boy with long silver-blond hair which he kept sweeping back with a quick, rather graceful movement of his cupped palm. "Just as plain as day. They were waving colored scarfs or—you know, rebozos or something; and pointing. They kept pointing north toward the old Spanish barracks, up the road toward Ritidian . . ."

"I see," Massengale said. "What about troop movements?"

The boy frowned. He was wearing the inevitable crash bracelet on his right wrist; his sleeves were tightly rolled high above the biceps, and his arms were covered with a soft golden down of hair. "Well, it's pretty hard to see much down there. Except on the highway. I was down to fifty, sixty feet a lot of the time. I got one glimpse of a small column—"

"What do you mean, a *small* column?" The pilot glanced at him in mild alarm, and Massengale realized his voice was sharper than he'd intended it to be. This was silly: it would only rattle the boy. "I mean, what would you estimate it to be, son?" he amended in a persuasive, fatherly tone. "Battalion strength, would you say? or greater?"

"Oh, no." The flier slapped his baseball cap against his knee. "Less. A company, maybe two. They were pretty disorganized, you see—all strung out, running around and scattering . . . It's awfully tough to get a clear picture through all that spinach."

"Of course it is."

"But this matter of the Filipinos, General," Fowler interjected. "It's my opinion they're trying to tell us the Japanese are pulling out, starting a general retreat toward the north."

"Yes. It's possible." Massengale asked the pilot a few more questions, listening to him with a semblance of complete calm. The heat was fierce; Fowler's face was brick red and streaming sweat from every pore. All the decent dwellings in Dalomo had been shelled to bits before the landing, and Ewing had set up the CP in the ruins of the old Del Monte office near the beach; but it was completely inadequate. Here on the east side of the island below the hills, blocked off from the life-giving trades, it was breathless and stifling. He would have to change his headquarters as soon as practicable, get out of this glaring furnace. His chest burned with prickly heat; he lifted the shirt and undershirt away from his skin with distaste.

Ryetower and Prengle came in and he nodded to them. After a few moments he got to his feet, and Fowler and the pilot rose. "Well, that's fine, son," he said. "I think that's all, then. I won't detain you any longer." He smiled and nodded in the overcourteous formality that he had made a hallmark of his and that had become known as the Massengale Manner. Then he put out his hand and said, "Good boy."

"Thank you, sir." The boy's awkwardness was touching; he turned to go, turned back. "I just thought you'd want to know about that, sir."

"I do. I do indeed. I'm always grateful for any information, no matter how trivial or irrelevant it may seem. Thank you, Lieutenant."

The pilot left and he went over to the map, which occupied the entire east wall of the room and where every landmark, every activity was recorded. He was conscious of Ryetower and Fowler in the room behind him, watching him with deference, waiting on his formulations, and the thought afforded him, even in the midst of his vast impatience, a certain pleasure. The very contemplation of a map always gave him great comfort. The world was erected on symbols: flags, wedding rings, mourning bands, stars and bars and evening gowns and automobiles. Those rectangles with their intersecting lines—symbolic of the crossed chest straps of the infantry—embodied companies and battalions of men moving through the jungle, pressing against the Japanese defenses guarding the airfield. All the vast complexity of war was represented: the patrols moving silently and then pausing, while the point knelt behind a tree, tapping his rifle stock, the sound like a gourd in the tense, damp stillness; the wire companies stringing communications wire along the trails, the 105 batteries lunging and recoiling in their sweaty, iron pavane around the guns, the engineers perched on their shuddering cats and graders, grinding out roads and clearings for supplies. All of it was here under his eye. At one word from him all these tens of thousands of toiling men would stop, and move again in some other manner . . .

God, it was hot. Heat—the very element itself—seemed to emanate from under his flesh, like some noxious and flammable gas. Not a breath of air stirred the huge acacia beyond the window. Sound swelled in the heat—the grating mutter of radio voices, the pulsing thud of the tele-type machines in the message center in the next room, struck him as abnormally loud and oppressive. Perhaps he'd made a mistake—perhaps he should have set up his Corps Headquarters over on the Babuyan side, with Damon. Swanson was malleable enough. All he had was radio contact with the Night Clerk; and he'd had no report from him in nearly two hours now.

He felt a quick thrust of anger, remembering the quarrel at Damon's quarters the day before. Unseemly. Unseemly and ineffective. Of course he could *command*—but that was no satisfaction, or at best a very minor one: the triumph lay in the ability to *convince*, to bring the doubtful or hostile nature under the sway of his own logic. And with Damon he'd failed, palpably: Damon was like that crab he'd tried to capture on the beach at Newport, when he was a child: no matter how he dodged and feinted, no matter what ruses he employed, there it was, facing him, fighting claws up and flaring—until at last in a flash of frustration and rage he'd picked up a stone and smashed it into a feebly groping. blue-and-yellow pulp—

He inserted a cigarette in the long jade holder and lighted it, keeping his back to the two staff officers, running his eyes absently over hills and streams and trails already familiar past cognition. They were behind schedule. The estimates of enemy strength had been way off base; apparently Ochikubo had concentrated many more of his people in that central area astride the airstrip and the highway junction than anyone had foreseen. If they didn't get a move on and nail that strip down within two days, Murtaugh would complain to Kincaid that he couldn't get away, and Kincaid would protest to MacArthur—and a few hours after that MacArthur would be calling *him*. Luzon was the baby, the cherished operation: whatever interfered with that, drew off power or support from that, would arouse the Supreme Commander's wrath.

He went over to his desk and picked up the phone and said: "Get me MANGO." There was the customary ear-splitting crackle and flurry of voices, and then Riemen came on, and after that Swanson's measured, rather sepulchral voice.

"Archibald? Massengale here. How are you progressing?"

"Quite well, General. Quite well. All things considered. MUSLIN just got in to Hasugbu Village."

"What about the ridge?"

"There's increasing resistance in the ridge area, General. The Nip is touchy as hell there. Evans has patrols out—"

"How about the bridge over the Lanoba? Is it still in?"

"I believe so, sir."

"We've got to get across there, you know. It's key. Keep pushing hard. What about Grossing's battalion—has he taken Hill 307?"

"I'm expecting it momentarily, sir. He sounded full of confidence this morning. I'll check on that right away if you'd like."

"Good. Keep pushing now, Archibald. Try swinging west of that bend in the Laguac." He rapidly gave the thrust line co-ordinates—he held them all in his mind with perfect clarity. "That alternate we talked about. Keep maximum pressure on the ridge."

"Yes, General, I will. The Jap's putting up a terrific fight for Noguete, we've had very heavy casualties—"

"I know. Keep thinking aggressively. Time is of the very essence. We *must* take that airdrome by tomorrow noon."

"Yes, sir. We're giving it everything we have."

Massengale replaced the phone in its jacket and leaning back in the swivel chair closed his eyes.

"Have they taken D Ridge, General?" Ryetower asked.

He shook his head. "Not as yet. Has there been anything from CUT-LASS?"

"Nothing since that first report at eleven hundred hours, sir."

"I see." He felt suddenly exasperated and depressed. The great map, with its neat, threadlike lines and symbols, mocked him. It was fraudulent, it didn't tell you what was really happening; and neither did anything else. You could tear around and shake up divisional and regimental commanders, oversee bridging and supply operations, exude confidence or offer reprimand; you could issue orders and even (rarely) knock heads together, or sit here in this hotbox and pick up reports and note the changes—but you couldn't really *know* what had happened. You couldn't be sure. Men lied to you: they told you what they thought was happening, like Ryetower, or—like Swanson—what they felt you wanted to hear. Out of fear or confusion or sycophancy or guilt or ambition they spun their false versions of that one adamantine *actuality* that was being acted out in the tangle of rain forest and cogon grass and ravine, and you sat and tried to weave this fanciful tangle into a smooth, comprehensible fabric you could work with . . .

He got up and began walking back and forth, dwelling on the pilot's report. What had they been signaling? Reina Blanca. That little jewel of a city on its high green plain, twenty-five miles away, like a barbaric white citadel, an exotic dream of a city. Before the war he had walked its teeming streets, marveling at the ferocious mélange of alien races—Moros and Sulus and Tagalogs and Bajaos and Samals and the proud Spanish faces, the girls with their fluttering ternos, the handsome park with its mosaic fountain and the birds dancing in the flame trees. It had repelled and attracted him, like everything in these impudently sensuous islands—the men with their short, muscular bodies, their laughter and singing, the women whose eyes rolled up at you so dark and mischievous. Children: they were children—willful, wayward, headlong, amusing and appealing as children always were. Once during the Garfield days Asunta had failed to come back to prepare an important dinner until it was nearly too late, and he'd upbraided her. "Oh but sir," she pleaded, "I was at mass, at Malate Church—a mass in memory of my mother." "*No*," he'd said angrily, and gripped her arm. "I am more important than mass. Do you understand?" "Oh sir—!" What a strange look she'd given him! And then Emily had walked up to him and said: "No. You are not more important, Courtney. You may be one day, but you are not right now." And she had smiled that simple, constrained Boston smile that had always enraged him, and turned away. To go back to her poppy and mandragora, her drowsy syrups of the world that had been for so many years her solace and escape.

Now—curiously, for there had been no catalytic episode he'd been able to find—she had changed. Her letters were full and informative, her thoughts ordered and vigorous. She had busied herself with USO work and enlisted men's clubs; she was—it was utterly amazing!—even speaking at war bond rallies, at which she'd become apparently very adept: he'd heard enthusiastic reports from Uncle Schuyler and officers still with OPD. It was maddening: why couldn't she have acted this way years ago, when it would have helped him professionally? Well, one ought to be grateful for small favors as well as large ones—she was beyond question a credit to him now, keeping his name before the public eye, balancing the periodic communiqués in which he was now beginning to figure prominently . . . and yet there was something upsetting about this—as though it was his *absence* that had freed her from the drug; and—nearly as disconcerting—that she had managed this renascence without his help, almost in defiance of it. She seemed even to have effected a better relationship with Jinny, who was living in New York City with two other girls, and whose letters, infrequent and brief, gave evidence of a mounting wildness and rebellion, a serious loss of control—

"Lyal," he said suddenly.

"Yes, sir?" Ryetower was gazing at him with his chubby, round face and large blue eyes: an infantile expectancy, as though hoping for a bottle. A perfectly prosaic, pedestrian mind, incapable of creative impulsion; but an extraordinary memory, and a workhorse. And utterly loyal, which was the paramount thing.

"Lyal, what's the highway to Reina Blanca like?"

The Chief of Staff pursed his lips. "Excellent, General. Well surfaced, two lanes, good shoulders. The Japs kept it up pretty well. There may be a few bad spots—bomb craters and so on. It's a first-class road."

"Just over sixteen miles, isn't it?"

"That's right, sir. Sixteen-point-two."

"And the rest is crushed coral and limestone."

"Yes, sir."

"I wonder . . . I wonder if a battalion of armor could smash through at Apolete and roll on in and nail the place down."

"Reina Blanca itself? Yes sir, I imagine so . . ." Ryetower's baby blue eyes were troubled. Massengale knew what he was thinking: that column of armor, sitting there in the town while the Japanese reserve elements around the uncompleted airstrip and south of the city regrouped, and assaulted, and wiped them out. But he said nothing more. With a smile he looked away.

It would require a quick, violent blow. The Japanese would certainly blow up the town if they were given time: they were not in the habit of declaring cities open for any reason—least of all a city on high ground, flanked by a river, which would afford good defensive possibilities.

He looked out at the beach, where vehicles beetled over the churned-up ground, and antlike men struggled and gesticulated, their cries as faint as memory. Beyond that frantic activity lay the flat, dark water of the Sulu Sea, where the transports rode at anchor, disgorging supplies.

A quick, violent blow. To ride into a conquered city—no, more than that, a *liberated* city; gliding through the golden streets to the Plaza Grande, where the mosaic tiles gleamed and the populace surged and swayed, and screamed their thanks, pelting his command car with orchids and lilies and cadeña de amor in a petaled rain. The magic of it! Gerow and Barton had had all of Paris at their feet, the whole vast City of Light half-mad with rejoicing. Even Eisenhower and that stodgy methodical Bradley had got in on the festivities. Wayne Clark had had his short-lived triumph in the city of the Caesars, and later Florence . . .

MacArthur would never take Manila intact: the distances were too great, the approach down the valley from Lingayen Gulf too thorny, the Japanese too vindictive and demented . . . Which would leave Reina Blanca as the first, most important Philippine city to be freed. And the Islanders would never forget it, either—their gratitude would be boundless. Focus: it would give a focus to the whole campaign, a bejeweled little climax. No Pacific city had yet been taken intact. New Guinea and the Solomons had held nothing but wretched little nipa-hut villages, the Navy had smashed Garapan and Agaña beyond recognition, the Japanese had fired Tacloban. It would make headlines in the stateside papers. Why shouldn't it?—now that Patton and Hodges were stalled in the Vosges and the Italian Front was dead . . . ?

It would put the cork in the bottle.

"Sir?"

He started, smiled at Ryetower's expression of cherubic inquiry: he must have spoken out loud. He gave his attention to the map again. Of course he could mount another amphibious landing farther up the coast—

at Patnong, say. But it would take too long, and it would mean going back to the Navy to beg ships, and more air cover; and he didn't want that. It would cause talk of the kind that was exceedingly dangerous. He could imagine the conversations at CINCPAC, at the Hawaiian Department, back in Washington. "Who is it—Massengale? My God, he's got three divisions to play with, all the naval support in the theater, what more does he want? Can't he wind it up with what he's got?"

It seemed to be even hotter in the long, white-walled room. His head ached dully, and his chest burned with this hellish rash. Stolidly he smoked, his eyes narrowed. No. He had chosen this operation with all the cunning three years with Operations had given him, and he had chosen well. It had suited all his requirements: an island in the Philippines campaign, large enough for maneuver, involving two vetted divisions and a third he could for various reasons control as if it were his own. He was not going to risk criticism now. It was simply a matter of staying firmly on top of the situation, maintaining a flexible posture, and seizing such opportunities as arose. This was going to be the operation that would establish his reputation as a brilliant tactician, throw him into prominence as the leading corps commander for the Japanese home islands assaults. With luck he might even secure an Army command. With a little more than luck he might even—

"Radio from CUTLASS, General." Mincher, standing at his desk, with the decoded slip. He took hold of it and read it.

TIME: 1438 PYLON UNDERWAY AS ORDERED X LEADING ELEMENTS 2378 WEST FANEGAYAN X ASSAULT PLATOON STRENGTH REPULSED X CUTLASS

He wanted to laugh out loud. He smiled at Ryetower and handed him the radio, said: "What did I tell you? Two-three-seven-eight—that's more than half of the pivot, isn't it? that's almost two-thirds of the way . . ."

"Yes sir, it is."

"Didn't I tell you?" he demanded happily.

"Yes, you did, sir." Both Ryetower and Fowler were beaming at him.

"Damon's got himself all exercised over nothing at all. It'll run off like clockwork. The Orientals are too bewitched, bothered and bewildered to do anything about it." Two forty. In another four hours they'd be virtually in position, and ready to start the assault on the airstrip tomorrow, bright and early. They'd have it by noon. He was flooded with certainty, with vigor; all his depression had vanished.

He jumped to his feet. "Lyal," he said. "Contact Bannerman and order him to execute ROTUNDA at once. Get hold of Preston and tell him to commit his armor above Apolete at sixteen thirty hours. Issue attack order for Reina Blanca on the axis Pandada-Aguinaldo Highway-Limpoc. Tell Preston he must expect that the enemy will attempt to outflank to the east, and impress on him that his primary mission is to block the highway to the south and the Sabag Valley to the east. Inform

Bannerman that his cardinal mission is the capture of the city, intact—stress the fact that he will have the enemy both front and rear, and that the necessity for all-around defense is obvious. And advise him that I am moving the Five forty-first, less one battalion, to Noquete without delay. Now have you got all that?"

Ryetower was staring at him, his mouth ajar, eyes darting nervously. "You mean—that is, right away, General?"

"When did you think?" he snapped. "Easter morning?"

"Yes, sir. Of course."

"Get on it, now. We're going to wind it up with a flourish. I'm running over to MANGO to see about that bridge."

"Yes, sir."

Their eyes followed him as he strode across the room—a comical mixture of apprehension and awe. It struck him that there are only two kinds of men—the worried and the certain; and that all human intercourse was dominated by this division. It might be an intriguing thought to explore in his journal that evening, after the dust settled. "Come along, Edward," he said, and Prengle leaped to his feet and hurried over to him. Standing at the room's entrance watching Ryetower and Fowler, he laughed softly. "To horse, gentlemen," he said. "In war there is only one favorable moment; genius seizes it. Napoleon, Maxim XCV."

Still laughing softly he went down the steps to his waiting scout car.

It began subtly, like a spring rain: a distant popping, toylike and faint, the individual shots coming so fast they finally blended into a steady, crackling roar, punctuated by the sonorous thump of mortar shells. Damon raised his head, saw Feltner and Brand and the others listening too, spoons and canteens and ration tins frozen below their faces. A moment of waiting, paced by the groan of a weapons carrier coming up the trail from the beach and the tart Yankee intonations of Dickinson, who was inside the tent talking on the phone to Division Artillery.

"Where's that, Fotgon?" Spaulding, the G-3, said to nobody in particular.

"No." Brand tossed his head toward the north. "That's up there. Fanegayan."

It was: there wasn't the slightest doubt about it. A dry gust of breeze passed through the palms and they clattered fitfully and subsided. The headquarters area seemed all at once empty, without purpose.

"God damn *flies*," Pritchard said. He had his mess gear in his lap and was passing one hand rapidly over it and eating with the other. The flies were fierce: they came in blue-black swarms, weaving about heavy-bodied, as though already engorged, and settled on your food, crawling over it and one another until they looked like shreds of some furry, animate, glistening mat. And when you thought about where they'd probably been just before—

"They bother you, do they, Harry?" Spaulding asked the aide amiably.

"By God, they do, Colonel. I don't mind their *eating* my chow, I can put up with that, they're hungry right along with everybody else; it's when they lie in it and spit in it and wipe their God damn feet in it that gets me riled . . ."

Damon smiled at the low ritual laughter. He hated the flies more than almost anything else. Of all the trials and miseries of jungle warfare—rain and mosquitoes and malaria and jungle crud and heat—the flies with their black furry swarming were the worst. They seemed to presage some terrible day when man would have lost control, succumbed utterly to his propensity for violence and self-destruction; when all cities were razed, all farms in ruins, all fields gone back to swamp or scrub forest—and the insects alone, the multitudinous insects, had taken over.

He felt the prefatory clutch in his bowels, set down his canteen cup and wiped his hands and mouth with his red cotton handkerchief. This had been bothering him ever since the start of the operation: a swollen, painful pressure low in his belly right after eating, followed by cramps. He was conscious of sweat popping out on his neck and forearms. Brand was watching him; he winked without expression, got to his feet and went down the trail behind the tents. The firing in the direction of Fanegayan had continued steady—it had increased, if anything. A regular fire fight; no platoon probe this time, that was for sure.

He stepped inside the latrine. It was the one luxury of the headquarters bivouac he'd permitted, and it was modest enough: a green cheesecloth structure over a two-by-four frame and roofed with a tarpaulin. But the flies had got in here, too—they got in everywhere—and the air inside the cheesecloth was stifling. Captain Preveau of G-1 and Lieutenant McGovern from Operations were seated at the far end of one of the two planks. Their heads turned, they spoke in greeting.

"Hello, boys." He lowered his trousers and eased himself onto the rough two-inch plank—gasped softly as the hot streaming began. Runs again. Or was it something more than that? He'd have to go see Weintraub. The tart stench of chlorine stung his nostrils. Preveau and McGovern, who had been talking animatedly, had fallen silent with his entrance and he offered a few observations in an effort to put them at their ease. Preveau answered with curt deference. Rank. Well, he was damned if he would waste the time and energy of good men putting up separate latrines or messes until operations were over and the situation warranted such foolishness.

Rank. His bowels let go again with a burning rush that made him snort through his nose. What he needed was a good slug of paregoric. He thought of Lin Tso-han in the plain, worn blue tunic and cap, helping himself from the iron cauldron with the others. All men are brothers. Though he, Damon, had two stars and the power of life and death over fifteen thousand men, he was nonetheless constrained to crouch in the perennial simian squat, his buttocks whitely exposed and traversed by flies, and evacuate his bowels as readily as the meanest company messman or ammunition carrier. A vigorous incitement to humility—yet the rich and powerful never seemed to reflect on this fact unduly. What conclusions did Charles de Gaulle draw from his recurrent need to take a crap, as the saying went? or MacArthur, or Massengale?

"It's a snap," McGovern was saying in his breezy Irish voice. "Hell, they're all through, Sid. Campaign'll be over in three days, four at the outside."

"I don't know," Preveau answered somberly. "There's a million of 'em out there, and they're all dug in . . ."

"Oh, you sad-sack pessimist. I'm telling you, I'm going to be drinking Philippine beer and chasing quail through the streets of Reina Blanca a week from today."

Preveau chewed at his nails. "You remember you said the Germans were going to surrender by October first. Remember that?"

"Oh, that's different. The Krauts—they're smart. Real pros, always figuring the angles, doping out ways to beat you while you're sleeping. These dumb slopies don't know the time of day . . . Aren't we going to wrap it up quick, General? Three more days, right?"

He grinned at them tightly, wanting to strain and trying not to. What did you say? that McGovern was an irrepressible optimist, that Preveau was a hopeless pessimist? The gunfire around Fanegayan had mounted now, into a stuttering, pulsing uproar of sound. Whatever you said—the merest aside—tore through the Division with the speed of light and came racing back, rearing, hydra-headed, distended beyond all recognition, mocking you before you'd got your trap shut. The perils of overconfidence could be almost as great as those of gloom. There was a day he would have said, "Sure—we'll take 'em in a walk," there was a day he'd have muttered, "Don't make any mistake about it, we're a long way from wrapping this one up." Now he smiled with a confidence he did not feel, pulling up his trousers, and said: "To tell the truth, boys, I'm working under a handicap—I haven't read my George Fielding Eliot for today. When I have I'll know just how we'll do."

They laughed together easily, watching him. As he stepped out into the blaze of light, the cooler air, he saw Pritchard hurrying down the path toward him, his face strained. "General—"

Aware of the concern on his aide's face, knowing that Preveau and

McGovern could hear them, he shook his head once, sternly. Pritchard frowned but fell silent. Damon came up to him and said: "What is it?"

"It's General Krisler, sir. With the Four Seventy-seventh. They've been hit in force . . ."

He nodded, walking rapidly, sweating, his guts still griping rudely, along the trail, across the little clearing and into the CP. Stinson handed him the phone and he said, "CUTLASS."

"Sam, it's rough as a cob." Ben's voice, terse and flat over a background of dusty crackling, underlaid with hisses and booms. "Carefully planned assault preceded by mortar barrage. They've poured through Fletcher's company already."

"What strength?"

"Regiment at least, maybe more."

"Regiment! Ben, are you sure of that?"

"Christ Almighty yes, I'm sure . . ."

"How's Johnny taking it?"

"He's been hit, Sam. I've taken over. I thought I'd better—things are not in too good shape right now. Look, I'm falling back to the little ridge below the village, try to establish a line, L 86-32. Give me everything you can just beyond the ridge right away."

"—Have you got it in hand, Benjy?"

"I don't know. They're all over the place, they just keep right on coming. They're giving us a very rough time. You better—" There was a thump and then a wild crackling.

"*Ben?*"

"Yeah. You better plaster everything above Umatoc—that banana grove we talked about, the woods at the base of the hills. That's where they're staging."

"Right. Hold on. Hold on, now. I'll get up there with a fire brigade."

He hung up and looked at his hand. Timed it perfectly: just past maximum swing of the arc. Of course. Why shouldn't he? He said: "Dick, tell Fuglister to get his people up there without delay."

"Right, General."

"Vinnie," he said to Sergeant De Luca.

"Yes, sir."

"Get this off at once. Top priority. 'From CUTLASS to SPANNER. Execute BACKSTOP THREE immediately. Acknowledge.' End message. Got that?"

"Yes, sir."

"Now another one. Top priority. 'CUTLASS to CONDOR. PYLON counterattacked in at least regimental strength. Situation critical. Am ordering SPANNER ashore at once. Request air strikes north Umatoc 600–1000 yards. Extremely urgent.' End message."

For the next twenty minutes he busied himself with fire missions to artillery; he rushed the reserve battalion of the 484th to the bend in the Kalahe below Umatoc, alerted Frenchy Beaupré, who was on the 477th's left, and talked with Dickinson and Spaulding about trail net and supply problems as soon as Bannerman's people were ashore. There was another brief report from Jack Brozzi, the regiment's exec, screaming for artillery. Damon tried to calm him down, but without much success. The Double Seven was falling back from L Ridge, apparently, under increasing pressure. Damon fiddled with his penknife, cursing this lunatic system of radio communications. Which was better—to go up front and buck up Ben and the Regiment, or run down to the beach? He decided on the latter: Ben was steady enough, and he could communicate a sense of urgency more forcibly to Porky if he met him in person; and there would be problems as to how to deploy the 49th.

"Sir, message from SPANNER," De Luca said. He took the slip of paper from the radioman and read it.

CANNOT COMPLY X PREVIOUSLY ORDERED EXECUTE ROTUNDA X ADVANCE ELEMENTS DEBARKING DALOMO 1630 X SPANNER

A fly had settled on De Luca's sweaty cheek; its hind legs stroked briskly over its blued iridescent wings: left, then right, then both. Stroked grossly, over and over. The radioman's eyes were staring wide.

"—They're my reserve," he said savagely. "*Mine . . . !*" He put his lips together. Dickinson's bony, professorial face was full of alarm. This God damned double-beachhead foolishness. He should be in direct telephonic contact with Massengale and Swanson both, not this antediluvian radio mummery. And Bannerman wandering around now, out at sea, heading for Dalomo—

"Are they gone?" he heard himself saying importunately. "Really gone?"

"Who, General?"

"Mitch," he said to the Signals Officer. "Send someone down to the beach at once to check out SPANNER, see if he can spot them."

"Yes, sir."

"And Vinnie . . ."

"Yes, General?"

He said bitterly, "Send one more. Just one. Top priority. 'CUTLASS to CONDOR. Request immediate return of SPANNER to execute BACKSTOP as agreed—repeat—agreed. Blue Beachhead in jeopardy.' End message."

He felt actively sick. The realization that fifteen thousand men at his back no longer existed, that they were miles and miles away and preparing even now to debark where they were not needed at all; that he had nothing but two battalions in reserve, both of them already past weariness, with which to oppose twenty thousand Japanese—all this was like a blade driven deep in his belly. He could go chasing Porky in a PT boat, but it wouldn't do any good, it wouldn't bring the 49th back. It would only waste time. The son of a bitch: the stupid, power-drunk, one-way son of a bitch! Desperately he struggled for balance, a semblance of calm, beating down panic. He had to *think*—

When CROSSBOW came on again he picked up the phone with dread.

"Sam? Benjy. We've caught it big. They've thrown in the kitchen stove too, now." His voice was tense, high-pitched, almost incoherent. "The boys are wonderful. They're—I can't tell you all they've done. Jackson is—"

"Ben—"

"But we're in a bad way, Sam. A very bad way. Four hundred effectives."

"—*Four hundred . . . !*"

"Yes. If that. I'm out of communication with Fred. Can you lay everything on L 84. L 84."

"But—that's where you *are . . .*"

"They pushed us off the ridge. We're on the west side of the valley, those two little mounds we looked at, remember? Lay on every—" There was a commotion on the line, a ripping crackle and crash.

"Ben!" he shouted.

"Yeah. I'm here. Still. Sam, look, we can't hold 'em. They're coming in waves, any old way. It's a division. A division at least. Can you get us a drop? Thirty-caliber ammo. They're filtering, then rushing—flanking rushes. This is no banzai. Watch out for—" The crackling was so dense now Damon couldn't get a word.

"Ben," he shouted, "—look, you pull back, now! Pull out of there while you can . . ."

"No question of that, Dad. We're in all-around defense now. It's Little Big Horn time on Pala. You better get set, he's shooting his wad on this. Full commitment. Tell Frenchy he better—"

The line went dead. In place of the hisses and thumps and crackling, absolute stillness. Cut. They'd cut it. Or mortar fire had broken it, no way of knowing. He set the phone back in its jacket gently and got to his feet. The tent was quiet.

"Line gone?" Brand asked.

He nodded. "De Luca," he said, "get on CROSSBOW wave length and stay with it."

"Yes, sir."

It was very clear now, the burgeoning roar of battle, the hellish, orchestrated cacophony whose every effect he knew so well: sweeping nearer. A forest fire, bearing down, preparing to burn them all. He began to walk back and forth across the tent's entrance. What would Murasse do? He could consolidate his gain and make a holding action of it. He could swing west below Fotgon and try to roll up Frenchy and release pressure on the airstrip. He could run back west along the highway and hit Swanson in force and clear his own escape hatch to the north.

Or he could keep right on coming down the alley for the beachhead. Full commitment, Ben had said. Of course you could always be mistaken—in combat three hundred men could look like an army corps. But Ben wouldn't be wrong about that. And what was he going to say Frenchy had better do? refuse his flank? pull out? attack toward Fanegayan?

They were all watching him, a ring of faces—fearful, impatient, angry, confused. Waiting. The way he had waited in other days. Waiting for the word that would deliver them all from this new menace, deliver them from death and maiming. For him to act, quickly and correctly, in the face of onrushing catastrophe. Standing there, one hand gripped in the other, sweating, silent, swept with remorse and the sense of betrayal, half-stunned with the awful realization that a gaping hole half a mile wide existed where his beloved 477th had been only a few hours ago, a hole through which the Japanese could even now be pouring, that he had no patrols or communications net to warn him of the movements of what could be the better part of three enemy divisions, and no appreciable reserves to contain a major attack when it did fall upon him—standing at the entrance to the Operations tent thinking all this, he felt the terrible weight of absolute power and responsibility. He must do it—and he must be right the first time. There would not be another chance.

Which way would Murasse go?

He found himself staring at the G-2 tent where under the rolled flaps Dan Hanida was interrogating a prisoner. He was one of the few Japanese who had been captured, and he had been taken unconscious; a superior private from the 39th Division. Odd—he'd been wounded in almost exactly the same way Ben had on Lolobiti: a bullet had traveled the length of his arm. His closely cropped head was thrust forward, he was watching his interrogator with an almost myopic intensity. Hanida asked him something and he nodded and said, "Haee." Hanida spoke again and the prisoner looked back coldly and scowled, then burst into a little torrent of speech. Damon caught the phrase *yamato damashi*. Unconquerable, unreckoning will. Well, they had that to burn, all right. Dan smiled softly and spoke still again, and this time the Japanese stared at the intelligence officer blankly, in silence. Hanida handed him something to eat, perhaps a piece of tropical chocolate; the Japanese prisoner made a short, quick bow, seized the food almost fearfully and began to eat with desperate ardor, throwing it about in his mouth like a hound chewing.

Damon turned. Murasse would go for the beach. For the supplies stacked in tiers under the palms, the angular mountains of rations and ammunition and medical supplies. Cut off from these things for days, he would sacrifice anything to reach them. It was not sound tactics—what he *should* do was turn on Swanson full force, drive him back on Dalomo and withdraw toward Reina Blanca and the north with the mountains on his left flank. But the lure of the beachhead would be too great: hungry, harassed, desperate, he would not be able to resist it. Perhaps he had already given up hope of withdrawal, perhaps—as with Toyada on Wokai—it had never really entered his mind. Yamato damashi. If he could reach the beach he would shoot up the LSTs and smaller craft, burn what he could not use, and either run down into Tanag Peninsula or fall back into the parched and unprofitable ground toward Kalao. It would mean abandoning the airstrip, but he would risk that: they had no planes left anyway, and denying the Americans the use of the strip would count as nothing beside the possible destruction of the principal beachhead. It would also mean splitting their forces and abandoning Ochikubo's people at the airstrip to the nutcracker between Swanson and Frenchy, and that didn't make sense from a tactical standpoint. Would Murasse merely feint here and then drive back on Fotgon, into the hole left by Frenchy's sideslip right, and fall on Swanny's flank?

No. There were the transports: his people would have seen them rounding Facpi Point, heading north—he may even have got word of the landing at Dalomo Bay. There were Japanese dressed in Filipino clothing moving around everywhere. Murasse would know he was stripped of reserves, and he would feel his own avenue of withdrawal to Reina Blanca and North Point was about to be blocked.

He went back to his field chair and got his belt and helmet and field glasses, while their eyes followed him. "Bob," he said to Spaulding, "round them up."

"Sir?"

"Everybody. Communications people, QM, clerks, cooks and bakers. Strip all rear echelon outfits. We're going to need everybody—and I mean everybody. You have my authority to sweep it out." He moved over to the map. "We're going to set up a line here, at Umatoc, right above Grassy Hollow."

Little Feltner was looking at him in amazement. "But Chief, what about the Regiment—aren't we going up there?"

"Out of the question. We've got troubles of our own. Dick, tell Frenchy to break off his attack and push northeast on Fanegayan with everything he's got."

"Yes, sir."

"I'm going on up there and get set up. Dick, I want you to hold the fort. Set up a line back here at Ilig, on the high ground, just ahead of the bivouac area, blocking the trail."

"Right, General."

He looked around the room. Their faces expressed apprehension, uncertainty, disbelief: he was the nerveless, flint-hearted son of a bitch, leaving the Regiment to its fate. Well, that didn't matter. But this other thing did.

"They're going to try to come right through here," he said sternly. "Right down the trail. And we're going to stop them. No excuses, no holding back, understand? We're going to make them pay for every yard." They watched him—grave and troubled. He had to get them up for this. He smiled grimly at them. "I'll tell you one thing: if they *are* ever lucky enough to reach the beach, there won't be enough of them left to get up a ball game."

A rose-and-orange light that glowed softly under the canopy of trees; the tips of the cogon grass swayed weakly, rippling, and figures bent and straightened, hacking at the rich, moist earth. Up ahead a machine gun spoke its short, heavy piece. *Dod dod dod.* And from Babuyan shells climbed overhead in pulsing, dying-away freight-train cadences and exploded thunderously. Then the silence came back. Damon walked among the foxholes, now and then stopping to talk, thinking, It'll be dark soon; quite soon now. A swarthy man with a black growth of beard called, "What you say, Damon?" Rossini, he remembered. From Worcester, Massachusetts. A cook striking for mess sergeant. He smiled.

"All set, Rossini?"

"You bet your life."

"That's the pitch." Farther on, two men from recon setting up a light caliber thirty. Speer, a quartermaster officer talking to three signals men about grenades. The tropic day slipping toward dusk: the foliage looked lighter than the sky now, more lambent, as though the world had been turned neatly upside down. He moved along, checking gun positions, fields of fire. A boy was watching him. In the onrushing dusk his face, foreshortened, with its deep, large eyes, reminded him of Donny. A replacement; he didn't know his name.

"How you making out, son?"

"Okay, sir. I guess." The boy paused, glanced apprehensively at the adjoining foxholes. "I've never"—he paused again—"I've never been in combat before."

"Everybody's got to start sometime."

"I guess so."

"What's your name?"

"Norris, sir. Private, 1371408."

"Sure. You'll do all right." Damon knelt by his hole. "You'll do fine. Just keep squeezing them off when you get the word. Did you open a couple of flaps?"

"Flaps?"

"Sure. On your belt. So you can get at your clips quicker if you need them. Like this, see?"

"Oh. Yes. I see." The boy grinned shyly. "Gee, I never thought of that."

He patted him on the shoulder and moved along. It was like the night at Brigny. All over again. He was going along the line checking, reassuring, joking, half a world and a quarter of a century away, in the face of an attacking enemy. That had been his first battle. How curious to come back to this. There was nothing else to do now. His dispositions had been made. Frenchy was moving his gang over as fast as he could to plug some of the hole; all his reserves were committed; he had called for naval gunfire and air strikes, brought up ammunition and chow and strung a few strands of wire. If he had guessed wrong, there would be a disaster and the entire island campaign would be in deep jeopardy; if he had guessed correctly, a lot of these boys digging in and cleaning weapons around him in the deep, roseate light would be killed. And he had guessed correctly: he knew it. Now there was nothing to do but wait, and move around like this, to show some frightened GIs a two-star general wasn't too good to put his ass on the line with the rest of them.

"Hey, when are the Nips coming, General?" a fat, jovial company clerk named Heffinglarner called out in his soft Alabama drawl.

Damon peered ostentatiously at his watch. "They'll be on the seven forty-eight, I believe. If it's on time."

"By Judas, we'll derail the bastards . . ."

"You're telling me."

Abruptly, like the falling of a dusty mantle, it was deep twilight: the faces around him faded into pale blurs, flat and indistinguishable.

"You better get into your hole, General," someone said, "or find you a neon sign, one. Somebody's liable to mistake you for a Jap and shoot you square in the ass."

"Anybody shoots me in the ass will get reduced two grades," he told them solemnly.

This sent several of them into fits and another voice called: "What you going to do about me? I'm a buck-ass p-v-t as it stands . . ."

The silence was like a weight you tried to push to one side, only to find it had shifted with your effort—a gas-filled bag that swelled and compressed in eerie patterns. There was no moon. In the partial clearing beyond the perimeter—Pritchard could hear it now, unmistakably, in spite of the sporadic firing south of Fanegayan—was the rhythmic rustling of figures crawling through jungle. He glanced at Damon, but the General, who was standing up in the big Command Post hole beside Major Scholes, made no sound or sign. Pritchard brushed the mosquitoes from his face irritably; he could feel his heart beating. They were out there in that black wall. They were coming. At Lolobiti he had taken over a platoon that had lost its officer and noncoms and had handled it with some competence; but this was different. Until dark he had been running errands for the General, helping string wire along the riverbank on their left, organizing and deploying this Coxey's army, and then on the telephone, taking reports on the progress of elements of the 484th hurrying to plug the gap west of the Kalahe. But there had been no time to do anything right. That was the trouble with war—there was never enough time for what you had to do . . .

Beside him Brand murmured softly, "Staging, Chief."

"Not yet," the General answered. "Not for a little while."

Pritchard kept peering at Damon's face, though he could see nothing at all beyond the tall, blocklike form solid against the patterned murk of jungle. In a tight. They were in a tight, now. He'd been with the General long enough to know he was worried—under the free-and-easy manner there was a terse, tight-lipped constraint in Damon beyond anything he'd noticed before, even on Lolo. Several holes away someone was digging softly—short, jabbing strokes: probably cutting a shelf for grenades and spare clips.

Three men had come into the line just before dark, a corporal and two privates from Bowcher's battalion—had sprawled on the ground, sitting and lying in the apathetic, head-lolling attitudes of utter exhaustion. Two of them were wounded, and while the medics worked on them they answered the General's queries in brief, monosyllabic phrases. The first they knew was when knee mortars began dropping into them from the right and rear. Then the Nambus opened up and all of a sudden they were everywhere. Martin was killed. Ainoura was killed. They fell back, tried to set up a line, fell back again. By that time they'd been broken up into isolate clots of men, out of communication, out of ammo. Later they had slipped away, hunting for the outfit, anybody. But there had only been the dead.

The corporal, a thin, narrow-shouldered man with dark wavy hair, leaned back against a tree trunk. "I want to tell you boys," he muttered. "It was one hell of a shit storm up there."

Damon said, "Did you see Krisler? or Colonel Ross?"

The corporal shook his head wearily. "Breger said Krisler was killed. Mortar burst."

The Old Man's face barely moved. "Are you sure of that?"

"No, General. I ain't sure of anything at all. I ain't even sure I'm here."

"Well, *I* am," one of the privates, a short, blond boy named Budjany, said. "And by Jesus, I'm staying here."

"You want to stay with us?" Damon asked him. "In the line?"

"You're a fuckin-A," Budjany answered tightly. "They killed my bunky Tommy Speier, I been with him since basic. I saw him get it and there wasn't a thing I could do about it. *I* ain't through with them, I'll tell you that." He was holding his wounded arm close against his side, but his eyes in the fitful flashlight glow were black and hard. "Give me a couple bandoleers." He was out there now on the left, in charge of an anomalous detail of permanent KPs and clerks. The corporal, who had been hit in the back, had gone off down the trail toward—

"—Hey, you guys . . ."

The voice was high and tense, words hissed from the jungle depths before them. Pritchard had started violently. There was a rippling click of safeties pressed forward to the off position all over the perimeter.

"Hey, are you there?" the voice went on, thin with urgency. "You guys—?"

"Lorelei," someone called.

"Look, I don't know the God damn password—"

"Who are you?" Pritchard recognized First Sergeant Lattimer's voice in one of the forward holes.

"We're from Bowcher's battalion. There's five of us. Let us come in, will you?"

Sergeant Lattimer called back toward the CP hole, "How about a flare at eleven o'clock?" and Pritchard picked up a flare shell.

"Christ, no—no flares. There's Japs all around us. Look, we got a wounded guy with us. Just hold your fire . . ."

"Who are *you?*" Lattimer called softly.

"Rodriguez, Lou Rodriguez . . ." Then quickly, angrily: "What the hell difference does it make who I am? For Christ sake, let us come on in, now. We've had a rough time up there . . ."

"Okay," Lattimer answered. "Come ahead."

There was a hurried, stealthy rustling, and the empty ration cans and rifle clips on the strands of wire tinkled merrily, like distant off-key cowbells.

"Fire."

Pritchard turned in amazement. Damon had his hand on the shoulder of the machine gunner at the leading edge of the hole. "Open fire."

The gunner's helmet swung around. "What? But look, they're—"

Damon jabbed the gunner smartly in the neck. "Do as I *say!*"

The gun jumped, a blast of blue flame half a foot long leaped from the muzzle in a sudden, stunning roar, and tracers floated like eerie orange balls into the night. Pritchard heard the thunk of a flare shell hitting the bottom of the tube, as the General moved. He gazed front. The Old Man's cracked up, he thought with sudden horror, he's blown his top. Someone was screaming, "Hold your *fire*, you stupid bastards—!" Then the flare burst with a sharp crack, in a wild diffusion of light that made his eyeballs smart. He saw a flurry of commotion at the wire: two figures lay on the ground, another was holding his head, and a voice was screaming in Japanese—quick, explosive syllables that made no sense. Rifles were roaring now, two more were down, the last man flitted away, a wild, scarecrow wraith, into the sea of vines. Then the machine gun stopped, and the rifle fire fell away to a chorus of voices calling, "Cease firing! Cease firing . . ."

"Trick," the General was saying crisply. "Couldn't know Rodriguez has called himself Tico for years. Hates his first name."

"I see," Pritchard answered shakily. The suddenness of the incident, the utterly unforeseen turn of events, and now the return of silence and darkness, had left him jangled, half out of breath. Still, there was something that bothered him. "But if he used Rodriguez' name—and Major Bowcher's—"

"Yes. That's right." Damon's voice was completely without inflection.

The perimeter was bathed in quiet again. One of the Japanese was moaning softly. Pritchard stood there with the flare in his hand. Oh the bastards, he murmured, half-aloud. The rotten bastards—to pull a trick like that, take advantage of a man that way . . . Again he heard the thick, deliberate sibilance of men moving. They were coming forward again, in the filthy dark they loved so, the jungle was crawling with them. He felt his head and shoulders shiver once, uncontrollably. With the death of the flare all his vision had deserted him; he could see nothing but gray splotches drifting and sinking in a black field. He rubbed his eyes. The air was close and foul; the odor of earth and damp rot and offal sank into the base of his nose and lodged there. Mosquitoes kept bumping against his cheeks and forehead. By Christ, he wasn't going to be late with a flare next time, he'd have the place looking like Broadway, he'd keep a—

"Hello, Yankee Doodle."

The voice was feline, tremulous, as if poised on the edge of laughter; but tensed now for anything out there beyond the perimeter Pritchard remained calm, listening intently.

"Oh, boy. Now you're going to get it . . . You know that? Soldier-boy?" In the dense, close air the words sounded extra-human, as if a hideous, epicene statue had been given voice. It's not the same man, Pritchard thought quietly—not the same one who tried to impersonate Rodriguez; they've got two men who can speak English that well. They certainly have got it all over us in the matter of languages.

"Soldier-boy, you're going to die very soon. You know that? Oh yes. Very soon, now." But as the voice went on, taunting, mocking them, it seemed less frightening. "Not much fun, is it, Yankee Doodle? Sitting there waiting to die?"

"—You eat shit, Tojo!" someone shouted hoarsely on the left.

"Thank you, soldier-boy," the voice simpered. "Thank you so much."

"Keep the frigging change!"

"All right," Damon called mildly. "That's enough of that . . ."

"How about it?" Major Scholes said. "Work them over now?"

"No," the General answered. He might have been discussing a requisition to Corps for blankets or tentage. "They're not all there yet. This is just to get us to fire prematurely, show them where our automatic weapons are. Won't be long now." And leaning forward Pritchard felt he could hear a dense, feathery rustling along the whole line. He was quivering with impatience, with exasperation.

"Why don't we—"

There came a soaring, mounting shriek, grinding away into the jungle depths. Siren. He realized he had jumped, that even the General had started. It went on and on, rising and falling, piercing the last recesses of the brain, evoking memories of times back home with the cars pulling over and faces turning, and a night when the apartment house diagonally across from theirs had caught fire. People were standing in dressing gowns out on the sidewalk, gazing upward where firemen clung antlike to swaying ladders and here and there figures moved at the windows; flickering, gesticulating shadows.

"Wonder where in hell they got that?" Major Scholes was saying to the General.

"Siren for the fire brigade. Pulling everything in the book, aren't they?" Pritchard felt Damon's hand on his arm. "They're coming up now. Hear them?"

"I can't hear *anything* with that God damn thing going . . ." All the same, in spite of the siren's wail and the firing off to the west, he could hear the crunch and susurrus of many men making their way through brush. And now the siren itself descended to a craking growl, and subsided. The taunting, feline voice had stopped. This is why they make you wait, Pritchard thought; wait and hurry, wait and hurry—to get ready for a rotten, stupid, maddening wait like this . . .

"Mortars," the General said crisply. Major Scholes relayed the order, and from behind them came the muffled pop-pop-pop and then in the jungle out ahead the crash of the shells exploding. Now screams and hoarse cries were audible.

"Good," Pritchard heard himself say. "Take it, you bastards. Take it!" He felt a taut, quivering rage against every Japanese who ever lived.

There was a torch flaring, a blinding blue-white blaze of light, and he flinched, saw the clean red wires of tracers; they seemed to float straight at him and then curve up and away, gaining speed, burning their way through the night overhead. Now another one was firing in long, shuttling bursts. Trying for the gun got the five at the wire, he thought. He averted his head now, peering out sideways at the flickering glare.

A hand tapped him on the arm and he looked up. "Flares," Damon was calling to him. "Continuous."

He wheeled obediently and dropped the projectile into the tube, swung away from the painful air-compressed *whunk!* of the propellant, reached out and picked up his carbine. The General, his hands cupped to his mouth, swung his head from left to right and roared, "Commence firing! Commence fi—"

His voice was drowned in the crash of gunfire. The night was laced in a crazy-quilt of tracers and the white darts of muzzle blasts: a terrible carnival, close at hand. Then with a flat crack the flare burst, the area was shot with light—and there they were, coming silently and steadily, their faces smooth and dark and glistening as if part of their helmets, their eyes incredibly long, theatrical slits in the inverted dawn of the flare. Coming in clots and clumps against the wire, hurling their bodies at it or slashing at it feverishly, their bayonets flickering, and here and there the short, fiery red arcs of thrown grenades. They were everywhere. For a wild, interminable instant Pritchard felt utterly paralyzed, defenseless, constrained to crouch helplessly in a hole and watch this brute, stubborn force sweep over them, destroy them all. It was too much, too much. Then the scene broke into a thousand crazy zebra stripes and colophons as the flare—Jesus the flare!—swaying, reached the trees; in an agony of dread he dropped in another shell, snatched up still another.

"Not too fast, Harry," Damon was saying, his face very close. "Pace them out, now."

"Right." He turned and raised his carbine. The machine gun beside him clattered like a riveting machine drilling at an anvil, the Japanese danced and scuttled and came on with that terrible menacing intention, and the concerted fire from the perimeter brought them down. It was very hard to think. Think clearly in all this bedlam of screams and roars and swaying underwater glare. But he was free now: he was able to move. He raised his carbine, held it centered on a huge man in a nearly black uniform who had just snapped his fist against his helmet. Grenade. He'd hit him, he was certain he'd hit him but the big Imperial Marine armed another grenade with that quick flexing of his arm, the blow against his helmet, and threw again. Then all at once he fell as if caught on a trip wire and went down out of sight. Pritchard remembered the flare this time, got off another and went on firing, emptied the magazine. The Japanese had reached the first line of holes and were shooting into some of them, tossing grenades, but he felt no fear now, only an anger dry as dust and a tight, vengeful exhilaration, a sense of being mildly out of wind. Two men were locked together like kids wrestling in a playground, swaying and scuffling, and an officer in a tightly fitting tunic with a burnished helmet and a sword held levelly in his two hands was racing up to them. He fired, saw the officer jerk from the impact, right himself and continue past the two struggling figures, raising the sword above his head, a fearfully quick gesture; then tracers slanted into his chest and he sank gently to his knees, his teeth flashing in an anguished grimace, like a man mired in quicksand. Pritchard swung left to another group of four or five who were driving their bayonets down at a hole. A hand gripped his shoulder, hard. Damon, pointing behind him and to their right, where several men were running through the splotched shadows.

"Stop them! Bring them back!"

He understood instantly and nodded. Taking off. That was bad. Thing like that could turn into a rout, mustn't happen. He leaped out of the hole, catching in the corner of his eye Brand feeding a belt into the machine gun, Scholes huddled in the forward edge of the pit, both hands cupped over the phone. Even as he got to his feet he could see another man scuttling off into the shadows.

"You!" he yelled. "Come back here!" It was curious: he'd never been much as a runner—he'd been rather slow of foot, preferring sports where his solid bulk could have free play, such as wrestling and the hammer throw, at which he'd excelled. But now he overtook the stragglers as though they were chained to the trees. He snatched at a man's collar and stopped him, caught another by the belt, and cried: "Where do you think *you're* going?"

The second man's eyes rolled wildly. "—We can't stay here, can't *stay—!*"

"Of course you can. You can and you will!"

"No, no—we've got to pull back, I heard them say—"

"You heard nothing of the kind! You were taking off. Now you cut that out, all of you . . ." They stood watching him, agitated and indecisive; he recognized one of them as a drafting clerk in G-2. "And you a sergeant!" he said hotly. The inanity, the sheer banality of his remarks astonished him. "Come on, now—get back to your holes!" One of the group started to run again, but he had worked his way around behind them and he stopped the soldier with a gesture. Tracers showered into the trees over their heads. The man who had spoken before gave an exclamation of uneasiness and started to move away again.

"God damn your asses," Pritchard roared, "—go back to your holes!" He waved his carbine at them. He wanted to howl with laughter, and at the same time he was filled with rage, standing here in the dark with all manner of ferocious destruction whining and moaning around them. "By Jesus, you're in the Double Five and you'd better act like it . . ." Something struck a tree trunk immediately behind him with a monstrous crash and fragments sang through the air around them; the little group trembled and fluttered. *There is no excuse for malingering or cowardice during battle. It is the task of leadership to stop it, by whatever means would seem to be the surest cure, always making certain that in so doing it will not make a bad matter worse.* Paragraph 23.

"Now I said get *back* there . . . !" He thought, I could shoot one of them right now, just like that—and the realization frightened him. The safety on his carbine was in the off position. "Come on now, God damn it—move!" Slowly he raised the carbine, keeping his finger well outside the trigger guard.

"Ooh, don't shoot, Cap," a short, fat man with thick lips cried with fearful concern, holding up one hand. "No, don't shoot, now . . ."

"Then get going! They're *counting* on you here—all of you . . ." He was pushing them now, a counselor with some reluctant kids on a hike through the rain. "All right, let's move out." At that moment a figure staggered out of the shadows, hand to his head. He was completely silent but in the fitful, splashed light of the flares they saw the side of his face and throat were coated slickly with blood. He threw them a single agonized glance and wandered away; but with the sight of him the little group went all to pieces again. The thin soldier who had spoken earlier murmured something and started backward. Pritchard seized him by the front of his fatigue jacket and shook him. "Where the hell are you going?" he demanded savagely. "Look, there's another defense line a hundred yards down that trail with orders to blast anything that moves. Anything! So you can forget *that* . . ."

It wasn't working: they looked at him with terrified entreaty, wavering. All the starch was out of them. "All right then—fuck you," he snarled, "I don't need you, nobody does—you no-good sons of bitches . . . You want to stay right here and get killed?" he taunted them bitterly, turning away now, leaving them. "Good! Go ahead—stay here, let *everybody* down. But by Christ, just wait till Sad Sam hears about *this* shit . . . !"

They were following him. Incredibly! Stumbling after him through the crashing, burdensome dark. They associated him with safety now, that was it—they didn't want him to leave them. Or was it Damon? "All right, now. That's more like it," he remarked. His words were lost in a perfect uproar of gunfire. The line up ahead looked like some devilish beach alive with fireworks displays, bonfires, figures that capered and shrieked with unholy glee. Faces looked up at them as they hurried past—faces that were angry, immensely surprised. He could hear someone cursing wildly.

They were at their holes now, were jumping down into them; the fat boy was hunting feverishly for his rifle. A tall, bearded man with his helmet cocked crazily on the side of his head was shouting at them.

"You in charge?" Pritchard yelled at him. "In charge of this detail?"

"Yeah, that's right. Dizzy bastards took off on me—"

"Then why didn't you go after them? Now you keep them here, Mac—I'm not going to go chasing after them again . . ."

"Ain't you going to stay here?" the scrawny kid called up to him.

"What? Don't you think I've got better things to do than *this?*" But the boy's face, drawn now with remorse and supplication, touched him. "I'll be back," he shouted. "You hold on tight, now . . ."

He whirled away and broke into a low, crouching run toward the CP; he was filled with a laughing exultation. I got them, he thought. I went and got them and brought them back. That's something, that's at least a—

He was down. On his side, sprawled. How had he got here? He tried to raise his arm to push himself off the ground and could not. He felt no pain at all: that was good. Stupid, he must have tripped over a root. That was the trouble with running around in the dark—

He was conscious of a warm, sick, flooding sensation; wires and arcs of radiance swooped around him. Slowly he reached back with his left hand—encountered a long rent, moist and deep, under his side. Very deep. Hit. He knew a boundless slow surprise that gave way all at once to fright. "Chief!" he cried. But his voice he knew was no more than a murmur under the wire-shot din. The hot, sick flooding was worse: his back hurt now, and his side; but dully, remotely. It was drifting away. Something brushed against his face like stiff feathers. He had to get back to Damon. Had to. An aide's place—

He made the most mighty effort of his life to get up. The flooding rushed to a pouring torrent. The lights swept up tightly, swept down and away where he could not follow; and then darkness rushed in, and a vast silence.

"I'm just putting it up to you, boys," Damon said. "I know you're all ticketed, I know you've already done more than most. You know I won't stop a single man if he wants to go down . . ."

The wounded lay or crouched in little groups under the long tent, whose ripped and tattered canvas threw over them a fitful light. Here and there medics were working with stoic haste. The rows of men watched him, most of them too weary, too sick, too weak, too empty to hold any emotion whatever. So many: there always seemed to be more wounded than there actually were—as though misery could multiply itself in ways health could not. A high-velocity 47 exploded with a tumultuous crash twenty-five yards away, and the eyes of the wounded men shifted rapidly in the direction of the shell burst and then back to him again.

"I'm asking for volunteers to go back up there with me. We need every man we can get up on the line and that's God's truth. If the line goes the beachhead goes, boys. And that'll be all she wrote."

There was no response. A stocky, curly-haired boy with a compress on his neck looked at him, and then looked away. Doctor Siebert, the center of a compact knot of corpsmen working on a man's thigh, threw Damon a quick, exasperated glance and went on working.

It had gone hard with them all night long; very hard. They'd held twice; then around 2 A.M. the Japanese had broken through in company strength on the extreme right flank, against the jungle wall. He'd shifted some of Young's people over there, the mortars had laid down a ferocious barrage, and finally they'd been able to contain it, and plug the hole. There were snipers all over the area now, hidden in trees or holes or piles of gear, but that was the least of their troubles. Then just after four the Japanese hit again and overran the left flank along the Kalahe.

With first light he'd dropped back down the trail to Dick's reserve line at Ilig.

"We've got to hold on," he said. "Just a little longer, boys. That's all I'm asking you. Just those that feel they can make it." He walked slowly through the tent, the points of sunlight raining on him in the dim, glaucous gloom. His guts clutched at him fiercely; he could feel the sweat glands on his forehead burn. His head ached from the incessant pounding of artillery fire. And at the back of his mind was the constant, burdensome sense of a mass of water mounting, cresting, exerting its sure, inexorable force against a worn and crumbling wall . . .

"You mean we don't get to sack in, General? After all we been through?"

Sergeant Levinson, a mortarman, his left hand a bloody club of gauze, his handsome face compressed in a wry, twisted grin.

"Hello, Levinson. How you making it?"

"Can't complain, General. Well, I *can*, but I guess it wouldn't do one hell of a lot of good."

He made himself grin: a poor substitute. "No rest for the weary. How about it? Will you come back up with me?"

Levinson watched him a moment. All at once he said very softly: "Is it that bad up there?"

Everything was point of view. Levinson sat here among his fellow sufferers and waited mutely for the white, immaculate stillness of the hospital ship, the mugs of coffee, the soothing roar of the blowers. For them the battle was over: they had done what they could, someone else would have to worry about who did what and how. They knew only that they had been hit, that they were weak and in some pain, and that other men like themselves were on the line fighting this numberless, hated enemy who held all the land, all the cards, who would never let them alone. Only he, Damon, knew that there would be more assaults in force, that he'd committed nearly everything he had, that they were fearfully low on 60s for the mortars and 105s, that more than half the radios were knocked out, and that it would be four long hours before the armor could get over from the far end of Blue One.

"Yes," he answered. "It's that bad."

Levinson looked away and sighed. "Oi weh." He clucked his tongue like a forbidding housewife. "So much trouble on the house, and I been so good." He got to his feet. The front of his jacket was spattered with his own blood. "Well—I can see *somebody's* got to be Guinea Pig Number One." He gave his wry, lopsided grin again. "All right. Give me a rifle. If some silly son of a bitch'll come up and play first loader for me, I'll fire it."

Damon felt a quick, deep surge of relief; he clapped the mortarman gently on the shoulder. "I'll get you a case of beer when we secure this operation. That's a solemn promise."

Levinson grinned. "I'm going to hold you to that.—All right, who's up?" he demanded, looking around the tent. "I'll be God damned if I'm going up there alone."

There was a little pause and then all at once the stocky boy with the curly hair got up, yanked the casualty tag off the front of his jacket and said savagely: "All right, let's go, let's get it over with—Jesus Christ, they never leave you alone in this frigging lash-up . . ."

"What are you bitching about, Becker?" a rifleman named Saunders with both legs splinted called to him. "You been goldbricking your way all over the Pacific for two years and a half . . ."

"Yeah, what do you know about it?" Becker demanded hotly, but several other men grinned, and a thin, gangling soldier with glasses Damon didn't know, whose chest was heavily bandaged, got to his feet and said doubtfully, "I'll give it a try but I don't know."

"Good boy." Damon turned to Siebert. "Can he make it?"

The doctor gave him the same sharp, hostile glance. "How in hell should *I* know? All it can do is hemorrhage . . ." But now others were moving up around him, he was speaking their names, those that he remembered. Siebert was still staring at him angrily. He had to do this: he had to. There was no other way.

A field telephone man named Tampler was sitting on the ground; no wound was visible on him. "How about it, Tampler?" he asked. "Will you come along?"

Tampler looked up at him tearfully; his big frame seemed actually to have shrunk, and his hands were shaking in that tight, palsied tremor Damon knew all too well. "I can't, General," he murmured. "I'll just— I won't be able to cut it. I know I won't . . ."

"All right, Tampler. You don't have to." He moved on through the tent, entreating, exhorting, explaining, while the sound of firing crackled and thumped up the trail, building again, and still more wounded were brought in from outside, crowding the ragged tent further. He had guessed right: Murasse was pouring everything into the Babuyan assault.

"Hey, Damon!" He turned. Rossini, his belly and groin a mass of gauze, a bottle of plasma above his head, his thick, dirty face dreamy with morphine. "Hey, what do you think of the frigging cooks and bakers now?"

Harden your heart. "I think they're fine, Rossini. The best. I'll put them up against any outfit in the Pacific, any day."

There they stood, over thirty of them, swaying on their feet, while young Ward of G-1 talked to them. Walking wounded, going back up because he had asked them to go. Because he had asked them to. They were filthy, the older ones had beards, they looked like half-starved old men—and not one of them was over twenty-seven. They were terrible, they were pitiful, they were magnificent; he was filled with awe and a kind of heartsick fright, watching them creep out of the tent to pick up weapons and ammunition.

He put his hand to his face. Christ, he was tired. They had to hold. They had to. Frenchy had pulled off his sideslip beautifully, the alley west of the Kalahe was solid. A bunch had broken through Agee's crowd just before dawn and were still wandering around somewhere behind them, but it was less than platoon strength; they weren't enough to do any real harm. The main thing was to break the back of the main force, chew them up as an effective unit. Anyway, he had guessed right. All they had to do was hold on, now. He'd have to make sure of adequate protection for the ammo parties. The recon company ought to be shifted—

"Filthy ghoul."

A wan, white face on a cot behind him, the lower part of the body covered with a blanket, only one foot protruding. Only one. A plasma bottle with its tube feeding down to a slender, white arm. A supply corporal, what was his name? Bright blue eyes fixed on him with glassy force. "Had to come in here to get us, I notice . . ."

Damon stared at him in silence.

"—Not enough to slaughter everyone in sight—no,"—his voice was rising shrilly—"you've got to come in here and drag us out again—"

"Look, soldier—"

"—a filthy, bloody ghoul and I don't care who knows it—you think *I* care? *I'll* tell you, I'll tell the whole stupid world what a dirty, bullying ghoul—"

Damon took a step toward him. "Be silent!" he said with all the threat he could muster. He turned to a medic, conscious of the long battery of eyes. "Shut this man up, you hear? *Shut him up! . . .*"

He went out of the tent trembling with dread, holding his belly openly with one hand, unable to stop thinking now of Westy, trying to drive it out of his mind.

They were shouting deep in the jungle: a single high-pitched voice, haranguing, and now and then an answering bark of approval, like some devil's litany. Brand, sitting behind the machine gun, thought savagely, Getting ready to try it again, getting up their nerve—and was filled with cold rage. Crouched near him in the long rectangular CP hole, the Old Man was saying to Cuddles Dickinson and Major Falk, the headquarters commandant:

"We've got to hold this line. Right here. There must be no faltering, no second thoughts, no talk of falling back. Impress that on your people."

"Think they'll try it in broad daylight?" Falk asked.

"Yes. He's got to. He's got to keep going. He's in just as deep as we are, now . . ."

Brand kept watching the General. He looked completely whipped; his shoulders sagged, his face was grimy and hollow and gray pouches of exhaustion lay under his eyes. He was sick, Brand knew—he'd gone and got him some more paregoric from Corrazzo, but he was still running badly. My God, he was tough; even when Brand himself had sunk into a brief, fitful, nap around three he'd wakened to find the Old Man gazing out into the jungle and talking to someone on the phone and giving the word to a runner. But now he looked all through: his eyes had receded under his brows to sharp, white points, and the heavy gray stubble on his cheeks made him look old and sad. But he was still functioning. He'd had the shakes after the fire fight up at the Hollow—the bad one, just before dawn; but here he was now, deftly loading a BAR magazine, forcing down the spring with his thumb, engaging a cartridge base, another, another, listening to Deacon Feltner, who was saying they were dangerously low on fifty-caliber ammunition and mortar shells.

Moisture dripped soddenly from the trees. Over by the river the spell was broken by scattered shots and the muffled crash of a grenade. If they hit us again, Brand thought tiredly, I don't know. Looking back southward from the gentle rise he could see through the screen of palms a slice of the sea beyond Babuyan and a transport, riding at anchor. "Lousy Navy bastards," he muttered, and ground his teeth. With their dry sacks and three hots a day and movies and ship's stores and their freshwater showers . . . He thought of the afternoon on Benapei when the Old Man had come in sweaty and tired from that deal up at the Horseshoe to find the weird shower Brand had rigged for him out of a halved oil drum punctured and slung from a tree branch and two buckets full of water that tilted on ropes slung from other branches. The Old Man had stood under it soaping himself up and singing "Love Me and the World Is Mine."

"Joe," he'd said, "I'm going to put you in for the Navy Cross. Valor beyond the last call of duty. By God, the three guys I'd like to shake hands with are the three guys that invented the wheel, the mosquito net, and the shower."

"How about gunpowder?" he'd asked, and Damon had grinned at him and made an obscene gesture, boyishly.

"Bugger all gunpowder. To the end of time." And then he'd gone on singing. Well, the world wasn't his, not by a long shot; but she loved him all right, if he was any judge. Lieutenant Tanahill. He'd been surprised beyond all measure that night back at Dizzy Spa when he'd come back to get the Old Man's laundry and heard them talking inside the tent. For a moment he'd hung there, listening avidly—then had slipped away in confusion, a little guilty for having listened at all. It had upset him at first: Damon had struck him as way above something like that—open-handed with beer and passes, and he liked a drink himself when he could get one. But he hadn't seemed to need liquor or women the way most of the men out here did; as though he could shove it on the back burner where it couldn't get in his way—as though real fear or loneliness or nameless hunger could never reach him. Now he knew differently. The

Old Man just didn't show it, that was all: he felt it, all right. He'd observed him once, reading his son's letters one night late, the visored fatigue cap low over his eyes. Watching, Brand had seen him pass a hand across his brow and eyes and go on reading. He kept them in a leather-cased envelope his daughter had given him for a birthday present. It was all cracked now, green and feathery from mildew, and several times Brand had been tempted to clean and soap it for him; but he was afraid the Old Man might be sore if he brought it up . . . and now Lieutenant Tanahill had been sent stateside. That bastard Massengale. More of his work.

Damon had come up beside him. "Still holding the convention?"

He nodded. "Thinking up some devilment."

The perimeter was very quiet. Sunlight burned through the foliage, glinted now on a helmet, now on an empty case of belt ammunition, rifle swung. A shadow—some noncom—knelt by someone's hole, talking urgently; straightened and moved along. It was hard to imagine that so many men were here around him, motionless, sweating, waiting for the tiger to spring. Unlike most soldiers, Brand did not hate the jungle: its murky tangle concealed him as well as the Japanese that sought his life, and he could use cover better than the next man. But the waiting was hard. Perspiration crawled through his eyebrows and streaked his chest.

De Luca said: "Message for you, General."

Damon turned and took it, read it softly aloud. "*CONDOR to CUT-LASS. Phase Line Orange must be held at all costs. Any further withdrawal expressly forbidden. Am confident you can hold on. 629th RCT embarking Dalomo for Blue Beachhead at once.* Sent it in clear, did he?"

"Yes, sir."

"Ain't that fine. So the Japs could monitor it and know just what to expect, I suppose."

No one said anything for a bit and Brand asked, "Where's Phase Line Orange?"

"First two days' objective. Right where we are now, as a matter of fact." He handed the radio to Dickinson and glared at the jungle wall. "*Any further withdrawal.* What does he think—I'm going to try to set up a line out in the water?" His lips curled mirthlessly. "Jesus, it's good to know he's got confidence in us, isn't it? If we don't hold here we might as well start swimming back to Benapei . . ."

"That's a long swim," Brand murmured.

"Isn't it, though." The General's face was working.

"What did he do," Dickinson said, "—get cold feet?"

"Maybe. Wants to cover himself with Army. Get it on the books in case the roof falls in."

"They can't possibly get here in time, can they?"

"Sixty-five miles by water? Not a chance. But pass the word on this one that help is on the way."

"But why, General? If they can't even—"

"Because men have got to have things to hold on to," Damon snapped at him, his face tight with exasperation. "Especially at miserable, fucked-up, rotten times like this one . . ." Cuddles' sober Yankee face looked blank and startled. The Old Man smiled wearily. "I'm sorry, Dick. It's been a long night." He slapped the Chief of Staff on the shoulder. "Take it easy, now. Go on back to the novelties counter. We'll get out of this yet, you'll see."

It's Krisler, Brand thought. That's what's got to him. Old Paprika Ben. He's afraid Krisler's packed it in, along with the rest of them, up there. God, he'll take it hard if Krisler's stopped one: it'll cut him to the heart.

"Win?" the General was saying over the phone in even, level tones. "No matter how hard they hit on the right, *don't* pull over there. It will be a feint. What he wants is the trail . . . Yes. That's right . . . No, they're steady: they'll hold. I'll be in touch . . ."

Brand smiled softly, listening. By God, there wasn't a thing the Old Man couldn't cope with: artillery, demolitions, tactics, first aid—he knew his trade from muzzle to butt plate. How many of the rajahs could make that claim? Brand remembered during a lull last night, some kid yelling from a nearby hole, "She won't work! My rifle—the operating rod won't move . . ." And Damon roaring at him: "Piss on it!" and then the kid's voice, thin and incredulous: "—on my *rifle?*" By Jesus, he was the kind of general to serve under, they could say anything they wanted to. Even now, exhausted and outgunned, there he was, loading magazines and sending off runners, figuring how to beat the bastards . . . Watching the iron gray face Brand was swept with a surge of affection that seeped, warm and pervasive, into the hard center of his heart and made his hands tremble.

. . . If you hurt the Old Man, he said silently, traversing the gun a few degrees, peering through the thin screen of guava bushes and vines, if you so much as touch a hair of his head I'll kill you myself, all of you. With my hands. Till the black end of time. "And that's a promise."

"What?" Whelan, a headquarters company casual who was serving as his loader, was gazing at him in surprise.

"Nothing."

The high, haranguing voice was louder now; or there were others. Mortar shells began to fall in the groves to the right, moving nearer like approaching thunder. He picked up his M1 and checked the clip and bayonet studs, then the row of grenades in the shelf at the forward edge of the emplacement, thinking vaguely of the evening back at Dizzy playing cards with several other NCOs and Goethals saying to Enright, "Of course he's shacking with her. What do you think they're doing—

playing cribbage? Santosky saw them at the beach near Tafua swimming one afternoon." Goethals' narrow little eyes had rolled around to him. "How about it, Joe-Joe? Isn't he humping that gash?"

He'd looked at the thick, low forehead, the cunning grin. He'd never liked Goethals much. "What gives you that idea?" he'd countered.

"Ah, come off it, buddy-ro. What is he—some kind of a sacred bull or something? How about it? Give us the skinnay."

He knew it was a lie but he couldn't help it. Goethals' tone, the intimation that it was nothing more than a cheap-and-easy roll in the hay, had forced his hand. "As a matter of fact there isn't anything there," he said. "And I ought to know if anybody does."

He stared them all down, but Goethals grinned his thick, lewd grin and said: "Who you conning, Joe-Joe—you expect us to believe that? Santosky *saw* them . . ."

"And anyway, his business is his business, when it isn't yours."

"Hey, are we playing cards or what?" Higgins demanded; but Goethals went on, more loudly:

"What? It's everybody's business if anybody's there to see it. What's Damon that he's so special?"

Right then Brand knew he'd have to fight him. He was down nearly fifteen pounds, his arm was barely healed, he felt tired and defeated at the very idea; but if that was how it had to be, all right. "He's worth a dozen of you," he said slowly.

Goethals laughed. "More than that—several hundred. He runs the Double Five: sergeants are a dime a dozen."

"I mean he's ten times the man you are. Rank aside."

The platoon sergeant's brows rose. "Maybe so, maybe no. He doesn't have to sit on his ass in the boondocks in the rain, take out patrols."

"He'll do anything you will, twice. And do it better."

"I wouldn't exactly say that."

"Take it easy, Walt," Tech Sergeant Luria said. "Damon's all right and you know it. Give me two cards."

"Sure. I never said anything against him as a DC. I'll vote for him—if they allowed me to vote. We're talking about this other thing, that's all."

"You're not talking about it," Brand retorted, "you're making up a lot of crap about it."

Goethals grinned again. "Hey, that shower you fixed up for him, Joe-Joe: has it got duckboards and handles? is it screened off, for playing—you know: drop the soap?"

The others all laughed. That was the trouble with Goethals: he had this sly way of saying things—you couldn't always be sure whether he was kidding or not. He'd *seemed* to be kidding—and then maybe he wasn't at all: it was hard to say.

"Have your fun," he muttered.

"What's the matter, Joe-Joe? Your feelings hurt? You got that tired, mashed-down sensation? Hell, you'd think he was your father."

"You'd be lucky to have a father like him." And then, baffled and angry, he had a little inspiration. He added: "In fact, I don't even know if you *have* a father . . ."

It got quiet all at once in the tent. Goethals' face turned set and very hard. He ran his thumb along the edge of the deck of cards. "That's not so funny, Brand."

He smiled now. "It isn't?"

"No. It isn't. Let's check this out: are you kidding or not kidding?"

Brand put down his hand and looked straight into Goethals' gray-green eyes. "It's up to you, buddy," he said levelly. "If you're kidding about the Old Man I'm kidding about your father."

Goethals said nothing for a moment. "You're not in very good shape, Joe-Joe. And you're spotting me twenty pounds."

"I'll work that out."

They locked eyes for another few seconds, and then Higgins said, "Let it alone, Walt. Don't you know better than to get going on that?" and at the same time Luria demanded:

"Look, are we playing cards or aren't we? What the frig is this all about? Or are we going to fight over something none of you knows anything about? Is that it?" And it had blown over; but neither Goethals nor any of the others had ever brought the matter up in his presence again.

The voices had subsided; there was only a sporadic yelling behind the tossing green sea of jungle. Braced tensely now, listening, Brand caught the ear-splitting crack of knee mortars just ahead and he shouted, "Here they come!" and ducked in the hole. He was showered with dirt and bits of débris. He pressed his helmeted head against the damp earth, watching the Old Man, already huddled against the forward edge of the pit, talking to the radio, his words coming in remote, disjointed snatches of phrase:

"—never mind that, *now is the time* . . . call for you, but you can't fire as separate . . . range one-eight-hundred, deflection as indicated . . . a big rush. Now lay it in as close as you can . . . until the tanks get—"

The mortar bursts moved ponderously off left, toward the river. Brand raised his head quickly. Dirt snapped just beyond his eye, and he ducked again; he felt pummeled and feverish—and yet at the same time oddly alert and prescient, on the edge of anger. He swung up again and there they were, in clumps and clusters, their mustard-brown uniforms like dirty patches against the rich green of the jungle; and they were screaming. Last night they had seemed to make no sound at all, but now they were giving this high, unearthly cry, their mouths round and black and wide; leaping and stumbling over their own dead, waving rifles, swords, grenades, looking clumsy and ineffectual and as strange as creatures from some remote planet. Around him the firing rose to one solid, all-engulfing roar. He pumped the cocking handle twice and fired, the gun bucking against the heel of his hand, deafening him. He watched his tracers converge with others into the chests and bellies of the enemy who faltered, slid forward, sank weakly away or kept on running, full of savage purpose, releasing their grenades like little tin cans and then fell in their turn, transformed into headless, limbless, lumpy sacks. And still they came on, screaming at the top of their lungs, words or names or cries of pain that all merged into the one, unearthly, incantatory *aaaaiiiii—!* Whelan fell against him, one arm outflung, struck him in the head and face, and collapsed in the bottom of the hole. The belt shivered and buckled and he swung the gun left, right again, firing in short bursts, wherever the clumps were largest, cursing, panting, hating with all his might this stupid, blind bravery that cared for nothing, had no end, that was going to engulf them all. Too many. There were far too many. They weren't going to be able to hold them. They were at the lead foxholes now, shrieking and wailing, lofting more grenades—

There was a series of thunderclaps that seemed to strike at the base of his forehead: the air before him turned malignant and hard—hard as sheet iron, wreathed in towers of smoke and dust. The pressure waves beat him with the force of a piece of planking; his vision went dark, he sank into an eerie twilight of puny, cringing powerlessness. He found he was crouched under the gun, hands over his head, buffeted and gasping. "Too fast!" he heard himself cry—but his voice was as faint as an asthmatic old man's. He had no idea what he was saying. "*Too—fast!*" Still it came, in rolling walls, in vast shattering blows—a hand pressing on his skull, squeezing out of it sight and sound and all coherent thought. It could not last, could not go on like this. But it did. The tops of trees dissolved in dreamy, floating fragments like the petals of some monstrous flower unfolding underwater. A leg—part of a leg with its boot and wraparound puttee—lay against his arm. Someone screamed vividly and long, and a body slammed into the pit beside him, confronted him with a scarlet pulsing fruit that he dully realized was the man's face; from the center of the pulpy fruit the screams came, but lower now and hoarser, dwindling. His senses deserted him. No more of this; no more! In sudden importunate terror he looked for the Old Man—saw him doubled over, his hand against his ear, and realized, with stunned slow amazement, that he was talking on the phone.

"Oh my Jesus," he panted. "Oh my good Jesus—"

Abruptly the crushing hand lifted, the belaboring plank vanished, sliding away. His sight cleared to a gray twilight flecked with drifting chains of blue. He reached up again, his hands shaking, and there they were still, unbelievably, unbearably, crawling, groping, stumbling over the high, careless windrows of their dead; moving like silly, deadly, drunken marionettes. He went on firing, watching them trip and falter. They were all around now, in among the foxholes, pressing on through sheer weight of numbers in a churned wilderness of mangled bodies and equipment and torn earth, slashing and firing. The gun stopped, shockingly. He snatched at the bolt, saw the belt had run out. A glance revealed the pit unmanned except for the Old Man, who was firing the BAR, his great shoulders shaking with the recoil, in perfect rolling bursts of four. Falk was down. So was De Luca. But they were nearer now, all at once, squat and bandy-legged, screaming their limbo battle cry: the hated, the enemy. He reached for a belt, saw there was no time, caught up his rifle instead and fired at two men running stride for stride, another, three more behind them, shouting himself, the numb fury of his rage astride him now, the dry white unreckoning rage that he could always trust, that never failed to carry him through when bone and muscle and nerve were gone. The empty clip whirled upward past his eye. He reached for another in his belt, and beheld in front of him an officer—a short, heavy man with a saber held at his shoulder, long and blue as ice in shadow. No time. He leaped forward out of the hole, slipped and went to one knee, flung up his rifle like a man on point signaling, watched angrily the sword come down and strike just below the stock ferrule with an impact that stung his hands. The officer, his face flat with exertion, terribly near, sweating, raised the sword again in his two hands, his thick body coiling with great celerity. Brand heaved upward with the bayonet, saw it go home, followed it right into the belly under a belt buckle adorned with the imperial chrysanthemum. Something struck him on the shoulder and back and drove him to his knees again. He looked up, thrusting. The officer was gripping the handguard of his rifle, his face flooded slowly with confusion, a kind of shame; and Brand saw he was an old man, sick and very frightened. A long jungle ulcer on his upper lip was oozing yellow mucus. Then he fell on Brand, his weight dragging the rifle down and away, and his body stank of fish and damp-rot and stale sweat.

Gasping, Brand let go of the rifle and flung the dead man to one side. His left arm hurt, a numbed tingling; but he could flex the fingers. He turned, saw Damon slumped against the back edge of the pit, fumbling awkwardly with a shiny black trapezoidal magazine, trying to reload the BAR; a crimson stain was slowly seeping through his jacket. Hit. The Old Man was hit.

"Chief!" he cried. He looked back to see four more—ah Christ, so many!—coming toward them now with implacable intent, shunning the other holes, their hands raised. They've figured it out, the thought reached him; they've doped it out: we're the ones they want. The bastards. Oh the bastards! Rage caught him up again, he wrenched at his impaled rifle in a transport of agony, yanked it free at last, knowing he was too late, there was nothing to be done now, nothing at all on this earth, yet constrained nonetheless to raise the rifle and bayonet, interpose his body.

He started to his feet. Behind him there was the deafening air blast of a Thompson gun: the oncoming Japanese whirled this way and that, tumbling headlong. A grenade rolled free, spinning on the ground. He turned and saw Colonel Feltner standing behind the pit, helmetless, his eyes slitted, firing in a frenzy. He screamed, "*Cover!—*" and plunged headlong into the hole. The grenade exploded with a sharp, flat crash and fragments moaned through the air like plucked harp strings. Feltner was gone, as though the earth had swallowed him. Brand straightened, snatched up Whelan's rifle and fired at an officer, a slender, willowy figure who was aiming carefully with a pistol at the message-center hole where Cuddles and some more of the headquarters people were. Brand hit him again and again, and still the officer continued doggedly to aim—finally clutched at his face and throat and fell, turning. Behind him came a short man in a fatigue cap, running with his head down, holding what looked like a saki bottle in one outstretched hand. Fire converged on him; he staggered but kept hurrying forward. His hand holding the bottle burst into flame that raced like an aureole over his head and shoulders. His hands were on fire, his tunic and cap; he turned sharply— a swift, agitated gesture as though he'd forgotten something—and darted off to the left, toward the river, uttering thin, harsh cries and fell at last in a faint, floating glide, the flames flaring from his hair and neck.

A towering, arching crash to the right: again. There were no more. No more of them. Only heaps of dead and dying, and the new-found silence was flooded with screams and moans. The artillery was going high now, searching the woods beyond. Behind him he could hear an automatic rifle hammering away in short bursts. They had held them! Sweet Christ, they had stopped them again—

A man was walking toward them: a man where none had been scant seconds before. Wandering leisurely, a drifting, wavering walk. He fired without thought. The Japanese went down, rose again in his terrible somnambulistic waver, again went down. Brand glanced at the Old Man, who was sitting down now at the base of the hole, trying one-handed to insert a fresh magazine into the guides. His face was like new wax; blood had soaked the sleeve, the whole side of his jacket.

"Medic!" Brand called hoarsely. "For Christ sake *medic*—!"

A fierce struggle was going on not thirty feet away, hand-to-hand: a flurry of gesticulating, lunging figures, shouts and screams. The gun. He flipped the snap on a case, flung back the oblong metal cover, snatched out a belt and set it in the lips; glanced again at the Old Man—and saw the shiny black-and-porcelain cylinder, like a huge corrugated spark plug, rolling on the tamped earth at the bottom of the hole. No time. He gazed at it in deepening terror—an expanding white eternity of instant in which he knew there was no purpose in shouting a warning, in which he knew he could leap out of the hole but that Damon, slumped there with the BAR across his lap, could never make it. Never. A thousand years of instant during which he saw Whelan's grotesquely twisted body, the angular bulk of the radio, and the Old Man now frankly holding his arm and shoulder and staring down at the terrible shiny corrugated engine which had stopped rolling now and lay there just out of reach, giving off a fitful little shower of sparks.

No time.

He flung away the belt and threw himself on the grenade.

. . . Cold. A still world, ringing and half-asleep, high on a mesa with the earth swinging ponderously below his body. Rocking and swinging. But he had no body, it had melted in the cold—blown clean, and his sight was dulled. Odd, because it was so clear out here, high on the mesa. Ah Mother of God, he'd made it, he'd made it home where the frost lay on the mountains in the fine dawn chill and the smell of woodsmoke from the morning fires was salt and heady—

But the Old Man. The Old Man was looking down at him, saying, "Joe, Joe . . ." He couldn't hear him but he could see his lips moving. The Old Man's face was all crinkled up; he looked scared, he looked as if he was going to cry.

All done. Home—

It was like the end of the world by violence. The valley made a long, lazy curve toward the northeast, trampled kunai grass and banana and coconut and ifil trees, stripped and scarred by gunfire. Around them the bodies lay in heaps, in vast ropelike mounds and windrows, strewn through a tattered junkland of smashed and abandoned war gear. The smell of death, which had reached out to them in brief waves on their way up the trail in the weapons carrier, was almost overpowering now. Colonel Beaupré rubbed his mouth and glanced sharply at Damon who, his arm bound close to his body by bandages and an improvised sling of webbing, was moving through this terrible wasteland with an obsessive fury, plodding ahead of the groups of medics and graves registration details and recon people, who kept peering fearfully into the impenetrable rain forest that was massed along the right flank of the valley. Once the General stumbled and almost fell. He was half-supporting himself with a Japanese rifle he held crutchlike under his good arm. He cursed and crept along among the dead, his eyes wild and wrathful under the fatigue cap; the lines in his face looked as if they had been cut in the flesh with a burin. Beaupré remembered an evening back in Devon Bay, after Moapora, with everyone moderately drunk, and Ben saying, "Sam, the lines in that craglike phiz of yours would hold three days of rain, do you realize that?" and Beaupré himself had scoffed, "Hell, that's no phiz—that's a God damn relief map of the Bitterroot Range!" But now it wasn't funny, remembering; not funny at all.

All morning, after the Japanese had broken off contact and fled north, and exhausted tatters of Ben's old regiment had come drifting into the lines, Sam had been in a torment to get back up here. It was stupid, it was how detachments ran into trouble, indulging in stunts like this, with handfuls of half-crazed Japanese with grenades, hiding in holes; which was why Beaupré had insisted on their taking a recon platoon with them. But there had been nothing: the enemy—what was left of him— was in full retreat toward Kalao and the mountains. There were no fire fights, no snipers, no incidents; just this vast and hideous graveyard of many, many men . . .

There was very little talk in the clearing. With such monstrous carnage the voices of the searchers had sunk away to monosyllabic whispers. Near them a sweating, buck-toothed medic kept muttering, "Holy Jesus Christ. Holy Jesus Christ . . ."

"Keep looking," Damon snapped at him.

"Yes sir," the corpsman answered nervously, and shied away.

It was hard to know where to look. The valley was interrupted by two small mounds to their left, just off the trail, and Beaupré moved toward it, his eyes darting over the corpses that had fallen in clumps and series, in tangles, and now lay in bizarre postures, sprawled forward over their heads, or flung back on their legs, or flat on their backs with both knees drawn up, as if squashed against a wall by some rude celestial hand. About a regiment, his mind registered automatically; a regiment at least. But the cold professional estimate broke down under the impact of such losses, such violence and death. The need to avert one's eyes, stop up all the bodily orifices in a single spasm of revulsion, was immense. Battle—yes, sure: he was used to battle and its odious consequences. But a vast thresher had done this—some sort of devilish combine and disk harrow bigger than a battleship had passed through this curving valley, grinding up trees and weapons and tentage and human beings and flinging them blithely aside. The peculiar stench of blood and putrefaction and damp-rot and burning grew heavier and heavier in the heat, clinging like a caveful of bats to the roof of one's senses, drowning sight and hearing and even thought. Beaupré felt his stomach churn, churn again, and then the sour rush of saliva into his mouth. He was going to be sick. No. He would not be. He would not. He had never been sick before and he would not be sick now.

Someone across the clearing gave a muffled cry of protest, but he could not tell who it was. It was impossible to walk without stepping on the bodies—this tumult of crushed heads and sheared-off legs and tight bouquets of guts flowering from ruptured bellies. Flies clung in loose, weaving masses, like slick blued bees swarming; the whole valley hummed with their odious presence. Maggots worked in gross struggling chains at the gaping wounds, bloated and intent. The buck-toothed corpsman near him became sick, a choked rhythmic coughing that went on and on. There were no voices now at all.

If you could bottle it, Beaupré thought savagely, swallowing, fighting the hot clutch of nausea with all his might, trying not to breathe, trying to look without seeing. This smell. If you could bottle it, store it in

some tanks just outside Washington or New York City or Chicago; and
then when the drums began to beat, when the eminent statesmen rose in
all their righteous choler and the news rags and radio networks started
their impassioned chant, if you could release a few dozen carboys on
the senate floor, the executive offices of Du Pont de Nemours, Boeing
and Ford and Firestone, the trading posts on Wall Street; and seal off
the exits. Repeat every three hours as needed. Rx. By God, that would
take some of the fun out of it. If you could only bottle it and feed it to
the fire-eating sons of bitches, jam it down their throats. . .

No, he thought, raging, looking down at an American still gripping
the slender bayonet that had run him through, his hands congealed in his
own blood; stepping over a Japanese lying on his back, spread-eagled,
thick open hands clutching nothing, his belly and thighs already swelling monstrously in his clothes; no, the greedy moronic bastards would
only launch one of their clean-up campaigns, underwrite funds, solicit
contributions for scientific research. Stamp Out Stink. They'd invent
something—trust them—some antidote compounded of Chanel and
coffee beans and beer; and then, safely delivered of such distressing
reminders, they could hurry right back to the quickened pulse, the
speeches, the righteous wrath—

Across the glade voices rose in muffled exclamation. He turned
dumbly, saw the medics urgently extracting from a pile of wreckage a
limp scarecrow dark with blood: they had found a soldier not quite
dead. Someone who was alive here: actually alive. Beaupré looked away
and went on walking, gagging frankly now, though without tangible
result.

Hades, the word rose in his mind. That trip made by—who was it?
Odysseus? Aeneas? had they both gone?—to the land of the dead. It
seemed callous, sacrilegious, almost obscene to be walking around, still
living, when all these men had died. War is so untidy, he thought, and
smiled grimly. A southern boy, impetuous, hot-tempered, a bit spoiled,
nursed on a pleasant, sunset gentility, he had never been very tidy
himself. The Army had created an order for him, punctilious and severe, and he'd welcomed it. Life passed more serenely, with less friction
and misunderstanding and waste, if there was order. You attended to
your duties, which were moderately exacting and healthful and well
defined; you played two hard sets of tennis in the afternoon and made
your courtesy calls or attended post functions or poker sessions in the
evenings. A well-ordered round . . . and it was all—he saw for the first
time with a quick, angry shock—nothing more or less than preparation
for this: this valley of death and wild disorder.

Stooping, he picked up a piece of paper, one of the multifarious scraps
you always saw in battle. There were so many—snapshots and chits and
money and letters from home; and lying here and there among them the
foolish, trivial things soldiers always picked up and carried around with
them, in spite of the grinding weight of packs and weapons and extra

bandoleers: souvenir penknives and cowrie shells and postcards of Balboa Park Zoo or Diamond Head, subway tokens and Australian shillings, and carnival trophies such as monkey hand puppets and harmonicas and handkerchiefs embroidered with legends like HOME IS WHERE THE HEART IS or *Count Your Blessings*. He was always running across them in men's footlockers during inspection. They had puzzled and amused him, once he had even tried to talk several NCOs out of lugging so much junk around with them. Now, with a single throb of rage and pity, he saw the desperate importance of these things: they provided an assurance of a man's particularity in the midst of a murderous, press-drill uniformity, an uncaring system that was forced to treat him, willy-nilly, like one more white chip in an interminable poker game. "Death is not an individual matter," Sam had said that last night aboard ship before the Wokai landing. "We like to think it is, but it isn't." Beaupré had fought the idea then, but now he understood. All dead were alike: all emptied, putrescent flesh was one. It was life that gave individuality, a bright sacredness . . .

He was at the top of the second little mound, where the remains of a nipa hut stood, now only two thatched walls. Someone had hastily rigged a shelter half like a tent fly to ward off sun or rain, but it had been ripped to shreds and hung gaping from the poles. Without reasoning he knew this was where the CP would be, and paused. A vast tangle of bodies, like flotsam left by a high-tide mark, the smooth earth floor sticky with blood; a battered radio; a message-center man Beaupré remembered named Kraenpuhl, with a great hole in his chest, through which bits of bone and gristle protruded like slender white sticks and wires. A map lay on the floor in a sea of papers, rusty with blood and dust; a split-toed Japanese zori had left its firm, clear print on the area below Fanegayan. Another welter of Japanese and three Americans pierced with terrible bayonet wounds. One with his head almost severed, cropped black hair and a big hooked nose, and patches of purple dye staining the cheeks and scalp.

Ben. Beaupré crouched, put out a hand. Yes. Ben. They'd stripped him of that crazy yellow scarf of his and torn the tin star from his collar but there was his helmet not two feet away, with the ITC monogram stenciled just above the brim, and a star riveted at the apex of the T. His '03 was gone, there were no clips left in the dirty cloth bandoleer over his shoulder. His eyelids were slightly raised, revealing blued whites, giving him a mean, sly look. Flies crawled at his open mouth.

Beaupré looked around fearfully, as if discovered at something shameful—reached down and pressed his fingers against the lids; but they would not close any further. He straightened then and stepped to the edge of the hut and called softly: "General . . ." Heads turned as if on strings, and Damon stared at him, mute and wild. "General," he repeated, "Over here, if you will . . ." The buck-toothed medic started over and he snapped, "No. Not you." The corpsman paused and turned away. Beaupré watched Sam come toward him with a heaving, ponderous gait, his face contorted with the effort. When the General had reached him he murmured: "It's Ben, Chief."

Sam gave him a quick, frightened glance—for an instant he looked as if he were going to hobble away. Then he sank to his knees and started to touch the nearly severed head, the cruelly ripped and shattered body that now looked puny and absurd, no longer human. No longer anything at all.

"—Oh," Damon said in a low, shaken voice. "*Oh.*" With his good arm he made a swift, petulant gesture to drive away the flies, which rose grossly and then began to settle again in lusting swarms; their clamor filled the air. "Ah God," he said. His eyes filled and his lips moved numbly. "Ah my God . . ." He threw Beaupré another swift, agonized glance, then suddenly began to try to lift the body with his arm—a clumsy, straining, ineffectual motion.

"Sam—" Beaupré said.

The General fell back, panting. Scarlet began to seep freshly through the layers of gauze at his shoulder; he fell against one of the poles, his face drained of color.

"Sam!" Beaupré cried in alarm. "Now God damn it, cut that out!"

"—Frenchy," Damon whispered, "Frenchy, we—"

"No—now stop it! You're going down. I'm going to send you down . . ."

Sam made another clumsy movement toward the corpse. Beaupré leaned down and held him by the good shoulder and said, "Sam—*no!* Over. It's over! You've had enough. Now let it go, now . . ."

The General looked up at him—a beaten, desperate, awful gaze. Then he nodded dumbly and dropped his head on his chest; and his shoulders began to shake rhythmically.

"Find anything, Colonel?"

Beaupré whirled around. The buck-toothed medic was gazing at them with bovine solicitude.

"Beat it!" Beaupré snarled. "Take your ass out of here!"

"Yes *sir* . . ." The corpsman backed away into the light. Beaupré stood in the humming silence, gripping his belt hard with both hands; his stomach heaved. There was nothing to do but watch Sam slumped against the house pole, weeping quietly.

There was a long wait after they rang, and Emily Massengale glanced at Tommy, who for answer rolled her eyes toward the foyer ceiling and said: "RHIP. A suitable interval will be maintained."

"Now, you promised," Emily reminded her.

"Okay, okay." Tommy gave her wry grin. "But don't think I don't know why she's throwing this bash."

Emily had started to ask her, when the door was flung open violently and Irene Keller stood before them in a flaming orange-and-black hostess gown and gold earrings whose chased oval balls flailed against her cheeks.

"Darlings!" she cried; she embraced them both passionately, Emily first. Emily was half-smothered in perfume. "What took you so long? But then, you were never very punctual, were you, Emmy dear?"

"No," Emily said with a calm smile, "I never was. Though I've improved."

"So I've heard. Come on in and have some Yuletide cheer. Most of the clan's already gathered . . ."

Irene Keller had blossomed out. Her hair was an almost feverish platinum blond; some big assiduous Finn had pounded her body nicely into shape. Her capped teeth gleamed porcelain between her wide orange lips. This was her night, and she was dressed for it.

"I thought it would be fun," she was saying to Emily, "—just us camp followers. No kids, no dogs. While the men are all overseas. Just a good chance to let our hair down."

She led the way into a great pink shell of a living room where a superfluous fire was roaring. A Christmas tree towered in a far corner, and the women Emily had known for years sat or stood in little groups, chattering with one another, while a phonograph brayed carols through the smoke-burdened air. She heard Tommy mutter something inaudible, and then Irene had called, "Girls: Emily Massengale and Tommy Damon," and had turned back to them with a prideful glint in her eyes, her head thrown back, her hair gleaming.

"Well," Emily said. She stared: she was unprepared for what she saw. These were not merely the habiliments and furnishings picked up on foreign tours and purchased over the years with calculated care. This was something quite different. There were porcelains from Alsace and Limoges, a French provincial secretary on delicately turned legs, an octagonal Moorish table inlaid with mother-of-pearl; there was a silver tureen filled with fruit and a silver figurine of a nymph reclining on a silver rock, there was a huge tapestry in faded blues and golds of huntsmen ringing a boar, and a chest whose lace-edged runner revealed the fine, gleaming wood. But above and beyond everything else was the glassware: goblets and stem glasses, pale green Arabic decanters with the necks of serpents, ruby vases and matching figures—they were ranged all about the room, on sideboards, on the mantel, in two handsome glassed cupboards. Some of the baubles on the tree were ingeniously blown globes and spirals, their gilt sparkling in the candlelight.

"Well," Emily repeated, in some confusion. She decided she'd better not look at Tommy. "Well, what a surprise, Reeny . . ."

"Oh, you haven't been by, have you, darling? Bart's got the nicest man on his staff, in G-2 Section—very social, professor of art history at Yale. Reserve, of course; but wonderfully cultured."

"And such a *profusion!*" Tommy exclaimed; her eyes had begun to shine. "The very heart and soul of Europe . . ."

"It's been fun. I never know what Bart will send home next."

"Every day must be like Christmas!"

"Bart says things are breaking so fast now he has to refer to his aide's journal just to hold it all."

"But just think—he'll have this lovely little treasure trove to remind him."

Irene's eyes narrowed, though she was still smiling complacently. "Don't be bitter, darling. Luck of the draw, you know."

"Bitter—how could I be bitter, Reeny?—seeing all *this?* And it's so right for you, dear. Why, it all looks like that castle in *Citizen Kane*— what was it called, Em?"

"Xanadu," Emily said dryly.

"Xanadu. Exactly! It does . . ."

For some reason Irene appeared mollified. "You're so sweet. Bart's always saying he was so lucky to be in on TORCH and OVERLORD and now this new command. Rather than various other assignments he might have drawn."

"Nonsense, dear—it's talent and capability and nothing else that placed him there . . ."

Emily glanced warningly at Tommy, but her face displayed nothing but interest and delight. She decided she'd better keep an eye on her. Tommy had remained essentially the same little girl who at the age of eight had walked out to the exact center of the parade ground at Fort Sill at two o'clock in the morning and on a band trumpet, holding the first two valves down, had blown fire call—and then had raced over to the headquarters building to watch the excitement. For months now Emily had taken her under her wing and kept her going. By spring Tommy had been moving on a fairly even keel—and then in late August her father had turned up as head of a decoying mission in connection with DRAGOON, and she'd started to come apart all over again. Her oscillations in mood had become more violent and abrupt: at times she seemed devoured by a need to scourge everyone—friends, tradespeople, her own tormented spirit.

She turned and said: "Peace on earth, good will toward men, Tommy."

Tommy looked at her from under her brows. "Oh boy!"

"All right, now."

Elaine Kneeland came up then and embraced her; Irene had gone off toward the door. Someone handed her a glass of eggnog and she let the greetings and gossip sweep over her, swallow her up in their easy, comforting turbulence.

"—I told her, 'No more of that for me, I brought up you and the twins in the middle of centipedes and snakes and God knows what else, and that's my quota.' Of course I didn't mean it for a moment—but my God, I hadn't any idea she was going to go to work in a war plant!"

". . . and Spider sent for Jerry and told him: 'All right now, you're out here and you're going to toe the line just the same as any other replacement officer. Also you're going to be the last shavetail in the whole command to get promoted, because I'm not going to have anybody out here saying Spider Spofford's favoring his son over the others. Now have you got that?' And he said Jerry popped to and answered, 'Very good, sir," just as if Spider had been his Tac. Spider said he almost burst out laughing. Then he grinned at him and said, 'All right, now that we understand each other, sit down and relax.' And he got out that bottle of Old Fitzgerald I gave him when his orders were cut for TORCH—"

"—asked for an audience with him and in they came, all feathers and loincloths and blowguns and things. And the chief outlined a plan for a raid on this other tribe on the other side of the mountains. Told Mac if he'd come in with him on this private operation with the RCT, he'd agree to a fifty-fifty split with him over this other tribe's livestock and women. I wrote him he must have been a bit tempted after all those months in the jungles and he wrote back, 'My God, Ella, you haven't seen these old crows!' . . ."

Nodding, smiling, Emily looked around the room. Our class reunion, she thought wryly; the only kind we'll ever know. They were nearly all here: Elaine, whose husband was G-1 on Lucian's staff in DRAGOON, and Betty Baird, whose husband was with PBS at Naples, and Maggie Vinzent, whose husband had been sent home after that awful business at Sidi Bou Noura; Jane Cross, whose husband had wrenched his back when a Jacob's ladder had let go off Attu and stuck him with a limited duty out in the desert at Huachuca, and Jenny Spofford, whose husband was on Krueger's staff on Luzon . . .

Good girls. They were good girls. They had done what they could, had skimped and saved during the lean years, worried over their men's careers and brought up the kids, helped one another out with food and dishes on the evenings they entertained the CO and his wife, and maybe even flirted with one another's husbands after a post party; and here they were, at the grand climax of the greatest war in history, their sons at the Point or in service, their daughters married or off to school, their husbands away in foreign lands running the big show—and all it meant for them now was separation and dogged cheerfulness and incessant strain. Even now, crowded together at this artificial conclave, wearing the suits and dresses of two years past, feverish and a little unsteady with drink, a somber dignity seemed to flow from them. They had paid, some of them, in very hard coin. There was Mae Lee Cleghorne, who was a widow, and Jean Mayberry, who—God help her—didn't know after two and a half years whether she was one or not; there was Iris Walters, whose husband was a POW in Germany, and Jane Holtzman, whose husband had been so terribly burned at Salerno; Enid Groat and Tommy had both lost sons, and now Sam was wounded. Thank God Marge Krisler wasn't here; she couldn't face Marge tonight. Not now, not here at this overstuffed Saturnalia Irene Keller had got together to celebrate Bart's fourth star and show off his plunder. It was bad enough that Courtney had been Corps Commander when it happened. His last letter had been brief—a few words about the Gold Dust Twins and their fatal impetuosity, and field commanders who never got over the Jeb Stuart mentality; and then he'd passed on to other matters. It had given her a shiver of apprehension, but she'd beaten it down. Of course they had both taken terrible chances, Ben and Sam. You had to if the command was endangered, she could understand that; but you couldn't go on exposing yourself time after time, unscathed . . .

"I just adore hors d'oeuvres," Elaine was saying, her taut, muscular jaws working rapidly. "Emmy, remember the party at Malacañan Palace where they served the raw octopus or whatever it was?"

"Indeed I do."

"Have you tasted these?" She held up what looked like an exfoliate green button. "What *are* they?"

"I think they're miniature artichokes."

"And pickled. How divine! Where do you suppose Reeny got them?"

Same place she got everything else, dear, she was moved to say tartly; but she bit it off. Good will toward men. The carols—some sort of girls' choir now—were still mooing through the room. She started to go and get herself another drink, thought better of it. She and Tommy and a few others would leave after a decent interval and eat dinner out somewhere; and they would have got through another day. It was hard living alone—even for those, like her, for whom marriage hadn't been all it might have been.

"—dizzy little fool," Elaine was saying, "I swear these young girls don't have their heads on straight. Jim got word to her he was going to be able to stop off on his way through and I thought she was going to go right out of her mind. Flying around cleaning up and shopping for things, and then at eleven she got that home permanent goo mixed up with the contraceptive jelly, the tubes do look alike—and of course she was *on fire.*"

Several of them laughed boisterously and Tommy said, "But what did you *do?*"

Elaine rolled her eyes at them. "Called the doc and kept flushing her out. What else was there to do? Jim got in around three, the flight was delayed at Gander. I thought it better under the circumstances if I'd retired, don't you know. I refrained from any inquiry as to how things went—but I want to tell you, Jim had one strange and mystified expression on his face at breakfast . . ."

There was a commotion at the entrance to the room, and looking past Elaine's head Emily saw Marge Krisler, standing there a bit diffidently, talking to Mae Lee. Oh no, she thought, not here, not tonight—and then she was moving quickly through the room in time to hear Irene say: "Why, darling! I thought you'd gone home to Wisconsin . . ."

Marge shook her head. "I started for home. But then I came back." Her face looked puffy and faded and covered with pink blotches. The buxom prettiness that men always found so attractive had gone slack; her eyes, usually so clear and wide and bubbling with enthusiasm, were whipped and apprehensive now. "I couldn't go," she went on, "—I wanted to be here, where I could—hear from Joey . . ." Some of the gabble and chatter had died away with her entrance, and now she opened her hands, and her eyes filled. "You're all I've got," she cried softly to them, and her shoulders began to shake, though her voice was steady. "It's true—you *are* . . ."

They surrounded her then, quickly, with the special warm benevolence given to the bereaved; they asked her about the children and her mother and wanted to know if there was anything they could do, and someone brought her a drink. The groups broke up under the pressure of Marge's presence: she was an army wife and she was the most recently afflicted of their number. They were—even Irene Keller—as tender as they knew how to be.

Nevertheless a curious constraint had fallen on the party. The world, which had been for a few sentimental moments a rather pleasurable arena of family and unity and heroism and nostalgia, stood revealed as a yawning pit of loneliness and terrors; Marge's presence made them feel, instead of relief, an increased sense of their own losses and dangers . . . And yet what, Emily wondered, were they to do? Go back to their worn, empty rooms, their jigsaw puzzles and detective novels and tomato sandwiches, one ear cocked for the relentless, hourly bulletins that meant triumph or death or maiming for their men . . . ?

It's utterly absurd, she thought, with her slow, wintry smile, this life we're leading; it's a wonder we're not all of us stark, raving mad. Maybe we are—we certainly were to come to this place.

It was time to leave; the women were all stirring restively now, glancing at the overladen Christmas tree, the array of glassware. They all wanted to go, despite Irene's strident blandishments. As the wife of the ranking officer present, except for Reeny, it was up to Emily to lead the procession. She signaled Tommy with her eyes, excused herself and went to the bathroom, a lavish blue-tile affair adorned with scatological mementoes obviously taken from the walls of Wehrmacht and Schutz Staffel barracks and pillboxes. One lusty Teutonic maiden bore an astonishing resemblance to Reeny; Emily laughed, studying it.

She came back into the room to hear their hostess's booming, clarion voice: "—and Bart told her, 'Maybe the Comte de Crémoire *used* to ride here but he doesn't anymore. You just take it up with SHAEF, lady.' And that was that. The most gorgeous horses! The Germans bred them to their own studs to break down the strain but they got some of them away, magnificent animals. Bart says they've been riding every minute they get the chance . . ."

"Oh stop it!"

They all turned, shocked into silence. Marge was sitting on the central couch, her face streaming. "Do you think we care about that—*any* of that? Don't be such a hard-nosed bitch . . ."

Irene's eyes dilated in anger; then she smiled her flat, condescending smile. Calmly she walked over to Marge. "Perhaps you'd better run along home, sweety," she said. "I'll have Arthur rustle you up a cab. *You've* had a little too much to drink, my girl."

"All right, maybe she has," Tommy Damon said fiercely. "And who's got a better right? Who wouldn't want to get swacked, surrounded by this—!"

Irene reared back. "Just what do you mean by that?"

"Just what I said—this disgusting God damn pirate's cave. Haven't you made a delicious thing out of it, though?"

"Tommy—" Emily said warningly, but Tommy was beyond listening.

"What fun it's all been, hasn't it? playing Lady Bountiful, smothered in the stolen treasures of dear old Europe." She laughed harshly. "God rest you merry gentlemen, let nothing you dismay . . ."

"Now listen, Tommy—"

"And all under the sweet, sanctimonious banner of old-times' sake. Who the hell do you think you're fooling, anyhow?"

Emily touched her arm. "That's enough, Tommy."

"I'll say that's enough . . . Who the hell are you to criticize what I do or don't do?" Irene stared at the flush, impassioned faces, the women she'd flouted and outmaneuvered for years; and Emily saw her mouth harden. Then her eyes came back to Tommy, the woman she hated more than all the others because Tommy was prettier and more charming, because she had always spoken up to her, and most of all because— Emily realized now with a little thrill of pleasure—Sam had never once given the sexy Reeny Keller a second glance.

Emily looked at Marge Krisler on the couch, weeping softly, her mouth drawn down with anguish, Irene's flushed and angry face, Tommy facing her defiantly; listening to the terse, angry voices that rose over the phonograph, which was now emitting a raucous swing version of "Jingle Bells." She should end it now; she could—break this off, say their good-byes and go, the others would all follow her lead. Yet she hesitated, caught up in the fitness of the moment—and her own furtive delight in this unmasking and discomfiture of the Post Menace. After all these years . . .

"—simply a question of decency," Tommy was saying tightly, "when people—"

"Decency! You dare to talk to me of decency? *You*—?"

"—when people everywhere have been making sacrifices—"

"Sacrifices!" Reeny Keller laughed her high, harsh laugh. "My dear, name a soul in this town who is doing without a single thing . . ."

"Not you, I know . . . Wouldn't it please Ben to see this room?—to know that he'd given his life so a Washington flat could be stuffed with gimcracks and plunder—"

"Tommy!" Emily said sharply. Marge had broken down completely now and she moved over to her.

"Ben!" Irene Keller cried all at once, and her great blue eyes glittered with malice. "Yes—Ben! Would you like to know something about him, my dears? Would you?"

"There is nothing you could tell me about Ben that would interest me," Tommy said in a cold, stern tone. "Or anybody else here."

"No?" Irene shrilled. "No? What would you think if I told you Ben didn't even have to die—what would you think of that? Or Sam get wounded, either . . . Yes, go ahead and comfort her, Emily, comfort them both for all you're worth—because *he*"—she pointed a long scarlet nail at Emily—"caused it! Yes, Court! Now what do you think of that—?"

Emily would always remember this moment: herself crouched above Marge's silent, huddled figure, gazing, speechless with consternation, at Irene and Tommy confronting each other, rigid and embattled before the frieze of shocked, still faces. Her dismay swept to deepest dread. It was true: every premonitory fiber of her being knew it was true. She tried to say something, could not.

"—*You lie*," Tommy gasped.

"Do I? Ask Don Grayson, then—Marv Farrier wrote him from Leyte—they were under attack and called for reinforcements and Court didn't send them any for days, let them get slaughtered like sheep! *Now* how about all your noble sacrifices!"

Emily moved then, but it was too late. With all the lithe violent grace of which she was capable Tommy stepped forward and struck Irene, a resounding, full-armed slap. Reeny was twice Tommy's size but the blow spun her almost completely around; she fell heavily against a table, her hand to her face. Then the women all moved at once and cut off Emily's view of them. Marge had her head in her hands, sobbing wildly, and Emily put her arm around her, saying, "It's all right, dear, it's all right now, don't you mind," as much to quiet her own fears as to comfort Marge in her anguish.

But Irene had broken away from the others now, was watching them all again, her breasts heaving, her eyes cold and implacable; the side of her face was a deep red from the blow. "Well, I guess the party's over, girls," she said. "Let's forget it. It wasn't such a hot idea, anyway, now that I think of it." She turned and walked quickly into one of the bedrooms.

Outside it was cold and damp, with a light snow falling. Emily and Tommy walked on each side of Marge, who kept weeping and shaking her head.

"I'm sorry I broke down like that. Stupid. I know. He's been in danger for years, he's always up front. I've known that . . . I just can't seem to keep from crying all the time."

"I know, honey," Tommy was saying. "Don't you worry about it now . . ."

The snow continued to fall fitfully, melting as it touched the pavement. They finally found a cab that had only one passenger, an effeminate, rather nervous young man who insisted on getting up front with the driver. Marge fell silent for a while and Emily sat watching the lights flow past, yellow against the snowflakes. Another year of war ending, another one beginning, already soaked in blood. In the Islands, Poland, the Ardennes, the Apennines. People must love it or they wouldn't cling to it for so long.

"—If I could have *seen* him," Marge was saying in a broken little voice. "Just once. Not since the summer of '42. The last time . . ."

"I know, dear." He wouldn't do that, Emily told herself desperately; he's capable of cruel things, terrible things, I know: but he wouldn't do something like that. He couldn't. No one could.

"Battle after battle, campaign after campaign—there's just no end to it. It's not fair . . ."

Life is unfair, Emily thought. But she remained silent. If I'd only moved faster, she told herself; got them out of there. The effeminate young man was looking studiously out of the window. Three generals' wives on a toot in little old D.C.

"—It's not true," Marge cried all at once. "How could she *say* that—? How could she say such a thing? . . ."

"She's a bitch," Tommy said tersely. "That's how. A total rotten lousy bitch on wheels." The effeminate young man glanced back at them in alarm.

"It isn't true, is it? Is it, Tommy?" Marge pleaded. "It can't be true . . ."

"Of course not," Tommy snapped. "She said the first nasty thing that came into her vicious little peanut brain." Her eyes flashed once, met Emily's over Marge's bowed head; and Emily knew that true or false, confirmed or denied, aired or suppressed, the possibility would always be there, between them. Nothing would ever be the same again. Bravely she tried to smile, but Tommy's gaze was stark and remote. He couldn't, she thought again, with real fear. He couldn't—no one could do something like that: for any reason at all, for anything on this earth . . .

But if it were possible—

They slid on through the chill, wet night, Marge sobbing quietly and hopelessly between them.

The press conference was held in the reception room of the palace. The old Sultan of Palamangao, now deceased, had lived there with his twenty-three wives and concubines and children in an atmosphere of cockfights and feasts and fishing expeditions to Cagayan or Tubbataha. All that had vanished with the coming of the Japanese, and now his eldest son, a slender, dark man who had been hidden by the guerrillas, sat on the left side of the broad dais, wearing wrinkled khaki and looking bright-eyed and tubercular, and stared at nothing. The room was high-ceilinged and cool; a second-story verandah thrust out from it, Spanish-style, framed in a running filigree of carved bayong wood. Bougainvillea and cadeña de amor swarmed in lush profusion over the slender columns and hung from the eaves, and now and then a breeze blew through the sala, rustling papers on the long desk behind which Lieutenant General Massengale stood in a freshly starched khaki uniform, the ivory-tipped pointer in his right hand, and waited for the last correspondents to file in. His public relations officer, Colonel Sickles, sat beside the young Sultan with some of the Civil Affairs people. On the other side sat Generals Bannerman and Swanson and most of the Corps staff, their arms folded, looking attentive and cheerful. The whole atmosphere was one of happy expectancy. Standing below the dais with the crowd of correspondents and photographers, David Shifkin was reminded of high school graduation exercises, or awards day at summer camp.

"Hello, Shif," Randall said, easing his way over to him. Like most of the correspondents he was wearing clean khaki, and he cocked an eyebrow and grinned at Shifkin's dirty, sweat-rimed fatigues. "You look pretty seedy, son. Pretty seedy."

Shifkin gazed at him without expression. "Lost all my gear."

"Pretty rough over there?" Meade asked him earnestly.

"Pretty rough, yes."

Behind them the great mahogany doors banged shut and two GIs with sidearms swung in front of them with the somber professional austerity MPs always had. Technical Sergeant Hartje called: "No smoking, please—General's orders," and walked over to the door at the far left side of the dais. Shifkin massaged his eyes and forehead, thinking, By the numbers. All by the numbers. And now the prizes and awards.

". . . At the heart of the Japanese debacle lay the problem of a unified command," Massengale was saying in his crisp, flawless voice. "Admiral Ochikubo seems to have been placed in charge of the over-all defense of the island. But General Yamashita at Imperial Headquarters on Luzon

had given General Kolusai command of *all ground forces* on Palamangao—and we have only recently learned from captured Japanese
documents that General Murasse considered *himself* to be in charge of
the defense line around Fotgon and the airstrip. In addition to all this
muddle was the fact that Kolusai and Murasse disliked and distrusted
each other intensely—not exactly the most auspicious basis for the effective conduct of military operations on unfriendly soil. Not that we
weren't grateful for such favors."

He smiled, and there was a low, appreciative murmur. "So that when
we struck at Dalomo, the Japanese were presented with the maddening
dilemma commanders in a defensive position often face: which was the
main assault force? Ochikubo had established fixed defenses to hold the
airstrip at all cost. But Kolusai apparently sought a more fluid solution—
he wanted to be able to withdraw on the axis Reina Blanca–Terauen–
Nabolos if the heat got too great, possibly setting up a last-ditch defense
line here." He drew the pointer across the cockatoo's bony neck.
"Murasse, on the other hand, was never fooled by the Dalomo landing:
he believed the Babuyan assault was the main one, and he advocated
large-scale attacks with all available forces against it, with the end in
view of driving it into the sea . . .

"Then General Bannerman's lightning advance on Reina Blanca
caught them all completely flatfooted. Kolusai decided—independently,
it appears—to withdraw northeast along the Aguinaldo Highway to
Nabolos anyway. Ochikubo very helpfully committed hara-kiri. Murasse, who had been cleverly containing the Babuyan beachhead, panicked and threw all the forces at his disposal in a series of headlong
assaults on the Fanegayan-Umatoc line—but without notifying either
Kolusai's or Ochikubo's headquarters, or making any effort to coordinate his attacks. He of course made some appreciable gains in real estate,
but in the end succeeded only in shattering his forces hopelessly . . . It
was the old sad story of Japanese inflexibility, rivalries carried to the
point of insubordination, and failure of nerve in the crucial places. I
sadly fear that what General MacArthur has often said is only too true:
they simply aren't good enough to play in the big leagues."

The laughter this time was fairly general. Shifkin looked around him.
Most of the correspondents were writing rapidly, following the ivory-
tipped pointer as it moved along the fine red and blue lines, gliding
eastward now around the tightly scored whorls of the mountain chain.

"As a consequence, the enemy garrison is now eliminated as an effective fighting force. Advance elements of the Forty-ninth Division are
within six miles of Nabolos and seventeen of North Cape, here"—the
pointer tapped the cockatoo's screaming head—"and the Eighteenth is
swinging around the southern road, below Mount Limpon. First-light
reports today placed elements of the Five ninety-eighth Regiment about
ten miles from Kalao, encountering only sporadic and very disorganized
resistance." Massengale straightened and faced his audience. "The cam-

paign is over—a good sixteen days ahead of the timetable. Mere mopping up remains. The latest count of enemy dead has reached 43,461. Is
that correct, Sherwin?"

"Yes, sir," Colonel Fowler answered, starting. "That is correct."

"I believe that's all I have to say. In conclusion, I'd like to read a radio
General Ryetower just handed me before this conference." He pulled a
slip of paper from his pocket. *"Please accept for yourself and extend to
all officers and men involved my heartiest commendation for your brilliant
execution of the Palamangao Campaign. It is nothing less than a model
of what an imaginative and aggressive command can accomplish in rapid
exploitation. It can serve as an inspiration to all commands, and has
brought us all hearteningly nearer that longed-for day.* It is signed:
Douglas MacArthur."

There was a quick spatter of applause from the press. Massengale
nodded and said: "Thank you, gentlemen, on behalf of Twenty-ninth
Corps. PALLADIUM, I think we can say, without fear or favor, has
been a success, to put it mildly. Now are there any questions?"

Randall called: "How does it feel to enter a city in style, General?"

Massengale smiled but his eyes, fixed on the gardens and the distant
sea, were serious. "It was—very stirring. The populace, as some of you
who were with me know, were out in force, and touchingly happy to be
free again after so much privation. We were thoroughly pelted with
flowers—which was a welcome change from missiles of the denser vari-
ety, I can assure you." The staff officers joined in the laughter this time.
"Representatives from the two guerrilla forces, Colonel Herrera and
Captain Tomás, were on hand, and we were delighted to greet them—
some of you were there for that, I remember. We have, as you know,
relied on much of their information during the campaign. There will be
a ceremony in a few days in which I shall personally decorate these very
brave men."

Shifkin glanced at Randall, who was grinning, his eyes glinting happily behind his glasses, and murmured: "A popular win at the Garden."

Randall frowned. "Come off it, Shif. It's a big day."

"I see we're not talking about the Double Five."

Randall shrugged and Meade said, "Why? What's there to say?"

"Plenty," he answered. "Plenty . . ." He listened with rising exasperation to the queries and answers, the random conviviality in the fine, tiled
room. The contrasts: he could never get used to them. The abrupt shift
from that land of heart-quaking, dry-mouthed fear and mud and high
explosive to places like this where no one was anxious or desperate or
remorseful or raging, where the game of talk pattered through the soft,
light air, never failed to shock him, anger him. He could listen to the AP
man Yortney asking about the condition of the harbor at Kalao, but he
could see only the look on a Negro stretcher-bearer's face when he
learned that the man he had just brought in was dead, or the buck
sergeant with the big red beard laughing and firing into the jungle. He

knew a good deal about discomfort, and toil, and fear; he had not been prepared for the confusion, the disintegration of orderly units and lines, the shattering of all communications and supply—and the absolutely astonishing iron nerve of one man in the face of it. At dawn that second day, when he could tell from the way men moved and dug and urinated that things were perilous beyond conjecture and even the calmest souls began to act tight-lipped and abrupt, he remembered Damon saying cheerfully to a shaken captain, "Why go to them when you can get them to come to you? At least we're not having to dig them out of the ground," and some time later—or was it earlier?—calling to a mortar platoon: "Cheer up, boys—we're sucking 'em into slingshot range . . ."

Long before then Shifkin had stopped asking questions, had given up all thought of remaining an observer and found himself staggering along at one end of a stretcher, panting and straining, his shoulders feeling as if they were being pried bluntly out of their sockets. Back and forth along a trail where things of immeasurable menace crashed and howled and whined and now and then blew him off his feet. You went down with wounded and came back up with ammunition and grenades and water. Hour after hour, until men fell where they walked, half-naked, and slept the iron sleep of the desperately weary; and when at last it was over and he came up to the haggard, bearded men he'd served, hastily cleaning weapons and stringing wire, he shared a quick, fierce affection he'd never known anywhere in his life before.

"What you say, Shif," they called, although he was old enough to be father to most of them, and grabbed his arm or clapped him on the back. "Hey, you made out okay! . . . Hey, the shit really hit the old fan there for a while, didn't it? I mean . . . Christ, the Old Man was the glue . . . Old Sad Sam stopped the sons of bitches . . ."

"The Old Man got it," he told them.

"Oh no . . ." They stared at him in consternation, in anger, in fear and grief; their eyes filled. "No—not the Old Man . . . Where? Where did he get it?"

"The trail block, at Ilig."

"No, for-Christ-sake—where was he *hit!*"

"Oh. In the chest and shoulder and arm."

"Then he's alive?—he's still alive?"

"I think so."

And then—unbelievably—they rejoiced, masking their relief in a torrent of obscenity. "He'll be back . . . Listen, Shif—you don't know the Old Man, he's a fucking ring-tailed tiger . . . Hell, if he had an arm blown off he'd stick it back on with concertina wire and smear it with oil and the fucker better work, I'm telling you! . . . He'll be back."

"I hope so."

"No hope-so about it. You wait and see."

Shifkin hadn't approached Damon before they'd loaded for the operation. He'd been mildly astonished at the odd currents of fate—he'd been

transferred from the European Theater after the liberation of Paris—
that had dropped him in such close proximity to the father of the boy
his daughter had so very nearly married. Grotesque, he had thought,
back on Désespoir, watching Damon talk to a group of junior officers;
grotesque, to be related—even by marriage—to a general, a Regular
Army man at that. Fantastic. He had risked it nevertheless aboard ship, a
brief opportunity just after evening chow when he'd found Damon
standing by himself, leaning against the rail.

"General, I'm David Shifkin. One of the correspondents attached to
the Double Five."

"How are you." They had shaken hands rather formally although
Lawrence the Press Officer had introduced them several weeks before;
the General had smiled, though the correspondent knew Damon's eyes
were measuring him carefully.

He paused, and then said: "I'm Marion's father."

The General's eyes had widened a trifle. "Oh, yes. I wondered if you
might be—Donny once mentioned you were a correspondent. I ought
to know more about such things. There never seems to be enough time
in this business to attend to half the things you should."

There was a brief silence then, while they both watched the emerald
water boiling astern and the sedate little ships of clouds turning rose and
lavender on their hulls. Damon seemed to have nothing more to offer;
but Shifkin felt he couldn't leave it there.

"General, I wanted to say how very sorry I was to learn about—your
son." He felt suddenly to use the boy's name would sound presumptu-
ous, the more so since he had seen him more recently than Damon. "It
must have been a terrible loss for you."

"Thank you." The General's voice was gracious but his face was
unapproachable and stern. "Yes. It was. I imagine it was very hard on
Marion. I wrote her."

Shifkin had looked down, and gripped the rough iron with his fingers.
Jesus, what a cold fish. Most of them were like that, basically—cold,
inexorable beings marching along just outside the human race, bound up
in sports and weapons and that harsh litany of punishment and punctilio. Probably they had to be. Why should they blanch or blubber at
death, any more than a surgeon's hand should falter as it laid open the
layers of fat and flesh and muscle, clamped off the blood vessels? Yet the
men were for him—they liked and respected him more than any other
divisional commander he'd seen, except perhaps Middleton or Terry
Allen.

The Army: that hard, alien world he'd always feared and distrusted
so deeply. The boy himself had been so different—he'd seen him for
part of an evening in New York between assignments: quick and lively
and reflective. The mother, probably. How strange life was! Here he
was on this ship of war, heading for an island swarming with death
and destruction, one more step in a long and sanguinary parade he

wanted with all his heart and guts and soul to forsake as soon as possible—and for this man standing beside him it was his life, his *trade*—

Still, he had written to Marion . . .

It was only during the past days ashore, watching Damon moving about imperturbably, exhorting, advising, crouched in a hole talking in casual earnest to someone while black geysers yawned everywhere; and later, assisted by a medic, tottering down the trail to the field hospital, hollow-cheeked and broken with grief but still pridefully moving under his own power—it was not until then that Shifkin had seen what he was like: and the awareness caught at his heart. They were bound together by loss, by unrealized possibility. Damon's boy was dead, and his own daughter was desolate with grief.

It's funny, Dad, I can say now I guess I always knew it, somehow. Did he? Does that sound cruel, or crazy? Our will and fates do so contrary run, that our something still are overthrown. Our thoughts are ours, their ends none of our own. Is that what it's all about, the best answer a person can hope for? I suppose so. I suppose that's why Shakespeare is so horribly great, he knew all this and everything else, too. I wish we could have a long talk now. Right this minute, while the sleet is banging against the window and a ship is hooting away out on the river. I've gone through so many crazy moods since I heard about Don: I wanted to kill every German on earth. Then I wanted to kill myself. Then I just felt numb and brainless. Now I feel as if everything has been scooped out of me, one colossal hollow ache. I wish we could sit and talk. You've seen so much of fear and death; and the powerful ones, the ones who say only one word, and make us all so wretched. Are they like us, Dad? Do they look at anything, I mean anything, *the way we do? I doubt it somehow. How can they? Oh Dad, I am so unhappy. I never thought a human being could feel like this. So full of misery . . .*

Earnshaw, the UPI man, was saying brightly: "Where to now, General?"

"We will go where we are assigned, gentlemen." Massengale revealed the charming, urbane smile. "But I think I can safely say the word is: Northward, ho."

There was some easy laughter. Then Bingham, the *Trib* reporter and unofficial dean of the correspondents in the theater, a big man with a full blond mustache and disconcertingly large, round, baby blue eyes and a fine, deep voice: "General, you've just concluded a little masterpiece of amphibious war—"

Massengale's eyes sparkled as he interrupted: "Remember, *you* said it, I didn't!—"

When the laughter had subsided again, Bingham went on, smiling gravely: "—and the most remarkable thing about it is that—correct me if I'm wrong—you never held a field command before. I know it sounds absurd to ask a question like this today, but tell us: Were you at all apprehensive when you came out here to take over your first combat command?"

Massengale frowned, hefting the pointer in his long fingers. "Not really. Oh, you worry—worry is the lot of the commander, of course: the unexpected, the unforeseen that might rise up and undo all your plans. This kamikaze threat—it's primarily the Navy's burden, thank the good Lord—is a case in point. But no: to answer your question, Mr. Bingham, I wasn't unduly concerned. Successful warfare is a matter of principles correctly applied, sound preparation—and above all, never doing what the enemy wants you to do. I think we did that, all right. After all, a very good general once said that war is compounded of nothing but accidents, and the alert commander loses no opportunity to profit by them. Messrs. Ochikubo, Kolusai and Murasse handed us a golden opportunity here."

Again there was the gentle murmur, laudatory, acquiescent. Shifkin bit his lip. He himself was comparatively new in the theater and heretofore he'd let the others ask the questions. But if nobody was going to say a single, solitary word—

"General—" he was startled at the force in his voice "—how is General Damon, could you tell us?"

"He's fine, Mr. Shifkin. Coming along superbly. My senior aide was over there and got a full report from Colonel Weintraub not two hours ago." Massengale's eyes left his and passed over the group. "I hope none of you are worried about the Night Clerk. He's a grand old war horse, you know." His lips parted in the crusty smile of the old soldier. "He'd be right here with us now but he couldn't resist playing Sergeant York for a little while."

The appreciative chuckles around the room angered Shifkin all at once. "It was my understanding General Damon entered the line at Umatoc in an effort to save the beachhead, after the Four-seventy-seventh had been hit on the flank and overrun—the action in which General Krisler was killed . . ."

The Corps Commander frowned. "It was hardly as grave as that, I think. Perhaps you're not too familiar with the Night Clerk's exploits at Moapora and Wokai, Mr. Shifkin. He's often a good deal farther front than might be most efficacious, and it's been a source of distress to me; but with the kind of impetuous, aggressive field commander such as General Damon you have to give him his head. I'm sure his presence did much to rally flagging spirits in the crucial places."

Massengale's eyes were running out over the room expectantly, looking for another questioner. Shifkin said quickly: "General, we've been talking about the Eighteenth and Forty-ninth Divisions. Could you give us a little information on the Fifty-fifth?"

"Why certainly—I'd be happy to do so. I thought it was already pretty much a matter of record. The Double Five bore the brunt of

Murasse's headlong attacks, fought magnificently, and is credited with chewing up the better part of two Japanese divisions, the Thirty-ninth and Ninety-second. Its performance was in keeping with the highest traditions of the service."

"Is the Fifty-fifth participating in the drive on Kalao?"

"No, it's not. The Division was pretty severely handled, as you all know, and the general consensus was it needed a rest from its gallant labors."

Shifkin clenched his hand. All right, then: all right. If that was how it was going to be. "Isn't it true, General, that if General Bannerman's division had been used in support of the Fifty-fifth, at Fanegayan and Umatoc, the Salamanders would not have suffered such heavy casualties?"

There was a stir in the room; Shifkin was conscious of several faces turning toward him. At his side Randall muttered something he couldn't hear. General Massengale was staring down at him gravely from the dais. "Elements of the Forty-ninth were dispatched to the Babuyan Beachhead in support of the Fifty-fifth, Mr. Shifkin."

"Yes, but not until oh-five-thirty hours on Friday, and from Dalomo, so that they arrived too late to be of any help."

Massengale's face took on a certain hard intensity. "I'm afraid you've been misinformed on that point."

"I was at the Ilig trail block when the Japanese broke off contact and began their retreat, General."

The Corps Commander's eyebrows rose. "What do you want me to say? A calculated risk was involved. The mobility of the reserve force was essential to the success of the operation, its rapid development. So that when the opportunity presented itself for the drive on Reina Blanca—"

"But isn't it true, sir, that the Forty-ninth Division was General Damon's reserve on Blue Beach?"

There was a short silence. Shifkin swallowed once; Massengale's eyes were boring into his—the large amber pupils, the tiny black points at their centers.

"Dave, I think"—it was Bingham's sonorous baritone, Shifkin could tell without turning—"I don't think any point will be served by going into a lot of conjecture and—"

"Bing, I'd like to get this clarified." He had not taken his eyes off Massengale. "Isn't that true, General?"

"Where did you obtain that information, Mr. Shifkin?"

The correspondent was filled with astonishment. "Why, the plan of battle, General—the briefing we received back at Walewa Heights . . ."

"I'm afraid you're mistaken about that. The floating reserve, designated as SPANNER, was on call by Blue Beach force *subject to the Corps Commander's approval*."

"But then in that case—"

"One moment. Please." Massengale's voice was suddenly hard and peremptory; running his eyes over the rest of the correspondents, he turned to the map again. "The situation involving the Fifty-fifth Division on the eighth and ninth, was regrettable, extremely regrettable; but there was no help for it. General Damon was in the process of effecting a pivoting movement—a sound maneuver though one of course involving some risks—below Fanegayan in an effort to envelop the airstrip above Fotgon, here. There seemed every reason to believe he would complete it without impediment. Whether through faulty intelligence or inadequate patroling, or blind chance—and chance *is* a mighty factor in battle, and one the commander must learn perforce to live with—the Four-seventy-seventh was unprepared for the attack that struck it on that exposed flank at fourteen-fifty on the eighth. As you know, two battalions were overrun and very severely mauled, contact was lost, and Murasse, surprised and elated—and badly misled—by this initial success, decided on his own authority to exploit the breakthrough and committed his two divisions en masse. It was a gambler's throw, it was absurd, it was perfectly characteristic of the temper of Japanese operations in this war. I was confident that the Fifty-fifth could and would contain this rash assault; and my confidence was more than sustained. The attack failed lamentably. Murasse's losses were staggering, the airstrip was left with insufficient forces to protect it, and Kolusai was unable to beat off the interdicting pressure of General Bannerman's forces on the Aguinaldo Highway north of Reina Blanca, and consequently to effect any kind of orderly withdrawal to Nabolos. The enemy was beaten on the twenty-fifth of last month, when the two beachheads had reached their first phase lines; but it was the PYLON maneuver and this astonishing tactical lapse of Murasse's—and our prompt exploitation of it—that enabled us to wind up PALLADIUM so swiftly and adroitly."

Shifkin felt his face growing warm. He ought to give up the floor now, fall silent and give up. If that was how it was going to be, who was he, a mere scribe, to beard the mighty in their marble halls? But something—the stubborn passion that had impelled him into journalism and later made him throw over a comfortable desk job in '37 for the Briguete front in Spain—or was it those haggard faces on the line at Ilig?—wouldn't let him. It was stupid, it was ruinous, it would serve no practical purpose at all. But he had to ask the question. It concerned the truth; and the truth was what he cared about more than anything else.

"Just a moment, General—let me understand you clearly. Did General Damon notify you that he had *completed* the PYLON maneuver?"

Massengale's eyes were steady and piercing. For the briefest of instants something seemed to flicker in their centers; then it vanished. "That is correct," he said.

"And you did not order the Forty-ninth Division to Dalomo until you had received that message?"

"That is correct. You will treat that information as classified, how-

ever." The General's eyes left him and ranged along his staff. "Censor-
ship officers will please take note of that fact. No purpose will be served
by querulous post mortems over the details of this operation, and no
obloquy should attach to either General Damon or the Fifty-fifth Division. On the contrary, their role was nothing less than valorous.
PYLON was a calculated risk, executed with my full approval. And the
results have, I think we can all agree, more than justified its employ-
ment."

"If by justified you mean to include the decimation of one of the
finest divisions I've seen in nearly three years of—"

"Mr. Shifkin," Massengale broke in, and now the correspondent could
see he was angry; a vein just to the right of the widow's peak stood out
like a slender, ruddy thread. "I realize you are relatively new to the
Theater. But I feel I should remind you that your movements and
expressions are subject to Army jurisdiction."

"I'm fully aware of that, General. I was assigned to Africa and Europe for over two years."

"Then surely you are familiar with the character and extent of your
privileges and obligations. This was a hard-fought battle: in hard-fought
battles one suffers losses. That is all I will say." He looked at the assembled audience, and his lean, white face brightened again. "I have no wish
to mar what is an occasion of great felicity; and I don't believe this will.
A great victory has been won by American arms. Let us all be humbly
grateful, and gird ourselves for the somber trials to come." He handed
the pointer to Sergeant Hartje. "I think that's all, then. Good afternoon,
gentlemen, and good luck to you."

There was a brisk pattering of applause. The Corps Commander
nodded, smiling, and headed toward the side entrance that led into the
living quarters of the palace. Shifkin watched the MP spring to attention
by the quickly opened door, the tall form pass through into the interior
gloom, followed by his staff and the divisional commanders.

Someone had a hand on his sleeve. Meade, his round face perplexed.
"What's the matter, Dave? What the hell's eating you?"

He stared at Meade for a moment. "Nothing," he muttered. "Just
shooting off my mouth."

They moved out into the high, broad verandah, and the breeze fretted
gently at the perspiration on his neck and forehead. Far out, the Sulu
Sea was like a vast blue plate. Bingham gave him a short, blandly disapproving glance, and passed on.

"What's the matter, Shif?" Randall said. "You nervous in the service?
You want to get sent home? Boy, you're going to be doing yourself
color pieces of jigaboo labor battalions down in Hollandia if you keep
that up."

"That's what I was going to tell him," Meade said.

He looked at them in cold outrage. "Look, Charlie, you know as well
as I—"

"All right, all right . . ." Meade's face was petulant with annoyance. "What are you going to do—fight city hall? You've been around."

"Yeah," he said sullenly, "I've been around."

"Well, then," Randall intervened, "relax. Massengale is going to be a big name in these parts. Old Dugout doesn't send congratulatory radios like that unless he means them. You know what I mean?"

"I know what you mean."

"What do you want to go roaring off at the mouth about Damon for?"

"Because he's getting the slimy end of the stick, that's why . . ."

"Oh Jesus, don't talk to me about Damon: I've seen him do things on Wokai that would turn your stomach. He's a blood-drinker, hard as nails."

"He is like hell."

"Sure he is—he's a nut, like all the rest of them. Only worse. You've missed the rough stuff, Shif. You've got out here for the peaches and cream."

"Yes, I can see that."

They sauntered along the fine, broad streets, past the houses with their fanciful grillwork and second-story porches framed in tangles of vines. Ahead of them some children were playing; one of them was riding a captured Japanese bicycle which was wobbling all over the road, and fowl scattered here and there in a torrent of cackles and dust. Two women passed with a stately, undulant walk, carrying great calabashes on their heads; their skirts were lovely diagonal stripes of red and green and yellow. Was it better? to rescue a little city, even if it meant the death of many American soldiers? No, it wasn't better. It was purchased at a breach of faith—and if trust went, a man's word, his promise, there was nothing left to rely on in this world . . .

"Cebu's next," Randall was saying pleasantly, squinting in the sunlight. "Then Panay and Zamboanga. Probably just in time for the grand old rainy season. This place has got it all over Leyte and Luzon. Bobby Blake just got over from Lingayen—he says they're living like animals . . . That's one of the distinct advantages of blitzing your way into cities—the billets and officers' clubs are all ready for the opening."

Shifkin stopped all at once and started back toward the harbor.

"What are you going to do *now?*" Meade demanded.

"I'll join you in an hour or so. There's a little errand I've got to do, at the hospital."

"Don't get into trouble, now," Meade warned him. "This isn't the ETO, you know. This is the Pacific."

"I'm getting the picture."

"Tell you what, Shif," Randall called after him with his broad, malicious grin. "How's for trotting around to see Massengale tomorrow, tendering your apologies? You could tell him you've got war nerves.

Tell him you were out of your head with dengue, didn't know what you were doing."

"Grand idea." He turned and looked at the two men, who were gazing at him uncertainly. "Maybe it's just dengue fever coming on."

"It's mending," Dr. Terwilliger said, peering balefully at the crusty, oozing flesh, his eyes bugging. "Coming along. You're a tough bastard, Damon. Even if you are the world's prize God damned fool." He took a probe that looked like a miniature lance with a tiny mace attached to the business end and bent forward again. "Three rounds. The Nipponese was either a superb marksman—which I'm inclined to doubt—or he must have been about ten feet away when he decided to send you to Avernus." Damon, breathing thickly through his nose, said nothing. "But *that's* a grenade fragment," Terwilliger went on. "Piece of scrap iron from a Chicago girder that's been rusting merrily away lo, these many years in a junkyard in South Gary, Indiana . . . The little yellow perils knew what to do with it, though." He handed the probe to a nurse, a big, pleasant girl with deep red hair named Eunice Hogan, and selected another while Damon opened his eyes and sighed. "Of course it's going to take a while. Scapular's affected, trapezium's all smashed to hell and gone. You can hardly expect everything to glue itself together again in five minutes, like some nineteen-year-old."

"I suppose not," Damon answered, watching Terwilliger reach toward his chest with the probe again.

"You're damned well right not. When are you going to stop playing Gustavus Adolphus? *Ill-weav'd ambition, how much art thou shrunk!*" he declaimed. "How long do you expect to get away with this particular game of Russian roulette? You must eat rabbits' feet for breakfast."

"Old—French franc," Damon muttered tightly.

"From Flanders. How bloody quaint. You better find yourself a Greek drachma. Or a God damn Buddhist prayer wheel. Half an inch lower and to the left and you'd be food for worms. *For worms, brave Percy!*"

The Tweaker, now a bird colonel, had lost all his hair and his face had thickened, which gave his upcurving satanic eyebrows all the more force. Staring at the place where one of the grenade fragments had entered, he chanted lustily: "*They come like sacrifices in their trim, and to the fire-ey'd maid of smoky war . . . will we—will we . . .*" He faltered. "Jesus, I've forgotten the lines. Would you believe it!"

"All—hot and bleeding," Damon gasped.

The Tweaker looked up in outrage. His breath smelled of peppermint and hay. "Damn! Yes. *All hot and bleeding will we offer them.* Can't imagine why you remember *that.* Call yourself an Army man, do you? Call yourself a mustang—and reading Shakespeare? Ah, times have changed," he went on, studying the wound, probing with deft care. "Time was when you could count on an RA right down to the wire: bridge and poker and the sports page and now and then the *Infantry Journal*. There's no consistency anymore: fecklessness, depravity is the order of the day . . . Spotted a boy in surgical when the carnage was at its height, lying there white as the belly of the sacred cod. Going right out on us, could tell by the lips. 'But we're giving him whole blood,' his misguided samaritans informed me. 'Put it in the femoral,' I told them, 'it'll go in faster through the groin. Don't you know *anything?*' Then of course they couldn't find it and I had to do *that* for them. Jesus. And all that time Margulis and I were sweating out a wicked abdominal. Fourteen resections. Hell, we don't need all those tripes down there . . ."

"Doctor, you're just saying that," Hogan protested.

"I was never in more deadly earnest. And women!" The Tweaker chortled in demonic glee. "A labyrinth of absurdities. I could tell you tales of the operating room that would curl your lovely hair—"

"Not mine," Hogan retorted.

"It's hilarious. Look at our teeth—why couldn't they have been made of something even faintly durable? and our arms and legs—why aren't they self-replacing, like crustaceans' limbs? Look at our joints: a riot of inflexibility. And fragile! One good puff and back we go to dust. Don't talk to me about the human form divine. It's a junk heap conceived by a clumsy, uninventive idiot . . ."

"But it's all we've got," Damon murmured. The Tweaker had finished probing during this last Jeremiad, and he lay back against the pillows, breathing heavily, sweat crawling in his brows, and looked dutifully at the bent, spiculate piece of old iron the Tweaker held before him.

"Well, it's not good enough. We ought to start over again. Limulus polyphemus, Damon! Put your money on the lowly horseshoe crab: he'll outlast us all, and more power to him." He cocked an eye at the Nebraskan and sighed. "*You* ought to go home, old-timer. You've had enough, you know that? Next time I'm going to refuse to patch you up at all . . ."

It was lonely in the private room after the Tweaker had gone. Damon had liked it better in the tent ward at Babuyan, where he was ranged with all the others, cloaked in the fine anonymity of pain; at night the voices came slowly and impersonally, the voices of men who have nothing but time. Time to pass, to outlast.

". . . Jiggs Reardon was killed."

"The hell you say."

"I saw him, Harry. He was lying there all busted up. All he could do was wink at me."

"Look, you can't kill Jiggs Reardon by degrees. If he wasn't killed outright he'll make it back all the way."

". . . I can't understand it. I was writing down a message for Swede

Lund, the runner was right there beside me. And the next thing I knew I was in here. I can't figure it out . . ."

". . . There's at least a foot of snow now. Maybe more. We always get a good heavy fall first week in December or thereabouts, and another sockdollager just before the holidays. Then it eases off for a while."

"Screw the holidays."

"Don't say that. Remember when the first real cold snap comes, and the ponds and swamps freeze solid, and clear as glass? You can look down and see all the leaves and branches and things, just as though they've been preserved . . ."

". . . I wonder if we get to get some ice cream."

"*Ice cream—!*"

"Sure. When I got hit on Wokai they ran us out to the hospital ship and we had ice cream the day after. Mixed chocolate and vanilla. I'll never forget the way that ice cream tasted."

"Well, you won't get any on *this* rock . . ."

Now, alone in the little room (I'm segregated, he thought wryly) in the hospital that had been converted from the old Spanish barracks in Reina Blanca, he lay patiently, confined in pain, and dozed, and stared at the ceiling, and tried not to think of the past thirty days and nights. Carefully he would thrust away the images and dwell on days back in Walt Whitman, barn raisings and church suppers and picnics, recall a frieze of faces, voices, gestures of school friends or grownups or girls. But inevitably, with the soft persistence of a tide's turning, memories of Benning or Dormer or Luzon would seep in, and then thoughts of field problems or evenings in the beat-up, flimsy, peeling sets, and a homely, bony face with a beak of a nose and quick, twinkling, mischievous eyes—and in spite of himself his own would fill with tears and he would grip the sheet with his good hand in a transport of rage and shame. He should never have agreed to carry out that pivot; never. He'd known it was wrong. He should have refused, categorically . . . Then Massengale would have put Ryetower in and rammed it through anyway. And the Division wouldn't have battled for Ryetower the way they had for him—they'd have been beaten back, overrun, busted all apart and brushed aside. Murasse would have reached the beach, turned Frenchy's flank and burned and blasted and butchered his way along their rear all the way to Facpi . . .

But maybe Ben would have quit, too: in which case—

He closed his eyes. So many good men gone. So many! Bowcher, Jackson, Frohman, Stankula, Cavallon, Dougherty, Rodriguez—all the Old Indomitables from the night at the river. Joe Brand and Harry Pritchard. Ray Feltner badly hurt by a grenade: if he lived he was certainly going to lose his manhood. Tom Spaulding had lost a leg. Vinnie De Luca was hit in both legs and Jack McGovern had been burned in the face and throat. Levinson, Lilje, Goethals dead. They were not a division anymore. A few of the survivors had come by to see him on one pretext or another; had sat, constrained and attentive, in the chair beside his cot. But there had been so little to say. They were not a division any longer, and they knew it: they were a slender collection of broken, exhausted old soldiers, and nothing could alter that. So far! To come so far!—and then wind up like this. And Ben—

There was the sound of movement, a brisk step, and he opened his eyes. Courtney Massengale was standing at the foot of his cot, watching him intently. There was no one with him. Had he been asleep? He scowled at the Corps Commander, blinking.

"Well—Samuel. How are you getting along?"

"Can't complain," he answered after a moment. "Well I could, but I imagine the Tweaker would turn a deaf ear."

"Yes, Terwilliger's a terror, isn't he? I was just talking to him about you: he's obsessed with the idea that you've about emptied your barrel of good luck. I told him, 'Audentes fortuna juvat,' and quick as a whip he retorted, 'Ben Jonson says it's *fools* that fortune favors, General,' and he gave me his satan's-imp grin. I declare, we're getting wonderfully cultured out here: next thing we'll be writing sonnets in Latin, and conversing in iambics." He swung the canvas folding chair around and sat astride it lightly. "I've meant to get by before this but things have been lively. Well: how are they treating you?"

Damon gestured with the good hand. "As you see." He pulled a cigarette out of the pack beside the bed and lighted it with Ben's silver-plated Zippo. The salamander crouched amid the flames, his tongue licking out defiantly, his webbed foot on the sword. The Corps Commander's eyes rested on it briefly, darted away again. He came alone, Damon thought; it's the first time I've seen him alone since Luzon.

"How's the operation going?" he asked flatly.

"Piece of cake, Samuel. Some of Archibald's people are in Kalao. It's all over—token resistance, a few road blocks, delaying actions purely. The rest of them are starving to death in the jungle. Just a case of mopping up. MacArthur's very pleased."

"Is he."

"Didn't you see the congratulatory radio? I had it posted and read to all units."

"Yes. I saw it."

Massengale bent down out of sight beside the cot, straightened again; and Damon saw the samurai sword lying across his knees, the purple whipping on the hilt studded with the garnet and emerald glow of gems, the delicate chasing on the naked blade. "It's Murasse's. Barbaric weapon, isn't it? I want you to have it, Samuel. It's yours, clearly."

"No," he said. "It's yours, General." He remembered Jackson in the teeming dark at the Watubu, gaunt and wild, with the sword in his hands. *Oh, didn't we nail the sons of bitches! After all these months . . .*

"Where's Murasse?" he asked.

Massengale smiled tightly. "Safe in a ditch he bides, with twenty trenchéd gashes on his head, as Terwilliger would say. Not fifty yards from your reserve line at Ilig. They never did find the scabbard."

So Murasse had gone all out, too: leading a last forlorn charge on that endless morning. And now he was starting to molder in the black earth, along with Ben and Bowcher and Joe and all the others. He watched Massengale's fingers running along the curved blade and rage began to beat in his head, making his hands tremble.

"Samuel, that was a magnificent job you did. Magnificent. Really."

"The Division did it, General."

"Well now, I'd hardly—"

"Oh, yes. The Division." His voice was tense and unsteady, and it angered him. "Knowledge of terrain, you know?" he went on. "I hammered it into them: *know your terrain.* And they've got it now, you see. Perfect familiarity. Half of them will never leave the filthy place . . ." All at once he thrust himself forward in the bed, although the pain made him grunt.

"—Why did you do it?" he whispered, despairing and enraged. "*Why—?* For headlines, for a phony Roman triumph?"

Massengale's face had gone very white, the thin lips more bloodless than ever. "Samuel, I don't think an operational misunderstanding over—"

"No," he said softly, and shook his head. "No. It won't wear, General. It won't wash and it won't wear. I've got your radios and I've got copies of mine. And there are a few witnesses left around. A couple of them. Too bad I didn't get starched too, isn't it? along with nearly everybody else? Then you'd have had it *all* your own way. No problems, no questions asked . . ."

"Samuel, those are hard words."

"Are they? I'm sorry—they're the very softest I can muster right now. The very softest, meechingest words I can come up with. Believe me."

Massengale examined his nails briefly. "I hope we won't conclude this gallant campaign in a spirit of acrimony—"

"Don't use that word!" Damon snapped.

"What word?"

"Gallant. Don't use that word in here. It makes me want to puke. You have no right to use that word, or several others. You profane them."

"Samuel, I know you don't mean that—any of it."

"Don't I? You're going to find out how much I mean it."

There was a short silence, while the Corps Commander's eyes widened, and the vein began to beat high on his forehead. "Surely you wouldn't throw away a career of nearly thirty years . . ."

He tried to laugh, but it didn't come off. "Massengale, I'd shove this arm"—he raised the good one—"in a pot of boiling oil if it would put you out of reach of even a *squad* of GIs . . . But I won't be throwing my career away. No."

"You're sure, Samuel? You're quite sure you want it that way?" The amber eyes were very pale and wide, the points of the pupils almost invisible. "You yourself have changed your plans when circumstances indicated. You even disobeyed orders on Moapora—"

"The only difference being that I did it to *save* lives—and I put my own ass on the line . . ."

"Ah, but there was more than that, wasn't there?" That thin, indulgent smile wreathed the Corps Commander's lips. "A certain indefinable pleasure in breaking away on your own—confounding the audience, carving a new triumph out of the blank rock of the future . . . ? And as you yourself are fond of saying—it's one of the Sad Sam trademarks by now: All's well that ends well."

Rage filled him again, thick as gas; he gripped the edge of the sheet. "You're a monster," he said, and his eyes filled. "You're a dirty, cold-blooded monster—you'd feed on your own mother's flesh for another rung in the golden ladder. You're worse than Benoît-Guesclin—at least he didn't know any better: but you—!"

"You're not yourself, Samuel."

"No. I'm not. I'm certainly not. If I were *half* the man I should be—just half!—I'd climb off this sack and beat your teeth down your filthy lying throat . . ."

Massengale got to his feet and began to walk back and forth at the foot of the cot, holding the sword close at his side. "You make it very difficult for me, Samuel. Very difficult indeed."

"That's one consolation."

"I certainly hope we can avoid the rigors of litigation, now the hurly-burly's done. I don't believe in a public airing of grievances, particularly within the family."

"What family?"

Massengale turned in sharp surprise. "The family of the Officer Corps. What did you think I was talking about? Of which you are a member, Samuel: an honored member. I had hoped you'd be a good soldier about this." He resumed his pacing. "You've been out here a long time, Samuel. Twenty-eight months, isn't it? That's a long time away from home and family, the ties that keep a man from wavering out of the line of march. I know what loneliness can do to a man under strain, a lot of us do. It's perfectly understandable. But they won't understand back in Washington—and the dear, bovine, misguided, straitlaced American public won't understand at all . . ."

"—You bastard," he breathed. "You'd haul that out too, wouldn't you?" Massengale's face remained perfectly expressionless. "Yes: you would. It wasn't enough that you shipped her back to the States—you'd wreck her life right along with mine, if you could—you'd wreck anybody or anything that threatened the exalted career of Courtney Schuyler Massengale. Sure." He clenched his fist, fighting to steady his voice. "Well, stand by for a blast, mister. If it comes to that, then so be it. I'm not backing off."

"I see." The Corps Commander nodded and resumed his pacing, his lips pursed. "This is regrettable. I wish I could bring you to see it. The larger issue."

"The larger issue."

"Yes. There's so much still to do. Such a long, long road, and a rough one . . ."

"Do tell."

"I wish you'd reconsider. Samuel, the Division needs you."

". . . *What* Division?" he cried softly. He was perilously close to weeping now, and the fear of breaking down filled him with raging mortification. If only he were on his feet! "What Division is that? They're all back at Fanegayan and Umatoc and Ilig, on the trail, under six feet of shit—and you put them there! . . . I've got some advice for you, Massengale. A few words. Don't be found out there after dark without your retinue." He felt weak with wrath. "They know, mister. Oh yes. Make no mistake. They know."

Massengale smiled his charming smile. "In point of fact I don't care *what* they think of me as long as they fear me. That's the driving gear that turns the wheels of war."

Damon felt a despair that sank into the marrow of his bones. "You poor son of a bitch," he said slowly. "You don't know anything, do you? Not anything at all." He started to go on and stopped himself: there was nothing to say. Massengale's sin—there was none greater—was that he had decided neither grace nor nobility nor love existed in this world. It was hateful to believe this in the wet, dark, desperate sewer's end of 1944. Hateful and demeaning of that fellow at the sink . . .

"Of course I'm sorry to hear that," Massengale was saying crisply. "I have nothing but praise for the troops of the Fifty-fifth Division. In all truth, that was one of the cardinal reasons for my stopping by today. I've been thinking we might put them in for a Presidential Unit Citation. I'm fairly confident that under the circumstances we could get it."

Damon smiled sadly and lowered his eyes. Of course. Massengale had known better than to try to bribe him with a decoration. He had put it on the Division—but left it nicely in the conditional. Might, could. Of course.

For the good of the service.

He studied his free hand. Well: why shouldn't they be cited? Who deserved it more than they did?—what was left of them . . . They were still the Double Five, the Scrofulous Salamanders. The ranks would be filled again, inexorably, in the replacement drafts from Pearl Harbor, Nouméa, Désespoir; the training schedule would crank itself up, range and assault problems and speed marches and scouting-and-patroling, the ammunition would be issued, the gear stenciled and strapped and sweated aboard the attack transports and LSTs. There was still Mindanao and then Formosa, and the Ryukyus; and then lay Dai Nippon herself, and the terrible Kwanto Plain. And who would protect the kids? Who would be left to show them how to file the stacking swivels off their M1s so they wouldn't catch in the creepers, how to tape their dogtags so they wouldn't jingle, how to wear their grenades on the sides of their belts so they wouldn't get in their way while crawling? With him out of the way, Massengale would be ruthless: they'd be given the dirty end of every operation, every logistics detail. Who would fight for them? Dick would merely acquiesce, Winslow was too young and inexperienced, Frenchy would blow his top and slug Massengale in front of thirty correspondents and a three-star admiral . . .

For the good of the service. He had done it over and over again. He had backed down with Hangfire Townsend at Hardee, he'd given way in the ruckus over a mixed regiment in '42 on old Hosmer's urging, he'd abandoned his campaign for the participation of enlisted men on courts-martial, he had let that shattering, portentous China experience bleed away in two voluminous reports, now carefully deep-sixed in some abandoned office in the old Munitions Building. For the good of the service. Was he turning into a circumspect subaltern, loyal to the point of subservience, drowning moral principle in the common good, a perfect tool for the arrogant and conniving—was he becoming the kind of soldier he'd always hated and despised? Ben—Ben would tell Massengale to go and fornicate with himself, Ben would already have beaten him to jelly with one arm . . .

But what would George Caldwell have done? What was wisdom here, in the face of such unscrupulous design? He didn't know. Sick, weak, crushed with grief and worn beyond weariness, he honestly didn't know.

He raised his eyes. Massengale was still watching him with perfect impassivity, the high cheekbones smooth, the amber eyes implacable: waiting. There is no gulf so great as that between the injured and the able-bodied, Damon thought unhappily, chafing the edge of the cast with his thumbnail. Christ, was he condemned for half his life to face this man—and always on unequal terms? There Massengale stood, with his khaki pressed in razor creases and his three stars, his visored barracks hat with the brim crumpled like MacArthur's—though without the golden filigree. So certain. So terribly certain in his seven-league strides toward high command. He was here to stay, now. MacArthur had recommended him for the DSM, he was scheduled to appear on the cover of *Time* magazine the following week, a feature story in *Colliers* was planned. Shifkin had come by two days ago, outraged and choleric, and told him: that, and other things.

And Massengale would fight too, he knew: he would spare nothing to protect himself if he, Damon, asked to be relieved and requested a court-martial. A man who would break his word to a trusted subordinate and then lie to the press about it would not stop in the suppression or falsification of messages, the destruction of reputations or the disastrous involvement of the innocent. And he had great political power behind him in Washington—that uncle of his in the Senate; and a smashing victory under his belt. Damon could hear a very exalted personage in the soft, still rooms of the Pentagon: "What's all this wrangle out there? A brilliant victory, brilliant, what's this Damon after, anyway? Always been a stormy petrel anyway, hasn't he? Maybe he'd better come on home and cool off for a while, get someone on that, will you, Harbison?"

Slowly, watching Massengale, he nodded. Barely moving his lips he said: "I hope you will be able to secure a Distinguished Unit Citation for the Salamanders, General. They deserve every bit of it, and more."

The Corps Commander permitted himself the faintest of smiles. "They certainly do, Samuel. They do indeed. I'm sure Washington will look favorably on a strong recommendation from this Headquarters."

He nodded again. "And now, with your permission, sir, I'll try to get a little sleep."

"Of course, Samuel . . . We'll put this behind us, then?"

Damon stared at him hard. "I would certainly like to, General. If the Citation were to be approved I would be inclined to do so."

Massengale started to say something, checked himself. "Very well. We'll consider this incident closed." At the doorway he paused, and extended Murasse's sword; the jeweled hilt glittered in the soft light. "You're quite sure you won't accept it?"

"Quite sure, General. As you say, it's a barbaric weapon. I want you to keep it."

"Just as you like." The Corps Commander turned away. "Good afternoon, Samuel."

"Good afternoon, sir."

He closed his eyes, but he could not sleep. For a long time after Massengale had left he lay gazing out at the tossing feathery green canopy of the acacia trees.

"Oh, well—*chance*," Bill Bowdoin called into the wind. "If you think it's all just a matter of chance . . ."

"Of course I do!" Tommy Damon laughed. "What else is there?"

The wind blew chill and wild from the African shore, a darkened world away, and the waves swept looping chains of green foam along the beach; above their heads sea birds whirled and dipped and uttered their pinched slatterns' cries.

"You're just cynical and rich," she taunted him.

"You bet. And I'm going to get richer."

"Well, I'm not—I believe in everything . . ." Smiling she broke away from him and ran along the beach. Sandpipers leaped into flight ahead of her, scattering like checkered fans. Glancing back she saw that Bill had decided not to pursue her but she ran harder anyway, the air cold and raw in her throat, her feet thudding on the damp, hard shore, until she was completely out of wind and threw herself down on a little shelf of sand. After a moment he approached and sat beside her.

"Do you know what you are?" he demanded. "You're a spiritual pirate."

"Pirates aren't spiritual—!"

"Spiritual as anybody else." He watched her for a moment with his shrewd, gray-blue eyes. "American women are so *docile*, under all the armor and pretensions. So cozy-coy. That's why you're unique—do you know that? You're willing to take risks."

She hugged her knees, watching the terns beating their way upwind, wheeling and diving. "I did the best I could with what I drew," she said evenly.

"You did better than that. You couldn't help it if you were brought up in a medieval atmosphere."

"Everybody's got to live by some kind of rules."

"Of course—it depends on what the rules are . . ." He smiled a sardonic smile. "You army brats. You're such puritans under all the tough talk. You should have lived with a dozen men, a hundred. You've got something to give every one of them."

"Bushwah," she retorted; but it was fun to hear on a Long Island beach, shivering in the sea wind, watching the breakers in their slow furling. The easy, calm assertion of his voice—the voice of the Eastern Seaboard, of inherited wealth and favored education and the steady generations of authority and power, redolent of summer homes on the water and annual voyages to St. Moritz or the Greek Islands and the car waiting outside the office in midtown at 4:30, chauffeur at the wheel—had plucked her out of the tight little vortex of the Army world. Until she'd met him at an OWI function three months before, she'd never really left it for an instant. Worlds might be crumbling and the heart wrung dry with anguish, but one dressed smartly, appeared poised, well groomed and in control, and feigned an interest in the topics of the day, cataclysmic or trivial. Even the news that Poppa had been wounded by shell fragments in the Huertgen Forest had not thrown her too badly off stride; it was merely one more boulder in an avalanche of calamity. He was shipped home some weeks later, limping badly and looking old and infirm—he promptly crept into bed and slept for hours and hours.

From Butch Rieser she learned that he had been wounded—and one of his aides had been killed—by our own artillery; a revelation that thrust to the front of her mind that vicious disclosure of Irene Keller's at Christmas. Marge had gone home to Wisconsin, and neither Tommy nor Emily had ever referred to it again; but it continued to torment her. If it were true, if Court had actually done something like that . . . Sam's letters were infrequent now, and they were noncommittal and brief. The Salamander had taken a terrible mauling, its survivors had been awarded the Presidential Unit Citation in a ceremony at the old Spanish barracks in Reina Blanca; he himself was on his feet again, and beginning to regain the use of his left arm. The only reference to Ben's death had been in one terse line.

One evening, while she was serving her father his dinner in bed, she told him about the cocktail party, and asked him if he'd heard anything.

He shook his head irritably. "War is the seat of confusion, ignorance and cross-purpose. If I were to tell you a tithe of the mix-ups and muddles—"

"But this isn't muddles, Poppa—this is hideous . . ."

"I should be very surprised if anything remotely like that happened. Bart Keller's wife is not celebrated for her veracity. Or some other conjugal qualities I could name."

"But she said Don Grayson heard it from—"

"I don't care who heard what from who. The Army's got its gossips and troublemakers, just like anything else."

"Well, couldn't you call up Ritchie Collis or someone like that?—find out if there's anything to it?"

"What good would it do? The Chief doesn't want his people bothered with that kind of thing. They're trying to get on with the war."

"But Poppa, if something like this could actually happen—"

"It's no good, Tommy." His worn blue eyes flashed out at her with a querulous appeal. "No constructive purpose will be served by raking up dead ashes. Look—I'm a poor old man, as full of grief as age. And sick into the bargain. Old men shouldn't get involved in such shenanigans. Old men lack the requisite ambition . . ."

He would not say anything more; he pushed the pillows up behind him and busied himself translating the memoirs of General Marbot. She knew then, or thought she knew. She swallowed her womanly—and therefore incompetent—objections, and went on cooking and caring for him, working with disabled veterans out at Walter Reed, putting in her time at the USO; doing the things that somebody—the Army, the country, the world—expected of her.

Bill Bowdoin had changed all that; his hard, indulgent cynicism laughed at her credulity. Shocked, fascinated, half-angry, she listened to his sardonic dissertations on the war—the chances missed, the duels of will, the conniving, the sly expropriation of supplies, even men. It was incredible: these men she'd known not long ago as happy-go-lucky, dutiful shavetails and captains were now squabbling like greedy little boys at a birthday party while the troops sweated and froze in the mud, the cold rain. Bill however seemed to regard it all as a kind of preposterous practical joke, all the more effective for its very outrageousness. Impatiently he would brush her consternation aside.

"You're so full of chivalry. The lot of you. Do you know there's a three-star general in the ETO who rises every morning from the bed of a particularly notorious countess, downs three ounces of Bourbon neat— and then kneels for twenty minutes in fevered, ardent prayer?"

She'd laughed weakly. "Yes, and I know who he is, too."

"Sure you do. You've all been stabbed to death by the twelfth century. You don't see how things operate. Every war has to be a gleaming crusade, with a hovering Grail of Joseph of Arimathea for only the holiest eyes to behold. When the plain fact of the matter is the war resembles nothing so much as a big corporation going full blast, with its board of directors meetings and reports and prospectuses, its graphs and charts and shipping sections, layout and advertising—right down to the final product."

His lips curving in the hard, disdainful smile he would sketch in the patterns and counterpatterns of intrigue and antipathy and long design. Churchill with his Balkan obsession, forever scheming for a Yugoslavian landing, invasion up the Danube to forestall the Russians—anything, anywhere to forestall the Russians; old Cord Hull gripped in his implacable hatred of De Gaulle, who on his part smoldered with an undying thirst for vengeance against Britain and America only an Alsatian could sustain; Chiang Kai-shek feuding with the British—and, rid of poor old Joe Stilwell at last, scheming to secure still more American aid to stuff the pockets of his favorites. And America? Now we were into Germany— and with perfect aplomb we were engaging Nazi officials to run things for us. We were no sword of the Lord and of Gideon, we were simply a great power—the dominant world power, now—emerging in a torrent of aggressiveness and expediency.

"Wait'll you see what's in the cards for Japan. Oh, my. All four islands aflame from sea to shining sea. The Hamburg raids are going to look like the feeble sputterings of a cigarette lighter . . ."

She supposed it was true. Bill sat in on some of the grand councils; he had gone to school with Hopkins, he'd been present at the Darlan negotiations in North Africa from start to finish. He had left his field of corporation law for the post of special assistant to the Secretary of War, and she knew he expected a federal judgeship or a seat on one of the war crimes commissions at the end of hostilities. He knew the world—and apparently the world was not what she'd thought it was.

Not that she cared so terribly—the very texture of her life had altered with his appearance. He had been twice married and twice divorced, and to the expensive, assured women of the rotogravures; and he wanted her. He *wanted* her, and his urbane attentiveness, his tough-fibered certainty was formidable. They met at his apartment on K Street, or at the flat of a friend of his who ran the Bureau of Statistics; occasionally they went to the beach or up into the mountains, riding along the smoky, somnolent trails where the sunlight flowed in a copper skein over the horses' flanks. She had found herself gliding toward his quick insistence like a native diver rising toward the surface of the sea, her lungs bursting with eagerness. She wanted to bask in his presence. On the far side of the moment was—she didn't like to think about what was on the far side. On this side, where she was, there was flight, the bubble-surge of sensation, the dense chafe of flesh. Time continued to crumble away—past and present continued to melt like salt pillars and left only the present to swoop through, sink through, founder upon. Avidly she sought the lash of rain in her face, the spongy feel of moist earth, the thunderous roll and crash of big band swing, the yellow sway of leaves against the sun. At such times her body seemed to her as vast as the earth, bombarded by a million sights and nuances, flayed by them . . .

Now in this second week in April he had persuaded her to come and stay for several days at his place in East Hampton, a great square house with columns and tortured ancient locust trees and a green sea of lawn that sloped toward the Atlantic. It was a discreet sojourn; he had closed the place down after he'd gone to Washington and it was opened just for the holidays, when the children flocked in from half a dozen prep schools and colleges. There was only a dour, uncommunicative Yankee who worked on the grounds. They camped in the master bedroom, and Tommy cooked their meals in the huge kitchen. Sitting where she was on this shoal of sand, turning, she could just catch the upper stories and the roof, with its massive chimney flanking each end; it looked awesome and durable, built to last for scores of generations.

"It's raining," he said.

They walked back hand in hand, arguing happily about chance and causality; and after that mounted to the great bedroom and took each other with a quick, sure passion. Where Sam had been restrained, a bit diffident in his lovemaking, Bill was abrupt, almost fierce—an approach she welcomed now. She wanted to be invaded, plundered and tossed about, she wanted to plunge into the act of love like a naked foot in moss, conscious of nothing but the grip of flesh and the tightening surge and scald of sensation, until at last all thought, all memory were swept away . . .

"Did you actually go on a bond tour?"

She smiled indolently. He had gone over to the table beside the long window to get his cigarettes. Every time his body broke away from hers in this abrupt way she felt a curious, not unpleasant numbness. He did what he wanted, too; not like Sam, but in another way.

"No," she answered. "I spoke at a rally. Once. It was absolutely disastrous. Emily Massengale talked me into it. It was supposed to keep me from brooding and things like that. I don't know what I could have been thinking of—I must have been out of my mind."

He came back to the bed and lay down beside her. "That old hovering Grail again."

"Yes, well—maybe. I had the speech all prepared, all carefully written out. Awful. I'm not much of a literary soul. And I put on my good blue gabardine and got up there on the platform with Em and some civic potentate and two kids, CMH winners, and one of them—well, never mind about that . . ."

"Looked just the *teeniest* bit like Donny." She glanced at him sharply, caught between resentment and admiration. "Look, you might as well start facing it, you know. Nothing is going to be improved by making a mystic technicolor production out of it." His voice was kind, however; maybe she needed to be talked to like that.

"All right, then—yes," she said. "He did. But it wasn't just that. It was this whole bovine herd out there, with their fish-eyes goggling up at me so expectantly, looking for something, hoping for something: what? Another circus? And yet it was more humble than that, it wasn't that feverish and greedy. You know what I mean . . . Bill, they were so pitiful!"

"Oh Jesus."

"No—I mean it. They didn't know *anything* and they wanted to, they really did. All those poor slobs, with their sweaty underwear and dandruff and unknown diseases—every bit as stupid and lost and mixed up as I was. What the hell was I *doing* up there? The local potentate introduced me, there was some polite applause, I started to speak—and I couldn't. Not a word. I just looked at them. I had my pretty little dull little speech right there in my hand and I couldn't use it. All I could think of was Donny and these silly, hopeful, expectant people and *their* kids, and what was going to happen to us all, and what a long, slow, hideous thing war is. Worse than anyone can imagine, because each person sees only one small, nasty part of it, but the war is like the ocean, roaring away everywhere, turning us all into cowards or tigers or slaves or sinners. I don't know how long I stood there looking at them. And then I said, 'You've got to buy bonds . . . because you've just *got* to!'—and then I burst into tears."

"And it brought down the house."

"Yes. That was the worst part of it. The very worst. They all jumped to their feet and yowled and howled and blew kisses at me and bought bonds till they were coming out of their ears. And those damned photographers, and everyone hovering around me on the platform as if I were a mental basket case, or pregnant out of wedlock or something. Ghastly."

"It served its purpose. What happened then?"

"Nothing happened. Who could follow *that?* Emily took me home in a cab and gave me a good stiff drink and put me to bed."

He put his hand over hers. "You're extraordinary," he said. "Do you know that? Really and truly extraordinary . . . Why don't you marry me?"

She looked at him in amazement. "*Marry* you?"

"Why not? It's done, you know."

She smiled, still held in surprise. "You'd get tired of me in half a year. Like the others."

"Oh, no I wouldn't. I want continuity now. One rhythm. I want someone with force, with discipline. Someone just like you."

"Good lord." It astonished her beyond measure that he could see her that way.

"I mean it . . . marry me," he repeated. "What's holding you? You know it's all gone to hell between you and Damon."

"Sam was a good husband to me," she replied stoutly—and only then realized with a pang the tense she'd used.

"I'm sure he was. But he's given up—you've told me so yourself." His gaze was confident and piercing. "You're more than he can handle. You always were, only neither of you saw it."

She shook her head. The clouds kept streaming in from the sea, all silver above and charcoal-dark on their bellies. "I couldn't, Bill. It wouldn't be right. With him out there . . ."

"What difference does that make? He knows it's all over. He's a professional soldier, with a war to win, a kingdom to take—do you think he'll resign and come home to mope? Or do you think he'll put his pistol in his mouth?"

"Bill, for Christ sake—!"

"You think he'll pine away and die of a broken heart? You know how he's been passing his lonely hours."

She stared at him. "What? What do you mean?"

"That nurse he's been playing around with out there . . ." His eyes were very wide. "You mean you didn't know about that? For God's sake—I thought you Army types knew everything that's going on everywhere . . ."

We do, she thought angrily; everybody but the goat. So that was what it was. God, it was just like him—go along like a stick for twenty years, a perfect stick, never even *looking* at anything in skirts—and then take up with some blowzy, giggling bedpan wielder in a way that would splash it all over the Army inside of a month. The big, dumb lame-brain. She was all at once furious and vengeful—then the incongruity implicit in this attitude turned her derisive.

"Well, that's up to him," she muttered. "If he wants to be the laughing stock of the Theater . . ."

"Gee, I'm sorry, Tom-Tom." Bill looked abashed—an expression she'd never seen on his face before. "I thought you knew, no kidding. Brad Parry over in Somervell's office told me he had it from—"

"Never mind," she said crossly. "I don't want to know any more. It's none of my business, anyway." Though it was her business, of course. If it wasn't hers, who in hell else's was it? But she was still struck with consternation: if *Sam*—steady old rocklike Sam—could fumble his way into a perfectly witless liaison like that . . .

All men had feet of clay, as Court Massengale once said; it was only necessary to discover the particular weakness and play upon it artfully—

Bill was scowling at his nails. "Damn. Just my luck. Now you'll think I threw that at you just to strengthen my case."

"Don't be silly," she said. "I know you better than that."

"Good. Marry me, then."

"Bill, it still doesn't alter the fact that he's out there in the wretched boondocks."

"Of course he is: he chose it, it's his life. That's a hopelessly sentimental attitude."

"I'm a sentimental gal."

"No, you're not. You're romantic—but you're not sentimental."

Her arms behind her head she considered this, while the clouds shouldered implacably overhead and the locust branches dashed up and down just beyond the window. She was romantic, all right: and here it was, at her feet—a life she had yearned for through five thousand dusty, sweltering afternoons, listening to the terse cries of command, the rippling pop of range gunfire, the hard, silvery bugle calls: the world of leisure and position . . . And yet here, now, she found herself shrinking from it. What was the matter with her? You had one life, one voyage—why not seize this moment, follow it wherever it led? Bill was right: the thing with Sam was over, he was through with her and she with him—he'd even found someone else, it seemed. To coin a phrase. And they could never bridge the marsh of recrimination and estrangement of the past two years. What was there to hold them? Donny was dead, Peggy didn't need her, she was happy on that Quaker farm project in Flemington, there was even a boy interested in her now; Poppa had immersed himself in his own concerns—what ties did she have left from that old, worn life? Here was a forceful, attractive, wealthy man offering her his hand, a new life fixed in the web of the present; a dalliance that could laugh at time . . . And if there wasn't love, not love exactly, there was affection, a lively interest in the partner, respect—why shouldn't she do it? Why this dismay, and a stealthy sense of loss?

All it meant was cutting a few frayed and unraveling hawsers, summoning up her courage and willing the change. Why shouldn't she?

She would: she would do it.

She opened her mouth to answer and the telephone rang. He bounded out of bed and went over to the table and picked up the receiver while she watched him; his trim, stocky figure, still nicely muscled and flat-bellied at forty-eight, his smooth silver hair pleasantly disarranged. Teeth pressed on her lower lip she carried her gaze around the room, which now looked as strange as some Arthurian castle—and as familiar as her father's old set at Fort Sam.

"Yes." He winked at her, his hand on his naked hip, the wrist cocked. "Yes, speaking." Then his whole manner changed. The confident, faintly amused air was gone, his face looked exasperated and tense; his eyes roamed blankly over her body. "It's confirmed, then?—definitely confirmed? Jesus. Yes. Jesus, yes. All right. All right, I'll get down there as fast as I can make it. Right."

He put down the phone as if it were a rare porcelain.

"What's the matter?" she asked.

"Oh my," he muttered. "My oh my." He was still staring at the phone. "The President," he said after a moment. "The President has just died. Massive cerebral hemorrhage."

"Oh," she heard herself murmur. "Then he won't live to see it."

"Not very likely. See what?"

"Why, the victory . . ." It was her first thought.

"Yeah." He was already dressing hurriedly. "I've got to get back right away. Do you want to go back with me or stay on here?"

"There's not much point in my staying on alone." She smiled at him, but his mind was already back in Washington.

"Boy oh boy." He was tugging savagely at his laces. "Now the walls'll come tumbling down. Steve Early said he was tired almost to death—I guess that's what he meant, all right."

"Truman'll be President," she said.

"Won't he, though? Won't he just." He snorted. "Too bad I never learned how to play poker. Think you could teach me on the way down? Cram course? Oh my God, what a royal changing of the guard there'll be. Probably get back just in time to find I'm out on my ear."

"They won't do that, will they?"

"I really couldn't tell you, sweet. Your guess is very bit as good as mine. Harry doesn't like us New York slickers, I know that much. Yes sir, he's one scared chicken right about now."

"What do you mean?" She was up now and throwing on her clothes.

"The President was carrying everything in his hands. *Everything.* Now the fat will be in the fire, along with everything else."

She felt her eyes fill all at once. "He was so brave," she murmured.

"FDR? Baloney. He was a power-drunk egocentric and the prince of political manipulators. But he knew how things worked, and he could make them go the way he wanted. Now watch old Naval Person take over, lock-stock-and-barrel. The Indomitable Cigar." She gathered dimly that he meant Churchill. "Stand by for the Red Menace. War at the Elbe."

"What?"

"Sure Mike. The New Hundred Years' War. 1914 to 2020 or so. Hadn't you heard? And this one will be a daisy. And after the Russkies comes China, and after China—who knows? Africa, I suppose . . ."

She stared at him, wordless. His flat, wry tone filled her with such desolation she felt rooted to the floor of this room forever.

". . . I don't believe it," she said.

"Don't. See if I care." He completed his Duke of Windsor knot with a flourish, cinched the foulard against his perfectly fitting collar. "That's what's going to happen, though. And now we haven't got anybody who knows the combination to the safe."

"—It can't be," she protested. "Not after all this . . ."

"Anything can be. Anything old homo sapiens decides to put his dirty, devilish little mind to. Anything at all . . . He's a beast," he declared with sudden declamatory heat, shrugging into his jacket. "Your fallen god, the master of his fate. He loves it: he *loves* slaughter and waste and the torture of his fellows. Wait'll you see what we find in the glorious Thousand Year Reich."

"Yes, the Nazis—"

"Nazis, hell—they've only done what we all of us dream of doing. There's nothing the human animal gets a greater kick out of than smashing all the glass in the palace, ripping open a few bellies, slurping up his own vomit—he's a hairless ape with a taste for flesh and devilment. Can't you see that?"

"No," she said fearfully, "—he's not a beast. Not just a beast."

"Oh God. And you've been hanging out in Washington for the past three years. Oh, you crippled, maudlin romantics . . ."

They were back on that again. Raising her head, she watched the rain driving in out of the Atlantic under the ragged canopy of cloud. Suddenly she knew she couldn't marry him—if only for the reason that she *was* a crippled, maudlin romantic at heart. There was something impassable in this argument. She could not agree with him; she couldn't. Man was not a beast, simply—he had captured glorious visions, he had chained the lightning, fashioned things of great beauty, grappled with the awful mysteries of the Universe: he was the only creature who had burst the bonds of the moment—

With quick surprise she glanced at Bill. But he had no further interest in the discussion, if discussion it was; he was packing swiftly and deftly, frowning, humming to himself. Perhaps that was as good an indication as any other. Well: the President was dead, his own future was vitally affected; but even so . . .

She felt a quick rush of concern for Sam, so forceful it was like an object held in her hand: what he might be doing at that moment, what he was thinking; what his opinion might be about this war, and the world that would emerge from the fire and rubble . . . The Second Hundred Years' War. Snatching up her pajama bottoms, she glanced at the rumpled bed with a mild aversion. I lie to myself, she thought; all the time. To *think*—to reflect, to speculate, to remember was to re- nounce the claims of the moment, thrust out in time. That was what it meant to be a man.

It was the hairless ape who drowned in the moment.

"Bill," she said quietly, "I don't believe you."

"I gathered that." He looked up then, and saw what she meant. His brows drew down; she had wrenched him back to the problem of the two of them, here on Long Island, and he resented it. "What are you talking about?"

"I mean—Bill, it's no go," she said lamely. "It won't be right. I can't do it."

He snapped his suitcase shut and straightened, watching her—a slow, measuring glance, his lower lip thrust out, his clear, cool eyes narrowed; and for an instant she felt a curious fear.

"Maybe you're right," he said. "Maybe you ought to go back to him. Just think what it would do for your martyrdom. All the things you could do—walk in with a grief-stricken countenance and drop onto the living-room couch and charge him with the death of the boy. Really stick him with it. A nice, raw wound lined with salt . . ."

She gazed at him, shocked into silence, half-stunned. His face was wearing a thin smile, but there was a dark red flush at each side of his throat; he was angrier than she'd ever seen him. Was this how she seemed—was this what she really wanted?

"You'd love it, wouldn't you? Mope around all day, jigsaw puzzles and hen sessions. The brave little army wife bearing up so nobly under this dreadful burden. Just think—you could be a conscience to him all day—and half the night, too; what a thrill that would give you. The Masochist's Delight."

She stammered: "Bill, that's not fair—"

"Isn't it? Think about it. Isn't that what you'd like better than any- thing else? A Gold Star Mama With a Cause. Oh boy." He pointed to the floor at his feet. "I just offered you—I'm not sure the offer still stands—a positive new life. A real break-out. Maybe it isn't exactly the life your romantic soul wanted when you were fifteen. But a real life, with dignity and purpose, and respect. No medals or reviews, but re- spect. There isn't an awful lot of that these days. And you could be a help to me, too—we could carve out something together. I think you know that."

"Bill, if you'd let me—"

"But no—you can't wait to get back to that good old rack. The agonies of the Catherine wheel, with an audience of thousands. This

Martyred Matron. Else what's a soldier husband for? Why, it's better than a twenty-year annuity! Jesus, won't it be a pity if he gets himself starched in the Honshu invasion—"

"All right, Bill! . . ." She was angry herself now, but it was dulled by confusion and a growing alarm. She should be able to laugh at this, it ought to be a source of amusement: what in God's name was the matter with her? She had a sudden image of Sam back at Hardee, long ago, sitting on the edge of her cot, his eyes tormented and pleading. *I'm that man, honey. Don't you see?*

"We're talking about identity," Bill was going on implacably. He was holding an unlighted cigarette between his finger and thumb, like a piece of chalk, and was pointing it at her. "Yours. Now you have a choice: a good clear one. Either you can make your life serve a positive and relatively normal function—or you can turn in on yourself and put on the weeds of the professional griever, the perennial man-punisher, feeding on the stones of bereavement and vengeance. Maybe you'll enjoy that more than anything else—maybe your sado-masochism synchromeshes perfectly, for all I know." He pointed the cigarette at her throat. "Now which road do you want to travel down?"

She shook her head; she was still full of alarm. "It isn't that simple . . ."

"No. Nothing is. But you better think about it: you better find out what's running you, sweet. What you really want."

She finished packing in silence, nervously. What was running her? Her mind appeared to her as a small room crammed with cast-off furniture, outworn garments and appliances. What did she want? Did she want to punish Sam? did she want to forsake him?

The Cormorants, Poppa had used to call them—perhaps because they held themselves with such stiff pride, their heads suspended on corded necks; or perhaps because they exuded an atmosphere of such blackness. They stood forbiddingly at the ends of reception lines, or sat at tea sets pouring with icy correctness, or leaned forward, conversing with one another in a fierce, taut complicity . . . Was she on the way to becoming a Cormorant? That was ridiculous—she was madcap Tommy Damon, who had introduced the Lindy Hop to Fort Beyliss, whose imitation of Tallulah Bankhead was famous from Fort Myer to Manila Bay . . .

She closed her bag, feeling defeated and apprehensive and angry. A little while ago she had become aware of the prison of the moment, and resolved to flee it. But Sam was her past, and a lien on her future. Donny was the core of that past, Donny was what they had together, they and they alone—promise and memory: to leave Sam was to destroy Donny all over again, more cruelly than the German fighter planes had done . . .

"All set?" Bill said from the doorway.

"All set."

As she descended the stairs the rain threw soft, transparent stains down the panes of glass.

"They did it just to get rid of me," Vicky Varden declared, and her smooth, lovely face tightened in a scowl. "They can put it any way they want, that's what it adds up to."

"Now sweetie, try to look at it another way," Al Hambro said.

"What other way is there to look at it?"

The press agent opened his hands. "You're doing yourself a world of good out here. Your publicity has been terrific, I've told you that . . ."

"Well, I hope it's scoring points for me in heaven," she retorted, "because it sure as hell isn't doing anything for me here on the ground." Her eyes were snapping. "The chance of a lifetime down the drain and here I sit on my aching fanny, ten thousand miles away from home plate. It's all T.L.'s fault. That foul-mouthed son of a bitch—"

"Now, Vee-Vee," Lew Pfyzer chided her. Like most comedians he was soft-spoken and shy when he wasn't on stage; he looked like a competent CPA with a stubborn, rather stupid client. "General Massengale has been wonderfully hospitable to us and I don't think he's all that interested in a lot of Hollywood shop talk. Do you?"

"—Oh, I'm sorry, General!" Vicky Varden turned toward the Corps Commander. Every trace of displeasure was gone; her face was alive with the winsome, eager smile that had gleamed from screens and billboards and GI footlocker covers for three years. "I'm sorry, I really am. This is honestly the sweetest reception I've been given since General Ike's place outside of Paris, at—what was the name of it, Lew?"

"Marnesse la Coquette."

"Oh, yes. How did I ever forget that?"

"I can't imagine, lover."

The star shivered her shoulders pleasurably. "I love palaces: they always make me want to do crazy, impossible things—have affairs with sultans and torture people in dungeons and throw myself around . . ."

"You don't need a palace for all that, sweetie," Pfyzer told her.

"Lew, you're a crummy sadist." She ran her fine hazel eyes around the ceiling filigree. "A castle like this tells you all the things you want to be. Do you know?"

Sitting at the head of the long table Courtney Massengale nodded gravely. Well, it did something like that, and a little more; he was pleased with the effect. The private dining room with its own balcony, where the USO troupe and his senior staff officers were now eating and drinking, was separate from the officers' club proper but connected by a narrow passageway, so that the music and laughter from the main room lent a distant air of frivolity to the smaller party. Yet it was understood that aside from barboys and messmen no one was to enter here, except for the most exceptional reasons. His guests as they came through Reina Blanca—correspondents, congressmen, entertainers—always sensed this; it never failed to make them a touch more respectful and subdued. All except Miss Varden, whom apparently nothing ever subdued.

"Forgive me for being in such a brutal mood, General," she pleaded; her face broke into a winsome little pout. "I'm standing right in the middle of the crisis of my life, I really am. And I need your help."

He smiled his most charming smile. "Anything within my humble powers, Miss Varden."

Her face brightened like a little girl's; there were actually tiny stars at the centers of her pupils. "Please call me Vicky."

"I'm afraid I couldn't do that," he answered. "I never address people by their nicknames, you know."

"But why not? I said you could . . ."

"In my opinion it's both vulgar and unnecessary."

"Oh."

There was a funny pause. Both Pfyzer and Hambro were staring at him blankly. Pleased with the effect he smiled again and said: "But I'll call you Victoria, if I may."

She straightened in her chair, fluttering a little. "Oh, I love that," she cried. Abruptly she aimed a bright vermilion fingernail across the table at Pfyzer's throat. "You see, Lew? There's gallantry. Something *you'll* never know . . . Jesus H, why can't men hang on to their gallantry anymore?"

"We've lost it all escorting you around the fighting fronts, darling," the comedian answered.

Vicky Varden ignored him; all her attention was focused on Massengale again. "It's just that I'm in danger of losing the role of my career. Absolutely. They're casting right now. *Tess of the D'Urbervilles.*" She put her teeth neatly on her ripe little lower lip. "It's a novel by Thomas Harding."

Massengale nodded again. "Oh. Of course. Do they hang her at the end?"

"I don't know—I haven't read the script. It's just the chance of a lifetime and the studio roped me into this mucking tour, every damn palm tree in the Pacific Ocean—and now I'm supposed to find Chet and be *reconciled* with him. Of all the God damn loony ideas!"

"Now, Vee-Vee," Hambro murmured.

"Well, it is. It's fantastic. In this heat . . . Of course you expect it to be hot anywhere in August," she said to Massengale. "Except L.A., I mean.—Can I call you Court?" she asked him. "It sounds so—I don't know: so strong and savage. Ruthless, sort of. General Court . . ." Her face went suddenly blank. "Oh: I guess I better not say it that way, should I?"

"Ah, but imagine if my last name had been Marshall."

Captain Graulet of the G-2 Section had entered from the corridor

that connected the private dining room with the Corps offices and now
was leaning over Fowler, speaking rapidly and urgently. Fowler had
turned in his seat and was staring up at Graulet with a quizzical, irritated
expression on his sober, scholarly face. Massengale watched them for a
moment, and then Bucky Warren, holding forth for the dancer Diana
Speers, who was shrieking happily, a hand at her throat. Ryetower and
Burckhardt were both convulsed with mirth. Lowering his eyes Massengale sipped at his wine and felt the old interior laughter. These USO
tours in particular amused him: the parade of stars and comedians and
dancers with their little packs of attendants and advisers, their false,
breezy camaraderie, their rituals of presentation and self-pretense, their
demands, the lamentable vulgarity that sheathed them like chain mail.
But the Varden girl intrigued him. Watching her from his screened
booth at the rear of the audience the evening before, standing so straight
and demure in the clinging blue gown, holding the microphone, her
head inclined prettily to one side, he'd been conscious of a quick, electric brightness reminiscent of Tommy Damon: that mirror flash of eyes,
and a vibrant, faintly husky voice that promised intimacy, dalliance, a
triumphant surrender.

> "... We'll ride a silver balloon
> To the Taj Mahal and Cathay ...
> Darling, it can't be too soon
> Till we've found that heavenly, golden day ..."

And there they sat below him in their dreary, starved, unwashed thousands, their faces following her every gesture with the blind, degrading
hunger that never failed to fill their eyes every time they glimpsed a
woman from home. The poor, pitiful clods—chained to a myth that
would never cease to mock them—

"You're lonely, aren't you, Court?"

The impertinence of these people was something marvelous. He knew
his face showed nothing. He turned to her, aware of a sudden, sharp
constraint among the others. They are afraid of her, he thought with
stealthy pleasure—and still more afraid of me: they are caught between
fears.

"*Command* is lonely," he answered.

Smiling she shook her head. "Not what I meant. Never mind." She
emptied her glass—she had scarcely touched her food, although most of
the others had exclaimed over the cuisine—and leaned toward him, her
eyes wide and challenging. "Timing—is—everything," she pronounced,
and tapped the table with her nails. "*Everything* ..."

"I know," he said.

"I know you do. That's why I admire you: you've never made a
mistake." She nodded, watching him steadily from under her brows.

"That's why I need your help. Will you come to the aid of a damsel in distress?"

He gave his slow, deprecatory nod—part of the Massengale Manner. All the old terms had been reversed. This star sitting here beside him was a law unto herself—her scowl could send panic through her entire retinue, her moods were the stuff of national press releases; but now, here, one word from him and she would be banished from his command like any courtier fallen out of favor in a Tudor realm. There was a curious sort of gratification in the thought. Gazing at the soft, eager face, those lightly parted lips, he thought again of Tommy and felt the germ of an old fantasy rise, tremulous and sly . . .

Then he suppressed it. This was his world: and it would increase. The Cagayan Valley campaign would be wound up by the end of the month; Damon's division had taken Lagum on the third. By September Swanson's people could start training for the Honshu landings. CORONET. The likeness of a kingly crown. He would have it then—Twelfth Army and his fourth star, and the broad Kwanto Plain on which to deploy his legions. Japan would fall, slowly, fanatically, and then would come the delights of occupation. There might even be—who knew?—mighty annexations, his old dream of an America-dominated East Asian Periphery; there would be a need for proconsuls who could rule with force and ingenuity. But not long: a year at most. Then back to Washington, and Plans. And then—

Fowler had left the table and gone quickly into the offices wing, followed by an anxious Graulet. Massengale wondered idly what it might be. Could Yamashita possibly have sent a surrender overture? Had Kurita made some final suicide sortie out of Brunei Bay? Both were unlikely—more probable was some enemy transfer of troops from China to the home islands.

"The whole thing is perfectly ridiculous," Vicky Varden was telling him. "The studio got this bug about me going out and looking up Chet, and you know, building it up a little. That it would help both our Hoopers. Where in hell is Lubagang?"

"Luabagán," Massengale corrected her automatically. "It's a well-demolished town on the west bank of the Chico River, up in the northern end of Luzon."

"God. Last time I went near the front lines I got sick as a dog. Galloping case of the trots. Damn it all, I *can't* go up there again," she wailed. "Eating hash out of an old tin dish, dragging my fanny through the mud and trying to find a—"

"Vee-Vee, honey, this is a battle zone," Hambro protested. "You know they said—"

"Oh dry up, Al . . . If only it weren't for the *bugs!*" she exclaimed in sudden exasperation. "And all the crazy diseases . . ."

"Who is *Chet?*" Massengale asked her.

"Chet Belgrade. He's my husband—my ex-husband, actually. He got filled full of patriotism as a Christmas turkey right after Pearl Harbor and joined up, there wasn't the slightest need for it, and he's been out here for years and years." She gave a sharp little cluck of distress. "I didn't know he was out in the *jungle*, for Pete sake. Fighting . . . I got Bert Lawson to see if they couldn't send him here, or to Manila. But nothing doing. They told Bert he's too essential. It's the first time anybody's ever called him that in twenty-six years. What's his rank, Al?"

"First Lieutenant."

"First Lieutenant. And I wondered, Court—they'd listen to you, wouldn't they? I mean, if you phoned them up? If he couldn't be detached or separated or whatever they do, and I could meet him here in Reina Blanca. Or up in Manila." Her eyes fastened on him, moist and beseeching, filled with stars. "Couldn't you, Court? Have them fly him down?"

Damon's division. All his troubles seemed to begin and end with the Night Clerk—even something perfectly frivolous such as this. Maybe he'd made a mistake in going so far with him. Bradley had sacked Terry Allen in Sicily for arrogance and insubordination, and it hadn't caused him any trouble. Well, he'd see how things went during the Honshu operation, hold a tight rein on him. Yet in all truth there was an undeniable satisfaction in keeping Damon on . . .

"Do you realize what you're asking, Victoria?" He let his gaze rest on her with the expression of tolerant rebuke he knew was particularly disconcerting. "Since you're *not* his wife the Army can hardly be expected to recognize any priority here. And furthermore—"

"General . . ."

He turned. Fowler was standing beside him, looking very odd. A faint sense of foreboding stole upon him. "Yes, Sherwin?"

"Could I see you a moment, sir?"

Fowler would never break in on him at a time like this if it wasn't important; the staff man's agitation was palpable. Suppressing his annoyance Massengale smiled lightly at the others and said: "Duty calls, it seems. I'll be with you presently." He led the way down the cool dim hallway to the war room, turned left and entered the G-2 Section. "What is it?" He held his voice perfectly calm, but the irritant tremor was still there.

"Graulet's just called me out about this, General. We thought it was necessary to let you know immediately. We've dropped a bomb on Japan."

Massengale's first thought was that Fowler, who was not the type at all, had gone dotty. He felt a spasm of anger: all Intelligence people were unstable, given to wild flights of fancy at unpredictable times. He said: "Is that *news*, Sherwin?"

"This is a fantastic bomb, sir. Graulet just got the TWX from Manila. It is in excess of twenty thousand tons of TNT."

He stared at them. "*One bomb?*"

"Yes, General. An atomic bomb, it says—a harnessing of the basic power of the universe. Here's the dispatch."

He read it with numb fingers; handed it back and went over to the window, his back to the others.

One bomb.

It was over. Clearly it was over. The Japanese would surrender now. Banzai, kamikazi, bushido, yamato damashi—nothing would keep them going. There would be no invasion of the home islands. He would not command an army. He was flooded with a sense of boundless loss—then with a rage that nearly choked him.

"There's another dispatch, sir—an Intelligence report that the Soviet Union is deploying forces along the Siberian border," Graulet said. And then Fowler, bright with elation: "This means they'll throw in the towel, doesn't it, sir?"

"Quite definitely." His voice was perfectly steady; his voice had never failed him. "Of course they may need to drop a dozen or so."

"A dozen more—!" Graulet exclaimed.

"Certainly." He turned. "Why not? I'd say we can expect overtures in a matter of days, two weeks at most."

". . . It seems fantastic, doesn't it, General?" Fowler said.

"Yes, it does."

"A whole city in a single bomb . . ."

Abortive, the thought reached out to him. The traditional forms of victory had been destroyed in a thunderclap. Abortive. He felt actually weak with rage and frustration. Why hadn't Schuyler told him about this, prepared him for it? They must have known back there—*somebody* in an influential position must have known . . . If he'd even been up in Manila! The world was altered: all the counters, the flat, familiar counters one passed one's days learning to manipulate, were gone. He had the sensation of a gambler who is condemned to see everything— fortune and home and family and future—all swept away in the relentless glide of the croupier's little wooden rake. It was unendurable, it was unthinkable. Filthy, vicious scientists! If they had been here in this room, any or all of their company, he could have shot them with the greatest pleasure. The taut jubilation on Graulet's tanned hatchet face filled him with loathing. He raised his eyes to the great map of Japan, the tortuous chain of islands like the bleached bones of some archaeological find: flat-capped Hokkaido, and Honshu slung hammock-like southwest, little Shikoku fitted against the Inland Sea like a metacarpal, and below it the thick Kyushu pendant. CORONET. The Choshi and Katsuta coastal areas he had studied for a hundred hours. All for nothing, now. For nothing.

It was the worst moment of his life.

When he turned back to the members of his staff his expression was alert, composed. "Well. That will affect our operational planning. To put it mildly."

"Yes, General. It certainly will."

"Well, I don't think we need to stand here, unhonored and unsung. Sherwin, would you convey my regrets to Miss Varden and her entourage."

Fowler blinked at him. "You—you won't be returning to the party, sir?"

There were times when the sheer bovine obtusity in the human cranium was utterly maddening. He clenched his fingers on the jade holder and said icily: "You have my permission to inform that pack of indecorous louts that I have work to do. Is that sufficiently clear, Sherwin?"

"Yes, General."

"Very good." He swung out of the G-2 room and hurried, almost running, down the dim corridor—and at the first corner came all at once against Master Technical Sergeant Hartje with an impact that nearly knocked the breath out of him. Hartje staggered back with a grunt, and several file folders slipped from his hands and spilled their contents on the floor.

"—God damn it," Massengale gasped. The shaking, vengeful rage had come back with the rush of nausea. *"Will you look where you're going—!"*

"Yes sir, General," Hartje stammered. "I'm sorry, sir—"

The Sergeant stood rigid in front of him; the skin was peeling high on his forehead and perspiration stood in a chain of tiny bubbles at the edge of his stiff black hair. I could kill this man, the thought thrummed into the Corps Commander's mind like an arrow: he is mine, completely—I could despoil him, crush him with a word, a single act . . . And as he intently watched the pinpoint of naked fear in the center of Hartje's eye, the old trembling exultation he'd first known as an upperclassman at the Point caught at him like the breath of fever; then it receded as swiftly, leaving a foul and empty wake. It wasn't enough now: not nearly enough.

"Carry on, Hartje," he said flatly. "Don't leave important papers lying on the floor, man . . ."

"Yes, sir."

Later he sat, perfectly immobile, in his room, once the bishop's quarters, and smoked. On his desk lay Burckhardt's report on the Order of Battle and the forward- and rear-echelon replacement depots. He averted his eyes in a spasm of exasperation. All for nothing. That a crew of effete eggheads should have concocted a device that could destroy the very scale of his triumph, rob him of all sense of fruition—it was contemptible! And now the filthy Russians were going to get in on it. There must be some way to stop them, roll them back; didn't they have *any* control of things back there? He would have to get in touch with Schuyler without delay.

There was a shriek of soprano laughter, muted and faraway, as though

issuing from deep underground; then silence again. *Timing—is—
everything*. He realized suddenly he was very near tears. He drove his
gaze around the room—the shelves of books with their slips for annotations, the rows of uniforms, the glass case of medals and decorations, the
detail map of Honshu.

In the far corner of the room stood Murasse's naked sword.

(16)

The cottonwoods and willows had turned a rusty gold, and the river
was low; it had been a dry summer. The corn was in—the big field
behind Timruds' looked barbaric and dense. There were curbs and a
slab sidewalk now, all the way out to Gus Hormel's place. Clausen's
Forge was gone, replaced by a Mobil Station, slick in reds and blues;
three cars were up on the hydraulic lifts, but no one was working under
them. A figure in the office caught sight of the little motorcade and
waved once, and the car ahead of theirs, the one Sam Damon's brother
Ty was driving, sounded its horn. Damon waved back, though he didn't
know who it was.

"That's Dick Tupper's boy Gene," Ted Barlow said, turning back
from the wheel to where Sam and Tommy sat together. "He'll be along
in a little while."

Banning's Feed and Grain store was closed, and so was Nisbet's Dry
Goods Emporium, the shades drawn against the light and a placard in
the window.

"Place is certainly quiet," Damon said.

"Everybody's at the Green," his sister Peg said. "They'd better be, if
they aren't!" They were riding in Ted's Buick convertible with the top
down, and she had her hand to the back of her head to hold her hat on;
its brim fluttered in the wind. "Civic ordinance. This is your day, Sam."

"No, it's not," he corrected her amiably. "But I'm glad to be here just
the same."

"Oh, don't be so stiff and modest!" She turned to Tommy, "Honestly—
can't he be maddening, though?"

Smiling faintly, Tommy nodded. "Yes. He can be maddening."

Her glance rose to his, held an instant and slipped away again; and he
clasped his hands in his lap. She was disappointed in him: his appearance.
As well as the other thing. She on the other hand looked as lovely as
ever—her chin up, her green eyes sparkling and wide; she was wearing
her hair shorter, swept up on one side in a pleasing little effect of curls.
He started to say something and stopped himself. Peg's daughter Nancy,
seventeen now and full of the devil, looked back at him through the rear

window of Ty's Pontiac and stuck out her tongue at him, and he grinned back. They glided along the shaded streets, turned up Merivale, then along Lincoln. There were people now, a lot of them, all moving toward the center of town, the kids running in and out around their elders, playing tag. Flags were hanging from the staffs, from the second-story windows above the front doors. Sheldon Kimball, in a gray linen suit—Damon recognized him instantly—raised both arms and shouted: "And there he is now!" and he waved and called, "Hello, Shelley . . ."

Homecoming. They turned right on to Main Street, and now he could see the signs in the shop windows, the blown-up photographs. His face stared back at him, trebled, quadrupled—younger, rather stern and forbidding, full of confidence; the picture Tommy'd got him to have taken when he'd made bird colonel, back at Ord. So terribly, unreachably long ago. The old Grand Western was now the Whitman Arms, with two modern plate-glass doors and a little marquee, and on one side a discreet neon sign that said *coffee shop* in lower case script.

"I suppose they've moved the second-floor reception desk," he said.

Ted Barlow laughed. "Hell, yes—it's all modernistical: formica counters and Muzak piped in on weekends. The old bar's a snazzy cocktail lounge where the drinks cost seventy cents a throw. Thoroughly renovated. I don't know what you'd do about Big Tim Riley now . . ."

"Oh, now I'd get out a Special Order."

The two men laughed together and Tommy said: "Who is Big Tim Riley?"

"Didn't he ever tell you about that?" Ted demanded. "Why, Tim Riley was the biggest man in the county, a hell-raiser and tough as nails. He dared Sam to throw him out of the hotel and Sam knocked him all the way down the stairs, through the front door and across the street. With one punch."

"Legends," Damon murmured. "How legends get born. Honey, you don't want to believe everything you hear around here."

"Oh, I won't—I never do!" She laughed, and as their eyes met again his heart caught at him with that quick, delectable pain; but he could not tell what she was thinking. They were together again—but as strangers, with a thousand questions there had been no time to answer since he'd stepped out of the C-54 at the field at Kearney and seen her standing on the asphalt, a little apart from the others, her feet together, looking small and trim and lonely and unflinching. He still loved her, he knew it even at that moment of greetings and confusion; he wanted her, he needed her . . . But you couldn't go back. Once certain things had happened, certain kinds of calamity, there was no returning.

And yet he was conscious of her nearness as a very bright, almost stultifying thing, like a beacon; she added to the strangeness of the day, this leisurely procession through the streets of his boyhood where old faces, on catching sight of him, brightened and called hello. He could think of nothing to say—his mind picked up snips and scraps of vanished moments and dropped them like a magpie, without reflection. He was still in Kobe—no, worse, he was still on Luzon glancing at routine patrol and operations reports and planning for the terrible Honshu assault . . . It came too fast, he thought; the peace. I wasn't ready for it, wasn't prepared for homecoming.

"How does it look to you, Sam?" Ted was asking him. "Now you've been to all those places and done all those things . . ."

"It looks pretty good," he answered, watching the familiar homes slide toward him, letting the warm, dense, dusty odor of mown hay and burning leaves and sage sweep over him again. Ted had never been east of Chicago except for a summer's drive to the New York World's Fair in '39; while he had marched down the Champs Elysées, stood in the courtyards of Rhenish castles, watched the feathered dawn creep over La Napoule; he had walked through the palm green isles and the gaunt blue mountains of far Cathay . . . I was right to go, he thought, encountering the diffident, wistful eyes of his old friend in the driver's mirror, I could never have stayed here, I'd have gone half crazy; and yet you could do a lot worse than pass your days in a little tank town on the Platte. "It looks pretty wonderful," he amended. "Pretty damned wonderful, let me tell you."

"I'll bet it does."

There ahead of them was the Green, and the big painted sign hanging across Main Street from Snow's Bakery to Winnott's Drug Store, now renamed the Paramount: WALT WHITMAN WELCOMES HER FAVORITE SON. And beyond that, WELCOME HOME SAM DAMON. And there was the town hall, set back at the far end of the Green, with the parking spaces all cleared and Ed Herkenthaler, now Chief of Police, standing there in full regalia, motioning them briskly past. There was a bandstand draped in bunting, the sidewalks were crowded thickly, and now everybody was calling to him, waving and pressing toward the car.

"For God's sake, stand up, Sam," Ted said. "What do you think they picked my convertible for?"

"They can see all of me they want to," he replied; reaching out now, taking hands, recalling with a slow surge of recognition the names and faces, while the cars eased around the square. The square they'd named for him so many years ago. They stopped, he helped Tommy out. There was a pleasant confusion; everyone was shouting, laughing, gripping his hands and arms. Ty had come up, and Peg's husband Frank with his slow, puzzled grin; and then his mother, who hadn't been at the airport, looking small and birdlike and very calm. Her body felt strangely puny when he hugged her.

"Sam," she said in her firm, musical voice; her voice hadn't changed. "It's good to have you back home."

"It's good to be home, Ma."

Her quick, dark gaze passed over his six banks of ribbons. They meant absolutely nothing to her and that pleased him; they never had. Her oldest boy was home safe. Her eyes searched his face. "Is it better now? Your arm?"

"Oh, sure, Ma. All fixed up."

"I wish your Uncle Billy could be here," she said. He could scarcely hear her. "It would have meant so much to him."

"So do I," he answered. "And Mr. Verney. And Pa." He embraced her again. Someone thumped him on the shoulder and he turned. Old Man Harrodsen, looking not a day older than he had in 1929, cried: "How does it feel to be back in God's own country, boy?" And behind him, wonder of wonders, stood Celia Shurtleff in a handsome low-cut lemon yellow dress and a big hat, stout now but very pretty all the same. And Fred beside her in a raw silk suit.

"Couldn't miss this day!" Celia was calling through the tumult of voices. "Fred had to be in Council Bluffs, and when Daddy said you were coming home—"

And then she had embraced him, laughing, and he thought of that evening by the gate when she'd reached up and kissed him, and then had broken away and run into the house. When she'd teased him about his destiny. He introduced her to Tommy, watching them both, still bound in strangeness; it was impossible to think in the midst of the hooting and hollering and well-wishing going on all around him. He wanted to put his arms around Tommy, hold her to him until they could hear their hearts beating. He turned away.

Emil Clausen, Fritz's brother and now mayor, looking very German and important and sweaty in a dark suit and white shirt and broad-striped maroon tie, was guiding him through the crowd to the band-stand, where twenty-odd GIs were standing in a row, wearing their uniforms. The ones who had come home. He moved along the line, repeating the names as Emil introduced them, fixing faces and rank and branch the way he'd done ever since France, catching resemblances now and then. There was Dick Tupper's oldest boy Harold, and John Stacy, a paratrooper with the 82nd Airborne, and Otto Skorny's son Bill, a ser-geant with the silver star and the Red Arrow of the 32nd Division; and an Air Force T-3 whose name he didn't know, and a lieutenant with one arm and the Tropic Lightning patch, and Peg's boy Alan who had been a corporal with the Third Marine Division, and Ted Barlow's nephew Ralph Lyons, a gunner's mate in the Navy. He shook their hands and spoke with each of them briefly. Here they were—pilots and boat han-dlers and riflemen and signalers: they had done what they had been asked to do—some of them a good deal more than that—and that was why they were all here on this bright new bandstand, with the country— this wonderful, precious, erring, troublesome old republic of theirs— free to go on being what it might be, if given half a chance . . .

Ed Herkenthaler was asking them to please be seated, if they would please be seated, please. Below them on the Green the townspeople were settling into the bamboo-yellow folding chairs borrowed for the occasion, Sam knew, from the Congregational Church basement and the VFW hall; rustling themselves into silence. The new minister was a plump, round-faced young man named Eckert. He composed his face in dogged, earnest lines and talked about the last full measure of devotion and keeping faith and treasure heaped in heaven. Its sole virtue was its brevity, and the Green rustled in relief when the concluding prayer was ended. Damon raised his head and looked down at the new memorial, covered now in white muslin. Then Emil Clausen was speaking again, nervously and unsurely, and Walter Harrodsen walked to the edge of the platform as though it were the portals of his bank, and pressed his bulk against the bunting-draped boards.

"We're gathered here today to unveil the new memorial tablet honoring our sons who've fallen in this war," he began. His voice was still full and powerful at seventy-six, without the trace of a tremor, and his hair was thick and blond on the top of his head. "This is a solemn day for us, and an important day. And there's no one we'd rather have here for this ceremony than the man I've been asked to introduce—the most illustrious of Walt Whitman's sons, who left his home over on Merivale Street some years ago and went out into the world and made it his very own. I knew this boy when he was that high, when he was a schoolboy, a brilliant athlete and a fine student; when he worked sixteen hours a day for Cyrus Timrud, and as night clerk at the hotel. He was a good field hand and a good night clerk, too—kept the books straight and got folks the rooms they liked, and he even kept order down there when it was needed."

There was a low, appreciative murmur from some of the older members of the audience and Walter Harrodsen grinned and shoved his hands in his coat pockets. "There was even a time when my Celia was just a mite sweet on him, as we used to say. But then she changed her mind. I told her she was making a terrible mistake, but you know what Walt Whitman girls are like." He waited until the laughter died away. "Yes, he seemed pretty much like the rest of us—maybe a mite quicker, a mite stronger than most boys his age. But under this easy, quiet exterior lay something none of us knew about: a sense of sacrifice, of love and devotion to this great country of ours, a burning patriotism that wanted nothing more than to uphold the honor of these United States in a time of trial . . ."

Sitting behind and to the right of Harrodsen, Sam composed himself, letting the big round words bowl on through his head. Why couldn't people steer a little closer to reality, especially at times like this? Stand a man up before his fellows and let him open his mouth—and God alone knew what would come tumbling out. He remembered Donny one evening back at Beyliss, during dinner, when they'd been talking about crotchety old Colonel Statts.

"But Dad, if it's not the truth, why does he say it?"

"—Because he's a silly, pompous, vain old man," his mother had interjected.

"Yes, but if he knows he's telling a lie . . ."

"It's not quite as simple as that," he'd said to the boy. "Sometimes your memory plays you tricks. Often when we think back on something we change it around to the way we wish it had been, rather than the way it really was."

"But why do we do that? if it's wrong . . . ?"

He had put down his knife and fork. "Well, for one thing, men don't like to remember times when they were inadequate, or miserable, or frightened; they'd rather remember times when they were brave and resourceful and good. So they—sort of swivel things around a bit. It's a human failing, and we're all human beings."

Donny had made no reply to this; Sam remembered the boy's quick, dark, terribly intense gaze. You never knew what a kid would take to heart. He stole a glance at Tommy but her expression showed only a polite interest.

"You all know how this boy went over to France and won this nation's highest decoration, in a deed of heroism unparalleled in the AEF; how he rose from private to the rank of major; how he was wounded leading a charge on enemy positions. And how this same deep sense of sacrifice and duty prompted him to stay on in the Army. I remember once when he was home here on leave he confided to me his fears that Germany had not been rendered a peace-loving nation, that Japan posed a continuous and stealthy threat to our shores. And he told me how he wanted to be ready if ever the need—how remote it all seemed then!—arose. And then like a thunderclap it did arise, and once again he went out to do what he had to do, to save this splendid democracy of ours. Not words but gallant deeds . . ."

It was curious hearing about yourself this way, the subject of such headlong, flagrant falsifications and inventions; curious, and not very pleasant. Old Man Harrodsen's version. What would George Caldwell, bedridden in a room in Rock Creek Park, laboriously translating the memoirs of General Marbot—what would he tell these Nebraskans about their native son, this lovely fall Friday at the end of a war? What would Ben have said about him, or little Brewster, now a senior member of the most venerable of New York law firms? or Reb Raebyrne, farming a strip somewhere in the North Carolina hills? or Dev? He shivered once in the silken sunlight and crossed his arms. A man was only one man, one meager entity, but he was so many divergent things to other men. Watching the back of Harrodsen's neck, half-listening to the parade of pompous phrases, he felt a slow, subtle anger.

"And you all know how he rallied a faltering, beaten army, and breathed courage into it, and hope, and led it to victory singlehanded over a savage and arrogant enemy, and won this nation's second highest award for that. And then personally knocked out a battalion of enemy tanks, and was asked to take over the finest division in the Pacific Theater of War. And how in the Philippines, a major general now, with the line crumbling all around him under the onslaught of the Jap hordes, he must have thought, like another hero of another immortal republic:

> *'And how can man die better*
> *Than facing fearful odds,*
> *For the ashes of his fathers*
> *And the temples of his gods?'*

But Sam Damon didn't die. He was gravely wounded, and for the second time in his life; but the line held. And his division was personally cited by no one less than the President of the United States. And I know all you sons and daughters of Walt Whitman and Buffalo County gathered here today join me in saying: 'Well done, Sam Damon. We haven't seen as much of you over the years as we'd like, but we claim you nonetheless: your nation is proud of you, your Army is proud of you— and last and by no means least, your old hometown is proudest of all! . . .' "

There was applause in a rising pattern, and the band began to play "The Stars and Stripes Forever." Damon, shaking hands again with Walter Harrodsen, remembered the swing band at the repple depple at Fort Ord, seated beside the tracks as the replacements shipped out, playing "Somebody Else Is Taking My Place," and the kids grinning ruefully, giving one another nervous sidelong glances. And the Salamanders on Dizzy Spa, drinking beer and chanting out their lean-and-mean war cry: "*Moa!—pora! Man—alive . . .*"

Emil Clausen had said something inaudible and gestured toward him, and he rose and went forward to the edge of the bandstand. The wood had the clean, spiritous odor of new-cut pine. He thought of the improvised stand at Moapora, at the cemetery, in the still heat. Below him they were clapping and cheering, their faces red and strained, heaving about, and he waved at them. He felt stirred, but not toward tears. It was strange what he felt now—a little numb, and weightless, as though he were falling slowly through space and seeking something to catch hold of—a hook, a plank, the wing of some great bird . . .

He had broken down only once, five days ago, when he had turned over the Division to Frenchy Beaupré at Kobe. The last review. Then it had been the faces he hadn't seen out ahead of him. Now it was the faces he could see—family and friends of his childhood and youth. He waved again, and gave himself a little shake; but the numbness persisted. Time had played him tricks: the past was more vivid than the present—it rose up and swamped this sunlit tumult. There in the center of the Green was the plaque from World War I, the war to end all war, and he had been closer to Dev and Raebyrne and Brewster than to any of these friends of his youth. And beside it, obscured by its cloth canopy, was the bronze-and-marble reason for their convocation, with its list of names for this war—the war to end all peace, Frenchy had wrathfully called it one evening—and there had been no man in his life, nor would there ever be, to compare with Ben.

Emil Clausen was waving his hands over his head for quiet and grinning at him apologetically. Well: let them roar their relief, their jubilation. It was over. Again. Over. But—and the slow, deep anger stirred him again—these Americans there below him would never know: that was the one thing that was insupportable in this long, exultant moment. None of them would really know. The papers had ranted and roared for four years, there had been the newsreels—now and then some spare, honest efforts among the combat cameramen and correspondents; and now and then one of the returned veterans seated here behind him might, huddled by the fire or in a darkened bar, seek to tell his wife or girl or parents something of it. But it would be only the feeblest approximation of the truth, deflected by desire, forgetfulness, sorrow, by a thousand thousand stealthy, affectionate censors. And maybe—who could say?—it was better that way . . .

But for the dead, in their tens of thousands, there had been no newsreels, no papers, no grand strategy, no jubilation. There had been only that one cataclysmic moment of terror and pain—the shock of realization that for them time had stopped, all things had rushed to a halt in the chill dark. They were the ones he would speak for, then: for all their hopes and dreams, their terrible fragility before that iron moment. Not *for* them exactly, because it was the living who bore life forward; but in their name. Now, while the wounds were raw, the memories bright and hard, he would speak a few words of truth about the war: a few honest words—as honest as he could make them, anyway—and then he would step off into the wings again.

They were quiet now, looking up at him; waiting for him to say something. He raised his head and gripped the rough pine railing and began to speak.

Sitting on the platform beside Emil Clausen and Walter Harrodsen, Tommy Damon watched her husband standing at the edge of the railing. He looked thinner than she'd ever seen him, thinner even than Cannes. He looked old all at once, his lined face shadowed like the faces in Brady's Civil War photographs. What was he? Forty-seven: two years older than the century. That wasn't old. The crowd would not be still, and Sam watched them with his calm, mournful gaze. She pressed her skirt forward over her knees and thought, Why did I come? What am I doing here? She was cloaked in confusion, a welter of memories and conjectures.

Their meeting at the airport at Kearney had been awkward. He had come down the ramp and spotted her instantly—his face underwent a strange little quiver, then flared into a smile of pure joy. Reporters and photographers had closed around him, he had broken through them and swung up to her, his arms outstretched: his embrace was at once familiar and alien. She was trembling; her hat had fallen off.

"Sam," she said.

"Oh, honey. Thank you for coming."

"I wanted to come," she answered. But that wasn't entirely true: she'd had to come, but it wasn't just desire. She was not sure what had impelled her. Sam had written her that he'd been asked to speak at the dedication of the new war memorial at Walt Whitman on his way back to Washington, and that he was leaving Kobe on the 17th. She had answered carefully that she would be glad to appear with him there if he wanted her to. His reply had been brief: he wanted her to; and she had flown out here, confused and full of misgivings, the night before and stayed with Sam's sister Peg and her family.

There had been no chance to say anything more; only a brief, uncertain colloquy of eyes, and then family and friends swept around them both in a pleasant confusion. Sam's brother Ty had handed her her hat, and she thanked him. After that the press took over—she was surprised to see a man from the Chicago *Tribune*—and the photographers moved them around like puppets.

"General, would you turn toward her more, would you mind looking at each other—like that, yes, that's fine, that's fine . . ."

She was filled with chagrin—confused, angry, laughing a little. This was not at all what she'd imagined their first meeting in over three years would be like, yet it was perfectly predictable: he was home, he was in the Army, they were on parade again . . .

The crowd was quiet now. Sam put his hands on the railing and gazed out at them intently, as if he wanted to memorize them, fix this instant for a long time.

"I hope you'll forgive me if I sound a little confused," he said. "Five short days ago I was in Japan, walking along the shore of the Inland Sea. It used to take five days to drive from here to Big Spring in a buckboard, when I was a boy . . . I've been away a long time—almost thirty years—and the world has shifted under my feet. Under all our feet. It is not the world we knew in 1916."

She remembered—she had not thought of it for a long time—that moment at the Casino, with the sunlight playing over the water in scales of pure gold. "I must apologize for staring," he'd said. His gaze had been so steady and diffident and trusting, in spite of the web of fine lines around his eyes. "It's just that you reminded me of—people back home . . ."

"You have asked me," he was saying now, "to assist in the dedication of this memorial; and I am greatly honored. But I know you will understand if I avoid the use of words like gallantry or valor or glory. I will leave them to those who have not had to add up the ledger of violence and misery. My own heart is too full of losses today. We are assembled here to honor the men whose names are inscribed on this tablet. Let us, then, do them the simple honor of honesty. This war"—and his voice was suddenly very harsh—"was a long, lonely, dirty job, as these men seated here behind me can attest. They fought it with courage and fortitude and the hope of better days, and what they did cannot and will not be forgotten. But there is nothing glorious about killing one's fellow man, or being killed by him, or passing many, many days in hatred and misery and fear. And whoever says it is a matter for glory lies in his teeth . . ."

Once in '42 at Ord they had drawn up at a station in Monterey for gas and the pumps on both sides were blocked because an armored forces corporal had left his car, a battered old black Chevrolet, and was leaning in the window of the other one, talking to a girl. She and Sam had been hiking under the redwoods up in the Corral de Tierra, and Sam was wearing a pullover sweater and no hat. He had turned off the engine and sat there idly, watching. Impulsively she had leaned over and pumped the horn twice. The corporal, a stocky, slope-shouldered man with great bushy black eyebrows, withdrew his head and turned and glared at them and said, "Keep your shirt on, buddy," then leaned in the window again.

"Oh honestly, Sam," she'd protested when he'd made no response, "this is ridiculous. Why doesn't he take her in the back seat and be done with it?"

"We're in no hurry."

"He's doing that simply because he doesn't know who you are."

"Of course he doesn't."

"Well, go on over to him and let him know . . ."

He had turned to her then, his eyes very steady and piercing. "Look, Tommy: in not too long a time he's going to be in some lousy place trying just to save his ass. Let him have his fun. We can wait."

She'd subsided, sulking. "You're hopeless. You just let them walk all over you."

"We like to say that war is cruel," he was saying now. "But no one knows how cruel it is—how deeply, monstrously cruel—unless he has himself walked through the fire and felt it sear him. The men recorded on this tablet have done that. Many of them died horribly, some of them needlessly. Yes, needlessly," he repeated. It was very quiet down on the Green. "Because what is most hideous about war is its waste: destruction of goods and homes, waste of life and hope and that dream of individual dignity we cherish as the particular achievement of America. A country's treasure is in its young men, and their loss is terrible beyond measure because it is irreparable. It is as shocking as the loss of innocence, or self-respect. And more often than not it is the good man who goes: the large act, the spendthrift heart. The medic who goes out to bring in the wounded man, the automatic rifleman who covers his patrol's withdrawal, the officer trying to prevent panic, the gunner who throws himself on the grenade menacing his friends . . ."

His face was somber, rather forbidding—as though he wanted to fight them with his fists but knew he wasn't allowed to. The crowd below was still, but it was, Tommy knew, the apprehensive quiet of an audience that feared what its speaker would say next. The poor, dear, wonderful, impossible man: couldn't he see they didn't want to hear any of this? that what they wanted was hymns to glory? He would never change.

"There they are, arrayed on the face of the stone. All that is left of their eager faces, their dreams, their inviolable souls. They are dead now. They were singularly trusting. They asked no collateral on the prompt surrender of their lives, they demanded no social privileges, no distinctions, no seats of power or influence as they walked steadily into the valley. They demanded nothing. What about us, the beneficiaries of such profligate bounty? Will we be so callous as to scheme and despoil for these things again—and mock their death, their slow, immeasurable agony?

"Power," he was saying, nodding at them grimly. "We have it now. In our two hands. A new world, a clean slate. These young men have made the down payment on it—and it was a bitter payment, I can assure you. Bitter as gall. And they did not make that payment for a world of rockets and bombs and barbed wire, or for a world of overseas markets and a favorable gold balance and the wolfish gutting of what we are pleased to call the underdeveloped nations. Old friends, we can build a new Jerusalem—but we will reach only what we seek . . ."

She found she was gripping her hands together tightly. It was true. Man was a beast, as Court had said, as Bill Bowdoin had said: he was weak, he pursued false gods, he had a positive genius for creeping out of one self-inflicted calamity only to fall headlong into one still worse; he was selfish and faithless and cruel . . . But one still had to hope. Hope for peace, for love, for generosity, for the sunlit riverbank where old men could sit and dream and children play without fear. Even in defeat, in the most chill despair, in the most boundless of cynicism, there had to be hope . . .

Tears stung her eyelids; she blinked, staring at the thin, worn figure. He was wearing his A uniform, and it was nicely pressed, though well worn at the elbows and shoulders. He was even wearing his ribbons, except for the Distinguished Unit bar. Beside her Mayor Clausen was listening with an almost fierce intensity; the man named Harrodsen and a companion of his who looked like a real estate broker were scowling down at their feet, their arms crossed. Dear Sam. If they wanted to hate him for saying these things, let them. Somebody ought to say them.

"Let us remember, then. They would want us to remember—if only because it may cause us to strengthen our resolve not to sow the dragon's teeth again. The naked sword we hold so proudly is two-edged: it is as dangerous for the wielder as for the recipient.

"We stand at an immense fork in the road. One way is the path of generosity, dignity and a respect for other races and customs; the other leads most certainly to greed, suspicion, hatred and the old, bloody course of violence and waste—and now, God help us, to the very destruction of all the struggles and triumphs of the human race on this earth. My old friends and fellow townsmen: which will it be?"

For a moment he was silent, measuring them; then he put his hand to his forehead. "Forgive me, if you can, for so somber an address on this beautiful September day, when the whole land echoes with cries of triumph; but I am weighed down with losses—I am constrained to cry, like another soldier sick of slaughter and folly: *The weight of this sad time we must obey; Speak what we feel, not what we ought to say . . .*"

He had stopped speaking and turned from the bunting-wrapped railing, looking sad and stern and defeated. All around her there was a brief, astonished, fearful silence—then an uncertain clatter of applause. Mayor Clausen was dabbing at his eyes with the back of one big red hand; Walter Harrodsen was watching Sam with a tight, exasperated grin. Sam took no notice of him and sat down beside her.

There was the unveiling then, the stone memorial looking absurdly commonplace and small; the Reverend Eckert led them in prayer, and then the veteran from the 32nd Division stepped forward with a bugle and blew taps, the notes falling in light, clean globes of sound through the still air. And then it was over, everyone was on his feet, several of the GIs had surrounded Sam and were shaking his hand, talking to him. And still she didn't know what she felt, why she had come or what she ought to do or say.

On the grass beside the stand people milled around endlessly; no one seemed to know what to do—there was the facetious relief of children let out of some burdensome duty, and it angered her suddenly. Sam's brother Ty was calling to them all to get in the cars, it was time to go home for a drink and dinner.

"We're going to have your favorite," his mother was saying to Sam. "Broiler chicken."

He smiled at her gently. "Lead me to it."

"Sad, bad old Sam," his sister Peg said to Tommy, and winked. "Stirred them all up, gave them something to think about. Hasn't changed any, has he?"

"No," she answered, "he hasn't changed."

"Come on, Sam," Ty called, "let's go. Nobody'll move till you do."

"You go on ahead." He reached out and took her hand, deep in his, the way he'd used to in Cannes, on La Croisette; she looked at him, startled. "We'll see you back at the house."

"But look, we ought to get back—there's no sense in hanging around here . . ."

"We'll see you there. We'll walk it."

"Wants to show off his girl to the town," Ted Barlow said. "Who wouldn't?"

Ty looked full of consternation. His hair, thinning, was parted neatly in the exact center of his scalp. "We've got room—it's half a mile, Sam . . ."

"We can swing it. Go ahead," he said with a mock glower, "be off with you . . ."

The streets were crowded and people kept calling to him, stopping them to chat and wish him well; they all wanted to utter his name, over and over, like a talisman; like the old franc piece he always carried in his right-hand trousers pocket, with his bone-handled penknife. "Sam," their voices floated through the fine fall air, "Sam . . . Sam Damon . . ."

Then they had turned up a hill past a large white house with columns and a greenhouse and a high wrought-iron gate, and then they were alone at the edge of a field that swept down toward the river's edge, where a big gray dog was circling, its nose to the ground.

"Sam," she said, "they'll throw the book at you for that speech."

"Yes. Damned good chance."

"Those reporters were taking it all down."

"I thought I'd give them a good reason for hanging me. What the hell—I've kept my mouth shut for four years. Nobody listens to two-star generals, anyway."

"It was a good speech," she said. "I'm glad you said what you did. Though I don't imagine they'll look on it too joyfully in the AG's office."

He snorted. "After Captious Court gets through with my efficiency rating they won't give me the Service Depot at Snoqualmie Junction."

"—Oh, but he can't do that," she protested, "not after the Citation—"

"Can't he, though. You just watch him. He can do just about anything he wants. He's MacArthur's fair-haired boy out there." He smiled grimly. "They understand each other."

From far off, down among the cottonwoods and thickets at the river, there came a solitary gunshot. The dog had vanished.

"Well, anyway," she said, "it's over."

"No. It's not over."

"What?" She glanced at him in alarm.

"The biggest battles are still to be fought."

She thought of Bill Bowdoin tucking his shirt into his trousers at East Hampton, the rain drumming against the glass. She felt utterly sick at heart. "Russia?" she murmured.

He shook his head. "No. I don't know. That's not the problem. It's us. Here. It's got to come to a head. Between those who want us to be a democracy—a real one, not a show-window one—and those who want us to be a Great Power. In caps and with all the trimmings." The gun fired again, its report echoing and reechoing along the river. "Some kid with a shotgun," he said absently, staring. "No—it's never over. I'm catching on. There's no discharge in this war."

She lowered her head. "That's an insupportable thought to me right now."

"I know. It was for me, once. But that's how it goes. People are going to go on being scared and vindictive and greedy and forgetful and everything else they happen to be. And all you can do is keep on going yourself, do what you can and hope for the best. That's a pretty drab philosophy, isn't it?—when you compare it with someone like Massengale. Sitting on his pinnacle, molding the minds of millions."

"No, it's not," she said with some distress. "It's just that you get so *tired*—there doesn't seem to be any end to it . . ."

He swung back to her. "Well: say not the struggle naught availeth. Perseverance keeps honor bright, they say."

She smiled awkwardly. "You said you weren't going to use any of those words."

"That's right—I did, didn't I?" He smiled, but his eyes were full of shadows. "Tommy." He had taken her hand again, but differently. "Tommy, I hope you'll come home with me. I want you to—if you want to, of course. I don't know how you feel about things . . ."

Wordless, she watched his face, feeling the firm, warm grip of his hand, the old pull to compliance, submission to what he wanted. But there were also the despairs and fevers of the past three years. His hand let go of hers and came up around her waist; that slow, gentle pressure. There were so many things she wanted to say and she couldn't seem to say any of them. Trembling with agitation she pulled away and turned to face him. "A lot of things have happened, Sam . . ."

"I know. That's true for me, too. Look, there are certain things that are more important than anything else." She had never seen him this confused. "Sometimes the most important thing is just to keep on going, doing what you have to, hewing to the line . . . I need you, Tommy. I do. I know I don't always act like it—I know I've done a lot of things badly, I've been a troublemaker and stubborn—but it's because I believe in things, in people. You do understand that, don't you? I never did one single thing for the hell of it . . ."

His face was very close to hers: he looked so old and worn. He's tired, she thought suddenly, he's so tired he's going to get sick if he doesn't take care of himself; if somebody doesn't take care of him . . . Her mind swayed like kelp in deep undertow. No discharge. She wanted to be a person of responsibility; didn't she? That's what Sam was: the kind of man people said they'd want to have with them in a rough deal, when all the chips were down, the kind of man they always went to when they were in trouble—she'd heard them at Hardee, at Ord, on Luzon. He hadn't had the rank, but he'd had this other thing, and that was what they all wanted, what they all leaned on.

". . . I need you, honey. You don't know how much." He gripped his hands together in that old gesture she remembered. "Honey, about Donny—I never influenced him about enlisting. I tried to dissuade him. You've got to believe that. Tommy, he was a *man*—his mind was made up, it was what he had to do, don't you see? You can't keep a man from doing a thing like that . . ."

"I know," she said. "He was old enough to know what he wanted. I know that now." She put her hand on his arm to stop him. Bill was wrong, she saw; dead wrong. She didn't want to lash Sam with the boy's death, she had no desire to play the Cormorant, roweling him with vengeance. The realization gave her a swift little surge of relief. She wanted—she wanted to be complete, a person of responsibility. There was a virtue simply in having begun together, in having struggled through the arduous years, neglected, unvalued, sharing the hopes and wonders of parenthood. All those years: was she to turn her back on them now, betray them, belittle them?

And more than that, too: he had said he needed her. He had never said that before, never exactly that, in all those years—

"We'll do it the way you want it," he was saying, "the way you'd like it to be, from now on. That's a promise. Will you try it with me? once more?"

She smiled at him gravely. Dear funny old Sam: he could no more change what he was than he could sprout wings and fly out over the river, the willows and cottonwoods huddled against its banks. She nodded once.

"All right," she said. "I'll give it a try."

His gaze softened still more, turned inward. "Ben used to say that: *it's worth a try* . . . Fair enough," he said, and embraced her gently; his lapel insigne scraped her forehead. She felt calm, and resigned, and hopeful and a little sad. Behind him at the turn in the road she saw two boys watching them, and thought of the sailors that afternoon on the parapet at Le Suquet. She had been crying then.

(V)
DELTA

1

"What they've *got* is a blasted menagerie," Gertrude Woodruff declared. "It seems they have to have a baby sitter—imagine two kids thirteen and fifteen needing a baby sitter!—and they got this girl, blue jeans and a nice sweet smile, and the next thing they knew she turned up in a motel outside Miami with two men. Not one but two. And so they engaged—I guess that's the word—another one, blue jeans and a nice sweet smile, and a week later when they were staying overnight with friends on St. Catherine's, that's one of the Sea Islands, this new one took it upon herself to throw a beer party right in the living room. And after a while they got bored with doing the Limbo and drinking beer and began to throw toys and odds and ends of furniture down the front stairs."

"Couldn't have been just beer," Tommy Damon said.

"You bet. And it wasn't. *Pot*, they call it. Goodness knows why." Gertrude gave her short, cackling laugh. "Do they take it out of a pot to make the cigarettes with it?"

"Tea," Tommy said, musing. "They call it tea, too. They used to call them reefers. And muggles and vipers and Mary Jane."

"Goodness, how do you know all that?" Jean Mayberry asked.

"Fascination, I guess. All the sinful delights have hundreds of names, have you ever noticed?"

"I guess that's so. It never occurred to me."

"Then what happened?" Tommy prompted Gertrude.

"The police got calls from next door and broke in. And there they were, our rising generation, hurling Ellie's platters and chairs end over end and singing some crazy dirge of a song. And there were Bobby and Karen in their pajamas, hurling and singing right along with them. And did any of the little dears take to the windows or cower in the closets? Not one. It was all a lark. It seems the ringleader, the sitter's boy friend, told the cops he was going into the Army in three days and couldn't care less. 'Khotiane, bing, bang!' he said. 'I'm in no hurry to get zapped. No hurry at all.' The words they use! It isn't true at all, of course. It's just advisory teams out there, isn't it? Career personnel."

"Not entirely," Tommy said.

"Anyway, that's what they came home to. I swear, the kids these days are a mystery to me. *I* don't understand them . . ."

(747)

"I do," Tommy answered slowly. "They feel just the way we did in
'19, only they don't *have* to go through it. They can see it all coming
and they know just what it's going to be like, and why."

They both were gazing at her, startled and blinking.

"Tommy," Gertrude said, "you don't mean that . . ."

"I do. I do indeed."

"But we can't let them just—run all over us. Norm says if Khotiane
goes—"

"Southeast Asia goes. Then Hawaii. Then the world. I know."
Tommy sighed. "I wonder if it's true—really true, the way they tell us
it is. Personally I'm inclined to doubt it." Gertrude was still watching
her with that troubled expression, and she gave a quick, easy smile and
tossed her head; she didn't want to quarrel with these two friends, and
over politics at that. "Well, it's their problem, not mine," she added
lightly. "I've put in my time on the old rock pile. And so have both of
you."

"Amen to that, and carry one," Jean said.

They all laughed, and looked idly away. The three women were
dressed in slacks and blouses and reclining in tube-aluminum folding
chairs on the cramped sun deck behind the Damons' house. The sun was
warm through the pines, but every now and then wraiths and scarves of
fog would drift gently overhead, and they would shiver and pull their
sweaters over their shoulders. On the redwood coffee table between
them was a welter of empty highball glasses and coffee cups and a box
of candy whose scalloped wrappers fluttered in the light breeze. From the
front of the house, muffled, came the hollow clank of something heavy
dropped in a wheelbarrow.

"What's he doing?" Gertrude asked.

"A walk. He got these redwood sections for a dollar apiece. A bargain, apparently. Then he's going to plant dichondra all around them."

"Oh, for a ground cover. I wish Norm would get interested in gar-
dening. All he does is talk golf over at the club and watch TV all
evening long. The Late Late Show. It's getting like your reefers. The
other night I said, 'For God sake, come to bed, Norm—you're acting
like a nine-year-old!' And he said, 'Just a couple more minutes. I didn't
realize all the movies I missed out on.' Last week he said his eyes were
hurting, he wanted to know if I had any idea why. I said hell no, I
couldn't imagine—I told him maybe if he got a little closer to the set
they might improve . . . I wish Sam played golf. If he did it would get
Norm out more."

"Sam won't play golf. I talked him into getting a set of clubs when we
first came out here, and he played a few times, quite respectably for a
beginner. But then he lost interest. He's suspicious of the game."

"Suspicious?"

"That's right. He's got it all hooked up with finance capitalists in
linen caps living it up while the laboring children look out of the barred

mill windows. Et cetera. Same thing with tennis—he can't forgive it for being connected with the idle rich. Unlike baseball or swimming. Only he can't play baseball anymore."

"Norm and Jerry used to play golf every chance they got, when they pulled duty together . . ." Reminded all at once that this might not be too tactful a subject in the face of Jean Mayberry's widowed state, Gertrude bit off the rest of what she had been going to say and picked at the lint on her slacks, frowning.

"Tommy," she said after a moment, "do you really think that?"

"Think what?"

"About Khotiane. Do you really think it's not—necessary?"

Tommy turned and looked at the lined, vigorous face, the nicely waved gray hair. Gertrude Woodruff had been a handsome woman and a fine army wife. It wasn't her fault that Norm had been on Packy Vinzent's staff when Packy'd been relieved after Sidi Bou Noura and nobody seemed to want him for a while. For an instant Tommy was tempted to turn the question aside; but something wouldn't let her. If Gert really wanted her opinion she would have it.

"I don't know what you mean by necessary," she said. "As far as I'm concerned it's about as necessary as theft or prostitution."

"Yes, but the spread of Communist terror—"

"Look: if this struggle in Khotiane is so important, so vital to us, why don't we get with it? Why don't we *declare* war and get behind it, then, put ourselves on the line and make the necessary sacrifices? Why all this furtive pussyfooting?"

Gertrude frowned. "It's not furtive, it's the way things are done nowadays."

"Yes, I can see that."

"Tommy," Jean intervened, "I don't see how we can judge—we don't know what they know back in Washington."

"Yes, that's what the Germans said in '33. Papa knows best. Well, maybe he doesn't know best. Had you ever thought of that? Maybe he's every bit as confused and guessing as the rest of us."

Gertrude was staring at her hard, but Jean was grinning indulgently, her head back. "Oh, Tommy, you always were such a maverick!"

"Wasn't I, though? And now school's out, girls." She sipped at her coffee, cold now, and watched the sun roll lazily through the streamers of fog. That was one advantage to having a reputation: people made allowances for you (if they felt like making allowances) in advance. At any rate, she had decided to say what she pleased from now on, within reason. She had kept her mouth closed—most of the time, anyway—for years and years, and now that was over. Sam had stood his last review, back at Beyliss, standing straight as a ramrod, taking the salute with perfect precision, his face hard, the tears slick on his cheeks; and they had come out here to Monterey and bought a home. He didn't like Carmel, where the Hammerstroms and Woodruffs and Jean Mayberry lived—its casual opulence and hoked-up rusticity offended him; so they had come over the hill and settled on a pleasant little redwood-and-stucco house in Monte Vista, deep in the pines, looking out toward Mount Toro and the Bay.

From over in Seaside where they were building the new express highway came the dense boom of blasting, and she thought of Hardee and the interminable crump of demolitions, and Major Bowers' wife. Well, this wasn't an awful lot, but at least they couldn't be ranked out of it. It had been pleasant enough. They had made some friends outside the military circles—a musician and his wife, a former rancher from Montana, a retired professor from Berkeley; but not many. They were still bound by the narrow channel of their lives. For a time Tommy had fought it, but after some months she had acquiesced to the casual round of bridge evenings and movie going. She started to paint, bought herself a set of oils and a collapsible easel at Oliver's Art Store and daubed at fanciful scenes of fishing boats anchored in the harbor or horses cantering through sunlit fields; but she couldn't get the effects she wanted. She dabbled in adult education courses at the high school on Tuesday nights, and finally settled on weaving, turning out place mats and curtains and napkins in blue-and-yellow designs. Then the restlessness would take hold of her again, and she would walk through the dry, sepulchral woods behind the house, assaulted by the scent of heather and manzanita.

Her life was over: was it? She was sixty-two, astonishingly, and one of Peggy's boys was in college. All those years had fled like shadows, in the dust and bugle clarions of two continents. Her father had died on the second anniversary of VJ Day, peacefully enough, after passing a few tart observations on the reluctance of certain highly placed military personages to accept the unified command, and had been buried at Arlington with full military honors. They had been transferred to Benning right after that. Her life had slipped away in a thousand teas and hops and receptions, her father and her son were dead, and all that was left were two grandsons, big, genial louts she saw perhaps once a year, a house they had barely started paying for, and a husband she wanted to love . . .

She did want to love him: she did love him, but they were such different people. Washing dishes or working at her loom, she would listen to the whine of the lathe or the power saw down in the cellar. He went on making things slowly and persistently—a chess set in lemon wood and walnut, two stools, a driftwood coffee table, an oak bread board. It was like a hunger with him, getting his hands on wood, planing it, fashioning it with slow care. After lunch he couldn't wait to get down to the shop again. His tools were all neatly arranged on hooks and brackets on the wall above the bench.

Evenings he sat in the second bedroom he'd made into a study, reading, his old fatigue cap pulled low to shade his eyes. The Far East still absorbed him; even in retirement he couldn't turn his back on it. He read Abend and Lacouture and Mao Tse-tung, he plowed through Fall, Guillain and the *Shui Hu Chuan.* All at once he was looked on as an expert on guerrilla warfare: events in Malaysia, Cuba, Algeria and Khotiane had aroused interest, the service journals besieged him for articles. "My God—I tramped all over North China for the better part of two years and handed them a thirty-five-thousand-word report, and they used it for toilet paper. And now they're dying to find out how the hell they did it." With a certain wry amusement he sent in the pieces on Sun Tzu and Lawrence and Francis Marion and the operations of Lin Tso-han—the same pieces that had been blandly rejected fifteen years before—and watched them featured, analyzed, praised to the skies. "The secret of success is longevity," he told Tommy, his eyes twinkling. "Just hang on long enough, and you'll see all your crazy notions turned into genius."

She tried to talk him into writing his memoirs.

"Honey, I'm no *writer*. If it had been Dad—"

"But you've had an interesting life, Sam. An important one. People want to hear about it."

"Nobody wants to read the muddled reminiscences of a divisional commander. Ike, Marshall, Georgie Patton, the movers and shakers—that's what they want."

"Or your journal with annotations. I should think that would make fascinating reading . . ."

He'd laughed once. "You'd see flames going up over the Pentagon all the way out here at Point Lobos. They'd boil me in crude oil."

"Well, you'd probably have to edit it a little."

"*Edit* it!—they'd have to print it on asbestos and bind it in lead."

Nevertheless he did a lot of writing. He corresponded voluminously with Jimmy Hoyt, now a two-star general with Plans, and Joey Krisler, who'd lived with them for a while at Benning, and who was currently fretting at a staff job up at Lewis; and several other men he'd served with. His arm hurt him nights—she would catch him kneading it gently, or doping himself up with aspirin or pain killer. His life was over too, but he didn't act as though it was; he seemed to feel none of the feverish resentment that gripped her at times.

"—Don't you get sick of this?" she'd demanded one evening as they were driving home from the Hammerstroms'. "All this silly old round—the same old games, the same old stories . . ."

"Chink can get tiresome, I'll admit."

"No, but I mean don't you wish you were doing something else—living in some other way?"

He had glanced at her then, with his faint, sad smile. "Poor kid. It isn't the gayest thing in the world for you, is it?"

"I didn't say that. I've no complaints."

"There's one thing I wish," he said. "I wish Dad were still alive: I'd like to sit around and listen to him for a while, three or four nights a week. He always made sense, and he could be witty about it, too. You felt—I don't know: attuned to things. More intelligent than you knew you really were."

She had started to remonstrate, a reflex action, then to her surprise had nodded. It was true. She'd fought her father, the oppressive force of his intellect, his incredible equanimity—but it was true. He could quicken your appetite for things. And now that she finally appreciated it and could value it, he was gone . . .

"He was remarkable, wasn't he?" she heard herself murmur. "It was funny, what he had. He was—"

"He had character," Sam said simply.

"Yes—I guess he did, didn't he? I never thought of him like that."

"That's what he had, though. He was always aware of consequences: he never forgot about them and he never deceived himself about them. That's very rare."

"I suppose so." She was reminded for no reason she could see of evenings in that bedraggled old set at Benning with Marge and Ben. "Remember the night Butch Batchelder came by and made that pass at Marge? and Ben wanted to fight him and you had to tackle him out on the back line and sit on him?" Silently he nodded; neon lights from a passing roadhouse glowed red on his face and then faded. "It seems funny thinking about that now. All that fuss . . ."

He would never talk about Palamangao: not one word. She had respected that, but later when they were down at Benning she had wormed it out of Frenchy Beaupré one evening when he was visiting them and Sam was held late at the headquarters building. Frenchy assumed she knew, and by pretending to ask for certain details she got the whole story. She could feel her face change as he told her; she'd suspected it was true—and yet something inside her had refused to accept the fact. But here it was, in all its vicious, murderous force. It had happened; it was true.

"It's hideous," she exclaimed. For the first time in her life—and this was strange, after so many years in the company of soldiers—she felt something of the terrible mental anguish in war. Before this she had thought of it only as physical agony, death and wounds and lesser privations; now she saw what exquisite torment a moment like this, with a man like Court, must mean. Damn him, she thought, and ground her teeth; damn him straight down to hell. "It's worse than hideous. It's outside the human race . . ."

"Yes, I'll sign that," Frenchy said.

She looked at him. "But how about you?—didn't you want to—I don't know: expose the whole thing, blow it all apart?"

"You're damned well right I did, Tommy. I argued with Sam about it, but his mind was made up. You know how that is."

"Indeed I do."

"God Himself couldn't change it. That was the way he wanted it, and that was the way it went. That's how the Double Five got the Distinguished Unit Citation. Sam made a deal with our friend—he wouldn't say anything if Massengale wangled the citation."

"—But they were dead!" she burst out. "All his friends . . ."

"No kidding," he came back hotly. "You think for one minute he didn't know that? There were plenty of sad sons of bitches coming right along behind them. The dear old dirty old war had to go on, didn't it? Don't be so God damned stupidly sanctimonious . . ."

She pressed her hand against her knee. "I'm not," she said softly. "I'm sorry, Frenchy; I don't mean to be." She paused. "That's why he won't wear the ribbon."

He stared irately up at the ceiling. "You're catching on."

She had never brought it up again with Sam. She could only guess at the violence of the struggle that had gone on in his heart, the burning mortification he must have felt at striking that bargain. It was odd—he'd been right about Court all along. For all his cranky, unpopular attitudes he'd been right about a lot of things. She remembered one night at the club at Ord, during the furor over the activation of the Negro divisions, and Maury Odom saying:

"Sam, you know as well as I do that I haven't got prejudice-one about this. But the sad fact of the matter is the Negro just can't think fast enough to fight well."

Sam had smiled. "Henry Armstrong and Sugar Ray Robinson seem to do pretty well."

"Oh, sure—prize fighting. I'm talking about aptitudes, reacting to the unexpected. You never worked with them, Sam. Talk to Jeff Barker— he's had them to here. Barracks a mess, automatic weapons frozen up, and vehicles—Jesus!"

"Maybe they feel it doesn't matter whether they take care of their gear or not."

"What do you mean? They're in the Army, aren't they? They're supposed to take care of their equipment like anybody else."

Sam had shifted in his seat. "I mean maybe if the Negro were treated like an equal—really like an equal—his attitude would change."

"Oh, come on, Sam," Jim Ravenel broke in with his soft drawl. "The nigger can't be treated like an equal for the simple reason that he *isn't* one. He never was and never will be. His skull is different, his brain is smaller, he's from an inferior race. I don't know whether that's good, bad or indifferent, but it happens to be a fact."

"I rather doubt that," Sam had said, and she could see his face settling in that stubborn look. "I rather doubt that a good deal."

"Sam, the trouble with you is, you're a dreamer," Maury said. "Seriously now, would you take orders from a colored officer?"

Sam looked at him in surprise. "Of course I would. And so would you, and so would Jim."

"Never!" Ravenel said, and his eyes were slits in his drawn, handsome face. "Never! I'd resign from the service before I'd do that . . ."

"Why?" Sam pursued. "Let's face it—we've all served under some complete and utter sons of bitches: incompetents and idiots and sadists and God knows what else. But they've given orders and we obeyed them. What's the difference? You're a good soldier—"

"This has nothing whatsoever to do with soldiering," Ravenel said in a frosty tone. "This is something else entirely. If you can't understand it I can't explain it to you."

Their corner of the room had turned silent and uncomfortable. She had signaled Sam furiously with her eyes, but he had said, without a trace of heat: "It's got to come, gentlemen; no matter what any of us thinks. Sooner or later it's got to come—if only so we're a bit closer to being that great democracy we're pleased to call ourselves. And the Army is just the place to begin."

"Why, in God's name?" Maury demanded crossly.

"Because we all do things we don't like, for the good of the service. All the time. Because we're trained to respect principle above person, rank over failings. And if an AGO comes down from Washington saying, '*You will*, regardless of your own personal feelings in the matter,' we will. And maybe we'll all be the better for it."

"Well, I'm here to tell you I hope and pray to Almighty God that day never comes," Jim Ravenel retorted, and drained his glass.

But the day had come, she thought, gazing up at the fog sifting grayly above the tops of the pines. The order *had* come down from the Adjutant General's Office, and Negro and white bunked together, and white men served under Negro officers; and the Jim Ravenels could resign from the service or make the best of it. Enlisted men could serve on courts-martial, as Sam had argued that they should, so long ago at Hardee; and a legally trained law officer presided over all general courts. Maybe the dreamers and the fools were right, over the long haul—more than the shrewd, practical ones. Maybe the troublemakers—

Inside, the phone was ringing, insistent and clear. She snapped back to the soft sunlight, Gertrude Woodruff's flat Ohio voice. With a groan she started to get to her feet, saw Sam in a dirty T-shirt moving through the kitchen. He called, "I'll take it," and she waved and nodded.

"I've got to be on my horse," Gertrude declared. "Come on, Jean."

"Why?" Tommy demanded. "What've you got that's so special?"

"Not a blessed thing. That's the trouble. Laundry and letters. The garden. A silly old woman's pastimes.—I'm getting fat," she said, and pushed at her midriff, which swelled against her blouse. "Look at that. Look at that. I've got to do something about it."

"Why don't you take up these Yoga drills?"

"Sit there holding my breath with my toes curled up under my armpits? No thanks."

"They're easy," Tommy protested, "—they're fun, in fact. I can show you in twenty minutes, Gert."

"No—I'll go along my weak and weary way: Canadian Club and a hot bath." She and Jean rose and moved toward the door that led through the living room, Tommy following them. "It's on for Friday, then?"

"Sure thing."

"Swell. Lord, it'll be good to get up to some decent shops, bright lights and things. This bucolic splendor goes a long way with little Gertie. We'll pick you up around eight?"

"Fine."

Tommy watched them walk off along the redwood sections. Sam had set them in too far apart for a woman's stride, and the effort to step in the center of each section threw them both into an extravagant, lurching gait.

"Beautiful!" Jean called, and pointed down. "You're going to have a showplace . . ."

"If we don't drop dead from exhaustion first."

In the kitchen Tommy paused, listening to the clatter of their departure. The Woodruffs had a British Ford, and it sounded exactly like an overloud sewing machine. She couldn't hear Sam's voice, so presumably the phone call was ended. Yet he hadn't gone out again. It was so quiet: why was that? She walked into the bedroom. Sam was sitting by the bed table, his thumb at his chin.

"Who was it, dear?"

He turned and looked at her. She could see where he'd scribbled two pages of notes on the telephone scratch pad. "It was Skip Burleson," he said. "The Chief's office. They want me to go to Khotiane."

"Khotiane!" she exclaimed. "What on earth for?"

He got to his feet. He was covered with adobe dust, and there was a smear of dirt low across his forehead. "There's a lot going on over there. More than meets the eye. It seems. It would be a special mission." His face was solemn and preoccupied, but there was that curious fugitive gleam in his eyes. *China*, she thought with a quick pang of jealousy, of outrage; oh my God, it's China all over again.

"The Chief wants me to head it," he went on.

She stared at him. "Now? Right away?"

"Well, yes. As soon as possible."

"You mean they're going to call you back into service?"

"That's what I gather."

"But why you? You're retired . . ." She made a brief sound of distress. "Besides, you've done enough—you've already done more than any baker's dozen of them together. Forty-three years—"

"I know."

He'd made up his mind, then: he'd decided to go. There was no sense in saying anything more. She folded her arms. "You're going, then?"

He frowned and looked at his dirty nails. "The Chief must have a reason. A particular one."

She sighed inaudibly and turned away. They had been pursued by war. VJ Day, the smoky, sunlit September afternoon on the Green at Walt Whitman and their most fervent hopes had meant nothing at all. Instead of the years of peace she had dreamed of, that rational, open-hearted community of peoples she'd felt must come, war had kept breaking out: in Indonesia, in Greece, in Palestine and Indo-China. There had very nearly been war over Berlin. Sam hadn't gone to Korea— Bradley had wanted him to take over the Infantry School at Benning. He had followed events closely, agonizing over the Pusan Perimeter where Joey Krisler had a company, rejoicing at the Inchon landings. But he had not requested a transfer: he would serve where he was sent. He would not change. He could not conceal his apprehension when MacArthur went north to the Yalu. "It won't work," he'd said grimly. "I don't care what he or Willoughby or any of the rest of his G-2 wizards say, it won't work. The Chinese are going to come in, and it's going to go very hard with us." During the truce negotiations he had been quietly jubilant. "Why all the wailing and gnashing of teeth? Total victory—that idea's as dead as the dodo bird. It was an impossible concept anyway. Look—we have checked armed aggression: let it rest there." Meanwhile war kept on breaking out—in Pakistan, Suez, Hungary, Cuba, Algeria, Laos, Khotiane. Sam had got his third star and been transferred back to Beyliss . . .

He was looking up flight schedules to San Francisco and writing down lists of things to do, talking to himself in an undertone: he had to shoot off a wire to Joey, he would have to take a physical at the Presidio, he ought to see Slattery and Spike Robinson who were just back from there and get all the dope he could, he wondered if Gene Villarette was available—

She said: "But Court Massengale's out there, isn't he?"

He nodded. "He's COMMACK."

"Bliss Farnham's out there, too. Fowler, Graulet, the whole gang. What makes you think you can make any headway against that crew?"

He frowned at her, but not in irritation. "Well, they're with the Military Advisory Corps. This would be different. It's a political mission."

"But you said everything's essentially political out there, anyway. Look at Laos. Where does one leave off and the other begin? Everything's political—and then it's military, and then it's political again." Her voice had risen a note and she depressed it. "It sounds to me as though you're just walking into a hornet's nest. And for what? What'll it accomplish? You'll just go out there and wear yourself out and in six months they'll be blowing each other up all over again . . ."

He sat down on the bed and passed his hand slowly over his face. "Somebody's got to do it."

"All right, but why you? Let someone else do it. Somebody"—she started to say "younger" and switched in midsentence—"who hasn't always been on Court Massengale's spit-list . . . Why in God's name did they pick *you?*" she cried. "Can't they see it's hopeless? He'll trick you and trap you every step of the way . . ."

He winked once. "Maybe I'll sidestep him."

"Don't be facetious," she snapped. "You're not thirty-five anymore, Sam. I don't want you out there, wallowing around in rice paddies and jungle. You'll come down with something horrible."

"I've already got everything horrible you can get."

"No you haven't, and you know it." Her agitation had grown with her talk rather than being diminished by it. "Probably they want a sacrificial lamb. Someone they won't miss—that's why they're calling you back. If it's a political thing . . ."

He eyed her askance, soberly. "That's possible. I thought of that. But I don't believe the Chief would do something like that."

"You sound awfully sure of yourself . . . How long will it be for?"

"Honey, I don't know."

She began to walk up and down in the bedroom. "—I don't see why you have to do this," she explained. "Jesus, war is vile . . ."

"Isn't it."

"I know I'm too old and foolish for it, but there are times when I wish I were a pacifist. An out-and-out pacifist. Sometimes I think the only truth is in peace. You know—what they say: Speak truth to power."

He nodded. "Yes. Sometimes I do, too. The only trouble is, power exists in the world. There it is—and the only way is to deal with it, face it out . . . Or anyway, that's the crummy old way I see it."

"No," she said after a moment. "I don't suppose there's any other way."

His eyes shot up to hers—a startled, anxious glance, almost frightened.

"What's the matter?"

"Nothing. Nothing."

Standing at the foot of the bed she watched him as he took off his field shoes, yellowed now with the adobe clay the house sat on. She could tell: it was going to be an adventure; he was going to go forth to do great deeds. The idiot! But she loved him: he was all she had and she loved him. It was wrong, all wrong—they had *left* the Army, they had bought this house on a home loan, they had found new friends and old friends and a new rhythm—and now it was all to be torn apart because some officious, misguided fool in the office of the Chief of Staff had had a brainstorm. Ridiculous. He drew off his sweaty T-shirt and her eyes darted swiftly over the scars: the scorched and puckered skin, foreign and rubescent, above the breast, the unpleasantly smooth purple grooves and triangles on the shoulder and back. His left arm and shoulder were thinner, more pinched than his right. He will be killed, the thought struck her like an open hand; if he goes this time he won't come back. She remembered the crazy masked ball at Garfield and Ben in the outlandish bummer's costume, and the quarrel with Massengale, and her sudden, awful premonition, prevision, whatever it was. But Ben had been only a friend—

"—Don't go."

She had never said anything like this before; anger and pride had always checked her. But now she didn't care. She thought of Jean Mayberry, and Mae Lee, and her own long, desolate war years, with a shiver of revulsion: she didn't want to be separated ever again from this worn, silly, earnest, lovable, maddening old man. She came up to him and put her hand deliberately on the slick, lacerated flesh. "Don't go, Sam. Please. I don't care who's a Communist or Fascist-imperialist or necrophilist or any damned thing else. Tell them you're not going. Please . . ."

He gazed at her very somberly for a moment, chewing at the inside of his cheek. "Honey, on Pala when I was hit, an Imperial Marine dumped a grenade in the CP hole and all I could do was lie there and look at it. And the only reason I'm sitting here right now looking at you is because a boy threw himself on it to save my beat-up old hide. And his name was Joe Brand."

"Oh," she said faintly. "You never told me that."

"No . . . So if they want me now, do you think I've got the right to sit back and let things float along? after that?"

"—But he wanted you to *live*," she protested.

"Yes. He must have." His voice was hard as flint, without inflection. "And frankly, I doubt very much if I was worth it." He stared off at the tortured black limbs of the pines above the canyon. "It involves China," he said. "The two Chinas, I mean . . . It's a very explosive situation they've got out there."

"Oh," she murmured. "China . . ."

"Yes. The Chief was talking to me for a minute or two himself."

She locked her fingers together. "*China*—" she burst out, "—do you mean to tell me they're actually—"

"All right," he answered, in the tone she'd heard him use with troops, the tone that nobody went on arguing against. Smiling faintly he patted her on the hip. "Now I've already told you more than I should have. And only because I know you're such a good, disciplined little camp follower." Pressing down on his thighs he heaved himself to his feet. "Honey, it's a pretty crucial affair, I think. I've got to go—and I've got to give it all I've got."

She put her hand to his cheek. "Zu Befehl, Herr old General."

"That's the pitch."

Listening to his voice on the phone she got out his Valpac and B-bag and his service suntans, and began transferring the ribbons with deft care, as she'd done for years. There were so many: the baby-blue rectangle of the Medal of Honor with its five staggered white stars, all by itself at the top; the Distinguished Service Cross with cluster, the Silver Star three times, the Purple Heart with cluster, the decorations from France and Great Britain and Italy and Portugal; the festive little parade of service and theater medals. The Presidential Unit Citation alone he would not wear: because of Court Massengale. Court was there now in Khotiane as head of the advisory groups, surrounded by his retinue of sycophants and hatchet men.

"Lion's den," she muttered crossly, working: apprehension had always made her sullen. "Walking into a lion's den. Cobra pit, more likely."

From the bathroom he called: "You say something, honey?"

"No. Nothing . . ."

She was rummaging around for underwear and skivvy shirts and socks when she came upon the piece of twisted iron, lying in a little box among some belts and shoelaces; black as lava, contorted. The Tweaker had dug it out of his back on Palamangao, probably to the tune of some esoteric and ribald remark. Scrap iron from the good old USA, Sam had said, come home to roost. She thought of Bert MacConnadin standing spraddle-legged in the middle of the croquet lawn that sunny December morning, his round, red face defiant and amused. What had he said? He'd wanted a return on his investments, *that* was what he cared about: now: today.

Sam was in the shower now; he started to sing—he had always loved to sing in the shower—and then broke off, as though he realized that she would hear him and construe it as high spirits.

"Go ahead," she called in bleak distress, knowing he could not hear her, "I don't care, go ahead and sing . . ." Laying out his green fatigues, pale with wear and launderings, his gleaming field shoes, groping deep in the back of his closet for his web belt and canteens and poncho and mosquito net. She felt stiff with resentment and fear. There was no end to it, no end at all, and they didn't care. There on the other side of the world in some dripping nipa hut her counterpart was sorting out *her* man's gear with a desolate, frantic heart. What did it matter whether Khotiane was controlled by Communists or a Fascist junta or an imperialist viceroy or a sun worshipers' convention? All *they* wanted—she and that wiry little Khotianese woman—were their men, safe at home, sweaty, carefree, singing in the shower . . .

The bottom drawer of his dresser held some khaki shirts. He'd been using them for work shirts, but three or four were still in good condition and nicely laundered. She lifted them out—and saw in the far corner of the drawer the little pink-and-blue papier-mâché marshal's baton from the Jongleur Ivre, crushed and half-unraveled at one end. Gazing at it she began soundlessly to weep, her tears staining the starched khaki.

The hills were a deep green; far below they heaved and sank like the backs of restless animals and in the valleys the rice paddies lay in feathery, pale lime patterns, flashing silver when the sun struck the water. Listening through the earphones Wodtke the crew chief had given him, Joey Krisler heard a voice say: "Tango Tiger, this is Three-zero-five. I am thuh-ree minutes from target. Over . . ." He looked up, encountered the leathery, wrinkled face of Sam Damon, who winked at him somberly. He winked back, and over the shuttling roar of the rotor mouthed the phrase: *Here—goes—nothin'* . . .

No matter how many times you did it, jungle or fir forests or barren, frozen hills, there was always that sharp, electric surge deep in your chest, like a blast of cold air; the old adrenalin pumping hard. And hard on that the pictures came racing the way they always did: Karas with his hands over his belly and his mouth wide, gasping: Ogline's back laid open, jacket and sweater and shirt and flesh and bone in a raw, streaming crater: the little medic sitting in the doorway staring in silent terrible awe at where his leg no longer was, Jensen on fire from his own flamethrower, rolling and writhing in the snow, turning it black—and through and over and inside all these the utterly stupefying blows on his arm, in his face, like the blunt end of an axe—and the searing pain and then the great, weak, liquid flooding. All the things that could happen to a man at war: all the rending possibilities. He knew so many of them now.

Wodtke clapped the little Khotianese squad leader on the shoulder, then turned to Damon and held up two fingers. The Old Man nodded once and picked up the '03, which looked slender and antiquated in the company of all the newer, grosser weapons. Krisler watched the General's hands lift a clip from his belt, tap the points once, smartly, on the stock, and insert it, his fingers flowing over the nicely templed bolt. Old Sad Sam, he thought: going to another war. No end to them.

He had spent half his convalescent leave from Korea with the Damons, waiting to find out what his face would look like, trying not to worry, telling himself it didn't matter: what was a chewed-up cheek and jaw compared to the loss of a leg or an arm, or a piece of your jewelry? Before then Tommy had always made him nervous—her quick, mordant wit had hit him on his blind side, so to speak; she seemed always to be judging him. He knew what it was—she was measuring him against Donny and finding him wanting more than a little. Which was natural enough: Donny had been tall and graceful and he had a terrific mind, whereas he himself was short and had never looked very special—and what was he going to look like now? But down at Benning, then, he'd come to be very fond of her: most of that wild, cantankerous side had vanished. She'd fed him, fattened him up, changed his dressings; it had been she who had driven him home after the plastic surgery bouts and bucked him up when the results weren't all they might have been. "They'll get it next time, you'll see—it's a hundred per cent better." And when he'd gloomily protested, she had straightened him out: "What do you expect to look like—Tyrone Power? They can't improve you that much. You'll never make it in the movies, anyway—none of you Krislers ever had any dramatic talent . . ."

Which wasn't so, to hear Sam tell it: according to Sam, his father was a fantastic actor with troops. After the arm had healed and the plastic surgery was over, they had gone on some great pack trips together up in Canada and out in the Cascades, fishing mostly. Sam had told him about Moapora and the native outriggers, and the ruckus over the ITC stenciling, and the yellow scarf, and the time on Wokai when the whole regiment was pinned down under some of the heaviest fire Sam had ever seen and his father had said to Bowcher, in his best parade-ground voice: "Stan, there's a raft of saki in those caves and if we don't get up there and take 'em the greedy little muff-divers are going to drink it all up . . ." His father had had color to spare—which was more than he could say. He could make it on his own, get a job done; and that was about all. Like Paprika Ben, he hated routine; he'd been delighted when Sam had asked for him for this mission. There were times when all the Army seemed to be full of was school or passing papers around. Jane hadn't liked it very much, but she was a sensible gal: she knew it was what *he* wanted, and that was good enough for her. It wouldn't be long, and the experience on a politico-military junket like this would be invaluable . . .

Some of the invaluable experience was rising toward him now. The helicopter began to vibrate sharply as the rotor shifted to maximum pitch. The Khotianese were peering through the open door, their mouths open, doubled over their weapons. Krisler took off the earphones, zippered up his armored vest and picking up his carbine inserted a banana clip in the breech. They were dropping fast now, slipping down a vast mountainside; the effect was of sinking, heavily weighted and pulled by a strong current, through water. The green blur on their left became high jungle. Sergeant Wodtke snapped himself into the long safety belt that was made fast to the helicopter door and picked up the wicked-looking M-14 with its blocky pistol grip and tubular flash hider at the end of the barrel. Krisler just had time to think of a guerrilla team sprawled behind an automatic weapon bore-sighted for the landing-zone approach, and to feel the curiously unpleasant sense between his legs, of descending so indolently, of being *above* fire. Then they were sweeping in low over the tall trees, a valley fanned out below them green and marshy, and a clearing. They sank like autumn leaves on a windless day and hit with a jar, and the high swamp grass swept back from the blast of the rotor, a tiny hurricane. Wodtke tapped the shoulder of the squad leader; he dropped out of sight, another, another, gripping their rifles high. Krisler moved forward behind the Old Man, and jumped. His feet went deep into muck, a big splash. He straightened, and moving away from the chopper he heard the old, familiar uproar of gunfire. Sam was standing perfectly motionless, waiting, as Gene Villarette, their interpreter, and Bob Forbes, the Old Man's junior aide, hurried toward them from Three-oh-seven.

"Did you see it?" Forbes asked. "That gun?"

"No," he answered. "Where?"

"Low on the hillside. Near that little creek. Four or five rounds. Like a BAR on slow rate."

There were huts in a dense cluster, their palm thatching withered and white against the rain forest. Soldiers were moving through them in a line, firing. Near one hut some Khotianese women stood in a tight, small group as though, huddled together, they could protect one another, render themselves immune to danger. They wore the typical ankle-length dresses of black or brown homespun, with a single broad hem of red-and-white embroidery. Captain Desautels, one of the MACK advisers on the sweep, was shouting something and pointing, and up ahead Krisler could hear the thinner snap of a small-caliber weapon. On the left there was a hue and cry, and turning he saw a slight figure splashing through the far end of the paddy, arms flailing, the water dancing around him in high, bright sheets. There was a burst of firing but the boy—it looked like a young boy—slipped into the reeds bordering the edge of the paddy, scrambled up the bank and vanished into the forest.

Krisler frowned. Damon was walking along behind the line of Khotianese soldiers, his rifle held easily in one hand. Ahead now there was the cough of grenades, but muffled, as though discharged underground. They had reached the huts; the women, some of them with babies at their breasts, were crowded around Desautels now, moaning and wailing. He was shaking his head at them sternly, his hand moving in peremptory demurral. A body lay nearby in the grass and mud, face down; a thin, wiry body in a long-sleeved jacket and loose black trousers. He was wearing sandals of tires held by thongs made from inner tubes. There was a narrow piece of webbing around his waist, and hanging from it what looked like a large ball of suet. There was no weapon. Krisler bent down and turned him over; the man's face was blunt and sturdy; so much blood was streaming from his nose and mouth it was impossible to tell where he had been hit. Krisler picked up the ball of suet and found it was a lump of glutinous rice wrapped in parachute nylon.

"He dead?" Kettelson, another of the advisers, was standing above him. He nodded, rose and moved on. The sweep was moving quickly through the huts now. A soldier just ahead of him called, "La dai, la dai!" and a bent old man with a white beard came out of the hut nearest them, his eyes narrowed. The soldier motioned him away sharply, slipped a grenade from his belt and pulled the pin. The old farmer's eyes went wide; he croaked something inaudible and waved his arms. The soldier lobbed the grenade into the entrance and ducked away quickly. The old man shouted something that sounded like, "Po ban nah!" and started back for the hut, coming right past Krisler, who stared at him in amazement—then caught him around the waist and flung him to the ground as gently as a gesture that violent could be, falling with him, watching the soldier scuttle away from the entrance. At that instant there came the thin, choked squalling of a baby from the hut. Lying there on his belly, Krisler thought with the brevity of dread, Four second lag—nothing to do; then: Oh Jesus—that's why he wanted to get back in there; then: Maybe it's a dud, it might be a dud, if only it's a—

The explosion was sharp and violent. Dust boiled sluggishly and bits of mud and earth spattered out of the entrance. Silence. He ran forward, stepped inside. In the center of the hut was a funny little bunker, like a squat beehive of dried mud; its side had been blown out by the grenade, and he peered in. Several forms in a dark tangle of limbs and strips of clothing and bits of pottery and a great deal of blood. The small bodies were mangled and limp. None of them moved. He stepped back.

"What is it?" It was Sam, behind him in the dim light.

"Two children—it looks like two children—and the mother and a baby."

They glanced at each other tensely, looked away. Then the General turned and they went out—to run against another soldier holding a flaming stick to the thatched eaves.

"What are *you* doing?" Damon demanded.

The Khotianese obviously knew no English. Nervously he smiled, and his free hand rose all at once in a graceful pantomime of conflagration. Then he darted off down the row. Several of the huts were already on fire; smoke rolled thickly around them, foul and stifling. Krisler could hear more shouted commands and the troops kept moving on quickly, grenading the huts and burning them; the wailing of the women and children rose still higher. Krisler swallowed and wiped his mouth. The old farmer was on his knees where Krisler had tackled him, facing his blazing hut, his thick, gnarled hands pressed together at his temples. With a curious deliberateness he rocked up and down from the waist, his seamed face convulsed with grief. His long white hair ruffled in the wind.

Jesus Christ, Krisler thought. He hurried after Sam, who was walking quickly toward two of the American advisers.

"*Captain*," the Old Man called. His face was fearsome. He did not shout, but his voice carried clearly against the wind and explosions. "*Captain . . .*"

Desautels broke away from the other officer and said, "Yes, General?"

"You are firing these huts."

"Yes, sir. Those are my orders. All hooches containing bunkers."

Damon stared at him. "Bunkers—those pitiful little mud shelters. . . ?"

"Yes, General. They are to be considered of an offensive nature."

"But you're firing their clothes, too—their food, their rice—how are they going to live?"

Desautels frowned. "They're to be relocated, General. The whole village."

"Who authorized this action?"

"General Tho Huc, sir. And General Bannerman concurs."

The Old Man closed his mouth. "I see. Carry on."

"Very good, sir." Desautels trotted off toward what looked like a storage shed at the far side of the village.

Sam shot Krisler and the others a quick, furious glance and said, "Come on. Let's see it all . . ." They went on. Nearly all the huts seemed to be on fire, their roofs seething in a crackling roar through which showers of sparks swirled and rained like mica. Everywhere there was the rancid stench of burned food and clothing.

In the clearing before the storage shed a man was crouching on the hard dirt, a boy of perhaps seventeen or eighteen. He was squatting on his thighs; he was naked to the waist and his hands were tied behind his back. A Khotianese regular was bent over him, speaking to him imperiously and persistently. The boy made no reply. At the end of each sentence the soldier would strike him across the face with a slender bamboo strip, and a fiery red welt would rise on his face or neck. The others stood watching, in silence. Finally the boy said something, and looked down.

"What did he say, Gene?" Sam asked Villarette.

"He says he is a rice farmer, he knows nothing about the Hai Minh."

"—He is a liar and a pig," the interrogator said. He was a sergeant, a short, powerfully built man with a heavy jaw and a small, pinched mouth. He said something in Khotianese, took his bayonet out of the scabbard and repeated the question. Then with a deft, tantalizingly casual motion he drew the point across the prisoner's chest. Blood leaped out in a lazy curve of bubbles and the boy winced, then stiffened again.

"For Christ's sake," Forbes said angrily.

The sergeant smiled; lowering the point of the bayonet he held it against the boy's belly, very low, his fingers pressing gently on the haft, and repeated the question. The boy said nothing. The interrogator pressed a little harder, and the blade entered the flesh. Sweat was running in great streams down the prisoner's lacerated face, and now blood began to seep into his trousers, staining the dark cloth; his teeth were bared.

Krisler averted his eyes. The firing had stopped almost entirely, and he could hear the boy's slow, labored breathing. God Almighty, he thought. He had seen some bad things; some pretty bad things in seventeen years of soldiering. Done them, too. At Werbomont, on the northern shoulder of the Bulge, he had helped the shattered remnant of an engineer company blow the bridge over the Amblève in the very face of the German armor, and then had crouched behind a pile of rubble and watched in helpless rage as the SS had routed two dozen women and children out of their homes on the far bank and shot them down amid curses and laughter. Schrecklichkeit, and then some. And the next afternoon, shivering behind a wall in the snow above Stoumont, with the sound of tank engines clattering hollowly through the fog, he had paid them back. Nothing like that had ever happened to him before; a genial, easygoing boy—he was his mother's son—he'd rarely lost his temper. But now as the black-uniformed figures came on through the fog he had shot them down in a cold fury, in exultant defiance. *Here* was the enemy, these SS monsters with their death's-head insignia and their gospel of terror and brutality: here they were. He had no wish to run anymore. This was it. He stayed, and he made the others stay with him. Forty-one of them, with four bazookas and half a dozen satchel charges and two machine guns—and that was as far along the road to Liège as the Wehrmacht got that day, or any other day. So much for Schrecklichkeit.

In Korea too he had seen some sights that sickened him: mutilated bodies, prisoners shot down in windrows, children blown to bloody rags by artillery fire. He had seen German prisoners threatened and roughed up for information. Blows struck in rage, in desperation, yes. But this kind of thing—the deliberate and indiscriminate butchery of helpless civilians, the depraved, malignant torturing of prisoners such as he was now witnessing, he had never seen. This was not war: this was not the destruction of enemy forces in the field, nor was it ambush, nor even reprisal. This was running exceedingly close to Schrecklichkeit . . .

With slow consternation he looked at Sam Damon, whose features were set in a noncommittal mask. Desautels had come up during this little scene, and the Old Man turned to him.

"And the guerrilla force, Captain?"

"We've got three of them. Two killed, and this prisoner here . . ."

"Who will apparently soon be dead himself."

The prisoner was doubled over on his thighs, gasping and trying with all his might not to cry out.

"It's the only way to deal with them, General." Desautels was a tall, blond man with heavy eyebrows, and he looked very serious and intent. "I was—disconcerted by some of the counterinsurgency measures employed here, at first. But it's the only way to get information, sometimes."

Sam gestured. "*He* didn't give us much, did he?"

"Some of them are very intransigent. The hard-core type."

"Was he armed when he was captured?"

Desautels shook his head. "They ditch them when they're about to be captured—it's SOP with them. So as not to be caught with the evidence. Then they pick up a straw hat and a hoe and they're right back down on the farm. That's the kind of war we've got." He grinned and added brightly: "We did capture a weapon, though."

"What type?"

"An M-1 carbine."

The Old Man's upper lip curled. "I see. You mean you've succeeded in recovering one of our own, then."

"That's about the size of it, General. They're pretty tough to nail down out here. Over in the real paddy country around Nanh Kep you can put the screws on them and track them down. Here, they break into the jungle and they're gone for good. They're masters of the easy fadeout."

"How about the blocking operation on the other side of the ridge there?"

"They must have had some trouble with it, sir. We just got the word on it—that drop was scrubbed."

"I see."

Desautels pawed at the earth a moment with his jungle boot. "I'm sorry this mission wasn't more rewarding, General. We often have better luck than this. Though to tell you the truth, sometimes we don't corral any of them." He made a curt, deprecatory gesture with his thumb and little finger. "Maybe this little son of a bitch will give us something we can use."

Krisler's eyes moved involuntarily back to the prisoner. Four or five soldiers were now crowded around him tightly and he couldn't make out what they were doing. Finally he was able to see that the boy's head was being held in a bucket full of water. He looked away again.

"*That* 'little son of a bitch' isn't going to tell anybody anything," Sam was saying in a flat, hard voice. "I'll bet you five hundred dollars.— When are they scheduled to pick us up?"

Desautels glanced smartly at his watch. "Eight minutes exact, General. They'll be right on the button, you'll see."

The Old Man looked down at his field shoes thoughtfully. Smoke from the burned huts swept low around them, turning the moving men to shadows. The crying of the women and children went on unabated. "I'm certainly gratified to hear that," he said.

16 *May* 62:   It is all very complicated, it seems. Hai Minh control most of country by night, Vu Khoi's people by day. Government forces have all kinds of American equipment and supplies, but they are being slowly forced back on Cau Luong. Insurgents have mostly old French and homemade weapons (when they have any at all, that is), but they are winning. Slowly, painfully, falteringly, but they are winning. Current crisis seems to have been created by Hoanh-Trac, a disaffected general from previous (Ngo Hieu) regime, who is apparently sulking in his tents like Achilles up at Plei Hoa, and who has been recently making noises about deserting his status as a sort of half-ass 3rd force and going over to the side of the Hai Minh. This, I was told almost tearfully by Starling at the Embassy, would certainly tip scales in favor of insurgents.

But of course the insurgents are not exactly insurgents. *They* call themselves People's Liberation Army (or some such) and many of them were leading lights in booting out French (which most of the jazzy types down at Cau Luong definitely were NOT).

And then there is the matter of those 3 Chinese Nationalist Divs which Hoanh-Trac wants to boot out of the country, too.

Flew back to Cau Luong Tuesday with my retinue. Joey and Bob Forbes playing 10-second chess, Gene perusing the *Upanishads* (in the ORIGINAL), Tony Giandoli keeping us in an uproar all the way. "Man, I feel like a presidential candidate. When I get home I'm going to run for office. On a sex-and-electronics ticket. Hello, out there! . . ." Waving grandly out of the window. "You greasy grunts with your never-jamming automatic weapons: Why crawl on your leech-infested bellies when you can do the ozone caper! Hey you know, this is the first time I've ever been in an aree-o-plane. . . ?" Rain clouds like great pewter dream-surf over the mountains. Thought of the flight in to Moapora with Ben that afternoon. Another Fast Trip to Big Trouble.

Cau Luong like a Fifth Avenue fag window dresser's idea of the Mysterious East. Pedicab drivers all right out of Charlie Chan, shop-keepers out of Mr. Moto. GIs cruising streets in pairs trying to appear casual about it all, arms full of purchases. Debouched (that should certainly be the word) at Régence, entrance guarded by 2 spit-'n'-polish Khotianese PFCs. The grand syndrome, as Tommy would say: lobby like the Statler, dining room on the right with white tablecloths and smiling Khotianese waiters, bar on left, nice and dimly lit and sultry. Already packed with liquid standbys and long-time shack jobs of the brass, attired in skin-tight dresses and false bosoms and lots and lots of

western type make-up. Just as American as Mom's applejack. Everything air conditioned, streamlined, sealed tight against bugs, dust,
vermin, reality. Home away from home in little old Kho-T.

Blix Wissocker the center of a festive group of lesser lights and twit-
tering maidens. Rigors of duty in Porky's overswollen headquarters.
"Sam! What'd they do—grab you in the draft? I'll write that mean old
son of a bitch Hershey myself. *You're* not what we want . . ." "No," I
said, "I can see that." Watching me shrewdly with his jolly fat man's
eyes: a little disdain, a little fear. "No kidding, what are you doing out
here? Man, we must be in real trouble if they're calling on the fire
brigade . . ." Some laughter from the celebrants—but cautious: no
knowing which way the beat-up old alley cat will jump. "Special mission for the IG's office, Blix," I said. "The Chief wants me to give a
good, hard look at the rear echelons, particularly Services of Supply."
He threw back his head, laughing: jolly fat man with a fat finger in
the pie. "Don't josh a josher, Sam—they'd never have an old groundhog
like you combing through records." His hand resting on the bare shoulder of a girl with elaborately piled black hair and skin like silk over spun
glass. "Come on down and have a drink when you get settled in." Felt
like the minister's son who's entered the town brothel by mistake.
Everybody happy as Larry. The perpetual freeload at the Big PX.

17 May 62:   Over to see C. S. Massengale this afternoon. Ensconced in
the old palace (what WOULD CSM do without a palace?) looking
out over the Bay. Flunkies and anterooms abounding. Let me walk ¾s of
way to his desk over soundless carpet, then rose and waited. A trifle
awkward. I came to attention and saluted. Why not? He returned the
salute carelessly and then shook hands. "Well, Samuel. We meet again."
How true. A bit off-balance himself, for all his savoir faire. "By Jupiter,
you don't look a day older." Not true at all: true of him, though. Same
old imperious, hawklike glance, the charming smile. Same voice without
a human flaw. He has arrested time. How? Four stars now, all kinds of
eerie decorations from Cambodian potentates. Four stars. I thought,
*Thou hast it now—king, Cawdor, Glamis, all as the weird women prom-
ised; and, I fear,* etc. Well, not quite: there's still the Chief's post he
hasn't quite nailed down. But give him time. (Which he's running out
of.)

Slouched back in his chair—that deceptive indolence. "Well, I'd have
thought you had enough service to last you three times around. Just
couldn't bear to stay out of things, eh?" "No, I've had enough, General." My turn to smile now. "The Chief called me back for this mission." Thought I might as well let him know how things stand right
away. "So I've heard."

A few pleasantries, no reminiscences. He said: "I ought to get out of
harness myself. It's getting to be too much for an old trooper.—The

world has changed since we were youngsters, Samuel, do you realize that?" "I'll sign that," I said. "Yes. I keep wondering what it's all for, do you know? I mean, just what are we busting our old guts for, out in this turbulent, unhappy land?" Hoped he'd go on but he didn't. Captious Courtney disillusioned, ready to relinquish ambition, let slip the baton? I think not. And under it was that easy, guileless smile.

But what, then? After a decent interval I said how sorry I was to hear about Emily's death. "Yes. Thank you for your note—it was good of you to write. You and Tommy." "She was a fine person," I said. "Yes— she was a gallant lady. Her only fault was that she was too vulnerable, too inflexible for this world." Sighing, gazing out at the magnificent gardens of the Empress Te-Phuong, who died of a broken heart when her young lord was killed in that witless expedition against Mandalay. Decided I'd better not ask after Jinny, not after that fantastic court case. God alone knows what she's doing now—and He better not tell.

He said softly: "And how's Tommy?" "Fine," I answered, "she needed a little time to get her feet under her. She's taken up weaving: I found her an old Shaker blanket loom with an overhead beater, and repaired it myself." "Penelope," he said, and smiled, "—the perfect occupation for a warrior's wife." "I'm not a warrior anymore," I said. "Wanderer, then. You're still wandering. Aren't you?" I didn't say anything. He gave me his long, low, significant look. "All's well that ends well, eh? You always said that." "Yes," I answered slowly, "it's sometimes true, General."

Then we got down to roofing nails. "Paul Bannerman tells me you've been observing some of our vertical-envelopment sweeps in the Delta. Tell me your impressions." That meant he already knew them, he's got his spies everywhere, I suppose. Told him I didn't feel I'd really seen enough to be a competent judge—of the three ops I watched, two were almost total failures and the third aborted.

He was on his feet now, pacing up and down. "Washington doesn't realize what we're up against out here. They're still operating on a World War II psychology—a monolithic enemy, fixed lines of battle, the whole mystique." He went off into a long dissertation involving what he called the New Diplomacy, the need for a more sophisticated, less sentimental approach to international relations, a return to the methods of Cardinal Mazarin (Jesus Christ, MAZARIN) in this new arena where indirection and subversion are the leading motifs, and a psychological preparation of the body politic is the paramount issue. I listened politely—nay, attentively. Couldn't help thinking of that audience with MacArthur at Lennon's. So long ago. Why do these types always need to have *you* seated while *they* pace and fulminate?

"Samuel, we've taken six hundred and forty-seven casualties in the last two months alone, do you realize that? *Six hundred and forty-seven.* That's including helicopter pilots and crews as well as ground advisers and the new Mobile Forces units we've just activated—I suppose you know about those." I said I did. "I know you think I don't give a brass farthing for the hoplites, but I do, believe me. Gehring was out here two weeks ago, full of righteous wrath. 'You're bombing civilians! You're destroying the organic fabric of the country!' The God damned fool—can't he see that the insurgents are the people and the people are the insurgents? They're one and the same thing . . . Oh sure—a few hard-core Moscow-trained cadres here and there, but they could never function if the populace weren't with them. How do you think they're warned, where they hide their weapons, where they get their food?" "So the answer is mass deportation," I said finally. "Samuel, I'll tell you something." Standing right above me, his eyes narrowed. "The *answer* is what Chiang Kai-shek did in Hupeh and Honan. Yes. If the peasants support the insurgents—hide them, feed them, supply their manpower—then the answer is perfectly logical. Destroy that base of the insurgents."

I could only stare at him. But he'd already turned away. "Well, there's no question about that, of course. We're too mired in a nineteenth century ground-rules morality to absorb any of that . . ." He went ranting on about Hoanh-Trac, who he said is playing footsie with the Hai Minh and screaming to the UN about territorial integrity. "Integrity! They don't know the meaning of the word . . ." I finally dove into the current and asked him if he'd talked to Hoanh-Trac. He looked at me with the expression of an exasperated saint. "I've invited him down here twice, and each time he's put me off with the most transparent of pretexts. Death of a sister! I tell you they are the very epitome of sinuosity. Simpering, faithless little creatures—God knows how the French put up with them as long as they did." "The silk and the rubber eased the pain," I said, "—not to mention all that copper and tin." He blinked at me with distaste. "That old bromide. Wait till you've seen a little more of them . . . It's obvious he's playing a double game, using us as a counterweight." He took out that perennial jade holder of his and fitted a cigarette into it neatly. "In any event, it's merely a case of waiting." "Sir?" I said, startled; he had me there. "For the right signal. The one that will signify his willingness to come to terms with us and stop this preposterous monkey business. You'll find out how things work after you've been out here a while, Samuel. It may come as an overture about economic aid, or one of their eerie religious ceremonies, or even a conference on agricultural development. But you can be sure it will be totally irrelevant to the problem at issue. That's the way the game is played out here. It's precisely *that* that they don't understand back in Washington. They like to think they do, but they don't. It's lamentable."

I said my understanding was that Hoanh-Trac quite simply wanted those Chinese Kuomintang divisions off his back, where they'd been ever since the Burmese booted them out, after footing the bill for them as long as *they* could. He tossed his head. "Pure poppycock, Samuel.

Feints and falderal. It's merely a pretext for bringing the Chinese Reds in, en masse: that's what he wants. He's only been deterred from that because of our presence here in Cau Luong. I want you to talk" to Frederick Brokaw, he's our top CIA man here and a crackerjack." The smile again. "I take it you have no objections to talking with him?" "Of course not," I said; one good smile deserves another. "I'll listen to anybody." He nodded. "Yes. You always would. It's your gravest fault. No: next gravest." I nobly resisted the temptation. He went around behind his desk and rested his knuckles on the blotter as a symbolic gesture that the interview was being brought to a close. I got up. He gave me the quick, piercing glance—the one that Ben used to call the Jehovah-Daddy Look, then all at once tilted the jade holder skyward between his teeth, like FDR in a facetious mood. "Only this time, Samuel, don't make up your mind too fast." "I won't, General," I said.

The briefing over at MACK Hq just about what I expected. Graulet handled it. He has changed. Most of the humorless officiousness is gone: he is smoother, more circuitous and deft. He's learned a lot. Nothing much I hadn't dug up on my own hook except for a whole bagful of personal data on some of the principals. Hoanh-Trac is something of a hedonist, according to reports: opium and women. Rather depressing sensation in those gloomy old French barracks: cool and dim, blinds shuttered against the harsh light, officers in quiet rows, smoking, participants and viewers of a film that bears very little relation to the life it is seeking to depict. But everyone fervently agreed on its being a great picture: colossal, gigantic.

A relief to get out into the streets afterward, moving through the crowds, the girls like the most exotic birds in their white silk trousers and gold and green jackets, the pedicab drivers gliding solemnly, the women haggling crablike with the fish vendors in the crazy stalls. It made me think of Manila, those lean years. The teeter-totter, with Massengale at one end and Joe Brand at the other. The years when my life changed. Colonel Fahrquahrson and Monk Metcalfe. Jarreyl and Lin Tso-han. All the opposites. Past and future, acceptance and denial, yang and yin.

But this too was wrong: it felt all wrong in another way—as unreal as the briefing room in the old French barracks. The chic, slender girls in their ao-dais, the rich kids, sons of Vu Khoi's clique, batting around in their Renaults (why aren't they up north, on patrol? or even doing guard duty in the Delta? It's *their* regime that's keeping them on top of the heap), the big brass in their Chryslers and Citroëns. On the spur of the moment took a pedicab out the Cao Binh Tra road toward the airfield, past the paddies, with the farmers bent under their limpet hats, barelegged, working, the golden light pouring over the fields and water, the carabaos moving like black ponderous engines and the kids prancing around them waving bamboo switches. The real world. Felt a seething, despondent rage at all of us with our plans for them—Communists and counterinsurgents, guerrillas and Mobile Forces: all of us seeking to bend things our way. Even now, hours later, sitting here writing in this overupholstered, air-conditioned brothel I feel it: the despondency, the rage. Who the hell do we think we're fooling? We are just like the French: sitting jauntily in our sand castles, prattling of vertical-envelopment and strategic hamlets and logistics patterns, while the tide sweeps gently, remorselessly around us. We give up nothing. We are so certain, so utterly certain . . .

Being alone in a vastly foreign town fills you with melancholy. So far from home. You see all your faults so clearly, so implacably. Tommy, I want to cry, forgive me my inflexibility, my predilection for judgment, my romantic extravagance, my willfulness—above all my unabated conviction that I must do great things—

An explosion. Two, three hundred yards away, maybe more. That dense, reverberant *crump* that only means trouble. Plastique, probably. Someone is dead, someone else is hideously disfigured, someone else is trying desperately to make his escape.

War is cruelty and you cannot refine it. W. T. Sherman.

Or is it someone trying to steal some medical supplies?

Have made up my mind to go north to see Hoanh-Trac on my own. CSM will not be overjoyed. But I am going anyway.

The rain battered down tremendously. It was exactly like a wall, curtaining the room from the rest of the world; another set of walls of teeming water, streaming in silvered sheets from tiled eaves, glittering in the light from the lamps. Like the lamplight back home, Damon thought, glowing in the kitchen and dining room windows on Merivale Street. But this interior was very spare. In place of the sofa, the platform rocker with its antimacassars, the chairs and cabinets and huge oak table, there was only a low couch in lemon brocade, a small table of inlaid teak, the mat he and his host sat on, and a screen depicting cranes flying above a marsh. The screen bore a pleasing relationship to the couch and table; and placed on the table was a striking little figurine traced in an electric blue on a pure white base. A sparse room: one couch, one mat, one table, one screen, one piece of statuary. But placed with care, with a love for beauty and order. Everything is placement, he thought absently. Furniture, forces, ideas, affections. Everything.

His bowels convulsed again in a series of mounting spasms and he tensed himself, waiting for them to subside. Aloud he said: "Very beautiful. Yüan Dynasty, is it?"

Hoanh-Trac inclined his head with the quick, delighted smile of the

Indo-Chinese. "A copy, merely—work of the Annamese sculptor Heng-Bo. But he studied with the Yüan masters." He was a little man of perhaps fifty-five with a lithe body and a birdlike, volatile manner. He was dressed in an open-necked army shirt of tropical worsted and a pair of slacks; he wore no ribbons or insignia. "How is it that you know Chinese sculpture?"

Damon smiled. "I don't know it, really; it was just a guess."

"But an extraordinarily good one." Hoanh-Trac gazed at the American thoughtfully. "That was a long journey you have made up here to Plei Hoa. You must be quite weary."

"A little, yes. I'm not a young man any longer. Not even middle-aged."

"That is true." The Khotianese General's face was perfectly bland now, without expression. "It is so far up here." He cocked his head again, and his voice fell into a whimsical, crooning tone, as though he were tracing the route in his mind's eye. "Up the great Hong Cua River across the Dai Pha Plateau, where the Kor live, and the Meos. Very fierce." His gaze became all at once ingenuous and bright. "Were you not afraid, General Damon?"

The tea was murderously hot. Damon kept his lips from quivering by an effort of will, and carefully set the little porcelain cup down on the tray beside him. He knew he was being interrogated, tested, perhaps baited a bit. All during the meal, whose rigors he had only just survived, Hoanh-Trac had been frivolous and reserved by turns, and the talk had been general. Now that the two of them had retired to Hoanh's private room and left the others, it was only to be expected that the Khotianese leader's manner would change. But it was not pleasant.

Damon said quietly: "In my life I have only known one man who was afraid of nothing; and in my opinion he was worthless as a human being."

Hoanh-Trac clapped his hands in glee. "That is pleasing," he exclaimed softly. For a moment he rocked back and forth, his eyes narrowed, his head cocked in that comical, avuncular manner. "Curious that you should say that. You are a very curious sort of American soldier, are you not?"

Damon smiled. "Yes. Fairly curious."

"I know some things about you. A few things. You have been in trouble with your superiors a great deal during your career. You have even been called"—Hoanh's lips curled in quick glee—"a Bolshevik. Are you one, in truth?"

"No. I can't say that I am. Sorry."

"Do you know that you are the only American officer who has come to Plei Hoa to confer with me? A singular circumstance, wouldn't you say? A Lieutenant General, one not connected with either the Embassy or the Military Advisory Group. A brave soldier, I am informed—but not a particularly favored one . . ." His large oval eyes took on a mischievous glint. "Why do you suppose they sent you all the way out here, to this wretched, inhospitable corner of the world?"

Damon took a deep breath and expelled it slowly. A prankster. He had flown and ridden and walked and waded and climbed two hundred and seventy-five miles to meet up with a jungle comic, facetious and nasty. Graulet was right: what was facing him was an epicene mama's boy with delusions of grandeur, who was currently amusing himself— hugely, it appeared—with the cumbersome white man, whose day was past. Well: maybe it was. His mission was already a total failure and he knew it. And his gut was griping at him again, more insistently. Gastroenteritis, with bells. He'd taken a bucketful of this new Polymagma and this was all the good it had been; he'd have done better to stick to the old standby paregoric. In one of the other rooms he could hear laughter as Gene Villarette told a story in Khotianese to some of Hoanh-Trac's staff. The Khotianese General was still watching him with that sly, gleeful expression. Of all the rotten, blasted, filthy, no-good, miserable luck. He resisted the temptation to get up and walk out of the room and hunt up a toilet where he could relieve his misery, at least temporarily.

Instead he shook his head slowly and said, "I don't know. I really don't know. I've never had any experience of a diplomatic nature, I've never drawn any assignments as an attaché . . . Perhaps I was chosen because of a tour I served as an observer in China, a long time ago."

"Ah." Hoanh nodded, as though that solved everything. "The Yangtze front?" he asked politely.

"No, General. In the North. With guerrilla groups, mostly."

"I see. And what conclusions did you draw from your observations?"

Damon folded his arms, watching the faintly derisive smile. "That Japan would never subdue the inhabitants of Shansi. That their fight was a just fight, and one involving new and immensely important tactics. And that they would ultimately be the victors."

"You said those things in your report?"

"I did."

"But the Japanese held the towns, the strong points, the railroads. They had all the weapons and equipment."

"That's true."

"And your own nation was supplying them with munitions."

"Unfortunately, yes."

"And still you thought that . . ." Hoanh shook his head in delighted bewilderment. "General Damon, you are a very, very singular American soldier."

"—Yes," the Nebraskan said, finally stung to anger by the air of mischievous raillery, "yes, I'm singular enough to believe that power has its obligations, and that a soldier—provided he *is* a soldier—owes a certain allegiance to his countrymen."

"Ah. That is interesting." Hoanh-Trac straightened, and the mobile, mocking features slowly turned solemn. The impression was of another, tougher man's face melting through the dandy's: a man capable of great determination and fortitude. "General, you are a soldier, you have gone to war again and again. I too have been at war for a long, long time. Longer than I would have believed possible. When the Japanese came I did not run away to Karachi and Paris and Antibes, like certain others of my class. I stayed in the Beng Lau and fought them. And when the Japanese left and the French came back I went on fighting the French. For my countrymen. And after Lap Khe, when we were fleeing across the Hong Cua, the French came over in planes and bombed and strafed us as we paddled. The Hong Cua is very wide, as you know. Very few of us reached the far shore. And those of us who did bore souvenirs of the crossing. Such as this." With a quick, angry gesture he wrenched the open-necked shirt from his shoulder and twisted where he sat, revealing a great jagged scar that ran down the side of his neck and into his back. He nodded, replaced the shirt and drew up his trousers, and Damon saw a maze of healed cuts and the dead white oval scars of yaws. "My only decorations from that war. Oh yes, I am a soldier." He picked up his teacup, set it down untouched. "I am sick of war—sick unto death of stealth and violence and fear and vengeance. Only . . . I am not quite so sick of it as I am of certain other things.—Tell me: do you think it was right for the French to come in and gut our country?"

Damon shook his head. "No, I don't. But the French are gone."

"Yes. The French are gone." Hoanh-Trac raised his hands before his face—a strange gesture, half-priestly, half-professorial. "Yes. Over one hundred years ago Prince Naphong was sorely pressed in his struggle against the Emperor Tu Duc, and the French asked him if they could be of service. And Prince Naphong in his fear and pride said yes. One word. And we had the French on our necks until at last we drove them out. With our blood . . . Now you are offering *your* services."

"But not for territorial concessions, political control—only to assist in the establishment of a free government . . ."

The smile reappeared. "For nothing, General? Out of pure altruism? For no advantage whatever?"

"None. For a free Khotiane. Free of Communist control. To put an end to a disastrous civil war."

"Perhaps . . . But it is *our* civil war!" the little man cried softly. "Ours. To settle *our* way, for better or for worse. In 1863 the British were eager to help your Confederacy. For reasons that were not completely altruistic. They came perilously close to intervening—do you remember? And what would have happened? The North would still have won—and you would never have forgiven Great Britain. Never. That was *your* civil war, to fight to bloody conclusion. And you did. Without 'assistance.'" He paused and rubbed the side of his face. "And Ch'en Pu Kou with his Chinese stragglers, in the hills—he would like to help us, too. Even Marshal Thanarat of Thailand has expressed *his* concern. How engaging it is: all these foreign powers so anxious to assist us in our hour of trial . . ." He dropped his hands and there was a short silence. "General, what would you have me do?"

Damon said: "Sir, I would hope that you could maintain your position of neutrality with regard to the civil war now raging in Khotiane."

"Neutrality." Hoanh-Trac peered skeptically out at the silvery curtain of rain. "Your government is preparing to fight the Hai Minh on an ever broader scale, but you wish me to remain neutral. But you see, it becomes increasingly more difficult to remain neutral. Sooner or later, one is forced to choose." He watched the American officer calmly. "Surely you can understand that? . . ."

Damon took a breath. The clutch in his belly had come back, redoubled, and with it now a faint surge of nausea. "General, I have none of the diplomatic graces, such as they are. I'd like to talk with you, if you will permit it, about these Chinese divisions. My government earnestly hopes that you will not move to oust them from Pao Xieng. My government's feeling is that they pose a—"

Hoanh-Trac stopped him with a sharp, peremptory gesture. "I know what your government thinks. And what it hopes. And even what it plans, perhaps . . . Do you know a man named Lyman Beemis?" Damon shook his head. "Pity . . .

"We do not like the Chinese," he went on in the calm, implacable voice. "We do not like them within our borders. We Khotianese have been invaded from the north times without number. The Emperor Wu Ti conquered us at the beginning of your Christian era. We ousted him two centuries later, and Ma Yüan came down and put us under the yoke for nearly a thousand years." He gave an exasperated laugh. "You had troops stationed on your soil for less than seven years—your own countrymen at that!—and you rose in revolt. You possess such a summary attitude about war, about international relations, you Americans. A republic not two centuries old, you have never gone to war for more than six years—and that was only once, your own war for independence— and you have never lost a war . . . though you have had a few rather uncomfortable scrapes. So brief! Of course you seek the quick solution, the apocalyptic victory. Whereas we have been invaded by the Hindus, the Chinese, the Mongols and Chams and Khmers. And the French . . . And they always wanted something. Something of ours. And they took it, too."

He paused and looked directly at his guest. "And you, General Damon: what do you yourself want?"

Damon set down his cup. Why was Khotianese tea always so *bitter*—? He clasped his hands together, fingers over knuckles. All these past days of hiking along the dark trails, over mountains, up the riverbeds over stones greasy with moisture and débris, like round, treacherous stairways for some agile fifteen-foot giant; the little green leeches dropping on your arms and neck from the branches as you swung by, like stealthy drops of water; the touch of a cigarette's coal would dislodge them, but only if you located them, and then only after they'd sucked an unbelievable amount of blood swiftly and painlessly from your sweating body. On over the rickety, swaying bamboo bridges with their handrails of creepers, the streams roaring away thirty feet below. Across the paddies where the rice thrust upward in a furry, pale green stipple, over which the dawn light flung a shimmering mosaic of azure and emerald and marble dust . . . A wild goose chase: was it? He thought he had seen heavy jungle in Papua and Palamangao, but he'd seen nothing to match this. Here was jungle so high, so deep the sky itself did not exist; time itself hung in confusion and the only metronome was the occasional bird that shrieked his metallic two-note cry, hour after hour after hour . . . So vast. He had not encountered such distances since China—and in China you knew at least where you were: there you were above the land, moving on its broad brown earth, the high blue mountains. Here you were an insect among insects, sunk deep in the grasses, plodding nowhere . . .

Yet he *was* here at last, in the private living quarters of this sly, ingenuous, epicene, harsh Khotianese soldier who was still watching him politely and implacably. Footsore, half-stupefied with heat and exhaustion, fighting the pain of gastroenteritis with every breath, willing his sphincter to hold, his nausea to subside, he was here nonetheless; and he would not give up on it now. With the quick, unhesitant prescience he had known ever since his boyhood he could sense the importance of this moment—the concurrence of forces bent on a collision course. The civil war intensifying in fury, COMMACK pressing for increased participation (whatever that meant in this wilderness of mountains and delta), those three Nationalist divisions near the border, and this astonishing, mercurial, very determined little man. All these rivers rushing pell-mell together and here he was, in midchannel—in a role for which he was ill prepared, to put it mildly. Bitter tea.

"—*I want to find out the truth*," he heard himself say with surprising vehemence.

The Khotianese straightened, raised his chin and looked very hard at him for several seconds. "The truth," he echoed softly; but there was no mockery in his voice. "Well. And what will you do with that truth when you find it?"

"I will act on it."

"Even if it should happen to be in conflict with the desires of your government?"

Now it was Damon's turn to stiffen and stare. This man was not what he'd thought he was at all. "Yes," he said quietly, after a pause. "If I am convinced that it is the truth. Yes."

There was a silence, dominated by the squattering thunder of the endless rain. Hoanh's eyes had not left his face. "Perhaps you would," he said finally. "Perhaps you do really want the truth. You are certainly a most singular American general . . . Very well, I will tell you the truth," he went on rapidly, "some of it. You know a good many things, I imagine. You have been well briefed, and I have the feeling there was not too much that the briefing could tell you. Certain things, that is. You probably know about the war against the Japanese in the Beng Lau and the work of your OSS agents, and the formation of the Hai Minh and the War of Liberation; you may even know that when the Japanese came the big landlords fled to Calcutta and Karachi and Nice—and that when the Japanese left they came back and claimed their holdings."

"Yes, I knew that."

"But did you know that they demanded backtaxes of the peasants who had stayed and suffered under the Japanese? Yes!—taxes retroactive to the day *they* slipped away to comfort and idleness? Make no mistake: I am of the mandarin class, and the peasants were never any of my concern. But I would not leave my country. And when my brother came back and took part in this vicious demand I told him: 'You are not fit to be a Khotianese. Leave this land in three days or I will not answer for your life.' And for that I was a traitor to my country. I, who have led an assault on Lap Ke through the rockets and artillery fire, who have hung to the side of a chuluc in the Hong Cua, while my men sank all around me and the water turned pink with our blood . . . Yes, and did you know that when Vu Khoi came to power, his people rounded up all those who had fought in the War of Liberation and shot some out of hand, and sent others to Dao Ba Mun, to the terrible French fortress where so many of us had died for a hundred years? That is new to your ears, is it not? To have fought the French is treason now. Why? As for me, I dislike the Communists: to give over one's mind to a series of ideas without question is odious. I was reared to study and reflection and I am skeptical of all panaceas, all quick and easy solutions, from whatever quarter. But some of the things they are willing to die for have an undeniable appeal: Khotiane for the Khotianese. Land to those who till it. I like those thoughts."

"Yankee-Go-Home," Damon said.

"Yes—possibly even Yankee-Go-Home." He smiled, turned serious again. "You say you want the truth. The truth is that what we finally evolve here must be our own. It may not be what *you* like, but it will be our own, and not Peking's or Washington's or Bangkok's solution. We want to create our own nation, free of *any* foreign assistance." Abruptly he said: "You must go to Pao Xieng, General."

"To see Ch'en Pu Kou?"

"More importantly, his *army*." His voice was heavy with irony. "This army in which your own government has placed such high hopes."

"My government?" Damon asked in surprise. "High hopes?"

Hoanh-Trac nodded rapidly. "Oh yes. The *truth* is that your government is supplying Ch'en's people with weapons and uniforms and supplies."

Damon gazed at him. "It can't be—I would have been informed . . ."

"Go and see, then. See for yourself. I can arrange a safe passage for you, if you are willing to risk it. They will seek to hide things from you, but you will see them anyway. It cannot be hidden. You will see why the Burmese drove them from their country four years ago, and why we have appealed to the United Nations, calling for their disarming and extradition. And why I have despaired of UN intervention, and have decided I must take things into my own hands."

"Will I really see all that?" Damon asked.

"Oh yes. I have great confidence in you." In Chinese he said: "For him who seeks the truth it will not long be hidden."

"And heaven will not delay a traveler," he answered in the same language.

Hoanh-Trac uttered his high, facetious laugh. "You are an extraordinary person: you know strange tongues, you seek out barbarian officers in the rain forest, you want to find out the truth . . . You would have made a good revolutionary, General Damon."

"Do you think so?" the American asked, amused himself.

"Oh yes. You have a very rare capacity for empathy, and a deep sense of justice. Like others of your countrymen. Other good revolutionaries. Like Adams and Jefferson and Hancock. Paul Revere. They met secretly, in rooms above coffee houses, I am told; they even belonged to revolutionary cells. The Sons of Liberty, they called themselves. A good name. Sons—of—Liberty . . . They wanted to get rid of the hated foreign soldiery, they wanted the freedom to control their own destinies, they didn't want to be exploited anymore. Fair enough, wouldn't you say? An honorable series of desires. Well, some of us feel we are the Sons of Liberty for Khotiane. Let us hope that we will also achieve it."

Abruptly he rose, and Damon got carefully to his feet. The change in position sent another series of spasms through his bowels; he wiped his face with his handkerchief.

"Would you like me to arrange for your trip to Pao Xieng?"

"If you would, please."

Hoanh-Troc nodded. "Good. This has been a distinct pleasure, meeting you, General. You are a courageous man—really courageous. I know a little of what you are suffering at this moment."

"It will pass."

"Oh yes. Everything passes, even the venerable dynasties. But that is scant consolation to the beleaguered soul." He offered his hand, and his slender, fragile face broke into the mischievous smile. "It seems—we were both wrong about each other!"

Damon laughed. "Yes. I know *I* was." He paused, said: "Will you hold off action against Ch'en until I have seen him and his people?"

"Yes, General. I give my word." Again he stared out at the relentless rain beyond the windows. "We have waited over a thousand years: I imagine we can compose our souls for another few weeks." He turned toward the American again, and his face was grave with entreaty. "I only beg of you to remember one thing: there are many roads to liberty. Many. Not just the high road of the Thirteen Embattled Colonies." He bowed. "Good night, General."

"Good night, sir," Damon said.

"Reports from my field managers have been uniformly alarming," Lyman Beemis said. He was a thick, bald man with pudgy hands that kept fretting with the reports on the desk in front of him, pushing them back and forth rhythmically; but his voice was calm. "Terrorist activity is increasing, especially in Bac Hoa and Vinh Yen Provinces. Production is virtually stopped." He looked at the other faces around the long table, his lips moving. "I have no hesitation in stating that Competrin is facing a crisis, and a grave one. The spokesman for the French investors' group has just informed me that they are seriously considering a cancellation of credits."

"Can't that be weathered, Bee?" the Undersecretary asked from the head of the table. "I wouldn't think they're all that important . . ."

"It might be weathered in itself," Beemis replied in the same measured tones. "But as soon as it became known there would be the market reaction. The New York speculators would undoubtedly take a short position on Competrin, with results that are not very pleasant to contemplate."

"How about the mines? What's the situation up there?"

"Substantially the same," a man Damon hadn't seen before named Frazier answered in a rather hollow, nasal voice. "All operations shut down. The ore is standing in the cars."

There was a short silence. The Undersecretary consulted the sheaf of papers under his left elbow. He was quite young—forty-six or -seven— but his hair was thinning and a very full, drooping blond mustache and bad posture combined to give him a weary, mournful expression, an aura of indecisiveness only partly offset by the sharply aquiline nose and close-set gray eyes. Yet his face had that look of righteous candor that only the exclusive preparatory schools north of Boston can give a man. His suit was of a British cut, with narrow lapels and double pleats, and his shirt was French, with wide cuffs and a stiff short collar. Customarily he wore glasses, but he never seemed to need them—one earpiece dangled now from the corner of his mouth.

"Well," he said with an air of vigor, and coughed. "It's the Secretary's feeling that a firm line ought to be taken here. But needless to say it behooves us to explore all the possibilities with care." He looked alertly down the table. "General Damon, is it your opinion that Hoanh-Trac intends to move against the Chinese units in the near future?"

"I would say not, sir. That is if you mean by the near future the next two weeks or so. He assured me that he would not start military operations until this current protest has been brought before the United Nations General Assembly. But I cannot guarantee it."

"Then there *is* the possibility of military action."

Damon stared at him. "Yes sir, there is. But I think it is negligible for the near future."

"The Generalissimo," Massengale interjected crisply, "has told me emphatically that he will construe any such action as an act of aggression against the Nationalist Republic of China."

Damon made no reply. The Undersecretary frowned, which made him look still more mournful. "It's an extremely awkward situation . . ."

"In my opinion it's an unparalleled opportunity, sir," Massengale rejoined. "General Ch'en Pu Kou's divisions afford the requisite force for the opening phase of operations. They know the terrain well, they're superbly trained—as you probably know, many of their officers and NCOs were in the X Force trained by Stilwell's people at Ramgarh for the Burma campaign in '44. The Generalissimo himself has assured me that he would consider himself obligated to come to their assistance in the event of a clash between General Ch'en's forces and the Chinese Communists."

Damon looked around him in sudden consternation. The problem before them was *Hoanh-Trac's* action: how did the Chinese come in here? Opening phase of *what* operations? But the faces around the table were merely interested, speculative, unperturbed, following the authoritative voice. For the smallest part of a moment Damon had the sensation of having fallen victim to one of those nightmares in which the protagonist, alone of all the grouped participants, senses the approaching catastrophe and tries to warn them all—a series of frantic, futile admonitions through which burns at last the awareness that he alone is the intended and unsuspecting victim, disregarded, helpless, overpowered—

But no: it was no dream. Here all around him was the Staff conference room with its slick cream walls, its portentously draped windows with the air conditioners soughing their muted, fluttering roar. There sat the Undersecretary with his attentive, mournful face, the glasses hanging from his nearly invisible lips, and around him the others, military and civilian, that he had called together for this meeting: all of them clear-eyed, reflective, acquiescent . . .

"Taipei has assured me that they would be prepared to field nine divisions immediately," Massengale was saying, "with fifteen to follow within sixty to ninety days. This is an iron-clad guarantee. It lends itself to several very intriguing possibilites." Rising he moved to the great map of Southeast Asia that covered one of the walls. "For instance, it would be eminently feasible to mount a two-pronged attack, one from Binh Quai into the Lung River Valley, here, and the other as a series of amphibious assaults on Peihai and Anp'u from the Gulf of Tonkin. Preliminary bombardment and covering strikes could easily be undertaken by Admiral Farnham's carrier force off Trucphong, as well as from the Mariannas and Vietnam bases. The beachhead could be built up slowly and surely across the Yü and Hsün River basins, with the primary objective Liuchow, and anchored on the flank points Dong Van and Chap'o, here and here. In effect this operation would be analogous to the Normandy beachhead, with the Luichow Peninsula playing the role of the Cotentin, the core of a powerful buildup preparatory to a major breakout, either toward Kweilin and Changsha, here, or eastward toward Canton and Changchow . . ."

Except that there will be no Paris, Damon thought, staring, listening to the clear, persuasive voice. No FFI, no local population who will welcome these invaders with open arms and vin rouge; no Soviet armies applying relentless pressure on another front. It would be a good deal easier to try to invade Russia from the Crimea . . . He caught himself up then with angry amazement. Was this contemplated? Was this assault, invasion—was this *war* actually and rationally under consideration—?

"The fact of the matter is we've got to come to grips with them sooner or later." Massengale had returned to his seat. "It must come—I think we can all agree on that point without any difficulty. And with that premise, where could a more adroit point of leverage and penetration be found than in a military force that has gallantly refused to give up the battle, that wants nothing more than to fight its way back to its homeland? This Ch'en Force is an inspiring element, and a golden opportunity. To fail them now is to sacrifice thirty thousand supremely loyal troops with counterinsurgency capabilities to the Khotianese insurrectionary forces. We will in effect simply be supporting an ally. I've no doubt the ROK and Philippine units could be induced to participate; and there are our units in Japan. Our current capabilities would include eight assault divisions, plus perhaps thirty supporting engineer and other-type battalions. That would be at the discretion of the Joint Chiefs, of course."

The Undersecretary had taken the earpiece out of the corner of his mouth. He turned to Farnham and said: "What's your opinion, Bliss?"

The Admiral examined his nails. Unlike Massengale he had aged substantially since '44, but the change was flattering: his lean, tanned face still looked aristocratic and capable. "I would be inclined to concur, sir. The Fleet is in an excellent state of readiness. Strikes could be coordinated with maximum effectiveness from both the carriers and the Cochin fields. The entire coast from Macao to Tunghsing would be extremely vulnerable to air and naval bombardment."

The Undersecretary nodded and looked at Brokaw. "Fred, what is your feeling about the extent and intensity of Chinese Communist reaction?"

The CIA man, who had a grave, scholarly look and the shoulders of a fullback, answered easily, "All reports indicate there is considerable unrest in both Kwangsi and Kwangtung provinces, with the consequent breakdown in various civil and constabulary functions. I'd say a military operation of this type would stand an excellent chance of success."

Again there was a brief pause. The Undersecretary fiddled with his glasses, staring sadly at the papers in front of him. He had obviously come out here prepared to do something momentous and firm; but this appeared to be a bit more than he had bargained for. "This is a very serious undertaking you've outlined, Courtney," he said carefully. "One fraught with a high ratio of risk."

"Sir, it has been my experience that nothing worthwhile is ever accomplished without taking a few risks along the way."

"If I may be forgiven for interjecting a note of urgency into the discussion," Beemis offered in his flat, unruffled voice, "Competrin and Tonkalloy will most certainly go under unless some positive and aggressive steps are taken to control the campaign of destruction and terror carried on by the Hai Minh. It's obvious that the government forces are totally inadequate to cope with them. A plan such as General Massengale has outlined would afford us the very means for rolling back Communist subversion. If we are to do anything in behalf of our overseas interests here, we must do it now or not at all."

Damon kept watching the faces. Incredulity had him like a fist. So neat. It was all so neat. Those Kuomintang divisions—if divisions you could call them—up at Pao Xieng; the official Khotiane protest, and Hoanh-Trac's declaration of intention; Chiang Kai-shek's ultimatum—a face-saving gesture pure and simple, any fool could see that (how on earth could the Peanut, sitting on his island citadel twelve hundred miles away, insist on a demilitarized zone of ten kilometers width between the tatterdemalion remnants of his army and Hoanh-Trac's forces, as a *final* condition? It was patently absurd); Massengale's flying trips to Taipei to confer with the G-mo; the Ninth Fleet off Trucphong; Brokaw's twilight operations over the border in China and Thailand; Competrin's massive rubber and mining interests in jeopardy. Interests—they were compulsions. Trade follows the flag, he had read somewhere long ago; now it seemed to be the other way around—the flag was expected to come fluttering in and wrap itself around the massive interests. Or maybe it always had . . .

There was more discussion of Competrin's predicament, and a lengthy exchange between Massengale and Farnham over the alternative possibility of the seizure of the island of Hainan as a buildup area for a subsequent assault on the China coast. Massengale disagreed vehemently: Hainan was largely rice paddy or mountainous country, there were no adequate facilities for training and supply areas; they would merely be repeating the Taiwan predicament all over again. Bliss replied coolly that the Japanese had found Yülin and the south coast adequate enough for their purposes in the forties. Massengale said that in any event they would only have alerted the Chinese to the threat of invasion, without effecting the desired objective, which was to reestablish the Generalis-

simo on the Chinese mainland. With raging admiration Damon watched
him at the map, discussing distances, logistics problems, terrain. Brilliant: they would still say he was brilliant, inventive, tireless. No topo-
graphical wrinkle had not been examined, no eventuality had not been
explored. Nothing ever changes, he thought bitterly. He had been
caught in a malevolent time bubble of steel—the clean, stately, cool
room, the long table, Massengale at the map (though without the ivory-
tipped pointer), everybody else obediently nodding. Though note the
undeniable advantages of increased rank, he told himself. Then we only
kept the wars going; now we can plan out how to start them . . .

All the threads, all the ingredients. So pat. The show was in the
works, the skids were greased, everything was set to roll for a fine,
spanking war against the dirty Chinese Reds. And here he sat—the only
one of this august company who had crawled through the boondocks to
talk to Hoanh-Trac, who had prowled around the wretched camps at
Pao Xieng, nodding earnestly to the bland offerings of the Chinese
interpreter while he listened to the squad and company commanders
talking among themselves; the only one for that matter who had ever
talked and hiked and fought with these same dirty Chinese Reds—here
he sat, far down at the end of the table, with Porky Bannerman and
Toddles Carrick, the jet carrier wizard, and the man named Frazier, and
two of the Undersecretary's staff.

"Emphatically, sir," Massengale was saying to the Undersecretary.
"The Generalissimo gave me the most solemn personal guarantee that he
was ready to throw all his resources into this operation. He is convinced
that the timing is right, and that it cannot fail."

The Undersecretary nodded and chewed at his glasses frame. His face
still bore the impassive, intent expression, but Damon could tell: he was
being won over. It all sounded so right, so necessary, so inevitable—

"General Bannerman, what is your opinion?"

"Most emphatically affirmative, sir!" Porky had held his body weight
down pretty well, but his face betrayed him. There had been so many
extracurricular attractions at Kyoto and Bad Godesburg and Paris and
Ankara and Seoul: and now here in Cau Luong. "All of that patishery!"
Raebyrne had used to say, watching the little midinettes hurrying home,
their dark eyes flashing. "Just feast your eyes on 'em, Skipper . . ."
Porky had found the patisserie—both culinary and feminine—irresistible during the lush years of occupation duty and overseas missions. It
was said he kept two Khotianese beauties—each in a separate apartment
—here in Cau Luong, and that his stag parties were awesome things,
even among the Mobile Forces revels. Now he stared eagerly down the
table at the Undersecretary, blinking with thought. His face had swollen
hugely, almost as though the bone itself had thickened, and then deepened to a choleric red stitched with fine purple veins, so that now he
looked not so much like a petulant baby as a rather bright, handsome
little pig—one of Ulysses' argonauts, perhaps, caught in midtransmogrifi-

cation in Circe's palace, just tapped by the malignant wand. But he knew
what he wanted—or what was expected of him. "It's a perfect multiple
solution, sir," he declared in his thin, hoarse voice. "This would settle
once and for all the problem of Communist infiltration from China: we
could seal off all points of ingress to the entire Indochinese complex,
without fear or favor. If you want my opinion it's time we started
carrying the fire to these people, instead of falling back into a defeatist
pattern, waiting for them to hit us before we move . . ."

There was a rustle of amusement around the table. The Undersecretary smiled, which made his face look suddenly boyish and winsome. "I
can share your impatience, General."

Porky licked his lips; two tiny beads of sweat glistened at the corners
of his nose. "I didn't mean to sound so frantic," he added. "But it gets to
you, taking losses the way we have. My boys have been carrying the
load, and with damned little support, too. It seems to me we've got to
begin to get somewhere in this hassle."

"I couldn't agree with you more." The cool gray eyes came to rest on
Damon. "How about you, General?"

It was a curious moment. The Undersecretary had spoken, but it was
Massengale's gaze he felt constrained to meet. All these years; and always his junior in grade, leading from weakness, not strength. Always
the outlaw, the heretic voice. The bad soldier . . . Only this time he
wasn't lying smashed to pieces on a cot, and there were no Salamanders
he felt himself personally responsible for.

He drew a breath and said: "Sir, I am solidly opposed."

The Undersecretary blinked as though he'd just been awakened in the
middle of the night. "You are? To what?"

"To the entire idea."

"Oh balls, Sam," Porky exclaimed with an air of humorous exasperation; but the others were silent.

"Your reasons, General?"

Damon leaned forward. Here goes nothing, as Joey would say. In
with both feet. "First of all: at the operational level, General Ch'en's
forces are utterly unreliable."

There was a low murmur at this. Massengale laughed lightly and said:
"Whatever you've got, the Night Clerk's against it! . . . Samuel, on
precisely what do you base that conclusion?"

"Five days at Pao Xieng, General."

They were all looking at him in surprise. The Undersecretary said,
"You were there? You inspected the army?"

"I observed this force right down to company and squad level. On
several occasions I got away from the staff watchdogs and talked with
both officers and men. They are completely demoralized, and they are
demoralizing and enraging the Khotianese among whom they are living.
They are subsisting mainly by brigandage and the opium trade: there
are ample evidences of both. The field-grade officers are every bit as

corrupt as they were during the war against Japan. Discipline is almost nonexistent, there are no training schedules, their weapons and equipment—*our* weapons and equipment, I should say"—he shot Brokaw a swift, sharp glance—"are in fearful condition. General Ch'en's 'army' has no value as an effective fighting force."

There was a short, embarrassed silence. Porky was apoplectic; Beemis was watching him with irritation and distaste, Massengale's expression was the old one he remembered—a steady, baleful speculation; Farnham was inspecting his cuticles; Brokaw's face was impervious, but his ice blue eyes held the faintest trace of contemptuous amusement; the Undersecretary was tugging at his glasses, his mouth open in disbelief. All right, then: the hell with all of them. They'd get reality if they choked on it.

"That is your considered professional opinion, Damon?"

"It is, sir. Far from being of top-caliber assault quality, these soldiers— I am using the word rashly—would crumble like chalk at the first organized resistance, and blow away. Also, I have talked at good length with General Hoanh-Trac at Plei Hoa, and two other of the northern commanders. I can say without hesitation that not only would they refuse to support a venture such as that outlined here today, they would be unalterably opposed to any operation in conjunction with or in support of these lawless divisions. They merely want them out of their country, in the same way that we would seek the removal of some renegade Mexican force bivouacked in the Gila Bend."

"The Generalissimo will never acquiesce to such an eventuality," Massengale said sharply.

Little old Peanut will acquiesce to what the United Nations directs, Damon thought; or to what Hoanh-Trac sets in motion. But he made no reply.

Brokaw smiled his thin, secret smile. "Do you mean to say that they are *opposed* to the Chinese Communists, Damon?"

"Yes. They are. But they will not support the idea of serving as the front line in a war of aggression."

"But if it should simply come about? They would have no choice."

"Don't worry," Beemis broke in, "they'd fall in line. They know which side their bread is buttered on."

"They're not eating bread in Plei Hoa, Mr. Beemis," Damon answered. "They're eating rice." He said to Brokaw: "Everyone always has a choice. It may be very narrow but there is still a choice. And I maintain they will not support any such scheme—in fact they are quite likely to take military action against it." He turned to the Undersecretary again. "And thirdly, I know a little about the Chinese partisan and guerrilla warfare. I traveled with several columns in Shansi and Hopei Provinces in the late 1930s, and I learned a good deal about their tactics and their morale." He put his hands flat on the polished wood. "I can tell you this: they will no more engage in the conventional forms of warfare—as we are pleased to wage it—than the Khotianese insurgents have; they will not be cast down by the most grievous losses in territory, matériel or human life; and they will never, never give up." He swept his eyes around the table. "Are we seriously contemplating this kind of war—a vast, interminable ground war—on the Asiatic mainland?"

Massengale said sharply, "Look here, Samuel, you came out here a scant two months ago on an impromptu junket—"

"I came out here to Asia twenty-four years ago, and I didn't sit around sipping Scotch-and-sodas in Shanghai or the Legation, either. I learned about the people's war at first hand. And I've spent nearly six weeks this time in the field, talking to the Khotianese on all levels. Listening to them, too. Have you gentlemen?"

"For pete's sake, Damon," Beemis broke in, "—whose side are you on, anyway?"

"I'm on the side of reality, and against the side of horse shit and wishful thinking."

"Reality—the reality of it is they're the *enemy*, those people up there. They're completely opposed to our way of life—our efforts to modernize their country, industrialize it, raise their standard of living. Are you in any doubt about that? Damned if I know what your persuasions are, but I guess it's true what they say about you . . ."

"What do they say about me, Mr. Beemis?" Damon said in a quiet voice.

The industrialist glanced at him savagely, twisting his neck inside his collar; but he volunteered nothing more. "I don't think my loyalty needs to be questioned here," Damon went on. "I don't think anyone will. I have served my country in fair weather and foul for forty-three years, and that is a good deal more than you can say, Mr. Beemis. But I can respect the patriotism of men from other lands—who are every bit as loyal and self-sacrificing and earnest as we are ourselves. They do not happen to believe what we believe; but have we been given some irrefutable proof that our way is the *only* way for all the rest of the world?—a world that is not as much in awe of us as we'd like to think. Not nearly as respectful and friendly toward us as it was fifteen short years ago . . ."

"Samuel," Massengale said in the icy, menacing tone he remembered, "if you find that you shrink from the necessary means—"

"Yes, I shrink from them," he answered, and now he could not keep the heat out of his voice. "I shrink from them . . ."

"That isn't the way you operated on New Guinea," Brokaw observed with a quick sardonic laugh. "I read Marv Randall's column—he said there wasn't anything in the book or out of it you wouldn't pull . . ."

Randall: yes, he would read Randall like holy writ. Beemis and Brokaw. God, they ought to be a vaudeville act. "Yes: once you are in battle all means are at hand. Who is going to debate niceties of design, degrees of ferocity then? Flamethrowers, napalm, phosphorus, crossbows, poisoned stakes, shu-mines—don't expect men caught in the desperate straits of war, crushed with a thousand hellish decisions, to resort to Marquis of Queensberry tactics then, Mr. Brokaw. Once that word is said—that one, final, utterly irrecoverable word—then there is no turning back: the wraps are off, the game is on, all manner of deviltry is unleashed . . . And so I shrink from the saying of that word. Yes. *I know everything it means*." He turned and faced the Undersecretary, whose face now showed a marked agitation. Damon suddenly remembered he had been a communications officer with the Fifth Army in Italy. Very softly he asked: "Do you want to be the one to say that word, sir?"

The Undersecretary pulled feverishly at one drooping wing of his mustache. "That's not for me to do," he said in some confusion. "You must realize that. Of course I can recommend certain courses of action . . ."

"This is getting us exactly nowhere at all," Beemis came in hotly. "Talk about prima donnas! You figure you're too good for it all, Damon, is that it? Look, we've all got a job to do. Mine is to run Competrin. Yours is to carry out what's been decided."

"Correction," Damon retorted. "My job is to give advice. I'm giving it."

"Samuel." Massengale was chewing on his jade holder, waggling it up and down rapidly between his teeth. "Are you trying to advance the theory that Communist China is *not* an enemy of the United States?"

He looked back levelly, his chin on his thumb. All these years: ever since St. Durance, in the blood-red sunlight, by the well. Ever since Dormer, when Tommy had danced with him, and over Irene Keller's shoulder he could see her lovely little face flushed with excitement—and watching, he had felt suddenly afraid. Here Massengale was still, brandishing the authority, the charm, the verbal facility, the astonishing intellectual prowess like some jeweled sword. He would always be there: he would always be in command.

But it didn't matter. This crazy, trumped-up assault on the Chinese mainland, using Chiang's demoralized, superannuated, tatterdemalion army wasn't for the good of the service, or the country, or the world.

"I don't know, General," he said quietly. "It's so hard to keep abreast of things. Back in 1950 you and Bliss and Mr. Beemis here were all telling us the Soviet Union was the real enemy—you were calling for war with them, predicting the terrible disasters that would befall us if we didn't bomb Moscow. We didn't take your advice; and the disasters didn't take place. Now you tell me that *China* is the real enemy, the blackhearted aggressor we must battle, right down to the last GI . . ." He glanced around the ring of faces, letting the scorn show in his eyes. "What a pity, gentlemen, if we had all of us died in a preventive war against the Russians in 1951—a war that obviously didn't need to take place at all! . . ."

They were all silent: he was a magnet, drawing their hatred toward him, polarizing them all. But none of them spoke. What was it Tommy had always said: "Nobody can say no to you, Sam . . ." A kind of loving despair in her voice as she said it. Well, so be it, then. He would make one more try.

"Sir," he turned to the Undersecretary, "I beg you to reconsider all of this most carefully. This venture General Massengale is proposing will not prosper; it will undo us. Taipei will use us coolly for their own purposes, the Chinese will fight skillfully and bravely. We will be drawn into a sea of sacrifice and blood: two divisions, ten divisions, forty divisions and what will be gained? There will be no end to it, and we will wither away like the Japanese in the great Hwang Ho Valley . . . This is not a heaven-sent opportunity: it is a siren song. It is still, as a very fine soldier said some years ago, the wrong war in the wrong place at the wrong time. It will be the greatest catastrophe our country has ever known."

He sat back and locked his fingers at the edge of the table, and looked at the others. Some avoided his eye, others glowered at him. Massengale smiled—though Damon knew it was not a smile at all—and said:

"Have you finished your peroration, Samuel?"

"Yes," he said, "I've finished."

They went on talking about strategic hamlets, economic reforms, the problems of security in Cau Luong. He stared at the blank pad in front of him, and drew a circle, and inside it a square, and inside it a circle, and inside it a square; and surrounded the figure with a crazy scrawl of concertina wire. Swan song. Famous last words. Well, at least he'd had them. He would be recalled now, without fanfare: a rather dim, dull ending, his only souvenir a galloping case of gastroenteritis, now fortunately more or less under control. Only the Undersecretary's face was unmarked by anger or resentment; the narrow-set gray eyes were pensive, absorbed. His glance rose thoughtfully once to Damon's, slipped away.

Well: he was tired. He was too old for all this Jungle Jim jazz, as Tony Giandoli put it. He'd had his day in court and to hell with them: let them whip up their artful, murderous little folly. It was time to go home, anyway.

In the center of the monotonous colophon he placed a tiny five-pointed star.

"It was quite bad," the Undersecretary said. "Really quite bad." He raised the white linen handkerchief to his mustache and patted it gently. "The whole front of the building was smashed in. They had them laid out on the street outside. Nine dead, eighty-four injured. Weren't those the figures, Gil?"

"Yes, sir," one of his assistants answered quickly. "But they said they hadn't finished digging out."

"It's amazing what two hundred pounds of plastique can do," Massengale observed, looking off at the trees at the edge of the pool, drooping now in the still heat of noon. "Amazing and shocking. When it's in the wrong hands."

"Isn't it possible to set up tighter security measures?" the Undersecretary asked, with a trace of irritation. "We talked about that at the conference Tuesday, I know." The dawn bombing of the Rigord, which he had passed on his way in from the airport, had apparently shaken him up a good deal. Massengale could imagine the scene readily enough: the fine white French colonial facade pocked and blackened, the wailing ambulances, the medics groping around in the rubble, the heaps of pulverized glass that gritted savagely underfoot, the supine figures, the blood. All this in the soft rose-and-lavender light.

"We've increased guards and set up new posts in various places," he answered, "and we've taken various other security precautions. But three or four members of a Hai Minh suicide club bent on taking out a restaurant or hotel are pretty hard to stop. With fanaticism of that caliber there's not an awful lot one can do. We're still here in what's little more than an advisory capacity. If we were here in force, with the corresponding authority . . ."

He let the phrase hang in the air and signaled to Phat to bring them all another round. It would be good to let the air clear a little. Graulet was on tenterhooks and he threw him a covert, forbidding glance. Overanxiety was the death of the diplomatic process. There was some inconsequential small talk and then Massengale asked lightly, "And what was the decision about our little Chinese excursion?" although he sensed what the answer would be.

". . . The decision was no." The Undersecretary seemed oddly apologetic. "The Secretary felt it would involve us in a greater commitment than we could sustain at this time. The current thinking is that Russia and China are at present nonimminent enemies, and that it would be ill advised to bring one or both of them in as active belligerents, particularly with regard to an operation involving so many intangibles." The Undersecretary paused thoughtfully. "Actually it's considered more important at the moment to negotiate with General Hoanh-Trac and secure his support, if we can. Our government will support a UN resolution to expedite the removal of the Chinese Nationalist divisions." The Undersecretary seemed still more apologetic. "In point of fact I've been instructed to pick Damon up at Pnom Du and fly on up to Plei Hoa—or as near as we can get to Plei Hoa—to confer with Hoanh-Trac tomorrow."

Massengale studied the end of his jade holder intently for a moment.

DELTA (791)

So there it was. Fantastic. That bastard Damon. They were going to pass up a crystal opportunity like this because that sanctimonious old woman had started invoking doom and destruction. Disgusting! He puffed swiftly at his cigarette, sent smoke swirling around him.

"The Generalissimo will take a very grave view of that," he permitted himself to say.

"I know." The Undersecretary smiled ruefully. "So did Vu Khoi. I've just spent most of the morning squaring it with him." He set down his drink and leaned forward. "I hope you won't be put out at not being brought in on these negotiations, Courtney. It was felt that your—uh, concern for the Generalissimo's position might militate against a favorable settlement."

"I quite understand." That was that. It was out. That filthy swine Damon. Rusticating away nicely in Carmel and then dropping in here out of the blue and wrecking everything, in one stupid swipe. *Everything*. And so they were going to knuckle under to the milksops and mollycoddles in the Administration. The idiots! A priceless chance to put Chiang back on the mainland, throw the Communists off balance, seal off Indochina in toto. What the devil did it matter if that simpering little monkey was or was not drifting into the hands of the Reds? Tell the world he *was* one, and let him worry about it. If they were to mount an attack in force he'd see the light soon enough, never fear. But no—they were all wound up in scruples and panics over that damned bomb. God, what a red herring. What earthly difference did it make? In war, as in diplomacy, you used what means would accomplish your purposes. But they were scared witless of the namby-pamby liberals, the ADA types who read the *New Republic* and the *Nation*, who wanted to integrate schools and worship the Negroes and—

But that Damon should have done this! That stolid, quixotic, stubborn numbskull . . .

Never kick over the pail: you might need the milk for breakfast yourself. Uncle Schuyler's line: nice and folksy. Well, he was probably right at that. Perhaps something could still be salvaged. It was possible: it was always possible.

He suppressed his rage without a tremor. "Well," he said, and gave a regretful smile, "that's it, then. I won't pretend I'm delighted—you know me better than that."

"I realize how much confidence you had in the plan."

"In point of fact I'm a touch mortified—I've always looked on myself as a rather persuasive type. But Damon seems to have put me in the shade . . ."

The Undersecretary twisted in his chair. "Well, the decision was necessarily—and quite properly—the Secretary's, of course."

"Of course. But I imagine the phrasing of the report had something to do with it, too."

Had he gone too far? The Undersecretary's glance was filled with

resentful candor—the sixth-form boy accused of coming unprepared to
recitation. "I think I can say it was a substantially impartial report,
General," he said a bit stiffly.

Massengale laughed and nodded. "I'm sure it was. See it as the measure of my confidence—I was so certain this plan of mine would solve so
many problems for us. At one blow. Well, opportunity once forsaken is
opportunity lost forever, as the adage goes." The Undersecretary
looked mollified, and a bit guilty. "Of course this will place Competrin
in a very serious situation."

"There's a good deal of concern over that."

"I earnestly hope so. The rate of infiltration from the north is increasing alarmingly—have you talked to Brokaw?"

The Undersecretary nodded. "There's a good deal of discussion going
on about that now. If the negotiations with Hoanh-Trac fail to accomplish the desired results, there is every indication we will increase our
troop commitment in Khotiane."

"I see."

"We may in any event. But we certainly will if Hoanh-Trac proves
difficult."

Something could be salvaged, then. Yes, there was always the chance:
it only needed the timing, the wit to find and exploit the moment.

He rose nimbly and threw open his hands. "Come and have lunch
with us and we can go into things further."

The Undersecretary looked at his watch. "Oh, I can't, Courtney. I'd
like to. I've arranged to meet Damon at Pnom Du at four."

"Ah, but you must . . ." Massengale put his hand on the younger
man's arm. "I've laid on a delightful little lunch for you. Nothing elaborate, but I want to show off my chef—he's first rate, really. It'll be a lot
more convenable than some catch-as-catch-can mouthful at the Splen-
dide, or the Rigord. But nobody will be eating at the Rigord for quite a
while, I suppose." He paused. "Have you had the drippy tummy yet?"

The Undersecretary, still thinking of the Rigord, shook his head
somberly.

"You don't want to get it. Does he, Stuart?"

"No, sir," Graulet said with a grin, "he certainly doesn't."

"Say you'll join us," Massengale went on, his hand under his guest's
arm, easing him toward the dining room. "You can leave whenever you
like. It's the least you can do after dashing all my hopes so cruelly . . ."
Subtly he changed tone. "And you really ought to let me give you a
quick briefing on the Night Clerk, since you're going up into the wilds
with him. We're old comrades-in-arms, you know."

There: that had iced it. When all else failed, one had only to proffer
power—or knowledge, which was power. The Undersecretary had
paused in surprise. "Oh, did he serve with you, Courtney?"

"Oh my, yes. Indeed he did. Indeed he did.—Sit over there, won't you? I want you to have the view of the Bay. I must apologize—my domestic ménage has been rather informal since my wife passed on."

He indicated places for the Undersecretary's two assistants, nodded to Graulet and seated himself, and rang for Phat. Cau Luong was what he had sought and not found in the Islands. The Bay swept away in a pretty little circle of the purest white sand, and the trees were feathery and towering, the most plangent green against the blues of sea and sky; the fine resort buildings of the French occupation—the Cham Bau section of Cau Luong had been a playground for the Parisian planters and bankers—gleamed like alabaster in the still, flat air: festive, exotic, beguiling. Massengale's suite was at the top of the old Dauphin—he was far too wise to use the Palace for anything but his working headquarters— and possessed a stout, imperturbable Khotianese chef who was a Cordon Bleu graduate and whose cuisine Massengale could not fault; a Borzoi named Alexander; and a Khotianese girl named Tuyet, who kept to her own quarters on occasions such as this. The apartment was completely air-conditioned: he'd had some of his choicer pieces of furniture and much of his library shipped out from the States. But it was the French heritage that delighted him about Cau Luong: a charming little Gallic island in the farouche Indochina sea. One evening, sitting before the great window, brandy glass in one hand, watching the fishing chulucs drifting toward the harbor like frail caravels discovering a continent, while the sky exploded in flamboyant streaks and whorls of vermilion and amethyst and ultramarine and the sea sank rapidly toward infinity, he was surprised to discover that he almost didn't want to go home. Almost . . .

"The thing you want to bear in mind with Samuel is that he's a mustang," he was saying, between spoonfuls of an excellent caviar madrilene. "He went in as a private, and he was a buck sergeant at the Marne. Old Caldwell, his father-in-law, got him a field commission. This set the pattern for the early part of his career, and dominated his attitudes: he's always been an EM at heart. He was forever in and out of hot water between the wars—on the cliff-hanging edge of insubordination half a dozen times: highly unorthodox positions balanced by that astonishing combat record. Don't misunderstand me—he was a splendid field commander. First rate. He served under me in the Visayas and on Luzon, and as Graulet can tell you, incompetent line officers in my command don't last very long. But like most strictly combat types he lacks political savoir faire."

He took a sip of wine. "Alas, it's not Bernkasteler Doktor, but it will have to suffice."

"It's extraordinarily good," the Undersecretary murmured.

"It's a pleasant little Moselle and that's about all you can say.—That brings us to the second stage," he went on, "and it's the only part of Samuel's life I can't figure out precisely." He paused and raised his spoon—something he never did. Graulet was watching him in astonishment and it amused him. "Something happened to Samuel on that China tour. I never found out what it was, and I should be surprised if anyone else did. It was nothing so trivial as a woman—Samuel never looked at another woman, not in *those* days—and it wasn't simply that he contracted trachoma and some undiagnosable fever, and had a couple of bad brushes with Japanese patrols. But he came back another man—changed utterly."

"In what way?" the Undersecretary asked with interest.

"It's hard to put simply." He was in his element now. Things could always be retrieved, where there was the requisite skill and imagination. He said: "He seemed to have—lost his sense of proportion. His awareness of how things work. The art of the possible, as the worn old phrase goes. I don't know how to put it better. It just didn't seem to have any meaning for him anymore. Oh, a smart psychoanalyst would call it anxiety neurosis or incipient paranoia or God knows what evacuation tag—and he'd be right, as far as he went. Though to tell the truth *I* don't think it was anything more or less than an early onset of the male climacteric. This malady seems to hit army people earlier than their civilian counterparts. I've often wondered why that is—the isolation perhaps, or maybe the incessant drain on the adrenalin. I suppose there are physiological reasons galore. I've been brushed by it myself: a mountainous weariness laced with a trembling, almost tearful exasperation—then it passes nearly as quickly as a yawn. And usually the problem resolves itself fairly readily: you catch your wind, so to speak, and go on."

Phat had served with unobtrusive deftness the sole aux amandes. The Undersecretary—an inveterate gourmet, he knew—praised it without reservation; and pleased, he acknowledged it, and signaled to Phat to refill their wine glasses.

"But with Samuel it effected a permanent change: he became irascible, choleric, rebellious without point. He got embroiled in two ungodly rows at Ord, then snatched at that regimental command under Westerfeldt. His coup at Moapora, as you probably know, was the result of direct disobedience of orders. He seemed to need to purge himself—his very soul, punish himself with a hundred and one acts of defiance. On Désespoir he got himself involved in a way I'm not going to tell you about; but suffice it to say it was very much part of the syndrome, and caused his superiors a lot of worry.

"And then came Palamangao, and the invasion, and the pivoting movement, which I imagine you've heard something about. Samuel had, as I say, these fixations and furies. Well, to make a long and highly complicated story less so—there is nothing simple about battle, no matter what armchair genius may advance the thought—he failed to get away with the maneuver. The Japanese hit him in great strength, and naturally he started screaming for reinforcements. Fair enough. Only the unpleasant part of it was he claimed that they should have been his *all along*—that I, his commanding officer, had no right to use them on the other flank of the operation, and he had the effrontery to radio me—"

It was astonishing: he had been running along at full speed, almost as though he couldn't check himself if he'd wanted to . . . and now, unbelievably, he had stopped. Dead. He could not go forward. He could not think what came next.

He blinked in surprise. The Undersecretary was still listening to him with that faintly scholarly, mournful air, his mustaches drooping; Graulet was staring at him in consternation. He felt tears come to his eyes. Ridiculous. It was ridiculous! He had the slow, drifting, naked dream sensation of an actor caught mindless and unsupported in the vast stage glare, before an astonished and accusatory audience. He coughed into his hand, squeezed his eyes shut. What in God's name had happened? And still he could not remember what he had been going to say.

"General," Graulet was saying gently, "you mustn't torture yourself over that grim time, it will only upset you . . ." His long, triangular face, his colorless eyes were suffused with just the proper concern and deference. "Don't go over it again, General. Damon was simply succumbing to the pressure of the breached line when he sent those radios to SPANNER that afternoon. He was simply afraid he'd be overrun, and he panicked."

Good boy. He knew, then: he'd read it. Good boy. Massengale held his forefinger and thumb pressed to his eyes. Now he remembered, he had it all again. "Silly," he murmured aloud. "The events we never really put behind us, the emotional undertow that's always there, looping up around our ankles . . . Well, it turned out all right, of course," he said with his old smile. "We won in a walk, as the saying goes; the battle and the campaign and the war, and went into proud Nippon. And then Samuel and I went our separate ways: MacArthur never thought very much of him. But of course I kept in touch. You meet people who served with old comrades, or you hear things at the club. You know how it goes. And now Samuel seemed to go into his third phase. It started—I guess it started—with a post-VJ Day speech to his hometown in Nebraska, which provoked a typically Damonesque flurry. What I call the Utopia complex: man is good, his instincts are noble, the world would fuse with the Elysian Fields if everybody would just step forward and join hands. You're familiar with this gestalt, I presume—even some of your eminent colleagues in State have not been completely immune . . ."

The Undersecretary smiled his scarcely perceptible, mustache-obscured smile; his teeth leaped into view like a nervous rabbit's.

"But I trust you'll take all that yowling and howling on the part of Beemis and Paul Bannerman with a good deal of salt," he went on. "All that about Samuel's being a Red, and so forth. Nothing could be further from the truth. Of course he's always been a maverick, a wild man—eating out of iron pots with coolies, defending perennial stockade types, the downtrodden, crossing swords with his superiors. But he's not a renegade. It's a case of misplaced loyalties, excessive sentimentality, the echo of those early years." He smiled fondly. "Samuel feels people are good because he wants them to be. A pleasant failing, but a lamentable one. Like this Hoanh-Trac. Now you know and I know he's a shrewd, tough, self-seeking old bandit who wants to advance his own personal position here in Cau Luong any way he can. I know for a fact that he has political ambitions—his nose was badly out of joint when Vu Khoi took over last summer . . ."

For several minutes he elaborated on the nice intricacies involving the quasi-military coup that had ousted Prince Vouna Sai and his clique, while he watched his visitor with covert care. The food and drink—especially the drink—were having their effect. Kimh had topped off his meal with pêches flambées and Cognac. The Undersecretary sat just as erectly as before, but the candid gray eyes looked dense and vague; perspiration was beading the high, narrow forehead below the wisps of hair. How easy it was to play on the vanities of the Eastern Seaboard! For all the centuries of authority, of grace and bestowal, their slender blood nonetheless yearned for the reassurance that they *were* able, they *were* tough-fibered and forceful, capable of the pitiless decisions that engendered triumph. Realists, in short.

"Realism," he said aloud, and snorted. "It's so fashionable to kick that term around now, isn't it? To equate it with cynicism, savagery, inhumanity . . . The fact is, war has come to us here in Khotiane. And since it *has* come, since it has been forced on us this way, why not let it work to our advantage? prepare us for the conflicts that lie ahead?"

The war would be expanded, he knew in his heart of hearts; it had to be expanded because it was the only logical step in the national pattern. The consumer market was nearing saturation, industry was hamstrung by costs and labor demands, the balance-of-payments deficit was becoming serious. All this liberal talk about war no longer serving as the instrumentation of policy was so much claptrap. In actual fact, a massive intervention in Khotiane was just what the doctor ordered, if only Washington had the brains to see it: here was John Hay's "splendid little war" revived in midtwentieth century, the perfect extension of the American martial tradition—a war the populace need not commit itself about, supported by big industry and the universal military obligation—now legalized and perpetuated—carried on at the far end of the world, and with little or none of the risks of a big power conflict. In some ways it was even preferable to the China venture . . .

"It's hard to avoid the conclusion that we are drifting," he said aloud. "Drifting into recession, drifting into complacency, stagnation, timidity.

The country lacks unity, cohesion, a sense of destiny. There's a very real question as to whether participation in an ideological conflict like this one here in Khotiane might not serve as a partial and much-needed mobilization of the nation's resources, as a focus for American concerns, economic and psychological, you know? . . ."

He stopped and sipped his Cognac. He would go no further than that; see what it elicited. That was the weakness of most military men—they never could resist uttering the additional word that brought the roof of the temple down on their bullet heads. That fellow Walker was a glowing example, with his loony covenants with Almighty God. MacArthur was his own worst enemy—he should never, never have issued that unfortunate statement about its being a new and dangerous concept that the soldier owed his primary allegiance to his country and the Constitution rather than to those who temporarily exercised the authority of the Executive. Disastrous. From that moment on MacArthur was dead as a political power in America. It was all right to think it, but he should never have said it aloud. And Patton—!

The Undersecretary had glanced at his watch. "Good heavens, it's after three. Well after." He got rapidly to his feet, and his assistants followed suit. He removed his glasses and delicately patted his brows and mustache; his broad French collar was stained. "It's a tribute to your eloquence and cuisine, Courtney. But I must run." Moving toward the entrance he said, "If American participation in the Khotianese conflict were to be expanded, can you give us assurances that the Chinese Communist government will not actively intervene?"

"Categorically," Massengale answered. "The most significant information our Intelligence has secured out here over the past three years is the knowledge that China will not march in such an eventuality. Of that we're certain."

The Undersecretary nodded, the glasses' stem in a corner of his mouth. "That was, of course, the contention of MacArthur's headquarters before the Yalu operation . . ."

"That is true. But the situation is not at all analogous. I'm sure Frederick Brokaw will bear me out on this."

"What do you feel would be the position of our SEATO allies?"

"I believe they would support it wholeheartedly. Especially the Philippines and Australia."

The Undersecretary nodded. "That's interesting. Would you work up a memorandum on this for me on my way through again?"

"I'd be happy to do so."

"And thank you very much for the most royal repast, Courtney. I haven't eaten like this since my salad days in the embassy in Paris."

Massengale took his hand. "I'll tell Kimh—he'll be overjoyed."

"I'm very grateful to you for the extensive briefing."

"My pleasure entirely." Massengale swung open the door. "God speed, Mr. Secretary. I will hope for your rapid and successful return . . ."

In Tuyet's room he lay on the broad, low bed and frowned at the ceiling. It was a quiet time of day. Far below in the street he heard two voices calling, then silence. Indolently he turned his head and watched Tuyet who was bent forward doing her nails, her lovely lacquered profile so delicate it seemed that the faintest gesture, the faintest sound, would shatter it. Aware of his gaze after a while, she turned and looked at him and smiled—the quick, childlike, empty smile of the Khotianese. A simple people. He sighed. Her body was slender, almost breastless, suggestive of some very fragile, beautiful young boy, but her lips were full and moist in the soft saffron light.

His rage had subsided; he felt in its place a gross, immovable weight, like a physical obstruction in the defile of his mind. He had lost; when he had been so certain. That credulous, stubborn, sentimental fool Damon. After all these years. The deep apocalyptic assault he'd dreamed of, that giant thrust into the heartland of China, would not come about. Not for a good long while, anyway. With luck they might ease their way into large-scale participation here, but that was not what he sought. He was facing retirement unless he could secure the post of Chief of Staff or some other executive intercession. That swine Velanger—he and that wretched little clique of his had blocked him. Now he could only reach it through a thunderbolt, some dazzling coup that would rivet attention on him out here, ten thousand miles from that blasted Pentagon.

Of course there was politics: he could go to the conventions, make the rounds and sound out the committeemen and ward heelers, the grubby, venal souls who carried on the errant business of the Republic. But he doubted if he would ever be able to stick it. An appointment, yes—such as Marshall had got, and Maxwell Taylor before the Administration had recalled him to active duty; but to curry favor with the flabby-faced men and strident, aggressive women . . .

Or he could go up to the old home at Rensselaer, listen to the snow stinging the storm sash, hire himself a housekeeper and tread out the dreary round of an old man's regimen, assembling his papers, writing letters to the editors of the New York papers. But he could never endure that after this—not after Fort Myer and Paris and Reina Blanca and Cau Luong: what he could not bear, he knew, was to fall back into obscurity, into solitude—

There was a distant boom, then another: muffled, stealthy, persistent. Artillery, up near Hua Ngai. What were they firing at? He opened his eyes. Tuyet had put down her stylus and brush and was gazing at the sea. She was so still. A longing urgent as breath swept over him. He said: "Tuyet."

She looked up, her flaring cheekbones and short, broad nose accentuated by the sun's low rays.

"Come here," he said in French. "Come to me."

Obediently she rose and came over and sat on the edge of the bed. There was in her movements the small, fastidious grace of a cat. "Will there be a film tonight?" she asked softly.

"I don't see why not." He put his hand on her thigh, her belly, feeling the young, firm flesh under the light chartreuse fabric; and a faint tremor of rage, of desolation, shook him.

"What is the matter?"

"Nothing. Nothing is the matter."

"Oh." She looked down at him, neither kindly nor fearfully. A simple, receptive look. Children, they were all children. But no matter what he did, in the end he always had to ask her.

"Serve me," he said in French.

Slowly, with infinite grace she undressed—he insisted on this although there was no actual need for it—and kneeling beside him began the ministration he needed now with the desperate, resurgent hunger of an opium smoker. He raised his head: he needed to watch her. It was sweet, the control of another being, the possession of this supine form, maculate flesh serving him, dependent on him, only him; it was this that was sweet, seething, tensing, caught in tumbling orange and indigo light that spread swiftly, tightened, released in joy, in joy, in spurting flaccid loss.

So brief.

It was so trivial, so brief. But it was what he had to have, now. He had to, he didn't quite know why . . . The urgency was gone, as usual. Its fulfillment was only for himself, that was paramount—but he could only enjoy that fleet fulfillment if he were with another. That was what was humiliating even while it gave him gratification—the need of another.

He looked up at her with utter hatred. "How strange it is," he said in French. "You have no sense of shame about it, have you? None at all . . ."

"Why should I?" She seemed merely surprised. "It is what you want. It is what you enjoy."

They said she was of good family; her parents had been killed in an air raid by the French. Her brother was in the North now, with the Hai Minh. She had been the lover of a Khotianese colonel who had been shot or exiled or imprisoned—purged, anyway—when Vu Khoi had taken over; she never spoke of him. Emptily he watched her dressing, her lithe, slender legs slipping into her trousers.

It is what you want. Yes. But that was not enough. Not nearly enough.

"The name of the game is: Bounce the Chinks!" Tony Giandoli declared. With a flick of his thumb he snapped open the cuff of his left sleeve and whipped out a wicked-looking Malaysian throwing knife strapped to his forearm. "All right, you Hai Minh hotshots—come on out of that folding bed! It's zapping time in old Khotiane . . ."

"Put it away, Gee, before you cut yourself and we have to leave you here as a line company replacement," Colonel Krisler told him.

"I just want 'em to see I'm ready, that's all. There's no front lines out here, you know. Got to be ready to fight at three hundred and sixty degrees. Right around the clock."

"What do you know about guerrilla warfare?" Captain Forbes taunted him lazily. "You've never heard a shot fired in anger."

"I can wait," Corporal Giandoli said. "I mean, let them work down the list till they get to me. You know?" He moved the blade along his bared forearm, staring in fascination as the thick black hair lifted away in tight rolls. "Look at that. What a gook-stabber . . . Hey, Chief," he said to Damon, "hey, when we wrap up this high-level diplomatic caper, how about us making it over to Hong Kong for a quick Rape and Ruin?"

"What do you want in Hong Kong?" Sam asked him.

"That crew chief Wodtke was telling me about a jazzo place called the Blue Phoenix, where they give you a menu—only the menu hasn't got chow on it but tail. Yeah!" His big, liquid eyes gleamed. "You draw a circle around the names you like and *choong!*—there they are, right at your table, rubbing up against you like they meant it."

"Come off it, Gee," Forbes said.

"He's right, Bob," Joey Krisler said with a grin. "Only thing: you'll have to pay four bucks an hour taxi-dance rental for each girl."

"Yeah, but while it lasts—heaven can wait!"

The four of them were sitting in a seedy little café near the airfield at Pnom Du. The sinking sun poured gold over the metal tables, the half-reclining customers, the faded pink and yellow façades of the tin shacks across the street. Dust rose in quick eddies on the gusts of wind, and bits of paper and leaves tumbled past as stealthily as forest animals. Now and then a plane took off in a shuddering, straining roar, and all talk ceased; then it was gone, fading up the sky, and the dust and poured molten light returned, and the smell of the cooking fires, strange with iodine and mold and fish and old brass. Sam Damon, slumped in one of the wire chairs, worn with heat and the interminable waiting, was reminded of the smells in Pasay, and then the long room at Charmevillers, above the

Marne: there was that same beguiling odor sharp with outlandish ways, which had always drawn him on—all the fantastic worlds beyond Walt Whitman, the island valleys filled with people in burnooses, pantaloons, barongs, loinskins, ao dais . . .

But this tawdry little midway of bars and cribs and laundries did not make the heart leap.

"Probably picked up a case of drippy tummy and changed his mind," Joey was saying crossly. "God damn politicians—I wouldn't trust them as far as I could throw one of these water buffaloes."

Damon looked at his watch. Five twenty. "They could have had plane trouble, I suppose."

"I don't like this, Chief. It feels goofy. Let me go over to the message center and check it out."

"We'll give them a little longer," he answered.

"You're the general."

He finished the dregs of his drink. The others had wanted brandy and soda, but on an impulse he'd ordered a vermouth-cassis—and with the first sip of the sweet, flat, dense apéritif the Riviera had swept back, and with it the first twinges of the melancholy that now gripped him. He had sat at a café then with the father, filled with bitterness and confusion; now he sat with the son in another café halfway around the world, and the comparisons and contrasts were unavoidable. Rock-and-roll music blasted from radios across the street, two different tunes competing stridently, and shoeshine boys in ragged yellow T-shirts ran beside a passing soldier, begging cigarettes; he mopped his face with the big red handkerchief he always carried, and picked at his nails.

He could not shake off the depression that had dogged him all afternoon. Earlier, on receiving the coded radio from the Undersecretary, he had been elated. He had—somehow, unpredictably and in complete defiance of all the odds—stopped this lunatic design for a mammoth war on China, at least temporarily. Now, a day later, killing time, still wobbly from dysentery and waiting for the plane, he was assailed by doubts and despondencies. He had said what he had to; he'd spoken his piece and retarded the ominous drift of things. But he was unable to escape the sense that wily and powerful forces were moving against him with sure stealth, while he sat here twiddling his thumbs. Massengale would get rid of him one way or another, and they'd crank up the Khotiane war to their hearts' content. Only the other day he'd overheard Usher on Fowler's staff telling reporters—off the record, of course—that from one point of view it wasn't desirable to be too successful here; that the invaluable lessons to be learned by troops up to battalion level made it well worth prolonging things . . .

Well: they didn't have a thing to worry about. It would prolong itself just as long as those in power wanted it to.

"—swung around this bunch of rocks and there it was—a jeep and two trucks and an M-39, all squashed together," Forbes was saying to

Joey. "And that did it. The minute we stopped all hell broke loose—machine guns, automatic rifles, mortars, the works. The Chinks had it interdicted from the west slope. And cold! I want to tell you, it was a bitch. They died in the road, in the trucks, on the tanks, they were hiding behind boulders and running up and down the road screaming. And the fire just kept right on pouring down."

"Man, that's bug-out time!" Giandoli chortled.

"Shut up, Gee," Krisler told him.

"Yes-sir."

"It was awful," Forbes went on, his smooth, rather handsome features pinched with reminiscence. "I could see one of the Chinks up there, directing fire, waving his arm and hollering. I thought: There's only one thing to do. We've got to go up and get those guns. I crawled over to where three or four GIs were lying in a gully and said: 'Let's go. Let's go get the sons of bitches. Who'll come with me?' No reaction. Then one of them said, 'You want it, you go get it, Jack.' I said: 'You want to lay here and get slaughtered, is that it? What's the matter with you people?' No answer. And then another one—a thin guy with a lot of teeth gone on one side of his mouth—said: 'You go take it and then shove it up your ass . . .' "

"Interesting command problem," Joey said. "How'd you play it?"

Forbes spread his hands on the table. "It's not in *The Armed Forces Officer*, I can tell you that. I had this pint of bourbon I'd been saving for two months. I figured now was the time. I hauled it out and took a good long slug and then I said to the guy without the teeth: 'Here's twenty minutes' worth of courage, you stupid bastard. Pass it around. And then God damn it, let's go!' " The two officers laughed. "And it worked. I got them up and we started climbing that pass. Some other people had got the same idea, and we got one gun with grenades. They all wanted to sit down and call it a day then, the bottle was gone and I had a hell of a time. But I signed up three more warriors with a promise of another drink after we'd got the gun—I guess that comes under the heading of flagrant misrepresentation—and we dragged ourselves on up. It got colder every step of the way, it was so cold you couldn't think. Literally. And on top of all that it started snowing. About halfway up, the gun quit. He's sucking us in, I figured, he's running low and he's waiting. Well, I could see the gun's muzzle stuck in a little notch in the rocks, and that was all. Perfect field of fire, just about no cover at all for the last fifteen, twenty yards. I still had two heroes with me and we got up as close as the cover lasted. By now it was snowing like a bastard. I was so cold I couldn't lie there any longer, I just couldn't, and I waved the other guys up and we rushed it. Utterly ridiculous. Still no fire. I came up over the rocks, stumbling and staggering like an old drunk—and there he was, all alone, sitting straight as a ramrod, his hands on the grip, staring right at me, the snow in his nose and mouth. Frozen stiff." He shook his head, staring. "The guts that took! Up there in that wind in that ragged beat-up old quilted jacket, no gloves, canvas shoes. Stayed right at the gun till he froze to death. I remember I thought: Jesus, we're going to be lucky to get out of this—any of us at all . . ."

Damon felt his lips move in a wry, sad smile. Fifty years ago he had sat and listened to the old soldiers; now he was listening to the young ones. He had traced the great circle, as Tommy called it. Some things had remained the same; but more had changed. On Memorial Day back home there had been the parade, led by George Verney and Old Emil Clausen in their fine, broad-brimmed hats and dark blue uniforms, striding right behind the band. Old Emil had walked very stiffly, carrying his sword with his forearm hooked under the hilt, but Mr. Verney had smiled around him, and now and then waved to friends. Behind them came the Spanish War veterans, the First Nebraska Volunteers, and there was Uncle Bill, if he was home, sweating in his tight-fitting khaki and looking bowlegged in his gaiters; and then the horse-drawn float from Shurtleff's with several of the prettiest girls sitting on the heaped banks of flowers, giggling furtively. And later, back at the house, the veterans would gather on the porch and George Verney would set out the big dark square bottle—he only got it out twice a year, Memorial Day afternoon and Christmas Eve—and the little glasses with the knobs all over them, and offer them all a drink. They would seat themselves deliberately, the older men and the officers on the chairs and settee, the younger men on the steps, their choke collars unbuttoned, their hats tilted back. The ridges where their hats had been made firm red lines low across their foreheads. Mr. Verney would stand in the center of the porch then and raise his glass—he called it a pony—and say, "Here's to the Republic, boys—may she always have men worthy of her in her hour of need." And they would all solemnly down their drinks. After a suitable interval George Verney would pass the bottle along, and the talk would begin, brief and monosyllabic at first, and then gathering pace and passion in reminiscence. He himself would be sent up to bed then, but for hours afterward he would lie awake, listening to the voices drifting up to him with the cigar smoke and the sharp, burned-clean odor of whiskey, talking of Shiloh and Missionary Ridge and El Caney and Balangiga and Punta Grande.

Those had been the voices, the names that had set his blood to dancing, that had molded him and thrust him off along his own long, tortuous, troubled road.

Destiny . . .

He rubbed his jaw, watching these younger, firmer faces, not listening. The world had changed: the world he had grown up in. He remembered his father sitting at the kitchen table, his face dark and block-like just outside the soft flood of light from the kerosene lamp, saying, "No, I couldn't do that. I couldn't do anything like that." That was because a man named Fryeburg had come by to return some tools he couldn't keep paying for because he'd lost his crop of winter wheat.

That had been when Carl Damon had owned the hardware store. He needed the money, but he knew the man needed the tools more. After half an hour and two steins of beer he'd been able to talk Fryeburg out of it and sent him home. And then when his father was sick, legless and wasting away, Fryeburg, who had moved out to Keith County near Ogallala, drove all the way to Walt Whitman in a buckboard in bitter weather, bringing a side of beef and two great hams. And other neighbors had come around with eggs and vegetables, and sat and talked softly in the overheated kitchen. It was right. It was the straight thing to do . . .

"You know what your grandfather did once?" he broke in on Joey, who was talking about the night assault across the Roer River. Their faces turned toward him, startled, deferential. "Some old friends, there were four of them, I think, came to him and asked him to invest some money for them, and he did. And later the company folded—it was one of those Great Lakes mining ventures, I believe—and they lost all their investment. And your grandfather insisted on paying for it. To the nickel. It strapped him for years, nearly broke him; but he did it."

"Yes, I remember something about that," Krisler answered. "Dad said they'd have been pretty well fixed if Grampa hadn't decided to pay them all off like that. He was an impulsive man, Grampa."

"But it was a personal obligation, Joey . . ." He stopped; he had spoken with more heat than he'd meant to. Their faces were grave, a bit constrained; they watched him levelly. They thought he was a tiresome old fool who had to be humored. Did they? Well, Rank Hath Its Pomposities, as Ben had used to say. Or should it read: Paralysis?

"I know, Chief, but it seems to me his first obligation should have been to his own family. He wasn't legally obligated to reimburse them— they knew the chance they were taking."

"You miss the point." He felt nettled and professorial. "You weren't in danger of starving. Don't you see?—he saw it as a matter of responsibility, a point of honor . . .

"I'll tell you what I mean," he went on. It suddenly seemed like a very important argument. "When we were driving to Erie in '29—that was right after your Dad and I had completed the Company Officers' Course at Benning—I stopped to get gas at a little town outside of Cincinnati. Sharonville, its name was. The owner said my left rear was soft, and offered to check it. I'd had a lot of tire trouble that day, and I thought he was making something out of nothing, maybe trying for a little extra work for himself, and I said it didn't matter, let it go. And he told me he'd take it off and check it, and if he didn't find a nail he'd put it back without charge. I said okay to that; and he found the nail and patched the tire . . . Now who does anything like that nowadays?"

"People still do things like that, General," Forbes said. "Or they want to."

"Maybe they want to . . ."

"But there isn't time for that kind of thing anymore. The personal touch—"

"There's always time. It's the will that's lacking. If there isn't time for the personal touch, as you call it, we might as well give up and go home . . ." He subsided again, folded his hands. The light was copper now, a burnished copper on the walls, the thatched huts just beyond the squalid midway. The younger officers were quiet, a kind of deference. Responsibility was what it was. Yes, and more than that—pride. Pride in the thing itself, a sober reverence for intrinsic truth, for a task secretly met and mastered. How did those great lines of Yeats go? *Be secret and exult, Because of all things known That is most difficult.* Magnificent. They thought he was big and easy: a sentimental old man. Maybe he was. Sorry about that, the GIs said now, in flat, sardonic intonation, not even bothering to smile; sorry about that, baby. In the Pacific they had said: Screw you, Jack, I got mine!—grinning like cats, half-meaning it. Now they seemed to mean it entirely . . . And who, knowing what they were asked to do, could take it on himself to blame them?

"He's not coming, General." Joey had risen and was standing at a sort of easy attention, looking down at him; Joey always observed the military proprieties when there were other soldiers around. "With your permission, sir, I think we ought to go back to the compound. The security is none too great around here, and it's getting late."

He studied Joey for a few seconds: the square, sturdy, snub-nosed face with its scar of slick, ruddy flesh that ran like a gross, misplaced lip from his nostril upward across his cheek into his hair; the mild brown eyes that measured everything with a slow, easy competence. Joey was a professional, more of a soldier than he'd ever been. Silver star, three bronze stars, Legion of Merit, DSM. Never once in trouble: no courts-martial, excellent efficiency reports, a nice clean 201 file. A good soldier. He would always be easy to get along with, he would never step out of line.

"Keep your shirt on, Joey," he said. "He'd have notified us before this if he'd been detained for any length of time. Bob, would you go over and check in with the message center, see if there's anything? And take Gee with you."

"Right with it, General."

He watched Forbes and Giandoli move off down the street—beset immediately by a cluster of girls in bright silk slacks or skirts and blouses; their hands reached out like petals in the deepening bronze light. The soldiers shook their heads, pushing on through them—Gee a bit reluctantly, with a funny little embarrassed wave of his hand. Damon sighed: he felt defeated, thwarted and cast aside. It wasn't plane trouble; Massengale had waylaid the Undersecretary or there had been a last-minute change of plans. They were going to relieve him, perhaps. Yes, that was most likely; because of the conference. But he was the man Hoanh-Trac wanted to work with . . .

He encountered Joey Krisler's eyes: the two men looked at each other for a short, silent moment.

"I know what you mean," Joey said, as though no time or talk had intervened. "But there isn't a place for that kind of thing, anymore. Maybe when you and Dad were young, sure. But now there's too many people, too much is going on. Everything's become too complicated. That guy in Sharonville is probably working in a GM garage in Cincy, doing nothing but carburetor overhaul. The corporations are running it all now. And the PR people."

"There was a public relations man on Oom Paul Thiemann's staff," Damon said. "Gilfoyle. How your Dad hated him! He got up once after Wokai and gave one of those mealy-mouthed speeches on casualty figures, and Ben asked him if he was planning to declare a dividend."

Joey nodded. "Typical. The trouble with Dad was he let his heart ride his head."

"Is that bad?"

"Oh, nobody wants to be thought of as a walking computer. But he *ran* on his emotions—he was always fighting everybody. You know that. Christ, what a chip he carried! He was his own worst enemy."

"And everyone else's best friend."

"Yeah, maybe. Except the people that counted—the ones who wrote up his fitness reports. Boy, you should have seen the reaction when I used to report in at a new post. 'Krisler? Paprika Ben's boy? Son, you want to walk mighty careful around here.' And then the stories. I guess they expected me to punch the adjutant in the nose and toss a chair through the picture window at the club. Or cop a feel with the CO's wife."

"Benjy would never have stopped with a feel."

Joey laughed. "I know. Don't I know . . . Oh, he made a fine record— of its kind; only I've always had to live it down, Sam. Dad made a religion of fighting City Hall. Which was great therapy for him, but rough enough on the rest of us. Hell, if it hadn't been for you he'd have wound up in Leavenworth stockade."

"I never bailed him out of a thing," Sam said.

"That isn't the way Mother tells it. Sure, when I was a kid I thought it was great, his telling some stuffed-shirt instructor where to get off. But where did it get him? I mean all the romantic malarkey aside. A 201 file that must have read like some GCM findings, and the longest lieutenancy since Homer. The only reason he got his chance to go out to Papua with you was because they were desperate to get rid of him down at Tarleton—and nobody else wanted any part of New Guinea at that stage of the game."

"That's for sure," Damon murmured.

"Don't get me wrong. I think he was one hell of a combat leader. But that isn't everything—there's a lot more to being a first-rate officer than that."

"That's true."

"Now you take Courtney Massengale. I know you don't like him, and Dad hated his very guts because of some row he got into with him at Garfield when he was tight. I was up at Baguio in school and I never got the full story on that, though Mom was awfully mad at him for a while. But that's neither here nor there. Massengale's a great military leader in my book. Not just with troops but in the full sense of the word. I know: they say he's cold as a witch's tit in December and he's used political influence, all that. Who wouldn't, in his shoes? That argument's always struck me as sour grapes, tell you the truth. It's the jokers without any connections who are always hollering foul. If I had an uncle in the United States Senate, I'm here to tell you I'd bend his ear till it dropped off." He scrubbed his scalp once, briskly. "The point is, Massengale isn't guilty of any waste motion: he never lets sentiment or personal feelings get in his way. He zeroes in on the primary objective and that's it. He doesn't let anything deflect him."

"No, he certainly doesn't."

"Well, by God, that's the way to be. The old hell-for-leather, hell-around, don't-give-a-damn days are over, as far as I can see. Everything's complicated now; everybody's a specialist. And the guy that knows where he's going and how to get there is the guy that's going to make himself felt. That's why Massengale's effective."

"No argument there," Damon agreed. "Only thing is: is this primary objective of his the best one?"

"It's what he wants."

"Sure. But is it going to be good for all the rest of us confused, emotional, mixed-up people?" He studied the younger man's face a moment, leaned forward and said: "Joey: did you ever disobey a direct order?"

"Only once. At Stoumont. The word was to pull out, drop back to Hamoir; and I couldn't see it. I'd been running for two days and two nights and I was sick of it—I guess I was afraid if I kept on running anymore I'd never be able to stop." He stared at the rows of bottles massed behind the bar. "Well, it was more than that, too—I guess I'd better level about it. There was this sunken road up from the river and they had to come single file—I figured if we could only get one of the bastards that'd be all she wrote, because there just wasn't any place to push it out of the way. It was nature's perfect roadblock. I knew if they ever got out on those fields behind us nothing would ever stop them."

"And you got the lead tank."

Joey nodded. "At fifteen yards. I never want to do that again, I can tell you. It was a highly emotional operation: just like the Old Man."

"And because you and a couple thousand guys like you indulged in a highly emotional operation, Peiper never made it into Liège."

"Yeah, sure, and I got a medal out of it and all that crap. Because it worked. But if it hadn't, I'd have got court-martialed. Of course if it hadn't worked I'd be dead anyway, so I guess that doesn't apply. Well, an extreme situation like that . . . But I'll never do it again. What's the percentage? You only get called on the carpet.

"A good friend of mine threw away a really promising career a few years ago—he took a pretty strong position in that hassle over arming the Krauts with tactical nuclear weapons. Maybe he was right, too: but what good did it do him? Now he's selling athletic goods in Long Island City . . ." He pushed his short legs out straight and crossed them. "Don't get me wrong, Sam. I don't hold for this dumb-blind-automaton stuff; a man ought to think for himself. But I'm not going to step out of line. Hell, I'm no hero, I know that—I'm no tactical genius like you, and I'm not a hotshot fireball like Dad, either; I'm just an average character who does what he's told and keeps his nose clean. And that isn't always easy . . ."

No, it wasn't always easy. What was it Raebyrne had said, that long-ago rainy afternoon in Lorraine? "But supposing the hoosier giving the commands is giving the wrong ones?" The Colonel's words about Massengale had surprised him. He knew the kind of man Joey was, the cast and scope of his mind, from half a hundred casual conversations around campfires and in drifting rowboats; but hearing them now, at this moment, had shaken him subtly, added to his sense of depression.

"Joey," he said slowly, "if this mission should run into any kind of trouble—if anything should happen to me . . ." He paused; his senior aide was looking at him in frank surprise. Generals didn't talk this way—at least successful ones didn't. He thought old Sad Sam had gone dotty: senile. Well, maybe he was. Maybe after slogging the length and breadth of two world wars and the vagaries of the peacetime Army, he had a right to be . . .

He grinned nevertheless, and shook his head. "No, I didn't mean anything like that. No histrionics. But I may be derricked without much fanfare; rendered hors de combat one way or another." He tapped the zinc table. "And I want you to go ahead and wind it up. No matter what. There's a great deal at stake here, Joey. More than you know." He paused. The Light Colonel was watching him now—attentive, thoughtful, a little wary. He said: "Massengale would like to torpedo this whole mission. In fact he may be doing something along those lines right now."

Krisler was looking at him blankly. "Why would he want to do that?"

"Because he's after something else. Something very different. Joey, I want you to go ahead with it. Nail it down, get those Chinese out of there. Just as quickly as possible. You can handle it, you've talked with Hoanh, you've talked with Ch'en's people. No matter what Massengale decrees."

"But Sam, he's COMMACK . . ."

"I know. He's a lot of things."

The younger man frowned. "Gee, I don't know, Sam. I wouldn't want to step out of line on a thing like this . . ."

Damon paused. "Joey, he's planning an invasion of China."

"China! But I heard him myself once—he said we ought never to—"

"So did I. Once. But things are different now. That's what's in the works."

"But—with what units?"

"That God damned hopeless Chinese rabble—first. Then US forces in support. They're talking about eight assault divisions, with twelve to follow."

"Wow . . ."

"Yes. By that time the money will be in the pot, with everyone raising against the opener."

Joey scratched his scalp—the sudden, arduous gesture that reminded him so of Ben. But the son's eyes when he raised his face were constrained and puzzled. "I can't believe it, Sam. He wouldn't do a thing like that: he just wouldn't. It runs counter to everything he's said . . . Are you sure, Sam?"

He saw it then: Joey was straining to accept this, believe this—but he couldn't. It ran contrary to his practical, credent view of the world; he suspected the source—his father's old friend and fellow rebel. Damon thought of Congressman Matt Bullen, biting on his cigar, his hands on the big oak desk. "Son, you still got to learn what the world runs on." Well: he'd learned, all right; he'd learned; but that didn't make it any more palatable . . .

"Joey, I'm going to tell you something." He took a deep breath and clasped his hands together. He had sworn he would never speak of it again, to anyone. Ever. He hadn't even told Tommy—not even when she'd pressed him that night.

But this was different. He would have to speak of it now.

"Massengale caused your dad's death, Joey. On Pala."

The battalion commander stared at him.

"Yes. And I aided and abetted him. In a manner of speaking." It was hard. He had not realized how hard it would be to say this out loud; after all this time. But he told it, slowly, evenly, while the jeeps roared up and down the squalid, noisy midway and the girls in their silk slacks called to the fitful parade of suntans and olive drab: PYLON, and the promise of the reserve, the angry conference in his headquarters tent, the attack, and the loss of contact, and standing there holding that radio from Porky Bannerman—the hollow, awful realization; and the others all looking at him in the silence . . .

"I see." Krisler nodded rapidly, his face stiff. "I see."

"Didn't you know anything about it, Joey? You never heard anything?" The younger man shook his head. It was what Tommy always said: Everybody always heard about it but the goat.

"—It seems impossible!" Joey burst out.

"Yes. It does, at times."

"It all—it really happened like that?"

He looked at the Light Colonel, whose eyes still held a shade of distrust. "You don't think I'd make up something like this, do you?" he asked quietly.

"No. No, of course not . . . But why—couldn't you have told him to go shit in his hat?"

"Yes. I could have. I thought about it. But he'd have loved that—he'd have shoved Ryetower in and run it off, anyway. I thought we might get away with it. And then of course"—and he could feel his lip curl—"I was under the impression I had Porky out there if anything did go wrong . . ."

"The bastard." Joey's face had turned very hard and plain, all ridges; he no longer looked like his mother at all. "But then why didn't you tear it open?" he cried hotly. "A thing that low, that rotten—why didn't you demand a court. . . ?"

He shifted his feet. "Probably I should have. I guess that was where I was weak. I didn't have an airtight case—some of my radios got lost when Dick moved the headquarters. Massengale had only given me his word about the Forty-ninth, there was nothing in writing." He smiled grimly. "Only his word as an officer and a gentleman. He had all those powerful connections you know about, in Congress, the AG's office—and he had a sparkling victory behind him, remember. He'd have come out all right; and they'd have burned me bad. To no purpose that I could see."

"But you *owe* a man that much—at least that much! To square it . . ."

He sighed. "You're probably right. I know . . . It was all over and done by then. The Salamanders were gone: your dad, Ray, Joe, Stan Bowcher, Jackson. All the old men, the good ones . . . You've got to remember"—his voice had taken on a supplicant note that distressed him—"the Kyushu and Honshu operations were still hanging over us: we didn't know how Luzon and Mindanao were going to turn out. Leyte and Pala were grim beyond belief. I figured I could be of more help to the Divison as its CO, fighting for it, than I could as a cashiered invalid holding down a cot at Walter Reed . . ."

He fell silent, thinking. When his eyes met Joey's he saw, behind the outrage and anger, a flicker of the bitter disappointment a man feels on finding a revered superior afflicted with feet of clay. Rugged old Uncle Sam, holder of the CMH, who had saved whole beachheads single-handed, who never flinched from a point of honor, had succumbed to expediency in this vicious incident like any grubby little staff conniver. He was just like all the rest, then: no better and no worse—

He lowered his eyes and picked at the callus on his thumb. He'd seen that look in Donny's face once, back at Garfield; that time he'd told the boy all men (himself included) were afraid . . . The Tweaker had glared at him in the harsh light of the corridor, his pixie satan's brows quivering, and demanded: "What did you expect: Damon?—an arachnid? a cephalopod?" Now Donny was dead nearly twenty years, and he, bereft, had served as surrogate father to a fatherless Joey—who now thought less of him. Well, that was only fair enough; he'd thought a good deal less of himself ever since that afternoon in the hospital at Reina Blanca. Maybe that was simply the price you paid for the truth: you exposed your own frailties along with those of others . . .

He felt all at once bleak and defeated, enormously tired. He longed with all his heart to be home in Monterey, working downstairs in the shop or walking along the shore at Point Piños with the sea swirling through the black pinnacles of rock and the seals' heads bobbing in the swells. Old men shouldn't try to run things: the young, with their boundless confidence, their naked credulity and hope, should do it . . . It was so important, so desperately important for Joey to see what was at stake here! But the Colonel sat staring into his empty glass, his short, square face closed and hard. Why in God's name had he brought up PYLON? What good had it done? He'd only upset the boy; wounded him deeply, and for no good reason. "Bête," Michele had said with still, implacable wrath. "You hurt everyone you touch. You are hateful." And he had suffered, and suffered again, and thought about it all the while—and it hadn't done him much good, truth to tell. He hadn't learned much of anything . . .

The flat, stark edges of the day were softening: it was late. One of those two-wheeled carts was coming down the road, pulled by a Khotianese farmer, his shoulders twisting at the shafts; and behind him another. At the sight of them Damon's heart sank. Why this sense of despondency that mounted and mounted, and hung over him like a cloud? He was afraid. Sitting here in the onrushing tropic twilight he shivered. Two guards passed the entrance to the café, swinging in stride, carbines at sling: the indolent, time-eating swagger of the soldier on guard duty in any era, any land. He frowned at his hands. A soldier. All his life a soldier. A narrow, topsy-turvy kind of trade—bound to scorn in days of peace, flung into the most terrible power in time of war. Westy, sick and beaten, had looked up at him helplessly and moaned, "I can't look at them. My boys. I can't look at them anymore!" and so he had taken matters into his own hands, made the ruthless decisions as to who should live, who should die. He had hardened his heart, lashed his command into a capacity for killing, ordered the death of others of his fellowmen by steel, by hunger, by fire. In order that it might be got over; and Joyce Tanahill, lying beside him with one arm behind her head, had murmured, "No, I don't suppose there's any other way."

In order that it might be got over. But it was never over—each conflict he'd struggled so arduously to end had led only to another, and another. The hot, fugitive hope he'd felt all around him in '45 was gone: war was ascendant everywhere, the threat of war was even grimmer; these younger men sitting at tables near him were swallowed up in it, exchanging tales of the rigors of the Pusan Perimeter, the Bulge, the fight for Duc Trang-na . . .

A soldier. He thought of Lin Tso-han, and the old Chinese proverb about good iron and the nail . . . And yet that wasn't all of it, either. It wasn't only flint hearts and slaughter. It was worth remembering, wasn't it, here in the hot red dust, that the hero of the Bhagavad Gita was a warrior, that old King David had been a soldier first and foremost, that it was of a Roman Centurion the Nazarene said: "I have not found so great faith, no, not in Israel" . . . ? The real hero of the *Iliad* was Hector, that bulwark of a doomed city; Othello had been a military leader of merit, but desperately led astray—he hadn't understood women any better than the rest of them; there was Roland, and Harry Plantagenet, and the persevering Aeneas, and Prince Andrei, whose luck finally ran out at Borodino—

He reached in his right cargo pocket, felt for and found the worn one-franc piece and took it out and looked at it. The girl in her Phrygian cap and oakleaf garland was nearly effaced now; he could barely make out the profile and the line of the eye. She had reminded him of Michele—that same long, straight nose, the suggestion of fullness at the chin, the vif glance. Was that why he'd chosen it? Luck. He'd carried it ever since the afternoon of the Paris Parade, guided by the old soldier's essentially humble knowledge that you did all you could, as long and as well as you could—but that even then you needed a little luck. Just a little.

Well, he'd had luck: a lot of it, if the truth were known. He put the coin on the table and spun it smartly with his thumb: it stood in a pulsing yellow meniscus, slowed, wobbling; settled and was still.

Tails. On the reverse the doubled cornucopias were clearly visible, and so were those three magic words that had electrified two centuries, and turned the world inside out. He put his hand over his mouth, watching absently several Khotianese unloading sacks of rice from one of the carts, which had stopped across the street. *Liberté, égalité, fraternité.* Now these Indochinese farmers and fishermen wanted them, too; but there were those abroad who, like the landed aristocracy of the ancien régime, didn't want them to have them—or wanted them to have them only under certain very special conditions. "But they're *Asiatics,* Damon," Colonel Fahrquahrson had informed him with patronizing congeniality; "separate is better." Lin Tso-han had wiggled his comical Groucho Marx eyebrows and observed: "It is curious how the Western World sees us," and in the spare, graceful room up in Plei Hoa, Hoanh-Trac held his joined hands before his face and cried softly, "But it is *our* civil war! . . ."

Forbes and Giandoli were coming back from the message center, again besieged by prostitutes; Tony Gee blew one of them a kiss, slipped his arm around another, a plump girl with her silky black hair in bangs, and began to walk along with her. Forbes scowled at him and said something and Tony, grinning, shrugged and reluctantly disengaged.

What had George Caldwell said at Angers? "Wonders are many, and none is more wonderful than man." He had meant to look it up and never had. *None more wonderful than man.* How intriguing it would be to escape time, hang in some exalted celestial net and watch the faltering, interminable passage of this earthly primate, with his perfectly apposable thumb and mighty cerebrum; following him as he developed speech, mastered tools and then engines and finally electrical impulses and radio waves—and never, for all his lordly capacity for wonder and reflection, overcame his need to lead, dominate, tyrannize over his fellows—

"General—"

Forbes was speaking to him. Joey had got to his feet, their faces swung toward the southeast; and turning he heard the pulsing bass drone, saw the long, low silhouette like some predatory bird hanging just above the purple mass of hills, its riding lights winking, stately and festive. Troubled, he watched its creeping descent. Why did man seek power so ardently? It meant so much to him: he was willing to give over so many glories, so much simple happiness, to its pursuit. And there was a palpable hook to its achievement, too—like facing the sphinx. The slave served the tyrant with his body: the slave, once his duties were discharged, was free to dream of other worlds, indulge in political heresies, even write poetry if he chose. The tyrant was the prisoner of his own design: he could not deviate, he could not afford the luxury of heresy. Too much was at stake: he must hew to the line, come what may . . .

"And about time," Joey was saying tersely. "What's he been doing—holding a God damn press conference?"

The big plane was landing, sinking gently down through the warm twilight air, melting into the dun and violet earth, merging with it. And with its thundering approach a sense of perfect dread slipped over Damon like a noisome cloak. It's going to crash, he thought unhappily. Jesus. It's going to crash and burn right there on the end of the runway, before anyone can get to it. But still he sat there, inert, imprisoned by foreboding and despair, remembering his father-in-law standing at the rain-soaked window, his face stern, saying: "Let's make sure it *is* the last argument . . ." Wonders are many. And what conclusions could a half-way earnest man draw from his more than three-score years—

No. It had landed, bounced once, gently, again, and twin plumes of dust spurted from its tires; it was rolling, ghostly and vast, toward the squat cluster of buildings at the far end of the field. Inside the cabin the lights were on. It wasn't going to crash at all, it was going to taxi up to the administration building and the Undersecretary was going to get out, supported by his little retinue. And he would have to gird himself, get ready to do battle once more.

"Mahogany bar, home movies, blonds in the upper berths ready and aching to spread," Corporal Giandoli marveled, following the smooth, dark hulk down the runway, his eyes shining. "Man, that's living! Hey Chief, what do you say we—"

He was in a globe of light and sound. Light and sound that passed beyond human sensibility. He was on the ground, sitting on the ground, and bits of unrelated movement slipped past him in too bright panels. *Bomb*, the thought sank into him. But his mind could go no farther. How had he got here? His ears were ringing, he heard sounds like midnight echoes in deserted streets. Dumbly he watched Joey crawl to his feet, gripping his carbine; his cap was gone, his face was blackened, blood was running in a neat little trickle down his neck. His entire left sleeve was gone. Bomb, the thought came again. That handcart. Yes. Now he could hear firing, the sudden chatter of automatic weapons. *Brrrrappppapppappp!* Joey was returning the fire deliberately, very calm, the slender brass shells spilling gaily on the table's surface, spinning. What the hell was he *doing* here? on his duff? He started to get to his feet, and pain came in a long, bright wave. He felt hollow and sticky and all apart. Hollowed all apart. Carefully he looked down. The front of his shirt was blown away, his trousers; there was a slick blue furrow right where his belt had been.

Oh, he said; or thought he said. He was hit. Hit past mending this time. A warm seeping through his body, his legs. What was it Lin Tso-han had said? "Once in the arm, once in the leg; but the third time will be fatal." Three times and out. He gripped his belly gently in both hands and looked around. Tables and chairs, splintered and upended; the bar was a sodden mass of shattered glass. Someone was shouting something. A body lay near him, the face pressed against the floor, a cratered nest like an inverted rose behind one ear. Tony Gee. He tried to move again, and barely repressed a shriek. Above him, directly ahead of his gaze Joey reversed the taped-together banana clip with perfect precision, fired five more rounds. With an immense effort he twisted his head to the right and saw a man in black jacket and trousers, slumped near the entrance, reaching for a grenade that lay not two feet away. The ring was still in it, however; it wasn't armed. Odd: that grenade. Joey fired again and again, and still the gnarled brown hand strained to reach the smooth shiny metal egg, stretched and strained. Then the body all at once contracted, but the fingers continued to scratch at the worn wood.

The firing had stopped: there was a great commotion that made no sense. His guts slipped and slithered wetly through his fingers; all of him sliding away. Got a general, he thought numbly; got themselves a three-star general. Big deal.

"Sam. *Sam—!*"

Joey's voice, Joey bending down; his cap was gone, he had a towel around his neck, splotched with red. The too-bright globe had lowered itself around him, set him afire, bubbling. This was serious. Quite serious. Without warning.

"Joey," he said. "You've got to do it now. By yourself. What I told you."

It's all right, Chief. Take it easy. He could see Joey's lips moving. Chief. What Joe Brand had called him, the other Joe. Reb had called him Skipper, or sometimes Cap. Ben had called him Chief, too. Or Sam. What Dev had called him. Old Dev. Took it where you did, in the gut.

"No, Joey, I mean it—you've got to go up there . . ."

The boy had turned away, was looking past him somewhere. Why wouldn't he *listen* to him! God damn it, this was important. The huge globe was fading, in its place black rings began coiling out from the center of his forehead and the pain swelled higher; it came on wires, in darts, in flaring windblown torches and seared him.

"Joey," he said. "Joey, they say we're only robots and yes-men. Stupid, no minds of our own. It isn't so. Give the lie to it—go on up there and block those bastards. What does one man's career matter if he can stop the black drift of things for a while, even the shortest while . . .?" Jesus, it was hard to talk. To keep his mind on things. It kept slithering away from him, hooking and sliding. "Joey, the only thing I've learned in sixty-five years, only one: the romantic, spendthrift moral act is ultimately the practical one—the practical, expedient, cozy-dog move is the one that comes to grief. Yes. Remember that. Joey, if it comes to a choice between being a good soldier and a good human being—try to be a good human being . . ."

Had he said that? any of it? Joey had looked away again. He wasn't going to do it; he could tell from the look in his eyes. Didn't he see what this meant? For the whole yearning, waking world, for the fellow at the sink? The most important thing that had ever happened to them, and he couldn't make the boy see it. "You drive right on," Dev had murmured, watching him with fearful, desolate eyes. "You're that kind of guy, you see a thing and that's the only way it can be. Nobody can say no to you . . ." Now it was the only really important time: and he had failed.

The voices went on above him, but they had changed subtly: instead of angry, urgent cries they were cold and terse, shuttling back and forth. Things incredibly sharp, incredibly jagged tugged at him, stabbed at him: it wasn't possible to suffer this much and still be here to suffer. The rings were much blacker, coiling. Joey was nowhere to be seen. He made another effort and twisted his head, and again saw the Hai Minh guerrilla, the blood-soaked head and chest, the fiercely outstretched arm whose fingers twitched and quivered.

He looked away. The rings had melted into a great murky circle; a swollen, chaotic whirling that frightened him more than the pain. Luck had run out. All run out. The one-franc piece was still there. On the table. Somewhere here. Like Lin he hadn't survived his war. *Tommy*, he thought with a start of pure agony, you knew. Funny Cassandra girl. He felt weaker suddenly, really sick: his head kept falling back and back through greasy, hollow spheres.

"Joey!" he cried at the top of his voice—knew he'd made no sound. He had to make him understand this! The pain was worse again, screeching in on its wires, fanning the flames, and the great dirty circle kept wheeling. "I want to see Joey. Lieutenant Colonel Krisler." Why didn't they obey him! He had to talk to him; he had to get up. But his footing was so unstable. He was sliding in water, sliding down through the murky water. *No.* He gathered himself together in one great, convulsive effort to rise over it. It wasn't good enough, he knew: he was emptied out, he was going, slipping under—

"There wasn't anything we could have done anyway, Colonel," Major Schultz said. He tapped the notations on the clipboard briskly. "He didn't have anything left to work with. And with that liver perforation . . ."

"Yes," Colonel Krisler answered. He was standing at the foot of the bed, staring at the General's body. His arm and neck were bandaged and his solid, snub-nosed face was expressionless. "I see."

"He had the constitution of a horse," Captain Delaney offered.

Schultz scowled at him. Of all the tactless comments! To cover it he asked, "How old was he?"

"Sixty-five," Krisler said. He seemed unable to take his eyes from Damon's face. "He was a great combat commander," he said in a hard, suddenly ominous tone.

"Yes, sir," Schultz replied. "He certainly was. It's most regrettable."

"Yes."

"Well," Delaney sighed, "chalk up another scalp to the Hai Minh."

Schultz threw his assistant another warning glance at this, but Krisler only nodded.

"They'll pay for this." The Colonel's voice was low but there was an edge in it that made Schultz's scalp prickle. "They're going to pay, and pay . . ." Slowly he walked up to the edge of the bed and stared hard at the worn, bloodless face. "He was the greatest combat commander the fucking U.S. Army ever saw. They can say anything they like."

He turned quickly and went out of the room. The two doctors exchanged a glance. Schultz blew out his cheeks. "Boy, *now* watch the end product hit the fan." Pulling back the sheet, he shook his head in wonder. "Look at him, Dan. Look at that thigh—looks as though the lateralis was nearly severed. Look at his shoulder and chest . . ." He leaned down, his eyes narrowing critically. "Good job. Wonder who did that."

"Weintraub was out there then. So was Terwilliger."

"That old windbag? I wouldn't let him touch me with a butterknife." Bending still closer he followed the grooves and stars of lacerated flesh. "It's a wonder that lowest round didn't nick the lung. He was lucky."

"That's the trouble with these old war-horses," Delaney said. "After a while they get to feel they're immortal. Like Achilles or somebody. And then they push their luck too far."

"Yeah, he was too old for this kind of fun-and-games." Whistling between his teeth Schultz drew the sheet up over the General's head, and they left the room.